Chan Sin-wai

A Chinese-English Dictionary of the Human Body

陳善偉

漢英翻譯詞典

身體用語匯編

商務印書館

A Chinese-English Dictionary of the Human Body

漢英翻譯詞典 —— 身體用語匯編

作者　陳善偉
Author　Chan Sin-wai

責任編輯　黃家麗　郭肇敏
Editors　Betty Wong　Skyle Kwok

封面設計　楊啟業
Graphic Designer　K. Y. Yeung

出版　商務印書館（香港）有限公司
Published by　The Commercial Press (H.K.) Limited
香港筲箕灣耀興道 3 號東滙廣場 8 樓
8/F, Eastern Central Plaza, 3 Yiu Hing Road, Shau Kei Wan, Hong Kong
http://www.commercialpress.com.hk

發行　香港聯合書刊物流有限公司
Distributed by　The SUP Publishing Logistics (HK) Limited
香港新界大埔汀麗路 36 號中華商務印刷大廈 3 字樓
3/F, C & C Building, 36 Ting Lai Road, Tai Po, N.T., Hong Kong

印刷　中華商務彩色印刷有限公司
Printed by　C & C Joint Printing Co., (H.K.) Ltd.
香港新界大浦汀麗路 36 號中華商務印刷大廈 14 字樓
14/F, C & C Building, 36 Ting Lai Road, Tai Po, N. T., Hong Kong

版次　2011 年 7 月第 1 版第 1 次印刷
Edition　First Edition, First Printing, July 2011

ISBN 978 96207 0318 8（平）
ISBN 978 96207 0309 6（精）

Printed in Hong Kong

Table of Contents

序言

《漢英翻譯詞典——身體用語匯編》的編纂由構思到完成經歷多年，今終面世，實在感到無比的欣慰。出版這本詞典的目的並非在漢英詞典汗牛充棟的市場中提供多一個選擇，而是創造一本題材新穎、內容永恒、詞匯貼身、譯法多樣、分類明確、物有所值的雙語參考書。

題材新穎

市場上的各類雙語詞典，據不完全的統計，總數應在三百多種以上。除了一般通用詞典外，專門詞典集中於金融財經及科技理工範疇。但與我們有密切關係的身體用語，卻未有雙語詞典出現。這本詞典就是希望補苴罅漏，在題材方面另闢溪徑，開創先河。

內容永恒

詞典編纂最大的考驗就是時間，雙語詞典尤其如是。編輯詞典需時，翻譯詞典需時，出版詞典需時，再版詞典需時。在在需時，結果詞典詞滙往往失去時效，與流行用語相去甚遠。電子詞典雖然相對靈活，但選詞標準及範疇各有不同，對於日新月異的領域亦難以處理。

身體用語則相對永恒，不會因時而異。人的眼耳口鼻、心肝肺臟的詞滙及用語基本上變化不大，歷久長青。因此這本詞典亦不需經常更新或再版。

詞匯貼身

這本詞典與同類詞典的最大分別是：選詞貼身。詞典中所有的條目都與我們息息相關，幫助用者用英語表達漢語身體用語的原義及轉義。學習語文的人都知道，由於文化、習俗、傳統等原因，要用地道語言表達身體的動作、狀況、疾病及情緒變化至為困難。這本詞典所收錄的常用語及醫學詞滙，相信對增進表達能力會有幫助。

譯法多樣

通用漢英詞典一般衹提供幾個對等詞。專門詞典則着重一對一的對應。這本詞典採取譯法多樣的概念，除了提供一個或幾個最常用的對等詞之外，亦以符號分隔並按字母次序列出同義詞，方便譯者就不同語境選擇不同的對應詞。由於翻譯著重上下文、語境及語域，所以對應詞不是以常用率排序，而是以字母排序，方便檢索。

分類明確

這本詞典將身體分為四十一個部份。這種分類並不是根據學術或醫學觀點而作出的，主要是以人體各主要部份、漢語詞滙的身體用語及編纂過程來決定。人體主要部份包括眼耳口鼻等，漢語詞滙包括肝和膽，編纂過程包括唇及皮膚。最後的分類數目，則經過不斷的分合與重組而確定。清晰精密的分類是條目歸類的基礎。

物有所值

通用詞典大概有三分之二的條目非日常用語，專門詞典亦涉及很多範疇，常用的條目相信衹有一半。身體用語詞典的常用率則非常高，雖然部份醫學詞滙使用率會低些，但具有很高認知作用，所以這本雙語身體用語詞典應該物有所值。

以上都是詞典的特色，也是我要編纂這本詞典的原因。

這本詞典得以面世，要多謝以下各位人士的幫忙：商務印書館董事總經理陸國燊博士、黃家麗及郭肇敏責任編輯、香港中文大學翻譯系講座教授黃國彬教授、同事李穎儀、劉翔宇、譚善圓及 Jenny Eagleton。亦要多謝慧莉、啟新、玉君、潤全的支持與鼓勵。

陳善偉

Introduction

This dictionary is the first Chinese-English dictionary of the human body ever published. According to a study on bilingual subject dictionaries for translators carried out by me a few years ago, 346 subjects were found to have bilingual or multilingual dictionaries that could help translators in their work. There are many dictionaries on "language," "medicine," "science," "technology," "idioms," "finance," and even "military science," yet there is not a single dictionary on the human body, whether monolingual (Chinese / English) or bilingual (Chinese-English / English-Chinese). It occurred to me that the compilation of a bilingual dictionary on the human body should be of great benefit to language learners and translators. It serves to add an important subject to specialized bilingual dictionaries.

This dictionary is also the most comprehensive Chinese-English dictionary of the human body ever produced. It has 28,600 entries with many translation equivalents. It contains both the medical terminology contained in specialist dictionaries and the figurative language about the body found in general purpose dictionaries. It is targeted at language learners, literary translators, and medical translators. For language learners, this dictionary shows very clearly the words and terms that they need to know to express what they do and how they feel. It is found that close to 7,500 of the 28,600 entries of body terms, or 27%, are related to the entire body (*shen ti* 身體), covering appearance, manners, personality, and abilities. Terms relating to the mouth (*kou* 口) come next, at 14% (or 4,000 entries), to be followed by those relating to the heart (*xin* 心) (3,300 entries, around 12%), the eye (2,000 entries, around 7%), and the hand (1,500 entries, around 5%). For literary translators, as this dictionary provides reliable translations of many cultural terms relating to different parts of the body, it serves as an indispensable reference where the cultural connotations of body terms in translation are concerned. For medical translators, this dictionary has a large number of terms relating to diseases of the entire body and its various parts. Medical terms relating to the human body of both the Chinese and Western traditions are included. Many people find it difficult to express their physical conditions when they see their doctors or to understand the terms that doctors use to describe their illnesses. All Chinese and Western medical terms are put under the parts they belong to, such as *dan guan gan yan* 膽管肝炎 (cholangiohepatitis) under *gan* 肝 (liver) and *shen kui* 腎虧 (asthenia of kidney) under *shen* 腎 (kidney).

What is of great significance is that this dictionary helps to demonstrate the idea of timelessness in dictionary-making. Most dictionaries on the market soon become outdated upon their publication. This is due mainly to the huge time gap between the preparation of the manuscript and the publication of the dictionary. By the time dictionaries are published, some of their entries have become the language of yesteryear, and they cannot be used to cope with the texts of today. For body terms, since all humans are physically alike, they never become outdated. Only minimal revisions are required to include body neologisms that crop up in various language communities.

In the arrangement of terms, this dictionary demonstrates how practical experience is more important than theoretical categorization. The classification of entries in this dictionary is mainly lexical and cultural rather than medical, physiological or academic. Terms in this dictionary have been divided into 41 parts, starting with *bei* 背 (back) and ending with *zi gong* 子宮 (womb). It must be mentioned that it was through a long period of trial and error before the present arrangement was made. The best classification method is one that leaves not a single term unaccounted for.

In providing English equivalents, this dictionary works on the principle of multiple contextual equivalence. It offers not just one or two equivalents for its entries, but a large number of English synonyms and near-synonyms of Chinese expressions that can be used as equivalents in translation. It should be noted that bilingual dictionaries and language dictionaries are different. Language dictionaries are not produced with the specific needs of the translator in mind. To explain a word in another language is not necessarily the same as providing a translation equivalent, least of all one which is usable in different contexts. What is also noteworthy is that most bilingual dictionaries give only a limited number of equivalents but not a comprehensive list of possible translations. To put down the first English equivalent that one comes across in a Chinese-English dictionary often leads to awkwardness in the target text if not mistranslation. In this dictionary, strenuous efforts have been made to provide as many equivalents as possible for the translator to choose from, so that an optimal equivalent can be used in context. A special effort has also been made to ensure that the equivalents given in the dictionary can be used in actual translation and not as explanations and descriptions for use as footnotes. It is for this reason that all equivalents have been listed in alphabetical order, unlike "definitions" in language dictionaries which are based on frequency of usage. It is also for the same reason that examples will not be included as they demonstrate only one or two contexts in which equivalents are used, whereas translation is about the selection of equivalents for a variety of contexts.

It is hoped that this dictionary will not only benefit language learners, literary translators and medical translators, but also anyone who is interested in learning or translating expressions relating to the human body.

Chan Sin-wai

Guide to the Use of the Dictionary

(a) All headwords are grouped under the 41 categories listed in the Table of Contents.

(b) All headwords under each category are arranged in the order of the Hanyu Pinyin romanization according to the four tones, which are indicated by numerals 1,2,3, and 4, such as *yue*4 悦 . Headwords with the same tones will be arranged according to the number of strokes in ascending order.

(c) Equivalents of a headword, which are used in different contexts, are alphabetically arranged and separated by slashes (/).

(d) For entries with many equivalents, the most common ones are placed at the beginning, separated from other equivalents by a double vertical line (‖).

(e) Words with meanings belonging to different parts of the body are cross-listed, such as *ai kei* 挨剋 appearing under *Kou* (Mouth) when it means "be scolded," and under *Shen ti* (Body) when it means "be beaten."

(f) Grammatical labels for entries and their translation equivalents are not given as most of them are verbs, nouns, adjectives, adverbs, phrases or sentences, all of which are separated by double slashes (//).

Bei 背 Back

ao1 bei bing 凹背病
swayback;

bei1 揹
(1) carry on the back;
(2) bear / shoulder;

bei bao fu 揹包袱
(1) carry a backpack on the back / carry a rucksack on one's back;
(2) have a load on one's mind / take on a mental burden;

bei hei guo 揹黑鍋
be made a scapegoat / bear the blame for others;

bei4 背
(1) back of the body;
(2) do sth behind sb's back / hide sth from;
(3) carry on the back;
(4) bear / shoulder;
ca bei 擦背
rub one's back / scrub one's back;
chui bei 搥背
massage the back by pounding with fists;
long bei 隆背
humpback / hunchback;
lu bei 露背
backless;
sao bei 搔背
scratch the back;

bei bu dong 背不動
unable to bear it on the back — too heavy;

bei bu 背部
back;

bei di li 背地裏
behind one's back / on the sly / privately / secretly;

bei dui bei 背對背
back to back;

bei fu 背負
(1) carry on the back;
(2) bear / have on one's shoulder / shoulder;

bei hou 背後
(1) at the back / behind / in the background;
(2) behind one's back;

bei hou gao gui 背後搗鬼
play underhand tricks;

bei ji 背脊
back;
niu shang bei ji 扭傷背脊
strain one's back;

bei kao bei 背靠背
back to back;

bei ruo mang ci 背若芒刺
feel uncomfortable / like having prickles on the back;

bei shang 背上
on the back / put on the back for carrying;

bei shi tou shang shan — yue bei yue zhong 背石頭上山——越背越重
going uphill carrying rocks on one's back — getting heavier and heavier;

bei tong 背痛
back pain / backache / dorsodynia;

bei zhe 背着
carry on the back;

bei zhe hai zi zhao hai zi — tou nao hun le 背着孩子找孩子——頭腦昏了
looking for a child while carrying the child on one's back — absent-minded / muddle-headed;

bei zhe mi tao fan — zhuang qiong 背着米討飯——裝窮
begging while carrying rice on one's back — pretending to be poor;

ca1 bei 擦背
rub one's back / scrub one's back / touch one's back;

chui2 bei 捶背
pound sb's back;

chui2 bei 搥背
massage the back by pounding with fists / pound one's back;

dian4 bei 墊背
play the scapegoat / suffer for the faults of others;

fu4 負
have at one's back;

gong3 jian suo bei 拱肩縮背
be all hunched up / shrink one's shoulder and bow one's back;

han4 liu jia bei 汗流浹背
be soaked with sweat ‖ all of a sweat; be running with sweat; perspire all over; pouring with sweat; stream with sweat; sweat like a pig; sweat like a trooper; wet through with perspiration; with perspiration running down his back; wringing wet;

hu3 bei xiong yao 虎背熊腰
of powerful build ‖ boxer's sinuous posture; of a stocky and imposing build; strong as a bear in the hips and with a back supple as a tiger's strapping; thick, powerful back and shoulders; tiger-backed and bear-loined — stalwart;

ji3 zhu 脊柱
back bone / spine;

ju1 痀
humpback / hunchback;

kai1 bei 揩背
scrub sb's back;

kong1 bei 空背
hollow-back;

liang3 shou cha bei 兩手叉背
with one's hands behind one's back;

long2 bei 隆背
humpback / hunchback;

lou2 僂
hunchbacked;

lou4 bei 露背
backless / sunback;

nian2 lao bei qu 年老背曲
be bent with age / one's shoulders bow with age;

niu3 shang bei ji 扭傷背脊
strain one's back;

qu1 bei er xing 曲背而行
stoop in walking;

sao1 bei 搔背
scratch the back;

tuo2 bei 駝背
crookback / humpback / hunchback / rachiokyphosis;

wan1 yao qu bei 彎腰曲背
crooked // with one's back bent;

yan3 偃
fall on one's back / lie on one's back;

yan pu 偃仆
fall down flat / fall on one's back;

yan wo 偃臥
lie on one's back / lie supine // supination;

yang3 wo 仰臥
lie on the back / lie supine // supination;

yu3 傴
hunchbacked // with one's back bent;

yu lou 傴僂
hunchbacked // with one's back bent;

zhuan3 bei 轉背
as soon as one turns one's back;

Bi 臂 Arm

ba3 bi 把臂
arm in arm / holding arms;

ban1 shou wan 扳手腕
arm wrestle / do arm wrestling // arm wrestling;

ban wan zi 扳腕子
arm wrestle / do arm wrestling // arm wrestling;

bang3 膀
arm / upper arm;

bang bi 膀臂
arms;

bang da yao yuan 膀大腰圓
beefy / hefty / hulky / husky / stout;

bang kuo yao yuan 膀闊腰圓
beefy / broad-shouldered and solidly built / hefty / husky / stout;

bang zi 膀子
upper arm;

bao4 抱
carry in one's arms / embrace / enfold / hold in one's arms / hug;

bao cheng yi tuan 抱成一團
hang together / stick together ‖ gang together; gang up; hold together to form a clique;

bao jin 抱緊
hold tightly in one's arms / hug;

bao zhe 抱着
embrace / hold in one's arms;

bao zhu 抱住
(1) hold in one's arms;
(2) hold on to;

bao zhu bu fang 抱住不放
hang on / stick to;

bao zi nong sun 抱子弄孫
carry one's grandson in arms and play with him / play with one's grandson while carrying him;

bi4 臂
(1) arm;
(2) upper arm;

ju bi 巨臂
macrobrachia;

bi bang 臂膀
arms;

bi bu 臂部
arm;

bi li 臂力
arm strength / strength of one's arm;

bi tong 臂痛
brachialgia / pain in the arm;

bi wan 臂彎
crook of the arm;

bi wan qu 臂彎曲
brachiocyllosis;

bi wan 臂腕
wrist;

bi zhi shi zhi 臂之使指
as easy as the arm using the fingers / easily controlled;

bi zhou 臂肘
elbow;

bi zhu 臂助
assist / give a helping hand / help;

cha1 shou er li 叉手而立
stand with folded arms;

chan1 攙
help by the arm / support with one's hand;

dao3 zai huai li 倒在懷裏
fall into sb's arms / lie back on sb's breast;

diao4 bi bu gu 掉臂不顧
walk out on sb;

fen4 bi 奮臂
lift up one's arms / raise one's arms;

fen bi gao hu 奮臂高呼
cheer with uplifted arms / raise one's arms and shout;

fen bi yi hu 奮臂一呼
raise one's arms and shout;

fen mei 奮袂
flap up one's sleeves for action / roll up one's sleeves for action / throw up one's sleeves for action;

fu2 xiu 拂袖
flick one's sleeve / give a flick of one's sleeve;

fu xiu er qu 拂袖而去
go off in a huff || flick the sleeve and go away — leave in displeasure; fling off; fling out of; go out abruptly; leave in a huff; storm out; storm out of the room; turn on one's heel; walk out on sb;

ge1 胳
arm;

ge bang 胳膀
upper arm;

ge bi 胳臂
arm;

ge bo 胳膊
arm;

ge bo wan zi 胳膊腕子
wrist;

ge bo zhou zi 胳膊肘子
elbow;

ge sao 胳臊
armpit odour;

ge1 胳
armpit;

ge bi 胳臂
arm;

ge bo 胳膊
arm;

ge bo cu 胳膊粗
have strong and muscular arms;

ge bo zhou er 胳膊肘儿
elbow;

ge zhi wo 胳肢窝
armpit;

gong1 肱
forearm;

gong gu 肱骨
bone of the upper arm;

guai3 zhou 拐肘
elbow;

hui1 wu shou bi 揮舞手臂
flap one's arms / saw the air / wave one's arms about;

jin3 bao 緊抱
hold tightly in one's arms / hug;

ju4 bi 巨臂
macrobrachia;

liang3 shou jiao bi 兩手交臂
have one's arms folded;

lou3 摟
embrace / hold in the arms / hug;

lou bao 摟抱
cuddle / embrace / hold in one's arms / hug;

lou lou bao bao 摟摟抱抱
hug and embrace;

lou zhe 摟着
embrace / press to one's chest;

lou zhu 摟住
embrace / enclasp / hold in the arms / hug;

luo1 ge bo 捋胳膊
roll up one's sleeves and show the arms;

nie4 bi 齧臂
bite one's arm / gnaw one's arm;

nu4 bi 怒臂
raise one's arms in anger;

qian2 bi 前臂
antibrachium / forearm;

qin1 qie yong bao 親切擁抱
have an affectionate embrace;

rang2 bi 攘臂
push up one's sleeves and bare one's arms / roll up one's sleeves and reveal one's arms;

rang bi chen mu 攘臂嗔目
push up one's sleeves, bare one's arms, and stare with wide open eyes / roll up one's sleeves and stare angrily || fly into a rage; see red;

rang bi er qi 攘臂而起
roll up one's sleeves and spring to one's feet || be excited and ready for action;

rang bi gao hu 攘臂高呼
raise one's hands and shout;

ru2 bi shi zhi 如臂使指
like the arms directing the fingers — in complete control of sth;

san3 tou liu bi 三頭六臂
resourceful and capable man || exceptionally capable; extraordinarily able person; three heads and six arms — superhuman;

shang4 bi 上臂
upper arm;

shang zhi gu 上肢骨
arm bone;

shou3 bi 手臂
arm;

shu1 yao shen bi 舒腰伸臂
lean back and stretch one's arms;

shuai1 shou 摔手
swing the arms;

tan3 bi yi hu 袒臂一呼
wave one's arm and shout;

wan3 bi er xing 挽臂而行
walk arm in arm;

wan shou 挽手
arm in arm / hand in hand / hold hands;

wo4 bi 握臂
grasp the arm of an old friend;

xia4 bo 下膊
lower arm / forearm;

xian1 bang zi 先膀子
bare-breasted // be stripped to the waist;

xiang1 bao er ku 相抱而哭
weep in each other's arms;

xiu4 shou pang guan 袖手旁觀
look on with folded arms / look on and do nothing || fold one's arms and look on; hold the ring; look on indifferently; praise the sea but stay on land; put one's hands in one's sleeves and look on; remain an indifferent spectator; sit around with folded arms; sit out; stand aside; stand by; stand by with folded arms; stand idle; stand idly by; watch indifferently without lending a hand; watch with folded arms;

xuan2 wan 懸腕
keep the arm off the desk;

ye4 腋
armpit;

ye chou 腋臭
foul-smelling sweat / osmidrosis;

ye mao 腋毛
armpit hair / underarm hair;

ye wo 腋窩
armpit;

ye xia 腋下
armpit // under the arms;

yi1 bao 一抱
an armful of;

yi bi zhi li 一臂之力
lend sb a hand || a hand's turn; a helping hand; a lift in life; assistance; help; offer a knee to sb;

yi bi zhi zhu 一臂之助
give sb a leg up / give sb a lift / lend a hand;

yong1 擁
(1) embrace / hold in one's arms / hug;
(2) crowd around / gather around;
(3) have / own / possess;

yong bao 擁抱
clasp / embrace / hold in one's arms / hug;

you4 bi 右臂
right arm;

yu4 bi 玉臂
girl's arms / pretty woman's arms;

zhen4 bi 振臂
raise one's arms;

zhen bi gao hu 振臂高呼
raise one's arm and shout;

zhen bi yi hu 振臂一呼
arouse to action || raise one's arm and cry for action — issue a call for action; sound the trumpet call of action;

zhou3 肘
(1) elbow;
(2) catch one by the elbow;

zhou fan she 肘反射
elbow reflex;

zhou guan jie 肘關節
elbow joint;

zhou ye 肘腋
close by / near at hand;

zhou ye zhi huan 肘腋之患
disturbances coming from those closest / trouble from one's nearest and dearest;

zhou zi 肘子
elbow;

zhu4 yi bi zhi li 助一臂之力
give a hand / give a helping hand / lend a hand / lend a helping hand;

zuo bi 左臂
left arm;

Bi 鼻 Nose

ai2 bi tou 挨鼻頭
suffer a criticism;

an1 bei bi 鞍背鼻
saddleback nose;

an bi 鞍鼻
saddle nose;

bai2 bi zi 白鼻子
crafty person;

bi2 鼻
nose;
an bei bi 鞍背鼻
saddleback nose;
an bi 鞍鼻
saddle nose;
bian ta bi 扁蹋鼻
snub nose;
chao tian bi 朝天鼻
short nose / upturn nose;
jiu zao bi 酒糟鼻
bottlenose || a nose to light candles at;
jiu zha bi 酒渣鼻
rosacea;
ju bi 巨鼻
macrorhinia;
shi zi bi 獅子鼻
pug nose / snub nose;
suan tou bi 蒜頭鼻
bullbous nose / pug nose / snub nose;
ta bi 塌鼻
flat nose / snub nose;
xiao bi 小鼻
congenitally small nose / microrhinia;
ying gou bi 鷹鈎鼻
acquiline nose / beak nose / hooknose / Roman nose;

bi ai 鼻癌
nasal carcinoma / nasopharyngeal carcinoma / rhinocarcinoma;

bi bai hou 鼻白喉
nasal diphtheria;

bi bei 鼻背
dorsum nasi;

bi bing 鼻病
rhinopathia / rhinopathy;

bi bu jie he 鼻部結核
tuberculosis of nose;

bi chu xue 鼻出血
epistaxie / nasal phemorrhage / nosebleed / rhinorrhagia;

bi chun gou 鼻唇溝
nasolabial fold;

bi dao 鼻道
nasal duct || meatus of nose;
shang bi dao 上鼻道
upper nasal duct;
xia bi dao 下鼻道
lower nasal duct;
zhong bi dao 中鼻道
middle nasal duct;

bi dou 鼻竇
paranasal sinus;

bi dou yan 鼻竇炎
nasosinusitis / nasal sinusitis / sinusitis;
hang kong xing bi dou yan 航空性鼻竇炎
aerosinusitis;
hua nong bi dou yan 化膿鼻竇炎
suppurative sinusitis;
qi ya xing bi dou yan 氣壓性鼻竇炎
barosinusitis;
quan bi dou yan 全鼻竇炎
pansinuitis;

bi du se 鼻堵塞
nasal obstruction / obstruction of nose;

bi duan 鼻端
tip of the nose;

bi fan she 鼻反射
nasal reflex;

bi feng 鼻峰
bridge of the nose;

bi gan 鼻乾
dry nose;

bi gen 鼻根
root of nose;

bi gu 鼻骨
nasal bone;

bi gu kong 鼻骨孔
nasal foramina;

bi hou yan 鼻喉炎
rhinolaryngitis;

bi hou kong 鼻後孔
choana;

bi jia 鼻甲
nasal concha / turbinal;
quan bi jia 全鼻甲
panturbinate;
shang bi jia 上鼻甲
superior nasal concha;

bi jia yan 鼻甲炎
conchitis;

bi jian 鼻尖
apex nasi / tip of the nose;

bi jie 鼻癤
furuncle of nose;

bi jing 鼻鏡
rhinoscope;

bi ju 鼻疽
glander;
ri ben bi ju 日本鼻疽
Japanese glander;

bi ke ji bing 鼻科疾病
nose diseases;

bi ke xue jia 鼻科學家
rhinologist;

bi kong 鼻孔
nostrils || nares;
qian bi kong 前鼻孔
prenares;
wa bi kong 挖鼻孔
pick one's nose;

bi kong bi se 鼻孔閉塞
have a stuffy nose // stuffed-up nose;

bi liang 鼻樑
bridge of the nose / nose bridge;
gao bi liang 高鼻樑
high nose;
ta bi liang 塌鼻樑
flat nose;

bi mao 鼻毛
nasal hair / nose hair / vibrissae;

bi nian mo 鼻黏膜
nasal mucous membrane;

bi niu er 鼻牛兒
nose dirt / nose wax;

bi nü 鼻衄
rhinorrhagia / nosebleed;

bi pang dou 鼻旁竇
paranasal sinus;

bi qi guan yan 鼻氣管炎
bovine rhinotracheitis;
chuan ran xing bi qi guan yan 傳染性鼻氣管炎
infectious bovine rhinotracheitis / infectious rhinotracheitis;

bi qiang 鼻腔
nasal cavity;

bi qing lian zhong 鼻青臉腫
a bloody nose and a swollen face ‖ badly battered; get a bloody nose;

bi ruan gu 鼻軟骨
cartilage of nose;

bi sai 鼻塞
nasal congestion / snuffle;
ying er bi sai 嬰兒鼻塞
snuffle;

bi sai bu tong 鼻塞不通
nasal congestion;

bi sai qian tong 鼻塞欠通
nasal congestion;

bi sai wu qie 鼻塞無歇
nasal congestion;

bi shi 鼻石
rhinolith;

bi shi 鼻屎
nasal secretion;

bi suan 鼻酸
have a twinge in one's nose;

bi ta zui wai 鼻塌嘴歪
with a snub nose and a wry mouth;

bi ti 鼻涕
nasal mucus / snivel;
liu bi ti 流鼻涕
have a runny nose / run at the nose;
xing bi ti 擤鼻涕
blow the nose;

bi tong 鼻痛
rhinalgia;

bi tou 鼻頭
nose;
da bi tou 大鼻頭
big nose;

bi tu 鼻突
nasal process;
wai ce bi tu 外側鼻突
lateral nasal process;

bi wo 鼻窩
nasal pit;

bi xi 鼻息
breath;

bi xi rou 鼻息肉
nasal polyp;

bi xi ru lei 鼻息如雷
snore like thunder / snore terribly;

bi xue 鼻血
nasal hemorrhage / nosebleed;

bi yan 鼻咽
nasopharynx;

bi yan ai 鼻咽癌
cancer of nasopharynx / nasopharyngeal carcinoma;

bi yan yan 鼻咽炎
nasopharyngitis;

bi yan 鼻炎
inflammation of the nose / rhinitis;
bian ying xing bi yan 變應性鼻炎
allergic rhinitis;
chuan ran xing bi yan 傳染性鼻炎
infectious rhinitis;
fei hou xing bi yan 肥厚性鼻炎
hypertrophic rhinitis;

guo min xing bi yan 過敏性鼻炎
allergic rhinitis;
huai ju xing bi yan 壞疽性鼻炎
gangrenous rhinitis;
huai si xing bi yan 壞死性鼻炎
necrotic rhinitis;
ji xing bi yan 急性鼻炎
acute rhinitis;
jie he xing bi yan 結核性鼻炎
tuberculous rhinitis;
man xing bi yan 慢性鼻炎
chronic rhinitis;
mei du xing bi yan 梅毒性鼻炎
syphilitic rhinitis;
mo xing bi yan 膜性鼻炎
membranous rhinitis;
te ying xing bi yan 特應性鼻炎
atopic rhinitis;
wei suo xing bi yan 萎縮性鼻炎
atrophic rhinitis;

bi yan rou 鼻炎肉
nasal polyp;

bi yang 鼻癢
itching in the nose / nose itch;

bi yi 鼻翼
wings of nose;

bi yin 鼻音
nasal / nasal sound / rhinolalia / through the nose;
hou bi yin 後鼻音
back nasal;
kai fang xing bi yin 開放性鼻音
open rhinolalia;
qian bi yin 前鼻音
front nasal;

bi yin guo shao 鼻音過少
denasality;

bi yin guo zhong 鼻音過重
hypernasality;

bi yuan 鼻淵
deep source nasal congestion;

bi yuan tou tong 鼻淵頭痛
headache of nasosinusitis / sinus headache;

bi zao 鼻燥
dry nose;

bi zhong ge 鼻中隔
nasal septum / septum of the nose;
mo xing bi zhong ge 膜性鼻中隔
membranous nasal septum;
ruan gu xing bi zhong ge 軟骨性鼻中隔
cartilaginous nasal septum;

bi zhong ge wan qu 鼻中隔彎曲
deviated septum / deviation of nasal septum;

bi zhu 鼻柱
columna nasi;

bi zhun 鼻準
tip of the nose;

bi zi 鼻子
nose;
ca bi zi 擦鼻子
wipe one's nose;
ca po bi zi 擦破鼻子
bark one's nose;
da bi zi 大鼻子
big nose ‖ bottle nose / high-bridged nose;
gua bi zi 刮鼻子
(1) rub sb's nose in it / rub sb's nose in the dirt;
(2) reprimand;
ji zhong bi zi 擊中鼻子
catch sb on the nose;
qiang bi zi 嗆鼻子
choke one's nose;
rou bi zi 肉鼻子
dumpy nose / fleshy nose / meaty nose;
ta bi zi 蹋鼻子
button nose / flat nose;
zao bi zi 糟鼻子
drunkard's nose;

bi zi bu ling 鼻子不靈
have a bad nose;

bi zi bu shi bi zi, lian bu shi lian 鼻子不是鼻子，臉不是臉
angry looks / unpleasant look;

bi zi bu tong 鼻子不通
clogged-up nose / stuffed-up nose;

鼻 *Nose*

bi zi bu tong qi 鼻子不通氣
nasal congestion;

bi zi ling 鼻子靈
have a good nose;

bi zi yan er 鼻子眼兒
nostrils;

bi zi yi suan 鼻子一酸
a lump comes into one's throat // get a lump in one's throat;

bi4 qi 閉氣
(1) feel suffocated / unable to breathe;
(2) stop breathing;

bian3 ta bi 扁蹋鼻
snub nose;

bian4 ying xing bi yan 變應性鼻炎
allergic rhinitis;

ca1 bi zi 擦鼻子
wipe one's nose;

ca po bi zi 擦破鼻子
bark one's nose;

chao2 tian bi 朝天鼻
short nose / upturn nose;

chi1 zhi yi bi 嗤之以鼻
show one's contempt with a snort || bite one's thumb at; contemptuous of; cook a snook at; despise; draw a snicker from; give a snort of contempt; make a long nose at sb; make a wry mouth at sb in scorn; pooh-pooh; scorn; sneeze at; sniff at; sniffy; thumb one's nose at sb; treat with contempt; turn up one's nose at; utter a sneer through the nose to show contempt;

chou1 bi zi 抽鼻子
sniffle / snivel / snuffle / take a deep breath by the nose;

chou4 bi zheng 臭鼻症
ozena;

chuan2 ran xing bi qi guan yan 傳染性鼻氣管炎
infectious bovine rhinotracheitis / infectious rhinotracheitis;

chuan ran xing bi yan 傳染性鼻炎
infectious rhinitis;

chuang1 shang xing dou dao 創傷性竇道
traumatic sinus;

ci4 bi 刺鼻
irritate the nose;

da3 e 打呃
hiccough / hiccup;

da ge er 打嗝儿
burp / hiccup;

da han 打鼾
snore;

da hu lu 打呼嚕
snore;

da pen ti 打噴嚏
sneeze;

da4 bi tou 大鼻頭
big nose;

da bi zi 大鼻子
big nose || bottle nose; high-bridged nose;

di1 bi yin 低鼻音
hyponasality;

dou4 dao 竇道
sinus;

chuang shang xing dou dao 創傷性竇道
traumatic sinus;

e2 bi ban 額鼻板
frontonasal plate;

e bi fa yu bu liang 額鼻發育不良
frontonasal dysplasla;

e bi guan 額鼻管
frontonasal duct;

e bi long qi 額鼻隆起
frontonasal prominence;

e bi tu 額鼻突
frontonasal process;

fei2 da xing jiu zha bi 肥大性酒渣鼻
rhinophyma;

fei hou xing bi yan 肥厚性鼻炎
hypertrophic rhinitis;

gao1 bi liang 高鼻樑
high nose;

ge1 bi wa yan 割鼻挖眼
cut off the nose and gouge out the eyes;

ge2 嗝
hiccough / hiccup;

gu3 bi zhong ge 骨鼻中隔
bony septum of nose;

gu xing bi zhong ge 骨性鼻中隔
bony nasal septum;

gua1 bi zi 刮鼻子
(1) rub sb's nose in it / rub sb's nose in the dirt;
(2) reprimand;

guo4 min xing bi yan 過敏性鼻炎
allergic rhinitis;

han1 鼾
snore;

han hou ru lei 鼾齁如雷
snore like thunder / snore thunderously // thunderous snoring;

han kong 鼾孔
snore-hole;

han sheng 鼾聲
snore / sound of snoring;

han sheng da zuo 鼾聲大作
snore terribly ‖ drive one's pigs to market; stertorous breathing;

han sheng hu xi 鼾聲呼吸
stertorous breathing;

han sheng ru lei 鼾聲如雷
snore like thunder ‖ one's snores drone like the distant roll of thunder; snore thunderously; thunderous snores;

han sheng ru zhu 鼾聲如豬
snore like a pig;

han shui 鼾睡
snoring sleep ‖ heavy sleep;

han yin 鼾音
snorous rale;

hang2 kong xing bi dou yan 航空性鼻竇炎
aerosinusitis;

heng2 tiao bi zi shu tiao yan 橫挑鼻子豎挑眼
find faults in every possible way ‖ find faults in a petty manner; look for flaws; nit-pick; pick faults right and left; pick faults with sb in various ways; pick holes in;

hou1 齁
snoring / snorting;

hou hou shu shui 齁齁熟睡
lie gently breathing in a sound sleep;

hou sheng 齁聲
snore / sound of snoring;

hou4 bi chu xue 後鼻出血
posterior epistaxis;

hou bi kong 後鼻孔
postnaris;

hou bi kong xi rou 後鼻孔息肉
choanal polyp;

hou bi yin 後鼻音
back nasal;

hu1 xi 呼吸
breathe / inhale and exhale / respire // breath / respiration;

nei hu xi 內呼吸
internal respiration;

qiang li hu xi 強力呼吸
forced respiration;

ren gong hu xi 人工呼吸
artificial respiration;

shen hu xi 深呼吸
deep breathing;

xu yang hu xi 需氧呼吸
aerobic respiration;

zhou qi xing hu xi 周期性呼吸
periodic respiration;

hu xi bu zu 呼吸不足
hypopnea;

hu xi chi huan 呼吸遲緩
abnormally infrequent respiration / oligopnea;

hu xi guo du 呼吸過度
abnormally fast breathing / hyperpnea;

hu xi guo huan 呼吸過緩
abnormally slow breathing / bradypnea;

hu xi guo man 呼吸過慢
abnormally slow breathing / bradypnea;

鼻 *Nose*

hu xi huan man 呼吸緩慢
abnormally slow breathing / bradypnea;

hu xi ji chu 呼吸急促
panting / polypnea / rapid breathing;

hu xi jian rou 呼吸減弱
abnormally shallow and slow breathing / hypopnea;

hu xi kun nan 呼吸困難
dyspnea // breathe with difficulty;
shen xing hu xi kun nan 腎形呼吸困難
renal dyspnea;
xin xing hu xi kun nan 心形呼吸困難
cardiac dyspnea;
xin zang xing hu xi kun nan 心臟性呼吸困難
cardiac dyspnea;
ye fa xing hu xi kun nan 夜發性呼吸困難
nocturnal dyspnea;
zhi li xing hu xi kun nan 直立性呼吸困難
orthostatic dyspnea;

hu xi xiang tong 呼吸相通
be intimately bound up with;

hua4 nong bi dou yan 化膿鼻竇炎
suppurative sinusitis;

huai4 ju xing bi yan 壞疽性鼻炎
gangrenous rhinitis;

huai si xing bi yan 壞死性鼻炎
necrotic rhinitis;

huan4 xiu 幻嗅
olfactory hallucination / phantosmia;

huo1 bi zi 豁鼻子
reveal sb's secret;

ji2 xing bi yan 急性鼻炎
acute rhinitis;

ji2 zhong bi zi 擊中鼻子
catch sb on the nose;

jia3 xiu jue 假嗅覺
pseudosmia / subjective sensation of an odour that is not present;

jie2 he xing bi yan 結核性鼻炎
tuberculous rhinitis;

jing4 luan xing pen ti 痙攣性噴嚏
ptarmus / spasmodic sneezing;

jiu3 zha bi 酒渣鼻
acne / rosacea;
fei da xing jiu zha bi 肥大性酒渣鼻
rhinophyma;
lang chuang zhuang jiu zha bi 狼瘡狀酒渣鼻
lupoid rosacea;
qiu zhen xing jiu zha bi 丘疹性酒渣鼻
papular rosacea;
rou ya zhong xing jiu zha bi 肉芽腫性酒渣鼻
granlomatous rosacea;

jiu zao bi 酒糟鼻
bottlenose || a nose to light candles at;

ju4 bi 巨鼻
macrorhinia;

kai1 fang xing bi yin 開放性鼻音
open rhinolalia;

lang2 chuang zhuang jiu zha bi 狼瘡狀酒渣鼻
lupoid rosacea;

lie4 bi 裂鼻
cleft nose;

ling4 ren suan bi 令人酸鼻
cause sb's heart to ache / cause a lump to come into one's throat / cause to get a lump in one's throat / make sb want to cry out of pity;

liu2 bi shui 流鼻水
drivel / snivel / snot;

liu bi ti 流鼻涕
drivel / have a running nose / run at the nose / snivel;

man4 xing bi yan 慢性鼻炎
chronic rhinitis;

mei2 ba bi 沒把鼻
groundless / without a basis;

mei2 du xing bi yan 梅毒性鼻炎
syphilitic rhinitis;

mo2 xing bi yan 膜性鼻炎
membranous rhinitis;

mo xing bi zhong ge 膜性鼻中隔
membranous nasal septum;

mo3 yi bi zi hui 抹一鼻子灰
suffer a snub || get rebuffed when trying to please; meet with a rebuff;

nan2 wen 難聞
malodorous / stinking;

nei4 hu xi 內呼吸
internal respiration;

nie1 bi zi 捏鼻子
(1) hold one's nose;
(2) suffer patiently and silently;

nü 衄
(1) nose bleeding;
(2) be given a bloody nose;

nü bi 衄鼻
bleed at the nose;

nü xue 衄血
epistaxis / nose bleeding;

pen1 ti 噴嚏
sneezing;
da pen ti 打噴嚏
sneeze;
jing luan xing pen ti 痙攣性噴嚏
ptarmus / spasmodic sneezing;

peng4 yi bi zi hui 碰一鼻子灰
suffer a snub || be sent off with a flea in one's ear; be snubbed; cold shoulder; get rebuffed; knock one's nose into ashes; meet with a rebuff; singe one's feathers;

pu1 bi 撲鼻
assail the nostrils / come suddenly into one's nostrils;

qi4 ya xing bi dou yan 氣壓性鼻竇炎
barosinusitis;

qian1 zhe bi zi zou 牽着鼻子走
lead sb by the nose || be led by the nose; have sb on the string; get sb on the string; keep sb on the string;

qian2 bi chu xue 前鼻出血
anterior epistaxis;

qian bi kong 前鼻孔
prenares;

qian bi yin 前鼻音
front nasal;

qiang2 li hu xi 強力呼吸
forced respiration;

qiang4 嗆
choking;

qiang bi zi 嗆鼻子
choke one's nose;

qiao4 qi bi zi 翹起鼻子
cock one's nose;

qing1 bi bing 青鼻病
bluenose disease;

qing1 xiang pu bi 清香撲鼻
be met by a waft of fragrance || a perfume particularly pleasant to the sense of smell; a sweet scent assails the nostrils; a waft of fragrance salutes the nostrils;

qiu1 zhen xing jiu zha bi 丘疹性酒渣鼻
papular rosacea;

quan2 bi dou yan 全鼻竇炎
pansinuitis;

quan bi jia 全鼻甲
panturbinate;

ren2 gong hu xi 人工呼吸
artificial respiration;

ren zhong 人中
philtrum / the raphe of one's lip;

ri4 ben bi ju 日本鼻疽
Japanese glander;

rou4 bi zi 肉鼻子
dumpy nose / fleshy nose / meaty nose;

rou ya zhong xing jiu zha bi 肉芽腫性酒渣鼻
granlomatous rosacea;

ruan3 gu xing bi zhong ge 軟骨性鼻中隔
cartilaginous nasal septum;

shang4 bi dao 上鼻道
upper nasal duct;

shang bi jia 上鼻甲
superior nasal concha;

shang hu xi dao 上呼吸道
the upper respiratory tract;

shang hu xi dao gan ran 上呼吸道感染
infection of the upper respiratory tract;

shen1 hu xi 深呼吸
deep breathing;

shen4 xing hu xi kun nan 腎形呼吸困難
renal dyspnea;

shi1 zi bi 獅子鼻
pug nose / snub nose;

shi2 ren ti tuo 拾人涕唾
pick up what others have said / pick up what others have written / repeat what others have said;

suan1 bi 酸鼻
feel like crying / grieved;

suan4 tou bi 蒜頭鼻
bullbous nose / pug nose / snub nose;

ta1 bi 塌鼻
button nose / flat nose / snub nose;

ta bi liang 塌鼻樑
flat nose;

ta bi zi 蹋鼻子
button nose / flat nose / snub nose;

te4 ying xing bi yan 特應性鼻炎
atopic rhinitis;

ti4 涕
mucus of the nose / snivel / snot;

ti4 嚏
sneeze;

ti pen 嚏噴
sneeze;

tong2 yi bi kong chu qi 同一鼻孔出氣
(1) breathe through the same nostrils;
(2) hold same opinions || conspire with sb; in tune with; talk exactly one like the other;

wa1 bi kong 挖鼻孔
pick one's nose;

wai4 bi 外鼻
external nose;

wai ce bi tu 外側鼻突
lateral nasal process;

wang1 ran chu ti 汪然出涕
weep profusely;

wei3 suo xing bi yan 萎縮性鼻炎
atrophic rhinitis;

wen2 聞
smell;

wen bu de 聞不得
too strong to be smelled;

wen bu jian 聞不見
cannot sense the smell;

weng4 bi 齆鼻
blocked-up nose;

wu2 ba bi 無巴鼻
have nothing to hold on / unreal;

wu bi 無鼻
arrhinia / congenital absence of the nose;

xi3 bi qi 洗鼻器
nose syringe;

xia4 bi dao 下鼻道
lower nasal duct;

xiao3 bi 小鼻
congenitally small nose / microrhinia;

xin1 xing hu xi kun nan 心形呼吸困難
cardiac dyspnea;

xin zang xing hu xi kun nan 心臟性呼吸困難
cardiac dyspnea;

xing3 擤
blow one's nose;

xing bi ti 擤鼻涕
blow one's nose / sniff one's nose;

xing bi zi 擤鼻子
blow one's nose / sniff one's nose;

xiu4 嗅
smell / sniff;

xiu jue 嗅覺
smell;

jia xiu jue 假嗅覺
pseudosmia / subjective sensation of an odour that is not present;

xiu jue bu quan 嗅覺不全
merosmia / partial loss of smell;

xiu jue dao cuo 嗅覺倒錯
paraosmia;

xiu jue guo min 嗅覺過敏
hyperosphresia / supersensitivity of smells;

鼻 *Nose*

xiu jue jian tui 嗅覺減退
hyposmia / impairment of the sense of smell;

xiu jue que fa 嗅覺缺乏
absence of the sense of smell / anosmia / loss of the sense of smell;

xiu jue que shi zheng 嗅覺缺失症
anosmia;

xiu jue sang shi 嗅覺喪失
anosmia;

xiu jue yi chang 嗅覺異常
allotriosmia;

xiu jue zhang ai 嗅覺障礙
dysosmia;

xiu jue zheng chang 嗅覺正常
euosmia;

xiu mi lu 嗅迷路
olfactory labyrinth;

xiu4 齅
smell;

xu1 yang hu xi 需氧呼吸
aerobic respiration;

yan3 bi er chang 掩鼻而嚐
hold one's breath while eating;

yan bi er guo 掩鼻而過
cover the nose and hurry away / cover the nose and pass by / hold one's nose and pass by / pass by holding one's nose;

yang3 ren bi xi 仰人鼻息
at sb's beck and call / live at sb's mercy ‖ curry to sb's every whim; depend on another's whims and pleasures; depend on others; dependent on the pleasure of others; dependent on the whims of others; rely on others and have to watch their every expression; slavishly dependent on others; under sb's thumb;

ye4 fa xing hu xi kun nan 夜發性呼吸困難
difficulty of breathing at night / nocturnal dyspnea;

yi1 bi kong chu qi 一鼻孔出氣
hold the same opinions ‖ breathe in the same way; conspire with sb; echo one another's opinion; hold identical opinions; in conformity with; in league with sb; in tune with; say exactly the same thing; side with; sing the same tune; talk exactly one like the other; toe the line of;

yi bi zhi cha 一鼻之差
by a nose / by a short margin;

yi bi zi hui 一鼻子灰
be rebuffed / meet frustration / meet humiliation / meet rejection / run into a stone wall;

yi2 洟
nasal mucus / snivel / snot;

yi ti 洟涕
nasal mucus / snivel / snot;

yi4 劓
cut off the nose;

ying1 er bi sai 嬰兒鼻塞
snuffle;

ying1 ge bi 鸚哥鼻
hooked nose;

ying1 gou bi 鷹鈎鼻
acquiline nose / beak nose / hooknose / Roman nose;

yong1 bi 擁鼻
hold one's nose;

you3 bi zi you yan er 有鼻子有眼兒
convincing / plausible;

yu4 yu 鬱鬱
strong fragrance;

zao1 bi zi 糟鼻子
drunkard's nose;

zao bi zi bu chi jiu, wang dan xu ming 糟鼻子不吃酒，枉擔虛名
have a bad reputation one doesn't deserve like a teetotaller with a red nose;

zhi2 li xing hu xi kun nan 直立性呼吸困難
orthostatic dyspnea;

zhong1 bi dao 中鼻道
middle nasal duct;

zhong bi jia 中鼻甲
middle nasal concha;

zhong bi jia gu 中鼻甲骨
middle turbinate bone;

zhou1 qi xing hu xi 周期性呼吸
periodic respiration;

zhou4 bi zi 皺鼻子
wrinkle one's nose;

Chang 腸 Bowel

a1 mi ba li ji 阿米巴痢疾
amoebic dysentery;

ai2 xing chang geng zu 癌性腸梗阻
carcinomatous ileus;

ba3 niao 把尿
help a small child pass water by holding his legs apart;

bao4 fa xing li ji 爆發性痢疾
fulminant dysentery;

bian4 便
stool;

pai bian 排便
defecation;

bian mi 便秘
constipation || astriction;

jing luan xing bian mi 痙攣性便秘
spastic constipation;

xi guan xing bian mi 習慣性便秘
habitual constipation;

zhi chang xing bian mi 直腸性便秘
proctogenous constipation;

bian mi jiao tong 便秘絞痛
stercoral colic;

bian ni 便溺
empty the bowels and urinate / relieve the bowls / urinate and defecate;

bian xue 便血
hematochezia || have blood in one's stool; occult blood in the faeces;

bing4 du xing li ji 病毒性痢疾
viral dysentery;

chang2 jie chang 長結腸
an abnormally long colon / dolichocolon;

chang2 腸
bowels / gut / intestines;

chang ai 腸癌
bowel cancer / cancer of the intestines / intestinal cancer;

chang bi se 腸閉塞
enterocleisis;

chang bing 腸病
bowel disease / enteropathy;
que xue xing chang bing 缺血性腸病
ischemic bowel disease;
yan xing chang bing 炎性腸病
inflammatory bowel disease;

chang bing fa sheng 腸病發生
enteropathogenesis;

chang bing xing guan jie yan 腸病性關節炎
enteropathic arthritis;

chang chong xing lan wei yan 腸蟲性闌尾炎
helminthic appendictis / verminous appendictis;

chang chu xue 腸出血
enterorrhagia;

chang chuan ci 腸穿刺
enterocentesis;

chang chuan kong 腸穿孔
enterobrosis / intestinal perforation;

chang dao 腸道
gut / intestinal tract;

chang dong 腸動
enterokinesia;

chang dong mai 腸動脈
arteriae intestinales;

chang du 腸肚
intestines and the belly;

chang duan 腸斷
heartbroken / deeply grieved;

chang fei nao man 腸肥腦滿
with a fair round belly and swelled head;

chang fu mo 腸腹膜
intestinal peritoneum;

chang fu mo yan 腸腹膜炎
exenteritis;

chang geng zu 腸梗阻
ileus / intestinal obstruction;
ai xing chang geng zu 癌性腸梗阻
carcinomatous ileus;
ji xing chang geng zu 急性腸梗阻
acute ileus;
jing luan xing chang geng zu 痙攣性腸梗阻
spastic ileus;
ma bi xing chang geng zu 麻痺性腸梗阻
paralyhtic ileus;
zu se xing chang geng zu 阻塞性腸梗阻
occlusive ileus;

chang jiao tong 腸絞痛
intestinal angina / tormina;
ying er chang jiao tong 嬰兒腸絞痛
infantile colic;

chang jie 腸節
enteromere;

chang jie shan 腸節疝
enteromerocele;

chang jie chang yan 腸結腸炎
entercolitis;

chang jie he 腸結核
tuberculosis of intestine;

chang jing luan 腸痙攣
enterospasm;

chang kui yang 腸潰瘍
enterelcosis;

chang kuo zhang 腸擴張
enterectasis;

chang liu 腸瘤
enteroncus;

chang niu jie 腸扭結
volvulus;

chang re bing 腸熱病
enteric fever;

chang shan 腸疝
enterocele;
pang guang chang shan 膀胱腸疝
cystoenterocele;

chang shen jing yan 腸神經炎
enteroneuritis;

chang shi 腸石
intestinal calculus;

chang shi bing 腸石病
enterolithiasis;

chang tao die 腸套疊
intussusception;

chang tong 腸痛
enterodynia;

chang wei 腸胃
intestines and the stomach;

chang wei bing 腸胃病
digestive ailment;

chang wei yan 腸胃炎
enterogastritis;

chang yan 腸炎
enteritis;

huai si xing chang yan 壞死性腸炎
enteritis necroticans;

jie duan xing chang yan 節段性腸炎
segmental enteritis;

jie he xing chang yan 結核性腸炎
tuberculous enteritis;

jie jie xing chang yan 結節性腸炎
enteritis nodularis;

ju bu xing chang yan 局部性腸炎
regional enteritis;

lian qiu jun xing chang yan 鏈球菌性腸炎
streptococcus enteritis;

rou ya zhong xing chang yan 肉芽腫性腸炎
granulomatous enteritis;

xi rou xing chang yan 息肉性腸炎
enteritis polyposa;

yuan chong xing chang yan 原蟲性腸炎
protozoan enteritis;

chang zhou yan 腸周炎
perienteritis;

chang zi 腸子
gut / intestines;

chang zu se 腸阻塞
intestinal obstruction;

chou2 chang 愁腸
pent-up sadness;

chou chang bai jie 愁腸百結
with anxiety gnawing at one's heart ‖ be overwhelmed with sorrow and longing; be weighed down with anxiety; brokenhearted; suffer great agonies of the mind;

chou chang cun duan 愁腸寸斷
eat one's heart out // one's anxious heart is broken // heartbroken;

chu1 xue xing jie chang yan 出血性結腸炎
hemorrhagic colitis;

chu xue xing xiao chang jie chang yan 出血性小腸結腸炎
hemorrhagic enterocolitis;

chuan1 kong xing lan wei yan 穿孔性闌尾炎
perforating appendicitis;

chuan2 ran xing jie chang yan 傳染性結腸炎
infectious colitis;

chuang1 shang xing lan wei yan 創傷性闌尾炎
traumatic appendicitis;

cun4 chang 寸腸
innermost feelings;

da4 bian 大便
(1) stool ‖ defecate; discharge; dump; egest; eject; empty; empty one's bowels; evacuate the bowels; expel; go boom-boom; go number one; go potty; go to the bank; have a bowel movement; loose one's bowels; make little soldiers; move the bowels; post a letter; relax the bowels; relieve oneself; relieve one's bowels; shit; sit on the throne; take a shit; the bowel moves; void excrement;
(2) motion ‖ bowel movement; faeces; human excrement; shit; stool;

yan da bian 驗大便
stool test;

yao da bian 要大便
the bowels are open / the bowels move;

da bian bu tong 大便不通
constipated;

da bian bu zheng chang 大便不正常
irregular bowel movements;

da bian kun nan 大便困難
(1) have difficulty in passing one's motions;
(2) dyschesia / dyschezia;

da bian shi jin 大便失禁
fecal incontinence / incontinence of faeces / unable to hold one's motions;

da bian xiao bian yi qi lai — shuang guan qi xia 大便小便一起來——雙管齊下
defecating and urinating at the same time — working along both lines at the same time;

腸 *Bowel*

da chang 大腸
large bowels / large intestines;

da chang re jie 大腸熱結
heat-evil accumulating in the large intestine;

da chang yan 大腸炎
inflammation of the large intestine;

duan4 chang 斷腸
break the heart // extremely sad / heartbroken;

duo1 niao zheng 多尿症
excessive urine output / polyuria;

e1 niao 阿尿
urinate;

e shi 阿屎
defecate / move the bowels;

e1 屙
discharge excrement / discharge urine;

e du 屙肚
diarrhoea;

e shi 屙屎
defecate / move the bowels;

e4 xing li ji 惡性痢疾
malignant dysentery;

er4 bian bu li 二便不利
difficulty in urination and defecation;

fang4 pi 放屁
(1) break wind / fart || backfire; beef-hearts; break wind backwards; break wind downwards; breezer; cut one's finger; drop a rose; have gas; lay fart; let one fly; make a noise; pass air; pass flatus; pass wind; raspberry tart; rip off a fart; set a fart; shoot rabbits; sneeze; there's a smell of touch bone and whistle;
(2) nonsense / what a crap;

fen4 糞
(1) droppings / dung / excrement / faeces;
(2) apply manure;

fen bian 糞便
dung / excrement || excrement and urine; faeces; feces; fecia; night-soil; ordure pellet; stool;

fen men 糞門
anus;

fen niao 糞尿
fecaluria;

fen niao zheng 糞尿症
enteruria;

gan1 chang cun duan 肝腸寸斷
be deeply grieved || be overwhelmed by grief; deep affliction; emotionally upset; sorrow-stricken; the liver and intestines seem broken into inches — heartbroken;

gang1 肛
anus;

tuo gang 脱肛
anal prolapse / prolapse of anus;

gang guan 肛管
anal canal;

gang lie 肛裂
anal fissure;

gang lou 肛瘻
anal fistula;

gang men 肛門
anus;

gang men fan she 肛門反射
anal reflex;

gang men guan 肛門管
rectal pipe;

gang men lie 肛門裂
anal fissure;

gang men sao yang 肛門瘙癢
pruritus ani;

gang men sao yang zheng 肛門瘙癢症
pruritus ani;

gang men sheng zhi qi yang zheng 肛門生殖器癢症
anogenital pruritus;

gang men shi jin 肛門失禁
copracrasia;

gang men wei 肛門痿
anal fistula;

gang men xian 肛門腺
anal glands;

gang men yan 肛門炎
anusitis;

gang men zhi chang 肛門直腸
anorectum;

gang men zhi chang yan 肛門直腸炎
anorectitis;

gang men zhi zhen 肛門指診
rectal touch;

gang mo 肛膜
anal membrane;

ge1 du qian chang 割肚牽腸
be deeply concerned / feel anxious || be kept in suspense;

gou1 chong bing 鈎蟲病
ancylostomiasis;

gu3 dao re chang 古道熱腸
warmhearted and compassionate || considerate and warmhearted; sympathetic;

guan4 chang 灌腸
enema / clyster;
xiao chang guan chang 小腸灌腸
small bowel enema;

hei1 bian 黑便
tarry stool;

hei fen 黑糞
melena;
jia xing hei fen 假性黑糞
melena spuria;
zhen xing hei fen 真性黑糞
melena vera;

hei niao bing 黑尿病
blackwater fever;

hou4 chang 後腸
epigaster;

hou chang guan 後腸管
metagaster;

hou chang men 後腸門
posterior intestinal portal;

huai4 ju xing lan wei yan 壞疽性闌尾炎
gangrenous appendictis;

huai si xing chang yan 壞死性腸炎
enteritis necroticans;

huai si xing xiao chang jie chang yan 壞死性小腸結腸炎
necrotizing enterocolitis;

huai xue bing xing li ji 壞血病性痢疾
scorbutic dysentery;

hui2 chang dang qi 迴腸盪氣
very touching;

hui2 chong 蛔蟲
ascarid / roundworm;

hui chong bing 蛔蟲病
ascariasis;

ji2 xing chang geng zu 急性腸梗阻
acute ileus;

ji xing lan wei yan 急性闌尾炎
acute appendictis;

ji4 sheng chong xing jia lan wei yan 寄生蟲性假闌尾炎
pseudoappendicitis zooparasitica;

jia3 lan wei yan 假闌尾炎
pseudoappendicitis;
ji sheng chong xing jia lan wei yan 寄生蟲性假闌尾炎
pseudoappendicitis zooparasitica;

jia li ji 假痢疾
pseudodysentery;

jia xing hei fen 假性黑糞
melena spuria;

jie1 chu xing lan wei yan 接觸性闌尾炎
appendicitis by contiguity;

jie2 chang 結腸
colon;
chang jie chang 長結腸
dolichocolon;
jing luan xing jie chang 痙攣性結腸
spastic colon;
ju jie chang 巨結腸
giant colon;
qian guan zhuang jie chang 鉛管狀結腸
lead-pipe colon;
you jie chang 右結腸
right colon;

jie chang ai 結腸癌
colon cancer;

jie chang bing 結腸病
colonopathy / disease of the colon;

jie chang chu xue 結腸出血
bleeding from the colon / colonorrhagia;

jie chang yan 結腸炎
colitis;

chu xue xing jie chang yan 出血性結腸炎
hemorrhagic colitis;

chuan ran xing jie chang yan 傳染性結腸炎
infectious colitis;

jie duan xing jie chang yan 節段性結腸炎
segmental colitis;

ju xian xing jie chang yan 局限性結腸炎
regional colitis;

kui yang xing jie chang yan 潰瘍性結腸炎
ulcerative colitis;

mo xing jie chang yan 膜性結腸炎
membranous conjunctivitis;

niao du zheng jie chang yan 尿毒症結腸炎
uremic colitis;

quan jie chang yan 全結腸炎
pancolitis;

que xue xing jie chang yan 缺血性結腸炎
ischemic colitis;

rou ya zhong xing jie chang yan 肉芽腫性結腸炎
granulomatous colitis;

xi rou zhuang jie chang yan 息肉狀結腸炎
colitis polyposa;

jie he xing chang yan 結核性腸炎
tuberculous enteritis;

jie jie xing chang yan 結節性腸炎
enteritis nodularis;

jie2 duan xing chang yan 節段性腸炎
segmental enteritis;

jie duan xing jie chang yan 節段性結腸炎
segmental colitis;

jie duan xing lan wei yan 節段性闌尾炎
segmental appendicitis;

jing4 luan xing bian mi 痙攣性便秘
spastic constipation;

jing luan xing chang geng zu 痙攣性腸梗阻
spastic ileus;

jing luan xing jie chang 痙攣性結腸
spastic colon;

ju2 bu xing chang yan 局部性腸炎
regional enteritis;

ju xian xing jie chang yan 局限性結腸炎
regional colitis;

ju xian xing xiao chang jie chang yan 局限性小腸結腸炎
regional enterocolitis;

ju4 jie chang 巨結腸
giant colon;

ju mang chang 巨盲腸
megacecum;

ju zhi chang 巨直腸
megarectum;

kong1 chang 空腸
empty intestine;

kong chang kui yang 空腸潰瘍
jejunal ulcer;

kong chang yan 空腸炎
jejunitis;

kuan1 chang 寬腸
relax the intestine;

kui4 yang xing jie chang yan 潰瘍性結腸炎
ulcerative colitis;

kui yang xing zhi chang yan 潰瘍性直腸炎
ulcerative proctitis;

la1 du zi 拉肚子
have diarrhoea / have loose bowels / suffer from diarrhoea;

la ni 拉溺
pass water / urinate;

la niao 拉尿
urinate;

la shi 拉屎
empty the bowels || deposit; go to stool; have a bowel movement; move one's bowels; shit;

la xi 拉稀
have diarrhoea / have loose bowels / suffer from diarrhoea;

lan2 wei 闌尾
epityphlon;

lan wei bing 闌尾病
appendicopathy;

lan wei ji shui 闌尾積水
hydroappendix;

lan wei jiao tong 闌尾絞痛
appendicular colic;

lan wei jie shi 闌尾結石
appendicular lithiasis;

lan wei jie shi zheng 闌尾結石症
appendicolithiasis;

lan wei lin ba jie 闌尾淋巴結
appendicular lymph nodes;

lan wei nei mo yan 闌尾內膜炎
endoappendictis;

lan wei nong zhong 闌尾膿腫
appendiceal abscess;

lan wei shan 闌尾疝
appendicocele;

lan wei shi bing 闌尾石病
appendolithiasis;

lan wei xi mo yan 闌尾系膜炎
meso-appendicitis;

lan wei yan 闌尾炎

chang chong xing lan wei yan 腸蟲性闌尾炎
helminthic appendictis / verminous appendictis;

chuan kong xing lan wei yan 穿孔性闌尾炎
perforating appendicitis;

chuang shang xing lan wei yan 創傷性闌尾炎
traumatic appendicitis;

huai ju xing lan wei yan 壞疽性闌尾炎
gangrenous appendictis;

ji xing lan wei yan 急性闌尾炎
acute appendictis;

jia lan wei yan 假闌尾炎
pseudoappendicitis;

jie chu xing lan wei yan 接觸性闌尾炎
appendicitis by contiguity;

jie duan xing lan wei yan 節段性闌尾炎
segmental appendicitis;

man xing lan wei yan 慢性闌尾炎
chronic appendicitis;

tiao yue xing lan wei yan 跳躍性闌尾炎
skip appendicitis;

lan wei yan xing xiao hua bu liang 闌尾炎性消化不良
appendicular dyspepsia;

lan wei zhou wei yan 闌尾周圍炎
periappendicitis;

li4 ji 痢疾
dysentery;

a mi ba li ji 阿米巴痢疾
amoebic dysentery;

bao fa xing li ji 爆發性痢疾
fulminant dysentery;

bing du xing li ji 病毒性痢疾
viral dysentery;

e xing li ji 惡性痢疾
malignant dysentery;

huai xue bing xing li ji 壞血病性痢疾
scorbutic dysentery;

jia li ji 假痢疾
pseudodysentery;

liu xing xing li ji 流行性痢疾
epidemic dysentery;

ri ben li ji 日本痢疾
Japanese dysentery;

xi jun xing li ji 細菌性痢疾
bacillary dysentery;

yuan chong xing li ji 原蟲性痢疾
protozoal dysentery;

lian4 qiu jun xing chang yan 鏈球菌性腸炎
streptococcus enteritis;

liu2 xing xing li ji 流行性痢疾
epidemic dysentery;

ma2 bi xing chang geng zu 麻痺性腸梗阻
paralyhtic ileus;

man4 xing lan wei yan 慢性闌尾炎
chronic appendicitis;

mang2 chang 盲腸
caecum;

腸 *Bowel*

ju mang chang 巨盲腸
megacecum;

mang chang jie chang 盲腸結腸
cecocolon;

mang chang peng zhang 盲腸膨脹
typhlectasis;

mang chang shan 盲腸疝
cecal hernia;

mang chang yan 盲腸炎
appendicitis;

mo4 xing jie chang yan 膜性結腸炎
membranous conjunctivitis;

nao4 du zi 鬧肚子
have diarrhoea / suffer from diarrhoea;

nei4 zang 內臟
internal organs;

nei zang fan she 內臟反射
viceral reflex;

nei zang fei da 內臟肥大
visceromegaly;

nei zang guo xiao 內臟過小
splanchnomicria;

nei zang ji bing 內臟疾病
splanchnopathy;

nei zang shi 內臟石
splanchnolith;

nei zang tong 內臟痛
visceral pain;

nei zang tong feng 內臟痛風
visceral gout;

nei zang yan 內臟炎
coelitis;

nei zang ying hua 內臟硬化
splanchnosclerosis;

nei zang zeng da 內臟增大
visceromegaly;

nei zang zheng chang 內臟正常
eusplanchnia;

nei4 zhi 內痔
internal hgemorrhoids / internal piles;

ni4 wei 膩胃
kill one's appetite;

niao4 du zheng jie chang yan 尿毒症結腸炎
uremic colitis;

nong2 niao 膿尿
pyuria;

nong xing fen 膿性糞
pyofecia;

pai2 bian 排便
defecate / void excrement // defecation;

pai bian fan she 排便反射
defecation reflex;

pai bian jie zhi 排便節制
fecal continence;

pai bian kong bu 排便恐怖
coprophobia;

pai bian shi jin 排便失禁
acathexia;

pang2 guang chang shan 膀胱腸疝
cystoenterocele;

qian1 chang gua du 牽腸掛肚
be deeply concerned / be very worried about sth || be kept in painful suspense; cause deep personal concern; feel constant anxiety about sth; feel deep anxiety; full of anxiety and worry; in an agony of anxiety; in deep distress and feel anxiety; in great anxiety; in great suspense; infinite longing; miss a great deal; on tenterhooks; wait in great suspense; with deep concern;

qian xin gua chang 牽心掛腸
be concerned / be very worried;

qian1 guan zhuang jie chang 鉛管狀結腸
lead-pipe colon;

quan2 jie chang yan 全結腸炎
pancolitis;

quan shan 全疝
complete hernia;

que1 xue xing chang bing 缺血性腸病
ischemic bowel disease;

que xue xing jie chang yan 缺血性結腸炎
ischemic colitis;

re4 chang 熱腸
ardent / enthusiastic / zealous;

ri4 ben li ji 日本痢疾
Japanese dysentery;

rou2 chang bai zhuan 柔腸百轉
deeply sorrowed over // deeply sorrowful;

rou chang cun duan 柔腸寸斷
brokenhearted // be overcome with great sadness;

rou4 ya zhong xing chang yan 肉芽腫性腸炎
granulomatous enteritis;

rou ya zhong xing jie chang yan 肉芽腫性結腸炎
granulomatous colitis;

ruan3 xin chang 軟心腸
softhearted;

sa1 fen 撒糞
empty the bowels ‖ defecate; evacuate the bowels; loose bowels; move the bowels; relieve bowels; shit; take a shit;

shan4 疝
hernia;
chang jie shan 腸節疝
enteromerocele;
chang shan 腸疝
enterocele;
pang guang shan 膀胱疝
vesical hernia;
quan shan 全疝
complete hernia;

shan qi 疝氣
hernia;

shan tong 疝痛
abnormal pain caused by spasm / colic;

shi2 er zhi chang 十二指腸
duodenum;

shi er zhi chang kui yang 十二指腸潰瘍
duodenal ulcer;

shi er zhi chang yan 十二指腸炎
duodenitis;

shi3 屎
excrement;

shi niao 屎尿
excrement and urine;

shui3 xie 水瀉
diarrhoea;

tao1 chong 絛蟲
tape worm;

tao chong bing 絛蟲病
tape worm disease // cestodiasis / taeniasis;

tiao4 yue xing lan wei yan 跳躍性闌尾炎
skip appendicitis;

tong1 bian 通便
purging / relief of constipation;

tong bian ji 通便劑
cathartic / laxative;

tuo1 chang 脱腸
hernia / prolapsus of the rectum;

tuo gang 脱肛
anal prolapse / prolapse of anus;

wai4 zhi 外痔
external hemorrhoid;

wu2 gang 無肛
aproctia / congenital absence of the anus / congenital imperfection of the anus;

xi1 rou xing chang yan 息肉性腸炎
enteritis polyposa;

xi rou zhuang jie chang yan 息肉狀結腸炎
colitis polyposa;

xi2 guan xing bian mi 習慣性便秘
chronic constipation / habitual constipation;

xi3 chang 洗腸
purge the bowels;

xi4 jun xing li ji 細菌性痢疾
bacillary dysentery;

xiao3 chang 小腸
small bowels / small intestines;

xiao chang guan chang 小腸灌腸
small bowel enema;

xiao chang jie chang yan 小腸結腸炎
enterocolitis;
chu xue xing xiao chang jie chang yan 出血性小腸結腸炎
hemorrhagic enterocolitis;

huai si xing xiao chang jie chang yan 壞死性小腸結腸炎
necrotizing enterocolitis;
ju xian xing xiao chang jie chang yan 局限性小腸結腸炎
regional enterocolitis;

xiao chang qi 小腸氣
hernia;

xiao chang xu han 小腸虛寒
asthenia-cold of small intestine;

xiao chang yan 小腸炎
enteritis / inflamation of the small intestine;

xie4 xie 泄瀉
diarrhoea / have loose bowels;

xie4 du 瀉肚
diarrhoea / have diarrhoea / have loose bowels;

xie li 瀉痢
diarrhoea;

xue4 bian 血便
bloody stool;

yan2 xing chang bing 炎性腸病
inflammatory bowel disease;

yan4 da bian 驗大便
stool test;

yao4 da bian 要大便
the bowels are open / the bowels move;

ye4 niao zheng 夜尿症
nocturia;

yi2 niao 遺尿
bed-wetting / incontinence of urine;

ying1 er chang jiao tong 嬰兒腸絞痛
infantile colic;

you4 jie chang 右結腸
right colon;

yuan2 chong xing chang yan 原蟲性腸炎
protozoan enteritis;

yuan chong xing li ji 原蟲性痢疾
protozoal dysentery;

zhen1 xing hei fen 真性黑糞
melena vera;

zhi2 chang 直腸
rectum;
ju zhi chang 巨直腸
megarectum;

zhi chang ai 直腸癌
cancer of the rectum / rectal cancer;

zhi chang chu xue 直腸出血
hemoproctia;

zhi chang fan she 直腸反射
rectal reflex;

zhi chang jing luan 直腸痙攣
proctospasm;

zhi chang kuo zhang 直腸擴張
proctectasia;

zhi chang ma bi 直腸麻痺
paralysis of the anus / proctoparalysis;

zhi chang qie chu 直腸切除
proctectomy / surgical resention of the rectum;

zhi chang shi jin 直腸失禁
rectal incontinence;

zhi chang tong 直腸痛
pain at the anus / pain in the rectum / rectalgia;

zhi chang xi rou 直腸息肉
polyp of rectum;

zhi chang xing bian mi 直腸性便秘
proctogenous constipation;

zhi chang yan 直腸炎
inflammation of the rectum / proctitis;
kui yang xing zhi chang yan 潰瘍性直腸炎
ulcerative proctitis;

zhi chang zhi du 直腸直肚
frank / outspoken / straightforward;

zhi chang zhou wei yan 直腸周圍炎
inflammation around the rectum / paraproctitis;

zhi3 xie 止瀉
stop diarrhoea;

zhi4 痔
piles || hemorrhoids;

nei zhi 內痔
internal piles;

wai zhi 外痔
external piles;

zhi chuang 痔瘡
piles || hemorrhoids;

zhi he 痔核
blind piles;

zhi lou 痔漏
anal fistula;

zhi qie chu 痔切除
hemorrhoidectomy;

zhui4 du 墜肚
have loose bowels;

zou3 du zi 走肚子
have diarrhoea / have loose bowels;

zu3 se xing chang geng zu 阻塞性腸梗阻
occlusive ileus;

Chun 唇 Lip

ba1 da zhe zui 吧嗒着嘴
smack one's lips // with a smack of the lips;

bai2 fei chun she 白費唇舌
waste one's breath / waste one's words || speak to the wind; whistle down the wind;

bie3 zui 癟嘴
drawn and retracted lips;

bo1 tuo xing chun yan 剝脫性唇炎
cheilitis exfoliativa;

chun2 唇
lip // labrum;

ju chun 巨唇
macrochilia;

ling chun 菱唇
rhombic lip;

run chun 潤唇
moisturize the lips;

xia chun 下唇
lower lip;

chun ai 唇癌
cheilocarcinoma;

chun chi gou 唇齒溝
labiodental sulcus;

chun chi xiang yi 唇齒相依
as close as lips and teeth / as close to each other as lips to teeth || as close to each other as the lips are to the teeth; as closely related as the lips and the teeth; as interdependent as lips and teeth; closely related and mutually dependent; closely related to each other like lips and teeth; mutually depend on each other as lips and teeth;

chun chuang 唇瘡
cold sore / fever sore;

chun er 唇兒
lips;

chun fa yu bu liang 唇發育不良
atelocheilia;

chun fa yu bu quan 唇發育不全
atelocheilia;

chun fan she 唇反射
lip reflex;

chun fei hou 唇肥厚
pachycheilia;

chun gan kou zao 唇乾口燥
one's lips are dry and one's mouth parched;

chun gan lie 唇乾裂
cheilosis;

chun gan she zao 唇乾舌燥
one's lips are dry and one's tongue parched;

chun gao 唇膏
lipstick;

chun gou 唇溝
labial groove;

chun hong chi bai 唇紅齒白
have rosy lips and pretty white teeth // red lips and white teeth;

chun jian 唇尖
procheilon;

chun jiao 唇角
labial angles;

chun jie jie 唇結節
labial tubercle;

chun ku she jiao 唇枯舌焦
one's lips and tongue become parched;

chun ku she lan 唇枯舌爛
talk oneself hoarse;

chun lie 唇裂
cleft lip / harelip;

chun ma bi 唇麻痺
labial paralysis / paralysis of the lips;

chun mian 唇面
labial surface / surface of the lips;

chun pao zhen 唇泡疹
cold sore;

chun pao zhen 唇疱疹
herpes labialis;

chun qiang she jian 唇槍舌劍
engage in a battle of words ‖ a battle of repartee; a battle of wits; cross verbal swords; exchange heated words; have tit-for-tat argument with sharp words;

chun qiang she zhan 唇槍舌戰
engage in a battle of words ‖ a battle of words; a fierce battle of tongue; a heated dispute; go at it hammer and tongs; have a verbal battle with sb;

chun ruo tu zhi 唇若塗脂
have rich red lips;

chun she 唇舌
(1) lips and tongue;
(2) argument ‖ persuasion; plausible speech; talking round; words;

chun wang chi han 唇亡齒寒
if one falls, the other is in danger ‖ be immediately threatened; if the lips are gone, the teeth are exposed; share a common lot; the teeth are cold when the lips are cold; when the lips are lost the teeth will be exposed to the cold;

chun yan 唇炎
cheilitis / inflammation of the lips;
bo tuo xing chun yan 剝脫性唇炎
cheilitis exfoliativa;
nong pao xing chun yan 膿疱性唇炎
impetiginous chelitis;
nong zhong xing chun yan 膿腫性唇炎
apostematous cheilitis;
ri guang xing chun yan 日光性唇炎
solar cheilitis;
rou ya zhong xing chun yan 肉芽腫性唇炎
granulomatous cheilitis;
xian xing chun yan 腺性唇炎
cheilitis glandularis;

chun yin 唇印
lip print;

da4 fei chun she 大費唇舌
exhaust one's eloquence / make a long harangue ‖ a long harangue; a lot of talking; take a lot of talking to convince;

da hou zui 大厚嘴
thick lips;

da hu zi 大鬍子
(1) full beard / long beard;
(2) heavily-bearded man;

duan3 chun 短唇
abnormally short lips / brachycheilia;

fan3 chun xiang ji 反唇相譏
answer back sarcastically / bicker with each other || answer with sarcastic rebuttal; back talk; dispute with each other; retort like for like; throw back an insinutation;

fan chun xiang ji 反唇相稽
answer back / rebuke with sarcastic remakrs || retort; retort like for like; turn against sb in mutual recrimination;

fei4 chun she 費唇舌
require a lot of talking;

fei jin chun she 費盡唇舌
have wasted all one's breath;

fei she lao chun 費舌勞唇
talk oneself out of breath / talk till one is out of breath;

guan1 jie chun 關節唇
articular lip;

hao4 chi zhu chun 皓齒朱唇
have pearly white teeth and crimson lips || one's teeth are very white and one's lips vermillion; white teeth and red lips;

hou4 chun 厚唇
abnormal thickness of lips / pachycheilia;

huo1 zui 豁嘴
(1) harelip;
(2) harelipped person;

jiang4 chun 絳唇
red lips;

jie1 wen 接吻
kiss;

ju4 chun 巨唇
macrochilia;

jue1 qi zui chun 撅起嘴唇
curl up ones lips / pout one's lips / pucker one's lips / purse one's lips // with pouting lips;

kou3 chun 口唇
lips;

kou gan chun zao 口乾唇燥
dry mouth and lips;

kou zao chun gan 口燥唇乾
lips are dry and mouth is parched / talk one's tongue dry;

lao2 chun fa she 勞唇乏舌
waste one's words;

lie3 zhe zui 咧着嘴
grinning;

lie4 chun 裂唇
cleft lip;

ling2 chun 菱唇
rhombic lip;

nong2 pao xing chun yan 膿疱性唇炎
impetiginous chelitis;

nong zhong xing chun yan 膿腫性唇炎
apostematous cheilitis;

nu2 chun pi she 奴唇婢舌
loose-tongued like a slave or maid / talkable like a slave or maid;

pie3 zui 撇嘴
pout / shoot out the lips;

qiao2 zui jue chun 翹嘴撅唇
pout one's lips in displeasure / pout one's mouth in anger;

qiao zui ta bi 翹嘴塌鼻
protruding lips and a snub nose;

qin1 wen 親吻
kiss;

qin zui 親嘴
kiss / smack on the lips;

que1 chun 缺唇
cleft lip / harelip;

ri4 guang xing chun yan 日光性唇炎
solar cheilitis;

rou4 ya zhong xing chun yan 肉芽腫性唇炎
granulomatous cheilitis;

run4 chun 潤唇
moisturize the lips;

run shi zui chun 潤濕嘴唇
moisten one's lips;

san1 ban zui er 三瓣嘴兒
harelipped;

shang4 chun 上唇
upper lip;

唇 *Lip*

shuang gu xing shang chun 雙弧形上唇
Cupid's bow;

shang zui chun 上嘴唇
upper lip;

she2 wen 舌吻
deep kiss / tongue kiss;

shen1 qing yi wen 深情一吻
an affectionate kiss;

shi4 shi zui chun 舐舐嘴唇
moisten one's lips;

shuang1 chun zheng 雙唇症
double lip;

shuang gu xing shang chun 雙弧形上唇
Cupid's bow;

song4 fei wen 送飛吻
blow sb a kiss / throw a kiss;

tan2 kou ying chun 檀口櫻唇
the red lips of a pretty girl / the small and reddish mouth of a woman;

tian3 chun za zui 舔唇咂嘴
lick one's lips and smack one's tongue;

tian zui chun 舔嘴唇
lick one's lips / smack one's lips;

tou1 wen 偷吻
snatch a kiss / steal a kiss;

tu4 chun 兔唇
cheiloschisis / cleft lip / harelip;

wang3 fei chun she 枉費唇舌
mere waste of breath / waste one's breath;

wen3 吻
(1) lip;
(2) the tone of one's speech;
(3) kiss;

wen bie 吻別
kiss sb goodbye;

wen he 吻合
coincide / fit / tally // identical;

wen3 脗
(1) kiss;
(2) join together / match / tally;
(3) lips;

wu2 chun 無唇
acheilia / congenital absence of the lips;

xia4 chun 下唇
lower lip;

xia zui chun 下嘴唇
lower lip;

xian1 chun 掀唇
open the mouth / speak;

xian4 xing chun yan 腺性唇炎
cheilitis glandularis;

xiao3 bo zui 小薄嘴
slim lips / thin lips;

yao2 chun gu she 搖唇鼓舌
instigate by talking || flap one's lips and beat one's tongue — engage in loose talk; flaunt one's red; persuade sb by sweet talk; wag one's tongue;

yao3 chi jiao chun 咬齒嚼唇
grind one's teeth and bite one's lips;

yao zui chun 咬嘴唇
bite one's lip;

yi1 zhi zui chun liang zhang pi, fan lai fu qu quan shi ni 一隻嘴唇兩張皮，翻來覆去全是你
your tongue is a double-edged sword;

ying1 chun 櫻唇
the small, beautiful mouth of a woman;

ying chun hao chi 櫻唇皓齒
cherry lips and gleaming teeth;

ying tao zui 櫻桃嘴
cherry lips / rosebud lips;

zao4 wen 燥吻
dry lips;

zhan1 chun 沾唇
touch the lips;

zhu1 chun hao chi 朱唇皓齒
red lips and white teeth / rosy lips and ivory white teeth;

zui3 嘴
lips;
bie zui 癟嘴
drawn and retracted lips;

da hou zui 大厚嘴
thick lips;
lie zhe zui 咧着嘴
grin / grinning;
pie zui 撇嘴
pout / shoot out the lips;
xiao bo zui 小薄嘴
slim lips / thin lips;
ying tao zui 櫻桃嘴
cherry lips / rosebud lips;

zui chun 嘴唇
lip;
bo zui chun 薄嘴唇
thin lips;
hou zui chun 厚嘴唇
thick lips;
jue qi zui chun 撅起嘴唇
curl up one's lips / pout one's lips / pucker one's lips / purse one's lips one's lips // with pouting lips;
run shi zui chun 潤濕嘴唇
moisten one's lips;
shang zui chun 上嘴唇
upper lip;
tian zui chun 舔嘴唇
lick one's lips / smack one's lips;
xia zui chun 下嘴唇
lower lip;
yao zui chun 咬嘴唇
bite one's lip;

zui chun you hua 嘴唇油滑
eloquent in speech / with one's tongue in one's cheek;

Dan 膽 Gall

chi4 dan 赤膽
sincere loyalty;

chi dan zhong xin 赤膽忠心
sincere loyalty / wholeheartedness;

chu1 xue xing dan nang yan 出血性膽囊炎
hemocholecystitis;

cou4 dan zi 湊膽子
seek company so as to boost courage;

da4 dan 大膽
audacious / bold / daring // have a nerve;

da dan chang shi 大膽嘗試
make a bold trial / take a long shot;

da dan po la 大膽潑辣
bold and vigorous / termagant;

dan3 膽
(1) gallbladder;
(2) courage / guts;
(3) bladder-like inner container;

dan chan xin jing 膽顫心驚
tremble with fright || one's heart beats with fear; strike terror into the heart of;

dan da 膽大
audacious / bold;

dan da bao tian 膽大包天
audacious in the extreme / daring;

dan da wang wei 膽大妄為
be undaunted and reckless || act in a foolhardy manner; daredevil; impudent; rush in where angels fear to tread; unscrupulous;

dan da xin xi 膽大心細
bold but cautious / be cautious and bold || brave but not reckless; courageous and wise;

dan dao 膽道
biliary tract;

dan dao chu xue 膽道出血
bleeding in the biliary tract and gallbladder / hematobilia;

dan dao nong zhong 膽道膿腫
biliary abscess;

dan gan 膽敢
dare / have the audacity to;

dan gu chun 膽固醇
cholesterol;

dan gu chun guo duo 膽固醇過多
excess cholesterol / hypercholesterolia;

dan gu chun jie shi 膽固醇結石
cholesterol calculus / cholesterol stone;

dan gu chun xue zheng 膽固醇血症
hypercholesterolemia;

dan guan 膽管
gall duct ‖ bile duct; bile vessels; biliary duct;

dan guan ai 膽管癌
bile duct carcinoma;

dan guan bing 膽管病
cholepathy / disease of the gallbladder;

dan guan gan yan 膽管肝炎
cholangiohepatitis;

dan guan jie shi 膽管結石
bile duct calculus;

dan guan kuo zhang 膽管擴張
cholangiectasis;

dan guan liu 膽管瘤
cholangioma;

dan guan yan 膽管炎
cholangitis;

dan han 膽寒
lose one's nerve;

dan hui chong bing 膽蛔蟲病
biliary ascariasis;

dan jiao tong 膽絞痛
billary colic;

dan jie shi 膽結石
cholelithiasis;

dan li 膽力
bravery / courage;

dan liang 膽量
boldness / courage / grit / guts / pluck / spunk // plucky / spunky;

dan liang guo ren 膽量過人
bolder than all the rest;

dan lie 膽裂
scared to death;

dan lie hun fei 膽裂魂飛
be frightened out of one's wits;

dan lüe 膽略
courage and resourcefulness / daring and resolute;

dan lüe guo ren 膽略過人
have unusual courage and resourcefulness;

dan luo 膽落
extremely frightened;

dan nang 膽囊
gallbladder;

dan nang bing 膽囊病
cholecystopathy / disease of the gallbladder;

zeng sheng xing dan nang bing 增生性膽囊病
hyperplastic cholecystosis;

dan nang dong mai 膽囊動脈
cystic artery;

dan nang guan 膽囊管
cystic duct;

dan nang jie shi bing 膽囊結石病
cholecystolithiasis;

dan nang jing mai 膽囊靜脈
cystic vein;

dan nang kuo zhang 膽囊擴張
cholecystectasia;

dan nang lin ba jie 膽囊淋巴結
cystic lymph node;

dan nang lou 膽囊瘻
amphibolic fistula;

dan nang qie chu 膽囊切除
cholecystectomy / removal of the gallbladder;

dan nang tong 膽囊痛
cholecystalgia;

dan nang yan 膽囊炎
cholecystitis / inflammation of the gallbladder;

chu xue xing dan nang yan 出血性膽囊炎
hemocholecystitis;

lü pao xing dan nang yan 濾泡性膽囊炎
follicular cholecystitis;

man xing dan nang yan 慢性膽囊炎
chronic cholecystitis;

nong qi xing dan nang yan 膿氣性膽囊炎
pyopneumocholecystitis;

qi zhong xing dan nang yan 氣腫性膽囊炎
cholecystitis emphysematosa;

dan nang yi wei 膽囊移位
gallbladder displacement;

dan nang zhou wei yan 膽囊周圍炎
perichlecystitis;

dan nang zhou yan 膽囊周炎
pericholecystitis;

qi zhong xing dan nang zhou yan 氣腫性膽囊周炎
gaseous pericholecystitis;

dan po 膽破
be frightened to death / be scared to death;

dan qi 膽氣
courage;

dan qie 膽怯
have cold feet / lose one's nerve / show the white feather // cold feet / diffidence // diffident / mousy / timid / timorous;

dan re duo shui 膽熱多睡
somnolence due to gallbladder heat;

dan shi 膽石
cholelith / gallstone;

dan shi bing 膽石病
biliary calculus / gallstone;

dan shi qie chu 膽石切除
cholelithotomy;

dan shi rong jie yao 膽石溶解藥
anticholelithogenic;

dan shi zheng 膽石症
cholelithiasis / gallstone;

dan shi 膽識
courage and insight;

dan shi guo ren 膽識過人
exceed the rest in bravery and wisdom / surpass others in intelligence and determination;

dan xiao 膽小
chicken-hearted / chicken-livered / cowardly / gutless / pusillanimous / timid / timid and overcautious / yellow-bellied;

dan xiao pa shi 膽小怕事
chicken-hearted / chicken-livered / cowardly / timid / timid and overcautious / yellow-bellied;

dan xiao ru shu 膽小如鼠
as timid as a hare || afraid of one's shadow; as bold as an Essex lion; as timid as a mouse; be a coward; cannot say boo to a goose; chicken-hearted; mouselike timidity;

dan xu 膽虛
jittery / nervous / scared;

dan zhan xin jing 膽戰心驚
be terror-stricken || be mortally frightened; be prostrated with fear; funky; in constant dread; in holy terror; in terror; nervous and jumpy; one's heart beats with fear; strike terror into the heart of; tremble with fear;

dan zhi 膽汁
bile // fearless / full of courage;

dan zhuang 膽壯
fearless / full of courage;

dan zi 膽子
courage / nerve;

dan zong guan 膽總管
common bile duct;

dou3 dan 斗膽
make bold || of great courage; venture;

fang4 dan 放膽
act boldly and with confidence / get bold;

gan1 dan 肝膽
(1) liver and gall;
(2) courage / heroic spirit;
(3) open-heartedness / sincerity;

gan dan guo ren 肝膽過人
exceed others in courage || a person of no ordinary spunk; far surpass others in daring; unsurpassed in valour; unusually courageous;

gan dan ju lie 肝膽俱裂
be heartbroken || one's liver and gall both seem torn from within — extremely frightened; overwhelmed by grief; terror-stricken;

gan dan xiang zhao 肝膽相照
open one's heart to sb || a genuine meeting of minds between friends; be open-hearted to each other; friends devoted to each other heart and soul; loyal-hearted; show utter devotion to a friend; treat each other with all sincerity;

han2 ren xin dan 寒人心膽
make one's blood cold / make one's blood run cold;

hun2 shen shi dan 渾身是膽
be filled with courage / full of courage || every inch a hero; one's whole body is valour; the very embodiment of valour;

jing1 xin diao dan 驚心掉膽
be frightened out of one's wits;

jing xin dong po 驚心動魄
soul-stirring and breathtaking;

jing xin po dan 驚心破膽
heart startled and gallbladder broken — be extremely frightened;

ku3 dan 苦膽
gall bladder;

li4 dan 瀝膽
manifest great bravery;

li dan pi gan 瀝膽披肝
absolutely sincere and loyal;

lie4 dan 裂膽
extremely frightened / extremely scared;

luo4 dan 落膽
be frightened out of one's wits // very scared;

lü4 pao xing dan nang yan 濾泡性膽囊炎
follicular cholecystitis;

man4 xing dan nang yan 慢性膽囊炎
chronic cholecystitis;

ming2 mu zhang dan 明目張膽
in a barefaced manner || before one's very eye; brazen; daringly; fearlessly; in a flagrant way; openly and wantonly; without caring for any on-lookers;

nong2 qi xing dan nang yan 膿氣性膽囊炎
pyopneumocholecystitis;

ou3 tan ji 嘔膽汁
cholemesis / the vomiting of bile;

pi1 gan li dan 披肝瀝膽
(1) bare one's heart / disclose one's secret feelings || hang one's heart on one's sleeve; lay bare one's mind; lay open one's heart; open one's heart to sb; open and sincere; unbosom oneself; unbutton one's soul;
(2) loyal and faithful // show a loyal heart;

pi gan lu dan 披肝露膽
lay bare one's heart / lay open one's heart to show loyalty;

pi li gan dan 披瀝肝膽
open up one's heart / open-hearted;

po4 dan 破膽
be scared out of one's wits;

pou1 gan li dan 剖肝瀝膽
lay bare one's mind / be open and sincere || open up one's heart; show sb one's inmost feelings; speak one's whole mind; unbosom oneself; unbutton one's soul;

qi4 zhong xing dan nang yan 氣腫性膽囊炎
cholecystitis emphysematosa;

qi zhong xing dan nang zhou yan 氣腫性膽囊周炎
gaseous pericholecystitis;

ren2 da dan xiao 人大膽小
though one's frame is large, one's character is timid;

ren duo dan zhuang 人多膽壯
gather courage on the strength of numbers / sheer numbers can pluck up one's courage;

sang4 dan 喪膽
be frightened out of one's wits / panic-stricken || break one's spirit; lose nerve // disheartened; terror-stricken;

se4 dan bao tian 色膽包天
extremely daring in lewdness;

shu1 dan guan 輸膽管
ductus biliferi;

shu3 dan 鼠膽
cowardice;

ti2 xin diao dan 提心吊膽
cautious and anxious || always on tenterhooks; be filled with anxiety; be haunted with fear; have one's heart in one's mouth; in a state of suspense; in great terror; live in constant fear; on tenterhooks; restless and anxious; scared; terror-stricken; terror-struck;

wen2 feng sang dan 聞風喪膽
become terror-stricken at the news;

wu2 dan ji 無膽汁
Acholia;

xia4 po le dan 嚇破了膽
be scared out of one's wits / panic-stricken || be psyched out; strike terror into the hearts of;

yi1 shen shi dan 一身是膽
very brave || absolutely fearless; be filled with courage; brave all through; every inch a hero; full of courage; have plenty of guts; know no fear; the very embodiment of valour; the whole body is one mass of courage;

you3 dan liang 有膽量
have the courage / have the guts;

zeng1 sheng xing dan nang bing 增生性膽囊病
hyperplastic cholecystosis;

zhong1 gan yi dan 忠肝義膽
having good faith, virtue, and patriotism;

zhuang4 dan 壯膽
embolden / screw up one's courage / strengthen one's courage;

Du 肚 Stomach

ai2 dong shou e 挨凍受餓
be beaten and starved;

ai e 挨餓
be starved / endure hunger / go hungry / suffer from hunger;

ai ji shou dong 挨飢受凍
suffer cold and hunger;

bai2 chi 白吃
eat without paying / have a free meal;

bai4 wei 敗胃
spoil one's appetite;

ban4 bao 半飽
half full;

ban ji ban bao 半飢半飽
underfed;

bao3 飽
full;

bao can 飽餐
eat to one's heart's content || be gorged with food; be replete with food; be stuffed with food; eat one's fill;

bao can yi dun 飽餐一頓
eat and drink one's fill || eat heartily of the meal; get one's whack; play a knife and fork; take a hearty meal;

bao chang 飽嘗
taste to the full / taste to the fullest extent;

bao han bu zhi e han ji 飽漢不知餓漢飢
one who is in comfortable circumstances does not know the bitterness of misfortune / the well-fed don't know how the starving suffer;

bao nuan 飽暖
more than enough to eat and wear / well-fed and well-clad;

bao4 shi 暴食
eat too much at one meal / overeat;

bian4 ying xing wei chang bing 變應性胃腸病
allergic gastroenteropahty;

bie3 zhe du zi 癟着肚子
with an empty stomach;

bo1 tuo xing wei yan 剝脫性胃炎
exfoliative gastritis;

bu4 bao zheng 不飽症
acoria / aplesia;

bu quan shan 不全疝
incomplete hernia;

chang2 wei 腸胃
belly / intestines and stomach;

chang wei bing 腸胃病
digestive ailment / disease of stomach and bowels / intestines and stomach trouble;

chang wei bu hao 腸胃不好
suffer from indigestion;

chang wei chong qi 腸胃充氣
flatulence / gas / wind;

chang wei yan 腸胃炎
enterogastritis;

chang3 kai du zi 敞開肚子
eat without inhibition;

cheng1 chang zhu fu 撐腸拄腹
excessive eating // fill the stomach;

chong1 ji 充飢
allay one's hunger with sth;

chong ji yu han 充飢禦寒
allay one's hunger and keep out the cold / stop hunger or resist cold;

chong ji zhi ke 充飢止渴
satisfy hunger or thirst;

chong xue xing pi da 充血性脾大
congestive splenomegaly;

chu1 xue xing wei yan 出血性胃炎
hemorrhagic gastritis;

cui1 xie 催瀉
purgation;

da4 du pi 大肚皮
paunch / pot-belly;

da du zi 大肚子
(1) big eater;
(2) paunch / pot-belly // pot-bellied;

dao3 wei kou 倒胃口
(1) spoil one's appetite ‖ curb one's appetite; cloy the appetite; feel like vomiting; feel sick; make one nauseous; ruin one's appetite; turn one's stomach;
(2) get fed up ‖ fed up to the teeth; get tired of someone or sth; have no interest in someone or sth;

di1 wei suan zheng 低胃酸症
hypochlorhydria;

diao4 wei kou 調胃口
whet one's appetite;

du4 肚
abdomen / stomach ‖ Aunt Nelly; belly; tripe;
pi jiu du 啤酒肚
beer belly;

du bao si shui 肚飽思睡
when the belly is full, the bones will be at rest;

du chang 肚腸
bowels;

du li ming bai 肚裏明白
clear to oneself // know in one's heart;

du li xun si 肚裏尋思
think within oneself;

du li you shu 肚裏有數
know in one's heart ‖ have a pretty good idea; know very well in one's mind; know what's what;

du liang 肚量
magnanimity / tolerance;

du pi 肚皮
belly;

du qi 肚臍
belly button / navel;

du qi yan 肚臍眼
belly button / navel;

du tong 肚痛
collywobbles;

du zi 肚子
stomach ‖ abdomen; belly; innards; tripe; tum; tummy;

du zi e 肚子餓
hungry;

du zi teng 肚子疼
bellyache // have a pain in one's belly / have a pain in one's innards / suffer from abdominal pain;

du zi tong 肚子痛
bellyache / collywobbles / stomach cramps / stomachache // have a pain in one's belly / have a pain in one's innards;

dui4 wei kou 對胃口
(1) appetizing / palatable;
(2) to sb's liking / to sb's taste;

e4 呃
hiccough / hiccup;

e ni 呃逆
hiccough / hiccup;
jing luan xing e ni 痙攣性呃逆
spasmolygmus;
liu xing xing e ni 流行性呃逆
epidemic hiccup;

e4 xing wei kui yang 惡性胃潰瘍
gastric malignancy;

e4 餓
hungry // starve;

e bian du zi 餓扁肚子
gaunt with hunger;

e de du zi jiao 餓得肚子叫
cry cupboard / have a wolf in the stomach / so hungry that the stomach rumbles;

e de si lan han, e bu si qiong han 餓得死懶漢，餓不死窮漢
a lazy man can starve to death, a poor man won't;

e hu pu shi 餓虎撲食
a hungry tiger at its prey ‖ a hungry tiger pouncing on its prey; the hungry tiger sprang on the sheep; prey on victim like a famished tiger;

e ru hu lang 餓如虎狼
hungry as a hawk;

e si 餓死
starve to death;

e si gui 餓死鬼
starveling;

e si shi xiao, shi jie shi da 餓死事小，失節事大
to be starved to death is a trifling thing, but to lose one's virtue is a serious matter;

fan1 wei 翻胃
feel nausea / nauseating;

fan3 wei 反胃
retch // nausea / regurgitation / regurgitation of food;

fei2 hou xing wei yan 肥厚性胃炎
hypertrophic gastritis;

fu4 tong 腹痛
abdominal pain;

fu tong ru jiao 腹痛如絞
have an excuriating pain in the belly;

fu zhong cang dao 腹中藏刀
a dagger hidden in the belly — a treacherous person;

ge1 du qian chang 割肚牽腸
be deeply concerned / be kept in suspense / feel anxious;

guan3 脘
inside of the stomach;

guo3 fu 果腹
fill the stomach;

guo4 bao 過飽
full to bursting / overeaten;

guo bao bing 過飽病
overeating disease;

han2 bu gu fu 含哺鼓腹
with food in the mouth and belly well-filled ‖ feed food and fill the stomach to the full — a scene of lightheartedness of the people in times of peace;

he2 wei kou 合胃口
suit one's taste / to one's taste;

he2 yu fu zhi 河魚腹疾
have loose bowels / suffer from diarrhoea // stomach ailment;

ji1 飢
(1) hungry // starve;
(2) crop failure / famine;

ji bao lao lu 飢飽勞碌
starve all day long with no assurance when the next meal will come;

ji bing jiao jia 飢病交加
suffer from hunger and disease;

ji bu na yan 飢不納言
hungry bellies have no ears / the belly has no ears;

ji bu ze shi 飢不擇食
a hungry person is not picky and choosy || a good appetite is a good sauce; a hungry person is not choosy about his food; a hungry person will eat anything given him; all food is delicious to the starving; beggars cannot be choosers; beggars must not be choosers; hunger finds no fault with the cookery; hunger gives relish to any food; hunger has always a good cook; hunger is the best sauce; hunger sweetens beans; hungry dogs will eat dirty puddings; hungry people are not particular about their food; nothing comes amiss to a hungry person; nothing is unwelcome to the hungry; the best sauce is hunger; when hungry, one takes any food that is ready;

ji bu ze shi, han bu ze yi 飢不擇食，寒不擇衣
when one is hungry, one eats what there is; when one is cold, one wears what one has;

ji can ke yin 飢餐渴飲
eat when hungry and drink when thirsty / when one is hungry, one eats and when thirsty, one drinks;

ji chang 飢腸
empty stomach;

ji chang lu lu 飢腸轆轆
one's stomach cries out for food || as hungry as a hawk; as hungry as a hunter; as hungry as a wolf; famishing; feel a vacuum in the lower regions; have a wolf in the stomach; one's belly is rumbling with hunger; one's inside rumbles for want of food; one's stomach rumbles with hunger; so hungry that the stomach is beginning to gurgle; the belly thinks the throat is cut;

ji e 飢餓
hunger / starvation;

ji e bing 飢餓病
malnutrition;

ji e tong 飢餓痛
hunger pain / hunger pangs;

ji e xing gu bing 飢餓性骨病
hunger osteopathy;

ji e xing shui zhong 飢餓性水腫
hunger swelling;

ji han jiao po 飢寒交迫
suffer from cold and hunger || a life of cold and hunger; be poverty-stricken; be pressed by hunger and cold; be wedged in between hunger and cold; go cold and hungry; lack of proper food and warmth; live in hunger and cold; suffer hunger and cold;

ji han suo bi 飢寒所逼
be driven by hunger and cold;

ji han qi dao xin 飢寒起盜心
an empty belly hears nobody / hunger and cold tempt men to steal;

ji huo zhong shao 飢火中燒
burning desire for food || acute hunger;

ji zhe yi wei shi 飢者易為食
hunger makes hard beans sweet || a good appetite is a good sauce; all food is delicious to the starving; hunger finds no fault with the cookery; hunger is the best sauce; the cat is hungry when a crust contents her; the first dish pleases all;

ji zhe yi wei shi, ke zhe yi wei yin 飢者易為食，渴者易為飲
the hungry man is easily satisfied with food and the thirsty man with drink;

ji2 fu tong 急腹痛
colic;

ji xing wei chang yan 急性胃腸炎
acute gastroenteritis;

ji xing wei yan 急性胃炎
acute gastritis;

ji4 fa xing wei qi zhang 繼發性胃氣脹
secondary ruminal tympany;

jian4 wei 健胃
good for the health of the stomach;

jing4 luan xing e ni 痙攣性呃逆
spasmolygmus;

jiu3 xie bu zhi 久瀉不止
chronic diarrhoea;

ju4 wei 巨胃
enlarged stomach / gastromegaly;

kou3 fu zhi yu 口腹之欲
the desire for good food || bodily desires; the bodily wants of food and drink;

liu2 xing xing e ni 流行性呃逆
epidemic hiccup;

lü4 pao xing wei yan 濾泡性胃炎
follicular gastritis;

man3 du zi 滿肚子
crop-full;

man du zi huai zhu yi 滿肚子壞主意
whirlpool of evil ideas;

man4 xing wei yan 慢性胃炎
chronic gastritis;

mei2 wei kou 沒胃口
have no appetite / not to one's liking;

mi2 lan xing wei yan 糜爛性胃炎
erosive gastritis;

nao4 du zi 鬧肚子
have loose bowels;

pi2 jiu du 啤酒肚
beer belly;

pi2 脾
spleen;

pi bing 脾病
lienopathy;

pi chong xue 脾充血
splenemphraxis;

pi chu xue 脾出血
splenorrhagia;

pi da 脾大
splenomegaly;
chong xue xing pi da 充血性脾大
congestive splenomegaly;
re dai pi da 熱帶脾大
tropical splenomegaly;
rong xue xing pi da 溶血性脾大
hemolytic splenomegaly;

pi guo da 脾過大
enlarged spleen / splenoparectasis;

pi guo xiao 脾過小
microsplenia;

pi kui yang 脾潰瘍
splenelcosis;

pi qie chu 脾切除
removal of the spleen / splenectomy;

pi ruo fei xu 脾弱肺虛
asthenia of the spleen and lung;

pi tou 脾頭
head of spleen;

pi wei 脾尾
tail of spleen;

pi wei 脾胃
spleen and stomach;

pi wei bu he 脾胃不和
incoordination between spleen and stomach;

pi wei bu jia 脾胃不佳
antipathetic // have a poor appetite / lack appetite;

pi wei she re 脾胃濕熱
wetness-heat accumulated in the spleen and stomach;

pi wei xiang tou 脾胃相投
have similar likes and dislikes / have similar tastes;

pi xia chui 脾下垂
splenoptosis;

pi xu 脾虛
asthenia of the spleen / spleen-asthenia;

pi yan 脾炎
inflammation of the spleen / lienitis;

pi ying hua 脾硬化
splenokeratosi;

pi zhang da 脾脹大
enlargement of spleen;

pi zhong da 脾腫大
enlargement of the spleen / splenomegalia / splenomegaly;

pi zhong liu 脾腫瘤
splenoma;

ping2 wei 平胃
settle the stomach;

qian2 wei 前胃
forestomach;

re4 dai pi da 熱帶脾大
tropical splenomegaly;

ren3 ji ai e 忍飢挨餓
suffer hunger;

rong2 xue xing pi da 溶血性脾大
hemolytic splenomegaly;

shan4 疝
hernia;
bu quan shan 不全疝
incomplete hernia;

shan xiu bu shu 疝修補術
hernia repair / herniorrhaphy;

shen1 shang fa guang, du li fa huang 身上發光，肚裏發慌
silks and satins put out the fire in the kitchen / silks and satins put out the kitchen fire;

shi2 bu guo fu 食不果腹
not to have enough food to eat || have little food to eat; have not enough to eat; have not sufficient food to eat; insufficient food at meals;

shi bu guo fu, yi bu bi ti 食不果腹，衣不蔽體
have not enough food and clothes;

shi wu zhong du 食物中毒
food poisoning;

shi yu 食慾
appetite;

shi yu bu zheng 食慾不振
anorexia / poor appetite // off one's oats;

shi yu guo sheng 食慾過盛
bulimia;

shi yu yi zhi yao 食慾抑制藥
anorexic;

suan1 xing xiao hua bu liang 酸性消化不良
acid dyspepsia;

wei3 suo xing wei yan 萎縮性胃炎
atrophic gastritis;

wei4 胃
stomach / tummy;
bai wei 敗胃
spoil one's appetite;
fan wei 反胃
nausea / regurgitation / regurgitation of food;
ju wei 巨胃
enlarged stomach / gastromegaly;
ping wei 平胃
settle the stomach;
qian wei 前胃
forestomach;
wen wei 溫胃
warm the stomach;
xi wei 洗胃
gastric lavage;
yi wei 益胃
reinforcing the stomach / tonifying stomach;
zhi wei 滯胃
indigestion || lie heavy on sb's stomach; lie heavy on sb's stomach;

wei ai 胃癌
cancer of the stomach / gastric cancer;

wei an 胃安
centrine;

wei bing 胃病
gastric disease / gastropathy / stomach trouble;
zhou qi xing wei bing 周期性胃病
gastroperiodynia;

wei chang 胃腸
stomach and intestines;

wei chang bing 胃腸病
gastroenteropathy;
bian ying xing wei chang bing 變應性胃腸病
allergic gastroenteropahty;

wei chang shen jing guan neng zheng 胃腸神經官能症
gastrointestinal neurosis;

wei chang tong 胃腸痛
gastroenteralgia;

wei chang yan 胃腸炎
gastroenteritis;
ji xing wei chang yan 急性胃腸炎
acute gastroenteritis;

wei chu xue 胃出血
bleeding from the stomach / gastrorrhagia;

wei chuan kong 胃穿孔
gastric perforation / stomach perforation;

wei da wan 胃大彎
greater curvature;

wei di 胃底
fundus of stomach;

wei gan yan 胃肝炎
gastrohepatitis;

wei guo min 胃過敏
irritability of the stomach // have a sensitive stomach;

wei huo 胃火
stomach fire;

wei huo shang sheng 胃火上昇
rising up of stomach fire;

wei jiao tong 胃絞痛
gastric colic;

wei jie chang fan she 胃結腸反射
gastrocolic reflex;

wei jing 胃鏡
gastroscope;

wei kong tong 胃空痛
gastralgokenosis;

wei kou 胃口
(1) appetite / belly;
(2) liking;
mei wei kou 沒胃口
have no appetite // loss of appetite;

wei kou bu hao 胃口不好
have a poor appetite / have no desire for food / have not much appetite / have not much of an appetite / off one's feed;

wei kui yang 胃潰瘍
gastric ulcer;
e xing wei kui yang 惡性胃潰瘍
gastric malignancy;

wei kuo zhang 胃擴張
dilatation of stomach;

wei pi 胃皮
gastrodermis;

wei po lie 胃破裂
gastrorrhexis;

wei qi 胃氣
stomach energy;

wei qi bu he 胃氣不和
disorder of stomach energy;

wei qi zhang 胃氣脹
ruminal tympany;
ji fa xing wei qi zhang 繼發性胃氣脹
secondary ruminal tympany;
yuan fa xing wei qi zhang 原發性胃氣脹
primary ruminal tympany;

wei qie chu 胃切除
gastrectomy / surgical removal of the stomach;

wei re 胃熱
gastric fever / stomach heat;

wei re shang ni 胃熱上逆
adverse rising of stomach heat;

wei ruan hua 胃軟化
gastromalacia;

wei sheng jing tong 胃神經痛
gastralgia;

wei shi er zhi chang yan 胃十二指腸炎
gastroduodenitis;

wei shi bing 胃石病
gastrolithiasis;

wei suan 胃酸
gastric acid / hydrochloric acid in gastric juice;

wei suan guo duo 胃酸過多
gastric hyperacidity / hyperacidity / sour stomach / superacidity;

wei suan guo shao 胃酸過少
gastric hyporacidity;

wei suan que fa 胃酸缺乏
absence of hydrochloric acid in the gastric secretions of the stomach / achlorhydria;

wei tan 胃癱
gastroplegia;

wei teng 胃疼
stomach pain / stomachache;

wei tong 胃痛
stomachache;

wei wei suo 胃萎縮
gastric atrophy;

wei xia zhai 胃狹窄
gastrostenosis;

wei xia chui 胃下垂
gastroptosis;

wei xia kou qian 胃下口鉗
pylorus clamp;

wei xiao hua 胃消化
gastric digestion;

wei xiao hua bu liang 胃消化不良
gastric dyspepsia;

wei xiao wan 胃小彎
lesser curvature of the stomach;

wei yan 胃炎
gastritis;
bo tuo xing wei yan 剝脫性胃炎
exfoliative gastritis;
chu xue xing wei yan 出血性胃炎
hemorrhagic gastritis;
fei hou xing wei yan 肥厚性胃炎
hypertrophic gastritis;
ji xing wei yan 急性胃炎
acute gastritis;
lü pao xing wei yan 濾泡性胃炎
follicular gastritis;
man xing wei yan 慢性胃炎
chronic gastritis;
mi lan xing wei yan 糜爛性胃炎
erosive gastritis;
wei suo xing wei yan 萎縮性胃炎
atrophic gastritis;
xi rou xing wei yan 息肉性胃炎
polypous gastritis;
ying hua xing wei yan 硬化性胃炎
cirrhotic gastritis;
zhong du xing wei yan 中毒性胃炎
toxic gastritis;

wei ye 胃液
gastric juice;

wei zang 胃臟
stomach;

wei zhi 胃汁
gastric juice;

wen1 bao 溫飽
adequately fed and clothed;

wen wei 溫胃
warm the stomach;

wu2 pi 無脾
asplenia / congenital absence of the spleen;

wu wei 無胃
agastria / congenital absence of the stomach;

xi1 rou xing wei yan 息肉性胃炎
polypous gastritis;

xi2 guan xing yin shi shi tiao zheng 習慣性飲食失調症
bulimia nervosa;

xi3 wei 洗胃
gastric lavage;

xiao1 hua 消化
digestion;

xiao hua bu liang 消化不良
dyspepsia / indigestion / stomach upset;
lan wei yan xing xiao hua bu liang 闌尾炎性消化不良
appendicular dyspepsia;
suan xing xiao hua bu liang 酸性消化不良
acid dyspepsia;

xiao hua dao chu xue 消化道出血
alimentary canal haemorrhage;

xiao hua li 消化力
digestion;

xiao hua liang hao 消化良好
eupepsia;

xiao hua qi guan 消化器官
digestive organs;

xiao hua ye 消化液
digestive juice;

xiao hua zheng chang 消化正常
eupepsia;

xiao3 du zi 小肚子
lower abdomen;

xiao fu 小腹
lower abdomen;

yan4 shi zheng 厭食症
anorexia;

yi1 du zi 一肚子
a stomachful of;

yi du zi huo 一肚子火
have a stomachful of anger;

yi du zi qi 一肚子氣
a stomachful of grudge || full of complaints; full of grievances; strong emotions;

yi4 wei 益胃
reinforcing the stomach / tonifying stomach;

yin3 shi shi tiao zheng 飲食失調症
bulimia;

xi guan xing yin shi shi tiao zheng 習慣性飲食失調症
bulimia nervosa;

ying4 hua wei 硬化胃
sclerotic stomach;

ying hua xing wei yan 硬化性胃炎
cirrhotic gastritis;

you2 zou pi 游走脾
displacement of the spleen / splenectopia;

you4 ji you ke 又飢又渴
hungry and thirsty;

yuan2 fa xing wei qi zhang 原發性胃氣脹
primary ruminal tympany;

yun4 pi 運脾
activate the spleen energy;

zhang4 脹
(1) full-stomached / glutted;
(2) swelling of skin;

zhang bao 脹飽
fullness of the stomach from overeating;

zhang man 脹滿
full / glutted / inflated;

zhang men 脹悶
tightness of the stomach;

zhi3 xie yao 止瀉藥
antidiarrhoeal;

zhi4 wei 滯胃
indigestion // lie heavy on sb's stomach;

zhong4 du xing wei yan 中毒性胃炎
toxic gastritis;

zhou1 qi xing wei bing 周期性胃病
gastroperiodynia;

zhou4 wei 皺胃
abomasum;

zhou wei qi zhang 皺胃氣脹
abomasal bloat;

zhou wei shi zhang li 皺胃失張力
abomasal atony;

zhou wei yan 皺胃炎
abomasitis;

Er 耳 Ear

ai4 da ting 愛打聽
(1) snoopy;
(2) inquisitive;

bai3 ting bu yan 百聽不厭
worth hearing a hundred times // never get tired of hearing;

bai wen bu ru yi jian 百聞不如一見
seeing is believing || a thousand words of hearsay are not worth a single glance at the reality; better seeing once than hearing a hundred times; hearsays are no substitutes for seeing with one's own eyes; it is better to see sth once than hear about it a hundred times; seeing for oneself is a hundred times better than hearing from others; seeing for oneself is better than all hearsays; there is nothing like seeing for oneself; to see is to believe; to see it once is better than to hear a hundred times;

bai4 ling 拜聆
have the honour to hear;

bei4 背
hard of hearing;

bo2 dong xing er ming 搏動性耳鳴
pulsatile tinnitus;

bu4 chi bu long 不痴不聾
blind and deaf / indifferent // pretend not to see and hear;

bu kan ru er 不堪入耳
offensive to the ear || disgusting; intolerable to the ear; revolting;

bu ren zu ting 不忍卒聽
heartbreaking to hear;

bu ru er 不入耳
not worth listening to // unpleasant to the ear;

bu sheng bu xiang 不聲不響
furtively / stealthily;

bu wen bu wen 不聞不問
indifferent to sth / pay no attention to || leave out of account; not bother to ask questions or listen to what's said; pass over in silence; remain indifferent to sth; show no interest in sth;

bu wen 不問
ignore / pay no attention to;

bu zhong ting 不中聽
grating;

can3 bu ren wen 慘不忍聞
too horrified to learn / too sad and shocking to hear / too sad and shocking to the ear;

cao2 za guo er 嘈雜聒耳
jar on one's ears;

ce4 er qing ting 側耳傾聽
incline one's ear and listen attentively || crane one's neck to listen; devour every word; harken to; incline the ear to listen; incline the head and listen attentively; prick up one's ears; strain one's ears;

ce er xi ting 側耳細聽
incline the head and listen attentively || prick up one's ears; split sb's ears; strain one's ears;

ce ting 側聽
eavesdrop / listen in / listen without permission / overhear;

ce wen 側聞
learn of sth from others;

chao1 ren de ting li 超人的聽力
clairaudience / the power to hear sounds beyond ordinary experience;

chi1 er guang 吃耳光
be slapped in the face / cuff sb on the ear / slap in the face // a slap in the face;

chong1 er bu wen 充耳不聞
turn a deaf ear to || close one's ears to; stop one's ears to; shut one's ears to; stuff one's ears and refuse to listen; stuff up one's ears and refuse to hear;

chuan1 er 穿耳
pierce the ears;

chuan2 dao xing long 傳導性聾
conduction deafness / transmission deafness;

chuan dao xing ting li sang shi 傳導性聽力喪失
conductive hearing loss / transmission hearing loss;

chui2 shou tie er 垂首帖耳
docile and obedient;

chui2 gu 錘骨
malleus;

chui gu ci 錘骨刺
spur of malleus;

ci4 er 刺耳
ear-piercing || grate on the ear; harsh; hurt the ear; irritating to the ear; jar upon the ear; jarring; unpleasant to the ear // grating;

ci er de hua 刺耳的話
a flea in one's ear / a flea in the ear / harsh words / sarcastic remarks / words that irritate the ears;

cuan2 tou jie er 攢頭接耳
(1) whisper;
(2) put heads together;

da1 耷
big ears;

da la 耷拉
droop / hang down;

da3 er guang 打耳光
box sb's ears || get a flap in the face; get a slap in the face; give sb a blow in the ears; give sb a box on the ears; give sb a sweet one on the ears; give sb a thick ear; hit sb in the face; slap sb across the face; slap sb in the face; slap sb on the face; slap sb's face;

dai4 戴
put on / wear;

dai er huan 戴耳環
wear earrings;

dan1 er ting jue 單耳聽覺
monaural hearing;

dang4 er bian feng 當耳邊風
regard as nothing but a wind blowing past the ear;

dao4 ting 盜聽
(1) eavesdrop;
(2) bug / tap a phone / wiretap;

de2 xi 得悉
hear of / learn about;

de xian 得閒
at leisure / free / have leisure;

deng1 gu 鐙骨
stapes / stirrup / stirrup bone;

deng gu fan she 鐙骨反射
stapedial reflex;

di4 ting 諦聽
listen attentively;

dong4 ren er mu 動人耳目
make one's ears and eyes tingle;

dong ting 動聽
pleasing to the ear || interesting to listen to; moving; pleasant to listen to;

duo1 jian duo wen 多見多聞
experienced;

duo ting shao shuo 多聽少說
keep your mouth shut and your ears open / swift to hear, slow to speak;

duo wen duo jian 多聞多見
widely experienced // have seen it all / have seen the elephant;

duo yan guo er 多言聒耳
make a din in one's ears;

e4 xing wai er dao yan 惡性外耳道炎
malignant otitis externa;

er3 耳
(1) ear || auris;
(2) ears / flaps;

er an mo 耳按摩
otomassage;

er ao 耳凹
ear pit;

er ban 耳斑
ear plaque;

er bei 耳背
cloth-eared / hard of hearing || cloth ears;

er bi hou ke 耳鼻喉科
otolaryngological department;

er bi suo 耳閉鎖
aural atresia;

er bian feng 耳邊風
(1) a matter of no concern / words of no importance;
(2) sth one hears but pays little attention

to || flit by like a breeze; go in at one ear and out at the other; like water off a duck's back;

er bian xi yu 耳邊細語
whisper in one's ear;

er bin si mo 耳鬢廝磨
intimate and innocent playmates || close association during childhood; ear to ear and temple to temple — have always been together; have close childhood friendship;

er bing 耳病
disease of the ear / otopathy;
re dai er bing 熱帶耳病
tropical ear;
you yong chi er bing 游泳池耳病
tank ear;
you yong zhe er bing 游泳者耳病
swimmer's ear;

er bing xing xuan yun 耳病性眩暈
aural vertigo;

er bu shen jing tong 耳部神經痛
otic neuralgia;

er chang 耳長
ear length;

er chi 耳匙
ear spoon || auriscalpium;

er chu xue 耳出血
otorrhagia;

er chuang 耳窗
ear window;

er chui 耳垂
earlobe || lobe of the ear; lobule; lobulus auriculae;

er cong mu ming 耳聰目明
able to see and hear clearly / have good ears and eyes || can hear and see well; have good sight and an exquisite sense of hearing; have sharp ears and eyes — have a clear understanding of the situation; quick at hearing and seeing;

er da shen jing 耳大神經
great auricular nerve / nervus auricularis magnus;

er dao 耳道
auditory meatus || duct; meatus acusticus;
wai er dao 外耳道
external auditory meatus;

er dao bi he 耳道閉合
otocleisis;

er dao ruan gu 耳道軟骨
meatal cartilage;

er di 耳底
inner part of the ear;

er di gu 耳底骨
basiotic;

er dian 耳點
auriculare / broca's point;

er duo 耳朵
ear;
la er duo 拉耳朵
drag by the ear / pull by the ear;
ning er duo 擰耳朵
pinch sb's ear;
wa er duo 挖耳朵
cleanse one's ears / pick one's ear;

er duo chang 耳朵長
capable of hearing much;

er duo fa shao 耳朵發燒
the ears burnt;

er duo jian 耳朵尖
have sharp ears;

er duo ling min 耳朵靈敏
have a quick ear;

er duo qing zhong 耳朵青腫
have a thick ear;

er duo ruan 耳朵軟
soft ear // susceptible to flattery;

er duo weng ming 耳朵嗡鳴
buzzing in one's ears;

er feng 耳風
hearsay;

er gao 耳高
auricular height;

er gen qing jing 耳根清靜
peace to one's ears || hear no more about; free from noise and dirt; there will be no more complaints; there will be peace to one's ears;

er gou 耳垢
cerumen / earwax;

er gu 耳骨
ear bones / otica;

er gu 耳鼓
eardrum / tympanum;

er guang 耳光
a box on the ear / a slap on the face;
da er guang 打耳光
box sb's ears;
shan er guang 搧耳光
box the ear;

er guo 耳廓
auricle / pinna;

er guo fan she 耳廓反射
auricle reflex;

er hong mian chi 耳紅面赤
be flushed / red in the face;

er ji 耳肌
auricularis;

er ji shui 耳積水
hydrotis;

er jie 耳癤
ear furuncle;

er jie 耳界
earshot / hearing distance;

er jie qing jing 耳界清淨
free from noise / quiet;

er ke 耳科
otology;

er ke 耳殼
auricle / concha;

er kong 耳孔
earhole;

er la 耳蠟
earwax;

er li 耳力
audition / power of hearing / sense of hearing;

er ling xin yue 耳聆心悅
both the ears and mind are pleased;

er ling yan jian 耳靈眼尖
can hear and see well // quick of hearing and sight;

er liu nong 耳流膿
discharging ear;

er long 耳聾
deaf;
fei xian tian xing er long 非先天性耳聾
adventitious deafness;
shen jing xing er long 神經性耳聾
nerve deafness;
zao sheng xing er long 噪聲性耳聾
deafness due to noise;

er long mu xuan 耳聾目眩
become both dazed and deaf;

er long yan hua 耳聾眼花
deafness and failing eyesight / one's eyes are faded and one's ears deaf;

er long yan xia 耳聾眼瞎
deaf and blind;

er lou 耳漏
otorrhea;

er lun 耳輪
helix;

er mao 耳毛
barbula hirsi / tragus;

er men 耳門
earlap / external ear / pinna;

er ming 耳鳴
tinnitus || a drumming in the ears; aurium; buzzing in the ears; have a ringing sound in the ear; have a singing in one's ear; one's ears are singing; ring in the ear;
bo dong xing er ming 搏動性耳鳴
pulsatile tinnitus;
zhen dong xing er ming 振動性耳鳴
vibratory tinnitus;

er ming mu xuan 耳鳴目眩
one's ears rang and spots danced before one's eyes;

er mo 耳膜
eardrum;

耳 *Ear*

er mu 耳目
(1) what one sees and hears;
(2) ears and eyes / one who spies for sb else;

er mu bi se 耳目閉塞
ignorant / ill-informed / uninformed;

er mu bu ling 耳目不靈
ill-informed;

er mu qing jing 耳目清靜
free from noise and dirt;

er mu suo ji 耳目所及
from all one hears and sees / from what one knows / from what one sees and hears;

er mu yi xin 耳目一新
find everything fresh and new || all is new before one's eyes 一 a great change for the better; find oneself in an entirely new world; refreshing;

er mu zhao zhang 耳目昭彰
known to all / universally known;

er mu zhi yu 耳目之娛
pleasures of the senses;

er mu zhong duo 耳目眾多
all ears and eyes || eyes and ears everywhere; too many people around;

er nang 耳囊
ear vesicle / otic capsule / statocyst;

er nei liu nong 耳內流膿
purulent ear;

er ping 耳屏
tragus;

er re 耳熱
have a burning sensation in the ears / have burning ears;

er ru mu ran 耳濡目染
be coloured by what one sees and hears constantly / be influenced by what one sees and hears;

er ruan xin huo 耳軟心活
credulous and pliable / easily influenced by others;

er sai 耳塞
cerumen / earwax;

er shen jing 耳神經
auricularis;

er sheng 耳生
strange-sounding / unfamiliar to the ear;

er shi 耳食
taste food with ears;

er shi bu hua 耳食不化
hear instruction without comprehending its import / hearing without digesting what is heard;

er shi 耳屎
cerumen / earwax;

er shi mu ting 耳視目聽
use one's ears to see and one's eyes to hear;

er shu 耳熟
familiar to the ear / sound familiar;

er shu neng xiang 耳熟能詳
what is familiar to the ears is on the tip of one's tongue / what has been often heard can be retold in detail;

er shu 耳屬
eavesdrop / listen with effort and attention;

er shun zhi nian 耳順之年
sixty years of age;

er ti mian ming 耳提面命
give earnest exhortations || pour exhortations into sb's ears; give orders personally; give personal advice sincerely; instruct with authority and sincerity; talk to sb like a Dutch uncle;

er ting ba fang 耳聽八方
extraordinarily alert;

er tong 耳痛
earache / otalgia // have a pain in the ear;
ji fa xing er tong 繼發性耳痛
secondary otalgia;
jian xie xing er tong 間歇性耳痛
otalgia intermittens;
ya xing er tong 牙性耳痛
otalgia dentalis;

er wen 耳聞
hear about / hear of // by hearsy / through hearsay;

er wen bu ru mu jian 耳聞不如目見
seeing for oneself is better than hearing from others / seeing is believing / what we hear is not as reliable as what we see;

er wen mu du 耳聞目睹
what one sees and hears || an eye finds more truth than two ears; fall under one's observation; hear with one's own ears and see with one's own eyes; hear with the ears is not so good as to see with the eyes; hearsay is not equal to observation; see and hear for oneself; seeing for oneself is better than hearing from others; seeing is believing; what is heard and seen;

er wen wei xu, yan jian wei shi 耳聞為虛，眼見為實
hearing can be vague, but seeing is definite || one eyewitness is better than two hearsays; one eyewitness is worth ten earwitness; seeing is believing; what you hear about may be false, what you see is true; what you see is real, what you hear are empty words; words are but wind, but seeing's believing;

er wo 耳蝸
cochlea;

er xi rou 耳息肉
aural polyp / otopolyus;

er xia xian 耳下腺
parotid gland;

er xia xian yan 耳下腺炎
parotitis;

er xue guan yan 耳血管炎
angiotitis;

er yan 耳炎
otitis;
hang kong xing er yan 航空性耳炎
aviation otitis;
ji sheng chong xing er yan 寄生蟲性耳炎
parasitic otitis;
jie xing er yan 癤性耳炎
furuncular otitis;
qi ya xing er yan 氣壓性耳炎
barotitis;
quan er yan 全耳炎
panotitis;
tuo xie xing er yan 脱屑性耳炎
otitis desquamativa;

er yan guan 耳咽管
auditory tube / ear canal / eustachian canal / eustachian tube;

er yang 耳癢
ear itching / itchy ear;

er yi 耳溢
otorrhea;

er ying hua zheng 耳硬化症
otosclerosis / otospongiosis;

er yu 耳語
whisper / whisper in sb's ear;

er yuan xing nao mo yan 耳原性腦膜炎
otogenic meningitis;

er yuan xing nao nong zhong 耳原性腦膿腫
otogenic brain abscess;

er yuan xing shen jing ma zui 耳原性神經麻醉
otogenic facial paralysis;

er zhi 耳脂
earwax;

er zhi 耳治
hear;

er zhu 耳珠
tragus;

fa1 kui zhen long 發聵振聾
awaken the deaf / awaken the unhearing and rouse the deaf / enlighten the benighted;

fa long zhen kui 發聾振聵
awaken the deaf / enlighten the benighted / rouse the deaf and the unhearing;

fa meng zhen kui 發蒙振聵
awaken the blind and rouse the deaf / enlighten the benighted / enlighten the blind and stir the deaf / make a deaf man hear and a blind man see;

fang mian da er 方面大耳
a square face with large ears / a handsome man have a dignified face and big ears;

fei1 xian tian xing er long 非先天性耳聾
adventitious deafness;

fei2 tou da er 肥頭大耳
large head and big ears — signs of a

prosperous man;

fu2 er 拂耳
grating on the ear;

fu3 shou tie er 俯首帖耳
submissive and obedient || all obedience and servility; docile and obedient; docilely obey; in complete obedience; obey with servility; servile like a dog; subservient to;

fu4 zhi wang wen 付之罔聞
give no heed to / turn a deaf ear to;

fu4 er 附耳
move close to sb's ear / whisper in one's ear;

fu er di yu 附耳低語
whisper in sb's ear;

fu er er yan 附耳而言
put one's mouth to sb's ear and say sth / speak into sb's ear;

fu er shou ji 附耳授計
whisper into sb's ear certain secret orders;

ge2 qiang you er 隔墻有耳
walls have ears / pitchers have ears;

gong1 neng xing ting li sang shi 功能性聽力喪失
functional hearing loss;

gu1 lou gua wen 孤陋寡聞
ignorant;

gu1 wang ting zhi 姑妄聽之
see no harm in hearing what sb has to say || just listen leisurely and by no means seriously; just listen to sth without taking it seriously; let him talk and let's just listen; take sth for what it is worth; take sth with a grain of salt; to hear is not to believe;

gu wang yan zhi 姑妄言之
just talk for the sake of talking || just talk for talking's sake; just venture an opinion; tell sb sth for what it is worth;

gu3 xing nei er dao 骨性內耳道
bony internal auditory meatus;

gu xing wai er dao 骨性外耳道
bony external auditory meatus;

gu3 mo 鼓膜
eardrum / tympanic membrance;

gu mo yan 鼓膜炎
inflammation of the tympanic membrance / myringitis;
mei jun xing gu mo yan 霉菌性鼓膜炎
mycomyringitis;

gu shi 鼓室
tympanic cavity;

gua3 jian shao wen 寡見少聞
have limited knowledge / have seen few and heard little // ignorant and ill-informed;

gua wen 寡聞
having little knowledge;

guan4 er 貫耳
hear;

gui4 er jian mu 貴耳賤目
value what one hears and despise what one sees || easily accept others' words and decline to see with one's own eyes; trust one's ears rather than one's eyes — rely on hearsay;

guo1 聒
clamorous;

guo er 聒耳
din in sb's ears // offensive to the ear;

guo guo 聒聒
clamorous / noisy;

guo rao 聒擾
make a din;

guo xu 聒絮
keep talking noisily;

guo zao 聒噪
noisy / uproarious;

guo4 er zhi yan, bu ke ting xin 過耳之言，不可聽信
hearsay is not reliable / words overheard are not to be trusted;

hai4 ren ting wen 駭人聽聞
appalling / astounding / frightful to the ear / horrid / horrifying / shocking / startling / terrifying;

han3 wen 罕聞
seldom heard of;

hang2 kong xing er yan 航空性耳炎
aviation otitis;

hang kong xing zhong er yan 航空性中耳炎
aerotitis media;

hao3 ting 好聽
(1) pleasant to hear / pleasant to listen to / pleasing to the ear;
(2) high-sounding;

hu1 wen 忽聞
hear suddenly;

huai4 si xing wai er yan 壞死性外耳炎
necrotizing otitis externa;

huan4 ting 幻聽
phonism;

ji2 xing hua nong xing zhong er yan 急性化膿性中耳炎
acute suppurative otitis media;

ji xing ka ta xing zhong er yan 急性卡他性中耳炎
acute catarrhal otitis media;

ji xing wai er yan 急性外耳炎
acute otitis externa;

ji4 sheng chong xing er yan 寄生蟲性耳炎
parasitic otitis;

ji4 fa xing er tong 繼發性耳痛
secondary otalgia;

jian1 ting 兼聽
listen to both sides;

jian1 ting 監聽
monitor;

jian4 xie xing er tong 間歇性耳痛
otalgia intermittens;

jiao1 tou jie er 交頭接耳
speak in each other's ears / whisper to each other || bill and coo; exchange confidential whispers; head to head; heads together and ears stretched out; secret conversations; talk confidentially; talk mouth to ear; whisper into each other's ears; whispering;

jie1 xing er yan 癤性耳炎
furuncular otitis;

jie2 he xing zhong er yan 結核性中耳炎
tuberculosis otitis media;

jin3 ting 謹聽
listen attentively;

jing1 shen xing long 精神性聾
functional deafness;

jing4 ting 靜聽
listen quietly;

jiu1 er duo 揪耳朵
hold sb by the ear / seize another's ear;

ju2 xian xing wai er yan 局限性外耳炎
circumscribed otitis externa;

kou3 bu jie er bu ting 口不捷耳不聽
slow of speech and hard of hearing;

kou er xiang chuan 口耳相傳
teach orally;

kui4 聵
deaf / hard of hearing;

la1 chang er duo 拉長耳朵
prick up one's ears;

la er duo 拉耳朵
drag by the ear / pull by the ear;

lao3 nian long 老年聾
presbycusis;

lao nian xing long 老年性聾
presbycusis;

le4 wen 樂聞
happy to hear about;

liang3 er bu wen chuang wai shi 兩耳不聞窗外事
be unaware of the outside world;

liang er sai dou 兩耳塞豆
close one's ears to anything / shut one's ears to sth / turn a deaf ear to;

liang er shi cong 兩耳失聰
stone-deaf;

liang er tong hong 兩耳通紅
one's ears turn red;

liao2 rao er ji 繚繞耳際
ringing in sb's ears;

ling2 聆
hear / listen;

ling jiao 聆教
listen to one's instructions;

ling qu 聆取
listen to;

ling ting 聆聽
listen to;

ling xi 聆悉
hear / learn;

long2 聾
deaf / hard of hearing;
chuan dao xing long 傳導性聾
conduction deafness / transmission deafness;
jing shen xing long 精神性聾
functional deafness;
lao nian xing long 老年性聾
presbycusis;
mi lu xing long 迷路性聾
labyrinthine deafness;
pi zhi xing long 皮質性聾
cortical deafness;
pian ce long 偏側聾
hemianacusia;
qi zhi xing long 器質性聾
organic deafness;
quan long 全聾
anakusis;
shen jing xing long 神經性聾
nerve deafness;
zhong nao xing long 中腦性聾
midbrain deafness;
zhong du xing long 中毒性聾
toxic deafness;

long kui 聾聵
deaf;

long ya 聾啞
deaf and dumb / deaf-mute;

long ya zheng 聾啞症
deaf mutism / partimutism;

long zheng 聾症
deafness;

long zi 聾子
deaf person;

long zi fang pao — san le 聾子放炮 —— 散了
a deaf person firing a cannon — no explosion;

ma3 er dong feng 馬耳東風
in at one ear and out at the other // pay no attention to what one says / take no heed to;

man3 er 滿耳
have one's ears filled with;

man4 xing ka ta xing zhong er yan 慢性卡他性中耳炎
chronic catarrhal otitis media;

man xing hua nong xing zhong er yan 慢性化膿性中耳炎
chronic suppurative otitis media;

mei2 ting ti 沒聽提
pay no attention to / take no notice of;

mei2 jun xing gu mo yan 霉菌性鼓膜炎
mycomyringitis;

mi2 lu xing long 迷路性聾
labyrinthine deafness;

mi lu yan 迷路炎
labyrinthitis;
xi jun xing mi lu yan 細菌性迷路炎
bacterial labyrinthitis;
zhong du xing mi lu yan 中毒性迷路炎
toxic labyrinthitis;

mi2 man xing wai er dao yan 彌漫性外耳道炎
diffused otitis externa;

mi man xing wai er yan 彌漫性外耳炎
diffuse otitis externa;

nan2 ting 難聽
grate on the ear // unpleasant to hear;

nei4 er 內耳
inner ear / internal ear;

nei er dao 內耳道
internal auditory meatus;
gu xing nei er dao 骨性內耳道
bony internal auditory meatus;

nei er mei zheng 內耳霉症
otomycosis;

nei er men 內耳門
internal acoustic pore;

nei er yan 內耳炎
inner ear infection / labyrinthitis / otitis interna;

ni4 er 逆耳
grate on the ear / offend the ear;

ni er li xing 逆耳利行
faithful words offend the ear but are good for improving one's conduct / honest advice, though unpleasant to the ear, benefit conduct;

nian2 lian xing zhong er yan 黏連性中耳炎
adhesive otitis media;

nie4 聶
whisper into another's ear;

ning2 er duo 擰耳朵
pinch sb's ear;

nuan3 er 暖耳
earmuffs;

pang2 ting 旁聽
audit;

pang2 ting 傍聽
audit;

pi2 zhi xing long 皮質性聾
cortical deafness;

pian1 ce long 偏側聾
hemianacusia;

pian ting pian xin 偏聽偏信
heed and believe in one side // biased;

qi2 wen 奇聞
sth unheard of;

qi4 ya xing er yan 氣壓性耳炎
barotitis;

qi ya xing zhong er yan 氣壓性中耳炎
baro-otitis media;

qi4 zhi xing long 器質性聾
organic deafness;

qia4 wen 洽聞
learned / widely read;

qian2 suo wei wen 前所未聞
have never heard of before;

qian ting 前庭
vestibule;

qian ting fan she 前庭反射
vestibular reflex;

qian ting gan jue 前庭感覺
vestibular sense;

qian ting yan 前庭炎
vestibulitis;

qie4 ting 竊聽
bug / eavesdrop / intercept / overhear / tap / tune in / wiretap;

qin1 er 親耳
with one's own ears;

qin er suo wen 親耳所聞
hear it oneself / hear with one's own ears;

qing1 ting 清聽
your kind listening;

qing1 er er ting 傾耳而聽
lend an attentive ear to / listen attentively / listen with all one's ears;

qing ting 傾聽
(1) listen attentively to || all ears for; give an ear to; give ear to; hear out; incline one's ear to; lend an ear to; listen carefully; pin one's ears back; prick up one's ears;
(2) turn a willing ear to;

qing ting yi jian 傾聽意見
listen attentively to different opinions;

qiu1 feng guo er 秋風過耳
turn a deaf ear to / like an autumn breeze passing the ear || like wind whistling past one's ears; of no importance; pay no heed to; unheeded like a passing autumnal breeze;

quan2 er yan 全耳炎
inflammation of the entire ear / panotitis;

quan long 全聾
anakusis;

re4 dai er bing 熱帶耳病
tropical ear;

ren2 xiao er jian 人小耳尖
little pitchers have long ears;

ru2 feng guo er 如風過耳
turn a deaf ear to;

ru lei guan er 如雷貫耳
it strikes one's ears like the roar of thunder || like the sound of thunder in one's ears; reverberate like thunder;

ru4 er 入耳
(1) hear;
(2) pleasing to the ear;

ruan3 gu xing wai er dao 軟骨性外耳道
cartilaginous external auditory meatus;

sai1 er 塞耳
aurula;

sai er bu wen 塞耳不聞
ignore / turn a deaf ear to;

shan1 er guang 搧耳光
box the ear;

shen2 jing xing er long 神經性耳聾
nerve deafness;

shen jing xing long 神經性聾
nerve deafness;

shi1 ting jue 失聽覺
auditory agnosia;

shi2 long 石聾
stone-deaf;

shou1 ting 收聽
listen in / tune in;

shu4 er qing ting 豎耳傾聽
keep one's ears flapping;

shu qi er duo 豎起耳朵
prick up one's ears;

shun4 er 順耳
pleasant to the ear / pleasing to the ear;

song3 dong shi ting 聳動視聽
create a sensation;

song er qing ting 聳耳傾聽
prick up one's ears;

song ren er mu 聳人耳目
arrest public attention / deliberately exaggerate so as to create a sensation;

song ren ting wen 聳人聽聞
arrest public attention || cause false alarm; electrify; make a sensation; sensational;

song ting 聳聽
alarm others with sth sensational / stimulate others;

su2 er 俗耳
vulgar ears;

su4 wen 素聞
have been frequently told / have often heard;

suo3 wen suo jian 所聞所見
what one sees and hears;

suo3 wen 瑣聞
bits of news / scraps of information;

tan4 ting 探聽
investigate secretly / try to find out;

tan ting mi mi 探聽秘密
pry a secret out of sb;

tan ting xiao xi 探聽消息
make inquiries about sb or sth;

tan ting xu shi 探聽虛實
try to ascertain the strength of the enemy;

tan xi 探悉
learn after investigating;

tang2 niao bing er 糖尿病耳
diabetic ear;

tao1 er duo 掏耳朵
clean the ears / pick the ears;

ti1 er 擿耳
cleanse the ears – listen attentively;

tie1 er 帖耳
droop one's ears like a dog — submissive;

tie1 er 貼耳
ready to listen;

ting1 聽
(1) hear / listen / listen to;
(2) do as / follow / heed / obey;
(3) allow / let;

ting ban 聽斑
acoustic spot;

ting ban 聽板
auditory plate;

ting bu de 聽不得
should not be heard;

ting bu jian 聽不見
cannot hear // inaudible;

ting bu jin 聽不進
close one's ears / refuse to listen to;

ting bu ming bai 聽不明白
cannot understand;

ting bu qing 聽不清
unable to hear clearly / unable to hear distinctly;

ting cong 聽從
comply with / obey || accept; heed; listen and follow; listen to;

ting cong diao qian 聽從調遣
accept an assignment;

ting cong fen fu 聽從吩咐
at sb's beck and call // do sb's bidding;

ting cuo 聽錯
hear incorrectly;

ting dao 聽到
hear / listen in || meet the ear; notice;

ting dao 聽道
auditory canal / ear canal;

ting dao ruan gu 聽道軟骨
cartilage of acoustic meatus;

ting de chu shen 聽得出神
be completely absorbed / listen with an open mouth;

ting de jian de 聽得見的
actually heard / audible / capable of being heard;

ting de ru shen 聽得入神
completely absorbed;

ting dong 聽懂
take / understand;

ting du bu neng 聽讀不能
aphemesthesia;

ting er bu wen 聽而不聞
hear but pay no attention / hear without understanding / listen but not hear / turn a deaf ear to;

ting fan she 聽反射
auditory reflex;

ting guan 聽管
auditory canal;

ting guan 聽慣
get used to hearing;

ting hua 聽話
(1) obedient;
(2) do as one is told;

ting hua ting sheng, luo gu ting yin 聽話聽聲，鑼鼓聽音
when you listen to someone talk, listen to their tone || the words are the criterion of the man; when you listen, listen to speaker's tone of voice;

ting hua ting yin 聽話聽音
when you listen, listen to speaker's tone of voice || listen for the meaning behind sb's words; when you hear people talk, listen to their tone;

ting jian 聽見
catch / hear // audible;

ting jian feng, jiu shi yu 聽見風，就是雨
catch at shadows / run after a shadow;

ting jiang 聽講
attend a lecture / listen to a talk;

ting jue 聽覺
auditory sense / sense of hearing;
shi ting jue 失聽覺
auditory agnosia;

ting jue bu liang 聽覺不良
hearing defect;

ting jue chi dun 聽覺遲鈍
bradyacusia / dullness of hearing;

ting jue fan she 聽覺反射
acoustic reflex;

ting jue guo min 聽覺過敏
abnormal acuteness of hearing / hyperacousia;

ting jue jian tui 聽覺減退
hypacusia / partial loss of hearing;

ting jue que xian 聽覺缺陷
hearing defect;

ting jue min rui 聽覺敏銳
oxyecoia;

ting jun yi xi hua, sheng du shi nian shu 聽君一席話，勝讀十年書
I profit more from one consultation with you than from ten years of reading;

ting ke 聽課
(1) attend a lecture / sit in on a class;
(2) visit a class / visit classroom;

ting li 聽力
(1) sense of hearing;
(2) aural comprehension;
chao ren de ting li 超人的聽力
clairaudience / the power to hear sounds beyond ordinary experience;

ting li jian tui 聽力減退
hypoacusis / partial loss of hearing;

ting li sang shi 聽力喪失
hearing loss;
chuan dao xing ting li sang shi 傳導性聽力喪失
conductive hearing loss / transmission hearing loss;
gong neng xing ting li sang shi 功能性聽力喪失
functional hearing loss;

ting neng 聽能
sense of hearing;

ting qi yan er guan qi xing 聽其言而觀其行
listen to what a man says and watch what he does ‖ hear their words and judge them by their deeds; hear what a man says and see how he acts; judge people by their deeds, not by their words; listen to a man's words and watch his deeds;

ting qi lai 聽起來
ring / sound;

ting qing 聽清
make out;

ting qu 聽取
hear / listen to;

ting shuo 聽説
be told / it is said;

ting wen 聽聞
(1) hear;
(2) what one hears;

ting xie 聽寫
dictate;

ting xin 聽信
(1) wait for information;
(2) believe what one hears / listen to and believe;

ting xin chan yan 聽信讒言
lend a ready ear to slander;

ting xin yao yan 聽信謠言
listen to and believe rumours;

tou1 ting 偷聽
bug / eavesdrop / listen in / listen in on / overhear / tap / tune in;

tou2 yun er ming 頭暈耳鳴
dizziness and tinnitus;

tuo1 xie xing er yan 脱屑性耳炎
otitis desquamativa;

wa1 er duo 挖耳朵
cleanse one's ears / pick one's ear;

wai4 er 外耳
external ear / outer ear;

wai er dao 外耳道
external auditory meatus;
gu xing wai er dao 骨性外耳道
bony external auditory meatus;
ruan gu xing wai er dao 軟骨性外耳道
cartilaginous external auditory meatus;

wai er dao fan she 外耳道反射
external auditory meatus reflex;

wai er dao jie 外耳道癤
furuncle of the external auditory canal;

wai er dao yan 外耳道炎
otitis externa;
e xing wai er dao yan 惡性外耳道炎
malignant otitis externa;
mi man xing wai er dao yan 彌漫性外耳道炎
diffused otitis externa;

wai er dao yi wu 外耳道異物
foreign body in the external auditory canal;

wai er kong 外耳孔
external auditory foramen;

wai er men 外耳門
external acoustic pore / porus acusticus externus;

wai er shi zhen 外耳濕疹
eczema of the external ear;

wai er yan 外耳炎
otitis externa;
huai si xing wai er yan 壞死性外耳炎
necrotizing otitis externa;
ji xing wai er yan 急性外耳炎
acute otitis externa;
jie xing wai er yan 癤性外耳炎
furuncular otitis externa;
ju xian xing wai er yan 局限性外耳炎
circumscribed otitis externa;
mi man xing wai er yan 彌漫性外耳炎
diffuse otitis externa;

wei3 wei dong ting 娓娓動聽
pleasing to the ear || rattle out the most attractive rhetoric; smooth-spoken; speak with absorbing interest; talk in an impressive way;

wen2 聞
(1) hear;
(2) learn / understand;

wen bao 聞報
hear it reported / learn of;

wen feng sang dan 聞風喪膽
become terror-stricken at the news;

wen feng tao cuan 聞風逃竄
run away upon hearing the news;

wen feng xiang ying 聞風響應
hear the news and rise up in response;

wen jian 聞見
have learned by hearing or seeing;

wen ming 聞名
(1) hear of sb's name;
(2) famous;

wen ming bu ru jian mian 聞名不如見面
knowing sb by name is not as good as meeting him in person;

wen ming quan guo 聞名全國
well known throughout the country;

wen ming si fang 聞名四方
become famous throughout the land;

wen ming tian xia 聞名天下
known far and wide / world-famous;

wen suo wei wen 聞所未聞
be unheard of || have never even heard of it; have never heard of such a thing; hear of sth extremely unusual;

wen xun 聞訊
hear the news / learn of the news;

wen yi zhi shi 聞一知十
hear one point and know the ten sequences / infer the whole matter after hearing but one point;

wen zhi 聞知
hear / know from others / learn;

wu2 er 無耳
anotia / congenital absence of the ear;

wu3 er 忤耳
grate on the ear;

wu3 zhe er duo 捂着耳朵
cover one's ears;

wu4 ting 誤聽
mishear;

xi3 er gong ting 洗耳恭聽
strain one's ears to listen || be all ears; bend an ear; clean one's ears; cock one's ears to listen; one is all ears; listen respectfully; listen with all one's ears; prick up one's ears; with open ears;

xi3 wen le jian 喜聞樂見
delighted to hear and see / like to hear and see / love to see and hear / receive with pleasure;

xi4 jun xing mi lu yan 細菌性迷路炎
bacterial labyrinthitis;

xian1 sheng duo ren 先聲奪人
overawe others by a display of one's strength;

xiao3 er 小耳
congenital small ears / microtia;

xiao3 wen 謏聞
known only to a small circle;

xin1 xi 欣悉
delighted to hear / delighted to learn;

xuan4 er zhi sheng 炫耳之聲
words that brighten the ears / words that make you sit up and notice;

ya2 xing er tong 牙性耳痛
otalgia dentalis;

yan3 er bu wen 掩耳不聞
close one's ear to / stop one's ears to / shut one's ears to / turn a deaf ear to;

yan er dao ling 掩耳盜鈴
close up one's own ears and steal a bell || bury one's head in the sand; plug one's ears while stealing a bell — deceive oneself; run away from one's own shadow; stuff the ears when stealing a bell — self-deceit; the cat shuts its eyes when stealing cream; the cat shuts its eyes while it steals cream;

yao3 er duo 咬耳朵
whisper / whisper in sb's ear;

yi1 er jin yi er chu 一耳進一耳出
in one ear and out the other // not pay attention to;

yi ji er guang 一記耳光
a slap in the face / box sb's ear / give sb a box on the ear / plant a blow on sb's ear;

yi shou yan jin tian xia ren er mu 一手掩盡天下人耳目
hide from public knowledge the errors committed by sb;

yi xin er mu 一新耳目
present a new appearance;

yi zhi er duo jin, yi zhi er duo chu 一隻耳朵進，一隻耳朵出
go in one ear and out the other // not pay attention to;

yi3 er dai mu 以耳代目
depend on hearsay instead of seeing for oneself || rely upon hearsay instead of seeing for oneself — understanding of sth not from personal investigation but from hearsay;

yi zheng shi ting 以正視聽
ensure a correct understanding of the facts / in order to ensure a correct understanding of the facts || so as to clarify matters to the public; so that the public may know the facts;

yin3 ting 隱聽
eavesdrop / keep quiet and listen;

you2 er duo 油耳朵
ceruminosis / excessive formation of cerumen;

you2 yong chi er bing 游泳池耳病
tank ear;

you yong zhe er bing 游泳者耳病
swimmer's ear;

you2 yan zai er 猶言在耳
ring in one's ears;

you4 long you ya 又聾又啞
deaf and dumb;

yue4 er 悅耳
easy on the ear / mellifluous / pleasing to the ear / sweet-sounding;

yue er dong ting 悅耳動聽
easy on the ear / melodious;

zao4 sheng xing er long 噪聲性耳聾
deafness due to noise;

zha1 er duo 扎耳朵
grate // unpleasant to the ear;

zha4 ting zhi xia 乍聽之下
at first hearing;

zha wen 乍聞
suddenly learn for the first time;

zhao1 feng er 招風耳
cauliflower ears / jug ears / protruding ears;

zhen1 gu 砧骨
anvil;

zhen1 ting 偵聽
intercept;

zhen4 dong xing er ming 振動性耳鳴
vibratory tinnitus;

zhen long fa kui 振聾發聵
rouse the deaf and awaken the unhearing || awaken the deaf; enlighten the benighted; make a deaf man hear and a blind man see; open the ears of the deaf and the eyes of the blind — enlighten another's ignorance;

zhen4 er yu long 震耳欲聾
deafening / ear-shattering || ear-splitting; enough to wake the dead; fit to wake the dead; make the ear tingle; raise the roof; split sb's ear; there is a deafening din of;

zhi1 leng 支愣
prick up one's ears;

zhi2 er er ting 植耳而聽
prick up one's ears to listen — listen attentively;

zhi4 ruo wang wen 置若罔聞
disregard completely / pay no heed to / turn a deaf ear to;

zhong1 er 中耳
middle ear;

zhong er ai 中耳癌
cancer of middle ear;

zhong er gu shi 中耳鼓室
mesotympanum;

zhong er yan 中耳炎
inflammation of the middle ear / otitis media;

hang kong xing zhong er yan 航空性中耳炎
aerotitis media;

ji xing hua nong xing zhong er yan 急性化膿性中耳炎
acute suppurative otitis media;

ji xing ka ta xing zhong er yan 急性卡他性中耳炎
acute catarrhal otitis media;

jie he xing zhong er yan 結核性中耳炎
tuberculosis otitis media;

man xing hua nong xing zhong er yan 慢性化膿性中耳炎
chronic suppurative otitis media;

man xing ka ta xing zhong er yan 慢性卡他性中耳炎
chronic catarrhal otitis media;

nian lian xing zhong er yan 黏連性中耳炎
adhesive otitis media;

qi ya xing zhong er yan 氣壓性中耳炎
baro-otitis media;

zhong nao xing long 中腦性聾
midbrain deafness;

zhong ting 中聽
agreeable to the hearer / pleasant to the ear;

zhong4 du xing long 中毒性聾
toxic deafness;

zhong du xing mi lu yan 中毒性迷路炎
toxic labyrinthitis;

zhong1 yan ni er 忠言逆耳
honest advice is often grating on the ear;

zhua1 er nao sai 抓耳撓腮
scratch one's ears / tweak one's ears and scratch one's cheeks;

zhuan1 xin qing ting 專心傾聽
be all ears / listen attentively / listen intently;

zhuan3 囀
pleasing to the ear;

zhuang1 long zuo sha 裝聾作傻
pretend to be ignorant of sth / pretend to know nothing and hear nothing;

zhuang long zuo ya 裝聾作啞
play deaf and dumb / pretend ignorance ‖ pretend to be deaf and dumb; pretend to be ignorant of sth; pretend to hear and know nothing; sham Abraham;

zi4 da er guang 自打耳光
box one's own ears / contradict oneself / slap one's own face;

zuo3 er ru, you er chu 左耳入，右耳出
go in one ear and out of the other;

Fei 肺 Lung

bai2 fei 白肺
white lung;

bai3 ri ke 百日咳
chain cough / pertussis / whooping cough;

bei4 guo qi 背過氣
gasp for breath // out of breath;

bian4 ying xing xiao chuan bing 變應性哮喘病
allergic asthma;

bing3 qi 屏氣
bate one's breath / hold one's breath;

bing xi 屏息
catch one's breath / hold one's breath;

chen2 fei 塵肺
mason's lung / pneumokoniosis;

chu1 qi jie he bing 初期結核病
pretuberculosis;

chuan2 ran xing fei dian xing fei yan 傳染性非典型肺炎
infectious atypical pneumonia;

chuan3 喘
(1) breathe heavily / gasp for breath / pant;
(2) asthma;

chuan chuan qi 喘喘氣
catch one's breath / pause for breath;

chuan qi 喘氣
gasp / pant;

chuan xi 喘息
(1) gasp for breath / pant / puff / wheeze;
(2) breather / breathing spell / respite;

chuan xi chu ding 喘息初定
(1) just as one recovers one's breath;
(2) recover from fear and confusion;

chuan xi wei ding 喘息未定
before catching one's breath / before one has a chance to catch one's breath || before one is oneself again; pant and be still out of breath;

chuan xi yu xia 喘息餘暇
breathing time;

chuan xu xu 喘吁吁
puff and blow;

chuang1 shang xing fei yan 創傷性肺炎
traumatic pneumonia;

chuang shang xing qi xiong 創傷性氣胸
traumatic pneumothorax;

chuang shang xing qi zhong 創傷性氣腫
traumatic emphysema;

fei1 dian xing jie he 非典型結核
atypical tuberculosis;

fei dian xing xing fei yan 非典型性肺炎
atypical pneumonia;

fei4 肺
lung;

ren zao fei 人造肺
aqualung;

run fei 潤肺
nourish the lung;

xin bing fei 心病肺
cardiac lung;

yi fei 宜肺
open the inhibited lung-energy;

fei ai 肺癌
cancer of the lung / lung cancer / pulmonary cancer;

fei bao 肺胞
pulmonary vesicle;

fei bing 肺病
lung ailment / lung trouble / pulmonary tuberculosis / tuberculosis;

xian zhi xing fei bing 限制性肺病
restrictive lung disease;

zhi qi guan fei bing 支氣管肺病
bronchopneumopathy;

fei bu 肺部
lung;

fei bu zhang 肺不張
atelectasis;

nian lian xing fei bu zhang 黏連性肺不張
adhesive atelectasis;

pan zhuang fei bu zhang 盤狀肺不張
patelike atelectasis;

ya po xing fei bu zhang 壓迫性肺不張
compression atelectasis;

yuan fa xing fei bu zhang 原發性肺不張
primary atelectasis;
yuan xing fei bu zhang 圓形肺不張
round atelectasis;
zu se xing fei bu zhang 阻塞性肺不張
obstructive atelectasis;

fei chang yan 肺腸炎
pneumoenteritis;

fei chen ai chen zhuo bing 肺塵埃沉着病
pneumonoconiosis chalicotica;

fei chen bing 肺塵病
pneumoconoiosis;

fei chong xue 肺充血
pulmonary congestion;

fei chu xue 肺出血
pulmonary hemorrhage;

fei di 肺底
base of the lung;

fei dian xing fei yan 非典型肺炎
atypical pneumonia / atypical pneumonitis;
chuan ran xing fei dian xing fei yan 傳染性非典型肺炎
infectious atypical pneumonia;
yuan fa xing fei dian xing fei yan 原發性非典型肺炎
primary atypical pneumonia;

fei dong mai 肺動脈
pulmonary artery;

fei dong mai ban 肺動脈瓣
pulmonary valve;

fei dong mai shuan se 肺動脈栓塞
pulmonary embolism;

fei fu 肺腑
bottom of one's heart;

fei fu zhi jiao 肺腑之交
bosom friend / deep and sincere friendship;

fei fu zhi yan 肺腑之言
speak from the bottom of one's heart || hearty talk; most reliable words; talk from the heart; the words from one's heart; words from the depths of one's heart;

fei gan 肺肝
lungs and liver;

fei geng se 肺梗塞
pulmonary impaction;

fei huai ju 肺壞疽
gangrene of the lung;

fei jian 肺尖
apex of the lung;

fei jie he 肺結核
consumption / pulmonary tuberculosis / TB / tuberculosis;

fei jie he bing 肺結核病
consumption / pulmonary tuberculosis / TB / tuberculosis;

fei jing mai 肺靜脈
pulmonary vein;

fei kuo zhang bu quan 肺擴張不全
pulmonary atelectasis;

fei lao 肺癆
consumption / phthisis / tuberculosis;

fei men 肺門
hilus of the lung;

fei men jie he 肺門結核
hilus tuberculosis;

fei men lin ba jie 肺門淋巴結
hilar lymph nodes;

fei mo 肺膜
pleura;

fei mo yan 肺膜炎
pulmonary pleurisy;

fei nong zhong 肺膿腫
lung abscess / suppuration of the lung;

fei pao 肺泡
lung alveolus;

fei pao ai 肺泡癌
alveolar carcinoma;

fei pao kong 肺泡孔
lung alveolar pores;

fei pao yan 肺泡炎
alveolitis;
bian ying xing fei pao yan 變應性肺泡炎
allergic alveolitis;

fei qi xu 肺氣虛
deficiency of lung-energy;

肺 *Lung*

fei qi zhong 肺氣腫
emphysema / pneumonectasis / pulmonary emphysema;
ju xian xing fei qi zhong 局限性肺氣腫
focal emphysema;
lao nian fei qi zhong 老年肺氣腫
senile emphysema;
mi man xing fei qi zhong 彌漫性肺氣腫
diffuse emphysema;
nang xing fei qi zhong 囊性肺氣腫
cystic emphysema;
wei suo xing fei qi zhong 萎縮性肺氣腫
atrophic emphysema;
zu se xing fei qi zhong 阻塞性肺氣腫
obstructive emphysema;

fei qie chu 肺切除
pneumonectomy / surgical removal of the lung;

fei re chuan ke 肺熱喘咳
dyspnea and cough due to lung-heat;

fei ruan gu 肺軟骨
pulmonary cartilage;

fei ruan hua 肺軟化
pneumomalacia;

fei shi 肺石
pneumolith;

fei shui zhong 肺水腫
oedema pulmonary / pulmonary oedema;
shi zhi fei shui zhong 實質肺水腫
solid pulmonary oedema;
zhen fa xing fei shui zhong 陣發性肺水腫
paroxysmal pulmonary oedema;

fei xi chong bing 肺吸蟲病
paragonimiasis;

fei yan 肺炎
pneumonia;
bai se fei yan 白色肺炎
white pneumonia / pneumonia alba;
bing du xing fei yan 病毒性肺炎
viral pneumonia;
chuang shang xing fei yan 創傷性肺炎
traumatic pneumonia;
da ye xing fei yan 大葉性肺炎
lobar pneumonia;
fei dian xing xing fei yan 非典型性肺炎
atypical pneumonia;
feng shi xing fei yan 風濕性肺炎
rheumatic pneumonia;
gan lao xing fei yan 乾酪性肺炎
caseous pneumonia;
gong nei fei yan 宮內肺炎
intrauterine pneumonia;
gong xing fei yan 汞性肺炎
mercury pneumonitis;
guo min xing fei yan 過敏性肺炎
hypersensitivity pneumonitis;
huai ju xing fei yan 壞疽性肺炎
gangrenous pneumonia;
huai si xing fei yan 壞死性肺炎
recrotising pneumonia;
ji hua xing fei yan 機化性肺炎
organizing pneumonia;
ji xing fei yan 急性肺炎
acute pneumonia;
ji fa xing fei yan 繼發性肺炎
secondary pneumonia;
jia fei yan 假肺炎
pseudopneumonia;
jie he xing fei yan 結核性肺炎
tuberculous pneumonia;
jiu du xing fei yan 酒毒性肺炎
alcoholic pneumonia;
ju xian xing fei yan 局限性肺炎
pneumonitis;
lian qiu jun xing fei yan 鏈球菌性肺炎
streptococcal pneumonia;
nian zhu jun xing fei yan 念珠菌性肺炎
candida pneumonia;
niao du zheng xing fei yan 尿毒症性肺炎
uremic pneumonitis;
rou ya zhong xing fei yan 肉芽腫性肺炎
granulomatous pneumonitis;
ru chong xing fei yan 蠕蟲性肺炎
verminous pneumonia;
shu yi xing fei yan 鼠疫性肺炎
plague pneumonia;
tan ju xing fei yan 炭疽性肺炎
anthrax pneumonia;

xi jun xing fei yan 細菌性肺炎
bacterial pneumonia;

xiao ye xing fei yan 小葉性肺炎
lobular pneumonia;

you zou xing fei yan 游走性肺炎
wandering pneumonia;

zhi qi guan fei yan 支氣管肺炎
bronchopneumonia;

zhi zhi xing fei yan 脂質性肺炎
pneumonolipidosis;

zhong yang fei yan 中央肺炎
central pneumonia;

zhong mo qi fei yan 終末期肺炎
terminal pneumonia;

zhuan yi xing fei yan 轉移性肺炎
metastatic pneumonia;

zu se xing fei yan 阻塞性肺炎
obstructive pneumonia;

fei ye 肺葉
lobe;

shang fei ye 上肺葉
upper lobe;

xia fei ye 下肺葉
lower lobe;

fei zang 肺臟
lungs;

fei zhang 肺脹
emphysema;

gong3 xing fei yan 汞性肺炎
mercury pneumonitis;

gui1 fei 硅肺
pneumosilicosis;

gui fei jie he 硅肺結核
silicotuberculosis;

guo4 min xing fei yan 過敏性肺炎
hypersensitivity pneumonitis;

hei1 fei bing 黑肺病
black lung;

hua4 tan 化痰
disperse phlegm / reduce sputum;

hua tan zhi ke 化痰止咳
disperse phlegm and prevent coughing;

huai4 ju xing fei yan 壞疽性肺炎
gangrenous pneumonia;

huai si xing fei yan 壞死性肺炎
recrotising pneumonia;

huo2 dong xing jie he 活動性結核
active tuberculosis;

ji1 hua xing fei yan 機化性肺炎
organizing pneumonia;

ji2 xing fei yan 急性肺炎
acute pneumonia;

ji4 fa xing fei yan 繼發性肺炎
secondary pneumonia;

ji fa xing jie he 繼發性結核
secondary tuberculosis;

jia3 fei yan 假肺炎
pseudopneumonia;

jia xing qi zhong 假性氣腫
false emphysema;

jian4 pi yi fei 健脾益肺
strengthening spleen and tonifying lung;

jie2 he 結核
consumption / TB / tuberculosis;

bo san xing jie he 播散性結核
disseminated tuberculosis;

fei dian xing jie he 非典型結核
atypical tuberculosis;

fei jie he 肺結核
consumption / TB / tuberculosis / pulmonary tuberculosis;

fei men jie he 肺門結核
hilus tuberculosis;

gu jie he 骨結核
bone tuberculosis;

gui fei jie he 硅肺結核
silicotuberculosis;

ji fa xing jie he 繼發性結核
secondary tuberculosis;

kai fang xing jie he 開放性結核
open tuberculosis;

pang guang jie he 膀胱結核
cystophthisis;

shen chu xing jie he 滲出性結核
exudative tuberculosis;

xi fei jie he 矽肺結核
silicotuberculosis;
yuan fa xing jie he 原發型結核
primary tuberculous complex;
yuan fa xing jie he 原發性結核
primary tuberculosis;
zeng sheng xing jie he 增生性結核
productive tuberculosis;

jie he bing 結核病
TB / tuberculosis;
chu qi jie he bing 初期結核病
pretuberculosis;

jie he liu 結核瘤
tuberculoma;

jie he xing fei yan 結核性肺炎
tuberculous pneumonia;

jing4 luan xing xiao chuan 痙攣性哮喘
spasmodic asthma;

jiu3 du xing fei yan 酒毒性肺炎
alcoholic pneumonia;

ju2 xian xing fei qi zhong 局限性肺氣腫
focal emphysema;

ju xian xing fei yan 局限性肺炎
pneumonitis;

ka3 tan 咯痰
cough up phlegm;

kai1 fang xing qi xiong 開放性氣胸
open pneumothorax;

ke2 咳
cough;
gan ke 乾咳
dry cough; tussiculation;
qing ke 輕咳
tussicula;
zhi ke 止咳
relieve cough;

lao2 bing 癆病
consumptive disease / phthisis / tuberculosis;

lao3 nian fei qi zhong 老年肺氣腫
senile emphysema;

lian4 fei zhi ke 斂肺止咳
stop cough with styptic pectorals;

lian4 qiu jun xing fei yan 鏈球菌性肺炎
streptococcal pneumonia;

lü4 se tan 綠色痰
green sputum;

mi2 man xing fei qi zhong 彌漫性肺氣腫
diffuse emphysema;

ming2 zhu fei fu 銘諸肺腑
be deeply impressed / engrave on one's memory / engrave on one's mind;

nang2 xing fei qi zhong 囊性肺氣腫
cystic emphysema;

nian2 lian xing fei bu zhang 黏連性肺不張
adhesive atelectasis;

nian4 zhu jun xing fei yan 念珠菌性肺炎
candida pneumonia;

niao4 du zheng xing fei yan 尿毒症性肺炎
uremic pneumonitis;

pan2 zhuang fei bu zhang 盤狀肺不張
patelike atelectasis;

pi2 ruo fei xu 脾弱肺虛
asthenia of the spleen and lung;

ping2 chuan yao 平喘藥
anti-asthmatic;

qi4 chuan 氣喘
gasp;

qi chuan bing 氣喘病
heaves;

qi geng 氣哽
choking;

qi men 氣悶
chagrin / feel oppressed / feel suffocated // in low spirits;

qi tong 氣痛
gas pain;

qi xiong 氣胸
collapsed lung / pneumothorax;
chuang shang xing qi xiong 創傷性氣胸
traumatic pneumothorax;
kai fang xing qi xiong 開放性氣胸
open pneumothorax;
ren gong qi xiong 人工氣胸
artificial pneumothorax;

wai shang xing qi xiong 外傷性氣胸
traumatic pneumothorax;
ya li xing qi xiong 壓力性氣胸
pressure pneumothorax;
yue jing xing qi xiong 月經性氣胸
catamenial pneumothorax;
zhang li xing qi xiong 張力性氣胸
tension pneumothorax;
zhen duan xing qi xiong 診斷性氣胸
diagnostic pneumotrorax;

qi zhang 氣脹
flatulence / gas / wind;

qi zhang bing 氣脹病
bloat;

qi zhang tong 氣脹痛
gas pains;

qi zhong 氣腫
emphysema;
chuang shang xing qi zhong 創傷性氣腫
traumatic emphysema;
fei qi zhong 肺氣腫
pulmonary emphysema / emphysema / pneumonectasis;
jia xing qi zhong 假性氣腫
false emphysema;
wai shang xing qi zhong 外傷性氣腫
traumatic emphysema;

qing1 fei re 清肺熱
clear away lung-heat;

qing1 ke 輕咳
tussicula;

qu1 tan 祛痰
eliminate the phlegm;

ren2 gong qi xiong 人工氣胸
artificial pneumothorax;

ren zao fei 人造肺
aqualung;

rou4 ya zhong xing fei yan 肉芽腫性肺炎
granulomatous pneumonitis;

ru2 chong xing fei yan 蠕蟲性肺炎
verminous pneumonia;

shen4 chu xing jie he 滲出性結核
exudative tuberculosis;

shi1 fei 濕肺
wet lung;

shi ke 濕咳
wet cough;

shi2 ji tan sou 食積痰嗽
productive cough due to indigestion;

shi2 zhi fei shui zhong 實質肺水腫
solid pulmonary oedema;

shu3 yi xing fei yan 鼠疫性肺炎
plague pneumonia;

tan2 痰
phlegm / sputum;
hua tan 化痰
disperse phlegm / reduce sputum;
ka tan 咯痰
cough up phlegm;
lü se tan 綠色痰
green sputum;
qu tan 祛痰
eliminate the phlegm;
wu geng tan 五更痰
cough before dawn;
yan tan 驗痰
sputum test;

tan huo 痰火
phlegm-fire;

tan yin 痰飲
phlegm-retention disease;

tan4 fei 炭肺
anthracosis;

tan ju xing fei yan 炭疽性肺炎
anthrax pneumonia;

te4 ying xing xiao chuan 特應性哮喘
atopic asthma;

wai4 shang xing qi xiong 外傷性氣胸
traumatic pneumothorax;

wai shang xing qi zhong 外傷性氣腫
traumatic emphysema;

wai yuan xing xiao chuan 外源性哮喘
extrinsic asthma;

wei3 suo xing fei qi zhong 萎縮性肺氣腫
atrophic emphysema;

wu2 fei 無肺
apneumia;

wu3 geng tan 五更痰
cough before dawn;

xi1 fei 矽肺
silicosis;

xi fei jie he 矽肺結核
silicotuberculosis;

xi4 jun xing fei yan 細菌性肺炎
bacterial pneumonia;

xian4 zhi xing fei bing 限制性肺病
restrictive lung disease;

xiao4 chuan 哮喘
asthma;
jing luan xing xiao chuan 痙攣性哮喘
spasmodic asthma;
te ying xing xiao chuan 特應性哮喘
atopic asthma;
wai yuan xing xiao chuan 外源性哮喘
extrinsic asthma;
xin xing xiao chuan 心性哮喘
cardiac asthma;
xin yuan xing xiao chuan 心源性哮喘
cardiac asthma;
yin yuan xing xiao chuan 隱源性哮喘
cryptogenic asthma;
zhi ye xing xiao chuan 職業性哮喘
occupational asthma;

xiao chuan bing 哮喘病
asthma;
bian ying xing xiao chuan bing 變應性哮喘病
allergic asthma;

xiao chuan bing fa zuo 哮喘病發作
access of asthma;

xin1 bing fei 心病肺
cardiac lung;

xin xing xiao chuan 心性哮喘
cardiac asthma;

xin yuan xing xiao chuan 心源性哮喘
cardiac asthma;

xue4 tan 血痰
bloody sputum;

ya1 li xing qi xiong 壓力性氣胸
pressure pneumothorax;

ya po xing fei bu zhang 壓迫性肺不張
compression atelectasis;

yan4 tan 驗痰
sputum test;

yin3 yuan xing xiao chuan 隱源性哮喘
cryptogenic asthma;

you2 zou xing fei yan 游走性肺炎
wandering pneumonia;

you4 fei 右肺
right lung;

yuan2 fa xing jie he 原發型結核
primary tuberculous complex;

yuan fa xing fei bu zhang 原發性肺不張
primary atelectasis;

yuan fa xing jie he 原發性結核
primary tuberculosis;

yuan2 xing fei bu zhang 圓形肺不張
round atelectasis;

yue4 jing xing qi xiong 月經性氣胸
catamenial pneumothorax;

zeng1 sheng xing jie he 增生性結核
productive tuberculosis;

zhang1 li xing qi xiong 張力性氣胸
tension pneumothorax;

zhen3 duan xing qi xiong 診斷性氣胸
diagnostic pneumotrorax;

zhen4 fa xing fei shui zhong 陣發性肺水腫
paroxysmal pulmonary oedema;

zhi1 qi guan fei bing 支氣管肺病
bronchopneumopathy;

zhi qi guan fei yan 支氣管肺炎
alveobronchiolitis;

zhi1 zhi xing fei yan 脂質性肺炎
pneumonolipidosis;

zhi2 ye xing xiao chuan 職業性哮喘
occupational asthma;

zhi3 ke 止咳
stop coughing;

zhong1 yang fei yan 中央肺炎
central pneumonia;

zhong1 mo qi fei yan 終末期肺炎
terminal pneumonia;

zhuan3 yi xing fei yan 轉移性肺炎
metastatic pneumonia;

zu3 se xing fei bu zhang 阻塞性肺不張
obstructive atelectasis;

zu se xing fei qi zhong 阻塞性肺氣腫
obstructive emphysema;

zu se xing fei yan 阻塞性肺炎
obstructive pneumonia;

zuo3 fei 左肺
left lung;

Fu 腹 Abdomen

bing4 du xing fu xie 病毒性腹瀉
virus diarrhoea;

chan3 hou fu mo yan 產後腹膜炎
puerperal peritonitis;

chang2 fu mo yan 腸腹膜炎
exenteritis;

chen2 qi fu xie 晨起腹瀉
morning diarrhoea;

chou1 fu shui 抽腹水
tapping the abdomen;

chu1 xue xing fu mo yan 出血性腹膜炎
hemorrhagic peritonitis;

chuan1 kong xing fu mo yan 穿孔性腹膜炎
perforative peritonitis;

chuang1 shang xing fu mo yan 創傷性腹膜炎
traumatic peritonitis;

chuang shang xing wang fu mo yan 創傷性網腹膜炎
traumatic reticuloperitonitis;

ci4 ji xing fu xie 刺激性腹瀉
irritative diarrhoea;

da4 du nan 大肚腩
pot-belly || spare tyre;

da fu pian pian 大腹便便
(1) big-bellied / pot-bellied || as plump as a partridge; as round as a barrel; barrel-bellied; fat and heavy belly; paunchy; with a big belly; with a huge belly; with a pot-belly;
(2) pregnant;

du4 nan 肚腩
belly;

du qi 肚臍
navel / belly button;

fei2 hou xing fu mo yan 肥厚性腹膜炎
pachyperitonitis;

fu4 腹
abdomen / belly / stomach;

fu bei 腹背
in front and behind;

fu bei shou di 腹背受敵
be attacked both from behind and in front || be caught between two fires; between the devil and the deep blue sea; between the hammer and the anvil; have enemies in front and rear;

fu bei xiang qin 腹背相親
very intimate;

fu bu 腹部
abdomen;

fu bu qu zhi shu 腹部去脂術
abdominoplasty;

fu bu teng tong 腹部疼痛
a pain in one's abdomen;

fu cang ji mou 腹藏機謀
one's breast conceals tactics;

fu cang jian mou 腹藏奸謀
harbour a sinister design;

fu cang liang mou 腹藏良謀
conceal a good stratagem deep in one's heart / have smart ideas up one's sleeve;

fu fei 腹誹
unspoken criticisms;

fu ji 腹肌
abdominal muscle;

fu ji tong 腹肌痛
myocelialgia;

fu ji yan 腹肌炎
laparomyitis;

fu jiao tong 腹絞痛
angina abdominis / cramps;

fu li cang dao 腹裏藏刀
hiding a sword in the bossom // very treacherous;

fu lie 腹裂
celoschisis;

fu liu 腹瘤
celioma;

fu ming 腹鳴
borborygmus;

fu mo 腹膜
abdominal membrane;

fu mo bing 腹膜病
peritoneopathy;

fu mo yan 腹膜炎
peritonitis;

chan hou fu mo yan 產後腹膜炎
puerperal peritonitis;

chang fu mo yan 腸腹膜炎
exenteritis;

chu xue xing fu mo yan 出血性腹膜炎
hemorrhagic peritonitis;

chuan kong xing fu mo yan 穿孔性腹膜炎
perforative peritonitis;

chuang shang xing fu mo yan 創傷性腹膜炎
traumatic peritonitis;

fei hou xing fu mo yan 肥厚性腹膜炎
pachyperitonitis;

jia fu mo yan 假腹膜炎
pseudoperitonitis;

jie he xing fu mo yan 結核性腹膜炎
tuberculous peritonitis;

ju xian xing fu mo yan 局限性腹膜炎
circumscribed peritoritis / localized peritonitis;

mi man xing fu mo yan 彌漫性腹膜炎
diffuse peritonitis;

nian lian xing fu mo yan 黏連性腹膜炎
adhesive peritonitis;

nian zhu jun xing fu mo yan 念珠菌性腹膜炎
candida peritonitis;

nong du xing fu mo yan 膿毒性腹膜炎
septic peritonitis;

nong qi xing fu mo yan 膿氣性腹膜炎
pyopneumoperitonitis;

qi xing fu mo yan 氣性腹膜炎
pneumoperitonitis;

qian fu xing fu mo yan 潛伏性腹膜炎
silent peritonitis;

xi jun xing fu mo yan 細菌性腹膜炎
bacterial peritonitis;

ying hua xing fu mo yan 硬化性腹膜炎
sclerosing peritonitis;

zhong qi fu mo yan 終期腹膜炎
terminal peritonitis;

zhou qi xing fu mo yan 周期性腹膜炎
periodic peritonitis;
zi gong fu mo yan 子宮腹膜炎
metroperitonitis;

fu nei zhong kuai 腹內腫塊
abdominal mass;

fu qi zhang 腹氣脹
tympanites;

fu qiang 腹腔
abdominal cavity;

fu re xin jian 腹熱心煎
look forward to sth very eagerly;

fu shui 腹水
ascites / ascitic fluid;
chou fu shui 抽腹水
tapping the abdomen;
zao fa xing fu shui 早發性腹水
ascites praecox;

fu tong 腹痛
abdominal pain / stomachache;

fu tong ru jiao 腹痛如絞
have an excruciating pain in the belly;

fu wai xie ji 腹外斜肌
oblique abdominal muscle;

fu wu di mo 腹無滴墨
there is not a single drop of ink in the bosom // utterly uneducated;

fu xie 腹瀉
diarrhoea // have loose bowels;
bing du xing fu xie 病毒性腹瀉
virus diarrhoea;
chen qi fu xie 晨起腹瀉
morning diarrhoea;
ci ji xing fu xie 刺激性腹瀉
irritative diarrhoea;
ji xie xing fu xie 機械性腹瀉
mechanical diarrhoea;
ji xing fu xie 急性腹瀉
sudden onset of diarrhoea;
ji bian xing fu xie 積便性腹瀉
paradoxical diarrhoea;
ji fen xing fu xie 積糞性腹瀉
paradoxical diarrhoea;
re dai fu xie 熱帶腹瀉
tropical diarrhoea;
shen tou xing fu xie 滲透性腹瀉
osmotic diarrhoea;
te fa xing fu xie 特發性腹瀉
idiopathic diarrhoea;
xia ji fu xie 夏季腹瀉
summer diarrhoea;
xiao hua bu liang xing fu xie 消化不良性腹瀉
lienteric;
yan xing fu xie 炎性腹瀉
inflammatory diarrhoea;
ying er fu xie 嬰兒腹瀉
infantile diarrhoea;

fu xin 腹心
belly and the heart;

fu xin zhi huan 腹心之患
danger from within;

fu yi 腹議
criticize in one's mind;

fu you lin jia 腹有鱗甲
one's mind is treacherous and evil || harbour evil intentions and be unapproachable; treacherous;

fu zhang 腹脹
abdominal distension / meteorism;

fu zhang ru gu 腹脹如鼓
one's belly is tight as a drum — well fed and content;

fu zhi ji 腹直肌
straight abdominal muscle;

fu zhong cang dao 腹中藏刀
a dagger hidden in the belly — a treacherous person;

gu3 fu 鼓腹
(1) eating well and living well / well-fed and unoccupied;
(2) beat one's belly as a drum;

han2 bu gu fu 含哺鼓腹
with food in the mouth and belly well-filled || feed food and fill the stomach to the full — a scene of light-heartedness of the people in times of peace;

hu2 fu 壺腹
ampulla;

hu fu ai 壺腹癌
ampullary carcinoma;

hu fu yan 壺腹炎
ampullitis;

hu fu zhou ai 壺腹周癌
periampullary carcinoma;

ji1 bian xing fu xie 積便性腹瀉
paradoxical diarrhoea;

ji fen xing fu xie 積糞性腹瀉
paradoxical diarrhoea;

ji2 fu zheng 急腹症
acute abdominal disease;

ji xing fu xie 急性腹瀉
sudden onset of diarrhoea;

jia3 fu mo yan 假腹膜炎
pseudoperitonitis;

jie2 he xing fu mo yan 結核性腹膜炎
tuberculous peritonitis;

ju2 xian xing fu mo yan 局限性腹膜炎
circumscribed peritoritis / localized peritonitis;

kai1 fu shu 開腹術
abdominal operation / abdominal section;

kong1 fu 空腹
empty stomach;

ling4 ren peng fu 令人捧腹
make one burst out laughing / make sb hold his sides with laughter / set people roaring with laughter ‖ sidesplitting; throw sb into convulsions;

man3 fu hao qing 滿腹豪情
be filled with pride;

man fu jing lun 滿腹經綸
full of learning / profoundly learned;

man fu lao sao 滿腹牢騷
full of complaints / full of dissatisfaction / full of grievances ‖ have a bellyful of complaints; querulous; have a grudge against everything;

man fu wen zhang 滿腹文章
full of learning / profoundly learned;

man fu yi tuan 滿腹疑團
full of doubts and suspicious;

man fu you lü 滿腹憂慮
full of sorrow / one's heart is filled with sorrow and anxiety;

man fu yuan qi 滿腹怨氣
a chestful of hate / full of grievances on account of wrongs;

man fu zhu ji 滿腹珠璣
have a well-stored mind / one's mind is full of valuable ideas — extensive knowledge;

mi2 man xing fu mo yan 彌漫性腹膜炎
diffuse peritonitis;

nian2 lian xing fu mo yan 黏連性腹膜炎
adhesive peritonitis;

nian4 zhu jun xing fu mo yan 念珠菌性腹膜炎
candida peritonitis;

nong2 du xing fu mo yan 膿毒性腹膜炎
septic peritonitis;

nong qi xing fu mo yan 膿氣性腹膜炎
pyopneumoperitonitis;

pai1 xiong fu 拍胸脯
pat one's chest;

peng3 fu 捧腹
hold one's sides with laughter / split one's sides with laughter;

peng fu da xiao 捧腹大笑
be convulsed with laughter / burst one's sides with laughter / burst with laughing / crack up / kill oneself laughing / kill oneself with laughter; shake one's sides with laughter;

peng fu jue dao 捧腹絕倒
split one's sides with laughter ‖ fold up; in convulsions of laughter;

pi1 lu xin fu 披露心腹
disclose a secret / tell one's innermost thoughts;

po4 fu 破腹
diarrhoea;

pou1 fu 剖腹
cut open the stomach / make an abdominal incision;

pou fu cang zhu 剖腹藏珠
cut open one's stomach to hide the pearl — sacrifice one's own life to conceal one's treasured possession;

pou fu tan cha 剖腹探查
abdominal laparotomy;

pou fu ming xin 剖腹明心
bare one's heart in all sincerity / disclose one's real feelings ‖ make a clean breast of; slit one's belly to show loyalty — lay open one's heart; tear the heart out of one's breast and show it to sb;

pou fu shu 剖腹術
laparotomy;

pou fu wan xin 剖腹剜心
cut open sb's side and dig out his heart / disembowel sb and have his heart torn out;

qi4 fu 氣腹
aeroperitoneum;

qi fu yan 氣腹炎
pneumoperitonitis;

qi xing fu mo yan 氣性腹膜炎
pneumoperitonitis;

qian2 fu xing fu mo yan 潛伏性腹膜炎
silent peritonitis;

qie1 fu zi sha 切腹自殺
happy dispatch;

re4 dai fu xie 熱帶腹瀉
tropical diarrhoea;

shang4 fu bu 上腹部
epigastrium / midriff;

shang fu bu tong 上腹部痛
epigastralgia;

shang fu tong 上腹痛
pain in the upper abdomen;

shen4 tou xing fu xie 滲透性腹瀉
osmotic diarrhoea;

tan3 fu dong chuang 坦腹東牀
worthy son-in-law of sb;

tan xiong lu fu 坦胸露腹
bare-chested;

te4 fa xing fu xie 特發性腹瀉
idiopathic diarrhoea;

ting3 xiong tu du 挺胸突肚
high breast and big belly // puff up one's chest ‖ stand straight in a gesture of self-confidence; stick out one's chest; stretch the chest and expand the belly; with one's chest stuck out;

tui1 xin zhi fu 推心置腹
confide in sb / lay bare one's heart / open one's heart to / pour out all one's inmost feeling ‖ put every trust in; repose full confidence in sb;

wai4 ke ji fu zheng 外科急腹症
surgical acute abdomen;

wang3 fu mo yan 網腹膜炎
reticuloperitonitis;

chuang shang xing wang fu mo yan 創傷性網腹膜炎
traumatic reticuloperitonitis;

xi4 jun xing fu mo yan 細菌性腹膜炎
bacterial peritonitis;

xia4 fu 下腹
lower abdomen / underbelly;

xia4 ji fu xie 夏季腹瀉
summer diarrhoea;

xiao1 hua bu liang xing fu xie 消化不良性腹瀉
lienteric;

xiao3 fu 小腹
lower abdomen;

yan2 xing fu xie 炎性腹瀉
inflammatory diarrhoea;

ying1 er fu xie 嬰兒腹瀉
infantile diarrhoea;

ying4 hua xing fu mo yan 硬化性腹膜炎
sclerosing peritonitis;

zao3 fa xing fu shui 早發性腹水
ascites praecox;

zhong1 qi fu mo yan 終期腹膜炎
terminal peritonitis;

zhou1 qi xing fu mo yan 周期性腹膜炎
periodic peritonitis;

zi3 gong fu mo yan 子宮腹膜炎
metroperitonitis;

Gan 肝 Liver

a1 mi ba gan nong zhong 阿米巴肝膿腫
amoebic abscess / liver abscess;

a mi ba gan yan 阿米巴肝炎
hepatic amoebiasis;

bao3 gan 保肝
protect the liver;

bao4 fa xing gan yan 爆發性肝炎
fulminant hephatitis;

bing3 xing gan yan 丙型肝炎
hepatitis C;

bing xing gan yan bing du 丙型肝炎病毒
hepatitis C virus;

bing4 du xing gan yan 病毒性肝炎
viral hepatitis;

chong1 xue xing gan ying bian 充血性肝硬變
congestive cirrhosis;

chong xue xing gan ying hua 充血性肝硬化
congestive cirrhosis;

chuan1 ran xing gan yan 傳染性肝炎
infective hepatitis;

chuan ran xing huang dan 傳染性黃疸
infectious jaundice;

da4 dong gan huo 大動肝火
fly into a rage / get into a rage || go into one's tantrums; stir the gorge; up in arms;

diao1 gan zhuo shen 雕肝琢腎
exhaust physical and mental energy;

dong4 gan huo 動肝火
lose temper;

fen1 ye gan 分葉肝
degraded liver;

gan1 肝
liver;

bao gan 保肝
protect the liver;

he gan 和肝
regulate the liver-energy;

qing tong se gan 青銅色肝
bronze liver;

yang gan 養肝
nourish the liver;

gan ai 肝癌
cancer of the liver / hepatocarcinoma;

gan bian ying 肝變硬
cirrhosis of the liver;

jie jie xing gan bian ying 結節性肝變硬
hobnail liver;

gan bing 肝病
hepatopathy / liver ailment / liver trouble;

zhi fang gan bing 脂肪肝病
fatty liver disease;

gan bing kou chou 肝病口臭
liver breath;

gan bing mian rong 肝病面容
facies hepatica;

gan bing xing kou chou 肝病性口臭
fetor hepaticus;

gan bing xing shui zhong 肝病性水腫
hepatic oedema;

gan chang 肝腸
liver and intestines;

gan chang cun duan 肝腸寸斷
be deeply grieved / be overwhelmed by grief || deep affliction; emotionally upset; sorrow-stricken; the liver and intestines seem broken into inches — heartbroken;

gan chuan ci 肝穿刺
liver puncture;

gan da 肝大
hepatomegalia;

gan dan 肝膽
(1) liver and gall;
(2) courage / heroic spirit;
(3) open-heartedness / sincerity;

gan dan guo ren 肝膽過人
exceed others in courage || a man of no ordinary spunk; far surpass others in daring; unsurpassed in valour; unusually courageous;

gan dan ju lie 肝膽俱裂
be overwhelmed by grief / heartborken || one's liver and gall both seem torn from within — extremely frightened;

肝 *Liver*

terror-stricken;

gan dan shi re 肝膽濕熱
damp-heat of liver and gallbladder;

gan dan xiang zhao 肝膽相照
a genuine meeting of minds between friends // be open-hearted to each other / friends devoted to each other heart and soul || loyal-hearted; show utter devotion to a friend; treat each other with all sincerity;

gan gong neng 肝功能
liver function;

gan guan 肝管
hepatic duct;

gan guan xi tong 肝管系統
heptatic duct system;

gan huai si 肝壞死
hepatic necrosis;

yin shi xing gan huai si 飲食性肝壞死
dietary hepatic necrosis;

gan hun mi 肝昏迷
hepatic coma;

gan huo 肝火
(1) liver-fire;
(2) irascibility;

qing gan huo 清肝火
clear away liver-fire;

gan huo er ming 肝火耳鳴
tinnitus due to the dominant liver-fire;

gan huo wang 肝火旺
hot-tempered; irascible;

gan nao tu di 肝腦塗地
die the cruelest death || ready to dash one's brains out against the ground in doing homage to; ready to die the cruelest death for principles; suffer any form of death; the liver and brains split on the ground — lay down one's life; willing to repay a favour with extreme sacrifice;

gan nong zhong 肝膿腫
liver abscess;

gan po lie 肝破裂
rupture of the liver;

gan qi 肝氣
liver-energy;

gan qi bu he 肝氣不和
disorder of liver-energy;

gan qie chu 肝切除
hepatectomy / surgical removal of the liver;

gan qie kai 肝切開
hepathomy;

gan shen 肝腎
liver and kidney;

gan shen da 肝腎大
hepatonephromegaly;

gan shen kui shun 肝腎虧損
asthenia of liver and kidney;

gan shen yan 肝腎炎
hepatonephritis;

gan shen zhong da 肝腎腫大
hepatonephromegaly;

gan shi 肝石
hepatolith;

gan shi bing 肝石病
hepathlithiasis;

gan tong 肝痛
hepatodynia;

gan wei suo 肝萎縮
hepatatrophia;

gan xing nao bing 肝性腦病
hepatic encephalopathy;

gan xue 肝血
liver-blood;

gan xue xu 肝血虛
deficiency of liver-blood;

gan yan 肝炎
hepatitis;

bao fa xing gan yan 爆發性肝炎
fulminant hepatitis;

bing xing gan yan 丙型肝炎
hepatitis C;

bing du xing gan yan 病毒性肝炎
viral hepatitis;

chuan ran xing gan yan 傳染性肝炎
infective hepatitis;

dan guan gan yan 膽管肝炎
cholangiohepatitis;
ji xing tu fa xing gan yan 急性突發型肝炎
acute fulminating hepatitis;
jia xing gan yan 甲型肝炎
hepatitis A;
jia zu xing gan yan 家族性肝炎
familial hepatitis;
jie zhong hou gan yan 接種後肝炎
inoculation hepatitis;
jiu jing xing gan yan 酒精性肝炎
alcoholic hepatitis;
liu xing xing gan yan 流行性肝炎
epidemic hepatitis;
nong qi xing gan yan 膿氣性肝炎
pyopneumohepatitis;
shu xue hou gan yan 輸血後肝炎
post-transfusion hepatitis;
shu xue xing gan yan 輸血性肝炎
transfusion hepatitis;
wu huang dan xing gan yan 無黃疸型肝炎
anicteric hepatitis;
xue qing gan yan 血清肝炎
serum hepatitis;
yi xing gan yan 乙型肝炎
hepatitis B;
zhi fang gan xing gan yan 脂肪肝性肝炎
fatty liver hepatitis;
zhi fang gan yan 脂肪肝炎
steatohepatitis;
zhong du xing gan yan 中毒性肝炎
toxic hepatitis;

gan yan bing du 肝炎病毒
hepatitis virus;
bing xing gan yan bing du 丙型肝炎病毒
hepatitis C virus;
jia xing gan yan bing du 甲型肝炎病毒
hepatitis A virus;
yi xing gan yan bing du 乙型肝炎病毒
hepatitis B virus;

gan yang bian 肝樣變
hepatization;

gan ye 肝葉
hepatic lobes;

gan ye qie chu 肝葉切除
hepalobectomy;

gan yi zang 肝胰臟
hepatopancreas;

gan ying bian 肝硬變
cirrhosis;
chong xue xing gan ying bian 充血性肝硬變
congestive cirrhosis;

gan ying hua 肝硬化
cirrhosis;
chong xue xing gan ying hua 充血性肝硬化
congestive cirrhosis;
jiu jing xing gan ying hua 酒精性肝硬化
alcoholic cirrhosis;
mei du xing gan ying hua 梅毒性肝硬化
syphilitic cirrhosis;
wei suo xing gan ying hua 萎縮性肝硬化
atrophic cirrhosis;
xi jun xing gan ying hua 細菌性肝硬化
bacterial cirrhosis;
xin xing gan ying hua 心形肝硬化
cardiocirrhosis;
xin yuan xing gan ying hua 心源性肝硬化
cardiac cirrhosis;
zhi fang xing gan ying hua 脂肪性肝硬化
fatty cirhosis;
zhi xing gan ying hua 脂性肝硬化
fatty cirrhosis;
zhong du xing gan ying hua 中毒性肝硬化
toxic cirrhosis;

gan you ye 肝右葉
right lobe of the liver;

gan zang 肝臟
liver;

gan zang tuo chu 肝臟脱出
hepatocele;

gan zang ying hua 肝臟硬化
cirrhosis of liver;

gan zhong da 肝腫大
hepatomegaly / enlargement of the liver;

gan zuo ye 肝左葉
left lobe of the liver;

he2 gan 和肝
regulate the liver-energy;

huang2 dan 黃疸
jaundice;
chuan ran xing huang dan 傳染性黃疸
infectious jaundice;
ji xie xing huang dan 機械性黃疸
mechanical jaundice;
liu xing xing huang dan 流行性黃疸
epidemic jaundice;
qian fu xing huang dan 潛伏性黃疸
latent jaundice;
rong xue xing huang dan 溶血性黃疸
hemolytic jaundice;
sheng li xing huang dan 生理性黃疸
physiologic jaundice;
yin xing huang dan 隱性黃疸
latent jaundice;
zao fa xing huang dan 早發性黃疸
icterus praecox;
zhong du xing huang dan 中毒性黃疸
toxic jaundice;
zu se xing huang dan 阻塞性黃疸
obstructive jaundice;

ji1 xie xing huang dan 機械性黃疸
mechanical jaundice;

ji2 xing tu fa xing gan yan 急性突發型肝炎
acute fulminating hepatitis;

jia1 zu xing gan yan 家族性肝炎
familial hepatitis;

jia3 xing gan yan 甲型肝炎
hepatitis A;

jia xing gan yan bing du 甲型肝炎病毒
hepatitis A virus;

jie1 zhong hou gan yan 接種後肝炎
inoculation hepatitis;

jie1 jie xing gan bian ying 結節性肝變硬
hobnail liver;

jiu3 jing xing gan yan 酒精性肝炎
alcoholic hepatitis;

jiu jing xing gan ying hua 酒精性肝硬化
alcoholic cirrhosis;

liao2 dong gan huo 撩動肝火
stir up anger;

liu2 xing xing gan yan 流行性肝炎
epidemic hepatitis;

liu xing xing huang dan 流行性黃疸
epidemic jaundice;

mei2 du xing gan ying hua 梅毒性肝硬化
syphilitic cirrhosis;

nong2 qi xing gan yan 膿氣性肝炎
pyopneumohepatitis;

pi1 gan li dan 披肝瀝膽
(1) bare one's heart / disclose one's secret feelings || hang one's heart on one's sleeve; lay bare one's mind; lay open one's heart; open one's heart to sb; open and sincere; unbosom oneself; unbutton one's soul;
(2) loyal and faithful // show a loyal heart;

pi gan lu dan 披肝露膽
lay bare one's heart / lay open one's heart to show loyalty;

pi li gan dan 披瀝肝膽
open up one's heart / open-hearted;

pou3 gan li dan 剖肝瀝膽
lay bare one's mind / unbosom oneself || open and sincere; open up one's heart; show sb one's inmost feelings; speak one's whole mind; unbutton one's soul;

pou gan qi xue 剖肝泣血
extremely sad;

pou xin lu gan 剖心露肝
bare one's heart / open one's heart to sb;

qian2 fu xing huang dan 潛伏性黃疸
latent jaundice;

qing1 tong se gan 青銅色肝
bronze liver;

rong2 xue xing huang dan 溶血性黃疸
hemolytic jaundice;

sheng1 li xing huang dan 生理性黃疸
physiologic jaundice;

shu1 xue hou gan yan 輸血後肝炎
post-transfusion hepatitis;

shu xue xing gan yan 輸血性肝炎
transfusion hepatitis;

wei3 suo xing gan ying hua 萎縮性肝硬化
atrophic cirrhosis;

wu2 huang dan xing gan yan 無黃疸型肝炎
anicteric hepatitis;

xi4 jun xing gan ying hua 細菌性肝硬化
bacterial cirrhosis;

xiao3 er gan 小兒肝
infantile liver;

xin1 xing gan ying hua 心形肝硬化
cardiocirrhosis;

xin yuan xing gan ying hua 心源性肝硬化
cardiac cirrhosis;

xue qing gan yan 血清肝炎
serum hepatitis;

yang3 gan 養肝
nourish the liver;

yi3 xing gan yan 乙型肝炎
hepatitis B;

yi xing gan yan bing du 乙型肝炎病毒
hepatitis B virus;

yi4 dong gan huo 易動肝火
have an inflammable temper;

yin3 shi xing gan huai si 飲食性肝壞死
dietary hepatic necrosis;

yin3 xing huang dan 隱性黃疸
latent jaundice;

ying4 bian gan 硬變肝
cirrhotic liver;

ying hua gan 硬化肝
cirrhotic liver;

you2 zou gan 游走肝
wandering liver;

zao3 fa xing huang dan 早發性黃疸
icterus praecox;

zhi1 fang gan 脂肪肝
adiposis hepatica / fatty liver;

zhi fang gan bing 脂肪肝病
fatty liver disease;

zhi fang gan xing gan yan 脂肪肝性肝炎
fatty liver hepatitis;

zhi fang gan yan 脂肪肝炎
steatohepatitis;

zhi fang xing gan ying hua 脂肪性肝硬化
fatty cirhosis;

zhi xing gan ying hua 脂性肝硬化
fatty cirrhosis;

zhi4 huang dan ji 治黃疸劑
icteric;

zhong1 gan yi dan 忠肝義膽
having good faith, virtue, and patriotism;

zhong4 du xing gan yan 中毒性肝炎
toxic hepatitis;

zhong du xing gan ying hua 中毒性肝硬化
toxic cirrhosis;

zhong du xing huang dan 中毒性黃疸
toxic jaundice;

zu3 se xing huang dan 阻塞性黃疸
obstructive jaundice;

Gu 骨 Bone

ao1 xian gu zhe 凹陷骨折
depressed fracture;

ao4 gu 傲骨
lofty character / lofty and unyielding character || proud bones; self-esteem;

bai2 gu 白骨
bones of the dead;

ban4 tuo wei 半脫位
semi-dislocation;

bi2 gu 鼻骨
nasal bone;

bi4 he xing gu zhe 閉合性骨折
closed fracture;

bi4 髀
(1) buttocks;
(2) hipbone / innominate bone;

bi gu 髀骨
hipbone / innominate bone;

bian1 gu 砭骨
pierce the bone;

bian ren ji gu 砭人肌骨
bone-piercing;

bian3 gu 扁骨
flat bone;

bian4 xing guan jie yan 變性關節炎
degenerative arthritis;

bin4 gu 髕骨
kneecap || patella;

bing4 du xing guan jie yan 病毒性關節炎
viral arthritis;

bing du xing ji sui yan 病毒性脊髓炎
viral myelitis;

bing li xing tuo wei 病理性脫位
pathologic dislocation;

bo1 li gu zhe 剝離骨折
cleavage fracture;

bo tuo xing gu ruan gu yan 剝脫性骨軟骨炎
osteochondritis dissecans;

bo4 san xing ji sui yan 播散性脊髓炎
disseminated myelitis;

bu3 gu yao 補骨藥
osteoprastics;

bu4 quan tuo wei 不全脫位
incomplete dislocation;

bu wan quan gu zhe 不完全骨折
incomplete fracture;

bu4 fen tuo wei 部份脫位
partial dislocation;

chang2 gu 長骨
long bone;

chang xing gu pen 長型骨盆
dolichopellic pelvis;

chang2 bing xing guan jie yan 腸病性關節炎
enteropathic arthritis;

chang gu 腸骨
ilium;

che4 gu 徹骨
to the bone;

cheng2 gu 成骨
ossification;

cheng nian gou lou bing 成年佝僂病
adult rickets;

chi2 gu 尺骨
ulna;

chi2 fa xing gu zhe 遲發性骨折
deferred fracture;

chi3 gu 恥骨
public bone / pubis;

chi gu lian he 恥骨聯合
pubic symphysis;

chi gu qie kai 恥骨切開
pubiotomy;

chu1 xue xing gu mo yan 出血性骨膜炎
hemorrhagic periostitis;

chu xue xing guan jie 出血性關節
bleeder's joint / hemophilic joint;

chu xue xing ji sui bing 出血性脊髓病
hemorrhagic myelopahty;

chu1 qi tuo wei 初期脫位
primitive dislocation;

chuan1 kong gu zhe 穿孔骨折
perforating fracture;

chuang1 shang hou gu wei suo 創傷後骨萎縮
post-traumatic atrophy of bone;

chuang shang hou gu zhi shu song 創傷後骨質疏鬆
post-traumatic osteoporosis;

chuang shang hou ji zhui yan 創傷後脊椎炎
post-traumatic spondylitis;

chuang shang xing gu nang zhong 創傷性骨囊腫
traumatic bone cyst;

chuang shang xing gu ruan hua 創傷性骨軟化
malacia traumatica;

chuang shang xing ji sui bing 創傷性脊髓病
traumatic myelopathy;

chuang shang xing ji sui ruan hua 創傷性脊髓軟化
spondylomalacia traumatica;

chuang shang xing ji sui yan 創傷性脊髓炎
traumatic spondylitis;

chuang shang xing ji zhui bing 創傷性脊椎病
traumatic spondylopathy;

chuang shang xing tuo wei 創傷性脫位
traumatic dislocation;

chui2 gu 錘骨
malleus;

ci4 gu 次骨
to the bone / piercing to the bones || biting; cut to the bones; piercing;

ci4 gu 刺骨
to the bone / piercing to the bone || biting; cut to the bone; piercing;

cui4 gu 脆骨
brittle bones / gristle;

cui gu bing 脆骨病
brittle bone disease;

cui xing gu yan 脆性骨炎
osteitis fragilitans;

da4 wan gu 大腕骨
great carpal bone;

dan1 chun tuo wei 單純脫位
simple dislocation;

dan chun xing gu zhe 單純性骨折
simple fracture;

dan guan jie 單關節
simple joint;

dan guan jie yan 單關節炎
monarthritis;

deng1 gu 鐙骨
stapes / stirrup bone;

di3 ban 骶斑
sacral spot;

di gu 骶骨
sacrum;

di gu tong 骶骨痛
sacralgia;

di tong 骶痛
sacrodynia;

di4 fang xing gu guan jie yan 地方性骨關節炎
endemic osteoarthritis;

dian3 xing xing gu rou liu 典型性骨肉瘤
classical osteosarcoma;

die2 gu 蝶骨
sphenoid bone;

ding3 gu 頂骨
parietal bone;

dou4 fu li tiao gu tou 豆腐裏挑骨頭
picky / trying to find bones in bean curd;

duan3 gu 短骨
short bone;

duo1 guan jie yan 多關節炎
polyarthritis;

jie he xing duo guan jie yan 結核性多關節炎
tuberculous polyarthritis;

liu xing xing duo guan jie yan 流行性多關節炎
epidemic polyarthritis;

zhou wei xing duo guan jie yan 周圍性多關節炎
peripheral polyarthritis;

e2 gu 額骨
frontal bone;

e4 gu 顎骨
jawbone;

fa1 xiao gu 發笑骨
funny bone;

fan2 gu 凡骨
mortal bones / ordinary person;

fan3 ying xing guan jie yan 反應性關節炎
reactive arthritis;

fei2 da xing guan jie yan 肥大性關節炎
hypertrophic arthritis;

fei da xing ji zhui yan 肥大性脊椎炎
hypertrophic spondylitis;

fei hou xing gu mo yan 肥厚性骨膜炎
pachyperiostitis;

fei2 gu 腓骨
fibula;

fen3 shen sui gu 粉身碎骨
have one's body smashed to pieces ‖ be beaten till one's bones are broken; be crushed to powder; be crushed to pulp; be dashed to pieces; be hacked to pieces; be smashed to pieces; die the most cruel death; grind someone's bones to powder and make mincemeat of one's flesh; have one's body pounded to pieces and one's bones ground to powder; one's bones are ground to powder;

fen sui xing gu zhe 粉碎性骨折
comminuted fracture;

feng1 shi 風濕
rheumatism;

feng shi bing 風濕病
rheumatism;
guan jie feng shi bing 關節風濕病
articular rheumatism;
jia feng shi bing 假風濕病
pseudorheumatism;
lei feng shi bing 類風濕病
rheumatoid disease;
lin bing xing feng shi bing 淋病性風濕病
gonorrheal rheumatism;
yan xing feng shi bing 炎性風濕病
inflammatory rheumatism;

feng shi guan jie yan 風濕關節炎
rheumarthritis;

feng shi re 風濕熱
rheumatic fever;

feng shi tong 風濕痛
rheumatalgia;

feng shi xing dong mai yan 風濕性動脈炎
rheumatic arteritis;

feng shi xing fei yan 風濕性肺炎
rheumatic pneumonia;

feng shi xing guan jie yan 風濕性關節炎
rheumatic arthritis;
ji xing feng shi xing guan jie yan 急性風濕性關節炎
acute rheumatic arthritis;
lei feng shi xing guan jie yan 類風濕性關節炎
rheumatoid arthritis;

feng shi xing ji wei suo 風濕性肌萎縮
rheumatic atrophy;

feng shi xing shui zhong 風濕性水腫
rheumatismal oedema;

feng shi xing xin bao yan 風濕性心包炎
rheumatic pericarditis;

feng shi xing xin ji yan 風濕性心肌炎
rheumatic myocarditis;

feng shi xing xin yan 風濕性心炎
rheumatic carditis;

feng shi xing xin zang bing 風濕性心臟病
rheumatic heart disease;

feng shi xing zhu dong mai yan 風濕性主動脈炎
rheumatic aortitis;

feng shi xing zi dian 風濕性紫癜
purpura rheumatica;

feng shi zhen 風濕疹
rheumatid;

fu1 gu 跗骨
tarsal bone / tarsus;

fu gu tong 跗骨痛
pain in the foot / tarsalgia;

fu gu yan 跗骨炎
inflammation of the tarsus of the foot / tarsitis;

fu2 lei 浮肋
floating ribs;

fu3 gu 腐骨
sequestrum;

fu4 he gu zhe 複合骨折
compound fracture;

gan4 骭
shinbone;

ge2 骼
bone / skeleton;

ge gu 骼骨
ilium;

gen1 gu 跟骨
calcaneum / heel bone;

ju gen gu 巨跟骨
tarsomegaly;

gen gu ao 跟骨凹
calcaneal fovea;

gen gu ci 跟骨刺
calcaneal spur;

gen gu jie jie 跟骨結節
calcaneal tubercle;

gen gu yan 跟骨炎
calcaneitis;

gen tong 跟痛
calcaneodynia;

gong1 gu 肱骨
humerus;

gou1 lou 佝僂
rickets;

gou lou bing 佝僂病
rickets;

cheng nian gou lou bing 成年佝僂病
adult rickets;

shen xing gou lou bing 腎形佝僂病
renal rickets;

gu3 gu 股骨
femur / tighbone;

gu guan jie 股關節
hip joint;

gu guan jie yan 股關節炎
coxarthritis;

gu shan qi 股疝氣
crural hernia;

gu3 骨
bone;

jie gu 接骨
set a broken bone / set a fracture;

ru gu 入骨
to the bones;

zheng gu 正骨
(1) bonesetting;
(2) set a broken bone / set a fracture;

gu ai 骨癌
cancer of the bone / osteocarcinoma;

gu bi 骨痺
heumatism;

gu bing 骨病
bone disease / osteopathia / osteopathy;

ji e xing gu bing 飢餓性骨病
hunger osteopathy;

niao du zheng gu bing 尿毒症骨病
uremic bone disease;

yin shi xing gu bing 飲食性骨病
alimentary osteopathy;

ying yang bu liang xing gu bing 營養不良性骨病
hypertrophic osteopathy;

gu chu xue 骨出血
osteorrhagia;

gu ci 骨刺
bony spur / spur;

gu cui zheng 骨脆症
fragile fern / fragilitas ossium;

gu cuo 骨銼
bone file;

gu duan 骨端
extremitas;

gu fa sheng 骨發生
osteogenesis / ostosis;

gu fa yu bu liang 骨發育不良
anostosis;

gu fa yu bu quan 骨發育不全
dyosteogenesis;

gu fa yu zhang ai 骨發育障礙
dysosteogenesis;

gu fan she 骨反射
bone reflex;

gu fei hou 骨肥厚
hyperostosis;

gu feng 骨縫
sutura;

gu fu wei 骨復位
reduction;

gu gan jue 骨感覺
bone sensitivity;

gu gan 骨幹
diaphysis;

gu gan fa yu bu liang 骨幹發育不良
diaphyseal dysphlasia;

gu gan fa yu yi chang 骨幹發育異常
diaphyseal sclerosis;

gu gan yan 骨幹炎
diaphysitis;

gu gan ying hua 骨幹硬化
diaphyseal sclerosis;

gu ge 骨隔
scleroseptum;

gu ge 骨骼
ossature / skeleton;

ying hua gu ge 硬化骨骼
scleroskeleton;

gu ge fa sheng 骨骼發生
skeletogeny;

gu ge fa yu bu liang 骨骼發育不良
ostemyelodysphlasia;

gu ge ji 骨骼肌
skeletal muscle;

gu geng 骨骾
bone sticking;

gu geng zai hou 骨鯁在喉
a lump in the throat / have a fishbone stuck in one's throat || having a fishbone in one's throat; having an opinion one cannot suppress; voice certain sentiments which one can no longer repress;

gu geng zhi qi 骨骾之氣
have the spirit of open frankness;

gu gu mo yan 骨骨膜炎
osteoperiostitis;

gu gua 骨刮
raspatory / scalprum;

gu guan jie bing 骨關節病
osteoarthritis;

gu guan jie jie he 骨關節結核
osteoarticular tuberculosis;

gu guan jie wo 骨關節窩
socket;

gu guan jie yan 骨關節炎
osteoarthritis;

di fang xing gu guan jie yan 地方性骨關節炎
endemic osteoarthritis;

you nian xing gu guan jie yan 幼年性骨關節炎
osteoarthrosis juvenilis;

zeng zhi xing gu guan jie yan 增殖性骨關節炎
hyperplastic osteoarthritis;

gu hou 骨骺
apophysis ossium;

gu hou fa sheng bu quan 骨骺發生不全
epiphyseal dysgenesis;

gu hua 骨化
ossification / sclerotization;

mi lu yan xing gu hua 迷路炎性骨化
labyrinthitis ossificans;

pi fu gu hua 皮膚骨化
osteodermia;

gu hua bing 骨化病
osteosis;

pi fu gu hua bing 皮膚骨化病
osteosis cutis;

gu hua bu quan 骨化不全
defective formation of bone / dysostosis;

gu hua guo du 骨化過度
excessive ossification of bone / pleonosteosis;

gu hua guo zao 骨化過早
excessive ossification of bone / pleonosteosis;

gu hua ruan gu 骨化軟骨
ossifying cartilage;

gu hua xing gu yan 骨化性骨炎
osteitis ossificans;

gu hua xing ji yan 骨化性肌炎
myositis ossificans;

gu hua yi chang 骨化異常
osthexia / osthexy;

gu huai si 骨壞死
osteonecrosis / recrosis of bone;

gu hui 骨灰
(1) bone ash / bone char;
(2) ashes of the dead / cremains;

gu ji xing 骨畸形
bone malformation;

gu ji bing 骨疾病
bone disease;

gu ji 骨極
bone exhaustion;

gu jia 骨痂
callus / osteotylus / poroma;
zan shi gu jia 暫時骨痂
provisional callus;

gu jia 骨架
(1) skeleton;
(2) bone / frame || armature; carcass; framework; scaffolding;

gu jiao 骨膠
bone glue || lime glue; pastern; osseocolla;

gu jie he 骨結核
bone tuberculosis / tuberculosis of bones;

gu jie 骨節
osteocomma / scleromere;

gu jie cu da 骨節粗大
gnarl;

gu jie teng tong 骨節疼痛
arthralgia / pain in a joint;

gu jing mai yan 骨靜脈炎
inflammation of the veins of a bone / osteophlebitis;

gu jiu 骨臼
bone socket;

gu ju 骨疽
caries / decay;

gu ju xing huai si 骨疽性壞死
carionecrosis;

gu kang 骨抗
fracture;

gu lao 骨癆
bone and joint tuberculosis;

gu lian he 骨聯合
synostosis;

gu liu 骨瘤
bone tumour;
pi fu gu liu 皮膚骨瘤
osteoma cutis;
xiang ya yang gu liu 象牙樣骨瘤
ivory osteoma;

gu lou 骨瘻
bone fistula;

gu lu 骨顱
osteocranium;

gu mo 骨膜
periost / periosteum;

gu mo fan she 骨膜反射
periosteal reflex;

gu mo fan ying 骨膜反應
periosteal reaction;

gu mo gu 骨膜骨
periosteal bone;

gu mo gu hua 骨膜骨化
periosteal ossification;

gu mo gu sui yan 骨膜骨髓炎
periosteomyelitis;

gu mo gu yan 骨膜骨炎
periostosteitis;

骨 *Bone*

gu mo ji bing 骨膜疾病
periosteous disease;

gu mo liu 骨膜瘤
periosteoma;

gu mo shui zhong 骨膜水腫
periosteodema;

gu mo yan 骨膜炎
periostitis;

chu xue xing gu mo yan 出血性骨膜炎
hemorrhagic periostitis;

fei hou xing gu mo yan 肥厚性骨膜炎
pachyperiostitis;

zao fa xing gu mo yan 早發性骨膜炎
precocious periostitis;

zeng sheng xing gu mo yan 增生性骨膜炎
periostitis hyperplastica;

gu nang zhong 骨囊腫
bone cyst;

chuang shang xing gu nang zhong 創傷性骨囊腫
traumatic bone cyst;

gu nei ai 骨內癌
introsseous carcinoma;

yuan fa xing gu nei ai 原發性骨內癌
primary intraosseous carcinoma;

gu pen 骨盆
pelvis;

chang xing gu pen 長型骨盆
dolichopellic pelvis;

gu pen gu 骨盆骨
pelvic bone;

gu pen guan 骨盆管
pelvic canal;

gu pen yan 骨盆炎
pelvic inflammation;

gu rou 骨肉
flesh and blood / kindred;

gu rou liu 骨肉瘤
osteosarcoma;

dian xing xing gu rou liu 典型性骨肉瘤
classical osteosarcoma;

gu rou liu bing 骨肉瘤病
osteosarcomatosis;

gu rou qing yi 骨肉情誼
feelings of kinship / kindred feelings;

gu rou tong bao 骨肉同胞
kith and kin / one's own flesh and blood;

gu rou tuan ju 骨肉團聚
family reunion;

gu rou xiang lian 骨肉相連
as close and dear as blood relatives || as closely linked as flesh and blood; near to each other as bone and flesh; very closely related;

gu rou xiong di 骨肉兄弟
blood brothers / one's own brothers;

gu rou zhi qin 骨肉之親
blood relations || blood relationship; near of kin;

gu rou zhi qing 骨肉之情
family relationship and feeling / kindred feelings / the ties of blood;

gu ruan gu bing 骨軟骨病
osteochondrosis;

gu ruan gu guan jie yan 骨軟骨關節炎
osteochondroarthritis;

gu ruan gu liu 骨軟骨瘤
osteochondroma;

gu ruan gu yan 骨軟骨炎
osteochondrosis;

bo tuo xing gu ruan gu yan 剝脱性骨軟骨炎
osteochondritis dissecans;

huai si xing gu ruan gu yan 壞死性骨軟骨炎
osteochondritis necroticans;

gu ruan hua 骨軟化
halisteresis;

chuang shang xing gu ruan hua 創傷性骨軟化
malacia traumatica;

jia gu ruan hua 假骨軟化
pseudo-osteomalacia;

lao nian xing gu ruan hua 老年性骨軟化
senile osteomalacia;

gu ruan hua zheng 骨軟化症
osteomalacia;

gu ruan jin ma 骨軟筋麻
enervated / paralyzed // one's bones are weak and one's muscles numbed;

gu shang 骨傷
bone fracture;

gu shen jing tong 骨神經痛
osteoneuralgia;

gu shen bing 骨腎病
osteonephropathy;

gu sheng cheng 骨生成
ostosis;

gu shou ru chai 骨瘦如柴
a mere bag of bones / a mere skeleton || angular; as thin as a lath; as thin as a rail; as thin as a rake; as thin as a threadpaper; as thin as a whipping post; as thin as sticks; bare-boned; be reduced to a skeleton; be reduced to a show; become as emaciated as a fowl; bone-thin; lean and skinny; raw-boned; skin and bones; skinny; worn to a shadow;

gu shou xing xiao 骨瘦形銷
grow greatly emaciated;

gu sui 骨髓
bone marrow / marrow / medulla;

gu sui bing 骨髓病
myelopathy;
quan gu sui bing 全骨髓病
panmyelopathy;

gu sui fa yu bu liang 骨髓發育不良
myelodysplasia;

gu sui hua 骨髓化
medullization;

gu sui lao 骨髓癆
myelophthisis;

gu sui liu 骨髓瘤
myeloma;
ju xian xing gu sui liu 局限性骨髓瘤
localized myeloma;
ying hua xing gu sui liu 硬化性骨髓瘤
sclerosing myeloma;

gu sui yan 骨髓炎
osteomyelitis;
hua nong xing gu sui yan 化膿性骨髓炎
purulent osteomyelitis;

gu sui yi zhi 骨髓移植
bone marrow transplantation;

gu sui lie 骨碎裂
osteomiosis;

gu sun shang 骨損傷
bone injury;

gu teng rou fei 骨騰肉飛
be fascinated by sb's compelling beauty / go off into ecstasies;

gu tong 骨痛
ostalgia;

gu tou 骨頭
bone;
ken gu tou 啃骨頭
gnaw on bones;

gu tou geng zai hou long kou — yan bu xia, tu bu chu 骨頭鯁在喉嚨口——咽不下，吐不出
a bone wedge in one's throat — can't get rid of sth in any way;

gu tou jia zi 骨頭架子
(1) skeleton;
(2) bag of bones / skin and bones;

gu tou li zha you 骨頭裏搾油
squeeze fat from bones / take sth out of nothing;

gu tou qing 骨頭輕
light bones;

gu tou tong 骨頭痛
pain in the bones;

gu tou ying 骨頭硬
hard bone // a dauntless, unyielding person;

gu tu 骨突
apophysis;

gu tu bing 骨突病
apophytseopathy;

gu wai 骨歪
displacement of the fractured end of a bone;

gu wan qu 骨彎曲
cyrtosis;

gu wei suo 骨萎縮
bone atrophy / osteanabrosis;
chuang shang hou gu wei suo 創傷後骨萎縮
post-traumatic atrophy of bone;

gu xiao guan 骨小管
bone canalicules;

gu xiao liang 骨小梁
bone trabecula;

gu xing guan jie yan 骨性關節炎
osteoarthritis;

gu xing liu 骨性瘤
osteocele;

gu yan 骨炎
inflammation of the bone / osteitis;
cui xing gu yan 脆性骨炎
osteitis fragilitans;
gu hua xing gu yan 骨化性骨炎
osteitis ossificans;
huai si xing gu yan 壞死性骨炎
necrotic osteitis;
ji xing gu yan 急性骨炎
acute ostetitis;
man xing gu yan 慢性骨炎
chronic osteitis;
mei du liu xing gu yan 梅毒瘤性骨炎
gummatous osteitis;
quan gu yan 全骨炎
panosteitis;
rou ya xing gu yan 肉芽性骨炎
osteitis granulosa;
ying hua xing gu yan 硬化性骨炎
sclerosing osteitis;
zeng sheng xing gu yan 增生性骨炎
productive osteitis;

gu ying hua 骨硬化
osteosclerosis;

gu zhe 骨折
fracture;
ao xian gu zhe 凹陷骨折
depressed fracture;
bi he xing gu zhe 閉合性骨折
closed fracture;
bo li gu zhe 剝離骨折
cleavage fracture;
bu wan quan gu zhe 不完全骨折
incomplete fracture;
chi fa xing gu zhe 遲發性骨折
deferred fracture;
chuan kong gu zhe 穿孔骨折
perforating fracture;
dan chun xing gu zhe 單純性骨折
simple fracture;
fen sui xing gu zhe 粉碎性骨折
comminuted fracture;
fu he gu zhe 複合骨折
compound fracture;
gong nei gu zhe 宮內骨折
intrauterine fracture;
hou gu zhe 骺骨折
epiphyseal fracture;
ji fa xing gu zhe 繼發性骨折
secondary fracture;
jia gu zhe 假骨折
pseudofracture;
jie duan xing gu zhe 節段性骨折
segmental fracture;
kai fang xing gu zhe 開放性骨折
open fracture;
nei fen mi xing gu zhe 內分泌性骨折
endocrine fracture;
pi lao gu zhe 疲勞骨折
fatigue fracture;
qian guan gu zhe 鉛管骨折
lead pipe fracture;
qian ru gu zhe 嵌入骨折
impacted fracture;
qing zhi gu zhe 青枝骨折
greenstick fracture;
shang han gu zhe 上頜骨折
maxillary fracture;
shen jing yuan xing gu zhe 神經源性骨折
neurogenic fracture;
tui bu gu zhe 腿部骨折
fracture in the leg;
wan quan gu zhe 完全骨折
complete fracture;

wan quan xing gu zhe 完全性骨折
complete fracture;
wei suo xing gu zhe 萎縮性骨折
atrophic fracture;
yan xing gu zhe 炎性骨折
inflammatory fracture;
ying yang xing gu zhe 營養性骨折
trophic fracture;
zhong liu xing gu zhe 腫瘤性骨折
neoplastic fracture;
zi fa xing gu zhe 自發性骨折
spontaneous fracture;

gu zhe fu wei 骨折復位
reduction of the fracture;

gu zheng xing shu 骨整形術
osteoplasticity;

gu zhi ruan hua zheng 骨質軟化症
osteomalacia;

gu zhi shu song 骨質疏鬆
osteoporosis;
chuang shang hou gu zhi shu song 創傷後骨質疏鬆
post-traumatic osteoporosis;
lao nian xing gu zhi shu song 老年性骨質疏鬆
senile osteoporosis;

gu zhi shu song zheng 骨質疏鬆症
brittle-bone disease / osteoporosis;

gu zhi zeng sheng 骨質增生
hyperplasia;

gu zi li 骨子裏
(1) in one's heart of hearts;
(2) in essence;
(3) in private / personally;

gu zu zhi 骨組織
bone tissue;

guan1 jie 關節
articulus / joint / juncture / knuckle;
chu xue xing guan jie 出血性關節
bleeder's joint / hemophilic joint;
dan guan jie 單關節
simple joint;
jia guan jie 假關節
false joint / pseudoarthrosis;
mian guan jie 面關節
facet joint;

guan jie bing 關節病
arthropathy / arthrosis / articular disease;
kai fang xing guan jie bing 開放性關節病
open joint;
mei du xing guan jie bing 梅毒性關節病
syphilitic arthropathy;
shen jing bing xing guan jie bing 神經病性關節病
neuropathic arthropathy;
shen jing xing guan jie bing 神經性關節病
neuroarthropathy;
shen jing yuan xing guan jie bing 神經源性關節病
neurogenic arthropathy;
yan xing guan jie bing 炎性關節病
inflammatory arthropathy;
yin xiao bing xing guan jie bing 銀屑病性關節病
psoriatic arthropathy;

guan jie fa yu bu liang 關節發育不良
arthrodysplasia;

guan jie fa yu bu quan 關節發育不全
arthrodysplasia;

guan jie feng shi bing 關節風濕病
articular rheumatism;
ji xing guan jie feng shi bing 急性關節風濕病
acute articular rheumatism;
man xing guan jie feng shi bing 慢性關節風濕病
chronic articular rheumatism;

guan jie gu ding shu 關節固定術
arthrodesis;

guan jie gu zhe 關節骨折
joint fracture;

guan jie ji shui 關節積水
hydrarthrosis;
jian xie xing guan jie ji shui 間歇性關節積水
intermittent hydrarthrosis;

guan jie jie he 關節結核
tuberculosis of joints;

guan jie ruan gu 關節軟骨
arthrodial cartilage;

guan jie ruan gu liu 關節軟骨瘤
joint chondroma;

guan jie ruan gu yan 關節軟骨炎
arthrochondritis;

guan jie song chi 關節鬆弛
arthrochalasis;

guan jie tong 關節痛
arthralgia / joint pains / pain in a joint;

qian du xing guan jie tong 鉛毒性關節痛
arthralgia saturnina;

guan jie tong feng 關節痛風
articular gout;

guan jie tuo wei 關節脫位
abarticulation;

guan jie yan 關節炎
arthritis;

bian xing guan jie yan 變性關節炎
degenerative arthritis;

bing du xing guan jie yan 病毒性關節炎
viral arthritis;

chang bing xing guan jie yan 腸病性關節炎
enteropathic arthritis;

dan guan jie yan 單關節炎
monarthritis;

fan ying xing guan jie yan 反應性關節炎
reactive arthritis;

fei da xing guan jie yan 肥大性關節炎
hypertrophic arthritis;

feng shi guan jie yan 風濕關節炎
rheumarthritis;

feng shi xing guan jie yan 風濕性關節炎
rheumatic arthritis;

gu xing guan jie yan 骨性關節炎
osteoarthritis;

gu guan jie yan 股關節炎
coxarthritis;

ji xing guan jie yan 急性關節炎
acute arthritis;

jian guan jie yan 肩關節炎
omarthritis;

lei feng shi xing guan jie yan 類風濕性關節炎
rheumatoid arthritis;

lin bing xing guan jie yan 淋病性關節炎
gonorrheal arthritis;

lin qiu jun xing guan jie yan 淋球菌性關節炎
gonococcal arthritis;

mei du xing guan jie yan 梅毒性關節炎
syphilitic arthritis;

mei jun xing guan jie yan 霉菌性關節炎
mycotic arthritis;

nong du xing guan jie yan 膿毒性關節炎
septic arthritis;

pi fu bing guan jie yan 皮膚病關節炎
dermatoarthritis;

quan shen guan jie yan 全身關節炎
panarthritis;

shao guan jie yan 少關節炎
oligoarthritis;

shen jing bing xing guan jie yan 神經病性關節炎
neuropathic arthritis;

shen chu xing guan jie yan 滲出性關節炎
exudative arthritis;

shou guan jie yan 手關節炎
cheirarthritis;

tong feng xing guan jie yan 痛風性關節炎
gouty arthritis;

xi jun xing guan jie yan 細菌性關節炎
bacterial arthritis;

xing bing guan jie yan 性病關節炎
venereal arthritis;

yin xiao bing guan jie yan 銀屑病關節炎
psoriatic arthritis;

you nian xing guan jie yan 幼年性關節炎
juvenile chronic arthritis;

zeng sheng xing guan jie yan 增生性關節炎
proliferative arthritis;

zeng zhi xing guan jie yan 增殖性關節炎
hypertrophic arthritis;

zhi guan jie yan 肢關節炎
acroarthritis;

zu guan jie yan 足關節炎
podarthritis;

guan jie ying hua 關節硬化
arthrosclerosis;

guan jie zhong da 關節腫大
arthrophyma;

hai2 ge 骸骼
dry bones;

hai gu 骸骨
femur / human bones;

han2 feng che gu 寒風徹骨
be chilled to the bone;

he4 gu ji fu 鶴骨雞膚
like a crane's bone and a fowl's skin — thin and weak;

hen4 zhi ru gu 恨之入骨
hate sb to the marrow || be consumed with hatred for; bear a bitter hatred for; cherish bitter hatred; harbour an intense hatred; hate sb like poison; hate sth like poison; hate sb to the core; hate sb's guts; hate with all one's soul; nurse an inveterate hatred for;

hou2 骺
epiphysis;

hou bing 骺病
epiphysiometer;

hou fa yu bu liang 骺發育不良
epiphyseal dysplasia;

hou fa yu bu quan 骺發育不全
epiphyseal dysplasia;

hou gu zhe 骺骨折
epiphyseal fracture;

hou yan 骺炎
epiphysitis;

qing shao nian hou yan 青少年骺炎
epiphysitis juvenilis;

hou4 die gu 後蝶骨
postsphenoid;

hou huai 後踝
hock;

hua4 nong xing gu sui yan 化膿性骨髓炎
purulent osteomyelitis;

huai2 gu 踝骨
anklebone;

huai zi gu 踝子骨
anklebone;

huai4 si xing gu ruan gu yan 壞死性骨軟骨炎
osteochondritis necroticans;

huai si xing gu yan 壞死性骨炎
necrotic osteitis;

huai si xing ji sui bing 壞死性脊髓病
necrotizing myelopathy;

ji1 gu 肌骨
muscles and bones;

ji2 xing feng shi xing guan jie yan 急性風濕性關節炎
acute rheumatic arthritis;

ji xing gu yan 急性骨炎
acute ostetitis;

ji xing guan jie feng shi bing 急性關節風濕病
acute articular rheumatism;

ji xing guan jie yan 急性關節炎
acute arthritis;

ji3 脊
(1) spinal column / spine;
(2) ridge;

ji liang 脊梁
back of the human body;

ji liang gu 脊梁骨
backbone / spine;

ji mo ji sui yan 脊膜脊髓炎
meningomyelitis;

ji mo yan 脊膜炎
spinal meningitis;

ji sui 脊髓
spinal cord / spinal marrow;

ji sui bing 脊髓病
myelopathy;

chu xue xing ji sui bing 出血性脊髓病
hemorrhagic myelopahty;

chuang shang xing ji sui bing 創傷性脊髓

病
traumatic myelopathy;
huai si xing ji sui bing 壞死性脊髓病
necrotizing myelopathy;
wai shang xing ji sui bing 外傷性脊髓病
traumatic myelopathy;
xi tong xing ji sui bing 系統性脊髓病
systemic myelopathy;
ya po xing ji sui bing 壓迫性脊髓病
compression myelopathy;

ji sui hui zhi yan 脊髓灰質炎
poliomyelitis;

ji sui ma zui 脊髓麻醉
spinal anaesthesia;

ji sui ruan hua 脊髓軟化
spondylomalacia;
chuang shang xing ji sui ruan hua 創傷性脊髓軟化
spondylomalacia traumatica;

ji sui shen jing 脊髓神經
spinal nerve;

ji sui yan 脊髓炎
myelitis;
bing du xing ji sui yan 病毒性脊髓炎
viral myelitis;
bo san xing ji sui yan 播散性脊髓炎
disseminated myelitis;
ji mo ji sui yan 脊膜脊髓炎
meningomyelitis;
jie zhong hou ji sui yan 接種後脊髓炎
postvaccinal myelitis;
man xing ji sui yan 慢性脊髓炎
chronic myelitis;
mei du xing ji sui yan 梅毒性脊髓炎
syphilitic myelitis;
mi san xing ji sui yan 彌散性脊髓炎
diffuse myelitis;
ya po xing ji sui yan 壓迫性脊髓炎
compression myelitis;
zhen dang xing ji sui yan 震蕩性脊髓炎
concussion myelitis;

ji zhu 脊柱
spine / vertebral column;
lie ji zhu 裂脊柱
cleft spine;

ji zhu bing 脊柱病
rachiopathy;

ji zhu fa yu bu liang 脊柱發育不良
atelorachidia;

ji zhu fa yu bu quan 脊柱發育不全
atelorachidia;

ji zhu tong 脊柱痛
rachialgia;

ji zhu yan 脊柱炎
rachitis;

ji zhui bing 脊椎病
spondylopathy;
chuang shang xing ji zhui bing 創傷性脊椎病
traumatic spondylopathy;

ji zhui gu 脊椎骨
vertebra || spine;

ji zhui tong 脊椎痛
spondylitis;

ji zhui yan 脊椎炎
spondylitis;
chuang shang hou ji zhui yan 創傷後脊椎炎
post-traumatic spondylitis;
chuang shang xing ji sui yan 創傷性脊髓炎
traumatic spondylitis;
fei da xing ji zhui yan 肥大性脊椎炎
hypertrophic spondylitis;

ji4 fa xing gu zhe 繼發性骨折
secondary fracture;

jia2 gu 頰骨
cheekbone;

jia3 gu 胛骨
scapula / shoulder blade;

jia3 feng shi bing 假風濕病
pseudorheumatism;

jia gu ruan hua 假骨軟化
pseudo-osteomalacia;

jia gu zhe 假骨折
pseudofracture;

jia guan jie 假關節
false joint / pseudoarthrosis;

jia lei 假肋
false ribs;

jia ruan gu 假軟骨
pseudocartilage;

jian1 jia gu 肩胛骨
shoulder blade / scapula;

jian1 xie xing guan jie ji shui 間歇性關節積水
intermittent hydrarthrosis;

jian4 tu gu 劍突骨
xiphoid bone;

jian tu ruan gu 劍突軟骨
ensiform cartilage;

jian tu tong 劍突痛
xiphodynia;

jian tu yan 劍突炎
xiphoiditis;

jian4 gu tou 賤骨頭
contemptible wretch;

jian4 gu 薦骨
sacrum;

jie1 gu 接骨
(1) synthesis;
(2) set broken bones / unite a fractured bone;

jie zhong hou ji sui yan 接種後脊髓炎
postvaccinal myelitis;

jie2 he xing duo guan jie yan 結核性多關節炎
tuberculous polyarthritis;

jie jie zhuang ruan gu bing 結節狀軟骨病
chondropathia tuberosa;

jie2 duan xing gu zhe 節段性骨折
segmental fracture;

jin1 gu 筋骨
(1) bones and muscles;
(2) physique;

jing4 脛
shin;

jing ban 脛斑
shin spot;

jing bu 脛部
shin;

jing gu 脛骨
shin bone / tibia;

jing gu yan 脛骨炎
cnemitis;

jing xia gu 脛下骨
os subtibiale;

ju2 xian xing gu sui liu 局限性骨髓瘤
localized myeloma;

ju4 gen gu 巨跟骨
tarsomegaly;

kai1 fang xing gu zhe 開放性骨折
open fracture;

kai fang xing guan jie bing 開放性關節病
open joint;

kai fang xing tuo wei 開放性脫位
open dislocation;

ke1 髁
(1) hipbone / innominate bone;
(2) kneecap / kneepan;

ke4 gu 刻骨
deeply ingrained / deeply rooted;

ken3 gu tou 啃骨頭
gnaw on bones;

kua4 gu 胯骨
hipbone / innominate bone;

kuan1 髖
coxa;

kuan gu 髖骨
hipbone / innominate bone;

kuan guan jie 髖關節
coxal joint;

lao3 nian xing gu ruan hua 老年性骨軟化
senile osteomalacia;

lao nian xing gu zhi shu song 老年性骨質疏鬆
senile osteoporosis;

lei4 肋
ribs;

fu lei 浮肋
floating ribs;

jia lei 假肋
false ribs;

zhen lei 真肋
sterual ribs;

lei gu 肋骨
ribs;

zhuang lei gu 壯肋骨
strengthen the bone, tendon and muscle;

lei ruan gu 肋軟骨
cartilage ribs;

lei4 gu 淚骨
lachrymal bone;

lei4 feng shi bing 類風濕病
rheumatoid disease;

lei feng shi guan jie yan 類風濕關節炎
rheumatoid arthritis;

you nian xing lei feng shi guan jie yan 幼年型類風濕關節炎
juvenile rheumatoid arthritis;

lei feng shi xing guan jie yan 類風濕性關節炎
rheumatoid arthritis;

li2 gu 犁骨
vomer;

lie4 ji zhu 裂脊柱
cleft spine;

lin2 bing xing feng shi bing 淋病性風濕病
gonorrheal rheumatism;

lin bing xing guan jie yan 淋病性關節炎
gonorrheal arthritis;

lin qiu jun xing guan jie yan 淋球菌性關節炎
gonococcal arthritis;

liu1 gu sui 溜骨髓
drain bone marrow – indulge in sex / lewd;

liu2 xing xing duo guan jie yan 流行性多關節炎
epidemic polyarthritis;

lou4 gu ming xin 鏤骨銘心
engrave on the bones and imprint on the heart — remember forever with gratitude / wholeheartedly grateful to sb;

lou xin ke gu 鏤心刻骨
inscribe a debt of gratitude on one's mind;

lou4 gu 露骨
barefaced / undisguised;

lu2 gu 顱骨
skull;

lu gu guan jie 顱骨關節
articulationes cranli;

lu gu ruan hua 顱骨軟化
craniosclerosis;

lu gu yan 顱骨炎
cranitis;

lu gu zeng sheng 顱骨增生
hyperostosis cranli;

lü3 膂
backbone / spinal column;

lü li 膂力
brawn / muscular strength / physical strength;

lü li fang gang 膂力方剛
while one's backbone retains its strength;

lü li guo ren 膂力過人
possessing extraordinary physical strength;

man4 xing gu yan 慢性骨炎
chronic osteitis;

man xing ji sui yan 慢性脊髓炎
chronic myelitis;

mao2 gu song ran 毛骨悚然
be absolutely terrified / be frightened from the tips of one's hair to the marrow of his very bones ‖ be overcome with horror; bloodcurdling; give sb the creeps; have gooseflesh; make one's blood run cold; make one's flesh creep; send chills up sb's spine; with one's hair standing on end;

mei2 gu tou 沒骨頭
have no backbone // chicken-hearted / spineless;

mei2 du liu xing gu yan 梅毒瘤性骨炎
gummatous osteitis;

mei du xing guan jie bing 梅毒性關節病
syphilitic arthropathy;

mei du xing guan jie yan 梅毒性關節炎
syphilitic arthritis;

mei du xing ji sui yan 梅毒性脊髓炎
syphilitic myelitis;

mei2 jun xing guan jie yan 霉菌性關節炎
mycotic arthritis;

mei4 gu 媚骨
obsequiousness;

mi2 lu yan xing gu hua 迷路炎性骨化
labyrinthitis ossificans;

mian4 gu 面骨
facial bone;

mian guan jie 面關節
facet joint;

mo1 gu tan xiang 摸骨談相
read one's character and tell their fortune by studying their bone structure / tell a person's fortune by feeling their bones;

nao3 gai gu 腦蓋骨
cranium;

nei4 fen mi xing gu zhe 內分泌性骨折
endocrine fracture;

nei gu ge 內骨骼
endoskeleton;

nian2 ye ruan gu 黏液軟骨
mucocartilage;

nian ye ruan gu liu 黏液軟骨瘤
myxoenchondroma;

niao4 du zheng gu bing 尿毒症骨病
uremic bone disease;

nie4 gu 顳骨
temporal bone;

nong2 du xing guan jie yan 膿毒性關節炎
septic arthritis;

pan2 zhuang ruan gu 盤狀軟骨
discoid meniscus;

pi2 fu bing guan jie yan 皮膚病關節炎
dermatoarthritis;

pi2 lao gu zhe 疲勞骨折
fatigue fracture;

qian1 du xing guan jie tong 鉛毒性關節痛
arthralgia saturnina;

qian guan gu zhe 鉛管骨折
lead pipe fracture;

qian2 bi gu 前臂骨
focil;

qian4 ru gu zhe 嵌入骨折
impacted fracture;

qiao1 gu xi sui 敲骨吸髓
break the bones and suck the marrow || beat sb's bones flat for the marrow inside / bleed sb white; bloodsucking exploitation; enforce the most relentless oppression and exploitation; exploit cruelly; milk sb dry; ruthless economic exploitation; suck the lifeblood; wring every ounce of sweat and blood out of sb;

qie1 gu 切骨
in bitter hatred of || bitter; deep; intense; strongly felt;

qie gu tong hen 切骨痛恨
hate like poison / hate with particular venom;

qie gu zhi chou 切骨之仇
hate to the very marrow of one's bones;

qing1 shao nian hou yan 青少年骺炎
epiphysitis juvenilis;

qing zhi gu zhe 青枝骨折
greenstick fracture;

qing1 gu tou 輕骨頭
(1) base / lowly / mean;
(2) frivolous;

qing2 tong gu rou 情同骨肉
as dear to sb as one's own flesh and blood / as fast and indissoluble as flesh and bone;

qing yu gu rou 情逾骨肉
as dear as one's own flesh and blood / dearer than one's own flesh and blood;

quan2 gu sui bing 全骨髓病
panmyelopathy;

quan gu yan 全骨炎
panosteitis;

quan shen guan jie yan 全身關節炎
panarthritis;

quan2 gu 權骨
cheekbone;

quan2 gu 顴骨
cheekbone;

rao2 gu 橈骨
radius;

rou2 ruo wu gu 柔若無骨
soft as soap;

rou xin ruo gu 柔心弱骨
as mild as a dove by nature / tender conscience;

rou4 ya xing gu yan 肉芽性骨炎
osteitis granulosa;

ru4 gu 入骨
to the bones / to the marrow;

ruan3 gu 軟骨
cartilage;
jia ruan gu 假軟骨
pseudocartilage;
jian ruan gu 瞼軟骨
ciliary cartilages;
jian tu ruan gu 劍突軟骨
ensiform cartilage;
jian ruan gu 腱軟骨
tendon cartilage;
nian ye ruan gu 黏液軟骨
mucocartilage;
pan zhuang ruan gu 盤狀軟骨
discoid meniscus;
shi zhi ruan gu 實質軟骨
parenchymatous cartilage;
ting dao ruan gu 聽道軟骨
cartilage of acoustic meatus;
ting guan ruan gu 聽管軟骨
cartilage of auditory tube;
wai er dao ruan gu 外耳道軟骨
cartilago meatus acustici;
zan shi xing ruan gu 暫時性軟骨
temporary cartilage;

ruan gu bing 軟骨病
cartilage;
jie jie zhuang ruan gu bing 結節狀軟骨病
chondropathia tuberosa;

ruan gu cheng gu 軟骨成骨
cartilage bone;

ruan gu fa yu bu liang 軟骨發育不良
achondroplasia;

ruan gu fa yu bu quan 軟骨發育不全
dyschondroplasia;

ruan gu liu 軟骨瘤
cartilaginous tumour / chondroma;
nian ye ruan gu liu 黏液軟骨瘤
myxoenchondroma;
zhen xing ruan gu liu 真性軟骨瘤
true chondroma;
zhi fang ruan gu liu 脂肪軟骨瘤
lipochondroma;

ruan gu tou 軟骨頭
weak-kneed;

ruan gu you 軟骨疣
chondrophyte;

shai1 gu 篩骨
ethmoid / ethmoid bone;

shang4 han gu zhe 上頜骨折
maxillary fracture;

shao3 guan jie yan 少關節炎
oligoarthritis;

she2 gu 舌骨
tongue bone;

shen2 jing bing xing guan jie bing 神經病性關節病
neuropathic arthropathy;

shen jing bing xing guan jie yan 神經病性關節炎
neuropathic arthritis;

shen jing xing guan jie bing 神經性關節病
neuroarthropathy;

shen jing yuan xing gu zhe 神經源性骨折
neurogenic fracture;

shen jing yuan xing guan jie bing 神經源性關節病
neurogenic arthropathy;

shen4 xing gou lou bing 腎形佝僂病
renal rickets;

shen4 chu xing guan jie yan 滲出性關節炎
exudative arthritis;

shi1 gu 屍骨
skeleton;

shi2 zhi ruan gu 實質軟骨
parenchymatous cartilage;

shou3 gu 手骨
bones of the human forelimbs;

shou guan jie 手關節
articulations of the hand;

shou guan jie yan 手關節炎
cheirarthritis;

shou zhi gu 手指骨
bones of digits of hand;

shou zhi gu ti 手指骨體
corpus phalangis manus;

shou zhi gu tou 手指骨頭
caput phalangis manus;

shou zhi guan jie 手指關節
articulations of digits of hand;

shua3 gu tou 耍骨頭
irritate sb with sarcastic remarks;

sui3 髓
marrow;

suo3 gu 鎖骨
clavicle / collarbone;

te4 fa xing tong feng 特發性痛風
idiopathic gout;

tie3 gu hong xin 鐵骨紅心
bones of iron and a red heart;

ting1 gu 聽骨
auditory ossicle / ear bones / ossicula auditus;

ting xiao gu 聽小骨
ossicles;

ting xiao gu guan jie 聽小骨關節
joints of auditory ossicles;

tong4 feng 痛風
gout;

cao suan zhong du xing tong feng 草酸中毒性痛風
oxalic gout;

dian xing tong feng 典型痛風
regular gout;

fei dian xing tong feng 非典型痛風
irregular gout;

guan jie tong feng 關節痛風
articular gout;

ji fa xing tong feng 繼發性痛風
secondary gout;

jia tong feng 假痛風
pseudogout;

jia xing tong feng 假性痛風
pseudogout;

jian tong feng 肩痛風
omagra;

nei zang tong feng 內臟痛風
visceral gout;

qian du xing tong feng 鉛毒性痛風
saturnine gout;

qian zhong du xing tong feng 鉛中毒性痛風
lead gout;

qian fu xing tong feng 潛伏性痛風
latent gout;

shou tong feng 手痛風
cheiragra;

te fa xing tong feng 特發性痛風
idiopathic gout;

tong feng shi xing tong feng 痛風石性痛風
tophaceous gout;

yuan fa xing tong feng 原發性痛風
primary gout;

zhou tong feng 肘痛風
anconagra;

zu tong feng 足痛風
podagra;

tong feng shi xing tong feng 痛風石性痛風
tophaceous gout;

tong feng xing guan jie yan 痛風性關節炎
gouty arthritis;

tong ru gu sui 痛入骨髓
the pain penetrates into the marrow;

tou2 gai gu 頭蓋骨
skull;

tou gu 頭骨
cranium / skull;

tou4 gu 透骨
chilled to the bone / piercing;

tui3 bu gu zhe 腿部骨折
fracture in the leg / leg fracture;

tuo1 wei 脫位
dislocation;

ban tuo wei 半脫位
semi-dislocation;

bing li xing tuo wei 病理性脫位
pathologic dislocation;

bu quan tuo wei 不全脫位
incomplete dislocation;

bu fen tuo wei 部份脫位
partial dislocation;

chu qi tuo wei 初期脫位
primitive dislocation;

chuang shang xing tuo wei 創傷性脫位
traumatic dislocation;

dan chun tuo wei 單純脫位
simple dislocation;

gong nei tuo wei 宮內脫位
intrauterine dislocation;

guan jie tuo wei 關節脫位
abarticulation;

kai fang xing tuo wei 開放性脫位
open dislocation;

wai shang xing tuo wei 外傷性脫位
traumatic dislocation;

wan quan tuo wei 完全脫位
complete dislocation;

wai4 er dao ruan gu 外耳道軟骨
cartilago meatus acustici;

wai shang xing ji sui bing 外傷性脊髓病
traumatic myelopathy;

wai shang xing tuo wei 外傷性脫位
traumatic dislocation;

wan2 quan gu zhe 完全骨折
complete fracture;

wan quan tuo wei 完全脫位
complete dislocation;

wan quan xing gu zhe 完全性骨折
complete fracture;

wan4 腕
carpus;

wan gu 腕骨
carpal bone / carpus;

wan gu zhe 腕骨折
carpal fracture;

wan guan jie 腕關節
carpal joint;

wei3 gu 尾骨
coccyx / tail bone;

wei3 suo xing gu zhe 萎縮性骨折
atrophic fracture;

xi1 gai gu 膝蓋骨
kneecap / patella;

xi guan jie 膝關節
knee joint;

xi guan jie bing 膝關節病
gonarthrosis;

xi guan jie yan 膝關節炎
gonarthritis;

xi4 tong xing ji sui bing 系統性脊髓病
systemic myelopathy;

xi4 jun xing guan jie yan 細菌性關節炎
bacterial arthritis;

xia4 zhi gu 下肢骨
leg bone;

xiang4 ya yang gu liu 象牙樣骨瘤
ivory osteoma;

xing4 bing guan jie yan 性病關節炎
venereal arthritis;

xiong1 gu 胸骨
breastbone / sternum;

xiu3 gu 朽骨
decaying bones;

ya1 po xing ji sui bing 壓迫性脊髓病
compression myelopathy;

ya po xing ji sui yan 壓迫性脊髓炎
compression myelitis;

yan2 xing feng shi bing 炎性風濕病
inflammatory rheumatism;

yan xing gu zhe 炎性骨折
inflammatory fracture;

yan xing guan jie bing 炎性關節病
inflammatory arthropathy;

yao1 zhui 腰椎
lumbar vertebrae;

yi1 ba gu tou 一把骨頭
a bag of bones / all bones;

yin2 xiao bing guan jie yan 銀屑病關節炎
psoriatic arthritis;

yin xiao bing xing guan jie bing 銀屑病性關節病
psoriatic arthropathy;

yin3 shi xing gu bing 飲食性骨病
alimentary osteopathy;

ying2 yang bu liang xing gu bing 營養不良性骨病
hypertrophic osteopathy;

ying4 gu tou 硬骨頭
dauntless, unyielding person;

ying hua gu ge 硬化骨骼
scleroskeleton;

ying hua xing gu sui liu 硬化性骨髓瘤
sclerosing myeloma;

ying hua xing gu yan 硬化性骨炎
sclerosing osteitis;

you3 gu qi 有骨氣
have integrity;

you gu tou 有骨頭
indomitable / manly;

you4 nian xing gu guan jie yan 幼年性骨關節炎
osteoarthrosis juvenilis;

you nian xing guan jie yan 幼年性關節炎
juvenile chronic arthritis;

you nian xing lei feng shi guan jie yan 幼年型類風濕關節炎
juvenile rheumatoid arthritis;

yu4 gu bing ji 玉骨冰肌
bones of jade and flesh of ice — purity of character / jade bones and ice skin — an elegant demeanour and high personality;

yuan2 fa xing gu nei ai 原發性骨內癌
primary intraosseous carcinoma;

yuan fa xing tong feng 原發性痛風
primary gout;

yuan4 ru gu sui 怨入骨髓
hate to the very marrow;

zao3 fa xing gu mo yan 早發性骨膜炎
precocious periostitis;

zeng1 sheng xing gu mo yan 增生性骨膜炎
periostitis hyperplastica;

zeng sheng xing gu yan 增生性骨炎
productive osteitis;

zeng sheng xing guan jie yan 增生性關節炎
proliferative arthritis;

zeng zhi xing gu guan jie yan 增殖性骨關節炎
hyperplastic osteoarthritis;

zeng zhi xing guan jie yan 增殖性關節炎
hypertrophic arthritis;

zan4 shi gu jia 暫時骨痂
provisional callus;

zan shi xing ruan gu 暫時性軟骨
temporary cartilage;

zhang3 gu 掌骨
metacarpal bone;

zhen1 lei 真肋
sterual ribs;

zhen xing ruan gu liu 真性軟骨瘤
true chondroma;

zhen1 gu 砧骨
anvil / incus;

zhen3 gu 枕骨
occipital bone;

zhen4 dang xing ji sui yan 震蕩性脊髓炎
concussion myelitis;

zheng4 gu 正骨
(1) bonesetting;
(2) set a broken bone / set a fracture;

zhi1 gu 肢骨
bones of one's limbs;

zhi gu tong 肢骨痛
acrostealgia;

zhi guan jie yan 肢關節炎
acroarthritis;

zhi1 fang ruan gu liu 脂肪軟骨瘤
lipochondroma;

zhi2 gu 蹠骨
metatarsal bones;

zhi3 gu 指骨
phalanx;

zhi3 gu 趾骨
toe bone / phalanges;

zhong3 liu xing gu zhe 腫瘤性骨折
neoplastic fracture;

zhou1 wei xing duo guan jie yan 周圍性多關節炎
peripheral polyarthritis;

zhou3 tong feng 肘痛風
anconagra;

zhu3 xin gu 主心骨
backbone;

zhuang4 lei gu 壯肋骨
strengthen the bone, tendon and muscle;

zhui1 gu 椎骨
vertebra;

zhuo2 gu 灼骨
burn the bones;

zi4 fa xing gu zhe 自發性骨折
spontaneous fracture;

zu2 gu 足骨
ossa pedis;

zu gu yan 足骨炎
pedal osteitis;

zu guan jie 足關節
articulationes pedis;

zu guan jie yan 足關節炎
podarthritis;

zu jia 足痂
foot scab;

zuo4 gu 坐骨
ischium / sciatic nerve;

zuo gu jie jie 坐骨結節
tuber ischiale;

zuo gu shan 坐骨疝
ischiatic hernia;

zuo gu shen jing tong 坐骨神經痛
sciatica;

Guan mai 管脈 Arteries and Veins

an4 mai 按脈
feel the pulse / take the pulse;

ba3 mai 把脈
feel sb's pulse / take sb's pulse;

bian4 ying xing mai guan yan 變應性脈管炎
allergic vasculitis;

bing4 du xing shi guan yan 病毒性食管炎
viral esophagitis;

chan3 luan guan 產卵管
ovipositor;

chan4 mai 顫脈
running pulse;

chang2 dao 腸道
intestinal tract;

chang dong mai 腸動脈
arteriae intestinales;

chi2 dong mai 尺動脈
ulnar artery;

chi2 mai 遲脈
retarded pulse;

chu1 qiu dong mai 出球動脈
revehent artery;

chu qiu jing mai 出球靜脈
revehent veins;

chu xue xing zhi qi guan yan 出血性支氣管炎
hemorrhagic bronchitis;

chuan2 dao dong mai 傳導動脈
conducting arteries;

chuan dao qi guan 傳導氣管
conducting airway;

chuang1 shang xing dong mai liu 創傷性動脈瘤
traumatic aneurysm;

da4 dong mai 大動脈
main artery;

da yin jing mai 大隱靜脈
great saphenous vein;

dong4 mai 動脈
artery;

chu qiu dong mai 出球動脈
revehent artery;

chang dong mai 腸動脈
arteriae intestinales;

chuan dao dong mai 傳導動脈
conducting arteries;

da dong mai 大動脈
main artery;

dan nang dong mai 膽囊動脈
cystic artery;

fei dong mai 腓動脈
peroneal artery;

fei dong mai 肺動脈
pulmonary artery;

fu qiang dong mai 腹腔動脈
abdominal artery;

gao wan dong mai 睪丸動脈
arteria testicularis;

ge nei dong mai 骼內動脈
internal iliac artery;

gong dong mai 肱動脈
brachial artery;

gu dong mai 股動脈
femoral artery;

guan zhuang dong mai 冠狀動脈
coronary artery;

jing dong mai 頸動脈
carotid artery;

mi lu dong mai 迷路動脈
labyrinthine artery;

mian dong mai 面動脈
facial artery; frontal artery;

nie dong mai 顳動脈
temporal artery;

pi dong mai 脾動脈
arteria splenica;

qian ting dong mai 前庭動脈
vestibular arteries;

rao dong mai 橈動脈
radial artery;

shen dong mai 腎動脈
renal artery;

tun shang dong mai 臀上動脈
superior gluteal artery;

tun xia dong mai 臀下動脈
inferior gluteal artery;

xi jiang dong mai 膝降動脈
descending genicular artery;
xi zhong dong mai 膝中動脈
middle genicular artery;
xia chun dong mai 下唇動脈
inferior labial artery;
xiao chang dong mai 小腸動脈
intestinal arteries;
xiao dong mai 小動脈
arteriole;
yin bu nei dong mai 陰部內動脈
internal pudendal artery;
yin dao dong mai 陰道動脈
vaginal artery;
zhu dong mai 主動脈
aorta;

dong mai chu xue 動脈出血
arterial hemorrhage;

dong mai huai si 動脈壞死
arterionecrosis;

dong mai jie shi 動脈結石
arteriolith;

dong mai liu 動脈瘤
aneurysm;
chuang shang xing dong mai liu 創傷性動脈瘤
traumatic aneurysm;
ji sheng chong xing dong mai liu 寄生蟲性動脈瘤
verminous aneurysm;
jia xing dong mai liu 假性動脈瘤
spurious aneurysm;
mei du xing dong mai liu 梅毒性動脈瘤
syphilitic aneurysm;
pian ce dong mai liu 偏側動脈瘤
lateral aneurysm;
ru chong xing dong mai liu 蠕蟲性動脈瘤
worm aneurysm;
shen dong mai liu 腎動脈瘤
renal aneurysm;
wai shang xing dong mai liu 外傷性動脈瘤
traumatic aneurysm;
xi jun xing dong mai liu 細菌性動脈瘤
bacterial aneurysm;
zhen xing dong mai liu 真性動脈瘤
true aneurysm;

dong mai yan 動脈炎
arteritis;
feng shi xing dong mai yan 風濕性動脈炎
rheumatic arteritis;
huai si xing dong mai yan 壞死性動脈炎
necrotizing arteritis;
jie he xing dong mai yan 結核性動脈炎
tuberculous arteritis;
mei du xing dong mai yan 梅毒性動脈炎
syphilitic arteritis;
quan shen dong mai yan 全身動脈炎
panarteritis;
ying er dong mai yan 嬰兒動脈炎
infantile arteritis;

dong mai ying hua 動脈硬化
arterial sclerosis / hardening of arteries;
ying er dong mai ying hua 嬰兒動脈硬化
infantile arteriosclerosis;

duan3 mai 短脈
short pulse;

fei2 dong mai 腓動脈
peroneal artery;

fei4 dong mai 肺動脈
pulmonary artery;

fei jing mai 肺靜脈
pulmonary vein;

fu4 qiang dong mai 腹腔動脈
abdominal artery;

fu zhu dong mai 腹主動脈
abdominal aorta;

ge2 nei dong mai 髂內動脈
internal iliac artery;

ge nei jing mai 髂內靜脈
internal iliac vein;

gong1 dong mai 肱動脈
brachial artery;

gu3 dong mai 股動脈
femoral artery;

gu jing mai 股靜脈
femoral vein;

guan1 zhuang dong mai 冠狀動脈
coronary artery;

gui4 yao jing mai 貴要靜脈
basilic vein;

guo2 mai min ming 國脈民命
existence as a nation and people;

hao4 mai 號脈
feel sb's pulse / take sb's pulse;

hong2 mai 洪脈
full pulse;

huai4 si xing dong mai yan 壞死性動脈炎
necrotizing arteritis;

ji2 xing zhi qi guan yan 急性支氣管炎
acute bronchitis;

ji4 sheng chong xing dong mai liu 寄生蟲性動脈瘤
verminous aneurysm;

ji sheng chong xing zhi qi guan yan 寄生蟲性支氣管炎
parasitic bronchitis;

jia3 xing dong mai liu 假性動脈瘤
spurious aneurysm;

jian4 xie mai 間歇脈
intermittent pulse;

jie1 he xing dong mai yan 結核性動脈炎
tuberculous arteritis;

jing3 dong mai 頸動脈
carotid artery;

jing nei jing mai 頸內靜脈
internal jugular vein;

jing wai jing mai 頸外靜脈
external jugular vein;

jing zong dong mai 頸總動脈
common carotid artery;

jing4 mai 靜脈
veins;

chu qiu jing mai 出球靜脈
revehent veins;

da yin jing mai 大隱靜脈
great saphenous vein;

dan nang jing mai 膽囊靜脈
cystic vein;

ge nei jing mai 骼內靜脈
internal iliac vein;

gu jing mai 股靜脈
femoral vein;

men jing mai 門靜脈
portal vein;

mi lu jing mai 迷路靜脈
labyrinthine vein;

mian jing mai 面靜脈
facial vein; frontal vein;

nie jing mai 顳靜脈
temporal vein;

pang guang jing mai 膀胱靜脈
vesical veins;

pi jing mai 脾靜脈
vena splenica;

qian ting jing mai 前庭靜脈
vestibular veins;

rao jing mai 橈靜脈
radial vein;

shang qiang jing mai 上腔靜脈
superior vena cava;

shen jing mai 腎靜脈
renal vein;

tou jing mai 頭靜脈
cephalic vein;

tun shang jing mai 臀上靜脈
superior gluteal veins;

tun xia jing mai 臀下靜脈
inferior gluteal veins;

xi jing mai 膝靜脈
genicular vein;

xia chun jing mai 下唇靜脈
inferior labial vein;

xia qiang jing mai 下腔靜脈
inferior vena cava;

ye jing mai 腋靜脈
axillary vein;

yin bu nei jing mai 陰部內靜脈
internal pudendal vein;

jing mai ban 靜脈瓣
venous valve;

jing mai bing 靜脈病
inflammation of a vein / phlebosis;

管脈 *Arteries and Veins*

jing mai bo 靜脈搏
venous pulse;

jing mai chong xue 靜脈充血
venous congestion;

jing mai chu xue 靜脈出血
venous hemorrhage;

jing mai fa yu bu liang 靜脈發育不良
hypovenosity;

jing mai fa yu bu quan 靜脈發育不全
hypovenosity;

jing mai fan she 靜脈反射
venous reflux;

jing mai qie kai 靜脈切開
venesection;

jing mai qu zhang bing 靜脈曲張病
varicosis;

jing mai yan 靜脈炎
inflammation of a vein / phlebitis;

lan se jing mai yan 藍色靜脈炎
blue phlebitis;

nian lian xing jing mai yan 黏連性靜脈炎
adhesive plebitis;

nong du xing jing mai yan 膿毒性靜脈炎
septic phlebitis;

xue shuan xing jing mai yan 血栓性靜脈炎
thrombophlebitis;

zeng sheng xing jing mai yan 增生性靜脈炎
proliferative phlebitis;

jing mai zhou yan 靜脈周炎
periphlebitis;

ying hua xing jing mai zhou yan 硬化性靜脈周炎
sclerosing periphlebitis;

lan2 se jing mai yan 藍色靜脈炎
blue phlebitis;

lao3 nian xing shi guan 老年性食管
presbyesophagus;

lei4 guan 淚管
dacryosyrinx;

lei guan bi se 淚管閉塞
dacryagogatresia;

lei guan lou 淚管瘻
dacryosyrinx;

lei guan xia zhai 淚管狹窄
dacryostenosis;

lei guan yan 淚管炎
dacryosolenitis;

lei xiao guan 淚小管
lacrimal canal;

lei xiao guan yan 淚小管炎
canaliculitis;

lin2 ba guan 淋巴管
lymphatic vessel;

lin ba guan kuo zhang 淋巴管擴張
lymphangiectasis;

lin ba guan liu 淋巴管瘤
lymphangioma;

dan chun xing lin ba guan liu 單純性淋巴管瘤
simple lymphangioma;

lin ba guan yan 淋巴管炎
lymphangitis;

kui yang xing lin ba guan yan 潰瘍性淋巴管炎
ulcerative lymphangitis;

lou4 瘻
fistula;

dan nang lou 膽囊瘻
amphibolic fistula;

gang lou 肛瘻
anal fistula;

gu lou 骨瘻
bone fistula;

lei guan lou 淚管瘻
dacryosyrinx;

mi lu lou 迷路瘻
labyrinthine fistula;

qian ting lou 前庭瘻
vestibular fistula;

mai4 脈
artery / pulse;

an mai 按脈
feel the pulse / take the pulse;

ba mai 把脈
feel sb's pulse / take sb's pulse;

hao mai 號脈
feel sb's pulse / take sb's pulse;

qie mai 切脈
feel a patient's pulse;

zhen mai 診脈
feel sb's pulse / take sb's pulse;

mai bo 脈搏
pulse;

mai bo duan chu 脈搏短絀
pulse deficit;

mai bo guo huan 脈搏過緩
bradysphygmia;

mai bo ting zhi 脈搏停止
cessation of pulsation;

mai bo wei ruo 脈博微弱
acrotism;

mai bo xiao shi 脈搏消失
asphygmia;

mai chong 脈沖
pulse;

mai guan 脈管
angiologia / pulse artery;

mai guan tong 脈管痛
vasalgia;

mai guan yan 脈管炎
angiitis / vasculitis;

bian ying xing mai guan yan 變應性脈管炎
allergic vasculitis;

mai ruo 脈弱
weak pulse;

mai su 脈速
rapid pulse;

mai ya 脈壓
pulse pressure;

man4 xing zhi qi guan yan 慢性支氣管炎
chronic bronchitis;

mao2 xi guan 毛細管
capillary;

mao xi xue guan 毛細血管
blood capillary;

mei2 du xing dong mai liu 梅毒性動脈瘤
syphilitic aneurysm;

mei du xing dong mai yan 梅毒性動脈炎
syphilitic arteritis;

men2 jing mai 門靜脈
portal vein;

mi2 lu dong mai 迷路動脈
labyrinthine artery;

mi lu jing mai 迷路靜脈
labyrinthine vein;

mi lu lou 迷路瘻
labyrinthine fistula;

mi2 man xing shi guan jing lun 彌漫性食管痙攣
diffuse esophageal spasm;

mian4 dong mai 面動脈
facial artery;

mian jing mai 面靜脈
facial vein;

ming4 mai 命脈
lifeblood / lifeline;

mo4 xing zhi qi guan yan 膜性支氣管炎
membranous bronchitis;

nian2 lian xing jing mai yan 黏連性靜脈炎
adhesive plebitis;

nian4 zhu jun xing shi guan yan 念珠菌性食管炎
candida esophagitis;

nie4 dong mai 顳動脈
temporal artery;

nie jing mai 顳靜脈
temporal vein;

nong2 du xing jing mai yan 膿毒性靜脈炎
septic phlebitis;

pang2 guang jing mai 膀胱靜脈
vesical veins;

pi2 dong mai 脾動脈
arteria splenica;

pi jing mai 脾靜脈
vena splenica;

pian1 ce dong mai liu 偏側動脈瘤
lateral aneurysm;

qi4 guan 氣管
trachea / windpipe;

chuan dao qi guan 傳導氣管
conducting airway;

qi guan bing 氣管病
tracheopathy;

qi guan chu xue 氣管出血
tracheorrhagia;

qi guan yan 氣管炎
tracheitis;

bi qi guan yan 鼻氣管炎
bovine rhinotracheitis;

hou qi guan yan 喉氣管炎
laryngotracheitis;

xi jun xing qi guan yan 細菌性氣管炎
bacterial tracheitis;

qian2 ting dong mai 前庭動脈
vestibular arteries;

qian ting guan 前庭管
vestibular canal;

qian ting jing mai 前庭靜脈
vestibular veins;

qian ting lou 前庭瘻
vestibular fistula;

qie1 mai 切脈
feel a patient's pulse;

qing1 jin 青筋
blue veins;

quan2 shen dong mai yan 全身動脈炎
panarteritis;

rao2 dong mai 橈動脈
radial artery;

rao jing mai 橈靜脈
radial vein;

re4 bing mai 熱病脈
febrile pulse;

ru2 chong xing dong mai liu 蠕蟲性動脈瘤
worm aneurysm;

ru chong xing zhi qi guan yan 蠕蟲性支氣管炎
verminous bronchitis;

sai1 xian jing mai 腮腺靜脈
parotid veins;

sai xian yan 腮腺炎
parotiditis;

shan4 guan 疝管
hernial canal;

shang4 qiang jing mai 上腔靜脈
superior vena cava;

she2 bei dong mai 舌背動脈
dorsal artery of tongue;

she bei jing mai 舌背靜脈
dorsal lingual vein;

she guan 舌管
lingual duct;

shen2 jing guan 神經管
neurocanal;

shen jing guan jie 神經管節
neural segment;

shen4 dong mai 腎動脈
renal artery;

shen dong mai liu 腎動脈瘤
renal aneurysm;

shen guan 腎管
nephric duct;

shen xiao guan 腎小管
renal tubules;

shen xiao guan bing bian 腎小管病變
tubulopathy;

shen xiao guan po lie 腎小管破裂
tubulorrhexis;

shen xiao guan shen yan 腎小管腎炎
tubal nephritis;

shen4 chu xing zhi qi guan yan 滲出性支氣管炎
exudative bronchitis;

shi2 dao ai 食道癌
cancer of the esophagus / carcinoma esophagi;

zao qi shi dao ai 早期食道癌
early stage of carcinoma esophagi;

shi dao yan 食道炎
esophagitis / inflammation of the esophagus;

shi guan 食管
esophagus / gullet;

lao nian xing shi guan 老年性食管
presbyesophagus;

shi guan bu fen qie chu 食管部份切除
esophagectomy / surgical removal of the esophagectomy;

shi guan jing luan 食管痙攣
esophageal spasm;

mi man xing shi guan jing lun 彌漫性食管痙攣
diffuse esophageal spasm;

shi guan xia zhai 食管狹窄
stenosis of the esophagus;

shi guan yan 食管炎
esophagitis / inflammation of the esophagus;

bing du xing shi guan yan 病毒性食管炎
viral esophagitis;

nian zhu jun xing shi guan yan 念珠菌性食管炎
candida esophagitis;

shi4 shen jing guan 視神經管
optic canal;

shu1 jin huo luo 舒筋活絡
stimulate the circulation of the blood and cause the muscles and joints to relax;

shu jin huo xue 舒筋活血
relax the muscles and enliven the blood / relax the muscles and stimulate the blood circulation;

shu1 niao guan 輸尿管
ureter;

shu niao guan bing 輸尿管病
ureteropathy;

su4 mai 速脈
quick pulse / racing pulse / rapid pulse;

suo3 gu xia dong mai 鎖骨下動脈
subclavian artery;

suo gu xia jing mai 鎖骨下靜脈
subclavian vein;

ting1 guan 聽管
acoustic duct;

ting guan ruan gu 聽管軟骨
cartilage of auditory tube;

tou2 jing mai 頭靜脈
cephalic vein;

tun2 shang dong mai 臀上動脈
superior gluteal artery;

tun shang jing mai 臀上靜脈
superior gluteal veins;

tun xia dong mai 臀下動脈
inferior gluteal artery;

tun xia jing mai 臀下靜脈
inferior gluteal veins;

wai4 shang xing dong mai liu 外傷性動脈瘤
traumatic aneurysm;

wei1 xue guan 微血管
capillaries;

wei4 guan 胃管
stomach tube;

wu2 mai 無脈
absence of the pulse / acrotism / weakness of the pulse;

wu mai bing 無脈病
pulseless disease / takayasu disease;

xi1 jiang dong mai 膝降動脈
descending genicular artery;

xi jing mai 膝靜脈
genicular vein;

xi zhong dong mai 膝中動脈
middle genicular artery;

xi4 jun xing dong mai liu 細菌性動脈瘤
bacterial aneurysm;

xia4 chun dong mai 下唇動脈
inferior labial artery;

xia chun jing mai 下唇靜脈
inferior labial vein;

xia qiang jing mai 下腔靜脈
inferior vena cava;

xia zhi jing mai qu zhang 下肢靜脈曲張
varicose vein of the leg;

xian4 guan 腺管
crypta;

xiao3 chang dong mai 小腸動脈
intestinal arteries;

xiao dong mai 小動脈
arteriole;

xiao dong mai bing 小動脈病
arteriolopathy;

xiao dong mai yan 小動脈炎
arteriolitis;

xiao dong mai ying hua 小動脈硬化
arteriolar sclerosis;

xiao zhi qi guan 小支氣管
bronchus;

xin1 jing mai 心靜脈
cardiac vein;

xue4 mai liu tong 血脈流通
blood circulation;

xue shuan xing jing mai yan 血栓性靜脈炎
thrombophlebitis;

ye4 jing mai 腋靜脈
axillary vein;

yi1 mai xiang cheng 一脈相承
come down from the same origin / in direct line of descent || a true disciple of; be imbued with the same spirit; in the same strain;

yi mai xiang chuan 一脈相傳
derived from the same origin;

yi mai xiang tong 一脈相通
be intimately tied up with / kindred to;

yin1 bu guan 陰部管
pudendal canal;

yin bu nei dong mai 陰部內動脈
internal pudendal artery;

yin bu nei jing mai 陰部內靜脈
internal pudendal vein;

yin dao dong mai 陰道動脈
vaginal artery;

ying1 er dong mai yan 嬰兒動脈炎
infantile arteritis;

ying er dong mai ying hua 嬰兒動脈硬化
infantile arteriosclerosis;

ying2 yang xue guan 營養血管
nutrient vessel;

ying4 hua xing jing mai zhou yan 硬化性靜脈周炎
sclerosing periphlebitis;

zao3 qi shi dao ai 早期食道癌
early stage of carcinoma esophagi;

zeng1 sheng xing jing mai yan 增生性靜脈炎
proliferative phlebitis;

zhen1 xing dong mai liu 真性動脈瘤
true aneurysm;

zhen3 mai 診脈
feel sb's pulse / take sb's pulse;

zhi1 qi guan 支氣管
bronchus;

xiao zhi qi guan 小支氣管
bronchus;

zhi qi guan ai 支氣管癌
bronchogenic carcinoma;

zhi qi guan bing 支氣管病
bronchopathy / disease of the bronchial tubes;

zhi qi guan kuo zhang 支氣管擴張
bronchiectasis;

zhi qi guan kuo zhang yao 支氣管擴張藥
bronchodilator;

zhi qi guan kuo zhang zheng 支氣管擴張症
bronchiectasis;

zhi qi guan nang zhong 支氣管囊腫
brochocele;

zhi qi guan qi chuan 支氣管氣喘
bronchial asthma;

zhi qi guan xiao chuan 支氣管哮喘
bronchial asthmas;

zhi qi guan yan 支氣管炎
bronchitis / inflammation of the bronchial tubes;

chu xue xing zhi qi guan yan 出血性支氣管炎
hemorrhagic bronchitis;

ji xing zhi qi guan yan 急性支氣管炎
acute bronchitis;
ji sheng chong xing zhi qi guan yan 寄生蟲性支氣管炎
parasitic bronchitis;
man xing zhi qi guan yan 慢性支氣管炎
chronic bronchitis;
mo xing zhi qi guan yan 膜性支氣管炎
membranous bronchitis;
ru chong xing zhi qi guan yan 蠕蟲性支氣管炎
verminous bronchitis;
shen chu xing zhi qi guan yan 滲出性支氣管炎
exudative bronchitis;

zhou3 zheng zhong jing mai 肘正中靜脈
median basilic vein;

zhu3 dong mai 主動脈
aorta;

zhu dong mai gong 主動脈弓
aortic arch;

zhu dong mai yan 主動脈炎
aortitis;
feng shi xing zhu dong mai yan 風濕性主動脈炎
rheumatic aortitis;

Hou 喉 Throat

bai2 hou 白喉
diphtheria;
jia bai hou 假白喉
diphtheroid / pesudodiphtheria;
pi fu bai hou 皮膚白喉
cutaneous diphtheria;

bai hou du su 白喉毒素
diphtheria toxin;

bai hou mo 白喉膜
diphtheritic membrane;

bai hou xing bian tao ti yan 白喉性扁桃體炎
diphtherial tonsillitis;

bai hou xing kui yang 白喉性潰瘍
diphtheritic ulcer;

bai hou xing ma bi 白喉性麻痺
diphtheritic paralysis;

bai hou xing yan yan 白喉性咽炎
diphtheritic pharyngitis;

bai3 ri ke 百日咳
pertusis / whooping cough;
qing bai re ke 輕百日咳
parapertussis;

bian3 tao ti 扁桃體
tonsil;
xian yang bian tao ti 腺樣扁桃體
adenoid tonsil;
xiao chang bian tao ti 小腸扁桃體
intestinal tonsil;
xiao nao bian tao ti 小腦扁桃體
tonsil of cerebellum;
yan bian tao ti 咽扁桃體
pharyngeal tonsil;

bian tao ti qie chu 扁桃體切除
tonsillectomy;

bian tao ti yan 扁桃體炎
tonsillitis;
bai hou xing bian tao ti yan 白喉性扁桃體炎
diphtherial tonsillitis;
ji xing bian tao ti yan 急性扁桃體炎
acute tonsillitis;

lian qiu jun xing bian tao ti yan 鏈球菌性扁桃體炎
streptococcal tonsillitis;

lü pao xing bian tao ti yan 濾泡性扁桃體炎
follicular tonsillitis;

man xing bian tao ti yan 慢性扁桃體炎
chronic tonsillitis;

mei jun xing bian tao ti yan 霉菌性扁桃體炎
mycotic tonsilitis;

pao zhen xing bian tao ti yan 疱疹性扁桃體炎
herpetic tonsillitis;

qian yan xing bian tao ti yan 遷延性扁桃體炎
tonsillitis lenta;

bian tao ti zhou wei nong zhong 扁桃體周圍膿腫
peritonsillar abscess;

chuan2 ran xing hou qi guan yan 傳染性喉氣管炎
infectious laryngotracheitis;

chuan3 ming 喘鳴
stridor;

chuan ming xing hou jing luan 喘鳴性喉痙攣
laryngismus stridulus;

chuan ming xing hou yan 喘鳴性喉炎
laryngitis stridulosa;

cu1 sang zi 粗嗓子
husky voice;

diao4 sang zi 吊嗓子
exercise one's voice / train one's voice;

e4 hou fu bei 扼喉撫背
hold the best strategic positions;

e sha 扼殺
choke the life out of / nip in the bud || catch by the throat; have by the throat; hold by the throat; nip; seize by the throat; smother; strangle; strangle in the cradle; take by the throat; throttle;

fan3 she xing ke 反射性咳
reflex cough;

fei2 da xing yan yan 肥大性咽炎
hypertrophic pharyngitis;

fei hou xing hou yan 肥厚性喉炎
hypertrophic laryngitis;

fei4 jin hou she 費盡喉舌
do a lot of talking / have wasted all one's breath;

gan1 ke 乾咳
dry cough / hacking cough;

geng3 zai hou tou 哽在喉頭
stick in sb's throat;

hou2 喉
larynx / throat;

hou bai hou 喉白喉
laryngeal diphtheria;

hou ban dian 喉斑點
stigma;

hou bing 喉病
laryngopathy;

hou chu xue 喉出血
laryngorrhagia;

hou dou 喉竇
laryngeal sinus;

hou e xing zhong liu 喉惡性腫瘤
malignant tumour of larynx;

hou fan she 喉反射
laryngeal reflex;

hou jie 喉結
Adam's apple / laryngeal protuberance;

hou jie he 喉結核
laryngeal tuberculosis / tuberculosis of larynx;

hou jing luan 喉痙攣
laryngismus;

chuan ming xing hou jing luan 喘鳴性喉痙攣
laryngismus stridulus;

ma bi xing hou jing luan 麻痺性喉痙攣
laryngismus paralyticus;

hou liang xing zhong liu 喉良性腫瘤
benign tumour of larynx;

hou long 喉嚨
gullet / throat;

hou ma bi 喉麻痺
laryngoplegia;

hou men 喉門
glottis;

hou nong zhong 喉膿腫
laryngeal abscess;

hou qi guan yan 喉氣管炎
laryngotracheitis;
chuan ran xing hou qi guan yan 傳染性喉氣管炎
infectious laryngotracheitis;

hou qiang 喉腔
cavitas laryngis;

hou ruan gu 喉軟骨
cartilagines laryngeales;

hou tong 喉痛
laryngalgia / sore throat;

hou tou 喉頭
larynx;

hou tou yan 喉頭炎
laryngitis;

hou tu 喉突
laryngeal protuberance;

hou xi rou 喉息肉
laryngeal polyp;

hou xia chui 喉下垂
laryngoptosis;

hou xia zhai 喉狹窄
laryngeal stenosis;

hou yan 喉咽
laryngopharynx;

hou yan qiang 喉咽腔
laryngopharyngeal cavity;

hou yan 喉炎
inflammation of the larynx / laryngitis;
chuan ming xing hou yan 喘鳴性喉炎
laryngitis stridulosa;
fei hou xing hou yan 肥厚性喉炎
hypertrophic laryngitis;
huai ju xing hou yan 壞疽性喉炎
gangrinous laryngitis;
huai si xing hou yan 壞死性喉炎
necrotic laryngitis;
ji xing hou yan 急性喉炎
acute laryngitis;
man xing hou yan 慢性喉炎
chronic laryngitis / clergyman's throat;
mei du xing hou yan 梅毒性喉炎
syphilitic laryngitis;
mo xing hou yan 膜性喉炎
membranous laryngitis;
qian ting hou yan 前庭喉炎
vestibular laryngitis;
wei suo xing hou yan 萎縮性喉炎
atrophic laryngitis;

hou yi wu 喉異物
foreign body of larynx;

hou yin 喉音
guttural sound;

hou zu se 喉阻塞
laryngeal obstruction;

hua4 tan ji 化痰劑
expectorant;

huai4 ju xing hou yan 壞疽性喉炎
gangrinous laryngitis;

huai ju xing yan hou tong 壞疽性咽喉痛
ulcerated sore throat;

huai ju xing yan yan 壞疽性咽炎
gangrenous pharyngitis;

huai si xing hou yan 壞死性喉炎
necrotic laryngitis;

ji2 xing bian tao ti yan 急性扁桃體炎
acute tonsillitis;

ji xing hou yan 急性喉炎
acute laryngitis;

ji xing yan yan 急性咽炎
acute pharyngitis;

jia3 bai hou 假白喉
diphtheroid / pesudodiphtheria;

jie1 hou 結喉
Adam's apple;

ju4 ke 劇咳
bad cough;

ke2 咳
cough / cough up;
ju ke 劇咳
bad cough;

ke ning 咳寧
bechisan;

ke sou 咳嗽
cough;

ke sou fan she 咳嗽反射
cough reflex;

ke tan 咳痰
cough up phlegm;

ke xue 咳血
cough up blood;

kou3 chuang xing yan yan 口瘡性咽炎
aphthous pharyngitis;

kou da hou long xiao 口大喉嚨小
bite off more than one can chew;

lei1 bo zi 勒脖子
seize sb by the throat;

lian4 qiu jun xing bian tao ti yan 鏈球菌性扁桃體炎
streptococcal tonsillitis;

lian qiu jun xing yan hou tong 鏈球菌性咽喉痛
streptococcal sore throat;
liu xing xing lian qiu jun xing yan hou tong 流行性鏈球菌性咽喉痛
epidemic streptococcal sore throat;

lian qiu jun xing yan yan 鏈球菌性咽炎
streptococcal pharyngitis;

liu2 xing xing lian qiu jun xing yan hou tong 流行性鏈球菌性咽喉痛
epidemic streptococcal sore throat;

long2 嚨
throat;

lü4 pao xing bian tao ti yan 濾泡性扁桃體炎
follicular tonsillitis;

lü pao xing yan hou tong 濾泡性咽喉痛
spotted sore throat;

ma2 bi xing hou jing luan 麻痺性喉痙攣
laryngismus paralyticus;

man4 xing bian tao ti yan 慢性扁桃體炎
chronic tonsillitis;

man xing hou yan 慢性喉炎
chronic laryngitis / clergyman's throat;

man xing yan yan 慢性咽炎
chronic pharyngitis;

mei2 du xing hou yan 梅毒性喉炎
syphilitic laryngitis;

mei2 jun xing bian tao ti yan 霉菌性扁桃體炎
mycotic tonsilitis;

mo4 xing hou yan 膜性喉炎
membranous laryngitis;

mo xing yan yan 膜性咽炎
membranous pharyngitis;

nong2 tan 濃痰
purulent sputum;

nong2 du xing yan hou tong 膿毒性咽喉痛
septic sore throat;

pao4 zhuang yan yan 泡狀咽炎
vesicular pharyngitis;

pao4 zhen xing bian tao ti yan 疱疹性扁桃體炎
herpetic tonsillitis;

pao zhen xing yan yan 疱疹性咽炎
pharyngitis herpetica;

pin2 ke 頻咳
hacking cough;

qi4 chuan 氣喘
asthma / short of breath;

qia1 bo zi 掐脖子
seize sb by the throat;

qia hou long 掐喉嚨
seize sb by the throat;

qian1 yan xing bian tao ti yan 遷延性扁桃體炎
tonsillitis lenta;

qian2 ting hou yan 前庭喉炎
vestibular laryngitis;

qing1 sang zi 清嗓子
clear one's throat;

喉 *Throat*

qing1 bai re ke 輕百日咳
parapertussis;

ru2 geng zai hou 如鯁在喉
as if one has a fishbone in one's throat / like a fishbone getting stuck in the throat || give vent to one's pent-up feelings;

ru gu geng hou, yi tu fang kuai 如骨鯁喉，一吐方快
feel suffocated if one doesn't speak out / have a criticism that one must express;

sang3 嗓
one's voice / throat;

sang men er 嗓門兒
one's voice;

sang men han po 嗓門喊破
shout oneself hoarse;

sang men sha ya 嗓門沙啞
have a thick voice;

sang yin 嗓音
one's voice;

sang zi 嗓子
(1) larynx / throat;
(2) one's voice;
diao sang zi 吊嗓子
exercise one's voice / train one's voice;
qing sang zi 清嗓子
clear one's throat;

sang zi da 嗓子大
have a loud voice;

shu3 yi xing yan yan 鼠疫性咽炎
plague pharyngitis;

shu4 hou long 漱喉嚨
gargle one's throat;

tan2 痰
sputum;
ke tan 咳痰
cough up phlegm;
nong tan 濃痰
purulent sputum;

wei3 suo xing hou yan 萎縮性喉炎
atrophic laryngitis;

wei suo xing yan yan 萎縮性咽炎
atrophic pharyngitis;

wei4 min hou she 為民喉舌
speak for the people;

wen3 刎
cut one's throat;

wen jing zhi jiao 刎頸之交
bosom friends who are willing to die for one another || a friendship to the death; Damon and Pythias friendship; friends sworn to death; friends that are ready to die for each other;

wen jing zi lu 刎頸自戮
commit suicide by cutting one's throat;

xian4 yang bian tao ti 腺樣扁桃體
adenoid tonsil;

xiao3 chang bian tao ti 小腸扁桃體
intestinal tonsil;

xiao nao bian tao ti 小腦扁桃體
tonsil of cerebellum;

yan1 咽
pharynx / gullet / larynx / throat;

yan bai hou 咽白喉
pharyngeal diphtheria;

yan bian tao ti 咽扁桃體
pharyngeal tonsil;

yan bu chong xue 咽部充血
congested throat;

yan e xing zhong liu 咽惡性腫瘤
malignant tumour of pharynx;

yan hou 咽喉
larynx / throat;

yan hou tong 咽喉痛
sore throat;
huai ju xing yan hou tong 壞疽性咽喉痛
ulcerated sore throat;
lian qiu jun xing yan hou tong 鏈球菌性咽喉痛
streptococcal sore throat;
lü pao xing yan hou tong 濾泡性咽喉痛
spotted sore throat;
nong du xing yan hou tong 膿毒性咽喉痛
septic sore throat;

yan hou zhong tong 咽喉腫痛
swelling and pain in the throat;

yan hou nong zhong 咽後膿腫
retropharyngeal abscess;

yan liang xing zhong liu 咽良性腫瘤
benign tumour of pharynx;

yan tong 咽痛
pharyngalgia;

yan tou 咽頭
pharynx / throat;

yan xia yan 咽峽炎
angina;

yan yan 咽炎
pharyngitis;

bai hou xing yan yan 白喉性咽炎
diphtheritic pharyngitis;

fei da xing yan yan 肥大性咽炎
hypertrophic pharyngitis;

huai ju xing yan yan 壞疽性咽炎
gangrenous pharyngitis;

ji xing yan yan 急性咽炎
acute pharyngitis;

kou chuang xing yan yan 口瘡性咽炎
aphthous pharyngitis;

lian qiu jun xing yan yan 鏈球菌性咽炎
streptococcal pharyngitis;

man xing yan yan 慢性咽炎
chronic pharyngitis;

mo xing yan yan 膜性咽炎
membranous pharyngitis;

pao zhuang yan yan 泡狀咽炎
vesicular pharyngitis;

pao zhen xing yan yan 疱疹性咽炎
pharyngitis herpetica;

shu yi xing yan yan 鼠疫性咽炎
plague pharyngitis;

wei suo xing yan yan 萎縮性咽炎
atrophic pharyngitis;

zhen4 ke 陣咳
paroxysmal cough;

zhi3 ke 止咳
relieve a cough / stop coughing;

zhi ke sheng jin 止渴生津
quench thirst and help produce saliva;

zhi ke xiao lao 止渴消勞
relieve thirst and fatigue;

Ji rou 肌肉 Muscle

bai2 ji 白肌
white muscle;

bai ji bing 白肌病
white muscle disease;

bei4 kuo ji 背闊肌
latissimus dorsi;

bi3 mu yu ji 比目魚肌
soleus;

biao3 qing ji 表情肌
muscles of expression;

biao qing ji ma bi 表情肌麻痺
mimetic paralysis;

bu4 sui yi ji 不隨意肌
involuntary muscle;

chan3 hou xin ji bing 產後心肌病
postpartum cardiomyopathy;

chou1 chu 抽搐
convulsion / tic;
ju bu xing chou chu 局部性抽搐
local tic;
mian ji chou chu 面肌抽搐
facial tic;
wu dao chou chu 舞蹈抽搐
tic de sommeil;

chou chu bing 抽搐病
maladie des tics;

chuan ran xing jian qiao yan 傳染性腱鞘炎
infectious tenosynovitis;

cui1 dong ji 催動肌
agonistic muscle;

da4 yuan ji 大圓肌
teres major;

e2 ji 額肌
frontal muscle / frontalis;

fang1 xing ji 方形肌
musculus quadratus;

fei2 hou xing jian qiao yan 肥厚性腱鞘炎
tenosynovitis hypertrophica;

fei hou xing xin ji bing 肥厚性心肌病
hypertrophic cardiomyopathy;

fei3 chang ji 腓腸肌
gastrocnemius;

fei gu chang ji 腓骨長肌
long peroneal muscle;

feng2 jiang ji 縫匠肌
sartorius;

fu4 ji 腹肌
abdominal muscle;

fu wai xie ji 腹外斜肌
external oblique / oblique abdominal muscle / obliqnus abdominis;

fu zhi ji 腹直肌
straight abdominal muscle / transversus abdominis;

gen1 jian 跟腱
Achilles' tendon / heel string / tendo calcanaeus;

gong1 er tou ji 肱二頭肌
biceps / biceps brachii;

gong rao ji 肱橈肌
trachio radialis;

gong san tou ji 肱三頭肌
triceps / triceps brachii;

gu3 er tou ji 股二頭肌
biceps femoris / femoral biceps;

gu nei ji 股內肌
vastus medialis;

gu si tou ji 股四頭肌
quadriceps femoris;

gu wai ji 股外肌
vastus lateralis;

gu3 ge ji 骨骼肌
skeletal muscle;

he2 zuo ji 合作肌
synergistic muscle;

heng2 ji 橫肌
transversalis;

heng wen ji 橫紋肌
striated muscle;

hua4 nong xing jian qiao yan 化膿性腱鞘炎
purulent tendovaginitis;

ji1 肌
muscle;
bai ji 白肌
white muscle;
bei kuo ji 背闊肌
latissimus dorsi;
bi mu yu ji 比目魚肌
soleus;
biao qing ji 表情肌
muscle of expression;
bu sui yi ji 不隨意肌
involuntary muscle;
cui dong ji 催動肌
agonistic muscle;
da yuan ji 大圓肌
teres major;
e ji 額肌
frontal muscle / frontalis;
fang xing ji 方形肌
musculus quadratus;
fei chang ji 腓腸肌
gastrocnemius;
feng jiang ji 縫匠肌
sartorius;
fu ji 腹肌
abdominal muscle;
fu zhi ji 腹直肌
straight abdominal muscle / transversus abdominis;
gong er tou ji 肱二頭肌
biceps / biceps brachii;
gong rao ji 肱橈肌
trachio radialis;
gong san tou ji 肱三頭肌
triceps / triceps brachii;
gu er tou ji 股二頭肌
biceps femoris / femoral biceps;
gu ge ji 骨骼肌
skeletal muscle;
gu nei ji 股內肌
vastus medialis;
gu si tou ji 股四頭肌
quadriceps femoris;
gu wai ji 股外肌
vastus lateralis;
he zuo ji 合作肌
synergistic muscle;
heng ji 橫肌
transversalis;
heng wen ji 橫紋肌
striated muscle;
jiang ji 降肌
depressor muscle;
jie kang ji 拮抗肌
antagonistic muscle;
jing gu qian ji 脛骨前肌
anterior tibial muscle;
jing ji 頸肌
cervical muscle;
jing kuo ji 頸闊肌
neck muscle / platysma;
ju jue ji 咀嚼肌
masticatory muscle;
ke ji 頦肌
mentalis;
kou lun za ji 口輪匝肌
orbicularis oris;
kuai ji 快肌
fast muscle;
kuo zhang ji 擴張肌
dilator muscle;
man ji 慢肌
slow muscle;
mian ji 面肌
facial muscle;
nie ji 顳肌
temporal muscle / temporalis;
pang guang bi niao ji 膀胱逼尿肌
detrusor urinae muscle;
pi ji 皮肌
cutaneous muscle;
ping hua ji 平滑肌
smooth muscle;
qian ju ji 前鋸肌
serratus anterior;
qian lie xian ji 前列腺肌
musculus prostaticus;
rao ze wan ju ji 橈側腕屈肌
flexor carpi radialis;

san jiao ji 三角肌
deltoid / deltoid muscle;
sui yi ji 隨意肌
voluntary muscle;
tun da ji 臀大肌
gluteus maximus;
tun xiao ji 臀小肌
musculus gluteus minimus;
tun zhong ji 臀中肌
mesogluteus;
tun zui xiao ji 臀最小肌
least gluteal muscle;
wai bu ji 外部肌
extrinsic muscle;
xiao yuan ji 小圓肌
teres minor;
xie fang ji 斜方肌
trapezius;
xin ji 心肌
cardiac muscle;
xiong da ji 胸大肌
greater pectoral muscle / pectoralis major / pectoris major;
xiong ji 胸肌
pectoral muscle;
xiong suo ru tu ji 胸鎖乳突肌
amuent muscle / sternocleidom-astoid;
yan ji 眼肌
eye muscle;
yan lun za ji 眼輪匝肌
orbicularis oculi;
yao ji 咬肌
great masticatory muscle / masseter;
yu ji ji 魚際肌
thenar muscle;
zhang ji 張肌
tensor;
zhen ji 枕肌
occipital muscle / occipitalis;
zhi chang shen ji 趾長伸肌
extensor digitorum;

ji bing 肌病
myopathy;
zhi zhi xing ji bing 脂質性肌病
lipid myopathy;

ji jian 肌腱
tendon;

ji jue 肌覺
muscle sense;

ji liu 肌瘤
muscular tumour / myama / myoma;

ji rou 肌肉
brawn / muscle;
la shang ji rou 拉傷肌肉
pull a muscle;

ji rou chou chu 肌肉抽搐
tic;

ji rou fa da 肌肉發達
brawny / muscular;

ji rou wei suo zheng 肌肉萎縮症
muscular dystrophy;

ji rou zhu she 肌肉注射
intramuscular injection;

ji song chi 肌鬆弛
muscular relaxation;

ji tong 肌痛
muscular rheumatism / myalgia / pain in the muscles;
liu xing xing ji tong 流行性肌痛
epidemic myalgia;

ji wei suo 肌萎縮
muscular atrophy;
feng shi xing ji wei suo 風濕性肌萎縮
rheumatic atrophy;
jin xing xing ji wei suo 進行性肌萎縮
progressive muscular atrophy;
que xue xing ji wei suo 缺血性肌萎縮
ischemic muscular atrophy;
shen jing bing xing ji wei suo 神經病性肌萎縮
neuropathic atrophy;
shen jing yan xing ji wei suo 神經炎性肌萎縮
neuritic muscular atropathy;
shen jing yuan xing ji wei suo 神經源性肌萎縮
neural atrophy;

tang niao bing ji wei suo 糖尿病肌萎縮
diabetic amyotrophy;
te fa xing ji wei suo 特發性肌萎縮
idiopathic muscular atrophy;

ji wu li zheng 肌無力症
myasthenia;

ji xian wei 肌纖維
muscle fibre;

ji yan 肌炎
infammation of a muscle / myositis;
nong xing ji yan 膿性肌炎
pyomyositis;
shi zhi xing ji yan 實質性肌炎
parenchymatous myositis;
shou han xing ji yan 受寒性肌炎
myositis a frigore;
zeng sheng xing ji yan 增生性肌炎
proliferative myositis;

ji4 fa xing xin ji bing 繼發性心肌病
secondary cardiomyopathy;

jia2 ji 夾肌
great-toe flexor;

jian4 腱
sinew / tendon;

jian duan lie 腱斷裂
disinsertion;

jian fan she 腱反射
tendon jerk / tendon reflex;

jian fan ying 腱反應
tendon reaction;

jian qiao 腱鞘
tendon sheath;

jian qiao nang zhong 腱鞘囊腫
ganglion;
mi man xing jian qiao nang zhong 彌漫性腱鞘囊腫
diffuse ganglion;
yuan fa xing jian qiao nang zhong 原發性腱鞘囊腫
primary ganglion;

jian qiao yan 腱鞘炎
tenosynovitis / tenovaginitis;
chuan ran xing jian qiao yan 傳染性腱鞘炎
infectious tenosynovitis;
fei hou xing jian qiao yan 肥厚性腱鞘炎
tenosynovitis hypertrophica;
hua nong xing jian qiao yan 化膿性腱鞘炎
purulent tenovaginitis;
jie jie xing jian qiao yan 結節性腱鞘炎
nodular tenosynovitis;
lin bing xing jian qiao yan 淋病性腱鞘炎
gonorrheal tenosynovitis;
lin qiu jun xing jian qiao yan 淋球菌性腱鞘炎
gonococcic tenosynovitis;
rou ya xing jian qiao yan 肉芽性腱鞘炎
tenosynovitis granulosa;

jian qiao zhong 腱鞘腫
onkinocele;

jian ruan gu 腱軟骨
tendon cartilage;

jian yan 腱炎
tendinitis;

jiang4 ji 降肌
depressor muscle;

jie2 kang ji 拮抗肌
antagonistic muscle;

jie2 jie xing jian qiao yan 結節性腱鞘炎
nodular tenosynovitis;

jin1 筋
(1) muscle;
(2) sinew / tendon;
(3) veins that stand out under the skin;
(4) anything resembling a tendon or vein;

jin gu 筋骨
muscles and bones;

jin jie 筋節
muscles and joints;

jin mo 筋膜
aponeurosis;

jin mo yan 筋膜炎
fascitis;

jin pi li jin 筋疲力盡
be extremely fatigued / be utterly exhausted / be worn out ‖ all in; all tuckered out; be

beaten out; be clapped out; be exhausted with toil; dead on one's dead; dead-beat; dog-tired; down and out; exhausted; fagged out; give out; jacked up; knock up; knocked out; overspent; pumped out; run down; run out of steam; run sb ragged; spend oneself; tire out; used up // exhaustion;

jin4 xing xing ji wei suo 進行性肌萎縮
progressive muscular atrophy;

jing3 ji 頸肌
cervical muscle;

jing kuo ji 頸闊肌
neck muscle / platysma;

jing4 gu qian ji 脛骨前肌
anterior tibial muscle;

ju2 bu xing chou chu 局部性抽搐
local tic;

ju3 jue ji 咀嚼肌
masticatory muscle;
ju jue ji ma bi 咀嚼肌麻痺
masticatory paralysis;

ju jue ji ma bi 咀嚼肌麻痺
masticatory paralysis;

ke1 ji 頦肌
mentalis;

kou3 lun za ji 口輪匝肌
orbicularis oris;

kuai4 ji 快肌
fast muscle;

kuo4 zhang ji 擴張肌
dilator muscle;

la1 shang ji rou 拉傷肌肉
pull a muscle;

lin2 bing xing jian qiao yan 淋病性腱鞘炎
gonorrheal tenosynovitis;

lin qiu jun xing jian qiao yan 淋球菌性腱鞘炎
gonococcic tenosynovitis;

liu2 xing xing ji tong 流行性肌痛
epidemic myalgia;

man4 ji 慢肌
slow muscle;

mi2 man xing jian qiao nang zhong 彌漫性腱鞘囊腫
diffuse ganglion;

mian4 ji 面肌
facial muscle;

mian ji chou chu 面肌抽搐
facial tic;

mian ji jing luan 面肌痙攣
mimetic convulsion;

mian ji ma bi 面肌麻痺
mimetic paralysis;

nie4 ji 顳肌
temporal muscle / temporalis;

nong2 xing ji yan 膿性肌炎
pyomyositis;

pang2 guang bi niao ji 膀胱逼尿肌
detrusor urinae muscle;

pi2 ji 皮肌
cutaneous muscle;

pi ji yan 皮肌炎
dermatomyositis;

ping2 hua ji 平滑肌
smooth muscle;

qian2 bi qu ji qun 前臂屈肌羣
forearm flexor group;

qian bi shen ji qun 前臂伸肌羣
forearm extensor group;

qian ju ji 前鋸肌
serratus anterior;

qian lie xian ji 前列腺肌
musculus prostaticus;

que1 xue xing ji wei suo 缺血性肌萎縮
ischemic muscular atrophy;

rao2 ze wan ju ji 橈側腕屈肌
flexor carpi radialis;

rou4 ya xing jian qiao yan 肉芽性腱鞘炎
tenosynovitis granulosa;

san1 jiao ji 三角肌
deltoid / deltoid muscle;

shen2 jing bing xing ji wei suo 神經病性肌萎縮
neuropathic atrophy;

shen jing ji bing 神經肌病
neuromyopathy;

shen jing yan xing ji wei suo 神經炎性肌萎縮
neuritic muscular atropathy;

shen jing yuan xing ji wei suo 神經源性肌萎縮
neural atrophy;

shi2 zhi xing ji yan 實質性肌炎
parenchymatous myositis;

shou4 han xing ji yan 受寒性肌炎
myositis a frigore;

shu1 jin huo luo 舒筋活絡
relax and activate the tendons;

sui2 yi ji 隨意肌
voluntary muscle;

tang2 niao bing ji wei suo 糖尿病肌萎縮
diabetic amyotrophy;

te4 fa xing ji wei suo 特發性肌萎縮
idiopathic muscular atrophy;

tong2 jin tie gu 銅筋鐵骨
tough and strong as iron and steel || an iron constitution; brass muscles and iron bones — a strong and solid body; with vigorous sines and bones and strengthened muscles;

tun2 da ji 臀大肌
gluteus maximus / great gluteal muscle;

tun ji yan 臀肌炎
glutitis / inflammation of the musculus of the buttock;

tun xiao ji 臀小肌
musculus gluteus minimus;

tun zhong ji 臀中肌
mesogluteus;

tun zui xiao ji 臀最小肌
least gluteal muscle;

wai4 bu ji 外部肌
extrinsic muscle;

wei4 ji ceng 胃肌層
tunica muscularis gastris;

wei ji wu li 胃肌無力
myasthenia gastrica;

wu3 dao chou chu 舞蹈抽搐
tic de sommeil;

xian4 ji liu 腺肌瘤
adenomyoma;

xian ji liu bing 腺肌瘤病
adenomyomatosis;

xian ji rou liu 腺肌肉瘤
adenomyosarcoma;

xiao3 yuan ji 小圓肌
teres minor;

xie2 fang ji 斜方肌
trapezius;

xin1 ji 心肌
cardiac muscle;

xin ji bing 心肌病
cardiomyopathy / disease of the heart muscle;

chan hou xin ji bing 產後心肌病
postpartum cardiomyopathy;

fei hou xing xin ji bing 肥厚性心肌病
hypertrophic cardiomyopathy;

ji fa xing xin ji bing 繼發性心肌病
secondary cardiomyopathy;

yuan fa xing xin ji bing 原發性心肌病
primary cardiomyopathy;

zhong du xing xin ji bing 中毒性心肌病
toxic cardiomyopathy;

xiong1 da ji 胸大肌
greater pectoral muscle / pectoralis major / pectoris major;

xiong ji 胸肌
pectoral muscle;

xiong suo ru tu ji 胸鎖乳突肌
amuent muscle / sternocleidom-astoid;

yan3 ji 眼肌
eye muscle;

yan ji bing 眼肌病
ocular myopathy;

yan ji tan huan 眼肌癱瘓
ophtalmoplegia;

yan ji yan 眼肌炎
ophthalmomyositis;

yan lun za ji 眼輪匝肌
orbicularis oculi;

yao3 ji 咬肌
great masticatory muscle / masseter;

yin1 dao ji ceng 陰道肌層
tunica muscularis vaginae;

yin dao ji ceng yan 陰道肌層炎
myocolpitis;

yu2 ji ji 魚際肌
thenar muscle;

yuan2 fa xing jian qiao nang zhong 原發性腱鞘囊腫
primary ganglion;

yuan2 fa xing xin ji bing 原發性心肌病
primary cardiomyopathy;

zeng1 sheng xing ji yan 增生性肌炎
proliferative myositis;

zhang1 ji 張肌
tensor;

zhen3 ji 枕肌
occipital muscle / occipitalis;

zhi1 zhi xing ji bing 脂質性肌病
lipid myopathy;

zhi3 chang shen ji 趾長伸肌
extensor digitorum;

zhong4 du xing xin ji bing 中毒性心肌病
toxic cardiomyopathy;

Jian 肩 Shoulder

ai2 jian 挨肩
sit shoulder to shoulder / stand should to shoulder;

ai jian ca bang 挨肩擦膀
rub shoulders;

ai jian ca bei 挨肩擦背
follow closely / go in a jostling crowd / rub shoulders;

ai jian da bei 挨肩搭背
shoulder to shoulder and arm in arm;

ai jian die bei 挨肩疊背
shoulder against shoulder and chest against chest;

ai jian er guo 挨肩而過
make one's way through the crowd;

bang3 膀
shoulder;

bang zi 膀子
shoulder;

bei4 背
bear / carry on the back / shoulder;

bei fu 背負
bear / carry on the back / have on one's shoulder;

bi3 jian 比肩
shoulder to shoulder / side by side;

bi jian bing jin 比肩並進
advance shoulder to shoulder;

bi jian er li 比肩而立
stand shoulder to shoulder / very near;

bi jian er shi 比肩而事
work together;

bi jian ji zhong 比肩繼踵
one follows on the heels of another || be overcrowded with people; follow closely one after another;

bing4 jian 並肩
shoulder to shoulder / side by side || abreast; stand beside; stand side by side;

bing jian er xing 並肩而行
walk shoulder to shoulder / walk side by

side || walk abreast;

bing jian er zuo 並肩而坐
sit side by side;

bing jian qian jin 並肩前進
advance shoulder to shoulder / march forward shoulder to shoulder;

bing jian zuo zhan 並肩作戰
fight side by side;

ca1 jian er guo 擦肩而過
brush past sb || brush against sb; brush by sb;

chi4 bo 赤膊
barebacked / stripped to the waist;

chi bo shang zhen 赤膊上陣
step forward in person without any disguise || come out into the open; come out pugnaciously; come out without any disguise; emerge into the open; go into battle stripped to the waist; go into battle with bared shoulders; strip off all disguise and come to the fore; take the field oneself undisguisedly; throw away all disguise;

dan1 擔
carry on a shoulder pole;

fu4 負
carry on the back or shoulder / shoulder;

gong3 jian suo bei 拱肩縮背
shrink one's shoulder and bow one's back (due to cold weather);

gou1 jian da bei 鉤肩搭背
hold each other's arms while walking side by side;

gu1 ji jian mo 轂擊肩摩
hubs hit hubs and shoulders rub shoulders // with jamming vehicles and pedestrians;

ji2 jian 及肩
come up to the shoulder;

jia3 胛
shoulder / shoulder blade;

jia gu 胛骨
shoulder blade;

jian1 肩
shoulder;

qiao luo jian 敲落肩
knocked-down shoulder;

song jian 聳肩
hump up one's shoulders / shrug one's shoulders;

xi jian 息肩
be relieved of a responsibility / put down one's burden;

xie jian 歇肩
remove the load from one's shoulder for a rest;

xie jian 脅肩
shrug the shoulders;

jian bang 肩膀
shoulder;

jian bei 肩背
shoulders and the back;

jian bu neng dan dan, shou bu neng ti lan 肩不能擔擔，手不能提籃
unable to carry anything, either on one's shoulders or in one's hands;

jian chui bing 肩垂病
drop shoulder;

jian fen li 肩分離
shoulder separation;

jian fu 肩負
bear / shoulder / take on / undertake;

jian fu zhong ren 肩負重任
bear heavy responsibilities || hold an important position; sustain great responsibilities; take up the heavy responsibility;

jian guan jie yan 肩關節炎
inflammation of the shoulder joint / omarthritis;

jian he 肩荷
carry on the shoulder / shoulder;

jian jia 肩胛
shoulder;

jian jia gu 肩胛骨
shoulder blade;

jian kang shou ti 肩扛手提
carry on one's shoulders or with one's hands;

jian kuan ti zhuang 肩寬體壯
have broad shoulders;

jian mo gu ji 肩摩轂擊
be overcrowded with people and traffic || go in a jostling crowd; shoulders rubbing and carriages knocking at each other — busy traffic;

jian mo zhong jie 肩摩踵接
rub the shoulder and follow the steps || crowded;

jian tiao bei fu 肩挑背負
carry on the shoulders and back;

jian tong 肩痛
omalgia / pain in the shoulder / shoulder pain;

jian tong feng 肩痛風
gout in the shoulder / omagra;

jian tou 肩頭
shoulder;

kang2 zai jian shang 扛在肩上
carry on the shoulder;

liu1 jian bang 溜肩膀
sloping shoulders;

mo2 jian ca bei 摩肩擦背
go in a jostling crowd;

mo jian ji gu 摩肩擊轂
shoulder to shoulder and hub to hub || be crowded with people and carriages; be overcrowded with people and traffic;

mo jian jie zhong 摩肩接踵
shoulder to shoulder and closely upon heels || be jam-packed with people; jostle each other in a crowd; jostle one another on the way; rubbing the shoulders and following the steps;

qiao1 luo jian 敲落肩
knocked-down shoulder;

shuang1 jian 雙肩
both shoulders / the two shoulders;

song3 jian 聳肩
hump up one's shoulders / shrug one's shoulders;

song jian ha yao 聳肩哈腰
hump up one's shoulders and offer an ingratiating smile / shrug one's shoulders and offer an ingratiating smile;

tan3 jian lu bi 袒肩露臂
expose one's neck and shoulders;

tiao1 挑
carry things with a pole on one's shoulder / shoulder;

tiao bu dong 挑不動
too heavy to shoulder it;

tuo1 jian 脱肩
relinquish one's responsibility / shirk one's responsibility;

xi1 jian 息肩
be relieved of a responsibility / put down one's burden;

xie1 jian 歇肩
remove the load from one's shoulder for a rest;

xie2 脅
shrug shoulders;

xie jian 脅肩
shrug shoulders;

xie jian chan xiao 脅肩諂笑
act obsequiously / sycophantic;

xie jian lei zu 脅肩累足
apprehensive and nervous / frightened / jittery;

xie4 jian 卸肩
lay down responsibilities;

xue1 jian 削肩
sloping shoulders;

ya1 jian die bei 壓肩迭背
press breast to back and shoulder to shoulder;

yi1 jian xing li liang xiu qing feng 一肩行李兩袖清風
own nothing but one's personal belongings;

肩 *Shoulder*

Jiao 腳 Foot

ai4 shou ai jiao 礙手礙腳
very much in the way;

ai shou jiao 礙手腳
(1) hinder the movement of sb's hand and feet / stand in the way;
(2) drag / nuisance;

an1 bu 安步
go leisurely on foot;

an bu dang che 安步當車
go leisurely on foot is as good as riding in a chariot / go on shank's mare / walk instead of taking vehicles / walk rather than ride;

ang2 ran er ru 昂然而入
come walking in proudly ‖ come in walking proudly; enter in a stately manner; step grandly into;

ao2 xi 遨嬉
make merry ‖ play; ramble; travel for pleasure;

ao you 遨遊
ramble / roam / travel;

ba1 zi bu 八字步
splayfoot walking;

ba zi jiao 八字腳
splayfoot;

ba1 yi zi tui 扒一字腿
do the splits;

ba2 bu chu tui lai 拔不出腿來
cannot get away from sth;

ba bu 拔步
take to one's heels ‖ lift the foot (and begin to run); march forward; move forward quickly; walk with big and quick strides;

ba jiao jiu zou 拔腳就走
get off at once / leave at once ‖ scurry away; scuttle away; scuttle off;

ba tui 拔腿
lift the foot and begin to run / light out / stir one's stump / take to one's heels;

ba tui jiu pao 拔腿就跑
immediately take to one's heels ‖ beat it as fast as one can; light out; make the best use of one's legs; make tracks; show a clean pair of heels; start running away at once; stir one's stump; take to one's legs; take to one's legs as fast as one can; turn and scamper off;

ba2 lü shan chuan 跋履山川
travel across hills and rivers;

ba shan she shui 跋山涉水
across mountains and rivers / travel over mountains and rivers ‖ over the hills and through the rivers; scale mountains and ford streams; travel across mountains and rivers; travel by climbing up hills and wading over rivers; travel over land and water;

ba shan she ye 跋山涉野
roam over hills and dales;

ba she 跋涉
make a long, tiring journey / travel over land and water ‖ make a weary journey; tramp; trek; trudge; wade;

ba she shan chuan 跋涉山川
travel by climbing up hills and wading across rivers;

ba she xiang ye 跋涉鄉野
trudge through the countryside;

ba she zhi lao 跋涉之勞
the hardship of journeying over land and across water / the troubles of climbing and wading;

bai2 pao 白跑
be on a fool's errand;

bai pao yi tang 白跑一趟
make a fruitless trip / make a futile trip;

bai4 dao zu xia 拜倒足下
prostrate oneself before sb ‖ grovel at sb's feet; lie prostrate before sb; prostrate oneself and kowtow at sb's feet; throw oneself at sb's feet;

bai4 zou 敗走
flee after defeat;

ban1 qi shi tou za zi ji de jiao 搬起石頭砸自己的腳
intend to do harm to others but only hurt oneself / lift a rock only to drop it on one's own feet / pick up a strone only to drop it on one's own feet;

腳 *Foot*

ban4 絆
(1) be in the way // hindrance;
(2) cause to trip / cause to stumble / stumble / trip;

ban ban ke ke 絆絆坷坷
stagger along;

ban dao 絆倒
stumble / trip / trip over;

ban jiao 絆腳
(1) tie up a person's movements / trip;
(2) fettered / hindered;

ban jiao shi 絆腳石
obstacle / stumbling block;

ban ma suo 絆馬索
ropes for tripping the enemy's horses;

ban shou ban jiao 絆手絆腳
encumber the free movement of one's limbs / in the way;

ban zhu 絆住
be detained / be held back || entangle; successfully hinder movement;

ban4 zu 瓣足
lobed foot;

bang3 tui 綁腿
leg wrappings;

bang4 di zou 傍地走
run closely on the ground;

bang hu er li 傍戶而立
stand close to the door;

bao4 cu tui 抱粗腿
cling to the rich and powerful / curry favour with sb || flatter; latch on to the rich and powerful; throw oneself under the protection of someone of influence;

bao fo jiao 抱佛腳
make a last-minute effort;

bao tui qiu rao 抱腿求饒
embrace sb's legs and plead for mercy;

bao4 趵
jump / leap;

bao bao 趵趵
noise of tramping feet;

bao4 tiao ru lei 暴跳如雷
stamp the feet with fury;

bei4 qu 背屈
dorsiflexion;

ben1 奔
(1) run quickly || gallop; hasten; hurry move quickly; rush; rush about;
(2) flee || run away; run for one's life;
(3) go straight towards / head for;
(4) approach / getting on for;
(5) elope;

ben bo 奔波
rush about || busy running about; on constant run; on the run;

ben chi 奔馳
run quickly / scoot;

ben cuan 奔竄
flee in disorder / run helter-skelter;

ben fu 奔赴
hasten to / hurry off to || go to; hurry off for; hurry to a place; rush to;

ben pao 奔跑
run in great hurry / scoot;

ben tao 奔逃
flee off / run away;

ben zhu 奔逐
chase / run after;

ben zou 奔走
busy running about || do a job on order; run; rush about; solicit help;

ben zou hu hao 奔走呼號
go around campaigning for a cause / go around crying for help;

ben zou xiang gao 奔走相告
rush about telling the news / run around spreading the news || lose no time in telling each other the news; pass the news from mouth to mouth; pass the news from one person to another;

beng4 san 迸散
flee in all directions;

beng tiao 迸跳
jump about;

beng4 蹦
jump / leap || caper; skip; spring; trip;

beng beng tiao tiao 蹦蹦跳跳
bounce about || bouncing and vivacious; capering; cut a caper; cut capers; frolicsome; jump like parched peas; prance about to romp; romping; skipping; tripping;

bi3 shou hua jiao 比手劃腳
illustrate with the help of gestures / make lively gestures;

bi4 躄
crippled in both legs / having both legs disabled;

bi yong 躄踊
stamp the feet with grief;

bian1 zou bian tan 邊走邊談
talk while walking;

bian3 ping zu 扁平足
flatfoot;
jing luan xing bian ping zu 痙攣性扁平足
spastic flatfoot;

bian4 bu 便步
(1) walk at ease;
(2) route step;

bian bu zou 便步走
march at ease;

bie2 蹩
limp;

bie jiao 蹩腳
lame;

bing4 li 並立
stand side by side / stand together;

bing lie 並列
stand side by side;

bing4 zhi 併趾
losyndactyly;
duo bing zhi 多併趾
polysyndactyly;
ju bing zhi 巨併趾
megalosyndactyly;

bo2 踣
stumble and fall;

bo3 跛
crippled / lame // lameness;

bo bi 跛躄
crippled / lame;

bo jian 跛蹇
crippled / lame;

bo jiao 跛腳
(1) walk with a limp;
(2) crippled / lame // have a lame foot;

bo jue 跛蹶
stumble and fall;

bo tui 跛腿
crippled / lame;

bo xing 跛行
(1) limp / walk lamely / walk with a limp || have a limp;
(2) claudication / lameness;
jian xie xing bo xing 間歇性跛行
intermittent claudication;
shen jing yuan xing bo xing 神經源性跛行
neurogenic claudication;

bo xing zheng 跛行症
string-halt;

bo zi 跛子
cripple;

bo zi pa lou ti — nan shang nan 跛子爬樓梯——難上難
a cripple climbing a stairway — harder and harder;

bo zu 跛足
crippled / crooked-foot / lame;

bu4 liang yu xing 不良於行
have difficulty in walking;

bu liang li 不量力
do not consider one's ability to do a job;

bu4 步
(1) pace / step;
(2) stage / step;
(3) go on foot / walk;

bu bu 步步
(1) at every step;
(2) step by step;

bu bu deng gao 步步登高
rise step by step in the world;

bu bu jin bi 步步緊逼
press forward steadily;

bu bu liu shen 步步留神
be careful of every step / watch every step || act with the utmost prudence and circumspection; pick one's steps;

bu bu tui que 步步退卻
incessant retreats;

bu bu wei ying 步步為營
move carefully every step on the way || a bastion at every step; act cautiously; advance gradually and entrench oneself at every step; consolidate at every step; make a stand at every step; raise a fort at every step;

bu diao 步調
pace / step / tempo;

bu diao yi zhi 步調一致
in step with;

bu fa 步伐
pace / step;

bu fu 步幅
the width of stride;

bu lü 步履
walk;

bu lü chen zhong 步履沈重
heavy-footed;

bu lü jiao jie 步履矯捷
fleet of foot // at a cracking pace / in great speed;

bu lü qing ying 步履輕盈
walk with a light step / walk with a lightsome step // light-footed;

bu lü ru fei 步履如飛
walk very quickly / with flying feet;

bu lü sheng feng 步履生風
stride jubilantly;

bu lü wei jian 步履維艱
hard to move one's feet / have difficulty walking || a little too heavy for one's feet to carry; difficult to go on foot; hobble along; trudge; very hard to walk; walk with difficulty; walking in a difficult manner;

bu lü wen luan 步履紊亂
in disorder || walk out of step — in great confusion;

bu lü wen jian 步履穩健
sure-footed;

bu ren hou chen 步人後塵
follow in sb's footsteps / tread in the footsteps of || dog the steps of others; follow in the wake of; step into sb's shoes; trail along behind others; tread in the footprints of;

bu ru 步入
step into;

bu ru qi tu 步入歧途
take the wrong turning;

bu tai 步態
gait / manner of walking;
pian tan bu tai 偏癱步態
hemiplegic gait;

bu tai jiao jin 步態驕矜
have a proud walk;

bu tai niao nuo 步態裊娜
walk with a mincing step;

bu tai pan shan 步態蹣跚
one's gait is unsteady // staggering;

bu tai you ya 步態優雅
walk gracefully;

bu wu xian xian 步武先賢
tread in the footsteps of ancient worthies;

bu xing 步行
go afoot / go on foot / walk;

bu xing bu neng 步行不能
abasia;
ma bi xing bu xing bu neng 麻痺性步行不能
paralytic abasia;

bu xing kun nan 步行困難
difficulty in walking / dysbasia;

bu zi 步子
footstep / step;

cai3 踩
(1) trample / tread on;
(2) chase / pursue;

cai bian 踹扁
trample sth flat;

cai chu 踹出
tread;

cai fang 踹訪
search and arrest a criminal;

cai huai 踹壞
break or damage by trampling / trample and break;

cai shi 踹實
(1) tread / tread down;
(2) mat down;

cai shui 踹水
tread water;

cai ta 踹踏
tread;

cai zhu 踹住
keep the feet upon;

cai zuo cai you 踹左踹右
at odds with;

cai3 踩
step on / trample / tread on / tread upon;

cai hu 踩乎
bully / oppress || deprecate; disparage; tread upon;

cai shi 踩實
mat / trample down / tread down;

cai shui 踩水
tread water;

cai xian 踩線
step on line;

ceng4 蹭
stroll;

cha1 zu 插足
put one's foot in;

chan2 jiao 纏腳
bind the feet // foot-binding;

chan zu 纏足
foot-binding;

chang2 shou chang jiao 長手長腳
all legs;

chang zu 長足
by leaps and bounds;

chang zu jin bu 長足進步
marked progress // come a long way;

chang4 du jiao xi 唱獨腳戲
one doing work all by oneself;

che3 hou tui 扯後腿
pull the hind leg || a drag on sb; a hindrance to sb; hold sb back from action; pull sb back from action;

cheng3 bu 騁步
rush / speed;

cheng chi 騁馳
go at full speed;

cheng zu ji chi 騁足疾馳
run quickly — in a quick manner;

chi4 jiao 赤腳
barefoot / go barefoot // barefooted;

chi zu 赤足
with bare feet / without shoes;

chi4 彳
go on one leg;

chong1 chu lai 衝出來
belt out;

chou1 jin 抽筋
(1) pull out a tendon;
(2) clonus / cramp;

chou jin bo pi 抽筋剝皮
peel off the skin and pluck out the sinews / pull out sb's rendons and tear his skin off;

chou shang 抽傷
sprain;

chuai4 踹
trample / tread;

chuai ta 踹踏
trample / tread;

chuai zu er nu 踹足而怒
tramp one's foot with rage;

chuan1 穿
cross / go through / pass through;

chuan da jie, zou xiao xiang 穿大街，走小巷
through a maze of streets and crooked lanes;

chuan hua du liu 穿花度柳
go through the flowers and willows;

chuan jie guo xiang 穿街過巷
go through streets and alleys;

chuan lin du shui 穿林度水
through the trees and across the water;

chuan suo lai wang 穿梭來往
busy comings and goings // shuttle back and forth;

chuan tang ru shi 穿堂入室
go everywhere as one pleases;

chuan xie 穿鞋
put on shoes;

chuan4 jie you xiang 串街游鄉
make one's rounds of the streets and villages;

chuan jie zou xiang 串街走巷
make one's rounds of the streets and lanes;

chuan you 串遊
amble / saunter / stroll;

ci3 跐
tiptoe;

ci zhe jiao 跐着腳
on tiptoe;

cong2 tou dao jiao 從頭到腳
from head to foot ‖ from face to foot; from the sole of the foot to the crown of the head; from top to toe;

cu4 蹴
(1) tread on;
(2) kick;

cu qu 蹴去
kick away;

cu ta 蹴踏
tread underfoot;

cu ti 蹴踢
trample on;

cuan1 躥
leap up ‖ go up suddenly; hike up; rise quickly;

cuan fang yue ji 躥房越脊
jump onto the roof and descend into rooms — a thief;

cuan shang tiao xia 躥上跳下
bounce up and down;

cun4 bu 寸步
single step / tiny step;

cun bu bu li 寸步不離
follow sb closely ‖ cup and can; finger and thumb; keep close to; move in pairs; never move a step from; not let sb out of one's sight; not to budge an inch from one's side; not to take an inch leave of sb; not to leave sb at any time; stay without leaving a step;

cun bu bu rang 寸步不讓
not to make the slightest concession ‖ dispute every inch of ground; fight every inch of the way; give not an inch; hold one's ground; never to give away one inch; not to surrender one inch of land; not to yield a single step; not yield an inch; refuse to yield an inch;

cun bu nan xing 寸步難行
difficult to move even one step ‖ cannot do anything; cannot go a step; cannot move a single step; difficult for sb to move a single step; find it hard to make a single move; forced into a strait; unable to do a thing; unable to move one inch forward;

cun bu nan yi 寸步難移
can hardly move a step ‖ bogged down and cannot move a step; hard to walk even an inch; in a difficult pass; stumble at every step;

da1 da jiao 搭搭腳
rest one's feet;

da jiao 搭腳
get a foothold;

da3 chi jiao 打赤腳
(1) bare the feet;
(2) go barefooted;

da dao 打道
clear the way;

da dao hui fu 打道回府
direct one's step toword home;

da4 shou da jiao 大手大腳
extravagant;

da ta bu 大踏步
in big strides;

da tui 大腿
thigh;

da zhi 大趾
big toe;

da zhi tong 大趾痛
hallux dolorosus / pain in the big toe;

dai4 bu 代步
ride instead of walk;

dao3 蹈
(1) step / tread;
(2) skip / trip;

dao hai 蹈海
plunge oneself into the sea to commit suicide;

dao xi 蹈襲
follow slavishly;

dao xi fu zhe 蹈襲覆轍
follow the same old disastrous road / follow the tracks of an overthrown chariot;

dao xi qian ren 蹈襲前人
slavishly follow one's predecessors;

dao4 chu zou dong 到處走動
get about;

deng1 登
(1) ascend / climb;
(2) employ / take;
(3) board / wear;

deng cheng 登程
set out on a journey / start off on a journey;

deng gao 登高
ascend a height;

deng gao yi hu 登高一呼
make a public appeal || make a clarion call; mount a stone and cry;

deng gao yuan tiao 登高遠眺
ascend a height to enjoy a distant view;

deng gao zi bei 登高自卑
in order to climb up high, one must begin from the bottom;

deng lu 登陸
go to debarkation / land;

deng men 登門
call at sb's house;

deng men bai fang 登門拜訪
call on sb in person || call at sb's house; come on a visit to sb's house; pay sb a visit;

deng men bai xie 登門拜謝
call at sb's house to express one's thanks / go to sb's house and offer thanks;

deng men bao xi 登門報喜
announce good news at the house door / call on sb to announce happy news / go to sb's house to report success;

deng men ci bie 登門辭別
personally pay a farewell call;

deng men da xie 登門答謝
call on sb to express gratitude;

deng men dao he 登門道賀
call on sb to offer one's congratulations / go to pay sb a congratulatory call;

deng men dao qian 登門道歉
go to sb's home and apologize;

deng men dao xie 登門道謝
go to sb's house and offer thanks;

deng men diao yan 登門吊唁
go to sb's house to offer one's condolences / pay a visit of condolence on the death of sb;

deng men gao bie 登門告別
call on sb to say goodbye;

deng men qing zui 登門請罪
go to sb's house and make apologies;

deng men qiu jiao 登門求教
go to sb for advice || call on sb for counsel; come to seek advice;

deng men qiu yi 登門求醫
go to the doctor for treatment;

deng men zao fu 登門造府
call on a person at his house;

deng men zi jian 登門自薦
present oneself at the door;

deng pan 登攀
climb / scale;

deng shan 登山
(1) climb a mountain;
(2) mountaineering;

腳 Foot

deng shan she shui 登山涉水
climb mountains and wade through rivers / go over mountains and cross streams / scale mountains and cross rivers / traverse mountains and wade through rivers;

deng shan yuan wang 登山遠望
ascend a hill to have a wide view / climb a mountain and gaze for afield;

deng tang ru shi 登堂入室
(1) pass through the hall into the inner chamber / reach the hall and enter the chamber;
(2) gain the mastery of;

deng4 蹬
step on / tread on;

di4 er zhi 第二趾
second toe;

dian4 踮
stand on tiptoe;

dian zhe jiao 踮着腳
on tiptoe;

die2 jiao chui xiong 跌腳捶胸
stamp one's feet and beat one's chest in bitterness;

die jiao jiao ku 跌腳叫苦
stamp one's feet and cry out one's bitterness;

die zu 跌足
stamp one's foot;

die2 蹀
stamp the feet;

die die 蹀蹀
walk in mincing gait;

die xie 蹀躞
(1) pace about / pace up and down;
(2) walk in small steps;

die zu 蹀足
stamp the feet;

dong1 ben xi cuan 東奔西竄
disperse helter-skelter / flee in all directions;

dong ben xi pao 東奔西跑
rush around || bat around; bustle about; bustle around; bustle in and out; dash about; drive from post to pillar and from pillar to post; move from post to pillar and from pillar to post; run about; run around; run around here and there; run hither and thither; run this way and that; run to and fro; rush about; tear around; wander from place to place;

dong ben xi zou 東奔西走
rush hither and thither || dash about; in all directions; run about; run around; run to and fro;

dong pao xi cuan 東跑西竄
dash about / fool about / fool around / run about / run around;

dong pao xi dian 東跑西顛
run hither and thither || dash about; keep on the run; run about busily;

dong pao xi liu 東跑西蹓
gad about / gad around;

du2 bu 獨步
peerless / unrivaled / without match;

du bu gu jin 獨步古今
be equaled neither in ancient times nor in modern times;

du bu yi shi 獨步一時
be unequalled in one's generation;

du jiao xi 獨腳戲
one-man show;

duan3 bu 短步
brachybasia;

dun1 蹲
(1) hunker down / sit on one's haunch / squat / squat on one's haunchn / squat on one's hunkers / squat on the heels;
(2) crouched;
(3) stray;

dun bu xia qu 蹲不下去
unable to squat || unable to crouch;

dun fu 蹲伏
crouch in hiding / hunker down;

dun ju 蹲踞
squat || crouch;

dun keng bu la shi 蹲坑不拉屎
squat over a latrine pit without releasing oneself;

dun xia qu 蹲下去
hunker down / squat;

dun zhe 蹲着
squatting || crouching;

dun zuo 蹲坐
squat on the heels || crouch on the heels;

dun4 zu 頓足
stamp one's feet;

dun zu bu qian 頓足不前
come to a standstill;

dun zu chui xiong 頓足捶胸
stamp one's feet and beat one's breast / stamp one's feet and pound one's breast;

dun zu hao ku 頓足號哭
cry stamping one's feet;

dun4 qu 遁去
run away / take to one's heels;

dun zou 遁走
flee / take to one's heels;

duo1 bing zhi 多併趾
polysyndactyly;

duo2 踱
pace / stroll;

duo bu 踱步
pace / walk slowly;

duo fang bu 踱方步
walk with measured tread;

duo lai duo qu 踱來踱去
pace back and forth || be on the prowl; pace the floor; pace to and fro; pace up and down; scout about; tramp back and forth; walk to and fro; walking hither and thither; walk up and down;

duo4 跺
stamp one's foot;

duo jiao 跺腳
stamp one's foot;

e2 xing ya bu 鵝行鴨步
walk with a swagger || go as slowly as ducks or geese do; waddle along like a duck or a goose;

er4 lang tui 二郎腿
sit cross-legged || with ankle on knee;

er zhi 二趾
second toe;

fang4 kai shou jiao 放開手腳
have one's hands and feet unfettered;

fang shou fang jiao 放手放腳
with hands and feet unfettered;

fei1 ben 飛奔
belt down / gallop / run at full speed / run like mad / run like the wind;

fei ben er qu 飛奔而去
fly off / take a flight / take wing;

fei jiao 飛腳
flying kick;

fei mao tui 飛毛腿
(1) fleet-footed;
(2) fast runner / fleet-footed runner;

fei yue 飛躍
advance rapidly / by leaps and bounds;

fei4 shou jiao 費手腳
take much handwork and footwork / take much physical labour;

fen1 zhi ta lai 紛至沓來
flock in;

fu1 趺
(1) back of the foot;
(2) sit cross-legged;

fu zuo 趺坐
sit cross-legged;

fu2 zhang er xing 扶仗而行
walk on crutches / walk with a cane / walk with the help of a staff;

fu4 赴
go to;

fu hui 赴會
go to a meeting;

fu yan 赴宴
go to a banquet;

fu yue 赴約
go to an appointment;

gan3 shang 趕上
catch up / come up with / keep pace with;

gao1 fei yuan zou 高飛遠走
abscond;

gao gong zu 高弓足
pes cavus;

gen1 bu shang 跟不上
unable to catch up with / unable to keep pace with;

gen shang 跟上
catch up with / keep pace with / overtake;

gen sui 跟隨
follow / go closely behind;

gen wo zou 跟我走
follow me;

gen zong 跟踪
follow others' footsteps / follow others' tracks / shadow;

gen zong 跟蹤
keep track of / shadow / tail;

gong1 xing tui 弓形腿
bandy leg / bowleg;

gong xing zu 弓形足
cavus;

gong3 li 拱立
stand in a reverent posture;

gu3 gu 股骨
femur / thigh bone;

gu4 bu zi feng 固步自封
rest content with old practice ‖ continue walking in the old steps and seclude oneself; limit one's own progress; remain where one is, without desire to advance further; rest complacently on one's laurels; stand still and refuse to make progress; stick to the beaten track; unwilling to move forward;

gu4 bu zi feng 故步自封
rest content with old practice ‖ a standpatter and be proud of it; be satisfied with old practices; complacent and conservative; confine oneself to the old method; confine oneself to the traditional way; content with staying where one is; do not want to move a step forward; hold fast to one's established ideas; limit one's own progress; remain where one is; rest complacently on one's laurels; self-satisfaction and conservatism; self-satisfied with being a stick-in-the-mud; stand still and cease to make progress; stand still and refuse to make progress; ultraconservative and self-satisfied; unwilling to move forward; without desire to advance further;

guang1 jiao 光腳
barefooted;

guang zhe jiao 光着腳
barefooted;

guang4 逛
ramble / roam / stroll;

guang da jie 逛大街
strolling around the streets ‖ go shopping; window-shopping;

guang jie 逛街
stroll around the streets ‖ go shopping; window-shopping;

guang shang dian 逛商店
go shopping;

guang dang 逛蕩
gad about / linger idly / loaf about / loiter;

guang lai guang qu 逛來逛去
hang around;

gui1 xing ju bu 規行矩步
act strictly according to accepted practices / act strictly according to rules / follow the beaten track;

guo3 jiao 裹腳
bind the feet;

guo zu 裹足
(1) bind the feet of women;
(2) hesitate for fear of danger;

guo zu bu qian 裹足不前
come to a standstill / not step forward ‖ drag one's feet; halt in hesitation; hesitate to move forward; hesitate to proceed; mark time; put down one's feet; refuse to go further; stop from proceeding; unwilling to go further;

han2 tui 寒腿
rheumatoid-arthritis in the legs;

han4 jiao 汗腳
feet that tend to perspire;

hong2 zu zheng 紅足症
redfoot;

hou4 jiao 後腳
rear foot;

hou tui 後腿
hind leg;

hou zu 後足
hindfoot;

hua2 jiao 滑跤
have a slip when walking / slip;

hua le yi jiao 滑了一跤
have a slip when walking / slip;

huai2 踝
ankle / malleolus;
nei huai 內踝
internal malleolus;
wai huai 外踝
external malleolus;
you huai 右踝
right ankle;
zuo huai 左踝
left ankle;

huai fan she 踝反射
ankle jerk;

huai gu 踝骨
anklebone;

huai guan jie 踝關節
ankle joint;

huai zi gu 踝子骨
anklebone;

huan1 beng luan tiao 歡蹦亂跳
jumping about with joy / gambolling / skipping about with joy;

huan xin que yue 歡欣雀躍
jump up and down with excitement;

huan yue 歡躍
dance with joy / jump for joy;

huan3 bu 緩步
ramble / stroll / walk slowly;

huan bu dang che 緩步當車
have a slow walk instead of riding on a carriage;

huan bu er xing 緩步而行
walk at a foot's pace / walk at a snail's pace / walk unhurriedly;

huan4 bu 換步
change step;

huang1 le shou jiao 慌了手腳
be thrown off one's balance || be greatly alarmed; be seized with a panic; be thrown into a panic; become panicky;

huang shou huang jiao 慌手慌腳
in a great flurry;

ji1 xing zu 畸形足
clubfoot;

ji1 蹟
footprint / trace;

ji1 躋
ascend / go up / rise;

ji2 de duo jiao 急得跺腳
stamp one's foot with worry || make sb jump up with nervousness;

ji xing wu dao zheng 急性舞蹈症
acute chorea;

ji zou 急走
go quicky;

ji2 zou 疾走
trot;

ji zou ru fei 疾走如飛
run so fast as if flying / speed on flying feet;

ji zu xian deng 疾足先登
one who acts fast will succeed first / the hasty foot gets there first;

ji2 踖
trample / tread upon;

ji2 蹐
walk with small steps;

ji3 踦
(1) shin;
(2) lean against;

jia1 kuai bu fa 加快步伐
mend one's pace / move ahead faster;

jia2 跲
stumble;

腳 *Foot*

jian3 蹇
crippled / lame;

jian bu 蹇步
slow and clumsy steps;

jian4 xie xing bo xing 間歇性跛行
intermittent claudication;

jian4 bu 健步
walk with vigorous strides;

jian bu ru fei 健步如飛
walk with springy steps || at a good bat; fleet of foot; swift of foot; walk as if on wings; walk fast and vigorously; walk with much bounce; with flying feet;

jian xing 健行
hike // hiking;

jian4 踐
trample / tread upon;

jian lü 踐履
trample;

jian ta 踐踏
trample / tread on;

jiao1 跤
fall / stumble;

jiao3 腳
foot;

jiao ban 腳板
sole of the foot;

jiao bei 腳背
instep;

jiao bing 腳病
pedopathy;

yun dong yuan jiao bing 運動員腳病
athlete's foot;

jiao bu 腳步
footstep / step || pace; tread;

jiao bu liang qiang 腳步踉蹌
staggering / with unsteady steps || dotty;

jiao bu qing kuai 腳步輕快
light of foot;

jiao bu sheng 腳步聲
footfall;

jiao di 腳底
sole;

jiao di ban er 腳底板兒
sole of the foot;

jiao di xia 腳底下
under the feet;

jiao gen 腳跟
back part of the foot / heel;

jiao hou gen 腳後跟
back part of the foot / heel;

jiao huai 腳踝
ankle;

cui ruo de jiao huai 脆弱的腳踝
delicate ankle;

niu shang de jiao huai 扭傷的腳踝
sprained ankle;

niu shang jiao huai 扭傷腳踝
sprain one's ankle / strain one's ankle / twist one's ankle / wrench one's ankle;

shang le jiao huai 傷了腳踝
hurt one's ankle;

zhong zhang de jiao huai 腫脹的腳踝
swollen ankle;

jiao ji 腳跡
footmark / footprint;

jiao jian 腳尖
tip of a toe / tiptoe;

jiao li 腳力
strength of one's legs;

jiao li jin jian 腳力勁健
get strong legs;

jiao mian 腳面
back of a foot / instep;

jiao pao 腳泡
blisters on the feet;

jiao qi 腳氣
(1) beriberi;
(2) athlete's foot;

jiao qi bing 腳氣病
(1) beriberi;
(2) athlete's foot;

ma bi xing jiao qi bing 麻痺性腳氣病
paralytic beriberi;

shi xing jiao qi bing 濕性腳氣病
wet beriberi;

wei suo xing jiao qi bing 萎縮性腳氣病
atrophic beriberi;

jiao suan tui ruan 腳酸腿軟
one's feet give way and one's legs are without strength // footsore;

jiao ta liang zhi chuan 腳踏兩隻船
have it both ways / sit on two chairs / straddle the fence // undecided;

jiao ta shi di 腳踏實地
do solid work // down-to-earth || earnest and down to earth; have one's feet firmly planted on solid ground; have one's feet on the ground; on firm ground; stand on solid ground; work without bluster and ostentation;

jiao ti 腳踢
kick;

jiao wan zi 腳腕子
ankle;

jiao xia 腳下
under one's feet;

jiao xian 腳癬
athlete's foot / ringworm of the foot / tinea pedis;

jiao xin 腳心
arch;

jiao yin 腳印
footstep / pedograph || footmark; footprint; step; track;

jiao zhang 腳掌
sole / sole of the foot;

jiao zheng bu pa xie wai 腳正不怕鞋歪
a clear conscience is a sure card / a straight foot is not afraid of a crooked shoe;

jiao zheng bu pa xie wai, shen zheng bu pa ying xie 腳正不怕鞋歪，身正不怕影斜
a clean hand wants no washing / a clear conscience laughs at false accusations / a good conscience is a continual feast;

jiao zhi 腳指
toe;

jiao zhi feng er 腳指縫儿
the space between two toes;

jiao zhi jia 腳指甲
toenail;

jiao zhi 腳趾
toe;

jiao zhi tou 腳趾頭
toe;

jiao3 jian bu fa 矯健步伐
vigorous strides;

jie1 zhong 接踵
come one after another / follow on sb's heels;

jie zhong er lai 接踵而來
arrive in quick succession || arrive one after another in rapid succession; be rapidly followed by; come in quick succession; come one after another; come one on the heels of the other; follow close on another; in the train of; tread on the heels of;

jie zhong er qi 接踵而起
arise after another || follow on the heels of;

jie zhong er xing 接踵而行
follow at one's heels;

jie2 li 孑立
stand in isolation;

jie2 zu xian de 捷足先得
the nimble foot gets first || it's the early bird that catches the worm; the early bird catches the worm;

jie zu xian deng 捷足先登
the fastest reaches the goal first || he that runs fastest gets the ring; if you are quick, you get ahead of others; outstrip all others; outstrip everyone else; the nimble foot gets there first; the nimble-footed get up first; the quick-footed mount first; the race is to the swiftest; the swift-footed arrive first; victory to the swift-footed;

jie2 jue 蹶蹶
stagger / totter;

jie2 zhi shi ju 截趾適屨
cut one's toes to fit the shoes — a foolish measure;

jin4 yi bu 進一步
move further ahead / take one step ahead;

jing1 zou 驚走
(1) run away in fright;
(2) scare away;

jiong3 bu 窘步
walk awkwardly because of being hard pressed;

ju2 跼
(1) bent;
(2) confined / cramped;

ju cu 跼促
ill at ease;

ju ji 跼蹐
confined / restricted;

ju tian ji di 跼天蹐地
confined / restricted;

ju zhu 跼躅
faltering / halting;

ju3 bu 舉步
take strides;

ju zhong 舉踵
on tiptoe;

ju zu qing zhong 舉足輕重
play a decisive role;

ju3 踽
walk alone;

ju ju 踽踽
walk alone;

ju ju du xing 踽踽獨行
walk alone / walk in solitude;

ju4 bing zhi 巨併趾
megalosyndactyly;

ju tui 巨腿
macroscelia;

ju zhi 巨趾
dactylomegaly;

ju zhi jia 巨趾甲
megalonychia;

ju zu 巨足
sciopody;

ju4 踞
squat ‖ crouch;

ju zuo 踞坐
squat ‖ crouch;

ju4 bu 遽步
walk hastily / walk hurriedly;

jue2 蹶
(1) tread;
(2) stumble and fall;

jue zhi 蹶躓
stumble and fall;

jue3 蹶
kick backward;

kai1 bu zou 開步走
forward march;

kang4 zu 抗足
stand on tiptoe;

kua4 胯
groin / space between the legs;

kua xia zhi ru 胯下之辱
crawl between another's legs — drain the cup of humiliation;

kua4 跨
(1) stride / take a stride;
(2) sit astride on / straddle;
(3) cut across / extend across / go beyond;

kuai4 bu 快步
half step;

kuai bu zou 快步走
quick march;

kuai pao 快跑
run fast;

kuai shou kuai jiao 快手快腳
do things quickly ‖ agile; do things with celerity; nimble; nimble of hands and fast of feet;

kuan3 bu 款步
walk in slow steps;

kuang2 ben 狂奔
run about madly / run about wildly / rush like mad / rush madly;

kuang zou 狂走
run about madly / run about wildly;

kui3 跬
half a pace;

kui bu bu li 跬步不離
not move even a half step from sb || follow sb closely; keep close to; not let sb out of sight;

kui bu nan xing 跬步難行
difficult to move even a short step;

kui bu qian li 跬步千里
even small steps may carry one a thousand miles;

kuo4 bu 闊步
make great strides / take big strides / walk in big strides;

kuo bu er xing 闊步而行
stride along at a great pace / stride with a dignified gait / walk with big strides;

kuo bu gao lun 闊步高論
indulge in oratory when walking / take big strides and give a high-flown talk;

kuo bu gao shi 闊步高視
swagger / take big strides and look high — put on airs;

kuo bu gao tan 闊步高談
take big strides and give a high-flown talk;

kuo bu qian jin 闊步前進
advance in giant strides / advance with giant strides / march on in big strides / stride ahead / stride forward / take big strides forward;

la1 hou tui 拉後腿
pull sb back || a drag on sb; a hindrance to sb; hinder sb; hold sb back;

la kua 拉跨
limp / walk lamely;

lan2 qiu zu 籃球足
basketball foot;

lao3 nian xing wu dao zheng 老年性舞蹈症
senile chorea;

li4 jiao 立腳
have a footing;

lian2 beng dai tiao 連蹦帶跳
hopping and skipping;

lian ti dai da 連踢帶打
knock and kick || beat severely with both hands and feet;

lian2 bu 蓮步
steps of a beautiful woman;

lian3 bu 斂步
hesitate to advance further / hold back from going / slow down one's steps / withdraw one's footstep;

lian zu 斂足
hesitate to advance further / hold back from going / slow down one's steps / withdraw one's footstep;

lian zu bu qian 斂足不前
hold back from going further / hold one's steps and refuse to go further;

liang3 jiao chao tian 兩腳朝天
lie with legs pointing up;

liang tiao tui zou lu 兩條腿走路
walk on two legs;

liang tui fa dou 兩腿發抖
quake // one's knees knock together;

liang tui fa ruan 兩腿發軟
one's legs feel like jelly / one's legs give way;

liang4 踉
limp / stagger / totter / walk unsteadily;

liang liang qiang qiang 踉踉蹌蹌
stumble along || press on hurriedly — advance with speed; roll from side to side as a drunken man; stagger; stagger about in all directions; stumbling and wavering; teeter; totter;

liang qiang 踉蹌
stagger / teeter / totter;

liang qiang er xing 踉蹌而行
stagger along;

lie4 躐
overstep / transgress;

lie deng 躐等
skip steps;

lin2 bing xing zu gen 淋病性足跟
gonorrheal heel;

lin4 躪
trample;

lin li 躪轢
trample and hurt;

liu1 da 溜達
ramble / stroll;

liu zhi da ji 溜之大吉
leave stealthily / mike off / slip out;

liu zou 溜走
slip away || leave stealthily; slink; slip off;

liu2 bu 留步
please do not trouble yourself by accompanying me to the door;

liu tui bu 留退步
leave ground for retreat;

liu4 zhi 六趾
hexadactyly;

liu4 遛
roam / saunter / stroll / walk slowly;

liu da 遛達
(1) go for a walk / have a short walk / muck about / muck around / take a stroll / take a walk;
(2) stretch one's legs;

liu da liu da 遛達遛達
(1) go for a walk / have a short walk / muck about / muck around / take a stroll / take a walk;
(2) stretch one's legs;

liu liu 遛遛
take a stroll / take a walk;

liu liu tui 遛遛腿
(1) take a walk;
(2) stretch one's legs;

liu ma 遛馬
take a walk;

liu wan er 遛彎兒
go for a stroll / take a walk;

long2 xing hu bu 龍行虎步
majestic gait || one's step is like a dragon's gambol and a tiger's walk;

luan2 qi shou zu 攣其手足
hands and feet crooked;

luo4 jiao 落腳
put up / put up at / stay at / stay with / stop / stop at;

ma2 bi xing bu xing bun eng 麻痺性步行不能
paralytic abasia;

ma bi xing jiao qi bing 麻痺性腳氣病
paralytic beriberi;

ma3 jiao 馬腳
sth that gives the game away;

ma jiao bi lu 馬腳畢露
show one's true colours;

mai4 tou mai jiao 賣頭賣腳
show one's face in public;

mai4 bu 邁步
make a step / step forward / take a step;

mai bu kai bu 邁不開步
unable to take a step;

mai bu qian jin 邁步前進
make great strides forward / take a step and go forward;

mai da bu zou 邁大步走
long stride // stride out;

mai fang bu 邁方步
take slow, swinging steps / walk slowly;

man4 bu 慢步
jog / trot / walk slowly;

man pao 慢跑
jog / trot // jogging;

man xing 慢行
walk slowly;

man zou 慢走
(1) goodbye // take care;
(1) don't go yet / stay / wait a minute;

man4 bu 漫步
take a stroll || loiter; pad; permenade; ramble; roam; saunter; stroll; wander;

mao2 shou mao jiao 毛手毛腳
(1) clumsily || brash and clumsy; rough-handed;
(2) careless / recklessly;

mu3 zhi 拇趾
big toe / great toe;

mu zhi qiu 拇趾球
ball of the foot;

na4 lü zhong jue 納履踵決
down at the heel / out at the elbows;

nei4 fan zhi 內翻趾
digitus varus;

nei fan zu 內翻足
crossfoot;

nei huai 內踝
internal malleolus;

ni2 zu shen xian 泥足深陷
sink deep in the mire ‖ get into real trouble;

nie1 shou nie jiao 捏手捏腳
move around lightly ‖ let one's hand and foot take too great liberties; walk gingerly; walk on tiptoe; walk with light steps; with light steps and soft movements of one's hands;

nie4 躡
(1) lighten one's step / walk on tiptoe;
(2) step on / walk with;

nie bu er ru 躡步而入
enter noiselessly / enter with careful steps;

nie deng 躡登
go up;

nie die 躡蹀
walking with mincing steps;

nie jue dan deng 躡屩擔簦
make a long journey / take a long journey / undertake a long journey;

nie shou nie jiao 躡手躡腳
walk gingerly ‖ do things stealthily; make one's way noiselessly to; pussyfoot; sneak up; tiptoe; walk on tiptoe; walk stealthily / with light steps and soft movements of one's hands;

nie ying zhui zong 躡影追蹤
locate / look for / trace;

nie zong 躡蹤
follow along behind sb / track;

nie zu 躡足
step on another's foot;

nie zu bu qian 躡足不前
not to move a step forward;

nie zu fu er 躡足附耳
press the foot and whisper in the ear — tell a secret;

nie zu qi jian 躡足其間
(1) associate with a certain type of people;
(2) follow a trade;
(3) join a profession;

nie zu qian zong 躡足潛蹤
walk stealthily;

nie zu xiang qian 躡足向前
go forward softly;

niu3 shang jiao huai 扭傷腳踝
sprain one's ankle / strain one's ankle / twist one's ankle / wrench one's ankle;

pa1 趴
lie face downwards / lie on one's stomach / prostrate oneself;

pa xia 趴下
(1) grovel / lie face downwards / prostrate oneself;
(2) fall flat on the ground;

pan2 tui 盤腿
cross one's legs;

pan2 蹣
(1) jump over;
(2) dodder / limp;

pan shan 蹣跚
stagger / stumble ‖ blunder; dodder; falter; flounder; gangle; hobble; joll dodder; limp; lurch; stump; titubate; totter; walk haltingly;

pan shan er xing 蹣跚而行
drag one's feet slowly along ‖ dodder; gangle; hobble along; lurch along; teeter; totter; walk lamely;

pao3 跑
(1) run;
(2) escape / run away;
(3) bustle about / go around ‖ on the go; run about doing sth; run errands;
(4) go;

pao bu 跑步
(1) run;
(2) double march ‖ double time march; march at the double; on the double;

pao bu qian jin 跑步前進
double time;

pao bu zou 跑步走
march double time;

pao chu qu 跑出去
run out / run out of / rush off / rush out;

pao jin 跑進
run in / run into;

pao kai 跑開
make off / run away / run off / run out;

pao lai pao qu 跑來跑去
bustle about / dash here and there / run back and forth;

pao ru 跑入
run into;

pao xiang 跑向
run to;

peng3 chou jiao 捧臭腳
hold with respect an odorous foot – act obsequiously;

pi1 fa xian zu 披髮跣足
with dishevelled hair and bare feet;

pi1 yi zi tui 劈一字腿
do the splits;

pian1 ce wu dao zheng 偏側舞蹈症
hemilateral chorea;

pian shen wu dao zheng 偏身舞蹈症
chorea dimidiata;

pian tan bu tai 偏癱步態
hemiplegic gait;

pian tan hou wu dao zheng 偏癱後舞蹈症
posthemiplegic chorea;

pian2 shou zhi zu 胼手胝足
work hard || with hand and feet becoming callous;

pian2 蹁
limping / walking unsteadily;

ping2 zu 平足
flat-footed;

ping2 tou lun zu 評頭論足
carp at;

qi1 shou ba jiao 七手八腳
in a bustle || all flurry and confusion; all hitching in; all lend a hand to; bustle about; great hurry and bustle; helter-skelter; hurriedly; in great haste; many people doing sth at the same time in a disorganized manner; serve hand and foot; several people engaged in a scuffle; take all together; too many cooks spoil the broth; with everybody lending a hand; with many people taking part; with seven hands and eight feet;

qi2 bu 齊步
fall into step // in step // uniform steps;

qi bu bing jin 齊步并進
keep pace with;

qi bu zou 齊步走
forward march / quick march / quick step;

qi3 企
stand on tiptoe;

qi li 企立
stand on tiptoe;

qi zhong 企踵
stand on tiptoe;

qi zhong yan jing 企踵延頸
stand on tiptoe and crane the neck — on the very tiptop of expectation;

qi zu er dai 企足而待
be on the very tiptoe of expectancy / expect with eagerness / wait on tiptoe;

qi zu er wang 企足而望
look forward to on tiptoe / stand on tiptoe to see;

qi zu yi dai 企足以待
wait on tiptoe;

qi3 bu 起步
(1) start;
(2) get moving / get off the mark / get underway;

qi4 de duo jiao 氣得跺腳
stamp one's feet with anger;

qi4 跂
stand on tiptoe / tiptoe;

qi wang 跂望
earnestly wait for / look forward with eagerness / wait on tiptoe;

qi wang yuan zhu 跂望援助
earnestly wait for help / stand on tiptoe

longing for assistance;

qi zhong er wang 跂踵而望
look forward to anxiously / look forward to on tiptoe;

qi zhong hou jia 跂踵候駕
stand on tiptoe longing for your presence;

qi zu yi dai 跂足以待
stand on tiptoe in wait for / wait / wait for;

qi zuo 跂坐
sit with legs hanging above the ground;

qian1 li zhi xing, shi yu zu xia 千里之行，始於足下
a thousand mile's journey begins with the first step;

qian1 jiao 扦腳
pedicure / trim toenails;

qian2 jiao 前腳
front foot;

qian tui 前腿
foreleg;

qian zhi 前肢
(1) forelimb;
(2) foreleg;

qiang1 蹌
bustle about / limp / stagger / walk rapidly / walk unsteadily;

qiang liang 蹌踉
stagger;

qiang qiang 蹌蹌
walk in rhythm;

qiang qiang dian dian 蹌蹌顛顛
bustle about / on the go;

qiang1 蹡
in motion / walking;

qiang qiang 蹡蹡
walking;

qiang3 xian yi bu 搶先一步
get a march on sb / steal a march on sb;

qiang4 蹡
limp;

qiao1 zu 蹺足
raise a foot;

qiao zu er dai 蹺足以待
sit down cozily and wait at ease;

qiao1 蹺
(1) raise the feet;
(2) on tiptoe;

qiao2 zu yi dai 翹足以待
stand on tiptoe in expectation / wait on tiptoe;

qiao zu yin ling 翹足引領
eagerly look forward to / raise one's head and crane one's neck;

qiao4 bu xu xing 俏步徐行
mincing gait;

qie4 踥
in motion / walk;

qie die 踥蹀
in motion / walk;

qie qie 踥踥
moving back and forth;

qing1 ying bu lü 輕盈步履
airy steps;

qing3 bu 頃步
half a step;

qiong2 跫
footsteps / sound of steps;

qiong ran 跫然
sound of footsteps;

qiong yin 跫音
footsteps / sound of steps;

qu1 bei er xing 曲背而行
stoop in walking;

qu4 去
(1) depart / go || go away; leave; make sb go; quit; send sth;
(2) abandon / discard || cast aside; clear away; do away with; eradicate; exterminate; get rid of; put off; reject; remove; throw out;
(3) apart from;

qu4 bu 覷步
spy on;

que1 zhi 缺趾
ectrodactyly;

脚 *Foot*

que2 瘸
(1) cripple;
(2) lame;

que tui 瘸腿
crippled / lame;

que zi shang shan — jin tui liang nan 瘸子上山—進退兩難
a lame person climbing up a mountain — in a dilemma;

que4 bu 卻步
step back || flinch from; hang back from; ink back at the sight of; retreat; shrink back from; withdraw;

que li 卻立
stand back;

que zou 卻走
run backward / turn away;

que4 yue 雀躍
jump for joy / leap with joy;

rang4 bu 讓步
back down / make a concession || back out of; compromise; give in; give way; yield;

rou2 ruo zu 柔弱足
weak foot;

rou2 蹂
(1) trample / trample on / tread upon;
(2) tread out grain;

rou jian 蹂踐
trample / tread upon;

rou lin 蹂躪
trample on || crush under one's feet; devastate; make havoc of; ravage;

rou ruo 蹂若
trample / tread on;

ru2 lü bo bing 如履薄冰
as if treading on thin ice / like walking on thin ice // on thin ice;

ruan3 jiao bing 軟腳病
beriberi;

sa1 jiao 撒腳
take to one's heels;

sa tui 撒腿
run / start running / take to one's heels;

sa tui jiu pao 撒腿就跑
make off at once / scamper;

sa4 趿
pick up with the foot;

san1 zhi 三趾
third toe;

san zu ding li 三足鼎立
stand like the three legs of a tripod / tripartite confrontation;

san4 guang 散逛
loaf about;

san bu 散步
go for a stroll / take a walk || go for a walk; have a stroll; have a walk; ramble; stretch one's legs; take a ramble;

sha4 jiao 煞腳
halt / stop;

sha zhe bu er 煞着步兒
halt one's pace;

shan1 跚
stagger / walk unsteadily;

shang4 cuan xia tiao 上竄下跳
run around on sinister errands;

she4 ji er shang 拾級而上
go up a flight of steps;

she4 zu 涉足
set foot in;

she zu hua cong 涉足花叢
(1) fool around with women;
(2) visit brothels;

she zu qi jian 涉足其間
set foot there;

she zu shi tu 涉足仕途
join the civil service / start an official career;

shen1 tui 伸腿
(1) stretch one's legs;
(2) step in;
(3) die / kick the bucket / turn up one's toes;

shen tui deng yan 伸腿瞪眼
dead;

shen2 jing yuan xing bo xing 神經源性跛行
neurogenic claudication;

shi1 jiao 失腳
lose one's footing / slip / slip on the ground;

shi zu 失足
(1) lose one's footing / miss one's foot / slip // false step / misstep;
(2) commit a mistake / take a wrong step in life;

shi zu luo shui 失足落水
slip and fall into the water;

shi1 xing jiao qi bing 濕性腳氣病
wet beriberi;

shou1 bu zhu jiao 收不住腳
unable to come to a quick stop;

shou4 chang shuang tui 瘦長雙腿
long gangling legs;

shu4 fu shou jiao 束縛手腳
bind sb hand and foot;

shuang1 jiao 雙腳
both feet / the two feet;

shuang shou shuang jiao 雙手雙腳
all fours;

si4 chu ben mang 四處奔忙
flutter about;

si jiao chao tian 四腳朝天
fall on one's back ‖ fall backwards with hands and legs in the air; fall down on one's back with legs pointing up;

si zhi 四趾
(1) tetradactyly;
(2) fourth toe;

sui4 bu 碎步
mince // quick short steps;

ta1 趿
wear shoes in a casual way;

ta4 踏
(1) step on / tread on;
(2) go to the spot;

ta bu 踏步
mark time;

ta bu bu qian 踏步不前
cease to advance / mark time and make no headway;

ta bu zou 踏步走
mark time, march;

ta ge 踏歌
beat time to a song with the feet;

ta jian 踏踐
trample upon / tread on;

ta pian 踏遍
traverse the length and breadth of a place;

ta po tie xie 踏破鐵鞋
wear out the iron shoes — search painstakingly everywhere;

ta po tie xie wu mi chu, de lai quan bu fei gong fu 踏破鐵鞋無覓處，得來全不費工夫
find sth accidentally after tracking miles in vain for it / find sb by chance after a painstaking search;

ta qing 踏青
go hiking on a spring day ‖ a spring outing; go for a walk in the country in spring; have an outing in spring;

ta qing shang chun 踏青賞春
go out to enjoy the beautiful scenery in spring time;

ta qing shang hua 踏青賞花
enjoy flowers in a spring outing / go for a walk in the country in spring and enjoy the beauty of the flowers;

ta sheng xun you 踏勝尋幽
choose places of scenic beauty;

ta xue xun mei 踏雪尋梅
go over the snow in search of plums;

ta yue 踏月
walk in the moonlight;

ta4 蹋
slip / stumble;

ta dao 蹋倒
slip and fall;

ta zu 蹋足
slide;

tan1 huan xing wu dao zheng 癱瘓性舞蹈症
paralytic chorea;

tang1 蹚
(1) tread / tread on;

腳 Foot

(2) wade / walk through mud or water;

tang shui 蹚水
tread water / wade water;

tang shui guo he 蹚水過河
wade a stream;

tao2 pao 逃跑
run off || abscond; betake oneself to flight; break away; buzz off; copa heel; cut and run; cut away; cut loose; cut one's stick; decamp; duck; escape; flee; get away; get out; give leg bail; make good one's escape; make off; make one's escape; make one's getaway; move off; run away; show a clean pair of heels; show legs; show one's heels; sling one's hook; slip away; take flight; take leg bail; take one's hook; take to flight; take to one's heels; take to one's legs;

ti1 踢
kick;

ti chu qu 踢出去
kick out;

ti kai 踢開
(1) kick open;
(2) kick sth out of the way;

ti qiu 踢球
(1) kick a ball;
(2) play football;

ti si 踢死
kick to death;

ti teng 踢騰
kick at random;

ti wu 踢舞
bouncing movement / tittup;

ti2 shou nie jiao 提手躡腳
walk on tiptoe;

tian1 zu 天足
natural feet;

tiao4 跳
(1) bounce / hop / jump / leap / spring;
(2) beat / move up and down / pulsate / throb / twitch;
(3) make omissions / skip;

tiao chu 跳出
jump out / leap out;

tiao jiao 跳腳
stamp one's feet;

tiao jin 跳進
jump into;

tiao lai tiao qu 跳來跳去
jump about;

tiao li 跳離
jump off // jump-off;

tiao lou 跳樓
commit suicide by jumping off a building;

tiao shang tiao xia 跳上跳下
bounce up and down / jump up and down;

tiao tiao beng beng 跳跳蹦蹦
cut a caper / skip and jump about;

tiao xia qu 跳下去
jump down / leap down;

tiao yue 跳躍
dance / hop / jump / leap;

ting2 bu bu qian 停步不前
cease to advance / come to a halt / mark time / stay;

tu2 徒
go on foot;

tu bu 徒步
go afoot / go on foot / use shank's pony;

tu bu ba she 徒步跋涉
march;

tu she 徒涉
wade cross a stream;

tu xi 徒裼
barefooted and bare-breasted;

tu xian 徒跣
move on one's bare feet;

tu xing 徒行
go on foot / hike / walk;

tui3 腿
(1) leg;
(2) leglike support;

gong xing tui 弓形腿
bandy leg / bowleg;

ju tui 巨腿
macroscelia;

qian tui 前腿
foreleg;

tui ce wan 腿側彎
cnemoscoliosis;

tui gan zi 腿杆子
lower leg / shank;

tui gen 腿跟
heel;

tui gu 腿骨
leg bone;

tui jiao 腿腳
capable of walking;

tui jiao bu li luo 腿腳不俐落
walk with difficulty;

tui jiao bu ling bian 腿腳不靈便
have difficulty walking / walk with difficulty;

tui jiao li luo 腿腳俐落
walk briskly;

tui jin 腿筋
sinews of one's legs;

tui ma 腿麻
one's leg has gone numb;

tui mao 腿毛
hair on legs / leg hair;

tui san jiao 腿三角
crural triangle;

tui suan 腿酸
one's legs are tired;

tui suan jiao ruan 腿酸腳軟
one's legs are tired from walking for a long time;

tui tong 腿痛
skelalgia;

tui wu li 腿無力
skelasthenia;

tui zi 腿子
henchman / hired thug / lackey;

tui4 bu 退步
(1) fall back / suffer a relapse;
(2) retreat;

tuo1 zu 托足
have a foothold / have a place to live in;

tuo1 hou tui 拖後腿
hold sb back || a drag on sb; hinder sb; turn sth into a break on;

tuo zhe jiao bu 拖着腳步
shuffle;

wai4 huai 外踝
external malleolus;

wan3 踠
crooked leg;

wang3 hou tui 往後退
back off / backstep;

wei3 suo xing jiao qi bing 萎縮性腳氣病
atrophic beriberi;

wen3 bu 穩步
steadily / with steady steps;

wen bu bu qian 穩步不前
mark time and make no advance;

wen bu qian jin 穩步前進
advance steadily / make steady progress || proceed by steady steps; progress steadily; steer a steady course;

wen bu zeng zhang 穩步增長
steady-state growth;

wu1 jiao bing 烏腳病
black foot disease;

wu2 suo cuo shou zu 無所措手足
not to know what to do || at a loss what to do; find no place to put one's hands and feet; have nowhere to put hand or foot — at a loss to know how to conduct oneself;

wu zu 無足
apodia / congenital absence of feet;

wu3 shi bu xiao bai bu 五十步笑百步
the pot calling the kettle black || one who retreats fifty paces mocks one who retreats a hundred — different in degrees but the same in essence; Satan reproves sin; the frying-pan said to the kettle: Avaunt, black brows; the pot calls the kettle black;

wu3 bu 舞步
dance step;

wu dao 舞蹈
dance;

wu dao zheng 舞蹈症
chorea;

ji xing wu dao zheng 急性舞蹈症
acute chorea;

lao nian xing wu dao zheng 老年性舞蹈症
senile chorea;

pian ce wu dao zheng 偏側舞蹈症
hemilateral chorea;

pian shen wu dao zheng 偏身舞蹈症
chorea dimidiata;

pian tan hou wu dao zheng 偏癱後舞蹈症
posthemiplegic chorea;

tan huan xing wu dao zheng 癱瘓性舞蹈症
paralytic chorea;

tiao yue xing wu dao zheng 跳躍性舞蹈症
dancing chorea;

xian tian xing wu dao zheng 先天性舞蹈症
chorea;

xin zang xing wu dao zheng 心臟型舞蹈症
chorea cordis;

ye fa xing wu dao zheng 夜發性舞蹈症
chorea nocturna;

wu shou nong jiao 舞手弄腳
play gestures;

wu4 li 兀立
stand rigidly without motion;

xi3 jiao 洗腳
wash one's feet;

xia4 chui zu 下垂足
dangle foot / drop foot;

xia jiao 下腳
get a foothold / make a short stay;

xia zhi gu 下肢骨
leg bone;

xia4 le yi tiao 嚇了一跳
give a jump / give sb a turn;

xia pao 嚇跑
scare away / scare sb off / scare off;

xian1 tian xing wu dao zheng 先天性舞蹈症
chorea;

xian2 bu 閒步
roam at leisure / stroll without a destination;

xian3 跣
barefooted;

xian zi 跣子
slippers;

xian zu 跣足
barefooted;

xiang1 gang jiao 香港腳
athelete's foot / Hong Kong foot;

xiao3 bu 小步
(1) half step;
(2) stroll;

xiao tui 小腿
cnemis / lower leg / shank;

xiao tui guo duan 小腿過短
microcnemia;

xiao tui jin 小腿脛
lower part of the leg;

xiao tui jing tan 小腿痙癱
scelotyrbe;

xiao tui tong 小腿痛
scelalgia;

xiao zhi 小趾
little toe / microdactyly;

xiao zu 小足
micropodia;

xie1 jiao 歇腳
rest the feet after walking / stop on the way for a rest;

xie tui er 歇腿兒
rest one's feet after a long walk;

xie2 jian lei zu 脅肩纍足
apprehensive and nervous / frightened / jittery;

xie4 蹀
walking;

xie die 蹀蹀
walking;

xin1 zang xing wu dao zheng 心臟型舞蹈症
chorea cordis;

xin4 bu 信步
stroll aimlessly || ramble; stroll; take a leisurely walk; walk aimlessly; wander;

xin bu lai dao 信步來到
come to a place in aimlessly wandering;

xin bu xian duo 信步閒踱
walk about aimlessly || roam about without definite objective; take a leisurely walk;

xin bu xian you 信步閒遊
walk aimlessly || ramble; roam about without definitive objective;

xing2 bu ru fei 行步如飛
go like a streak / go like blazes;

xing lu 行路
walk on the road;

xing zou 行走
go on foot / walk;

xiu1 jiao 修腳
pedicure;

xu2 bu 徐步
stroll / walk leisurely / walk slowly;

xu bu er xing 徐步而行
walk with slow steps;

xue1 zu shi lü 削足適履
an impractical solution of a problem || act in a Procrustean manner; cut the feet to fit the shoes; make fit the Procrustean bed; mince the facts to fit a Procrustean bed; place on the Procrustean bed; stretch on the Procrustean bed; stretch the facts to fit a Procrustean bed; trim the toes to fit the shoes; use an unreasonable and imparactical method; whittle down the feet to fit the shoes;

xun4 zou 迅走
go fast / hurry on;

ya3 bu 雅步
leisurely and graceful steps;

ye4 zu er xing 曳足而行
walk with a shuffling gait;

ye4 fa xing wu dao zheng 夜發性舞蹈症
chorea nocturna;

yi1 beng yi tiao 一蹦一跳
skipping and hopping;

yi bu 一步
a single step / a step;

yi bu bu rang 一步不讓
fight every inch of the way / not to yield a step;

yi bu deng tian 一步登天
a meteoric rise to fame || a sudden rise in life; fast advancement in one's career; have a meteoric rise; have a sudden success; reach Heavens at a single bound — have a meteoric rise; reach the sky in a single bound — attain the highest level in one step;

yi bu san hui tou 一步三回頭
with every step one looks back three times;

yi bu yi dian 一步一顛
one's head nodding with every stride / stagger along;

yi bu yi ge jiao yin 一步一個腳印
leave one's footmark with every step || every step leaves its print — work steadily and make solid progress; one step leaves one footmark — do things in a down-to-earth manner;

yi bu yi gui 一步一鬼
a suspicious heart will see imaginary ghosts;

yi bu yi kan 一步一看
take one step and look around before taking another;

yi bu yi qu 一步一趨
follow in sb's footsteps / follow others at every step / follow suit blindly;

yi cu er jiu 一蹴而就
reach the goal in one step || accomplish in one move; accomplish one's aim in one move; at a heat; at one stroke; expect results overnight; gain success in one step; reach at a single leap; succeed in doing sth at the first try; win an easy success; with one bound;

yi dian yi bo 一顛一跛
limp along / walk with a limp;

yi jiao 一腳
(1) a kick;
(2) take part in sth;

yi jiao gao yi jiao di 一腳高，一腳低
up-and-down;

yi jiao ti fan 一腳踢翻
knock sb down with one's foot ‖ send sb sprawling with one kick; shoot up a foot to send sb sprawling;

yi jiao ti kai 一腳踢開
kick aside / kick away / kick out ‖ spurn away;

yi liu wai xie 一溜歪斜
stagger / walk unsteadily in a zigzag;

yi quan lai, yi jiao qu 一拳來，一腳去
a blow for a blow / a Roland for an Oliver / retaliation equal to its provocation / retort equal to its provocation;

yi quan yi jiao 一拳一腳
with a blow of one's fist and a kick from one's foot;

yi que yi guai 一瘸一拐
limp / walk jerkily and unevenly;

yi shi zu cheng qian gu hen 一失足成千古恨
a false step becomes the regret of a lifetime ‖ a moment's error can bring a lifelong regret; a moment's error will bring about sorrow for a thousand years; a single error can cause incalculable suffering; a single slip may cause lasting sorrow; a wrong step results in eternal regret; do wrong once and you'll never hear the end of it; old sin makes new shame; one false step brings everlasting grief; one pitfall leads to endless misery and regret; the error of a moment bcomes the regret of a lifetime;

yi yue er guo 一躍而過
jump...at one bound / jump across / leap over...at one bound / take a leap over;

yi yue er qi 一躍而起
get up with a jump / jump to one's feet / jump up all of a sudden / nip-up;

yi zou liao zhi 一走了之
evade the solution of a problem by walking away from it;

yi4 bu yi qu 亦步亦趨
follow in sb's footsteps ‖ ape sb at every step; dance after sb's pipe; dance after sb's whistle; dance to sb's music; dance to sb's pipe; dance to sb's tune; follow sb's walking; follow the example of another person at each move; perform to sb's baton; slavish imitation;

yi4 zu 逸足
fleet-footed / walking very fast;

yi4 zu 義足
artificial leg;

yong1 rong ya bu 雍容雅步
peaceful and mild steps;

yong3 踊
jump / leap;

you4 huai 右踝
right ankle;

yu1 xing 紆行
proceed through a winding and twisting path;

yu4 bu 玉步
(1) your footsteps;
(2) footsteps of a pretty girl;

yu zhi 玉趾
your footsteps;

yu zhi guang lin 玉趾光臨
the approach of your footsteps;

yu4 xing you zhi 欲行又止
start to walk, then stop;

yuan3 zou gao fei 遠走高飛
flee far away ‖ fly far and high; fly high and go away; go far away; off to distant parts; slip away to distant place; take it on the lam; take wing; take wing and fly away;

yuan zou ta xiang 遠走他鄉
off to a place far away from home / travel in distant parts;

yuan zu 遠足
(1) hike ‖ excursion; outing; pleasure trip on foot; walking tour;
(2) take long hikes;

yue4 刖
cut off the feet as a punishment;

yue4 躍
bound / jump / leap / spring;

yue bu 躍步
galloping;

yue dong 躍動
in lively motion / move actively;

yue guo 躍過
jump across / leap over;

yue jin 躍進
leap forward / make a leap;

yue qi 躍起
jump up / leap up;

yue sheng 躍升
zoom;

yun4 dong yuan jiao bing 運動員腳病
athlete's foot;

zhan4 站
stand;

zhan bu qi lai 站不起來
unable to stand up;

zhan bu wen 站不穩
unable to stand firmly;

zhan bu zhu 站不住
unable to keep standing;

zhan bu zhu jiao 站不住腳
unable to hold one's position // ill-founded;

zhan chu lai 站出來
come forward;

zhan de zhu 站得住
able to stand;

zhan de zhu jiao 站得住腳
hold water;

zhan ding 站定
stand still;

zhan kai 站開
stand aside;

zhan li 站立
stand;

zhan qi lai 站起來
rise / pull oneself up / stand up / straighten up;

zhan wen jiao gen 站穩腳根
get a firm foothold;

zhan zhu 站住
halt / hold there / stand where you are;

zhan zhu jiao 站住腳
(1) halt / stop;
(2) consolidate one's position / hold one's ground;

zhe2 zu fu su 折足覆餗
break the leg of a tripod and overturn the food — without the required ability to undertake a given task / not equal to the task;

zheng4 bu 正步
goose step / parade step;

zhi2 gu 跖骨
metatarsal bone;

zhi gu guan jie 跖骨關節
articulations of metatarsal bones;

zhi2 躑
falter / hesitate;

zhi zhu 躑躅
loiter around / walk to and fro;

zhi zhu er xing 躑躅而行
(1) stagger || shuffle along; walk with a mincing step; walk with a shuffling gait;
(2) uncertain whether to advance or retire;

zhi zhu jie tou 躑躅街頭
wander about the streets || on the pavement; tramp the streets;

zhi3 bu 止步
halt || go no further; stand still; stop;

zhi bu bu qian 止步不前
cease to advance / go no further || halt; make no headway; stand still;

zhi3 指
toe;
mu zhi 拇指
big toe / great toe;

zhi3 趾
(1) toe;
(2) foot;
(3) footprint / track;
bing zhi 併趾
losyndactyly;
er zhi 二趾
second toe;
ju zhi 巨趾
dactylomegaly;

nei fan zhi 內翻趾
digitus varus;

san zhi 三趾
third toe;

si zhi 四趾
fourth toe;

xiao zhi 小趾
little toe;

zhi fei da 趾肥大
pachydactyly;

zhi gao qi yang 趾高氣揚
above oneself / be bloated with arrogance || arrogant; as proud as a peacock; as proud as Punch; carry one's head high; cocky; crow over; drag oneself up; draw oneself up; get a swelled head; get on one's high horse; give oneself airs and swagger about; high and mighty; hold one's head high; in all one's splendour; lift one's head high; on one's high horse; on stilts; proud as a peacock; proud as a stack on fire; puff one's chest out; put on an elated look; put on the ritz; raise the horn; ride one's high horse; step high and look proud; swagger about and give oneself airs; with one's head in the air;

zhi gu 趾骨
phalanx of the foot;

zhi gu guo duan 趾骨過短
brachyphalangia;

zhi gu yan 趾骨炎
phalangitis;

zhi guan jie 趾關節
digital joints;

zhi jia 趾甲
nail / toenail;

ju zhi jia 巨趾甲
megalonychia;

zhi jia guo xiao 趾甲過小
micronychia;

zhi jia ying hua 趾甲硬化
scleronychia;

zhi jian 趾尖
tiptoe;

zhi jian bi 趾間襞
interdigital fold;

zhi jian kui yang 趾間潰瘍
interdigital ulcer;

zhi jian pi yan 趾間皮炎
interdigital dermatitis;

zhi jing luan 趾痙攣
dactylospasm;

zhi lie 趾裂
toe crack;

zhi nong zhong 趾膿腫
toe abscess;

zhi shui zhong 趾水腫
dactyledema;

zhi tuo luo 趾脫落
dactylolysis;

zi fa xing zhi tuo luo 自發性趾脫落
dactylolysis spontanea;

zhi wan qu 趾彎曲
clinodactyly;

zhi yan 趾炎
dactylitis / inflammation of a toe;

zhi4 shou zhi jiao 窒手窒腳
obstructing hand and foot / troublesome;

zhi4 躓
stumble / trip;

zhi dun 躓頓
stumble and stop;

zhi jue 躓蹶
stumble and fall;

zhi jue bu qi 躓蹶不起
stumble and unable to rise;

zhong3 踵
(1) heel;
(2) call in person;
(3) follow close behind;

zhong jian 踵見
call repeatedly in person;

zhong jue zhou xian 踵決肘見
down at the heels and elbows — tattered dress / out at the heels and the elbows;

zhong men 踵門
call at another's house in person;

zhong men bai bei 踵門拜別
personally pay a farewell call;

zhong men dao xie 踵門道謝
call in person to express one's thanks;

zhong men qiu jian 踵門求見
call on sb at his abode / seek an interview at sb's house;

zhong qi hou chen 踵其後塵
follow sb's footsteps;

zhong xie 踵謝
thank in person;

zhong zhi xiang jie 踵趾相接
follow the footsteps;

zhong zhi 踵至
arrive upon the heels of another / arrive just behind;

zhu2 bu 逐步
gradually / step by step;

zhu2 躅
falter;

zhu3 佇
stand for a long time;

zhu hou 佇候
stand and wait;

zhu li 佇立
stand still;

zhuai3 跩
waddle;

zhuai4 kai shuang jiao 拽開雙腳
let free one's steps — walk quickly;

zhuo2 li 卓立
stand alone / stand upright;

zi1 趑
falter;

zi ju 趑趄
(1) plough one's way / walk with difficulty;
(2) hesitate to advance;

zi ju bu qian 趑趄不前
hesitate to advance ‖ hang back; hesitate to act or choose one's course; hesitating whether to go forward or not; hobble along;

zi4 fa xing zhi tuo luo 自發性趾脫落
dactylolysis spontanea;

zong1 踪
footprint / traces;

zong1 蹤
footprint / traces;

zong ji 蹤跡
traces;

zong ying 蹤影
traces;

zong4 bu 縱步
(1) stride;
(2) bound / jump;

zou3 走
(1) go on foot / walk;
(2) go swiftly / move / run;
(3) depart / go away / leave;
(4) call on / visit;
(5) get going;

zou bi 走避
evade / run away from / shun;

zou bian 走遍
travel all over an area;

zou bian quan guo 走遍全國
travel all over the country / travel the length and breadth of the whole country;

zou bian tian xia 走遍天下
travel all over the world / wander through the world;

zou bu dao 走不到
unable to go as far as / unable to walk as far as;

zou bu de 走不得
(1) not safe to travel / unfit to travel;
(2) not allowed to leave;

zou bu dong le 走不動了
unable to walk;

zou bu guo qu 走不過去
not able to go over;

zou bu kai 走不開
not able to get away / not able to leave;

zou bu liao 走不了
not able to leave / not likely to leave;

zou bu 走步
walk with the ball;

zou cuo yi bu lu 走錯一步路
mak a wrong move;

zou cuo yi zhao, quan pan jie shu 走錯一着，全盤皆輸
a trip in one point would have spoiled all;

zou dao er 走道兒
on the road / travel;

zou dao tou 走到頭
walk to the end of the road;

zou de kuai 走得快
go fast / walk fast;

zou de man 走得慢
go slowly / walk slowly;

zou dong 走動
(1) go for a stroll / stretch one's leg / walk about;
(2) visit each other;

zou fang bu 走方步
exercise caution // prudent;

zou fang 走訪
(1) interview / have an interview with;
(2) go and see / pay a visit to / visit;

zou hou men 走後門
get in by the back door / go through the back door / take the back door ‖ double upon one's steps; enter by the back door — secure advantages through influence; pull strings; pull wires; reverse one's course; secure advantages through pull;

zou hui tou lu 走回頭路
take the road back ‖ backtrack; retrace one's steps; turn the clock back;

zou jin zou chu 走進走出
go in and out;

zou kai 走開
get out / get out of the way ‖ beat it; buzz off; go and chase oneself; go chase oneself; naff off; run along;

zou lai zou qu 走來走去
(1) walk back and forth;
(2) pace in anxiety;

zou lu 走路
go on foot / walk;

zou lu bu zhang yan jing 走路不長眼睛
jaywalk;

zou nan chuang bei 走南闖北
roam all over the country ‖ journey north and south; travel everywhere; travel widely; wander up and down the country;

zou ren 走人
leave;

zou ru qi tu 走入歧途
deviate from the right path / go astray ‖ go off at a tangent; jump the track; take the wrong turning;

zou san 走散
(1) walk away in different directions;
(2) get separated from other travelers;

zou shang po lu 走上坡路
go uphill ‖ make steady progress; on the up-and-up; upgrade;

zou shang que lu 走上絕路
head for one's doom / head toward disaster;

zou shang xie lu 走上邪路
follow the wrong track / go astray / take to evil ways;

zou shang zheng gui 走上正軌
get onto the right path / set on the correct path;

zou shi 走失
be lost / wander away ‖ lose the original shape, flavour, etc.; missing;

zou tou wu lu 走投無路
at the end of one's rope / have no way out ‖ at the end of one's tether; be driven from pillar to post; be driven into a corner; be driven to desperation; be driven to the wall; be locked in the horns of a dilemma; between the hammer and the anvil; between the upper and nether millstone; can find no way out; come to a dead end; come to the end of one's tether; drive sb to the last shifts; drive sb to the wall; feel oneself concerned; find oneself

cornered; from pillar to post; go down a dead alley; go to the wall; have no one to turn to; have no way to turn for help; in a tight corner; in an impasse; land in an impasse; not know which way to turn;

zou wan lu 走彎路
take a wrong path || do sth in a wrong way; follow a zigzag course; make a detour; take a roundabout route; take a tortuous course; travel a tortuous road;

zou xia po lu 走下坡路
(1) go downhill || hit the skids; over the hill;
(2) on the decline / on the downgrade;

zou xiang 走向
(1) run / trend;
(2) head for / move toward / on the way for;

zou xiang fan mian 走向反面
change into one's opposite / go over to the opposite side;

zou yi bu kan yi bu 走一步看一步
do as one sees fit / take one step and look around before taking another — proceed without a long-range plan;

zou yi zou 走一走
stretch one's legs / take a walk;

zou yuan wang lu 走冤枉路
go the long way;

zou zai qian mian 走在前面
get ahead;

zou zhe qiao 走着瞧
see who's right / wait and see;

zou zou 走走
take a walk / take an airing;

zu2 足
foot / leg;
ju zu 巨足
sciopody;

zu bei 足背
dorsum of foot;

zu bei fan she 足背反射
dorsocuboidal reflex;

zu bing 足病
pedopathy;

zu bu chu hu 足不出戶
confine oneself within doors / stay in || keep the house; keep to the house; keep within doors; never to go out; never to leave one's home; never to step out of door; refrain from stepping outside the house; remain quietly at home behind closed doors // housebound;

zu chang 足長
foot length;

zu di 足底
footplate;

zu di fan she 足底反射
plantar reflex;

zu di kui yang 足底潰瘍
plantar ulcer;

zu di tong 足底痛
plantalgia;

zu di you 足底疣
plantar wart;

zu fa yu bu liang 足發育不良
atelopodia;

zu fa yu bu quan 足發育不全
atelopodia;

zu gen 足跟
heel;
lin bing xing zu gen 淋病性足跟
gonorrheal heel;

zu gen tong 足跟痛
painful heel / talagia;

zu guo xiao 足過小
micropodia;

zu ji 足蹟
footmarks / footprints / tracks;

zu jiao tong 足絞痛
angina cruris;

zu shui zhong 足水腫
podedema;

zu tong 足痛
pain in the sole of the foot / pododynia;

zu tong feng 足痛風
gouty inflammation of the great toe / podagra;

zu tu 足突
foot process;

zu tu bing 足突病
foot process disease;

zu wai fan 足外翻
strephexopodia;

zu xia chui 足下垂
footdrop;

zu xian 足癬
tinea of the foot / tinea pedis;

zu xin 足心
sole of the foot;

zu yin 足印
footmark / footprint;

zu zhen luan 足陣攣
foot clonus;

zu zhi 足趾
toe;

zu zhi gu 足趾骨
bones of the digits of the foot;

zu zhong duan 足中段
midfoot;

zu zhong bing 足腫病
cryptopodia;

zui4 bu 醉步
reeling steps of a drunkard;

zuo3 huai 左踝
left ankle;

zuo4 li bu an 坐立不安
restless;

Jing 頸 Neck

bian3 tao xian 扁桃腺
tonsil;

bian tao xian zhong da 扁桃腺腫大
hypertrophy of tonsils;

bo2 脖
neck;

bo jing er 脖頸兒
back of the neck / nape;

bo jing zi 脖頸子
neck;

bo zi 脖子
neck;
da bo zi 大脖子
goitre;
lou zhu bo zi 摟住脖子
fall upon sb's neck;
niu le bo zi 扭了脖子
have sprained the neck;
rao bo zi 繞脖子
beat about the bush / speak in a roundabout way;
shen chang bo zi 伸長脖子
crane one's neck / stretch out one's neck;

che3 zhe bo zi 扯着脖子
strain the neck in shouting;

cu1 bo zi 粗脖子
overgrown neck;

da4 bo zi 大脖子
goitre;

da bo zi bing 大脖子病
goitre / struma;

dou4 脰
neck;

duan3 jing 短頸
brevicollis;

jia3 xing xie jing 假性斜頸
spurious torticollis;

jian4 xie xing xie jing 間歇性斜頸
intermittent torticollis;

jiao1 jing 交頸
fondle each other;

jie1 jing jiao bi 接頸交臂
(1) neck;
(2) make love with / very intimate with;

jin3 zhang xing jing fan she 緊張性頸反射
tonic neck reflex;

jing1 shen xing xie jing 精神性斜頸
mental torticollis;

jing3 剄
cut the throat;

jing3 頸
neck;
duan jing 短頸
brevicollis;
pang guang jing 膀胱頸
cervix vesicae / bladder neck;

jing bei 頸背
nape;

jing bi tong 頸臂痛
cervicobrachialgia;

jing bu 頸部
cervix;

jing bu bai ban bing 頸部白斑病
leukoderma colli;

jing bu nang zhong 頸部囊腫
cervical cyst;

jing bu nong zhong 頸部膿腫
cervical abscess;

jing bu peng da 頸部膨大
cervical enlargement;

jing fan she 頸反射
neck reflex;
jin zhang xing jing fan she 緊張性頸反射
tonic neck reflex;

jing ji 頸肌
cervical muscle;

jing ji tong 頸肌痛
myalgia cervicalis;

jing jiang ying 頸僵硬
stiff neck;

jing nei jing mai 頸內靜脈
internal jugular vein;

jing wai jing mai 頸外靜脈
external jugular vein;

jing xiang 頸項
nape of the neck / scruff of the neck;

jing zhui 頸椎
cervical vertebrae;
di er jing zhui 第二頸椎
epistropheus;

jing zhui bing 頸椎病
cervical spondylosis;

jing4 luan xing xie jing 痙攣性斜頸
spasmodic torticollis;

ke1 頦
chin;

ke fan she 頦反射
chin reflex;

lou1 zhu bo zi 摟住脖子
fall upon sb's neck;

mi2 lu xing xie jing 迷路性斜頸
labyrinthine torticollis;

mo3 bo zi 抹脖子
commit suicide by slicing one's throat;

mo jing 抹頸
commit suicide by slicing one's throat;

nan3 yan chi jing 赧顏赤頸
blush down to one's neck;

niu3 le bo zi 扭了脖子
have sprained the neck;

pang2 guang jing 膀胱頸
bladder neck / cervix vesicae;

pang guang jing yan 膀胱頸炎
cystauchenitis;

rao4 bo zi 繞脖子
beat about the bush / speak in a roundabout way;

shen1 chang bo zi 伸長脖子
crane one's neck / make a long neck / stretch out one's neck;

shen2 jing yuan xing xie jing 神經源性斜頸
neurogenic torticollis;

xiang4 項
back of the neck / nape;

xiang bei 項背
a person's neck and back;

xiang bei xiang wang 項背相望
neck to back / one after another in close succession — a huge jostling crowd;

xie2 jing 斜頸
torticollis;

jia xing xie jing 假性斜頸
spurious torticollis;

jian xie xing xie jing 間歇性斜頸
intermittent torticollis;

jing shen xing xie jing 精神性斜頸
mental torticollis;

jing luan xing xie jing 痙攣性斜頸
spasmodic torticollis;

mi lu xing xie jing 迷路性斜頸
labyrinthine torticollis;

shen jing yuan xing xie jing 神經源性斜頸
neurogenic torticollis;

xing4 bing jing 性病頸
venereal collar;

yan2 jing ju zhong 延頸舉踵
look forward anxiously;

yi4 jing 縊頸
hang oneself;

yin3 jing 引頸
crane one's neck to look forward;

yin jing chang ming 引頸長鳴
stretch the neck and utter a cry;

yin jing er pan 引頸而盼
crane one's neck to wait;

yin jing er wang 引頸而望
crane one's neck to watch for / stretch the neck to look;

yin jing jiu lu 引頸就戮
crane one's neck to be executed / meet one's death without resistance ‖ bare one's neck to the sword; extend one's neck for the final stroke; stick one's neck out to have one's head chopped off; stretch the neck to be beheaded;

yin jing qi zu 引頸企足
raise one's head and stand on tiptop — eagerly looking foward to;

yin jing zi wen 引頸自刎
commit suicide by slashing one's own neck / cut one's throat in suicide;

yin ling 引領
crane one's neck to look into the distance ‖ eagerly look forward to sth / stretch the neck in order to have a better look;

yin ling er wang 引領而望
crane one's neck to look forward ‖ crane one's neck for a look — eagerly look forward to; stretch out one's neck and look after;

zuo2 jing 捽頸
seize by the throat;

Kou 口 Mouth

ai1 gao 哀告
(1) beg piteously / implore / supplicate;
(2) announce sb's death;
(3) speak about one's grievances;

ai hao 哀號
cry mournfully / wail / yammer;

ai hao zhen tian 哀號震天
the wail shakes the heaven;

ai hao 哀嚎
(1) howl;
(2) wail || cry; cry bitterly; cry piteously; lament; wail of woe; whine in despair;

ai hu 哀呼
cry piteously / cry sadly / wail;

ai jiao 哀叫
cry sadly;

ai ken 哀懇
beg for mercy / entreat / implore / sorrowfully request;

ai ku 哀哭
wail / weep in sorrow / whine;

ai li 哀厲
heartbreaking voice;

ai ming 哀鳴
wail / woeful cry || doleful cry; give mournful cries; lamentations; moan; plaintive cry; plaintive whine; whine; whine plaintively;

ai qi 哀泣
mourn || cry sorrowfully; keen; sob; weep plaintively; weep with sorrow;

ai qiu 哀求
beg piteously || appeal pathetically; beg; beg humbly; beg pitifully; beseech; entreat; grovel; implore;

ai qiu kai en 哀求開恩
beseech sb for mercy;

ai quan 哀勸
admonish in a tearful voice;

ai su 哀訴
bleat / whimper / whine;

ai tan 哀歎
bemoan / bewail / lament;

ai1 sheng tan qi 唉聲歎氣
heave a sigh of frustration / heave deep sighs / heave great sighs / moan and groan / mope and sigh / sigh and groan / sigh and moan / sigh in despair;

ai2 kei 挨剋
be scolded / scold;

ai ma 挨罵
be scolded || be called names; be reproached; be told off; catch it; get a dressing down; get a scolding; get into a row; get scolded; give sb gyp; receive a scolding;

ai ma shou qi 挨罵受氣
be scolded and suffer indignity;

ai yi dun chou ma 挨一頓臭罵
get a good talking-to / get an earful / receive a good dressing down;

ai4 ai 艾艾
stammer / stutter;

ai ai nan yan 艾艾難言
stutter and speak with difficulty;

ai4 cheng 愛稱
hypocorism / pet name / term of endearment;

ai chi cu 愛吃醋
easy to get jealous;

ai chi hao he 愛吃好喝
love to eat and drink and enjoy oneself;

ai chi la 愛吃辣
have a liking for hot food / love spicy food;

ai da bu li 愛搭不理
give sb the cold shoulder / turn a cold shoulder // cold and different / lukewarm towards sb / standoffish;

ai kai wan xiao 愛開玩笑
fond of jesting;

ai wen chang wen duan 愛問長問短
like to rubberneck;

ai4 kou 礙口
too embarassing to mention / unpleasant to talk about;

ai4 qi 噯氣
belch / hiccup // belching / eructation / ructus;

ai suan 噯酸
have an acid belch // acid eructation / ructus;

an1 jing 安靜
noiseless / quiet;

an sheng 安聲
quiet / silent;

an1 song 諳誦
recite from memory;

an4 ci fa yan 按次發言
speak in due order;

an4 chao 暗嘲
laugh in secret / ridicule;

an feng 暗諷
(1) insinuate // innuendo;
(2) allusive / implicative / ironic;

an xiao 暗笑
laugh in one's heart / laugh in one's sleeve || chuckle; laugh behind sb's back; laugh up one's sleeve; snicker; snigger;

ao2 嗷
cry of hunger;

ao jiao 嗷叫
cry / scream || sing out; squeal; yell;

ao2 謷
defame / discredit / slander / vilify;

ao ao 謷謷
abusive / slanderous;

ao chou 謷醜
abuse / defame / slander;

ao4 拗
awkward-sounding / hard to pronounce;

ao kou 拗口
twist the tongue || awkward-sounding; hard to pronounce; tongue-twisting;

ao kou ling 拗口令
tongue twister;

ba1 ba jie jie 巴巴結結
splutter / stammer / stutter;

ba1 ba 吧吧
loquacious / talkative;

ba da 吧嗒
(1) smack one's lips;
(2) pull at;

ba da zui 吧嗒嘴
smack one's lips over food, drink, etc;

ba er ba er 吧兒吧兒
clear, flowing-voiced;

ba ji 吧唧
move one's jaws up and down as in eating;

ba ya 吧呀
(1) big-mouthed;
(2) quarrel;

ba3 hua shuo ming 把話說明
strike a light;

ba jiu 把酒
hold a wineglass – to drink;

ba zhan 把盞
hold wine cups – to drink;

bai2 chi 白吃
eat without payment / have a free meal;

bai chi bai he 白吃白喝
food and drink are served gratis;

bai fei kou she 白費口舌
speak to the wind / waste one's breath / waste one's words;

bai huo 白話
(1) blah-blah / make empty talk / talk big / talk nonsense;
(2) promise that cannot be kept;

bai mo 白沫
foam / frothy saliva;

bai shuo 白說
speak in vain / waste one's breath;

bai3 ban chao xiao 百般嘲笑
heap scorn and abuse on;

bai ban quan shuo 百般勸說
try to persuade sb in every possible way;

bai ban ru ma 百般辱罵
abuse in every possible way || assail sb with every possible kind of abuse; call all kinds of names; hurl every sort of insult at sb; indulge in scurrilities; shout all sorts of abuse; yell every form of insult;

bai ban zhou ma 百般咒罵
abuse in every possible way / heap abuse;

bai hui mo bian 百喙莫辯
beyond dispute ‖ a hundred mouths can't explain it away; even a hundred mouths cannot absolve guilt; no one can argue it away;

bai kou mo bian 百口莫辯
beyond dispute ‖ even a hundred tongues fail to excuse; inexcusable; the ready tongue permits of no excuse; there is no room for verbal defense;

bai ren chi bai wei 百人吃百味
everyone to his own taste / tastes differ;

bai wen bu yan 百問不厭
not to lose one's temper no matter how often others ask / patiently answer any questions sb asks;

bai3 擺
lay bare / state clearly;

bai long men zhen 擺龍門陣
engage in chitchat ‖ chat; chat together and gossip; get together and spin a yarn; get together and tell yarns; tell a story;

bai4 bai 拜拜
bye-bye;

bai bei 拜別
say farewell / say good-bye / take leave;

bai ci 拜辭
say good-bye / take leave;

bai ken 拜懇
beg bumbly / implore / request;

ban1 chun di she 搬脣遞舌
tell tales;

ban kou nong she 搬口弄舌
make mischief / tell tales;

ban nong shi fei 搬弄是非
gossip / sow discord ‖ carry tales; create troubles and dissensions; indulge in tittle-tattle; make mischief; make mischief through tittle-tattle; sow discord though gossip; stir up trouble by gossip; tell tales;

ban4 han 半酣
half drunk ‖ besotted; in one's cups; slightly drunk; tipsy;

ban ji ban bao 半飢半飽
half-fed, half-starving / underfed;

ban jie hua 半截話
half-finished speech;

ban tun ban tu 半吞半吐
hum and haw;

ban zui 半醉
half-drunk;

ban4 chang 伴唱
(1) vocal accompaniment;
(2) accompanying singer;

ban jiu 伴酒
drink in company of sb / drink in company with sb / drink with sb;

ban4 拌
bicker / quarrel / squabble;

ban zui 拌嘴
bicker / quarrel / squabble ‖ words of a sort; wrangle;

bang1 qiang 幫腔
back sb / speak in support of sb ‖ chime in with sb; echo sb; give verbal support to a person;

bang zui 幫嘴
help in an altercation / speak for another;

bang4 he 棒喝
a blow and shout to waken one from error;

bang4 謗
defame ‖ condemn; denounce publicly; libel; slander; smear; vilify;

bang fei 謗誹
defame ‖ condemn; denounce publicly; libel; slander; smear; vilify;

bang ji 謗譏
denounce / impeach;

bang seng hui dao 謗僧毀道
have no respect for pious bonzes and holy Daoist priests;

bang seng ma dao 謗僧罵道
abuse Buddhist and Taoist priests / attack Daoism and Buddhism;

bang wen 謗聞
malicious gossip;

bang yan 謗言
(1) libel / slander;
(2) defamatory remark;

bang yi 謗議
criticize / libel / slander;

bao1 褒
commend / extol / praise;

bao bian 褒貶
pass judgment on || appraise; comment; praise and disparage;

bao jiang 褒獎
commend and award || praise and cite; praise and honour;

bao jiu bian xin 褒舊貶新
glorify the old and belittle the new;

bao mei 褒美
honour with praise / laud;

bao shan bian e 褒善貶惡
glorify virtue and censure vice;

bao yang 褒揚
cite / commend / praise;

bao3 chi chen mo 保持沉默
be mute / bite the tongue / hold one's peace / hush / keep a still tongue in one's head / keep one's peace / remain silent;

bao chi jian mo 保持緘默
button up one's mouth / hold one's tongue / keep one's mouth shut || keep a still tongue in one's head; keep one's mouth closed; keep one's peace;

bao3 飽
be full / have eaten one's fill;

bao chi 飽食
eat one's fill / eat to one's heart's content / glut;

bao4 報
(1) announce / declare || inform; report; tell;
(2) reciprocate / reply / respond;

bao an 報案
report a case to the police;

bao4 shi 暴食
eat excessively at one meal / glut / gorge;

bao yin 暴飲
drink excessively / drink hard;

bao yin bao shi 暴飲暴食
eat and drink excessively / eat and drink too much at one meal / make a pig of oneself // gluttony;

bei1 ge 悲歌
elegy / song of lament;

bei1 ge kang kai 悲歌慷慨
sing with solemn fervour to express one's feeling of oppression;

bei ming 悲鳴
cry mournfully;

bei sheng 悲聲
plaintive cries / sad voice;

bei tan 悲歎
deplore / lament / sigh mournfully / sigh over;

bei tan bu yi 悲歎不已
sigh with sadness without stopping;

bei ti 悲啼
cry mournfully;

bei4 man 悖謾
arrogantly impolite / disrespectful;

bei miu 悖謬
absurd / irrational / perverse / preposterous;

bei4 hou di gu 背後嘀咕
gossip about sb behind their back;

bei hou fei bang 背後誹謗
slander people behind their backs / stab sb in the back;

bei hou jiang ren huai hua 背後講人壞話
tell tales;

bei hou ma ren 背後罵人
curse sb behind their back;

bei hou yi lun 背後議論
talk of people behind their backs;

bei kou zhi yan 背口之言
talk behind one's back;

bei ren fei yi 背人非議
speak ill of a person behind their back;

bei song 背誦
parrot off / recite / repeat from memory / say by heart / say by rote;

bei song ru liu 背誦如流
rattle off / reel off;

bei tai ci 背台詞
say one's part / speak one's part;

ben4 kou zhuo she 笨口拙舌
awkward in speech / clumsy of speech / inarticulate / slow of speech;

bi1 wen 逼問
force sb to answer / press for an answer;

bi3 fang shuo 比方說
for example / for instance;

bi wen 比聞
hear recently;

bi3 xiao 鄙笑
jeer / mock / ridicule / scoff at / taunt;

bi4 kou 閉口
button one's lip / shut up;

bi kou bu tan 閉口不談
avoid mentioning / keep one's mouth shut || keep silent; make no mention of; keep one's tongue between one's teeth; not to say a way about; never talk about; refuse to say anything about;

bi kou bu yan 閉口不言
avoid mentioning / keep one's mouth shut || button one's lip; keep one's tongue between one's teeth; shut one's mouth and say nothing;

bi kou wu yan 閉口無言
be left speechless / button one's lip / keep one's mouth shut || not utter a single word; refrain from speaking; remain silent; shut one's mouth and say nothing; tongue-tied; zip one's lip;

bi zui 閉嘴
keep one's mouth shut || button one's lip; clam up; close one's mouth; hold your tongue; keep one's peace; shut one's mouth; shut shop; shut up; shut your mouth; shut your shop; zip one's lip;

bi4 ci 詖辭
biased remarks / partial statements;

bi lun 詖論
erroneous statements in which the speaker is unable to see the error;

bi4 yan 辟言
go away because of an offensive statement;

bi4 bu zuo da 避不作答
decline answering a question / parry a question;

bi er bu da 避而不答
avoid answering / avoid answering a question / avoid giving an answer / avoid making any reply || be evasive; decline answering a question; parry a question; slide over without answering; take the Fifth;

bi er bu tan 避而不談
avoid any mention / avoid mentioning || deliberately not to touch the point; draw a veil over; evade a question; keep away from the subject; keep from talking about; not to touch on the question of;

bi4 jian 愎諫
deaf to remonstrances;

bian1 zao huang yan 編造謊言
fabricate lies;

bian zao jie kou 編造借口
cook up an excuse / fabricate an excuse;

bian1 chi bian tan 邊吃邊談
talk while eating;

bian3 chi 貶斥
demote / denounce;

bian ze 貶責
reprimand / reproach;

bian4 ying xing kou yan 變應性口炎
allergic stomatitis;

bian4 辯
argue / debate / dispute;

bian bai 辯白
(1) offer an explanation;
(2) plead innocence / try to defend oneself;

bian bo 辯駁
defend oneself verbally / dispute / refute;

bian cai 辯才
ability as a debater / eloquence;

bian cai wu ai 辯才無礙
very eloquent;

bian hu 辯護
argue in favour of / defend / speak in defence of / take up the gauntlet;

bian jie 辯解
argue that / provide an explanation;

bian kou 辯口
eloquence;

bian lun 辯論
argue / debate;

bian ming 辨明
argue out;

bian nan 辯難
debate / defend and question / retort with challenging questions;

bian shou 辯説
argue / debate;

bian wu 辯誣
defend sb falsely accused;

bian zheng 辯證
(1) analyze and verify a point;
(2) dialectical;

biao3 bai 表白
bare one's heart / express clearly;

biao da 表達
express / make known / voice;

biao yang 表揚
commend / praise / praise in public;

biao zhang 表彰
commend / honour;

bie2 chui niu 別吹牛
don't boast ‖ come off it; don't brag; don't shoot a line; don't talk big; don't talk horse;

bie dui wai ren jiang 別對外人講
between ourselves / between you and me;

bie hu che 別胡扯
come off it / get off it;

bie hu zou le 別胡謅了
stop talking nonsense;

bie ti 別提
it's not necessary to say;

bing4 cong kou ru 病從口入
disease enters by the mouth / diseases come in at the mouth / illness finds its way in by the mouth;

bing cong kou ru, huo cong kou chu 病從口入，禍從口出
a closed mouth catches no flies / disease goes in by the mouth and trouble comes out of the mouth;

bo2 駁
argue / contradict / refute;

bo bian 駁辯
argue / debate / dispute;

bo chi 駁斥
argue against ‖ contradict; denounce; disprove; gainsay; rebut; refute;

bo dao 駁倒
argue down / refute ‖ confute; defeat in a debate; demolish sb's argument; disprove; outargue; put to silence; reduce sb to silence; score off;

bo de ya kou wu yan 駁得啞口無言
argue sb down ‖ jump down sb's throat; leave sb flat; make scores off sb; put sb to silence; reduce sb to silence; shut up;

bo huan 駁還
reject;

bo jia 駁價
argue over prices / haggle;

bo jie 駁詰
question persistently / refute and question;

bo nan 駁難
refute and blame / retort and blame;

bo yi 駁議
dispute / refute;

bu1 餔
eat / feed;

bu chuo 餔啜
eat and drink;

bu chuo wu shi 餔啜無時
have no time to eat and drink;

bu4 cha bu fan 不茶不飯
neither drink nor eat || be laden with anxiety; not want to eat;

bu cheng hua 不成話
absurd / rediculous;

bu chi xia wen 不恥下問
ask for advice from those beneath oneself / not feel ashamed to consult inferiors || modest enough to consult one's inferiors; not consider it beneath one's dignity to learn sth from one's subordinates by asking about it; not feel ashamed to ask and learn from one's subordinates; not feel ashamed to seek advice from those beneath one's station in life; not mind seeking advice from the rank and file; stoop to ask advice from the common run of people;

bu dai shuo 不待說
it goes without saying / needless to say;

bu dai zhui yan 不待贅言
it would be superfluous to dwell on the matter any more;

bu gan shuo ban ge bu zi 不敢說半個不字
dare even mutter dissent;

bu gen zhi tan 不根之談
mere talk / unfounded statement;

bu gou yan xiao 不苟言笑
discreet in speech and manner / not frivolous in talking and joking / not inclined to talk and laugh;

bu he jiu 不喝酒
teetotal;

bu huang xia shi 不遑暇食
so busy as to have no time for eating;

bu huang zhi hui 不遑置喙
too late to put in a word;

bu jin shi xiao 不禁失笑
cannot forbear laughing / cannot refrain from laughing;

bu jin yu yan 不盡欲言
cannot express all one wishes to say;

bu jing zhi tan 不經之談
absurd statement;

bu ke jiu jie 不可究詰
cannot be explained;

bu ke sheng yan 不可勝言
beyond description / it cannot be told;

bu ke tong ri er yu 不可同日而語
cannot be mentioned in the same breath || not to be brought into comparison; there is no comparison between;

bu ke yan chuan 不可言傳
it cannot be related by language;

bu ke yan zhuang 不可言狀
ineffable;

bu lu kou feng 不露口風
not breathe a word about;

bu ming ze yi, yi ming jing ren 不鳴則已，一鳴驚人
in for a penny, in for a pound;

bu ping ze ming 不平則鳴
where there is injustice, there will be an outcry || man will cry out against injustice;

bu rong fen shuo 不容分說
do not wait for an explanation;

bu rong zheng bian 不容爭辯
beyond debate / beyond dispute / without dispute // incontestable / indisputable / irrefragable / unarguable;

bu rong zheng yi 不容爭議
beyond debate / beyond dispute / without dispute // incontestable / indisputable;

bu rong zhi bian 不容置辯
beyond dispute / indisputable / undeniable;

bu rong zhi hui 不容置喙
allow no interruption / brook no intervention / refuse to let others talk;

bu shan ci ling 不擅詞令
lack facility in polite speech // inarticulate;

bu sheng bu xiang 不聲不響
make no reply / mute / not making a sound / not utter a word / without saying a word;

bu shun kou 不順口
not easy to say;

bu shuo 不說
don't say / no comment;

bu shuo wei miao 不說為妙
be better left unsaid;

bu shuo zi ming 不說自明
tell its own tale;

bu tu bu kuai 不吐不快
have to get it off one's chest / have to speak out;

bu wen bu wen 不聞不問
indifferent to sth || leave out of account; not bother to ask questions or listen to what's said; pass over in silence; pay no attention to; remain indifferent to sth; show no interest in sth;

bu wen 不問
(1) disregard / ignore / not consider / pay no attention to;
(2) let off;

bu wen hao dai 不問好歹
come what may / no matter whether it is good or bad / whether good or bad;

bu wen pin fu 不問貧富
make no distinction between the rich and the poor;

bu wen qing you 不問情由
without asking about the circumstances or causes / without first asking about what happened;

bu wen shi fei qu zhi 不問是非曲直
not to bother to look into the rights and wrongs of a case;

bu xian ci fei 不嫌詞費
talk at length;

bu xiang wen wen 不相聞問
not on speaking terms;

bu xiang hua 不像話
(1) absurd / unreasonable;
(2) outrageous;

bu xiao shuo 不消說
needless to say;

bu yan bu yu 不言不語
keep silent / utter not a single word;

bu yan er yu 不言而喻
go without saying || it is self-evident; speak for itself; taken for granted; tell its own story; understand without explanation;

bu yong shuo 不用說
it goes without saying / needless to say;

bu you fen shuo 不由分說
allowing no explanation || give no chance to explain; not allowing sb to speak; not waiting for an explanation; without giving sb the opportunity to explain; without listening to sb's protests; without stopping for an explanation;

bu zai hua xia 不在話下
nothing difficult;

bu zan yi ci 不贊一詞
do not make any comment;

bu zhi suo da 不知所答
be puzzled how to answer;

bu zhi suo yun 不知所云
cannot make out what sb is driving at || make neither head nor tail of what's been said; neither rhyme nor reason; not realizing hat one has said; not to know what is talked about; not to know what it means; not to know what sb is driving at; not to mean a thing; not to understand what sb is driving at; scarcely know what one has said; unintelligible; without rhyme or reason;

bu zhi yi bo 不值一駁
not fit to be refuted / not worth refuting;

bu zhi yi tan 一值一談
nothing to speak of;

bu zhi yi ti 不值一提
not much to be particular about / not worth mentioning / unworthy of being mentioned;

bu zhi yi xiao 不值一笑
beneath contempt / not worth a laugh / not worth despising;

bu zhi ke fou 不置可否
avoiding saying yes or no / noncommittal || decline to comment; give no opinion whether or not it will do; hedge; indicate neither consent nor dissent; not express an opinion; not to express any opinion; not to say yes or no; prevaricate; refuse to comment; say neither buff nor stye; show neither approval nor disapproval; without giving an affirmative or negative

answer; yea and nay;

bu zhi yi ci 不置一詞
not utter a comment / say not a single word;

bu zu dao 不足道
do not deserve mentioning / not worth mentioning || not worth saying anything of; of no consequence;

bu zu wei wai ren dao 不足為外人道
no need to let others know || not worth telling it to outsiders; off the record; strictly between ourselves;

bu zu wei xun 不足為訓
not to be taken as a guide;

bu zuo sheng 不作聲
keep silence / not to say anything;

cai3 fang 採訪
interview;

cai na liang yan 採納良言
accept good counsel;

can3 bu ren yan 慘不忍言
too deplorable to describe;

can jiao 慘叫
give out sad cries / screech;

can jiao yi sheng 慘叫一聲
utter a heartrending cry;

can xiao 慘笑
bitter smiles from a heavy heart;

can4 粲
laugh / smile;

can ran 粲然
laugh / smile;

can ran yi xiao 粲然一笑
give a beaming smile / grin with delight;

cao1 操
speak (a language or dialect);

cao2 嘈
clamourous / noisy;

cao nao 嘈鬧
tumultuous / turbulent;

cha1 插
get a word in edgeways / interrupt;

cha bu jin hua 插不進話
cannot get a word in;

cha bu shang zui 插不上嘴
cannot get a word in edgeways / cannot put a word in conversation;

cha hua 插話
chime in / chip in / chuck out / interrupt / strike in / throw in;

cha yi zui 插一嘴
chime in / chip in / interrupt / strike in;

cha zui 插嘴
chip in / put in a word || barge in; break in; break in upon; burst in; burst in on; burst in upon; butt in; butt in with a remark; chime in; chop in; cut in; cut into; get a word in; get a word in edgeways; horn in; interpolate; interpose; interrupt; nip in; nip into; put in; snap sb up; strike in; take up; throw in;

cha2 wen 查問
inquire / interrogate / question;

cha xun 查詢
inquire about;

chan2 讒
backbite / calumniate / defame / misrepresent / slander;

chan bang 讒謗
calumniate / defame / slander;

chan hai 讒害
incriminate by false charges;

chan kou jiao jia 讒口交加
beset by slander;

chan ren 讒人
slanderer;

chan xian yu di 讒涎欲滴
mouth drooling with greed;

chan yan 讒言
malicious talk;

chan yan re huo 讒言惹禍
slander brings trouble;

chan2 饞
gluttonous / greedy / piggish;

chan gui 饞鬼
gourmet;

chan shi 饞食
greedy and voracious;

chan zui 饞嘴
gluttonous / voracious;

chan3 諂
fawn / flatter;

chan mei 諂媚
curry favour / fawn on / flatter / toady // flattery // soapy;

chan ning 諂佞
flatter / toady;

chan shang qi xia 諂上欺下
fawn on those above and bully those below;

chan xiao 諂笑
ingratiating smile;

chan yu 諂諛
curry favour / flatter;

chan3 闡
elaborate || elucidate; explain; expound; make clear;

chan fa 闡發
clarify / elucidate / explain / make clear;

chan ming 闡明
clarify / elucidate / expound || illustrate; shed light on; throw light on;

chan ming guan dian 闡明觀點
clarify one's views / explain one's position;

chan shi 闡釋
elucidate / explain / expound / interpret;

chan shu 闡述
elaborate / expound / set forth;

chan yang 闡揚
expound and propagate;

chang2 hua duan shuo 長話短說
to cut a long story short / to make a long story short / to make short of long;

chang pian da lun 長篇大論
long speech / pondrous talk;

chang tan 長談
long chat / long conversation / long discussion / long talk;

chang tan 長歎
have a deep sigh / sigh deeply // deep sigh;

chang tan yi sheng 長歎一聲
give a long sigh / heave a deep sigh / let out a long sigh;

chang xu 長吁
heave a long sigh;

chang xu duan tan 長吁短歎
moan and groan // sighs and groans;

chang2 tan 常談
commonplace talks / platitudes;

chang2 嚐
taste;

chang3 zui 敞嘴
unguarded in one's talk;

chang4 yan 倡言
initiate / propose;

chang yi 倡議
initiate / the first to propose;

chang4 唱
sing;

chang du jiao xi 唱獨腳戲
one doing work all by oneself;

chang fan diao 唱反調
take a contrary action || deliberately speak or act contrary to; harp on an opposite tune; sing a different tune; strike up a tune that runs counter to;

chang gao diao 唱高調
utter high-sounding words without putting them into practice || affect a high moral tone; use high-flown words;

chang ge 唱歌
sing a song / troll;

chang ge tiao wu 唱歌跳舞
singing and dancing;

chang he 唱和
(1) one singing a song and the others joining in the chorus;
(2) an exchange of poems;

chang lao diao 唱老調
harp on the same string / sing the same old song;

chang shuang huang 唱雙簧
collaborate with each other;

chang shuai 唱衰
bad-mouth;

chang xi 唱戲
sing and act in a Chinese opera;

chang xi de he cai — zi chui zi lei 唱戲的喝彩——自吹自擂
actors cheering — self-glorification;

chang4 suo yu yan 暢所欲言
air one's views freely / express one's opinions freely / speak out freely || express oneself with zest and gusto; have one's say; pour out all that one wishes to say; say exactly as the mind dictates; say freely what one thinks without reserve; say one's say; say one's piece; say out one's say; speak one's mind freely; speak without any inhibitions; talk to one's heart's content;

chang tan 暢談
talk freely and to one's heart's content || have a delightful talk; speak glowingly of; talk freely;

chang xu 暢敘
chat cheerfully / converse joyfully;

chang yin 暢飲
drink one's fill / drink to one's heart's content / quaff;

chao2 嘲
deride / jeer / mock / ridicule / scoff / sneer;

chao feng 嘲諷
sneer at / taunt // a smack in the eye / a smack in the face / taunt;

chao feng nong yue 嘲風弄月
sport with the wind and play with the moon — seek pleasure;

chao ma 嘲罵
jeer and abuse;

chao nie 嘲謔
make fun of / poke fun at;

chao nong 嘲弄
jape / mock / palter / poke fun at;

chao shan 嘲訕
deride / sneer at;

chao xi 嘲戲
make fun of / poke fun at;

chao xiao 嘲笑
ridicule || banter; chaff; deride; fleer; flout at; gibe; hold sb up to mockery; hold sth up to mockery; jeer at; jest; jibe; joke; laugh at; laugh to scorn; make a butt of; make a mock of; make a mockery of; make mock; make sport of; mock; palter; poke fun at; rally; razz; scoff; scoff at; scorn; sneer at; twist // mockery / scoff;

chao3 吵
(1) make a noise;
(2) quarrel / squabble / wrangle;
(3) annoy / disturb;

chao chao 吵吵
make a noise || talk rapidly at the same time; twitter;

chao chao nao nao 吵吵鬧鬧
raise a great hue and cry || create noisy disturbance; cut up; hubble-bubble; hurly-burly; in a bustle; kick up a cloud of dust; make a noise; raise a racket; raise jack;

chao chao rang rang 吵吵嚷嚷
boisterous || clamorous; hullabaloo; in an uproar; make a noise; raise a hue and cry;

chao jia 吵架
quarrel || a bull and cow; have a row; wrangle;

chao nao 吵鬧
(1) pick up a row / raise jack / tear up jack / wrangle;
(2) din / hubbub / hubbub-bubble;

chao nao bu xiu 吵鬧不休
kick up a great deal of fuss about / make a great noise;

chao rang 吵嚷
clamour / make a racket / shout in confusion;

chao rao 吵擾
annoy / disturb;

chao ren 吵人
disturb others by noise;

chao si le 吵死了
boisterous;

chao zui 吵嘴
bicker / quarrel;

che3 扯
chat / gossip;

che bai 扯白
talk nonsense;

che che la la 扯扯拉拉
ramble in talk;

che dan 扯淡
(1) chat;
(2) talk nonsense;

che huang 扯謊
lie / tell a lie;

che jia chang 扯家常
chat about everyday family affairs / chitchat / engage in small talk;

che kai sang zi 扯開嗓子
shout at the top of one's voice;

che pi 扯皮
argue back and forth / dispute over trifles / wrangle;

chen1 guai 嗔怪
blame / rebuke;

chen he 嗔喝
yell at in rage;

chen nu 嗔怒
get angry;

chen2 mo 沈默
(1) reticent / taciturn;
(2) silent;

chen mo bu yan 沈默不言
keep silent;

chen mo bu yu 沈默不語
as dumb as a fish / as dumb as an ox / as dumb as an oyster;

chen mo gua yan 沈默寡言
quiet and taciturn in disposition / reticence || a person of few words; a regular oyster; a reticent person; buttoned-up; close-mouthed; not to be given to much speech; of few words; reticent; scanty of words; sparingly of words / taciturn;

chen mo shi jin 沈默是金
silence is golden;

chen yin 沈飲
drink heavily;

chen2 ci lan diao 陳詞濫調
hackneyed expressions / hackneyed remarks / platitude;

chen shu 陳述
declare definitely / state;

chen shuo 陳説
explain / state;

chen shuo li hai 陳説利害
explain the advantages and disadvantages;

chen su 陳訴
complaint;

chen yan 陳言
hackneyed expressions / stale expressions;

chen4 kou hu shuo 趁口胡説
speak thoughtlessly;

chen4 yu 讖語
a prophetic remark made casually which later comes true;

cheng1 稱
call / nominate;

cheng de qi 稱得起
deserve to be called;

cheng dao 稱道
commend / praise || speak approvingly of;

cheng hao 稱號
(1) address / call;
(2) a form of address;

cheng he 稱賀
congratulate;

cheng hu 稱呼
address / call / name;

cheng mei 稱美
praise;

cheng shang 稱賞
praise and extol / speak highly of;

cheng shuo 稱説
name sth when speaking;

cheng song 稱頌
eulogize / extol / praise;

cheng tan 稱歎
acclaim / praise;

cheng wei 稱謂
appellation / title;

cheng xie 稱謝
express one's thanks / thank;

cheng xu 稱許
commendation / praise;

cheng yang 稱揚
praise and extol;

cheng yin 稱引
quote;

cheng yu 稱譽
acclaim / praise / sing the praises of;

cheng zan 稱讚
acclaim / commend / praise || pat sb on the back; slap sb on the back;

cheng2 nuo 承諾
(1) agree / promise;
(2) promise;

cheng ren 承認
acknowledge / admit / concede / profess;

cheng3 qi kou she 逞其口舌
swear like a bargee;

chi1 吃
(1) eat / take || get one's teeth into; have sth (to eat); nosh; sink tooth into;
(2) eat / have one's meal;

chi bai fan 吃白飯
live off others || be supported by others; eat for free;

chi bai shi 吃白食
live off others || be supported by others; eat for free;

chi bao 吃飽
full / have eaten one's fill;

chi bao chuan nuan 吃飽穿暖
eat one's fill and wear warm clothes;

chi bao he zu 吃飽喝足
eat and drink one's fill / eat and drink to one's heart's content || eat and drink to one's satisfaction; eat and drink to the limit of one's capacity; have a good long drink of water and a hearty meal;

chi bao shui zu 吃飽睡足
stoke up on food and get plenty of sleep;

chi bu de 吃不得
not edible / not good to eat;

chi bu fu 吃不服
be unaccustomed to eat sth;

chi bu kai 吃不開
unpopular;

chi bu lai 吃不來
not fond of eating sth;

chi bu liao 吃不了
cannot finish eating so much food;

chi bu shang 吃不上
have nothing to live on;

chi bu xia 吃不下
(1) not feel like eating;
(2) unable to eat any more;

chi bu xiao 吃不消
unable to bear;

chi bu zhu 吃不住
(1) be unable to control;
(2) be unable to support;

chi chi he he 吃吃喝喝
eat and drink / wine and dine with sb;

chi chuan 吃穿
food and clothing;

chi chuan bu chou 吃穿不愁
need not worry about food and clothing / there is plenty to eat and wear;

chi de hen duo 吃得很多
eat like a horse;

chi de ji shao 吃得極少
eat like a bird;

chi de kai 吃得開
popular;

chi de kuai 吃得快
rush one's food;

chi de lai 吃得來
able to eat;

chi de shang 吃得上
(1) can afford to eat;
(2) able to get meal;
(3) in time for a meal;

chi de xia 吃得下
able to eat;

chi de xiao 吃得消
bearable / tolerable;

chi de zhu 吃得住
(1) be able to support;
(2) be able to control;

chi dong xi 吃東西
eat sth;
chi dou fu 吃豆腐
eat bean curd;

chi fa 吃法
how to eat;

chi fan 吃飯
eat / feed one's face / have a meal;

chi fan bu gei qian 吃飯不給錢
eat a meal without paying;

chi fan le 吃飯了
come and get it;

chi guo hai xiang chi 吃過還想吃
want to eat again what has been eaten before;

chi he bu chou 吃喝不愁
have enough to eat and drink / want neither eat nor drink || enough to live on for life;

chi he wan le 吃喝玩樂
feasting and reveling || beer and skittles; cakes and ale; eat, drink and be merry; eating, drinking, and making merry; gluttony and pleasure-seeking; idle away one's time in pleasure-seeking;

chi hua jiu 吃花酒
drink and eat at a girlie bar;

chi huang lian 吃黃蓮
swallow a bitter pill / take an infusion of bitter herbs;

chi hun 吃葷
eat meat and other food produced by fowls or animals;

chi huo guo 吃火鍋
hot-pot meal;

chi ling zui 吃零嘴
nibble between meals / nibble tidbit / take snacks between meals;

chi feng mi, shuo hao hua — tian yan mi yu 吃蜂蜜，說好話——甜言蜜語
speaking fine words while eating honey — sweet words and honeyed phrases;

chi guang 吃光
eat up;

chi ling shi 吃零食
eat snacks;

chi mian tiao 吃麵條
eat noodles;

chi ni le 吃膩了
cloy the appetite with;

chi pian fan 吃偏飯
get a special help / receive a particular treatment;

chi qing 吃請
(1) be invited to a dinner;
(2) treat sb to a meal at public expense;

chi shi 吃食
feed;

chi shui 吃水
(1) drinking water;
(2) absorb water;

chi su 吃素
vegetarian;

chi su de 吃素的
easy / easygoing / easy to deal with;

chi wu fan 吃午飯
have lunch;

chi xi fan 吃稀飯
eat porridge;

chi yao 吃藥
take medicine;

chi ye xiao 吃夜宵
have a midnight snack;

chi zhuo bu jin 吃着不盡
have as much food and clothing as one wants;

chi zhuo wan li, qiao zhe guo li 吃着碗裏，瞧着鍋裏
peep in my cabbage pot, stare in my cupboard / while eating one dish, one keeps watching for next;

chi1 ma 笞罵
whip and revile;

chi1 嗤
laugh sneeringly / sneer;

chi chi xiao sheng 嗤嗤笑聲
peals of laughter;

chi di 嗤詆
laugh at / mock;

chi xiao 嗤笑
laugh at / laugh sneeringly / sneer at / snigger;

chi1 xiao 痴笑
giggle / simper / titter // gelasmus / hysterical laughter / silly smile;

chi2 lun 持論
express a view / present an argument / put a case;

chi lun gong ping 持論公平
express a view impartially / state a case fairly;

chi ping er lun 持平而論
give the devil his due;

chi ping zhi lun 持平之論
conciliative views / fair and square views / fair argument / unbiased views;

chi yi yi 持異議
maintain an opposite view;

chi2 bian 馳辯
exercise one's eloquence;

chi kou wang tan 馳口妄談
talk at random without restrain / talk quickly and wildly;

chi3 lun 侈論
(1) exaggerated talk;
(2) prate about / prattle about / talk glibly about;

chi tan 侈談
(1) prate about / prattle about / talk glibly about;
(2) unpractical hyperbole;

chi yan 侈言
exaggerated talk;

chi3 xiao 恥笑
hold sb to ridicule / mock / sneer at;

chi3 leng 齒冷
laugh sb to scorn;

chi4 叱
loudly rebuke / shout at / yell;

chi he 叱喝
bawl at / shout at;

chi ma 叱罵
abuse / curse / scold roundly;

chi ze 叱責
jump all over / rebuke / scold / upbraid;

chi4 斥
denounce / reprimand / scold / upbraid;

chi he 斥喝
scold;

chi ma 斥罵
reproach / scold / upbraid;

chi ze 斥責
reprimand || chastise; chew out; denounce; denunciate; objurgate; rebuke;

chi4 kou bai she 赤口白舌
talk nonsense // tawdry squabble over nothing;

chi kou du she 赤口毒舌
slander venomously / speak bitingly;

chong1 ji 充飢
appease one's hunger / assuage one's hunger / satisfy one's hunger;

chong1 kou er chu 沖口而出
blurt out / say sth without thinking;

chong2 shen 重申
ingeminate / reaffirm / reassert / reiterate / restate;

chong ti 重提
bring up again / mention again;

chong ti jiu shi 重提舊事
bring up an old case / rake over old ashes || rake up; rake up the past; recall past events;

chong2 lun hong yi 崇論宏議
an exalted discussion and extensive statement / a great essay or lofty exposition of point of view;

chou1 chou da da 抽抽嗒嗒
sob and sniffle || emit intermittent sobs; sob intermittently;

chou yan 抽煙
smoke a cigarette;

chou ye 抽噎
sob;

chou2 tan 愁歎
give sighs of distress;

chou yin 愁吟
grieving and worrying;

chou2 wen 讎問
ask difficult questions;

chou3 di 醜詆
abuse / revile;

chou hua 醜話
harmful gossip;

chou yu 醜語
abusive words / vile language;

chou4 ma 臭罵
curse roundly / scold angrily and abusively;

chou jiao 臭嚼
chatter on and on meaninglessly / keep on jawing nonsense;

chu1 kou 出口
speak / utter;

chu kou cheng zhang 出口成章
make polished impromptu speech || have the gift of the gab; speak like a ready orater whenever one speaks; talk beautifully; toss off smart remarks; words flow from the mouth as from the pen of a master;

chu kou cu ye 出口粗野
swear like a trooper;

chu kou ma ren 出口罵人
shout out abuse;

chu kou shang ren 出口傷人
use bad language to insult people || give sb the rough side of one's tongue; offend by rude remarks; speak bitingly // a hurtful tongue;

chu sheng 出聲
speak / utter a sound || make a sound;

chu yan 出言
speak;

chu yan bu xun 出言不遜
make impertinent remarks || drop a clanger; rough it; speak insolently; utter impolitely;

chu yan cu lu 出言粗魯
speak in a harsh tone;

chu yan tang tu 出言唐突
make a blunt remark;

chu yan wei he 出言威嚇
speak daggers to sb;

chu yan wu zhuang 出言無狀
speak rudely / use rude language;

chu yu bu su 出語不俗
speak in a lofty manner / speak in an uncommon way;

chu4 jue xing shi yu zheng 觸覺性失語症
tactile aphasia;

chu jue yu chan 觸覺語顫
tactile fremitus;

chuan2 dao xing shi yu zheng 傳導性失語症
conduction aphasia;

chuan e 傳訛
pass on wrong reports;

chuan hu 傳呼
notify sb by phone message;

chuan hua 傳話
pass on a message;

chuan ran xing kou jiao yan 傳染性口角炎
angulus infectiosus;

chuan ran xing kou yan 傳染性口炎
infectious stomatitis;

chuan song 傳誦
pass from mouth to mouth;

chuan wei hua bing 傳為話柄
become a subject for ridicule;

chuan wei jia hua 傳為佳話
become a favourite tale / everybody is telling the story of...;

chuan wei mei tan 傳為美談
be told from mouth to mouth with approbation;

chuan wei xiao bing 傳為笑柄
a laughing stock through the ages || be considered material for ridicule; it is all the more a laughting stock;

chuan wei xiao tan 傳為笑談
become a standing joke / pass into a proverb;

chuan wen 傳聞
hearsay / rumour;

chuan wen shi shi 傳聞失實
the rumour is unfounded;

chuan yan 傳言
(1) hearsay / rumour;
(2) pass on a message;
(3) make a statement / speak;

chuan yan fei xu 傳言非虛
it's not just hearsay;

chuan yang 傳揚
spread from mouth to mouth;

chuan yang si fang 傳揚四方
spread far and wide;

chuan yi 傳譯
interpret;

chuan3 喘
(1) huff / huff and puff / pant;
(2) asthma;

chuan qi 喘氣
(1) gasp / huff / huff and puff / pant;
(2) take a breather;

chuan xi 喘息
(1) gasp / huff / huff and puff / pant;
(2) take a breather;

chuang2 di zhi yan 牀第之言
intimate words said in bed / pillow talk / private talks between husband and wife;

chui1 吹
(1) blow / puff;
(2) boast / brag || talk big;

chui chui pai pai 吹吹拍拍
boasting and toadying;

chui de tian hua luan zhui 吹得天花亂墜
make a wild boast about / boast in the most fantastic terms || flatter up to the nines; give an extravagant account of; laud to the skies;

chui fa luo 吹法螺
boast / brag;

chui huo 吹火
blow a fire;

chui kou shao 吹口哨
whistle;

chui la ba 吹喇叭
(1) wind a trumpet;
(2) boast / praise / puff up;

chui mie 吹滅
blow out;

chui niu 吹牛
boast / brag / shoot a line / shoot one's mouth off / talk big // big talk // blowhard;

chui niu pai ma 吹牛拍馬
boast and flatter;

chui niu pi 吹牛皮
boast / brag || act the braggadocio; draw the long bow; shoot aline; shoot crap; shoot one's mouth off; shoot the bull; shoot the shit; stick it on; talk big; talk horse; talk in high language; talk through one's hat;

chui pai 吹拍
boast;

chui peng 吹捧
flatter / laud to the skies / lavish praise on;

chui qi 吹氣
huff;

chui qi ru lan 吹氣如蘭
give out fragrant smell / have a breath like a lily;

chui qu 吹去
blow away;

chui shao zi 吹哨子
blow a whistle;

chui xi 吹熄
blow off;

chui xiao nong di 吹簫弄笛
play the flute;

chui xu 吹噓
boast || advertise oneself; blow one's own trumpet; boast about oneself; boost up; crow about; glibly profess; lavish praise on oneself or others;

chui xu peng chang 吹噓捧場
laud / lavish and sing the praises of others;

chui yi kou qi 吹一口氣
give a puff;

chui zhi 吹指
whistle with fingers in the mouth;

chui zou 吹奏
play wind instruments;

chui1 jin zhuan yu 炊金饌玉
eat luxurious food;

chui2 xian 垂涎
covet || drool; gloat over; hanker over; slaver;

chui xian san chi 垂涎三尺
drool with envy || bring the water to one's mouth; cast a covetous eye at sth; cast greedy eyes at; cannot hide one's greed; gape after; gape for; hanker for; have one's mouth made up for; lick one's chops; lick one's lips; make sb's mouth water; one's mouth waters after; smack one's lips;

chui xian yi jiu 垂涎已久
have coveted sth for a long time / one's mouth has long been watering for...;

chui xian yu di 垂涎欲滴
have the mouth water / keep a covetous eye on / make sb's mouth water;

chui xun 垂詢
make gracious enquiries;

chun3 hua 蠢話
feeble-minded remarks / malarkey / silly remarks;

chuo2 歠
drink / sip / suck;

chuo4 啜
(1) sip / suck;
(2) sob;

chuo cha pin ming 啜茶品茗
sip tea;

chuo cha qing tan 啜茶清談
sip tea as they talk;

chuo ming 啜茗
drink tea;

chuo qi 啜泣
sob;

ci2 詞
speak / talk / tell;

ci feng 詞鋒
the sharpness of one's tongue;

ci qiong 詞窮
exhaust arguments // nothing more to say;

ci qiong li zhuo 詞窮理拙
poor in expression and perverted in logic;

ci qiong yu se 詞窮語塞
close one's mouth for want of words;

ci2 se 辭色
one's speech and facial expression;

ci tu ya zhi 辭吐雅致
refined conversation;

ci yan se li 辭嚴色厲
harsh speech and stern countenance;

ci yan yi zheng 辭嚴義正
severity in speech and fairness in principle;

ci3 chang bi he 此唱彼和
when one starts singing, another joins in;

ci4 ci bu xiu 刺刺不休
chatter without stop || chatter like a magpie; chatter on and on; gabble on and on; go nineteen to the dozen; keep on clamouring; repeat endlessly; run nineteen to the dozen; run off at the mouth; speak nineteen to the dozen; talk a leg off a dog; talk a leg off a donkey; talk a leg off a horse; talk incessantly; talk nineteen to the dozen; talk one's head off; talk without cease;

ci kou lun shi 刺口論事
remark frankly and criticize openly;

cong2 jian ru liu 從諫如流
follow good advice like the flowing of the river;

cu1 hua 粗話
coarse language / obscence language / vulgar language;

cu lu hua 粗魯話
coarse tongue / rough tongue;

cu sheng cu qi 粗聲粗氣
speak in an injured voice / with a deep, gruff voice;

cu sheng da qi 粗聲大氣
deep and gruff voice;

cu shi jian can 粗食簡餐
have coarse rice and simple dishes for one's meals;

cu yan e yu 粗言惡語
dirty words / four-letter words / the rough side of the tongue;

cu4 xi tan xin 促膝談心
have a heart-to-heart talk ‖ sit closely together and have an intimate chat; sit side by side and talk intimately; talk head and head;

cui1 tu fa 催吐法
vomit-inducing method;

cui tu yao 催吐藥
emetic;

cui4 啐
(1) sip / taste;
(2) spit;

cui yi kou tan 啐一口痰
spit phlegm;

cun2 wen 存問
send a messenger to inquire after sb;

cuo1 shang 磋商
discuss;

cuo4 hua 錯話
improper remarks;

cuo yu 錯語
paraphasia;

cuo yu zheng 錯語症
heterophasia;

da1 答
answer / reply / respond;

da li 答理
acknowledge / respond;

da qiang 答腔
answer / respond;

da ying 答應
(1) answer / reply / respond;
(2) accede to / agree / allow / comply with / permit / promise;

da yun 答允
undertake;

da2 答
(1) answer / reply / respond;
(2) reciprocate / return a visit;

da bian 答辯
reply in support of one's ideas / reply to a charge;

da bu shang lai 答不上來
at a loss how to answer;

da ci 答詞
answering speech / reply / speech in reply;

da dui 答對
answer / reply;

da fei suo wen 答非所問
an answer wide of the mark / an irrelevant answer / give an irrelevant answer ‖ answer beyond the question; answer what is not asked; dodge the question; give an answer wide off the mark; the answer evades the question; the answer is beside the question;

da fu 答覆
answer / reply;

da hua 答話
answer / reply;

da wen 答問
questions and answers;

da xie 答謝
gratefully acknowledge;

da yi wei xiao 答以微笑
respond with a smile;

da yu 答語
words of a reply;

da1 huo 搭伙
eat regularly in a place;

da qiang 搭腔
(1) answer / respond;
(2) talk to each other;

da shan 搭訕
accost sb / try to strike up a conversation with sb;

da tan 搭談
have conversation with / talk to;

da3 bao ge er 打飽嗝兒
belch after a solid meal;

da cha 打岔
cut in / interrupt a conversation;

da da nao nao 打打鬧鬧
(1) boisterous;
(2) fight in jest;

da da tan tan 打打談談
fight and talk alternately;

da dian hua 打電話
make a phone call / call sb || call sb up; contact sb by phone; give sb a bell; give sb a buzz; give sb a call; give sb a ring; give sb a shout; make a call; phone; phone sb up; ring sb up; telephone sb;

da dian hua liao da tian 打電話聊大天
have a long chat over the phone;

da duan 打斷
(1) break / break-in;
(2) cut short / interrupt;

da duan hua tou 打斷話頭
cut sb short / interrupt sb;

da ha ha 打哈哈
crack a joke || joke; joke about; make fun; poke fun at;

da ha qian 打哈欠
yawn;

da kai hua xia zi 打開話匣子
start a conversation || begin to talk; plunge into one's spiel; turn on the gas;

da kai tian chuang shuo liang hua 打開天窗説亮話
have a frank talk || come out flatfooted; frankly speaking; have a straight talk; place all one's cards on the table; let's be frank and put our cards on the table; let's not mince matters; not to mince matters; speak out without the slightest hesitation; talk frankly without hedging about; talk turkey;

da ma 打罵
beat and scold / maltreat;

da quan zi 打圈子
(1) banter / make fun of / tease;
(2) beat about the bush / speak in a roundabout way;

da ren ma ren 打人罵人
beat or scold sb / hit and swear at people / strike and curse sb;

da wen 打問
interrogate with torture / torture sb during interrogation;

da ya shuai zui 打牙涮嘴
chat / gossip / tattle;

da zui ba 打嘴巴
box sb in the ear || give a good talk to; take sb to task;

da zui zhang 打嘴仗
argue / dispute;

da4 bu wei ran 大不謂然
hold an entirely different view;

da chang fan diao 大唱反調
come out with a different tune / sing a different tune / strike up an entirely different tune;

da chang gao diao 大唱高調
claim in high-sounding language / play up the theme of;

da chao da nao 大吵大鬧
create a scene / raise a hue and cry || barney; create a noisy disurbance; cut up bad; cut up nasty; cut up rough; cut up savage; cut up stiff; cut up ugly; have a big row with sb; kick up a fuss; kick up a row; kick up a shine; make a great wrangle and quarrel; make a hell of a noise; make a scene; make a tremendous row; make the feathers fly; raise a big uproar; raise Cain; raise havoc;

raise hell; raise the devil; raise the roof; yell bloody murder;

da chao da rang 大吵大嚷
bluster / make a great hue and cry;

da chi 大吃
tuck away / tuck in;

da chi da he 大吃大喝
eat and drink to one's heart's content || eat and drink immoderately; excessive feasting; extravagant; guzzle; make a glutton of oneself; make a pig of oneself; on the spree; overeating and overdrinking; spendthrift in feasting;

da chi yi dun 大吃一頓
(1) stoke;
(2) have a square meal // on the spree;

da chui da lei 大吹大擂
trumpet loudly about || a high-pitched loose talk; ballyhoo for; beat the drum; blow a loud blast on the trumpet; blow one's own trumpet; blow the trumpet and beat the drum; brag; brag and blare about one's success; fuss and feathers; hue and cry; make a big noise; make a great fanfare; put up a big show; raise a great fanfare; talk big // ballyhoo;

da chui niu pi 大吹牛皮
pitch it strong / talk big;

da fa hong lun 大發宏論
express one's intelligent views freely || get on one's soapbox; pour forth wisdom;

da fa yi lun 大發議論
speak at great length / talk a lot;

da fang jue ci 大放厥詞
talk wildly || engage in a wild talk; hold forth; let out a torrent of abuse; loose one's tongue; spout a stream of empty rhetoric; talk a lot of drivel; talk a lot of nonsense; talk drivel;

da fei chun she 大費唇舌
make a long harangue || a long harangue; a lot of talking; take a lot of talking to convince;

da han da jiao 大喊大叫
shout at the top of one's voice || cheer and shout; cry and scream; raise a great hue and cry; shout and bellow loudly;

da he ha jiao 大喝大嚼
eat and drink one's fill;

da he chang 大合唱
cantata / chorus;

da hong long 大轟隆
all talk but no action;

da hu xiao jiao 大呼小叫
shout and wrangle;

da hua 大話
big talk / tall talk || boast; bragging; overstatement;

da jiao 大叫
(1) yell;
(2) ululate;

da jiao da rang 大叫大嚷
bawl and shout / cry at the top of one's voice || make a fuss about; raise a hue and cry;

da jiao jiu ming 大叫救命
yell for help;

da jiao yi sheng 大叫一聲
give a cry / shout out loud / utter a cry;

da kou tun yan 大口吞咽
gollop / swill;

da ma 大罵
bawl sb out / rail at;

da ma yi dun 大罵一頓
break into a torrent of abuse;

da miu bu ran 大謬不然
entirely wrong;

da sheng 大聲
loud / in a loud voice;

da sheng ji hu 大聲疾呼
call out with a loud voice / raise a cry of warning || appeal loudly; cry as loud as possible; cry out; lift up one's voice; sound out;

da sheng shuo chu 大聲說出
shout out;

da shua zui pi zi 大耍嘴皮子
talk gibly;

da tan te tan 大談特談
keep on talking about / talk at length;

da xiao 大笑
laughter;

da xiao qi lai 大笑起來
break out in laughter;

da xiao yi sheng 大笑一聲
give a loud laugh / laugh loudly;

da yan bu can 大言不慚
boast without shame / brag unblushingly / brag without feeling shame // shamelessly boastful;

da zui ru ni 大醉如泥
as drunk as a lord / blind drunk / dead drunk / smashed;

dai1 xiao 呆笑
fatuous grin / imbecile smile;

dai1 hua 獃話
stupid nonsense;

dai4 ren shuo xiang 代人說項
put in a good word for sb || intercede for sb; make intercession; speak for sb;

dai yan ren 代言人
mouthpiece / spokesperson;

dai4 bu 待哺
wait for feeding;

dai4 tou fa yan 帶頭發言
the first to speak;

dai xiao 帶笑
smilingly / wearing a smile;

dan4 shuo wu fang 但說無妨
it does not matter to say what is in one's mind;

dan4 啖
eat / feed;

dan4 dan yi xiao 淡淡一笑
with a faint smile;

dan hua 淡話
insipid conversation / insipid talk;

dang mian yan ming 當面言明
state clearly in one's presence;

dang3 讜
speak out boldly;

dang ci 讜辭
outspoken words;

dang lun 讜論
outspoken statements;

dang yan 讜言
outspoken remarks;

dang yan gao lun 讜言高論
honest and wise counsel;

dao1 zi zui, dou fu xin 刀子嘴，豆腐心
a good heart, but a sharp tongue || his bark is worse than his bite; his tongue is as sharp as a knife, his heart is as soft as bean curd; more bark than bite;

dao1 叨
(1) chatterbox;
(2) garrulous / talkative;

dao dao 叨叨
chatter away / rattle / talk on and on // garrulous;

dao dao nian nian 叨叨念念
mutter and grumble;

dao deng 叨登
(1) turn sth over and over;
(2) harp on an old story;

dao jiao 叨教
thank you for favouring us with your advice / trouble you by requesting your instructions;

dao lao 叨嘮
chatter away / complain / nag / talk on and on // talkative;

dao nian 叨念
chatter incessantly / talk about again and again in recollection;

dao xu bu xiu 叨絮不休
talk endlessly;

dao4 chou yi kou qi 倒抽一口氣
hold one's breath;

dao ku shui 倒苦水
grumble / pour out one's grievances;

dao xu 倒敘
narrate an incident in inverted order

chronologically;

dao4 ci 悼詞
memorial speech;

dao ge 悼歌
dirge / funeral hymn;

dao4 he 道賀
congratulate;

dao po 道破
lay bare / point out frankly / reveal;

dao qian 道歉
apologize / make an apology;

dao san bu zhuo liang 道三不着兩
(1) not see reason;
(2) talk irrelevantly;

dao ting tu shuo 道聽途説
get by hearsay / listen to gossip / pick up hearsay knowledge // gossip / hearsay / rumour;

dao xi 道喜
congratulate sb on a happy occasion;

dao xie 道謝
express one's thanks / thank;

de2 yi wang yan 得意忘言
an understanding without words;

di1 diao 低調
low-key // mild remarks;

di sheng 低聲
in a low voice / under one's breath;

di sheng chang 低聲唱
sing small;

di sheng xi yu 低聲細語
in a whisper;

di sheng xia qi 低聲下氣
speak humbly and in a low voice || have a servile manner; humble oneself; lower one's voice and stifle one's anger; meek and subservient; obsequitous; soft-spoken and submissive; speak humbly and under one's breath; speak low and repress one's feelings of revolt;

di ya 低啞
low and hoarse (voice);

di2 嘀
babble;

di di gu gu 嘀嘀咕咕
babble on and on / jabber-jabber / keep on growling / mumble to oneself / mutter to oneself // grousing / grumbling;

di gu 嘀咕
talk in whispers / whisper;

di3 zhang er tan 抵掌而談
chat leisurely / have a close, intimate talk / have a pleasant conversation;

di3 詆
defame / denigrate / slander;

di bang guan si 詆謗官司
libel case;

di he 詆訶
defame / disparage / slander;

di hui 詆毀
calumniate / defame / denigrate / dispraise / slander / vilify // defamation / vilification;

di lan 詆讕
cover up with lies;

di man 詆謾
slander and insult;

di zi 詆訾
defame / denigrate / dispraise / slander;

die2 喋
blah-blah / chatter / chirp / gibberish / incessant chattering / twitter;

die die 喋喋
garrulous / talkative;

die die bu xiu 喋喋不休
chatter without stop || blah-blah; chatter away; chatter like a magpie; clack; gabble away; gabble on and on; go nineteen to the dozen; keep clamouring; of many words; rattle away; rattle on; run nineteen to the dozen; run on; talk an arm off; talk away; talk endlessly about; talk nineteen to the dozen; talk one's head off; talk sb's ear off // garrulous;

die nie 喋囁
whisper;

die2 諜
garrulous / glib;

die die bu xiu 諜諜不休
chatter without stop || blah-blah; chatter away; chatter like a magpie; gabble on and on; go nineteen to the dozen; keep clamouring; of many words; rattle away; rattle on; run nineteen to the dozen; run on; talk an arm off; talk endlessly about; talk nineteen to the dozen; talk one's head off; talk sb's ear off;

ding1 叮
(1) bite / sting;
(2) say or ask again to make sure;

ding ning 叮嚀
exhort || give repeated injunctions; repeatedly advise; urge again and again; warn;

ding zhu 叮囑
exhort / repeatedly advise / urge again and again / warn;

ding3 gang 頂槓
argue;

ding zui 頂嘴
answer back / argue back / back talk / mouth off / reply defiantly / talk back;

ding3 yan 鼎言
important statements / words of importance;

ding4 yi 定議
closed decision;

dong1 la xi che 東拉西扯
drag in irrelevant matters / talk incoherently // bitty;

dong yi ju, si yi ju 東一句，西一句
talk incoherently;

dong4 kou bu dong shou 動口不動手
argue without coming to blows;

dong wen 動問
offer a question;

dong zhe da ma 動輒打罵
beat sb and swear at him on the least pretext;

dong zhe xun ren 動輒訓人
only too ready to lecture others / reprove others at every turn;

dou1 quan zi 兜圈子
beat about the bush;

dou4 ren xiao 逗人笑
crack sb up;

dou zui 逗嘴
set each other laughing by funny remarks;

dou zui pian zi 逗嘴片子
cross words with sb / quarrel with sb;

dou4 hua 鬬話
argue / debate;

dou zui 鬬嘴
bicker / cross talk / squabble / tiff;

du1 嘟
(1) pout;
(2) honk / toot;

du du nang nang 嘟嘟囔囔
mumble and sputter;

du du nong nong 嘟嘟噥噥
mumble in whispers / mutter to oneself;

du du sheng 嘟嘟聲
beep / blare / toot;

du lu 嘟嚕
(1) bunch / cluster;
(2) trill;

du nang 嘟囔
mumble / mutter to oneself;

du nong bu ping 嘟噥不平
complain ceaselessly / say the devil's paternoster;

du qi zui ba 嘟起嘴巴
pout one's lips in displeasure;

du2 ma 毒罵
scold ferociously and maliciously;

du2 chang 獨唱
solo;

du2 讀
(1) read / read aloud;
(2) attend school;

du chu 讀出
read out;

du shu 讀書
(1) read / study;

(2) attend school;

du shu 讀熟
learn by heart;

du3 sang 堵喪
talk back;

du zui 堵嘴
gag sb / shut sb's mouth / silence sb;

du4 jian 杜諫
advise / persuade;

du jue yan lu 杜絕言路
not let others express their views / stifle criticism;

du jue yao yan 杜絕謠言
stop rumours;

du kou 杜口
shut one's mouth and say nothing;

du kou bu yan 杜口不言
keep silent / shut up;

duan4 jiu 斷酒
abstain from alcohol;

duan shi 斷食
starve to death voluntarily;

duan yan 斷言
affirm / allege / assert categorically / aver / declare / say with certainty / state with certainty;

duan yu 斷語
conclusion / judgment;

dui4 bai 對白
dialogue;

dui da 對答
answer / reply;

dui da ru liu 對答如流
glib reply ‖ answer as quickly as the flowing of water; answer fluently; answer glibly; answer readily without stopping; answer up to every question; answer without a hitch; answer without any hesitation; be ready at repartee; fluent repartee; give fluent replies; have a ready tongue; quick in answer; ready answer; reply in a stream of eloquence; reply in a stream of eloguence;

dui hua 對話
conversation / dialogue // have a conversation / have a dialogue;

dui kou 對口
speak or sing alternately;

dui kou chang 對口唱
antiphonal singing;

dui kou hui tan 對口會談
counterpart conversations;

dui ma 對罵
abuse each other / scold each other;

dui zhi 對質
face each other and exchange questions;

dun4 zui zhuo she 鈍嘴拙舌
one does not shine in conversation;

dun4 kou wu yan 頓口無言
be completed silenced / have nothing to say in reply;

duo1 can shao shi 多餐少食
have many meals but little food at each;

duo chi duo zhan 多吃多佔
eat or take more than one's share ‖ consume and take more than one's due; grab more than one's share; sponge and take more than one's share; take more than one is entitled to;

duo hua 多話
big mouth;

duo yan guo er 多言聒耳
make a din in one's ears;

duo zui 多嘴
gossipy ‖ gabby; long-tongued; loquacious; shoot off one's mouth; speak out of turn; talk out of place; talk too much;

duo zui duo she 多嘴多舌
gossipy and meddlesome ‖ gabby; have a loose tongue; long-tongued; loquacious; run off at the mouth; shoot one's mouth off; talkative;

duo zuo shi, shao shuo hua 多做事，少說話
more cider and less talk / work more and talk less;

duo1 咄
(1) angry cry;

(2) scold in a loud voice;

duo duo bi ren 咄咄逼人
overbearing;

duo jie 咄嗟
cry out;

e1 hao zhi yan 阿好之言
a statement to please one side;

e2 chuan 訛傳
false rumour / groundless rumour / unfounded rumour;

e yan 訛言
idle talk / rumour;

e yan e yu 訛言訛語
erroneous and irresponsible talk;

e4 du zhou ma 惡毒咒罵
vicious vilification || scurrilous asperson; vile ravings; virulent abuse;

e kou 惡口
abusive tongue / bad language;

e kou shang ren 惡口傷人
say libelous things about sb / use bad language to insult people;

e ma 惡罵
abuse / vicious abuse / vilification;

e ren kou du 惡人口毒
a vicious person has a slanderous mouth;

e shan 惡訕
libel / slander;

e sheng 惡聲
(1) abusive language / angry curses / bad language;
(2) inauspicious sound;

e yan 惡言
abusive words / vicious remarks;

e yan du yu 惡言毒語
malicious language / malicious remarks / vicious remarks;

e yan e shi 惡言惡食
poor clothing and poor food / poor clothing, meagre meal;

e yan e yu 惡言惡語
the rough side of the tongue;

e yan po yu 惡言潑語
malicious remarks / vicious remarks;

e yan shang ren 惡言傷人
use bad language to insult people / make disparaging remarks about others;

e yan xiang xiang 惡言相向
cast an evil eye on sb;

e yi shan bang 惡意訕謗
spread vicious gossip;

e yu 惡語
malicious remarks;

e yu shang ren 惡語傷人
use bad language to insult sb || give sb the rough side of one's tongue; make disparaging remarks about sb; malicious remarks hurt people to the quick;

e yu shang ren hen bu xiao 惡語傷人恨不消
slander always leaves a slur / slander leaves a scar behind it / the wicked words hurting others cause unperishable hatred;

e yu shang ren liu yue han 惡語傷人六月寒
vicious slander makes one feel cold even in the hotest time || slander is hurtful;

e yu zhong shang 惡語中傷
use bad language to insult people || attack with vicious words; calumniate; cast aspersions on sb; malign sb viciously; say malicious remark to hurt sb; slander with malicious language; speak ill of sb; use abusive words to hurt others; viciously slander;

e zui du she 惡嘴毒舌
have a vicious tongue || bad tongue; biting tongue; bitter tongue; caustic tongue; dangerous tongue; sharp tongue; venomous tongue; wicked tongue;

e4 腭
roof of the mouth;

e lie 腭裂
cleft palate;

e4 諤
honest speech / frank comments;

e4 顎
(1) the cheek / jowl;

(2) jaw;
(3) high cheek-bone;

e gu 顎骨
jawbone;

e gu gu zhe 顎骨骨折
jaw fracture;

e gu sui yan 顎骨髓炎
osteomyelitis of the jaw;

er2 ge 兒歌
children's song / nursery rhyme / songs for children;

er yu 兒語
baby language;

er4 hua 二話
(1) demur;
(2) objection;

er hua xiu ti 二話休提
that's flat;

er4 yan 貳言
different views;

fa1 sheng guo qiang 發聲過強
superenergetic phonation;

fa sheng guo ruo 發聲過弱
subenergetic phonation;

fa sheng kun nan 發聲困難
dysphonia;
jing luan xing fa sheng kun nan 痙攣性發聲困難
spasmodic dysphonia;

fa sheng wu li 發聲無力
phonasthenia;

fa shi 發誓
cross one's heart / make an oath / pledge / swear / take an oath / take one's dick / vow;

fa wen 發問
ask a question / raise a question ‖ fire off; pose a question; put a question;

fa xiao 發笑
chuckle / giggle / laugh;

fa yan 發言
have the floor / make a speech / make a statement / speak / take the floor;

fa yan fan dui 發言反對
speak against;

fa yan quan 發言權
right to speak;

fa yan ren 發言人
spokesperson;

fa yan zhong ken 發言中肯
hit the mark / hit the right nail on the head / make a pertinent speech / speak to the point / strike the right note;

fa yin 發音
articulate;

fa yin guo qiang 發音過強
hyperphonia;

fa yin guo ruo 發音過弱
hypophonia;

fa yin jing luan 發音痙攣
phonatory spasm;

fa yin kun nan 發音困難
dysphonia;

fa yin zheng chang 發音正常
orthophony;

fan2 yan 煩言
(1) complaint / grievance // complain about / grumble;
(2) gossip / tedious remarks / tedious words;

fan3 bian 反辯
refute;

fan bo 反駁
controvert / disprove / refute / retort / snap back at sb;

fan fu yin yong 反復吟詠
recite again and again in appreciation;

fan gong zi wen 反躬自問
ask oneself ‖ examine oneself; hold communion with oneself; search one's conscience; search one's heart; search one's soul; turn back and question oneself; the examining of oneself;

fan hua 反話
irony;

fan jie 反詰
ask in retort;

fan kou 反口
go back on one's words;

fan kou xiang jie 反口相詰
ask in retort / counter with a question;

fan wen 反問
(1) ask in reply;
(2) rhetorical question;

fan yao 反咬
bite back;

fan yao yi kou 反咬一口
do harm to one's benefactor ‖ make a false countercharge; make false countercharges; shift the blame to sb; trump up a countercharge against one's accuser; turn around and charge the victim;

fan yu 反語
irony;

fan4 fan er tan 泛泛而談
speak in general terms / talk in generalities;

fan lun 泛論
general discussion;

fan lun shi qing 泛論世情
discuss vaguely about the worldly affairs;

fan wen 泛問
general question;

fan4 lai kai kou 飯來開口
eat but not work / live like a parasite;

fan liang 飯量
appetite / capacity for eating;

fang4 da pao 放大炮
talk big / talk boldly;

fang ge 放歌
sing with uninhibited loudness;

fang hua 放話
create public opinion / spread news / spread rumours;

fang kong pao 放空炮
indulge in idle boasting / talk big;

fang ma hou pao 放馬後炮
comment on sth when it is over;

fang sheng 放聲
sing out // sound reproduction;

fang sheng da ku 放聲大哭
cry loudly ‖ burst into loud sobbing; burst out crying; burst out sobbing; cry loudly and bitterly; cry without restraint; lift up one's voice and wail; raise one's voice in loud weeping; set up loud lamentations; sob loudly; utter a great cry; wail at the top of one's voice; weep aloud; weep in a loud voice / weep with noisy abandon // outburst of weeping;

fang sheng da xiao 放聲大笑
give a noisy laugh / guffaw / laugh like a drain // outburst of laughter / screams of laughter;

fang sheng ge chang 放聲歌唱
sing at the top of one's voice / sing loudly / sing out / sing up;

fang sheng tong ku 放聲痛哭
raise one's voice in great weeping / weep bitterly with abandon;

fang yan gao lun 放言高論
give a free speech and boasting // highflown talk;

fei1 nan 非難
blame and reproach // adverse criticism;

fei xiao 非笑
laugh at / ridicule;

fei yi 非議
censure / dispute / reproach;

fei1 duan liu chang 飛短流長
flying rumours / spread embroidered stories and malicious gossip;

fei1 duan liu chang 蜚短流長
flying rumours ‖ spread embroidered stories and malicious gossip; spread rumours; talk behind sb's back; tell tales;

fei yu 蜚語
gossip / rumour;

fei3 hua 匪話
thief's slang;

fei3 誹
defame / libel / slander;

fei bang 誹謗
libel ‖ asperse; calumniate; defame; denigrate; fling dirt at; slander; sling mud at;

smear; throw mud at;

fei bang ming yu 誹謗名譽
libel;

fei bang xing wei 誹謗行為
act of libel;

fei guo qi shi 誹過其實
paint the devil blacker than he is;

fei4 fu zhi yan 肺腑之言
speak from the bottom of one's heart || hearty talk; most reliable words; talk from the heart; the words from one's heart; words from the depths of one's heart;

fei4 tuo mo 費唾沫
waste one's breath;

fei zui pi zi 費嘴皮子
talk nonsense;

fei4 hua 廢話
talk rubbish || crap; flapdoodle; flimflam; hogwash; nonsense; rubbish; stuff and nonsense; superfluous words; verbiage; waffle;

fei hua lian pian 廢話連篇
talk rubbish || beat one's gums; empty phrases; it's all moonshine; multiply words; pages of nonsense; reams of rubbish; talk downright nonsense;

fei qin wang shi 廢寢忘食
too busy to eat or sleep || disregard meal times and go without sleep; do sth almost to the gross neglect of one's health; forget food and rest; forget meals and sleep; lose sleep and forget to eat; neglect one's meals and sleep;

fen1 bang 分謗
share blame;

fen bian 分辯
make excuses / explain;

fen1 吩
direct / instruct;

fen fu 吩咐
instruct / tell;

fen1 fen yi lun 紛紛議論
opinions are widely divided;

fen4 yan 忿言
angry words;

fen4 tu zhi yan 糞土之言
talk of refuse / valueless talk;

feng1 zhu zui ba 封住嘴巴
gag one's mouth / shut sb up || one's lips are sealed; shut one's mouth; silence the voice of; stop sb's mouth;

feng zui 封嘴
hush up / refuse to say anything / prevent sb from talking;

feng zui qian 封嘴錢
bribe / hush money;

feng1 liang hua 風涼話
irresponsible and sarcastic remarks / sarcastic comments;

feng1 hua 瘋話
gibberish / jargon;

feng2 ren dan shuo san fen hua, mo ba zhen xin yi guo duan 逢人但説三分話，莫把真心一鍋端
think before you speak and then talk with reservation;

feng ren qie shuo san fen hua, wei ke quan pao yi pian xin 逢人且説三分話，未可全抛一片心
all truths are not to be told; all truths must not be told at all times;

feng ren shuo xiang 逢人説項
tell everybody of a person's virtue || praise a person before everybody; publish abroad a person's good acts;

feng ying 逢迎
curry favour with / fawn on / make up to;

feng ying ba jie 逢迎巴結
bootlick / suck;

feng ying e yu 逢迎阿諛
bootlick / dance attendance on / flatter and toady;

feng ying gan dai 逢迎感戴
bootlick / fawn on and servilely thank;

feng ying pai ma 逢迎拍馬
excessively fawning / unctuous;

feng3 唪
chant / recite;

feng jing 唪經
chant liturgies / recite scriptures;

feng4 shang shang shou 奉觴上壽
drink a toast of longevity / a toast to long life;

feng4 諷
(1) mock / satirize;
(2) chant / intone;

feng ci 諷刺
make a crack / mock / satirize // sarcastic / sardonic // sarcasm / satire;

feng jian 諷諫
admonish in a roundable way;

feng shi 諷示
admonish in a roundable way;

feng song 諷誦
read with intonation and expression;

feng yi quan bai 諷一勸百
satirize one in order to admonish a hundred;

feng yu 諷喻
allegory / parable;

fo2 kou she xin 佛口蛇心
say sweet things but do evil things;

fou3 ren 否認
deny || disaffirm; disavow; disclaim; give a denial to sth; make a denial of; negate; reject; repudiate // denial / disaffirmation / disavowal;

fu2 服
take medicine;

fu du 服毒
take poison;

fu du er si 服毒而死
die of poison;

fu du zi sha 服毒自殺
destroy oneself by taking poison / poison oneself / swallow poison purposely to commit suicide;

fu shi 服食
take;

fu yao 服藥
take medicine;

fu yong 服用
take medicine;

fu2 kua yan lun 浮誇言論
bombast;

fu shuo 浮說
groundless remarks;

fu yan 浮言
groundless statements / unfounded remarks;

fu3 zhang da xiao 撫掌大笑
clap one's hands and laugh aloud / laugh loud and clap one's hands;

fu3 shou wu yan 俯首無言
bend one's head in silence;

fu4 zhi yi xiao 付之一笑
dismiss with a laugh / laugh off || afford to laugh at; carry off with a laugh; laugh and forget about it; laugh away;

fu4 訃
obituary;

fu gao 訃告
obituary notice;

fu wen 訃聞
obituary notice;

gai1 shuo bu shuo 該說不說
button up one's lips / button up one's mouth;

gai3 kou 改口
eat one's words / correct oneself;

gan1 yan 甘言
honeyed words;

gan yan mi yu 甘言蜜語
honeyed tongue and sugary words / honeyed words;

gan1 bei 乾杯
bottom up / drink to / here's mud in your eye;

gan1 ke 乾渴
very thirsty;

gan xiao 乾笑
hollow laugh / laugh without mirth;

gan ye 乾咽
sob / weep;

gan3 nu er bu gan yan 敢怒而不敢言
feel angry but not dare to speak out || be

forced to keep one's resentment to oneself; furious but not dare to say anything; choke with silent fury; not dare to express one's inner anger or discontent; suppress one's rage;

gan qing 敢請
venture to request;

gan wen 敢問
venture to ask;

gan yan 敢言
courageous enough to express one's beliefs;

gan3 zui 趕嘴
uninvited guest at dinner;

gan4 shi xiao yi 旰食宵衣
eat late and get up early;

gao1 chang 高唱
(1) sing loudly / sing with spirit;
(2) call out loudly for / talk glibly about;

gao chang ru yun 高唱入雲
sing so loud as to reach the clouds / sing with a resounding voice;

gao ge 高歌
sing loudly / sing with a resounding voice;

gao ge meng jin 高歌猛進
advance boldly with songs on one's lips / advance triumphantly / stride forward singing militant songs;

gao ge shu huai 高歌抒懷
express one's heart's feelings by a song;

gao ge yi qu 高歌一曲
chant a melody / raise one's voice to sing a song / sing a song loudly;

gao lun 高論
original remarks / outstanding statement;

gao sheng 高聲
in a raised voice // sing loudly / speak loudly;

gao sheng da xiao 高聲大笑
roar with laughter;

gao sheng lang song 高聲朗誦
recite aloud;

gao tan kuo lun 高談闊論
talk with eloquence ‖ set the world to rights; talk incessantly; very articulate speech;

gao4 告
(1) tell;
(2) accuse;

gao bang 告幫
ask for assistance;

gao ci 告辭
bid farewell / say goodbye / take leave;

gao fa 告發
delate / inform against sb / peach against sb / peach on sb // delation;

gao jie 告誡
admonish / exhort ‖ adjure; counsel; dissuade from; enjoin; warn // exhortation;

gao mi 告密
blow the gab / inform against sb / tip off;

gao rao 告饒
apologize;

gao su 告訴
let sb know / make clear to sb / tell sb;

gao zhi 告知
impart / inform / notify;

ge1 咯
cough;

ge ge xiao 咯咯笑
chortle / giggle;

ge1 ge xiao 格格笑
cackle;

ge1 歌
(1) song;
(2) chant / sing;
(3) praise;

ge chang 歌唱
(1) sing;
(2) praise / sing in praise of;

ge gong song de 歌功頌德
chant one's praises and sing of sb's virtue ‖ eulogize sb's virtue and achievements; eulogize the deeds and virtues of; flattery and exaggerated praise; glorification of; glorify sb's character and accomplishments; heap praises and eulogies on; praise and eulogy; sing the praise of; sing the praise of sb's achievements and virtue;

ge hou 歌喉
singer's voice / singing voice / voice;

ge hou wan zhuan 歌喉婉轉
sing in a beautiful voice // sweet singing; sweet voice;

ge sheng 歌聲
singing / sound of singing;

ge sheng liao liang 歌聲嘹亮
the singing is loud and clear;

ge sheng liao rao 歌聲繚繞
the song lingers in the air;

ge sheng rao liang 歌聲繞梁
the voice of singing reverberates round the beams of a house for days;

ge sheng ru chao 歌聲如潮
the sound of songs rising and falling like waves;

ge sheng si qi 歌聲四起
sounds of singing are heard from all around;

ge sheng ying er 歌聲盈耳
the sound of singing fills the ear;

ge song 歌頌
eulogize / extol / praise / sing the praises of;

ge yao 歌謠
ballad / ditty / folk song / rustic song;

ge yin 歌吟
sing;

ge yong 歌詠
singing;

ge4 zhi yi ci 各執一詞
cling to one's own interpretation || each holds to his own statement; each one has his own words; each sticks to his own version;

gen1 zhe chang 跟着唱
sing after sb;

geng3 哽
choke;

geng bu cheng sheng 哽不成聲
one's voice fails one;

geng geng ye ye 哽哽咽咽
groan in sorrow and tears;

geng ye 哽咽
choke with sobs // suppressed sob;

geng ye nan yan 哽咽難言
choke with sobs and be unable to speak;

geng3 jie zhi yan 骾訐直言
blunt speech;

geng3 lun 鯁論
outspoken statement;

gong1 lun 公論
public opinion;

gong shuo gong you li, po shuo po you li 公說公有理，婆說婆有理
both parties claim to be in the right || each of the two quarreling parties insists that he is right; each says he is right; the Old Man says he is right, the Old Lady says she is right — hard to judge; there is much to be said on both sides; wranglers never want words;

gong1 neng xing shi yu zheng 功能性失語症
functional aphasia;

gong1 wei 恭維
compliment / flatter;

gong wei hua 恭維話
goo;

gong3 du xing kou yan 汞毒性口炎
mercurial stomatitis;

gong3 mo 拱默
salute in silence;

gou3 yan 苟言
careless speech / rash remarks;

gou4 詬
(1) humiliation / shame;
(2) revile / talk abusively;

gou bing 詬病
castigate / denounce;

gou li 詬詈
berate / vituperate;

gou ma 詬罵
abuse / revile / vilify;

gou ru 詬辱
insult / shame // insult / mortification;

gou sui yao zhuo 詬誶謠諑
be whispered about and secretly discussed everywhere;

gu1 qie bu lun 姑且不論
leave sth aside for the moment;

gu qie bu tan 姑且不談
leave sth aside for the moment;

gu wang yan zhi 姑妄言之
say sth as a gossip;

gu1 咕
(1) cluck;
(2) coo;
(3) murmur;

gu dong 咕咚
plump / splash / thud;

gu du 咕嘟
bubble / grugle;

gu lu 咕嚕
mumble / roll / rumble;

gu nong 咕噥
grumble / grunt / mumble / murmur / mutter;

gu rong 咕容
wriggle;

gu1 呱
cry;

gu da 呱嗒
clack / clip-clop;

gu gu 呱呱
(1) cry of a baby;
(2) croak;
(3) caw;

gu gu jiao 呱呱叫
excellent / first-rate ‖ A1; A one; gorgeous; great; superb; terrific; thumbs up; tiptop; top-notch;

gu gu zhui di 呱呱墮地
be born / be born crying / come into the world with a cry;

gu3 shuo 瞽說
wild talks;

gu yi 瞽議
groundless statements / wild talks;

gua4 詿
cheat / deceive;

guai3 wan mo jiao 拐彎抹角
beat about the bush / talk in a roundabout way;

guai4 han guai jiao 怪喊怪叫
bawl and squall;

guai hua 怪話
(1) strange tales;
(2) complaints / cynical remarks / grumbles;

guai lun 怪論
absurd talks / strange statements / wild talks;

guai qiang guai diao 怪腔怪調
speak in a queer way // queer tune;

guai sheng guai qi 怪聲怪氣
speak in a strange voice or an affected manner;

guai tan 怪談
weird talks;

guai xiao 怪笑
sardonic laughter;

guan4 mi tang 灌迷湯
bewitch sb by means of flattery;

guan yao 灌藥
force sb to take medicine;

guan zui 灌醉
force sb to drink until he is drunk;

guang1 shuo bu gan 光說不幹
be all mouth / be all mouth and trousers;

guang3 chang she 廣長舌
eloquence;

guang er yan zhi 廣而言之
general speaking;

gui1 jian 規諫
admonish / advise;

gui jie 規誡
admonish;

gui quan 規勸
admonish / give friendly advice;

gui3 hua 鬼話
deceptive remarks / flimflam / lies / nonsense / outright lies;

gui hua lian pian 鬼話連篇
a pack of lies / tell a whole series of lies;

gui3 bian 詭辯
quibbling / sophism / sophistry;

gui cheng 詭稱
falsely allege / pretend;

gui ci 詭辭
lies to cover up the truth;

guo4 hua 過話
talk with each other;

guo wen 過問
(1) ask about / make inquiry about;
(2) interfere with;

guo yu 過譽
acclaim excessively // excessive praise;

ha1 哈
(1) blow / blow one's breath / breathe out / exhale;
(2) (expressing satisfaction) aha / ha;
(3) (sound of laughter) ha-ha;
(4) bow;

ha ha 哈哈
ha-ha / haw-haw;

ha ha da xiao 哈哈大笑
burst into hearty laughter / roar with laughter || burst out into a fit of violent laughter; give a loud guffaw; laugh heartily // a full-mouthed laugh;

hai3 hua 海話
big talk / boasts / exaggerations / bragging;

han1 酣
drink to one's heart's content;

han chang 酣暢
drink to one's heart's content / drink as much as one can;

han ge 酣歌
sing in exhilaration from drinking;

han ge kuang wu 酣歌狂舞
sing and dance rapturously;

han xing 酣興
elation from drinking;

han yin 酣飲
drink to the full;

han yu 酣飫
intoxicated and satiated;

han zong 酣縱
indulge in excessive drinking;

han zui 酣醉
dead drunk / smashed // in one's cups;

han1 xiao 憨笑
(1) simper;
(2) smile fatuously;

han2 含
hold in the mouth;

han bei yin qi 含悲飲泣
sob pitifully / weep pitiful tears;

han hu qi ci 含糊其詞
mince one's words || ambiguous; equivocate; hum and haw; make sth very vague; mention vaguely; mince matters; slur over a matter; weasel word;

han xiao 含笑
wear a smile // with a smile || grin; have a smile on one's face; smilingly;

han xiao bu yu 含笑不語
smile without speaking;

han xiao dian tou 含笑點頭
nod with a smile;

han xiao jiu quan 含笑九泉
die with a smile on one's face / die with satisfaction / smile in one's grave;

han xiao zuo da 含笑作答
laugh in reply;

han xue pen ren 含血噴人
cast malicious words to injure sb || do wrong to sb; fling mud at; make slanderous accusations; make slanderous charges against others; make vicious attacks; mud-slinging; sling mud at; slur sb's good name; smite with the tongue; spit poison; throw dirt at sb; throw mud at;

han3 yan gua yu 罕言寡語
quiet and unexpressive;

han3 喊
(1) cry out / shout / yell;
(2) call;

han da 喊打
shout "beat him";

han dao hao 喊倒好
make catcall;

han hao 喊好
cheer and applaud;

han hua 喊話
shout through a loudspeaker;

han jiao 喊叫
cry out / shout / yell;

han jiu ming 喊救命
cry for help;

han ku 喊苦
bawl out pain;

han po sang men er 喊破嗓門兒
rave oneself hoarse;

han qiong jiao ku 喊窮叫苦
complain about one's lack of money || cry poor-mouth; poor-mouth; talk poor-mouth;

han sha lian tian 喊殺連天
the battle cry reached the heavens / the noise of battle filled the sky;

han sheng 喊聲
hubbub / yell;

han sheng lian tian 喊聲連天
the battle cry reaches the heaven;

han sheng zhen tian 喊聲震天
make the welkin ring / rend the welkin / shout to high heaven;

han tong 喊痛
yelp in pain;

han yuan jiao qu 喊冤叫屈
cry out for justice || call for redressing grievance; complain loudly about an alleged injustice; cry out about one's grievances;

han4 頷
chin;

hang2 hua 行話
buzz word / cant / jargon;

hang hua shi yu 行話市語
the language of every trade and business;

hao2 bu hui yan 毫不諱言
put it bluntly || call a spade a spade; candid; confess freely; declare in no uncertain terms; make no attempt to conceal the truth; make no secret of; outspoken;

hao wu yi wen 毫無疑問
as sure as eggs are eggs / as sure as death // beyond question / out of question / without doubt / without question // make no question about / make no question of;

hao wu yi yi 毫無異議
have no objection at all / there is no objection to;

hao wu yuan yan 毫無怨言
not to utter a word of complaint / not to utter any complaint;

hao2 yan zhuang yu 豪言壯語
brave words / heroic pledge / heroic utterance / splendid vow;

hao yin 豪飲
drink like a fish;

hao yu 豪語
brave words;

hao2 嚎
howl / wail;

hao jiao dao di 嚎叫倒地
fall with a howl;

hao jiao yi sheng 嚎叫一聲
give a howl;

hao ku 嚎哭
mourn bitterly / wail;

hao tao 嚎啕
cry loudly / wail;

hao tao da ku 嚎啕大哭
cry loudly with abandon || break into violent lamentations; burst into loud sobs; burst into tears; crack up; cry aloud; cry bitter tears; wail at the top of one's voice; wail bitterly;

hao tian dong di 嚎天動地
call upon Heaven and Earth;

hao3 chi 好吃
good to eat / delicious / moreish / palatable;

hao hua 好話
(1) good word / words of praise;
(2) fine words;

hao hua shuo jin, huai shi zuo jue 好話説盡，壞事做絕
say every fine word and do every foul deed || go to all lengths to flatter as well as commit the worst crime; mouth the nicest things while committing the most outrageous crimes; say all the fine things while doing all the vilest actions; say all the nice things while stopping at no crime;

hao sheng hao qi 好聲好氣
in a gentle voice || gently; in a good-natured way; in a kindly manner;

hao shi bu chu men, e shi chuan qian li 好事不出門，惡事傳千里
bad news has wings / bad news travels quickly / ill news comes apace / ill news flies fast;

hao shuo dai shuo 好說歹說
do a lot of talking to convince sb / plead with sb in every way one could / try every possible way to persuade sb;

hao shuo hao shuo 好說好說
it's nice for you to say so;

hao shuo hua er 好說話兒
easy to get along with || amiable; easy to deal with; good-natured;

hao xiao 好笑
funny / laughable / ridiculous;

hao yan xiang quan 好言相勸
plead with tactful words;

hao yan xiang wei 好言相慰
say sth nice to comfort sb / soothe sb with fair words;

hao4 chi hao he 好吃好喝
fond of food and drink;

hao chi lan zuo 好吃懶做
like to eat but not to work || caring for nothing but eating; eat one's head off; fond of eating and averse to work; gluttonous and lazy; lazy and fond of good food; piggish;

hao4 號
(1) howl / yell;
(2) wail;

hao han ti ji 號寒啼飢
cry from hunger and cold || cry out because of hunger and cold; howl for being hungry and cry for feeling cold;

hao jiao 號叫
howl / yell;

hao ku 號哭
cry loudly / wail;

hao sang 號喪
cry at funeral;

hao tao 號啕
cry loudly / wail;

hao tao tong ku 號啕痛哭
cry one's heart out || bewail mournfully; burst into a storm of tears; cry loudly; cry one's eyes out; utter a loud cry; wail loudly; weep and wail; weep with complete abandon;

hao tian da ku 號天大哭
weep loudly;

hao tian ku di 號天哭地
bewail loudly || weep and wail, calling on heaven and earth; weep to the very heaven and to the very earth;

he1 呵
(1) breathe out;
(2) scold;

he chi 呵斥
berate / exoriate / jump at / scold;

he he da xiao 呵呵大笑
laugh loudly || be convulsed in laughter; burst into peals of laughter; horse laugh; laugh a great ho-ho; roar out a great ho-ho of laughter; roar with laughter;

he he 呵喝
shout at sb;

he qian 呵欠
yawn and stretch;

he yi kou qi 呵一口氣
give a puff;

he ze 呵責
give sb a dressing down / scold sb severely;

he1 喝
(1) drink / imbibe;

口 Mouth

(2) drink alcoholic liquor;

he cha 喝茶
(1) drink tea;
(2) go to a restaurant;

he cha chou yan 喝茶抽煙
drink tea and smoke;

he cha liao tian 喝茶聊天
chat over a cup of tea / gossip over the teacups / sip tea and chat;

he gan 喝感
thirst;

he gan guo shao 喝感過少
oligodipsia;

he gan jian tui 喝感減退
abnormal absence of thirst / hypodipsia;

he gan zheng chang 喝感正常
eudipsia / ordinary normal thirst;

he guang 喝光
drain / drink off / drink up;

he jiu 喝酒
drink wine || bend an elbow; bend one's elbow; bend the elbow; crook an elbow; crook one's elbow; crook the elbow; knock over a drink; moisten one's clay; moisten one's lips; moisten one's throat;

he jiu cai quan 喝酒猜拳
drink and play finger-games;

he jiu jie chou 喝酒解愁
drown one's sorrows in wine;

he jiu tai duo 喝酒太多
drink too much || bend one's elbow; crook the elbow; lift the elbow; raise the elbow;

he shui 喝水
(1) drink water;
(2) suffer losses in business;

he shui bu wang jue jing ren 喝水不忘掘井人
don't forget the well-diggers when you drink from this well / when you drink the water, think of those who dug the well;

he xi bei feng 喝西北風
live on air || drink the northwest wind — have nothing to eat; feed on the winter's northwestern wind — suffer from cold and hunger; stay idle and out of work with no income to support oneself;

he yi bei 喝一杯
wet one's whistle;

he yi kou 喝一口
drink a mouthful of sth;

he zhou 喝粥
eat porridge;

he zui 喝醉
drunk || have a drop too much; in drink; in one's cups; in the sunshine; intoxicated; pickled; sottish; take a drop too much; the worse for drink; the worse of drink; tipsy; well in one's cup; well-oiled;

he1 訶
blame in a loud voice / scold in a loud voice;

he chi 訶叱
revile / scold in a loud voice / upbraid;

he qian 訶譴
blame / censure / reprimand / scold;

he ze 訶責
berate / give sb a dressing down / scold;

he2 bu long zui 合不攏嘴
grin from ear to ear;

he chang 合唱
sing in chorus;

he jin 合巹
drink the nuptial cup — get married;

he jin jiao huan 合巹交歡
drink the nuptial wine cup;

he kou 合口
delicious / palatable / savory / tasty;

he2 wei 何謂
what is known as / what is meant by;

he2 tan 和談
peace negotiations / peace talks;

he2 wen 劾問
investigate a person;

he2 yi 核議
decide after consideration;

he4 喝
shout loudly;

he cai 喝彩
acclaim / cheer / plaudit;

he cai jiao hao 喝彩叫好
(1) shout of applause;
(2) applaud to the echo;

he dao cai 喝倒彩
boo || boo and hoot; boot; give a Bronx cheer; give sb the bird; heckle; make catcalls; shout booing // slow handclap;

he4 嚇
sound of laughter;

he he 嚇嚇
ha ha;

he zha 嚇詐
take money by threat and deceit;

he zhu 嚇阻
stop sb by threat;

hei1 hua 黑話
argot / cant / double-talk / malicious words;

hen3 nan shuo 很難說
you never know;

heng1 哼
h'm || bat; but; hum; humph; ugh; yes;

heng chi 哼哧
puff hard;

heng er ha er 哼兒哈兒
hem and haw;

heng ha 哼哈
hum and haw;

heng heng 哼哼
groan continually;

heng heng ha ha 哼哼哈哈
hum and ha / hum and haw;

heng heng ji ji 哼哼唧唧
groan and moan;

heng ji 哼唧
make inaudible sounds / mumble / whisper;

heng le yi sheng 哼了一聲
give a snort of contempt;

heng sheng 哼聲
heave ho / yo-heave-ho / yo-ho;

heng xiao diao 哼小調
hum a song;

heng2 shuo shu shuo 横說豎說
exhaust oneself with persuasion / persuade repeatedly and insistently;

heng yi 横議
extreme views / far-fetched arguments / radical statements;

heng zhe shuo hua 横着說話
deliberately contrary;

heng4 hua 横話
harsh words / stiff and stern language;

hong1 哄
(1) roars of laughter;
(2) hubbub;

hong dong 哄動
cause a sensation / make a stir;

hong dong yi shi 哄動一時
cause a sensation // sensational;

hong han 哄喊
shout at;

hong quan 哄勸
coax;

hong ran 哄然
boisterous / uproarious;

hong ran er san 哄然而散
disperse with great noise and hubbub;

hong ran qi xiao 哄然起笑
go off into laughter;

hong tang 哄堂
bring the room down / fill the room with laughter;

hong tang da xiao 哄堂大笑
the whole room bursts out laughing || a volley of laughter; burst into a guffaw; burst into uproarious laughter; fall about laughing; laugh uproariously; roar with laughter; the whole room rocking with laughter;

hong tang jue dao 哄堂絕倒
all break out into a fit of laughter / the entire house is convulsed with laughter;

hong xiao yi zhen 哄笑一陣
burst into a peal of laughter;

hong2 bian 宏辯
well-supported argument;

hong liang 宏亮
loud and clear / sonorous;

hong lun 宏論
informed opinion;

hong2 liang 洪亮
loud and clear / sonorous;

hong3 pian 哄騙
bamboozle / blandish / cajole / coax / cod / delude / diddle / humbug / string along;

hou3 吼
howl / roar;

hou han 吼喊
shout at;

hou jiao 吼叫
bellow;

hou sheng 吼聲
roaring cry;

hou sheng ru lei 吼聲如雷
roar like thunder / roar with rage;

hu1 呼
(1) breathe out / exhale;
(2) shout;
(3) call;

hu chi 呼哧
(1) puff / wheeze // out of breath;
(2) the sound of puffing and blowing;

hu chi 呼叱
shout at;

hu die jiao niang 呼爹叫娘
cry "mamma" in distress;

hu han 呼喊
call out / shout;

hu hao 呼號
cry out in distress / wail;

hu he 呼喝
bawl at;

hu hu da shui 呼呼大睡
snore loudly in one's sleep;

hu hu ru shui 呼呼入睡
sink into a deep sleep;

hu huan 呼喚
call / shout to;

hu jiao 呼叫
(1) call out / shout;
(2) call / ring;

hu jiu jian zhuan 呼酒荐饌
call for wine and food;

hu jiu 呼救
call for help;

hu jiu wu men 呼救無門
nowhere to turn for help;

hu kou hao 呼口號
give password / shout slogans;

hu lu 呼嚕
snore;

hu lu sheng 呼嚕聲
snore;

hu men 呼門
call for opening the door;

hu niu hu ma 呼牛呼馬
let people call me what they will — disregard hostile opinion;

hu peng yin lei 呼朋引類
gang up / gather a clique / summon one's friends and pals;

hu qi 呼氣
exhale // breath / exhalation / expiration / exsufflation;

hu shao 呼哨
whistle;

hu sheng 呼聲
cry / loud cries / voice;

hu sheng shen gao 呼聲甚高
be favoured to win / great popular demand for sb to be elected;

hu sheng zhen tian 呼聲震天
rend the air;

hu sun 呼損
call loss;

hu tian huan di 呼天喚地
call to heaven and earth / cry to heaven;

hu tian qiang di 呼天搶地
cry bitterly and loudly in excessive grief / utter cries of anguish;

hu tong 呼痛
cry out in pain;

hu xiao 呼嘯
howl / roar / scream ‖ whistle; whizz;

hu xiao er guo 呼嘯而過
roar past;

hu xiong huan di 呼兄喚弟
address each other as brothers / call each other brother;

hu ying 呼應
act in cooperation with each other / echo / work in concert with;
hu yu 呼語
direct address / vocative expression;

hu yu 呼籲
appeal / petition;

hu yuan 呼冤
call for justice / cry one has been wronged;

hu yuan han qu 呼冤喊屈
complain about an injustice / complain and call for redress / cry for redress of a wrong / cry out for justice;

hu yun huan yu 呼雲喚雨
command the clouds and rains — control the forces of nature;

hu zao 呼噪
make loud, confused noise;

hu zhi ji lai, hui zhi ji qu 呼之即來，揮之即去
come at one's call and go at one's beck / have sb at one's beck and call / have sb at one's disposal;

hu zhi yu chu 呼之欲出
almost certain / obvious / seem ready to come out at one's call;

hu2 che 胡扯
talk rubbish ‖ aimless conversation; boloney; bosh; bullshit; drivel; fiddle–faddle; flimflam; gibberish; hogwash; prattle; rubbish; stuff and nonsense; talk nonsense; waffle about; wag one's tongue;

hu chui xia shuo 胡吹瞎說
brag groundlessly / drivel irresponsibly / prattle // hogwash;

hu chui yi qi 胡吹一氣
tell tall stories ‖ boast outrageously; bosh; talk big and irresponsibly;

hu hua 胡話
ravings / wild talk;

hu liao 胡聊
chat;

hu lu da xiao 胡盧大笑
roar with laughter;

hu shao 胡哨
whistle;

hu shuo 胡說
talk nonsense ‖ bilge water; blather; bunk; cobblers; cod; codswallop; cut the nonsense; don't talk rot; fiddlesticks; flapdoodle; hogwash; horseshift; humbug; nonsense; rats; rot it; rubbish; shit; stuff and nonsense; what crap;

hu shuo ba dao 胡說八道
talk nonsense ‖ a pile of shit; all balconey; all my eye; apple sauce; banana oil; blather; blithering; broad nonsense; bunk; cobblers; cod; drool; fiddle-de-dee; flubdub and gulf; full of hops; haver; hogwash; lie in one's teeth; lie in one's throat; mere humbug; prate nonsense; pure rubbish; rats; rubbish; sheer nonsense; shoot one's mouth off; sling the bull; speak through one's neck; speak through the back of one's neck; stuff and nonsense; talk balderdash; talk bosh; talk foolishly; talk gibberish; talk rot; talk rubbish; talk sheer nonsense; talk through one's hat; talk through one's neck; talk through the back of one's neck; talk wet; talk without truth; throw the bull // gammon and spinach;

hu shuo luan dao 胡說亂道
talk without restraint ‖ shoot one's mouth off; speak wildly like a fool; talk foolishly and wildly; talk in a wild disorderly manner;

hu yan 胡言
crap;

hu yan luan yu 胡言亂語

talk foolishly || babble; balderdash; blather; clotted nonsense; codswallop; crap; flimflam; full of hops; gibberish; jabberwocky; maunder; muck; nonsense; punk; ramble in one's speech; rave; ravings; rigmarole; shoot off one's mouth; shoot the bull; sling the bull; speak at a venture; talk through one's hat; talk wildly; throw the bull; wander in one's speech; wander in one's talk; wanderings;

hu zhuo 胡謅

cook up / fabricate wild tales / wild talk;

hu2 kou 糊口

live from hand to mouth / make a living / make both ends meet;

hua1 qiang 花腔

fancy vocalism;

hua yan qiao yu 花言巧語

fine and deceiving words || a lot of artful talk; banana oil; blandishments; do a snow job; fair words; fast talk; fine rhetoric; fine words; flannel-mouthed; flowery words and cunning statements; goo; honeyed words; make a sophisticated speech; mealy; mealy-mouthed; mouth fair words; plausible; pretty words; seductive speech; smooth talk; sweet chatter; sweet talk; talk clever stuff; use specious excuses;

hua1 嘩

clamour / hubbub / uproar;

hua ran 嘩然

outcry / in an uproar;

hua zhong qu chong 嘩眾取寵

try to please the public with claptrap;

hua2 yan 華言

impressive but insincere words;

hua2 ji ke xiao 滑稽可笑

funny / funny-ha-ha;

hua kou 滑口

glib / voluble;

hua2 譁

clamour / noise;

hua bian 譁變

mutiny;

hua ran 譁然

in an uproar / in commotion;

hua ran qi hong 譁然起哄

rising up in an uproar;

hua xiao 譁囂

noisy commotion / uproar;

hua xiao 譁笑

noisy laughter / uproarious laughter // roar with laughter;

hua zao 譁噪

noisy // hubbub;

hua zhong qu chong 譁眾取寵

talk big to impress people || court people's favour by saying sth impressive; curry favour by claptrap; gain notoriety by shocking statements; impress people by claptrap; play to the gallery; seek popularity by doing sth sensational; try to please the public with claptrap;

hua4 話

(1) talk;

(2) speak about / talk about;

hua bie 話別

say a few parting words / say goodbye;

hua bing 話柄

a subject for ridicule;

hua bu cheng yi 話不成意

the words make no sense;

hua bu li zong 話不離宗

speak exclusively of one's own business / talk shop;

hua bu tou ji 話不投機

disagreeable conversation || can't see eye to eye with sb; dissidence of opinion in talks; mistime one's remarks; not to talk to the point; resulting in estrangement;

hua bu tou ji ban ju duo 話不投機半句多

when the conversation gets disagreeable, to say one word more is a waste of breath || dissidence of opinions makes it useless to talk; if one argues with a disagreeable man, half a sentence is too much; if there's no common ground, a single word is a waste of breath; in a disagreeable conversation one word more is too many;

hua bu xu chuan 話不虛傳
that remark is true / there is truth to that;

hua dao she bian liu ban ju 話到舌邊留半句
hold back part of what one has to say when you're about to say it;

hua dao zui bian 話到嘴邊
at the tip of one's tongue / on the tip of sb's tongue // the words come to the tip of one's tongue / the word is just on one's lips / words rush to one's lips;

hua duo bu tian 話多不甜
too much talk is unpleasant;

hua feng 話鋒
topic of the conversation;

hua jia chang 話家常
chitchat / exchange small talk;

hua jiu 話舊
reminisce about old times / talk about the old days / talk of former times;

hua li ben ti 話離本題
talk away from the point / wander away from the proper question;

hua li dai ci 話裏帶刺
hidden barbs in one's words / one's words carry a sting / there is a touch of irony in one's speech;

hua li dai gu 話裏帶骨
hidden barbs in one's words;

hua li tao hua 話裏套話
touch upon other matters when discussion is centered on one topic;

hua li you hua 話裏有話
have one's tongue in one's cheek / there is more to it than what is said || put one's tongue in one's cheek; speak with one's tongue in one's cheek; sth one means but never says; the words mean more than they say; there is an insinuation in that remark; there is more to it than meets the ear; tongue-in-cheek;

hua li you wen zhang 話裏有文章
that's an insinuating remark / there is an insinuation in that remark;

hua li you yin 話裏有因
there is sth more implied than what is said;

hua shao huo shao 話少禍少
the least said, the soonest mended;

hua shuo san bian dan ru shui 話說三遍淡如水
a tale twice told is cabbage twice sold || don't take your harp to the party; not good is it to harp on the frayed string;

hua sui ru ci 話雖如此
be that as it may / having said that;

hua ti 話題
gambit / the subject of a talk / the topic of conversation;

hua ti yi zhuan 話題一轉
change the topic of conversation;

hua tou er 話頭兒
sth to open a conversation / sth to talk about;

hua wai zhi yi 話外之意
the meaning between the lines || idea not expressed in words; implied meaning; more is meant than meets the ear; what is actually meant;

hua yin 話音
(1) one's voice in speech;
(2) implication / tone;

hua yin gang luo 話音剛落
even as the sound of one's voice dies away || as soon as one stops; before the sound of one's voice has died away; hardly had one's voice faded away;

hua yin wei luo 話音未落
when one has hardly finished speaking;

hua yu 話語
utterance;

hua zai zui bian 話在嘴邊
on the tip of one's tongue;

hua zhong jian qing 話中見情
feelings expressed in one's words;

hua zhong you ci 話中有刺
hidden barbs in one's words;

hua zhong you hua 話中有話
with tongue in cheek;

hua zhong you yin 話中有因
sth left unsaid;

huai4 hua 壞話
slander;

huai ju xing kou yan 壞疽性口炎
gangrenous inflammation of the mouth / noma;

huai si xing kou yan 壞死性口炎
necrotic stomatitis;

huan1 hu 歡呼
acclaim / cheer ‖ hail; holler; jubilate;

huan hu que yue 歡呼雀躍
shout and jump for joy;

huan sheng 歡聲
cheers;

huan sheng bian ye 歡聲遍野
gladness fills the countryside;

huan sheng dong di 歡聲動地
the sound of rejoicing fills the land;

huan sheng ge chang 歡聲歌唱
sing with joy;

huan sheng lei dong 歡聲雷動
break into deafening cheers / break into thunderous applause ‖ give a great shout of approval; give thunderous cheers; cheers rent the air like thunder; cheers resound like peals of thunder;

huan sheng xiao yu 歡聲笑語
cheering and laughing;

huan xiao 歡笑
laugh heartily;

huan1 讙
noisy // clamour;

huan hu 讙呼
cheer / give a cheer;

huan2 kou 還口
retort / talk back;

huan yan 還言
retort;

huan zui 還嘴
answer back / retort / talk back;

huan4 喚
call out;

huan qi 喚起
(1) arouse;
(2) call / recall;
(3) evocation;

huan xing 喚醒
awaken / rouse up / wake up;

huan4 ju hua shuo 換句話說
in other words / put it in another way / say sth in other words / that is to say;

huan yan zhi 換言之
in other words / put it in another way / say sth in other words / that is to say;

huang1 qiang tuo ban 荒腔脱板
sing out of key;

huang2 lun qi ta 遑論其他
not to mention the others / let alone the other points;

huang3 謊
lie // lie;

huang hua 謊話
falsehood / lie;

huang pian 謊騙
cheat / deceive / hoax;

huang yan 謊言
lie ‖ a bit of fiddle; bunk; categorical inaccuracy; cover story; distort facts; embroider the truth; erroneous report; eyewash; fabrication; fib; fiddle-faddle; flannel; forked tongue; humbug; falsehood; misinform; mispresent the facts; plausible denial; prevaricate; selective facts; story; strain; stretch; swing the lamp; tale of a tub; tall tale; terminological inexactitude;

huang yan ke wei 謊言可畏
lies are terrible / untrue statements are frightful;

huang yan tui duan 謊言腿短
lies have short legs;

hui1 詼
(1) joke / ridicule;
(2) funny / humorous;

hui gui 詼詭
grotesquely funny / grotesquely hilarious;

hui nüe 詼謔
joke / jest / ridicule;

hui pai 詼俳
joke / jest / ridicule;

hui xie 詼諧
comical / funny / humorous // make humorous remarks / tell jokes;

hui xie bai chu 詼諧百出
very humorous;

hui1 yan 徽言
good advice;

hui2 bo 回駁
refute;

hui da 回答
answer / answer up / answer up to / in answer to / reply / respond / respond to // answer / reply / soft answer;

hui hua 回話
answer / bring back word / reply / talk back;

hui ma 回罵
answer defiantly and scold in return;

hui zui 回嘴
(1) answer back / retort / talk back;
(2) back answer / back chat / back talk // backchat / backtalk / backword;

hui3 qi 悔泣
cry of remorse;

hui3 bang 毀謗
caluminate / defame / malign / slander;

hui di 毀詆
libel / slander;

hui duan 毀短
denounce / disparage / run down / speak ill of;

hui4 can 會餐
dine together / have a dinner party;

hui chi hui he 會吃會喝
have a good plate for food;

hui hua 會話
chat / conversation / dialogue / talk;

hui tan 會談
talk;

hui4 誨
instruct / teach;

hui ren bu juan 誨人不倦
tireless in teaching others || indefatigable in teaching people; instruct without fatigue; never tired of teaching others; teach with tireless zeal; teach without weariness; untiring in the instruction of others;

hui4 諱
(1) avoid as taboo;
(2) forbidden word / taboo;

hui ji ci 諱忌詞
forbidden word / taboo;

hui yan 諱言
avoid mentioning sth / dare not speak up / would not speak up;

hui yan qi shi 諱言其事
forbid to mention the affair;

hun4 fan 混飯
eat at others' expense;

hun he xing shi yu zheng 混合性失語症
combined aphasia;

hun shuo 混說
talk nonsense;

hun wei yi tan 混為一談
confuse sth with sth else;

hun zhang hua 混帳話
impudent words;

hun4 shuo 溷説
use bad language;

hun4 諢
derision / jest / joke / ridicule;

huo4 cong kou chu 禍從口出
misfortunes come from the mouth || a ready tongue is an evil; all one's troubles are caused by his tongue; careless talk leads to trouble; out of the mouth comes evil; disaster emanates from careless talk; evil originates in the mouth; improper language brings sb ruin; out of the mouth comes evil; the tongue talks at the head's cost;

ji1 gu 唧咕
mutter / whisper;

ji nong 唧噥
talk in a low voice / whisper;

ji1 嘰
mutter / whisper;

ji gu 嘰咕
mutter / talk in a low voice / whisper;

ji ji ga ga 嘰嘰嘎嘎
cackle / creak;

ji ji gu gu 嘰嘰咕咕
babble on and on / jabber / mumble / murmur / mutter / whisper;

ji li gu lu 嘰哩咕嚕
talk in low whispers ‖ gabble; jabber; talk in an indistinct manner;

ji li zha la 嘰哩喳拉
make a confused noise;

ji1 bian 機辯
witty and sharp-tongued;

ji1 ang fa yan 激昂發言
speak in excitement;

ji bian 激辯
heated argument / heated debate;

ji lie zheng lun 激烈爭論
heated debate;

ji lun 激論
heated discussions;

ji1 譏
mock / ridicule / satirize;

ji cha 譏察
interrogate closely;

ji ci 譏刺
satirize / taunt;

ji feng 譏諷
ridicule / satirize ‖ throw out innuendoes against;

ji ping 譏評
make jeering comments;

ji qiao 譏誚
deride / jeer / mock / sneer at / taunt;

ji xiao 譏笑
deride / gibe / jeer / ridicule / sneer at / taunt // taunt;

ji2 xi fa yan 即席發言
extemporize;

ji2 kou ling 急口令
tongue twister;

ji2 hu 疾呼
call out loudly / shout;

ji yan li se 疾言厲色
with a severe countenance and a harsh voice ‖ a hard word and a black look; brusque; harsh words and stern looks; look fierce and talk boisterously; speak gruffly with a stern countenance; sudden outpourings and fierce looks;

ji yan ju se 疾言遽色
speaking hastily and looking flurried;

ji2 kou cheng yu 極口稱譽
loud in one's praise of / praise lavishly / utter one's approval;

ji4 jiu 忌酒
give up alcohol / quit drinking;

ji kou 忌口
avoid certain food / on a diet;

ji yan 忌煙
quit smoking;

ji zui 忌嘴
avoid certain food / on a diet;

ji4 yu 寄語
convey a message / send word;

jia1 yan 佳言
good words;

jia1 chang bian fan 家常便飯
ordinary plain meal;

jia chang hua 家常話
ordinary conversation;

jia1 嘉
commend / praise;

jia mian 嘉勉
praise and encourage;

jia na 嘉納
accept sb's view with admiration;

jia xu 嘉許
praise;

jia yan yi xing 嘉言懿行
fine words and deeds;

jia2 ran chang ming 戛然長鳴
long and loud cries;

jia3 hua 假話
lie;

jia kou yu ren 假口於人
put words into sb's mouth;

jia ku 假哭
mimic tears;

jia sang zi 假嗓子
falsetto;

jia sheng 假聲
falsetto;

jia xiao 假笑
feign a laugh / hokey laugh / smirk;

jian1 xiao 奸笑
sinister smile;

jian1 jiao 尖叫
scream / screech / shriek / shrill;

jian sheng jian qi 尖聲尖氣
in a shrill voice;

jian suan ke bo 尖酸刻薄
acrimonious / catty // acrimony;

jian zui bo she 尖嘴薄舌
catty // have a caustic and flippant tongue;

jian zui hou sai 尖嘴猴腮
one's mouth sticks and one has a chin like an ape's;

jian zui jiao she 尖嘴嚼舌
fond of gossip / have a sharp tongue;

jian1 cheng 堅稱
insist on saying;

jian1 ting 監聽
listen in;

jian ting tan hua 監聽談話
bug a conversation / monitor a conversation / tap a conversation;

jian1 kou 緘口
hold one's tongue / keep one's mouth shut / say nothing;

jian mo 緘默
keep silent / reticent;

jian mo bu yu 緘默不語
keep silent about sth or sb // as mute as a fish;

jian mo gua yan 緘默寡言
silent and speak little;

jian3 謇
(1) stammer / stutter;
(2) speak out boldly;

jian e 謇諤
candid / frank / outspoken;

jian jian zhi yan 謇謇直言
outspoken in speech;

jian3 er yan zhi 簡而言之
in short || briefly speaking; for shortness's sake; in a few words; in a nutshell; in brief; make a long story short; to put it in a nutshell; to sum up;

jian yan zhi 簡言之
in short || all things considered; briefly; by and large; first and last; in a few words; in a nutshell; in a word; in brief; in fine; in sum; in the lump; make a long story short; on the whole; take it all in all; the long and short of it;

jian4 ren shuo ren hua, jian gui shuo gui hua 見人說人話，見鬼說鬼話
scratch sb where he feels an itch || double-cross; double-faced;

jian xiao 見笑
(1) incur ridicule;
(2) laugh at;

jian xiao da fang 見笑大方
expose oneself to ridicule || be laughed at by experts; become a laughingstock of the educated; give an expert cause for laughter; incur the ridicule of experts; make a laughingstock of oneself before experts;

jian xiao yu ren 見笑於人
(1) laughingstock;
(2) be laughed at;

jian4 yi 建議
propose / suggest // proposal / suggestion;

jian4 tan 健談
(1) conversational / loquacious / talkative / voluble // volubleness;
(2) good talker;

jian4 nuo 踐諾
fulfill a pledge / keep a promise;

jian yan 踐言
fulfill a promise;

jian yan shi xing 踐言實行
fulfill a promise and put into operation;

jian4 諫
admonish / advise / caution / counsel against sth / remonstrate;

jian yan 諫言
admonition;

jian zheng 諫諍
criticize sb's faults frankly;

jian zhi 諫止
admonish against sth;

jiang3 講
(1) say / speak / talk about / tell;
(2) explain / interpret / make clear;

jiang dao 講道
give sermons / preach;

jiang dao li 講道理
give sermons / preach;

jiang ding 講定
settle sth by verbal agreement;

jiang fei hua 講廢話
bat one's gums / beat one's gums / bump one's gums;

jiang gu shi 講故事
tell stories;

jiang he 講和
settle a dispute;

jiang hua 講話
address / speak / talk // speech;

jiang jia 講價
bargain / haggle over the price;

jiang jie 講解
discuss and explain / explain / expound / interpret;

jiang ke 講課
give a lesson / give a lecture / lecture / teach;

jiang lai jiang qu 講來講去
talk repeatedly;

jiang li 講理
(1) argue things out / reason with sb;
(2) amenable to reason / appeal to reason / listen to reason;
(3) reasonable / sensible;

jiang li mao 講禮貌
do the civil;

jiang lun 講論
discuss / expound;

jiang ming 講明
explain / make clear / state explicitly;

jiang ping 講評
comment on and appraise;

jiang qing 講情
plead for sb;

jiang shou 講授
give a lecture / instruct / lecture / teach;

jiang shu 講述
give an account of / narrate / recount / relate / tell about;

jiang tiao jian 講條件
bargain over terms;

jiang xi 講習
lecture and study;

jiang xian hua 講閒話
dig up dirt about sb / take sb's name in vain;

jiang xiao hua 講笑話
crack a joke || break a jest; tell funny stories; tell jokes;

jiang xin li hua 講心裏話
bare one's heart / open one's mind;

jiang xin yong 講信用
keep a promise / keep one's words;

jiang xue 講學
discourse on an academic subject / give lectures;

jiang yan 講演
give a lecture / lecture / make a speech;

jiang4 zui 強嘴
answer back / reply defiantly / talk back;

jiao1 hong 交閧
quarrel;

jiao kou 交口
talk with each other;

jiao kou cheng yu 交口稱譽
be praised by one and all ‖ be held in public esteem; praise with one voice; vie in singing the praise of sb; unanimously praise;

jiao qian yan shen 交淺言深
have a hearty talk with a slight acquaintance / have a slight acquaintance with sb but talk intimately with him;

jiao tan 交談
converse;

jiao1 ke 焦渴
very anxous;

jiao1 chen 嬌嗔
get angry;

jiao chuan 嬌喘
gasp for breath for lack of strength;

jiao sheng 嬌聲
sweet girlish voice;

jiao sheng jiao qi 嬌聲嬌氣
with a sweet girlish voice ‖ in a winning tone; speak in a seductive tone;

jiao sheng nen yu 嬌聲嫩語
in a sweet voice;

jiao1 kua 驕誇
boast / brag;

jiao3 bian 狡辯
indulge in sophistry / quibble / resort to sophistry // artful self-defence;

jiao4 叫
(1) cry / shout;
(2) call / name;
(3) ask / order;

jiao cai 叫菜
order dishes;

jiao guo 叫聒
loud and shrill noises;

jiao han 叫喊
cry / howl / shout / yell // shouting;

jiao hao 叫好
applaud / shout "bravo";

jiao hao da qi 叫好打氣
cheer blatantly;

jiao huan 叫喚
call out / cry out;

jiao hui 叫回
recall;

jiao jin er 叫勁兒
(1) challenge / have a competition;
(2) dispute / oppose;

jiao jue 叫絕
shout bravo;

jiao ku 叫苦
complain of hardship / complain of suffering / moan and groan;

jiao ku bu die 叫苦不迭
keep complaining ‖ complain incessantly; complain of one's hard life over and over again; constantly complain; cry bitterness without cease; pour endless grievances;

jiao ku ku qiong 叫苦哭窮
make a mouth;

jiao ku lian sheng 叫苦連聲
howl in the bitterness of one's distress;

jiao ku lian tian 叫苦連天
complain bitterly ‖ complain to high heaven; cry to heaven; keep on pouring out one's hard lot; pour out endless grievances; showl out in pain;

jiao ma 叫罵
shout curses;

jiao mai 叫賣
hawk ‖ cry one's goods for sale; cry one's wares; hawk one's wares; peddle;

jiao men 叫門
call at the door to be let in;

jiao qu 叫屈
knock at the door ‖ complain of being wronged; protest against an injustice;

jiao rang 叫嚷
clamour ‖ howl; hue and cry; shout; vociferate;

jiao ren 叫人
cry for sb;

jiao tian tian bu ying, ru di di wu men 叫天天不應，入地地無門
nowhere to turn for help;

jiao xiao 叫囂
clamour / raise a hue and cry;

jiao xing 叫醒
wake up;

jiao zhen er 叫針兒
(1) argue / wrangle;
(2) conscientious and meticulous / finicky / inflexible;

jiao zuo 叫做
be called / be known as;

jiao4 訆
(1) call in a loud voice / scream / yell;
(2) talk wildly / tell a falsehood / tell a lie;

jiao4 dao 教導
instruct / teach and guide;

jiao hui 教誨
teach and admonish;

jiao suo 教唆
abet / incite / instigate / suborn;

jiao xun 教訓
admonish;

jiao4 噍
chew / munch / nibble;

jie1 chu xing kou yan 接觸性口炎
contact stomatitis;

jie kou 接口
go on to say sth immediately after sb has finished;

jie1 tan xiang yi 街談巷議
market gossip / street rumours / talk of the town;

jie yan xiang yu 街言巷語
talk of the thoroughfare;

jie1 tan 嗟歎
deplore / lament / sigh with grief;

jie2 yang 訐揚
expose the faults of another / reveal the faults of another;

jie zhi 訐直
blame sb bluntly for his faults;

jie2 gei 捷給
eloquent / glib;

jie kou 捷口
swift in verbal response;

jie2 jie ba ba 結結巴巴
stammer ‖ bumble; gibber; halt; have a speech impediment; have an impediment in speech; splutter; stammer out; stumble over; stutter // halting; hesitating in speaking; stuttering;

jie jie xing sheng dai yan 結節性聲帶炎
chorditis tuberosa;

jie2 詰
closely question / interrogate;

jie nan 詰難
censure / reproach;

jie wen 詰問
closely question / cross-examine / heckle / interrogate;

jie ze 詰責
censure / denounce / rebuke;

jie2 shi 節食
go on diet;

jie yi suo shi 節衣縮食
economize clothing and food / live a frugal life;

jie3 chan 解饞
greedy to satisfy an appetite for good food;

jie chao 解嘲
find excuses to save one's face;

jie e 解餓
satisfy one's hunger;

jie jiu 解酒
alleviate a hangover / neutralize the effect of alcoholic drinks;

jie ke 解渴
allay thirst / appease one's thirst / assuage one's thirst / quench thirst;

jie shuo 解説
explain;

jie yi 解頤
laugh / smile;

jie4 hun 戒葷
go on a vegetarian diet;

jie4 jiu 戒酒
abstain from alcohol / give up drinking // on the wagon // temperance;

jie yan 戒煙
quit smoking || cut out smoking; smoking cessation; stop smoking;

jie4 wen 借問
may I ask;

jie4 誡
(1) admonish / warn;
(2) commandment;

jin1 kou 金口
(1) little-uttered mouth;
(2) golden sayings;

jin kou yu yan 金口玉言
excellent advice || golden sayings; good news; precious words; valuable instructions;

jin ren jian kou 金人緘口
careful in speech / keep one's mouth shut;

jin yu liang yan 金玉良言
golden sayings / good counsels / invaluable advice / precious teaching / profitable advice;

jin yu zhi yan 金玉之言
precious words / valuable advice;

jin1 kua 矜誇
brag about one's accomplishments;

jin1 jin le dao 津津樂道
delight in talking about || dwell upon sth with great relish; gleefully dwell on; gush over; indulge in elaborating on; prattle to one's heart's content; talk with great relish; take delight in talking about; tell with unction;

jin3 yan shen xing 謹言慎行
be careful as to one's words or behaviour || be cautious with one's words and actions; be discreet in word and deed; be prudent in making statements and careful in personal conducts; mind one's P's and Q's; speak and act cautiously; watch your step and mind what you are saying;

jin4 jian 進諫
remonstrate with one's senior;

jin shi 進食
eat / feed / have one's meal / take food;

jin shi zhang ai 進食障礙
eating disorder;

jin yan 進言
offer advice;

jin4 jiu 禁酒
prohibit the use of alcoholic drinks;

jin shi 禁食
fast;

jin4 qing ge chang 盡情歌唱
sing to one's heart's content;

jin yan 盡言
(1) express oneself fully / say sth without reserve;
(2) speak bluntly;

jin4 噤
keep one's mouth shut / shut up;

jin ruo han chan 噤若寒蟬
keep quiet out of fear;

jing1 shen xun hua 精神訓話
pep talk;

jing1 hu 驚呼
cry out in alarm;

jing jiao 驚叫
cry in fear / scream;

jing tan 驚歎
exclaim / marvel;

jing3 警
(1) keep watch;
(2) alert / warn;

jing gao 警告
admonish / caution / warn // warning;

jing jie 警戒
alert / guard / stand guard / watch out for // on one's guard / on the alert // vigilant;

jing4 shuo bu gan 淨說不幹
all talk and no cider / all talk and no deed / all talk, no action;

jing shuo fei hua 淨說廢話
only talk nonsense;

jing4 gao 敬告
tell respectfully;

jing jiu 敬酒
drink a toast;

jing xie 敬謝
thank respectfully;

jing xie bu min 敬謝不敏
decline a request politely;

jing4 luan xing fa sheng kun nan 痙攣性發聲困難
spasmodic dysphonia;

jing luan xing shi sheng 痙攣性失聲
spastic aphonia;

jing luan xing shi yu 痙攣性失語
aphthongia;

jing luan xing tun yan kun nan 痙攣性吞咽困難
dysphagia spastica;

jing xiao 痙笑
cainine laugh / convulsive laughter;

jing yu 痙語
logoclonia;

jiong3 kou wu yan 窘口無言
a distressed mouth says nothing;

jiu1 gen wen di 究根問底
investigate exhaustively;

jiu jie 究詰
cross-examine / interrogate;

jiu wen 究問
cross-examine / study and question;

jiu3 hou shi yan 酒後失言
say sth wrong when drunk;

jiu hua 酒話
utterances of a drunkard;

jiu liang 酒量
one's capacity for drinking;

jiu shi 酒食
food and drink;

jiu yan jiu yu 酒言酒語
talk incoherently when drunk / unable to speak clearly when drunk;

jiu zui 酒醉
activated / drunk / intoxicated / tipsy;

jiu zui fan bao 酒醉飯飽
having drunk and eaten to one's heart's content;

jiu4 咎
blame;

jiu ze 咎責
be blamed for one's own faults;

ju3 咀
chew / masticate;

ju jue 咀嚼
mastication;

ju jue bing 咀嚼病
quidding;

ju jue li 咀嚼力
chewing force / masticatory force;

ju4 ju shi hua 句句實話
every word said is true;

ju4 shuo 據說
as the story goes / as the story runs / it is said;

ju4 yin 劇飲
drink with abandon;

jue1 zui 撅嘴
pout one's lips;

jue zui ban lian 撅嘴扳臉
have a fit of the pouts;

jue2 bu shi yan 決不食言
never to break a promise;

jue2 dao 絕倒
roar with laughter;

jue kou 絕口
(1) stop talking;
(2) keep one's mouth shut;

jue kou bu tan 絕口不談
not to say a word about || absolutely silent about; keep one's mouth shut and say nothing; keep one's mouth tight shut about; keep silent and say nothing; never to have a single word to say about; never to say a single word about; refuse to say anything about; seal one's lips and say nothing;

jue kou bu ti 絕口不提
never to say a single word about || avoid all mention of; avoid mentioning; make no mention whatsoever of;

jue shi 絕食
(1) absolute diet / fast;
(2) go on hunger strike;

jue wen 絕問
have no communication with;

jue2 噱
loud laughter;

jue2 jian 譎諫
admonish by hints / remonstrate with sb in indirect ways;

jue2 嚼
chew / munch;

jun1 heng yin shi 均衡飲食
balanced diet;

kai1 chang bai 開場白
gambit;

kai hua xia zi 開話匣子
keep on talking without stop;

kai huai da xiao 開懷大笑
belly-laugh;

kai huang qiang 開黃腔
make lewd utterances;

kai kai wan xiao 開開玩笑
have a little fun at sb / make fun of;

kai kou 開口
begin to speak / open one's mouth / start to talk;

kai kou bi kou 開口閉口
cannot open one's mouth without talking about / every time when one opens one's mouth / whenever one speaks;

kai kou ma ren 開口罵人
break into abuse / use abusive language;

kai kou shang ren 開口傷人
use bad language to insult people || offend by rude remarks;

kai kou shuo hua 開口説話
lift up one's voice / loose sb's tongue;

kai qiang 開腔
begin to speak / open one's mouth / speak out;

kai wan xiao 開玩笑
crack a joke || cut a joke; in joke; in play; jape; jest; joke; laugh at; make a joke; make fun of; make game of sb; make jests; make sport of sb; play a joke on; pull one's leg; tease;

kai yan 開言
speak / talk;

kai yan 開顏
beam / laugh / smile;

kai3 hu yan zhi 慨乎言之
say sth with a sigh;

kai tan 慨歎
deplore with sighs / lament with sighs;

kan3 kan 侃侃
speak freely and frankly;

kan kan er tan 侃侃而談
speak freely and frankly || speak with fervour and assurance; talk high, wide, and handsome; talk with ease and fluency;

kang1 kai bei ge 慷慨悲歌
chant in a heroic but mournful tone;

kang4 bian 抗辯
speak out in one's own defense / refute / retort;

kang lun 抗論
argue against / retort;

kang sheng 抗聲
raise one's voice;

kang yi 抗議
cry against / protest / raise one's voice against;

kao3 wen 考問
examine orally;

kao3 wen 拷問
extort information by means of torture;

ke1 ze 苛責
criticize severely / objurgate / rebuke;

ke3 kou 可口
delectable / delicious / moreish / palatable / pleasant to the palate;

ke wei 可謂
it may be called;

ke xiao 可笑
laughable / preposterous / ridiculous;

ke yi yi hui, bu ke yi yan chuan 可以意會，不可以言傳
can be understood but cannot be described;

ke4 qi hua 客氣話
polite remarks;

ke4 shou nuo yan 恪守諾言
hold by one's promise;

ken3 啃
bite / gnaw / munch / nibble;

ken3 jian 懇諫
admonish earnestly / admonish with sincerity;

ken qing 懇請
ask earnestly / beseech / entreat / implore / plead;

ken tan 懇談
have a sincere talk / talk in a sincere manner;

ken tuo 懇託
ask earnestly / make a sincere request;

kong1 hua 空話
empty words / hot air / waffle;

kong kou 空口
eat dishes without rice;

kong kou bai she 空口白舌
with mere words of mouth || pure bunk;

kong kou nan ping 空口難憑
an oral promise is not enough;

kong kou shuo bai hua 空口說白話
make empty promises || a mere high-sounding talk; all talk and no cider; an empty promise; an empty promise without substance; brag; speak without acting; talk big;

kong kou wu ping 空口無憑
an oral promise has no binding force;

kong lun 空論
empty talks;

kong shuo 空說
empty talks / useless talks;

kong tan 空談
claptrap / empty talk;

kong tan wu yi 空談無益
it is useless to make empty talks;

kong tan wu guo 空談誤國
empty talks jeopardize national interests;

kong yan 空言
empty talks / mere talks;

kou3 口
mouth;

kou ben she zhuo 口笨舌拙
awkward in speech;

kou bi mo 口鼻膜
oronasal membrane;

kou bu chuan qi, lian bu fan hong 口不喘氣，臉不泛紅
not be out of breath or even faintly flushed;

kou bu jie er bu ting 口不捷耳不聽
slow of speech and hard of hearing;

kou bu ying xin 口不應心
words not agreeing with the heart || carry fire in one hand and water in the other; not to have the courage of one's opinion; profess one thing, but mean another;

kou bu ze yan 口不擇言
talk recklessly;

kou cai 口才
eloquence / gift of the gab;

kou cheng 口稱
claim / say;

kou chi 口吃
dysphemia / stammer / stutter;

kou chi bing 口吃病
a chronic spasm that interferes with speech /

labiochorea;

kou chi 口齒
(1) enunciation;
(2) ability to speak;

kou chi bu qing 口齒不清
a twist in one's tongue / speak with a lisp / swallow one's words;

kou chi ling li 口齒伶俐
have a nimble tongue || a good talker; a ready tongue; clever and fluent; fluent of speech; have a ready tongue; one's tongue is very swift answer; quick of wit and eloquent;

kou chi liu xiang 口齒留香
the exquisite verses have left a lingering fragrance in one's mouth;

kou chi qing chu 口齒清楚
have clear enunciation / talk distinctly;

kou chou 口臭
bromopnea || bad breath; fetid oris; foul breath; halitosis; kakostomia;
gan bing kou chou 肝病口臭
liver breath;
gan bing xing kou chou 肝病性口臭
fetor hepaticus;
qian zhong du kou chou 鉛中毒口臭
lead breath;

kou chou zheng 口臭症
halitosis / ozostomia;

kou chu bu xun 口出不遜
make impertinent remarks / talk harshly;

kou chu da yan 口出大言
boast / brag / utter bold words;

kou chu kuang yan 口出狂言
cheek up / talk nonsense / talk wildly;

kou chu yuan yan 口出怨言
be discontented and speak resentfully;

kou chuan 口傳
by word of mouth / from mouth to mouth;

kou chuan xin shou 口傳心授
an oral teaching that inspires true understanding within;

kou chuang 口瘡
aphtha;

kou chuang bing 口瘡病
aphthosis;

kou chuang re 口瘡熱
aphthous fever;

kou chuang xing kou yan 口瘡性口炎
stomatitis aphthosa;

kou chuang xing kui yang 口瘡性潰瘍
aphthous ulcer;

kou da hou long xiao 口大喉嚨小
bite off more than one can chew;

kou dai wei xiao 口帶微笑
a smile plays on one's lips;

kou de 口德
propriety in one's remarks;

kou er xiang chuan 口耳相傳
teach orally;

kou fa 口伐
attack verbally;

kou fa yu bu liang 口發育不良
atelostomia;

kou fa yu bu quan 口發育不全
atelostomia;

kou feng 口風
one's intention as revealed in what one says;

kou fu 口服
(1) profess to be convinced;
(2) take orally;

kou fu xin bu fu 口服心不服
pretend to be convinced;

kou fu xin fu 口服心服
be convinced of / be sincerely convinced;

kou fu 口福
gourmet's luck || luck in having nice food; the luck to get sth nice to eat;

kou fu bu qian 口福不淺
luck of having good food || it is fortunate to eat such delicious things; luck of the mouth is not shallow;

kou fu 口腹
food;

kou fu zhi yu 口腹之欲
the desire for good food || bodily desires; the

bodily wants of food and drink;

kou gan 口乾
thirst;

kou gan she zao 口乾舌燥
mouth parched and tongue scorched;

kou gou 口垢
saburra;

kou hui 口惠
lip service || empty service;

kou hui er shi bu zhi 口惠而實不至
pay lip service || make a promise and not keep it; great promise with small performance; leaves without figs; promises given in words but not fulfilled;

kou jiang zhi hua 口講指畫
gesticulate;

kou jiao 口角
angle of mouth / angulus oris / corner of the mouth;

kou jiao chun feng 口角春風
speak in praise of || give verbal praise; lavish praise on others by word of mouth; pay compliments to; praise by word of mouth;

kou jiao chun yan 口角唇炎
angular cheilitis;

kou jiao gan lie 口角乾裂
angular cheilosis;

kou jiao liu jin 口角流津
saliva drops from the corners of one's mouth;

kou jiao yan 口角炎
angular stomatitis / aphatha;
chuan ran xing kou jiao yan 傳染性口角炎
angulus infectiosus;

kou jin 口緊
tight-lipped;

kou jin bu zhao huo 口緊不招禍
a closed mouth catches no flies;

kou jing bu he 口徑不合
what people say does not agree with one another;

kou jue 口角
quarrel / spat / squabble / wrangle;

kou ke 口渴
thirsty // have a cobweb in the throat // with one's tongue hanging out;

kou kou sheng sheng 口口聲聲
keep saying all the time || avow time and again; go on prating about; keep on proclaiming; keep prating about; make noisy professions about; pay lip service to; say again and again; talk glibly about;

kou kou xiang chuan 口口相傳
from mouth to mouth / pass from mouth to mouth;

kou kuai 口快
speak rashly;

kou kuai xin zhi 口快心直
wear one's heart on one's sleeve || blunt, outspoken, but honest; free from affectation and hesitation; open-hearted; what the heart thinks, the tongue speaks;

kou ling chi li 口伶齒俐
gifted with a quick tongue / have a numble tongue;

kou ling 口令
(1) command / word of command;
(2) password / shibboleth / watchword;

kou mi fu jian 口蜜腹劍
honey in mouth, dagger in heart || a cruel heart under the cover of sugar-coated words; a honey tongue, a heart of gall; a Judas kiss; a mouth that praises and a hand that kills; fair without, foul within; give sb sweet talk when there's hatred in the heart; have honey on one's lips and murder in one's heart; have sweet talk, but evil intentions; honey on one's lips and murder in one's heart; honey-mouthed and dagger-hearted; hypocrtical and malignant; one's honeyed words hide daggers; play a double game; velvet pans hide sharp claws; with an iron hand in a velvet glove; with peace on one's tongue and guns in one's pocket;

kou qi 口氣
(1) note / tone;
(2) implication / what is actually meant;
(3) manner of speaking;

kou qi ao man 口氣傲慢
take a high tone;

kou qiang 口腔
cavity of the mouth;

kou qiang ji bing 口腔疾病
disease in the oral cavity;

kou qiang tong 口腔痛
stomalgia;

yi chi xing kou qiang tong 義齒性口腔痛
denture sore mouth;

kou qiang yan 口腔炎
stomatitis;

nong xing kou qiang yan 膿性口腔炎
pyostomatitis;

kou qiao shou zhuo 口巧手拙
glib in tongue and clumsy of hands || those who are good at making excuses will be good at nothing else;

kou ruo xuan he 口若懸河
have a great flow of speech / pour forth || a glib; a great talker; a great talker made a torrent of words; eloquent; eloquent in speech; gift of the gab; have eloquence on tap; let loose a flood of eloquence; nimble of speech; one's mouth is like tumbling river — talk rapidly; one's words pour forth like a rushing river; speak incessantly like a stream; talk glibly; talk in a flood of eloquence; utter a torrent of words; voluble; with an easy flow of language;

kou she 口舌
(1) dispute / exchange of words / quarrel;
(2) talk / talk round;

kou she shi fei 口舌是非
dispute / wagging of tongues;

kou she zhi zheng 口舌之爭
a contention of mouth and tongue;

kou shi 口實
a cause for gossip;

kou shi feng, bi shi zong 口是風，筆是蹤
words fly, writing remains || words spoken are like the wind; the tracing of the pencil remains;

kou shi xin fei 口是心非
agree in words but disagree in heart || a hypocrite; affirm with one's lips but deny in one's heart; bear two faces under one hood; carry fire in one hand and water in the other; carry two faces under one hood; cry with one eye and laugh with the other; double-dealing; double-faced; duplicity; have two faces; hypocrisy; keep two faces under one hood; outwardly agree but inwardly disagree; pay lip service; play a double game; play the hypocrite; right with the mouth but wrong at heart; say one thing and mean another; say yes and mean no; show a false face; the mouth specious and the mind perverse; though one speaks well, one's heart is false;

kou shou 口授
(1) oral instruction / pass on through oral instruction;
(2) dictate;

kou shou bi lu 口授筆錄
dictate / talk down from dictation || one gives verbal instructions and the other records with a pen;

kou shu 口述
(1) oral account;
(2) dictate;

kou shui 口水
saliva / slobber / spittle;

kou shuo bu ru shen lin 口說不如身臨
to hear it told is not equal to experience;

kou shuo wu ping 口說無憑
words alone are no proof || a verbal arrangement should not furnish a substantial proof; oral expressions cannot be taken as evidence; oral promise is not enough; verbal promise is rather dubious; verbal statements are no guarantee; words don't carry conviction;

kou song xin wei 口誦心惟
read sth while pondering its meaning;

kou tian xin la 口甜心辣
honey on the lips and viciousness in the heart;

kou tou 口頭
(1) oral / verbal;

(2) by word of mouth || in speech; in words; on one's lips; verbal;

kou tou chan 口頭禪
pet expression || catchword; common saying; commonplace saying; conventional expressions; parrot cry; pet phrase; shibboleth; stock phrase;

kou tou tong zhi 口頭通知
inform orally / notify orally;

kou tou zhi jiao 口頭之交
a friendship which is outward and of the mouth;

kou tu du yan 口吐毒焰
speak daggers to;

kou tu kuang yan 口吐狂言
cheek up / talk nonsense / talk wildly;

kou tu lian hua 口吐蓮華
have the gift of the gab — good at speaking;

kou tu xian xue 口吐鮮血
spit blood || blood gushes from one's mouth;

kou wei 口味
(1) flavour of food;
(2) a person's taste;

kou wen 口吻
(1) muzzle / snout;
(2) note / tone;

kou wen shou xie 口問手寫
ask questions and take notes;

kou wu 口誤
a slip of the tongue / an error in speaking;

kou xin ru yi 口心如一
one means what one says / what one says is indeed what one thinks;

kou xin 口信
message / oral message;

kou xiong xin ruan 口兇心軟
his bark is worse than his bite;

kou xue wei gan 口血未乾
the blood in the mouth is not yet dried;

kou yan 口炎
stomatitis;
bian ying xing kou yan 變應性口炎
allergic stomatitis;
chuan ran xing kou yan 傳染性口炎
infectious stomatitis;
gong du xing kou yan 汞毒性口炎
mercurial stomatitis;
huai ju xing kou yan 壞疽性口炎
noma;
huai si xing kou yan 壞死性口炎
necrotic stomatitis;
huai xue bing kou yan 壞血病口炎
stomatitis scorbutica;
jie chu xing kou yan 接觸性口炎
contact stomatitis;
kou chuang xing kou yan 口瘡性口炎
stomatitis aphthosa;
kui yang xing kou yan 潰瘍性口炎
ulcerative stomatitis;
lin bing xing kou yan 淋病性口炎
gonorrheal stomatitis;
lin qiu jun xing kou yan 淋球菌性口炎
gonococcal stomatitis;
lü pao xing kou yan 濾泡性口炎
stomatitis follicularis;
mei du xing kou yan 梅毒性口炎
syphilitic stomatitis;
mei jun xing kou yan 霉菌性口炎
mycotic stomatitis;
mo xing kou yan 膜性口炎
membranous stomatitis;
niao du zheng kou yan 尿毒症口炎
uremic stomatitis;
nong xing kou yan 膿性口炎
pyostomatitis;
qian du xing kou yan 鉛毒性口炎
lead stomatitis;
re dai xing kou yan 熱帶性口炎
tropical stomatitis;
xing hong re xing kou yan 猩紅熱性口炎
stomatitis scarlatina;
yi chi xing kou yan 義齒性口炎
denture stomatitis;
zhong du xing kou yan 中毒性口炎
stomatitis venenata;

kou yin 口音
(1) voice;
(2) accent;

kou zao chun gan 口燥唇乾
lips are dry and mouth is parched / talk one's tongue dry;

kou zhi xin kuai 口直心快
talk bluntly;

kou zhu 口誅
tongue lashing;

kou zhu bi fa 口誅筆伐
condemn both by word of mouth and in writing / condemn both in speech and in writing / lash out at both by word of mouth and in writing;

kou4 叩
ask;

kou wen 叩問
ask / make enquiries;

kou4 wen 扣問
stop and ask;

ku1 哭
cry / sob / wail / weep;

ku bi zi 哭鼻子
snivel / weep;

ku bu cheng sheng 哭不成聲
unable to speak for weeping || break down entirely; sob too much to speak; weep too bitterly to speak;

ku bu de xiao bu de 哭不得笑不得
at a loss whether to cry or laugh / at one's wits' end;

ku cheng lei ren 哭成淚人
be drenched in tears || be dissolved in tears; one is all tears;

ku dao yu di 哭倒於地
fall to the ground with a great cry / throw oneself on the ground and weep;

ku die ku niang 哭爹哭娘
yell inordinately;

ku duan gan chang 哭斷肝腸
cry as if one's heart would break / cry one's eyes out / cry one's heart out;

ku gan yan lei 哭乾眼淚
cry until one has no more tears to shed;

ku ge bu ting 哭個不停
go on crying;

ku ge tong kuai 哭個痛快
cry one's heart out / weep one's fill;

ku han 哭喊
cry and shout;

ku ku nao nao 哭哭鬧鬧
make a tearful scene;

ku ku shuo shuo 哭哭説説
cry between the words;

ku ku ti ti 哭哭啼啼
lachrymose / weep and wail / weeping and wailing / whine with plaintive broken sounds;

ku ku xiao xiao 哭哭笑笑
cry one moment and laugh the next;

ku nao 哭鬧
cry and scream;

ku qi 哭泣
cry / sob / weep;

ku qiong 哭窮
complain of being short of money;

ku sang 哭喪
wail at a funeral;

ku sheng ai qi 哭聲哀悽
cry sadly // plaintive cries / sad cries;

ku sheng bian ye 哭聲遍野
long-drawn-out howls of misery are heard on every side / the air is rent for miles around with cries of weeping and lamentation;

ku sheng zai dao 哭聲載道
cries of misery are heard the whole length of the way;

ku sheng zhen tian 哭聲震天
the cries of lamentation rise to the skies || a wail of sorrow arises to the very sky; the noise of grief rises to Heaven;

ku su 哭訴
complain tearfully;

ku tian ku di 哭天哭地
wail bitterly;

ku tian mo lei 哭天抹淚
cry piteously / wail and whine;

ku xiao bu de 哭笑不得
not to know whether to laugh or to cry || able neither to cry nor to laugh; at a loss whether to cry or laugh; find sth both funny and annoying; one can neither cry nor laugh; unable either to laugh or to cry;

ku xiao wu chang 哭笑無常
weeping and laughing hysterically || cry and laugh by turns, without any apparent reason; now he laughs, then he cries;

ku ya sang men 哭啞嗓門
lose one's voice in tears;

ku zhe qiu rao 哭着求饒
whine for mercy;

ku zhong yan pi 哭腫眼皮
cry one's eyes out;

ku3 bu kan yan 苦不堪言
miserable beyond description / painful beyond description;

ku jian 苦諫
admonish earnestly // earnest admonition;

ku kou 苦口
(1) bitter to the taste;
(2) admonish earnestly / exhort earnestly;

ku kou po xin 苦口婆心
exhort with earnest words prompted by a kind heart;

ku quan 苦勸
advise earnestly / exhort earnestly // earnest exhortation;

ku wei 苦味
bitter taste;

ku xiao 苦笑
(1) bitter smile / forced smile / moody smile / wry smile;
(2) produce a forced smile;

kua1 夸
boast / brag / talk big;

kua dan 夸誕
boastful / bragging;

kua kua qi tan 夸夸其談
indulge in exaggeration / shoot one's mouth off // gas and gaiters // gassy / pompous;

kua1 誇
(1) exaggerate / boast / brag;
(2) praise;

kua da qi ci 誇大其詞
exaggerate;

kua dan 誇誕
exaggerating to an incredible extent;

kua gong 誇功
boast of one's contribution;

kua kou 誇口
boast / brag / talk big;

kua shi 誇示
flaunt / show off;

kua shi 誇飾
exaggerate;

kua xia hai kou 誇下海口
have boasted;

kua xu 誇詡
boast / exaggerate;

kua yao 誇耀
flaunt / show off;

kua zan 誇讚
extol / praise;

kua zui 誇嘴
boast / talk big;

kuai4 du 快讀
fast-reading / speed-reading;

kuai ren kuai yu 快人快語
straight talk of a straightforword person;

kuai shuo 快說
speak up;

kuai zui 快嘴
quick-tongued;

kuai zui kuai she 快嘴快舌
prone to talk rashly;

kuai4 zhi ren kou 膾炙人口
be oft-quoted and widely loved || enjoy great popularity; on everybody's lips; pleasant to all tastes; please all tastes; popular; popular and much praised; twice-told; widely quoted; win universal praise;

kuan3 jin 款襟
talk to one's heart's content;

kuan yan 款言
empty words;

kuan yu 款語
gentle and persuasive conversation;

kuang1 誆
cheat / deceive / delude / hoax / lie;

kuang hong 誆哄
cheat / deceive / hoax / lie;

kuang huo 誆惑
deceive / delude;

kuang pian 誆騙
cheat / deceive / delude / hoax / lie / swindle;

kuang yan 誆言
false words / lies;

kuang2 ge 狂歌
sing with wild joy;

kuang hu 狂呼
shout in wild excitement;

kuang xiao 狂笑
give wild laughter // deranged laugh / extravagant laughter;

kuang yan 狂言
boastful talks / wild words;

kuang yin 狂飲
quaff;

kuang2 誑
deceive / delude;

kuang dan 誑誕
deceive / delude;

kuang pian 誑騙
cheat / deceive / swindle;

kuang yan 誑言
falsehood / lie / wild talk;

kui4 yang xing kou yan 潰瘍性口炎
ulcerative stomatitis;

kui4 喟
sigh heavily;

kui ran 喟然
manner of sighing;

kui ran chang tan 喟然長歎
draw a long breath and sigh / heave a deep sigh / let out a long breath / sigh deeply;

kui ran xing tan 喟然興歎
give a sigh of disappointment / heave a sigh of regret // with a heavy sigh;

kui tan 喟歎
sigh with deep feeling;

la1 che 拉扯
indulge in aimless talks;

la hua 拉話
chat / talk;

la la che che 拉拉扯扯
(1) pull and drag a person, asking him to do sth against his will;
(2) digress in speaking;

lan2 讕
abuse / calumniate / libel / revile / slander;

lan yan 讕言
calumny / slander;

lan4 yan 濫言
too lavish of one's tongue;

lan4 zui 爛醉
dead drunk / stonkered // under the table;

lan zui ru ni 爛醉如泥
dead drunk / drunk as a lord / rotten drunk / stonkered // under the table;

lang2 tun hu yan 狼吞虎咽
devour ravenously / gobble up / gulp down / hoe in / ingurgitate / pig out / wolf down;

lang3 du 朗讀
read aloud / read out;

lang song 朗誦
read aloud / read out || declaim; deliver a recitation; read aloud with expression; recite;

lang yong 朗詠
chant verses;

lang4 yu 浪語
nonsensical joke;

lang zui qing she 浪嘴輕舌
wag one's tongue too freely;

口 *Mouth*

lao2 嘮
(1) chat / have a gab / talk;
(3) garrulous / loquacious / voluble;

lao dao 嘮叨
burble / chatter / chatter incessantly / clack / gabble / nag / prate // garrulous / mouthy / talkative;

lao dao bu xiu 嘮叨不休
babble on and on || burble without stop; gabble on and on; talk a dog's hind leg off; talk a donkey's hind leg off; talk a horse's hind leg off; talk the hind leg off a dog; talk the hind leg off a donkey; talk the hind leg off a horse // perpetual nagging;

lao ke 嘮嗑
burble / chat / talk;

lao lao 嘮嘮
babble on and on / nag at;

lao lao dao dao 嘮嘮叨叨
babble on and on || burble; go on about; nag; nag at; repeat over and over again; say over and over again; talk nineteen to the dozen;

lao nu 嘮呶
hubbub;

lao3 hua 老話
old saying;

lao sheng chang tan 老生常談
cliché // corny;

lao sheng lao qi 老聲老氣
the sound and look of an old person;

leng3 chao re feng 冷嘲熱諷
sarcasm and mockery;

leng hua 冷話
cool, sarcastic remarks;

leng leng yi xiao 冷冷一笑
(1) bleak smile / cold smile / wintry smile;
(2) give a bleak smile / give a sneering laugh;

leng xiao 冷笑
sneer || grin with dissatisfaction, helplessness, etc.; laugh grimly; sardonic grin;

leng yan leng yu 冷言冷語
sarcastic remarks || cold remarks; cold words; cool remarks; cynicism; ironic remarks; mocking words; sarcastic comments; shafts of ridicule;

leng4 shuo 愣說
allege / assert / insist;

li1 哩
speak indistinctly;

li li la la 哩哩啦啦
scattered / sporadic;

li li luo luo 哩哩囉囉
gab // rambling and indistinct / verbose and unclear in speech;

li2 ti 離題
digress / discursive // digression;

li3 kui yu se 理虧語塞
principles deficient and words blocked;

li qu ci qiong 理屈詞窮
on the wrong side and unable to say a word in self-defense;

li4 lun 立論
present one's argument // argumentation;

li tan zhi jian 立談之間
in a moment;

li yan 立言
achieve glory by writing;

li4 zui du she 利嘴毒舌
(1) sharp tongue;
(2) have a shrewd tongue;

li zui hua ya 利嘴花牙
(1) have a ready tongue;
(2) saponaceous;

li zui qiao she 利嘴巧舌
have the gift of the gab;

li4 詈
berate / revile / scold / upbraid;

li bang 詈謗
slander;

li ma 詈罵
abuse / scold;

li ru 詈辱
scold and insult;

li ru xie fen 詈辱洩憤
scold in order to ward off one's indignation;

li4 se zheng yan 厲色正言
speak with stern countenance;

li sheng 厲聲
shout angrily / talk harshly;

li sheng chi ze 厲聲斥責
scold with an irritating voice;

li sheng gao ma 厲聲高罵
keep up a stream of furious abuse;

lian2 ku dai ma 連哭帶罵
cry and swear / sobs and curses;

lian sheng 連聲
again and again / repeatedly;

lian sheng cheng zan 連聲稱讚
full of praise for / rain praises on;

lian sheng jiao ku 連聲叫苦
one cries out one's bitterness without ceasing;

lian sheng nuo nuo 連聲諾諾
say aye, aye;

lian sheng ren cuo 連聲認錯
hasten to acknowledge one's error;

lian shuo dai bi 連說帶比
gesticulate as one talks / talk and gesticulate;

lian shuo dai xiao 連說帶笑
laugh and talk;

lian zhu miao yu 連珠妙語
scintillate witticisms / sparkling discourse;

lian zu dai ma 連詛帶罵
alternate invective with curses;

lian2 謰
talk vaguely;

lian lou 謰謱
talk vaguely and aimlessly;

liang4 hua 亮話
frank remarks;

liang4 喨
clear and resonant sound;

liao2 聊
chat;

liao liao 聊聊
have a chat;

liao tian 聊天
chat / ramble;

liao2 liang 憀亮
loud and clear;

liao2 嘹
resonant;

liao liang 嘹喨
loud and clear / resonant;

lie1 咧
grin;

lie lie 咧咧
(1) gossip / speak carelessly;
(2) cry / sob;

lie3 咧
stretch the mouth horizontally;

lie kai zui xiao 咧開嘴笑
one's mouth widens in a smile;

lie zhe zui 咧着嘴
grin;

lie zui 咧嘴
grin;

lie zui da xiao 咧嘴大笑
laugh from ear to ear;

lie zui sha xiao 咧嘴傻笑
grin like a Cheshire cat;

lie4 e 裂顎
cleft palate;

lin2 bing xing kou yan 淋病性口炎
gonorrheal stomatitis;

lin qiu jun xing kou yan 淋球菌性口炎
gonococcal stomatitis;

lin2 bie zeng yan 臨別贈言
advice by one just before parting;

lin ke wa jing 臨渴挖井
dig a well when one feels thirsty;

ling2 chi 零吃
between-meal nibble;

ling shi 零食
refreshments / snacks;

ling zui 零嘴
refreshments / snacks;

ling4 ren fa xiao 令人發笑
(1) make one laugh / provoke laughter;
(2) ridiculous;

ling ren pen fan 令人噴飯
make people laugh;

ling ren ya kou wu yan 令人啞口無言
cause sb to be a loss for words / strike sb dumb;

ling ren ya ran 令人啞然
strike sb dumb;

ling ren zuo ou 令人作嘔
make sb's gorge rise // sick-making;

ling4 yi 另議
to be discussed separately;

liu1 hong 溜哄
flatter / please;

liu kou 溜口
a slip of the tongue / blurt out;

liu2 kou shui 流口水
dribble / drool / make one's mouth water / run at the mouth;

liu shuo 流說
heretical assertion;

liu yan 流言
gossip / rumour;

liu yan zhi yu zhi zhe 流言止於智者
a wise man does not believe in rumours;

liu2 hua 留話
leave a message;

liu yan 留言
leave a message;

lu1 嚕
(1) verbose / wordy;
(2) indistinct speech sound;

lu li lu su 嚕哩嚕蘇
talk endlessly / talk unnecessarily;

lu su 嚕蘇
long-winded;

lü4 pao xing kou yan 濾泡性口炎
stomatitis follicularis;

luan4 chi 亂吃
eat without caution;

luan han luan jiao 亂喊亂叫
talk wildly;

luan rang 亂嚷
clamour;

luan shuo 亂說
make irresponsible remarks / speak indiscreetly;

lüe4 shu 略述
give a short description of;

lüe shuo 略說
say a few words about;

lüe yan geng gai 略言梗概
simply tell the main points;

lüe yan zhi 略言之
in short;

lun4 論
(1) appraise / comment on / discuss / evaluate / talk about;
(2) argue / debate / dispute;
(3) consider / mention;

lun bian 論辯
argumentation;

lun dian 論點
point of discussion;

lun diao 論調
(1) tone of a speech;
(2) views;

lun duan 論斷
discuss and judge;

lun ji 論及
touch on;

lun ju 論據
grounds of an argument;

lun ping 論評
comment // commentary;

lun shu 論述
discuss / expound;

lun shuo 論說
theory / thought;

lun zhan 論戰
battle of words / controversy;

lun zheng 論爭
argument / debate / controversy;

lun zheng 論政
discuss politics;

lun zheng 論證
argumentation;

luo1 囉
chatter;

luo li luo suo 囉哩囉嗦
long-winded // verbal diarrhoea;

luo suo 囉嗦
gab / get on sb's back / prate / witter || long-winded; verbose; wordy;
ting zhi luo suo 停止囉嗦
get off / keep off sb's back;

ma2 bi xing tun yan kun nan 麻痺性吞咽困難
dysphagia paralytica;

ma4 罵
(1) abuse / curse / swear;
(2) condemn / rebuke / reprove / scold;

ma bu hui kou 罵不回口
remain silent when verbally abused;

ma bu jue kou 罵不絕口
cure unceasingly;

ma da jie 罵大街
call people names in public / shout abuses in the street;

ma die 罵爹
curse one's father;

ma jie 罵街
call people names in public / shout abuses in the street;

ma ma lie lie 罵罵咧咧
foul-mouthed / intersperse one's talk with violent abuse;

ma ren 罵人
scold || abuse; call sb names; condemn; curse; give a bad name to sb; give sb a good dressing down; give sb a good wigging; give sb a scolding; give sb a piece of one's mind; give sb the edge of one's tongue; haul sb over the coals; load sb with insults; mutter insults against; rake sb over the coals; reprove; revile; sail into; swear at; take sb to task; tell sb off;

ma ren qu le 罵人取樂
criticize others as a pastime;

ma yu 罵語
abusive language / cuss word / opprobrious language / opprobrious remarks;

mai4 chang 賣唱
live on singing;

mai nong kou she 賣弄口舌
show off one's glibness in speech;

mai zui 賣嘴
self-praise / show off one's skill or kind-heartedness by talking;

man2 謾
disdain / scorn;

man tian man di 謾天謾地
deceive everybody;

man yu 謾語
deceitful words;

man3 kou 滿口
speak profusely / speak unreservedly;

man kou bu jue 滿口不絕
simply flow from one's lips;

man kou cheng zan 滿口稱讚
praise profusely;

man kou chun feng 滿口春風
eloquent in speaking / one speaks eloquently and fluently;

man kou da ying 滿口答應
consented without any lengthy deliberation / readily promise;

man kou gong wei 滿口恭維
full of flattery / smarmy;

man kou hu shuo 滿口胡說
talk irresponsibly / talk nonsense;

man kou hu yan 滿口胡言
full of foolish talk;

man kou huang yan 滿口謊言
spout lies;

man kou kuang lan 滿口誑讕
tell a pack of lies;

man kou ying cheng 滿口應承
make profuse promises / promise readily / promise with great readiness;

man kou yu xiang 滿口餘香
leave a lingering fragrance in one's mouth;

man kou yuan yan 滿口怨言
one's mouth is full of resentful talk;

man zui 滿嘴
have a mouthful of;

man4 ma 漫罵
abuse wildly / curse / slander with;

man ping 漫評
rambling comments;

man shuo 漫說
let alone / say nothing of;

man tan 漫談
ramble // rambling talks;

man tian da huang 漫天大謊
monstrous lie;

man yan 漫言
unsupported remarks;

man yu 漫語
unfounded remarks;

man4 嫚
(1) despise / slight;
(2) arrogant / haughty;
(3) negligently / slowly;

man ma 嫚罵
slight and insult verbally;

man4 shi pi 慢食癖
bradyphagia;

man4 蔓說
windy talk;

man4 謾
deceive;

man ma 謾罵
abuse / call sb names / fling abuse / rail / revile scornfully // extravagant abuse / name-calling;

mao4 cheng 冒稱
claim falsely;

mei2 hua zhao hua 沒話找話
make conversation;

mei2 du xing kou yan 梅毒性口炎
syphilitic stomatitis;

mei2 jun xing kou yan 霉菌性口炎
mycotic stomatitis;

mei3 tan 美談
instructive anecdote;

mei wei 美味
delicious;

mei yan 美言
commending remarks;

men1 sheng bu xiang 悶聲不響
keep one's mouth shut / remain quiet / remain silent;

meng4 lang zhi yan 孟浪之言
reckless talk;

mi4 gao 密告
inform secretly / tip off;

mi tan 密談
have a secret conversation;

mi yi 密議
confidential discussion;

mian2 mian xu yu 綿綿絮語
whisper continually;

mian3 kai zun kou 免開尊口
you'd better shut up ‖ keep your opinion to yourself; please keep your mouth shut; you'd better keep your honourable mouth shut;

mian tan 免談
you might as well save your breath;

miao3 bu zu dao 渺不足道
too small for mention;

miao4 bu ke yan 妙不可言
too subtle to be described;

miao lun 妙論
clever remarks;

miao yu 妙語
quip / wisecrack / witticism;

miao yu jie yi 妙語解頤
wisecracks that really tickle;

miao yu ru zhu 妙語如珠
sparkling discourse;

mie4 kou 滅口
kill a person to prevent him from disclosing a secret;

min3 抿
purse up lips;

min zhe zui xiao 抿着嘴笑
smile with closed lips ‖ compress one's lips to smile; one's lips curling in a part smile; smile one's tight-lipped smile;

min zui er xiao 抿嘴而笑
purse one's lips up in a smile;

min zui ren xiao 抿嘴忍笑
purse one's lips to suppress laughter;

ming2 zheng yan shun 名正言順
have good reason / valid in name and in reason;

ming2 bu ping 鳴不平
complain against injustice / voice grievances;

ming yuan 鳴寃
air grievances / complain of unfairness;

ming yuan jiao qu 鳴寃叫屈
complain and call for redress / voice grievances;

ming3 酩
drunk / inebriate / intoxicated;

ming ding 酩酊
dead drunk / drunk / intoxicated / tipsy;

ming ding da zui 酩酊大醉
dead drunk / well oiled // inebriation;

ming4 ling 命令
command / order;

miu4 lun 謬論
absurd statement / fallacious argument;

mo2 xing kou yan 膜性口炎
membranous stomatitis;

mo2 po zui pi 磨破嘴皮
talk oneself hoarse;

mo zui pi zi 磨嘴皮子
(1) do a lot of talking;
(2) blah-blah / jabber;

mo4 嘿
(1) silent / speechless;
(2) quiet / still;

mo4 bu zuo sheng 默不作聲
silent / speechless;

mo dao 默禱
pray silently;

mo du 默讀
read silently;

mo mo 默默
quietly / silently;

mo mo wu yan 默默無言
in silence / silent / speechless / wordless;

mou2 yi 謀議
confer / meet and plan;

na2 wen 拿問
detain for questioning;

na4 吶
(1) cheer / cry out / shout / yell;
(2) speak hesitatingly;

na han 吶喊
cry out / loud shouts in support / shout loudly / yell;

na han zhu wei 吶喊助威
shout one's support ‖ cheer; shout encouragement; shout loudly to encourage;

na na 吶吶
speak haltingly;

na4 jian 納諫
accept an admonition / receive advice;

nan2 喃
murmur;

nan nan 喃喃
murmur / mutter;

nan nan bu ping 喃喃不平
express one's discontent by muttering to oneself;

nan nan bu xiu 喃喃不休
make endless speeches;

nan nan zi yu 喃喃自語
mumble to oneself / mutter under one's breath / utter one's thoughts unconciously;

nan2 諵
chatter / gabble;

nan nan 諵諵
loquacious / talkative;

nan2 chi 難吃
unbearable to palate / unpalatable;

nan jiang 難講
difficult to predict / hard to say;

nan yi chu kou 難以出口
difficult to speak out one's mind / too embarrassed to say it;

nan yi shuo ming 難以說明
unaccountable;

nan yi yan biao 難以言表
ineffable / inexpressible / unspeakable;

nao2 譊
argue;

nao nao 譊譊
arguing voices;

nao4 jiu 鬧酒
engage in a drunken brawl / start a drinking bout;

nao rang rang 鬧嚷嚷
clamorous / noisy;

nao xiao hua 鬧笑話
arouse ridicule;

ne4 訥
slow of speech / slow-tongued / stammer;

ne chi 訥吃
spasmophemia;

ne kou 訥口
slow of speech;

ne kou shao yan 訥口少言
not communicative / tight-lipped;

ne se 訥澀
slow of speech / stammer;

neng2 ge shan wu 能歌善舞
skilled in singing and dancing;

neng shuo hui dao 能說會道
very eloquent;

neng yan kuai yu 能言快語
eloquent and frank in speaking;

neng yan shan bian 能言善辯
eloquent and glib in argument / plausible;

ni2 呢
murmur;

ni2 zui 泥醉
dead drunk;

ni4 xiao 匿笑
laugh in secret;

nian4 唸
chant / read / recite;

nian fo 唸佛
chant the name of Buddha / pray to Buddha;

nian jing 唸經
chant scriptures / recite scriptures;

nian jing wen bu 唸經問卜
cast a horoscope and recite the sutra;

nian nian you ci 唸唸有詞
mumble some words || chant; incant; mumble about; mutter incantations;

nian shu 唸書
(1) read;
(2) attend school / study;

nian song 唸誦
read aloud / recite;

nian zhou 唸咒
chant a chant / intone a chant;

niang2 niang qiang 娘娘腔
sissy / nancy / womanish;

niao4 du zheng kou yan 尿毒症口炎
uremic stomatitis;

nie4 囁
(1) falter in speech;
(2) move the mouth;

nie ru 囁嚅
speak haltingly;

nie ru bu yan 囁嚅不言
move the mouth, but refrain from speaking;

ning2 嚀
enjoin / instruct;

ning2 xiao 獰笑
laugh malignantly;

niu2 yin 牛飲
drink gallons / drink like a fish / ingurgitate / swig;

niu4 bu guo 拗不過
fail to talk sb out of doing sth / unable to dissuade;

nong2 xing kou qiang yan 膿性口腔炎
pyostomatitis;

nong xing kou yan 膿性口炎
pyostomatitis;

nong4 kou 弄口
sow discord by making false statements;

nong zui nong she 弄嘴弄舌
talk idly;

nu3 zui 努嘴
purse up one's lips;

nu4 chi 怒叱
shout in rage;

nu chi 怒斥
angrily denounce / give sb a piece of one's mind / huff;

nu he 怒喝
fulminate;

nu hou 怒吼
bluster / sound off;

nu ma 怒罵
cure in rage;

nüe4 謔
(1) jest / joke;
(2) ridicule / satirize;

nüe er bu nüe 謔而不虐
joke without hurting anyone;

nüe lang 謔浪
make fun without restraint;

nüe lang xiao ao 謔浪笑傲
with scornful words and jeering smiles;

nüe nong 謔弄
make fun of / play tricks on;

nüe nüe 謔謔
cheerful / happy;

nuo4 諾
(1) assent;
(2) pledge / promise;

nuo yan 諾言
pledge / promise;

ou1 謳
chant / sing;

ou ge 謳歌
glorify / sing in praise;

ou3 嘔
throw up / vomit;

ou tu 嘔吐
vomit ‖ anabole; barf; cast up; cast up one's accounts; chuck up; puke; retch; shoot the cat; throw up;
ren shen ou tu 妊娠嘔吐
vomiting of pregnancy;
zhou qi xing ou tu 周期性嘔吐
periodic vomiting;
zi fa xing ou tu 自發性嘔吐
autemesia;

ou xie 嘔泄
vomiting and diarrhoea;

pa2 fan 爬飯
rake rice into the mouth with chopsticks;

pan1 tan 攀談
strike up a conversation / accost ‖ chat with; chitchat; drag another into conversation; engage in small talk with; have a free and easy talk;

pan2 cha 盤查
cross-examine ‖ examine thoroughly; grill; interrogate and examine; question;

pan jie 盤詰
cross-examine / grill / question;

pan jie jian gui 盤詰奸宄
cross-examine bad elements;

pan jiu 盤究
cross-examine and investigate / grill;

pan wen 盤問
cross-examine / grill / interrogate;

pao2 咆
bluster / rage / roar;

pao xiao 咆哮
bluster / growl / rage / roar;

pao xiao ru lei 咆哮如雷
roar like thunder || in a thundering rage; roar with rage;

pei2 bu shi 賠不是
apologize / ask forgiveness;

pei hua 陪話
apologize;

pei jiu 陪酒
accompany a patron in drinking;

pei xiao 陪笑
smile apologetically / smile dutifully;

pei zui 陪罪
apologize;

pei2 xiao 賠笑
smile apologetically / smile obsequiously;

pen1 fan 噴飯
laughable;

pen fen 噴糞
preposterous statements || curses;

pen yun tu wu 噴雲吐霧
smoke;

pi1 批
criticize;

pi1 du 披讀
read / open and read;

pi4 hua 屁話
baloney;

pi4 miu 闢謬
refute absurdities;

pi yao 闢謠
clarify rumoured reports / refute rumours;

pian1 shi 偏食
eat certain dishes only / monophagia;

pian2 諞
quibble;

pian yan 諞言
quibble;

pian3 諞
boast / brag / show off;

pian kuo 諞闊
show off // boastful;

pian neng 諞能
show off one's abilities;

pian4 mian zhi ci 片面之詞
one-sided remarks;

pian mian zhi yan 片面之言
one-sided remarks;

pian yan 片言
a few words;

pian yan jiu ding 片言九鼎
a solemn pledge / a solemn promise;

pian yan ke jue 片言可決
be settled by one word;

pian yan zhi ci 片言隻詞
a few words and phrases;

pian yan zhe yu 片言折獄
a single world uttered by a wise man can decide a legal case;

pie3 chi la zui 撇齒拉嘴
wear a contemptuous expression;

pie zui 撇嘴
curl one's lip || make a lip; make a mouth; make a wry mouth; make mouths; make up a lip; shoot out the lips; twitch one's mouth;

pin2 zui 貧嘴
garrulous / loquacious / talkative;

pin zui bo she 貧嘴薄舌
have a caustic and flippant tongue || be addicted to senseless talks; garrulous and sharp-tongued; light and airy utterance; wag one's tongue too freely;

pin zui jian she 貧嘴賤舌
be addicted to senseless talk / disgustingly talkative / make vulgar jokes;

pin zui lan she 貧嘴爛舌
be given to nasty talk / have a caustic and flippant tongue / like to say nasty things about people / love to gossip;

ping2 xin er lun 平心而論
discuss sth fairly / give the devil his due / to be fair;

ping yi 平議
fair and just discussion;

ping2 評
comment / criticize / review // comments / reviews;

ping lun 評論
comment / review // commentary / comments;

ping lun shi fei 評論是非
discuss the right and wrong;

ping yi 評議
discuss the right or wrong of sth;

ping yu 評語
comments / criticism;

ping2 kou shuo 憑口說
mere talk / make an unfounded assertion;

ping xin er lun 憑心而論
give the devil his due;

po1 kou da ma 潑口大罵
give vent to a torrent of abuse / let loose a flood of abuse / pour out a flood of abuse on;

po4 kou da ma 破口大罵
burst into a storm of abuse / let loose a torrent of abuse ‖ abuse roundly; bawl abuse; curse freely; give vent to a torrent of abuse; heap abuse on; hurl all kinds of abuse against; let loose a flood of abuse; pour out a whole ocean of abuse over; pour out torrents of abuse; raise hail Columbia; rave widely against; shout abuse; swear home; swear like a trooper; swear one's way through; swear one's way through a stone wall; swear through a two-inch board; vociferate oaths;

po ti wei xiao 破涕為笑
break into laughter while still crying;

pou2 yin 抔飲
drink out of the hands;

qi1 yan bay u 七言八語
all sorts of opinions / gossip;

qi zhang ba zui 七張八嘴
at sixes and sevens / in a state of disagreement;

qi zui ba she 七嘴八舌
everybody talking at the same time ‖ a babel of; a hubbub of voices; a scene of noisy and confused talking; all giving tongue together; all talking at once; all talking simultaneously producing great confusion; all talking together; confused talking; like a rattle-box; like a talkshot; lively discussion with everybody trying to get a word in; many diverse opinions; many men, many minds; with everybody eager to put in a word;

qi1 ren zhi tan 欺人之談
lie;

qi1 諆
cheat;

qi2 tan 奇談
strange story;

qi2 chang 齊唱
sing in unison;

qi kou tong sheng 齊口同聲
say in unison;

qi sheng 齊聲
in unison / with one voice;

qi3 shi 乞食
beg one's bread;

qi3 kou yu yan 啟口欲言
move one's lips in an attempt to speak;

qi4 hua 氣話
angry words;

qi4 yan 棄言
unable to keep one's promise;

qia4 shang 洽商
discuss;

qia tan 洽談
discuss and consult / talk;

qia yi 洽議
meet and discuss;

qian1 jin yi xiao 千金一笑
a smile of a beautiful lady is worth a thousand taels of gold;

qian yan wan yu 千言萬語
hard to express the many words in one's mind;

qian1 du xing kou yan 鉛毒性口炎
lead stomatitis;

qian zhong du kou chou 鉛中毒口臭
lead breath;

qian1 ci 謙辭
(1) humble expression || modest speech; self-depreciatory expression;
(2) decline out of modesty / decline out of humbleness;

qian2 jin 鉗噤
keep one's mouth shut / keep quiet;

qian kou 鉗口
(1) keep one's mouth shut / keep silent;
(2) prevent from talking;

qian kou bu yan 鉗口不言
keep mum / keep one's mouth shut;

qian kou jie she 鉗口結舌
be forced to keep silence / keep mum / keep one's mouth shut / tongue-tied;

qian2 kou 箝口
(1) keep one's mouth shut / keep silent;
(2) force to keep silent / gag / prevent from talking;

qian kou jie she 箝口結舌
(1) keep silent;
(2) be forced to keep silent;

qian kou wu yan 箝口無言
button up / shut up;

qian yu 箝語
restrict freedom of speech;

qian3 bai yan zhi 淺而言之
talk in a simple way;

qian xiao 淺笑
smile;

qian3 譴
(1) castigate || condemn; denounce; disparage; reprimand; reproach; scold; upbraid;
(2) punishment;

qian he 譴訶
reproach / scold;

qian nu 譴怒
reprove and anger;

qian ze 譴責
castigate || animadvert; censure; condemn; denounce; denunciate; disparage; flay; haul over the coals; lambaste; repudiate; take to task // animadversion / denunciation;

qiang2 diao 強調
emphasize / point up / stress / underline / underscore;

qiang3 bai 搶白
reprimand sb to one's face;

qiang zui 搶嘴
(1) try to beat others in being the first to talk;
(2) argumentative / assertive;

qiao1 bian gu 敲邊鼓
speak for sb in order to help him;

qiao3 bian 巧辯
ingenious argument;

qiao xiao 巧笑
artful smile / smile artfully;

qiao yan ling se 巧言令色
say smooth words to sb and wear a fair face before him / sweet words and insinuating manners;

qiao yan song ting 巧言聳聽
clever words that make one listen;

qiao zha 巧詐
artful / tricky // ingenious fraud;

qiao3 sheng 悄聲
quietly / talk in a low voice;

qiao yu 悄語
speak softly / talk in a low voice / whisper;

qiao4 pi hua 俏皮話
clever retort / jibe / one-liner / persiflage / quip / wisecrack;

qiao4 誚
blame / censure / reproach;

qiao he 誚呵
blame / censure / reproach;

qiao rang 誚讓
blame / censure / reproach;

qie4 kou 怯口
rustic accent;

qie4 qie 竊竊
(1) in a low voice / under one's breath;

(2) assume busily and brightly;

qie qie an xiao 竊竊暗笑
chuckle to oneself / laugh in one's sleeve;

qie qie jiao tan 竊竊交談
converse in whispers;

qie qie si yi 竊竊私議
discuss sth in secret ‖ a confidential conversation; comment on sth in whispers; discuss the matter privately in low tones; exhange views in private; exchange whispered comments; in a subdued voice; in a whisper; murmur secretly; mutter to each other; talk about sth in private;

qie qie si yu 竊竊私語
talk stealthily ‖ murmurous; speak to another in private in a whisper; talk in a low voice secretly; talk in whispers; the muffled sounds of a conversation; whisper;

qie xiao 竊笑
laugh up one's sleeve ‖ laugh behind sb's back; laugh in one's sleeve; laugh secretly; snicker; titter;

qin1 kou 親口
from sb's own lips ‖ in person; personally; right from one's own mouth; say sth personally; state personally;

qin kou da ying 親口答應
make a promise personally;

qin3 shi bu an 寢食不安
restless due to worries;

qin shi nan wang 寢食難忘
constantly in one's mind;

qing1 dan yin shi 清淡飲食
bland diet;

qing tan 清談
pure theoretical talks;

qing xiang shuang kou 清香爽口
pleasant to the palate;

qing1 su 傾訴
unbosom oneself ‖ make a clean breast of; pour forth; pour out; unburden oneself;

qing su ku qing 傾訴苦情
give full vent to one's feelings / pour out one's grievances ‖ the outpouring of the heart; unburden one's heart; unburden oneself of sorrows;

qing su xin qu 傾訴心曲
lay bare one's pent-up feelings / lay one's heart bare / pour out one's secret concern;

qing su zhong chang 傾訴衷腸
pour out one's heart / reveal one's innermost feelings;

qing su zhong qing 傾訴衷情
give full vent to one's feelings / pour out one's innermost feelings ‖ open one's heart to sb; reveal all one's innermost feelings; reveal one's heartfelt emotion; say what there is on one's mind without reservation; unbosom every bit of oneself; unburden one's heart; unburden oneself to;

qing tan 傾談
have a good talk ‖ get into intimate conversation with; have a good, heart-to-heart talk;

qing tu 傾吐
pour out one's heart ‖ reveal one's sorrows; say what is on one's mind without reservation; speak freely of one's thoughts;

qing tu fei fu 傾吐肺腑
lay one's heart bare ‖ have a confidential talk; unbosom oneself to; unbutton one's soul;

qing tu ku shui 傾吐苦水
unburden oneself of one's grievances;

qing tu zhong qing 傾吐衷情
pour out one's heart to sb / unbosom oneself;

qing tu zhong qu 傾吐衷曲
open one's heart to sb / pour out one's heart to sb ‖ pour out one's thoughts; talk to each other to their hearts' content;

qing1 ge man wu 輕歌曼舞
sing cheerfully and dance gracefully;

qing kou bo she 輕口薄舌
flippant ‖ like to say nasty things about people; loose-tongued; speak impolitely; speak rudely;

qing nuo gua xin 輕諾寡信
give it a promise easily and break it easily;

qing sheng 輕聲
(1) in a soft voice / softly;

(2) light tone;

qing sheng di yu 輕聲低語
speak softly / whisper;

qing yan 輕言
speak lightly / speak without thinking;

qing yan qing yu 輕言輕語
express oneself with a ready, shallow pertness || flippant; talk jestingly in regard to sth demanding more serious treatment;

qing yan xi yu 輕言細語
speak softly || say sth under one's breath; speak in a mild tone; talk in a soft voice;

qing yan zhao yuan 輕言招怨
cause hatred by reckless words;

qing zui bo she 輕嘴薄舌
make irresponsible remarks;

qing2 hua 情話
(1) lovers' prattle / sweet nothings / whispers of love;
(2) hearty talks;

qing hua mian mian 情話綿綿
endless whispers of love;

qing3 qiu 請求
ask / request / petition / solicit;

qing4 謦
(1) cough lightly;
(2) speak softly;

qing kai 謦欬
talking and laughing;

qu3 xiao 取笑
chaff / gibe / jape / laugh at / make a gibe at / make fun of / make sport of / pun fun at / razz / ridicule / take the mickey out of / tease;

quan2 chang he cai 全場喝彩
bring down the gallery / bring down the house / bring the house down;

quan4 勸
advise / exhort / try to persuade / urge;

quan dao 勸導
admonish / advise;

quan fu 勸服
induce / persuade / talk sb over / talk sb round // inducement;

quan gao 勸告
advise / counsel;

quan hui 勸誨
advise / exhort;

quan jian 勸諫
remonstrate;

quan jie 勸誡
admonish / exhort / expostulate;

quan mian 勸勉
encourage / urge;

quan ren wei shan 勸人為善
exhort people to do good;

quan shuo 勸説
advise / persuade;

quan wei 勸慰
console / soothe;

quan you 勸誘
console / soothe;

que1 shi 缺食
insufficiently fed;

que zui 缺嘴
(1) never stop eating;
(2) harelip;

rang1 嚷
call out loudly / complain / cry / shout;

rang rang 嚷嚷
(1) bawl || howl; make a noise; make an uproar; roar; shout; yell;
(2) bring before the public || give to the world; make public; make widely known;

rang2 gou 攘詬
cleanse oneself of dishonour / clear oneself of a dishonour;

rang3 kou 瓤口
taste;

rang3 嚷
shout / yell || bellow; call out loudly; create an uproar; cry; howl; make an uproar;

rang jiao 嚷叫
shout / yell || bellow; howl; make an uproar;

rang zui 嚷嘴
bicker / quarrel;

rao4 kou ling 繞口令
tongue twister;

rao zui 繞嘴
difficult to articulate;

re4 dai xing kou yan 熱帶性口炎
tropical stomatitis;

re lie tao lun 熱烈討論
heated discussion;

re lie zheng lun 熱烈爭論
heated argument;

ren2 duo zui za 人多嘴雜
a babel of voices || agreement is difficult if there are too many people; divided counsel; so many heads, so many opinions; the more people, the more talk; too many people, too many ideas;

ren gong hu xi 人工呼吸
artificial respiration;

ren hua 人話
reasonable statement;

ren sheng 人聲
voice;

ren sheng cao za 人聲嘈雜
a confusion of voices || a confused noise of voices; a tremendous hubbub;

ren sheng ding fei 人聲鼎沸
a hubbub of voices || a babel of voices; noise and shouts in great commotion; the clamour of the people bubble up;

ren wei yan qing 人微言輕
when a man is in a low position, his words carry little weight || a poor man's tale cannot be heard; as one is in a low position, one's words are of little effect; in one's humble position, one's words do not carry much weight; poor men's reasons are not heard; the poor man's reasons are of no weight; the reasons of the poor weigh not; the words of the lowly carry little weight;

ren yan 人言
(1) human speech;
(2) public opinion;

ren yan bu ke xin 人言不可信
don't believe rumours / gossips are not to be believed / words are but wind;

ren yan ding fei 人言鼎沸
many people talk together and the noise they make is like the bubbling of water boiling in a cauldron / tremendous hubbub;

ren yan ji ji 人言藉藉
gossips are rife / there is a great deal of gossip;

ren yan ke wei 人言可畏
gossip is a fearful thing / the voice of the people is sth to fear;

ren yan ren shu 人言人殊
the accounts are at variance among themselves;

ren yan ze ze 人言嘖嘖
complaints are whispered in a good-natured way || criticism of the people is evident; there are plenty of criticisms; there is a good deal of unfavourable comments;

ren yun yi yun 人云亦云
parrot what others say;

ren2 yan 仁言
kind words;

ren3 bu zhu xiao 忍不住笑
cannot refrain from laughing;

ren jun bu jin 忍俊不禁
cannot help laughing;

ren qi tun sheng 忍氣吞聲
eat dirt / eat humble pie / restrain one's temper and say nothing;

ren xiao 忍笑
hold back laughter / stifle a laugh;

ren4 訒
cautious in speech / difficult to speak out;

rou2 sheng 柔聲
soft voice // in a sweet and girlish voice;

rou sheng xi yu 柔聲細語
coo;

rou yan mi yu 柔言蜜語
speak in a melting voice;

ru2 chu yi kou 如出一口
in one voice || all say the same thing; everyone says so; unanimously; with one

voice;

ru2 嚅
talk indistinctly and falteringly;

ru dong 嚅動
move one's lips as if to say sth;

ru nie 嚅囁
falter in one's speech;

ru3 ma 辱罵
abuse / call sb names / hurl insults // invective / name-calling / opprobrium;

ru mo 辱沒
insult / disgrace;

ru4 kou 入口
enter the mouth;

ruan3 yu 軟語
gentle words;

sa1 huang 撒謊
lie / tell a lie;

sa zui 撒嘴
relax the bite;

san1 ban zui er 三瓣嘴兒
harelipped;

san jian qi kou 三緘其口
remain silent ‖ a tightly fastened-down mouth; hold one's peace; hold oneself back from saying a word; keep one's peace; reluctant to voice one's opinions; very reluctant to make comments; with one's lips sealed;

san ju bu li ben hang 三句不離本行
talk shop;

san yan liang yu 三言兩語
in a few words / a couple of words / a word or two / in one or two words;

san3 hua 散話
gossip / idle talk;

sang4 bang 喪謗
speak ill of;

sang sheng ai qi 喪聲唉氣
complaining and whining;

se4 ne 澀訥
slow of tongue;

se na yan yu 澀訥言語
blunt in speaking;

sha3 hua 傻話
drivel / foolish talk / nonsense;

sha xiao 傻笑
silly smile ‖ giggle; goofy grin; gormless grin; grin like a Cheshire cat; laugh foolishly; laugh for no conceivable reason; simper; smirk; titter;

sha4 嗄
hoarse voice;

shan1 xiao 姍笑
ridicule;

shan3 shuo qi ci 閃爍其詞
make an ambiguous speech / speak evasively;

shan4 訕
(1) laugh at / sneer;
(2) abuse / slander;
(3) awkward / embarrassed / shamefaced;

shan bang 訕謗
backbite / libel / slander;

shan shang 訕上
slander one's superiors;

shan xiao 訕笑
deride / laugh at / mock / ridicule / sneer at;

shan4 yan 善言
well-intentioned advice;

shan yan xiang quan 善言相勸
advise with good words // kind advice and persuasion;

shang1 商
discuss / exchange views;

shang ding 商定
agree on / decide after discussion;

shang liang 商量
consult / discuss / exchange opinions;

shang qia 商洽
consult and discuss;

shang que 商榷
discuss and consider;

shang tan 商談
exchange views;

shang tao 商討
discuss;

shang4 e 上顎
upper jaw || roof of the mouth;

shang e gu 上顎骨
upper jaw bone || maxilla;

shang e gu zhe 上顎骨折
maxillary fracture;

shang han 上頷
mandible;

shang kou 上口
easy to read / easy to speak;

shang su 上訴
state one's case to a superior;

shang tu xia xie 上吐下瀉
suffer from vomiting and diarrhoea / vomit and have watery stools / vomiting and purging;

shao3 shuo fei hua 少說癈話
stop talking nonsense;

shao wen 少問
refrain from asking;

she1 yan 奢言
extravagant talk;

she yu 奢語
extravagant talk;

shen1 bian 申辯
argue / contend / defend oneself / explain one's conduct;

shen chi 申斥
castigate / reprimand;

shen jie 申解
explain / state;

shen tao 申討
denounce / openly condemn;

shen1 呻
drone / groan / moan;

shen hu 呻呼
groan for pain;

shen huan 呻喚
groan for illness;

shen yin 呻吟
groan / moan;

shen1 tan 深談
intimate talk;

shen yan 深言
confidential talk;

shen yu 深語
intimate talk;

shen1 詵
(1) ask / question;
(2) address / speak to;

shen2 jing xing tan shi 神經性貪食
bulimia nervosa;

shen jing xing yan shi zheng 神經性厭食症
anorexia nervosa;

shen3 哂
give a sneering smile;

shen xiao 哂笑
laugh at with contempt;

shen3 諗
(1) announce / tell;
(2) remonstrate;

shen3 wen 審問
interrogate || examine; hear; question; try;

shen yi 審議
consideration / deliberation / discussion;

shen4 yan shen xing 慎言慎行
exercise caution in speech and conduct;

sheng1 jin 生津
promote salivation;

sheng1 cheng 聲稱
assert / claim / declare / profess;

sheng dai 聲帶
vocal cord;

sheng dai ma bi 聲帶麻痺
vocal cord paralysis;

sheng dai pi lao 聲帶疲勞
vocal fatigue;

sheng dai yan 聲帶炎
corditis;

jie jie xing sheng dai yan 結節性聲帶炎
chorditis tuberosa;

sheng diao 聲調
tone of a voice;

sheng diao di chen 聲調低沈
in a low and heavy tone;

sheng diao ji ang 聲調激昂
in an impassioned tone;

sheng dong ji xi 聲東擊西
make noise in the east while striking in the west;

sheng huan 聲喚
call aloud / shout;

sheng qing 聲請
make requests with reasons stated;

sheng rong 聲容
voices and appearances;

sheng ru hong zhong 聲如洪鐘
the voice sounds like a roaring bell;

sheng se 聲色
voice and the facial expression;

sheng se ju li 聲色俱厲
speak in a harsh tone and with a severe expression;

sheng shu 聲述
explain / tell;

sheng shuo 聲説
expound / narrate;

sheng si li jie 聲嘶力竭
the voice gets husky as a result of exhaustion;

sheng tao 聲討
condemn by words;

sheng yan 聲言
announce / claim / declare / profess;

sheng zhang 聲張
announce / publicize;

sheng4 zan 盛讚
pay high compliments / praise profusely;

shi1 kou 失口
a slip of the tongue / say sth improper;

shi sheng 失聲
(1) cry out involuntarily;
(2) lose one's voice;
jing luan xing shi sheng 痙攣性失聲
spastic aphonia;

shi sheng tong ku 失聲痛哭
burst out weeping || be choked with tears; cry in a sad voice; lose control and cry out loud;

shi xiao 失笑
cannot help laughing / laugh in spite of oneself;

shi yan 失言
a slip of the tongue || an improper remark; drop a clanger; make an indiscreet remark; make improper utterances; put one's foot in one's mouth; say what should not be said;

shi yan zhao yuan 失言招怨
cause hatred by reckless words;

shi yin 失音
aphonia;

shi yu 失語
aphasia;
jing luan xing shi yu 痙攣性失語
aphthongia;
yun dong xing shi yu 運動性失語
aphemia;

shi yu zheng 失語症
aphasia;
chu jue xing shi yu zheng 觸覺性失語症
tactile aphasia;
chuan dao xing shi yu zheng 傳導性失語症
conduction aphasia;
gong neng xing shi yu zheng 功能性失語症
functional aphasia;
hun he xing shi yu zheng 混合性失語症
combined aphasia;
ting jue xing shi yu zheng 聽覺性失語症
acoustic aphasia;
wan quan shi yu zheng 完全失語症
complete aphasia;
wan quan xing shi yu zheng 完全性失語症
total aphasia;
yi wang xing shi yu zheng 遺忘性失語症
amnesic aphasia;

yun dong xing shi yu zheng 運動性失語症
logaphasia;
za luan xing shi yu zheng 雜亂性失語症
jargonaphasia;
zhen xing shi yu zheng 真性失語症
true aphasia;
zhi neng xing shi yu zheng 智能性失語症
intellectual aphasia;

shi1 shi 施食
feed the poor;

shi2 xiao er 拾笑兒
join in laughter;

shi2 bu gan wei 食不甘味
eat food without knowing its taste;

shi bu guo fu 食不果腹
have not enough to eat;

shi bu yan jing 食不厭精
meticulous about fine food;

shi er bu hua 食而不化
eat without digesting;

shi liang 食量
quantity of food one consumes;

shi liao 食療
diet therapy / food therapy;

shi shao shi fan 食少事繁
eat little and work a lot;

shi yan 食言
eat one's own words || back out; break one's promise; break one's words; cop out on one's words; fink out; go back on one's word;

shi yan er fei 食言而肥
break faith with sb / break one's promise / fail to make good one's promise;

shi yu 食慾
appetite;

shi2 yan 碩言
boastful talks;

shi2 hua 實話
truth;

shi hua shi shuo 實話實説
talk straight || lay it on the line; not beat about the bush; not to mince words; put it on the line; speak frankly; tell the truth;

shi3 kou 矢口
assert positively || insist emphatically; state categorically; swear; vow;

shi kou bu yi 矢口不移
adhere to one's declaration / stick to one's original statement;

shi kou cheng yan 矢口成言
words uttered become a saying;

shi kou di lai 矢口抵賴
deny flatly || refuse pointblank to admit; refuse to admit even unto death;

shi kou fou ren 矢口否認
deny firmly / flatly deny;

shi kou jiao lai 矢口狡賴
refusing to admit one's guilt || persistently quibble and deny one's errors; quibble and prevaricate;

shi shi 矢誓
take an oath;

shi yan 矢言
make an oath;

shi3 huan 使喚
order others to do sth;

shi jiu 使酒
get drunk and behave irrationally;

shi4 shi sheng yu xiong bian 事實勝於雄辯
facts speak louder than eloquence / facts speak louder than words;

shi4 lun ping yun 恃論平允
pass a fair opinion;

shi4 chang 視唱
sightsinging;

shi4 jiu 嗜酒
be addicted to drinking;

shi4 kou 適口
agreeable to the taste / palatable / pleasant to the palate;

shi4 誓
(1) pledge / swear / vow;
(1) take an oath;

shi bu ba xiu 誓不罷休
swear not to stop;

shi bu gan xiu 誓不甘休
vow never to let the offender get away with it;

shi bu liang li 誓不兩立
vow to fight till oneself or the other party falls;

shi ci 誓詞
oath / pledge;

shi yan 誓言
solemn pledge;

shou3 kou ru ping 守口如瓶
tight-mouthed || as close as an oyster; as dumb as an oyster; as silent as the grave; as silent as the tomb; be buttoned up; be tight-mouthed; breathe not a word of a secret; button up one's lip; button up one's mouth; hold one's cards close to one's chest; keep a calm sough; keep a still tongue in one's head; keep dumb as an oyster; keep mum; keep one's lips buttoned; keep one's mouth closed; keep one's mouth shut; keep one's mouth tight as a jar; keep one's tongue between one's teeth; keep the mouth closed like a bottle; keep the mouth shut as that of a jar; one's lips are sealed; stay tight-lipped; tight-lipped;

shou kou ru ping, fang yi ru cheng 守口如瓶，防意如城
guard your mouth as though it were a vase and guard your thoughts as if you were a city wall;

shou4 ren ba bing 授人把柄
give a handle for / give a handle to / give others sth to talk about oneself;

shou ren kou shi 授人口實
give a handle for / give a handle to / give people a basis for gossip;

shu1 wen 淑問
skillful at questioning;

shu3 luo 數落
give sb a good scolding / hold forth;

shu ma 數罵
enumerate sb's faults / scold sb;

shu shuo 數說
(1) accuse / reproach;
(2) ascertain the number of / count / enumerate;

shu4 shuo 述說
give an account of / narrate / recount / state / tell;

shu4 漱
gargle / rinse;

shu kou 漱口
gargle the throat / rinse the mouth;

shua3 pin zui 耍貧嘴
(1) garrulous / talkative;
(2) joke a great deal;

shua xiao 耍笑
(1) have fun / joke / poke fun at;
(2) make fun of / play a joke on sb;

shua zui pi zi 耍嘴皮子
(1) talk glibly || slick talker; brag; show off one's eloquence;
(2) lip service || mere empty talk; play lip service; talk big;

shuai3 xian hua 甩閒話
complain / grumble;

shuang1 xia ba 雙下巴
double chin;

shuang3 kou 爽口
palatable / tasty / tasty and refreshing;

shui4 說
influence / persuade;

shui fu 說服
convince / persuade;

shun3 吮
lick / suck;

shun4 kou 順口
(1) read fluently / read smoothly;
(2) say without thinking || slip out of one's tongue; speak casually; speak without much thought; talk casually;

shun kou da ying 順口答應
promise casually / promise without hesitation;

shun kou liu 順口溜
doggerel / jingle;

shun zui er 順嘴兒
slip out of one's tongue / speak casually without much thought;

shuo1 說
(1) say / speak / talk / utter // utterance;
(2) clarify / explain;
(3) describe / narrate / state;
(3) teaching / theory;
(4) blame / criticize / scold / talk to;

shuo bai 說白
spoken parts in an opera;

shuo bai dao lü 說白道綠
comment on various things without restraint;

shuo bai le 說白了
put in plain language;

shuo bu chu hua 說不出話
words fail one || cannot utter a word; lose one's tongue; one's tongue fails one // tongue-tied;

shuo bu chu kou 說不出口
unable to speak out / unspeakable / unutterable;

shuo bu de 說不得
(1) unmentionable / unspeakable;
(2) scandalous;

shuo bu ding 說不定
maybe / perhaps / probably;

shuo bu guo 說不過
unable to out-debate / unable to outspeak;

shuo bu guo qu 說不過去
hardly justifiable || cannot be explained away; cannot be justified; doesn't make sense; have no excuse;

shuo bu kai 說不開
unable to reach a mutual understanding;

shuo bu lai 說不來
(1) cannot get along with sb;
(2) unable to speak / unable to utter;

shuo bu qi 說不齊
cannot say for sure;

shuo bu qing 說不清
cannot be explained clearly;

shuo bu qing, dao bu ming 說不清，道不明
it is not sth that one can explain clearly and make people understand;

shuo bu shang 說不上
(1) cannot say / cannot tell;
(2) do not fit the description / not worth mentioning;

shuo bu shang lai 說不上來
not know how to say it || cannot remember it now; cannot tell; unable to get the words out;

shuo bu xia qu 說不下去
(1) unable to continue one's speech;
(2) not acceptable to one's sense of propriety;

shuo chang dao duan 說長道短
gossip idly || backbite people; gossip about pople behind their backs; indulge in idle gossip; make captious comments; random talk; speak ill of a person who is absent;

shuo chang lun duan 說長論短
make captious comments || criticize others; discuss a variety of subjects; gossip idly; indulge in idle gossip;

shuo chu 說出
speak out || reveal; take the words out of sb's mouth; utter;

shuo chuan 說穿
reveal / unravel by some remarks;

shuo ci 說詞
excuse / plea / pretext;

shuo cuo 說錯
say the wrong thing / speak incorrectly;

shuo da hua 說大話
boast || brag; draw the long bow; talk big; talk tall; talk through one's hat; talk wet; tell exaggerated stories;

shuo dao 說到
as to / mention / refer to / speak of;

shuo dao di 說到底
at bottom / at the end of the day / in the final analysis;

shuo dao zuo dao 說到做到
the equal of one's word || as good as one's word; do what one says; live up to one's word; match one's deeds to one's words; match one's words with deeds; practise what one preaches; suit the action to the word;

shuo de bi chang de hao ting 說的比唱的好聽
make empty promises / mouth high-sounding words;

shuo de chu zuo de dao 說得出，做得到
mean what one says ‖ carry out one's pledge; speak and follow through in action;

shuo de dao rong yi 說得倒容易
it's easy to say;

shuo de guo qu 說得過去
acceptable / excusable / pardonable / passable;

shuo de hao 說得好
well said;

shuo de hao ting 說得好聽
use fine-sounding phrases ‖ fine words; make an unpleasant fact sound attractive; says you; talk fine;

shuo de huo ling huo xian 說得活靈活現
give a vivid description / make it come to life / tone sth up with colour and life;

shuo de lai 說得來
able to get along / on good terms;

shuo de shang 說得上
deserve mention;

shuo de tian hua luan zhui 說得天花亂墮
elaborate in high-flown phraseology / give an extravagantly colourful description / talk about sth in superlative terms;

shuo de xia qu 說得下去
passable;

shuo de yi tao, zuo de yi tao 說得一套，做得一套
say one thing but do quite another;

shuo de you li 說得有理
reasonable / sound;

shuo di tan tian 說地談天
(1) talk about everything under the sun;
(2) eloquent / skilled in speech;

shuo ding 說定
agree on / settle;

shuo dong dao xi 說東道西
talk about this and that ‖ chat of everything under the sun; chatter away on a variety of things; gossip; make all kinds of remarks; talk about all sorts of subjects without restraint;

shuo duan dao chang 說短道長
gossip ‖ criticize others; discussion as to who is right and who is wrong;

shuo er bu yi 說二不一
stand by one's word ‖ a man of his word; keep one's promise;

shuo fa 說法
(1) argument / the way of reasoning / the way of saying a thing;
(2) statement / version / wording;

shuo fan hua 說反話
speak an irony;

shuo fang bian 說方便
speak in favour of;

shuo feng liang hua 說風涼話
make sarcastic comments ‖ make cool, sly criticisms; make irresponsible and carping comments; talk like an unconcerned person;

shuo fu 說服
convince / persuade ‖ bring around; bring round; bring over; gain over; get round; prevail on; prevail upon; talk around; talk over; talk round;

shuo fu li 說服力
persuasion ‖ authority; convincingness; force; point; stringency;

shuo gan jiu gan 說幹就幹
act without delay ‖ a word and a blow; let no grasss grow under one's feet; no sooner said than done; not to let grass grow under one's feet;

shuo gao shuo di 說高說低
criticize others thoughtlessly;

shuo gu tan jin 說古談今
talk at random of things past and present / talk over past and present;

shuo gui gui jiu dao 說鬼鬼就到
speak of the devil / talk of the devil and he will appear;

shuo gui hua 說鬼話
lie / tell a fib / tell a lie;

shuo guo tou hua 說過頭話
make thoughtless statements;

shuo hao 說好
agree on / come to an agreement;

shuo hao hua 說好話
put in a good word for sb;

shuo hao shuo dai 說好說歹
use all means of persuasion;

shuo he 說合
(1) bring two parties together;
(2) discuss / talk over;

shuo he 說和
mediate a settlement ‖ act as a mediator; compromise a quarrel; mediate;

shuo hei dao bai 說黑道白
criticize others thoughtlessly / practise groundless criticism;

shuo hua 說話
(1) say / speak / talk;
(2) chat / talk;
(3) gossip / talk;

shuo hua bin bin you li 說話彬彬有禮
keep a civil tongue;

shuo hua bu de ti 說話不得體
sound a false note;

shuo hua bu suan shu 說話不算數
break one's word / fail to keep one's promise / go back on one's word;

shuo hua cu lu 說話粗魯
have a rough tongue;

shuo hua de ti 說話得體
strike the right note;

shuo hua ding yong 說話頂用
one's words carry weight;

shuo hua dou quan zi 說話兜圈子
beat about the bush;

shuo hua feng qu 說話風趣
speak in a humorous vein;

shuo hua jian ke 說話尖刻
have a sharp tongue / have an acid tongue / make aculeate remarks;

shuo hua man 說話慢
drawl;

shuo hua mao shi 說話冒失
have a big mouth;

shuo hua qing shuai 說話輕率
one's tongue is too long for one's teeth;

shuo hua suan shu 說話算數
keep one's word ‖ as good as one's word; honour one's own words; live up to one's word; one means what one says; put one's money where one's mouth is;

shuo hua ting yin, luo gu ting sheng 說話聽音，鑼鼓聽聲
the words are the mirror of one's mind;

shuo hua yuan hua 說話圓滑
have a glib tongue / have a smooth tongue;

shuo hua zhi jian 說話之間
in a short while / while talking;

shuo hua zhong ken 說話中肯
hit the nail on the head / speak to the point;

shuo hua zou huo 說話走火
go too far in what one says / shoot off one's mouth / talk without careful choice of words and overstep limits;

shuo huai hua 說壞話
badmouth sb / speak ill of sb;

shuo huang dao hei 說黃道黑
criticize others / tell lies about this and about that / wantonly slander others;

shuo huang 說謊
lie / tell a lie / tell wild tales;

shuo jiao 說教
(1) deliver a sermon / preach // homily;
(2) expound sth mechanically / talk rubbish;

shuo kai 說開
account for / explain;

shuo kong hua 說空話
empty talk / mere rhetoric / palaver;

shuo kou 說口
boast / exagerrate;

shuo ku dao nan 說苦道難
tell all one's woes;

shuo lai hua chang 說來話長
it's a long story;

shuo lai qi guai 說來奇怪
it's strange / oddly enough / strange to say;

shuo lai rong yi zuo lai nan 說來容易做來難
easier said than done / saying and doing are two things / saying is one thing and doing another;

shuo lai shuo qu 說來說去
after all is said and done ‖ no matter how you put it; say the same thing over and over again; when all is said, the fact remains that...;

shuo lao shi hua 說老實話
frankly speaking ‖ call a spade a spade; speak the truth; tell the truth; to be candid with you; to be frank with you;

shuo le bu suan 說了不算
eat one's words / fail to keep a promise / go back on one's word;

shuo le suan 說了算
have the final say / have the last word;

shuo le suan shu 說了算數
I mean what I say;

shuo li 說理
(1) argue / reason things out;
(2) reasonable;

shuo liang xin hua 說良心話
to be fair / to be frank;

shuo liu le zui 說溜了嘴
inadvertently blurt out / make a slip of the tongue ‖ blurt out; crack the bell; inadvertently blurt out; let slip; let the cat out of the bag; spill the beans;

shuo lou zui 說漏嘴
inadvertently blurt out;

shuo mei ying er de shi 說沒影兒的事
empty talk / mere rhetoric / palaver;

shuo meng hua 說夢話
(1) talk in one's dream / talk in one's sleep;
(2) talk nonsense;

shuo ming 說明
clarify / demonstrate / elucidate / explain / expound / illustrate / show / state;

shuo ming lai yi 說明來意
make clear what one has come for;

shuo ming yuan wei 說明原委
explain why and how;

shuo ming zhen xiang 說明真相
give the facts;

shuo piao liang hua 說漂亮話
offer lip-service // service by words only;

shuo po 說破
expose by some remarks / unravel by some remarks;

shuo po sang men 說破嗓門
talk oneself hoarse;

shuo qi 說起
as for / with regard to ‖ begin talking about; bring up;

shuo qi lai 說起來
as a matter of fact / in fact;

shuo qian dao wan 說千道萬
speak again and again;

shuo qiao pi hua 說俏皮話
jest / make witty remarks / wisecrack;

shuo qin dao re 說親道熱
sound very friendly / with mild and affectionate words;

shuo qing dao bai 說清道白
talk clearly;

shuo qing 說情
intercede for sb / plead for mercy for sb / solicit favour on behalf of others;

shuo san bu jie liang 說三不接兩
talk incoherently;

shuo san dao si 說三道四
make carping comments on / make irresponsible remarks / make thoughtless comments;

shuo shen mo hua 說甚麼話
what are you talking about;

shuo shi chi, na shi kuai 說時遲，那時快
quicker than words can tell ‖ before you can say knife; in less time than it takes to describe it;

shuo shi rong yi zuo shi nan 説時容易做時難
easier said than done;

shuo shi hua 説實話
if truth be told / to come clean with sb / to tell the truth;

shuo shi 説事
(1) negotiate / try to come to an agreement;
(2) explain an idea / expound a theory / make things clear;

shuo shi yi hui shi, zuo shi ling yi hui shi 説是一回事，做是另一回事
to say is one thing, to practise is another;

shuo shi zhe me shuo 説是這麼説
that's what we say;

shuo shu 説書
storytelling / tell stories;

shuo shuai 説要
jest / joke;

shuo shuo er yi 説説而已
just a few casual remarks;

shuo shuo xiao xiao 説説笑笑
have a pleasant talk together / joke and chat freely / jolly along;

shuo si 説死
make it definite;

shuo tian shuo di 説天説地
(1) boast / brag;
(2) be skilled in speech / eloquent;

shuo tong 説通
succeed in reaching an understanding;

shuo tou zhi wei 説頭知尾
if the head were spoken of in a matter, at once he knew the tail also;

shuo tuo 説妥
come to an agreement;

shuo wan 説完
finish speaking;

shuo wu dao liu 説五道六
make thoughtless comments;

shuo xian hua 説閒話
gossip / talk behind sb's back ‖ make idle talk; make unfavourable comments; talk scandal;

shuo xiang 説項
try to persuade ‖ ask leniency or special consideration; intercede for sb; put in a good word for sb;

shuo xiao 説笑
chat and laugh / jape / joke / kid / talk and laugh // persiflage;

shuo xiao da hun 説笑打諢
make all manner of quips and jokes;

shuo xiao hua 説笑話
jape / jest / tell jokes;

shuo xiao jie men 説笑解悶
be engaged in a lively conversation with sb;

shuo xiao qu le 説笑取樂
talk and laugh and seek to enjoy themselves;

shuo xin li hua 説心裏話
speak one's mind;

shuo ye qi guai 説也奇怪
for a wonder / oddly enough;

shuo yi bu er 説一不二
as good as one's word / mean what one says / stand by one's word;

shuo yi shi yi, shuo er shi er 説一是一，説二是二
to say one it is one and to say two it is two / whatever one says goes;

shuo yi xing nan 説易行難
easier said than done;

shuo zhang dao li 説張道李
gossip about this or that person;

shuo zhe shuo na 説這説那
say this and this;

shuo zhen de 説真的
no kidding;

shuo zhen hua 説真話
tell the truth;

shuo zhi bu jin 説之不盡
it is too long a story to tell;

shuo zhi 説知
inform / let sb know / notify;

shuo zhun 説準
it's settled;

shuo zou jiu zou 說走就走
announce the intention to leave and really mean it;

shuo zou le zui 說走了嘴
a slip of the tongue;

shuo zui 說嘴
(1) boast / brag;
(2) argue / quarrel;

si1 hua 私話
confidential talks / secret talks;

si1 tan 私談
talk in private // private talks / confidential talks;

si1 chao 廝吵
quarrel with each other over sth;

si1 嘶
hoarse;

si sheng ai jiao 嘶聲哀叫
cry sadly / wail sadly;

si si sheng 嘶嘶聲
fizz;

si ya 嘶啞
hoarse / hoarse-voiced / husky;

si3 shuo huo shuo 死說活說
persuade by all means;

si4 xiao fei xiao 似笑非笑
with a half-smile;

si4 kou 肆口
talk without much thought;

si kou da ma 肆口大罵
abuse sb outrageously and without any restraint;

si kou man ma 肆口漫罵
rail and swear at wildly || swear home; swear like a lord; swear one's way through a stone wall; use profane language freely;

si yan li ru 肆言詈辱
abuse outrageously and without any restraint / swear wildly;

si yin 肆飲
indulge in drinking;

song1 kou 鬆口
(1) relax a bite;
(2) show a degree of flexibility in negotiating;

song4 yan 訟言
announce / declare;

song4 頌
(1) acclaim / eulogize / extol / laud / praise;
(2) eulogy / hymn / ode;
(3) express good wishes;

song ci 頌詞
complimentary address / congratulatory speech / eulogy;

song ge 頌歌
hymn / ode / song;

song gu fei jin 頌古非今
eulogize the past and condemn the present || admire everything ancient and belittle present-day achievements; eulogize the ancient while disparaging the modern; eulogize the past at the expense of the present; extol the past to negate the present; praise the ancient and attack the present; praise the past and deplore the present;

song gu fei jin 頌古誹今
denounce the present and extol the past / praise the past to condemn the present;

song mei 頌美
acclaim / praise the achievements of others;

song sheng zai dao 頌聲載道
praises all along the way;

song shi 頌詩
eulogistic poem;

song yang 頌揚
acclaim / eulogize / exalt / extol / laud / praise / sing sb's praises // exaltation;

song yang bei zhi 頌揚備致
laud...to the skies / praise profusely;

song zan 頌讚
acclaim / praise;

song4 誦
(1) chant / intone / read aloud / recite;
(2) poem / song;

song du 誦讀
chant / intone / read aloud / recite;

song jing 誦經
recite passages from scriptures;

song shi 誦詩
intone a verse / recite a poem;

song shuo 誦説
read and explain;

song xi 誦習
learn by recitation;

sou4 漱
(1) gargle / rinse;
(2) wash;

sou di 漱滌
rinse / wash;

sou kou 漱口
gargle the throat / rinse the mouth;

su2 hua 俗話
common sayings;

su4 kou ma ren 素口罵人
eat vegetables but freely use abusive language || a religious man swears;

su4 zui 宿醉
hangover / morning after;

su4 da 速答
reply promptly;

su shi pi 速食癖
excessively fast eating / tachyphasia;

su4 訴
(1) inform / relate / tell;
(2) accuse / charge / complain / file a complaint;
(3) appeal to / petition / resort to;

su ku 訴苦
air one's grievances / complain about one's grievances / pour out grievance / pour out one's woes / vent one's grievances;

su ku qiong er 訴苦窮兒
tell others of one's state of poverty;

su ku su yuan 訴苦訴冤
voice one's grievances and state the wrong;

su ku su yuan 訴苦訴怨
air one's grievances / pour out one's discontent and grievances;

su shuo 訴説
air grievances / complain / narrate / recount / relate / whine;

su shuo ku zhong 訴説苦衷
recount one's worries and difficulties / tell one's troubles;

su yuan 訴冤
complain about grievances / state injustice;

su yuan tu hen 訴怨吐恨
complain of one's untold misery and pour out one's wrath;

su zhu 訴諸
appeal to / resort to;

su zhu gong lun 訴諸公論
appeal to public opinion / appeal to verdict of the masses;

su zhu wu li 訴諸武力
appeal to arms / resort to force || betake oneself to arms; have recourse to force; resort to the use of force; resort to violence;

sui2 kou 隨口
blurt out whatever comes into one's head / slip off one's tongue without much thought / speak without thinking;

sui kou da ying 隨口答應
agree without thinking / promise at once without hesitation;

sui kou er chu 隨口而出
escape sb's lips / fall from sb's lips;

sui sheng fu he 隨聲附和
agree to what other people say / echo what others say || chime in with others; echo this line; follow others' lead in voicing opinion; swell the chorus;

sui4 誶
reproach / scold / upbraid;

sui ma 誶罵
reproach / scold / upbraid;

suo1 唆
abet / incite / instigate;

suo nong 唆弄
incite / instigate;

suo nong shi fei 唆弄是非
sow discord;

suo ren zuo e 唆人作惡
instigate others to do evil things / lead people astray;

suo shi 唆使
abet / incite / instigate;

ta4 ta duo yan 沓沓多言
garrulous / talkative;

tai1 gang 擡槓
argue for the sake of arguing / bicker / quarrel / wrangle;

tan1 bei 貪杯
indulge in drinking // liquorish;

tan chi 貪吃
eat piggishly / make a pig of oneself // gluttonous;

tan chi lan zuo 貪吃懶做
greedy of eating and lazy in doing work / lazy glutton;

tan shi 貪食
bulimia;

shen jing xing tan shi 神經性貪食
bulimia nervosa;

tan shi pi 貪食癖
phagomania;

tan shi zheng 貪食症
bulimia;

tan zui 貪嘴
gluttonous / greedy / piggish;

tan2 談
(1) chat / discuss / talk;
(2) what is said or talked about;

tan bing 談柄
butt / joke;

tan bu dao 談不到
out of the question;

tan bu shang 談不上
out of the question;

tan dao 談到
refer to / speak of / talk about;

tan de lai 談得來
get along well with sb;

tan de tou ji 談得投機
have a nice chat / have a very pleasant talk;

tan feng 談鋒
eloquence ‖ incisiveness of speech; thread of discourse; volubility;

tan feng shen jian 談鋒甚健
have the gift of the gab ‖ a good talker; loquacious; talk volubly;

tan feng xi li 談鋒犀利
incisive in conversation;

tan gu shuo jin 談古說今
talk over past and present ‖ discourse at random of things past and present;

tan he rong yi 談何容易
by no means easy ‖ easier said than done; easy to talk, difficult to achieve; how easy it is to talk about it; it's no easy thing; not as easy as it sounds; not as easy as one thinks it to be;

tan hu se bian 談虎色變
pale even at the mention of the name of / turn pale at the mention of a tiger — become jittery at the mention of sth frightful;

tan hua 談話
chat / converse / converse with / state / talk // chat / colloquy / conversation / talk;

tan ji 談及
talk about;

tan jia chang 談家常
engage in small talk ‖ chitchat; talk about everyday matters;

tan kong shuo you 談空說有
get together and chat / talk speculative philosophy;

tan lian ai 談戀愛
in love;

tan lun 談論
discuss / speak about / talk about;

tan pan 談判
negotiation / talk;

tan pan tiao jian 談判條件
bargaining power;

tan qi 談起
mention / speak of;

tan qing shuo ai 談情說愛
be concerned with love and romance || bill and coo; chat intimately; love and romance; talk love;

tan si fang hua 談私房話
confide one's secrets to sb / exchange confidences;

tan tan 談談
have a chat;

tan tian 談天
chat / make conversation;

tan tian shuo di 談天說地
gossip and chat || bat the breeze; chat about all sorts of subjects; chat idly; fan the breeze; shoot the breeze; talk of anything under the sun;

tan tu 談吐
the manner of speaking / the style of conversation / the way a person talks;

tan tu ben zhuo 談吐笨拙
do not shine in conversation;

tan tu feng ya 談吐風雅
a person of pleasing address / an eloguent speaker;

tan tu gao ya 談吐高雅
have a refined style of conversation;

tan tu wen ya 談吐文雅
have a refined style of conversation / one's talk is elegant / talk in polite and cultivated language // fair-spoken;

tan tu you mo 談吐幽默
talk with a sense of humour;

tan xiao feng huo 談笑封侯
obtain a high rank easily / rise in the world with great ease;

tan xiao feng sheng 談笑風生
in merry conversation // talk cheerfully and humorously || a charming personality with a valuable humorous tongue and winsome blossom-like smiles; intersperse a speech with humorous remarks; joke and chat freely; needle a speech with humour; play the conversation in a gay manner; talk and laugh cheerfully; talk in a jovial mood; there is sth charming about the way one talks and smiles;

tan xiao ru qian 談笑如前
talk and laugh together precisely as in days gone by;

tan xiao xi xue 談笑戲謔
chat and jest;

tan xiao zhi zhong cun zhi li 談笑之中存至理
many a true word is spoken in a jest;

tan xiao zi ruo 談笑自若
be perfectly composed / go on talking and laughing as if nothing has happened;

tan xin 談心
have a heart-to-heart talk / have a serious and intimate discussion // heart-to-heart;

tan yan wei zhong 談言微中
be able to satirize aptly / make one's point through hints / speak tactfully but to the point;

tan2 kou 檀口
the red lips of a pretty girl;

tan4 wen 探問
inquire about / inquire after;

tan e 歎愕
exclaim in surprise / exclaim in wonder;

tan fu 歎服
praise and admire;

tan jia 歎嘉
eulogize / extol / glorify / praise;

tan mei 歎美
praise;

tan qi 歎氣
sigh;

tan shang 歎傷
lament;

tan shang 歎賞
praise and admire;

tan wan 歎惋
sigh in lamentation / sigh with regret;

tan xi 歎惜
sigh with regret;

tan xi 歎息
sigh;

tan yi kou qi 歎一口氣
heave a sigh;

tang3 kou shui 淌口水
drivel / drool;

tao1 tao bu jue 滔滔不絕
talk without cease || a flood of words; an unceasing flow of words; exhaust oneself by talking; flow on without stopping; hold forth; pour out words like a flood; shoot off one's mouth; spout eloquent speeches; talk a horse's hind legs off; talk away; talk fluently and endlessly; talk nineteen to the dozen; talk oneself out of breath;

tao tao shan bian 滔滔善辯
eloquent / skilled in debating;

tao tao xiong bian 滔滔雄辯
a torrent of eloquence // eloquent;

tao2 dan 陶誕
cheat / swindle;

tao3 fan 討飯
beg one's bread;

tao jia huan jia 討價還價
bargain / chaffer over price / dicker for / haggle over prices / palter;

tao lun 討論
discuss // discussion;

tao4 hua 套話
cliché;

tao wen 套問
tactfully sound sb out;

teng2 xiao 騰笑
arouse laughter;

teng xiao hai nei 騰笑海內
be laughed at in the whole country;

teng xiao wan fang 騰笑萬方
cause a laughter everywhere;

ti1 wen 擿問
interrogate;

ti2 啼
(1) cry / weep aloud;
(2) caw / crow;

ti ji hao han 啼飢號寒
cry out from hunger and cold || howl for being hungry and cry for feeling cold; lament in hunger and cold; wail with hunger and cold;

ti jiao 啼叫
scream / screech / wail;

ti qi 啼泣
sob / wail;

ti xiao jie fei 啼笑皆非
one does not know whether to laugh or to cry || between tears and laughter; choke sb up; find sth both funny and annoying; unable to cry or laugh;

ti2 提
bring forward / mention / propose / suggest;

ti chu 提出
propose / put forward / raise / suggest;

ti dao 提到
bring up / mention / put to;

ti ji 提及
mention;

ti qi 提起
bring up / mention / refer to / speak of;

ti qing 提請
propose;

ti wen 提問
ask a question / put questions to / quiz;

ti yi 提議
propose || move; propound; put forth suggestions; suggest // proposition;

tian1 fan 添飯
have another bowl of rice;

tian2 mei sang yin 甜美嗓音
sweet voice;

tian wei bing 甜味病
saccharine disease;

tian yan mi yu 甜言蜜語
sweet words and honeyed phrases || an oily tongue; coax with delusive promise; fine-sounding words; glib talk; goo; honeyed

words; honey-lipped; honey-mouthed; honey-sweet words; honey-tongued; smooth-tongued; soft words; sugar plum; sugary words; sweet talk; tidbits;

tian3 yan er yan 腆顏而言
speak with a bashful countenance;

tiao1 chi jian he 挑吃揀喝
choose one's food;

tiao2 kan 調侃
jeer / mock / scoff;

tiao suo 調唆
incite / instigate;

tiao suo shi fei 調唆是非
stir up trouble;

tiao xi 調息
regulate one's breath;

tiao xiao 調笑
make fun of / tease;

tiao xiao wei le 調笑為樂
take pleasure in jeering;

tiao zui xue she 調嘴學舌
carry tales / tell tales || cause alienation by spreading rumours; gossip; speak ill of sb behind his back; stir up enmity; tittle-tattle;

tie3 zui 鐵嘴
accurate judgment / accurate prediction;

ting1 jue xing shi yu zheng 聽覺性失語症
acoustic aphasia;

tong1 feng bao xin 通風報信
tip off // tip-off;

tong hua 通話
(1) call / communicate by telephone / message;
(2) converse / hold conversation / talk with sb;

tong su yu yan 通俗語言
lay language;

tong zhi 通知
inform / let sb know / notice / notify;

tong2 ri er yu 同日而語
mention in equal terms;

tong sheng xiang yin 同聲相應
act in unison;

tong sheng xiang yin, tong qi xiang qiu 同聲相應，同氣相求
like attracts like || like calls to like; like draws to like; like to like; like will to like; similar sounds echo one another, and the same odour merge together — people of an inclination fall into the same group;

tong sheng yi ku 同聲一哭
share the same feeling of grief;

tong4 chi 痛斥
give sb the rough edge of one's tongue / give sb the sharp edge of one's tongue / inveigh / light into / scathe / scold severely;

tong di 痛詆
berate / revile / vituperate;

tong feng yin shi 痛風飲食
gouty diet;

tong jia chi ze 痛加斥責
scold sharply / take sb to task;

tong ku 痛哭
weep bitterly;

tong ku liu ti 痛哭流涕
shed tears in bitter sorrow;

tong ma 痛罵
berate / burn sb's ears / execrate / give sb a good dressing down / revile / sail in // invective;

tong ma yi dun 痛罵一頓
break into a torrent of abuse at sb;

tong yin 痛飲
drink to one's heart's content / quaff / swig;

tong ze 痛責
lash out / scold severely;

tou1 zui 偷嘴
steal food / take food on the sly;

tou2 qi zhi tan 投契之談
congenial talk / heart-to-heart talk;

tu2 fei kou she 徒費口舌
waste one's breath;

tu ge 徒歌
sing without accompaniment of any musical instrument;

tu hu fu fu 徒呼負負
exclaim in disappointment for having achieved nothing;

tu tuo kong yan 徒託空言
render lip service;

tu4 吐
(1) utter;
(2) vomit;

tu chu 吐出
disgorge;

tu lu 吐露
confess / disclose / reveal / tell;

tu lu xin shi 吐露心事
pour out one's heart;

tu lu zhen qing 吐露真情
unbosom oneself || come out with the truth; tell the truth;

tu lu zhong qu 吐露衷曲
outpour one's heart / unbosom oneself || come out with the truth; come out with what is in one's heart of hearts;

tu tan 吐痰
spit / spit phlegm;

tu xie 吐瀉
vomiting and diarrhoea / vomiting and purging;
xia ji tu xie 夏季吐瀉
summer cholera;

tui1 ci 推辭
decline;

tui wei 推諉
make excuses // run-around;

tui wen 推問
interrogate;

tui xu 推許
praise;

tun1 吞
gulp / swallow;

tun fu 吞服
take medicine;

tun sheng 吞聲
gulp down one's sobs / swallow one's sobs;

tun sheng ren lei 吞聲忍淚
choke down one's tears;

tun sheng yin qi 吞聲飲泣
gulp down one's sobs / sob bitterly / swallow the voice and tears;

tun shi 吞食
devour / gollop / swallow;

tun shi 吞噬
devour / engulf / gobble up / swallow;

tun tu 吞吐
(1) swallow and spit;
(2) take in and send out in large quantities;

tun tun tu tu 吞吞吐吐
mince words || halt; hem and haw; hesitate in speech; hum and haw; mutter and mumble; prunes and prism; say hesitantly; speak in a halting way; speak of things with scruple; speak with reservation; stumble over one's words; tick over;

tun yan kun nan 吞咽困難
dysphagia;
jing luan xing tun yan kun nan 痙攣性吞咽困難
dysphagia spastica;
ma bi xing tun yan kun nan 麻痺性吞咽困難
dysphagia paralytica;
yan xing tun yan kun nan 炎性吞咽困難
dysphagia inflammatoria;

tun yun tu wu 吞雲吐霧
smoke tobacco || blow a cloud — smoke tabacco; puff; smoke; smoke opium; take puffs;

tuo1 ci 託辭
make excuses;

tuo yan 託言
make excuses;

tuo zhi kong yan 託之空言
give empty promises / pay lip service;

tuo1 kou cheng zhang 脱口成章
speak beautifully;

tuo kou er chu 脱口而出
slip out of one's lips || a ready tongue; being quick with one's tongue; blurt out; bolt; come

in pat; escape one's lips; let slip; one's tongue runs before one's wit; pass one's lips; say sth unwittingly; say the first thing that comes into one's head; speak by impulse;

tuo xia ba 脫下巴
dislocated jaw;

tuo2 詑
cheat;

tuo4 唾
(1) spittle / saliva;
(2) spit;

tuo ma 唾罵
revile / spit on and curse;

tuo mian zi gan 唾面自乾
drain the cup of humiliation;

tuo qi 唾棄
cast aside / disdain and reject;

tuo ye 唾液
saliva;

tuo ye guo duo 唾液過多
hypersalivation;

tuo ye guo shao 唾液過少
hyposialosis;

tuo ye jian shao 唾液減少
hyposalivation;

tuo ye que fa 唾液缺乏
aptyalism;

wa1 哇
(1) the sound of vomiting;
(2) cry / make a crying sound / the sound of crying by a child;

wa la 哇啦
din / hullabaloo / uproar;

wa la wa la 哇啦哇啦
a hubbub of voices / gabble away / make a hullabaloo / prate;

wa wa 哇哇
cry / make a crying sound;

wa wa da ku 哇哇大哭
cry very loudly;

wa1 ku 挖苦
ridicle / make sarcastic remarks;

wa ku hua 挖苦話
ironical remarks / verbal thrusts;

wai1 zui 歪嘴
(1) wry mouth;
(2) wry-mouthed;

wan2 quan shi yu zheng 完全失語症
complete aphasia;

wan2 er hua 玩兒話
joke;

wan hua 玩話
joke;

wan xiao 玩笑
joke;

wan xiao hua 玩笑話
persiflage;

wan3 ci 婉辭
(1) gentle wording;
(2) decline with great courtesy;

wan quan 婉勸
persuade gently;

wan shang 婉商
discuss with great courtesy;

wan xie 婉謝
decline with thanks;

wan yan 婉言
(1) gentle words / tactful expressions;
(2) speak tenderly;

wan yan ju jue 婉言拒絕
(1) polite refusal;
(2) decline with entreaties / refuse politely;

wan yan xiang quan 婉言相勸
gently persuade / plead tactfully;

wan yan xie jue 婉言謝絕
(1) polite refusal;
(2) decline...with thanks / graciously decline / politely refuse / refuse with thanks;

wan3 莞
smiling;

wan er 莞爾
smile;

wan er yi xiao 莞爾一笑
(1) slight smile;

(2) give a soft smile;

wang3 re ren xiao 枉惹人笑
this would make the people laugh at someone;

wang3 xia shuo 往下說
talk on;

wang4 kuo ba she 妄口巴舌
blasphemous talks / wild talks;

wang yan 妄言
(1) talk nonsense / tell lies;
(2) rant / wild talk;

wang yan wang ting 妄言妄聽
both to speak and hear absurdly / don't take it too seriously;

wang yu 妄語
(1) talk nonsense / tell lies;
(2) rant / wild talk;

wang yu xu ci 妄語虛詞
wild talks and vain words;

wang4 shi 忘食
so busy as to forget mealtime;

wei1 yan song ting 危言聳聽
exaggerate things just to scare people || an alarmist talk; make an inflammatory statement; raise a false alarm; say frightening things just to raise an alarm;

wei yan wei xing 危言危行
cautious speech and conduct;

wei1 bian 微辯
hint by sarcastic remarks;

wei bu zu dao 微不足道
nothing to speak of;

wei wei yi xiao 微微一笑
give a wee smile;

wei xiao 微笑
smile;

wei yan ta yi 微言大義
subtle words with profound meanings;

wei zui 微醉
be moist around the edges / have an edge on / have had a glass too much // slightly drunken / tiddly;

wei3 wan yu qi 委婉語氣
mild tone;

wei3 wei 娓娓
talk tirelessly;

wei wei er tan 娓娓而談
talk effusively / talk volubly || talk familiarly on and on;

wei3 wei lian sheng 唯唯連聲
assent meekly;

wei3 諉
evade / shirk;

wei guo 諉過
lay the blame on others;

wei wei bu zhi 諉為不知
pretend not to know;

wei4 ren shuo xiang 為人說項
say a good word for sb;

wen1 yan ruan yu 溫言軟語
with mild and affectionate words;

wen3 吻
kiss;

wen bie 吻別
kiss sb goodbye;

wen4 問
(1) ask;
(2) ask after / inquire after;
(3) examine / interrogate;
(4) hold responsible;

wen an 問安
pay one's respect / send greetings / wish sb good health;

wen an shi shan 問安視膳
take good care of one's parents;

wen an 問案
hear a case / hold court / try a case;

wen bu 問卜
consult fortunetellers / seek guidance from divination;

wen chang wen duan 問長問短
ask sb all sorts of questions / ask about this and that || ask a thousand and one things; ask all manner of questions; ask sb about the length and breadth of various things; ask sb

the whys and wherefores; inquisitive; make detailed inquires;

wen da 問答

(1) conversation;

(2) dialogue;

(3) questions and answers;

wen dao yu mang 問道於盲

ask a blind man for directions / ask the blind to show the way / the blind leading the blind;

wen dong wen xi 問東問西

ask all sorts of questions;

wen duan 問短

make sb unable to answer;

wen han wen nuan 問寒問暖

solicitous for sb's welfare || ask about sb's needs; ask after sb's health with deep concern; inquire with concern about sb's well-being; see to the comfort of sb;

wen hao 問好

send one's regards to || ask after; extend greetings to; say hello to;

wen hou 問候

ask after / extend greetings to / inquire after / send one's regards to;

wen hua 問話

ask questions;

wen ji 問疾

visit and console a patient;

wen jia 問價

shop around;

wen jin 問津

make inquiries;

wen ming 問明

ask for explicit answers / find out the details;

wen ming di xi 問明底細

find out the details of the case;

wen ming yuan wei 問明原委

find out the origin of an affair;

wen nan 問難

ask difficult questions in a debate / question and argue repeatedly;

wen qing di xi 問清底細

find out the exact details of the case / get to the bottom of the matter / make sure of every detail;

wen ti 問題

(1) case / issue / matter / point / problem / question / subject / thing ;

(2) defect / drawback / error / fault / mistake / trouble;

wen ti cheng dui 問題成堆

a batch of questions / be weighed down with all sorts of problems;

wen ti de he xin 問題的核心

heart of the matter;

wen ti er tong 問題兒童

problem child;

wen ti shao nian 問題少年

juvenile delinquent / problem youth;

wen ti xing wei 問題行為

problem behaviour;

wen xin wu kui 問心無愧

with a clear conscience || examine oneself and find nothing to be ashamed of; feel a twinge of conscience; feel guilty; feel no qualms about; free from any compunction; have a clear conscience; have a guilty conscience; have nothing to be ashamed of; have nothing on one's conscience; have sth on one's conscience; peace of conscience;

wen xin wu kui, gao zhen wu you 問心無愧，高枕無憂

a good conscience is a constant feast / a good conscience is a soft pillow;

wen xin you kui 問心有愧

feel guilty || feel a twinge of conscience; feel a twinge of remorse; have a guilty conscience; have sth on one's conscience; pangs of conscience for;

wen xun 問訊

(1) ask / enquire;

(2) send one's regards to;

wen zhe wen na 問這問那

ask about this and that;

wen zhen 問診

the method of interrogation in Chinese medical diagnosis;

wen zhu 問住
unable to answer a question asked;

wen zui 問罪
call a person to account || condemn; denounce; rebuke; reprimand; reprove;

wen zui zhi shi 問罪之師
an army for punitive purpose;

wu1 yan hui yu 污言穢語
bestial words / expletive / off-colour language;

wu1 zui hei mei 烏嘴黑眉
dark in complexion;

wu1 誣
accuse falsely / bring a false charge against sb;

wu bang 誣謗
libel / slander;

wu fu 誣服
plead guilty when one is not;

wu gao 誣告
accuse falsely / bring a false charge against;

wu hai 誣害
accuse falsely;

wu lai 誣賴
accuse falsely / incriminate falsely / slander;

wu liang wei chang 誣良為娼
charge a virtuous woman with prostitution;

wu liang wei dao 誣良為盜
bring a false charge of theft against an upright man / charge an innocent man with robbery;

wu mie 誣衊
caluminiate / libel / slander / smear / vilify;

wu mie gou xian 誣衊構陷
calumniate and implicate;

wu nie dao qie 誣捏盜竊
trump up a charge of burglary;

wu nie shi shi 誣捏事實
fabricate a false story;

wu ran 誣染
libel / slander;

wu wang 誣罔
accuse falsely;

wu xian 誣陷
frame sb / incriminate falsely;

wu zheng 誣證
(1) perjury;
(2) give false testimony;

wu2 yong hui yan 毋庸諱言
there's no need for reticence || it is no secret that; needless to cover up; no need for reticence; to be frank;

wu yong zhui shu 毋庸贅述
it is pointless to belabour the obvious / need not enlarge upon it / there is no need to go into details;

wu yong zhui yan 毋庸贅言
need not go into the details / no need to repeat it;

wu2 bing shen yin 無病呻吟
groan for no reason / complain without a cause;

wu chi lan yan 無恥讕言
shameless slander || brazen lie; impudent and tendentious allegations; shameless babblings;

wu hua bu tan 無話不談
chat with sb without reserve || in each other's confidence; keep no secrets from each other; tell one another everything;

wu hua ke da 無話可答
at a loss for words / have no fitting reply to make / have no words to answer / have nothing to say in reply;

wu hua ke shuo 無話可說
there is nothing one can say || can say nothing more; cannot think of anything to say; find nothing to say; have nothing to say;

wu hua ze duan, you hua ze chang 無話則短，有話則長
if nothing more happens the story will be short, if events come, it will be long;

wu ji zhi tan 無稽之談
sheer nonsense || absurd view; baseless gossip; Canterbury tale; clotted nonsense; cock-and-bull story; cooked-up story; fable; fabrication; false tale; fantastic talk; fiction; fishy story; groundless statement; groundless utterances; rumours; tale of a tub; traveller's tale; unfounded talk; wild talk;

wu ke bian bo 無可辯駁
beyond all dispute || incontrovertible; indisputable; irrefragable / irrefutable; unanswerable; unchallengeable;

wu ke ci yi 無可疵議
nothing to object to;

wu ke fei yi 無可非議
above reproach || beyond challenge; blameless; irreproachable; not blameworthy; reproachless; unimpeachable; unobjectionable; unquestionable; without rebuke;

wu ke feng gao 無可奉告
have nothing to say // no comment;

wu ke fou ren 無可否認
cannot be denied || it is not to be denied that; there is no denying // undeniable;

wu ke hui yan 無可諱言
beyond all question / beyond doubt || indisputable; past dispute; there's no denying the fact; there's no hiding the fact;

wu ke zheng bian 無可爭辯
admit of no dispute / beyond dispute || beyond all question; incontestable; indisputable; irrefutable; past dispute; unarguable; undeniable; unimpeachable; unquestionable; without dispute; without question;

wu ke zheng yi 無可爭議
beyond controversy / indisputable / unarguable;

wu ke zi yi 無可訾議
above criticism / unimpeachable;

wu kou 無口
astomia;

wu liao zhi tan 無聊之談
milk and water / silly talk // talk all the time about nonsense;

wu lun 無論
not to mention the fact that / to say nothing of;

wu rong hui yan 無容諱言
need not conceal mentioning / not to mince words / straightforward;

wu suo bu tan 無所不談
say one's say / talk about everything under the sun;

wu yan ke da 無言可答
nothing to say in reply || at a loss for word; can say no more and be silent; have no word to answer; have not a word to say in return; speechless with embarrassment;

wu yan ke hui 無言可諱
undeniable;

wu yan yi dui 無言以對
have nothing to say in reply;

wu yi wei da 無以為答
unable to answer;

wu yi wei dui 無以為對
do not know how to reply;

wu yi yi 無異議
unanimous / without a dissenting vocie;

wu yong duo yan 無庸多言
need scarcely say;

wu yong hui yan 無庸諱言
frank // no need for reticence;

wu yong xi shu 無庸細述
there is no need to go into details / this need not be related in detail;

wu yong zhi hui 無庸置喙
brook no intervention / not allow others to butt in / not be allowed to meddle in;

wu zheng zhi yan 無徵之言
unfounded assertion / baseless talk;

wu3 ma 侮罵
insult with words;

wu4 yi 物議
public censure / public criticisms;

wu yi fei teng 物議沸騰
popular cirticisms are boiling;

wu4 ge 晤歌
sing face to face;

wu shang 晤商
negotiate face to face;

wu tan 晤談
converse / discuss face to face / meet and talk;

wu yan 晤言
meet and talk;

wu4 du 誤讀
(1) mispronounce;
(2) misread;

wu yi 誤譯
mistranslate // mistranslation;

xi1 吸
absorb / breathe / inhale / suck;

xi du 吸毒
be addicted to narcotics / take acid // behind acid;

xi shi 吸食
suck / take in;

xi shun 吸吮
absorb / suck;

xi yan 吸煙
smoke;

xi1 bang 息謗
silence slanders;

xi chuan 息喘
pant;

xi1 luo 奚落
gibe / jeer at / laugh at / make a fool of / scoff at / taunt // a smack in the eye / a smack in the face;

xi luo yi fan 奚落一番
make sarcastic remarks against sb / scoff at sb / take a dig at sb;

xi1 xu 欷歔
sigh / sob;

xi xu liu ti 欷歔流涕
shed tears / sigh and sob;

xi1 xiao 熙笑
laugh happily;

xi1 嘻
laughing happily;

xi pi xiao lian 嘻皮笑臉
grin cheekily / laughing in a frolicsome manner;

xi xi 嘻嘻
laughing happily;

xi xi ha ha 嘻嘻哈哈
giggling / laughing and joking || laughing and talking happily; mirthful; run on; tittering with joy;

xi xiao 嬉笑
giggle / laugh merrily / laughing and playing / mischievous smile / playful / playsome / titter;

xi xiao nu ma 嬉笑怒罵
making fun of and cursing angrily — write freely;

xi xiao yan kai 嬉笑顏開
wild with joy;

xi xiao zi ruo 嬉笑自若
laughing and playing just as if one were in one's own home;

xi1
brawl / quarrel / squabble;

xi3 xiao yan kai 喜笑顏開
brimming with smiles;

xi3 諰
speak frankly;

xi4 du 細讀
read carefully;

xi jiang 細講
state in detail;

xi lun 細論
discuss in detail / elaborate;

xi sheng 細聲
a very low voice;

xi sheng si qi 細聲細氣
in a soft voice / soft-spoken;

xi shu 細述
give a detailed account / state in detail;

xi shuo 細説
give a detailed account / state in detail;

xi shuo ben mo 細説本末
recount the developments from the beginning;

xi tan 細談
talk in detail;

xi wen 細問
question in detail;

xi xu ku qing 細敘苦情
narrate one's bitter feeling in detail;

xi yu 細語
low and tender talk;

xi4 nüe 戲謔
jest / joke / persiflage / witticism;

xi yan 戲言
jest / joke / persiflage / witticism;

xia1 瞎
recklessly;

xia che 瞎扯
natter / talk recklessly // flapdoodle;

xia chui 瞎吹
brag;

xia hua 瞎話
flapdoodle / natter / nonsensical remarks;

xia liao 瞎聊
chat idly / natter;

xia peng 瞎捧
heap praises on sb blindly;

xia san hua si 瞎三話四
reckless talk / talk nonsense;

xia shuo 瞎說
speak groundlessly || blow it out your ear; natter; talk irresponsibly; talk nonsense; talk rubbish;

xia shuo ba dao 瞎說八道
make reckless utterances || talk nonsense; talk through one's hat; tell lies;

xia shuo yi dun 瞎說一頓
nonsensical talk / talk about sth useless / talk nonsense;

xia zou 瞎謅
natter / speak groundlessly;

xia4 ba 下巴
(1) lower jaw;
(2) chin;
shuang xia ba 雙下巴
double chin;
tuo xia ba 脫下巴
dislocated jaw;
xiang hou xue de xia ba 向後削的下巴
retreating chin;

xia ba wo 下巴窩
dimple in the chin;

xia e 下顎
lower jaw;

xia e gu 下顎骨
lower jaw bone / mandible;

xia e gu zhe 下顎骨折
mandibular;

xia e tuo wei 下顎脫位
dislocation of the lower jaw;

xia jiu 下酒
to go with wine;

xia wen 下問
learn from one's inferior;

xia yan 下嚥
gulp down / swallow;

xia ji tu xie 夏季吐瀉
summer cholera;

xia liu hua 下流話
dirty language / foul language / obscene language / vulgar language;

xian2 涎
saliva;

xian mo 涎沫
saliva;

xian2 che 閒扯
chat / chew the fat / engage in chit-chat / prattle // chat / chin music / chinwag;

xian hua 閒話
(1) chat / chinwag / chitchat / digression;
(2) complaint;
(3) gossip;
(4) chat about;

xian hua gu jin 閒話古今
talk casually about the past and present;

xian hua shao shuo 閒話少說
cut the cackle || let's get back to the subject; save your breath to cool your porridge;

xian hua shao shuo, yan gui zheng zhuan 閒話少說，言歸正傳
enough of this digression, and back to the true story || enough of this digression, let's return to our story; put aside all idle talk

and tell only the true story; return from a digression;

xian hua xiu ti 閒話休提
return from the digression;

xian ke da ya 閒磕打牙
chat without a purpose;

xian liao 閒聊
chat / chew the fat / chew the rag / natter // chitchat / gab / gabble / gossip / natter;

xian liao suo shi 閒聊瑣事
have a good gossip on trivial matters;

xian tan 閒談
chat || chew the fat; chinwag; chitchat; confabulate; engage in chitchat / gab / natter;

xian xiao 閒笑
pleasant chatter;

xian yan 閒言
(1) gossip / idle talk / small talk;
(2) balderdash;

xian yan shao xu 閒言少敘
make a long story;

xian yan sui yu 閒言碎語
gossip;

xian yan xian yu 閒言閒語
gossip / sarcastic complaints / sarcastic remarks / small talk;

xian yu 閒語
(1) personal talk;
(2) gossip / sarcastic remarks;

xian2 yu ci ling 嫻於辭令
eloquent / gifted with a silver tongue / skilled in speech;

xian4 bian xian chang 現編現唱
make up a song as one sings;

xiang1 gao 相告
pass information / tell;

xiang ma 相罵
abuse each other / revile each other;

xiang quan 相勸
offer advice / persuade;

xiang shang 相商
confer / consult / exchange views;

xiang tan 相談
converse / talk together;

xiang ti bing lun 相提並論
mention (two things or persons) in the same breath;

xiang1 yin 鄉音
local accent / one's native accent;

xiang2 tan 詳談
go into details / speak in detail;

xiang wen shi mo 詳問始末
enter into the details of the beginning and end;

xiang yan zhi 詳言之
state in detail and particular;

xiang3 liang 響亮
resonant / sonorous;

xiang4 hou xue de xia ba 向後削的下巴
retreating chin;

xiang4 sheng 相聲
comic dialogue / cross talk;

xiao1 囂
clamour / hubbub / noise;

xiao bang 囂謗
be slandered by others;

xiao3 ma da bang mang 小罵大幫忙
a few verbal attacks but a major help in deeds || attack on minor issues and support on major ones; criticize in a small way and help in a big way; minor attack but major help; minor attacks in words but major help in deeds;

xiao sheng 小聲
lower one's voice / speak low;

xiao zui 小嘴
hypostomia;

xiao4 笑
laugh || cachinnate; cackle; chortle; chuckle; crack one's face; deride; giggle; grin; guffaw; have them rolling in the aisle; horselaugh; knock them in the aisles; laugh one's head off; laugh up one's sleeve at; lay them in the aisles; mock; ridicule; roar; rock them in the aisles; roll them in the aisles; simper at; smile; smirk at; snicker; taunt; titter;

xiao bi he qing 笑比河清
to make sb smile is as difficult as to purify the river;

xiao bing 笑柄
butt / joke / laughingstock / mockingstock / standing joke / stock joke;

xiao bu he kou 笑不合口
keep on laughing / laugh so much that one cannot close the mouth;

xiao bu ke e 笑不可遏
cannot stop laughing / in an uncontrollable fit of laughter / roll with laughter;

xiao bu ke yang 笑不可仰
roll with laughter;

xiao bu xiu 笑不休
compulsive laughing / forced laughing;

xiao chu yan lei 笑出眼淚
laugh till one cries / laugh till the tears roll down one's cheeks;

xiao de he bu long zui 笑得合不攏嘴
grin from ear to ear;

xiao de tong kuai 笑得痛快
have a good laugh / laugh outright;

xiao de yao si 笑得要死
die with laughter / laugh oneself to death;

xiao diao da ya 笑掉大牙
double up in laughter / laugh one's head off / make one hold one's sides / make sb laugh his teeth off;

xiao duan du chang 笑斷肚腸
split one's sides with laughter;

xiao er bu da 笑而不答
only smile and make no reply / only smile but do not answer / smile but do not reply;

xiao er bu shuo 笑而不說
smile and say nothing;

xiao feng ao yue 笑風遨月
enjoy the breeze and moonlight;

xiao ha ha 笑哈哈
laugh heartily / laughingly / with a laugh;

xiao he he 笑呵呵
cheerful and gay / happy and gay;

xiao hua 笑話
jest / joke;

xiao hua bai chu 笑話百出
make many ridiculous mistakes;

xiao kuo chang kai 笑口常開
grinning all the time;

xiao li cang dao 笑裏藏刀
conceal a knife in one's smile || betray with a kiss; cloak and dagger; conceal a sword in a smile; hide a dagger in a smile; there is a hidden dagger behind his smiling face; there are daggers in one's smiles;

xiao liao 笑料
jape / jest / joke / laughingstock / ribtickler;

xiao ma 笑罵
deride / deride and taunt / mock and berate;

xiao ma you ta 笑罵由他
let others say what they like;

xiao ma you ren 笑罵由人
let them talk and criticize all they like / let others say what they like;

xiao mi le yan 笑眯了眼
all smiles / grin all over;

xiao mi mi 笑眯眯
all smiles / beaming / smilingly / with a smile on one's face;

xiao mian hu 笑面虎
a friendly-looking villain || a smiling tiger — an outwardly kind but inwardly cruel person; a tiger with a smiling face — a wicked person with a hypocritical smile; a treacherous fellow; a wolf in sheep's clothing;

xiao na 笑納
kindly accept;

xiao po bu xiao bu 笑破不笑補
better a clout than a hole out;

xiao po du pi 笑破肚皮
be overwhelmed with laughter / kill oneself laughing / kill oneself with laughter / laugh oneself into convulsions / roll with laughter / split one's sides with laughing;

xiao rong 笑容
smile // smiling expression;

xiao rong ke ju 笑容可掬
all smiles / radiant with smiles || show pleasant smiles; smile broadly; the face beams with a broad smile; with a charming smile;

xiao rong man mian 笑容滿面
be all smiles || a face radiating with smiles; a smile lit up one's face; grin from ear to ear; have a broad smile on one's face; with a beaming face; with a face all smiles;

xiao sheng 笑聲
laugh / laughter / sound of laughter;

xiao sheng ding fei 笑聲鼎沸
bubble with laughter;

xiao sheng shuang lang 笑聲爽朗
burst out in peals of laughter;

xiao sheng yang yi 笑聲洋溢
bursts of laughter keep floating out;

xiao si ren 笑死人
ludicrous to the utmost degree // make one laugh to death;

xiao tan 笑談
laughingstock / object of ridicule;

xiao tong du pi 笑痛肚皮
be thrown into convulsions of laughter / laugh oneself into convulsions;

xiao wai le zui 笑歪了嘴
laugh one's mouth crooked;

xiao wan le yao 笑彎了腰
double up with laughter / fold up / have sb in stitches / keep sb in stitches;

xiao wei wei 笑微微
smiling;

xiao xi xi 笑嘻嘻
all smiles / grinning / smiling broadly;

xiao ye 笑靨
dimples appearing with a smile;

xiao yi xiao 笑一笑
give a smile;

xiao yi xiao, shi nian sha; chou yi chou, bai le tou 笑一笑，十年少；愁一愁，白了頭
an ounce of mirth is worth a pound of sorrow / smiles make one young, worries make one aged;

xiao yin yin 笑吟吟
smiling happily;

xiao yu 笑語
talking and smiling;

xiao yu lian tian 笑語連天
talk and laugh merrily and incessantly;

xiao yu qing ying 笑語輕盈
chatter merrily / smile at each other as they whisper / talk and laugh merrily and light-heartedly / talk cheerfully;

xiao yu xuan hua 笑語喧嘩
uproarious talk and laughter;

xiao yu ying ying 笑語盈盈
chatter merrily / smiling at each other as they whisper / talk and laugh merrily and light-heartedly / talk cheerfully;

xiao zai lian shang, xi zai xin tou 笑在臉上，喜在心頭
with a smile on one's face and joy in one's heart;

xiao zhu yan kai 笑逐顏開
beam with smiles || a smile creeps across one's face; all smiles; be wreathed in smiles; beam with pleasure; give a broad smile; laugh cheerfully; one's face is beaming with smiles of joy; with a cheery smile;

xiao4 嘯
cry / roar;

xiao ao 嘯傲
talk and behave freely;

xie1 zui 歇嘴
shut up / stop talking;

xie2 jian chan xiao 脅肩諂笑
act obsequiously // sycophantic;

xie2 諧
jest / joke // funny / humorous;

xie nüe 諧謔
jest / joke / wisecrack;

xie xi 諧戲
jest / joke;

xie4 lu mi mi 泄露秘密
blow the gab / let the cat out of the bag;

xie mi 泄密
blow the gab;

xie4 謝
thank;

xie xie 謝謝
thanks;

xin1 fu hua 心腹話
confidential talk;

xin4 kou ci huang 信口雌黃
criticize freely without careful thought || free with one's tongue; lie in one's throat; make deceitful statements; make irresponsible remarks; make unfounded charges; talk sheer nonsense; wag one's tongue too freely;

xin kou ci huang, yi pai hu shuo 信口雌黃，一派胡說
irresponsible talk // this is sheer nonsnese;

xin kuo hu shuo 信口胡說
sheer nonsense || babble; barefaced falsehood; let out a stream of lies; speak thoughtlessly; talk recklessly; tattle;

xin kou hu zhou 信口胡謅
talk nonsense || fabricate wild tales; jabber about; speak thoughtlessly; speak wildly; talk at random; talk recklessly;

xin kou kai he 信口開河
talk irresponsibly || an aimless talk; an irresponsible chat; brag irresponsibly; have a loose tongue; let one's tongue run away with one; lie in one's teeth; lie in one's throat; loosen one's tongue; loosen up; open one's mouth wide; rambling blether; run off at the mouth; say whatever comes to one's mind; shoot at the mouth; shoot off; shoot off one's mouth; shoot one's mouth off; speak without measuring one's words; talk at random; talk drivel; talk in a loose kind of way; talk off the top of one's head; talk recklessly; talk through one's hat; talk through one's neck; talk through the back of one's neck; talk without forethought; unbridle the tongue; wag one's tongue too freely;

xin kou kai he, hu shuo ba dao 信口開河，胡說八道
speak at random and talk nonsense / talk at random and utter sheer nonsense;

xing1 hong re xing kou yan 猩紅熱性口炎
stomatitis scarlatina;

xing2 bu gu yan 行不顧言
not to practise what one preaches || act differently from what one says; not to act according to one's words; say one thing but do sth else;

xiong2 bian 雄辯
convincing argument / eloquence / forceful presentation of one's points in a debate;

xiong bian gao tan 雄辯高談
vigorous debate and high talk;

xiong bian shi yin, chen mo shi jin 雄辯是銀，沉默是金
speech is silver and silence is gold;

xiong bian tao tao 雄辯滔滔
argue eloquently // eloquent;

xiu1 kou nan kai 羞口難開
too embarrassed to say it / too embarrassed to speak out / too shy to speak;

xiu kui nan yan 羞愧難言
be ashamed beyond words;

xiu qie chen yan 羞怯陳言
narrate shyly and nervously;

xiu yu yan tan 羞於言談
coy of speech / modest of speech;

xu1 吁
sigh;

xu xu 吁吁
sound of panting;

xu1 訏
(1) boast / brag;
(2) sigh;

xu1 bang 虛謗
groundless accusation;

xu hua 虛話
empty talk / lie / unfounded statement;

xu ke 虛喝
give an empty scare;

xu kua 虛誇
boast / brag;

xu tan 虛談
empty talk / impractical suggestions;

xu wu 虛誣
accuse groundlessly;

xu yan 虛言
empty talk;

xu1 噓
(1) speak well of sb;
(2) deep sigh;
(3) boo / hiss;

xu han wen nuan 噓寒問暖
inquire after sb's well-being;

xu qi 噓氣
blow;

xu sheng 噓聲
breathe out slowly / catcalls;

xu sheng si qi 噓聲四起
a wave of hisses all round / hiss and boo everywhere / resound with catcalls;

xu xi 噓唏
sob;

xu xi yao tou 噓唏搖頭
shake the head with a deep sigh;

xu xu 噓噓
snore;

xu yin 噓音
hush;

xu3 許
(1) permit / promise;
(2) commend / praise;

xu nuo 許諾
promise;

xu3 詡
boast / brag / exaggerate;

xu xu 詡詡
boast / brag;

xu4 bie 敘別
get together for talk before parting / have a farewell talk / say goodbye to each other;

xu jia chang 敘家常
talk about daily life;

xu jiu 敘舊
talk about the old days;

xu shuo 敘說
narrate / tell;

xu tan 敘談
chat / chitchat / get together and chat / talk together;

xu tan qi kuo 敘談契濶
chat over the conditions which happened after separating from one another;

xu4 jiu 酗酒
indulge in excessive drinking // crapulent / liquorish // crapulence;

xu4 dao 絮叨
nag / talk endlessly // tiresomely talkative;

xu fan 絮煩
talkative / windy;

xu guo 絮聒
(1) chatter / windy and tiresome;
(2) bother sb / importune incessantly / trouble sb;

xu guo bu xiu 絮聒不休
annoyingly talkative // chatter / din / din in one's ears;

xu xu bu xiu 絮絮不休
jabber continuously || ceaseless chatter; long-winded; talk rapidly and trivially;

xu xu dao dao 絮絮叨叨
babble || harp on; hum about; repeat over and over again;

xu yu 絮語
garrulous / wordy // incessantly chatter;

xuan1 宣
announce;

xuan bu 宣佈
announce / declare / proclaim;

xuan cheng 宣稱
assert / claim;

xuan du 宣讀
read out in public;

xuan gao 宣告
announce / declare / proclaim / pronounce;

xuan jiang 宣講
deliver a speech / preach;

xuan shi 宣誓
swear / swear an oath / take an oath;

xuan yan 宣言
declaration / manifesto;

xuan1 喧
(1) talk noisily;
(2) noisy;

xuan rang 喧嚷
clamour / din;

xuan guo 喧聒
noisy;

xuan1 han 喧寒
greetings to one another;

xuan1 諠
bawl / shout;

xuan hua 諠譁
tumult / uproar;

xuan nu 諠呶
tumult / uproar;

xuan1 諼
(1) deceive;
(2) forget;

xuan2 tan 懸談
make a rambling talk;

xue4 kou pen ren 血口噴人
curse and slander / make false accusations against others;

xue pen da kou 血盆大口
gory mouth / large and fierce-looking mouth;

xun1 醺
drunk / intoxicated / tipsy;

xun xun 醺醺
inebriated / tipsy;

xun2 song 尋誦
peruse repeatedly;

xun2 詢
ask / inquire;

xun cha 詢察
investigate and inquire;

xun wen 詢問
ask about / inquire about / question;

xun4 chi 訓斥
berate / dress down / rebuke / reprimand;

xun chi 訓飭
admonish and censure a junior severely;

xun dao 訓導
teach and guide;

xun hua 訓話
exhort / lecture // exhortation / speech;

xun hui 訓誨
instruct / teach and exhort the younger generation;

xun jie 訓誡
admonish / exhort and warn // exhortation and warning;

xun mian 訓勉
exhort and encourage;

xun ren 訓人
exhort people;

xun yu 訓諭
instruct;

xun4 wen 訊問
cross-examine / interrogate;

ya2 ya 牙牙
babble;

ya ya xue yu 牙牙學語
learn to speak || babble; babble out one's first speech sounds; begin to babble;

ya3 啞
(1) dumb / mute;
(2) hoarse / husky;

ya ba kui 啞巴虧
one's grievances which are unable to speak out;

ya kou wu yan 啞口無言
be rendered speechless || be left without an argument; be reduced to silence; become speechless as a dumb person; dumbfounded; have nothing to say for oneself; inarticulate; put sb to silence; reduce sb to silence; remain dumb; silent as a dumb mouth; speechless; strike dumb; tongue-tied;

ya ran 啞然
(1) silent;
(2) describing of the sound of laughter;

ya ran shi xiao 啞然失笑
unable to stifle a laugh || a faint laugh escapes sb; can't help laughing; chuckle to oneself; guffaw; laugh involuntarily;

ya ran wu sheng 啞然無聲
mute / silence reigns / soundless;

ya3 yan 雅言
honest advice;

yan1 shuo 燕說
distorted remarks / slanted views / twisted interpretation;

yan1 ran 嫣然
smiling merrily;

yan ran yi xiao 嫣然一笑
give a captivating smile || a captivating smile; give a bewitching smile; give a charming smile; give a sweet smile; give a winsome smile;

yan2 言
(1) speech / words;
(2) express / mean / say / speak / talk;

yan bi xin, xing bi guo 言必信，行必果
always be true in word and resolute in deed || promises must be kept and action must be resolute; promises must be kept and actions resolutely taken; what is said must be done, and what is done must be carried to a result;

yan bi you xin 言必有信
as good as one's word;

yan bi you zhong 言必有中
hit the point whenever one speaks / whenever one says sth one hits the mark / whenever one speaks, one speaks to the point;

yan bu chu zhong, mao bu jing ren 言不出眾，貌不驚人
neither outstanding in speech nor impressive in appearance / one's conversation does not impress anybody, nor does one's presence inspire awe;

yan bu er jia 言不二價
the prices are fixed;

yan bu fu shi 言不符實
statements that do not tally with the facts;

yan bu gu xing 言不顧行
speeches are not in accordance with action;

yan bu ji xing 言不及行
words are not equal to practice;

yan bu ji yi 言不及義
never to talk about anything seriously || indulge in gossip without touching anything serious; make idle talks; talk frivolously;

yan bu jian xing 言不踐行
words are not equal to practice;

yan bu jin yi 言不盡意
words cannot express all one intends to say;

yan bu ying dian 言不應點
break one's word / give one's word which one does not keep;

yan bu you zhong 言不由衷
not to say frankly what one thinks || disingenuous; insincere in one's speech; not speaking one's mind; not to say what one thinks in one's mind; not to speak honestly; not to talk from the bottom of one's heart; say what one does not mean; speak affectedly; speak with one's tongue in one's cheek; speak without sincerity; talk insincerely; the words do not come from the heart;

yan bu zhong ken 言不中肯
not to speak to the point;

yan cha yu cuo 言差語錯
erroneous utterances / misunderstanding in verbal exchanges;

yan chu bi xing 言出必行
suit the action to the word;

yan chu fa sui 言出法隨
enforce the regulations to the letter / the order, once given, will be strictly enforced;

yan chu ji xing 言出即行
no sooner said than done;

yan chu ru shan 言出如山
a promise is a promise || one's words are as stable as mountains; promises must be kept; the word is said and can't be taken back;

yan chu shen zheng 言出身證
vouch one's words with one's deeds;

yan chuan 言傳
explain in words;

yan chuan shen jiao 言傳身教
teach by percept and example || instruct sb not only in words, but also by deeds; set up example for others with both precept and prctice; teach by personal example as well as verbal instruction;

yan ci 言詞
what one says || diction; expressions; one's words; statements; words;

yan ci bian lun 言詞辯論
verbal argument of litigants at a court of law;

yan ci bu ya 言詞不雅
use vulgar language;

yan ci feng li 言詞鋒利
speak daggers;

yan ci ken qie 言詞懇切
sincere in what one says // speak in an earnest tone;

yan ci shan shuo 言詞閃爍
incoherent speech / jumping from one subject to another;

yan dong 言動
words and conduct / speech and behaviour;

yan dong bu gou 言動不苟
careful words and practice / prudent in speech and behaviour;

yan dui 言對
(1) converse / meet and talk;
(2) coupling of words;

yan duo bi shi 言多必失
he that talks much errs much || loquacity brings mistakes; loquacity is sure to err; much babbling is not without offence; much talk leads to faults; one is bound to have a slip of the tongue if one talks too much; talkativeness induces error; too much talking leads to error;

yan duo you shi 言多有失
if you talk too much, you may say the wrong thing;

yan duo yu shi 言多語失
one is liable to make a slip of the tongue, if one talks a great deal;

yan er wu xin 言而無信
break one's word; eat one's words || fail to carry out one's promise; fail to keep faith; fail to keep one's word; fail to live up to one's promise; go back on one's word; one's words are not dependable;

yan er you xin 言而有信
true to one's word || as good as one's word; carry out one's word to fruition; faithful in word; keep a promise inviolate; make good one's promises;

yan fu qi shi 言符其實
what one speaks conforms to reality || don't take a mountain out of a molehill; the statement tallies with the fact;

yan fu yu xing 言浮於行
one's practice does not meet one's words || speak above one's abilities; words float above practice;

yan gui yu hao 言歸於好
be reconciled / become reconciled || bury the hatchet; bury the tomahwak; heal the breach; kiss and be friends; maintain amicable relations hereafter; make friends again; make it up with sb; make one's peace with sb; make peace with; make sb's peace with; make up a quarrel; on good terms again; put up the sword; reconcile; resume friendship; shake and be friends; sink a feud; smoke the calmet; smoke the pipe of peace; square oneself with; start with a clean slate;

yan gui zheng zhuan 言歸正傳
come back to our story || and now to be serious; come to business; get down to business; hark back to the subject; jesting apart; jesting aside; joking apart; joking aside; keep to the record; lead the conversation to serious things; let's resume the narration; resume the thread of one's discourse; return from the digression; return to one's muttons; return to the subject; return to the topic of discussion; revert to the original topic of conversation;

yan gui jian jie 言貴簡潔
brevity is the soul of wit;

yan gui jian jie, wen gui jing lian 言貴簡潔，文貴精練
brevity is the soul of wit;

yan guo qi shi 言過其實
overstate the fact ‖ boast; bombastic; brag; come it strong; draw the long bow; exaggerate; give a false colour; go it strong; hyperbolize; inflated; make a mountain out of a molehill; overshoot the truth; overstate; pile on the agony; pull the long bow; put it on thick; strain the truth; stretch a point; stretch the facts; turn geese into swans;

yan he 言和
become reconciled / bury the hatchet / make peace;

yan ji 言及
mention / talk about / touch on;

yan jian yi gai 言簡意賅
brief and to the point ‖ compendious; comprise much matter in few words; concise and comprehensive; give the essentials in simple language; impart a deep meaning with only a few words; terse but comprehensive; terse in language and comprehensive in meaning;

yan jiao 言教
give verbal directions / teach by precept / teach by word of mouth;

yan jiao bu ru shen jiao 言教不如身教
example is better than precept;

yan jin yu ci 言盡於此
have no more to say / have nothing more to say;

yan jin zhi yuan 言近指遠
simple in language but profound in meaning ‖ express far-reaching meaning in simple words; simple words but deep meaning; some simple words carry a profound meaning;

yan lai yu qu 言來語去
(1) argue;
(2) talk back and forth / talk over and over again;

yan lu 言路
channels through which criticisms and suggestions may be communicated to the leadership;

yan lun 言論
speech / views;

yan lun zi you 言論自由
freedom of speech;

yan ming 言明
declare / make a statement / state clearly;

yan mo nan yu 言莫難喻
beyond description;

yan qing xing zhuo 言清行濁
one's words are nice, but one's actions are dirty / one's words are pure and one's actions are vile / one's words are sweet, but one's actions are dirty;

yan ren ren shu 言人人殊
each person tells a different story ‖ different people, different versions; different people give different views; each person offers a different version; every man differs in his statement; everybody has a different story; everyone gives a different version;

yan ru jin shi 言如金石
one's words are as gold and precious stones;

yan san yu si 言三語四
criticize without much thinking;

yan shi ruo shen 言事若神
foresee with divine accuracy / foretell like a prophet / foretell things accurately;

yan tan 言談
(1) conversation / the way one speaks;
(2) words and speech;

yan tan ju zhi 言談舉止
speech and deportment;

yan tan wei zhong 言談微中
one's speech is subtle;

yan tan zhi jian 言談之間
during a conversation / from the way sb talks;

yan ting ji cong 言聽計從
always listen to sb's words and accept his advice ‖ act at sb's beck and call; act upon whatever sb says; always follow sb's advice; believe and act upon whatever sb suggests; have an unquestioning faith in sb; have full confidence in sb; have implicit faith in sb;

jump through a hoop for sb; listen to every word sb says; listen to sb's words and follow his counsels; readily listen to sb's advice and accept it; take sb's advice and adopt his plan; trust sb completely;

yan wai 言外
between the lines / beyond the words spoken;

yan wai you yi 言外有意
more is meant than meets the ear;

yan wai zhi yi 言外之意
the meaning between the lines || ideas not expressed in words; implication; implied meaning; overtones; the meaning beyond the literal words; the real meaning; what is actually meant;

yan wei xin sheng 言為心聲
what the heart thinks the tongue speaks || as a man's heart is, so does he speak; as the inner life is, so will be the language; one's words reflect one's thinking; speech is the picture of the mind; speech is the voice of one's heart; words are echoes of the heart; words are the voice of the mind; words express what is in the heart;

yan wu bu jin 言無不盡
say all without reserve;

yan wu jin ji 言無禁忌
say without taboo;

yan xiao 言笑
talk and laugh;

yan xiao zi ruo 言笑自若
talk and laugh imperturbably || completely at ease; go on talking and laughing as if nothing has happened; natural and calm; undisturbed;

yan xin xing guo 言信行果
truthful in speech and firm in action || promises must be kept and actions resolutely taken; true to one's word and firm in one's actions; trustworthy in word and resolute in action;

yan xing 言行
statements and actions / words and deeds;

yan xing bu fu 言行不符
words do not correspond with deeds || deeds not matching words; one does not do what one preaches; words and acts do not correspond;

yan xing bu yi 言行不一
words and actions do not match || actions repugnant to one's words; one does not do what one preaches; one's actions are not in keeping with one's promises; one's acts belie one's words; one's conduct disagrees with one's words; one's conduct is at variance with one's words; one's deeds do not match one's words; one's deeds do not square with one's words; one's doings belie one's commitments; one's words and deeds are at complete variance; one's words are at variance with one's deeds; one's words are not matched by deeds; say one thing do another; talk one way and behave another; what one does belies one's commitments; words and deeds contradict each other;

yan xing jin shen 言行謹慎
mind one's p's and q's;

yan xing ruo yi 言行若一
live up to one's words;

yan xing shi jian 言行失檢
blot one's copybook // indiscretion;

yan xing xiang bei 言行相悖
practise against what one preaches;

yan xing xiang gu 言行相顧
practise what one preaches;

yan xing xin du 言行信篤
faithful in word and deed;

yan xing yi zhi 言行一致
act in accordance with one's words || actions matching words; as good as one's word; deeds accord with words; fit one's deeds to one's words; live up to one's words; match one's deeds with one's words; match word to deed; match words with deeds; one's actions are in keeping with one's promises; one's deeds and words are in accord; one's deeds are consistent with one's words; one's words correspond with one's actions; square one's words with one's conduct; stand by one's word; suit one's actions to one's words; the deeds suit the words; the deeds match the words;

yan you jin er yi wu qiong 言有盡而意無窮
there's an end to the words, but not to their

口 *Mouth*

message;

yan you zai er 言猶在耳

while the words are still ringing in one's ears / the words still ring in one's ears;

yan yu 言語

speech / spoken language / words;

yan yu cu su 言語粗俗

coarse and vulgar in speech;

yan yu cu ye 言語粗野

expressions are coarse and wild;

yan yu wu wei 言語無味

insipid talk // keep on jawing;

yan yu zhi wu 言語支吾

mince words / prevaricate;

yan ze 言責

responsibility of offering advice;

yan zhe wu xin, ting zhe you yi 言者無心，聽者有意

a careless word may be important information to an attentive listener / a casual remark sounds deliberate to a suspicious listener;

yan zhe wu yi, ting zhe you xin 言者無意，聽者有心

a pair of good ears will drain dry a hundred tongues / one pair of ears draws dry a hundred tongues;

yan zhe wu zui, wen zhe zu jie 言者無罪，聞者足戒

do not blame the one who speaks but heed what you hear || blame not the critic, heed what he says; blame not the speaker but be warned by his words; don't blame the speaker but take his words as a warning; it is not the one who speaks who is culpable; it is up to the one who listens to exercise due caution;

yan zhe zhun zhun, ting zhe miao miao 言者諄諄，聽者藐藐

the words are earnest but they fall on deaf ears || the speaker is earnest but the hearer is casual; the speaker talks with great earnestness, but the audience pay little attention;

yan zhi bu xiang 言之不詳

be stated too briefly;

yan zhi cheng li 言之成理

what one says makes sense || be said with solid judgement; present in a reasonable way; sound reasonable; speak in a rational and convincing way; speak on the strength of reason; stand to reason; talk sense; well-reasoned;

yan zhi fa wei 言之乏味

be tired of what is said;

yan zhi guo shen 言之過甚

exaggerated statement // go too far / put it strong;

yan zhi guo zao 言之過早

it's too early to say || make a premature statement; premature to say; speak too soon; still too early to say;

yan zhi ke chi 言之可恥

it is disgraceful to speak of it;

yan zhi li li, ru zai yan qian 言之歷歷，如在眼前

give a glowing account;

yan zhi wu wen, xing er bu yuan 言之無文，行而不遠

non-elegant words will not become popular;

yan zhi wu wu 言之無物

empty talk || devoid of substance; hot air; make an inane remark; mere verbiage; talk endlessly with no substance at all;

yan zhi wu xin 言之無心

often says things one does not mean;

yan zhi you ju 言之有據

speak in good authority / speak on good grounds;

yan zhi you li 言之有理

it stands to reason || hold water; speak in a rational and convincing way;

yan zhi you wu 言之有物

have substance in a speech;

yan zhi you xin 言之有信

honour one's own words;

yan zhi zhong ken 言之中肯

the remark is to the point || the cap fits;

yan zhi zao zao 言之鑿鑿

say sth with certainty / say with definite

evidence;

yan zhong 言重
speak so seriously and strongly as to embarrass sb;

yan zhong jiu ding 言重九鼎
one's word carries the weight of nine tripods — weighty advice;

yan zhuang 言狀
describe;

yan2 xing tun yan kun nan 炎性吞咽困難
dysphagia inflammatoria;

yan2 ci 嚴詞
stern words / strong terms;

yan ci qian ze 嚴詞譴責
denounce in strong terms;

yan li pi ping 嚴厲批評
criticize severely / flay / wade into;

yan sheng li se 嚴聲厲色
with stern tones and severe countenance;

yan ze 嚴責
objurgate;

yan3 kou 掩口
cover one's mouth with one's hand;

yan kou er xiao 掩口而笑
laugh in secret || hide one's smile; put one's hand to one's mouth to hide one's laughter;

yan3 jiang 演講
(1) harangue / deliver a speech;
(2) harangue / speech;

yan shuo 演説
deliver a speech / give a speech / harangue // oration / speech // oratory;

yan4 yin 宴飲
dine and wine / feast;

yan4 shi 厭食
anorectic // anorexia / apocleisis / lack of appetite;

yan shi zheng 厭食症
anorexia;
shen jing xing yan shi zheng 神經性厭食症
anorexia nervosa;

yan4 yin 燕飲
feast;

yan4 嚥
swallow;

yan qi 嚥氣
breathe one's last;

yan qi zheng 嚥氣症
aerophagia;

yang1 央
request;

yang gao 央告
beg / beseech;

yang qing 央請
make a request;

yang qiu 央求
beg / entreat / implore / plead;

yang tuo 央託
request sb to do sth;

yang2 yan 佯言
lie / tell lies;

yang2 sheng 揚聲
raise one's voice;

yang yan 揚言
declare in public || exaggerate; pass the word that; spread words; threaten;

yang2 yan fan dui 颺言反對
speak against in a loud and speedy voice;

yang3 tian da xiao 仰天大笑
look up to the sky and laugh || laugh sardonically; lean back and laugh; lift one's head and guffaw;

yao1 吆
cry / shout;

yao he 吆喝
cry / shout;

yao1 sheng yao qi 妖聲妖氣
speak flirtatiously;

yao yan 妖言
absurd statements / heresies / fallacies;

yao yan huo zhong 妖言惑眾
spread fallacies to deceive people || arouse people with wild talk; cheat people with

sensational speeches; deceive people with fabulous stories; deluge people with strange legends; spread wild rumours to mislead the people; wild rumours mislead the masses;

yao2 謠
rumour;

yao chuan 謠傳
(1) rumour;
(2) it is rumoured / according to rumour / rumour has it that;

yao yan 謠言
groundless allegation / rumour;

yao yan fen yun 謠言紛紜
rumours are flourishing || alive with rumours; rumours and gossip are everywhere; there are many rumours doing the rounds;

yao yan huo zhong 謠言惑眾
delude the people with rumours / lying rumours lead astray the people / wild rumours mislead the masses;

yao yan man tian fei 謠言滿天飛
all sorts of rumours are going the rounds;

yao zhuo 謠諑
calumny / rumour / slander;

yao zhuo fen yun 謠諑紛紜
there are many rumours doing the rounds;

yao3 咬
bite / chew / gnaw / snap at;

yao diao 咬掉
bite off;

yao ding 咬定
insist;

yao4 yan 藥言
sincere admonitions;

yao yan ke qu 藥言可取
sincere admonitions are acceptable;

ye1 噎
(1) be choked with food;
(2) choke off;

ye zhu 噎住
be choked with food;

ye2 揶
jeer at / ridicule / tease;

ye yu 揶揄
jeer at / ridicule / tease;

ye4 咽
be choked / speak in a choked vocie / weep in a choked voice;

ye wu chou qi 咽嗚抽泣
be seized with convulsive sobbing;

ye wu ti ku 咽嗚啼哭
cry and sob softly;

ye ye wu wu 咽咽嗚嗚
break out into sobs;

yi1 chang bai he 一唱百和
meet with general approval || one leads, and the rest follow; one person proposes and a hundred others respond; one sings, all follow; when one starts singing, all the others join in;

yi chang san tan 一唱三歎
one sings and the other three joins in / sing or write with affected pathos;

yi chang yi he 一唱一和
one echoes the other || chime in with; echo each other; in perfect harmony; join in chorus; sing a duet with sb; sing in chorus with; sing to each other's tune;

yi chuan shi, shi chuan bai 一傳十，十傳百
(gossip, rumours) go fast / (gossip, rumours) travel fast;

yi da kou 一大口
a mouthful;

yi hu bai nuo 一呼百諾
one's summons are answered by a hundred voices || have hundreds at one's neck and call — a wealthy or influenctial person who has a large number of servants always waiting to obey his orders; one command draws a hundred answers;

yi hu bai ying 一呼百應
a hundred responses to a single call;

yi hu ji lai 一呼即來
come like a dog at a whistle;

yi ju hua 一句話
in a word / in short;

yi kou 一口
(1) flatly || readily; with certainty; promise

without hesitation;
(2) bite;
(3) a draught of / a morsel of / a mouthful of / a nip of / a sip of / a whiff of;

yi kou cha 一口茶
a mouthful of tea;

yi kou chi bu cheng ge pang zi 一口吃不成個胖子
you can't build up your constitution on one mouthful ‖ you can't get fat on one mouthful — you must keep at it;

yi kou chi guang 一口吃光
eat up at a mouthful;

yi kou cui lian 一口啐臉
spit in sb's face;

yi kou da ying 一口答應
readily agree ‖ consent without any lengthy deliberation; promise without hesitation; readily comply with;

yi kou duan ding 一口斷定
allege / arbitrarily assert / jump to the conclusion;

yi kou fou ren 一口否認
completely deny / flatly deny / repudiate flatly;

yi kou hui jue 一口回絕
flatly refuse;

yi kou qi 一口氣
(1) at a stretch ‖ at a gallop; at a whack; at one fling; at one go; at one go-off; at one sitting; in one breath; right off the reel; straight off the reed; without a break; without stopping;
(2) breath;

yi kou shui 一口水
a draught of water;

yi kou tun diao 一口吞掉
devour in one gulp / gobble up in one go;

yi kou yan 一口煙
a puff of a cigarette;

yi kou yao ding 一口咬定
assert categorically ‖ cling to one's view; insist emphatically; insist on saying sth; state categorically; stick to one's statement; stick to what one says; stubbornly assert that; the arbitrary assertion that;

yi kou yi sheng 一口一聲
without interruption;

yi mian zhi ci 一面之詞
one-sided statement;

yi ming jing ren 一鳴驚人
become famous overnight;

yi nuo qian jin 一諾千金
solemn promise;

yi pai hu yan 一派胡言
complete nonsense ‖ a bunch of malarkey; a load of rubbish; a lot of eyewash; a lot of malarkey; a pack of lies; a pack of nonsense; gross nonsense; sheer rubbish;

yi pai huang yan 一派謊言
a pack of lies;

yi pian huang yan 一片謊言
a pack of lies;

yi pian zui, liang pian she 一片嘴，兩片舌
double-talk;

yi pin yi xiao 一顰一笑
every twinkle and smile;

yi ren chao bu qi jia 一人吵不起架
it takes two to make a quarrel;

yi ren chuan shi, shi ren chuan bai 一人傳十，十人傳百
flow lip to lip / go from mouth to mouth / pass the news from person to person;

yi ren chuan xu, wan ren chuan shi 一人傳虛，萬人傳實
one man tells an idle story and it becomes fact in the mouths of ten thousand ‖ fling dirt enough and some will stick;

yi sheng bu keng 一聲不吭
without saying a word ‖ as mute as a fish; as mute as a statue; as mute as a stone; keep one's mouth shut; say neither ba nor bum; say nothing;

yi sheng bu xiang 一聲不響
not to utter a sound ‖ as dumb as a fish; as mute as a mouse; not to say a word; without many words;

yi sheng chang tan 一聲長歎
draw a deep sigh / heave a long sigh / let out a long heavy sigh;

yi sheng hao ling 一聲號令
issue an order;

yi sheng jiao han 一聲叫喊
call / cry;

yi sheng ling xia 一聲令下
as soon as the order is given / at the first call;

yi wen san bu zhi 一問三不知
(1) deny all knowledge of an event / not to know a thing // entirely ignorant;
(2) keep one's mouth shut;

yi wen yao tou san bu zhi 一問搖頭三不知
shake one's head in answer to all questions;

yi wen yi da 一問一答
ask and answer interchangeably / one asking and the other answering;

yi xi hua 一席話
a talk / a speech / a chat;

yi xiao dun shi 一笑頓釋
bring sb round with a laugh;

yi xiao er qu 一笑而去
leave with a smile;

yi xiao liao zhi 一笑了之
laugh away / laugh out of count;

yi xiao qian jin 一笑千金
(1) a smile is worth a thousand pieces of gold;
(2) enchanting smile;

yi xiao qing cheng 一笑傾城
a single smile would overthrow a city;

yi xiao zhi zhi 一笑置之
dismiss with a laugh / laugh off ‖ carry off with a laugh; chuckle at; chuckle over sth; dismiss with a smile; dispose of... with a smile; laugh away; laugh off as a joke; laugh out of court; pass the thing off with a laugh; smile at; smile away; with a sneer;

yi xiao zuo da 一笑作答
answer only by a smile;

yi xin 一新
fresh look / new look;

yi yan ban yu 一言半語
a word or two;

yi yan bi zhi 一言蔽之
in a word ‖ in a few words; in a nutshell; in short; sum up in a word;

yi yan bu da 一言不答
answer only by a smile;

yi yan bu fa 一言不發
without saying a word ‖ button up one's mouth; have nothing to say for oneself; keep one's mouth tightly shut; not a word is said; not to breathe a word; not to say a word; not to utter; say nothing;

yi yan bu he 一言不合
a single jarring note in conversation;

yi yan bu he, ba dao xiang xiang 一言不合，拔刀相向
a word and a blow;

yi yan bu liu 一言不留
not to leave a word;

yi yan bu xie 一言不泄
not to breathe a syllable about;

yi yan dao po 一言道破
lay bare its secret with one remark;

yi yan ji chu, si ma nan zhui 一言既出，駟馬難追
a word spoken is an arrow let fly / a promise cannot be taken back once it is made / a word spoken is past recalling / better the foot slip than the tongue trip;

yi yan jiu ding 一言九鼎
a solemn promise ‖ a solemn pledge; one word is as heavy as nine tripods; one's word carries the weight of nine tripods — weighty advice;

yi yan nan jin 一言難盡
it is hard to explain in a few words ‖ difficult to embody in a single sentence; difficult to put in a nutshell; it's a long story; that's a long, long story;

yi yan sang bang 一言喪邦
a single wrong statement may bring disaster to the nation / bring disaster to the nation by a mere word;

yi yan tang 一言堂
one person alone has the say;

yi yan wei ding 一言為定
reach a verbal agreement || a bargain is a bargain; a promise is a promise; call it a call; call it a deal; count it as settled; it's a whack; it is agreed; sth is settled; that's a bargain; that's a deal; that's a whack;

yi yan wei liao 一言未了
before one finishes speaking...;

yi yan xing bang 一言興邦
flourish the state by a mere word;

yi yan yi xing 一言一行
every word and deed || a word and an action; each word and act; in all that one says and does;

yi yan yi yu 一言一語
every word and phrase;

yi yan yi bi zhi 一言以蔽之
in a word || in a nutshell; in short; to make a long story short; to sum up;

yi yan zuo pi 一言作譬
have a parable for explaining sth;

yi yin er jin 一飲而盡
empty one's cup in one gulp || at one gulp; drain the cup with one gulp; drink at a draught; drink it clean at one gulp; drink it down in a breath; drink it off; drink up; empty the glass at one gulp; fetch off; gulp down a drink; toss off the cup;

yi yu cheng chen 一語成讖
a saying turns out to be a prophecy / the prophecy has unfortunately come true / a casual remark that turned out to be prophetic in a tragedy;

yi yu dao po 一語道破
puncture a fallacy with one remark || betray...in a statement; clear up the matter in a single sentence; get to the heart of the matter in a few words; hit the mark with a single comment; hit the nail on the head; lay bare the truth with one penetrating remark;

yi yu dao ti 一語到題
come to the point;

yi yu ji zhong 一語擊中
hit with one vivid expression / the word goes right to the heart of the matter;

yi yu jing si zuo 一語驚四座
one's remark gives everyone there a surprise;

yi yu po di 一語破的
hit the mark with a single comment || hit the exact point with a word; hit the nail on the head; hit the target with one remark;

yi yu xiang guan 一語雙關
pun || a double-edged remark; a single phrase with a double meaning;

yi zhang zui 一張嘴
(1) mouth / tongue;
(2) whenever one speaks;

yi zhen da xiao 一陣大笑
a roar of laughter;

yi zhen xiao sheng 一陣笑聲
a gust of laughter / an outburst of laughter;

yi2 sheng 怡聲
soft and tender voice that is pleasing;

yi2 xiao da fang 貽笑大方
make a laughing-stock of oneself;

yi2 bang 疑謗
suspected and slandered;

yi wen 疑問
doubt / question;

yi2 wang xing shi yu zheng 遺忘性失語症
amnesic aphasia;

yi4 yan zhi 易言之
in other words;

yi4 kou tong sheng 異口同聲
with one voice || cry out in one voice; in unanimous agreement; in unison; join in the chorus of; sing the same tune in different keys; speak with one voice; unanimously; with one accord;

yi shuo 異説
heresies;

yi yan 異言
dissenting words;

yi yi 異議
dissent / objections;

口 *Mouth*

yi4 hua 逸話
anecdote;

yi kou 逸口
make an indiscreet remark;

yi yan 逸言
extravagant talk;

yi4 mei 溢美
praise excessively;

yi mei zhi yan 溢美之言
words of fulsome praise;

yi wu 溢惡
excessively abusive;

yi yu yan biao 溢於言表
show clearly in one's utterances and manners;

yi yu 溢譽
excessive praises / flattery;

yi4 wei 意謂
it seems to say;

yi zai yan wai 意在言外
more is meant than meets the ear / the real meaning is not expressed but implied;

yi4 chi xing kou qiang tong 義齒性口腔痛
denture sore mouth;

yi chi xing kou yan 義齒性口炎
denture stomatitis;

yi4 議
(1) argue / debate / discuss / negotiate / talk over;
(2) comment / criticize;

yi ding 議定
arrive at a discussion after discussion / arrive at a discussion after negotiation;

yi he 議合
discuss together;

yi jia 議價
negotiate over the price;

yi jue 議決
pass a resolution;

yi lun 議論
(1) debate;
(2) comment / remark on / remark upon;
(3) discuss / speak / talk;

yi lun feng sheng 議論風生
create a lively atmosphere by one's talk;

yi4 囈
talk in sleep;

yi yu 囈語
(1) talk in one's sleep;
(2) crazy talk / ravings;

yi zhen 囈怔
talk in sleep;

yin1 rong 音容
(1) voice and countenance;
(2) the likeness of the deceased;

yin rong wan zai 音容宛在
as if the person were in the flesh ‖ as if the person were still alive; can see sb's smile and hear his voice today as clearly as if he were standing before us; one's voice and appearance seem to be still with us; voice and facial expression of the deceased are still vividly remembered;

yin rong xiao mao 音容笑貌
(1) one's voice and expression;
(2) the likeness of one's laughing face;

yin1 喑
(1) lose one's voice;
(2) keep silent;

yin long 喑聾
(1) deaf-and-mute;
(2) a deaf-mute;

yin ya 喑啞
dumb / mute / unable to talk;

yin1 瘖
dumb / mute;

yin ya 瘖啞
dumb / mute;

yin2 吟
(1) chant / intone / recite / sing;
(2) moan / sigh;

yin chang 吟唱
chant / sing;

yin e 吟哦
chant / recite poetry with a cadence;

yin shi 吟詩
hum verse / recite poems;

yin shi yong huai 吟詩詠懷
compose poems to express one's feelings / express one's feelings by verse;

yin shi zuo hua 吟詩作畫
chant poetry and paint pictures / write and sing poems or to draw;

yin song 吟誦
chant / intone / recite;

yin wei 吟味
recite with appreciation / recite with relish;

yin xiao 吟嘯
(1) sing in freedom / whistle in freedom;
(2) lament / sigh;

yin xiao e wan 吟嘯扼腕
wring one's hands and lament;

yin xiao zi ruo 吟嘯自若
whistle or shout in freedom;

yin xiao zi yu 吟嘯自娛
amuse oneself with loud singing;

yin yong 吟詠
chant / intone a verse / recite with a cadence;

yin2 sheng 淫聲
lewd songs;

yin tan 淫談
obscene talks;

yin yan hui yu 淫言穢語
profane and obscene language;

yin2 xiao 齗笑
laugh;

yin yin 齗齗
disputing;

yin3 hang gao ge 引吭高歌
sing at the top of one's voice || belt out songs; roar out a song; sing aloud; sing in a spirit of utter abandonment; sing joyfully in a loud voice; sing lustily; sing with outstretched neck; stretch one's neck and sing loudly;

yin hang kuang ge 引吭狂歌
sing with wild abandon;

yin ren fa xiao 引人發笑
induce sb to laugh / make sb laugh / raise a laugh // provocative of mirth;

yin3 飲
(1) drink;
(2) drinks;
(3) swallow;
(4) keep in the heart / nurse;
(5) be hit;

yin bing 飲冰
cool oneself down by gulping ice water;

yin bing ru bo 飲冰茹檗
drink ice water and eat the stump — the hard life of a widow;

yin cha 飲茶
drink tea;

yin cha jin dian 飲茶進點
have tea and snacks;

yin cha liao tian 飲茶聊天
talk over a cup of tea;

yin chun zi zui 飲醇自醉
win others' support with one's virtue;

yin feng can lu 飲風餐露
live a primitive and hard life || feed on wind and dew; take in wind and eat dew — a hard life of a monk or nun;

yin jian 飲餞
give a farewell party for a friend;

yin jin 飲盡
drain / drink off;

yin jiu 飲酒
drink wine || belt down; bend an elbow; crook one's little finger; crook the elbow; drink liquor; go on the batter; go on the spree; hit the bottle; imbibe; juice; life one's elbow; lift one's little finger; moisten one's clay; on the batter; raise an elbow; throw one's little finger; tip one's elbow; turn up one's little finger; wet; wet one's clay; wet one's whistle; wood up;

yin jiu fu shi 飲酒賦詩
drink and write poems;

yin jiu guo liang 飲酒過量
drink beyond one's capacity;

yin jiu jie chou 飲酒解愁
drown one's sorrows in wine / drink sorrow down;

yin jiu shang hua 飲酒賞花
drink wine and look at the flowers;

yin jiu shang yue 飲酒賞樂
feast and enjoy music;

yin jiu wu shi 飲酒誤事
liquor causes delay in one's business;

yin jiu zuo le 飲酒作樂
drink and amuse oneself || drink wine and make merry; enjoy oneself drinking; give oneself up to dissipation, spending days and nights in drinking and music; wine and music are the order of the day;

yin shi 飲食
(1) diet / food and drink;
(2) drink and eat;
jun heng yin shi 均衡飲食
balanced diet;
qing dan yin shi 清淡飲食
bland diet;
tong feng yin shi 痛風飲食
gouty diet;

yin shi bu jin 飲食不進
can neither eat nor drink / refuse food;

yin shi gai bian 飲食改變
metatrophy;

yin shi guo du 飲食過度
hyperphagia;

yin shi guo duo 飲食過多
hyperphagia;

yin shi liao fa 飲食療法
dietetic therapy / dietotherapy;

yin shi nan nü 飲食男女
food and drink and sex — man's natural instincts;

yin shi tan 飲食攤
food stall;

yin shi wu du 飲食無度
excessive eating and drinking;

yin shi wu wei 飲食無味
have no appetite for food or drink;

yin shi you du 飲食有度
abstemious / temperate in eating and drinking;

yin shui 飲水
(1) drinking water;
(2) drink water;

yin shui bu wang wa jing ren 飲水不忘挖井人
don't forget the well-diggers when you drink from this well / when you drink the water, think of those who dig the well;

yin shui dang si wa jing ren 飲水當思挖井人
let every man praise the bridge he goes over / let every man speak well of the bridge that carries him over;

yin shui guo duo 飲水過多
hyperposia;

yin shui guo shao 飲水過少
hypoposia;

yin shui si yuan 飲水思源
remember the source of one's blessings || cast no dirt into the well that hath given you water; gratitude for the source of benefit; let every man praise the bridge he goes over; let every man speak well of the bridge that carries him over; never cast dirt into that fountain of which thou hast sometimes drink; remember past kindness; when drinking water, think of its source — never to forget where one's happiness comes from; when one drinks water, one must not forget where it comes from — bear in mind where happiness comes from;

yin xue 飲血
(1) weep in deep sorrow;
(2) drink blood / hemoposia;

yin yong 飲用
drink;

yin yong shui 飲用水
drinking water / potable water;

yin zhen zhi ke 飲鴆止渴
drink poison to quench thirst — seek temporary relief regardless of the disastrous consequence || quench a thirst with poison — a supposed remedy having the opposite effect; stop thirst by drinking poison — temporary relief which results in disaster;

yin zui 飲醉
get drunk / get smashed;

ying1 tao xiao kou 櫻桃小口
small cherrylike mouth;

ying4 hua 硬話
defiant talk;

ying shuo 硬說
insist on saying;

ying ye 硬咽
choke down;

ying4 cheng 應承
(1) assent / consent;
(2) pledge;

ying da 應答
answer / reply / respond;

ying da ru liu 應答如流
give answers quickly and fluently || answer as quickly as the flowing of water; answer the question without any hitch; answer with a readiness equal to the flowing of water; give fluent replies; reply readily and fluently; one's replies flow like a stream; quick at repartee;

ying dui 應對
(1) answer questions;
(2) repartee;

ying dui ru liu 應對如流
answer questions fluently / answer the questions without any hitch / give fluent replies;

ying nuo 應諾
assent / consent / promise / undertake;

ying sheng 應聲
echo;

ying sheng er dao 應聲而倒
fall as soon as sth is heard;

ying xu 應許
assent / promise;

yong1 yan 庸言
cliché / platitude / trite remark;

yong yan yong xing 庸言庸行
commonplace words and deeds / ordinary and common words and acts;

yong2 喁
unison of sounds;

yong yong si yu 喁喁私語
coo / coo one's words / talk in whispers;

yong3 詠
chant / hum / sing;

yong chang 詠唱
chant;

yong shi 詠詩
chant poems;

yong tan 詠歎
chant / intone / sing;

yong tan diao 詠歎調
arias;

yong wu gan huai 詠物感懷
chant things recollecting past memories;

yong zan 詠贊
praise / sing the praises of;

yong4 fan 用飯
eat a meal / have lunch / take a meal;

you2 zhong yi xiao 由衷一笑
laugh a hearty laugh;

you zhong zhi yan 由衷之言
words which come from the bottom of one's heart || a talk straight from the heart; sincere words; words spoken from the bottom of one's heart; words uttered in sincerity;

you2 qiang hua diao 油腔滑調
mealy-mouthed || glib tongue; shifty argument; frivolous and insincere in speech; full of guile and cunning;

you zui 油嘴
(1) glib-tongued / oil-tongued;
(2) glib talker;

you zui hua she 油嘴滑舌
oily-mouthed || flattering tongue; smooth tongue; glib; glib-tongued; have a well-oiled tongue; mealy-mouthed; slimy-tongued; smooth-tongued;

you2 ci 游辭
unfounded remarks;

you shui 游說
canvass / lobby;

you tan 游談
play and talk;

you yan 游言
unfounded remarks;

you3 kou jie bei 有口皆碑
win universal praise || be praised by all; be universally acclaimed; enjoy great popularity among the people;

you kou nan bian 有口難辯
find it hard to vindicate oneself / hard to explain;

you kou nan fen 有口難分
find it difficult to vindicate oneself;

you kou nan yan 有口難言
find it hard to bring up a matter || cannot bring oneself to mention sth; dare not speak out;

you kou wu xin 有口無心
sharp-tongued but not malicious || not really mean what one says; one's bark is worse than one's bite; say what one does not mean; sharp in tongue but not malicious in mind;

you wen bi da 有問必答
answer all questions asked;

you yan zai xian 有言在先
as agreed before / as said before;

you zui wu xin 有嘴無心
say what one does not mean;

you3 yan 莠言
bad words / dirty words;

you4 da you ma 又打又罵
beat and curse at the same time;

you ku you xiao 又哭又笑
cry and laugh at the same time;

you long you ya 又聾又啞
deaf and dumb;

you shuo you xiao 又說又笑
talking and laughing at the same time;

you wen 又問
ask again;

you4 zhi ke xiao 幼稚可笑
ridiculously childish;

yu1 lun 迂論
impractical argument / unrealistic statement;

yu yan 迂言
absurd statement / impractical remarks;

yu2 諛
flatter / toady;

yu ci 諛詞
flattering words;

yu yan 諛言
flattering words;

yu3 語
(1) language / speech / tongue;
(2) say / speak / talk;
(3) proverb / saying / set phrase;

yu bing 語病
(1) faulty wording / illogical use of words;
(2) difficulty in speaking caused by vocal defects;

yu bu jing ren, mao bu ya zhong 語不驚人，貌不壓眾
nothing striking about the way he speaks, nor does he surpass others in looks || as a speaker he is just so-so, about his face there is nothing to atttract attention; for all his glib tongue, he can lay no claim to eloquence, his looks are ordinary with no marked features to speak of; in speech he has no remarkable address, in looks he has nothing that outstrips other men;

yu bu li zong 語不離宗
talk shop;

yu chan 語顫
fremitus;
chu jue yu chan 觸覺語顫
tactile fremitus;

yu dai xie xue 語帶諧謔
speak somewhat jokingly;

yu diao 語調
intonation;

yu duo guai li 語多乖戾
use absurd and offensive language;

yu jing si zuo 語驚四座
one's words electrify his listeners / one's words were received with raised eyebrows;

yu miao tian xia 語妙天下
unequalled in making wisecracks;

yu neng sang shi zheng 語能喪失症
aphasia;

yu qi 語氣
(1) the manner of speaking / tone;
(2) mood;

yu se 語塞
hesitate to make a response / unable to respond // tongue-tied;

yu wu lun ci 語無倫次
speak incoherently || babble in one's statement; babble like an idiot; go off at score; ramble in one's statement; use indecent language; want of order in one's speech;

yu yan bu xiang 語焉不詳
make only a bare of mention sth / not to go into details / not to speak in detail;

yu yan 語言
language / speech;

yu yan bu qing 語言不清
alalia / inability to speak clearly;

yu yan cu su 語言粗俗
one's language is vulgar;

yu yan wu wei 語言無味
drab language / insipid in language;

yu yan zhang ai 語言障碍
defect of speech / lalopathy;

yu yan zhi liao 語言治療
speech therapy;

yu yin zhen chan 語音震顫
vocal fremitus;

yu zhong xin chang 語重心長
sincere words and earnest wishes || meaningful; say in all earnestness; say with deep feeling;

yu4 yan you zhi 欲言又止
swallow back the words on the tip of one's tongue || about to speak, but say nothing; bite one's lip; hold back the words which spring to one's lips; wish to speak but not to do so on second thought;

yu4 譽
eulogize / praise;

yuan4 fei 怨誹
murmur against;

yuan sheng bu jue 怨聲不絕
always complaining / complain unceasingly;

yuan sheng zai dao 怨聲載道
voices of discontent are heard everywhere || complaints are heard everywhere; complaints rise all round; grumblings are heard all over; murmurs of discontent fill the streets; swamp with complaints;

yuan tan 怨歎
sigh with bitterness;

yuan yan 怨言
complaints / grumbles;

yue1 yan 約言
one's word / pledge / promises;

yue yan zhi 約言之
in a word / in brief / in short;

yue4 kou 悅口
palatable / savory / tasty;

yun4 yi 惲議
deliberate / discuss;

yun4 dong xing shi yu 運動性失語
aphemia;

yun dong xing shi yu zheng 運動性失語症
aphasia of articulation / logaphasia;

za1 咂
sip / suck;

za gan 咂乾
suck dry;

za zui 咂嘴
click the tongue / make clicks of praise;

za zui nong she 咂嘴弄舌
purse one's lips || make clicks of admiration; smack one's lips;

za2 luan xing shi yu zheng 雜亂性失語症
jargonaphasia;

za luan yu 雜亂語
jargon;

za tan 雜談
chat / rambling talk / random talk / tittle-tattle;

zai4 tan 再談
discuss later;

zai4 xiao zai yan 載笑載言
talking and laughing at the same time;

zan4 贊
commend / praise;

zan bu jue kou 贊不絕口
profuse in praise || admire incessantly; full of praise; heap praise upon praise; praise again and again; praise profusely; rain praise on; repeatedly speak in favour of; unstinting in one's praise;

zan cheng 贊成
agree with / consent to / hold with;

zan mei 贊美
eulogize / extol / glorify / laud / praise;

zan pei 贊佩
admire / esteem / think highly of;

zan shang 贊賞
admire / extol / praise;

zan song 贊頌
extol / eulogize / praise;

zan tan 贊歎
gasp in admiration / highly praise;

zan tong 贊同
agree / consent to / homologate;

zan xu 贊許
approve of;

zan yang 贊揚
exalt / praise;

zan yu 贊語
praises / words of praise;

zan4 讚
applaud / commend / eulogize / laud / praise;

zan bu jue kou 讚不絕口
profuse in praise || admire incessantly; full of praise; heap praise upon praise; praise again and again; praise profusely; rain praise on; repeatedly speak in favour of; unstinting in one's praise;

zan bu sheng zan 讚不勝讚
above praise / beyond praise;

zan ci 讚詞
words of praise;

zan ge 讚歌
song of praise;

zan mei 讚美
eulogize / extol / glorify / laud / praise;

zan mei bu jin 讚美不盡
appreciate sth without stopping // beyond praise;

zan pei 讚佩
admire / esteem / think highly of;

zan shang 讚賞
admire / appreciate / commend / praise;

zan song 讚頌
eulogize / extol / sing the praises of;

zan tan 讚歎
gasp in admiration / highly praise;

zan tan bu yi 讚歎不已
praise again and again / sing sb's praise without ceasing;

zan tan tai xi 讚歎太息
praise and sigh with admiration;

zan xu 讚許
praise || commend; deserve of high praise; give a high appraisal to; loud in the praise of; make sb a compliment; meet sb's approbation; pay high tribute to; praise; praise sb a compliment; praise sb up to the skies; set a high value on; sing sb's praises; sing the praise of; speak highly of; speak favourably of; win high praise;

zan yang 讚揚
praise || a pat on the back; commend; glorify; pat sb on the back; pay a tribute to; praise; speak highly of;

zan yang 讚仰
regard with admiration and respect;

zan yu 讚語
praise / words of praise;

zan yu 讚譽
commend / praise;

zang1 wu 臧誣
accuse falsely / slander;

zao1 ren fei yi 遭人非議
have one's name bandied about;

zao4 yao 造謠
cook up a story and spread it around / start a rumour;

zao yao huo zhong 造謠惑眾
confuse people with lies / fabricate rumours to mislead people / spread rumours to confuse people;

zao yao sheng shi 造謠生事
spread rumours to create trouble || cause trouble by false stories; cause trouble by rumour-mongering; start a rumour to create trouble; stir up trouble by rumour-mongering;

zao yao wu mie 造謠誣蔑
spread rumours and sling mud || lies and calumnies; make stories and hurl venmous shafts at; rumour-mongering and mud-slinging; rumours and slanders; spread lies and slanders;

zao yao xian hai 造謠陷害
fabricate rumours and trump up charges against sb;

zao yao zhong shang 造謠中傷
fabricate rumours to slander people || hurt sb by calumnious fabrication; make up stories to defame others; mudslinging; slander sb without the slightest excuse; spread rumours to injure others' reputation;

zao yao zuo sui 造謠作祟
rumours and tricks;

zao4 噪
noisy;

zao guo 噪聒
noisy;

zao4 ke 燥渴
very thirsty;

zao ke zhi ji 燥渴至極
parched with thirst to the utmost degree;

zao4 譟
abuse / slander;

zao rao 譟擾
disturb / make trouble;

ze2 咋
bite;

ze2 責
blame / reprimand / reproach / upbraid;

ze bei 責備
blame / chide / reprimand / reproach / reprove / scold / upbraid // a flea in one's ear / a flea in the ear;

ze guai 責怪
blame / give sb a piece of one's mind;

ze ma 責罵
dress down / reprimand / reprove / scold / tell off / upbraid // telling-off;

ze nan 責難
reprimand;

ze wen 責問
blame and demand an explanation / heckle;

ze xun 責詢
interpellate;

ze2 嘖
argue / dispute;

ze you fan yan 嘖有煩言
there are a lot of complaints / there are complaints all round;

ze ze 嘖嘖
the sound of approval or admiration;

ze2 shi 擇食
select one's food;

zen4 譖
charge falsely / slander;

zen ren 譖人
slander others;

zen yan 譖言
slanderous remarks;

zha4 吒
shout with anger;

zha4 咤
shout with anger;

zha4 cheng 詐稱
state falsely / tell a lie;

口 *Mouth*

zha hu 詐唬
bluff / bluster;

zha yu 詐語
fabrication / falsehood / lie;

zhan1 zui 霑醉
dead drunk;

zhang1 kou 張口
gape / open mouth;

zhang kou bing 張口病
gape;

zhang kou jie she 張口結舌
agape and tongue-tied || at a loss for words; gape with astonishment; gape with wonder; in open-mouthed astonishment; one's tongue glues itself to the roof of one's mouth; see a wolf; with open mouth;

zhang kou ning hi 張口凝視
stare with open mouth;

zhang kou qing ting 張口傾聽
listen with parted lips;

zhang kou tu she 張口吐舌
hang one's tongue out in astonishment / stick out one's tongue in amazement;

zhang kou yu yan 張口欲言
on the point of speaking // open one's mouth to speak;

zhang kou ze she 張口咋舌
cluck one's tongue in surprise;

zhang zui 張嘴
(1) gape / open one's mouth;
(2) ask for a favour / ask for a loan;

zhang3 kou chuang 長口瘡
have a thrush;

zhang4 yi zhi yan 仗義執言
speak boldly in defense of justice || speak in accordance with justice; speak out from a sense of justice; speak out to uphold justice; speak straightforwardly for justice;

zhao shuo 招說
(1) acknowledge / confess;
(2) annoying;

zhao1 xiao er 招笑兒
incur ridicule || funny; hilarious; incite laughter;

zhao4 huan 召喚
call / summon;

zhen1 hua 真話
true statements;

zhen xin hua 真心話
words from the bottom of one's heart;

zhen xing shi yu zheng 真性失語症
true aphasia;

zhen yan shi yu 真言實語
tell the truth / what one says is true;

zhen1 yan 箴言
admonitions / warning words;

zhen3 bian yan 枕邊言
pillow talk;

zhen4 zhen you ci 振振有詞
speak forcefully || say plausibly; speak plausibly and at length; speak plausibly and volubly; talk fluently and loudly;

zheng1 bian 爭辯
argue / debate / dispute / jangle;

zheng chao 爭吵
altercate / bicker / cause some fur fly / cause the fur fly / fall out / make some fur fly / make the fur fly / quarrel / squabble / tangle with / wrangle // shout-up / squabble;

zheng chao bu xiu 爭吵不休
become entangled in endless quarrels / bicker endlessly;

zheng lun 爭論
argue / debate / dispute / go to mat with // contention / controversy / disputation / passage at arms / passage of arms;

zheng lun bu xiu 爭論不休
argue ceaselessly || an endless debate; enter into endless arguments; keep on arguing; palter;

zheng ming 爭鳴
contend;

zheng song 爭訟
dispute through a lawsuit;

zheng xian qi 爭閒氣
argue trifles / dispute over trifles;

zheng yi 爭議
argue / dispute / engage in a controversy;

zheng zui 爭嘴
(1) fight for food;
(2) argue in self-defense;

zheng1 da 徵答
solicit answers to questions;

zheng1 諍
criticize sb's faults frankly;

zheng yan 諍言
expostulation / remonstrance;

zheng4 gao 正告
admonish severely / warn sternly;

zheng lun 正論
appropriate opinion / reasonable opinion / sound statement;

zheng yin 正音
correct pronunciation;

zhi1 wu 支吾
falter / hum and haw / speak haltingly;

zhi wu qi ci 支吾其詞
mince one's words || equivocate; hum and haw; make an ambiguous statement; mince matters; prevaricate; quibble; speak evasively; try to avoid giving a definite answer;

zhi zhi wu wu 支支吾吾
equivocate || falter; hum and haw; palter; prevaricate; speak with hesitation;

zhi1 ci man yu 枝辭蔓語
lengthy and confused talk;

zhi1 wu bu yan 知無不言
speak without reserve || have one's say without reserve; hide nothing; say all that one knows; speak one's mind; tell sb all that one knows without any reservation;

zhi wu bu yan, yan wu bu jin 知無不言，言無不盡
say all one knows and say it without reserve / tell the truth and the whole truth;

zhi xin hua 知心話
heart-to-heart talk / intimate words;

zhi yan 知言
words of wisdom;

zhi1 yan pian yu 隻言片語
a few words;

zhi2 chi bu wei 直斥不諱
reprimand without concealment;

zhi hua 直話
frank speech / outspoken remarks;

zhi jian 直諫
admonish without reserve;

zhi jiang 直講
explain in the vernacular;

zhi ren bu hui 直認不諱
plead guilty to a charge;

zhi sheng 直聲
shout aloud because of pains or fear;

zhi shuo 直說
say out;

zhi yan 直言
frank remarks / speak bluntly / state outright;

zhi yan bu hui 直言不諱
without mincing words || call a pikestaff a pikestaff; call a spade a spade; free one's mind; give it to sb straight; give sb a piece of one's mind; make no secret of; mince no words; not to mince words; plainspoken; speak bluntly; speak plainly and frankly; talk straight // free-spoken / plain-spoken / straight from the shoulder;

zhi yan gu huo 直言賈禍
straight talk brings trouble || be persecuted for one's frank criticism; be punished for having voiced one's critical opinions; frankness in speech causes trouble;

zhi yan quan jian 直言勸諫
use blunt words to remonstrate;

zhi yan wu hui 直言無諱
outspoken in one's remarks / speak one's mind out;

zhi yan wu yin 直言無隱
tell the truth without reservation || give sb a bit of one's mind; speak one's mind;

zhi yan xiang gao 直言相告
lay one's cards on the table;

zhi2 yan 執言
make positive assertions;

zhi3 bang 止謗
stop libel / stop slander;

zhi bang mo ruo zi xiu 止謗莫若自修
nothing stops gossip as correcting one's own way;

zhi he 止渴
quench thirst;

zhi ou 止嘔
stop vomiting;

zhi3 zhai 指摘
criticize || blame; censure; impugn; pick faults and criticize; point out the faults of others;

zhi4 ci 致辭
deliver a speech;

zhi xie 致謝
acknowledge;

zhi4 zhe gua yan 智者寡言
a still tongue makes a wise head;

zhi4 bian 置辯
argue / defend / explain / rebutt / refute;

zhi zhi bu da 置之不答
brush it aside / make no response to;

zhi zhi bu wen 置之不問
dismiss the subject || leave unnoticed; leave unquestioned; pass by;

zhi zhi yi xiao 置之一笑
carry off with a laugh / laugh out of court;

zhi neng xing shi yu zheng 智能性失語症
intellectual aphasia;

zhi4 質
call to account / question;

zhi nan 質難
blame / censure / rap / reproach;

zhi rang 質讓
admonish bluntly;

zhi wen 質問
call to account / grill / heckle / interrogate / query / question;

zhi xun 質詢
address inquiries to / ask for an explanation / interpellate / interrogate // interpellation / interrogation;

zhi yan 質言
honest talk / plain talk / truthful words;

zhi yan zhi 質言之
in other words / in short / put it bluntly / put it in plain language;

zhi yi 質疑
call in question / call into question / challenge / impugn / oppugn / query / question;

zhi yi wen nan 質疑問難
raise doubts and difficult questions for discussion / raise doubts to seek solutions;

zhi ze 質責
blame and demand an explanation righteously;

zhong1 duan jiao tan 中斷交談
break off a conversation / interrupt a conversation / terminate a conversation;

zhong1 gao 忠告
honest advice;

zhong gao shan dao 忠告善道
offer advice with sincerity and tact;

zhong yan 忠言
sincere advice;

zhong yan ni er 忠言逆耳
honest advice is often grating on the ear;

zhong4 du xing kou yan 中毒性口炎
stomatitis venenata;

zhong4 kou fen yun 眾口紛紜
everybody talking at once;

zhong kou jiao zhe 眾口交謫
be censured by everybody;

zhong kou nan tiao 眾口難調
it is hard to please all || it is difficult to cater for all tastes; it is difficult to cook it to suit everyone's taste; it is difficult to make everyone feel satisfied; no dish pleases all plates alike; no dish suits all tastes; tastes differ;

zhong kou ru yi 眾口如一
with one voice || all agree in saying; everyone

says so;

zhong kou shuo jin 眾口爍金

people's gossip is enough to melt metals ‖ if you throw mud enough, some of it will stick; public clamour can confound right and wrong; public clamour can melt metals; the voice of many people confuse right with wrong; when all men say you are an ass, it is time to bray;

zhong kou suo chuan 眾口所傳

in everybody's mouth;

zhong kou xiang chuan 眾口相傳

spread from mouth to mouth;

zhong kou yi ci 眾口一詞

with one voice ‖ all agree in saying; all tell the same story; everyone says so; in the same story; say of one accord; unanimously;

zhong shuo bu yi 眾說不一

there are many different versions of a story;

zhong shuo fen yun 眾說紛紜

accounts differ and opinions vary ‖ opinions are widely divided; opinions vary; public opinion is divergent;

zhong shuo fen yun, mo zhong yi shi 眾說紛紜，莫衷一是

as opinions vary, no decision can be reached ‖ as opinions vary, no unanimous conclusion can be drawn; there are so many contradictory views that it is difficult to decide which is right;

zhou1 qi xing ou tu 周期性嘔吐

periodic vomiting;

zhou4 咒

curse / damn / swear;

zhou ma 咒罵

abuse / curse / call names / inveigh / revile / swear at;

zhou ren 咒人

curse people;

zhou yu 咒語

curse / imprecation / incantation;

zhou yuan 咒願

oath / pledge;

zhou zu 咒詛

curse / swear at // imprecations;

zhu3 囑

direct / instruct;

zhu fu 囑咐

exhort / instruct;

zhu tuo 囑託

entrust sb to do sth;

zhu4 kou 住口

hold one's tongue / shut sb's mouth / shut up ‖ belt up; button it; button up; button up your lip; come off it; cut the cackle; dry up; hush up; not a word; not to say a word; pull in your ears; quit it out; quit your muttering; say no more; shut one's mouth; stop sb's mouth; stop talking; stop your gab; stow your gab;

zhu zui 住嘴

button up / come off it / hold your noise / hold your tongue / hush up / shut up / stop talking / stop your gab / stow your gab;

zhui2 gen wen di 追根問底

raise one question after another to get to the bottom of sth;

zhui wen 追問

question insistently;

zhui4 yan 贅言

say more than is needed ‖ unnecessary words; verbosity;

zhun1 諄

earnest;

zhun qie 諄切

advise sincerely and warmly;

zhun zhun 諄諄

earnest;

zhun zhun gao jie 諄諄告誡

admonish repeatedly;

zhun zhun jiao hui 諄諄教誨

teach and admonish with patience;

zhun zhun shan you 諄諄善誘

teach and admonish untiringly;

zhun3 hua 準話

honest words;

zhuo2 kou dun ci 拙口鈍辭
slow of tongue and clumsy of utterance;

zhuo zui ben sai 拙嘴笨腮
slow of tongue and clumsy of utterance;

zhuo2 jiu 酌酒
pour wine;

zhuo yi 酌議
consider and discuss;

zhuo2 kou 濁口
foul-mouthed;

zhuo2 諑
rumours;

zi1 咨
consult / inquire;

zi fang 咨訪
ask for advice / consult;

zi jie 咨嗟
sigh;

zi mou 咨謀
take counsel;

zi xun 咨詢
consult / inquire;

zi1 諮
confer / consult / inquire;

zi qu 諮諏
consult;

zi xun 諮詢
inquire and consult / seek advice;

zi yi 諮議
confer / discuss;

zi3 訾
attack / slander;

zi yi 訾議
criticize // criticism;

zi zi 訾訾
defame / slander;

zi3 訿
defame / slander;

zi4 cheng 自稱
call oneself / claim / style oneself;

zi chui fa luo 自吹法螺
blow one's own trumpet / toot one's own horn;

zi chui zi lei 自吹自擂
blow one's own trumpet / toot one's own horn || all his geese are swans; big talk; blow one's own horn; boast; brag; brag about; brag and boast; crack oneself up; cry roast meat; indulge in self-praise; lavish praise on oneself; praise one's own wares; praise oneself; ring one's own bell; self-advertisement; self-glorification; sing one's own praise; snow job; sound one's own trumpet; tall talk; toot one's own horns; vaunt; with a flourish of trumpets;

zi da zui ba 自打嘴巴
contradict oneself / slap one's own face;

zi fa xing ou tu 自發性嘔吐
autemesia;

zi jin 自矜
brag;

zi kua 自誇
boast / brag / crack oneself up / sing one's own praises;

zi kua zi shang 自誇自賞
establish one's own system / indulge in self-glorification;

zi kua zi zan 自誇自讚
brag and boast oneself / plume oneself || all one's geese are swans;

zi la zi chang 自拉自唱
do sth all by oneself / sing to one's own accompaniment || accompany one's own singing; hold forth all alone in defence of one's own views or proposals; play an instrument and sing by oneself; praise one's own effort; second one's own motion;

zi mai zi kua 自賣自誇
blow one's own trumpet || indulge in self-glorification; praise the goods one sells;

zi ming de yi 自鳴得意
be puffed up with pride / be very pleased with oneself || blow one's own horn; chuckle with pride; cock-a-hoop; complacent; crow over one's success; get too big for one's shoes; preen oneself; pride oneself on having

done sth smart; rub one's hands in glee; self-satisfied; sing one's own praises; with stars in one's eyes;

zi ming qing gao 自鳴清高
consider oneself morally superior to others || claim to be immaculate; imagine oneself to be superior to others; look down on others as vulgar or dishonest; profess to be above politics and worldly considerations;

zi shi qi guo 自食其果
as you brew, so shall you drink / drink as you have brewed / one must drink as one brews;

zi shu 自述
narrate one's own experience / narrate one's own story;

zi shuo zi hua 自說自話
say to oneself / talk to oneself;

zi wen 自問
ask oneself || examine oneself; search one's own soul;

zi wen liang xin 自問良心
ask one's own conscience / examine one's conscience;

zi wen wu kui 自問無愧
have nothing to be ashamed of;

zi wen zi da 自問自答
ask a question and answer it oneself / think to oneself;

zi xu 自詡
boast / brag and boast / crack oneself up / praise oneself;

zi yan zi yu 自言自語
say to oneself || soliloquize; speak to oneself; talk to oneself; think aloud; think out loud;

zi yuan qi shuo 自圓其說
justify one's argument || explain oneself away; fill up gaps in one's theory; give a satisfactory explanation for what one has said; justify oneself; make one's statement consistent; make one's story sound plausible; make out a good case for oneself; patch up the breach oneself;

zi zan 自贊
praise oneself;

zong3 de lai shuo 總的來說
all in all / by and large / on the whole || first and last; generally speaking; in general; make a generalization; on balance; overall; taking it all in all; taking it all round; taking it as a whole; taking one thing with another;

zong er yan zhi 總而言之
all things considered / by and large / in short / on the whole || at any rate; cut a long story short; first and last; in a few words; in a nutshell; in a word; in brief; in fine; in one word; in sum; in the lump; make a long story short; put it briefly; take it all in all; taking one thing with another; the long and the short of it; to make a long story short; to sum up;

zong4 jiu 縱酒
drink to excess;

zong sheng 縱聲
laugh at the top of one's voice / shout at the top of one's voice;

zong sheng da xiao 縱聲大笑
burst out laughing;

zong tan 縱談
speak freely / talk freely / talk without inhibition;

zong yan 縱言
continue an informal and free conversation;

zong yin 縱飲
drink uninhibitedly / indulge in drinking;

zou1 諏
(1) confer;
(2) consult / seek the advice of;

zou fang 諏訪
consult / seek the advice of;

zou1 謅
talk nonsense;

zou3 ban 走板
sing out of rhythm;

zou diao er 走調兒
out of tune;

zou yin 走音
clinker;

zou zui 走嘴
let slip an inadvertent remark / make a slip of

the tongue;

zu3 詛
(1) abuse / curse / imprecate / swear;
(2) make a vow / swear / take an oath / vow;

zu ma 詛罵
curse and berate;

zu meng 詛盟
oath / vow;

zu zhou 詛咒
curse / imprecate / swear / wish sb evil // imprecation;

zu zhou ta ren, ying zai zi shen 詛咒他人，應在自身
curses come home to roost;

zui3 嘴
mouth;

zui ba 嘴巴
mouth;

zui ba bu rao ren 嘴巴不饒人
sharp-tongued || be fond of making sarcastic remarks;

zui ba li hai 嘴巴利害
bitter in speech // sharp-tongued;

zui ben 嘴笨
clumsy of speech / inarticulate / not skilled in talking;

zui bi yan ming 嘴閉眼明
keep the mouth shut and the eyes open;

zui bu gan jing 嘴不乾淨
use dirty language;

zui bu rao ren 嘴不饒人
fond of making sarcastic remarks;

zui bu wen 嘴不穩
fond of talking and unable to keep a secret;

zui chan 嘴饞
fond of good food / gluttonous / inclined to eat greedily / lickerish;

zui chan du bao 嘴饞肚飽
greedy while the stomach is already full;

zui da ren 嘴打人
abuse people / ridicule people / slander people;

zui diao 嘴刁
particular about food;

zui guai 嘴乖
clever and pleasant when speaking to elders / given to sweet talking / soft-spoken;

zui guai she qiao 嘴乖舌巧
full of gibes and ready with one's tongue;

zui ji 嘴急
eager to eat;

zui jian 嘴尖
cutting in speech / sharp-tongued;

zui jian pi hou 嘴尖皮厚
sharp-tongued and thick-skinned;

zui jian she kuai 嘴尖舌快
fluent in speech // have a loose and sharp tongue;

zui jian she qiao 嘴尖舌巧
gifted with a quick and sharp tongue / have a capable tongue // sharp-tongued;

zui jian she suan 嘴尖舌酸
cutting in speech / sharp-tongued;

zui jiao 嘴角
corners of the mouth;

zui jiao dao gua 嘴角倒掛
pull down the corners of one's mouth;

zui jiao gua xiao 嘴角掛笑
a smile plays on one's lips / the trace of a smile appears at the corners of one's mouth;

zui jiao liu xian 嘴角流涎
the corners of one's mouth are drooping;

zui jin 嘴緊
close-mouthed / tight-lipped;

zui kuai 嘴快
have a loose tongue / incapable of keeping secrets // rash in speech;

zui kuai xin zhi 嘴快心直
be outspoken || frank; jaws are quick and heart is straight; sincere; straightforward;

zui lan 嘴懶
not inclined to talk much / taciturn;

zui leng 嘴冷
rough and plain in speech;

zui li fa ku 嘴裏發苦
have a bad taste in the mouth / have a bitter taste in the mouth;

zui li nian mi tuo, xin li du she wo 嘴裏念彌陀，心裏毒蛇窩
beads about the neck and the devil in the heart || crosses without and the devil within; the cross on the breast, and the devil in the heart;

zui li shuo dong, xin li xiang xi 嘴裏說東，心裏想西
saying one thing while one's mind is far away on sth else;

zui li tian tian, xin li yi ba ju ju lian 嘴裏甜甜，心裏一把鋸鋸鐮
honey in the mouth and poison in the heart || a honey tongue, a heart of gall; have honey on the lips but murder in the heart;

zui lian 嘴臉
face / look || countenance; features;

zui pi zi 嘴皮子
lips;

zui pin 嘴貧
chatty / talkative;

zui qiang 嘴強
(1) inclined to argue;
(2) talk toughly;

zui qiao she neng 嘴巧舌能
clever and plausible in speech / gifted with a quick and sharp tongue / shine in coversation;

zui qin 嘴勤
fond of talking / ready to talk;

zui shang gua xiao 嘴上掛笑
a smile is clinging to one's lips;

zui shang mei mao, ban shi bu lao 嘴上沒毛，辦事不牢
a man too young to grow a beard is not dependable || a man with downy lips is bound to make slips; downy lip make thoughtless slips; young people cannot be trusted with important tasks because they lack experience;

zui shang yi tao, xin li yi tao 嘴上一套，心裏一套
carry fire in one hand and water in the other;

zui sui 嘴碎
garrulous / loquacious / newsy / talkative;

zui sun 嘴損
cutting in speech / sharp-tongued;

zui tian 嘴甜
honey-mouthed / ingratiating in speech / smooth-tongued;

zui tian xin ku 嘴甜心苦
talk sweetly while harbouring evil thoughts;

zui tian xin la 嘴甜心辣
a cruel heart under the cover of sugar-coated words / sweet words and a bitter heart;

zui tou 嘴頭
mouth / tongue;

zui tou zi 嘴頭子
(1) ready tongue;
(2) lips;

zui wai guai cha bei lou 嘴歪怪茶杯漏
a bad shrearer never had a good sickle / a bungler cannot find good tools || a bad workman always blames hit tools;

zui wen 嘴穩
able to keep a secret / discreet in speech;

zui yan 嘴嚴
able to keep a secret || capable of keeping secrets; cautious about speech; discreet in speech;

zui ying 嘴硬
(1) refuse to admit a mistake || never say uncle; stubborn and reluctant to admit mistakes or defeats;
(2) talk toughly;

zui ying xin ruan 嘴硬心軟
firm in speech but soft in heart;

zui zhi 嘴直
speak frankly / speak out without reservation;

zui zi 嘴子
mouthpiece;

zui4 醉
drunk / intoxicated / off the nail / smashed / tipsy;

zui dao 醉倒
pass out / succumb to the effect of alcohol;

zui tai 醉態
state of being drunk;

zui xing 醉醒
regain presence of mind after getting drunk / sober up;

zui xun xun 醉醺醺
drunk / inebriated / soaked / sottish / / tipsy // under the influence of liquor;

zui yi 醉意
drunkenness;

zuo1 嘬
(1) bite;
(2) gobble up;

zuo3 shuo you shuo 左說右說
say sth over and over again;

zuo wen you wen 左問右問
ask everybody / question and question;

zuo zhi you wu 左支右吾
equivocate / prevaricate;

zuo4 ou 作嘔
(1) nauseate;
(2) disgusting;

zuo sheng 作聲
break silence / make noise / speak;

zuo4 shi 坐食
eat without toiling;

zuo4 sheng 做聲
make a sound / speak;

Lian 臉 Face

ai4 mian zi 爱面子
be afraid of losing face / be concerned with face-saving / be sensitive about one's reputation // vain // self-conscious;

ai4 mian zi 礙面子
be afraid of hurting sb's feeling;

ba1 lian 疤臉
scarred face;

bai2 lian 白臉
(1) white face;
(2) handsome young man;

ban3 qi lian kong 板起臉孔
keep a straight face ‖ as grave as a judge; as grave as an owl; draw a long face; keep a stiff face; keep one's face straight; look glum; make a long face; pull a long face; put on a long face; put on a solemn face; put on a stern expression; screw one's face up; wear a long face;

ban3 qi mian kong 板起面孔
keep a straight face ‖ as grave as a judge; as grave as an owl; draw a long face; keep a stiff face; keep one's face straight; look glum; make a long face; pull a long face; put on a long face; put on a solemn face; put on a stern expression; screw one's face up; wear a long face;

ban zhe lian 板着臉
pull a long face ‖ draw a long face; keep a straight face; look serious; make a long face; pull a long face; put on a long face; stop smiling; wear a long face; with a straight face;

ban4 guai lian 扮怪臉
make antic gestures / make faces;

ban gui lian 扮鬼臉
make faces ‖ grimace; mop and mow;

bao3 quan mian zi 保全面子
save one's face;

bei4 guo lian 背過臉
turn one's face away;

bei4 se 憊色
expression of fatigue / tired look;

beng3 zhe lian 繃着臉
pull a long face || assume a displeased look; assume a serious look; have a taut face; look displeased // with a long face; with a straight face // one's face is grim;

bi2 qing lian zhong 鼻青臉腫
a bloody nose and a swollen face || badly battered; get a bloody nose;

bi4 bu jian mian 避不見面
avoid meeting sb;

bi bu lou mian 避不露面
hide oneself out of the way;

bi mian 避面
avoid meeting sb;

bian3 lian 扁臉
chamaeprosopic;

bian ta lian 扁蹋臉
flat face;

bian4 lian 變臉
change one's countenance || change countenance; change one's facial expressions; get angry; suddenly turn hostile; turn angry; turn hostile; turn sulky;

bian se 變色
go red in the face;

bo2 ran bian se 勃然變色
turn red in the face || a sudden change in countenance; be visibly stung; go red in the face; show displeasure all of a sudden; turn red in the face;

bo ran se bian 勃然色變
show displeasure all of a sudden || a sudden change in countenance; change countenance suddenly;

bo2 mian zi 駁面子
have no consideration for sb's feeling;

bu4 gei mian zi 不給面子
not to give sb face;

bu lu xiao rong 不露笑容
keep a straight face / keep one's countenance;

bu yao lian 不要臉
without self-respect || have no sense of shame; shameless; what a nerve;

ca1 lian 擦臉
(1) dry one's face / wipe one's face;
(2) wash one's face;

cai2 mao 才貌
talent and appearance;

cai mao shuang quan 才貌雙全
beautiful and brainy / talented and good-looking;

can3 bai 慘白
deathly pale / dreadfully pale / pale;

can xiang 慘相
crestfallen look;

cang1 bai ru zhi 蒼白如紙
one's face is as white as paper // with an ashen-pale face / with a grey face;

ce2 mian 側面
aspect / flank / side;

chang2 fang lian 長方臉
long face;

chang4 bai lian 唱白臉
play the villain || pretend to be harsh and severe; wear the white mask of the villain;

chang hong bai lian 唱紅白臉
double dealings;

chang hong lian 唱紅臉
play the hero || prentend to be generous and kind; wear the red mask of the hero;

chen1 ni 嗔睨
look askance at sb with anger;

chen se 嗔色
angry look / sullen look;

cheng3 lian 逞臉
proud and self-indulgent because of being pampered;

chou2 rong 愁容
anxious expression / worried look;

chou rong man mian 愁容滿面
have a mournful countenance / look extremely worried;

chou3 醜
hideous / ugly / unsightly;

chou ba guai 醜八怪
very bad-looking person / very ugly person;

chou lou 醜陋
bad-looking / hideous / ugly;

chou ren duo zuo guai 醜人多作怪
there is never a foul face but there's a foul fancy;

chu1 mian 出面
do sth on behalf of a person or an organization;

chuang4 yan 愴顏
bitterly saddened look;

chun1 feng fu mian 春風拂面
a spring breeze stroking the face;

chun feng man mian 春風滿面
wear a broad smile || all smiles; full of joy; beaming with satisfction; one's face is lit up with joy; radiant with happiness; smile broadly;

chun feng pu mian 春風撲面
the spring wind caresses one's face;

ci2 yan 慈顏
(1) kindly face;
(2) face of one's mother;

ci2 se 辭色
one's speech and facial expression;

da1 la zhe lian 耷拉着臉
pull a long face;

da3 ge zhao mian 打個照面
come face to face with sb || meet face to face with sb; meet sb face to face; run into sb; show up;

da zhong lian chong pang zi 打腫臉充胖子
keep up appearances || a jackdaw in peacock feathers; an impudent attempt to represent the defeat as a victory; having one's face slapped until it is swollen to pretend that one has gotten fatter; keep up with the Jones; puff oneself up at one's own cost; put a bold face on the matter; put on a bold front; shabby gentility;

da4 shi ti tong 大失體統
great loss of face;

da shi yan mian 大失顏面
be utterly disgraced / make one lose face very badly;

dai1 xiang 獃相
silly look;

dan3 黵
tattoo the face;

dan mian 黵面
tattoo a criminal's face (an ancient punishment);

dan4 zhuang su miao 淡妝素描
have a simple makeup;

dang1 mian 當面
before sb's face || barefaced; face to face; in sb's presence; in the face of; in the presence of sb; personally; right in one's face; to sb's face; under sb's nose;

dang mian bo chi 當面駁斥
refute sb face to face;

dang mian bu shuo, bei hou luan shuo 當面不說，背後亂說
say nothing in one's face, but gossip a lot behind one's back;

dang mian chao xiao 當面嘲笑
laugh at sb's beard;

dang mian chi ze 當面斥責
rebuke sb to his face;

dang mian chui peng 當面吹捧
flatter sb to his face;

dang mian cuo guo 當面錯過
let slip the chance of;

dang mian di lai 當面抵賴
make a barefaced denial of;

dang mian dui zhi 當面對質
challenge sb face to face;

dang mian feng cheng 當面奉承
flatter sb to his face / speak nice things to sb's face;

dang mian jiao ge ge, bei hou mo jia huo 當面叫哥哥，背後摸傢伙
a mouth that praises and a hand that kills / honey on one's lips and murder in one's heart;

dang mian jiao zi, bei hou jiao qi 當面教子，背後教妻
you may admonish your children in the presence of others, but you wife, only in privacy;

dang mian jiao liang 當面較量
take sb on in a face-to-face encounter;

dang mian luo, dui mian gu 當面鑼，對面鼓
in one's presence / right in one's face;

dang mian pai xuan 當面排揎
give sb a piece of one's mind;

dang mian peng chang, bei hou ma niang 當面捧場，背後罵娘
pay compliments to someone's face but to curse and swear behind their back / praise sb to his face and abuse him behind their back;

dang mian qu xiao 當面取笑
laugh in one's face;

dang mian ren cuo 當面認錯
personally to admit one's mistakes before sb;

dang mian sa huang 當面撒謊
lie in one's throat / tell a barefaced lie;

dang mian shi ren, bui hou shi gui 當面是人，背後是鬼
act one way in public and another in private;

dang mian shuo de hao ting, bei hou you zai dao gui 當面説得好聽，背後又在搗鬼
speak fine words to sb's face while using dirty tricks behind their back / speak nice words to sb's face but resort to underhand means behind their back / speak plausibly in sb's presence but do mischief behind their back;

dang mian shuo hao, bei hou tong dao 當面説好，背後捅刀
say nice things to sb's face, then stab them in the back;

dang mian shuo hao hua, bei hou xia du shou 當面説好話，背後下毒手
say nice things to sb's face, then stab them in the back;

dang mian shuo ming 當面説明
state clearly in sb's presence;

dang mian xun chi 當面訓斥
reprove sb to their face;

dang mian yi tao, bei hou yi tao 當面一套，背後一套
act one way in public and another in private || act one way to sb's face and another behind sb's back; say all the proper things to sb's face but do exactly the opposite behind their back;

dang mian zao yao 當面造謠
lies are told point-blank / tell a barefaced lie;

dang mian ze nan 當面責難
fling sth in sb's face / throw sth in sb's face;

dang mian zhao xiao ren 當面嘲笑人
laugh in sb's face;

dang mian zhi yan 當面直言
say sth to one's face;

dang mian zhi kong 當面指控
charge with a crime face to face;

de2 lian 得臉
win sb's favour;

diao4 bei lian 掉背臉
turn one's face;

diu1 chou 丟醜
be disgraced / lose face / make an exhibition of oneself;

diu fen 丟份
disgraceful / embarrass oneself / lose face;

diu lian 丟臉
be disgraced / lose face || be humiliated; bring disgrace to; bring shame on oneself; disgrace; have egg on one's face; have egg over one's face // discreditable / disgraceful / humiliating / ignominious // a loss of face / dishonour / ignominy;

diu mian zi 丟面子
be disgraced / lose face || be humiliated; bring disgrace to; bring shame on oneself; disgrace; have egg on one's face; have egg over one's face // discreditable / disgraceful / humiliating / ignominious // a loss of face / dishonour / ignominy;

diu ren 丟人
be disgraced / lose face;

diu ren xian yan 丟人現眼
make a fool of oneself / make a spectacle of oneself || disgrace;

dong4 rong 動容
be visibly moved / change countenance;

duan1 fu yan rong 端服嚴容
one's dress is sober and one's face stern;

er4 pi lian 二皮臉
brazen-faced / thick-skinned;

fan1 lian 翻臉
fall out / turn hostile || break up; suddenly turn hostile;

fan lian bu ren ren 翻臉不認人
pretend not to know old friends / turn against a friend;

fan lian wu qing 翻臉無情
turn against a friend and show him no mercy || a word and a blow; be treacherous and ruthless; break up an old friendship; change colour and have no feeling; fall out with and turn a cold shoulder to sb;

fan3 lian 反臉
turn hostile suddenly;

fan yan xiang xiang 反顏相向
look with a turned countenance;

fang1 lian tu e 方臉突額
have a prominent forehead and a broad face;

fang mian da er 方面大耳
a square face with large ears || a handsome man has a dignified face and big ears;

fen3 mian 粉面
powdered face;

fen mian you tou 粉面油頭
powder the face and anoint the head / the fair sex / the ladies;

fo2 mian she xin 佛面蛇心
with a Buddha's face and the heart of a snake;

fu2 rong qi mian, she xie qi xin 芙蓉其面，蛇蝎其心
have a fair face, but a foul heart;

fu2 mian 拂面
caress the face lightly;

fu2 艴
look angry;

fu ran 艴然
(1) angry look;
(2) look angry;

gai3 guan 改觀
assume a new look / change the face;

gai rong yi mao 改容易貌
change one's looks and appearance / one's face changes its hue;

gai tou huan mian 改頭換面
change the appearance;

gan1 ku mian 乾枯面
a dead and dry face;

ge2 mian ge xin 革面革心
repent and reform oneself inside out;

ge mian xi xin 革面洗心
reform oneself thoroughly / turn over a new leaf;

ge mian xi xin, chong xin zuo ren 革面洗心，重新做人
reform oneself inside out and start life anew / repent genuinely and make a fresh start;

gei3 lian 給臉
save another's face;

gei lian bu yao lian 給臉不要臉
foolish enough to reject a face-saving offer;

gei mian zi 給面子
do sb proud / give face to sb / save sb's face;

gou4 mian zi 夠面子
gain enough recognition of one's rank / have favourable responses to one's request as a mark of recognition;

gu3 mao gu xin 古貌古心
dignified-looking;

gu4 lian hao ming 顧臉好名
care for one's face and take fancy for fame;

gu quan mian zi 顧全面子
keep up appearances as sth important / save one's face || mindful of the need for respectability; save appearances; spare sb's feelings;

gua1 zi lian 瓜子臉
oval face;

gua1 lian 刮臉
shave / shave the face;

gua lian pi 刮臉皮
point the finger of scorn at sb / rub the forefinger against one's own cheek;

guai4 xiang 怪相
grimace;

guan4 shu 盥漱
wash one's face and rinse out one's mouth;

gui3 lian 鬼臉
funny face / grimace / wry face;

han2 xiu 含羞
wear a bashful expression;

han4 liu man mian 汗流滿面
one's face streaming with perspiration / perspire all over one's face / sweat dripped from one's face / sweat like a trooper / sweat stream down one's face;

han yan 汗顏
perspire from embarrassment or shame;

hao2 bu 毫不
not in the least || devoid of; not...at all; not the least bit; nothing; without the slightest;

hao bu dong rong 毫不動容
not to move a muscle / without changing countenance;

hao3 bu yao lian 好不要臉
brazen;

he2 yan yue se 和顏悅色
cheerful countenance / smiling face;

heng2 rou 橫肉
fierce-looking;

hong2 guang man mian 紅光滿面
a healthy and hearty look || be aglow with health; glowing ruddy cheeks; have a fine colour in one's cheeks; have a high colour; in ruddy health; in the pink; one's face glowing with health; sanguine; wear a radiant face;

hong lian 紅臉
(1) blush;
(2) flush with anger / get angry;

hou4 lian 厚臉
brazen-faced / shameless / unblushing;

hou lian pi 厚臉皮
cheek || brazen; cheeky; have a thick skin; shameless; thick-skinned; unblushing;

hou yan 厚顏
shameless / thick-skinned / unblushing;

hou yan wu chi 厚顏無恥
barefaced impudence || brazen; brazen-faced; as bold as brass; barefaced; be dead to shame; be lost to shame; be past shame; be without shame; bold-faced; brass-visaged; gall; have a nerve; have no shame; have rubbed one's face with a brass candlestick; have the effrontery to; have the front to do sth; have the gall to do sth; have the hide to do sth; have the nerve for sth; impudent; shamelss beyond description; too impudent and shameless; unblushing // effrontery / impudence / impudicity;

hu2 mian cai se 鵠面菜色
look famished || emaciated; gaunt and emaciated; haggard face and vegetable colour; unnourished; pale;

hu mian jiu xing 鵠面鳩形
emaciated from hunger / haggard;

hu3 qi zui lian 唬起嘴臉
put on a solemn face;

huan1 rong yue se 歡容悅色
bright face / joyous and lively countenance;

huan yan 歡顏
happy appearance / happy looks;

hui3 rong 毀容
disfigure;

hui4 mian 會面
meet face to face;

hui4 靧
wash one's face;

ji1 se 飢色
hungry look;

jia2 頰
cheek;

jia fu 頰輔
flesh on the cheeks;

jia gu 頰骨
cheekbone;

jian4 mao bian se 鑒貌辨色
look at sb's face and distinguish its colour

— examine sb's countenance ‖ quick to see which way the wind blows — very shrewd; subtly react by noticing one's superior's countenance;

jiang3 mian zi 講面子
care about one's face;

jiao1 se 驕色
haughty expression / proud look;

jing4 mian 淨面
wash one's face;

jiu3 wo 酒窩
dimples;

jiu yun 酒暈
a flush on the face as a result of drinking;

ju4 se 懼色
look of fear;

juan4 rong 倦容
look tired / jaded look;

juan se 倦色
look tired / jaded look;

kai1 mian 揩面
wipe the face;

kou1 po lian 摳破臉
take actions in disregard of the face of the other party;

kou3 bu chuan qi, lian bu fan hong 口不喘氣，臉不泛紅
not be out of breath or even faintly flushed;

ku1 sang zhe lian 哭喪着臉
draw a long face ‖ a woe-begone look; disconsolately; go around with a long face; make a long face; one looks mournful as if in bereavement; one's face is glum; put on a long face; wear a long face;

ku3 xiang 苦相
face of misery;

ku yan 苦顏
look of distress;

kui4 se 愧色
expression of shame;

la1 bu xia lian 拉不下臉
cannot do sth for fear of hurting another person's feelings;

la chang lian 拉長臉
have a face as long as a fiddle / pull a long face // straight face // straight-faced;

la xia lian 拉下臉
look displeased / not to spare sb's sensibilities / pull a long face / put on a stern expression;

la xia lian lai 拉下臉來
look mean / make a long face;

lai4 lian 賴臉
shameless;

lao3 lian 老臉
(1) face / prestige;
(2) thick-skinned person;

lao lian pi 老臉皮
brazen-faced / thick-skinned;

lao mian pi 老面皮
brazen-faced / thick-skinned;

lao mian zi 老面子
out of respect of the aged;

lao zhe lian pi 老着臉皮
thick-skinned / unabashedly;

leng3 mian 冷面
poker face;

li4 se 厲色
look angry;

lian3 rong 斂容
assume a serious expression / put on a sober face;

lian3 臉
(1) countenance / face;
(2) front;

ban zhe lian 板着臉
keep a straight face / pull a long face / wear a long face;

beng zhe lian 繃着臉
pull a long face ‖ assume a displeased look; assume a serious look; have a taut face; with a long face; with a straight face;

chang fang lian 長方臉
long face;

gua zi lian 瓜子臉
oval face;

man yue lian 滿月臉
moon face;
meng zhe lian 蒙着臉
cover one's face;
si fang lian 四方臉
square face;
wa wa lian 娃娃臉
childish face;
ya dan lian 鴨蛋臉
oval face;
yuan he lian 圓核臉
round face;

lian bu gai se 臉不改色
keep a straight face / keep one's countenance;

lian da 臉大
big face;

lian dai xiao rong 臉帶笑容
a smile is on one's face;

lian dan er 臉蛋儿
cheeks / face;

lian dui xiao rong 臉堆笑容
one's face is wreathed with smiles;

lian fu xiao rong 臉浮笑容
one's face breaks into a smile;

lian han pi hou 臉憨皮厚
have a thick skin // shameless;

lian hong 臉紅
(1) blush / blush with shame;
(2) blush with anger || flush with anger; get excited; get worked up;

lian hong bo zi cu 臉紅脖子粗
one's face turns crimson with anger;

lian hong er chi 臉紅耳赤
become red in the face / flush crimson up to one's ears / flush up to one's ears;

lian ji 臉急
easily angered / excitable / hot-tempered;

lian jia 臉頰
cheeks;

lian kong 臉孔
face;

lian mian 臉面
(1) face;
(2) self-respect / sb's feelings;

lian nen 臉嫩
bashful / shy / timid;

lian pan zi 臉盤子
the shape of one's face;

lian pi 臉皮
cheek / face;
gua lian pi 刮臉皮
point the finger of scorn at sb / rub the forefinger against one's own cheek;
hou lian pi 厚臉皮
cheek || brazen; cheeky; have a thick skin; shameless; thick-skinned;

lian pi bo 臉皮薄
have a thin skin // thin-skinned;

lian pi hou 臉皮厚
have a thick skin // thick-skinned / unblushing;

lian qing bi zhong 臉青鼻腫
one's face has grown purple and one's nose is swollen;

lian rong 臉容
facial expression;

lian ru huang la 臉如黃臘
ashen-coloured || become waxen yellow in the face; one's face turns waxen;

lian ru si hui 臉如死灰
one's face turns ashen || one's face is like a death mask; one's face is the colour of wood ash; one's face turns pale;

lian ruan 臉軟
having too much consideration for sb's feelings;

lian ruan xin ci 臉軟心慈
faint-hearted and hesitant / shy and kind;

lian ruo fu rong 臉若芙蓉
with a face like hibiscus;

lian se 臉色
(1) complexion / look;
(2) countenance / expression / face / facial expression / puss;

lian se bu jia 臉色不佳
don't look very well // off-colour;

lian se can bai 臉色慘白
look deathly pale;

lian se cang bai 臉色蒼白
pale / peaky // with a grey face;

lian se chen yu 臉色沉鬱
look very sour;

lian se fa bai 臉色發白
become pale / lose colour / pale about the gills;

lian se fa qing 臉色發青
blue in the face;

lian se fa zi 臉色發紫
black in the face / blue in the face / one's face turns purple with anger / with a frightened face;

lian se hong run 臉色紅潤
rosy cheeks || a ruddy complexion; rosy about the gills;

lian se hui bai 臉色灰白
with a complexion like the colour of chalk;

lian se jiao huang 臉色焦黃
one's face is sallow / sallow face;

lian se la huang 臉色臘黃
one's face is like wax / waxen complexion;

lian se qing huang 臉色青黃
one's face is sallow;

lian se tie qing 臉色鐵青
one's face is ghastly pale / one's face turns deathly pale / turn livid;

lian se yan jun 臉色嚴竣
one's face is stern // stern-faced;

lian se yi chen 臉色一沉
harden one's face // one's face falls;

lian se yin chen 臉色陰沉
blue about the gills / have a sombre countenance / look glum;

lian se yin yu 臉色陰鬱
have a face like a fiddle;

lian shang 臉上
on the face;

lian shang fa guang 臉上發光
bright countenance // one's face shines;

lian shang fa shao 臉上發燒
have one's ears burn;

lian shang mo hei 臉上抹黑
cast manure on / fling manure on || sling mud at; throw mud at;

lian shang tie jin 臉上貼金
blow one's own trumpet / put feathers in the caps of sb;

lian shang wu guang 臉上無光
lose face / make sb lose face;

lian shang xie zi — biao mian wen zhang 臉上寫字，表面文章
writing on one's face — an essay on the face / superficial / no real substance;

lian tang er 臉膛兒
facial contour;

lian wu ren se 臉無人色
one's face is pale as death;

lian yi zhen hong, yi zhen bai 臉一陣紅，一陣白
flushing and turning pale alternately / turn white and red alternately;

lian yi zhen qing, yi zhen huang 臉一陣青，一陣黃
one's face becomes the colour of a green pumpkin, and then turns yellow;

lian ying 臉硬
flinty / ruthless;

lian you ji se 臉有飢色
hunger seems to be written on one's face;

lian you xi se 臉有喜色
happy expression on one's face;

lian zhang fei hong 臉漲緋紅
flush with embarrassment / turn red as a beetroot;

lian zhong 臉腫
blubber-faced;

liang3 jia ao xian 兩頰凹陷
have hollow cheeks;

liang jia fei hong 兩頰緋紅
a blush suffuses one's cheeks / a hot flush

spreads over one's face / get red in the face;

liang jia hong run 兩頰紅潤
with rosy cheeks;

liang jia liu lei 兩頰流淚
the tears fall down one's cheeks;

liang lian zi zhang 兩臉紫脹
one's face turns purple;

liao2 mian 獠面
fierce appearance / terrifying looks;

lou4 lian 露臉
appear / show one's face;

lou mian 露面
(1) make an appearance / show up || appear; appear on public occasions; put in an appearance; show a leg; show one's face; show one's head;
(2) do credit to / win honour for;

lou tou 露頭
appear / emerge / show one's head;

lu chu xi se 露出喜色
lighten;

lu chu xiao rong 露出笑容
reveal a smile;

lu chu xiong xiang 露出兇相
show one's horns;

lu chu zhen mian mu 露出真面目
show one's true colours;

lü2 lian 驢臉
donkey's face – long face;

lüe4 mian er guo 掠面而過
flit across one's face;

ma2 lian 麻臉
pitted face / pock-marked face;

ma mian 麻面
pock-marked face;

ma3 lian 馬臉
horsy face;

mai4 mian zi 賣面子
do sb a favour for the sake of friendship;

man3 lian 滿臉
all over the face;

man lian dui xiao 滿臉堆笑
a benign smile spreads over one's face / all smiles / one's face becomes suffused with smiles of joy / one's face is all smiles;

man lian fei hong 滿臉緋紅
as red as a turkey-cock / blush like a rose;

man lian feng chen 滿臉風塵
a faceful of travelling dust / weather-beaten countenance // the whole face covered with dust — hardship of travelling // travel-stained;

man lian han shui 滿臉汗水
one's face is bathed in sweat;

man lian heng rou 滿臉橫肉
cross-grained features / ugly, ferocious and pugnacious looks;

man lian hui qi 滿臉晦氣
have an ill-omened look / look very depressed;

man lian jiao qi 滿臉驕氣
swell with pride;

man lian lei hen 滿臉淚痕
a face bathed in tears / one's cheeks are tearstained / one's face is covered with traces of tears;

man lian sha qi 滿臉殺氣
look like one in a murderous mood;

man lian sheng hua 滿臉生花
smiling all over;

man lian shi lei 滿臉是淚
one's face is bathed in tears;

man lian su qi 滿臉俗氣
look very vulgar;

man lian tie qing 滿臉鐵青
one's face is darkening;

man lian tong hong 滿臉通紅
one's face reddens all over;

man lian xiao rong 滿臉笑容
all smiles;

man lian zhou wen 滿臉皺紋
have a wrinkly face;

man mian 滿面
have one's face covered with;

man mian chou rong 滿面愁容
full of worry on one's face / look extremely worried / one's face is covered with deep lines of care;

man mian chun feng 滿面春風
be all smiles / beam with satisfaction / look like a million dollars / one's face is full of joy / shine with happiness / smile from ear to ear;

man mian hong guang 滿面紅光
glow with health / have a fine colour in one's cheeks / radiant with vigour;

man mian huan rong 滿面歡容
beam with delight;

man mian lei hen 滿面淚痕
one's face is covered with tear stains / one's face is stained with tears;

man mian nu rong 滿面怒容
a face contorted with anger / one's face is ablaze with anger / red with anger;

man mian tong hong 滿面通紅
a blush overspreads one's face / flush red all over;

man mian xi se 滿面喜色
all smiles / grin from ear to ear / one's face is wreathed in smiles;

man mian xiao rong 滿面笑容
a smile lights up one's face / all smiles / grin from ear to ear / one's face is wreathed in smiles;

man mian xiu can 滿面羞慚
be overwhelmed with shame / blush with shame / extremely ashamed of oneself / flush crimson // shamefaced;

man mian xiu hen 滿面羞恨
one's face is filled with shame and remorse;

man mian you rong 滿面憂容
full of sorrow on one's face;

man yue lian 滿月臉
moon face;

mao4 貌
facial appearance;

mao bu jing ren 貌不驚人
look mediocre // unprepossessing;

mao chou 貌醜
ill-looking / ugly;

mao he shen li 貌合神離
seemingly in harmony but actually at odds;

mao mei 貌美
beautiful;

mao qin bu yang 貌寢不揚
very ugly face;

mei2 lian 沒臉
lose face // in disgrace;

mei lian jian ren 沒臉見人
too ashamed to face anyone;

mei pi lai lian 沒皮賴臉
brazen-faced || dead to shame; hang on without any sense of shame; shamelessly; thick-skinned and hard to shake off; unshamed;

mei pi mei lian 沒皮沒臉
have no shame || as bold as brass; shameless; thick-skinned and hard to shake off; unashamed; without shame;

mei3 mao 美貌
beautiful face;

mian4 面
(1) face;
(2) directly / face to face / personally;

mian ban 面般
shape of one's face;

mian bu gai rong 面不改容
not to change colour / without changing countenance || one's countenance betrays nothing; one's face is untroubled; remain calm; undismayed; without batting an eyelid; without turning a hair;

mian bu gai se 面不改色
not to change colour / remain composed / without batting an eyelid;

mian bu lu se 面不露色
not to allow one's feelings to be visible in one's face;

mian bu 面部
face;

mian bu biao qing 面部表情
facial expressions;

mian bu shen jing tong 面部神經痛
face-ache;

mian cong xin wei 面從心違
comply in appearance but oppose in heart;

mian dai 面帶
wear;

mian dai bing rong 面帶病容
look seedy / one's face assumes a sickly countenance;

mian dai chou rong 面帶愁容
wear a worried look || look blue; one's face shows a sad expression; one's face shows signs of worry; wear an air of sadness; with a sad air;

mian dai chun se 面帶春色
one's face is like the very bloom of health;

mian dai ji se 面帶飢色
hunger seems to be written on one's face;

mian dai juan rong 面帶倦容
look tired // jaded look;

mian dai nu se 面帶怒色
as black as thunder / wear an angry look;

mian dai xi se 面帶喜色
a happy expression on one's face / wear a happy expression;

mian dai xiao rong 面帶笑容
with a smiling face || one's face shows a smiling mood; wear a smile; with a smile on one's face;

mian dai yun se 面帶慍色
look disgruntled;

mian dou 面豆
smallpox;

mian dui 面對
confront / face;

mian dui shi shi 面對事實
face up to the facts;

mian dui xian shi 面對現實
face reality || face the facts; let's face it; realistic;

mian dui mian 面對面
face each other / face to face / nose to nose // face-to-face / one-on-one / one-to-one;

mian e 面額
denomination;

mian fa yu bu liang 面發育不良
ateloprosopia;

mian fa yu bu quan 面發育不全
ateloprosapia;

mian fan she 面反射
facial reflex;

mian gao 面高
facial height;

mian gou 面垢
dirty complexion;

mian he xin bu he 面和心不和
remain friendly in appearance but estranged at heart || only friends on the surface;

mian hong 面紅
blush;

mian hong er chi 面紅耳赤
one's face reddens to the ears || as red as a turkey-cook; blush to the roots; blush up to the ears; colour up; crimson with rage; flush red in the face; flush to the ears; flush with shame; get red in the face; red in the face;

mian hong er re 面紅耳熱
with one's face flushed and one's ears hot;

mian hong guo er 面紅過耳
flush up to one's ears;

mian huang ji shou 面黃肌瘦
lean and haggard || flesh emaciated and face yellow; pale and emaciated; pale and thin; thin and colourless; thin and sallow;

mian hui 面會
meet;

mian jia 面頰
cheek;

mian jiao 面交
deliver sth to sb in person;

mian jiao zhi you 面交之友
know each other by chance;

mian jing luan 面痙攣
facial spasm;

mian kong 面孔
face;

mian kong gan ga 面孔尷尬
embarrassment is written on one's face;

mian lin 面臨
be faced with / be confronted with / be up against;

mian lin ba jie 面淋巴結
facial lymph nodes;

mian ling jiao yi 面聆教益
benefit by your advice;

mian lu bu yue 面露不悅
one's face becomes clouded;

mian lu bu an 面露不安
an anxious expression comes into one's face;

mian lu juan rong 面露倦容
tired-looking;

mian lu sha ji 面露殺機
one's face is blazed with murderous hatred;

mian lu xi se 面露喜色
happiness shines from one's face / one's face is beamed with delight / one's face lights up;

mian mao 面貌
(1) face / features / looks / visage;
(2) appearance / aspects / looks;

mian mao chou e 面貌醜惡
ugly and evil countenance;

mian mao qing xiu 面貌清秀
delicately modelled features // have delicate looks;

mian mao yi xin 面貌一新
take on a completely new look / take on an entirely new aspect;

mian mian ju dao 面面俱到
attend to each and every aspect of a matter / take every aspect into consideration ‖ give mature consideration to all aspects of a question; not to miss a thing; think of every detail; well considered in every aspect;

mian mian xiang qu 面面相覷
look blankly into each other's face ‖ gaze at each other in speechless despair; look at each other helplessly; look at each other in astonishment, look at each other in blank dismay; look at each other in surprise;

mian ming 面命
instruct sb face-to-face;

mian mu 面目
(1) face / features / visage;
(2) appearance / aspects / looks;
(3) a sense of shame / face / honour / self-respect;

mian mu ke zeng 面目可憎
abominable countenance / detestable countenance / hateful countenance / repulsive in appearance / repulsive looks;

mian mu quan fei 面目全非
be changed beyond recognition ‖ beyond recognition; look entirely different; very different from the original;

mian mu quan xin 面目全新
a complete change / change beyond recognition;

mian mu yi xin 面目一新
assume a competely new appearance ‖ assume a new aspect; give an entirely new complexion to; impart a new spirit to; put a new face on; take on a new look; take on an entirely new aspect;

mian mu zheng ning 面目猙獰
sinister in appearance ‖ ferocious features; look fierce; vile visage; with grossly offensive features;

mian nen 面嫩
sensitive / timid;

mian pang 面龐
contours of the face / face / visage;

mian pi 面皮
face / face-skin;

mian pi bo 面皮薄
sensitive / with a sharp sense of shame;

mian pi hou 面皮厚
brazen / shameless / thick-skinned;

mian rong 面容
complexion ‖ face; facial features;

physiognomy;

mian rong qiao cui 面容憔悴
haggard // careworn look / scythropasmus;

mian rong shi ren zheng 面容失認症
face agnosia;

mian rong xiao shou 面容消瘦
look emaciated;

mian ru cai se 面如菜色
the pinched look of a hungry person;

mian ru fang tian 面如方田
a face presaging good fortune / one's face is as square as the character / square-faced;

mian ru fu fen 面如傅粉
the face looks white as if painted / the natural colour of one's cheeks triumphs over the artificial effect of powder and paint;

mian ru guan yu 面如冠玉
one's complexion is clear as jade;

mian ru huang la 面如黃臘
one's face is yellow as wax;

mian ru qi xin 面如其心
one's face reveals one's heart;

mian ru si hui 面如死灰
the face turns the colour of ashes || a white and bloodless complexion; one's face is as white as a sheet;

mian ru tao hua 面如桃花
rosy cheeks — said of a beautiful girl;

mian ru tao hua, mei ru xin yue 面如桃花，眉如新月
with a face of peach-blossom loveliness and two brows as finely curved as the sickle of the new moon — said of a beauty;

mian ru tu se 面如土色
look ashen / ghastly livid countenance / look pale // one's face is ashen pale;

mian ruo qiu yue 面若秋月
one's face is as bright as the mid-autumn moon;

mian ruo tao hua, xin ru she xie 面若桃花，心如蛇蝎
she has a fair face, but a foul heart;

mian se 面色
(1) complexion / the colour of the face;
(2) facial expressions;

mian se cang bai 面色蒼白
look pale;

mian se cang huang 面色蒼黃
have a sallow complexion;

mian se hong run 面色紅潤
have rosy cheeks // ruddy-cheeked;

mian se ru la 面色如臘
one's face is waxen // look sallow;

mian se ru sheng 面色如生
look as if still alive;

mian se you yu 面色憂鬱
have a melancholy look / look worried;

mian shan 面善
(1) look familiar;
(2) look kind in face;

mian shan bu shu 面善不熟
someone's face looks familiar but one is not acquainted with him;

mian shan xin e 面善心惡
a kind face but a wicked heart / bear the semblance of an angel but have the heart of a devil;

mian shan xin hen 面善心狠
innocent in appearance but a very wolf at heart; the cross on the breast and the devil in the heart;

mian shan xin zha 面善心詐
complacent look;

mian shang 面商
consult personally || discuss with sb face to face / take up a matter with sb personally;

mian shang wu guang 面上無光
feel ashamed / lose face // loss of prestige;

mian shang xiao he he, xin li du she wo 面上笑呵呵，心裏毒蛇窩
have a face wreathed in smiles and a heart filled with gall;

mian sheng 面生
look unfamiliar;

mian sheng xi se 面生喜色
look happy / wear a happy expression;

mian shou 面授
face to face teaching / mouth to ear instruction;

mian shou ji yi 面授機宜
give confidential instructions in person ‖ brief sb on sth; give a confidential briefing; give instructions in person as to how to proceed; give personal instructions on an important policy; instruct a policy personally;

mian shu 面熟
look familiar;

mian shu bu xiang 面熟不詳
that person looks familiar but I can't place him;

mian tan 面癱
facial paralysis;

mian tan 面談
speak to sb face to face / take up a matter with sb personally;

mian tuan tuan 面團團
full round face;

mian tuo 面託
ask sb to do sth in person;

mian wu biao qing 面無表情
expressionless / poker-faced;

mian wu ju se 面無懼色
look undaunted / not to look at all afraid / show no fear;

mian wu ren se 面無人色
pale-faced ‖ as pale as a ghost; as pale as ashes; as pale as death; ashen-faced; look ghastly pale;

mian wu 面晤
interview / meet;

mian xian 面癬
ringworm of the face;

mian xiang shang 面向上
faceup;

mian xiang xia 面向下
facedown;

mian xie 面謝
thank sb in person;

mian yi 面議
discuss personally;

mian you cai se 面有菜色
have a pale, anemic complexion / look famished;

mian you chou se 面有愁色
make a glum face / one's face looks worried;

mian you juan rong 面有倦容
look tired // jaded look;

mian you kui se 面有愧色
look ashamed;

mian you nan se 面有難色
appear to be reluctant / show signs of reluctance / with a look of disinclination;

mian you xi se 面有喜色
complacent look // wear a happy expression;

mian you yun se 面有慍色
pull a long face;

mian yu bei hui 面譽背毀
praise openly and slander secretly / praise sb to his face and abuse him behind his back;

mian zhe ren guo 面折人過
point out sb's mistake to his face;

mian zi 面子
(1) face / outer part / outside;
(2) face / prestige / reputation;

mian zi wen ti 面子問題
issue of face / point of honour;

mo3 xia lian lai 抹下臉來
show anger suddenly / show displeasure suddenly;

nu4 rong 怒容
angry look;

nu rong man mian 怒容滿面
a face contorted with anger ‖ look very angry; one's face darkens; the face flashes with rage;

nu se 怒色
angry look;

nu xing yu se 怒形於色
look angry;

peng2 tou gou mian 蓬頭垢面
disheveled hair and a dirty face;

peng4 mian 碰面
meet sb;

pi1 jia 批頰
slap sb in the face;

pi mian 批面
slap sb in the face;

pi1 lian 劈臉
right in the face;

pi2 lian 皮臉
brazen / shameless;

ping2 guo lian er 蘋果臉兒
rosy cheeks;

po4 lian 破臉
fall out / turn against sb;

po yan 破顏
break into a smile;

pu1 fen 撲粉
powder one's face;

pu mian 撲面
blow against one's face / blow on one's face / brush the face;

pu4 mian 暴面
make an appearance;

qi1 rong 戚容
sad look;

qi1 mao 慼貌
appearance of sorrow;

qi1 rong 慼容
sad look / sorrowful expression;

qi4 de lian fa huang 氣得臉發黃
yellow with rage;

qiang3 yan 強顏
force a smile;

qiang yan huan xiao 強顏歡笑
affected cheerfulness / constrained smile;

qiang zuo huan yan 強作歡顏
affected cheerfulness / constrained smile;

qing2 mian 情面
(1) face / feelings / personal consideration / sensibilities // face-saving;
(2) friendship / regard for others;

qing mian nan que 情面難卻
hard to decline for the sake of friendship / hard to refuse for the sake of friendship || it is difficult to break away from personal esteem for sb; the principle of friendship will not admit of a refusal;

qing2 黥
tattoo the face (ancient punishment);

qing mian 黥面
tattoo the face (ancient punishment);

qing mian yue zu 黥面刖足
have sb's kneecaps removed and his face tattooed;

qing shou yue zu 黥首刖足
brand sb's face and cut off his feet;

quan1 rong 悛容
look of repentance;

quan2 顴
cheekbone;

quan gu 顴骨
cheekbone / malar bone;

ren2 bu ke yi mao xiang 人不可以貌相
a person should not be judged by his looks;

ren mian 人面
human face;

ren mian shou xin 人面獸心
a fair face and a foul heart || a beast in human shape; a brute of a man; a brute under a human mask; a fair face may hide a foul heart; a fiend in human shape; a man's face but the heart of a beast; a wolf in sheep's clothing; bear the semblance of a man but have the heart of a beast; gentle in appearance but cruel at heart; have the face of a man but the heart of a beast; with a human face and the heart of a beast;

ren yao lian, shu yao pi 人要臉，樹要皮
face is as important to a person as the bark is to a tree;

ren you lian, shu you pi 人有臉，樹有皮
face is as important to a person as the bark is to a tree;

rong2 容
countenance / face;

rong guang 容光
dashing appearance;

rong guang huan fa 容光煥發
have a face radiant with well-being;

rong mao 容貌
appearance / countenance / features / looks;

rong mao duan zheng 容貌端正
have proper facial features;

rong mao liu pan 容貌流盼
have alluring eyes and exquisite features;

rong mao xiu li 容貌秀麗
charming appearance / pretty;

rong se 容色
peaceful and happy countenance;

rong se zi ruo 容色自若
keep an easy countenance;

rong yan 容顏
appearance / facial appearance / looks;

rong yan qiao cui 容顏憔悴
melancholy appearance / sorrowful look;

rong yan ru yu 容顏如玉
a face as beautiful as a flawless gem;

rong yan shi se 容顏失色
change of colour because of fear;

rong yan shuai lao 容顏衰老
lose one's good looks;

sai1 腮
cheek;

sai bang zi 腮幫子
cheek;

sai gu 腮骨
cheekbone;

sai jia 腮頰
cheek;

san1 tou er mian 三頭二面
cunning / double-faced;

sao4 lian 掃臉
lose face;

se4 li nei ren 色厲內荏
looking tough but scared at heart;

se xi 色喜
looking pleased;

se xiao 色笑
benign look;

shan4 lian 訕臉
brazen / shameless;

shang3 lian 賞臉
favour with one's presence;

shang mian zi 賞面子
do one the honour;

shang4 jing tou 上鏡頭
photogenic;

shen2 qing ai qie 神情哀切
sad and wretched;

shen qing you shang 神情憂傷
a melancholy air // with a sorrowful mien;

sheng4 yan 盛顏
one's look in the prime of life;

shi1 mian zi 失面子
lose face;

shou4 lian 瘦臉
angular face // hatchet-faced;

shu2 mian kong 熟面孔
familiar face;

shua3 lian zi 耍臉子
look at sb angrily;

shuai1 yan 衰顏
the face of an old person;

shuai3 lian zi 甩臉子
pull a long face / turn a hostile look;

shuang1 jia 雙頰
both cheeks;

si1 po lian 撕破臉
come to an open break in frendship with each other || have no consideration for sb's feelings; offend sb openly; rip open the face; shed all pretences of cordiality;

si po mian zi 撕破面子
cast aside all consideration of face / not to spare sb's sensibilities;

si3 bu yao lian 死不要臉
utterly shameless || brazen-faced; dead to all feelings of shame; dead to shame; devoid of shame; extremely shameless; lose all sense of shame; utterly devoid of shame;

si pi lai lian 死皮賴臉
as bold as brass / brazen-faced and unreasonable || doggedly and shamelessly; importune shamelessly; shamelessly; thick-skinned and hard to shake off; utterly shameless; with a brazen face;

si yao mian zi 死要面子
anxious to keep up appearances / dead determined to save face / try to preserve one's face at all cost;

si yao mian zi huo shou zui 死要面子活受罪
keep up appearance to cover up one's predicament / puff oneself up at one's own cost;

si4 fang lian 四方臉
square face;

ta4 ran 嗒然
looking dejected;

tao2 hua lian 桃花臉
rosy cheeks / the peach-blossom face of a beauty;

tao sai xing yan 桃腮杏眼
peach-red cheeks and almond-shaped eyes / rosy cheeks and almond eyes;

tian3 腆
bashful / blush;

tian mo 腆默
blush and keep silent;

tian yan er yan 腆顏而言
speak with a bashful countenance;

tian3 靦
ashamed and embarrassed;

tian lian 靦臉
brazen / shameless;

tian mao 靦冒
ashamed and embarrassed;

tian ran 靦然
blush for shame / come to blush with shame;

tian yan 靦顏
bashful / shy / timid;

tiao2 rong 齠容
youthful look;

tie3 mian wu qing 鐵面無情
inexorable / inflexibly just and fair / just and stern / relentless / unmoved by personal appeals;

tie mian wu si 鐵面無私
just and stern || impartial and incorruptible; integrity and justice; not to spare anyone's sensibilities; strict and impartial; strictly impartial;

tou2 mian 頭面
face;

tu2 zhi mo fen 塗脂抹粉
paint and powder oneself || apply cosmetics; apply facial makeup; apply powder and paint; deck oneself out; deck up; make up;

wa2 wa lian 娃娃臉
baby face / childish face // baby-faced;

wan3 hui mian zi 挽回面子
redeem one's reputation / save face;

wei1 lian 偎臉
put cheek and cheek together;

wei4 zhi dong rong 為之動容
become interested and show so in one's facial expression;

wen1 yan 溫顏
happy and agreeable look;

wu2 lian jian ren 無臉見人
feel too ashamed to face people || fly from the face of men; have no face to show to any person;

wu yan jian jiang dong fu lao 無顏見江東父老
have no face to go back home to see one's elders / too ashamed to go back home to see one's elders;

wu yan jian ren 無顏見人
too ashamed to face anyone || fly from the face of men; have no face to show to any person; not to have the face to appear in public;

wu3 guan 五官
(1) the five sense organs — ears, eyes, lips, nose and tongue;
(2) facial features;

wu guan bu zheng 五官不正
irregular features / one's features are not proper;

wu guan duan zheng 五官端正
have regular features // well-featured;

wu4 dui 晤對
meet face to face;

wu mian 晤面
meet / see each other;

xi1 pi lai lian 嬉皮賴臉
slobbering appearance // grinning cheekily // shameless;

xi pi xiao lian 嬉皮笑臉
grinning cheekily ‖ behave in a noisy, gay and boisterous manner; grinning and smiling; grinning mischievously; smiling and grimacing; with a cunning smile; with an oily smile;

xi3 lian 洗臉
wash one's face;

xi3 jian yu mian 喜見於面
face lit up with pleasure ‖ not disguise one's gladness; visibly pleased;

xi nu bu xing yu se 喜怒不形於色
show no emotion // poker-faced;

xi rong 喜容
happy look;

xi se 喜色
happy expression / joyful look;

xi xiao yan kai 喜笑顏開
a face lit up with pleasure ‖ a face wreathed in smiles; all smiles; an ear-to-ear grin; beaming with smiles; cheerful;

xi xing yu se 喜形於色
one's face is lit up / a face lit up with pleasure ‖ a happy expression in one's countenance; appear merry; beam with delight; beam with happiness; have an expression of delight; light up with pleasure; look happy; look very pleased; visibly pleased;

xi ying yu se 喜盈於色
radiant with joy;

xi zhu yan kai 喜逐顏開
beam with smiles ‖ be wreathed in smiles; joyful countenance; light up with pleasure;

xian2 lian 涎臉
brazen / shameless;

xian pi lai lian 涎皮賴臉
brazen / shameless;

xiang4 mao 相貌
appearance / countenance / face / facial features / looks / physiognomy;

xiang mao duan zheng 相貌端正
have regular features;

xiang mao kui wei 相貌魁偉
a man of stately and prepossesing appearance;

xiang mao ping ping 相貌平平
bland in appearance / not to be much to look at / singularly plain;

xiang mao tang tang 相貌堂堂
of splended appearance ‖ commanding appearance; handsome and highly esteemed; have a dignified appearance; have a majestic bearing;

xiang mao wei suo 相貌猥瑣
have a trifling appearance;

xiang4 像
resemble;

xiang mao 像貌
a person's looks;

xiang mao fei fan 像貌非凡
distinguished appearance;

xiao4 lian 笑臉
smiling face;

xiao lian pei hua 笑臉陪話
smile sheepishly and coax sb;

xiao lian xiang ying 笑臉相迎
give sb a welcoming look / meet sb with a smiling face ‖ give the glad eye; greet sb with a broad smile; receive sb with a smiling countenance; salute sb with a smile; smile one's welcome; welcome sb with a beaming

face; welcome sb with smiles;

xiao mao 笑貌
smiling expression / smiling face;

xiao yan 笑顏
crack one's face / smiling face;

xiao yan chang kai 笑顏常開
beam with smiles at all times;

xiao ye 笑靨
(1) dimple;
(2) smiling face;

xing2 rong qiao cui 形容憔悴
careworn look;

xing4 lian 杏臉
the beautiful face of a woman;

xing lian sheng chun 杏臉生春
have a cheerful look;

xing mian 杏面
the beautiful face of a girl;

xiu1 mian 修面
shave one's face;

xiu1 can man mian 羞慚滿面
be overwhelmed with shame || shamefaced; the flush of shame spreads over one's face;

xiu de lian hong 羞得臉紅
shame flushes one's cheeks;

xiu de mei lian jian ren 羞得沒臉見人
hide one's face in shame;

xiu mian jian ren 羞面見人
feel ashamed to see others;

ya1 dan lian 鴨蛋臉
oval face;

ya dan lian er 鴨蛋臉兒
oval face;

yan2 顏
(1) countenance / face;
(2) face / prestige / reputation;

yan hou 顏厚
(1) brazen / thick-skinned / unblushing;
(2) shamefaced;

yan mao 顏貌
features / looks;

yan mian 顏面
(1) countenance / face;
(2) face / honour / prestige;

yan mian sao di 顏面掃地
be thoroughly discredited / lose face altogether;

yan mian you guan 顏面攸關
have to do with one's face;

yan se 顏色
countenance / facial expression;

yan se zi ruo 顏色自若
calm and at ease in facial expression / composed in countenance;

yan3 mian 掩面
cover one's face;

yan mian ai qi 掩面哀泣
cover one's face and cry sadly;

yan mian da ku 掩面大哭
cover up one's face and begin to weep / bide one's face and sob bitterly;

yan mian er qi 掩面而泣
cover one's face and weep / put one's finger in one's eye;

yan mian shi se 掩面失色
cover one's eyes and turn pale;

yan mian tan xi 掩面歎息
over one's face and sigh;

yan mian wu ye 掩面嗚咽
(1) bury one's face in one's hands and begin to weep;
(2) faceup / upturned face;

yang3 mian chao tian 仰面朝天
fall flat on one's back / lie on one's back / with one's face towards the sky;

yang mian da xiao 仰面大笑
look up and begin to laugh loud / throw up one's head and laugh;

yang mian die zu 仰面跌足
stamp on the ground with irritation and in perplexity;

yang mian ning xiao 仰面獰笑
head high, one laughs ominously;

yang mian qiu ren 仰面求人
look up one's face and implore sb;

yao4 lian 要臉
anxious to keep up appearances / keen on face-saving;

yao mian zi 要面子
anxious to keep up appearances / keen on face-saving;

ye3 rong 冶容
(1) seductive looks;
(2) seductively made up;

ye rong hui yin 冶容誨淫
bewitching countenance invites lewdness / dress prettily invites adultery / seductive looks incite wantonness;

ye4 靨
dimples in the face;

ye zi 靨子
a mole on the cheek;

yi1 ge chang hong lian yi ge chang bai lian 一個唱紅臉一個唱白臉
one plays the gentleman and the other the villain;

yi lian e ba xiang, shi zu liu mang qiang 一臉惡霸相，十足流氓腔
acting the tyrant and talking gangster language / hundred per cent tyrant's features and gangster's logic;

yi lian heng rou 一臉橫肉
look ugly and ferocious // with a grim face;

yi lian ku xiang 一臉苦相
a glum look;

yi lian si xiang 一臉死相
have the seal for death on one's face;

yi lian xiong xiang 一臉兇相
a fierce countenance / a fierce look on one's face;

yi mian zhi jiao 一面之交
have a nodding acquaintance / have met but once;

yi2 se 怡色
pleasant look // look cheerful / look pleased;

yi yan 怡顏
pleasant look // smiling;

yi yan yue se 怡顏悅色
cheerful countenance and contented appearance;

yi4 se 意色
mental condition and facial expression;

ying2 mian 迎面
face to face / head-on || in one's face; right against one's face in the opposite direction;

ying mian pu lai 迎面撲來
spray into one's face;

ying4 lian 硬臉
let no personal feelings influence one's decision;

yong3 gan mian dui 勇敢面對
face squarely / face up to / outface;

you1 rong 憂容
sad look / worried look;

you xing yu se 憂形於色
wear a sad expression || draw a long face; look dismal and unhappy; make a long face; pull a long face; put on a long face; sadness is manifested on the countenance; wear a long face; wear a worried expression;

you3 lian 有臉
(1) honourable / respectable;
(2) favoured / loved;

you mian zi 有面子
gain face / have the honour;

you shi ti mian 有失體面
loss of face // lose face // beneath one's dignity;

you tou you mian er 有頭有面兒
(1) honoured / respected;
(2) presentable;

you yi mian zhi yuan 有一面之緣
happen to have met once;

you4 chang hong lian you chang bai lian 又唱紅臉又唱白臉
play the role of a gentleman and villian;

yu2 se 愉色
cheerful expression / pleased look;

yu4 mao 玉貌
(1) fair face / the face of a pretty girl;
(2) your face;

yu mian hu li 玉面狐狸
a pretty woman of loose morals;

yu mian zhu chun 玉面朱唇
a beautiful and fashionable woman;

yu rong 玉容
a beautiful face;

yu rong hua mao 玉容花貌
a fair face and elegant form // beautiful and charming;

yuan2 he lian 圓核臉
round face;

yuan lian 圓臉
moony face / round face;

yuan4 se 怨色
resentful look;

yue4 se 悦色
happy look;

yun2 lian 勻臉
powder and paint one's face evenly;

yun4 rong 慍容
angry appearance / displeased look / face of resentment;

yun se 慍色
angry appearance / displeased look / gloomy countenance;

zhang3 xiang 長相
appearances / features / looks;

zhang xiang xiang 長相像
be the image of ‖ a close resemblance between sb; a precise counterpart of; as like as peas; be a copy of; be alike; be an edition of; be the picture of; be the image of; bear close resemblance to; in the likeness of; in the similitude of; look alike; resemble; similar in appearance; take after; the spitting image of;

zhang4 hong le lian 漲紅了臉
turn red in the face;

zhao3 mian zi 找面子
try to save face;

zhao4 mian 照面
come face to face / meet;

zhe1 mian 遮面
cover the face / shade the face;

zhe tou gai mian 遮頭蓋面
cover one's head and face;

zhen1 mian mu 真面目
the real face;

zheng1 mian zi 爭面子
try to win for the sake of face;

zheng1 ning mian mu 猙獰面目
brutish features / diabolical face / forbidding countenance / grim visage / repulsive physiognomy;

zheng3 rong 整容
perform face-lifting / perform plastic surgery;

zheng4 se 正色
stern and serious facial expression;

zheng se li sheng 正色厲聲
with a severe countenance and a harsh voice;

zheng yan li se 正顏厲色
in a serious tone and with a solemn look ‖ a serious manner; keep a stern face; keep one's countenance; keep one's face straight; put on a stern countenance; with a severe look; with a straight face and in a serious tone of voice;

zhi1 yi 芝儀
your noble face;

zhi1 ren zhi mian bu zhi xin 知人知面不知心
a fair face may hide a foul heart ‖ appearances are deceitful; cats hide their claws; in knowing people, you may know their faces, but never their minds; it is impossible to judge a man's heart from his face; one may know a person for a long time without understanding his true nature;

zhu1 yan 朱顏
(1) the beautiful face of a young lady;
(2) the beautiful face of a youth;

zhu yan he fa 朱顏鶴髮
a fit old man / the hair is snow-white but the face is that of a young person;

zhu3 jia 拄頰
rest one's cheek in hand;

zhu4 yan 駐顏
preserve a youthful complexion / retaining youthful looks;

zhu yan wu shu 駐顏無術
no recipe for eternal youth;

zhu yan you shu 駐顏有術
have a recipe for eternal youth;

zhua1 po lian 抓破臉
(1) hurt the face by scratching;
(2) break off friendly relations;

zhuan3 lian 轉臉
(1) turn one's face;
(2) in a wink / in no time / in the twinkling of an eye;

zhuan mian wu qing 轉面無情
turn against a friend and show him no mercy;

zhuan mian zi 轉面子
regain lost face;

zhuang4 mao 狀貌
appearance / looks;

zi1 姿
(1) appearance / looks;
(2) bearing / gesture / manner / position;

zi mao 姿貌
woman's looks;

zi mei 姿媚
elegant and graceful manners;

zi rong 姿容
appearance / looks;

zi rong jue dai 姿容絕代
one's beauty is unparallelled;

zi rong wan li 姿容婉麗
have pretty and graceful features;

zi rong xiu mei 姿容秀美
good-looking / pretty;

zi se 姿色
beauty / charm / good looks;

zi shou 姿首
pretty face and beautiful hair;

zuo4 se 作色
change facial expression;

zuo4 gui lian 做鬼臉
make a face / make faces / mug / pull a face / pull a grimace;

zuo ku lian 做苦臉
make a wry face;

zuo lian 做臉
do sth for the sake of appearance / put up a pleasant front;

zuo mian zi 做面子
do sth for the sake of appearance / put up a pleasant front;

Mao fa 毛髮 Hair and Beard

ba1 zi hu 八字鬍
droopy moustache / handlebar moustache / moustache;

ba1 la bin 疤瘌鬢
birthmark at the temple;

ba2 diao bai fa 拔掉白髮
pluck grey hairs;

ba gen han mao, bi bie ren yao cu 拔根汗毛，比別人腰粗
one hair from one's body is thicker than sb's waist;

ba mao 拔毛
depilate / epilate / pluck out hairs;

ba mao fa pi 拔毛髮癖
trichotillomania;

bai2 fa 白髮
grey hair / white hair;
ba diao bai fa 拔掉白髮
pluck grey hairs;

bai fa cang cang 白髮蒼蒼
grey-haired / grey-headed / hoary-haired / white-haired / white-headed;

bai fa cang ran 白髮蒼髯
have white hair and a hoary beard / hoary-headed;

bai fa hong yan 白髮紅顏
marry a woman many years younger than oneself / an old man marrying a young lady;

bai fa po ran 白髮皤然
white-haired;

bai fa qi mei 白髮齊眉
remain a devoted couple to the end of their lives / with white hair and white eyebrows;

bai fa xie lao 白髮偕老
a married couple reaching old age together / live to a ripe old age in conjugal bliss / remain a devoted couple to the end of their lives;

bai fa zheng 白髮症
canities / poliosis;

ban1 bin 斑鬢
grey hair at the temples;

ban3 shua tou 板刷頭
crew cut;

bei4 er tou 背兒頭
all back;

bian1 fa 編髮
braid the hair;

bian1 fen 邊分
side parting;

bian4 辮
braid / pigtail / plait / queue;

bian fa 辮髮
(1) plaited hair;
(2) braid one's hair / plait one's hair;
(3) wear a queue;

bian zi 辮子
braid / pigtail / plait / queue;

bin4 鬢
hair on the temples;

bin ban 鬢斑
hair turning grey at the temples;

bin bian 鬢邊
temples;

bin fa 鬢髮
earlock / hair on the temples;

bin fa hui bai 鬢髮灰白
greying at the temples;

bin jiao 鬢角
(1) temples;
(2) sideburns;

bin jiao 鬢腳
sideburns;

bin luan chai heng 鬢亂釵橫
hair in disorder and hairpins out of place / unkempt appearance after sleep and before makeup;

bin mao 鬢毛
hair on the temples;

bin shuang 鬢霜
temples covered with white hair;

bo1 lang shi 波浪式
natural wave style;

bo tao shi 波濤式
irregular wave style;

bu4 dai jia fa 不戴假髮
wear one's own hair;

chan3 hou tuo fa 產後脫髮
postpartum alopecia;

chang2 fa 長髮
long hair;

che3 tou fa 扯頭髮
tear one's hair;

chi3 fa 齒髮
one's tooth and hair;

chi4 fa 赤髮
red hair;

chuang1 shang xing tuo fa 創傷性脫髮
traumatic alopecia;

chui1 hu zi deng yan 吹鬍子瞪眼
foam at the mouth and glare with rage;

chui2 fa 垂髮
have one's hair hanging down;

da3 bian zi 打辮子
knit a pigtail / wear a pigtail;

dai4 fa xiu xing 帶髮修行
submit to Buddhist discipline while still wearing one's hair;

dai4 jia fa 戴假髮
(1) periwig;
(2) wear a wig // wiggery;

dan1 hua shi 單花式
wavy;

dian1 mao 顛毛
hair on top of head;

ding3 tuo 頂脫
become bald;

duan3 fa 短髮
bob / hair in a bob / shingle / short hair // bob-haired / bobbed hair;

duo1 mao zheng 多毛症
hypertrichosis;
jia duo mao zheng 假多毛症
pseudohypertrichosis;
quan shen xing duo mao zheng 全身性多毛症
hypertrichosis universalis;

fa4 髮
hair;

fa bian 髮辮
braid / plait / tail;

fa duan xin chang 髮短心長
have sparse hair and an intelligent mind -- old in age but vigorous in mind;

fa fu 髮膚
one's hair and skin;

fa ji 髮際
hairline;

fa jie 髮髻
bun;

fa jia 髮夾
bobby pin / hairpin;

fa la 髮蠟
pomade;

fa ru 髮乳
hair cream;

fa shi 髮式
hair style;

fa shua 髮刷
hairbrush;

fa wang 髮網
hairnet;

fa xian 髮癬
porrigo;

fa xian 髮線
hairline;

fa xing 髮型
coiffure / hairstyle / hairdo;
ban shua tou 板刷頭
crew cut;
bei er tou 背兒頭
all back;
bian zi 辮子
braid / pigtail / plait / queue;
bian fen 邊分
side parting;

bo lang shi 波浪式
natural wave style;
bo tao shi 波濤式
irregular wave style;
chang fa 長髮
long hair;
dan hua shi 單花式
wavy;
duan fa 短髮
short hair / hair in a bob / shingle // bob-haired / bobbed hair;
fa jie 髮髻
bun;
fei yan shi 飛燕式
swept-back;
fen tou 分頭
hair partings;
feng liang shi 風涼式
cool style;
guang tou 光頭
shaven;
hu xing shi 弧形式
arc style;
hua ban er shi 花瓣兒式
petal style;
jiao xing shi 角形式
angular style;
luo xuan shi 螺旋式
spiral style;
ma wei bian 馬尾辮
ponytail;
peng song shi 蓬鬆式
bouffant style;
ping tou 平頭
close crop / crewcut / flat top;
ping zhi xing shi 平直形式
smooth style;
shuang hua shi 雙花式
symmetric waves;
tong hua shi 童花式
pageboy style;
xue sheng tou 學生頭
student's haircut;
yang jiao bian 羊角辮
ram's horns;
yuan tou 圓頭
pudding cut / round cut;
zhong chang fa 中長髮
medium-length hair;
zhong fen 中分
centre parting;

fa zhi 髮指
boil with anger / in a towering rage;

fei1 yan shi 飛燕式
swept-back;

fen1 tou 分頭
hair partings;

feng1 liang shi 風涼式
cool style;

ge1 xu 割鬚
cut off one's beard;

gua1 hu zi 刮鬍子
shave;

guang1 tou 光頭
shaven;

han2 mao 寒毛
downy hair;

hao2 fa 毫髮
the least bit / the slightest;

hao fa bu cha 毫髮不差
not deviate a hair's breadth / without the slightest difference || exactly the same; perfectly accurate; without a shade of difference; without the least difference;

hao fa bu shuang 毫髮不爽
exact to a tee / exact to a tittle / not the least error / not to deviate a hair's breath || perfectly accurate; there is not a fraction of difference; to a hair; to a hair's breadth; to the turn of a hair; without the slightest error;

hao fa zhi cha 毫髮之差
turn of a hair;

hao mao 毫毛
hair;

he4 fa 鶴髮
white air;

he fa ji pi 鶴髮雞皮
a hoary head with wrinkled skin / white hair and wrinkled skin;

he fa tong yan 鶴髮童顏
a hoary head and a fresh boyish complexion || hale and hearth; healthy and aged; healthy in old age; one's hair is white and one's complexion like a child's;

hong2 yan bai fa 紅顏白髮
a young lady married to an old man;

hu2 xing shi 弧形式
arc style;

hu2 鬍
beard;

hu shua 鬍刷
shaving brush;

hu xu hua bai 鬍鬚花白
have a grizzled beard;

hu xu jie shuang 鬍鬚結霜
one's beard frosts in the piercing winter wind;

hu xu man sai 鬍鬚滿腮
whiskers cover one's cheeks;

hu zi 鬍子
beard;
gua hu zi 刮鬍子
shave;
yi pie hu zi 一撇鬍子
moustache;

hu zi la cha de 鬍子拉碴的
much-bearded;

hu zi zhan shi – kai bu de kou 鬍子沾屎——開不得口
a beard sticky with dung – can't open one's mouth;

hu2 fa 鵠髮
grey hair / white hair;

hua1 ban er shi 花瓣兒式
petal style;

hua2 fa 華髮
grey hair;

huang2 fa chui tiao 黃髮垂髫
old and young / the aged and the young;

jia3 duo mao zheng 假多毛症
pseudohypertrichosis;

jia fa 假髮
wig || hairpiece / periwig / toupee;
bu dai jia fa 不戴假髮
wear one's own hair;
dai jia fa 戴假髮
wear a wig // wiggery;

jian3 fa 剪髮
cut hair / cut one's hair / have a haircut // hairdressing;

jian4 bu rong fa 間不容髮
by a hairbreadth || by a hair's breadth; not a hair's breath in between – the situation is extremely critical; within a hair of; with an ace of; within an inch of;

jiang4 jia 絳頰
flushed face / rosy cheeks;

jiao3 xing shi 角形式
angular style;

jing1 shen xing tuo fa 精神性脫髮
psychogenic alopecia;

jiu1 bian zi 揪辮子
(1) give sb a handle against oneself;
(2) to be hypercritical and seize upon sb's shortcomings;

ju2 xian xing tuo fa 局限性脫髮
alopecia areata;

juan3 fa 卷髮
(1) curly hair;
(2) curl one's hair;

kuo4 fa 括髮
tie up one's hair with hemp as a symbol of mourning;

li3 fa 理髮
have a haircut // haircut / hairdressing;

lian2 bin hu zi 連鬢鬍子
full beard;

lian2 鬑
hair hanging down the temples;

lian lian 鬑鬑
having sparse hair on the temples;

liang3 bin ban bai 兩鬢斑白
grey at the temples / with greying temples;

liang bin cang cang 兩鬢蒼蒼
greying at the temples;

liang bin ru shuang 兩鬢如霜
one's hair is greyishly white at the temples;

liao3 fa 燎髮
to singe hair — a thing that can be done very easily;

liao mao 燎毛
to singe hair — a thing that can be done very easily;

ling4 ren fa zhi 令人髮指
make one's hair stand on end ‖ get one's hackles up; make one bristle with anger; make one's blood boil; make one's hackles rise // heinous;

ling ren mao gu song ran 令人毛骨悚然
make sb's hair stand on end ‖ bloocurdling; make sb's flesh creep; make the flesh creep; send cold shivers down one's spine;

liu2 tou fa 留頭髮
allow the hair to grow;

liu xu 留鬚
grow a beard;

liu2 hai 劉海
bangs / fringe;

lü3 hu xu 捋鬍鬚
stroke one's beard;

luo2 xuan shi 螺旋式
spiral style;

luo4 sai hu zi 絡腮鬍子
whiskers;

luo4 fa 落髮
shave off one's hair / shave one's head;

luo sai hu zi 落腮鬍子
whiskers on one's cheeks;

ma3 wei bian 馬尾辮
ponytail;

mao2 fa 毛髮
hair;

mao fa dao shu 毛髮倒豎
gruesomely / with one's hair standing on end — absolutely terrified;

mao fa song ran 毛髮悚然
very scary;

mao fa tuo luo 毛髮脫落
falling off of hair;

mao fa wei li 毛髮蝟立
one's hair stands on end like the spines of a hedge boy;

mao fa zhi gong 毛髮之功
small contributions / tiny deeds;

mao gen 毛根
hair root;

mao gu song ran 毛骨悚然
with one's hair standing on end ‖ be absolutely terrified; be frightened from the tips of one's hair to the marrow of his very bones; be overcome with horror; bloodcurdling; give sb the creeps; have gooseflesh; make one's blood run cold; make one's flesh creep; send chills up sb's spine;

mao nang 毛囊
hair follicle;

mei du xing tuo fa 梅毒性脫髮
syphilitic alopecia;

min3 抿
caress one's hair / smooth one's hair / stroke one's hair;

min fa 抿髮
brush the hair;

min tou 抿頭
smooth one's hair;

mu4 fa 沐髮
shampoo;

nan2 xing xing tuo fa 男性型脫髮
male pattern alopecia;

nian1 xu 拈鬚
finger one's beard / stroke one's beard;

nian3 xu 撚鬚
stroke one's beard;

nong4 zhi tou fa 弄直頭髮
straighten sb's hair;

nu4 fa chong guan 怒髮衝冠
one's hairs stand on end with anger ‖ blow

one's top; boil over; bristle with anger; in a towering rage; make one's blood boil; so angry that one's hair lifts one's cap;

nu fa dao shu 怒髮倒豎
one's hair stands on end with anger;

pang2 mei hao fa 龐眉皓髮
shaggy eyebrows and hoary head — a healthy, aged person / with white hair and white eyebrows;

peng2 fa 蓬髮
disheveled hair // tow-headed / uncombed;

peng shou 蓬首
disheveled hair // tow-headed;

peng song shi 蓬鬆式
bouffant style;

pi1 fa 披髮
dishevelled hair;

pi1 fa xian zu 披髮跣足
with dishevelled hair and bare feet;

pi fa yang kuang 披髮佯狂
have shaggy hair to feign madness;

pi san 披散
with hair hanging down loosely;

pi san zhe tou 披散着頭
with dishevelled hair;

pi tou san fa 披頭散髮
have one's hair hanging loose // dishevelled / tousled / tow-headed / unkempt;

pi tou xian zu 披頭跣足
her hair is down and she is barefooted;

pi zhe tou fa 披着頭髮
in one's hair;

ping2 tou 平頭
close crop / crewcut / flat top;

ping zhi xing shi 平直形式
smooth style;

pu3 tong tuo fa 普通脫髮
common baldness;

qian1 jun yi fa 千均一髮
hang by a single hair ‖ a close thing; a hundred weight hanging by a hair; a near thing; at a crucial moment; by a hairbreadth; by the skin of one's teeth; extremely delicate and dangerous situation; hang by a hair; hang by a single thread; hang on by the eyelids; in a most dangerous situation; in an extremely critical situation; in grave danger; very critical situation;

qian1 yi fa er dong quan shen 牽一髮而動全身
a slight move in one part may affect the entire situation ‖ domino effect; pull a single hair and the whole body is affected — a slight partial move may affect the overall situation;

qiao4 bian zi 翹辮子
die / kick the bucket;

quan2 bu tuo fa 全部脫髮
alopecia totalis;

quan shen tuo mao 全身脫毛
alopecia universalis;

quan shen xing duo mao zheng 全身性多毛症
hypertrichosis universalis;

quan2 鬈
(1) fine hair;
(2) curled hair;

quan fa 鬈髮
crimps / kinky hair;

quan mao 鬈毛
frizzle;

quan qu 鬈曲
crimp / crinkle / curl;

ran2 髯
whiskers;

ran mao 髯毛
beard / beard hair;

ran3 fa 染髮
colour one's hair / dye one's hair;

rui4 fa 銳髮
stray hair before the ear;

san4 fa 散髮
disheveled hair / unkempt hair;

shang4 tou 上頭
put one's hair up // an up-do;

sheng1 zhang qi tuo fa 生長期脫髮
anagen effuvium;

sheng2 fa 繩髮
rope-like braids of hair;

shu1 li tou fa 梳理頭髮
arrange one's hair;

shu tou 梳頭
comb one's hair;

shu tou fa 梳頭髮
comb one's hair;

shu xi 梳洗
comb one's hair and wash up;

shu zheng tou fa 梳整頭髮
get up one's hair;

shu4 fa 束髮
reach boyhood;

shu4 mao 豎毛
the hair standing on end;

shuai3 fa 甩髮
a long, hanging wig;

shuang1 bing 霜鬢
greying at temples;

shuang1 hua shi 雙花式
symmetric waves;

si1 fa 絲髮
glossy, silky hair;

su1 fa 酥髮
lustrous hair;

su4 fa 素髮
white hair;

suan4 fa 蒜髮
premature white hair of a young person;

tai1 fa 胎髮
hair of a new-born baby;

tang4 fa 燙髮
give a permanent wave / have a permanent / perm / wave hair;

ti4 髢
wearing false hair;

ti4 薙
cut hair / shave hair;

ti fa 薙髮
haircut // cut hair / shave hair;

tong2 hua shi 童花式
pageboy style;

tong yan hao shou 童顏皓首
ruddy complexion and hoary head;

tong yan he fa 童顏鶴髮
have white hair and a ruddy complexion;

tou2 fa 頭髮
hair / hair on the human head / human hair;
che tou fa 扯頭髮
tear one's hair;
nong zhi tou fa 弄直頭髮
straighten sb's hair;
pi zhe tou fa 披着頭髮
in one's hair;
shu li tou fa 梳理頭髮
do up one's hair;
wan qi tou fa 綰起頭髮
coil up one's hair;
za qi tou fa 紮起頭髮
tie one's hair up;
zuo tou fa 做頭髮
do one's hair / set one's hair;

tou fa peng luan 頭髮蓬亂
shock-headed / tow-headed // towhead;

tou mao 頭毛
hair;

tu1 ding 禿頂
bald / baldheaded || bald at the top of the head; become bald;

tu fa 禿髮
alopecia;

tu fa zheng 禿髮症
alopecia;

tu tou 禿頭
bald / baldheaded;

tui1 tou 推頭
cut hair with clippers;

tui3 mao 腿毛
hair on legs;

tuo1 fa 脫髮
alopecia / baldness || falling out of hair; lose one's hair; trichomadesis;
chan hou tuo fa 產後脫髮
postpartum alopecia;

chuang shang xing tuo fa 創傷性脫髮
traumatic alopecia;
jing shen xing tuo fa 精神性脫髮
psychogenic alopecia;
ju xian xing tuo fa 局限性脫髮
alopecia areata;
mei du xing tuo fa 梅毒性脫髮
syphilitic alopecia;
nan xing xing tuo fa 男性型脫髮
male pattern alopecia;
pu tong tuo fa 普通脫髮
common baldness;
quan bu tuo fa 全部脫髮
alopecia totalis;
sheng zhang qi tuo fa 生長期脫髮
anagen effuvium;
ya po xing tuo fa 壓迫性脫髮
pressure alopecia;
ying ji xing tuo fa 應激性脫髮
stress alopecia;
zao lao xing tuo fa 早老性脫髮
premature alopecia;

tuo mao 脫毛
depilate || molt; shed; the falloff of old hair;
quan shen tuo mao 全身脫毛
alopecia universalis;

wan3 fa cheng ji 挽髮成髻
gather hair into a knot;

wan ji 挽髻
tie the hair into a knot;

wan3 qi tou fa 綰起頭髮
coil up one's hair;

wo4 fa 握髮
anxious to meet men of ability;

wu1 bin 烏鬢
young people;

wu fa 烏髮
(1) dark hair / raven hair;
(2) dye the hair black;

wu2 mao zheng 無毛症
atrichosis;

xi1 fa 晞髮
loosen the hair in order to dry it;

xi3 fa 洗髮
have hair washed / shampoo;

xi tou 洗頭
have one's hair washed / shampoo / wash one's hair;

xian1 ran 掀髯
the rising of the beard when laughing or smiling;

xie1 ding 歇頂
get bald as one gets older;

xie4 tou 卸頭
take off hair decorations;

xiong1 mao 胸毛
chest hair;

xiu1 fa 修髮
trim one's hair;

xu1 鬚
beard;
nian xu 拈鬚
finger one's beard / stroke one's beard;

xu fa 鬚髮
beard and hair;

xu mao 鬚毛
cirrus / tendril;

xu mei 鬚眉
beard and eyebrows;

xu mei jiao bai 鬚眉交白
grey-haired / white with age;

xu xian 鬚癬
tinea sycosis;

xu4 fa 蓄髮
cultivate long hair / grow long hair;

xue1 fa 削髮
shave the head;

xue fa pi zi 削髮披緇
shave one's head and become a monk;

xue fa wei seng 削髮為僧
make oneself a shaveling / shave one's head and be a monk;

xue fa xiu xing 削髮修行
tonsure one's head and enter the religious life;

xue2 sheng tou 學生頭
student's haircut;

ya1 bin 鴉鬢
raven black hair of a woman;

ya1 po xing tuo fa 壓迫性脫髮
pressure alopecia;

yang2 jiao bian 羊角辮
ram's horns;

yi1 ba tou fa 一把頭髮
a wisp of hair;

yi fa qian jun 一髮千鈞
hang on a hair || a close shave; a dangerous situation; a hundredweight hanging by a hair — in imminent peril; a thousand piculs suspended by a single hair — in a most precarious state; an impending disaster; hang by a thread; hang by the eyelids; the sword of Damocles;

yi fa zhi cha 一髮之差
by a hair // a hair's breadth;

yi liu tou fa 一綹頭髮
a lock of hair / a tuft of hair / a wisp of hair;

yi mao 一毛
a hair;

yi mao bu ba 一毛不拔
unwilling to sacrifice even a single hair;

yi pie hu zi 一撇鬍子
moustache;

yi4 ji 義髻
wig;

yin1 mao 陰毛
hair at the private part / pubes;

yin2 fa 銀髮
silver hair / snowy hair;

ying1 ji xing tuo fa 應激性脫髮
stress alopecia;

you2 tou fen mian 油頭粉面
heavily made up / sleek-haired and creamy-faced;

you tou hua nao 油頭滑腦
flippant / slick || frivolous and tricky; oily; shifty-looking;

yu3 gan 羽幹
hair shaft;

yu4 bing 玉鬢
white hair;

yuan2 tou 圓頭
pudding cut / round cut;

za1 qi tou fa 紮起頭髮
tie one's hair up;

zao3 lao xing tuo fa 早老性脫髮
premature alopecia;

zao tu 早禿
alopecia prematura;

zhang3 mao 長毛
get hairy / grow hair;

zhi2 mao 植毛
hair transplant;

zhong1 chang fa 中長髮
medium-length hair;

zhong fen 中分
centre parting;

zi1 髭
moustache;

zi kou 髭口
(1) bearded mouth;
(2) man's mouth;
zi mao er 髭毛兒
bristle up — get furious;
zi mian 髭面
hairy face / unshaven face;
zi nan 髭男
heavily bearded man;
zi xu 髭鬚
moustaches and beards;

zuo2 fa 捽髮
grasp by the hair;

zuo zhu tou fa 捽住頭髮
grasp by the hair;

zuo4 tou fa 做頭髮
do one's hair / set one's hair;

Nao 腦 Brain

ai1 si 哀思
sad memories;

ai2 xing nao mo yan 癌性腦膜炎
meningitis carcinomatosa;

an1 bu wang wei 安不忘危
be mindful of possible danger in times of peace;

an1 諳
know well;

an da 諳達
know well;

an ji 諳記
learn by heart;

an lian 諳練
know well;

an shi 諳事
sensible;

an shu 諳熟
conversant with / familiar with;

an song 諳誦
recite from memory;

an suan 諳算
calculate mentally;

an xi 諳悉
know well;

an4 按
contain || control; govern; keep under control; restrain;

an li 按理
according to reason || according to common practice; according to principle; according to simple reasoning; as things should be; be supposed to; generally speaking; in reason; in the ordinary course of events; it stands to reason; normal; normally, ought to;

an li shuo 按理説
according to reason || by right; in the ordinary course of events; normally;

an4 na 暗訥
quietly think over;

an xiang 暗想
think to oneself || foster an idea; muse; nurse an idea; nurture an idea; ponder; secret thoughts; think in secret; turn over in one's mind;

an zhong pan suan 暗中盤算
calculate in one's mind / figure on the sly;

an4 ji 闇記
commit to memory / recite in silence;

ba3 chi 把持
control / dominate / monopolize;

ba chi bu ding 把持不定
undecided / vacillating / wavering;

bai2 chi 白痴
(1) idiocy;
(2) idiot;

bai fei xin ji 白費心機
a sheer waste of brains || fail in one's designs; make plans to no avail; rack one's brains in vain; scheme in vain;

bai fei xin si 白費心思
bother one's head for nothing / make futile efforts / rack one's brains in vain;

bai ri meng 白日夢
daydream;

bai yong xin ji 白用心機
fail in one's designs / scheme in vain;

bai zhi nao bing 白質腦病
leukoencephalopathy;

bai zhi nao yan 白質腦炎
leukoencephalitis;

bai3 si bu de qi jie 百思不得其解
unable to find an answer even after much thinking || fail to understand even though one cudgels one's brain; incomprehensible; remain perplexed despite much thought; remain puzzled after pondering over sth a hundred times;

bai si bu jie 百思不解
unable to find an answer even after much thinking || fail to understand even though one cudgels one's brain; incomprehensible; remain perplexed despite much thought; remain puzzled after pondering over sth a

hundred times;

bai3 bu 擺佈
manipulate || arrange; push about; push around;

ban4 dong bu dong 半懂不懂
half being barely intelligible / not fully understand;

ban feng bu dian 半瘋不癲
crazy;

ban hun mi 半昏迷
semicoma;

ban xin ban yi 半信半疑
not quite believe / not quite convinced // take with a grain of salt / take with a pinch of salt;

bao3 chi leng jing 保持冷靜
keep one's cool || keep a cool head; keep cool; keep one's head; keep one's shirt on; maintain one's cool; play it cool; remain calm; remain composed; remain cool; remain imperturbable // cool-headed // presence of mind;

bao3 zhu nao dai 保住腦袋
save one's neck;

bao4 nian 抱念
remember / think of;

bei1 gong she ying 杯弓蛇影
extremely suspicious || imaginary fears; self-created suspicion; shy at a shadow;

bei1 bao fu 揹包袱
have a load on one's mind || carry a burden; have a weight on one's mind; take on a mental burden;

bei4 li 背理
go against good conscience / go against good reason;

bei4 li 悖理
absurd / irrational / unreasonable;

bi4 men si guo 閉門思過
reflect on one's faults in private;

bian1 yuan xing nao yan 邊緣性腦炎
limbic encephalitis;

bian4 辨
(1) differentiate / discern / discriminate / distinguish;
(2) identify / recognize;

bian bai 辨白
(1) distinguish clearly / identify clearly;
(2) account for;

bian bie 辨別
differentiate / discriminate / distinguish / make out sb / make out sth;

bian bie shi fei 辨別是非
discern what is right from what is wrong;

bian bie zhen wei 辨別真偽
discern the false from the genuine / distinguish the true from the false;

bian ming 辨明
distinguish between;

bian ming shi fei 辨明是非
distinguish between right and wrong;

bian ren 辨認
identify / make out / recognize;

bian se ce yan 辨色測驗
colour discrimination / colour vision test;

bian shi 辨識
(1) identification;
(2) recognize // discernible;

bian xi 辨析
differentiate and analyse / discriminate;

bian yi 辨異
distinguish differences between things;

bian zheng 辨證
discriminate;

bing1 xue cong ming 冰雪聰明
very clever;

bing4 du xing nao ji sui yan 病毒性腦脊髓炎
viral encephalomyelitis;

bing du xing nao mo yan 病毒性腦膜炎
viral meningitis;

bo2 shi 博識
erudite / learned;

bo wen guang shi 博聞廣識
extensive information and learning;

bo wen qiang ji 博聞強記
have wide learning and a retentive memory || have encyclopaedic knowledge;

have extensive knowledge and a powerful memory; have wide learning and a good memory; with a wide range of knowledge and a long memory;

bo xue 博學
erudite / learned || extensive study; knowledgeable; well-read; well-versed; wide range of studies or learning;

bo xue duo cai 博學多才
well-read and talented || erudite; learned; of extensive learning; savant; well-read;

bo xue duo neng 博學多能
have extensive learning and ability;

bo xue duo wen 博學多聞
learned and well-informed / wealthy in knowledge;

bo xue hong ci 博學宏詞
extensive learning and great literary talent;

bo xue hong ru 博學鴻儒
person of wide learning / profound scholar / well-informed scholar;

bo xue zhuo shi 博學卓識
have vast knowledge and experience;

bu4 bao huan xiang 不抱幻想
cherish no illusions / not to cherish fancies;

bu bao pian jian 不抱偏見
have no bias against / hold no prejudice;

bu bian shi fei 不辨是非
fail to make a distinction between right and wrong / not know chalk from cheese;

bu bian shu mai 不辨菽麥
not able to know beans from wheat || cannot tell beans from wheat; have no knowledge of practical matters; incapable of distinguishing between beans and wheat; not to know chalk from cheese;

bu bian zhen wei 不辨真偽
unable to tell the true from the false || fail to distinguish between truth and falsehood; not know chalk from cheese; unable to distinguish the genuine from the imitation;

bu bian zi ming 不辨自明
be made clear without debate / self-evident;

bu chu suo liao 不出所料
as expected || as anticipated; as foreseen; as might have been expected; as predicted; happen just as expected; it does not exceed one's expectations; just as expected; not at all surprising; not unexpected; things do not turn out beyond one's expectations; think as much; turn out just as expected; within expectation;

bu de er zhi 不得而知
do not know / there is no way to know;

bu dong ren shi 不懂人事
ignorant of the ways of the world / not to know the ways of the world || inexperienced in life;

bu dong shi 不懂事
naive;

bu dong zhuang dong 不懂裝懂
pretend to know when one does not know / smatter;

bu dong nao jin 不動腦筋
don't take the trouble to think / don't use one's brain;

bu he luo ji 不合邏輯
illogical;

bu jia si suo 不假思索
respond without thinking // offhand // off the top of one's head / without hesitation;

bu kan she xiang 不堪設想
unthinkable;

bu ke bian shi 不可辨識
indiscernible;

bu ke gu liang 不可估量
incalculable / inestimable;

bu ke li jie 不可理解
beyond one's comprehension / incomprehensible / inscrutable // defy comprehension / elude comprehension;

bu ke li yu 不可理喻
cannot be brought to reason / impervious to reason / not subject to reason / unreasonable / won't listen to reason;

bu ke si yi 不可思議
inconceivable || as if by magic; beyond comprehension; beyond conception; boggle

the mind; uncanny; unimaginable;

bu ke xiang xiang 不可想像
inconceivable || as if by magic; beyond comprehension; beyond conception; boggle the mind; uncanny; unimaginable;

bu ke xin 不可信
implausible / incredible;

bu li jie 不理解
incomprehensive;

bu liao jie 不了解
do not comprehend / do not understand;

bu liao 不料
never thought // unexpectedly;

bu liu yi 不留意
careless;

bu ming 不明
(1) fail to understand // unknown;
(2) not clear // unclear;

bu ming di yun 不明底蘊
ignorant to the true picture;

bu ming shi li 不明事理
lack of common sense // unreasonable;

bu ming shi fei 不明是非
confuse right and wrong;

bu ming zhen xiang 不明真相
not to understand the true situation || be kept in the dark; ignorant of the actual situation; ignorant of the facts; not to know the truth of the matter;

bu ming zhi 不明智
injudicious;

bu rong zhi yi 不容置疑
admit of no doubt / allow of no doubt / leave no room for doubt // incontrovertible / indisputable / indubitable / undisputed / undoubtable / undoubted // above suspicion / beyond doubt / beyond question;

bu shi zi 不識字
illiterate;

bu xin ren 不信任
mistrust;

bu yu kao lü 不予考慮
do not consider;

bu zhi bu jue 不知不覺
without knowing it / unconsciously;

bu zhi dao 不知道
do not know / have no idea / have no knowledge of / not have a clue // clueless;

bu zhi gan ku 不知甘苦
do not know the difficulty of doing sth;

bu zhi qing zhong 不知輕重
unable to tell the significane of a situation;

bu zhi qing 不知情
be in the dark / not to know about sth / out of the picture;

bu zhi tian gao di hou 不知天高地厚
think too much of one's abilities;

cai1 猜
(1) conjecture / draw the bow / guess / guess at / speculate;
(2) suspect // suspicion;

cai bu tou 猜不透
cannot read sb's mind / unable to guess / unable to make out;

cai bu zhao 猜不着
cannot guess || miss one's guess; unable to make out the right answer; unable to reach the right answer;

cai ce 猜測
(1) guess || conjecture; draw the bow; guestimate; speculate; surmise // speculation;
(2) suspect;

cai chu 猜出
dope out / guess at;

cai dao 猜到
guess;

cai dui 猜對
make a correct guess || hit it; right in one's guess;

cai duo 猜度
conjecture || draw the bow; guess and assess; speculate; surmise;

cai duo zai san 猜度再三
form a judgment again and again;

cai mei 猜枚
guessing game;

腦 *Brain*

cai po 猜破
make out;

cai tou 猜透
guess correctly / make a correct guess / outguess;

cai tou xin si 猜透心思
read sb's mind;

cai xian 猜嫌
suspicious and jealous;

cai xiang 猜想
guess / imagine / suppose / suspect / think;

cai yi 猜疑
suspect || harbour suspicions; have misgivings; suspicious;

cai zhong 猜中
guess right / make a right guess;

cai2 si 才思
brilliant thoughts;

cai si min jie 才思敏捷
have an agile imagination // nimble;

cai wu 才悟
aptitude / intelligence;

cai zhi 才智
gumption / intelligence;

can1 tou 參透
understand profundities;

can wu 參悟
understand from meditation;

can zhi huan jue 殘肢幻覺
stump hallucination;

chang3 xiong lu huai 敞胸露懷
bare the breast / frank / open-minded;

chen2 si 沈思
be immersed in thought / be lost in thought / meditate / ponder // in a brown study // contemplative / deliberating / meditative / pensive / ponderous / reflective;

chen si ban shang 沈思半晌
be wrapped in thought;

chen si chu shen 沈思出神
be lost in contemplation;

chen si ming xiang 沈思冥想
be in a brown study / cudgel one's brains / think long and hard;

chen si mo xiang 沈思默想
in a brown study / meditate insilence // meditation / rumination;

chen si ning xiang 沈思凝想
think deeply or profoundly;

chen yin 沈吟
meditate in silence / mutter to oneself / unable to make up one's mind;

chen yin ban xiang 沈吟半晌
meditate in perfect silence for a while / remain in deep thought for some time;

chen yin bu jue 沈吟不決
(1) hesitate / unable to make up one's mind;
(2) irresolute / undecided;

chen yin liang jiu 沈吟良久
mutter to oneself for a long while / ponder long in silence;

chen yin wei jue 沈吟未決
hesitant / irresolute / undecided;

cheng2 jian 成見
bias / preconceived idea / prejudice;

cheng zhu zai xiong 成竹在胸
know what to do in the mind || have an ace up one's sleeve; have definite ideas in one's mind; have the cards in one's own hands;

chi1 tou 吃透
ascertain thoroughly / have a thorough grasp / understand thoroughly;

chi tou liang tou 吃透兩頭
have a thorough grasp of the party's policies and a thorough understanding of the views of the masses;

chi1 痴
(1) idiotic / silly;
(2) crazy about;

chi dai 痴呆
(1) dull-witted / stupid;
(2) dementia;
chuang shang hou chi dai 創傷後痴呆
post-traumatic dementia;

jiu jing xing chi dai 酒精性痴呆
alcoholic dementia;
lao nian chi dai 老年痴呆
senile dementia;
ma bi xing chi dai 麻痺性痴呆
paralytic dementia;
zao fa xing chi dai 早發性痴呆
dementia praecox;
zao lao xing chi dai 早老性痴呆
presenile dementia;
zhong du xing chi dai 中毒性痴呆
toxic dementia;

chi dai zheng 痴呆症
dementia;

chi dai dai 痴呆呆
dumbfounded;

chi kuang 痴狂
crazy about / infatuated with;

chi mi 痴迷
crazy / infatuated / obsessed;

chi tou chi nao 痴頭痴腦
crazy / idiotic;

chi xiang 痴想
illusion / wishful thinking;

chi xiao xing dian xian 痴笑性癲癇
gelastic epilepsy;

chi yu 痴愚
imbecility / moronity;

chi2 xin pang wu 馳心旁騖
in an absent-minded sort of way / one's mind keeps wandering off;

chi2 踟
hesitate;

chi chu 踟躕
hesitate / waver;

chi chu bu jue 踟躕不決
remain in an undecided state;

chi chu bu qian 踟躕不前
falter to press forward / hesitate to move forward / tarry to go forward;

chi2 ben 遲笨
slow;

chi dun 遲鈍
obtuse / slow;

chi fa xing dian xian 遲發性癲癇
tardy epilepsy;

chi yi 遲疑
hesitate;

chi yi bu jue 遲疑不決
cannot make up one's mind || hesitate; hesitate to make a decision; irresolute; undecided;

chi yi zuo kun 遲疑坐困
hesitate and allow oneself to be tied down / hesitate in a self-imposed predicament;

chong1 hun tou nao 衝昏頭腦
be carried away || be eaten up; be lost in; become dizzy with; beside oneself with; dizzy with; get dizzy with; get swollen-headed; giddy with; go to sb's head; have one's head turned; in heaven; lose one's head in; lose one's mind; off one's head; out of one's mind; turn one's head;

chong2 shen ji jian 重申己見
reiterate one's views;

chong tan lao diao 重彈老調
harp on the same string / sing the same old tune / strike up an old tune;

chong xin kao lü 重新考慮
reconsider;

chong zhen jing shen 重振精神
second breath / second wind;

chou1 si bo jian 抽絲剝繭
make a painstaking investigation;

chou2 躊
(1) hesitant;
(2) complacent / confident;

chou chu 躊躇
dither / hesitate // shilly-shally;

chou chu ban shang 躊躇半晌
ponder for a while;

chou chu bu an 躊躇不安
have the fidgets // in fidgets;

chou chu bu jue 躊躇不決
think back and forth without end / uncertain

as to what decision or action to take;

chou chu bu qian 躊躇不前

hesitate to move forward || hang back; hesitate to make a move; hold back; jib at; show reluctance to go forward;

chou chu man zhi 躊躇滿志

be elated with success || be self-satisfied; complacent; enormously proud of one's success; erect one's crest; feel self-satisfied; puffed up with pride; smug;

chou chu pang huang 躊躇徬徨

dawdle and hesitate;

chu1 hu suo liao 出乎所料

beyond expectation / out of one's reckoning;

chu hu yi liao 出乎意料

beyond expectation / contrary to one's expectations || come from out in left field; cup the climax; exceed one's expectations; out of a clear sky; out of nowhere; outside of expectation; to one's amazement; to one's surprise; unexpectedly;

chu ren yi liao 出人意料

beyond everyone's expectation / contrary to everyone's expectations || cup the climax; exceed one's expectations; out of a clear sky; out of nowhere; outside of expectation; to one's amazement; to one's surprise; unexpectedly;

chu shen 出神

be lost in thought / in a muse / spellbound;

chu shen chen si 出神沉思

be buried in thought / be lost in thought;

chu xue xig nao yan 出血性腦炎

hemorrhagic encephalitis;

chu4 jue shi shi zheng 觸覺失識症

tactile agnosia;

chuai3 揣

(1) calculate / estimate / measure / reckon / weigh;

(2) probe;

chuai ce 揣測

conjecture / guess / reckon / surmise;

chuai duo 揣度

appraise / conjecture / estimate / reckon / surmise;

chuai duo di qing 揣度敵情

make an appraisal of the enemy's situation;

chuai mo 揣摩

try to fathom / try to figure out;

chuai mo hua yi 揣摩話意

figure out the hidden meaning of sb's words;

chuai qing duo li 揣情度理

consider the circumstances and judge by common sense || make a reasonable appraisal of the situation; reckon the situation; weigh the pros and cons;

chuai xiang 揣想

conjecture / imagine / make an intelligent guess;

chuan1 zao 穿鑿

give a far-fetched interpretation / read too much into sth;

chuan zao fu hui 穿鑿附會

twist or pervert the meaning of sth || bring in by head and shoulders; distorted conclusion; drag in by head and shoulders; fasten on an unwarranted conclusion; force words into a sense; give strained interpretations and draw farfetched analogies; make a forced interpretation; offer farfetched explanation; push in by the head and shoulders; strain the sense; stretch the meaning; thrust in by head and shoulders; wrest the sense;

chuang1 shang hou chi dai 創傷後痴呆

posttraumatic dementia;

chuang shang hou dian xian 創傷後癲癇

posttraumatic epilepsy;

chuang shang xing dian xian 創傷性癲癇

traumatic epilepsy;

chun1 ji nao yan 春季腦炎

vernal encephalitis;

chun3 蠢

(1) stupid || bog-ignorant; boneheaded; foolish; idiotic; silly;

(2) clumsy;

chun ben 蠢笨

awkward / bog-ignorant / clumsy / foolish / stupid;

chun ben ru niu 蠢笨如牛
dumb as oxen;

chun cai 蠢材
fool / idiot || blistering idiot; blockhead; bloody fool; bonehead; cabbagehead; dunce; pig-headed person; stupid person;

chun hua 蠢話
blather / foolish words / maladroit remark / nonsense / rubbish;

chun huo 蠢貨
blockhead / dunce / idiot;

chun lü 蠢驢
ass / donkey / idiot;

chun ren 蠢人
blockhead / fool;

chun shi 蠢事
fooly / tomfoolery;

chun zhu 蠢豬
ass / idiot / stupid swine;

cong1 hui 聰慧
astute / bright / clever / intelligent;

cong jun 聰俊
intelligent and attractive;

cong min 聰敏
clever and intelligent;

cong ming 聰明
clever || as sharp as a needle; astute; bright; intelligent; smart; wise;

cong ming cai zhi 聰明才智
wisdom and ability || ability and cleverness; intelligence and wisdom; wisdom and talents;

cong ming dong shi 聰明懂事
clever and sensible;

cong ming fan bei cong ming wu 聰明反被聰明誤
a wise man can be ruined by his own wisdom / fall victim to one's own cleverness || clever people may be victims of their own cleverness; cleverness may overreach itself; every man has a fool in his sleeve; suffer for one's wisdom;

cong ming guo ren 聰明過人
too clever by half;

cong ming hao xue 聰明好學
bright and diligent / clear and eager to learn / intelligent and fond of study;

cong ming huo po 聰明活潑
clever and active || intelligent and lively; wise and active;

cong ming jue ding 聰明絕頂
extremely clever / extremely intelligent;

cong ming ling li 聰明伶俐
clever and quick-witted || clever and sensible; intelligent and smart; quick on the uptake;

cong ming neng gan 聰明能幹
clever and capable || have a good head on one's shoulders; clever and capable;

cong ming rui zhi 聰明叡智
intellectual virtues;

cong ming tou ding 聰明透頂
clever to the extreme / extremely clever;

cong ming yi shi, hu tu yi shi 聰明一世，糊塗一時
a clever man has his stupid moments || a lifetime of cleverness can be interrupted by moments of stupidity; clever all one's life, but stupid this once; smart as a rule, but this time a fool;

cong ming yi shi, meng dong yi shi 聰明一世，懵懂一時
wise for a lifetime but foolish at a critical moment || quick-witted throughout one's life, but bewildered for a single moment;

cong ming you wei 聰明有為
intelligent and promising;

cong ming zhi hui 聰明智慧
sagacious / very intelligent;

cong ming zi wu 聰明自誤
be ruined by one's own cleverness || too smart;

cong rui 聰叡
bright and far-sighted;

cong ying 聰穎
as sharp as a needle / bright / clever / intelligent;

cun3 忖
ponder / speculate / turn over in one's mind;

cun duo 忖度
conjecture / presume / speculate / suppose / surmise;

cun liang 忖量
(1) think over / turn over in one's mind;
(2) conjecture / guess;

da2 guan 達觀
optimistic ‖ philosophical; take things philosophically;

da guan an ming 達觀安命
take things as they come;

da qing da li 達情達理
understanding and reasonable ‖ sensible; show good sense; stand to reason;

da tian zhi ming 達天知命
aware that all things depend upon the will of heaven;

da yi 達意
convey one's ideas / express one's ideas;

da yu shi li 達於事理
understanding and amenable to reason;

da3 ding zhu yi 打定主意
arrive at a decision ‖ hold firmly one's determination; make up one's mind; set one's heart on;

da duan si lu 打斷思路
interrupt sb's train of thought;

da ru yi suan pan 打如意算盤
expect things to turn out as one wishes / indulge in wishful thinking;

da suan 打算
intend ‖ be going to; have a mind to; have it in mind; mean; plan; set out; think // calculation / consideration / intention;

da tan 打探
ask about / inquire about ‖ investigate; reconnoitre;

da tan di qing 打探敵情
reconnoitre the enemy's position;

da tan xu shi 打探虛實
ascertain the actual situation;

da ting 打聽
inquire about ‖ ask about; find out; get a line on; pry;

da xiao 打消
dispel / get rid of / give up / remove;

da xiao gu lü 打消顧慮
dispel misgivings;

da xiao nian tou 打消念頭
dismiss the idea / drop the idea / give up the idea;

da zhu yi 打主意
(1) evolve an idea / make a decision / think of a plan;
(2) have ideas about ‖ plan; seek; try to obtain;

da4 bu wei ran 大不謂然
hold entirely different views ‖ definitely regard it as wrong; greatly differ;

da che da wu 大徹大悟
great awakening / greatly discerning and apprehending;

da chu suo liao 大出所料
well beyond expectations;

da chu suo wang 大出所望
well beyond one's expectations / well beyond one's hopes;

da fei zhou zhang 大費周章
make much ado / take great pains;

da huo bu jie 大惑不解
be greatly puzzled ‖ be not a little bewildered; unable to make head or tail of sth;

da nao 大腦
cerebrum / forebrain;

da nao ban qiu 大腦半球
cerebral hemisphere / hemicerebrum;

da nao bing 大腦病
cerebrosis;

da nao chu xue xing zhong feng 大腦出血性中風
haemorrhagia cerebri;

da nao feng shi bing 大腦風濕病
cerebral rheumatism;

da nao ma bi 大腦麻痺
cerebral paralysis;

da nao si wang 大腦死亡
cerebral death;

da nao yan 大腦炎
cerebritis;

da shang nao jin 大傷腦筋
put a great strain on sb's nerves || cudgel one's brains; puzzle one's brains; rack one's brains;

da zhi 大志
high aims / high aspirations / lofty aims;

da zhi ruo yu 大智若愚
the wisest person is often stupid-looking / an intelligent person looks dull || a man of great wisdom often appears slow-witted; a master mind looks like a fool; great wisdom takes the looks of folly; smooth water runs deep; still waters run deep; the greatest wisdom is like foolishness;

dai1 呆
(1) dull-witted || dim-witted; dull; dull of mind; dull-brained; slow-witted; stupid; unintelligent;
(2) empty-headed || blank; blank-minded; vacuous; wooden;

dai ban 呆板
(1) boring / dull || as dull as ditchwater; inflexible; rigid; stereotyped;
(2) stiff || rigid; starchy;

dai ban fa wei 呆板乏味
as dull as ditchwater / dull and uninteresting / very dull;

dai dai chu shen 呆呆出神
be absorbed in thought / be lost in one's own thoughts / in a brown study;

dai leng 呆楞
in a daze // stare blankly;

dai mu 呆木
dazed and numb;

dai ruo mu ji 呆若木雞
transfixed;

dai sha 呆傻
dazed / stupefied;

dai tou dai nao 呆頭呆腦
muddleheaded || a bit weak in the head; dull-looking; idiotic; idiotic-looking; pudding-headed; stupid; stupid-looking;

dai tou dai nao de yang zi 呆頭呆腦的樣子
look like a dummy / look like a stuffed dummy;

dai zheng 呆怔
in a daze // stare blankly;

dai zheng zheng 呆怔怔
be dazed;

dai zhi 呆滯
(1) dull / inert / lifeless;
(2) dull / idle / slack / sluggish / stagnant;

dai1 獃
(1) foolish / idiotic / silly / stupid;
(2) awkward / bungling / clumsy / maladroit;
(3) depressed / in low spirit;

dai dai di 獃獃地
idiotically / stupidly;

dai tou dai nao 獃頭獃腦
dull-looking;

dai3 nian 歹念
evil thoughts;

dan1 si 耽思
think deeply / ponder;

dan1 殫
exhaust / use up;

dan men 殫悶
faint / lose consciousness;

dan si ji lü 殫思極慮
rack one's brains;

dan4 wang 淡忘
fade from one's memory;

dang1 ji li duan 當機立斷
make a prompt decision || decide in the nick of time; decide on the moment; decide on the spot; decide promptly and opportunely; make a rapid appraisal; prompt decision at the right moment; take prompt action;

dao4 bei ru liu 倒背如流
can even recite sth backwards / know sth thoroughly by heart;

de2 chu 得出
obtain a result / reach a conclusion;

de chu jie lun 得出結論
arrive at a conclusion || come at a conclusion; come to a conclusion; draw a conclusion; reach a conclusion;

de ji 得計
have a winning hand;

de long wang shu 得隴望蜀
the more one gets, the more one wants || ambition grows with success; appetite comes with eating; give him an inch and he will take a mile;

di1 gu 低估
disappreciate / underestimate / underrate;

dian1 癲
insane / mentally deranged;

dian kuang 癲狂
demented / frivolous / insane / mad;

dian xian 癲癇
epilepsy;
chi xiao xing dian xian 痴笑性癲癇
gelastic epilepsy;
chi fa xing dian xian 遲發性癲癇
tardy epilepsy;
chuang shang hou dian xian 創傷後癲癇
posttraumatic epilepsy;
chuang shang xing dian xian 創傷性癲癇
traumatic epilepsy;
jing shen xing dian xian 精神性癲癇
psychic epilepsy;
quan shen xing dian xian 全身性癲癇
generalized epilepsy;
te fa xing dian xian 特發性癲癇
idiopathic epilepsy;

dian xian fa zuo 癲癇發作
suffer an epileptic seizure;

diao4 nao dai 掉腦袋
get beheaded;

diu1 zai nao hou 丟在腦後
completely ignore / let sth pass out of one's mind;

dong3 懂
comprehend / know / understand;

dong dao li 懂道理
considerate / reasonable;

dong de 懂得
grasp / know / understand // intelligible;

dong qing li 懂情理
reasonable and understanding;

dong ren qing 懂人情
have a heart / understand how to behave;

dong ren yi 懂人意
understand the ideas of people;

dong shi 懂事
intelligent / sensible;

dong4 cha 洞察
see clearly || discern; examine thoroughly; have an insight into; have penetrating insight; see through clearly;

dong cha li 洞察力
discernment;

dong cha min qing 洞察民情
know the popular feeling thoroughly;

dong cha qing shi 洞察情勢
make a thorough investigation of the circumstances;

dong cha shi fei 洞察是非
see clearly the rights and wrongs of the case;

dong cha wei lai 洞察未來
see into the future;

dong cha yi qie 洞察一切
have a deep insight into matters;

dong cha yu qing 洞察輿情
know the public sentiment well;

dong da 洞達
understand thoroughly;

dong da shi li 洞達事理
penetrating mind that grasps ideas / sensible;

dong ming shi gu 洞明世故
have seen the ways of the world;

dong xi 洞悉
know clearly / understand thoroughly;

dong xi di yun 洞悉底蘊
know clearly the inside information / know the details; know the ropes;

dong xi wu yi 洞悉無遺
be perfectly acquainted with || have thorough

knowledge of; see and know completely; understand thoroughly;

dong xi yuan wei 洞悉原委
know clearly the whole story / understand thoroughly all the details;

dong xiao 洞曉
have a clear knowledge of / know sth thoroughly;

dong4 nao jin 動腦筋
use one's brains || cudgel one's brains; deliberate; rack one's brains; ransack one's brains; set one's brains to work; take trouble over; think hard; use one's head; use one's wits;

dong nao jin, xiang ban fa 動腦筋，想辦法
use one's head to think of a way || beat one's brains to find a way out; cudgel one's brains to find a way out; puzzle one's brains to find a way out; rack one's wits to find a solution; rack one's brains to find ways and means;

dou4 zhi dou li 鬬智鬬力
fight a battle of wits and a contest of strength;

du2 chi yi yi 獨持異議
alone hold a different opinion / the only one to dissent;

du dao zhi jian 獨到之見
individual insight / original view;

du duan jian jie 獨斷見解
dogmatic view;

du li si kao 獨立思考
independent thinking // think independently / think things out for oneself;

du qing du xing 獨清獨醒
remain sane and sober and realize the lurking dangers in time of outward peace and prosperity when others live in a false sense of security;

duan1 nao 端腦
endbrain;

duan4 ding 斷定
conclude / decide / determine;

duan yi 斷疑
resolve doubts;

dun4 kai mao se 頓開茅塞
suddenly come to an understanding;

dun meng ta zhi 頓萌他志
have other ideas suddenly;

dun qi dai nian 頓起歹念
suddenly a wicked idea comes to mind / turn ungrateful suddenly;

dun sheng yi dou 頓生疑竇
suddenly feel suspicious;

dun wu 頓悟
realize suddenly // sudden enlightment;

dun wu qian fei 頓悟前非
suddenly recall to mind a previous fault;

duo1 mou gua cheng 多謀寡成
dogs that put up many hares kill none;

duo mou shan duan 多謀善斷
resourceful and decisive || full of wrinkes; sagacious and resolute;

duo yi 多疑
oversensitive / suspicious;

fa1 hun 發昏
(1) feel dizzy || faint; feel giddy;
(2) lose one's senses || become confused; beside oneself; go crazy; lose one's head;

fa ren shen xing 發人深省
set people thinking || call for deep thought; give sb sth to think about; make sb think; provide food for thought; prompt sb to deep thought; thought-provoking;

fan3 fu si kao 反覆思考
think over and over again // soul-searching;

fan fu si liang 反覆思量
think over and over again // soul-searching;

fan si 反思
review;

fei1 fei zhi xiang 非非之想
wishful thinking;

fei fen zhi xiang 非分之想
improper desire;

fei3 yi suo si 匪夷所思
unthinkable || sth one could never imagine; unimaginable;

fei4 jie 費解
hard to understand / obscure / unintelligible // obscurity;

fei ren si suo 費人思索
exhaust one's mind to think;

fen1 bie shan e 分別善惡
distinguish good from evil / separate the sheep from the goats;

fen qing 分清
distinguish / draw a clear distinction between / draw a clear line of demarcation between;

fen qing di wo 分清敵我
draw a clear distinction between ourselves and the enemy / draw a clearcut line between the enemy and ourselves / make a distinction between ourselves and the enemy;

fen qing di you 分清敵友
distinguish between friend and enemy / know a friend from an enemy;

fen qing liang you 分清良莠
separate the husk from the grain ‖ differentiate; distinguish;

fen qing shi fei 分清是非
distinguish between right and wrong ‖ differentiate between truth and falsehood; distinguish right from wrong; draw a clear distinction between right and wrong;

fen qing zhu ci 分清主次
differentiate what is primary from what is secondary;

feng1 瘋
crazy / insane / loony / loopy / lunatic / mad / mentally deranged;

feng dian 瘋癲
insane / mentally deranged;

fu2 xiang 浮想
thoughts flashing across one's mind / thoughts rising in one's mind;

fu xiang lian pian 浮想聯翩
many thoughts flash through one's mind / thoughts thronging one's mind;

fu3 gong zi wen 撫躬自問
examine oneself ‖ examine one's own conscience; examine the question through self-reflection; hold communication with oneself; search one's heart;

gan1 hun mi 肝昏迷
hepatic coma;

gan3 ran xing nao mo yan 感染性腦膜炎
infectious meningitis;

gong1 yu xin ji 工於心計
adept at scheming / calculating / designing;

gou3 tong 苟同
agree with sb against principle / agree without giving serious thought;

gou4 si 構思
(1) conception;
(2) work out the plot of a literary work;

gou xiang 構想
concept / conception / idea / plan / scheme;

gu1 liang 估量
assess / estimate / size up / weigh up;

gu1 lou 孤陋
ignorant;

gu3 guai nian tou 古怪念頭
cranky idea;

gu4 zhi ji jian 固執己見
hold stubbornly to one's own viewpoint ‖ abide by one's opinion; adhere stubbornly to one's own ideas; have a will of one's own; nail one's colours to the mast; stick to one's guns; stick to one's own view;

gu4 yi 故意
deliberately / on purpose ‖ by design; by intention; go out of one's way; intentionally; of set purpose; wilfully;

gu yi diao nan 故意刁難
deliberately make things difficult for others / deliberately place obstacles;

gu yi tiao xin 故意挑釁
trail one's coat;

gu yi tuo yan 故意拖延
drag one's feet / give sb the runaround;

gu4 lü 顧慮
apprehension / misgiving / scruple / worry;

gu lü chong chong 顧慮重重
full of worries ‖ be encumbered with personal

concerns; have no end of misgivings; have numerous scruples;

gu lü zhou xiang 顧慮周詳
consider sth down to the minutest details / thoughtful about everything;

guan4 shu 灌輸
imbue with / implant / inculcate / infuse / inoculate / instil in / instil into // infusion;

gui3 cong ming 鬼聰明
petty cleverness;

gui3 zhu yi 鬼主意
evil plan / evil plot / wicked idea;

gui3 ji 詭計
crafty plot / cunning scheme / scam / trick;

gui ji bai chu 詭計百出
present numerous artful tricks;

gui ji duo duan 詭計多端
full of tricks || as cunning as a fox; as tricky as monkey; be up to all the dodges; brimful of mischief; crafty; foxy and wily; full of craft; full of cunning manoeuvre; have a bag full of tricks; have a flair for intrigue; know every sort of wicked guile; play many deceitful tricks; use every cunning trick;

han1 meng 酣夢
sweet dream;

han1 tou han nao 憨頭憨腦
with a stupid head and a dull brain || doltish; foolhardy; foolish; silly;

hao3 bu jiang li 好不講理
totally impervious to reasoning;

hao4 qi 好奇
curious / inquisitive // curiosity;

heng2 liang 衡量
assess / consider / estimate / evaluate / judge / measure / weigh;

heng qing 衡情
consider the actual situations;

heng qing duo li 衡情度理
all things considered / considering the circumstances and judging by common sense;

hong2 tu 宏圖
ambitious plan;

hou4 nao 後腦
afterbrain / back of the head / hindbrain;

hou nao shao zi 後腦勺子
the back of one's head;

hou nao shao zi shang zhang chuang, zi ji kan bu jian 後腦勺子上長瘡，自己看不見
one has a boil on the back of one's head, one can't see it oneself;

hou nao tu chu 後腦突出
notencephalocele;

hu1 fa qi xiang 忽發奇想
suddenly hit on a wild idea;

hu2 cai luan xiang 胡猜亂想
make blind and disorderly conjectures / wild conjecture;

hu luan cai ce 胡亂猜測
make wild guesses;

hu si luan xiang 胡思亂想
be lost in various fancies and conjectures || be moved by confused, foolish reflections; confuse one's brain by foolish ideas; cranky; engage in fantasy; entertain all sorts of ideas; entertain foolish ideas; flights of fancy; flights of imagination; get ideas into one's head; give free play to one's imagination; go off into wild flights of fancy; go woolgathering; have a bee in one's bonnet; have a bee in one's head; have a maggot in one's brain; have a maggot in one's head; have irresponsible thoughts; indulge in flights of fancy; let one's fancy run wild; let one's imagination run wild; let one's mind wander; make fantasies; one's wits go a woolgathering; plunge in reverie; run woolgathering; spoil one's head by thinking nonsense; think confusedly; woolgathering;

hu2 li hu tu 糊裏糊塗
muddleheaded || act stupidly; bewildered; in disorderly fashion; mixed up; puzzled;

hu tu 糊塗
bewildered / confused / foolish / muddled;

hu tu chong 糊塗蟲
nitwit;

hu tu dong xi 糊塗東西
fool / idiot || muddled thing;

hu tu liao shi 糊塗了事
finish a job carelessly / wind up a case carelessly;

hu tu yi shi 糊塗一時
suddenly take leave of one's senses;

hu tu yi shi 糊塗一世
dream away one's life / sleep away one's life;

hua2 tou hua nao 滑頭滑腦
artful / crafty / slick;

huai4 xin yan er 壞心眼兒
evil intention / ill will;

huan4 jue 幻覺
hallucination;
can zhi huan jue 殘肢幻覺
stump hallucination;
jia xing huan jue 假性幻覺
pseudohallucination;
zhen dong huan jue 振動幻覺
oscillating vision;

huan jue fa sheng 幻覺發生
hallucinogenesis;

huan jue zheng 幻覺症
hallucinosis;
jiu jing xing huan jue zheng 酒精性幻覺症
alcoholic hallucinosis;
qi zhi xing huan jue zheng 器質性幻覺症
organic hallucinosis;

huan xiang 幻想
fancy / fantasy / illusion || make belief; square the circle;

huan4 de huan shi 患得患失
worry about personal gains and losses || anxious for a favour and worried lest one should lose it; be obsessed with worries about personal gain and loss; be swayed by considerations of gain and loss; mindful of personal gains and losses; one is never satisfied; think in terms of personal gain and loss;

huang3 ran da wu 恍然大悟
be suddenly enlightened / suddenly realize || a light breaks in upon one; come to understand suddenly; it is a revelation to one; it suddenly dawns on one; scales fall from one's eyes; see light suddenly; suddenly see the light; suddenly to become aware; take a tumble; tumble to;

hui2 xiang 回想
(1) bring back / call to mind / cast one's mind back / flash back / hark back / look back / recall / recollect / think back to;
(2) anamnesis;

hui yi 回憶
look back / recall / recollect;

hui4 wu 會悟
realize a truth;

hun1 dao 昏倒
faint || fall down in a faint; fall unconscious; swoon;

hun guo qu 昏過去
faint / fall down in a faint / fall into a swoon / lose consciousness / pass out;

hun jue 昏厥
faint / swoon;

hun kui 昏聵
decrepit and muddleheaded;

hun kui long zhong 昏聵龍鍾
a dim vision and dullness of senility;

hun kui wu neng 昏聵無能
decrepit and incompetent / decrepit and muddleheaded;

hun kui yu mei 昏聵愚昧
being stupefied and foolish;

hun mei 昏昧
stupid;

hun mi 昏迷
coma || knockdown; muzziness; stupor;
ban hun mi 半昏迷
semicoma;
gan hun mi 肝昏迷
hepatic coma;
jia hun mi 假昏迷
pseudocoma;
jiu jing xing hun mi 酒精性昏迷
alcoholic coma;
niao du zheng hun mi 尿毒症昏迷
uremic coma;

qing hun mi 輕昏迷
semicoma;
tang niao bing hun mi 糖尿病昏迷
diabetic coma;
tang niao bing xing hun mi 糖尿病性昏迷
diabetic coma;

hun mi bu xing 昏迷不省
in a coma;

hun mi bu xing 昏迷不醒
in a complete state of mental confusion // remain unconscious;

hun shui 昏睡
lethargic sleep / trance;

hun tou hun nao 昏頭昏腦
feel dizzy, confused and mixed up;

hun2 魂
(1) soul;
(2) mood / spirit;

hun bu fu ti 魂不附體
as if the soul has left the body / be frightened out of one's wits || be entranced with fear; be scared out of one's wits; be scared to death;

hun bu shou she 魂不守舍
out of one's mind || lose one's presence of mind; one's mind is somewhat unhinged;

hun fei dan lie 魂飛膽裂
be frightened out of one's wits / strike terror into sb's heart;

hun fei jiu xiao 魂飛九霄
one's spirit flows to heaven — be frightened to death / one's spiritual soul floats away into the ninth sphere of heaven;

hun fei po san 魂飛魄散
be frightened out of one's wits / one's heart almost stands still;

hun fei po sang 魂飛魄喪
in extreme fright / make the soul of sb almost leave the body in horror;

hun fei tian wai 魂飛天外
one's soul flows beyond the skies || one's spirits rise to the clouds; one's soul seems to leave one's body and fly beyond the confines of heaven;

hun gui tai xu 魂歸太虛
die || be removed by death; go to one's account;

hun li qu cun 魂離軀存
one's spirit has departed and only one's body remains;

hun ling 魂靈
soul || ghost; soul of the departed;

hun meng bu an 魂夢不安
on tenterhooks;

hun meng wei lao 魂夢為勞
be troubled with dreams / remember ... even in one's dreams;

hun mi po dang 魂迷魄蕩
bewitched / fascinated;

hun po 魂魄
soul || psyche; the spirits and animal forces of man;

hun qian meng rao 魂牽夢繞
be carried away into a region of dreams || be lost in a reverie; in a disturbed state of mind; in a state of mental confusion;

hun xiao po san 魂消魄散
it seems that their souls have melted away or evaporated like a mist;

hun4 xiao 混淆
confuse || blur; confound; mingle; mix up;

hun xiao di you 混淆敵友
confuse friend with foe;

hun xiao hei bai 混淆黑白
call white black || juggle black and white; mix up black and white; obliterate the difference between black and white; obliterate the difference between good and bad; the confounding of black and white; to call black white; turn black into white; turn things upside down;

hun xiao shi fei 混淆是非
confuse right and wrong || call right wrong and wrong right; confound the right with the wrong; confuse right and wrong; confuse the right with the wrong; confound the right with the wrong;

huo4 豁
clear / generous / open / open-minded;

huo da 豁達
(1) open and clear;
(2) broad-minded || generous; magnanimous; open-minded; sanguine;

huo da da du 豁達大度
generous and open-minded / open-minded and magnanimous;

huo ran 豁然
open and clear / suddenly enlightened;

huo ran guan tong 豁然貫通
suddenly see the whole thing in a clear light / understand the thorough meaning suddenly;

huo ran kai lang 豁然開朗
be suddenly enlightened / become clear-minded / suddenly see the light;

ji duan 機斷
act promptly and decisively in an emergency;

ji1 guan suan jin 機關算盡
use all sorts of intrigues and wiles || exhaust every power of one's mind; for all one's calculations and scheming; one's schemes rack one's brains in scheming; use up all one's tricks;

ji jie 機捷
clever / quick-witted / witty;

ji jing 機警
sharp and quick-witted;

ji ling 機伶
clever / quick-witted / readily responsive;

ji ling 機靈
clever / intelligent / sharp / shrewd / smart;

ji min 機敏
clever / quick-witted / sharp / shrewd;

ji mou 機謀
cunning / quick-witted / shrewd / tricky;

ji qiao 機巧
clever / shrewd / tactful;

ji wu 機悟
quick-witted;

ji zha 機詐
crafty / cunning / tricky;

ji zhi 機智
mercurial / perspicuous / quick-witted / resourceful // perspicuity;

ji zhi chen zhuo 機智沉着
composed and quick-witted / cool and resourceful;

ji zhi guo gan 機智果敢
with resourcefulness and determination;

ji zhi guo ren 機智過人
have a flashing wit;

ji zhi yong gan 機智勇敢
brilliant and resourceful, brave and steadfast / resourceful and brave;

ji1 zhi 齎志
cherish unfulfilled ambitions;

ji2 zhi 急智
nimbleness of mind in dealing with emergencies / quick-wittedness;

ji zhong sheng zhi 急中生智
a clever idea occurs to one's mind at the crucial moment || have a brainwave when in danger; have a sudden flash of inspiration; have quick wits in emergency; hit upon a plan in desperation; show resourcefulness in an emergency; suddenly hit on a way out of a predicament; wit comes to their rescue when people are in a critical situation;

ji4 計
plot / scheme / trick;

ji lü zhou mi 計慮周密
plan and consider thoroughly;

ji lüe 計略
deliberate / scheme // scheme;

ji mou 計謀
artifice / scheme;

ji qiong 計窮
at the end of one's rope;

ji qiong cai jie 計窮才竭
at the end of one's tether || at the end of one's row; come to the end of one's tether;

ji qiong li jie 計窮力竭
at the end of one's rope || come to the end of one's tether; one's schemes are poor and his strength is exhausted; with nothing much left up one's sleeves;

腦 *Brain*

ji qiong lü ji 計窮慮極
helpless and in the greatest straits;

ji qiong zhi jin 計窮智盡
at one's wit's end / on one's beam-ends;

ji shang xin lai 計上心來
a new idea flashes across one's mind || a plan comes into one's mind; a stratagem comes to mind; an idea comes across one's mind; bethink oneself of a good plan; concoct a plan; have a brainwave; hit upon an idea; one thinks out a plan; strike out a plan; stumble on a plot;

ji shen lü yuan 計深慮遠
a far-sighted plan that goes deep into the most probable changes in the years to come / the plan is deep-laid in terms of the distant future;

ji wu suo chu 計無所出
at a loss what to do / at one's wits' end / unable to think of a way;

ji wu suo shi 計無所施
at a loss as what to do / there is nothing one can do / up the creek;

ji yi 計議
negotiate / talk it over;

ji4 記
bear in mind / call to mind / keep in mind / remember;

ji bu de 記不得
unable to recall / unable to remember;

ji bu qi 記不起
cannot remember / cannot think of it // outside sb's recollection;

ji bu qing 記不清
unable to remember exactly;

ji chou 記仇
bear a grudge / harbour bitter resentment;

ji cuo 記錯
misremember / remember incorrectly;

ji de 記得
remember || call back to mind; keep in memory; recall; recollect; within sb's recollection;

ji de kuai, wang de kuai 記得快，忘得快
soon learnt, soon forgotten;

ji gua 記掛
be constantly on one's mind / remember and be anxious about;

ji hen 記恨
bear a grudge;

ji lao 記牢
commit to memory firmly;

ji nian 記念
commemorate / remember;

ji qi 記起
call to mind / put sb in mind of / recall / recollect // in mind of;

ji qu 記取
bear in mind / remember;

ji song 記誦
commit to memory / recite;

ji xing 記性
memory;

ji xing hao 記性好
powerful memory;

ji xing huai 記性壞
poor memory;

ji yi 記憶
(1) recall / remember;
(2) memory;
qian zai ji yi 潛在記憶
cryptomnesia;

ji yi hen ji 記憶痕跡
memory trace;

ji yi jian tui 記憶減退
hypomnesia;
lao nian xing ji yi jian tui 老年性記憶減退
dotage;

ji yi li 記憶力
anamnesis / faculty of memory / memory;

ji yi que shi zheng 記憶缺失症
amnesia;

ji yi que sun 記憶缺損
retention defect;

ji yi suo ji 記憶所及
as far as one can remember ‖ anything that one can remember; as far as one can recollect; if my memory serves me correctly; if my memory serves me right; if my memory serves me well; to the best of one's recollection;

ji yi you xin 記憶猶新
be still fresh in one's memory ‖ as fresh in one's memory; be very much alive in one's memory; be still green in one's memory; be still very much alive in one's memory; remain fresh in one's memories; the memory is still fresh;

ji yi zeng qiang 記憶增強
hypermnesia;

ji yi zhang ai 記憶障礙
dysmnesia;

ji zhu 記住
bear in mind / remember ‖ at the back of one's mind; carry sth in mind; commit to memory; fix in one's mind; get sth by heart; hold in one's head; impress on one's memory; keep at the back of one's mind; keep in mind; know sth by heart; learn by heart; make a mental note of; memorize; say sth by heart;

ji4 fa xing nao ji shui 繼發性腦積水
secondary hydrocephalus;

jia3 hun mi 假昏迷
pseudocoma;

jia xing huan jue 假性幻覺
pseudohallucination;

jia xing nao tu chu 假性腦突出
pseudocephalocele;

jia zhuang bu zhi 假裝不知
affect ignorance / feign ignorance;

jia zhuang hu tu 假裝糊塗
pretend ignorance / pretend to be ignorant;

jia zui yang kuang 假醉佯狂
pretend to be very drunk and act like a lunatic;

jia zuo zhen jing 假作鎮靜
pretend to be calm;

jian4 wang 健忘
absent-minded / forgetful / scatterbrained / scatty;

jian wang zheng 健忘症
amnesia;
ting jue xing jian wang zheng 聽覺性健忘症
acousmatamnesia;

jian4 鑑
examine / scrutinize;

jian bie 鑑別
discriminate / distinguish / make an appraisal of sth;

jian ding 鑑定
examine and determine;

jian shang 鑑賞
examine and appreciate;

jian shi 鑑識
discern / distinguish / judge / tell;

jian wang zhi lai 鑑往知來
foresee the future by reviewing the past;

jian4 鑒
examine;

jian cha 鑒察
examine and study;

jian he 鑒核
examine and make a decision;

jiao1 huan yi jian 交換意見
compare notes;

jiao3 zha 狡詐
crafty / cunning / deceitful;

jiao zha jian hua 狡詐奸滑
cunning and knavish;

jiao3 nao zhi 絞腦汁
rack one's brains;

jiao jin nao zhi 絞盡腦汁
rack one's brains ‖ beat one's brains; beat one's brains out; busy one's brains; cudgel one's brains; drag one's brains; puzzle one's brains; rack one's head; ransack one's brains;

jie2 he xing nao mo yan 結核性腦膜炎
meningitis tuberculosis;

jin3 ji 謹記
remember with reverence;

jing1 ming 精明
adroit / astute / bright / hard-headed / sagacious / sharp / shrewd / smart;

jing shen xing dian xian 精神性癲癇
psychic epilepsy;

jing3 jue 警覺
alert / vigilant / watchful;

jing jue xing 警覺性
alertness / vigilance / watchfulness;

jing wu 警悟
quick to realize / quick to understand;

jing xing 警醒
(1) quick to awake;
(2) vigilant;

jing4 ji si dong 靜極思動
when one remains idle for too long, one thinks of taking an active role in life;

jing ju si guo 靜居思過
live in seclusion and make self-examination;

jing si 靜思
contemplate quietly / meditate / think quietly;

jiu3 jing xing chi dai 酒精性痴呆
alcoholic dementia;

jiu jing xing huan jue zheng 酒精性幻覺症
alcoholic hallucinosis;

jiu jing xing hun mi 酒精性昏迷
alcoholic coma;

jiu4 guan nian 舊觀念
old ideas;

jiu nao jing 舊腦筋
conservative-minded;

ju1 an si wei 居安思危
when safe, don't forget danger;

ju2 xian xing nao wei suo 局限性腦萎縮
circumscribed cerebral atrophy;

ju xian xing yi wang zheng 局限性遺忘症
circumscribed amnesia;

ju4 jing hui shen 聚精會神
concentrate oneself / with attention;

ju song 聚訟
hold different views;

ju song fen yun 聚訟紛紜
opinions are divided;

jue2 ding 決定
decide / determine / resolve / settle;

jue duan 決斷
decide / make a decision;

jue duan guo gan 決斷果敢
decisive judgement;

jue duan li 決斷力
decision / the ability to decide and act accordingly;

jue2 ding cong ming 絕頂聰明
extremely clever / very intelligent;

jue2 譎
(1) cheat / deceive / swindle;
(2) artful / crafty / tricky;

jue er bu zheng 譎而不正
crafty and not upright;

jue gu 譎觚
artful / crafty / cunning / tricky;

jue zha 譎詐
deceitful / deceptive / dishonest / tricky;

jue4 tou jue nao 倔頭倔腦
blunt in manner and gruff of speech;

kai1 dong nao jin 開動腦筋
set one's wits to work / sharpen one's wits / use one's brains / use one's head;

kao3 lü 考慮
consider / deliberate / ponder / think over / weigh // consideration / deliberation;

kao lü qian zhou 考慮欠周
ill-considered / ill-advised;

ke3 yi 可疑
dubious / dubitable / questionable / suspectable / suspicious;

ke3 bing 渴病
diabetes;

ke nian 渴念
miss very much / yearn for;

ke wang 渴望
long for || ache for; aspire; be all agog to; be bursting to; be eager about; be eager after;

be eager for; crave; hanker after; hanker for; have a good mind to; hunger for / pine for; thirst for; yearn after; yearn for // craving / longing;

ke xiang 渴想
crave for / long for / miss very much;

ku3 ku si suo 苦苦思索
puzzle over;

ku si 苦思
cudgel one's brains / think hard;

ku si ming xiang 苦思冥想
cudgel one's brains;

kuai4 hua 獪猾
cunning;

kui2 揆
consider / estimate;

kui ce 揆測
calculate / estimate;

kui duo 揆度
observe and estimate;

kui qing duo li 揆情度理
measured by reason and common practice;

lao2 ji 牢記
hold fast in one's heart / keep firmly in mind / make a mental note of;

lao3 jian ju hua 老奸巨猾
shrewd and crafty;

lao mou shen suan 老謀深算
experienced and astute / scheming and calculating;

lao nao jin 老腦筋
stubborn old brain ‖ old ways of thinking; old-fashioned;

lao nian chi dai 老年痴呆
senile dementia;

lao nian chi dai zheng 老年痴呆症
Alzheimer's disease;

lao nian xing chi dai zheng 老年性痴呆症
senile dementia;

lao nian xing ji yi jian tui 老年性記憶減退
dotage;

le4 guan 樂觀
optimistic;

leng3 jing 冷靜
calm / phlegmatic / sober;

leng jing xia lai 冷靜下來
simmer down;

leng4 tou leng nao 愣頭愣腦
foolhardy ‖ hothead; impetuous; rash; reckless;

li3 jie 理解
comprehend / understand;

li jie li 理解力
faculty of comprehension / understanding;

li qu 理屈
cannot appeal to good reasoning // on the wrong side;

li zhi 理智
intellect / reason;

li4 ling zhi hun 利令智昏
be blinded by greed;

lian4 qiu jun xing nao mo yan 鏈球菌性腦膜炎
streptococcal meningitis;

liang2 zhi 良知
instinct / one's better self;

liang zhi liang neng 良知良能
innate knowledge and ability;

liang3 ge nao dai sheng yi ge 兩個腦袋勝一個
two heads are better than one;

liao3 jie 了解
comprehend / understand;

liao wu 了悟
comprehend / realize / understand / wake up to;

liao4 shi ru shen 料事如神
predict with miraculous accuracy;

ling2 nao 菱腦
afterbrain;

ling2 gan 靈感
inspiration;

ling hui 靈慧
very clever / very intelligent;

ling huo 靈活
active and clever / quick-minded / quick-witted;

ling huo min jie 靈活敏捷
active and intelligent;

ling ji 靈機
sudden inspiration;

ling ji yi dong 靈機一動
dawn on one suddenly / have a brain wave;

ling3 hui 領會
appreciate / understand;

ling wu 領悟
comprehend / understand;

ling4 ren fei jie 令人費解
elude understanding / pass comprehension // puzzling // beyond comprehension;

ling ren shen si 令人深思
call for deep thought / make one ponder / provide food for thought;

ling4 xiang ban fa 另想辦法
think of some other way;

liu2 xing xing nao ji sui mo yan 流行性腦脊髓膜炎
cerebrospinal meningitis;

liu xing xing nao mo yan 流行性腦膜炎
epidemic cerebrospinal meningitis;

liu xing xing nao yan 流行性腦炎
epidemic encephalitis;

liu xing xing yi xing nao yan 流行性乙型腦炎
epidemic encephalitis B;

liu2 yi 留意
pay attention to;

liu4 shen wu zhu 六神無主
out of one's wits;

lou4 jian 陋見
shallow views / vulgar views;

lu3 dun 魯鈍
dull / slow-witted;

lü4 慮
consider / take into account;

lü ji 慮及
anticipate / take into account;

lü shi 慮事
(1) make plans for a matter;
(2) have misgivings about a matter;

lü yuan 慮遠
plan for the distant future / think far ahead;

luo4 wu si xiang 落伍思想
backward ideas / backward thinking;

ma2 bi xing chi dai 麻痺性痴呆
paralytic dementia;

man3 fu 滿腹
have one's mind filled with;

man fu hu yi 滿腹狐疑
be filled with suspicion || extremely suspicious; full of misgiving; have all sorts of doubts and conjectures in one's mind; very suspicious;

man nao zi 滿腦子
have one's mind stuffed with;

man4 xing nao mo yan 慢性腦膜炎
chronic meningitis;

mang2 ran bu zhi 茫然不知
completely in the dark / helplessly ignorant;

mang wu tou xu 茫無頭緒
not knowing where or how to start;

mao2 tou mao nao 毛頭毛腦
impetuous / rush;

mao2 se 茅塞
obstacle in the mind to understanding;

mao se dun kai 茅塞頓開
come to an understanding all of a sudden;

mao4 si 耄思
confused thoughts;

mei2 dao li 沒道理
unreasonable;

mei tou mei nao 沒頭沒腦
absent-minded / listless / without clue / without rhyme or reason;

mei tou nao 沒頭腦
ignorant / stupid / without brains;

mei xiang dao 沒想到
have not expected;

mei zhu yi 沒主意
cannot make up one's mind / lose one's head;

mei2 du xing nao mo yan 梅毒性腦膜炎
syphilitic meningitis;

meng3 懵
confused / muddleheaded;

meng dong 懵懂
ignorant / muddleheaded / muddled;

mi2 xin 迷信
(1) superstition;
(2) blind faith / blind worship;
(3) have blind faith in;

mi zhu 迷住
be enthralled / enthral;

mi2 man xing nao ying hua 彌漫性腦硬化
diffuse cerebral sclerosis;

mi4 mou 密謀
plan secretly / plot;

mian2 si meng xiang 眠思夢想
long for sb even in dreams;

ming2 bian shi fei 明辨是非
know distinctly what is right and what is wrong / make a clear distinction between right and wrong;

ming da 明達
intelligent and broad-minded;

ming duan 明斷
unbiased and wise decision;

ming hui 明慧
intelligent;

ming li 明理
reasonable / understanding;

ming zhi 明智
judicious / politic / sagacious / sensible / wise;

ming2 xiang 冥想
deep meditation;

mo1 bu zhao tou nao 摸不着頭腦
be out of one's depth / cannot make head or tail of sth;

mo4 ming qi miao 莫明其妙
(1) inexplicable / odd / unaccountable / without rhyme or reason;
(2) unable to make head or tail of sth;

mo4 ji 默記
silently remember;

mo nian 默念
ponder / think;

mo shi 默識
memorize silently;

mo xiang 默想
contemplate / meditate / ponder;

mou2 謀
design / devise / plan / plot / scheme // conspiracy / plan / scheme / stratagem;

mou ding hou dong 謀定後動
devise first and then move;

mou fan 謀反
plot a revolt;

mou lü 謀慮
plan and contrive;

mou lüe 謀略
(1) plot / scheme / strategy;
(2) astute / resourceful;

mou pan 謀叛
plot a revolt;

na2 bu ding zhu yi 拿不定主意
halt between two opinions // hard to decide // in two minds ;

na zhu yi 拿主意
make a decision / make up one's mind;

nan2 dong 難懂
difficult to comprehend / hard to solve / hard to understand / impalpable / incomprehensible / opaque;

nan jie 難解
difficult to understand / hard to solve / impalpable / incomprehensible / opaque;

nan wang 難忘
difficult to forget / unforgettable;

nan yi duan ding 難以斷定
hard to decide // imponderable;

nan yi li jie 難以理解
above one's comprehension / beyond one's

comprehension / difficult to understand / hard to solve / impalpable / incomprehensible / opaque // defy comprehension / elude comprehension;

nan yi ni liao 難以逆料
hard to predict;

nan yi que ding 難以確定
hard to determine // indeterminable // indetermination;

nan yi xiang xin 難以相信
difficult to believe / hard to believe / implausible / incredible / unbelievable / unconvincing;

nan yi zhi xin 難以置信
difficult to believe / hard to believe / implausible / incredible / unbelievable / unconvincing;

nao3 腦
(1) brain ‖ think box; think tank; topstorey; upper storey; upstairs;
(2) mind;

nao ai 腦癌
cancer of the brain / cerebral cancer;

nao bing 腦病
cerebral disease / cerebrosis;
bai zhi nao bing 白質腦病
leukoencephalopathy;
da nao bing 大腦病
cerebrosis;
gan xing nao bing 肝性腦病
hepatic encephalopathy;
niao du zheng nao bing 尿毒症腦病
uremic encephalopathy;
qian du xing nao bing 鉛毒性腦病
lead encephalopathy;
wai shang xing nao bing 外傷性腦病
traumatic encephalopathy;

nao chong xue 腦充血
cerebral congestion / encephalemia;

nao chu xue 腦出血
cerebral hemorrhage;

nao dai 腦袋
garret / head / loaf / noddle;

nao fa yu bu liang 腦發育不良
atelencephalia;

nao fa yu bu quan 腦發育不全
atelencephalia;

nao fan she 腦反射
cranial reflex;

nao fei da 腦肥大
encephalauxe;

nao gai 腦蓋
top of the skull;

nao gai gu 腦蓋骨
cranium;

nao gan 腦幹
brain stem;

nao gan fan she 腦幹反射
brain stem reflex;

nao gua ding er 腦瓜頂兒
top of the head;

nao gua er 腦瓜兒
head;

nao guo xiao 腦過小
micrencephalon;

nao hai 腦海
brain / mind;

nao hai shen chu 腦海深處
at the back of sb's mind / in the back of sb's mind;

nao hou 腦後
disregard;

nao ji sui mo yan 腦脊髓膜炎
cerebrospinal meningitis;
liu xing xing nao ji sui mo yan 流行性腦脊髓膜炎
cerebrospinal meningitis;

nao ji sui shen jing 腦脊髓神經
cerebrovascular diseases;

nao ji sui yan 腦脊髓炎
encephalomyelitis;
bing du xing nao ji sui yan 病毒性腦脊髓炎
viral encephalomyelitis;

腦 *Brain*

nao ji ye 腦脊液
cerebrospinal fluid;

nao ji shui 腦積水
hydrocephalus;
ji fa xing nao ji shui 繼發性腦積水
secondary hydrocephalus;
yuan fa xing nao ji shui 原發性腦積水
primary hydrocephalus;
zhang li xing nao ji shui 張力性腦積水
tension hydrocephalus;
zhong er yan xing nao ji shui 中耳炎性腦積水
otitic hydrocephalus;

nao jiang 腦漿
brain;

nao jiang si jian 腦漿四濺
one's brains are scattered in all directions;

nao jin 腦筋
(1) brains / head / mind;
(2) ideas;

nao jin chi dun 腦筋遲鈍
have a slow wit / have slow wits; slow-witted;

nao jin jian dan 腦筋簡單
simple-minded;

nao jin ling huo 腦筋靈活
quick-witted ‖ have a quick wit; have a supple mind; have quick wits; keen and sharp in thinking;

nao jin ling min 腦筋靈敏
keen and sharp in thinking / quick-witted;

nao ke 腦殼
head;

nao li 腦力
brains / mental exertion;

nao man chang fei 腦滿腸肥
with fat cheeks and a big belly ‖ heavy-jowled and pot-bellied — said of the idle rich; with a fair round belly and a swelled head;

nao men zi 腦門子
forehead;

nao mo 腦膜
meninges;

nao mo nao yan 腦膜腦炎
meningoencephalitis;
rou ya zhong xing nao mo nao yan 肉芽腫性腦膜腦炎
granulomatous meningoencephalitis;

nao mo yan 腦膜炎
meningitis;
ai xing nao mo yan 癌性腦膜炎
meningitis carcinomatosa;
bing du xing nao mo yan 病毒性腦膜炎
viral meningitis;
gan ran xing nao mo yan 感染性腦膜炎
infectious meningitis;
jia xing nao mo yan 假性腦膜炎
meningism;
jie he xing nao mo yan 結核性腦膜炎
meningitis tuberculosis;
lian qiu jun xing nao mo yan 鏈球菌性腦膜炎
streptococcal meningitis;
liu xing xing nao mo yan 流行性腦膜炎
epidemic cerebrospinal meningitis;
man xing nao mo yan 慢性腦膜炎
chronic meningitis;
mei du xing nao mo yan 梅毒性腦膜炎
syphilitic meningitis;
shu yi xing nao mo yan 鼠疫性腦膜炎
plague meningitis;
xi jun xing nao mo yan 細菌性腦膜炎
bacterial maningitis;
zhong liu xing nao mo yan 腫瘤性腦膜炎
neoplastic meningitis;

nao nong zhong 腦膿腫
abscess;

nao piao er 腦瓢兒
top of the head;

nao pin xue 腦貧血
cerebral anemia;

nao qiao 腦橋
pons;

nao ruan hua 腦軟化
softening of the brain;

nao shao zi 腦勺子
back of the head;

nao shen jing 腦神經
cranial nerve;

nao shi 腦室
ventricle;

nao shuan se 腦栓塞
cerebral embolism / cerebromalacia;

nao si wang 腦死亡
brain death / cerebral death;

nao sui 腦髓
brain;

nao tong 腦痛
cerebralgia;

nao tu chu 腦突出
cephalocele;
jia xing nao tu chu 假性腦突出
pseudocephalocele;
nian lian xing nao tu chu 黏連性腦突出
synencephalocele;

nao wai shang 腦外傷
brain surgery;

nao wei suo 腦萎縮
cerebral atrophy;
ju xian xing nao wei suo 局限性腦萎縮
circumscribed cerebral atrophy;

nao xia chui ti 腦下垂體
pituitary gland;

nao xue shuan xing cheng 腦血栓形成
cerebral thrombosis;

nao yan 腦炎
brain fever / encephalitis;
bai zhi nao yan 白質腦炎
leukoencephalitis;
bian yuan xing nao yan 邊緣性腦炎
limbic encephalitis;
chu xue xig nao yan 出血性腦炎
hemorrhagic encephalitis;
chun ji nao yan 春季腦炎
vernal encephalitis;
liu xing xing nao yan 流行性腦炎
epidemic encephalitis;
liu xing xing yi xing nao yan 流行性乙型腦炎
epidemic encephalitis B;
pao zhen xing nao yan 疱疹性腦炎
herpetic encephalitis;
qian du xing nao yan 鉛毒性腦炎
lead encephalitis;
quan nao yan 全腦炎
panencephalitis;
ri ben nao yan 日本腦炎
Japanese encephalitis;
xia ji nao yan 夏季腦炎
summer encephalitis;
zhong er xing nao yan 中耳性腦炎
otoencephalitis;

nao yi xue 腦溢血
cerebral apoplexy / cerebral hemorrhage;

nao ying hua 腦硬化
cerebrosclerosis;
mi man xing nao ying hua 瀰漫性腦硬化
diffuse cerebral sclerosis;

nao zhang 腦脹
heavy feeling in the brain;

nao zhen dang 腦震蕩
cerebral concussion / concussion;

nao zhi 腦汁
mental effort;

nao zhi tu di 腦汁塗地
willing to repay a favour with extreme sacrifice;

nao zhong liu 腦腫瘤
brain tumour / encephaloma;

nao zhong feng 腦中風
stroke;

nao zi 腦子
(1) brains;
(2) head / intelligence / mental power / mind;

nao zi bu zheng chang 腦子不正常
have a cog loose / have a screw loose / have a screw missing // not quite right in the head;

nao zi huo 腦子活
clever;

nao zi ling huo 腦子靈活
have a quick wit // alert and active / clever /

keen and sharp in thinking;

ni4 ji 逆計
conjecture beforehand / reckon beforehand;

ni liao 逆料
anticipate / conjecture beforehand;

ni zhi 逆知
foresee / know beforehand;

nian2 lian xing nao tu chu 黏連性腦突出
synencephalocele;

nian4 ji jiu qing 念及舊情
for old times' sake;

niao4 du zheng hun mi 尿毒症昏迷
uremic coma;

niao du zheng nao bing 尿毒症腦病
uremic encephalopathy;

ning2 shen 凝神
concentrate one's thoughts on;

ning si 凝思
meditate;

ning xiang 凝想
meditate;

nong4 hu tu 弄糊塗
confuse / puzzle;

nong qing 弄清
fully understand / gain a clear idea of;

nong tong 弄通
get a good grasp of;

pan2 suan 盤算
calculate / consider and weigh / deliberate / figure / plan / premeditate;

pan4 duan 判斷
judge;

pao4 zhen xing nao yan 皰疹性腦炎
herpetic encephalitis;

pi1 pan 批判
appraise / judge;

pi ping 批評
comment / criticize;

ping2 評
judge;

ping bi 評比
appraise through comparison / compare and assess;

ping duan 評斷
arbitrate / decide;

ping duan shi fei 評斷是非
judge between right and wrong;

ping jia 評價
appraise / assess / estimate;

ping liang 評量
evaluate / weigh;

ping pan 評判
judge;

ping tou lun zu 評頭論足
carp at;

po4 hai wang xiang 迫害妄想
delusion of persecution;

qi1 wang 期望
desire / expect / hope / look forward to;

qi3 tu 企圖
attempt / intend / seek // motive;

qi3 si 綺思
beautiful thoughts;

qi xiang 綺想
beautiful thoughts;

qi4 器
think highly of;

qi zhi xing huan jue zheng 器質性幻覺症
organic hallucinosis;

qi zhong 器重
regard highly / think highly of;

qian1 si wan xiang 千思萬想
think over and over again;

qian1 du xing nao bing 鉛毒性腦病
lead encephalopathy;

qian du xing nao yan 鉛毒性腦炎
lead encephalitis;

qian2 nao 前腦
forebrain;

qian si hou xiang 前思後想
think over again and again;

qian2 yi shi 潛意識
subconsciousness;

qian zai ji yi 潛在記憶
cryptomnesia;

qian zai yi shi 潛在意識
subconsciousness;

qie4 ji 切記
be sure to remember / bear in mind / keep in mind;

qie4 tou qie nao 怯頭怯腦
nervous and clumsy / timid and unsophisticated;

qing1 xing 清醒
awake / come to one's senses // cool;

qing xu 清虛
high and mild;

qing1 ren 傾人
frame sb / implicate sb;

qing1 hun mi 輕昏迷
semicoma;

qing xin 輕信
believe lightly // gullible;

qing2 gan 情感
affection / emotions / feelings / sentiments;

qing li 情理
common sense / reason;

qing li nan rong 情理難容
contrary to common sense / contrary to reason;

qu1 jie 曲解
distort / misinterpret // misinterpretation;

quan2 nao yan 全腦炎
panencephalitis;

quan shen xing dian xian 全身性癲癇
generalized epilepsy;

quan shen guan zhu 全神貫注
pay undivided attention to // preoccupied // preoccupation;

quan zhi quan neng 全知全能
omniscient and omnipotent;

quan2 詮
explain / expound / illustrate;

quan shi 詮釋
interpret;

quan2 duo 權度
estimate;

quan heng 權衡
assess / consider / weigh;

quan liang 權量
assess / consider / weigh;

quan mou 權謀
schemes and power;

quan shi 權時
expedient;

quan zha 權詐
crafty and dishonest;

que4 xin 確信
be convinced / firmly believe // certitude;

ren2 nao 人腦
human brain;

ren4 chu 認出
identify / make out / recognize;

ren wei 認為
think // in one's mind / to sb's mind;

ren zhi si wang 認知死亡
cognitive death;

reng1 kai 扔開
dismiss from consideration;

ri4 ben nao yan 日本腦炎
Japanese encephalitis;

rou4 ya zhong xing nao mo nao yan 肉芽腫性腦膜腦炎
granulomatous meningoencephalitis;

rui4 睿
(1) understand thoroughly;
(2) mercurial / wise and clever;

rui zhe 睿哲
saintly wisdom;

rui zhi 睿智
mercurial wit / sagacity / superior intelligence;

ruo4 zhi 弱智
mental retardation // mentally retarded / weak-minded;

sha4 fei ku xin 煞費苦心
go to great pains || assiduous; at great pains; at the pains of; cudgel one's brains; from Dan to Beersheba; go through a lot of trouble; laborious; rack one's brains; take pains;

sha fei xin ji 煞費心計
beat one's brains / rack one's brains;

shang1 nao jin 傷腦筋
cause sb enough of a headache || beat one's brains; bothersome; harrowing; have a hard nut to crack; knotty; nuisance; task sb's mind; troublesome; trying to the nerves;

shang shen 傷神
beat one's brains out;

shang tou nao jin 傷透腦筋
cause sb enough of a headache / give sb a headache;

she1 wang 奢望
wild hope;

she xiang 奢想
think wishfully;

she yuan 奢願
wild wish;

she4 xian 涉嫌
come under suspicion;

she xiang 涉想
think about;

she4 xiang 設想
assume / conceive // idea / scheme;

shen1 mou yuan lü 深謀遠慮
think and plan far ahead;

shen si 深思
ponder deeply over || chew over; deep in contemplation; deep in thought; think deeply about;

shen si shu lü 深思熟慮
ponder deeply || careful consideration; chew the cud; consult with one's pillow; deliberation; give careful consideration to; think and contemplate thoroughly; think over carefully; turn sth over in one's mind; well-thought-out;

shen zhi bu qing 神智不清
light-headed // in a coma;

shen3 cha 審查
examine / investigate;

shen duo 審度
consider the pros and cons / deliberate;

shen duo qing li 審度情理
consider all the circumstances;

shen duo qing shi 審度情勢
study and weigh the conditions;

shen duan 審斷
examine and decide;

shen jue 審決
examine and decide;

shen shi duo shi 審時度勢
judge the hour and size up the situation;

shen4 si ming bian 慎思明辨
think carefully and clearly;

shi1 shi zheng 失識症
agnosia / inability to recognize objects by use of the senses;

chu jue shi shi zheng 觸覺失識症
tactile agnosia;

shi4 fei 是非
(1) right and wrong / right or wrong / yes and no;
(2) gossip / scandal;
(3) discord;

shi fei dian dao 是非顛倒
confound right and wrong;

shi fei qu zhi 是非曲直
right and wrong, proper and improper;

shu2 ji 熟記
commit to memory / memorize;

shu lü 熟慮
consider carefully;

shu si 熟思
consider carefully / deliberate / ponder deeply;

shu xi 熟悉
have an intimate knowledge of / very familiar with;

shu3 yi xing nao mo yan 鼠疫性腦膜炎
plague meningitis;

shu4 fu si xiang 束縛思想
straiten the mind;

si1 思
(1) consider / think;
(2) hope / wish;

si bian 思辨
speculate;

si bian neng li 思辨能力
analytical ability;

si chun 思春
(of a young girl) yearn for love;

si cun 思存
favour in heart;

si cun 思忖
deliberate / ponder / reflect;

si gu 思古
muse over the past / recall the past // nostalgic;

si guo 思過
repent || ponder over one's fault; reflect on one's fault;

si jiu 思舊
remember old times;

si kao 思考
plan for / ponder on / reflect on / think deeply;

si lian 思戀
cherish the memory of;

si liang 思量
consider / ruminate;

si lü 思慮
consider / turn sth over in one's mind;

si mu 思慕
(1) admire;
(2) remember;

si nian 思念
recall / remember;

si qi 思齊
wish to emulate;

si qian xiang hou 思前想後
ponder over sth;

si qin 思親
think of one's relatives;

si ru quan yong 思如泉湧
brimming with ideas and thoughts;

si shen lü yuan 思深慮遠
think deep and far ahead;

si suo 思索
deliberate / ponder / ponder over;

si wei 思維
thinking;

si wei min jie 思維敏捷
have a sharp mind;

si xiang 思鄉
think of one's home // homesick;

si xiang bing 思鄉病
homesickness / nostalgia;

si xiang 思想
idea / thinking / thought || ideology; mind;

si xiang kai ming 思想開明
one's mind is well informed;

si xiang luo wu 思想落伍
old-fashioned in thinking / outdated ideas;

si xiang min jie 思想敏捷
think on one's feet;

si xiang you zhi 思想幼稚
childish thinking;

si xu 思緒
one's state of mind;

si yi 思議
imaginable / thinkable;

si3 nao jin 死腦筋
one-track mind;

sou1 suo ku chang 搜索枯腸
rack one's brains || beat one's brains; beat one's brains out; cudgel one's brains; scratch through one's mind for sth; think hard;

su4 hui 宿慧
innate intelligence;

suan4 算
count / figure / reckon;

suan bu de 算不得
not to be counted / not to be regarded as;

suan bu qing 算不清
innumerable / uncountable;

suan de shen mo 算得甚麼
of no special consequence;

suan ji 算計
(1) consider / plan;
(2) plot against sb;

suan lai suan qu 算來算去
count over and over;

suan le 算了
forget about it;

suan qi lai 算起來
in all / in the aggregate / in total;

suan zhang 算賬
settle an account;

suo1 tou suo nao 縮頭縮腦
(1) cower from fear / shrink from fear || shrink from responsibility; timid;
(2) faint-hearted;

tan2 si 覃思
deep thought / meditation / profound thought // deep in thought;

tan si er xing 覃思而行
think deeply and move;

tan4 ming 探明
find out by inquiry;

tang2 niao bing hun mi 糖尿病昏迷
diabetic coma;

tang niao bing xing hun mi 糖尿病性昏迷
diabetic coma;

te4 fa xing dian xian 特發性癲癇
idiopathic epilepsy;

ting1 jue xing jian wang zheng 聽覺性健忘症
acousmatamnesia;

tong1 mou 通謀
conspire;

tong pan an pai 通盤安排
comprehensive arrangement;

tong pan gu ji 通盤估計
all-round estimate;

tong pan ji hua 通盤計劃
overall plan;

tong pan kao lü 通盤考慮
consider from every possible angle;

tong qing da li 通情達理
reasonable / sensible;

tou2 nao 頭腦
(1) brain / mind;
(2) clue / main thread;

tou nao bu qing 頭腦不清
mixed-up / muddleheaded;

tou nao bu qing xing 頭腦不清醒
insobriety;

tou nao bu zheng chang 頭腦不正常
have a button missing || be a button short; have a few buttons loose; have a few buttons missing; have a siren loose; have lost a button; not all there; not have all one's button on;

tou nao chi dun 頭腦遲鈍
have a slow wit / have slow wits // slow-witted;

tou nao dong hong 頭腦冬烘
badly read and extremely bigoted || die hard; ultraconservative; with musty ideas;

tou nao fa hun 頭腦發昏
addle one's head / lose one's head // addlebrained / addleheaded;

tou nao fa re 頭腦發熱
become hotheaded;

tou nao fa zhang 頭腦發脹
have a big head / have a swelled head / get a big head;

tou nao jian dan 頭腦簡單
simple-minded // light in the head / see things too simply;

tou nao leng jing 頭腦冷靜
cool-headed // have a cool head / have one's wits about one;

tou nao ling huo 頭腦靈活
quick-witted || have a mind like a steel trap; have a quick wit; have quick wits / have an active brain;

tou nao qing chu 頭腦清楚
clearheaded / quick-witted || with an alert mind;

tou nao qing xing 頭腦清醒
clearheaded / level-headed / right-minded / sober-minded // keep a cool head;

tou nao zheng chang 頭腦正常
have all buttons / have all one's button on;

tu3 tou tu nao 土頭土腦
countrified / rustic || hillbilly; hob-nailed; stupid and uncouth; unsophisticated;

tui1 推
deduce / infer / ponder // inference;

tui ce 推測
conjecture / guess / infer from / surmise;

tui ding 推定
deduce / infer // inference;

tui duan 推斷
infer / speculate // inference / speculation;

tui duo 推度
deduce / infer // inference;

tui jiu 推究
infer / reason out / study;

tui li 推理
infer / reason / reason out;

tui lun 推論
infer // argumentation;

tui qiao 推敲
examine carefully / investigate carefully;

tui qiu 推求
analyze and study;

tui suan 推算
calculate;

tui xiang 推想
deduce / infer;

tun4 tou suo nao 褪頭縮腦
slink away;

wa1 kong xin si 挖空心思
cudgel one's brains / rack one's brains / think hard / work one's head to the bone;

wai1 nian tou 歪念頭
crooked ideas / depraved thoughts / evil ideas;

wai xin 歪心
crooked mind / evil mind / twisted mind;

wai4 shang xing nao bing 外傷性腦病
traumatic encephalopathy;

wan1 kong xin si 剜空心思
exhaust one's ingenuity / exhaust one's wits;

wan4 nian ju hui 萬念俱灰
completely discouraged / extremely pessimistic;

wang3 gu 罔顧
despite / disregard / take no consideration of;

wang ran 罔然
at a loss // disconcerted;

wang yang 罔養
unable to make a decision;

wang3 fei xin ji 枉費心機
waste one's efforts || a fool for one's pains; bay at the moon; bark at the moon; bay the moon; beat the air; beat the wind; flog a dead horse; fruitless efforts; futile; go down the drain; go on a wild goose chase; in vain; make futile efforts; rack one's brains in vain; scheme in vain; scheme without avail; try in vain to; waste one's contrivances; waste one's labour; waste one's pains; wreck one's brain without results;

wang3 hao chu xiang 往好處想
think of the better possibilities of a situation;

wang huai chu xiang 往壞處想
think of the unfavourable possibilities of a situation;

wang4 nian 妄念
fancy // like / take a liking to / would like;

wang xiang 妄想
fancy // like / take a liking to / would like // delusion;

wang xiang chi dai 妄想痴呆
paraphrenia;

wang xiang kuang 妄想狂
paranoid delusion;

wang4 忘
(1) forget;
(2) neglect / overlook;

wang ben 忘本
ungrateful;

wang bu liao 忘不了
will not forget;

wang diao 忘掉
forget / put out of sb's mind / slip from one's mind;

wang hu suo yi 忘乎所以
be carried away;

wang huai 忘懷
dismiss from one's mind;

wang ji 忘記
(1) forget / put out of sb's mind;
(2) neglect;

wang le 忘了
forget;

wang qing 忘情
be unmoved;

wang que 忘卻
forget;

wang wo 忘我
selfless / unselfish;

wei2 惟
meditate / think;

wen1 tou wen nao 瘟頭瘟腦
go about in a daze;

wu2 yong zhi yi 毋庸置疑
admit of no doubt / allow of no doubt / leave no room for doubt // incontrovertible / indisputable / indubitable // above suspicion / beyond doubt / beyond question;

wu2 fa jie shi 無法解釋
unaccountable;

wu suo yong xin 無所用心
without applying one's mind to anything good || give one's thought to nothing; not to give serious thought to anything; remain idle; show one's concern to nothing;

wu tou wu nao 無頭無腦
completely without clue / disorderly and confused / muddled and mixed-up;

wu yi 無意
have no intention to // unintentional;

wu yi zhong 無意中
accidentally / unexpectedly / unintentionally;

wu yi shi 無意識
(1) unconsciousness;
(2) unintentional;

wu zhi 無知
ignorant // ignorance;

wu3 duan 武斷
arbitrary decision;

wu4 hui 誤會
misinterpret / misunderstand // misunderstanding;

wu jie 誤解
misconstrue / misunderstand // misundertstanding;

wu xin 誤信
misplace one's confidence;

xi1 nian tou 息念頭
give up one's idea;

xi3 nao 洗腦
brainwash / indoctrinate;

xi4 cha 細查
examine thoroughly;

xi cha 細察
examine thoroughly / observe carefully / observe in detail ;

xi cha jiu jing 細察究竟
examine the outcome minutely;

xi cha lai yi 細察來意
judge the motive of one's coming;

xi jun xing nao mo yan 細菌性腦膜炎
bacterial meningitis;

xi mi 細密
careful / detailed / meticulous;

xi wei 細味
reflect carefully / study carefully / think over carefully;

xi xin 細心
attentive / careful / cautious / circumspective;

xi xin chuai mo 細心揣摩
think of it carefully;

xia2 ai si lu 狹隘思路
one-track mind;

xia2 si 遐思
wild and fanciful thoughts;

xia xiang 遐想
wild and fanciful thoughts;

xia zhi 遐志
lofty ambition / lofty aspiration;

xia4 yi shi 下意識
subconsciousness;

xia4 ji nao yan 夏季腦炎
summer encephalitis;

xian1 zhi 先知
person of foresight;

xian zhi xian jue 先知先覺
(1) having foresight;
(2) a person of foresight;

xian4 ji 獻計
make suggestions / offer advice;

xiang1 xin 相信
believe / have faith in / trust;

xiang3 想
(1) consider / suppose / think;
(2) plan;
(3) want / would like to;

xiang ban fa 想辦法
think of a way;

xiang bu dao 想不到
to one's surprise / unexpectedly;

xiang bu kai 想不開
take things too hard;

xiang bu qi lai 想不起來
cannot remember / unable to call to mind;

xiang bu tong 想不通
beyond comprehension / can't figure it out;

xiang chu 想出
think up;

xiang dang ran 想當然
as may be taken for granted;

xiang dao 想到
hit upon an idea / think of;

xiang de dao 想得到
expect / imagine / think;

xiang de kai 想得開
not to take to heart;

xiang fa 想法
idea / notion / plan;

xiang fa yi zhi 想法一致
one's mind is sb's mind // of the same mind;

xiang fa zi 想法子
think of a way;

xiang fang she fa 想方設法
try everything possible;

xiang jin ban fa 想盡辦法
leave no stone unturned;

xiang kai le 想開了
not take to heart / stop worrying;

xiang lai 想來
it may be assumed;

xiang lai xiang qu 想來想去
ponder / think over sth again and again / turn a matter over and over;

xiang qi 想起
bring to mind / call to mind / come into sb's mind / come to mind / occur / put sb in mind of / recall / remember / think of;

xiang ru fei fei 想入非非
be lost in daydreams / indulge in wishful thinking;

xiang tong 想通
straighten out one's thinking;

xiang tou 想頭
(1) idea / notion / thought;
(2) expectation / hope;
(3) thinking;

xiang wang 想望
desire / expect / hope;

xiang xiang kan 想想看
think about it;

xiang xiang 想像
fancy / imagine / visualize;

xiang xiang li 想像力
imagination / imaginative power;

xiang yi xiang 想一想
pause to think / reflect a little;

xiao3 cong ming 小聰明
petty tricks // clear and smart in a small way;

xiao nao 小腦
cerebellum;

xiao nao ban qiu 小腦半球
cerebellar hemisphere;

xie2 ji 邪計
conspiracy / evil scheme;

xie mou 邪謀
conspiracy / evil scheme;

xin1 ji 心計
scheming ‖ calculation; designing; designs of the mind; planning;

xin ji du la 心計毒辣
one's clever schemes are poisonous and cruel;

xin zhi 心智
mentality / the abilities and powers of the mind;

xin zhi zheng chang 心智正常
sane // sanity;

xin4 信
(1) faithfulness;
(2) believing / true;
(3) believe / trust;

xin bu guo 信不過
have no trust in;

xin de guo 信得過
can be believed;

xin feng 信奉
believe in / worship;

xin fu 信服
believe in / trust;

xin kao 信靠
trust;

xin lai 信賴
trust;

xin nian 信念
belief / conviction;

xin ren 信任
have faith in // confidence / faith / trust;

xin shou 信守
abide by / keep a promise;

xing2 cheng yu si 行成於思
a goal is achieved through thinking carefully;

xu1 諝
(1) sagacity / wisdom;
(2) clear idea / stratagem;

xuan1 pi 軒闢
generous / open-minded;

xuan2 chuai 懸揣
conjecture / speculate;

xuan duan 懸斷
judge without any sufficient basis;

xuan xiang 懸想
conjecture / imagine / speculate;

xue2 tan 踅探
peep / spy / watch and investigate stealthily;

xun2 li 循理
in accordance with reason;

xun2 si 尋思
mediate / ponder / reflect;

yang2 zuo bu zhi 佯作不知
feign ignorance / pretend not to know;

yi1 ban ren de kan fa 一般人的看法
conventional wisdom;

yi nian jian 一念間
a fleeting thought;

yi nian zhi cha 一念之差
a false step / a wrong decision made in a moment of weakness;

yi shan nian 一閃念
a fleeting thought / an idea runs through one's mind;

yi wu suo zhi 一無所知
not to know anything about ‖ absolutely ignorant of; completely unaware; have no idea of; in the dark; know neither buff nor style; know nothing about; know nothing at all about sth; not have the least inkling of; not to have the least inkling of;

yi zhi ban jie 一知半解
a smack of knowledge / half knowledge of sth / incomplete comprehension;

yi2 wang zheng 遺忘症
amnesia;
chuang shang hou yi wang zheng 創傷後遺忘症
posttraumatic amnesia;
ju xian xing yi wang zheng 局限性遺忘症
circumscribed amnesia;
ying er qi yi wang zheng 嬰兒期遺忘症
infantile amnesia;

yi2 shen 頤神
have a mental relaxation / rest one's mind;

yi4 xiang tian kai 異想天開
have fantastic notions;

yi4 jian 意見
idea / opinion / suggestion / view;

yi jian yi zhi 意見一致
in full agreement // one's opinions jump with sb's;

yi liao zhi wai 意料之外
unexpected happening;

yi liao zhi zhong 意料之中
par for the course;

yi shi 意識
awareness / consciousness / sense;
qian yi shi 潛意識
subconsciousness;

yi4 ce 臆測
conjecture / guess / surmise;

yi duan 臆斷
assume / speculate / suppose // assumption / speculation / supposition;

yi duo 臆度
conjecture / guess / surmise;

yi shuo 臆説
assumption / supposition;

yi xiang 臆想
speculate // speculation;

yi4 si 繹思
think of continuously;

yin1 mou 陰謀
conspiracy / machination;

yin2 nian 淫念
carnal desires / lust;

ying1 er qi yi wang zheng 嬰兒期遺忘症
infantile amnesia;

you1 rou gua duan 優柔寡斷
faint-hearted / irresolute;

you2 yu bu jue 猶豫不決
hesitate / remain undecided // irresolute / off-again, on-again // in two minds;

you3 tou wu nao 有頭無腦
stupid;

you4 nao 右腦
the right side of one's brain;

you4 zhi 幼稚
immature / naïve;

you zhi bing 幼稚病
(1) infantile disorder;
(2) infantilism;

yu4 ce 預測
forecast / foretell / predict // prediction;

yu duan 預斷
prejudge;

yu gan 預感
premonition / presentiment;

yu ji 預計
calculate in advance / estimate / surmise;

yu liao 預料
anticipate / expect / predict / surmise;

yu mou 預謀
scheme beforehand;

yu xiang 預想
anticipate / expect;

yu yan 預言
foretell / predict / prognosticate // prediction / prognostication / prophecy;

yu zhi 預知
know beforehand / know in advance // foreknowledge;

yuan2 fa xing nao ji shui 原發性腦積水
primary hydrocephalus;

yuan3 lü 遠慮
worry and plan far ahead;

zai4 xin 在心
attentive / feel concerned / keep in mind;

zang1 pi 臧否
evaluate / pass judgment;

zang pi ren wu 臧否人物
pass judgment on people;

zao3 fa xing chi dai 早發性痴呆
dementia praecox;

zao lao xing chi dai 早老性痴呆
presenile dementia;

zha4 yi xiang 乍一想
at first blush;

zhang1 li xing nao ji shui 張力性腦積水
tension hydrocephalus;

zhang3 jian shi 長見識
gain experience / increase one's knowledge;

zhao1 si mu xiang 朝思暮想
yearn day and night;

zhao2 mi 着迷
be captivated / be fascinated / be infatuated / daft about;

zhao mo 着魔
be bewitched / be possessed;

zhao san bu zhao liang 着三不着兩
ill-considered / thoughtless;

zhen4 dong huan jue 振動幻覺
oscillating vision;

zhi1 知
aware of / know / understand;

zhi dao 知道
aware / know / learn / realize / understand;

zhi fei 知非
know one's mistakes;

zhi guo 知過
know one's mistakes;

zhi guo gai guo 知過改過
acknowledge one's faults and correct them;

zhi nan er jin 知難而進
press forward in spite of difficulties;

zhi nan er tui 知難而退
withdraw after learning of the difficulties;

zhi nan xing yi 知難行易
it is easier to do a thing than to know the why;

zhi qing 知情
in the know / in the picture;

zhi qing bu ju 知情不舉
know the condition and take no action;

zhi4 智
(1) clever / intelligent;
(2) prudence;

zhi hui 智慧
intelligence / wisdom;

zhi li 智力
intelligence / the exercise of reason;

zhi li di ruo 智力低弱
feeble-mindedness;

zhi li di xia 智力低下
mental retardation;

zhi li luo hou 智力落後
mental retardation;

zhi li que xian 智力缺陷
mental defect;

zhi lü 智慮
wisdom;

zhi lüe 智略
intellengence and tact;

zhi mou 智謀
cleverness / tactics;

zhi neng 智能
intelligence and capacity;

zhi neng bu zu 智能不足
mental retardation;

zhi neng que xian 智能缺陷
mental deficiency;

zhi qiao 智巧
brains and tact;

zhi yu 智愚
the wise and the foolish;

zhi4 xin 置信
believe;

zhi zhi du wai 置之度外
care nothing about / give no thought to;

zhi zhi nao hou 置之腦後
disregard it / forget it;

zhong1 er xing nao yan 中耳性腦炎
otoencephalitis;

zhong er yan xing nao ji shui 中耳炎性腦積水
otitic hydrocephalus;

zhong nao 中腦
mesencephalon / midbrain;

zhong nao yan 中腦炎
mesencephalitis;

zhong3 liu xing nao mo yan 腫瘤性腦膜炎
neoplastic meningitis;

zhong4 du xing chi dai 中毒性痴呆
toxic dementia;

zhuan3 nian 轉念
change one's mind / have second thoughts;

zhuang1 sha 裝傻
counterfeit folly / feign ignorance / feign stupidity;

zhuo2 ban 酌辦
handle by taking actual circumstances into consideration;

zhuo cai 酌裁
consider and decide;

zhuo ding 酌定
decide by taking circumstances into consideration;

zhuo duo 酌奪
make a considered decision;

zhuo liang 酌量
weigh and consider;

zhuo qing 酌情
take circumstances into consideration;

zi4 bi zhang ai 自閉障礙
autistic disorder;

zi bi zheng 自閉症
autism;

zi cha 自察
make self-examination;

zi jue 自決
(1) decide by oneself / solve a problem by oneself;
(2) self-determination;

zi jue 自覺
(1) self-consciousness / self-realization;
(2) aware / feel sth concerning oneself;

zi jue zi yuan 自覺自願
by one's own desire / voluntarily / willingly;

zi qi 自欺
(1) deceive oneself;
(2) self-deceit;

zi qi qi ren 自欺欺人
deceive oneself and others as well;

zi wo tao zui 自我陶醉
indulge in daydreaming;

zi xing 自省
examine oneself / introspect // introspection / self-examination;

zi zhao 自招
confess // confession;

zi zhi li que 自知理缺
realize that one is on the wrong side;

zi zhi zhi ming 自知之明
know oneself;

zi zhi 自制
self-restraint / self-discipline;

zu2 zhi duo mou 足智多謀
ingenious / resourceful / wise and full of stratagems;

zuo3 nao 左腦
the left side of one's brain;

zuo si you xiang 左思右想
think over from different angles || crack one's brains over; cudgel one's brains; deep in thought; keep thinking; muse on sth; ponder; rack one's brains; ruminate; think back and forth; think from different angles; think of this and that; think over and over; turn sth over in one's mind;

zuo4 meng 做夢
(1) dream / have a dream;
(2) have a pipe dream;

Pang guang 膀胱 Bladder

bai2 hou xing pang guang yan 白喉性膀胱炎
diphtheritic cystitis;

bai niao 白尿
albinuria;

bai xi bao niao 白細胞尿
leukocyturia;

beng1 lou 崩漏
uterine bleeding;

beng lou dai xia 崩漏帶下
uterine bleeding and vaginal discharge;

beng lou xia xue 崩漏下血
uterine bleeding;

bian4 ying xing pang guang yan 變應性膀胱炎
allergic cystitis;

bian ying xing qian lie xian yan 變應性前列腺炎
allergic prostatitis;

bie1 niao 憋尿
hold up one's urine;

bing4 li xing tang niao 病理性糖尿
pathologic glycosuria;

bo1 tuo xing pang guang yan 剝脫性膀胱炎
exfoliative cystitis;

can2 yu dan bai niao 殘餘蛋白尿
residual proteinuria;

can yu niao 殘餘尿
residual urine;

cheng2 nian xing tang niao bing 成年型糖尿病
adult-onset diabetes mellitus;

cheng shu xing tang niao bing 成熟型糖尿病
maturity-onset diabetes mellitus;

chu1 xue xing pang guang yan 出血性膀胱炎
hemorrhagic cystitis;

chuan1 ci xing tang niao bing 穿刺性糖尿病
puncture diabetes;

chui2 ti xing niao beng zheng 垂體性尿崩症
pituitary diabetes insipidus;

ci4 ji xing pang guang 刺激性膀胱
irritable bladder;

cui4 xing tang niao bing 脆性糖尿病
brittle diabetes;

da4 chang gan jun niao 大腸杆菌尿
colibacilluria;

da xiao bian 大小便
answer a call of nature / obey a call of nature / pay a call / pay a call of nature;

da xiao bian shi jin 大小便失禁
gatism / incontinence // incontinent;

dan1 chun xing niao dao yan 單純性尿道炎
simple urethritis;

dan chun xing pang guang kui yang 單純性膀胱潰瘍
ulcus implex vesicae;

dan4 bai niao 蛋白尿
albuminuria / proteinuria;

can yu dan bai niao 殘餘蛋白尿
redisual proteinuria;

fa re xing dan bai niao 發熱性蛋白尿
febrile proteinuria;

gong neng xing dan bai niao 功能性蛋白尿
functional proteinuria;

jia dan bai niao 假蛋白尿
pseudalbuminuria;

jian xie xing dan bai niao 間歇性蛋白尿
intermittent proteinuria;

nei yuan xing dan bai niao 內源性蛋白尿
intrinsic proteinuria;

nong xing dan bai niao 膿性蛋白尿
pyogenic proteinuria;

qing lian dan bai niao 輕鏈蛋白尿
light-chain proteinuria;

shen xing dan bai niao 腎形蛋白尿
renal proteinuria;

sheng li xing dan bai niao 生理性蛋白尿
physiologic proteinuria;

shuang dan bai niao 雙蛋白尿
diploalbuminuria;

te fa xing dan bai niao 特發性蛋白尿
essential proteinuria;

tiao jie xing dan bai niao 調節性蛋白尿
regulatory preteinuria;

tong feng xing dan bai niao 痛風性蛋白尿
gouty proteinuria;

tou ming dan bai niao 透明蛋白尿
hyalinuria;

xiao hua xing dan bai niao 消化性蛋白尿
digestive proteinuria;

xin xing dan bai niao 心形蛋白尿
cardiac proteinuria;

ye dan bai niao 夜蛋白尿
noctalluminuria;

yi chu xing dan bai niao 溢出性蛋白尿
overflow proteinuria;

yin shi xing dan bai niao 飲食性蛋白尿
dietetic proteinuria;

yuan fa xing dan bai niao 原發性蛋白尿
essential proteinuria;

yun dong xing dan bai niao 運動性蛋白尿
athletic proteinuria;

zhen xing dan bai niao 真性蛋白尿
true proteinuria;

zhen fa xing dan bai niao 陣發性蛋白尿
paroxysmal proteinuria;

zhi li xing dan bai niao 直立蛋白尿
orthostatic proteinuria;

zi fa xing dan bai niao 自發性蛋白尿
essential proteinuria;

dan bai niao zheng 蛋白尿症
proteinuria;

xin zang xing dan bai niao zheng 心臟性蛋白尿症
cardiac proteinuria;

dao3 niao 導尿
urethral catheterization;

di1 dan niao 低氮尿
hypoazoturia;

di dan niao zheng 低氮尿症
hypazoturia;

di dan zhi niao 低膽汁尿
hypocholuria;

di gai niao 低鈣尿
hypocalciuria;

di lü niao 低氯尿
hypochloruria;

di niao su xue zheng 低尿素血症
hypouremia;

di niao suan niao 低尿酸尿
hypouricuria;

di shen niao 低滲尿
hyposthenuria;

di4 fang xing xue niao 地方性血尿
endemic hematuria;

duo1 niao zheng 多尿症
polyuria;

er4 bian bu li 二便不利
difficulty in urination and defecation;

fa1 guang niao 發光尿
photuria;

fa re xing dan bai niao 發熱性蛋白尿
febrile proteinuria;

fan3 chang xing niao shi jin 反常性尿失禁
paradoxical incontinence;

fan she xing pang guang 反射性膀胱
reflex bladder;

gang1 men pai niao 肛門排尿
urochezia;

gao1 lü niao 高氯尿
hyperchloruria;

gao niao suan niao 高尿酸尿
hyperlithuria;

gao shen niao 高滲尿
hypersthenuria;

gao tong niao 高銅尿
hypercupriuria;

gong1 neng xing dan bai niao 功能性蛋白尿
functional proteinuria;

gong neng xing xue niao 功能性血尿
functional hematuria;

guang1 胱
bladder;

hei1 niao 黑尿
black urine;

hei niao re 黑尿熱
blackwater fever;

hong2 niao bing 紅尿病
redwater;

hong niao zheng 紅尿症
erythruria;

hou4 niao dao 後尿道
posterior urethra;

ji1 xie xing pang guang yan 機械性膀胱炎
mechanical cystitis;

ji2 po pai niao 急迫排尿
precipitant urination;

jia3 dan bai niao 假蛋白尿
pseudalbuminuria;

jia niao du zheng 假尿毒症
pseudouremia;

jia tang niao bing 假糖尿病
pseudodiabetes;

niao du zheng xing jia tang niao bing 尿毒症性假糖尿病
uremic psuedodiabetes mellitus;

jia xue niao 假血尿
pseudohematuria;

jian4 xie xing dan bai niao 間歇性蛋白尿
intermittent proteinuria;

jian xie xing niao shi jin 間歇性尿失禁
intermittent incontinence;

jian xie xing pai niao 間歇性排尿
stuttering urination;

jie2 jia xing pang guang yan 結痂性膀胱炎
incrusted cystitis;

jie jing niao 結晶尿
crystalluria;

jie shi niao 結石尿
uraturia;

jie shi xing wu niao 結石性無尿
calculous anuria;

jie3 shou 解手
do one's needs / ease nature / go to the toilet / pay a call of nature / relieve nature / relieve oneself // call of nature;

jin3 po xing niao shi jin 緊迫性尿失禁
urgency incontinence;

jing1 ye niao 精液尿
seminuria;

jing4 luan xing niao bi 痙攣性尿閉
ischuria spastica;

jing luan xing pai niao kun nan 痙攣性排尿困難
spastic dysuria;

jing luan xing pang guang 痙攣性膀胱
spastic bladder;

ju4 pang guang 巨膀胱
megabladder;

ju shu niao guan 巨輸尿管
megaloureter;

lan2 se niao 藍色尿
cyanuria;

li4 niao 利尿
diuresis;
shen tou xing li niao 滲透性利尿
osmotic diuresis;

li niao su 利尿素
diuretin;

li niao suan 利尿酸
etacrynic acid;

li niao yao 利尿藥
diuretics;

liang2 xing qian lie xian fei da 良性前列腺肥大
benign prostatic hypertrophy;

liang xing tang niao 良性糖尿
benign glycosuria;

lin2 bing xing niao dao yan 淋病性尿道炎
gonorrheal urethritis;

lin jun xing niao dao yan 淋菌性尿道炎
gonococcal urethritis;

lü4 pao xing pang guang yan 濾泡性膀胱炎
crstitis follicularis;

ma2 bi xing pang guang 麻痺性膀胱
paralytic bladder;

mao2 dun niao bi 矛盾尿閉
ischuria paradoxa;

mi4 niao 泌尿
uropoiesis;

mi niao dao 泌尿道
urinary tract;
sheng zhi mi niao dao 生殖泌尿道
genitourinary tract;

mi niao guan 泌尿管
urinary canal / uropoietic passage;

mi4 yue pang guang yan 蜜月膀胱炎
honeymoon cystitis;

nan2 niao dao 男尿道
urethra masculina;

nang2 xing niao dao yan 囊性尿道炎
urethritis cystica;

nang xing qian lie xian zeng sheng 囊性前列腺增生
cystic prostatic hyperplasia;

nang xing shu niao guan yan 囊性輸尿管炎
ureteritis cystica;

nang zhong xing pang guang yan 囊腫性膀胱炎
cystic cystitis;

nei4 yuan xing dan bai niao 內源性蛋白尿
intrinsic proteinuria;

nian2 ye niao 黏液尿
blennuria;

nian4 zhu jun niao 念珠菌尿
candiduria;

niao4 尿
(1) urine;
(2) make water / pass water / urinate;
bie niao 憋尿
hold up one's urine;
sa niao 撒尿
pass water / pee ‖ make water; pass urine; pass water; pee-pee; piddle; piss; spend a penny; urinate; wee-wee;

niao beng zheng 尿崩症
diabetes insipidus;
chui ti xing niao beng zheng 垂體性尿崩症
pituitary diabetes insipidus;
shen xing niao beng zheng 腎性尿崩症
nephrogenic diabetes insipidus;

niao beng ting 尿崩停
posterior pituitary insufflation;

niao bi 尿閉
anuria / ischuria / suppression of urine;

jing luan xing niao bi 痙攣性尿閉
ischuria spastica;
mao dun niao bi 矛盾尿閉
ischuria paradoxa;

niao chen dian 尿沉澱
urinary sediment;

niao chuang 尿牀
wet the bed;

niao dao 尿道
urethra;
hou niao dao 後尿道
posterior urethra;
nan niao dao 男尿道
urethra masculina;
nü niao dao 女尿道
urethra feminina;
qian lie xian niao dao 前列腺尿道
prostatic urethra;
qian niao dao 前尿道
anterior urethra;

niao dao chu xue 尿道出血
hemorrhage of the urethra / urethrorrhagia;

niao dao pang guang yan 尿道膀胱炎
urethrocystitis;

niao dao qie kai 尿道切開
urethrotomy;

niao dao tong 尿道痛
urethrodynia;

niao dao xing xue niao 尿道性血尿
urethral hematuria;

niao dao yan 尿道炎
urethritis;
dan chun xing niao dao yan 單純性尿道炎
simple urethritis;
lin bing xing niao dao yan 淋病性尿道炎
gonorrheal urethritis;
lin jun xing niao dao yan 淋菌性尿道炎
gonococcal urethritis;
nang xing niao dao yan 囊性尿道炎
urethritis cystica;
pang guang niao dao yan 膀胱尿道炎
cystourethritis;
qian niao dao yan 前尿道炎
preurethritis;
rou ya xing niao dao yan 肉芽性尿道炎
urethritis granulosa;
te yi xing niao dao yan 特異性尿道炎
specific urethritis;
tong feng xing niao dao yan 痛風性尿道炎
gouty urethritis;
xian xing niao dao yan 腺性尿道炎
urethritis glandularis;
xing bing niao dao yan 性病尿道炎
urethritis venerea;
yu fang xing niao dao yan 預防性尿道炎
prophylactic urethritis;

niao dao ye yi 尿道液溢
urethrorrhea;

niao dao yi 尿道溢
medorrhea;

niao du zheng 尿毒症
uremia;
jia niao du zheng 假尿毒症
pseudouremia;

niao du zheng xing jia tang niao bing 尿毒症性假糖尿病
uremic psuedodiabetes mellitus;

niao guo nong 尿過濃
oligohydruria;

niao guo shao 尿過少
uropenia;

niao han 尿汗
uridrosia;

niao han zheng 尿汗症
uridrosis;

niao hun zhuo 尿渾濁
cloudy urine;

niao ji 尿急
urgent urination;

niao ji gan 尿急感
stangury;

niao jie shi bing 尿結石病
lithiasis;

niao jin run 尿浸潤
urecchysis;

niao ku zi 尿褲子
wet the bed;

niao liang bu deng 尿量不等
anisuria;

niao liang jian shao 尿量減少
hypourocrinia;

niao liang zeng duo 尿量增多
hydrouria;

niao lou 尿瘻
urinary fistula;

niao lu 尿路
urinary tract;

niao lu bing 尿路病
urosis;

zu se xing niao lu bing 阻塞性尿路病
obstructive uropathy;

niao lu bing bian 尿路病變
uropathy;

niao lu jie shi 尿路結石
lithangiuria;

niao lu kui yang 尿路潰瘍
urelcosis;

niao lu shang pi 尿路上皮
urothelium;

niao pin 尿頻
frequent urination / pollakiuria / sychnuria;

niao shao zheng 尿少症
oliguria;

niao shi jin 尿失禁
incontinence;

fan chang xing niao shi jin 反常性尿失禁
paradoxical incontinence;

jian xie xing niao shi jin 間歇性尿失禁
intermittent incontinence;

jin po xing niao shi jin 緊迫性尿失禁
urgency incontinence;

yi liu xing niao shi jin 溢流性尿失禁
overflow incontinence;

ying ji xing niao shi jin 應激性尿失禁
stress incontinence;

niao shi 尿石
urolith;

niao shi zheng 尿石症
urinary calculus / urolithiasis;

niao su 尿素
urea;

niao suan 尿酸
uric acid;

niao suan geng si 尿酸梗死
uric acid infarct;

niao suan jie shi 尿酸結石
urate calculus;

niao suan jie shi bing 尿酸結石病
uric acid lithiasis;

niao suan niao 尿酸尿
uricaciduria;

di niao suan niao 低尿酸尿
hypouricuria;

gao niao suan niao 高尿酸尿
hyperlithuria;

zheng chang niao suan niao 正常尿酸尿
normouricuria;

niao tang guo duo 尿糖過多
hyperglycosuria;

niao xu ji 尿蓄積
retention of urine;

niao xue 尿血
blood in the urine / hematuria;

niao ye 尿液
chamber lye / urina / urine;

niao4 chuang 溺牀
wet the bed;

niao ku 溺褲
wet oneself;

niao niao 溺尿
make water / urinate;

nong2 niao 濃尿
pyuria;

nong2 niao 膿尿
pyuria;

nong xing dan bai niao 膿性蛋白尿
pyogenic proteinuria;

nü3 niao dao 女尿道
urethra feminina;

pai2 niao 排尿
micturate / urinate // micturition;
ji po pai niao 急迫排尿
precipitant urination;
jian xie xing pai niao 間歇性排尿
stuttering urination;
tong xing pai niao 痛性排尿
alginuresis;

pai niao fan she 排尿反射
micturition reflex;

pai niao guo huan 排尿過緩
bradyuria;

pai niao han zhan 排尿寒戰
urethral chill;

pai niao jian shao 排尿減少
hypouresis;

pai niao kun nan 排尿困難
difficult urination / dysuria;
jing luan xing pai niao kun nan 痙攣性排尿困難
spastic dysuria;

pai niao tong 排尿痛
urodynia;

pai niao tong gan 排尿痛感
painful urination;

pai niao wu li 排尿無力
acraturesis;

pai niao xu huan 排尿徐緩
bradyuria;

pai niao yi chang 排尿異常
paruria;

pai niao zheng chang 排尿正常
normosthenuria;

pai niao zhong shu 排尿中樞
micturition centre;

pang2 膀
bladder;

pang guang 膀胱
urinary bladder;
ci ji xing pang guang 刺激性膀胱
irritable bladder;
fan she xing pang guang 反射性膀胱
reflex bladder;
jing luan xing pang guang 痙攣性膀胱
spastic bladder;
ju pang guang 巨膀胱
megabladder;
ma bi xing pang guang 麻痺性膀胱
paralytic bladder;
shen jing xing pang guang 神經性膀胱
nervous bladder;
shen jing yuan xing pang guang 神經源性膀胱
neurogenic bladder;

pang guang ai 膀胱癌
bladder cancer;

pang guang bi 膀胱襞
fold;
zhi chang pang guang bi 直腸膀胱襞
rectovesical fold;

pang guang bi suo 膀胱閉鎖
atretocystia;

pang guang chu xue 膀胱出血
cystorrhagia;

pang guang fan she 膀胱反射
bladder reflex;

pang guang ge 膀胱隔
septum;
zhi chang pang guang ge 直腸膀胱隔
rectovesical septum;

pang guang guo du huo yue zong he zheng 膀胱過度活躍綜合症
overactive bladder;

pang guang guo min 膀胱過敏
cysterethism;

pang guang ji nong 膀胱積膿
pyocystis;

pang guang ji xue 膀胱積血
hematocyst;

pang guang jie he 膀胱結核
cystophthisis;

pang guang jie shi 膀胱結石
bladder stone / vesical calculus;

pang guang jie shi bing 膀胱結石病
cystolithiasis;

pang guang kou 膀胱口
opening of bladder;

pang guang kui yang 膀胱潰瘍
cystelcosis;
dan chun xing pang guang kui yang 單純性膀胱潰瘍
ulcus implex vesicae;

pang guang kuo zhang 膀胱擴張
megabladder;

pang guang niao dao kou 膀胱尿道口
vesicourethral orifice;

pang guang niao dao yan 膀胱尿道炎
cystourethritis;

pang guang shan 膀胱疝
vesical hernia;

pang guang shen xue 膀胱滲血
cystostaxis;

pang guang shi 膀胱石
vesical calculus || bladder stone;

pang guang tong 膀胱痛
cystalgia;

pang guang wei suo 膀胱萎縮
cystatrophia;

pang guang yan 膀胱炎
cystitis;
bai hou xing pang guang yan 白喉性膀胱炎
diphtheritic cystitis;
bian ying xing pang guang yan 變應性膀胱炎
allergic cystitis;
bo tuo xing pang guang yan 剝脱性膀胱炎
exfoliative cystitis;
chu xue xing pang guang yan 出血性膀胱炎
hemorrhagic cystitis;
ji xie xing pang guang yan 機械性膀胱炎
mechanical cystitis;
jie jia xing pang guang yan 結痂性膀胱炎
incrusted cystitis;
lü pao xing pang guang yan 濾泡性膀胱炎
crstitis follicularis;
mi yue pang guang yan 蜜月膀胱炎
honeymoon cystitis;
nang zhong xing pang guang yan 囊腫性膀胱炎
cystic cystitis;
niao dao pang guang yan 尿道膀胱炎
urethrocystitis;
qi zhong xing pang guang yan 氣腫性膀胱炎
cystitis emphysematosa;
qian lie xian pang guang yan 前列腺膀胱炎
prostatocystitis;
quan pang guang yan 全膀胱炎
pancystitis;
shen pang guang yan 腎膀胱炎
nephrocystitis;
shen yu pang guang yan 腎盂膀胱炎
pyelocystitis;
xi jun xing pang guang yan 細菌性膀胱炎
bacterial cystitis;
xian xing pang guang yan 腺性膀胱炎
cystitis glandularis;
yin dao pang guang yan 陰道膀胱炎
colpocystitis;

pao1 脬
bladder;

pi4 gun niao liu 屁滾尿流
be frightened out of one's wits / piss in one's pants / scare the shit out of sb / wet one's pants in terror;

pin2 niao 頻尿
pollakiuria;

qi4 zhong xing pang guang yan 氣腫性膀胱炎
cystitis emphysematosa;

qian2 lie xian 前列腺
prostate / prostate gland;

qian lie xian ai 前列腺癌
cancer of the prostate gland;

qian lie xian dou 前列腺竇
prostatic sinus;

qian lie xian fei da 前列腺肥大
prostatic hypertrophy;
liang xing qian lie xian fei da 良性前列腺肥大
benign prostatic hypertrophy;

qian lie xian pang guang yan 前列腺膀胱炎
prostatocystitis;

qian lie xian qie chu 前列腺切除
prostatectomy / removal of the prostate;

qian lie xian kui yang 前列腺潰瘍
prostatelcosis;

qian lie xian nang 前列腺囊
prostatic vesicle;

qian lie xian niao dao 前列腺尿道
prostatic urethra;

qian lie xian yan 前列腺炎
prostatitis;
bian ying xing qian lie xian yan 變應性前列腺炎
allergic prostatitis;

qian lie xian zeng sheng 前列腺增生
prostatic hyperplasia;
nang xing qian lie xian zeng sheng 囊性前列腺增生
cystic prostatic hyperplasia;

qian niao dao 前尿道
anterior urethra;

qian niao dao yan 前尿道炎
preurethritis;

qing1 niao zheng 青尿症
cyanuria;

qing tong se tang niao bing 青銅色糖尿病
bronze diabetes;

qing1 lian dan bai niao 輕鏈蛋白尿
light-chain proteinuria;

qing2 xu xing tang niao 情緒性糖尿
emotional glycosuria;

quan2 pang guang yan 全膀胱炎
pancystitis;

re4 bing xing niao 熱病性尿
febrile urine;

ren4 shen tang niao bing 妊娠糖尿病
gestational diabetes;

rou4 ya xing niao dao yan 肉芽性尿道炎
urethritis granulosa;

rou yan xue niao 肉眼血尿
gross hematuria;

ru3 mi niao 乳糜尿
chylous ruine / rina chyli;

ru zhuang niao 乳狀尿
milky urine / urina galactodes;

sa1 niao 撒尿
pass water / pee || make water; pass urine; pee-pee; piddle; piss; spend a penny; urinate; wee-wee;

shang4 ce suo 上廁所
go to toilet || answer a call of nature; ease nature; go to the washroom; obey a call of nature; pay a call; pay a call of nature; relieve nature; spend a penny;

shao3 niao 少尿
oliguresis;

shao niao zheng 少尿症
meagre urine output / oligoanuria;

shen2 jing xing pang guang 神經性膀胱
nervous bladder;

shen jing yuan xing pang guang 神經源性膀胱
neurogenic bladder;

shen4 xing tang niao bing 腎性糖尿病
renal diabetes;

shen xing dan bai niao 腎形蛋白尿
renal proteinuria;

shen xing niao beng zheng 腎性尿崩症
nephrogenic diabetes insipidus;

shen xing tang niao 腎性糖尿
renal glycosuria;

shen xing wu niao 腎性無尿
renal hermaturia;

shen yu pang guang yan 腎盂膀胱炎
pyelocystitis;

shen4 tou xing li niao 滲透性利尿
osmotic diuresis;

sheng1 li xing dan bai niao 生理性蛋白尿
physiologic proteinuria;

sheng zhang qi tang niao bing 生長期糖尿病
growth-onset diabetes mellitus;

sheng zhi mi niao dao 生殖泌尿道
genitourinary tract;

sheng4 yu niao 剩餘尿
residual urine;

shu1 niao guan 輸尿管
ureter;

ju shu niao guan 巨輸尿管
megaloureter;

shu niao guan shi qie chu 輸尿管石切除
ureterolighotomy;

shu niao guan yan 輸尿管炎
ureteritis;

nang xing shu niao guan yan 囊性輸尿管炎
ureteritis cystica;

xian xing shu niao guan yan 腺性輸尿管炎
ureteritis glandularis;

shuang1 dan bai niao 雙蛋白尿
diploalbuminuria;

shuang pang guang 雙膀胱
double bladder;

sou1 溲
(1) urinate;
(2) drench / immerse / soak;

sou bian 溲便
urinate / urine and feces;

sou ni 溲溺
urinate;

suan1 niao 酸尿
aciduria;

tang2 niao 糖尿
glucosuria;

bing li xing tang niao 病理性糖尿
pathologic glycosuria;

liang xing tang niao 良性糖尿
benign glycosuria;

qing xu xing tang niao 情緒性糖尿
emotional glycosuria;

shen xing tang niao 腎性糖尿
renal glycosuria;

xiao hua xing tang niao 消化性糖尿
digestive glycosuria;

yin shi xing tang niao 飲食性糖尿
alimentary glycosuria;

zhong du xing tang niao 中毒性糖尿
toxic glycosuria;

tang niao bing 糖尿病
diabetes;

cheng nian xing tang niao bing 成年型糖尿病
adult-onset diabetes mellitus;

cheng shu xing tang niao bing 成熟型糖尿病
maturity-onset diabetes mellitus;

chuan ci xing tang niao bing 穿刺性糖尿病
puncture diabetes;

cui xing tang niao bing 脆性糖尿病
brittle diabetes;

jia tang niao bing 假糖尿病
pseudodiabetes;

qing tong se tang niao bing 青銅色糖尿病
bronze diabetes;

ren shen tang niao bing 妊娠糖尿病
gestational diabetes;

shen xing tang niao bing 腎性糖尿病
renal diabetes;

sheng zhang qi tang niao bing 生長期糖尿病
growth-onset diabetes mellitus;

yin xing tang niao bing 隱性糖尿病
latent diabetes;

you nian xing tang niao bing 幼年型糖尿病
juvenile diabetes mellitus;

zai ti xing tang niao bing 甾體性糖尿病
steroid diabetes;

zai ti yuan xing tang niao bing 甾體源性糖尿病
steroidogenic diabetes;

tang niao bing huai ju 糖尿病壞疽
diabetic gangrene;

te4 fa xing dan bai niao 特發性蛋白尿
essential proteinuria;

te yi xing niao dao yan 特異性尿道炎
specific urethritis;

tiao2 jie xing dan bai niao 調節性蛋白尿
regulatory preteinuria;

tong2 niao 銅尿
cupruresis;

tong4 feng niao 痛風尿
gouty urine;

tong feng xing dan bai niao 痛風性蛋白尿
gouty proteinuria;

tong feng xing niao dao yan 痛風性尿道炎
gouty urethritis;

tong xing pai niao 痛性排尿
alginuresis;

tou4 ming dan bai niao 透明蛋白尿
hyalinuria;

wu2 niao 無尿
anuria;

jie shi xing wu niao 結石性無尿
calculous anuria;

shen xing wu niao 腎性無尿
renal hermaturia;

wu niao zheng 無尿症
absent urine output / oligoanuria;

wu pang guang 無膀胱
acystia;

wu se niao 無色尿
achromaturia;

xi4 jun niao 細菌尿
bacteriuria;

xi jun xing pang guang yan 細菌性膀胱炎
bacterial cystitis;

xian4 xing niao dao yan 腺性尿道炎
urethritis glandularis;

xian xing pang guang yan 腺性膀胱炎
cystitis glandularis;

xian xing shu niao guan yan 腺性輸尿管炎
ureteritis glandularis;

xiao1 hua bu liang xing niao 消化不良性尿
dyspeptic urine;

xiao hua xing dan bai niao 消化性蛋白尿
digestive proteinuria;

xiao hua xing tang niao 消化性糖尿
digestive glycosuria;

xiao3 bian 小便
pass water / pee ‖ apple and pip; burn the grass; dicky-diddle; do; drain one's radiator; drain one's snake; empty one's bladder; evacuate the bladder; go for a pee; go tap a kidney; have a pee; have a quickie; have a run off; life his leg; make number one; make salt water; make water; micturate; micturition; pass urine; piddle; pie and mash; piss; plant a sweet pea; point Percy at the porcelain; pump ship; retire; scatter; see a man about a dog; see one's aunt; shake hands with an old friend; shake the dew off the lily; shoot a lion; spend a penny; take a quickie; tap a keg; tinkle; urinate; water the lawn; water the stock; whiz;

yan xiao bian 驗小便
urine test;

xiao bian ci tong 小便刺痛
ardour urinae;

xiao bian kun nan 小便困難
have difficulty in passing water / have trouble urinating / urination difficulty;

xiao bian shi jin 小便失禁
aconuresis / urinary incontinence;

xiao bian zhuo tong 小便灼痛
ardour urinae / dysuria / painful urination;

xiao jie 小解
make water / pass water / pee / urinate;

xin1xing dan bai niao 心形蛋白尿
cardiac proteinuria;

xin zang xing dan bai niao zheng 心臟性蛋白尿症
cardiac proteinuria;

xing4 bing niao dao yan 性病尿道炎
urethritis venerea;

xue4 niao 血尿
blood urine / bloody urine / hematuria / urina cruenta;

di fang xing xue niao 地方性血尿
endemic hematuria;

gong neng xing xue niao 功能性血尿
functional hematuria;
jia xue niao 假血尿
pseudohematuria;
niao dao xing xue niao 尿道性血尿
urethral hematuria;
rou yan xue niao 肉眼血尿
gross hematuria;

yan4 xiao bian 驗小便
urine test;

ye4 dan bai niao 夜蛋白尿
noctalluminuria;

ye jian duo niao 夜間多尿
polyuria at night;

ye niao 夜尿
nocturia / nocturnal enuresis;

ye niao zheng 夜尿症
excessive urination at night / nycturia;

yi2 niao 遺尿
bedwetting / enuresis / urorrhea;

yi niao zheng 遺尿症
bedwetting / nocturnal enuresis;

yi4 chu xing dan bai niao 溢出性蛋白尿
overflow proteinuria;

yi liu xing niao shi jin 溢流性尿失禁
overflow incontinence;

yin3 shi xing dan bai niao 飲食性蛋白尿
dietetic proteinuria;

yin shi xing tang niao 飲食性糖尿
alimentary glycosuria;

yin3 xing tang niao bing 隱性糖尿病
latent diabetes;

you4 nian xing tang niao bing 幼年型糖尿病
juvenile diabetes mellitus;

yu4 fang xing niao dao yan 預防性尿道炎
prophylactic urethritis;

yuan2 fa xing dan bai niao 原發性蛋白尿
essential proteinuria;

yuan2 zhu niao 圓柱尿
cylindruria;

yun4 dong xing dan bai niao 運動性蛋白尿
athletic proteinuria;

zai1 ti xing tang niao bing 甾體性糖尿病
steroid diabetes;

zai ti yuan xing tang niao bing 甾體源性糖尿病
steroidogenic diabetes;

zhen1 xing dan bai niao 真性蛋白尿
true proteinuria;

zhen4 fa xing dan bai niao 陣發性蛋白尿
paroxysmal proteinuria;

zheng4 chang niao suan niao 正常尿酸尿
normouricuria;

zhi1 fang niao 脂肪尿
adiposuria;

zhi lei niao 脂類尿
lipiduria;

zhi mei niao 脂酶尿
lipasuria;

zhi niao zheng 脂尿症
pimeluria;

zhi suan niao 脂酸尿
lipaciduria;

zhi2 chang pang guang bi 直腸膀胱襞
rectovesical fold;

zhi chang pang guang yan 直腸膀胱炎
rectovesical septum;

zhi li xing dan bai niao 直立蛋白尿
orthostatic proteinuria;

zhong4 du xing tang niao 中毒性糖尿
toxic glycosuria;

zi4 fa xing dan bai niao 自發性蛋白尿
essential proteinuria;

zu3 se xing niao lu bing 阻塞性尿路病
obstructive uropathy;

Pi fu 皮膚 Skin

ai2 qian pi fu bing 癌前皮膚病
precancerous dermatosis;

ai qian pi yan 癌前皮炎
precancerous dermatitis;

ai qian qi pi fu bing 癌前期皮膚病
precancerous dermatosis;

ba1 pi 扒皮
peel off the skin;

ba1 疤
scar;

ba hen 疤痕
scar || pit; sore; spot;

ba la 疤瘌
scar;

bai2 ban 白斑
leucoma || leucoplakia; leukoplasia; white specks; white spots;
wei suo xing bai ban 萎縮性白斑
atrophic leukoplakia;

bai ban bing 白斑病
leucoderma / vitilago;
jing bu bai ban bing 頸部白斑病
leukoderma colli;
mei du xing bai ban bing 梅毒性白斑病
syphilitic leukoderma;
wai yin bai ban bing 外陰白斑病
leukoplakia vulvae;
yan zheng hou bai ban bing 炎症後白斑病
postinflammatory leukoderma;
zhi ye xing bai ban bing 職業性白斑病
occupational leukoderma;

bai fei 白痱
sudamina;

bai li tou hong 白裏透紅
milk and rose / peaches and cream;

bai nen 白嫩
(of skin) delicate / fair and clear;

bai pi bing 白皮病
whitle skin disease;

bai run 白潤
(of skin) fair and delicate;

ban1 斑
spot;
bai ban 白斑
leucoma || leucoplakia; leukoplasia; white specks; white spots;
han ban 汗斑
(1) sweat stain;
(2) tinea versicolour;
hei bai ban 黑白斑
melanoleukoderma;
hei ban 黑斑
eschar;
hong ban 紅斑
blotch;
huang ban 黃斑
macula lutea;
huang he ban 黃褐斑
cholasma;
lan ban 藍斑
blue spot;
lao nian ban 老年斑
senile lentigo;
lao ren ban 老人斑
age-mark;
lin bing xing ban 淋病性斑
macula gonorrhoeica;
qing ban 青斑
blue spot;
que ban 雀斑
freckle / ephelides;
ru bai ban 乳白斑
milk spot;
shai ban 曬斑
sunburn;
shang han ban 傷寒斑
typhoid spot;
shen jing yan xing ban 神經炎性斑
neuritic plaques;
si ban 死斑
livor;
yu ban 瘀斑
ecchymosis;
zi ban 紫斑
petechia;

ban ban 斑斑
spotted || full of spots; full of stains; mottled;

ban ban dian dian 斑斑點點
spotted || mottled; speckled;

ban dian 斑點
speck || dot; fleck; freckle; mottle; speckle; spot; stain;

ban tu 斑禿
alopecia areata;

ban1 瘢
flecks / rash || blotch; rash on skin; unhealthy marks on the skin;

ban1 瘢
freckle / scar;

dao ban 刀瘢
scar of a knife-cut;

ban dian 瘢點
black spot on the skin / scar;

ban hen 瘢痕
cicatrix / scar;

e xing ban hen 惡性瘢痕
vicious cicatrix;

fei hou xing ban hen 肥厚性瘢痕
hypertrophic scar;

bao4 fa xing cuo chuang 爆發性痤瘡
acne fulminans;

bian1 yuan xing hong ban 邊緣性紅斑
erythema marginatum;

bian3 ping shang pi 扁平上皮
pavement epithelium;

bian ping shi you 扁平濕疣
condyloma latum / flat condyloma;

bian ping shi zhen 扁平濕疹
moist papule / mucous papule;

bian ping tai xian 扁平台癬
lichen planus;

bian ping you 扁平疣
flat wart || plane wart; verruca plana; verruca plana juvenills;

bian4 ying xing pi yan 變應性皮炎
allergic dermatitis;

bian ying xing shi zhen 變應性濕疹
allergic eczema;

bian ying xing zi dian 變應性紫癜
allergic purpura;

biao3 pi 表皮
epidermis;

shang biao pi 上表皮
epicuticle;

biao pi fa yu bu liang 表皮發育不良
epidermodysplasia;

biao pi fa yu bu quan 表皮發育不全
epidermodysplasia;

biao pi shang 表皮傷
superficial wound;

biao pi yan 表皮炎
epidermitis;

shen chu xing biao pi yan 滲出性表皮炎
exudative epidermitis;

bing1 ji xue fu 冰肌雪膚
delicate skin;

bing ji yu gu 冰肌玉骨
spotless white and smooth skin;

bo1 fu zhi tong 剝膚之痛
the pain of being skinned;

bo pi 剝皮
peel off the skin || flay; skin;

bo tuo xing cuo chuang 剝脫性痤瘡
excoriated acne;

bo tuo xing pi yan 剝脫性皮炎
exfoliative dermatitis;

bo tuo xing yin xie bing 剝脫性銀屑病
exfoliative psoriasis;

ca1 han 擦汗
wipe off sweat;

ca huai 擦壞
graze;

ca lan 擦爛
inflammation caused by chafing / intertrigo;

ca lan hong ban 擦爛紅斑
erythema intertrigo;

ca lan xing shi zhen 擦爛性濕疹
eczema intertrigo;

ca po pi 擦破皮
raw;

ca shang 擦傷
chafe // abrasion;

ca zhuo shang 擦灼傷
brush burn / friction burn;

cao1 pi bing 糙皮病
pellagrosis;

cao3 di pi yan 草地皮炎
meadow dermatitis;

che3 pi 扯皮
argue over trifles;

chen2 ren ying pi zheng 陳人硬皮症
sclerema adultorum;

chou1 jin bo pi 抽筋剝皮
peel off the skin and pluck out the sinews / pull out sb's rendons and tear his skin off;

chou4 han 臭汗
bromidrosis / fetid sweat;

chou han zheng 臭汗症
bromidrosis / foul sweat;

chu1 han 出汗
(1) perspire / sweat;
(2) perspiration || diaphoresis; sudation; sweating;
pian ce chu han 偏側出汗
hemihidrosis;

chu han zhang ai 出汗障礙
dyshidrosis;

chu xue xing ma zhen 出血性麻疹
hemorrhagic measles;

chu xue xing zi dian 出血性紫癜
purpura hemorrhagica;

chu4 ran xing nong pao bing 觸染性膿疱病
impetigo contagiosa;

chuang1 hen 創痕
scar;

chuang shang xing pao zhen 創傷性疱疹
traumatic herpes;

chuang1 瘡
(1) skin ulcer / sore;
(2) wound;

chuang ba 瘡疤
(1) scar;
(2) sore;

chuang hen 瘡痕
wound scar;

chuang jia 瘡痂
scar;

chuang lao 瘡癆
chronic ulcer;

chuang yi 瘡痍
sores and wounds;

ci4 ji xing pi yan 刺激性皮炎
irritant dermatitis;

ci yang 刺癢
itch // itchy;

cuo2 chuang 痤瘡
acne;
bao fa xing cuo chuang 爆發性痤瘡
acne fulminans;
bo tuo xing cuo chuang 剝脱性痤瘡
excoriated acne;
jie chu xing cuo chuang 接觸性痤瘡
contact acne;
jie he xing cuo chuang 結核性痤瘡
acne scrofulosorum;
liu xing xing cuo chuang 流行性痤瘡
epidemic acne;
nang xing cuo chuang 囊性痤瘡
cystic acne;
nong pao xing cuo chuang 膿疱性痤瘡
acne pustulosa;
qiu zhen xing cuo chuang 丘疹性痤瘡
acne papulosa;
re dai cuo chuang 熱帶痤瘡
tropical acne;
wei suo xing cuo chuang 萎縮性痤瘡
acne atrophica;
xia ji cuo chuang 夏季痤瘡
acne estivalis;

ying er cuo chuang 嬰兒痤瘡
infantile acne;

ying jie xing cuo chuang 硬結性痤瘡
acne indurata;

yue jing qian cuo chuang 月經前痤瘡
premenstrual acne;

zhi ye xing cuo chuang 職業性痤瘡
occupational acne;

da4 han lin li 大汗淋漓
be bathed in perspiration / be drenched in sweat / be wet with perspiration / drip sweat / sweat like a pig / sweat profusely;

dai4 zhuang pao zhen 帶狀疱疹
herpes zoster;

dan1 du 丹毒
erysipelas;

lei dan du 類丹毒
erysipeloid;

dan1 chun pao zhen 單純疱疹
herpes simplex;

dan chun xing zi dian 單純性紫癜
purpura simplex;

dan chun you 單純疣
common wart;

dan3 疸
keratitis;

dao1 ban 刀瘢
scar of a knife-cut;

dao4 han 盜汗
night sweat;

de2 guo ma zhen 德國麻疹
German measles;

ding1 疔
boil / carbuncle;

ding chuang 疔瘡
malignant boil;

ding du 疔毒
carbuncular infection;

dong4 chuang 凍瘡
chilblain / frostbite / perniosis;

shen bu dong chuang 深部凍瘡
deep frostbite;

dong chuang hong ban 凍瘡紅斑
erythema pernio / suppurating frostbite;

dong chuang jiao jia 凍瘡焦痂
eschar frostbite;

dou4 chuang 痘瘡
pock mark;

duo1 han 多汗
hyperhidrosis;

pian ce duo han 偏側多汗
hemihyperidrosis;

qing xue xing duo han 情緒性多汗
emotional hyperhidrosis;

shou zhang duo han 手掌多汗
volar hyperhidrosis;

duo xing hong ban 多形紅斑
erythema multiforme;

e2 pi 鵝皮
cutis anserina / goose flesh;

e4 xing ban hen 惡性瘢痕
vicious cicatrix;

er4 du shao shang 二度燒傷
second degree burn;

fa1 han 發汗
make one perspire // diaphoresis / sweating;

fa re xing pao zhen 發熱性疱疹
herpes febrillis;

fa yan 發炎
inflammation;

fa yang 發癢
itch / tickle;

fang1 han 芳汗
perspiration (of a young woman);

fei1 dian xing ma zhen 非典型麻疹
atypical measles;

fei2 hou xing ban hen 肥厚性瘢痕
hypertrophic scar;

fei4 痱
heat rashes / heat spots / prickly heat;

fei zi 痱子
heat rashes / heat spots / miliaria / prickly heat;

fen3 ci 粉刺
acne;
hei tou fen ci 黑頭粉刺
comedo;
kai fang xing fen ci 開放性粉刺
open comedo;

fen ci ai 粉刺癌
comedo carcinoma;

fen ci zhi 粉刺痣
nevus comedonicus;

feng1 zhen 風疹
nettle rash;

fu1 膚
(1) skin || surface;
(2) skin-deep || shallow; superficial;
run fu 潤膚
moisturize the skin;

fu qian 膚淺
skin-deep / superficial;

fu ru ning zhi 膚如凝脂
creamy skin;

fu se 膚色
colour of skin || colour; complexion;

gan1 pi zheng 乾皮症
xeroderma;

gan xing pi fu 乾性皮膚
dry skin;

gan3 han 趕汗
induce sweat;

ge1 疙
keloid;

gong1 ye zhi ye xing pi fu bing 工業職業性皮膚病
industrial occupational dermatoses;

guang1 hua pi yan 光化皮炎
erythema solate;

guo4 min xing pi yan 過敏性皮炎
neurodermatitis;

guo min xing zi dian 過敏性紫癜
anaphylactic purpura;

hai4 han 駭汗
perspire as a result of fright;

han4 汗
perspiration / sweat;

han ban 汗斑
(1) sweat stain;
(2) hidroa / tinea versicolour;

han gou 汗垢
sweat mixed with dirt;

han guan 汗管
sweat duct;

han guan ai 汗管癌
porocarcinoma;

han kong 汗孔
pore / sweat pore;

han lin lin 汗淋淋
wet with sweat;

han liu ru yu 汗流如雨
perspire profusely // the perspiration pours down one's face;

han liu ru zhu 汗流如珠
the perspiration drips off sb like falling pearls;

han liu ru zhu 汗流如注
the perspiration runs off sb like a waterfall;

han liu shuang jia 汗流雙頰
sweat comes trickling down one's cheeks;

han mao 汗毛
down / fine hair on the human body;

han mao kong 汗毛孔
pores in the skin;

han pao 汗疱
cheiropompholyx;

han pao zhen 汗疱疹
dyshidrosis;

han re bing 汗熱病
sweating sickness;

han ru yu xia 汗如雨下
the sweat runs down like raindrops || sweat profusely;

han shui 汗水
perspiration / sweat;

han wei 汗味
stink with perspiration;

皮膚 *Skin*

han xian 汗腺
apocrine sweat gland / sweat gland;

han xian ai 汗腺癌
syringocarcinoma;

han xian guan 汗腺管
sudoriferous duct / sweat duct;

han xian yan 汗腺炎
hydradenitis;

han ye 汗液
perspiration / sweat;

han zhen 汗疹
miliaria;

han zhu zhi tang 汗珠直淌
beads of sweat have broken out profusely / the sweat rolls off in big drops;

han zhu zi 汗珠子
beads of sweat;

hei1 bai ban 黑白斑
melanoleukoderma;

hei bai pi bing 黑白皮病
melanoleukoderma;

hei ban 黑斑
eschar;

hei pi bing 黑皮病
melanoderma;

ji sheng xing hei pi bing 寄生性黑皮病
parasitic melanoderma;

lao nian xing hei pi bing 老年性黑皮病
senile melanoderma;

hei pi yan 黑皮炎
melanodermatitis;

hei tou fen ci 黑頭粉刺
blackhead / comedo;

hei zhi 黑痣
mole;

hong2 ban 紅斑
blotch / erythema;

bian yuan xing hong ban 邊緣性紅斑
erythema marginatum;

ca lan hong ban 擦爛紅斑
erythema intertrigo;

dong chuang hong ban 凍瘡紅斑
erythema pernio / suppurating frostbite;

duo xing hong ban 多形紅斑
erythema multiforme;

huai si xing hong ban 壞死性紅斑
erythema necroticans;

jie jie xing hong ban 結節性紅斑
erythema nodosum;

li zhuang hong ban 粒狀紅斑
pellagra;

lian qiu jun xing hong ban 鏈球菌性紅斑
erythema streptogenes;

liu xing xing hong ban 流行性紅斑
epidemic erythema;

niao bu hong ban 尿布紅斑
napkin erythema;

re ji xing hong ban 熱激性紅斑
erythema caloricum;

shou zhang hong ban 手掌紅斑
palmar erythema;

ying jie xing hong ban 硬結性紅斑
erythema induratum;

you zou xing hong ban 游走性紅斑
erythema migrans;

zan shi xing hong ban 暫時性紅斑
erythema fugax;

zeng zhi xing hong ban 增殖性紅斑
erythroplasia;

zhong du xing hong ban 中毒性紅斑
toxic erythema;

hong ban dian 紅斑點
rash;

hong ban lang chuang 紅斑狼瘡
lupus erythematosis;

pi fu hong ban lang chuang 皮膚紅斑狼瘡
cutaneous lupus erythematosus;

shen bu hong ban lang chuang 深部紅斑狼瘡
lupus erythematosus profundus;

xi tong xing hong ban lang chuang 系統性紅斑狼瘡
system lupus erythematosus;

zeng zhi xing hong ban lang chuang 增殖性紅斑狼瘡
hypertrophic lupus erythematosus;

zhong zhang xing hong ban lang chuang 腫脹性紅斑狼瘡
lupus erythematosus tumidus;

hong ban xing shi zhen 紅斑性濕疹
eczema erythematosum;

hong zhen 紅疹
rubeola;

hua1 ban bing 花斑病
piebaldism;

hua ban pi 花斑皮
piebald skin;

hua ban xian zhen 花斑癬疹
pityriasis versicolor;

hua4 nong 化膿
suppuration;

hua nong pi fu bing 化膿皮膚病
pyoderma;

huai4 ju xing pi yan 壞疽性皮炎
gangrenous dermatitis;

huai ju xing shui dou 壞疽性水痘
varicella gangrenosa;

huai si xing hong ban 壞死性紅斑
erythema necroticans;

huai si xing pi yan 壞死性皮炎
necrotic dermatitis;

huang2 ban 黃斑
macula lutea;

jia xing huang ban 假性黃斑
false macula;

jie mo huang ban 結膜黃斑
pinguicula;

huang ban bing bian 黃斑病變
maculopathy;

huang han zhi tang 黃汗直淌
sweat profusely;

huang he ban 黃褐斑
chloasma;

hui1 ban xian 灰斑癬
grey-patch ringworm;

hui se pi bing 灰色皮病
dermatosis cenicienta;

hui se pi yan 灰色皮炎
ashy dermatitis;

hui1 han cheng yu 揮汗成雨
wipe off perspiration enough to make a shower — referring to the large number of men;

hui han ru yu 揮汗如雨
perspiration comes down like raindrops || drip with sweat; sweat like a trooper; sweat profusely;

hun2 shen 渾身
all over / from head to foot;

hun shen chou han 渾身臭汗
be covered with smelly sweat || be in a muck of sweat; reek with sweat;

hun shen da han 渾身大汗
be covered with sweat || all of a muck of sweat; all of a sweat; be in a sweat all over; be steeped in sweat;

hun shen fa yang 渾身發癢
itch all over;

hun shen leng han 渾身冷汗
a cold sweat breaks forth on one's whole body / be bathed in a cold and clammy perspiration;

hun shen liu han 渾身流汗
one's whole body is dripping with sweat;

hun shen shi han 渾身是汗
be covered with sweat / be steeped in sweat / in a sweat all over;

ji1 fu 肌膚
skin and flesh;

ji li 肌理
texture of the skin;

ji li xi ni 肌理細膩
smooth fine skin // skin of fine texture;

ji1 pi ge da 雞皮疙瘩
goose bumps / goose-flesh / goose-pimples / goose-skin / lump / horripilation;

ji yan 雞眼
callosity / corn;

ji4 sheng xing hei pi bing 寄生性黑皮病
parasitic melanoderma;

ji sheng xing pi fu chu xue 寄生性皮膚出血
dermatorrhagia parasitica;

jia3 xing huang ban 假性黃斑
false macula;

jiao1 jia 焦痂
eschar;
dong chuang jiao jia 凍瘡焦痂
eschar frostbite;

jie1 chu xing cuo chuang 接觸性痤瘡
contact acne;

jie chu xing pi yan 接觸性皮炎
contact dermatitis;

jie2 he pi fu bing 結核皮膚病
tuberculosis cutis;

jie he xing cuo chuang 結核性痤瘡
acne scrofulosorum;

jie jia 結痂
incrustation;

jie jia xing jie chuang 結痂性疥瘡
crusted scabies;

jie jia xing shi zhen 結痂性濕疹
eczema crustosum;

jie jie 結節
tuber;
ma feng jie jie 麻瘋結節
leproma;
mei du jie jie 梅毒結節
syphilitic node;
mei du xing jie jie 梅毒性結節
tophus syphiliticus;
tong feng jie jie 痛風結節
gouty node;
tong xing jie jie 痛性結節
tuberculum dolorosum;

jie jie bing 結節病
nodule disease;

jie jie xing hong ban 結節性紅斑
erythema nodosum;

jie4 疥
sarcoptidosis / scabies;

jie chuang 疥瘡
scabies;

jie jia xing jie chuang 結痂性疥瘡
crusted scabies;

jie xian 疥癬
itch / mange / ringworm / scabies;

jie4 癤
furunculus;
re jie 熱癤
heat spots;

jie bing 癤病
furunculosis;

jing1 han 驚汗
cold perspiration / perspiration in fear;

ju2 xian xing shen jing xing pi yan 局限性神經性皮炎
localized neurodermatitis;

ju xian xing ying pi bing 局限性硬皮病
circumscribed scleroderma;

kai1 fang xing fen ci 開放性粉刺
open comedo;

kui4 han 愧汗
perspiration of shame;

kui4 yang xing pi fu bing 潰瘍性皮膚病
ulcerative dermatosis;

la1 pi zi 拉皮子
thick-skinned / unashamed;

lan2 ban 藍斑
blue spot;

lang2 chuang 狼瘡
lupus;
hong ban lang chuang 紅斑狼瘡
lupus erythematosis;
shen bu lang chuang 深部狼瘡
lupus profundus;
zeng zhi xing lang chuang 增殖性狼瘡
lupus hypertrophicus;
zhong zhang xing lang chuang 腫脹性狼瘡
lupus tumidus;

lao3 nian ban 老年斑
senile lentigo;

lao nian xing hei pi bing 老年性黑皮病
senile melanoderma;

lao nian xing zi dian 老年性紫癜
purpura senilis;

lao ren ban 老人斑
age spots / aged mark / old-age spots;

lei4 dan du 類丹毒
erysipeloid;

lei niu pi xian 類牛皮癬
parapsoriasis;

leng3 han 冷汗
cold sweat;

leng han bian shen 冷汗遍身
a cold sweat breaks out all over one's body;

leng han ru yu 冷汗如雨
a cold sweat drips from one's body like rain;

leng han yi shen 冷汗一身
wet with cold sweat;

li2 hei zhi rong 黧黑之容
dusty complexion;

li4 zhuang hong ban 粒狀紅斑
pellagra;

li zhong 粒腫
milium;

lian4 qiu jun xing hong ban 鏈球菌性紅斑
erythema streptogenes;

lie4 fu 裂膚
crack up the skin;

lin2 bing xing ban 淋病性斑
macula gonorrhoeica;

lin2 xie 鱗屑
scale;

lin xie xing shi zhen 鱗屑性濕疹
eczema squamosum;

lin4 痳
gonorrhea;

lin bing 痳病
gonorrhea;

lin zheng 痳症
gonorrhea;

ling2 xing pi fu bing 菱形皮膚病
diamond skin disease;

liu2 han 流汗
perspire / sweat;

liu xing xing cuo chuang 流行性痤瘡
epidemic acne;

liu xing xing hong ban 流行性紅斑
epidemic erythema;

luo1 han 捋汗
be embarrassed;

lü4 han zheng 綠汗症
green sweat;

ma2 feng 麻瘋
leprosy;

ma feng fan ying 麻瘋反應
lepra reaction;

ma feng jie jie 麻瘋結節
leproma;

ma pi 麻皮
pock-mark;

ma zhen 麻疹
measle / rubeola;
chu xue xing ma zhen 出血性麻疹
hemorrhagic measle;
de guo ma zhen 德國麻疹
German measle;
fei dian xing ma zhen 非典型麻疹
atypical measle;

ma zi 麻子
pock-mark;

ma2 痲
(1) measle;
(2) leprosy;
(3) anesthetize / benumb / paralyze / stupefy;
(4) pock-mark;

man3 shen da han 滿身大汗
all of a sweat ‖ all of a muck of sweat; perspire profusely; sweat all over;sweat like a pig;

man shen liu han 滿身流汗
perspire profusely;

man shen shi han 滿身是汗
sweat all over;

mao2 kong 毛孔
ositium / sweat pores;

mao nang yan 毛囊炎
folliculitis;

mei2 pi lai lian 沒皮賴臉
brazen-faced;

mei pi mei lian 沒皮沒臉
shameless;

mei2 gui kang zhen 玫瑰糠疹
pityriasis rose;

mei2 du shi you 梅毒濕疣
condyloma;

mei du xing bai ban bing 梅毒性白斑病
syphilitic leukoderma;

mei du xing jie jie 梅毒性結節
tophus syphiliticus;

mi2 man xing shang pi liu 彌漫性上皮瘤
diffuse epithelioma;

mi man xing ying pi bing 彌漫性硬皮病
diffuse scleroderma;

min3 gan xing pi fu 敏感性皮膚
sensitive skin;

nan3 yan han xia 赧顔汗下
extremely ashamed // flush with shame;

nang2 xing cuo chuang 囊性痤瘡
cystic acne;

nei4 pi 內皮
endothelium;

nei pi ai 內皮癌
endothelial cancer;

nei pi liu 內皮瘤
endothelioma;

nei pi liu bing 內皮瘤病
endotheliomatosis;

nei pi yan 內皮炎
endothelitis;

nei pi zeng sheng 內皮增生
endotheliosis;

nen4 pi 嫩皮
soft skin;

nian2 ye shang pi 黏液上皮
mucoepidermoid;

nian4 zhu jun bing 念珠菌病
candidiasis;
wei suo xing nian zhu jun bing 萎縮性念珠菌病
atrophic candidiasis;

niao4 bu hong ban 尿布紅斑
diaper rash / napkin erythema / napkin rash;

niao bu pi yan 尿布皮炎
diaper dermatitis;

niao bu zhen 尿布疹
nappy rash;

nie1 yi ba han 捏一把汗
break into a sweat with fright ‖ be seized with anxiety; be seized with deep concern; breathless with anxiety; breathless with tension; have one's heart in one's mouth; in a sweat; with one's heart in one's mouth;

nie yi ba leng han 捏一把冷汗
break into a cold sweat ‖ hold in one's palm a handful of perspiration; in a cold sweat of anxiety;

niu2 dou ba 牛痘疤
vaccination scar;

niu dou xing shi zhen 牛痘性濕疹
eczema vaccinatum;

niu pi xian 牛皮癬
psora / psoriasis / serpedo;
lei niu pi xian 類牛皮癬
parapsoriasis;
zhi yi xing niu pi xian 脂溢性牛皮癬
seborrhiasis;

nong2 ye zhi ye xing pi fu bing 農業職業性皮膚病
agricultural occupational dermatoses;

nong2 pao 膿疱
pimple / pustule;

nong pao bing 膿疱病
impetigo;
chu ran xing nong pao bing 觸染性膿疱病
impetigo contagiosa;

皮膚 *Skin*

nong pao chuang 膿疱瘡
impetigo;

nong pao xing cuo chuang 膿疱性痤瘡
acne pustulosa;

nong pao xing shi zhen 膿疱性濕疹
eczema pustulosum;

nong pi bing 膿皮病
pyoderma;
zeng zhi xing nong pi bing 增殖性膿皮病
pyoderma vegetans;

nong xian 膿癬
kerion;

nong xing shui pao 膿性水疱
vesicopustule;

pa4 yang 怕癢
afraid of tickling / ticklish;

pai2 han 排汗
perspire / sweat;

pan2 zhuang yin xie bing 盤狀銀屑病
discoid psoriasis;

pao4 疱
acne / bleb;

pao zhen 疱疹
(1) bleb;
(2) herpes;
chuang shang xing pao zhen 創傷性疱疹
traumatic herpes;
dai zhuang pao zhen 帶狀疱疹
herpes zoster;
dan chun pao zhen 單純疱疹
herpes simplex;
fa re xing pao zhen 發熱性疱疹
herpes febrillis;
jiao mo pao zhen 角膜疱疹
herpes corneae;
re bing xing pao zhen 熱病性疱疹
fever blister;
ren shen pao zhen 妊娠疱疹
herpes gestationis;
sheng zhi qi pao zhen 生殖器疱疹
genital herpes;
shui pao zhen 水疱疹
tetter;
wai shang xing pao zhen 外傷性疱疹
traumatic herpes;

pao zhen bing 疱疹病
vesicular exanthema;

pao zhen re 疱疹熱
herpetic fever;

pao zhen xing shi zhen 疱疹性濕疹
eczema herpeticum;

pao zhen yang pi yan 疱疹樣皮炎
dermatitis herpetiformis;

pao4 皰
pimple;

pi2 皮
skin;

pi bao gu 皮包骨
only skin and bones / skinny;

pi chen 皮層
cortex;

pi chu xue 皮出血
dermatorrhagia;

pi fei hou 皮肥厚
pachyderma;

pi fu 皮膚
skin;
gan xing pi fu 乾性皮膚
dry skin;
min gan xing pi fu 敏感性皮膚
sensitive skin;
you xing pi fu 油性皮膚
oily skin;

pi fu ai 皮膚癌
skin caner || cancer of the skin; cataneun carinoma;

pi fu bai hou 皮膚白喉
cutaneous diphtheria;

pi fu bian huang 皮膚變黃
xanthoderma;

pi fu bian se 皮膚變色
dyschromia;

pi fu bing 皮膚病
dermatosis / skin ailment / skin disease;

ai qian pi fu bing 癌前皮膚病
precancerous dermatosis;
ai qian qi pi fu bing 癌前期皮膚病
precancerous dermatosis;
gong ye zhi ye xing pi fu bing 工業職業性皮膚病
industrial occupational dermatoses;
hua nong pi fu bing 化膿皮膚病
pyoderma;
jie he pi fu bing 結核皮膚病
tuberculosis cutis;
kui yang xing pi fu bing 潰瘍性皮膚病
ulcerative dermatosis;
ling xing pi fu bing 菱形皮膚病
diamond skin disease;
nong ye zhi ye xing pi fu bing 農業職業性皮膚病
agricultural occupational dermatoses;
tang niao bing xing pi fu bing 糖尿病性皮膚病
diabetic dermopathy;
zhi ye xing pi fu bing 職業性皮膚病
occupational dermatosis;

pi fu bing bian 皮膚病變
dermopathy;
tang niao bing pi fu bing bian 糖尿病皮膚病變
diabetic dermopathy;

pi fu chu xue 皮膚出血
dermatorrhagia;
ji sheng xing pi fu chu xue 寄生性皮膚出血
dermatorrhagia parasitica;

pi fu fa yu bu liang 皮膚發育不良
dermatodysplasia;

pi fu fa yu bu quan 皮膚發育不全
adermogenesis;

pi fu fan she 皮膚反射
skin reflex;

pi fu fan ying 皮膚反應
demoreaction;

pi fu gan zao bing 皮膚乾燥病
exroderma;

pi fu gan zao zheng 皮膚乾燥症
xerosis cutis;

pi fu gu hua 皮膚骨化
osteodermia;

pi fu gu hua bing 皮膚骨化病
osteosis cutis;

pi fu gu liu 皮膚骨瘤
osteoma cutis;

pi fu hong ban lang chuang 皮膚紅斑狼瘡
cutaneous lupus erythematosus;

pi fu hu xi 皮膚呼吸
skin respiration;

pi fu jie 皮膚節
dermatomere;

pi fu jie he 皮膚結核
dermal tuberculosis / tuberculosis of skin;
ying hua xing pi fu jie he 硬化性皮膚結核
tuberculosis cutis indurativa;

pi fu jie he bing 皮膚結核病
dermal tuberculosis / tuberculosis of skin;

pi fu jie mo yan 皮膚結膜炎
dermatoconjunctivitis;

pi fu jie shi 皮膚結石
skin stone;

pi fu lin ba jie bing 皮膚淋巴結病
dermatopathic lymphadenopathy;

pi fu lin ba liu 皮膚淋巴瘤
lymphoma cutis;

pi fu mei jun bing 皮膚霉菌病
dermatophytosis;

pi fu qing zi 皮膚青紫
cyanosis;

pi fu song chi 皮膚鬆弛
dermatolysis;

pi fu song chi zheng 皮膚鬆弛症
cutis laxa;

pi fu song chui 皮膚鬆垂
anetoderma;

pi fu sun hai 皮膚損害
efflorescence;

pi fu wei suo 皮膚萎縮
atrophoderma;
ru chong yang pi fu wei suo 蠕蟲樣皮膚萎縮
atrophodermia vermiculata;
shen jing xing pi fu wei suo 神經性皮膚萎縮
atrophoderma neuriticum;

pi fu wei suo bing 皮膚萎縮症
atrophodermatosis;

pi fu xue guan yan 皮膚血管炎
angiodermatitis;

pi fu yan 皮膚炎
dermatitis;

pi fu yi zhi 皮膚移植
epidermization;

pi fu you 皮膚疣
thymian;

pi fu zhen jun bing 皮膚真菌病
dermatomycosis;

pi fu zhong kuai 皮膚腫塊
phyma;

pi hou 皮厚
thick-skinned;

pi kai rou zhan 皮開肉綻
with skin cut open and flesh torn || a mass of bruises; badly bruised; the skin is torn and the flesh gapes open;

pi li chou rou 皮裏抽肉
emaciated / skinny;

pi po xue liu 皮破血流
get bumped and bruised / run into bumps and bruises;

pi xia xue zhong 皮下血腫
ecchymoma;

pi xia zhu she 皮下注射
hypodermic injection;

pi xia zu zhi 皮下組織
subcutaneous tissue;

pi xiao rou bu xiao 皮笑肉不笑
(1) cold smile / false smile / skin-deep smile;
(2) put on a false smile / smile hypocritically / twist one's lips into a faint smile;

pi yan 皮炎
dermatitis;
bian ying xing pi yan 變應性皮炎
allergic dermatitis;
bo tuo xing pi yan 剝脫性皮炎
exfoliative dermatitis;
cao di pi yan 草地皮炎
meadow dermatitis;
ci ji xing pi yan 刺激性皮炎
irritant dermatitis;
guang hua pi yan 光化皮炎
erythema solate;
guo min xing pi yan 過敏性皮炎
neurodermatitis;
huai ju xing pi yan 壞疽性皮炎
gangrenous dermatitis;
huai si xing pi yan 壞死性皮炎
necrotic dermatitis;
hui se pi yan 灰色皮炎
ashy dermatitis;
jie chu xing pi yan 接觸性皮炎
contact dermatitis;
niao bu pi yan 尿布皮炎
diaper dermatitis;
pao zhen yang pi yan 疱疹樣皮炎
dermatitis herpetiformis;
pi zhi yi xing pi yan 皮脂溢性皮炎
dematitis seborrheica;
qing ban zhuang pi yan 青斑狀皮炎
livedoid dermatitis;
re ji xing pi yan 熱激性皮炎
dermatitis calorica;
ri guang xing pi yan 日光性皮炎
photodermatitis;
ru chong xing pi yan 蠕蟲性皮炎
verminous dermatitis;
shen jing xing pi yan 神經性皮炎
neurodermatitis;
shi zhen xing pi yan 濕疹性皮炎
eczematous dermatitis;
shui dao tian pi yan 水稻田皮炎
dematitis of the rice field;
te ying xing pi yan 特應性皮炎
atopic dermatitis;

yao wu xing pi yan 藥物性皮炎
dematitis medicamentosa;
you xing pi yan 疣性皮炎
verrucous dermatitis;
you zhuang pi yan 疣狀皮炎
verrucose dermatitis;
you yong zhe pi yan 游泳者皮炎
swimmers' dermatitis;
zeng sheng xing pi yan 增生性皮炎
proliferative dermatitis;
zeng zhi xing pi yan 增殖性皮炎
dermatitis vegetans;
zhi yi xing pi yan 脂溢性皮炎
seborrheic dermatitis;
zhi ye xing pi yan 職業性皮炎
occupational dermatitis;
zhi jian pi yan 指間皮炎
interdigital dermatitis;
zhi jian pi yan 趾間皮炎
interdigital dermatitis;
zu pi yan 足皮炎
pododermatitis;

pi zhi xian 皮脂腺
sebaceous gland;

pi zhi yi chu zheng 皮脂溢出症
seborrhea;

pi zhi yi xing pi yan 皮脂溢性皮炎
dematitis seborrheica;

pian1 ce chu han 偏側出汗
hemihidrosis;

pian ce duo han 偏側多汗
hemihyperidrosis;

pin2 xue xing zhi 貧血性痣
nevus anemicus;

po4 shang feng 破傷風
tetanus;
yin yuan xing po shang feng 隱源性破傷風
cryptogenic tetanus;

pu3 tong you 普通疣
common wart;

qi3 ji pi ge da 起雞皮疙瘩
be gooseflesh all over / come out in goosebumps // one's flesh creeps;

qie4 fu 切膚
be keenly felt / be very close to oneself;

qie fu zhi tong 切膚之痛
the pain which one has personally experienced || acute pain; bitter experience; deep sorrow; keenly felt pain; piercing sorrow; sharp pain; sorrow which cuts to the quick;

qing1 ban 青斑
blue spot;

qing ban zhuang pi yan 青斑狀皮炎
livedoid dermatitis;

qing chun dou 青春痘
acne / pimple;

qing nian you 青年疣
juvenile wart;

qing pi zheng 青皮症
cyanoderma;

qing2 xue xing duo han 情緒性多汗
emotional hyperhidrosis;

qiu1 zhen 丘疹
papule;

qiu zhen bing 丘疹病
papulosis;

qiu zhen xing cuo chuang 丘疹性痤瘡
acne papulosa;

qiu zhen xing shi zhen 丘疹性濕疹
eczema papulosum;

quan2 shen xing ying pi bing 全身性硬皮病
generalized scleroderma;

que4 ban 雀斑
ephelides / freckle;

re4 bing xing pao zhen 熱病性疱疹
fever blister;

re dai cuo chuang 熱帶痤瘡
tropical acne;

re ji xing hong ban 熱激性紅斑
erythema caloricum;

re ji xing pi yan 熱激性皮炎
dermatitis calorica;

re jie 熱癤
heat spots;

ri4 guang ban 日光斑
solar lentigo;

ri guang xing pi yan 日光性皮炎
photodermatitis;

rou4 zhong 肉腫
sarcoma;

ru2 chong xing pi yan 蠕蟲性皮炎
verminous dermatitis;

ru chong yang pi fu wei suo 蠕蟲樣皮膚萎縮
atrophodermia vermiculata;

ru3 bai ban 乳白斑
milk spot;

ru4 chuang 褥瘡
bedsore;

run4 fu 潤膚
(1) emollient;
(2) moisturize the skin;

sa3 han 灑汗
perspire / sweat;

san1 du shao shang 三度燒傷
third degree burn;

sao1 yang 搔癢
scratch the itching place;

sha1 zi 痧子
measle;

shai4 ban 曬斑
sunburn;

shang1 ba 傷疤
scar;

shang han ban 傷寒斑
typhoid spot;

shang hen 傷痕
bruise / scar;

shang shi zi han 傷濕自汗
spontaneous perspiration due to wetness-evil;

shang4 biao pi 上表皮
epicuticle;

shang pi 上皮
epithelium;
bian ping shang pi 扁平上皮
pavement epithelium;
nian ye shang pi 黏液上皮
mucoepidermoid;
shen jing shang pi 神經上皮
neurepithelium;
shen xiao qiu shang pi 腎小球上皮
glomerular epithelium;
sheng zhi shang pi 生殖上皮
germinal epithelium;

shang pi ai 上皮癌
epithelioma;

shang pi liu 上皮瘤
epithelioma;
mi man xing shang pi liu 彌漫性上皮瘤
diffuse epithelioma;
shen jing shang pi liu 神經上皮瘤
neuroepithelioma;

shao1 shang 燒傷
burn;
er du shao shang 二度燒傷
second degree burn;
san du shao shang 三度燒傷
third degree burn;
si du shao shang 四度燒傷
fourth degree burn;
yi du shao shang 一度燒傷
first degree burn;
yi zhi shao shang 醫治燒傷
healing of burns;

shao3 han 少汗
hypoidrosis;

she2 pi xian 蛇皮癬
pityriasis;

shen1 bu dong chuang 深部凍瘡
deep frostbite;

shen bu hong ban lang chuang 深部紅斑狼瘡
lupus erythematosus profundus;

shen bu lang chuang 深部狼瘡
lupus profundus;

shen2 jing shang pi 神經上皮
neurepithelium;

shen jing shang pi liu 神經上皮瘤
neuroepithelioma;

shen jing xing pi fu wei suo 神經性皮膚萎縮
atrophoderma neuriticum;

shen jing xing pi yan 神經性皮炎
neurodermatitis;
ju xian xing shen jing xing pi yan 局限性神經性皮炎
localized neurodermatitis;
shen chu xing shen jing xing pi yan 滲出性神經性皮炎
exudative neurodermatitis;

shen jing yan xing ban 神經炎性斑
neuritic plaques;

shen4 chu xing biao pi yan 滲出性表皮炎
exudative epidermitis;

shen chu xing shen jing xing pi yan 滲出性神經性皮炎
exudative neurodermatitis;

sheng1 zhi qi pao zhen 生殖器疱疹
genital herpes;

sheng zhi qi shi you 生殖器濕疣
genital wart;

sheng zhi shang pi 生殖上皮
germinal epithelium;

shi1 you 濕疣
condyloma;
bian ping shi you 扁平濕疣
flat condyloma / condyloma latum;
mei du shi you 梅毒濕疣
condyloma;
sheng zhi qi shi you 生殖器濕疣
genital wart;
xing bing shi you 性病濕疣
condyloma;

shi run xing shi zhen 濕潤性濕疹
eczema madidans;

shi zhen 濕疹
eczema;
bian ping shi zhen 扁平濕疹
moist papule / mucous papule;
bian ying xing shi zhen 變應性濕疹
allergic eczema;
ca lan xing shi zhen 擦爛性濕疹
eczema intertrigo;
hong ban xing shi zhen 紅斑性濕疹
eczema erythematosum;
jie jia xing shi zhen 結痂性濕疹
eczema crustosum;
lin xie xing shi zhen 鱗屑性濕疹
eczema squamosum;
niu dou xing shi zhen 牛痘性濕疹
eczema vaccinatum;
nong pao xing shi zhen 膿疱性濕疹
eczema pustulosum;
pao zhen xing shi zhen 疱疹性濕疹
eczema herpeticum;
qiu zhen xing shi zhen 丘疹性濕疹
eczema papulosum;
shi run xing shi zhen 濕潤性濕疹
eczema madidans;
shui pao xing shi zhen 水泡性濕疹
eczema vesiculosum;
te ying xing shi zhen 特應性濕疹
atopic eczema;
ying er shi zhen 嬰兒濕疹
infantile eczema;
zhi yi xing shi zhen 脂溢性濕疹
seborrheic eczema;

shi zhen xing pi yan 濕疹性皮炎
eczematous dermatitis;

shou3 xian 手癬
tinea manuum;

shou zhang duo han 手掌多汗
volar hyperhidrosis;

shou zhang hong ban 手掌紅斑
palmar erythema;

shui3 dao tian pi yan 水稻田皮炎
dematitis of the rice field;

shui dou 水痘
chickenpox / varicella;
huai ju xing shui dou 壞疽性水痘
varicella gangrenosa;

shui pao xing shi zhen 水泡性濕疹
eczema vesiculosum;

shui pao 水疱
blister / bulla;

nong xing shui pao 膿性水疱
vesicopustule;

shui pao zhen 水疱疹
tetter;

si1 po pi 撕破皮
excoriation;

si3 ban 死斑
livor;

si rou 死肉
gangrene;

si4 du shao shang 四度燒傷
fourth degree burn;

tai1 ban 胎斑
mongolian macula / mongolian spot;

tang2 niao bing pi fu bing bian 糖尿病皮膚病變
diabetic dermopathy;

tang niao bing xing pi fu bing 糖尿病性皮膚病
diabetic dermopathy;

tang3 han 淌汗
perspire / sweat;

te4 ying xing pi yan 特應性皮炎
atopic dermatitis;

te ying xing shi zhen 特應性濕疹
atopic eczema;

ti3 wu wan fu 體無完膚
(1) be torn to pieces ‖ a mass of bruises; be torn to shreds; have cuts and bruises all over the body;
(2) be thoroughly refuted ‖ be refuted down to the last point;

ti xian 體癬
ringworm of the body / tinea corporis;

tian1 pao chuang 天疱瘡
pemphigus;

tian2 yang bing 甜痒病
sweet itch;

tong4 feng jie jie 痛風結節
gouty node;

tong xing jie jie 痛性結節
tuberculum dolorosum;

tou2 xian 頭癬
tinea capitis;

tou4 han 透汗
perspire all over / sweat all over;

tuo1 pi 脫皮
ecdysis;

wai4 biao pi 外表皮
exocuticle;

wai shang xing pao zhen 外傷性疱疹
traumatic herpes;

wai yin bai ban bing 外陰白斑病
leukoplakia vulvae;

wan2 fu 完膚
unhurt skin / unscathed skin;

wan2 chuang 頑瘡
obstinate pyogenic skin infection;

wan xian 頑癬
stubborn dermatitis;

wei3 痏
scar;

wei3 suo ban 萎縮斑
maculae atrophicae;

wei suo xing bai ban 萎縮性白斑
atrophic leukoplakia;

wei suo xing cuo chuang 萎縮性痤瘡
acne atrophica;

wei suo xing nian zhu jun bing 萎縮性念珠菌病
atrophic candidiasis;

xi4 tong xing hong ban lang chuang 系統性紅斑狼瘡
system lupus erythematosus;

xia4 ji cuo chuang 夏季痤瘡
acne estivalis;

xian3 癬
ringworm / tinea;
niu pi xian 牛皮癬
psoriasis;
she pi xian 蛇皮癬
pityriasis;
shou xian 手癬
tinea manuum;

ti xian 體癬
ringworm of the body / tinea corporis;
tou xian 頭癬
tinea capitis;
zu xian 足癬
tinea of the foot / tinea pedis;

xiang4 pi bing 象皮病
elephantiasis;

xiao3 ba 小疤
pit;

xiao ban 小斑
patch;

xiao qiu zhen 小丘疹
pimple;

xin1 sheng er ying pi zheng 新生兒硬皮症
sclerema neonatorum;

xing4 bing shi you 性病濕疣
condyloma;

xu1 han 虛汗
cold sweat / night sweat;

xue3 fu 雪膚
snow-white skin;

xue fu hua mao 雪膚花貌
skin as white as snow and complexion as beautiful as flowers — a beauty;

xue ji 雪肌
snow-white skin;

xun2 ma zhen 蕁麻疹
urtica / urticana;

ya3 si bing 雅司病
yaws;

yan2 zheng hou bai ban bing 炎症後白斑病
postinflammatory leukoderma;

yang2 瘍
skin diseases / skin infections;

yang3 癢
itch;

yang zhen 癢疹
prurigo;
dan chun yang zhen 單純癢疹
prurigo simplex;

yao4 wu xing pi yan 藥物性皮炎
dematitis medicamentosa;

yi1 ba han 一把汗
breathless with anxiety;

yi du shao shang 一度燒傷
first degree burn;

yi shen leng han 一身冷汗
wet with cold sweat ‖ a cold sweat; be bathed in cold and clammy perspiration; cold sweat breaks out all over one's body; in a cold sweat;

yi shen shi han 一身是汗
be steeped in sweat / in a complete sweat / sweaty all over;

yi1 zhi shao shang 醫治燒傷
healing of burns;

yin2 xie bing 銀屑病
psoriasis;
bo tuo xing yin xie bing 剝脫性銀屑病
exfoliative psoriasis;
pan zhuang yin xie bing 盤狀銀屑病
discoid psoriasis;
zhi yi xing yin xie bing 脂溢性銀屑病
seborrhiasis;

yin3 yuan xing po shang feng 隱源性破傷風
cryptogenic tetanus;

ying1 er cuo chuang 嬰兒痤瘡
infantile acne;

ying er shi zhen 嬰兒濕疹
infantile eczema;

ying2 yang que fa ban 營養缺乏斑
plaques jaunes;

ying4 ban 硬斑
induration;

ying ban bing 硬斑病
morphea;

ying hua xing pi fu jie he 硬化性皮膚結核
tuberculosis cutis indurativa;

ying jie xing cuo chuang 硬結性痤瘡
acne indurata;

ying jie xing hong ban 硬結性紅斑
erythema induratum;

ying pi bing 硬皮病
scleroderma;
ju xian xing ying pi bing 局限性硬皮病
circumscribed scleroderma;
mi man xing ying pi bing 彌漫性硬皮病
diffuse scleroderma;
quan shen xing ying pi bing 全身性硬皮病
generalized scleroderma;

ying pi zheng 硬皮症
scleroderma;
xin sheng er ying pi zheng 新生兒硬皮症
sclerema neonatorum;
zhi fang xing ying pi zheng 脂肪性硬皮症
sclerema adiposum;

you2 xing pi fu 油性皮膚
oily skin;

you2 疣
wart;
bian ping you 扁平疣
flat wart || plane wart; verruca plana; verruca plana juvenills;
chu xue xing you 出血性疣
hemorrhagic pian;
dan chun you 單純疣
common wart;
pi fu you 皮膚疣
thymian;
pu tong you 普通疣
common wart;
qing nian you 青年疣
juvenile wart;
ruan gu you 軟骨疣
chondrophyte;
zan shi xing you 暫時性疣
fugitive wart;
zhen zhu you 珍珠疣
molluscum contagiosum;
zhi yi xing you 脂溢性疣
seborrheic wart;
zu di you 足底疣
plantar wart;

you bing 疣病
verrucuosis;

you xing pi yan 疣性皮炎
verrucous dermatitis;

you zhuang pi yan 疣狀皮炎
verrucose dermatitis;

you2 yong zhe pi yan 游泳者皮炎
swimmers' dermatitis;

you zou xing hong ban 游走性紅斑
erythema migrans;

yu1 ban 瘀斑
ecchymosis;

yu4 gu bing ji 玉骨冰肌
bones of jade and flesh of ice — purity of character / jade bones and ice skin — an elegant demeanour and high personality;

yu ji 玉肌
the pure, snow-white skin of a woman;

yu ji xue fu 玉肌雪膚
the pure, snow-white flesh of a woman;

yue4 jing qian cuo chuang 月經前痤瘡
premenstrual acne;

zai1 ti xing zi dian 甾體性紫癜
steroid purpura;

zan4 shi xing hong ban 暫時性紅斑
erythema fugax;

zan shi xing you 暫時性疣
fugitive wart;

zang1 chuang 髒瘡
syphilitic lesions of the skin;

zeng1 sheng xing pi yan 增生性皮炎
proliferative dermatitis;

zeng zhi xing hong ban 增殖性紅斑
erythroplasia;

zeng zhi xing hong ban lang chuang 增殖性紅斑狼瘡
hypertrophic lupus erythematosus;

zeng zhi xing lang chuang 增殖性狼瘡
lupus hypertrophicus;

zeng zhi xing nong pi bing 增殖性膿皮病
pyoderma vegetans;

zhen1 zhu you 珍珠疣
molluscum contagiosum;

zhen1 pi 真皮
corium / dermis;

zhen3 疹
exanthema;

zhen bing 疹病
exanthem;

zhi1 duan ying pi bing 肢端硬皮病
acroscleroderma;

zhi1 fang xing ying pi zheng 脂肪性硬皮症
sclerema adiposum;

zhi yi xing niu pi xian 脂溢性牛皮癬
seborrhiasis;

zhi yi xing pi yan 脂溢性皮炎
seborrheic dermatitis;

zhi yi xing shi zhen 脂溢性濕疹
seborrheic eczema;

zhi yi xing yin xie bing 脂溢性銀屑病
seborrhiasis;

zhi yi xing you 脂溢性疣
seborrheic wart;

zhi2 pi 植皮
skin-grafting;

zhi2 ye xing bai ban bing 職業性白斑病
occupational leukoderma;

zhi ye xing cuo chuang 職業性痤瘡
occupational acne;

zhi ye xing pi fu bing 職業性皮膚病
occupational dermatoses;

zhi ye xing pi yan 職業性皮炎
occupational dermatitis;

zhi3 han 止汗
hidroschesis;

zhi yang 止癢
alleviage itching / stop itching;

zhi3 jian pi yan 指間皮炎
interdigital dermatitis;

zhi4 痣
freckle / mole;
pin xue xing zhi 貧血性痣
nevus anemicus;

zhong3 zhang xing hong ban lang chuang 腫脹性紅斑狼瘡
lupus erythematosus tumidus;

zhong zhang xing lang chuang 腫脹性狼瘡
lupus tumidus;

zhong4 du xing hong ban 中毒性紅斑
toxic erythema;

zhu1 han 珠汗
beads of perspiration;

zhua1 po 抓破
injure skin by scratching;

zhua yang 抓癢
scratch an itchy part;

zi3 ban 紫斑
petechia;

zi ban bing 紫斑病
purpura;

zi dian 紫癜
peliosis ‖ pelioma; purpura; neonatorum;
bian ying xing zi dian 變應性紫癜
allergic purpura;
chu xue xing zi dian 出血性紫癜
purpura hemorrhagica;
dan chun xing zi dian 單純性紫癜
purpura simplex;
feng shi xing zi dian 風濕性紫癜
purpura rheumatica;
guo min xing zi dian 過敏性紫癜
anaphylactic purpura;
jing shen xing zi dian 精神性紫癜
psychogenic purpura;
lao nian xing zi dian 老年性紫癜
purpura senilis;
zai ti xing zi dian 甾體性紫癜
steroid purpura;

zi4 han 自汗
spontaneous perspiration;

zu2 pi yan 足皮炎
pododermatitis;

zu xian 足癬
tinea of the foot / tinea pedis;

zuo4 yang 作癢
itch;

She 舌 Tongue

bai2 fei chun she 白費唇舌
waste one's breath || speak to the wind; whistle down the wind;

ban1 she tou 搬舌頭
sow discord;

bian3 ping she 扁平舌
flat tongue;

bo1 tuo xing she tong 剝脫性舌痛
glossodynia exfoliativa;

bo2 chun qing yan 薄唇輕言
garrulous and sharp-tongued / thin lips speak freely;

bu4 lan zhi she 不爛之舌
glib tongue;

can4 hua miao she 粲花妙舌
glib tongue / the gift of the tongue;

chang2 she 長舌
fond of gossip // long-tongued // tongue enough for two sets of teeth;

chang she fu 長舌婦
garrulous woman / shrew;

cheng1 mu jie she 瞠目結舌
stare tongue-tied || be struck dumb; be wide-eyed and unable to speak; gape with astonishment; stare dumbfounded; stare tongue-tied; wide-eyed and tongue-tied;

cheng3 qi kou she 逞其口舌
swear like a bargee;

chi3 wang she cun 齒亡舌存
the hard is lost, while the weak and soft endure / the soft and flexible lasts longer than the hard;

chi4 kou bai she 赤口白舌
tawdry squabble over nothing;

chi kou du she 赤口毒舌
slander venomously / speak bitingly;

chi she shao cheng 赤舌燒城
a slanderous tongue can burn up a city || opinion sways the world; we are all slaves of opinion;

chuan2 she tou 傳舌頭
gossip / spread rumours / tell tales;

chuo1 she 戳舌
talk too much;

da4 fei chun she 大費唇舌
make a long harangue || a lot of talking; long harangue; take a lot of talking to convince;

da she tou 大舌頭
lisp;

diao4 she 掉舌
(1) eloquent;
(2) chatter;
(3) stir up ill will between others by loose gossip;

du2 she 毒舌
wicked tongue || bad tongue; biting tongue; bitter tongue; caustic tongue; dangerous tongue; venomous tongue;

dun4 she 鈍舌
ineloquence;

dun zui zhuo she 鈍嘴拙舌
not a good conversationist / one does not shine in conversation;

e4 zui du she 惡嘴毒舌
sharp-tongued;

fa1 yin 發音
get one's tongue round;

fei4 she lao chun 費舌勞唇
talk oneself out of breath;

fen1 cha she 分叉舌
bifid tongue;

fen ya she 分葉舌
lobulated tongue;

gu3 she ru huang 鼓舌如簧
talk glibly / wag one's tongue with honeyed words;

gu she yao chun 鼓舌搖唇
spread rumours || flatter; gossip;

gu zui nong she 鼓嘴弄舌
wag one's tongue;

hei1 she 黑舌
black tongue;

hei she bing 黑舌病
glossophytia;

hou4 she 厚舌
pachyglossia;

hou tai she 厚苔舌
encrusted tongue;

huan4 wei 幻味
gustatory hallucination;

jian1 zui bo she 尖嘴薄舌
have a caustic and flippant tongue // acid-tongued / acidulous;

jian zui hou sai 尖嘴猴腮
one's mouth sticks and one has a chin like an ape's;

jian zui jiao she 尖嘴嚼舌
fond of gossip // have a sharp tongue;

jiao2 she 嚼舌
(1) wag one's tongue || chatter; gossip;
(2) argue meaninglessly;

jiao she gen 嚼舌根
(1) gossip;
(2) argue meaninglessly;

jiao3 she 撟舌
raise the tongue in an effort to speak;

jie2 she 結舌
(1) unable to speak because of fear or groundlessness;
(2) tongue-tied;

jie she jin sheng 結舌禁聲
control one's tongue and keep silent;

jiu3 ru she chu 酒入舌出
when wine sinks, words swim;

ju4 she 巨舌
glossocele;

ju she zheng 巨舌症
macroglossia;

kou3 ben she zhuo 口笨舌拙
awkward in speech;

kou gan she zao 口乾舌燥
dry mouth and lips / mouth parched and tongue scorched;

kou she 口舌
(1) dispute / quarrel // exchange of words;
(2) talk / talk round;

kou she mi lan 口舌糜爛
erosion of mucous membrane in the oral cavity;

kou she shi fei 口舌是非
dispute // wagging of tongues;

kou she zhi zheng 口舌之爭
contention of mouth and tongue;

la1 she tou 拉舌頭
gossip / slander;

lan2 she bing 藍舌病
blue asbestos;

lang4 zui qing she 浪嘴輕舌
wag one's tongue too freely;

lao2 chun fa she 勞唇乏舌
waste one's words;

li4 zui du she 利嘴毒舌
sharp tongue // have a shrewd tongue;

li zui qiao she 利嘴巧舌
have the gift of the gab;

liang3 tou chuo she 兩頭戳舌
carry gossip;

ling4 ren zha she 令人咋舌
make one speechless / take one's breath away // horrendous;

mai4 nong kou she 賣弄口舌
show off one's glibness in speech;

mai she 賣舌
make sensational statements for the sake of publicity;

men2 she 捫舌
hold one's tongue;

nian2 lian she 黏連舌
adherent tongue;

nu2 chun bi she 奴唇婢舌
loose-tongued like a servant / talkable like a servant;

pian1 ce she fei da 偏側舌肥大
hemimacroglossia;

pian ce she wei suo 偏側舌萎縮
hemilingual atrophy;

pian ce she yan 偏側舌炎
hemiglossitis;

pin2 zui bo she 貧嘴薄舌
have a caustic and flippant tongue ‖ be addicted to senseless talks; garrulous and sharp-tongued; light and airy utterance; wag one's tongue too freely;

pin zui jian she 貧嘴賤舌
be addicted to senseless talk ‖ disgustingly talkative; make vulgar jokes; scurrility;

pin zui lan she 貧嘴爛舌
be given to nasty talk ‖ have a caustic and flippant tongue; like to say nasty things about people; love to gossip;

qi1 zui ba she 七嘴八舌
a babel of voices ‖ a hubbub of voices; a scene of noisy and confused talking; all giving tongue together; all talking at once; all talking simultaneously producing great confusion; all talking together; confused talking; everybody talking at the same time; like a rattle-box; like a talkshot; lively discussion with everybody trying to get a word in; many diverse opinions; many people, many minds; with everybody eager to put in a word;

舌 *Tongue*

qiao3 she 巧舌
false words / insincere words;

qiao she ru huang 巧舌如簧
have a slick tongue ‖ glib-tongued; have a glib tongue; have a ready tongue; have a reed-like, have a silver tongue; have a smooth tongue; have a voluble tongue; have an oily tongue; mealy-mouthed; plausible tongue; smooth-tongued; talk glibly; very plausible tongue;

qing1 zui bo she 輕嘴薄舌
make irresponsible remarks;

rao2 she 饒舌
(1) panglossia;
(2) long tongue ‖ chatter; garrulous; have a big mouth; have too much tongue; loquacious; naggish; too talkative; voluble;
(3) say more than is proper / shoot off one's mouth;

rao she pi 饒舌癖
verbomania;

rao she tiao chun 饒舌調唇
garrulous and insidious // gossip and sow dissension;

ru2 huang zhi she 如簧之舌
glib tongue;

san1 cun bu lan zhi she 三寸不爛之舌
eloquent tongue / glib tongue;

san cun zhi she 三寸之舌
eloquent tongue / glib tongue;

se4 ne 澀訥
slow of tongue;

she2 舌
(1) tongue;
(2) sth shaped like a tongue;
bian ping she 扁平舌
flat tongue;
ju she 巨舌
glossocele;

she ai 舌癌
tongue cancer;

she bai ban bing 舌白斑病
leukoplakia lingualis;

she ban 舌板
lingual plate;

she ban 舌瓣
lingual tongue flap;

she bei 舌背
dorsum of tongue;

she ben 舌本
back of the tongue / root of the tongue;

she bi chun jiao 舌敝唇焦
one's tongue and lips become parched / talk oneself hoarse ‖ talk till one's tongue and lips are parched; the tongue is weary and the lips are dry; wear oneself out in pleading;

she bi er long 舌敝耳聾
with discussions so many and diverse that the speakers' tongues are parched and the listeners' ears are deafened;

she fa yu bu liang 舌發育不良
ateloglossia;

she fa yu bu quan 舌發育不全
ateloglossia;

she fei da 舌肥大
macroglossia;
pian ce she fei da 偏側舌肥大
hemimacroglossia;

she fei dao jian, dan neng shang ren 舌非刀劍，但能傷人
the tongue is not steel, yet it cuts;

she fei hou 舌肥厚
pachyglossia;

she feng 舌鋒
eloquence;

she gen 舌根
root of the tongue;

she jian 舌尖
tip of the tongue;

she jian chun qiang 舌劍唇槍
acrimonious words used in a quarrel;

she jing luan 舌痙攣
glossospasm;

she ku chun jiao 舌枯唇焦
talk oneself hoarse;

she lie 舌裂
cleft tongue;

she long qi 舌隆起
lingual swelling;

she ma bi 舌麻痺
lingual paralysis;

she mian 舌面
lingual surface;

she qiao ru huang 舌巧如簧
have a tongue like a reed organ;

she ru li ren 舌如利刃
have a tongue like a razor / one's tongue is as sharp as a sword;

she sheng lian hua 舌生蓮花
have the gift of the gab;

she tai 舌苔
coated tongue / fur on the tongue / furred tongue;

she tan 舌癱
lingual paralysis;

she tong 舌痛
glossalgia;
bo tuo xing she tong 剝脱性舌痛
glossodynia exfoliativa;
tong feng xing she tong 痛風性舌痛
gouty glossagia;

she tou 舌頭
tongue;

she wei suo 舌萎縮
lingual atrophy;
pian ce she wei suo 偏側舌萎縮
hemilingual atrophy;

she xi dai qie kai 舌繫帶切開
frenotomy;

she xia chui 舌下垂
glossoptosis;

she xia shen jing 舌下神經
hypoglossal nerve;

she xia xian 舌下腺
sublingual gland;

she yan 舌咽
glossopharyngeum;

she yan shen jing 舌咽神經
glossopharygeal nerve;

she yan 舌炎
glossitis;
pian ce she yan 偏側舌炎
hemiglossitis;
te fa xing she yan 特發性舌炎
idiopathic glossitis;
wei suo xing she yan 萎縮性舌炎
atrophic glossitis;
you zou xing she yan 游走性舌炎
glossitis migrans;
zi fa xing she yan 自發性舌炎
idiopathic glossitis;

she zhan 舌戰
have a verbal battle with sb || argue heatedly; debate with verbal confrontation;

she zhan zhi dou 舌戰智斗
match wits and engage in a battle of words;

she zhong ge 舌中隔
septum of tongue;

she zhong 舌腫
glossoncus;

she zhou yan 舌周炎
periglossitis;

shen1 she tou 伸舌頭
loll out one's tongue / stick out the tongue;

shi4 舐
lick;

si4 bu ji she 駟不及舌
a word lightly spoken goes faster than a team of four horses / even a team of four horses cannot overtake and recover what is already said;

suo2 tou tu she 縮頭吐舌
shrug and stick out the tongue;

te4 fa xing she yan 特發性舌炎
idiopathic glossitis;

tian3 舔
lick / taste;

tian gan jing 舔乾淨
lick clean;

tian yi tian 舔一舔
taste by licking;

tong4 feng xing she tong 痛風性舌痛
gouty glossagia;

tu1 she 禿舌
bald tongue;

wei3 suo xing she yan 萎縮性舌炎
atrophic glossitis;

wei4 味
smell / taste;

wei dao 味道
(1) smell;
(2) taste;
(3) feeling;

wei jue 味覺
gustation / the faculty of taste;

wei jue chi dun 味覺遲鈍
amblygeustia;

wei jue dao cuo 味覺倒錯
parageusia;

wei jue guo min 味覺過敏
hypergeusia;

wei jue jian tui 味覺減退
hypogeusesthesia;

wei jue que shi 味覺缺失
ageustia;

wei jue que sun 味覺缺損
taste-blindness;

wei jue yi chang 味覺異常
allotriogeustia;

wei mang 味盲
taste blindness;

wei tong jue la 味同嚼蠟
insipid;

wu2 she 無舌
aglossia / congenital absence of the tongue;

xiao3 she 小舌
uvula;

yao2 chun gu she 搖唇鼓舌
instigate by talking || flay one's lips and beat one's tongue — engage in loose talk; flaunt one's red; persuade sb by sweet talk; wag one's tongue;

yao she 搖舌
talk glibly;

yao3 she 咬舌
have a lisp || lisp; speak imperfectly; speak with a lisp;

yi1 pian zui, liang pian she 一片嘴，兩片舌
double-talk;

you2 zui hua she 油嘴滑舌
smooth-tongued;

you2 zou xing she yan 游走性舌炎
glossitis migrans;

ze2 she 咋舌
be left breathless / be left speechless / bite the tongue;

ze2 ze 嘖嘖
(1) click of the tongue;
(2) remarks;

ze ze cheng shan 嘖嘖稱善
praise with a clicking of the tongue;

ze ze cheng xian 嘖嘖稱羨
click the tongue in admiration;

ze ze tan shang 嘖嘖歎賞
profuse in one's praise;

zhou4 bi she 皺襞舌
lingua plicata;

zhou lie she 皺裂舌
wrinkled tongue;

zhou suo she 皺縮舌
wrinkled tongue;

zi4 fa xing she yan 自發性舌炎
idiopathic glossitis;

Shen ti (zheng ti, yang zi he tai du, ge xing he neng li)
身體 (整體、樣子和態度、個性和能力)
Body (Entire Body, Appearance and Manners, Personality and Abilities)

Entire Body 整體

ai1 hui gu li 哀毀骨立
be emaciated by grief / be consumed with grief;

ai1 shen er ru 挨身而入
elbow one's way in / force one's way in / push one's way in / shoulder one's way in;

ai2 挨
(1) next to;
(2) touch;
(3) endure / struggle to pull through (hard times) / suffer;

ai bu zhu 挨不住
cannot endure any more;

ai da 挨打
get a beating / get a thrashing / suffer a beating / take a beating;

ai da shou ma 挨打受罵
put up with blows an scoldings / suffer beatings and receive scoldings;

ai da shou qi 挨打受氣
suffer beatings and insults;

ai dong 挨凍
go cold / endure cold / suffer from cold;

ai dong shou e 挨凍受餓
go cold and hungry / suffer from cold and hunger;

ai dou 挨鬥
be publicly criticized / be publicly denounced / be struggled / come under attack ;

ai fa 挨罰
(1) be fined;
(2) be punished / get it in the neck / get punished;

ai gun zi 挨棍子
(1) get the canning;
(2) to be criticized or attacked;

ai jin 挨近
cosy up to;

ai kei 挨剋
be beaten;

ai lin 挨淋
be caught in a pouring rain / be drenched;

ai pi 挨批
be criticized / be denounced;

ai ri ai ye 挨日挨夜
suffer by day and by night;

ai ri zi 挨日子
drag out a miserable existence / eke out a living / go through hard times / suffer day after day // through one's days in misery;

ai shou 挨受
endure / suffer;

ai shi jian 挨時間
procrastinate / stall for time;

ai zheng 挨整
be punished / be the target of criticism or attack;

ai zou er tong zong he zheng 挨揍兒童綜合症
battered child syndrome;

ai2 捱
(1) endure / suffer;
(2) put off;

ai bu zhu 捱不住
cannot endure any more;

ai guo 捱過
survive a crisis;

ai ku 捱苦
endure hardships;

ai yi hui 捱一會
endure a moment;

ai2 癌
cancer / carcinoma;

bi yan ai 鼻咽癌
cancer of nasopharynx / nasopharyngeal carcinoma;

chang ai 腸癌
bowel cancer / cancer of the intestines / intestinal cancer;

fang ai 防癌
prevent cancer;

gao wan ai 睪丸癌
cancer of the testis;

ji tai ai 畸胎癌
teratocarcinoma;

jie chang ai 結腸癌
colon cancer;

jie chu xing ai 接觸性癌
contact cancer;

lin ba xian ai 淋巴腺癌
cancer of the lymph glands;

pi fu ai 皮膚癌
cancer of the skin / cataneun carinoma / skin cancer;

qian qi ai 前期癌
precancer;

ru ai 乳癌
breast cancer / mammary cancer;

xian ai 腺癌
glandular cancer;

xue ai 血癌
leukaemia;

yan ai 眼癌
eye cancer;

yin xing ai 隱性癌
occult cancer;

ying ai 硬癌
scirrhous cancer;

yuan fa ai 原發癌
primary cancer;

yuan wei ai 原位癌
preinvasive cancer;

zi gong ai 子宮癌
cancer of the uterus / cancer of the womb / uterine cancer;

ai bian 癌變
become cancerous / cancerate / develop into cancer;

ai bing 癌病
carcinosis / carcinomatosis;

ai fa sheng 癌發生
carcinogenesis;

ai kuo san 癌擴散
metastasis of cancer / proliferation of cancer;

ai qian qi bing bian 癌前期病變
precancerous lesion;

ai qian zhuang tai 癌前狀態
precancerous condition;

ai rou liu 癌肉瘤
carcinosarcoma / sarcocarcinoma;

ai xing kui yang 癌性潰瘍
cancerous ulcer / carcinelcosis;

ai xing xi rou 癌性息肉
carcinopolypus;

ai yang zhong liu 癌樣腫瘤
cancerous tumour / cancroid tumour;

ai zheng 癌症
cancer;

ai zhong 癌腫
cancerous swelling;

ai4 zi 艾滋
AIDS (acquired immune deficiency syndrome / acquired immunodeficiency syndrome);

ai zi bing 艾滋病 / 愛滋病
AIDS;

ai zi bing du 艾滋病毒
AIDS virus / HIV (human immunodeficiency virus);

ai zi bing du kang ti 艾滋病毒抗體
antibody of AIDS virus / antibody of HIV;

ai zi bing huan zhe 艾滋病患者
AIDS patient;

ai zi bing chi dai zong he zheng 艾滋病痴呆綜合症
AIDS dementia complex;

ai zi bing xiang guan zong he zheng 艾滋病相關綜合症
AIDS-related complex;

ai4 guan xian shi 愛管閒事
have an oar in every man's barge / have an oar in every man's boat / like to poke one's nose into other people's business / love meddling in other people's affairs // officious / pushing;

ai4 mei 曖昧
(of attitude) ambiguous / equivocal || indefinite; indistinct; obscure; unclear;
tai du ai mei 態度曖昧
dubious / murky || shady;
guan xi ai mei 關係曖昧
have a dubious relationship with sb;

ai mei guan xi 曖昧關係
have an affair with sb;

an1 an jing jing 安安靜靜
peaceful and serene;

an an wen wen 安安穩穩
secure and stable;

an cha 安插
place sb in an organization;

an cha qin xin 安插親信
put one's trusted persons in key positions;

an chang chu shun 安常處順
take things as they are;

an ding 安定
stabilize;

an du wan nian 安度晚年
live one's latter days in peace;

an dun 安頓
(1) nestle in / nestle on / settle;
(2) put in a proper place;

an fu xu pin 安富恤貧
protect the rich and relieve the poor;

an fu zun rong 安富尊榮
enjoy wealth and honour;

an hao 安好
safe and sound;

an jia 安家
(1) nestle in / nestle on / settle down;
(2) set up a home;
(3) get married;

an le 安樂
peaceful and happy;

an le si 安樂死
euthanasia || assisted suicide; mercy killing; painless death;

an1 mian 安眠
sleep peacefully;

an pai 安排
arrange / make arrangements for;

an pai tuo dang 安排妥當
jack up / make proper arrangements;

an pin 安貧
content with poverty;

an quan 安全
safe / secure // safety / security;

an ran 安然
(1) safe;
(2) feel at ease;

an ran wu yang 安然無恙
safe and sound // without a scratch;

an shen 安身
make one's home / nestle in / nestle on / take shelter;

an shen li ming 安身立命
make a place one's refuge / settle down and get on with one's pursuit;

an sheng 安生
stable;

an shi 安適
peaceful and comfortable;

an shu 安舒
leisurely and comfortably;

an shui 安睡
go to sleep peacefully / sleep in peace / sleep soundly;

an tai 安泰
healthy / well;

an tian le ming 安天樂命
be content with one's lot;

an tian 安恬
peaceful;

an wei 安危
safety;

an wei yu gong 安危與共
stick together in security and danger;

an xi 安息
(1) go to sleep;
(2) rest in peace;

an xian 安閒
peaceful and carefree || live in ease; relaxed;

an xian wu shi 安閒無事
have no work;

an xiang 安祥
composed / serene;

an xiang 安享
enjoy in peace;

an xiang wan nian 安享晚年
enjoy one's old age in peace;

an xie 安歇
(1) go to bed / retire for the night / turn in for the night;
(2) take a rest;

an yi 安逸
easy and comfortable;

an zang 安葬
bury the dead;

an zhen 安枕
sleep in peace;

an zhi 安置
put in a proper place;

an zuo 安坐
sit idly;

an1 lian 諳練
familiar with / skilled in / versed in;

an shu 諳熟
familiar with;

an xi 諳習
be proficient in;

an xiao 諳曉
be well-versed in;

an4 na 按捺
control / hold back / restrain / suppress;

an4 bing 暗病
(1) hidden disease / latent disease;
(2) sexual disease;

an du chen cang 暗度陳倉
(1) do sth in secret;
(2) carry on a romantic intrigue;

an hai 暗害
assassinate / kill secretly;

an ji 暗疾
(1) latent disease;
(2) unmentionable disease;

an jian 暗箭
a stab in the back / an underhanded attack;

an jian nan fang 暗箭難防
a covert attack is hard to avoid || an arrow shot from hiding — a stab in the back; an unseen arrow is hard to guard against; hidden arrows are difficult to guard against; it is difficult to guard against the secret arrow; it is not easy to avoid a secret arrow;

an jian shang ren 暗箭傷人
stab sb in the back || a stab in the back; calumniate sb behind his back; hit sb below the belt; injure sb by underhand means; make a sniping attack; mill in the darkness; slander others behind their backs; stab sb in the back; wound sb with a sniping arrow; wound with a secret arrow;

an shi 暗示
give a hint / hint / suggest;

an suan 暗算
plot in secret;

an tong guan jie 暗通關節
make secret deals with sb;

an zhong 暗中
on the sly / secretly;

an zi 暗自
inwardly / to oneself / secretly;

an4 lie 闇劣
stupid and incompetent;

an mei 闇昧
ignorant and stupid;

an nuo 闇懦
ignorant and timid;

an qian 闇淺
shallow, ignorant and stupid;

an ran 闇然
concealed / obscure;

an ruo 闇弱
ignorant, stupid and cowardly / irresolute;

ang1 zang 骯髒
(1) dirty / filthy / squalid;
(2) foul / mean / vile;

ang2 ang 昂昂
bold and proud / brave-looking / high-spirited;

ao2 xi 遨嬉
make merry / travel for pleasure;

ao you 遨遊
go on a trip / tour about / travel;

ao2 熬
endure;

ao bu guo 熬不過
cannot survive a grave illness / unable to endure;

ao chu lai 熬出來
have gone through all sorts of ordeal;

ao jian 熬煎
suffer through unhappy days / torment / torture // suffering;

ao mo 熬磨
suffer with patience || bear; brave; endure; go through; hold out; pull through; stand; stick it out; suffer; sustain; take it;

ao ye 熬夜
burn the midnight oil / stay up all night;

ba1 疤
scar;

ba hen 疤痕
scar;

ba la 疤瘌
scar;

ba2 chu 拔除
pull out / remove / wipe out;

ba shen 拔身
break away from busy schedule / escape / get away;

ba2 shan she shui 跋山涉水
scale mountains and ford streams;

ba she 跋涉
trek / trudge;

ba3 chi 把持
dominate / monopolize;

ba lan 把攬
monopolize / seize control of;

ba shou 把守
guard;

ba wu 把晤
meet and shake hands;

ba4 罷
cease / stop;

ba4 chi 霸持
forcibly dominate;

ba zhan 霸佔
forcibly occupy;

bai2 fei qi li 白費氣力
a waste of efforts ‖ a fool for one's pains; a waste of breath; a wild-goose chase; beat the air; beat the wind; bite a file; bite on granite; blow at cold coal; cast water into the Thames; catch a shadow; catch at shadows; draw a blank; draw water in a sieve; fish in the air; flog a dead horse; force an open door; futile; gnaw a file; go on a wild-goose chase; in vain; knock at an open door; labour in vain; labour lost; lash the waves; lose one's labour; lose one's pains; plough the air; plough the sands; pour water into a sieve; run one's head against a brick wall; shoe a goose; sow beans in the wind; wash a blackamoor white; wash an ass's ears; wash an ass's head; waste effort on; waste one's breath; waste one's energy; waste one's words;

bai mang 白忙
busy oneself to no purpose;

bai3 bing 百病
all kinds of diseases;

bai bing chan shen 百病纏身
disease-ridden;

bai ke 百痾
all kinds of diseases;

bai mang zhong 百忙中
in the thick of things;

bai3 擺
put on;

bai bu 擺佈
manipulate / order about;

bai dong 擺動
sway / swing / swing back and forth;

bai3 jiu jie feng 擺酒接風
give a banquet to welcome visitors from afar;

bai mi hun zhen 擺迷魂陣
lay out a scheme to bewitch sb / muddle sb up / set a trap;

bai nong 擺弄
(1) fiddle with / play with / toy with;
(2) manipulate / order about;
(3) make fun of // trick;

bai ping 擺平
treat fairly;

bai pu 擺譜
show off one's wealth ‖ go in for extravagance; keep up appearance; take pains to show off; try to appear rich and elegant;

bai shi shi, jiang dao li 擺事實，講道理
set forth the facts and discuss them rationally ‖ adduce facts and use reasoned arguments; present the facts and reason things out;

bai tuo 擺脱
break away from ‖ break from; break off; break loose; cast off; clear of; clear off; clear sb of sth; cut loose from; do away with; extricate oneself from; find freedom from; free from; free of; free oneself from; free sth of; get rid of; get sth off one's hands; get out; get over; give sb a miss; give sth a miss; give sb the go-by; give sth the go-by; rid; rid of; rid oneself of; see the back of sb; shake off; wash one's hands of;

bai tuo kun jing 擺脱困境
escape from a predicament ‖ above water; extricate oneself from a predicament; get sb off the hook; out of hot water;

bai tuo yi lai 擺脱依賴
shake off dependence on;

bai4 拜
(1) do obeisance;
(2) congratulate;
(3) pay a visit / visit;

(4) acknowledge sb as one's master;

bai bai 拜拜
(1) bye-bye;
(2) break off a relationship;

bai bei 拜別
say farewell / say goodbye / take leave;

bai cha 拜茶
ask a guest to come in and have tea;

bai ci 拜辭
say goodbye / take leave;

bai dao 拜倒
fall on one's knees / grovel / prostrate oneself / prostrate oneself in worship / surrender / worship;

bai dao shi liu qun xia 拜倒石榴裙下
fall head over heels for a woman || at one's feet; throw oneself at sb's feet;

bai dao zai di 拜倒在地
be bowed to the ground;

bai fang 拜訪
pay a visit to sb || call around sb's house; call at; call at sb's house; call on; call on sb; call over; call round; call to see; call upon sb; come around; drop in; drop in on sb; drop in to see sb; give a visit to sb; give sb a visit; go to see; look in on sb; look sb up; make a visit to sb; make sb a visit; on a visit; pay an official call; pay sb a call; see; visit; visit with sb; wait on sb;

bai fo 拜佛
prostrate oneself before the image of Buddha / worship Buddha;

bai fu 拜服
greatly admire;

bai he 拜賀
congratulate / offer congratulations;

bai hou 拜候
call on / visit;

bai hui 拜會
call on || make an official visit; pay a courtesy call; pay an official call;

bai jian 拜見
(1) call to pay respect / pay a formal visit;
(2) meet one's senior or superior;

bai jie 拜節
extend holiday greetings / pay a visit on holidays;

bai ke 拜客
call on / pay a visit / visit;

bai ken 拜懇
beg humbly / implore / request;

bai lao shi 拜老師
become a pupil to a master in a ceremony;

bai ling 拜領
accept with thanks;

bai men 拜門
(1) pay thanks by personal visit;
(2) become a pupil or apprentice to a master;

bai meng 拜盟
become sworn brothers;

bai miao 拜廟
worship at a temple;

bai mu 拜墓
worship at the grave;

bai nian 拜年
make a New Year call / pay a New Year call;

bai ou xiang 拜偶像
idol-worshipping;

bai ren wei shi 拜人為師
acknowledge sb as one's tutor / sit at sb's feet and be his pupil;

bai shen 拜神
worship gods;

bai shi 拜師
sit at sb's feet / take sb as one's teacher;

bai shi qiu xue 拜師求學
pay respect to a master and seek for knowledge;

bai shou 拜壽
congratulate an elderly person on his or her birthday / offer birthday greetings;

bai tang 拜堂
perform the formal wedding ceremony;

bai tian di 拜天地
bow to heaven and earth as part of wedding ceremony;

bai tuo 拜託
request sb to do sth;

bai tuo dai lao 拜託代勞
request to do sth for another;

bai wang 拜望
call on / call to pay one's respects / visit;

bai xie 拜謝
express one's thanks / humbly thank;

bai ye 拜謁
(1) call to pay respects / pay a formal visit;
(2) pay homage;

bai zai men xia 拜在門下
become a pupil to sb;

bai zu 拜祖
ancestor worship;

ban1 zhen shang han 斑疹傷寒
typhus / typhus fever;
di fang xing ban zhen shang han 地方性斑疹傷寒
endemic typhus;
dian xing ban zhen shang han 典型斑疹傷寒
classic typhus;
liu xing xing ban zhen shang han 流行性斑疹傷寒
epidemic typhus;

ban1 搬
(1) remove;
(2) present;

ban dong xi 搬東西
move things;

ban dong 搬動
move / shift;

ban lai ban qu 搬來搬去
move here and there;

ban nong 搬弄
(1) show off;
(2) fiddle with;
(3) instigate / sow discord / stir up;

ban nong shi fei 搬弄是非
tell tales and sow discord;

ban yi 搬移
move;

ban yun 搬運
carry / move / transport;

ban4 bei zi 半輩子
half a lifetime / half part of one's life;

ban luo ti 半裸體
half-naked;

ban shen 半身
(1) one side of the body;
(2) half of the body;

ban shen bu sui 半身不遂
(1) semiphlegia;
(2) be half paralyzed // half-paralyzed;

ban shi 半世
half of a person's life span;

ban shui ban xing 半睡半醒
half asleep, half awake // drowsy / slumberous;

ban si 半死
half-dead;

ban si bu huo 半死不活
half-dead / more dead than alive / on the verge of death;

ban tan huan 半癱瘓
semiparalysis;

ban tui ban jiu 半推半就
yield with a show of reluctance;

ban wen mang 半文盲
semiliterate;

ban zheng ban jia 半真半假
partly true, partly false;

ban4 扮
(1) be dressed up as / disguise oneself as;
(2) play the part of;

ban xi 扮戲
play a role in a play;

ban yan 扮演
act the part of sb / play the role of sb || act; act sb; be dressed up to represent sb; carry off one's role of sb; dress up as sb; interpret the role of sb; in the character of sb; make oneself up as sb; play sb; take on the role of sb;

ban zhuang 扮裝
disguise / make up;

ban zuo 扮作
disguise as / dress up as / dress up to;

ban4 song 伴送
accompany / escort / see sb off;

ban tong 伴同
accompany / go along with;

ban wu 伴舞
(1) dance with;
(2) dance in the background;

ban you 伴遊
(1) travel in sb's company / travel with;
(2) traveling companion;

ban4 絆
cause to stumble / stumble / trip;

ban dao 絆倒
stumble / stumble down;

ban zhu 絆住
be bogged down / be detained / be held back;

ban4 辦
(1) do || apply for; attend to; deal with; handle; manage; settle; tackle;
(2) get sth ready / prepare;
(3) bring to justice;
(4) establish || manage; run; set up;

ban an 辦案
handle a case;

ban bu cheng 辦不成
unable to be accomplished;

ban bu dao 辦不到
impossible to accomplish / impossible to manage / unable to accomplish / unable to manage;

ban bu liao 辦不了
too much for one to accomplish / too much for one to finish;

ban bu wan 辦不完
too much for one to finish;

ban de bu hao 辦得不好
badly managed / bungled / mismanaged / poorly handled;

ban de hao 辦得好
well-done / well-handled / well-managed;

ban gong 辦公
attend to business / do office work;

ban jiao she 辦交涉
negotiate;

ban jiu xi 辦酒席
host a feast / prepare a banquet;

ban li 辦理
handle / manage / take care of;

ban sang shi 辦喪事
arrange funeral matters / handle funeral matters;

ban shi 辦事
(1) handle matters;
(2) do one's job;

ban shi gong dao 辦事公道
fair and just // play the game;

ban shi gong zheng 辦事公正
do one's job squarely;

ban shi lao lian 辦事老練
dispatch one's business with dexterity;

ban shi ren zhen 辦事認真
conscientious in one's work;

ban tuo 辦妥
finish doing sth properly;

ban xi shi 辦喜事
host a party on a joyous occasion / organize a wedding;

ban xue 辦學
run a school;

bang1 幫
aid / assist / help;

bang chu 幫廚
help with cooking;

bang cou 幫湊
contribute money to help sb;

bang dao mang 幫倒忙
counterproductive / more of impediment than of assistance;

bang fu 幫扶
aid / assist / help;

bang mang 幫忙
aid / assist / do a favour / give a hand / help / lend a hand;

bang zhu 幫助
aid / assist / do a favour / give a hand / help / lend a hand;

bao1 ban 包辦
undertake sth alone ‖ be manipulated by sb single-handedly; do sth all by oneself; keep everything in one's own hands; single-handedly; take everything on oneself;

bao bi 包庇
cover up for sb / screen / shield;

bao chao 包抄
envelop / outflank;

bao guan 包管
assure / guarantee;

bao lan 包攬
(1) monopolize;
(2) pocket;

bao1 bian 褒貶
praise and disparage;

bao jiang 褒獎
commend and award;

bao lai 褒賚
commend and reward;

bao mei 褒美
praise and cite;

bao yang 褒揚
commend / praise;

bao zan 褒贊
commend / extol / praise;

bao3 保
(1) defend / protect / safegurad;
(2) keep / maintain;

bao chi 保持
keep / maintain ‖ conserve; keep up; preserve; remain; retain; uphold;

bao chi zhong li 保持中立
sit on the fence / stand neuter;

bao cun 保存
preserve ‖ conserve; keep; save; store;

bao guan 保管
take care of / keep in custody ‖ hold in trust; keep in a safe place; store;

bao hu 保護
defend / preserve / protect / safeguard;

bao hu mo 保護膜
preservative membrane;

bao hu xing mian yi 保護性免疫
protective immunity;

bao liu 保留
(1) preserve / retain;
(2) reserve // reservation;

bao mi 保密
keep secret;

bao ming 保命
save one's life;

bao nuan 保暖
keep warm;

bao quan 保全
(1) preserve;
(2) keep in good condition;

bao shi 保釋
bail / release on bail;

bao wei 保衛
defend / guard against / safeguard;

bao yang 保養
(1) maintain;
(2) keep fit;

bao you 保佑
bless;

bao zhang 保障
safeguard;

bao zheng 保證
guarantee;

bao zhong 保重
look after oneself / take care;

bao zhu 保住
retain / save;

bao3 chang 飽嘗
endure one's fill of hardship / experience for long / experience to the fullest extent;

身體 *Body*

bao chang tong ku 飽嘗痛苦
have the black ox tread on one's foot;

bao chang xin suan 飽嘗辛酸
go through the mill / pass through the mill / taste to the full the bitterness of life;

bao jing cang sang 飽經滄桑
have experienced many vicissitudes of life;

bao jing feng shuang 飽經風霜
have experienced the hardships of life || endure all the hardship of exposure; have experienced years of wind and frost; have gone through all hardships of life; have weathered many storms; weather-beaten;

bao jing feng yu 飽經風雨
one's face furrowed by rain and wind;

bao jing shi gu 飽經世故
be well experienced in ways of the world / have seen the elephant;

bao jing you huan 飽經憂患
have suffered untold tribulations || be no stranger to sorrow; have gone through a good deal of misery;

bao nuan 飽暖
more than enough to eat and wear / well-fed and well-clad;

bao nuan si yin yu 飽暖思淫欲
when the belly is full, one's thoughts turn to sex || debauchery is a common vice among the wealthy; material comfort leads to sexual desire;

bao nuan si yin yu, ji han qi dao xin 飽暖思淫欲，飢寒起盜心
those who are well-fed and well-clad are inclined to be lustful, whereas hunger and cold breed the temptation to steal;

bao shou 飽受
suffer to the fullest extent;

bao3 dao wei lao 寶刀未老
old but still vigorous in mind and body;

bao4 bing 抱冰
train oneself to endure hardships;

bao bing 抱病
be ill / in bad health;

bao bing chu xi 抱病出席
come to the meeting despite one's illness;

bao bing gong zuo 抱病工作
carry on work while sick / go on working in spite of ill health;

bao bu ping 抱不平
be outraged by an injustice done to another person / take up the cudgels against an injustice || be the champion of the oppressed; champion the accuse of a wronged person; indignant at injustice;

bao can shou que 抱殘守缺
stick to the outmoded ways || a stickler of ancient ways and things; a traditionalist; be conservative; cherish the outmoded and preserve the outworn; cling to bygone values; retain what is old and outworn;

bao can han xiu 抱慚含羞
be overcome by shame;

bao cheng yi tuan 抱成一團
hang together || gang up; hold together to form a clique;

bao cu tui 抱粗腿
cling to the rich and powerful / curry favour with sb || flatter; latch on to the rich and powerful; throw oneself under the protection of someone of influence;

bao de yang he 抱德煬和
adhere to virtue and kindness / bosom virtue and blend kindness / stick to virtue and kindness;

bao ding jue xin 抱定決心
determined // hold on to one's determination;

bao fu 抱負
ambition / aspiration;

bao fu bu fan 抱負不凡
ambitious || cherish aspirations out of the common; entertain high aspirations; have great life ambition;

bao nian 抱念
remember / think of;

bao qian 抱歉
feel apologetic / feel sorry / regret;

bao qian zhi zhi 抱歉之至
feel very sorry / very sorry;

bao qu 抱屈
bear a grudge / feel wronged / harbour resentment;

bao qu han yuan 抱屈含冤
be wronged and aggrieved / bear a deep grudge;

bao tong xi he 抱痛西河
feel sorrow over the loss of one's son / mourn over the death of one's son / suffer the sorrow of losing one's son;

bao wa wa 抱娃娃
(1) give birth to a child;
(2) look after a child;

bao4 報
(1) report;
(2) respond;
(3) repay;

bao an 報案
report a case to (police);

bao chang 報償
recompense / repay;

bao chou 報仇
avenge / revenge ‖ be out for sb's scalp; get back at; get even with sb; get one's own back on sb; get square with sb; have one's own back on sb; have sb's scalp; pay back sb; pay off sb; pay out sb; serve out sb; take sb's scalp;

bao chou xue chi 報仇雪恥
settle an old score ‖ avenge a wrong and wipe out a humiliation; pay old scores; pay off old scores; take revenge and wipe out a disgrace; take revenge for an insult; wipe off old scores; wipe out an old score;

bao chou xue hen 報仇雪根
pay off old scores ‖ avenge a grievance; avenge oneself; get even with a hated enemy; glut one's revenge; hurt sb in return for a wrong; take revenge to wreak vengeance and redress hatred;

bao da 報答
repay / reward // requited;

bao dao 報到
report for duty;

bao de 報德
repay a kindness;

bao en 報恩
repay a debt of gratitude;

bao fu 報復
hit back / retaliate / revenge // retaliation / vengeance / vindication;

bao gao 報告
report;

bao jie 報捷
announce a victory / report a success;

bao jing 報警
call the police / report to the police;

bao kao 報考
register for an examination;

bao ming 報名
sign up;

bao shi 報失
report a loss;

bao xi 報喜
announce good news;

bao xie 報謝
acknowledge;

bao xin 報信
inform;

bao4 bi 暴斃
meet a sudden death;

bao bing 暴病
a sudden attack of a serious illness;

bao bing shen wang 暴病身亡
die from a sudden illness;

bao lu 暴露
come to light / expose / give away / lay bare / reveal / unmask;

bao pi qi 暴脾氣
hot temper // crabby / grumpy / hot-tempered / narky;

bao si 暴死
die a sudden death / die of a sudden disease / meet sudden death // die off;

bao tian qing sheng 暴殄輕生
commit suicide / make light of one's life;

bao xing zi 暴性子
hot temper;

bao zao 暴躁
irascible / irritable / short-tempered / tetchy;

bao zu 暴卒
die a violent death / die of a sudden illness / die suddenly;

bao4 fa xing tian hua 爆發型天花
fulminant smallpox;

bei4 fu 背負
bear / carry on the back / have on one's shoulder;

bei hei huo 背黑鍋
be made a scapegoat || be unjustly blamed; hold the bag; take the blame for another person; take the consequences on one's own;

bei ben 背本
bite the hand that feeds one;

bei dao er chi 背道而馳
run in the opposite direction || act counter to; act in direct contravention to; be diametrically opposed to; go against; go contrary to; go counter to; go in a diametrically opposite direction; heading in opposite directions; incompatible with; moving in the opposite direction; moving in the wrong direction; proceed in opposite directions; run counter to;

bei di li 背地裏
behind one's back / in secret / on the quiet / on the sly // clandestinely / furtively / privately / secretly;

bei di li gao gui 背地裏搞鬼
play a deep game;

bei hou dao gui 背後搗鬼
embark on conspiracy behind the scenes || instigate trouble behind sb's back; play underhand tricks; plot behind the scenes; scheme behind the scenes;

bei hou tong dao zi 背後捅刀子
stab sb in the back;

bei hou xia du shou 背後下毒手
stab sb in the back;

bei hou xing shi 背後行事
go behind sb's back;

bei hou zao yao 背後造謠
start rumours behind sb's back;

bei hou zhong shang 背後中傷
rip up the back / stab sb in the back;

bei meng 背盟
break a promise / break an agreement // breach of contract;

bei meng qi xin 背盟棄信
violate a treaty;

bei pan 背叛
apostatize / betray / defect / rebel // treacherous // treachery;

bei qi 背棄
betray / break faith with / renounce / turn one's back on;

bei shi li su 背世離俗
leave the world and its vulgarities;

bei xin 背信
break one's promise / break one's words // breach of faith / perfidy // faithless;

bei xin qi yi 背信棄義
break one's promise // bad faith / breach of faith / perfidy // perfidious;

bei yi qiu quan 背義求全
renounce honour and strive for existence;

bei yue 背約
breach of agreement // break an agreement / break one's promise / go back on one's word;

bei yun 背運
(1) in one's unlucky day / out of luck;
(2) unlucky fate;

bei zhu 背主
disloyal to one's master;

bei4 bi 被逼
be compelled / be forced;

bei bu 被捕
be arrested / under arrest;

bei fu 被俘
be captured / be taken prisoner;

bei hai 被害
be killed / be murdered;

bei jie 被劫
be kidnapped / be robbed;

bei jie gu 被解僱
be sacked || catch it in the neck; get it in the neck; get the hook; get the push; get the sack; give sb the push; knock off; take it in the neck;

bei kai chu 被開除
be sacked / get the push / get the sack / give sb the push / knock off;

bei pian 被騙
be fooled / be swindled;

bei po 被迫
be compelled / be constrained / be forced;

bei sha hai 被殺害
be killed / be murdered / get the works;

bei4 備
(1) get ready;
(2) prepare against;
(2) in full;

bei ban 備辦
get things ready / prepare;

bei chang gan ku 備嚐甘苦
have experienced good fortunes and adversities / have tasted the sweet and bitter / have tasted the sweetness and bitterness of life;

bei chang jian xin 備嚐艱辛
undergo hardships || drain the cup of sorrow to the dregs; suffer many privations; suffer untold hardships;

bei chang xin ku 備嚐辛苦
undergo all kinds of hardships;

bei chang xin lao 備嚐辛勞
have experienced hardships and difficulties;

bei chang xin suan 備嚐辛酸
have gone all kinds of hardships || drain the cup of bitterness to the dregs; have a rough time;

bei chang you huan 備嚐憂患
have undergone much worry and hardships;

bei er bu fang, fang er bu bei 備而不防，防而不備
preparedness averts peril;

bei er bu yong 備而不用
keep sth for possible future use;

bei huang 備荒
prepare against natural disasters;

bei ke 備課
prepare lessons;

bei ma 備馬
saddle a horse for riding;

bei qu 備取
on the waiting list / put on reserve;

bei shou huan yin 備受歡迎
be very popular / enjoy great popularity;

bei shou ling ru 備受淩辱
suffer wrongs and contumelies;

bei shou rou lin 備受蹂躪
under the hoof;

bei shu 備述
report completely;

bei xi 備悉
know the whole story / learn completely;

bei zhan 備戰
prepare for war;

bei4 憊
exhausted / fatigued / tired / weary;

bei juan 憊倦
exhausted / fatigued / tired / weary;

bei lan 憊懶
tired and indolent;

bei lei 憊累
exhausted / tired / weary;

ben1 奔
(1) hurry / move quickly / run;
(2) flee;
(3) elope;

ben bo 奔波
toil / work very hard;

ben chi 奔馳
run quickly / gallop || hasten; move along quickly; move fast; speed; speed on; travel quickly;

ben cuan 奔竄
flee about / flee and hide / scuttle off;

ben fang 奔放
bold and unrestrained / untrammelled ‖ expressive and unrestrained; moving and forceful;

ben jing 奔競
struggle for wealth and fame;

ben mang 奔忙
bustle about ‖ busy rushing about; in a great hurry; on the move constantly; toil;

ben ming 奔命
(1) be kept on the run ‖ in a desperate hurry; run for one's life; rush about on errands;
(2) do one's best / go all out;

ben sang 奔喪
hasten home on the death of one's parent ‖ hasten home for the funeral of a parent or grandparent;

ben3 fen 本分
keep to one's lot;

ben neng 本能
instinct;
fan yan ben neng 繁衍本能
sexual drive;
gong ji ben neng 攻擊本能
aggressive instinct;
xing ben neng 性本能
sexual instinct;

ben xin 本心
(1) one's conscience;
(2) one's true intention;

ben xing 本性
instincts / one's natural character / the real nature / what is bred in the bone;

ben xing bu bian 本性不變
the nature of sb never changes;

ben xing guai li 本性乖戾
be sullen by nature;

ben xing nan cang 本性難藏
one's true nature will always emerge / what's bred in the bone will come out in the flesh;

ben xing nan yi 本性難移
one's nature cannot be altered ‖ a leopard won't change its spots; it is difficult to alter one's character; what is bred in the bone will stick to the flesh;

beng1 崩
(1) collapse;
(2) die / pass away;

bi1 bu de yi 逼不得已
be compelled to / be forced to / have no alternative;

bi de zou tou wu lu 逼得走頭無路
leave sb no way out;

bi gong 逼供
extort a confession;

bi he 逼和
win a draw;

bi jia 逼嫁
force a woman to marry;

bi po 逼迫
coerce / compel / constrain / force;

bi qian 逼前
press forward;

bi qu 逼取
blackmail / extort / take by forcible means;

bi ren 逼人
pressing / threatening;

bi ren tai shen 逼人太甚
push sb too hard;

bi ru kun jing 逼入困境
drive sb into a corner ‖ drive sb to the wall; get sb cornered; push sb to the wall;

bi shang liang shan 逼上梁山
be forced to do sth desperate ‖ be driven to join the Liangshan Mountain rebels; be driven to revolt;

bi si 逼死
hound sb to death;

bi suo 逼索
force / obtain by force;

bi xia 逼狹
harsh / ungenerous;

bi xiao 逼肖
bear a close resemblance to / the very image of / with striking resemblance;

bi ya 逼壓
oppress;

bi zhai 逼債
demand payment of debt / press for payment of debts;

bi zhai le suo 逼債勒索
press for the repayment of debts and practise extortion;

bi zhe gong ji xia dan — ban bu dao 逼着公雞下蛋——辦不到
forcing a rooster to lay eggs — impossible to accomplish;

bi zhi jue jing 逼至絕境
drive sb to the wall / push sb to the wall;

bi zou 逼走
force to leave;

bi3 bu de 比不得
beyond all comparison / not to be compared;

bi bu shang 比不上
inferior to || no peer for; not hold a candle to; not so…as;

bi de shang 比得上
can compare with / compare favourably with;

bi dui 比對
collate / compare and check // comparison;

bi4 庇
protect || hide; conceal; harbour; shelter; shield;

bi duan 庇短
conceal a defect // partial and willing to overlook shortcomings;

bi hu 庇護
shelter || protect; put under one's protection; shield; take under one's wing;

bai ban bi hu 百般庇護
shelter by all possible means;

bi ni jian gui 庇匿奸宄
shelter a criminal;

bi shan fa e 庇善罰惡
heaven blesses the good and punishes the evil;

bi yin 庇蔭
(1) give shade;
(2) conceal / harbour / protect / shield;

bi you 庇佑
bless / prosper / protect;

bi4 ming 畢命
die / end one's life;

bi sheng 畢生
in one's whole life / all one's life / lifelong / lifetime / throughout one's lifetime;

bi sheng jing li 畢生精力
energy throughout one's life / the energies of a lifetime;

bi4 men xie ke 閉門謝客
refuse visitors;

bi se 閉塞
block;

bi kong bi se 鼻孔閉塞
have a stuffy nose;

bi4 xing 詖行
evil behaviour or conduct;

bi4 辟
(1) monarch;
(2) govern;
(3) avoid / escape / get rid of;

bi shi 辟世
live in seclusion / withdraw from the world;

bi xie 辟邪
ward off evil;

bi4 ti 蔽體
cover the body;

bi zhang 蔽障
keep in obscurity || an obstacle in the mind to understanding; an obstacle to faith;

bi4 斃
(1) die / get killed;
(2) execute by shooting / shoot to death;
(3) reject / veto / vote down;

bi di 斃敵
kill enemy troops;

bi ming 斃命
get killed / meet violent death;

bi4 避
(1) avoid / escape / evade / shun;

(2) keep away / prevent / repel;

bi feng tuo 避風頭
dodge the brunt / lie low until the critical time is over;

bi hai 避害
escape disaster / run away from a calamity;

bi han 避寒
escape cold / go to a winter resort;

bi hui 避諱
(1) a word or phrase to be avoided as taboo / taboo;
(2) dodge / evade;
(3) taboo on using the personal names of emperors, one's elders, etc.;

bi huo qu fu 避禍趨福
pursue good fortune and avoid disaster;

bi jing 避靜
retreat;

bi kai 避開
avoid / stay away from || evade; get away from; get out of the way; give sth a miss; keep away from; keep clear of; keep off sth; shun;

bi luan 避亂
run away from social upheaval;

bi mian 避免
avoid / refrain from || avert; forestall; prevent sth from happening; stave off;

bi mian chong tu 避免衝突
evade conflict / evade disagreement;

bi mian cuo wu 避免錯誤
avoid mistakes;

bi mian mao fan 避免冒犯
keep off the grass;

bi mian xian yi 避免嫌疑
save oneself from suspicion;

bi mian 避面
avoid meeting a person;

bi nan 避難
take refuge || avoid disaster; escape calamity; find refuge; seek asylum;

bi nan jiu yi 避難就易
evade the difficult and take the easy || follow the line of least resistance; shirk the hard matter and take up the easy ones;

bi ni 避匿
hide away / lie in hiding;

bi qiang da ruo 避強打弱
evade the strong and attack the weak;

bi ren er mu 避人耳目
escape the notice of others || avoid being noticed; avoid being observed; elude observation;

bi shi jiu xu 避實就虛
avoid the enemy's main force and strike at its weaknesses;

bi shi 避世
escape from the real world and live in isolation || lead a hermit's life; live as a recluse; retire from the world; retire from worldly affairs;

bi shi jue su 避世絕俗
withdraw from the society and live in solitude;

bi shi li su 避世離俗
try to escape reality / try to keep away from this world;

bi shu 避暑
avoid the summer heat / run away from summer heat || escape the summer heat; go away for summer holidays; go to a summer resort; take a summer vacation;

bi xi 避席
leave one's seat;

bi xian 避嫌
avoid arousing suspicion || avoid being suspected; avoid doing anything that may arouse suspicion; avoid suspicion;

bi xian yin tui 避嫌引退
withdraw from a post to avoid suspicion;

bi xiong qu ji 避凶趨吉
conduct oneself so as to avoid impending trouble and seek good luck / flee evil and strive to walk in fair fortune's way;

bi yi 避疫
escape from epidemics;

bi yu 避雨
find shelter against rain / take shelter from rain;

bi zai 避債
avoid creditors;

bi zhong jiu qing 避重就輕
take up minor issues to evade the major ones || avoid the important and dwell on the trivial; avoiding the main point; ride off on a side issue; shirk a difficult work and take an easy one; take the easier way out;

bi4 huan 璧還
return with thanks;

bi xie 璧謝
decline a gift with thanks;

bi4 lin 蹕臨
arrive / visit;

bian1 ce 鞭策
encourage / goad on / spur on / urge on;

bian ce luo hou 鞭策落後
spur those who are backward;

bian chang mo ji 鞭長莫及
beyond the reach of one's power || beyond one's influence; beyond one's reach; beyond the range of one's ability; cannot do it much as I would like to; out of range; too far away for one to be able to help;

bian chi tian xia 鞭笞天下
flog the world / make the people of the world at one's beck and call;

bian pi 鞭辟
urge and encourage;

bian pi ru li 鞭辟入裡
cut to the quick // deep-cutting / incisive / penetrating / trenchant;

bian3 ping tian hua 扁平天花
flat smallpox;

bian ping xi bao 扁平細胞
pavement cell;

bian3 ji 褊急
easily irritated / narrow-minded and short-tempered;

bian lou 褊陋
cramped and crude / narrow-minded and ignorant;

bian neng 褊能
of little ability;

bian qian 褊淺
narrow-minded and shallow;

bian4 wu 抃舞
cheer and dance / make merry;

bian yong 抃踴
cheer and dance;

bian4 shen 徧身
all over one's body;

bian ti lin shang 徧體鱗傷
suffer injuries all over one's body;

bian4 shen 遍身
all over the body;

bian ti 遍體
all over the body;

bian ti lin shang 遍體鱗傷
with wounds all over the body;

bian4 jie 變節
abandon one's belief and lose one's integrity under high pressure or torture / recant;

bian xing 變形
become deformed || change shape; deform; out of shape; trans-shape; transfigure;

biao1 彪
tall and big;

biao xing 彪形
tall and big;

biao1 xin li yi 標新立異
create sth new and original || do sth unconventional; do sth unorthodox; start sth new in order to be different; strain after novelty;

biao1 臕
fat;

biao fei ti zhuang 臕肥體壯
plump and sturdy;

biao hou 臕厚
fat thickness;

biao zhuang 臕壯
fat and strong;

biao3 li 表裏
both sides — inside and outside;

biao li bu yi 表裏不一
act a double part || have two faces; think in one way and behave in another; think one way and act another;

biao li ru yi 表裏如一
think and act in one and the same way || speak and act as one thinks; the same outside and inside; what one professes to be;

biao li wei jian 表裏為奸
conspiracy with people working inside;

biao li xiang ying 表裏相應
coordinated attack;

biao li yi zhi 表裏一致
honest and sincere;

biao tai 表態
declare where one stands / make known one's position towards an issue;

biao xian 表現
conduct oneself / demonstrate / display / exhibit / express / manifest / show / show off;

biao xian cha jin 表現差勁
give a poor account of oneself;

biao xian chu se 表現出色
acquit oneself / give a good account of oneself;

bin1 si 瀕死
near death / on the brink of death;

bin wei 瀕危
on the verge of death;

bin yu si wang 瀕於死亡
on the verge of death || at death's door; at one's last gasp; have one foot in the grave; nearing one's doom; on one's last legs; on the brink of death; totter on the brink of the grave;

bin4 擯
discard / expel / get rid of / oust / reject;

bin chi 擯斥
dismiss / expel / reject / repudiate;

bin chi yi ji 擯斥異己
dismiss those who hold different opinions / reject dissidents;

bin chu 擯除
discard / dispense with / get rid of;

bin er bu yong 擯而不用
reject;

bin luo 擯落
suffer rejection and downfall;

bin qi 擯棄
abandon / cast away / desert / discard / set aside;

bin qi bu yong 擯棄不用
dismiss sb and refrain from giving him an appointment / throw on the scrap-heap;

bin zhu men wai 擯諸門外
lock sb out / shut sb out;

bing3 chi 秉持
(1) adhere to / hold on to;
(2) hold in hand;

bing fu 秉賦
one's natural endowments;

bing gong 秉公
impartially / justly;

bing gong ban li 秉公辦理
handle a matter impartially;

bing gong er lun 秉公而論
in justice to;

bing yao zhi ben 秉要執本
grasp the essentials;

bing3 屏
abandon / discard / dismiss / get rid of / reject;

bing chu 屏除
banish / get rid of;

bing ji 屏跡
avoid / stay away from;

bing ju 屏居
live in retirement / out of public life;

bing jue 屏絕
stop having contact with;

bing qi 屏棄
brush aside / discard / reject / throw away;

bing tui 屏退
order sb to retire;

bing3 稟
(1) petition / report;
(2) be endowed with / receive;

bing bai 稟白
report to a superior;

bing chen 稟陳
report to a superior;

bing gao 稟告
report to one's superior;

bing ming 稟明
clarify a matter to a superior / explain to a superior;

bing ming 稟命
at the behest of / by order of;

bing shou 稟受
(1) endure;
(2) nature;

bing4 fa zheng 並發症
complication;

bing4 fa zheng 併發症
complication;

bing4 病
(1) disease / illness / sickness;
(2) feel unwell / ill / taken ill;
(3) ill / sick / sickly;
(4) defect / fault;
(5) worry;
(6) hate;

bing bian 病變
lesion;
huang ban bing bian 黄斑病變
maculopathy;
jiao mo bing bian 角膜病變
keratopathy;
niao lu bing bian 尿路病變
uropathy;
pi fu bing bian 皮膚病變
dermopathy;
shen bing bian 腎病變
nephropathy;
shen tou xing shen bing bian 滲透性腎病變
osmotic nephrosis;
shen xiao guan bing bian 腎小管病變
tubulopathy;
tang niao bing pi fu bing bian 糖尿病皮膚病變
diabetic dermopathy;
ying yang xing bing bian 營養性病變
trophic lesion;
you yang bing bian 疣樣病變
verruca;

bing dao 病倒
be struck down / come down with an illness / fall ill;

bing du 病毒
virus;

bing du bing 病毒病
virosis;

bing du 病篤
die of illness // critically ill / terminally ill;

bing fa 病發
fall ill;

bing fei 病廢
be disabled by disease;

bing ge 病革
about to die of an illness;

bing gen 病根
cause of a disease;

bing gu 病故
die of illness;

bing guo bing min 病國病民
injure both the state and the people;

bing guo yang min 病國殃民
injure both the state and the people;

bing ji 病疾
disease / illness / sickness;

bing kuang 病況
the condition of a patient;

bing lao gui xi 病老歸西
die of old age ‖ go to the paradise in the west;

bing mo 病魔
the curse of disease ‖ serious illness; the demon of ill health;

身體 *Body*

bing mo chan sheng 病魔纏身
be afflicted with a lingering disease / be prone to all kinds of sickness;

bing mo 病沒
die of illness / succumb to a disease;

bing qing 病情
the state of an illness || patient's condition;

bing qing hao zhuan 病情好轉
patient's condition takes a favourable turn / be on the mend;

bing qu 病軀
sick body;

bing rong 病容
emaciated look / sickly appearance / sickly look;

bing ru gao huang 病入膏肓
sick to the core || fatal disease; fatally sick; incurably ill; have no hope of recovery; past all hope;

bing ruo 病弱
sick and weak;

bing shi 病逝
die of an illness;

bing shi 病勢
patient's condition || the degree of seriousness of an illness;

bing shi wei dai 病勢危殆
dangerously ill;

bing si 病死
die of an illness;

bing tai 病態
morbid state;

bing tong 病痛
indisposition / slight illness;

bing tui 病退
resign one's job because of illness;

bing wang 病忘
amnesia;

bing wei 病危
at one's last gasp / critically ill / impending death / terminally ill;

bing xiang 病象
symptoms of a disease;

bing yin 病因
the cause of a disease / the origin of a disease;

bing yu 病癒
get well / recover from illness;

bing yuan 病原
the cause of a disease / the origin of a disease;

bing zai wei du 病在危篤
ill and failing fast;

bing zheng 病症
(1) ailment / disease;
(2) symptoms of a disease;

bing zhong 病終
die of disease;

bing zhong 病重
be severely indisposed / seriously ill // in a critical condition;

bing zhuang 病狀
symptoms of a disease;

bing4 摒
(1) expel / get rid of;
(2) arrange in order;

bing chu 摒除
get rid of / renounce;

bing dang 摒擋
arrange in order / pack up for travelling;

bing jue 摒絕
cut loose entirely;

bing qi 摒棄
abandon / get rid of;

bo1 剝
(1) peel || peel off; shell; skin;
(2) make bare / strip;

bo de jing guang 剝得精光
be stripped off all belongings / be stripped to the skin / strip sb to the skin;

bo duo 剝奪
deny / deprive of / divest sb of / expropriate / strip / take away;

bo lu 剝露
denudation;

bo1 kai wu mai 撥開霧霾
disperse the miasmal mist;

bo kai yun wu jian qing tian 撥開雲霧見青天
(1) dispel the clouds and see the sun;
(2) restore justice;

bo la 撥拉
move / stir;

bo luan fan zheng 撥亂反正
bring order out of chaos || clarify confusion and bring things back to order; restore things to order; set to right what has been thrown into disorder;

bo nong 撥弄
fiddle with / toy with;

bo nong shi fei 撥弄是非
sow discord / stir things up;

bo rong 撥冗
set aside a little time out of a tight schedule / find time in the midst of pressing affairs;

bo rong guang lin 撥冗光臨
please spare a little time and come;

bo yong 撥用
appropriate / set apart for a specific use;

bo yun jian ri 撥雲見日
(1) sweep away the dark clouds and bring sb the light;
(2) redress wrong and restore justice / remove the cloud of suspicion;

bo zheng 撥正
correct / set right;

bo1 nong 播弄
(1) order sb about;
(2) stir up;

bo nong shi fei 播弄是非
sow discord || sow dissension; stir things up; stir up trouble; tell tales;

bo san xing jian jin xing huai si 播散性漸進性壞死
diaspironecrobiosis;

bo san xing huai si 播散性壞死
diaspironecrosis;

bo2 qu 博取
contend for / court / try to gain;

bo qu xin ren 博取信任
win sb's confidence;

bo shi ji zhong 博施濟眾
help the public by bestowing generously;

bo2 搏
(1) combat / fight / struggle / wrestle;
(2) assault by preying / pounce on;
(3) beat / throb;

bo dong 搏動
beat rythmically / pulsate / throb;

bo dou 搏斗
combat || fight; struggle; tussle with; wrestle with;

bo ji 搏擊
strike || fight with hands; pound; strike violently;

bo sha 搏殺
fight and kill;

bo shou 搏手
at the end of one's wits / powerless;

bo xiang nong fen 搏香弄粉
apply a lot of make-up / doll oneself up;

bo ying 搏影
fight the shadow;

bo zhan 搏戰
box / combat / engage in hand-to-hand combat;

bo2 dai 薄待
treat sb rather badly / treat sb ungenerously;

bo jin mian li 薄盡綿力
exert my humble efforts || do my humble best; do what little I can; make my humble efforts;

bo ming 薄命
ill-fated || born under an unlucky star; fate is unkind to; ill-starred;

bu3 捕
arrest || apprehend; catch; seize;

bu chu 捕處
arrest and punish;

bu feng zhuo ying 捕風捉影
run after a shadow || act on hearsay evidence; catch at shadows — indulge in groundless suspicion;

bu huo 捕獲
(1) capture ‖ acquire; arrest; catch; seize; succeed in catching;
(2) trap;

bu lao 捕撈
fish for;

bu lie 捕獵
catch and hunt;

bu na 捕拿
arrest ‖ apprehend; capture; catch;

bu sha 捕殺
capture and kill / catch and kill;

bu zhuo 捕捉
catch / seize;

bu3 shen 補身
build up one's health;

bu yang 補養
take a tonic or nourishing food to build up one's health;

bu4 an shi gu 不諳世故
ignorant of worldly affairs / unworldly;

bu an shi shi 不諳世事
ignorant of worldly affairs / not familiar with the ways of the world;

bu an ben fen 不安本分
be dissatisfied with one's post / dislike to act one's part / not content in one's station;

bu an qi shi 不安其室
be discontented with one's home;

bu an yu shi 不安於室
have extramarital relations;

bu an yu wei 不安於位
dissatisfied with one's position / not content in one's job / unsteady in the chair;

bu bai zhi yuan 不白之冤
a case of being wrongly accused ‖ an innocence incapable of being vindicated; an unrighted wrong; be wronged; suffer wrong; to be pronounced guilty without being able to disprove the guilt; unredressed injustice; unrighted wrong;

bu bi jian xian 不避艱險
shrink from no difficulty or danger ‖ brave hardships and dangers; flinch from no difficulty or danger; make light of difficulties and dangers;

bu bie er qu 不別而去
go away without saying good-bye ‖ go away without a leave; leave without notice; leave without saying a word; take French leave; not uttering a word before one's departure;

bu cheng cai 不成材
good-for-nothing / useless / worthless;

bu cheng qi 不成器
good-for-nothing / useless / worthless;

bu cheng shi 不誠實
uncandid;

bu chuai mao mei 不揣冒昧
venture to ‖ make bold to; make free to; presume; take the liberty of;

bu ci er bie 不辭而別
leave without saying goodbye ‖ depart without taking leave; give one the slip; go away without saying a word; slip away; slip off; take French leave;

bu ci lao ku 不辭勞苦
make nothing of hardships ‖ does not mind the hardships; put oneself out; spare no pains; take the trouble;

bu ci shui huo 不辭水火
through thick and thin;

bu ci wan nan 不辭萬難
not to shirk all hardships / through thick and thin;

bu ci xin ku 不辭辛苦
not to shirk from toil and hardship ‖ not to shirk hardships; put oneself out of the way; spare no pains; take the trouble to; work tirelessly;

bu ci xin lao 不辭辛勞
not to shirk from toil and hardship ‖ not to shirk hardships; put oneself out of the way; spare no pains; take the trouble to; work tirelessly;

bu cun jie di 不存芥蒂
bear no grudge;

bu da bu xiang shi 不打不相識
it takes a fight for people to get to know each

身體 *Body*

other || by scratching and biting, cats and dogs come together; friends are often made after a fight; from an exchange of blows friendship grows; no discord, no concord; out of blows friendship grows;

bu da jin 不打緊

do not matter;

bu da zi zhao 不打自招

confess without being pressed || admit gratuitously; admit on one's own; be condemned out of one's own mouth; betray one's evil purpose through some indiscreet act or remarks; confess to a crime without being put on the grill; let the cat out of the bag without being pressed; make a confession without duress;

bu dao de 不道德

immoral / unethical;

bu de hao si 不得好死

die an unnatural death || die in one's boots; die in one's shoes; die with one's boots on; die with one's shoes on;

bu de qi fa 不得其法

do not know the right way to do sth;

bu de shan zhong 不得善終

may not die a natural death || impossible to acquire a peaceful end;

bu de ti 不得體

indecorous / infelicitous / uncomely // indecorum / infelicity;

bu de yao ling 不得要領

do not know what one is driving at || do not see the point of sth; fail to catch one's point; fail to grasp the main points; miss the main idea; miss the point; wide of the mark;

bu di 不敵

be defeated / no match for;

bu dong 不動

without any movement;

bu dong sheng se 不動聲色

without changing expression || display no sign of emotion; keep a straight face; keep one's countenance; keep one's feelings to oneself; keep one's peace and countenance; maintain one's composure; not to bat an eyelid; not to move a muscle; not to show one's feelings; not to turn a hair; shut one's pan; stay calm and collected; with a stiff upper lip; without batting an eyelash;

bu duan 不端

dishonorable / improper;

bu fa 不法

illegal / unlawful;

bu fan 不凡

exceptional / outstanding;

bu fei chui hui zhi li 不費吹灰之力

as easy as blowing off dust || able to do it on one's head; as easy as falling off a log; just a small effort; no skin off sb's nose; with minimum effort; without the least effort;

bu fei li 不費力

effortless // at an easy rate;

bu fen qin shu 不分親疏

regardless of relationship;

bu fen qing hong zao bai 不分青紅皂白

make no distinction between black and white / not to distinguish right and wrong // impetuous // indiscriminately;

bu fen shi fei 不分是非

confuse right and wrong / confuse truth and falsehood / fail to distinguish right from wrong;

bu fen xuan zhi 不分軒輊

equal / equally matched // on a par;

bu fen zao bai 不分皂白

make no distinction between right and wrong || indiscriminately; make no inquiries about the circumstances; unable to distinguish black from white; unable to distinguish right from wrong;

bu fu 不服

refuse to accept;

bu fu qi 不服氣

disobedient / recalcitrant / unwilling to submit;

bu fu shu 不服輸

refuse to concede defeat;

bu fu shui tu 不服水土

not acclimatized;

bu fu zhong wang 不孚眾望
fail to live up to public expectations / fall short of people's expectations || not popular with the people;

bu fu hou wang 不負厚望
live up to sb's great expectations / not to let sb down;

bu fu suo tuo 不負所託
merit sb's trust;

bu fu suo wang 不負所望
live up to expectations || answer one's expectation; come up to one's expectation; cut the buck; cut the mustard; deliver the goods; meet one's expectation; up to the mustard;

bu gan 不甘
not resigned to / unreconciled to / unwilling;

bu gan ci fu 不甘雌伏
unwilling to lie low;

bu gan hou ren 不甘後人
unwilling to lag behind || cannot bear playing second fiddle; hate to be outdone; not willing to let others outshine oneself; unwilling to take a back seat;

bu gan ji mo 不甘寂寞
hate to be neglected / hate to be overlooked;

bu gan luo hou 不甘落後
loathe to lag behind / unwilling to lag behind;

bu gan ren hou 不甘人後
unwilling to lag behind || desire to be second to none; hate to be outdone; not to reconcile oneself to falling behind; unwilling to yield to others;

bu gan shi ruo 不甘示弱
reluctant to show weakness || hate to show the white feather; refuse to admit being inferior; not to be outdone; unwilling to admit oneself outdone; unwilling to be outshone; unwilling to have one's weakness shown up;

bu gan 不敢
dare not;

bu gan bu cong 不敢不從
dare not disobey / dare not oppose;

bu gan bu fu 不敢不服
all the more ready to obey;

bu gan cong ming 不敢從命
I cannot do as you command me;

bu gan dang 不敢當
don't mention it / I really don't deserve this / you flatter me;

bu gan gao pan 不敢高攀
dare not aspire to sb's acquaintance / dare not aspire to sb's company;

bu gan gong wei 不敢恭維
cannot say much for;

bu gan gou tong 不敢苟同
beg to differ / cannot agree with sb;

bu gan hou ren 不敢後人
unwilling to fall behind others;

bu gan ling jiao 不敢領教
too bad to be accepted;

bu gan lüe mei 不敢掠美
can't claim credit due to others;

bu gan pang wu 不敢旁騖
dare not disperse one's attention;

bu gan shan mei 不敢擅美
dare not claim all credit to oneself;

bu gan wen jin 不敢問津
not dare to inquire || beyond the means of; dare not ask the way to the ford; dare not show any interest in;

bu gan yin man 不敢隱瞞
dare not conceal the truth;

bu gan yue lei chi yi bu 不敢越雷池一步
dare not go one step beyond the prescribed limit;

bu gan zao ci 不敢造次
dare not act rashly / not to venture;

bu gan 不幹
it's not acceptable / won't accept / won't do it;

bu gao er bie 不告而別
leave without saying goodbye / take French leave;

bu gao er qu 不告而去
leave without notice / leave without saying a

word / take French leave;

bu geng shi 不更事
inexperienced;

bu gong 不公
unfair / unjust;

bu gong 不恭
disrespectful;

bu gu fu ...qi wang 不辜負 ... 期望
live up to one's expectations || answer one's expectations; answer the expectations of sb; come up to one's expectations; come up to the expectations of sb; fulfil one's expectations; fulfil the expectations of sb; live up to the expectations of sb; meet one's expectations; meet the expectations of sb; not come short of one's expectations; not come short of the expectations of sb; not disappoint one's expectations; not disappoint the expectations of sb; not let sb down;

bu gu 不顧
without respect to || brush aside; in contempt of; in defiance of; in disregard of; in spite of; in the face of; in the teeth of; irrespective of; regardless of; with no respect to; without regard for; without regard to;

bu gu da ju 不顧大局
regardless of the whole situation || ignore the larger issues; lack of consideration for the whole; show no consideration for the general interest;

bu gu hou guo 不顧後果
give no heed to the consequences / reckless of the consequences;

bu gu qing mian 不顧情面
have no consideration for sb's feelings;

bu gu shi shi 不顧事實
ignore the facts || disregard facts; fly in the face of the facts; have no regard for the truth;

bu gu ta ren si huo 不顧他人死活
not to care whether live or die;

bu gu ti mian 不顧體面
regardless of reputation;

bu gu xin yi 不顧信義
guilty of bad faith;

bu gu yi qie 不顧一切
regardless of all consequences || desperately; neck or nothing; neck or nought; rain or shine; stick at nothing; stop at nothing; up hill and down dale;

bu guan tong yang 不關痛癢
a matter of no consequence || do not care a bit; have no compassion for others; insignificant; irrelevant; pointless; show no concern; without any bite;

bu guan xin 不關心
indifferent to / not concern oneself with;

bu guan cheng bai 不管成敗
sink or swim;

bu guan qing hong zao bai 不管青紅皂白
indiscriminately / irrespective of right or wrong / without finding out the truth;

bu guan san qi er shi yi 不管三七二十一
no matter how || casting all caution to the winds; chance the ducks; come what may; kill or cure; no matter what you may say; recklessly; regardless of the consequences;

bu guang cai 不光彩
inglorious;

bu hai xiu 不害羞
unabashed;

bu hao re 不好惹
not to be pushed around;

bu he shen 不合身
ill-fitting / unbecoming / unfitting;

bu he 不和
at odds with sb || at cross-purposes; at loggerheads with sb; at outs with sb; at sword's points with sb; at variance with sb; bad blood; get at cross-purposes; ill blood; not get along well; on bad terms;

bu he xie 不和諧
discord / disharmony / incompatibility;

bu huan er san 不歡而散
break up in disagreement || break up in discord; disperse with ill feelings; end in discord; end on an unpleasant note; part in dudgeon; part on bad terms;

bu ji qian xian 不計前嫌
wipe the slate clean;

bu jiang dao li 不講道理
impervious to reason / refuse to see reason // unreasonable;

bu jiang qing mian 不講情面
not to care to save the face of / without sparing anyone's sensibilities;

bu jiang xin yong 不講信用
not keep one's word;

bu jiao bu zao 不驕不躁
free from arrogance and rushness / guard against self-conceit and rushness / not proud or arrogant;

bu jin xi xing 不矜細行
pay no attention to trivial matters;

bu jing shi 不經事
inexperienced;

bu jing 不敬
disrespectful;

bu jiu ji wang 不咎既往
pardon sb for his past misdeeds;

bu ju li jie 不拘禮節
unceremonious;

bu ju xi su 不拘習俗
free from old customs and habits;

bu ju xiao jie 不拘小節
defy trivial conventions || neglect of minor points of conduct; not bother about small matters; not to stick at trifles;

bu juan 不倦
tireless;

bu ke jiu yao 不可救藥
incorrigible / incurable // beyond hope;

bu ke qi 不客氣
impolite;

bu ke yi shi 不可一世
be extremely arrogant;

bu ke zhong ri 不可終日
(1) be anxious throughout the day;
(2) in a desperate situation;

bu ke zhuo mo 不可捉摸
unpredictable;

bu lao er huo 不勞而獲
gain without effort;

bu li 不理
ignore / take no notice of || brush aside; pay no attention to; refuse to acknowledge; spurn; turn a deaf ear to; wave aside;

bu li bu cai 不理不睬
give sb the cold shoulder / ignore completely;

bu li cai 不理睬
turn a cold shoulder to sb || break with; brush off; close one's ears; cut sb dead; deaf to; fall on deaf ears; get shut of sb; get the go-by; give a cold shoulder to sb; give no heed to; give sb a brush; give sb the brush; give sb the cut direct; give sb the go-by; give the cold shoulder to sb; hide one's face from; ignore; leave sb alone; leave sb out in the cold; not give sb the time of day; pass by; pay no attention to; pay no heed to; see the back of sb; shut of sb; slam the door in sb's face; stop one's ears; spurn; take no heed of; take no notice of; turn a blind eye to; turn a deaf ear to; turn one's back on; turn one's blind eye to; turn the cold shoulder to sb; turn up one's nose at;

bu li hui 不理會
pay no attention to || inattentive; unmindful;

bu li 不力
go through the motions / work perfunctorily;

bu liao liao zhi 不了了之
end up with nothing definitive;

bu liu qing mian 不留情面
disregard to others' feelings or face;

bu lu feng mang 不露鋒芒
hide one's light under a bushel;

bu mai zhang 不賣賬
not go for it / not buy it;

bu man 不滿
discontent / disaffection / dissatisfaction;

bu mang 不忙
(1) take one's time;
(2) not in a hurry;

bu mian bu xiu 不眠不休
indefatigable / tireless / without rest;

bu mian zheng 不眠症
insomnia;

bu ming yi wen 不名一文
broke / on the rocks;

bu ming yu 不名譽
disreputable / scandalous;

bu mou er he 不謀而合
agree without prior consultation;

bu neng zi zhi 不能自制
have no control over oneself;

bu pa 不怕
not afraid;

bu pian bu dang 不偏不黨
fair to all / without wavering to one side or the other;

bu pian bu yi 不偏不依
(1) impartial ‖ avoid leaning to either side; even-handed; free from any bias; hold the scales even; not to take sides; not to throw one's weight either way; partial to one; show no partiality to either side; unbiased; without partiality;
(2) exact / just;

bu qiu wen da 不求聞達
do not seek fame or prestige;

bu qu 不屈
indefatigable / unbending / unyielding;

bu qu bu nao 不屈不撓
indefatigable / indomitable / unbending / unyielding;

bu qun 不群
outstanding;

bu ren dao 不人道
inhumane;

bu shan bu lü 不衫不履
dress slovenly;

bu shi da ti 不識大體
ignore the whole interest;

bu shi shi wu 不識時務
do not understand the times;

bu shi tai ju 不識擡舉
unappreciative;

bu shi 不適
ill / unwell;

bu shou ben fen 不守本份
fail to keep to one's own line / swerve from one's duty;

bu shou xin yong 不守信用
break one's promise ‖ back out; back out of one's promise; break faith with sb; break one's word; fail to keep a promise; fail to make good one's promise; forswear oneself; forsake oneself; go back from one's word; go back on one's word; go back upon one's word; not to keep one's word; worse than one's word;

bu shu fu 不舒服
feeling uncomfortable / feeling unwell / uncomfortable / unwell;

bu shu xi 不熟悉
unacquainted / unfamiliar with;

bu shuang 不爽
in a bad mood / out of sorts;

bu shuang kuai 不爽快
(1) not frank;
(2) out of sorts;

bu tan cheng 不坦誠
uncandid;

bu ting hua 不聽話
insubordinate;

bu xi guan 不習慣
unaccustomed;

bu xiang yang 不像樣
improper behaviour;

bu xiao 不孝
filial impiety / lack of filial piety // unfilial;

bu xing 不幸
infelicity / misfortune / mishap // infelicitous / misfortunate;

bu yan qi fan 不厭其煩
very patient // put oneself out;

bu yan qi xiang 不厭其詳
not to omit any detail;

bu yi yi li 不遺餘力
do one's utmost / spare no pains;

bu yong gong 不用功
not hardworking;

bu zai 不在
(1) dead / passed away;
(2) not in / out;

bu zai hu 不在乎
do not care / do not mind;

bu ze shou duan 不擇手段
stick at nothing // by fair means or foul;

bu zhang jin 不長進
good-for-nothing;

bu zhen 不貞
unchaste // infidelity;

bu zheng qi 不爭氣
let sb down;

bu zhi qu xiang 不知去向
disappear without a trace;

bu zhi si huo 不知死活
act recklessly and blindly;

bu zhi suo cuo 不知所措
at a loss / at a loss what to do;

bu zhi zi ai 不知自愛
act without self-respect;

bu zhi zi liang 不知自量
do sth beyond one's ability;

bu zhi zu 不知足
greedy / insatiable;

bu zhi 不治
die of illness despite treatment;

bu zhi zhi zheng 不治之症
incurable disease;

bu zi liang 不自量
overestimate one's abilities;

bu zi liang li 不自量力
kick against the pricks / overrate one's abilities / overreach oneself;

bu zi zai 不自在
feeling uneasy / feeling uncomfortable;

bu4 佈
(1) announce;
(2) arrange;

bu zhi 佈置
(1) make arrangements;
(2) decorate;

ca1 shen er guo 擦身而過
brush past / pass each other so close that they almost rub against each other;

ca zao 擦澡
rub oneself down with a wet towel;

cai2 de jian bei 才德兼備
have both talent and virtue;

cai fen 才分
natural talent;

cai gan 才幹
abilities / competence;

cai gao yi guang 才高意廣
have a brilliant mind and a broad vision;

cai hua 才華
talent;

cai hua chu zhong 才華出眾
of uncommon brilliance;

cai hua heng yi 才華橫溢
be full of coruscating wit / brim with talent / have superb talent;

cai lüe 才略
talent for scheming;

cai ming 才名
a reputation for talent;

cai neng 才能
abilities;

cai qi 才氣
brilliance / talent;

cai qi yang yi 才氣洋溢
brilliant intelligence;

cai shi 才識
ability and insight;

cai shu xue qian 才疏學淺
untalented and unlearned;

cai xue 才學
intelligence and scholarship;

cai2 jue 裁決
judge;

cai3 qu xing dong 採取行動
take action;

can1 參
(1) enter / join / take part in || get involved in; intervene;
(2) consult together / counsel / refer;
(3) collate / compare / consider;
(4) call to pay one's respect to / interview / visit;
(5) censure / impeach;
(6) recommend;

can bai 參拜
make a formal visit to || formally call on; pay a courtesy call; pay respects to;

can chan 參禪
practise meditation / try to reach understanding of Chan;

can guan 參觀
visit || inspect; look around; show around; show over; show round; watch; witness;

can guan xue xi 參觀學習
visit and learn from;

can guan you lan 參觀遊覽
go on a sightseeing tour / go sightseeing / visit places of interest;

can jia 參加
(1) attend / join / take part in || collaborate; enter; enter into; enter one's name for; enter oneself for; go in; go in for; have a hand in; join in; partake in; partake of; participate; participate in; present; present oneself for; show up; sit for; sit in;
(2) give advice;

can kao 參考
(1) collate / consult;
(2) examine and compare;
(3) read sth for reference / refer to;
(4) references;

can ye 參謁
(1) pay one's respects to sb;
(2) pay homage to sb;

can yu 參與
participate in / take part in || a party to; be active in; have a hand in; involve / involvement; join; partake; participation;

can yu qi shi 參與其事
be involved with sth || have a finger in the pie; have a hand in the matter; participate in an activity; take art and part in sth;

can zheng 參政
take part in politics || participate in government and political affairs; take part in government;

can zhuo 參酌
consider a matter in the light of actual conditions / consult and deliberate over / deliberate;

can2 bao 殘暴
brutal / cruel and heartless;

can hai 殘害
injure heartlessly / oppress cruelly;

can nian 殘年
the closing years of one's life / the evening of life;

can sha 殘殺
slaughter;

can3 si 慘死
die a tragic death / meet with a tragic death;

cang1 su 傖俗
vulgar;

cang1 lao 蒼老
hoary and old;

cang2 shen 藏身
go into hiding / hide oneself;

cang shen di 藏身地
lodging;

cang shen zhi chu 藏身之處
hiding place || a hole to conceal oneself in; a place to hide; a place to keep oneself out of sight; hideout;

cao3 cao 草草
carelessly / hastily;

cao cao liao shi 草草了事
dispose of a thing carelessly;

cao cao shou chang 草草收場
wind up the matter hastily;

cao shuai 草率
careless / perfunctory;

cao shuai cong shi 草率從事
do a job carelessly / do a job perfunctorily;

ce4 shen 側身
lean to one side // on one's side / sideways;

ce shen ai jin 側身挨近
incline near to / lean close to / side up to;

ce shui 側睡
sleep on the right / left ear;

ce wo 側臥
lie on the side;

cha1 插
insert / plant / take part in;

cha quan nong tao 插圈弄套
trap sb with tricks;

cha shen 插身
(1) edge in / squeeze in;
(2) get involved in / take part in;

cha shou gan yu 插手干預
interfere in / meddle and intervene in;

cha2 查
(1) check / examine / inspect;
(2) investigate / look into;
(3) consult / look up;

cha an 查案
investigate into a case;

cha ban 查辦
investigate and deal with accordingly;

cha chao 查抄
make an inventory of a criminal's possessions and confiscate them;

cha chu 查處
investigate and treat;

cha chu 查出
ferret out / trace;

cha dian 查點
check the amount of sth / check the number of sth / make an inventory of;

cha dui 查對
check / check off / verify;

cha dui wu wu 查對無誤
examine and find it correct;

cha fang 查房
make the rounds of the wards // ward rounds;

cha fang 查訪
go around and make inquiries / investigate;

cha feng 查封
close down / seal up;

cha ge shui le shi chu 查個水落石出
get to the botton of a matter / investiage sth thoroughly;

cha gen wen di 查根問底
investigate thoroughly;

cha he 查核
check;

cha he wu e 查核無訛
audited and found correct;

cha huo 查獲
discover and seize / ferret out / hunt down and seize / track down;

cha ji zou si 查緝走私
prevent and counter smuggling;

cha jin 查禁
ban / prohibit / put a ban on;

cha jiu 查究
investigate and ascertain;

cha jiu ze ren 查究責任
find out who should be held responsible;

cha kan 查勘
(1) explore;
(2) prospect / survey;

cha kao 查考
do research on / examine / try to ascertain;

cha kou 查扣
seize and hold in custody;

cha ming 查明
ascertain / find out / prove through investigation;

cha ming shu shi 查明屬實
prove to be true after investigation;

cha ming zhen xiang 查明真相
ascertain the facts / find out the truth;

cha piao 查票
check tickets / examine tickets;

cha po 查破
break a criminal case / investigate and unearth;

cha qi 查訖
checked;

cha qing 查清
check up on / make a thorough investigation of;

cha san wen si 查三問四
investigate thorough / make a wide-range investigation;

cha shi 查實
investigate and verify;

cha shou 查收
(1) find sth enclosed;
(2) check and accept;

cha ti 查體
physical examination;

cha wu shi ju 查無實據
no evidence is found after a thorough investigation;

cha yan 查驗
check / examine;

cha yue 查閱
consult / look up;

cha zhang 查帳
audit / audit accounts / check accounts / examine accounts;

cha zhao 查找
search out;

cha zhao 查照
note;

cha zheng 查證
check and testify / investigate and verify;

cha zheng shu shi 查證屬實
be checked and found to be true / be verified;

cha2 lai shen shou, fan lai zhang kou 茶來伸手，飯來張口
have a living without doing any work / live off without doing any work;

cha2 察
examine / look into / scrutinize;

cha ban 察辦
investigate a case and determine how to handle it;

cha fang 察訪
go about to find out / go around and make inquiries / investigate / make calls and investigate;

cha jue 察覺
be conscious of / become aware / perceive;

cha kan 察勘
examine / survey;

cha qi yan, guan qi xing 察其言，觀其行
check what one says against what one does / examine one's words and watch one's deeds / observe one's speech and behaviour;

chai1 拆
(1) take apart / tear down / tear open;
(2) analyze / scrutinize;

chai che 拆車
disassemble a car;

chai chu 拆除
demolish / dismantle / dismount / remove;

chai chu zhang ai wu 拆除障礙物
remove obstacles;

chai chu pian ju 拆除騙局
expose a fraud;

chai chuan huang yan 拆穿謊言
nail a lie / nail a lie to the counter;

chai chuan xi yang jing 拆穿西洋鏡
expose sb's tricks ‖ give away the show; give the show away; nail a lie; strip off the camouflage;

chai hui 拆毀
dismantle ‖ break down; demolish; destroy; knock down; tear down;

chai huo 拆伙
disband / dissolve a partnership / part company;

chai jian 拆建
dismantle and build / tear down and build;

chai kai 拆開
take apart ‖ break up; decollate; disconnect; open; separate; unpack;

chai ling 拆零
take apart and sell separately;

chai qian 拆遷
move a building to a new site / relocate after demolition;

chai qiang jiao 拆墻脚
pull away a prop / undermine;

chai san 拆散
break up;

chai tai 拆台
cut the ground from under sb's feet || cut the grass from under sb's feet; pull away a prop; pull the rug out from under;

chai xin 拆信
open a letter;

chai zhuang 拆裝
disassemble and reassemble;

chai1 差
dispatch / send on an errand;

chai lai chai qu 差來差去
order sb about;

chai lü 差旅
travel on official business;

chai qian 差遣
assign / dispatch / send sb on an errand;

chai wei 差委
appoint;

chan2 孱
feeble / frail / weak;

chan ruo 孱弱
delicate / frail / weak;

chan2 嬋
attractive / beautiful / graceful / pretty;

chan yuan 嬋媛
beautiful and graceful;

chan3 產
(1) be delivered of / give birth to;
(2) bring about / produce / yield;
(3) product;

chan sheng 產生
produce || come into being; emerge; engender;

chan4 顫
quiver / shake / tremble / vibrate;

chan chu 顫搐
twitch;

chan chu xing shou suo 顫搐性收縮
twitch contraction;

chan dong 顫動
quiver / vibrate;

chan dou 顫抖
shiver || quake; quiver; shake; shudder; tremble // tremulous // tremor;

chan dou bing 顫抖病
kuru;

chang2 mian 長眠
(1) die;
(2) death / eternal sleep;

chang mian bu qi 長眠不起
sleep the final sleep;

chang mian bu xing 長眠不醒
die;

chang mian di xia 長眠地下
dead and buried / sleep eternally underground;

chang ming 長命
long life / longevity;

chang ming bai sui 長命百歲
live to a ripe old age / live to be a hundred // a life of a hundred years / many happy returns of the day;

chang ming fu gui 長命富貴
a long life of abundance and respectability / longevity with wealth and honour;

chang sheng 長生
long life / longevity;

chang sheng bu lao 長生不老
live forever and never grow old || alive forever more; enjoy a long, long life without old age; live forever without getting old; never get old but live forever; perpetual rejuvenation;

chang shou 長壽
long life / longevity;

chang xiang si shou 長相廝守
keep each other company for life / stay married forever;

chang2 shi 嘗試
attempt / have a crack at / have a go at / make an effort / make an endeavour / take a crack at / try / venture;

chang2 ming 償命
a life for a life / pay with one's life;

chao1 qun 超群
head and shoulders above all others / preeminent / surpassing all others;

chao qun chu zhong 超群出眾
cut a conspicuous figure / rise above the herd;

chao qun jue lun 超群絕倫
far above the ordinary / far surpassing one's fellows / outshine all others / unequalled by contemporaries;

chao ran 超然
aloof / detached;

chao ran jue su 超然絕俗
stand aloof from the crowd;

chao ran shi shi 超然世事
hold aloof from the affairs of human life;

chao ran wu wai 超然物外
above worldly considerations / hold aloof from the world / stay away from the scene of contention;

chao sheng 超生
excuse from death / spare life;

chao tuo 超脱
(1) original / unconventional;
(2) detached // stand aloof / transcend worldliness;

chao tuo chen shi 超脱塵世
above worldly considerations / be detached from the world / stand aloof from this mortal life;

che3 pi 扯皮
pass the buck / shift responsibility to other people;

che4 撤
clear away / evacuate / remove / retreat / take away / take back / withdraw;

che chu 撤除
abolish / dismantle / do away with / remove;

che hui 撤回
take back / withdraw;

che qu 撤去
pull out / remove / withdraw;

che xiao 撤銷
abolish / do away with;

che zhi 撤職
remove from office;

chen2 bu zhu qi 沈不住氣
lose one's cool || blow one's cool; can hardly hold back; cannot remain calm;

chen de zhu qi 沈得住氣
keep one's composure;

chen mi 沈迷
indulge / wallow;

chen mi bu wu 沈迷不悟
indulge in error / refuse to come to one's senses;

chen mi bu xing 沈迷不醒
(1) be deeply addicted / be infatuated with;
(2) in a coma;

chen mian 沈緬
be given to / wallow in;

chen mian jiu se 沈緬酒色
be given to heavy drinking and sensual pleasures / indulge in wine and women / wallow in voluptuousness;

chen zhuo 沈着
calm / composed / cool-headed / steady;

chen zhuo guo gan 沈着果敢
iron nerves / nerves of iron / nerves of steel / steel nerves;

chen zhuo ji ling 沈着機靈
composed and smart / cool and clear;

chen zhuo ying bian 沈着應變
meet the danger calmly;

chen zhuo ying zhan 沈着應戰
accept a challenge composurely / meet the attack calmly;

chen zhuo zhen ding 沈着鎮定
sedate // presence of mind;

chen2 bing 陳病
chronic disease / old disease;

chen2 諶
candid / honest / sincere;

chen4 bian 趁便
take advantage of;

chen ji hui 趁機會
take advantage of an opportunity;

chen kong 趁空
avail oneself of leisure;

chen ren zhi wei 趁人之危
take advantage of others' weakness;

chen shi 趁食
make a living;

chen shi hou 趁時候
take advantage of the chance;

chen shi 趁勢
take advantage of the prevailing circumstances;

chen4 稱
fit / match / suit;

chen shen 稱身
fit;

chen ti cai yi 稱體裁衣
fit the dress to the figure;

cheng1 撐
(1) prop / support;
(2) keep up / maintain;

cheng bu zhu 撐不住
too weak to support;

cheng chang mian 撐場面
keep up appearances;

cheng chi 撐持
prop up / store up / sustain;

cheng de zhu 撐得住
strong enough to prop up;

cheng kai 撐開
prop open;

cheng qi lai 撐起來
prop up;

cheng zhu 撐住
prop from under;

cheng2 hun 成婚
get married;

cheng huo 成活
survive;

cheng jia 成家
have a family;

cheng jia li ye 成家立業
get married and start a career;

cheng jiu 成就
accomplishment / achievement;

cheng ming 成名
become famous / make a name for oneself / make one's mark / make one's name;

cheng nian xing fei pang 成年型肥胖
adult-onset obesity;

cheng qi 成器
become a useful person;

cheng qin 成親
get married;

cheng ren 成人
adult;

cheng zhang 成長
grow to maturity / grow up;

cheng2 乘
(1) ride;
(2) avail oneself of / take advantage of;

cheng liang 乘涼
cool oneself in the breeze / cool oneself in the shade / enjoy the cool air / relax in a cool place;

cheng2 dan 承擔
shoulder (responsibilities);

cheng2 fu 誠服
obey willingly / submit willingly;

chi1 bi men geng 吃閉門羹
be denied entrance || be left out in the cold; find the door slammed in sb's face; on the wrong side of the door; slam the door in sb's

face;

chi bu bao chuan bu nuan 吃不飽穿不暖
not have enough food and clothing || hardly able to keep body and soul together; lead a life of privation;

chi bu kai 吃不開
unpopular || not in the current demand; will not succeed; won't work;

chi bu xiao 吃不消
be too much for sb to do sth / more than one can bear / unable to stand;

chi bu zhu 吃不住
unable to bear or support;

chi de kai 吃得開
have a lot of pull || have a big drag with; make one's mark; much sought after; popular;

chi de ku zhong ku, fang wei ren shang ren 吃得苦中苦，方為人上人。
those who can bear the bitterness of hardship can then be a person above others || hardship increases stature; only after knowing real suffering can one have greater achievements than others;

chi dou fu 吃豆腐
flirt with a woman / take liberties with a woman;

chi he wan le 吃喝玩樂
eat, drink and make merry // convivial;

chi ku 吃苦
bear hardships;

chi ku nai lao 吃苦耐勞
hardworking and able to bear hardships || bear hardships and stand hard work; inured to hardships; work hard and endure hardship;

chi ku tou 吃苦頭
burn one's fingers / cost sb dear / cost sb dearly / get the works / run the gauntlet / suffer // to one's cost;

chi kui 吃虧
(1) get a beating || come to grief; get the worst of it; suffer losses; take a beating;
(2) at a disadvantage / in an unfavourable situation;

chi kui shang dang 吃虧上當
be fooled and get into trouble / have suffered and have been deceived;

chi lao ben 吃老本
rest on one's laurels || live off one's past gains; live on one's own fat; rest on past achievements;

chi li pa wai 吃裏爬外
live off one person while secretly helping another — work for the interest of an opposing group at the expense of one's own;

chi li 吃力
entail strenuous effort // laborious;

chi li bu tao hao 吃力不討好
do a hard but thankless job || a fool for one's pain; a thankless job; dirty work;

chi li gong zuo 吃力工作
wade through;

chi xian fan 吃閒飯
(1) lead an idle life / live in idleness;
(2) loafer / sponger;

chi xian cheng 吃現成
reap the profit;

chi xiang 吃香
be much sought after / find favour with sb / very popular / well-liked;

chi xiao kui zhan da pian yi 吃小虧佔大便宜
lose a little and gain much || take small losses for the sake of big gains; throw a sprat a catch a mackerel; venture a small fish to catch a great one;

chi ya ba kui 吃啞巴虧
be cheated but unable to talk about it || be forced to keep one's grievances to oneself; be unable to speak out about one's grievances; suffer a loss but unable to speak out;

chi yan qian kui 吃眼前虧
accept a present loss / suffer loss under one's nose;

chi yi qian, zhang yi zhi 吃一塹，長一智
a fall into the pit, a gain in your wit || adversity is a great schoolmaster; adversity is the school of wisdom; each time one takes a loss, one gains knowledge; experience bought by suffering teaches wisdom; experience is the mother of wisdom; experience must be bought; experience

teaches; I know it to my cost; learn from experience;

chi1 媸
ugly;

chi1 fei 痴肥
abnormally fat / obese;

chi2 持
(1) maintain / support;
(2) manage / run;
(3) oppose;

chi ai zhi yan 持愛直言
grasping your love for me, I take leave to speak without reservation;

chi jia 持家
keep house / run one's home;

chi jia you fang 持家有方
keep house in the right way / manage the affairs of the family methodically / run one's house with the proper method;

chi ping 持平
fair / unbiased;

chi shen 持身
conduct oneself;

chi shen she shi 持身涉世
exercise proper restraints in dealing with the world / maintain proper conduct in treading through the world;

chi shen yan zheng 持身嚴正
very exacting with regard to one's personal conduct;

chi wei fu qing 持危扶傾
(1) act as a champion of justice / uphold the tottering and support the falling;
(2) hold;

chi zhi yi heng 持之以恒
keep on with perseverence || have perseverance; keep it up; peg away at; persevere; perseveringly; stick to it;

chi zhi you gu 持之有故
have grounds for one's views / well-founded;

chi zhong 持重
prudent / cautious / dignified / discreet;

chi zhong lao cheng 持重老成
prudent and experienced;

chi3 ru 恥辱
disgrace / humiliation / ignominy / shame;

chi4 luo 赤裸
naked || in one's birthday suit; stark naked; without a stitch of clothing;

chi luo luo 赤裸裸
(1) naked as a jaybird / nude / stark-naked // in a state of nature / without a stitch of clothing;
(2) out-and-out / unadorned / undisguised;

chi shen 赤身
naked / nude;

chi shen lu ti 赤身露體
naked || as naked as my mother bore me; in a state of nature; in one's bare skin; in the raw; nature's garb; not wearing a stitch; without a piece of clothing;

chi shen luo ti 赤身裸體
naked || have not a stitch on; in a state of nature; in one's birth suit; in the buff; in the nude; nude; stark naked; to the raw;

chi tiao jing guang 赤條精光
completely naked / naked as a jaybird / stark naked / unclothed // in a state of nature / in the nude / without a shred of clothing on;

chi tiao tiao 赤條條
completely naked / naked as a jaybird / stark naked / unclothed // in a state of nature / without a shred of clothing on;

chi4 cha 飭查
order an investigation;

chi li 飭厲
exhort / instruct and encourage;

chi ling 飭令
direct / instruct / order;

chi na 飭拿
give orders for the arrest of;

chi zhi 飭知
inform a subordinate;

chong1 充
pretend;

chong dang 充當
act as / play the part of / serve as;

chong hao han 充好漢
play the hero;

chong1 chu 衝出
dash out / fight a way out / rush out;

chong ji 衝激
offend;

chong jin 衝進
burst in / rush in;

chong jue 衝決
burst open;

chong kua 衝垮
break down / burst / shatter;

chong po 衝破
breach / break through / smash;

chong ru 衝入
rush into;

chong san 衝散
break up / disperse;

chong xiang 衝向
run at;

chong xiao 衝霄
shoot up to the sky;

chong zhuang 衝撞
(1) collide;
(2) offend;

chong2 xin zhen zuo 重新振作
pull oneself together;

chong xin zuo ren 重新做人
begin one's life anew / start one's life afresh || lead a new life; make a fresh start in life; start with a new slate; turn over a new leaf;

chong xiu 重修
(1) rebuild / renovate;
(2) retake a course after failing to pass examination;

chong xiu jiu hao 重修舊好
become reconciled || bury the hatchet; make friends again; renew cordial relations;

chong xu jiu qing 重修舊情
renew one's acquaintance with / renew one's friendship / talk over old times;

chong2 bai 崇拜
adore / idolize / worship;

chong feng 崇奉
worship;

chong jing 崇敬
honour / regard with esteem / revere;

chong xin 崇信
worship;

chong3 ru 寵辱
favours and humiliation;

chou1 抽
(1) take out;
(2) take;
(3) put forth;
(4) obtain by drawing;
(5) shrink;
(6) lash / thrash / whip;

chou bu kai shen 抽不開身
cannot leave to do sth else;

chou cha 抽查
selective examination / spot check;

chou chou 抽抽
shrink;

chou chu 抽出
draw out / extract / select from a lot / withdraw;

chou da 抽打
(1) flog / lash / slash / thrash / whip;
(2) remove dust with a towel;

chou diao 抽調
transfer;

chou fei bu shou 抽肥補瘦
take from those with much and give to those with little || take from the fat to pad the lean; take from those who have too much and give to those who have too little;

chou kong 抽空
manage to find time;

chou kong tou xian 抽空偷閒
spare a few moments from work / take

身體 *Body*

advantage of any free time;

chou li 抽立
lose money;

chou shen 抽身
get away / leave one's work;

chou shen yin tui 抽身引退
leave one's work and resign || retire from active public life; withdraw from one's post;

chou zhi 抽脂
liposuction;

chou2 da 酬答
(1) thank sb with a gift;
(2) respond with a poem or speech;

chou da en de 酬答恩德
requite gratitde;

chou xie 酬謝
thank sb with a gift;

chou ying 酬應
have social intercourses with / social intercourse;

chou zuo 酬酢
(1) drink toasts to each other / exchange of toasts;
(2) have social intercourses with / treat with courtesy;

chou2 籌
plan / prepare;

chou ban 籌辦
make arrangements / make preparations / organize;

chou bei 籌備
make arrangements / make preparations || on the anvil; plan; prepare; upon the anvil;

chou cuo 籌措
raise money;

chou hua 籌劃
plan and prepare;

chou ji 籌集
raise money;

chou jian 籌建
prepare and establish / prepare to construct;

chou kuan 籌款
raise funds;

chou mou 籌謀
plan and prepare;

chou mu 籌募
collect funds;

chou shang 籌商
consult / discuss;

chou shang dui ce 籌商對策
discuss what counter-measures to take;

chou suan 籌算
count;

chou zu 籌組
plan and organize;

chou2 sha 讎殺
kill from hatred;

chou3 醜
disgraceful / scandalous / shameful;

chou hua 醜化
defame / smear / uglify / vilify;

chou tai 醜態
buffoonery / ugly performance;

chou tai bai chu 醜態百出
act like a buffoon / behave in a revolting manner / cut a contemptible figure;

chou4 臭
(1) disgraceful / disgusting;
(2) stupid;
(3) bad / inferior;
(4) disappointing;

chou da fen 臭大糞
low-grade / no good / stupid;

chou fu 臭腐
stinking and rotten;

chou mei 臭美
(1) beautify / dress up / make up;
(2) be stuck on oneself / give oneself airs // swell-headed;

chou mei niu 臭美妞
fussy about her appearance;

chou ming 臭名
ill fame / infamy / notorious reputation;

chou ming yuan bo 臭名遠播
infamous / notorious;

chou ming zhao zhu 臭名昭着
infamous / notorious / of ill repute // have an infamous character // foul reputation;

chou pi nang 臭皮囊
vile skin bag — the human body;

chou wei xiang tou 臭味相投
birds of a feather / two of a kind;

chu1 出
(1) come out / go out;
(2) exceed / go beyond;
(3) give / issue / offer / put up;
(4) produce / turn out;
(5) arise / happen / occur / take place;
(6) put forth / vent;
(7) rise well;
(8) expend / pay out;

chu ben 出奔
flee / leave / run away / take flight;

chu bin 出殯
carry a coffin to the cemetery / hold a funeral procession;

chu bing 出兵
dispatch troops / send an army into battle;

chu cai er 出彩兒
make a good show || brilliant; do brilliant things; exciting; put on a good play; splendid;

chu cai 出菜
achieve sth / make sth / produce a product;

chu cao 出操
go out to do exercises;

chu cha cuo 出差錯
go amiss / slip up;

chu cha zi 出岔子
run into trouble || go off the rails; go wrong; lead to no good; miss one's tip;

chu chai 出差
away on official business / on a business trip;

chu chan 出產
manufacture / produce;

chu chang 出場
(1) appear on the scene / come on the stage;
(2) enter;

chu chou 出醜
bring shame on oneself / make a fool of oneself;

chu chu jin jin 出出進進
coming and going;

chu cuo 出錯
make mistakes;

chu dong 出動
(1) set out / start off;
(2) call out / dispatch / send out;

chu er fan er 出爾反爾
go back on one's word || blow hot and cold; break one's word; contradict oneself; play fast and loose;

chu fa 出發
depart / take to the road;

chu fang 出訪
go abroad to visit / visit a foreign country;

chu feng tou 出風頭
be in the limelight || cut a dash; cut a smart figure; cut a swath; hold the limelight; in the spotlight; push oneself forward; seek the limelight; show off; steal the limelight;

chu ge 出格
(1) go too far || exceed proper limits for speech or action; exceed what is proper; overdo sth;
(2) differ from others // out of the ordinary;

chu ge 出閣
get married / marry;

chu gong 出工
(1) go to work || set out for work; show up for work; turn out for work;
(2) supply the labour;

chu gu zhang 出故障
go out of order / malfunctioning;

chu guai lu chou 出乖露丑
cut a very miserable figure / make a sight of oneself / make a spectacle of oneself;

chu gui 出軌
(1) be derailed / go off the rails / jump the rails;
(2) overstep the bounds;

chu guo 出國

go abroad / leave one's native land;

chu guo shen zao 出國深造

go abroad to further one's education || be sent to other countries for advanced studies; go abroad to continue one's studies;

chu hai 出海

go to sea / put out to sea;

chu hang 出航

(1) set out on a voyage / set sail;

(2) set out on a flight / take off;

chu hua er 出花儿

suffer from chicken pox;

chu huo 出活

yield results in work;

chu jia 出家

become a monk or a nun;

chu jia gui yi 出家皈依

give up one's home and practise religion;

chu jia 出價

bid / offer a price;

chu jia 出嫁

get married / marry;

chu jiang ru xiang 出將入相

as good a general as a minister;

chu jing 出境

emigrate || depart; exit; leave the country;

chu jing 出鏡

come on the camera / play a role in a film;

chu lai 出來

come out / emerge;

chu lei ba cui 出類拔萃

among the select best || cap all; distinguished from one's kind; far above the average; fill the bill; out of the common run; outstanding; pre-eminent; rise above the common herd; stand above the rest; stand out from one's fellows; stand out in the crowd; stand out from the rest; stand out in the crowd; stick out; top all of the others; tower above the rest; tower over;

chu li 出力

devote one's effort to / exert oneself || exert one's efforts; make great efforts; put forth one's strength;

chu li bu tao hao 出力不討好

do a thankless task;

chu liu 出溜

(1) slide / slip;

(2) degenerate / go downhill / sink low;

chu long 出籠

(1) come out of the steamer;

(2) appear / come forth / come out into the open;

chu lou zi 出漏子

blunder // in trouble;

chu luan zi 出亂子

get into trouble / go wrong;

chu luo 出落

grow prettier;

chu ma 出馬

go into action / take the field / take up a matter;

chu mai 出賣

barter away / betray / sell out;

chu mai ling hun 出賣靈魂

sell one's soul to;

chu mai peng you 出賣朋友

sell sb down the river / sell the pass;

chu mai yuan ze 出賣原則

barter away principles;

chu mai zi ji 出賣自己

sell oneself;

chu mao bing 出毛病

go out of order // out of order;

chu men 出門

go out / go on a journey // away from home;

chu men kan tian se, jin men guan lian se 出門看天色，進門觀臉色

look at a person's face when you step in / look at the weather when you step out;

chu men ying ya 出門迎迓

come out to greet sb at the gate / meet sb at the gate / step out to welcome sb / welcome sb at the gate;

chu mian 出面
act as / act in one's own capacity / appear personally / come forward;

chu ming 出名
famous || make a name for oneself; make one's mark; make one's name; renown; to a proverb; well-known; win a name for oneself;

chu mo 出沒
appear and disappear / haunt;

chu mo wu chang 出沒無常
come and go unexpectedly || appear at intervals; appear and disappear unexpectedly;

chu mo xian ce 出謀獻策
give advice and suggestions / offer advice;

chu nan ti 出難題
pose a difficult problem / set difficult questions / set sb a very difficult task;

chu pin 出品
make / manufacture / produce;

chu qi bu bei 出其不備
before one is prepared / catch one off guard / take one unaware;

chu qi bu yi 出其不意
take sb by surprise || all of a sudden; be taken unawares; catch sb napping; catch sb unawares; catch sb with his pants down; off one's guard; surprise sb; with one's pants down;

chu qi bu yi, gong qi wu bei 出其不意，攻其無備
do the unexpected, attack the unprepared || catch a weasel asleep; catch sb unprepared;

chu qi 出奇
extraordinarily / unusually;

chu qi zhi sheng 出奇制勝
win by means of a surprise attack || achieve success with original ideas; defeat one's opponent by a surprise move; defeat one's opponent by surprise tactics; win by novelty;

chu qi 出氣
blow off steam / give vent to one's anger / let off steam / vent one's spleen;

chu qi tong 出氣筒
take it out on sb;

chu qian 出錢
open one's purse;

chu qin 出勤
(1) turn out for work;
(2) out on duty;

chu qu 出去
get out / go out / pass out;

chu que 出缺
fall vacant;

chu rang 出讓
sell;

chu ren tou di 出人頭地
come to the fore || fill the bill; head and shoulders above others; make one's mark; put oneself on the map; rise head and shoulders above others; stand out among one's fellows;

chu ren yi biao 出人意表
to one's surprise || beyond all expectations; beyond one's expectation; come as a surprise; contrary to one's expections; exceeding all expectations;

chu ren 出任
take up the post of;

chu ru 出入
come in and go out / go out and come in;

chu ru xian heng 出入咸亨
abroad or at home || successful in everything;

chu ru xiang di 出入相抵
keep expenses within one's income / live within one's means / make both ends meet;

chu ru xiang you 出入相友
look for friends when one comes in and goes out — mutual help among the neighbours;

chu sai 出賽
compete / play in a match;

chu sang song bin 出喪送殯
follow the coffin on foot in the funeral procession;

chu se 出色
outstanding / remarkable / splendid;

chu shen 出身
(1) one's class origin / one's family background;

(2) one's previous experience / one's previous occupation;
(3) come from / rise from;

chu shen bei jian 出身卑賤
low-born;

chu shen fu gui 出身富貴
be born into wealth / be born with a silver spoon in one's mouth;

chu shen han jian 出身寒賤
come from humble origins || be born on the wrong side of the tracks; emerge from obscurity; of humble origins; rise from the gutter;

chu shen han men 出身寒門
come from humble origins || come from a humble home; of humble origins; of mean birth; rise from obscurity;

chu shen ming men 出身名門
be born in the purple || be sprung from noble ancestors; come out of the top drawer; from the top drawer; of good station;

chu shen qing bai 出身清白
one's family background is clear and clean;

chu shen wei han 出身微寒
be born of low extraction;

chu shen wei jian 出身微賤
a person of obscurity || one's origin is ignoble; rise from humble beginnings; rise from obscurity;

chu shen xian gui 出身顯貴
born into the purple;

chu shen yu 出身於
be born into || be born to; belong by birth to; come from; come of; descend from; spring from; stem from;

chu shen ru hua 出神入化
reach the acme of perfection || become spiritualized; miraculous; superb;

chu sheng 出生
be born || be sent into the world; come into the world; see the light of day;

chu sheng hou fa yu 出生後發育
postnatal development;

chu sheng qian fa yu 出生前發育
prenatal development;

chu sheng ru si 出生入死
at the risk of one's life || at the risk of life and limb; brave countless dangers; brave untold dangers; carry one's life in one's hands; defy all kinds of perils; go through fire and water; risk one's life; run the risk of life and disregard one's own safety;

chu shi 出師
(1) finish one's apprenticeship;
(2) dispatch troops to fight / send out an army;

chu shi bu li 出師不利
start off on the wrong foot || a bad beginning; be rebuffed in the first encounter; be thwarted at the very beginning; begin at the wrong side; get off on the wrong foot;

chu shi shun li 出師順利
get off on the right foot || without a hitch in the first encounter;

chu shi 出使
be sent on a diplomatic mission / serve as an envoy abroad;

chu shi 出示
produce / show;

chu shi 出世
(1) be born / come into the world;
(2) be produced / come into being;
(3) renounce the world / stand aloof from worldly affairs;

chu shi 出仕
become an official;

chu shi 出事
have an accident / meet with a mishap;

chu shou 出手
(1) dispose of / get off one's hands / sell;
(2) skills displayed in making opening moves;

chu shou 出售
sell || auction off sth; close out sth; for sale; offer for sale; on offer; on sale; on the block; on the market; put sth on the market; put sth up for auction; put sth up for sale; sell off sth;

chu shuang ru dui 出雙入對
go places together as a couple / go with each other all the time as lovers;

chu shui fu rong 出水芙蓉
pretty girl;

chu tan er 出攤兒
do business / set up a stall;

chu tao 出逃
escape / flee / run away;

chu ti 出題
(1) set a question || assign a topic; set a theme;
(2) make out questions;

chu ting 出庭
appear in court || before the court; enter an appearance;

chu tou 出頭
(1) lift one's head || free oneself; see daylight;
(2) appear in public / come forward;

chu tou lu jiao 出頭露角
come up in the world;

chu tou lu mian 出頭露面
appear in public || in the limelight; show oneself; show one's head;

chu tou zhi ri 出頭之日
have one's day;

chu tu 出土
(1) be excavated / be unearthed;
(2) come up / come up out of the ground;

chu tuo 出脫
(1) dispose of / manage to sell;
(2) grow prettier;
(3) absolve / acquit;

chu wai 出外
leave for another town;

chu xi 出席
attend / be present;

chu xi 出息
future / promise / prospects;

chu xian 出險
(1) get out of danger;
(2) be in danger / be threatened;

chu xian 出現
appear || appear on the scene; arise; come along; come into being; come on the scene; emerge; enter on the scene;

chu xue xing deng ge re 出血性登革熱
hemorrhagic dengue;

chu xue xing nang zhong 出血性囊腫
hmorrhagic cyst;

chu xue xing tian hua 出血性天花
hemorrhagic smallpox;

chu yang 出洋
go abroad;

chu yang xiang 出洋相
make a spectacle of oneself || cut a sorry figure; cut up; lay an egg; make a fool of oneself; make a money of; make a show of oneself; make a sight of oneself; make an ass of oneself; make an exhibition of oneself; make sb a laughing stock for all; play the fool; play the monkey; show up; wear the cap and bells;

chu you 出游
go on a tour;

chu yu 出於
due to / out of // proceed from / stem from;

chu yu wu nai 出於無奈
as it cannot be helped || no other course was open to sb; only because one can do no better; out of sheer necessity; there being no alternative;

chu yu wu zhi 出於無知
out of ignorance;

chu yu yi wai 出於意外
contrary to expectation || against one's expectation; out of one's reckoning;

chu yu zi yuan 出於自願
of one's own accord || by choice; by one's own volition; of one's free will; on a voluntary basis;

chu yu 出獄
be discharged from prison / be released from prison;

chu yuan 出院
leave hospital;

chu zhen 出診
make a house call / pay a home visit / visit a patient at home;

chu zhen 出陣
(1) go forth into battle;
(2) take part in an athletic contest;

chu zheng 出徵
go on an expedition / go out to battle;

chu zhong 出眾
out of the ordinary / outstanding;

chu zi fei fu 出自肺腑
from the depths of one's heart / straight from the heart;

chu zou 出走
flee / leave / run away;

chu zuo ru xi 出作入息
begin work at dawn and stop at dusk;

chu1 qi shi mian 初期失眠
initial insomnia;

chu2 除
eliminate / get rid of / remove;

chu bao an liang 除暴安良
weed out the tyrant and let people live in peace || champion the good and kill tyrants; drive out the rascals and protect the people; eliminate the evil and give peace to the good people; get rid of bullies and bring peace to good people; get rid of evil and give peace to the good; get rid of the cruel and pacify the good people; kill tyrants and champion the good people; remove despots and help the good people; run down the people's oppressors; weed out the wicked and let the law-abiding critizens live in peace;

chu gen 除根
(1) dig up the roots / grub / root out;
(2) cure once and for all / eradicate;

chu hai an liang 除害安良
remove the evil and quiet the good;

chu hai mie bing 除害滅病
wipe out pests and disease;

chu xie qu e 除邪驅惡
remove noxious influences and get rid of evil;

chu3 處
(1) get along;
(2) be situated in / in a certain condition;
(3) deal with / handle / manage;
(4) punish / sentence;

chu bian bu jing 處變不驚
with presence of mind in the face of disasters;

chu fa 處罰
penalize / punish;

chu fang 處方
prescribe / write out a prescription;

chu fen 處分
punish / take disciplinary action against;

chu ji wei ren 處己為人
put oneself in the place of others;

chu jing 處境
the circumstances one finds oneself in || plight; unfavourable situation;

chu jing gan ga 處境尷尬
in an awkward situation || be awkwardly situated; be hard put to it; in a dilemma; in a pickle; in an awkward position; in dead lumber; in difficulties; in Queer Street;

chu jing kun nan 處境困難
in an awkward predicament || hard up against it; in a difficult situation; in a predicament; in a scrape; in a sorry plight; in a spot; in a tight place; in the soup; live in difficult circumstances;

chu jing wei xian 處境危險
in a dangerous position || out on a limb; skate on the thin ice; touch and go;

chu jing xian e 處境險惡
in a perilous position;

chu jing xiang tong 處境相同
in the same boat / in the same box;

chu jue 處決
execute / put to death;

chu li 處理
address / deal with / dispose of / handle;

chu li bu dang 處理不當
mishandle / mismanage / not to handle properly;

chu li bu shan 處理不善
mishandle / mismanage / not to handle properly;

chu li cong kuan 處理從寬
be treated with leniency / lenient in handling the cases / lenient in measures;

chu li de dang 處理得當
deal with sth properly / run affairs in an appropriate way;

chu si 處死
executed / put to death / put to execution;

chu xing 處刑
sentence;

chu yi si xing 處以死刑
put to death / put to execution;

chu yu 處於
in a certain condition;

chu yu di chao 處於低潮
at a low ebb;

chu yu kun jing 處於困境
in predicament ‖ at bay; behind the eight ball; between wind and water; get into deep waters; get into hot water; get sb into chancery; have a wolf by the ears; in a bind; in a box; in a catch-22 situation; in a cleft stick; in a dilemma; in a fix; in a hole; in a nice fix; in a scrape; in a tight box; in a tight place; in an awkward predicament; in deep waters; in hot water; in Queer Street; in rough water; in the cart; in the soup; in the wrong box; into deep waters; on the horns of a dilemma; in troubled water; place sb in a dilemma; put sb in a dilemma; stick in the mud; up a creek; up a gum tree; up a tree; up the pole;

chu yu you li di wei 處於有利地位
hold all the aces / hold all the trumps;

chu zhi 處置
(1) deal with / dispose of / handle / manage;
(2) punish;

chu zhi bu dang 處置不當
mishandle / mismanage;

chu zhi shi dang 處置失當
mismanage ‖ badly managed; ill management; mishandle; not properly handled;

chu zhi shi yi 處置失宜
handle improperly;

chu3 儲
save / store;

chu cang 儲藏
(1) keep / lay by / save and preserve / store;
(2) deposit;

chu cun 儲存
accumulate / keep in reserve ‖ lay in; lay up; stockpile;

chuai3 he feng ying 揣合逢迎
try by tricks to find favour / try by various tricks to find favour with;

chuan1 穿
(1) be dressed in / have...on / put on / wear;
(2) cross / go through / pass through;

chuan bu de 穿不得
cannot be worn;

chuan bu qi 穿不起
cannot afford to wear it;

chuan bu zhu 穿不住
cannot wear it any longer;

chuan dai 穿戴
apparel / clothing dress / what one wears // wear;

chuan de fei chang shi mao 穿得非常時髦
be dressed to death / be dressed up to the nines;

chuan fan le 穿反了
wear sth inside out;

chuan hong zhuo lü 穿紅着綠
gaily dressed;

chuan kong xing kui yang 穿孔性潰瘍
diabrosis / perforating ulcer;

chuan luo zhuo duan 穿羅着緞
be dressed in silks and satins;

chuan tong xing kui yang 穿通性潰瘍
perforating ulcer;

chuan tou xing kui yang 穿透性潰瘍
penetrating ulcer;

chuan xiao 穿孝
in mourning / put into mourning / wear mourning;

chuan yi shang 穿衣裳
put on clothes;

chuan yue 穿越
cut across / pass through;

chuan zhuo 穿着
dress / apparel / what one wears;

chuan zhuo hua shao 穿着花哨
be dolled up / be dressed to kill;

chuan zhuo zheng qi 穿着整齊
be dressed up to the nines / be neatly dressed;

chuan2 傳
(1) pass on to;
(2) preach;

chuan bo 傳播
disseminate / spread;

chuan bu 傳佈
(1) disseminate;
(2) preach;

chuan dao ma zui 傳導麻醉
conduction anesthesia;

chuan dao 傳道
preach a religion;

chuan di 傳遞
forward / transmit;

chuan jiao 傳教
preach a religion;

chuan ran 傳染
infect // contagious / infectious // contagion / infection;

jiao cha chuan ran 交叉傳染
cross infection;
jie chu chuan ran 接觸傳染
contagion;
kong qi chuan ran 空氣傳染
airborne infection;

chuan ran bing 傳染病
communicable disease / contagious disease / infectious disease;
jie chu chuan ran bing 接觸傳染病
contagious disease / infectious disease;

chuan ran li 傳染力
infectivity;

chuan ran xing ji bing 傳染性疾病
infection;

chuan shou 傳授
teach / tutor;

chuan zong jie dai 傳宗接代
continue the family line by producing a male heir;

chuan2 si 遄死
die very quickly;

chuan4 men er 串門兒
call at sb's home || call on a friend's family; drop in on sb; drop around; drop round;

chuan men zi 串門子
call at sb's home / drop in;

chuan men zou hu 串門走戶
pass from house to house;

chuan pian 串騙
gang up and swindle sb;

chuan qi 串氣
collude with / gang up;

chuan tong 串通
collude with || collaborate; conspire with; gang up; in collusion with; work hand in glove with;

chuan tong yi qi 串通一氣
work in close collaboration with || collaborate; collude with; gang up; hand in glove with; in cahoots with; in league with; stand in with;

chuan tong zuo bi 串通作弊
in collusion over corrupt practices || conspire with sb for illegal acts; league together for some evil end; string together for evil purpose;

chuang1 shang 創傷
traumatism;
kai fang xing chuang shang 開放性創傷
open wound;
qian zai chuang shang 潛在創傷
potential trauma;

chuang shang hou ying yang bu liang 創傷後營

養不良
wound dystrophy;

chuang shang xing xiu ke 創傷性休克
traumatic shock;

chuang3 huo 闖禍
cause a disaster / cause a misfortune / get into trouble;

chui1 chui pai pai 吹吹拍拍
boasting and flattery / bragging and toadying / flattery and touting / fulsome flattery;

chui chui pai pai, la la che che 吹吹拍拍，拉拉扯扯
boasting and toadying // resort to boasting, flattery and touting;

chui le 吹了
break off / break off a relationship / break up;

chui lei 吹擂
boast / brag;

chui mao qiu ci 吹毛求疵
fastidious || blow aside the fur to seek for faults; blow upon the hair trying to discover a mole; captious; carp; carp at minor errors; censorious; deliberately to find fault; faultfinding; find fault with; find quarrel in a straw; finicky; hair-splitting; hypercritical; miminy-piminy; niggle about; nitpick; pernickety; pick flaws; pick holes in; pick on sth to find fault with; picksome; picky; pull ...to pieces; split hairs; squeamish; very fastidious;

chui niu pi 吹牛皮
boast || act the braggadocio; brag; draw the long bow; shoot aline; shoort crap; shoot the bull; shoot the shit; stick it on; talk big; talk horse; talk in high language; talk through one's hat; tell large stories;

chui peng 吹捧
flatter / laud to the skies / lavish praise on;

chui qiu 吹求
fastidious / hypercritical;

chui xu peng chang 吹噓捧場
laud / lavish and sing and the praises on others;

chui1 炊
cook a meal;

chui shi 炊事
kitchen work;

chui2 lao 垂老
in declining years;

chui mu zhi nian 垂暮之年
in declining years / in old age;

chui si 垂死
dying || at the last breath; expiring; fading fast; going; going belly up; going for your tea; have one foot in the grave; knocking on heaven's door; moribund; on one's last legs; receive notice to quit; sinking; slipping;

chui si zheng zha 垂死掙扎
flounder desperately before dying || conduct desperate struggles; deathbed struggle; give dying kicks; in one's death throes; in the throes of one's deathbed struggle; make a last desperate stand; on one's last legs; put up a last-ditch fight;

chui ti xing fei pang 垂體性肥胖
pituitary adiposity;

chui tiao 垂髫
(1) early childhood;
(2) children;

chui tiao zhi nian 垂髫之年
time of young childhood;

chui wei 垂危
critically ill || approaching death; at one's last gasp; close to death; near one's end; terminally ill;

chun1 feng de yi 春風得意
ride on the crest of success || extremely proud of one's success; look triumphant; the spring breeze has obtained its wish;

chun feng feng ren 春風風人
the spring breeze refreshes the minds of the people || give the people a timely and salutary education; the spring breeze brings the people to life;

chun feng hua yu 春風化雨
the stimulating influence of good teachers || the life-giving spring breeze and rain; the salutary influence of education; the stimulating influence of a good teacher can be compared to spring atmosphere;

chun qiu yi gao 春秋已高
advanced in years // have seen many summers;

chun qiu zheng fu 春秋正富
in the prime of youth;

chun1 椿
(1) father;
(2) cedrela;

chun ling 椿齡
great age / venerable;

chun ting 椿庭
father;

chuo1 si 戳死
stab to death;

chuo4 shu yin shui 啜菽飲水
have a simple diet // poor but filial;

ci2 雌
female / feminine / womanlike;

ci2 bie 辭別
bid farewell / say good-bye / take one's leave;

ci fu ju pin 辭富居貧
decline riches and prefer poverty;

ci gong tiao cao 辭工跳槽
from one employment to another / leave one's work and go to another;

ci ling 辭靈
bow to the coffin before leaving;

ci pin 辭聘
discharge an appointment / refuse a job offer;

ci rang 辭讓
politely decline;

ci rang xian neng 辭讓賢能
yield one's position to a more capable man;

ci shi 辭世
die / pass away;

ci sui 辭歲
bid farewell to the outgoing year / celebrate the lunar New Year's Eve;

ci tui 辭退
discharge / dismiss / turn away;

ci xie 辭謝
decline with thanks / politely decline / reject with thanks;

ci xing 辭行
say good-bye to sb before setting out on a journey / take one's leave;

ci xing gao bie 辭行告別
take leave of and bid farewell to;

ci zhi 辭職
hand in one's resignation || quit office; resign; send in one's jacket; send in one's papers; submit one's resignation;

ci zun ju bei 辭尊居卑
refuse to accept an honourable station and occupy a humble one;

ci3 hu bi ying 此呼彼應
echo each other || act in coordination with each other; echo one another; react on each other; responding to each other; take concerned action;

ci4 伺
serve;

ci hou 伺候
attend upon / serve / wait upon;

ci4 ji 刺激
(1) excite / stimulate;
(2) irritate / provoke / upset;

ci ji xing pi lao 刺激性疲勞
stimulation fatigue;

ci sha 刺殺
assassinate;

ci tan 刺探
make roundabout inquiries || detect; make secret inquiries; pry; spy;

ci tan jun qing 刺探軍情
gather military intelligence || pry about military intelligence; spy on the military movements; spy out military secrets;

ci4 賜
favour / grant by a superior / honour sb by giving sth;

ci fu 賜福
blessing;

ci fu 賜覆
kindly favour us with a reply / please favour me with a reply;

ci jiao 賜教
condescend to teach / grant instruction;

ci yu 賜予
bestow / grant;

cong1 cong 匆匆
hastily / hurriedly;

cong cong bu ji 匆匆不及
too much in a hurry to do sth;

cong cong chu ying 匆匆出迎
hurry out and greet sb;

cong cong er lai 匆匆而來
come in great haste;

cong cong er qu 匆匆而去
hurry away / leave in a hurry / pop off;

cong cong jiu zuo 匆匆就座
seat oneself in haste / take a seat in haste / take one's place with a rush;

cong cong li kai 匆匆離開
leave in a hurry || bundle away; bundle off; bundle out; dash off; get up and dig; get up and dust; hurry away; hurry off; leave in haste; make away; pop off;

cong cong mang mang 匆匆忙忙
head over heels || bustle up; heels over head; in a hurry / jammed for time;

cong cong tao ming 匆匆逃命
run for one's life;

cong cu 匆促
hastily / in a hurry;

cong cu 匆猝
hastily / in a hurry;

cong ju 匆遽
hastily / hurriedly;

cong mang 匆忙
hastily / in a hurry / in haste;

cong2 從
(1) easy / lax;
(2) abundant / plentiful;
(3) persuade / urge;

cong cong rong rong 從從容容
leisurely / without haste;

cong jian ru liu 從諫如流
able to accept advice from one's inferiors / ready to listen to advice;

cong qi suo hao 從其所好
follow what one desires / in accordance with one's taste / let one have one's way;

cong rong 從容
calm / unhurried // leisurely;

cong rong bu po 從容不迫
calm and unhurried || by easy stages; calmly; go easy; in a leisurely manner; leisurely; pull down one's vest; take it easy; take it leisurely and unoppressively; take one's time; unhurried; with poise and ease;

cong rong gan hao shi, xing ji sheng cha zi 從容幹好事，性急生岔子
more haste, less speed / slow and steady is the way to success;

cong rong jian ding 從容堅定
stand firm and keep cool-headed;

cong rong jiu yi 從容就義
meet one's death like a hero || die a martyr to one's principle; go to one's death unflinchingly; tread the path of virtue calmly;

cong rong zi ruo 從容自若
composed;

cong rong zi zai 從容自在
calm and at ease;

cong shan ru liu 從善如流
readily accept good advice || follow good advice as naturally as a river follows its course; follow good advice readily; give the ready ear to wise counsel;

cong sheng dao si 從生到死
from cradle to grave / from the womb to the tomb;

cong shi 從事
be engaged in || about; be bound up in; be occupied in; be occupied with; busy with; busy with devote oneself to; engage in; go in for; occupy oneself with; take up; work on;

cong shi zhu shu 從事著述
be engaged in writing scholarly works;

cong xiao dao da 從小到大
(1) from small to large || develop gradually;

身體 *Body*

expand from small to big;
(2) man and boy;

cong xin zuo ren 從新做人
start one's life anew / start with a clean slate / turn over a new leaf;

cong yan 從嚴
on the strict side / severely / strictly;

cong ye 從業
get a job / take up an occupation;

cong yi er zhong 從一而終
be faithful to one's husband unto death / marry one husband in her life;

cong zhe ru yun 從者如雲
have a large following;

cong zheng 從政
become a government official / enter politics;

cong zhong dao luan 從中搗亂
throw a spanner into the works;

cong zhong mou li 從中牟利
get advantage out of || get some advantage from the delicate position between; have an axe to grind; make a profit for oneself in some deal; make capital out of sth; play both ends against the middle; step in and take the advantage;

cong zhong shuo he 從中說合
settle through a middleman;

cong zhong tiao xuan 從中挑選
make a choice among;

cong zhong tiao jie 從中調解
act as an intermediary between...and...;

cong zhong wo xuan 從中斡旋
mediate between disputants;

cong zhong yu li 從中漁利
cash in on / make or reap profits from;

cong zhong zu ai 從中阻礙
lie in the way;

cong zhong zuo bao 從中作保
be sb's guarantor || go bail for; play the part of the sponsor;

cong zhong zuo fa 從中作伐
act as a matchmaker / play the part of the go-between;

cong zhong zuo geng 從中作梗
come between || create difficulties; hinder sb from carrying out a plan; make things difficult for sb; place obstacles in the way; put a spoke in sb's wheel;

cong zhong zuo sui 從中作祟
do mischief surreptitiously / play tricks in secret;

cou4 qian 湊錢
fork out / muck in / pool money;

cou re nao 湊熱鬧
(1) join in the fun || go along for the ride; take part in the merrymaking;
(2) add trouble to;

cu1 粗
(1) coarse / crude / rough;
(2) careless / negligent;
(3) rude / unrefined / vulgar;

cu bao dui dai 粗暴對待
kick in the teeth;

cu huo 粗活
heavy manual work / unskilled work;

cu lou 粗陋
coarse and crude;

cu shu 粗疏
inattentive;

cu shuai 粗率
(1) crude and coarse;
(2) rough and careless || careless; ill-considered; rash;

cu shuai cong shi 粗率從事
act without care;

cu su 粗俗
coarse / uncouth / vulgar;

cu su bu dang 粗俗不當
harsh and inappropriate;

cu ye 粗野
rough || boorish; coarse; rustic; unrefined; unpolished;

cu yi dan shi 粗衣淡食
coarse clothes and simple food / rough clothes and simple fare;

cu yi jian shi 粗衣簡食
rough clothes and simple fare;

cu zhi da ye 粗枝大葉
in a cursory fashion || be done in broad strokes; crude and careless; crude and perfunctory; crude and sketchy; in a slipshod manner; slap-dash; slipshod; sketchy; sloppy;

cu zhi yi er 粗知一二
have a rough idea about / know a little / know sth about;

cu zhuang 粗壯
(1) sturdy || brawny; muscular; robust; stout; thickset;
(2) deep and resonant;

cu zhuo 粗拙
(1) coarse / crude;
(2) clumsy / unskilled;

cu2 徂
(1) advance / go ahead / go to;
(2) die;

cu luo 徂落
die / pass away;

cu2 殂
death // die;

cu mo 殂沒
die / perish;

cu4 bing 促病
a sudden and violent disease;

cu cheng 促成
help to materialize / help to bring about;

cu4 猝
abrupt / hurried / sudden / unexpected;

cu bu ji fang 猝不及防
be caught off the guard / be caught unprepared / be taken by surprise / put off one's guard;

cu ran 猝然
abruptly / suddenly / unexpectedly;

cu ran jue ding 猝然決定
make a sudden decision;

cu si 猝死
sudden death;

xin zang xing cu si 心臟型猝死
sudden cardiac death;

cuan1 攛
(1) fling / throw;
(2) do in a hurry;

cuan duo 攛掇
egg on / urge;

cuan duo hai ren 攛掇害人
stir up harm for everyone;

cuan nong 攛弄
egg on / urge;

cuan2 攢
assemble / collect together;

cuan ju 攢聚
crowd together / gather closely together / huddle together;

cuan san ju wu 攢三聚五
gather in little knots / gather in threes and fours;

cuan4 篡
seize / usurp;

cuan duo 篡奪
seize / usurp;

cuan gai 篡改
distort / falsify / misrepresent / tamper with;

cuan quan 篡權
usurp power;

cuan quan jian wei 篡權僭位
usurp power and the throne;

cuan shi 篡弒
commit regicide / kill the ruler;

cuan wei 篡位
usurp the throne;

cuan4 竄
flee / run about / scurry;

cuan fan 竄犯
intrude into / invade / make an inroad into / raid;

cuan gai 竄改
alter / falsify / manipulate / tamper with;

cuan rao 竄擾
harass / invade and harass;

cuan tao 竄逃
flee in disorder / scurry off;

cui1 催
(1) hurry / press / urge;
(2) expedite / hasten / speed up;

cui ban 催辦
press for handling of a matter / press sb to do sth / urge sb into doing sth / urge sb to do sth;

cui bi 催逼
hasten / press;

cui cu 催促
hasten / press / prompt / urge;

cui mian 催眠
hypnotize / mesmerize;

cui mian ma zui 催眠麻醉
hypnosis anesthesia;

cui ming 催命
keep pressing sb to do sth;

cui qing 催請
urge;

cui1 摧
break / destroy / ruin;

cui can 摧殘
destroy / devastate / ruin / wreck;

cui can shen ti 摧殘身體
ruin one's health;

cui huai 摧壞
destroy;

cui hui 摧毀
damage || demolish; destroy; flatten; level; raze; smash; wreck;

cui zhe 摧折
break / destroy / smash;

cui4 yu yi shen 萃於一身
be embodied in sb;

cun2 mo jun gan 存歿均感
both the dead and living are grateful;

cun shen 存身
make one's home / take shelter;

cun wang 存亡
live or die / survive and downfall / survive or perish;

cun wang guan tou 存亡關頭
at a most critical moment;

cun wang jue xu 存亡絕續
either continue to exist or come to an end || at a most critical moment; critical juncture of life and death; survive or perish; the fate is at stake;

cun wang wei ji 存亡危急
at the critical juncture of life and death;

cun wang wei bu 存亡未卜
to preserve or to ruin cannot be foretold;

cun wang yu gong 存亡與共
throw in one's lot with;

cun wang zhi qiu 存亡之秋
a preservation or destruction crisis;

cun4 si bu gua 寸絲不掛
stark naked || in a state of nature; not a stitch of clothing on; totally nude;

cuo1 he 撮合
act as a go-between / bring together / make a match;

cuo nong 撮弄
(1) tease || juggle; make a fool of; make fun of; play a trick on;
(2) incite || abet; instigate;

cuo1 磋
polish;

cuo mo 磋磨
(1) polish;
(2) learn through discussions with others;

cuo qie qiu shan 磋切求善
seeking perfection through discussion with others;

cuo shang 磋商
consult / exchange views / hold a discussion;

cuo shang da ji 磋商大計
discuss a major plan;

cuo tuo 蹉跎
(1) slip and fall;
(2) miss a chance / waste time;

cuo tuo sui yue 蹉跎歲月
idle away one's time || dawdle one's life; dawdle one's time; fool away one's

time; fritter away one's time; idle about; lead an idle life; let time slip by without accomplishing anything; live an idle life; live in idleness; on the racket; profane the precious time; spend one's time in dissipation; spend one's time in frolic; trifle away one's time; waste time; while away one's time;

cuo2 矬
dwarf / shortie;

cuo zi 矬子
dwarf / shortie;

cuo4 挫
(1) defeat / frustrate;
(2) lower / subdue;

cuo bai 挫敗
defeat || foil; frustrate; suffer a setback; thwart;

cuo qi feng mang 挫其鋒芒
blunt the edge of one's advance;

cuo qi rui qi 挫其鋭氣
break sb's spirit || cut sb down to size; deflate sb's arrogance; take down a peg or two; take the edge off sb's spirit;

cuo ru 挫辱
humiliate / put to shame;

cuo shang 挫傷
dampen / discourage;

cuo zhe 挫折
setback || blow; frustration; reverse; subdue;

cuo4 ci 措辭
diction / wording;

cuo ci bu dang 措辭不當
inappropriate wording || improper use of words; use wrong words; wrong choice of words;

cuo ci de tang 措辭得當
appropriate wording // aptly worded;

cuo ci de ti 措辭得體
put it in approrpiate terms / proper wording / words employed are suitable and proper;

cuo ci qian tuo 措辭欠妥
not properly worded;

cuo ci qiang ying 措辭強硬
strongly worded;

cuo ci wan zhuan 措辭婉轉
put it tactfully;

cuo zhi 措置
arrange / handle / manage;

cuo zhi de dang 措置得當
be handled properly;

cuo zhi shi dang 措置失當
not properly handled / mismanage;

cuo zhi yu ru 措置裕如
deal with sth in a calm and adequate way || arrange leisurely; cope with the situation successfully; handle with ease; manage one's affairs easily and leisurely; take one's time in arranging sth;

da1 搭
(1) build / pitch / put up;
(2) hang over / put over;
(3) come into contact / join;
(4) add / throw in more;
(5) take / travel by;

da ban 搭班
(1) join a group in order to help in a task;
(2) join a theatrical troupe temporarily;

da ban 搭伴
in company || join sb on a trip; travel together;

da bian che 搭便車
thumb a lift / thumb a ride;

da che 搭車
(1) get a lift / give sb a lift / hitchhike;
(2) do sth at the same time / do sth along with someone else;

da cheng 搭乘
travel by...;

da cuo xian 搭錯線
make a mistake / misunderstand;

da dang 搭檔
collaborate / cooperate;

da gai 搭蓋
build / put up;

da huo 搭伙
(1) join as partner;
(2) eat regularly in a place;

da jia zi 搭架子
build a framework / get sth roughly into shape / make an outline of;

da jian 搭建
build / put up;

da jiao er 搭腳儿
hitchhike;

da jie 搭界
(1) border on;
(2) have sth to do with;

da jiu 搭救
go to the rescue of / rescue;

da ke 搭客
give sb a lift / take on passengers;

da li 搭理
pay attention to || acknowledge; answer; respond; take heed;

da pei 搭配
(1) sort in pairs || arrange in groups; combine; coordinate;
(2) collocate;

da peng 搭棚
(1) put up a shed;
(2) build a scaffold;

da qiao 搭橋
build bridges || act as a go-between; bring both sides together; mediate; put up a bridge;

da qiao pu lu 搭橋鋪路
facilitate / pave the way for / remove obstacles;

da qiao qian xian 搭橋牽線
bring both sides together / build bridges / mediate;

da shang guan xi 搭上關係
establish contact with / strike up a relationship with;

da shou 搭售
make a tie-in sale;

da xian 搭線
(1) make contact;
(2) act as a go-between / act as a matchmaker;

da zai 搭載
carry;

da2 答
reciprocate / return a visit;

da bai 答拜
pay a return visit / return a courtesy call;

da li 答禮
return a salute;

da xie 答謝
acknowledge / express appreciation / reciprocate;

da2 cheng 達成
achieve / conclude / reach;

da cheng jiao yi 達成交易
strike a bargain;

da cheng liang jie 達成諒解
come to an understanding;

da cheng tuo xie 達成妥協
reach a compromise;

da cheng xie yi 達成協議
reach an agreement || close a bargain; make a bargain; strike a bargain;

da dao 達到
achieve / reach || amount to; attain; to the amount of;

da dao biao zhun 達到標準
up to scratch / up to the mark;

da dao gao chao 達到高潮
come to a climax / reach a high tide;

da dao mu di 達到目的
achieve one's end / attain the goal / gain one's end / win one's end // home and dry;

da3 ba 打靶
practise shooting // rifle practice / target practice;

da bai zi 打擺子
have malaria / suffer from malaria;

da bai 打敗
(1) beat / defeat;
(2) be defeated || fail; lose; suffer a defeat;

da bai zhang 打敗仗
suffer a defeat;

da ban 打扮
deck out / dress / dress up / make up / perk up / preen / prettify / pretty up / primp / primp up / prink / prink up;

da ban zheng jie 打扮整潔
brush up;

da bao 打包
(1) bundle up / pack;
(2) unpack;

da bao bu ping 打抱不平
defend sb against an injustice || a champion of the weak; a champion of the oppressed; champion the cause of the justice; champion the wronged party against the offender; come out in defence of the weak; feel injustice done to another and wish to help; interfere on behalf of the injured party; intervene in cases of injustice for the benefit of the injured party; lend a helping hand to right a wrong; play the part of a gallant knight; ready to help the wronged party to redress grievances; stand up to a bully in defense of sb; take up the cudgels against the injustice done to sb; take up the cudgels for the injured party;

da bian gu 打邊鼓
drum up / incite / instigate;

da cao chen tian qing 打草趁天晴
make hay while the sun shines;

da cao jing she 打草驚蛇
shake the bush to rouse the serpent || act rashly and alert the enemy; beat the grass and drive the snake away; drumming is not the way to catch a hare; give a warning; stir the grass and alarm the snake; to frighten a bird is not the way to catch it; wake a sleeping wolf;

da che 打車
by taxi / hail a cab / take a taxi;

da cheng ping ju 打成平局
draw || break even; come out even; end in a draw; fight to a standoff; play even; tie it up; tie the score;

da cheng yi pian 打成一片
at one with || be fused with; be unified as one; become a harmonious whole; become integrated with; become one with; form an indivisible whole; identify oneself with; integrate oneself with; merge with; one with; unify as one;

da dao 打倒
down with / knock down / overthrow;

da de huo re 打得火熱
be passionately attached to each other || as thick as thieves; be infatuated with sb; carry on intimately with; cheek by jowl; chum up with; fraternize with; hob and nob; hobnob with; join in a love feast; on terms of intimacy; thick with each other;

da di 打的
take a taxi / travel by taxi;

da di pu 打地鋪
make a bed on the floor;

da di zi 打底子
(1) make a rough draft of / sketch;
(2) lay a foundation;

da dian 打點
(1) get one's belongings ready / get ready;
(2) offer a bribe / present a gift;

da diao 打掉
destroy / drive out / knock out / wipe out;

da dou 打鬥
fight || brawl; dust-up; exchange blows; fight and quarrel; tussle;

da du 打賭
bet || accept a bet; accept a wager; have a bet with sb; lay a wager; lay a wager with sb; make a bet with sb; make a wager; risk money on sth; take up a bet; take up a wager; wager;

da dun er 打盹兒
take a nap || catch forty winks; doze off; nod off; snatch forty winks;

da duo suo 打哆嗦
(1) shiver / tremble;
(2) shudder;

da fa 打發
(1) dispatch / send;
(2) dismiss / get rid of / send away;
(3) while away;

da fa shi jian 打發時間
while away one's time;

da fan 打翻
overturn / strike down;

da fan zai di 打翻在地
beat sb to the earth || beat sb down; strike sb down to the dust;

da fen 打分
(1) grade;
(2) mark;

da gang zi 打槓子
loot / plunder / rob;

da ge xi lan 打個稀爛
beat ... into a pulp;

da ge yuan chang 打個圓場
explain and smooth the matter over / help settle a quarrel;

da ge zhao hu 打個招呼
give sb notice / make one's salutation / salute sb // in salutation;

da gong zuo yi 打躬作揖
bow and scrape / make a deep bow with folded hands || beg humbly; bow and greet sb; bow and raise one's clasped hands in salute; do obeisance; fold the hands and make deep bows; make a deep bow; make an obeisance; salute with folded hands again and again; scrape a bow; scrape a leg;

da guan qiang 打官腔
speak in a bureaucratic tone || assume bureaucratic airs; speak with official jargon; stall with official jargon; talk like a bureaucrat;

da guan si 打官司
engage in a lawsuit || file a suit against sb; go to court; go to law; litigation; squabble;

da gun 打滾
roll about || roll on the ground;

da gun zi 打棍子
criticize / punish;

da han jin 打寒噤
shudder because of cold / tremble because of cold;

da ji chu 打基礎
do spade work;

da ji 打擊
attack || blow; crack down; deal a blow; hit; retaliate; strike; swash; trip;

da ji bie ren, tai gao zi ji 打擊別人，抬高自己
attack others so as to build up oneself;

da jia jie she 打家劫舍
raid homes and plunder houses || commit house robbery in packs; go in all directions to loot; loot; pillage and rob; plunder; raid and pillage; raven about;

da jia 打架
come to blows / fight || engage in a brawl; fall to cuffs; go to cuffs; scuffle // at cuffs with;

da jiang shan 打江山
seize political power by force;

da jiao dao 打交道
come into contact with || deal with; have contact with; have dealings with; make contact with; negotiate with; team up with;

da jiao 打攪
(1) break / disturb / interrupt;
(2) bother / trouble;

da jie 打劫
loot / plunder / rob;

da jin 打緊
(1) matter;
(2) critical / serious;

da jin 打進
make one's way into;

da jing 打井
sink a well;

da kai jiang ju 打開僵局
break the deadlock || break the ice; break the impasse; bring the deadlock to the end; find a way out of a stalement; find solution for a problem;

da kai que kou 打開缺口
make a breach;

da ke shui 打瞌睡
fall into a doze || catnap; doze; doze away; doze off; doze over; drop off; drowse; get a wink of sleep; go off; go off into a doze; have

a nap; nod; nod off; steal a nap; take a nap;

da kua 打跨
completely defeat / crush;

da lao 打撈
get out of water / salvage;

da lei tai 打雷台
accept the challenge / pick up the gauntlet / take up the challenge;

da leng qiang 打冷槍
fire a sniper's shot / stab in the back;

da leng zhan 打冷戰
(1) fight a cold war;
(2) shudder with cold;

da leng er 打愣兒
in a daze || in a trance; stare blankly;

da lie 打獵
go hunting;

da luan 打亂
disorganize / disrupt / throw into confusion / upset;

da luo shui gou 打落水狗
beat the dog in the water || beat the dog that has fallen in the water; completely crush a defeated enemy; hit a person who is down;

da ma jiang 打麻將
play mahjong;

da ma hu yan 打馬虎眼
act dumb;

da mai fu 打埋伏
(1) ambush / lie in ambush / set an ambush;
(2) hold sth back / keep under cover;

da mao yi 打毛衣
knit a sweater;

da men gun 打悶棍
take advantage of sb's unawareness to strike a heavy blow at him;

da men hu lu 打悶葫蘆
throw sb into bewilderment || guess sb's riddles; puzzle one's head over sb's silly riddles;

da men lei 打悶雷
brood / leave sb in suspense;

da mo 打磨
burnish / polish / shine;

da nao 打鬧
kick up a row / quarrel and fight noisily;

da nei zhan 打內戰
be engaged in a civil war / fight a civil war;

da ping huo 打平伙
go Dutch / go halves;

da po 打破
(1) break / break down / smash;
(2) break away from;

da po chang gui 打破常規
break away from conventions || break with normal procedure; break the routine; off the beaten track;

da po cu tan zi 打破醋壇子
break the jar of vinegar — burn with jealousy;

da po fan wan 打破飯碗
lose one's job // unemployed;

da po guan li 打破慣例
break fresh ground / break new ground;

da po ji lu 打破記錄
beat the record / break the record / cut the record / set a new record;

da po jiang ju 打破僵局
break a deadlock / break the ice / break the stalemate / find a way out of a stalemate;

da po kuang kuang 打破框框
break away from conventions / break through the sterotypes / break with conventions;

da po le wu wei ping er — shuo bu chu shen me wei dao 打破了五味瓶兒——說不出甚麼味道
mixed feelings / breaking a Chinese five-spice bottle — can't tell what flavour it is;

da po mi xin 打破迷信
destroy superstitions;

da po qian li 打破前例
depart from precedents;

da po qing mian 打破情面
do not attempt to spare anybody's feelings;

da po que kou 打破缺口
drive a wedge between / make a breach;

da po sha guo wen dao di 打破沙鍋問到底

get to the bottom of sth || breaking an earthenware pot and it cracks to the bottom — insisting on getting to the bottom of sth; inquire into the root of the matter; inquisitive; insist on getting to the bottom of a matter; keep on asking questions till one gets to the bottom of a matter; probe sth to the bottom; wish to know every detail of sth; interrogate thoroughly;

da qi jing shen 打起精神

brace up energy / buck up energy || cheer up; keep up one's spirit; pluck up courage; with chin up;

da qi 打氣

(1) inflate / pump up;

(2) boost the morale || bolster up; bolster up the morale; brace up; cheer up; encourage; pep up;

da qiang xin zhen 打強心針

stimulate;

da qing ma qiao 打情罵俏

flirt with sb || joke between a young couple; tease one's lover by showing false displeasure; trifle with sb in love;

da qiu feng 打秋風

get money;

da qiu qian 打秋千

get on a swing / have a swing / play on the swing;

da qiu qian 打鞦韆

get on a swing / have a swing / play on the swing;

da qiu 打球

play a ball game;

da qu 打趣

banter / joke with / make fun of / poke fun at / tease;

da qun jia 打群架

engage in a gang fight;

da rao 打擾

(1) disturb / trouble;

(2) be received;

da ru 打入

(1) banish to / throw into;

(2) infiltrate;

da ru di xia 打入地下

be driven underground;

da ru lao yu 打入牢獄

throw sb into prison;

da ru leng gong 打入冷宮

be left out in the cold || banish to the cold palace; consign sb to limbo; consign to the back shelf; fallen into disfavour; out of favour; out in the cold; put on the back shelf; relegate to limbo; throw into limbo; turn out in the cold;

da ru men hu lu 打入悶葫蘆

throw into bewilderment;

da ru shi ba ceng di yu 打入十八層地獄

banish sb to the uttermost depths of hell || banish to the lowest depths of hell; condemn to eternal damnation; shut sb in the eighteenth hell;

da san 打散

break up / scatter / thrashing;

da sao 打掃

clean up / sweep;

da sheng 打勝

defeat || bear off the palm; beat; best; carry off the palm; carry the day; conquer; down; gain the victory over; get sb down; get the better of sb; have it on sb; have it over sb; have the best of it; have the scale of; one too many for sb; prevail over; put a head on sb; put to rout; route; smash; triump over; win; win the day;

da sheng zhang 打勝仗

victorious // win a war;

da shi 打食

(1) hunt for food / seek food;

(2) help to digest and excrete / relieve indigestion with a drug;

da si 打死

(1) beat to death;

(2) shoot to death;

(3) dispatch;

(4) kill;

(5) stop;

(6) smite sb dead;

da tian xia 打天下
(1) seize power by force / struggle to seize state power;
(2) build up one's position / establish an enterprise || originate a cause; originate an undertaking; set up an enterprise; start an enterprise;

da tong 打通
(1) break through / get through / open up;
(2) dispel;

da tong guan jie 打通關節
break through key links / bribe officials in charge;

da tou pao 打頭炮
fire the first shot || lead the attack; take the lead; the first to act; the first to speak;

da tou zhen 打頭陣
(1) fight in the van / spearhead the attack;
(2) take the lead;

da tui 打退
beat back / beat off / repulse;

da tui tang gu 打退堂鼓
back down || back out; back up before sth is finished; back water; beat a retreat; chicken out; cry off; draw back; draw in one's horns; fink out; give up; haul in one's horns; pull in one's horns; retreat; take the water; withdraw from;

da xian feng 打先鋒
lead the way || fight in the van; lead the van; pioneer;

da xiao bao gao 打小報告
inform secretly on sb || whistle-blower; inform on sb to superiors; write small reports;

da ye ma niang 打爺罵娘
unfilial;

da ye zuo 打夜作
work overtime at night;

da yuan chang 打圓場
smooth things over || do peacemaking; ease a situation; help effect a compromise; help settle a quarrel; mediate a dispute; proffer one's good offices; smooth out a dispute;

da za 打雜
fix up odds and ends || do odds and ends; serve as a handy man;

da zhan 打戰
shiver / shudder / tremble;

da zhang 打仗
go to war || fight; fight a battle; make war;

da zhao hu 打招呼
(1) greet sb || say hello; tip one's hat;
(2) notify in advance || give a previous notice; inform; remind; warn;
(3) let sb know / notify;

da zhe kou 打折扣
(1) at a discount // give a discount / sell at a discount;
(2) fall short of a promise / fall short of a requirement;

da zhen 打針
give an injection / have an injection;

da zhong 打中
hit the mark / hit the target;

da zhong yao hai 打中要害
hit where it really hurts || deal a blow at the heart; drive the nail; hit home; hit on the vital spot; hit squarely on the chin; hit the mark; hit the nail on the head; hit the right nail on the head; press home; push home; shoot home; strike home; touch... to the quick; the thrust goes home;

da zhu 打住
bring to a halt / hold on / stop;

da zhuan 打轉
revolve / rotate / spin / turn round and round;

da4 bai yan xi 大擺筵席
make a feast / spread a feast;

da bai 大敗
(1) defeat utterly / put to rout;
(2) suffer a crashing defeat;

da bai er hui 大敗而回
suffer a crashing defeat;

da bai er tao 大敗而逃
suffer defeat and run away;

da ban bei zi 大半輩子
in the midst of life;

da bao da lan 大包大攬
monopolize the job and the responsibility / take responsibility on oneself;

da bing 大病
serious illness;

da bing xin yu 大病新愈
just recovered from a serious illness;

da bu liao 大不了
(1) at the worst // if the worst comes to the worst;
(2) not so remarkable / nothing serious;

da cai 大才
great talent;

da cai 大材
great talent;

da cai xiao yong 大材小用
waste one's talent on a petty job ‖ a capable person in a job too small for his talents; a large material for petty use; an able person given a small job; cut blocks with a razor; employ a steam-engine to crack a nut; great genius in little employment; misuse of fine materials; put fine timber to petty use; shoot sparrows with artillery; use a sledgehammer to crack a nut; use talented people for trivial tasks; waste of talent;

da chu feng tou 大出風頭
enjoy great popularity ‖ cut a dashing figure; in the limelight; make a hit;

da chu qi chou 大出其醜
put sb to shame ‖ hold sb up to ridicule; make an ass of oneself; make a monkey out of sb;

da chu yang xiang 大出洋相
make an exhibition of oneself ‖ cut a poor figure; cut a sorry figure; make a bad show; make a ridiculous figure;

da chu luo mo 大處落墨
concentrate on the key points ‖ concentrate on the major problems; keep the general goal in view; lay hand on the main thing; pay attention to the important points; write on the key points;

da chu zhuo yan 大處着眼
pay attention to the important points ‖ far-sighted; keep the general goal in sight;

da chun xiao ci 大醇小疵
sound on the whole though defective in details / with great purity and small flaw;

da cuo te cuo 大錯特錯
as wrong as wrong can be ‖ absolutely wrong; all wet; all wrong; be gravely mistaken; be grievously mistaken; can hardly be more mistaken; commit a grave error; completely mistaken; far from being in the right; make a big mistake; make a gross error; off base; totally wrong; wide of the mark;

da da chu shou 大打出手
get into a fight ‖ attack brutally; come to blows; fight brutally; get into a free-for-all fight; strike violently;

da da fang fang 大大方方
in excellent taste / very natural and poised;

da da lie lie 大大咧咧
careless / casual;

da dao kuo fu 大刀闊斧
do sth in a big way ‖ bold and resolute; boldly and resolutely; cut the Gordian knot; deal with a matter summarily without regard to details; drastic; handle without gloves; handle without mittens; make bold decisions; make drastic measures; make snap decisions; put the ax in the helve;

da du 大度
magnanimous;

da du bao rong 大度包容
magnanimous and tolerant // regard with kindly tolerance;

da fa lao sao 大發牢騷
dissipate one's grief extensively / pour out a stream of complaints;

da fa lei ting 大發雷霆
in a towering rage ‖ all on end; bawl at sb angrily; become very angry; blow a fuse; blow one's lid; blow one's lid off; blow one's stack; blow one's top at sb; break into a rage; flare up; flip one's lid; flip one's wig; fly into a passion; fly into a rage; fly off the handle; foam at the mouth; furious; go into a rage; go through the roof; have a fit; hit the roof; in a fit; in a flare of anger; in a flare of temper; in a towering passion; on the warpath; raise the

roof; show one's teeth; throw a fit; throw a huge tantrum; thunder against;

da fa pi qi 大發脾氣
blow one's top / blow up / go off the top || blow one's lid; blow one's lid off; do one's fruit; do one's nuts; flare up; flip one's lid; fly into one's tantrums; get into a temper; get one's dander up; grab for altitude; lose one's shirt; lose one's temper; throw a huge tantrum;

da fang 大方
(1) carry oneself with ease and grace // natural / natural and poised;
(2) generous / liberal;
(3) in good taste / tasteful;

da gong wu si 大公無私
impartial and act without thought of self || give no thought to self; impartial; selfless; unselfish;

da hong da zi 大紅大紫
celebrated / famous / well-known;

da jing shi se 大驚失色
be frightened and change colour || be greatly frightened; be pale with fear; grey-faced with fright; grow alarm and turn colour; have a blue fit; turn pale with fright;

da jing xiao guai 大驚小怪
make a fuss about nothing || a tempest in a teapot; bark at the noon; be surprised at; get excited over a little thing; great alarm at a little bogey; make a great ado over sth; make a rare fuss over sth; much cry and little wool;

da kai fang bian zhi men 大開方便之門
do everything to suit sb's convenience || facilitate sth; give the green light to; open the floodgates wide to sb; provide sb with easy access;

da li 大力
energetically / vigorously;

da li jing ying 大力經營
devote great efforts to the development of;

da li xuan chuan 大力宣傳
conduct vigorous propaganda;

da li xie zhu 大力協助
provide great help;

da ming ding ding 大名鼎鼎
celebrated / famous || enjoy a big name; enjoy great celebrity; well-known; widely known;

da mo da yang 大模大樣
in a showy manner || high-and-mighty airs; in an open manner; in an ostentatious manner; look big; pompously; proudly; with a swagger;

da na 大拿
(1) a person with power / boss / head;
(2) able person / expert;

da nan bu si 大難不死
escape from death in a great catastrophe / be delivered from a great danger / escape death from a calamity;

da nan bu si, bi you hou fu 大難不死，必有後福
those who do not die in great dangers are sure to come to good fortune later on;

da nan lin tou 大難臨頭
a great calamity is at hand / be faced with imminent disaster;

da ni bu dao 大逆不道
(1) treacherous;
(2) treason and heresy;

da qi pang bo 大氣磅礡
grand and magnificent || great vitality; have power and range; of great momentum; powerful;

da qi wan cheng 大器晚成
great talents flower late;

da qiao ruo zhuo 大巧若拙
an extremely intelligent person looks dull || a person of great skill is like an idiot; great art conceals itself; great wisdom appears stupid;

da quan 大權
authority;

da quan du lan 大權獨攬
take all power into one's hands || absolute control on; arrogate all authority to oneself; centralize power in one man's hands to deal with major issues; centralize power on major issues; grasp the central power in one's own hands;

da quan pang luo 大權旁落
let power pass into others' hands / power has fallen into the hands of others;

da quan zai wo 大權在握
hold real power in one's hands || hold the reins; the great power is within one's grasp; with power in one's hands;

da sha feng jing 大煞風景
dampen the spirit || disappointing; frustrating; put a wet blanket on; sink the spirits of; spoil the fun; spoil the pleasure; take all the fun out of; throw a wet blanket over;

da shang yuan qi 大傷元氣
knock the stuffing out of / sap one's vitality / take the stuffing out of / undermine one's constitution;

da shao ye zuo feng 大少爺作風
behaviour typical of the spoiled son of a rich family / extravagant ways;

da shi guan zhan 大失觀瞻
a great loss of prestige;

da shi wei feng 大施威風
throw one's weight about;

da shi 大事
(1) great event / important matter / major event / major issue;
(2) the overall situation;
(3) in a big way;

da shi gong ji 大事攻擊
an all-out attack || attack in a big way; hurl wild attacks against; lash out at;

da shi hua xiao 大事化小
reduce a big trouble into a small one;

da shi hua xiao, xiao shi hua wu 大事化小，小事化無
turn big problems into small ones and small ones into nothing;

da shi hui huo 大事揮霍
fritter away one's money / launch out into extravagance // spendthrift;

da shi pu zhang 大事鋪張
make much of a little / present with a great fanfare;

da shi xuan chuan 大事宣傳
give great publicity || a whoop and a holler; ballyhoo; play up;

da shou da jiao 大手大腳
spend extravagantly // wasteful;

da ti xiao zuo 大題小做
little about a major issue // make little of / treat major issues light;

da tou tou er 大頭頭儿
big guy;

da wei chi jing 大為吃驚
be greatly surprised / be quite taken aback / be utterly startled;

da wei gai guan 大為改觀
change greatly;

da wei sheng se 大為生色
give colour to;

da wei shi wang 大為失望
feel very disappointed;

da wei xun se 大為遜色
not in the same street with / throw...into the shade;

da wei zhen jing 大為震驚
be much shaken / be terribly shocked || have a fit; have a thousand fits; throw a fit; throw a thousand fits;

da wu wei 大無畏
dauntless / fearless / indomitable;

da xian shen shou 大顯身手
display one's skill to the full || bring one's talents into full play; come out strong; cut a dashing figure; display one's skill to the full; distinguish oneself; give a good account of oneself; give full play to one's abilities; play one's prize; show one's best; turn one's talents to full account;

da xian shen tong 大顯神通
give full play to one's remarkable skill || display all one's valour; make the mare go; show a great miracle; show one's magic power; show what one is capable of;

da xian yin qin 大獻殷勤
do everything to please sb || dance attendance on sb; do one's utmost to please and woo; pay one's addresses to sb; serve sb hand and

foot;

da xing wen zui zhi shi 大興問罪之師
bring sb to book || launch a punitive campaign; point an accusing finger at sb;

da yao da bai 大搖大擺
come swaggeringly / roister / swagger;

da yi 大義
cardinal principles of righteousness;

da yi lin ran 大義凜然
awe-inspring righteousness || with a strong sense of righteouness;with stern righteousness;

da yi mie qin 大義滅親
punish one's own relations in the cause of justice || kill one's blood relations to uphold justice; place righteousness above family loyalty;

da yi 大意
careless / inattentive / negligent;

da you cheng jiu 大有成就
make quite a success || come out on top; make good one's running;

da you chu xi 大有出息
of great promise;

da you hao chu 大有好處
of great benefit to / of much good;

da you jin bu 大有進步
make great strides || advance by rapid strides; have greatly improved; have taken great strides in one's progress;

da you ke wei 大有可為
be well worth doing || can accomplish great things; have a brilliant future; have bright prospects;

da you lai tou 大有來頭
have powerful backing // very influential socially;

da you qian tu 大有前途
bear watching;

da you qu bie 大有區別
entirely different / poles apart;

da you ren zai 大有人在
not the only pebble on the beach / such people are by no means rare;

da you suo huo 大有所獲
have obtained a great deal;

da you wen zhang 大有文章
there's more to it than meets the eye / there's much more to it than appears;

da you xi wang 大有希望
full of hope || bid fair; full of promise; give great promise; promise high hopes; show great promise; stand a chance; there is great hope for;

da you yong chu 大有用處
of great use;

da you zhi nian 大有之年
bumper year || a good year for crops; abundant year;

da you zuo wei 大有作為
able to develop one's ability to the full || go a long way; have full scope for one's talents; have great possibilities; much can be accomplished; there is plenty of room to develop one's talents to the full;

da zhan hong tu 大展鴻圖
carry out one's great plan / realize one's ambition / ride on the crest of success;

da zhan jing lun 大展經綸
put one's statecraft to full use;

da zhan shen shou 大展身手
fully display one's skill / give full play to one's talents / show one's capabilities;

da zhang qi gu 大張旗鼓
by great publicity || flags and drums in array; give wide publicity to; in a big way; on a grand scale; put up a pageantry; with a big display of flags and drums; with a flourish; with a great fanfare; with colours flying and the band playing;

da zhang sheng shi 大張聲勢
put on a big show // great pageantry;

da zhang ta fa 大張撻伐
declare war on a country to punish it for its iniquities;

da zhang fu neng qu neng shen 大丈夫能屈能伸
a great man knows when to yield and when not / a real man is able to stoop or stand up /

a true man can either stoop or stand;

da zhi 大志
great ambitions;

da zuo wen zhang 大做文章
make a big issue of sth || blow up; kick up a big fuss; kick up a rumpus about; make a big fanfare over; make a fuss; turn out much propaganda;

dai1 呆
(1) dull;
(2) blank;

dai li bu dong 呆立不動
stand transfixed to the ground;

dai ren you dai fu 呆人有呆福
fortune favours fools;

dai ruo mu ji 呆若木雞
be stupefied || as dumb as a piece of wood; as motionless as a wooden image; be insensate like a wooden chicken; be paralyzed with fear; be rooted to the spot; dumb as a wooden chicken; dumbfounded; dumbstruck; remain in a state of stupefaction; rivet to the ground; root to the ground; spaced-out; stand like a log; stand like a staute; stand still like a piece of wood; transfixed with fear;

dai3 tu 歹徒
evil-doer / hoodlum / ruffian / scoundrel;

dai3 逮
(1) reach;
(2) after / chase and make arrest / hunt;

dai bu 逮捕
make arrest;

dai xi 逮繫
arrest and detain;

dai zhu 逮住
catch (a thief, etc);

dai4 bao bu ping 代抱不平
take up the cudgel for another — against injustice;

dai lao 代勞
(1) ask sb to do sth for oneself;
(2) do sth for sb / take trouble on sb's behalf;

dai ren shou guo 代人受過
be made the scapegoat for sb / bear the blame for sb else || carry the can; suffer for the faults of another; take the blame for others; take the can back;

dai xing 代行
act on sb's behalf;

dai xing zhi wu 代行職務
fill the breach / step into the breach;

dai4 待
(1) deal with / treat;
(2) entertain;
(3) await / wait for;
(4) need;
(5) about to / going to;

dai bi 待斃
sitting duck // await death;

dai cha 待茶
offer tea / receive a guest with tea;

dai cha 待查
yet to be investigated;

dai ji 待機
await the opportune moment / bide one's time;

dai ji er dong 待機而動
wait for an opportunity to make a move / wait for the right time to take action;

dai ji er zuo 待機而作
wait for an opportune moment to act / wait for one's opportunity;

dai kao 待考
need checking / remain to be verified;

dai ke 待客
entertain guests / receive guests;

dai ke zhou dao 待客周到
keep a good house;

dai ling 帶領
wait to be called for;

dai ming 待命
await orders;

dai ming chu fa 待命出發
await orders to set off / be ready for orders to set out / wait for orders to start off;

dai ren 待人
treat people;

dai ren cheng ken 待人誠懇
sincere with people // treat people sincerely;

dai ren jie wu 待人接物
the manner of dealing with people / the way one conducts oneself in relation to others / the way one gets along with people;

dai ren ru ji 待人如己
treat others as oneself;

dai ren yi cheng 待人以誠
honest in dealing with people // treat people with sincerity;

dai ren yi kuan 待人以寬
act generously towards people;

dai ru 待如
treat sb as if …;

dai ru ji chu 待如己出
treat a child as if he were one's own;

dai ru shang bin 待如上賓
be treated as a guest of honour / treat sb as a highly honoured guest / treat sb as the most honoured guest / treat sb like a distinguished guest;

dai shi er dong 待時而動
bide one's time / wait for the right time to take action;

dai yue xi xiang 待月西廂
have a nocturnal rendezvous with one's lover / wait for one's lover in the night;

dai zhi yi li 待之以禮
treat with courtesy;

dai zi 待字
wait for a right man to marry;

dai zi gui zhong 待字閨中
a girl not betrothed yet || be still unmarried; one's daughter is still unmarried; waiting in the boudoir to be betrothed;

dai4 gong 怠工
go slow / mike / slow down;

dai4 帶
(1) bring / take;
(2) do sth incidentally;
(3) bear / contain / have;
(4) head / lead;
(5) bring up / look after;

dai bing 帶病
in spite of illness;

dai bing gong zuo 帶病工作
carry on one's work in spite of illness;

dai dao 帶到
bring / lead / take;

dai dong 帶動
(1) drive / set in motion;
(2) bring along / lead / spur on;

dai hui 帶壞
lead astray;

dai lai 帶來
bring about / produce;

dai lei 帶累
implicate / involve;

dai ling 帶領
guide / lead || head;

dai lu 帶路
lead the way / show the way || act as a guide;

dai tou 帶頭
set an example / take the lead / take up the running / the first;

dai xiao 帶孝
be in mourning / wear mourning for a parent or relative;

dai xiu 帶羞
look bashful;

dai zuo 帶座
show to a seat;

dai lü mao zi 戴綠帽子
be cuckolded;

dai zui li gong 戴罪立功
atone for one's crimes by doing good deeds / make up for the crime one has committed / redeem oneself by performing a good service;

dan1 耽
(1) delay;
(2) abandon oneself to / indulge in;

dan ge 耽擱
(1) stay / stop over;
(2) delay / fail to do sth in time / lose;

dan le 耽樂
indulge in pleasure;

dan mian 耽湎
be addicted to;

dan ni 耽溺
indulge in evil ways;

dan wu 耽誤
delay / detain / hold up / miss / obstruct;

dan wu gong fu 耽誤功夫
waste time;

dan1 chun xing fei da 單純性肥大
simple hypertrophy;

dan chun xing fei pang 單純性肥胖
simple obesity;

dan chun xing kui yang 單純性潰瘍
simple ulcer;

dan chun xing yan 單純性炎
simple inflammation;

dan shou 單瘦
skinny / thin;

dan tiao 單挑
do sth by oneself / work on one's own;

dan1 擔
take on / undertake;

dan bao 擔保
guarantee ‖ assurance; bail; bet; by gum; ensure; go bail for; surety; swear; take an oath; upon my honour; upon my name; upon my word; vouch for; vow; warrant;

dan bu shi 擔不是
take the blame;

dan dai bu qi 擔戴不起
not able to assume the responsibility;

dan dai 擔待
(1) take on / take the responsibility / undertake;
(2) excuse / forgive / pardon;

dan dang 擔當
(1) assume / take on / undertake;
(2) deserve / worthy of;

dan dang bu qi 擔當不起
cannot bear the responsibility / unable to bear the burden;

dan feng xian 擔風險
face danger / run risks / take the risk of;

dan feng xiu yue 擔風袖月
travel in the open / with the wind on one's back and the moonlight in one's sleeves;

dan fu 擔負
be charged with / bear / shoulder / take on / undertake;

dan fu zhong ren 擔負重任
take on heavy responsibilities / undertake an important business;

dan ren 擔任
assume the office of / hold the post of;

dan ren zhu xi 擔任主席
take the chair;

dan zhong dan 擔重擔
bear a heavy burden / carry the ball;

dan4 xi huo fu 旦夕禍福
fortune is fickle / sudden changes of fortune / unexpected good or bad fortune;

dan xi nan bao 旦夕難保
danger is imminent // in imminent peril;

dan4 qiu wu guo 但求無過
just try to avoid making mistakes;

dang1 jia zuo zhu 當家作主
master in one's own house;

dang ju zhe mi 當局者迷
blunt are those concerned / people are blind in their own cause / those closely involved cannot see clearly;

dang ju zhe mi, pang guan zhe qing 當局者迷，旁觀者清
lookers-on see more than players ‖ lookers-on see most of the game; one who is concerned in the matter has not been able to see so clearly as one who is not himself involved; one who is in the game is blind, while a bystander sees through everything; the doer is not clear about what he is doing while the onlooker sees it clearly; the onlooker sees most of the game; the onlooker sees the game best; the spectators see the chess game better than the players; those closely involved cannot see as clearly as

those outside;

dang ren bu rang 當仁不讓
not to leave to others what one ought to do oneself || not to decline to shoulder a responsibility; not to pass on to others what one is called upon to do; not to shirk what one's obliged to do; take sth as one's obligation;

dang zhong 當眾
before the public / in front of everybody / in public / in the presence of all / openly;

dang zhong chu chou 當眾出醜
bring shame on oneself in public / make an exhibition of oneself || make a fool of oneself before others; make a silly error; pull a boner;

dang zhong shen chi 當眾申斥
criticize sb in public / reprove sb before the public;

dang zhong shou ru 當眾受辱
be insulted before a large company / be insulted in the presence of others;

dang zhong wu ru 當眾侮辱
offer an affront to / put an affront upon a person // open insult;

dang zhong xie zui 當眾謝罪
apologize in public;

dang zhong xiu ru 當眾羞辱
humiliate sb in public / offer an affront to sb in public;

dang zhong xuan bu 當眾宣佈
announce publicly;

dang3 擋
impede / obstruct / resist / stop / ward off;

dang bu zhu 擋不住
hindering / impeding / incapable of blocking / incapable of stopping;

dang heng 擋橫
block / get in the way / hinder;

dang heng er 擋橫兒
guard sb from violence;

dang jia 擋駕
decline to receive a guest / turn away a visitor with some excuse || decline to receive a call;

dang lu 擋路
get in the way / in the way / obstruct traffic;

dang yu 擋雨
keep off the rain / shelter one from the rain;

dang zhu 擋住
(1) check / halt / hamper / stop;
(2) hide / obstruct / screen / shield;
(3) bar / block / stem;

dang4 dang you you 蕩蕩悠悠
moving to and fro / shake and move / swinging;

dang jian yu xian 蕩檢逾閑
break laws and overstep bounds || be broken from moral bonds; licentious in conduct;

dang lai dang qu 蕩來蕩去
hanging about / hanging around;

dao3 倒
(1) fall over / lie down;
(2) empty / pour out;

dao ba 倒把
engage in profiteering / speculate;

dao ban 倒班
change shifts / work by turns / work in shifts;

dao bi 倒斃
fall dead;

dao ge 倒戈
revolt against one's own side || change sides in a war; mutiny; turn one's coat; turn the gun around;

dao ge tou di 倒戈投敵
betray to the enemy || turn renegade; turncoat;

dao ge xiang xiang 倒戈相向
attack one's own men || become a turncoat; revolt against constituted authority; turn one's force against one's master;

dao mei 倒霉
(1) fall on evil days / fall on hard time;
(2) hard luck || as good luck as had the cow that stuck herself with her own horn; bad luck; down on one's luck; hard cheese; have bad luck; ill luck; just my luck; luck in a bag; luck out; luck up; off one's luck; out of luck; play into hard luck; rough luck; tough luck; unlucky;

(3) go through a bad patch / hit a bad patch / strike a bad patch;

dao yun 倒運
out of luck;

dao3 搗
(1) pound with a pestle;
(2) beat with stick;
(3) disturb / harass;

dao dan 搗蛋
(1) give sb a hard time;
(2) act up / do mischief / make trouble / mess about / mess around // mischief;

dao gui 搗鬼
do mischief / mess about / play tricks / pull off;

dao hui 搗毀
demolish / destroy / devastate / smash up;

dao luan 搗亂
create a disturbance / make trouble / mess about;

dao3 chang xi gu 蹈常襲故
follow a set routine / get into a rut / go on in the same old way;

dao huo fu tang 蹈火赴湯
brace all possible difficulties / go through fire and water;

dao yi 蹈義
die for a cause;

dao4 到
(1) arrive / get to / reach;
(2) go to / leave for;

dao chang 到場
present / show up / turn up;

dao chu 到處
everywhere || all about; all over; all over the place; all over the shop; all over the show; all round; at all places; from place to place; here and there; here, there and everywhere; high and low; hither and thither; in all directions; in every place; in every quarter; on all hands; on all sides; on every side; on every hand; right and left; up and down; up hill and down dale;

dao chu ben bo 到處奔波
rush about hither and thither / travel from place to place;

dao chu cha shou 到處插手
meddle in others' affairs everywhere / stretch tentacles to every corner;

dao chu da ting 到處打聽
shop around;

dao chu liu lang 到處流浪
lead a vagrant life / live a vagabond life / wander from place to place;

dao chu luan chuan 到處亂傳
bandy about;

dao chu luan cuan 到處亂竄
poke one's nose everywhere;

dao chu peng bi 到處碰壁
get into trouble hither and thither || from pillar to post; from post to pillar; run into snags everywhere; run one's head against stone walls everywhere;

dao chu shen shou 到處伸手
ask for help at all places || poke one's fingers everywhere; reach out in all directions; reach out one's hand everywhere; stretch one's tentacles everywhere;

dao chu shu di 到處樹敵
make enemies everywhere || arouse a nest of hornets; bring a hornet's nest about one's ears; pit oneself against the people everywhere; raise a nest of hornets;

dao chu sou cha 到處搜查
look up and down;

dao chu wei jia 到處為家
can settle down everywhere / find oneself at home everywhere;

dao chu zuan ying 到處鑽營
poke one's nose into every corner / worm one's way to every turn;

dao da 到達
arrive / arrive at / arrive in / get to / reach;

dao4 da yi pa 倒打一把
put the blame on one's victim || blame others while one is at fault oneself; bring a completely false accusation against; falsely accuse one's critic; lay the blame on others

while oneself is at fault; make false charge; make unfounded countercharges; recriminate; trump up a countercharge against one's accuser;

dao xi xiang ying 倒屣相迎

hearty welcome || greet a visitor with the shoes on back to front;

dao xi ying bin 倒屣迎賓

welcome sb with the greatest deference || greet a visitor with the shoes on back to front; meet friends with one's sandals upturned; put on slippers hurriedly to extend welcome; put one's shoes the wrong way in receiving one's guests; rush out in haste to receive the guests;

dao xing ni shi 倒行逆施

(1) act against the right principles || act in opposition to right principles; go against the historical trend; go against the tide of history; go against the trend of the times; push a reactionary policy; put the clock back; set back the clock; try to put the clock back; turn back the wheel of history;

(2) do things in a perverse way / perverse acts;

dao4 hui 盜毀

steal and damage / vandalize;

dao mai 盜賣

misappropriate / steal and sell;

dao ming 盜名

seek undeserved publicity / steal glory one does not deserve;

dao ming qi shi 盜名欺世

steal a reputation and deceive the world;

dao ming qi shi, hun xiao shi ting 盜名欺世，混淆視聽

hoodwink world public opinion by calling black white;

dao ming qie yu 盜名竊譽

seek fame by cheap means;

dao pian 盜騙

steal and cheat;

dao qie 盜竊

steal // burglary / pilferage // on the game;

dao qu 盜取

embezzle / steal;

dao yi you dao 盜亦有道

robbers also have their code of conduct / thieves have their code of honour;

dao yong 盜用

embezzle / usurp;

dao yong gong kuan 盜用公款

embezzle public funds;

dao yong ming yi 盜用名義

illegally use the name of / usurp a name;

dao yun 盜運

illegal transport;

dao zeng zhu ren 盜憎主人

robbers hate the owner of lost property;

dao4 de guan 道德觀

moral outlook;

dao gao bang zhi 道高謗至

when one's principles are high, defamation arises against one;

dao gao bu ai 道高不矮

neither too high nor too low / neither too tall nor too short;

dao mao an ran 道貌岸然

pose as a person of high morals || assume solemn airs; one's imposing bearing; sanctimonious; simulate solemnity;

de2 得

acquire / gain / get / obtain / win;

de bing 得病

contract a disease / fall ill || come down with an illness; ill;

de bu chang shi 得不償失

gains cannot make up for losses / the loss outweighs the gain || give a lark to catch a kite; it's not worth it; lose more than gain; more kicks than halfpence; not worth the candle; pay for one's whistle; pay too dear for one's whistle; the game is not worth the candle; too dear for the whistle; what is gained does not make up for what is lost;

de bu dao 得不到

cannot get;

de cheng 得逞
have one's way || prevail; succeed;

de cheng yi shi 得逞一時
have one's way for a time / succeed for a time;

de chong 得寵
find favour with sb || have an in; in sb's good graces;

de ci shi bi 得此失彼
gain in one thing and lose in another / you lose on the swings what you make on the roundabouts;

de cun jin chi 得寸進尺
give sb an inch and they will take a mile || give sb an inch and they will take an ell; much will have more; reach out for a yard after taking an inch; the more gets, the more wants;

de dang 得當
appropriate / proper;

de dao 得到
get / obtain / receive || come at; gain;

de dao 得道
attain enlightenment;

de dao duo zhu 得道多助
a just cause enjoys abundant support / one who upholds justice shall not be alone;

de dong shi xi 得東失西
you lose on the swings what you make on the roundabouts;

de er fu shi 得而復失
lose after having got it;

de fa 得法
do sth in the proper way / get the knack;

de guo qie guo 得過且過
drift along || get by however one can; if it can pass, pass it; let well enough alone;

de jiu 得救
be rescued / be saved;

de kong 得空
free / have leisure;

de kui men jing 得窺門徑
just learn the rudiments of the subject;

de lai bu yi 得來不易
hard earned // it has not come easily;

de li 得力
(1) able / competent;
(2) thanks to;
(3) profit from;

de nian 得年
die at an age before sixty;

de qi suo zai 得其所哉
be in one's element;

de ren chong ai 得人寵愛
find favour in sb's eyes;

de ren qian cai, yu ren xiao zai 得人錢財，與人消災
if one gives me money, I will avert the disaster for him;

de ren zhe chang, shi ren zhe wang 得人者昌，失人者亡
those who win people, prosper; those who lose them, fail;

de shao shi duo 得少失多
gain little and lose much;

de sheng 得勝
win a victory || bear away the bell; bear the bell; bring home the bacon; carry away the bell; carry off the bell; coast home; come through with flying colours; triumph; win;

de sheng er gui 得勝而歸
return in triumph || come back victorious; return with flying colours;

de shi 得失
(1) gain and loss / success and failure;
(2) advantages and disadvantages / merits and demerits;

de shi can ban 得失參半
half gained but half lost / success equals failure;

de shi nan liao 得失難料
whether gain or loss is beyond one's powers to foresee;

de shi rong ku 得失榮枯
the vicissitudes of life;

de shi xiang dang 得失相當
gains and losses balance each other || break

身體 *Body*

even; half loss, half gain; the gains offset the losses;

de shi 得時
in luck;

de shi 得勢
(1) in power;
(2) get the upper hand / in the ascendent;

de shou 得手
come off / do fine / go smoothly / succeeed;

de sui suo yuan 得遂所願
attain one's end / obtain one's heart's desire;

de ti 得體
appropriate / befitting one's position or suited to the occasion / decorous / well-mannered;

de tian du hou 得天獨厚
be richly endowed by nature || abound in the gifts of nature; be born with a lucky star; enjoy exceptional advantages;

de tou ming 得頭名
come out first || come first; come out on top; come out top; get the first place; head the list; stand first on the list; take first place; win first place;

de wei ceng you 得未曾有
unprecedented / without precedent;

de wei ping sheng 得慰平生
fulfil the hope of one's life || fulfil the hopes of a lifetime; gratify the desire of one's whole life; the desire of one's life is satisfied;

de xia 得暇
at leisure;

de xian 得閒
at leisure;

de xin yan jiu 得新厭舊
disdain the old when one gets the new;

de yi wang er 得一望二
have an insatiable desire to acquire more;

de yi 得宜
appropriate / proper / suitable;

de yi fei qian 得益非淺
profit much;

de yu wang quan 得魚忘筌
forget the trap as soon as the fish is caught;

de zhan wu yao 得沾勿藥
happily recovered from illness / recover from illness in good time;

de zhi 得知
be informed of;

de zhi 得志
achieve one's ambition;

de zui 得罪
cause offence to sb || cross sb; displease; get across sb; give offence to sb; in Dutch with sb; in sb's bad books; in sb's black books; offend; put up sb's pecker; run foul of sb; step on sb's toes; stroke sb the wrong way;

de2 德
(1) decency / morality / virtues;
(2) favours / repay kindness;
(3) behaviour / conduct;

de bo cai shu 德薄才疏
one's virtue is insignificant and one's ability meagre;

de bo neng xian 德薄能鮮
lack both virtue and ability;

de cai jian bei 德才兼備
combine ability with political integrity || equal stress on integrity and ability; graced with many virtues and talents; have both ability and principles; have both political integrity and ability; possess political integrity and professional competence;

de gao wang zhong 德高望重
be highly respected for one's lofty virtue || be of noble character and high prestige; enjoy high prestige and command universal respect; have a high virtue and a glorious name; with a lofty virtue worthy of respect;

de guang cai gao 德廣才高
of lofty virtue and great talent;

de wang 德望
a person's moral prestige;

de xing 德行
(1) moral conduct / moral integrity;
(2) disgusting / shameful;

deng1 登
ascend / climb / mount / scale;

deng ge re 登革熱
dengue fever;
chu xue xing deng ge re 出血性登革熱
hemorrhagic dengue;

deng ge re bing du 登革熱病毒
dengue virus;

deng long you shu 登龍有術
very skilful in finding a powerful patron to advance one's career;

deng shan 登山
climb a mountain;

deng3 dai 等待
wait / watch for;

deng shen 等身
equal to one's height;

deng yi deng 等一等
hold on / hold one's horses;

di1 san xia si 低三下四
(1) humble / lowly / mean;
(2) cringing / obsequious / servile;

di su 低俗
low in taste / trashy / vulgar;

di zi tai 低姿態
in a low profile;

di3 抵
(1) prop / support / sustain;
(2) resist / withstand;
(3) compensate for / make for a life;
(4) balance / set off;
(5) equal to;
(6) arrive at / reach;

di bu zhu 抵不住
unable to hold out;

di bu 抵補
compensate // compensation;

di chang 抵償
compensate for / give sth by way of payment for / make good;

di chu 抵觸
conflict / contradict / contravene;

di da 抵達
arrive / reach;

di dang 抵擋
fend off || check; keep out; resist; stand up against; ward off; withstand;

di fa 抵法
be punished by law;

di huan 抵換
substitute for / take the place of;

di kang 抵抗
oppose / resist / stand up to / withstand;

di lai 抵賴
deny || disavow; refuse to admit; renegue a promise;
bai ban di lai 百般抵賴
deny by every means;

di mao 抵冒
offend;

di ming 抵命
atone by life / pay for life with life;

di shi 抵事
effective // serve the purpose;

di si 抵死
defy death / fight desperately;

di si bu cong 抵死不從
refuse to submit, even unto death;

di xia dao xi 抵瑕蹈隙
attack sb's weak points / exploit the shortcomings of others / point out sb's flaws;

di xiao 抵消
cancel out || counteract; counterbalance; kill; neutralize; offset; set-off;

di ya 抵押
collateral || collateralize; hold in pledge; hypothecate; impawn; mortgage; pawn; pledge;

di yu 抵禦
resist / withstand;

di zhai 抵債
pay a debt by labour / pay a debt in kind;

di zhang 抵帳
repay a debt;

di zhi 抵制
boycott || resist;

di zhu 抵住
hold out / resist;

di3 觝
butt / push / resist;

di chu 觝觸
conflict / contradict;

di pai 觝排
get rid of / reject;

di wu 觝牾
conflict / contradict;

di4 fang bing 地方病
endemia / endemic disease;
quan di fang bing 全地方病
holoendemic disease;

di fang xing ban zhen shang han 地方性斑疹傷寒
endemic typhus;

di fang xing liu gan 地方性流感
endemic influenza;

di4 jie 締結
conclude / establish;

di jie liang yuan 締結良緣
form marital ties;

di4 jie 遞解
escort a criminal from one place to another;

di jie chu jing 遞解出境
compel to leave the country / deport / expel;

di jie hui ji 遞解回籍
escort a deported criminal back to his native place / send sb to his native place under escort;

dian1 jin bo liang 掂斤播兩
concentrate on details / make a fuss over trifles;

dian1 dao 顛倒
(1) put upside down || confound; inverse; overturn; reverse; transpose;
(2) confused / disordered // get hold of the wrong end of the stick;

dian dao di wo 顛倒敵我
reverse enemies and comrades / take enemies for comrades and comrades for enemies;

dian dao hei bai 顛倒黑白
call white black and black white / turn matters upside down || give a false account of the true facts; make black look white, and white blook black; overthrow justice; pass off black as white; prove that black is white; stand facts on their heads; swear black is white; talk black into white; transpose black and white;

dian dao qian kun 顛倒乾坤
reverse heaven and earth;

dian dao shi fei 顛倒是非
confound right and wrong || confuse truth and falsehood; distort truth; give a false account of the true facts; invert justice; lead people's error; reversal of right and wrong; reverse right and wrong; stand facts on their heads; the perversion of truth; turn right into wrong; turn things upside down; twist the facts;

dian dao shi shi 顛倒事實
give a false account of the facts / turn things upside down;

dian fu 顛覆
overthrow / overturn / subvert;

dian lai dao qu 顛來倒去
harp on / over and over / ring the changes on;

dian pei 顛沛
in destitution / suffer setbacks;

dian pei liu li 顛沛流離
lead a homeless life / wander from place to place, enduring many hardships;

dian pu bu po 顛撲不破
able to withstand heavy battering;

dian san dao si 顛三倒四
all in confusion / turn everything upside down || confused; disorderly; incoherent; put the cart before the horse; turn everything topsy-turvy;

dian1 攧
fall / stumble;

dian3 xing ban zhen shang han 典型斑疹傷寒
classic typhus;

dian3 ren shu 點人數
count noses;

dian4 痁
chronic malaria;

diao1 nan 刁難
make things difficult;

diao4 er lang dang 吊兒郎當
dilly-dally || bugger about; carelss and casual; do a milk; dodge the column; dog it; fool around; fuck about; goof off; idle about; on the mike; slovenly; take a devil-may-care attitude; take things easy; undisciplined; untidy; utterly carefree;

diao4 掉
(1) come off / drop / drop off / fall / fall off;
(2) lose / miss;
(3) fall behind;
(4) turn;
(5) drop / reduce;
(6) change / exchange;

diao4 ming qi shi 釣名欺世
gain a reputation by deception;

diao4 cha 調查
investigate || carry out a research; check into; examine into; go into; hold an inquiry into; inquire into; learn the facts about; look into; make an inquiry; make an investigation into; make an investigation of; make an investigation on; make a survey of; search into; see into; survey;

diao cha he shi 調查核實
verify through investigation;

diao cha yan jiu 調查研究
investigate and study;

diao dong 調動
bring into play / mobilize / transfer;

diao dong jue se 調動角色
shuffle positions / shuffle the cards;

diao du 調度
(1) dispatch;
(2) dispatcher;
(3) control / manage;
(4) scheduling;

diao du you fang 調度有方
arrange and operate methodically / manage in the right way // skilfully arranged;

diao li 調離
leave under order / separate / transfer;

diao pai 調派
assign / dispatch / send / send out;

diao pei 調配
allocate / deploy;

diao qian 調遣
assign / dispatch;

diao ren 調任
be transferred to another post;

diao ru 調入
call in;

diao xiu 調休
work on one's day off in exchange for a day off on one's work day;

diao yan 調研
investigation and study;

diao zhuan 調轉
(1) change / switch;
(2) transfer to another job;

die2 跌
(1) fall / tumble;
(2) drop;

die dao 跌倒
fall / trip / tumble;

die die zhuang zhuang 跌跌撞撞
dodder along / stagger along / stumbling along / totteringly;

die fen 跌份
cause yourself embarrassment / embarrass yourself;

die jiao 跌交
(1) fall / stumble and fall / trip and fall;
(2) make a mistake / meet with a setback;

die luo 跌落
drop / fall / go down / lapse;

die shang 跌傷
fall and get hurt / get injured by a fall;

die zhuang 跌撞
stumbling and bumping into things;

ding1 you 丁憂
bereavement of parents;

ding3 gang 頂槓
bear the blame for sb else;

ding ming 頂名
assume sb's name with the intent to cheat;

ding ming mao chong 頂名冒充
take the name of another;

ding ti 頂替
stand in;

ding zhuang 頂撞
contradict one's elder or superior;

ding3 li 鼎力
your kind effort;

ding li fu chi 鼎力扶持
use one's great strength to support;

ding li yu cheng 鼎力玉成
help accomplish this small task with your great power;

ding li zhi chi 鼎力支持
powerful support;

ding4 ju 定居
settle down / settle in;

diu1 丟
(1) lose / mislay;
(2) cast / throw;
(3) lay aside / put aside;

diu chou 丟醜
disgrace oneself;

diu diao 丟掉
(1) lose;
(2) cast away / discard / throw away;

diu fan wan 丟飯碗
lose one's job;

diu kai 丟開
forget for a while / leave it off;

diu san la si 丟三落四
forgetful;

dong4 洞
penetratingly / thoroughly;

dong4 shang 凍傷
suffer injury due to long exposure to cold weather;

dong si 凍死
freeze to death;

dong4 胴
(1) large intestine;
(2) body / trunk;

dong ti 胴體
body / trunk;

dong4 動
(1) move / stir;
(2) act / get moving;
(3) alter / change;
(4) use;
(5) arouse / touch;
(6) eat or drink;

dong cu 動粗
resort to violence;

dong shen 動身
set out on a journey ‖ begin a journey; depart; get cracking; go on a journey; hit the track; leave for a place; set off; set out; start out;

dong tan 動彈
move / stir;

dong tan bu de 動彈不得
cannot move ‖ cannot move a step; incapable of moving;

dong wu 動武
resort to violence;

dong xiang 動向
tendency / trend;

dong xiang bu ming 動向不明
it is uncertain which way one will go;

dong yao 動搖
falter / hover / shake / sway / waver;

dong yao bei guan 動搖悲觀
waver and grow pessimistic;

dong yao bu ding 動搖不定
go seesaw / vacillating / waver;

dong yao you yu 動搖猶豫
irresolute and wavering;

dong zhe 動輒
frequently ‖ at every turn; easily;

dong zhe de jiu 動輒得咎
be blamed for whatever one does ‖ be constantly taken to task; get blamed for every move; liable to be blamed at every move;

dong zuo 動作
(1) action / motion / movement;
(2) act / start moving;
(3) operation;

dong zuo min jie 動作敏捷
nimble / quick in one's movements // move with alacrity;

dong zuo yi zhi 動作一致
act in uniformity / keep strokes;

dou1 兜
solicit;

dou feng 兜風
go for a ride;

dou3 抖
(1) shiver / tremble;
(2) jerk / shake;
(3) rouse / stir up;
(4) get on in the world;

dou chu lai 抖出來
spill out;

dou dong 抖動
(1) chatter / shake / tremble / vibrate;
(2) agitation / joggling / whipping;

dou fan 抖翻
expose / turn up;

dou lou 抖摟
(1) shake off / shake out of sth;
(2) expose;
(3) squander / waste;

dou sou 抖擻
enliven / pluck up / rouse // hyped-up / in high spirits;

dou sou jing shen 抖擻精神
pull oneself together // hyped-up / in high spirits;

dou wei feng 抖威風
throw one's weight about;

dou4 鬥
struggle;

dou4 逗
(1) play with / tease;
(2) amuse / provoke laughter;
(3) funny;
(4) stay / stop;

dou ke sou 逗咳嗽
at each other's throats ‖ find fault; pick a fight; quarrel with someone on account of a person; grudge;

dou liu 逗留
stay / stop;

dou men zi 逗悶子
joke with / make fun of / tease in a playful way;

dou nong 逗弄
make fun of / tease // persiflage;

dou nü hai zi 逗女孩子
tease girls;

dou yin 逗引
tease;

dou4 鬭
(1) fight / tussle;
(2) denounce / struggle against;
(3) contend with / contest with;
(4) make animals fight;
(5) fit together;

dou bu guo 鬭不過
unable to win in the struggle;

dou fu 鬭富
vie in wealth;

dou hen 鬭狠
compete in atrocities;

dou jing 鬭勁
compete in strength;

dou li 鬭力
wrestle;

dou nong 鬭弄
(1) flirt with / seduce;
(2) make fun of / play jokes;

dou ou 鬭毆
brawl / fight / have a fight;

dou qi 鬪氣
quarrel on emotional grounds;

dou qu 鬪趣
joke;

dou quan 鬪拳
boxing;

dou xian qi 鬪閑氣
quarrel with trifles;

dou zheng 鬪爭
combat / fight / strive / struggle;

du1 li 督勵
spur on / urge and encourage;

du2 da 毒打
beat cruelly;

du hai 毒害
injure atrociously;

du hen 毒狠
atrocious / cruel;

du la 毒辣
cruel / malicious / spiteful;

du sha 毒殺
kill by poisoning;

du si 毒死
poison to death;

du li 獨力
single-handed // all by oneself / on one's own;

du li zhi chi 獨力支持
support single-handedly;

du shan qi shen 獨善其身
attend to one's own virtue in solitude || be righteous alone in a community where the general moral tone is low;

du shen 獨身
(1) be separated from one's family;
(2) celibate / single / unmarried // bachelorhood; celibacy; spinsterhood;

du shen nü zi 獨身女子
spinster;

du shen sheng huo 獨身生活
celibacy / single life;

du shen zhong sheng 獨身終生
pass one's life unmarried / remain single all one's life;

du zi 獨自
alone / single-handedly;

du2 髑
human skull;

du lou 髑髏
human skull;

du3 賭
(1) gamble;
(2) bet;

du bo 賭博
gamble // gambling;

du ming 賭命
gamble on one's life / gamble with one's life;

du qi 賭氣
get in a rage || cut off one's own nose to spite one's face; feel wronged and act rashly; in a fit of pique; in a huff;

du qian 賭錢
gamble for money;

du shu 賭輸
lose in gambling;

du zhai 賭債
gambling debt;

du3 篤
(1) earnest / sincere;
(2) critical / serious;

du xin 篤信
sincerely believe in || a devout believer in; believe truly;

du xing bu juan 篤行不倦
work diligently without any worries / work persistently without any worries;

du xue 篤學
devoted to study / diligent in study / studious;

du zhi li xing 篤志力行
earnestly resolving to carry it out;

du zhi yu xue 篤志於學
zealously striving to study;

身體 *Body*

du4 杜
prevent / shut out / stop;

du jian fang meng 杜漸防萌
nip the matter in the bud;

du jian fang wei 杜漸防微
check at the outset / nip in the bud || crush in the egg; destroy at an early stage, before any mischief is done; destroy evils before they become apparent;

du jue 杜絕
completely eradicate / put an end to / stop;

du jue bi duan 杜絕弊端
cut off all corruption / stop all corrupt practices;

du jue hou huan 杜絕後患
eliminate the cause of future trouble / impede a future disaster / remove seeds of future trouble;

du jue lang fei 杜絕浪費
eliminate waste / put an end to waste;

du jue liu bi 杜絕流弊
put a stop to corrupt practices / put an end to abuses;

du men bu chu 杜門不出
close the door and stay home || close the door and refrain from going out; shut the door and keep at home; shut the door without going out;

du men que sao 杜門卻掃
close the gate and keep oneself to oneself || sever communication with the outside world; withdraw from society and live in solitude;

du men xie ke 杜門謝客
close one's door to visitors || close the gate and shut out visitors; live in complete seclusion; shut one's door and decline seeing visitors; sport one's oak;

du zhuan 杜撰
fabricate / make up;

du4 度
pass / spend;

du ci can nian 度此殘年
pass the last days of the year / spend the evening of life;

du guo 度過
pass / spend;

du guo yi shi 度過一世
live out one's days;

du jia 度假
go vacationing / spend one's holidays;

du liang 度量
magnanimity / tolerance;

du ming 度命
drag out a miserable existence / live a miserable life;

du ri 度日
eke out an existence / make a living / pass the day / spend the day / subsist;

du ri huo ming 度日活命
manage to keep oneself alive with;

du ri ru nian 度日如年
every day is a year long / days wear on like years || every day appears like a year in length; lead a miserable life; pass a day as if it were a year; time hangs heavily on one's hands;

du ri wei jian 度日維艱
pass the day hardly / pass the day with difficulty / scratch along;

du4 渡
(1) cross;
(2) pull through / tide over;
(3) ferry across;

du guo 渡過
tide over / voyage;

du guo ku hai 渡過苦海
rescue from life of pains and misery and reach the other shore of salvation;

du guo nan guan 渡過難關
go through a difficult period || go through a difficult pass; pull through; tide over a difficulty; turn the corner;

du hai 渡海
sail across a sea;

du he 渡河
cross a river;

du shui deng shan 渡水登山
cross rivers and go up mountains;

duan1 zuo 端坐
sit bolt upright / sit erect;

duan3 ming 短命
die young // short-lived;

duan4 lian 鍛煉
(1) have physical training / take exercise;
(2) steel / temper / toughen;

duan lian cheng zhang 鍛煉成長
be steeled and tempered and grow up;

duan lian shen ti 鍛鍊身體
exercise the body;

duan4 ming 斷命
die;

duan qi 斷氣
breathe one's last / die // off the hooks;

duan qi shen wang 斷氣身亡
die ‖ with a last gasp of breath he gives up the ghost;

duan ran 斷然
(1) absolutely / categorically / flatly / simply;
(2) drastic / resolute;

duan ran bu tong 斷然不同
be not at all one and the same;

duan ran chu zhi 斷然處置
manage resolutely / take the bull by the horns;

duan ran fou ren 斷然否認
categorically deny;

duan ran ju jue 斷然拒絕
flatly reject ‖ a flat refusal; peremptorily dismiss; refuse point-blank; shoot down;

dui4 xian 兑現
fulfill sth;

dui4 da 對打
fight each other;

dui dai 對待
approach / deal with / treat;

dui fu 對付
(1) cope with / deal with / tackle;
(2) make do;
(3) answer counter / oppose;

dui kang 對抗
(1) antagonize / counter;
(2) oppose / resist;

dui zheng xia yao 對症下藥
prescribe the right remedy for an illness ‖ apply medicine according to indications; do what is appropriate; prescribe medicine for a patient according to his illness — solve problems according to objective realities; suit the medicine to the illness; suit the remedy to the case;

dun1 敦
honest / sincere;

dun cu 敦促
press / urge earnestly;

dun qing 敦請
earnest request / earnestly invite;

dun quan 敦勸
exhort earnestly / urge;

dun3 盹
doze / nap;

dun shui 盹睡
doze / nap;

dun4 gai qian fei 頓改前非
reform oneself suddenly;

dun4 遁
escape / flee / fly;

dun bi 遁避
withdraw into hiding;

dun cang 遁藏
conceal oneself;

dun ji 遁跡
live like a hermit / retire from public life / rusticate / withdraw from society and lead a hermit's life;

dun ji kong men 遁跡空門
become a monk ‖ conceal oneself in the holy door — become a monk; retire into a cloister; take the monastic vow;

dun ji shan lin 遁跡山林
live the life of a hermit in a mountain / flee to the mountains — retire from official life / retire to the mountains;

dun ru kong men 遁入空門
become a Buddhist monk / take the monastic vow;

dun shi mi dao 遁世覓道
leave the world and search for truth;

dun shi yin yi 遁世隱逸
retire in seclusion;

dun zhi yao yao 遁之夭夭
sneak abroad;

duo1 bing 多病
susceptible to diseases;

duo cai duo yi 多才多藝
versatile ‖ able to put one's hand to many things; gifted in many ways; have ability in many different ways; have much talent // many-sided // with much talent and much artistry;

duo fa zheng 多發症
frequently-occurring disease;

duo guan xian shi 多管閒事
meddle in / meddle with // meddlesome;

duo mian shou 多面手
all-rounder ‖ Jack-of-all-trades; man of many-sided abilities; many-sided person; versatile man; able to put one's hand to anything;

duo xing bu yi bi zi bi 多行不義必自斃
a wicked person is sure to bring about their own destruction ‖ give sb an enough rope and they will hang themselves; if one keeps on doing unrighteous deeds, one is bound to come to ruin; those who are unjust are doomed to destruction; to do evil deeds frequently will bring ruin to the doer; wicked people are sure to bring destruction to themselves;

duo1 哆
shiver / tremble;

duo luo duo suo 哆囉哆嗦
tremble with cold or fear;

duo suo 哆嗦
shiver / tremble;

duo2 奪
(1) seize / take by force / wrest;
(2) force one's way;
(3) compete for / contend for / strive for;
(4) deprive;
(5) decide;

duo biao 奪標
capture prize / win the first prize / win the title;

duo de 奪得
carry off / seize / take / win;

duo guan 奪冠
take the first place / win the championship;

duo hui 奪回
recapture / retake / seize back;

duo kui 奪魁
contend for championship / strive for the first place;

duo men er chu 奪門而出
force one's way out / force open the door and rush out / hasten out of the house in a great rush;

duo men er ru 奪門而入
force one's way into a house;

duo qu 奪取
(1) capture / seize / take by force / wrest;
(2) court / strive for;

duo qu 奪去
take away from;

duo quan 奪權
seize power / take over power;

duo ren sheng ji 奪人生計
take the bread out of sb's mouth;

duo wei er chu 奪圍而出
burst through the investing force;

duo zhan 奪佔
take possession of sth illegally;

duo3 躲
(1) go into hiding / hide;
(2) avoid / dodge / evade / get out of;

duo bi 躲避
(1) avoid / dodge / elude;
(2) hide oneself;

duo bu kai 躲不開
unable to dodge / unable to shun;

duo bu liao 躲不了
inescapable / unavoidable;

duo cang 躲藏
conceal oneself / go into hiding / hide oneself;

duo duo cang cang 躲躲藏藏
dare not show up openly;

duo duo shan shan 躲躲閃閃
dodge and hide || avoid being seen; dare not show up; evade any direct answer; play bopeep;

duo kai 躲開
get out of the way / stay away;

duo lan 躲懶
loaf on the job / shirk / shy away from work;

duo ni 躲匿
hide oneself;

duo shan 躲閃
dodge / evade / get out of the way;

duo shan bu ji 躲閃不及
too late to dodge;

duo yu 躲雨
find shelter from the rain || get out of the rain; run for cover; run for shelter; take cover from rain;

duo zai bi nan 躲災避難
avoid the coming trouble || escape with one's life and hide from danger; hide somewhere until the evil is past;

duo zhai 躲債
avoid a creditor;

duo4 惰
lazy / idle / indolent;

duo xie 惰懈
negligent;

duo xing 惰性
inertia / inertness / sluggishness;

duo4 墮
fall / sink;

duo luo 墮落
(1) degenerate || drop by the wayside; fall by the wayside; go downhill; go to the bad; go to the deuce; go to the devil; sink low;
(2) depravity;

duo luo feng chen 墮落風塵
be driven to prostitution / become a courtesan / become a prostitute;

duo luo fu hua 墮落腐化
decadent and licentious / degenerate and corrupt;

duo luo tui hua 墮落蛻化
demoralization and degeneration;

duo ru 墮入
fall into / land oneself in / sink into;

duo ru ai he 墮入愛河
fall head over heels in love;

duo ru ni keng 墮入泥坑
fall into the pit / sink into the quagmire of;

duo ru quan tao 墮入圈套
be caught in a trap;

duo ru wu zhong 墮入霧中
be completely lost at sea / be lost in a thick fog;

duo ru yan hai 墮入煙海
get lost in a fog / lose oneself in a fog;

e1 chan 阿諂
fawn upon / flatter / toady;

e fu 阿附
fawn on and echo / toady to and chime in with;

e fu quan gui 阿附權貴
curry favour with those in power || attach oneself to some authority; attach oneself to the powerful and influential persons; cling to the powerful; curry favour with influential officials; toady to and chime in with the influential officials;

e mei 阿媚
flatter / toady;

e yu 阿諛
curry flavour with / fawn on / flatter / play up to;

e yu chan ning 阿諛諂佞
curry favour with sb;

e yu chan xiao 阿諛諂笑
fulsome flattery // flatter and curry favour;

e yu feng cheng 阿諛奉承
curry favour with sb || act the yes-man; butter sb; butter up; compliment unduly; dance attendance on; eat sb's toads; fawn on sb; flatter and cajole; flatter and toady; flattery; ingratiate oneself into sb's favour; ingratiate oneself with sb; lay it on thick; make much of; make up to; oil one's tongue; polish the apple; praise insincerely in order to please another's vanity; stoop to flattery; tickle sb's ears; toady;

e yu ren ren xi, zhi yan ren ren xian 阿諛人人喜，直言人人嫌
everyone is pleased by flattery but annoyed by frank statements;

e yu you fu, zhi yan you huo 阿諛有福，直言有禍
flattering produces good fortune and frank statements court disaster;

e2 訛
(1) errors;
(2) deceive / extort / swindle;

e chuan 訛傳
false rumours / unfounded hearsay / wrong information;

e wu 訛誤
inaccurate / wrong // error / mistake;

e zha 訛詐
blackmail / extort under false pretences / intimidate;

e zha qian cai 訛詐錢財
extort money under false pretences;

e4 扼
clutch / control / grip;

e sha 扼殺
smother / strangle / throttle;

e si 扼死
strangle / throttle;

e4 bing 惡病
malignant disease;

e guan man ying 惡貫滿盈
have committed one's full share of crimes || be steeped in evil and deserve damnation; face retribution for a life of crimes; full of iniquities; guilty of countless crimes and deserve to come to judgement; have a long list of crimes; have committed countless crimes and deserve to come to judgement; have sunk in sin with a record full of crimes and misdeeds; one's crimes are inexpiable; replete with crimes; the measure of iniquities is full;

e lie xing jing 惡劣行徑
disgusting conduct;

e ming 惡名
bad name / bad reputation / ill fame / infamy / notoriety;

e mo e yang 惡模惡樣
fierce appearance;

e pi 惡癖
bad habit;

e ren 惡人
evil person / villain;

e ren dang dao 惡人當道
the evildoers are now in power;

e ren xian gao zhuang 惡人先告狀
the guilty party files the suit first / the villain sues the victim before being prosecuted;

e ren xu yi e fa zhi 惡人須以惡法治
an evil person must have strict controls / to a vicious dog, a short chain;

e ren zhi you e ren xiang 惡人衹有惡人降
a wicked person can be dealt with only by another wicked person;

e ren zi you e ren mo 惡人自有惡人磨
a fierce person of course has a fierce person to torment them || a villain will catch a tartar one of these days; a villain will encounter sb more than their match sooner or later; bad people always find their match; be afflicted by a similar personality; the great thieves punish the little ones; where vice is, vengeance follows;

e ren zi you e xiang 惡人自有惡相
a wicked man has ferocious features;

e xing gao re 惡性高熱
malignant hyperpyrexia;

e xing tian hua 惡性天花
malignant smallpox;

e xing ying yang bu liang 惡性營養不良
malignant malnutrition;

e xing zhong liu 惡性腫瘤
malignant tumour;

e yun 惡運
bad luck / ill luck;

e4 bing 遏病
check disease;

e e yang shan 遏惡揚善
refrain from talking about another's evildoing but cite his good points;

e jin 遏禁
restrain / stop;

e jue 遏絕
exterminate / suppress entirely;

e zhi 遏止
check / hold back / stop;

e zhi 遏制
check / curb / restrain / stop;

e zu 遏阻
curb / stop;

er3 yu wo zha 爾虞我詐
cheat and deceive each other || deceive and blackmail each other; deceive mutually; double-cross each other; each trying to cheat or outwit the other; mutual suspicion and deception; scheme against each other;

fa1 發
(1) deliver / give / send / send out;
(2) discharge / emit / shoot;
(3) deliver a speech / express / utter;
(4) develop / expand;
(5) rise or expand when fermented or soaked;
(6) come or bring into existence / produce;
(7) discover / open up;
(8) become / get into a certain state;
(9) show one's feeling;
(10) feel / have a feeling;
(11) set out / start / start off;
(12) distribute / issue;
(13) get rich;

fa bao 發報
transmit messages;

fa biao 發表
announce / deliver || air; express; issue; project; publish; report; voice;

fa biao sheng ming 發表聲明
issue a statement;

fa biao wen zhang 發表文章
publish an article;

fa biao yi jian 發表意見
air one's views / express an opinion || pass on; put in one's two cents worth; state one's views;

fa bing 發病
get sick / fall ill;

fa bing lü 發病率
morbidity;

fa bu 發布
issue / release;

fa bu xin wen 發布新聞
release news;

fa cai 發財
get rich / make a fortune || clean up; make a pile; make one's fortune;

fa cai zhi fu 發財致富
get rich || amass great fortunes; enrich; make one's fortune; make one's pile;

fa chu 發出
deliever / dispatch / emit / issue / send out;

fa da 發達
advanced / developed / flourishing / prosperous / thriving;

fa dai 發呆
dumbfounded || in a daze; in a trance; spellbound; stare blankly; stunned; stupefied;

fa dia 發嗲
act like a spoiled child;

fa dong 發動
(1) get going / get started / launch;
(2) arouse / call into action / mobilize;
(3) start (a machine);

fa dong qun zhong 發動群眾
arouse the masses to action / mobilize the masses;

身體 *Body*

fa dong zhan zheng 發動戰爭
start a war;

fa dou 發抖
quiver / shake / shiver / shudder / tremble;

fa duan 發端
inception / initiative // make a start;

fa fang 發放
give out / grant / hand out / issue / provide;

fa fen 發奮
bestir oneself / rouse oneself || exert oneself; make a determined effort; make a firm resolution; strive resolutely; work energetically; work hard;

fa fen gong zuo 發奮工作
pull all one's energies into one's work / work energetically;

fa fen tu qiang 發奮圖強
rise in great vigour || bring oneself to make the country strong; strive for national prosperity; with firm resolve to succeed; work hard and aim high; work with a will to make the country strong;

fa fen xue xi 發奮學習
put all one's energies into one's studies / stimulate oneself to study;

fa fen you wei 發奮有為
proving one's worth // with firm resolve to succeed;

fa fen 發憤
make a determined effort / make a firm resolution;

fa fen qiu xue 發憤求學
very eager in one's studies;

fa fen wang shi 發憤忘食
so immersed in work as to forget one's meals / study hard, neglecting one's meals / work so hard as to forget to eat;

fa fu 發福
put on weight || become plump; get fat; grow stout; plump;

fa gao shao 發高燒
be affected with high fever / have a high fever;

fa gao 發稿
send manuscripts to the press;

fa gong zi 發工資
pay salary / pay wages;

fa guang 發光
emit light;

fa hao shi ling 發號施令
give orders || boss; call the shots; call the tune; call the turn; command; dictate; dictate one's terms to; give law to; issue orders; lay down the law; order about; order around; order people about; order sb as one fancies;

fa hen 發狠
(1) make a determined effort;
(2) angry / be enraged / get rough / turn angry;

fa heng 發橫
become suddenly hard and harsh;

fa heng cai 發橫財
get a windfall || get rich by foul means; ill-gotten gains; make a fortune in a devious way; strike it rich; strike oil;

fa huan 發還
give back / return sth;

fa hui 發揮
(1) bring into play / give free rein to / give play to / give scope to;
(2) elaborate || air; amplify; develop; expound; express;

fa huo 發火
get angry / lose one's temper || fire up; fit to be tied; flare up;

fa ji 發跡
make a fortune || enrich oneself; gain fame and fortune; make a career; make one's way; rise in the world; rise to power and position;

fa ji 發急
become impatient;

fa jia zhi fu 發家致富
build up family fortunes || enrich one's family; enrich oneself; make one's family's fortune;

fa jiong 發窘
become embarrassed / feel embarrassed / ill

at ease;

fa jue 發掘

disinterment // excavate / explore / unearth;

fa jue 發覺

(1) aware of / come to know / get wind of;

(2) detect / discover / find / realize;

fa kan 發刊

issue / publish ‖ start the publication of a periodical;

fa kun 發睏

drowsy / sleepy;

fa lao sao 發牢騷

blow off steam ‖ beef; chew the rag; complain; grouch; grouse; grumble; grumble about; grumble at; grumble over; let off steam; make a sour remark; murmur; natter; say devil's paternoster; whine about; work off steam;

fa leng 發冷

chills // feel chilly; feel cold;

fa mao 發毛

(1) afraid of / scared / terrified;

(2) lose one's temper;

fa mei 發霉

become mildewed / go mouldy // mildew // mouldiness / mustiness;

fa meng qi zhi 發蒙啟滯

enlighten the young and open the minds of the dull;

fa meng zhen luo 發蒙振落

things easily accomplished without mental effort;

fa ming 發明

invent;

fa nan 發難

launch an attack / rise in revolt // the first to start revolt;

fa pang 發胖

get fat / put on weight ‖ burst one's buttons; gain flesh; put on flesh; round out;

fa pi qi 發脾氣

get angry ‖ be short-tempered; blow a fuse; blow a gasket; blow one's fuse; blow one's lid off; blow one's top; blow up; cut up rough; flare up; flay into a rage; fly into a temper; get into a tantrum; get one's dander up; get one's hackles up; get the grumps; have sb's hackles up; have the grumps; hit the ceiling; let oneself go; lose one's temper; make sb's hackles rise; vent one's spleen // in a tantrum; out of temper; under the dominion of grumps; with one's hackles rising; with one's hackles up;

fa qi 發起

get up / initiate / launch;

fa qiu 發球

serve / serve a ball // service;

fa shao 發燒

have a fever ‖ go down with a fever; have a fever; have a temperature; run a fever;

fa sheng 發生

(1) genesis;

(2) happen ‖ arise; come about; come over; come to pass; come up; fall out; go off; go on; occur; spring up; take place; turn up;

lin ba fa sheng 淋巴發生

lymphogenesis;

fa sheng bu quan 發生不全

dysgenesis;

gu hou fa sheng bu quan 骨骺發生不全

epiphyseal dysgenesis;

fa sheng xiao li 發生效力

do the trick;

fa shou 發售

put on sale / sell;

fa shu ji jian 發抒己見

express one's personal views;

fa xian 發現

detect / discover / find / find out / spot;

fa xiang 發祥

flourish / prosper;

fa xie 發洩

give vent to / let off;

fa xie bu man 發洩不滿

air one's grievances / express one's grievances;

fa xin 發薪

pay salary / pay wages;

fa xin 發信
post a letter;

fa xing 發行
distribute / issue / put on sale / release;

fa xue 發噱
amusing / funny;

fa yan 發炎
inflammation;

fa yang 發揚
(1) carry forward / carry on / develop / keep up / promote;
(2) bring into full play / give play to / make full use of / make the most of;

fa yang jiao feng 發羊角瘋
have an attack of epilepsy;

fa yang guang da 發揚光大
spread and flourish ‖ bring to a greater height of development; carry forward; develop; develop and shine with greater brilliance; develop to a higher stage; enhance; foster and enhance; give full play to; give greater scope to;

fa yao zi 發瘧子
suffer from malaria;

fa yu 發育
(1) development;
(2) engender / grow;
chu sheng hou fa yu 出生後發育
postnatal development;
chu sheng qian fa yu 出生前發育
prenatal development;

fa yu bu liang 發育不良
atelia / maldevelopment;
biao pi fa yu bu liang 表皮發育不良
epidermodysplasia;
chun fa yu bu liang 唇發育不良
atelocheilia;
e bi fa yu bu liang 額鼻發育不良
frontonasal dysplasla;
gong jing fa yu bu liang 宮頸發育不良
cervical dysphlasia;
gu fa yu bu liang 骨發育不良
anostosis;
gu gan fa yu bu liang 骨幹發育不良
diaphyseal dysphlasia;
gu ge fa yu bu liang 骨骼發育不良
ostemyelodysphlasia;
gu sui fa yu bu liang 骨髓發育不良
myelodysplasia;
guan jie fa yu bu liang 關節發育不良
arthrodysplasia;
hou fa yu bu liang 骺發育不良
epiphyseal dysplasia;
ji zhu fa yu bu liang 脊柱發育不良
atelorachidia;
kou fa yu bu liang 口發育不良
atelostomia;
lin ba fa yu bu liang 淋巴發育不良
alymphoplasia;
lu fa yu bu liang 顱發育不良
atelocephaly;
mian fa yu bu liang 面發育不良
ateloprosopia;
nao fa yu bu liang 腦發育不良
atelencephalia;
pi fu fa yu bu liang 皮膚發育不良
dermatodysplasia;
pian ce fa yu bu liang 偏側發育不良
hemihypoplasia;
ruan gu fa yu bu liang 軟骨發育不良
achondroplasia;
she fa yu bu liang 舌發育不良
ateloglossia;
shen ti fa yu bu liang 身體發育不良
hyposomia;
shen fa yu bu liang 腎發育不良
renal dysplasia;
shi wang mo fa yu bu liang 視網膜發育不良
retinal dysplasia;
shou fa yu bu liang 手發育不良
atelocheiria;
xin fa yu bu liang 心發育不良
atelocardia;
ya fa yu bu liang 牙發育不良
hypodontia;
zu fa yu bu liang 足發育不良
atelopodia;

fa yu bu quan 發育不全
aplasia;
biao pi fa yu bu quan 表皮發育不全
epidermodysplasia;
chun fa yu bu quan 唇發育不全
atelocheilia;
gong jing fa yu bu quan 宮頸發育不全
cervical dysphlasia;
gu fa yu bu quan 骨發育不全
dyosteogenesis;
guan jie fa yu bu quan 關節發育不全
arthrodysplasia;
hou fa yu bu quan 骺發育不全
epiphyseal dysplasia;
ji zhu fa yu bu quan 脊柱發育不全
atelorachidia;
kou fa yu bu quan 口發育不全
atelostomia;
lin ba fa yu bu quan 淋巴發育不全
alymphoplasia;
lu fa yu bu quan 顱發育不全
atelocephaly;
mian fa yu bu quan 面發育不全
ateloprosopia;
nao fa yu bu quan 腦發育不全
atelencephalia;
pi fu fa yu bu quan 皮膚發育不全
adermogenesis;
pian ce fa yu bu quan 偏側發育不全
hemihypoplasia;
ruan gu fa yu bu quan 軟骨發育不全
dyschondroplasia;
she fa yu bu quan 舌發育不全
ateloglossia;
shen ti fa yu bu quan 身體發育不全
hyposomia;
shen fa yu bu quan 腎發育不全
renal dysplasia;
sheng zhi qi fa yu bu quan 生殖器發育不全
agenosomia;
sheng zhi xian fa yu bu quan 生殖腺發育不全
gonadal dysgenesis;
shi wang mo fa yu bu quan 視網膜發育不全
retinal aplasia;
shou fa yu bu quan 手發育不全
atelocheiria;
xin fa yu bu quan 心發育不全
atelocardia;
xing xian fa yu bu quan 性腺發育不全
gonadal dysgenesis;
zi gong fa yu bu quan 子宮發育不全
uterine hypoplasia;
zu fa yu bu quan 足發育不全
atelopodia;

fa yu chi huan 發育遲緩
hypoevolutism;
gong nei fa yu chi huan 宮內發育遲緩
intrauterine growth retardation;

fa yu guo du 發育過度
hypergenesis;
pian ce fa yu guo du 偏側發育過度
hemihyperplasia;
sheng zhi qi fa yu guo du 生殖器發育過度
hypergenitalism;

fa yu guo huan 發育過緩
bradygenesis;

fa yu guo xiao 發育過小
microgenesis;

fa yu jun heng 發育均衡
eurhythmia;

fa yu jun yun 發育均勻
eurhythmia;

fa yu li 發育力
potency;

fa yu qi 發育期
maturity;

fa yu shi tiao 發育失調
dysmaturity;

fa yu ting dun 發育停頓
arrested development;

fa yu ting zhi 發育停止
developmental arrest;

fa yu yi chang 發育異常
dysplasia;

身體 *Body*

gu gan fa yu yi chang 骨幹發育異常
diaphyseal sclerosis;

fa yu zhang ai 發育障礙
developmental disorders;

gu fa yu zhang ai 骨發育障礙
dysosteogenesis;

pian ce fa yu zhang ai 偏側發育障礙
hemidystrophy;

sheng zhi qi fa yu zhang ai 生殖器發育障礙
dysgenitalism;

fa yuan 發源
have its source / originate / rise;

fa yun 發暈
faint / feel dizzy / feel giddy;

fa zhan 發展
(1) develop / expand / forge ahead / grow;
(2) admit / recruit;

fa zhan zhuang da 發展壯大
develop and grow in strength / expand / go from strength to strength;

fa zuo 發作
(1) break out / show effect / take effect;
(2) have a fit of anger / lose one's temper;

fa2 li 乏力
hypodynamia;

fan1 fu wu chang 翻覆無常
capricious / fickle-minded / whimsical;

fan gen dou 翻跟斗
turn a somersault;

fan lao zhang 翻老帳
bring up old scores again;

fan shen 翻身
(1) turn over;
(2) free oneself / stand up;

fan2 煩
(1) be annoyed / be irritated / be vexed;
(2) nag / trouble;

fan lao 煩勞
bother / trouble;

fan rao 煩擾
(1) bother / disturb / pester / trouble / vex;
(2) feel disturbed;

fan yan 煩厭
be fed up with;

fan3 chang 反常
abnormal;

fan dui 反對
be against ‖ argue against; be opposed to; buck against; combat; come out against; conspire against; cry against; cry out against; dead set against; declare against; decry; demonstrate against; demur; deprecate; fight; fight against; go against; have an objection to; make an objection to; have an opposition to; in opposition to; object to; oppose; protest against; raise one's back against; react against; set against; set one's face against; set oneself against; show opposition to; side against; speak against; stand against; take opposition to; thumbs-down; vote against;

fan she 反射
reflex;

bi fan she 鼻反射
nasal reflex;

bin fan she 髕反射
patellar reflex;

chun fan she 唇反射
lip reflex;

deng gu fan she 鐙骨反射
stapedial reflex;

er guo fan she 耳廓反射
auricle reflex;

gang men fan she 肛門反射
anal reflex;

gu fan she 骨反射
bone reflex;

gu mo fan she 骨膜反射
periosteal reflex;

hou fan she 喉反射
laryngeal reflex;

huai fan she 踝反射
ankle jerk;

jian fan she 腱反射
tendon reflex ‖ tendon jerk;

jiao cha fan she 交叉反射
crossed reflex;

jiao mo fan she 角膜反射
corneal reflex;

jie mo fan she 結膜反射
conjunctival reflex;

jin zhang fan she 緊張反射
tonic reflex;

jin shi fan she 近視反射
myopic reflex;

jing fan she 頸反射
neck reflex;

jing mai fan she 靜脈反射
venous reflux;

ju bu fan she 局部反射
local reflex;

ke fan she 頦反射
chin reflex;

ke sou fan she 咳嗽反射
cough reflex;

lao nian xing fan she 老年性反射
senile reflex;

lei fan she 淚反射
lacrimal reflex;

mi lu fan she 迷路反射
labyrinthine reflex;

mian fan she 面反射
facial reflex;

nao fan she 腦反射
cranial reflex;

nao gan fan she 腦幹反射
brain stem reflex;

nei zang fan she 內臟反射
visceral reflex;

pai bian fan she 排便反射
defecation reflex;

pai niao fan she 排尿反射
micturition reflex;

pang guang fan she 膀胱反射
bladder reflex;

pi fu fan she 皮膚反射
skin reflex;

qian ting fan she 前庭反射
vestibular reflex;

quan fan she 全反射
total reflection;

que xue xing fan she 缺血性反射
ischemic reflex;

shen ceng fan she 深層反射
deep reflex;

shui mian fan she 睡眠反射
hypnic jerk;

shun mu fan she 瞬目反射
blink reflex;

ting fan she 聽反射
auditory reflex;

ting jue fan she 聽覺反射
acoustic reflex;

tong kong fan she 瞳孔反射
pupillary reflex;

tun fan she 臀反射
gluteal reflex;

wai er dao fan she 外耳道反射
external auditory meatus reflex;

wei jie chang fan she 胃結腸反射
gastrocolic reflex;

xi fan she 膝反射
knee jerk / knee reflex / patellar;

xin fan she 心反射
heart reflex;

xing wei fan she 行為反射
behaviour reflex;

xing fan she 性反射
sexual reflex;

yao fan she 腰反射
lumbar reflex;

yin jing fan she 陰莖反射
penis reflex;

yin xing fan she 隱性反射
concealed reflex;

you nian xing fan she 幼年性反射
juvenile reflex;

zhang fan she 掌反射
palmar reflex;

zhi chang fan she 直腸反射
rectal reflex;

zhi fan she 指反射
digital reflex;

zhou fan she 肘反射
elbow reflex;

zi shi fan she 姿勢反射
postural reflex;

zu bei fan she 足背反射
dorsocuboidal reflex;
zu di fan she 足底反射
plantar reflex;

fan she wen luan 反射紊亂
parareflexia;

fan she yi chang 反射異常
dysreflexia;

fan xing 反省
reflect on // self-examination;

fan ying 反應
reaction;
guo min fan ying 過敏反應
anaphylactic reaction;
jia xing fan ying 假性反應
pseudoreaction;
jian fan ying 腱反應
tendon reaction;
ma feng fan ying 麻瘋反應
lepra reaction;
pi fu fan ying 皮膚反應
demoreaction;
tong kong fan ying 瞳孔反應
pupillary reflex;

fan ying ling min 反應靈敏
quick on the draw;

fan3 lao huan tong 返老還童
regain youth / rejuvenate oneself // rejuvenescence;

fan4 an 犯案
commit a crime / commit an offence;

fan bing 犯病
fall back into an old illness or a bad habit / have a relapse;

fan cuo wu 犯錯誤
commit an error / err / make a mistake;

fan fa 犯法
break the law; / violate the law;

fan gui 犯規
commit a foul / violate a rule;

fan ji 犯忌
violate a taboo;

fan ji wei 犯忌諱
violate a taboo;

fan jie 犯戒
violate a religious prohibition;

fan jin 犯禁
violate prohibitions;

fan ke 犯科
break the law / commit an offence;

fan nan 犯難
risk danger;

fan pi qi 犯脾氣
get one's dander up / lose one's temper;

fan shang 犯上
offend against one's superiors;

fan shang zuo luan 犯上作亂
rebel against authority;

fan zui 犯罪
commit a crime;

fang1 ling 芳齡
age (of a young lady);

fang2 ai 防癌
cancer prevention // prevent cancer;

fang shen 防身
guard personal safety // self-protection;

fang3 xiao 仿效
follow the example of sb;

fang3 訪
(1) call on / visit;
(2) find out;

fang qiu 訪求
look for / search for / seek;

fang wen 訪問
call on / pay a visit to / visit;

fang4 放
(1) let go / release / set free;
(2) give out / let off;
(3) put out to pasture;
(4) give way to / let oneself go;
(5) lend money for interest;
(6) expand / let out;
(7) blossom / open / open blossom;
(8) leave / lie / place / put;

(9) send away;
(10) play / show;

fang dang du ri 放蕩度日
pass the day recklessly;

fang diao 放刁
show villainy;

fang gong 放工
knock off;

fang jia 放假
take a leave;

fang kong qi 放空氣
put out feelers / send out trial balloons;

fang leng jian 放冷箭
injure others secretly;

fang qi 放棄
abandon / give up / relinquish / throw up;

fang ren 放任
leave alone / let sth take its own course;

fang song 放鬆
ease / lie back / loosen / relax / slacken;

fang xia 放下
lay down / put down;

fang xia bao fu 放下包袱
lay down one's burden || cast off mental burdens; get rid of the baggage; put down one's budren;

fang xia bu guan 放下不管
leave sb in the lurch;

fang xia chou jia zi 放下臭架子
drop pretentious airs / shed the ugly mantle of pretentiousness;

fang xia guan jia zi 放下官架子
discard bureaucratic airs / drop pretentious airs and graces;

fang xia jia zi 放下架子
discard one's haughty airs || come off one's high horse; come off one's perch; pocket one's dignity;

fang xia tu dao, li di cheng fo 放下屠刀，立地成佛
drop the butcher's knife and immediately become a Buddha || a butcher becomes a Buddha the moment he drops his cleaver; lay down the butcher knife and become a Buddha; throw away one's cleaver and become a Buddha;

fang yi ma 放一碼
let sb off || forgive; have mercy on; release;

fang zhu 放逐
banish / exile / send into exile;

fang zou 放走
let go / release / set free;

fei1 chang gao xing 非常高興
be tickled pink / be tickled to death // very happy;

fei li 非禮
sexual assault;

fei ren sheng huo 非人生活
miserable life;

fei1 huang teng da 飛黃騰達
have a meteoric rise in position || climb up the social ladder rapidly; come into one's kingdom; come up in the world; have the world at one's feet; make one's way; make rapid advance in one's career; rise high; rise in the world; sail before the wind; win one's spurs;

fei yan zou bi 飛簷走壁
fly over the eaves and run on the walls || climb walls and leap onto roofs; fly from house to house and walk on walls; leap onto roofs and vault over walls; make one's way into a house over walls and roofs;

fei1sheng 蜚聲
become famous / make a name;

fei sheng que qi 蜚聲鵲起
one's reputation suddenly becomes high and widespread;

fei ying teng mao 蜚英騰茂
reputed and rise up to prosperity;

fei2 肥
(1) fat;
(2) large / loose / loose-fitting;

fei bao si nang 肥飽私囊
line one's pockets;

fei chun 肥蠢
fat and stupid;

fei chun ru zhu 肥蠢如豬
fat and stupid as a pig;

fei da 肥大
(1) large / loose;
(2) fat / fat and big / plump;
dan chun xing fei da 單純性肥大
simple hypertrophy;
dan chun zhi jia fei da 單純指甲肥大
hyperonychia;
jia fei da 假肥大
false hypertrophy / pseudohypertrophy;
jia xing fei da 假性肥大
pseudohypertrophy;
liang xing qian lie xian fei da 良性前列腺肥大
benign prostatic hypertrophy;
nao fei da 腦肥大
encephalauxe;
nei zang fei da 內臟肥大
visceromegaly;
pian ce fei da 偏側肥大
hemihypertrophy;
shen fei da 腎肥大
nephromegaly;
sheng li xing fei da 生理性肥大
physiologic hypertrophy;
zhen xing fei da 真性肥大
true hypertrophy;
zhi fei da 指肥大
pachydactyly;
zhi jia fei da 指甲肥大
onychauxis;
zhi fei da 趾肥大
pachydactyly;

fei da xing fei pang 肥大性肥胖
hypertrophic obesity;

fei da zheng 肥大症
hypertrophy;

fei fei pang pang 肥肥胖胖
fat;

fei hou 肥厚
fleshy / plump / stout and strong;
hong mo fei hou 虹膜肥厚
iridauxesis;

fei ji 肥己
enrich oneself;

fei pang 肥胖
obesity ‖ adiposity; as fat as butter; corpulent; fat; fleshiness; obesitas; polypionia; polysarcia; stout; weight // obese;
cheng nian xing fei pang 成年型肥胖
adult-onset obesity;
chui ti xing fei pang 垂體性肥胖
pituitary adiposity;
dan chun xing fei pang 單純性肥胖
simple obesity;
fei da xing fei pang 肥大性肥胖
hypertrophic obesity;
nei yuan xing fei pang 內源性肥胖
endogenous obesity;
pian ce fei pang 偏側肥胖
hemiobesity;
pian shen fei pang 偏身肥胖
hemiobesity;
quan shen xing fei pang 全身性肥胖
adiposis universalis;
tong xing fei pang 痛性肥胖
adiposis dolorosa;
wai yuan xing fei pang 外源性肥胖
exogenous obesity;

fei pang guo du 肥胖過度
hyperadiposis;

fei pang zheng 肥胖症
obesity;

fei shi 肥實
big and corpulent;

fei shou 肥瘦
the fat and thin;

fei shou de zhong 肥瘦得中
good figure ‖ half lean; round without being plump, slender without being bony;

fei si nang 肥私囊
line one's pocket;

fei tou da er 肥頭大耳
large head and big ears — signs of a prosperous man;

fei4 jin jiu niu er hu zhi li 費盡九牛二虎之力
take a tremendous lot of work ‖ make

herculean efforts; spend a tremendous amount of labour; strain oneself to the limit; with all one's might and main; work overtime;

fei jin 費勁
strenuous // need great effort / put oneself out / take a lot of effort / use great effort;

fei li 費力
laborious / strenuous // need great effort / put oneself out / use great effort;

fei li bu tao hao 費力不討好
arduous but fruitless || a fool for one's pains; a fool to oneself; do a hard but thankless job; exacting but unrewarding; more kicks than halfpence; put in much hard work, but get very little result; tough but thankless; undertake a thankless task; work hard but get little result;

fei li qi 費力氣
do one's best;

fei4 廢
(1) abandon / abolish / give up;
(2) useless // waste;
(3) disabled / maimed;

fei chu 廢除
abolish || abrogate; annihilate; annul; cancel; do away with; nullify; repeal; revoke;

fei chu 廢黜
decrown / depose / dethrone;

fei er bu yong 廢而不用
fall into disuse || fall into oblivion; pass into disuse; put aside as useless; stop using;

fei qin wang shi 廢寢忘食
too busy to eat or sleep || disregard meal times and go without sleep; do sth almost to the gross neglect of one's health; forget food and rest; forget meals and sleep; lose sleep and forget to eat; neglect one's meals and sleep;

fei zhi 廢止
abolish / annul / put an end to;

fen1 cun 分寸
sense of propriety / sense of proportion;

fen cun gan 分寸感
sense of propriety / sense of proportion;

fen gan gong ku 分甘共苦
share the sweet and the bitter together || fare and share alike; go through thick and thin together; share comforts and hardships; share good luck and ill; share prosperity and adversity; share weal and woe;

fen shen 分身
spare time from one's main work to attend to sth else;

fen shen bu xia 分身不暇
unable to be in two places at a time / unable to disengage oneself;

fen shen 分神
(1) give some attention to;
(2) distraction;

fen1 rao 紛擾
(1) confuse / disturb;
(2) disturbance / turmoil;
(3) confused / disorderly;

fen zheng 紛爭
dispute / quarrel / wrangle;

fen2 gao ji gui 焚膏繼晷
burn the midnight oil || turn a candle to lengthen the day — sit up and study late at night;

fen shi mie ji 焚屍滅跡
burn the corpse in order to destroy all the traces || burn sb's body to cover up the crime; burn the corpse to destroy the evidence; reduce the corpse to ashes in order to destroy all traces of one's crime;

fen shi yang hui 焚屍揚灰
burn sb's corpse and scatter the ashes to the winds || destroy the corpse by fire and obliterate all the traces;

fen3 shen sui gu 粉身碎骨
have one's body smashed to pieces || be beaten till one's bones are broken; be crushed to powder; be crushed to pulp; be dashed to pieces; be hacked to pieces; be smashed to pieces; die the most cruel death; grind one's bones to powder and make mincemeat of one's flesh; have one's body pounded to pieces and one's bones ground to powder; one's bones are ground to powder;

fen shen sui gu, zai suo bu xi 粉身碎骨，在所不惜

not to flinch even if one is threatened with destruction;

fen4 bu gu shen 奮不顧身

be so dauntless as to forget one's own safety || be so eager for the safety of others as to forget about one's own; dash ahead regardless of one's safely; defy personal danger; regardless of personal danger;

fen dou 奮鬪

strive for / struggle;

fen fa 奮發

exert oneself / rouse oneself;

fen fa cong shi 奮發從事

direct one's efforts to;

fen fa nu li 奮發努力

put one's back into sth / put one's back to it;

fen fa tu qiang 奮發圖強

work with stamina and diligence || go all out to make the country strong; make efforts; rise in great vigour; strive to be strong; work hard for the prosperity of the country;

fen fa you wei 奮發有為

enthusiatic and press on / resolve to do some great things;

fen jin 奮進

advance bravely / press ahead / press forward / press on / push ahead;

fen li 奮力

do all one can / spare no effort;

fen li fan kang 奮力反抗

do all one can in resistance;

fen li tu cun 奮力圖存

keep one's head above water / put forth to maintain existence;

fen li zheng zha 奮力掙扎

struggle with all one's might;

fen qi 奮起

make a vigorous start || rise; rise up with ardour; rise with force and spirit;

fen qi kang di 奮起抗敵

rise against the enemy;

fen qi zhi zhui 奮起直追

do all one can to catch up || catch up assiduously; make high resolve to catch up with; press ahead to overtake; press forward to catch up with; pull up with a supreme effort; rise in great vigour so as to catch up with; rise up in a bounce and try to catch up with; rise up in pursuit straightaway;

fen yong 奮勇

summon up all one's courage and energy;

fen yong dang xian 奮勇當先

be brave and rush to the front / fight bravely in the van;

fen yong qian jin 奮勇前進

advance bravely || forge ahead courageously; forge valiantly ahead; march forward;

fen yong zhan dou 奮勇戰斗

act a good part;

fen yong zhi qian 奮勇直前

screw up one's courage and push forward;

fen zhan dao di 奮戰到底

fight to the bitter end / fight to the last ditch;

fen zhi bu xie 奮志不懈

determined and unwearied;

feng1 chen 風塵

(1) travel fatigue;

(2) hardships or uncertainties in an unstable society;

feng chen biao wu 風塵表物

one who rises above the common herd || one who rises above the winds and dust; one who rises from rank and file; one who transcends the secular world;

feng chen lu lu 風塵碌碌

busy with worldly affairs;

feng chen nü zi 風塵女子

prostitute || a lady of easy virtue; a lady of pleasure; a lady of the evening; a sporting lady; a street girl; a woman amidst winds and dust; a woman of pleasure; a woman of the street; a woman of the town; bachelor's wife; courtesan; cousin Betty; fancy girl; fancy lady; fancy woman;

feng chen pu pu 風塵僕僕

busy with travelling || be fatigued with the

journey; be worn out by one's journey; be travel-worn and weary; endure the hardships of a long journey; endure the hardships of travel; hard journey; look travel-stained; look travelweary; worn out by a long journey;

feng liu cai zi 風流才子
talented and romantic scholar;

feng liu jia shi 風流佳事
romance between man and woman;

feng liu ren wu 風流人物
(1) romantic person;
(2) original genius / truly great and noble-hearted men / truly great men;

feng liu yun san 風流雲散
go with the wind || be blown apart by the wind and scattered like the clouds — separated and scattered; be dispersed and evaporated into thin air; scatter and dissolve like wind-swept clouds; scatter like clouds before the wind; vanish without a trace;

feng liu yun shi 風流韻事
love affair / romance / romantic affair;

feng liu zui guo 風流罪過
blemishes;

feng qu 風趣
humorous / witty;

feng qu heng sheng 風趣橫生
sauced with wit;

feng qu you mo 風趣幽默
have a fine sense of humour;

feng ren mo ke 風人墨客
poets and literary people;

feng tou 風頭
(1) the trends of events;
(2) the publicity one receives;

feng tou shi zu 風頭十足
one's show is at its height;

feng tou zhu yi 風頭主義
showing off / striving for the limelight;

feng yu tong zhou 風雨同舟
stand together through thick and thin || cast one's lot with; go through storm and stress together; in the same boat; stand together through storm and stress — share a common fate;

feng yun ren wu 風雲人物
(1) celebrity / influential person;
(2) person in the news / person of the moment / person of the hour / person of the day;

feng yun tu bian 風雲突變
(1) a sudden burst of a storm; a sudden veer of wind and rain;
(2) a sudden change in the situation;

feng zhu can nian 風燭殘年
have one foot in the grave / old and ailing like a candle guttering in the wind / the decline of life;

feng1 kuang fan pu 瘋狂反撲
desperate counterattack / make a frenzied counterattack;

feng kuang zheng zha 瘋狂掙扎
frenzied and desperate kicks;

feng tan 瘋癱
paralysis;

feng1 meng 鋒芒
(1) spearhead / cutting edge;
(2) abilities / talent displayed;

feng mang bi ren 鋒芒逼人
display one's talent in an aggresive manner;

feng mang bi lu 鋒芒畢露
make a showy display of one's ability / show one's ability to the full extent;

feng mang chu lu 鋒芒初露
come to the fore / display one's talent for the first time;

feng mang suo xiang 鋒芒所向
the direction of an attack / the spearhead of / the target of attack;

feng mang tai lu 鋒芒太露
fail to show restraint / show too much of one's ability;

feng mang xiao shi 鋒芒小試
display only a small part of one's talent;

feng mang zhi xiang 鋒芒指向
direct the attack on / direct the sharp edge of struggle against / direct the spearhead against / focus the attack on;

feng1 er bu fei 豐而不肥
plump without being fat;

feng gong wei ji 豐功偉績
great achievements || gigantic contribution; great service to the country; heroic deeds; high merit and great achievements; immense merits;

feng2 chang zuo xi 逢場作戲
join in for the fun of it || act according to circumstance; along for the ride; find amusement when the occasion arises; join in the fun when there is a chance; seize a chance where there is merrymaking; want only a little excitement occasionally;

feng xiong hua ji 逢凶化吉
turn bad luck into good fortune;

feng ying 逢迎
flatter ; ingratiate;

feng ying chan mei 逢迎諂媚
adulate / seek to please superiors and curry favour with them // obsequious;

feng4 cheng 奉承
bow and scrape / butter up / fawn upon / flatter / lick the feet of sb / pay court on // obsequious / toady // flattery;

feng cheng pai ma 奉承拍馬
apple-polish || bootlick sb; bow the scrape; cajole sb with flattering words; fawn upon sb; flatter; kiss the hem of sb's garment; lick sb's boots; lick sb's feet / toady / tickle sb's ears;

feng cheng tao hao 奉承討好
fawn upon sb / flatter / lick the feet of sb / make up to / please / toady;

feng gao 奉告
inform / let sb know;

feng gong shou fa 奉公守法
dutiful and law-abiding || carry out official duties and observe the laws; conscientious and law-abiding; just and respect the law; respect justice and abide by the laws;

feng huan 奉還
return sth with thanks;

feng ling cheng jiao 奉令承教
obey commands and observe instructions;

feng ming 奉命
act under orders / receive orders;

feng ming wei jin 奉命唯謹
obey orders scrupulously / receive orders respectfully;

feng ming xing dong 奉命行動
act pursuant to the orders;

feng pei 奉陪
keep sb company;

feng pei dao di 奉陪到底
take on sb to the end || keep sb company to the end; keep sb company and fight to the finish; take sb on right to very end;

feng quan 奉勸
admonish / advise / give a piece of advice;

feng ruo shen ming 奉若神明
put sb on a pedestal || deify; laud...as sacrosanct; make a fetish of sth; regard...as a demigod; revere ... as sacred; sanctify; worship;

feng ruo zhi bao 奉若至寶
revere...as a priceless treasure / treat sth as most valuable treasure / value highly;

feng shang 奉上
have the honour to send;

feng song 奉送
give away free / offer as a gift;

feng tang song yao 奉湯送藥
dedicate oneself with touching devotion to nurse one's sick parent;

feng wei dian fan 奉為典範
look upon as a model;

feng wei gui nie 奉為圭臬
hold up as a model / look up to as the standard / take sth as the pattern;

feng wei jing dian 奉為經典
regard sth as canons;

feng wei kai mo 奉為楷模
hold up as a model / look upon sth as a pattern / regard sth as an example;

feng wei zhi bao 奉為至寶
value highly;

身體 *Body*

feng xian 奉獻
offer as a tribute / present with all respect;

feng xing 奉行
pursue a policy of;

feng xing bu dai 奉行不怠
carry out without negligence;

feng xing gu shi 奉行故事
act in accordance with practices and rules / follow established practice mechanically / follow the old routine;

feng yang 奉養
support and wait upon;

feng zhao bu wu 奉趙不誤
return a borrowed thing without delay;

feng zi cheng hun 奉子成婚
shotgun marriage / shotgun wedding;

fou3 否
deny / negate;

fou ding 否定
(1) deny / negate;
(2) negative;

fou jue 否決
reject / overrule / veto / vote down;

fou zheng 否證
falsify;

fu1 yan 敷衍
perfunctory || get by; go through the motions; skimp; whitewash;

fu yan ji ju 敷衍幾句
dismiss perfunctorily in a few words / make a few casual remarks;

fu yan liao shi 敷衍了事
do things in a perfunctory manner || attend to a matter negligently; do things carelessly; finish a job carelessly; give a lick and a promise; go through the motions; make a muddle of one's work; muddle through; play at; shuffle through one's work; skimp one's work; slight over; work perfunctorily;

fu yan se ze 敷衍塞責
be perfunctory in one's work || be half-hearted about; do just enough to get by; do things perfunctorily; give a lick and a promise; make a display and evade responsibility; make a show of doing one's duty; muddle with one's duty; perform one's duties as routine functions;

fu yan shou duan 敷衍手段
slovenly manner of attending to business;

fu2 扶
(1) support with the hand;
(2) help sb up / straighten sth up;
(3) help / relieve;

fu an shang ma 扶鞍上馬
get into the saddle / mount a horse;

fu bing 扶病
in spite of illness;

fu bing chu xi 扶病出席
present in spite of illness;

fu chi 扶持
support || give aid to; help sustain; place a hand on sb for support; support with the hand;

fu jiu gui ji 扶柩歸籍
escort sb's coffin back to his native place for burial / escort the coffin to the native place of the dead;

fu lao xie you 扶老攜幼
bring along the old and the young || carry the babes and support the old folk; help the aged and the young; help the elderly people and children; help the old and guide the young;

fu pin 扶貧
help the poor / support the poor;

fu pin ji kun 扶貧濟困
help poor rural households;

fu ruo ji wei 扶弱濟危
assist the weak and oppressed;

fu ruo yi qiang 扶弱抑強
fight for the weak against the strong || assist the weak and curb the violent; help the weak and curb the strong; help the weak and restrain the powerful; uphold the weak against the strong;

fu shan cheng e 扶善懲惡
support kindness, restrain evil;

fu shang jiu si 扶傷救死
heal the wounded and rescue the dying;

身體 *Body*

fu wei ding qing 扶危定傾
deliver the country from distress;

fu wei ji kun 扶危濟困
help poor people in distress || deliver the poor and all those who are oppressed; help the distressed and succour those in peril; help those in distress and aid those in peril; rescue the desperately poor and help those who are in difficulty; succour the poor and deliver those in distress and danger;

fu yang 扶養
bring up / foster / provide for;

fu yang cheng ren 扶養成人
bring sb up;

fu yao zhi shang 扶搖直上
on the rapid rise || be promoted quickly in official career; be successful in one's career; get up the social ladder quickly; rise directly to a high position;

fu ye 扶掖
help and support || support with one's hand;

fu you qu lie 扶優去劣
develop the good and eliminate the bad;

fu zhi 扶植
foster / groom sb to be / prop up;

fu zhi yang yu 扶植養育
groom and foster;

fu zhu 扶助
assist / help / support;

fu zhu lao ruo 扶助老弱
help the old and the weak;

fu2 服
(1) serve;
(2) be convinced / obey;
(3) be accustomed to;

fu cong 服從
obey || abide; be subordinated to; comply with; give way to; subject; submit to;

fu cong ming ling 服從命令
obey orders || hew the line; hew to the line; toe the line; toe the mark; toe the scratch;

fu2 hua bu shi 浮華不實
attractive on the surface but of no solid value || a meretricious style of writing; flowery language which lacks content;

fu hua sheng huo 浮華生活
a showy and luxurious life;

fu hua xu li 浮華虛禮
an empty show and pretentious ceremony;

fu jia fan zhai 浮家泛宅
a floating family and a drifting abode || dwell on boat; boat dwellers; those who make thier homes on boats;

fu kua zuo feng 浮誇作風
proneness to boasting and exaggeration;

fu ming 浮名
undeserved reputation;

fu ming bo li 浮名薄利
look down fame and gain;

fu ming xu li 浮名虛利
despise reputation;

fu qian 浮淺
shallow / superficial;

fu sheng 浮生
short and illusory life;

fu sheng ruo meng 浮生若夢
life is but a dream / life is like a dream;

fu sheng ruo meng, wei huan ji he 浮生若夢，為歡幾何？
our floating life is but a dream, how often can we enjoy ourselves?

fu yun zhao lu 浮雲朝露
life is as short as passing clouds and morning dew;

fu zao 浮躁
flighty and rash / impetuous / impulsive;

fu2 wu shuang zhi 福無雙至
the same person does not have the same luck twice || blessings do not come hand in hand; blessings never come in pairs; felicity never turns out in pairs; good fortune does not come in pairs; lightning never strikes twice in the same place;

fu wu shuang zhi, huo bu dan xing 福無雙至，禍不單行
good fortune does not come in pairs, and disasters do not come alone || blessings do not come in pairs; calamities never come

singly; joy comes never more than once but sorrows never come singly;

fu xing 福星

lucky star / mascot;

fu xing gao zhao 福星高照

a lucky star shines on high || be born under a lucky star; be in the ascendant; be under the smiles of fortune; bring sb good luck and success in life; come into luck; have one's star in the ascendant; ride the high tide of good luck;

fu zhong fu huo, huo zhong yu fu 福中伏禍，禍中寓福

in good fortune lurks calamity and in calamity lies good fortune;

fu3 俯

(1) bow down / come down / face down / stoop;

(2) condescend;

fu bai 俯拜

do obeisance to;

fu chong 俯衝

dive;

fu cong 俯從

follow sb's lead;

fu fu 俯伏

make obeisance to / prostrate;

fu jiu 俯就

deign;

fu3 bai 腐敗

(1) corrupt;

(2) decayed / putrid / rotten;

fu bai duo luo 腐敗墮落

become corrupt and degenerate;

fu bai wu neng 腐敗無能

corrupt and incompetent;

fu hua 腐化

(1) corrupt / degenerate / dissolute;

(2) decay / rot;

fu hua duo luo 腐化墮落

corrupt and degenerate / degenerate morally / dissolute and degenerate // corruption and degeneracy;

fu jiu 腐舊

old and worn-out / useless / worthless;

fu wu 腐惡

corrupt and evil;

fu3 wei 撫慰

comfort / console / dulcify / soothe;

bai ban fu wei 百般撫慰

try to soothe in every possible way;

fu xu 撫恤

comfort and compensate a bereaved family;

fu yang 撫養

foster / nurture / tend;

fu4 qian 付錢

pay / stump up;

fu4 he 附和

chime in with / echo;

fu hui chuan zao 附會穿鑿

draw farfetched analogies and give strained interpretations / make farfetched, unwarranted conclusions;

fu4 dan 負擔

bear a burden / load / shoulder;

fu dan bu chi 負擔不起

above one's weight / beyond one's capacity;

fu de 負德

against morality / against virtuous practice;

fu lei 負累

be dragged into trouble;

fu qi 負氣

in a fit of pique;

fu qu 負屈

suffer a wrong / suffer an injustice;

fu ze 負責

bear one's responsibility / in charge of / responsible for / take one's responsibility;

fu zhai 負債

in debt / incur debts;

fu zhai lei lei 負債纍纍

deeply in debt / head over ears in debt || get into debt; heavily in debt; in the red; over head and ears in debt; own lots of debts; run in debt; up to one's eyes in debt; up to one's neck in debt;

fu zhong 負重
carry a heavy load on one's back;

fu zhong zhi yuan 負重致遠
bear a heavy burden and cover a long distance — be able to shoulder important tasks;

fu4 nü bing 婦女病
gynaecological disease;

fu4 匐
lie prostrate / prostrate;

fu4 富
rich;

fu tai 富態
looking gentle and prosperous;

fu zu 富足
well-off / well-to-do;

fu4 xian 賦閒
unemployed / unwaged;

gai3 bian xi guan 改變習慣
break oneself of a habit / break sb of a habit;

gai e cong shan 改惡從善
turn from doing evil to good || abandon evil and do good; change from bad to good; mend one's ways; remove the evil and follow the good; turn over a new leaf;

gai guo 改過
correct one's mistakes / mend one's ways;

gai guo bu xian chi 改過不嫌遲
it is never too late to mend;

gai guo qian shan 改過遷善
convert from a bad life to a good one || change from sin to holiness; correct evil doings and revert to good deeds; repent and be good; reform errors and practise what is morally good;

gai guo zi xin 改過自新
mend one's ways and start anew || become a new person; convert from a bad life to a good one; correct one's errors and make a fresh start; correct one's mistakes and turn over a new leaf; live down; reform oneself; repent and reform; start with a clean slate; turn over a new leaf;

gai jin 改進
improve;

gai pi qi 改脾氣
change one's disposition;

gai xian geng zhang 改絃更張
adopt new ways || change over to new ways; change the course; cut loose from the past and make a new start; make a fresh start; mend one's ways; start a thorough reform; start afresh;

gai xian yi zhe 改絃易轍
make a new start || change one's direction; dance to another tune; strike out on a new path;

gai xie gui zheng 改邪歸正
give up evil and return to good || abandon the depraved way of life and return to the path of virtue; break away from evil ways and return to a virtuous way; forsake heresy and return to the truth; give up an evil way of life and reform oneself; give up one's evil ways and return to the right path; give up vice and return to virtue; go straight; on the straight; square it; stop doing evil and reform oneself; straight up; turn over a new leaf;

gan1 fan fa ji 干犯法紀
break the law and violate discipline;

gan1 bai xia feng 甘拜下風
acknowledge defeat || acknowledge the corn; admit defeat; admit oneself beaten; admit that sb has gained the upper hand; bow to sb's superiority; concede defeat willingly; confess oneself beaten; give in; give sb best; lower one's sail; lower one's flag; show the white feather; strike one's flag; throw in one's hand; throw in the towel; toss in the towel; willing to take an inferior position;

gan1 ga 尷尬
embarrassed / ill at ease;

gan3 chong gan da 敢衝敢打
have courage and the will to fight;

gan da gan pin 敢打敢拼
dare to fight and dare to risk all || dare to fight and dare to have a trail of strength; dare to fight and dare to take on the enemy;

gan zuo gan wei 敢作敢為
act with courage and determination || afraid of no difficulties; dare to do everything; decisive and bold in action; ready to take responsibility; take one's courage in both hands;

gan3 jue 感覺
sense // sensation;
gu gan jue 骨感覺
bone sensibility;
ji fa gan jue 繼發感覺
secondary sensation;
jia gan jue 假感覺
pseudoesthesia;
qian ting gan jue 前庭感覺
vestibular sense;
qian zai gan jue 潛在感覺
cryptesthesia;
quan bu gan jue 全部感覺
panesthesia;
shen bu gan jue 深部感覺
deep sensibility;

gan jue bo duo 感覺剝奪
sensory deprivation;

gan jue chi dun 感覺遲鈍
bradyesthesia;
pian ce gan jue chi dun 偏側感覺遲鈍
hemidysesthesia;
shen bu gan jue chi dun 深部感覺遲鈍
bathyhypesthesia;

gan jue guo min 感覺過敏
hyperesthesia;
pian ce gan jue guo min 偏側感覺過敏
hemihyperesthesia;
shen bu gan jue guo min 深部感覺過敏
bathyhyperesthesia;
shui meng xing gan jue guo min 睡夢性感覺過敏
oneiric hyperesthesia;

gan jue jian tui 感覺減退
hypoesthesia;
pian ce gan jue jian tui 偏側感覺減退
hemihypoesthesia;

gan jue ma bi 感覺麻痺
sensory paralysis;

gan jue neng li 感覺能力
sensibility;

gan jue qi guan 感覺器官
sensory organs;

gan jue que shi 感覺缺失
anesthesia;
pian ce gan jue que shi 偏側感覺缺失
hemianesthesia;
shen bu gan jue que shi 深部感覺缺失
bathyanesthesia;
tong xing gan jue que shi 痛性感覺缺失
anesthesia dolorosa;
wai zhou xing gan jue que shi 外周性感覺缺失
peripheral anesthesia;

gan jue xi bao 感覺細胞
seensory cell;

gan jue xiao shi 感覺消失
anesthesia;

gan jue yi chang 感覺異常
paresthesia;
pian ce gan jue yi chang 偏側感覺異常
hemiparesthesia;
shu hou gan jue yi chang 術後感覺異常
postoperative paresthesia;

gan jue zheng chang 感覺正常
eugnosia;

gan mao 感冒
(1) cold / common cold / influenza;
(2) catch a cold / have a cold / take cold;
liu xing xing gan mao 流行性感冒
influenza / flu;

gan mao chuang 感冒瘡
cold sore;

gan ran 感染
be infected / fester // infection;
ji hui xing gan ran 機會性感染
opportunistic infection;
ji fa gan ran 繼發感染
secondary infection;

ji sheng chong gan ran 寄生蟲感染
parasitization;
ji sheng wu gan ran 寄生物感染
parasitism;
jiao cha gan ran 交叉感染
cross infection;
jing shen gan ran 精神感染
psychic contagion;
liu chan gan ran 流產感染
septic abortion;
nei yuan xing gan ran 內源性感染
endogenous infection;
qian fu gan ran 潛伏感染
latent infection;
qian zai xing gan ran 潛在性感染
latent infection;
ru chong gan ran 蠕蟲感染
invermination;
wai yuan xing gan ran 外源性感染
exogenous infection;
xin li gan ran 心理感染
psychic contagion;
yin xing gan ran 隱性感染
latent infection;
yin yuan xing gan ran 隱源性感染
cryptogenic infection;

gan ran ai zi bing du 感染艾滋病毒
be infected with the AIDS virus / contract the AIDS virus;

gan ran ji bing 感染疾病
contract a disease;

gan3 bu ji 趕不及
unable to manage to be on time;

gan bu shang 趕不上
(1) unable to catch up with;
(2) miss;

gan che 趕車
catch a bus / catch a train;

gan chu qu 趕出去
drive out;

gan de shang 趕得上
(1) able to be in time for;
(2) able to catch up with;
(3) able to chance upon;

gan huo 趕活
hurry work;

gan kai 趕開
drive away;

gan kuai 趕快
hurry up;

gan kuai qi chuang 趕快起床
rise and shine;

gan lang tou 趕浪頭
follow the trend;

gan lu 趕路
hurry on with one's journey;

gan mang 趕忙
hurriedly / with haste;

gan shi mao 趕時髦
follow the fashion / try to be in the swim;

gan zou 趕走
drive away / expel ‖ drive sb out of the door; hunt; kick out of; kick sb downstairs; put sb to the door; see the back of sb; send sb packing; show sb the door; throw out; turn out sb; turn sb out of doors; turn sb out of the house;

gan4 幹
do / attend to business;

gan bu lai 幹不來
cannot be done / cannot be managed;

gan bu liao 幹不了
cannot be done or managed (due to lack of ability);

gan de lai 幹得來
can be done or managed;

gan de liao 幹得了
can be done or managed;

gan diao 幹掉
eliminate sb / kill sb;

gan huo 幹活
work ‖ labour; work on a job;

gan jin 幹勁
drive / enthusiasm / vigour;

gan jin chong tian 幹勁衝天
display rousing zeal / work with untiring energy ‖ show great enthusiasm; throw

oneself with rousing enthusiasm and boundless vigour into; with soaring enthusiasm;

gan jin shi zu 幹勁十足
full of energy / full of vigour ‖ full of drive; go all out; go at sth with a will;

gan lian 幹練
capable and experienced;

gan lüe 幹略
capable and full of ideas;

gao1 kong bing 高空病
altitude disease / altitude sickness / balloon sickness;

gao kong que yang 高空缺氧
altitude anoxia;

gao re 高熱
high fever / hyperpyrexia;
e xing gao re 惡性高熱
malignant hyperpyrexia;

gao ren yi chou 高人一籌
a notch better than average people;

gao ren yi deng 高人一等
a cut above other people;

gao shan bing 高山病
mountain disease / mountain sickness;
ji xing gao shan bing 急性高山病
acute mountain sickness;
man xing gao shan bing 慢性高山病
chronic mountain sickness;

gao shao 高燒
high fever;

身體 *Body*

gao tiao jing shou 高挑精瘦
stringy;

gao wen 高溫
high temperature / hyperthermy;

gao wen bing 高溫病
caloric disease;

gao xing 高興
delighted / glad / happy / pleased;

gao zi tai 高姿態
lofty stance;

gao3 搞
(1) cause trouble / stir up;
(2) be engaged in / engage;
(3) get / produce;
(4) carry out / organize / set up;

gao ba xi 搞把戲
play tricks;

gao gui 搞鬼
cause trouble / play underhand tricks;

gao hao 搞好
make a good job of;

gao hua yang 搞花樣
play tricks;

gao kua 搞垮
cause to fall;

gao luan 搞亂
screw up // screw-up;

gao qi gao ba 搞七搞八
cause mischief;

gao qian 搞錢
make money illegally;

gao qing chu 搞清楚
clarify / make clear;

gao yun dong 搞運動
start a campaign;

gao za 搞砸
flub;

gao zheng zhi 搞政治
play politics;

gao4 bie 告別
(1) leave / part with;
(2) bid farewell to / say goodbye to;

gao bie bai fang 告別拜訪
farewell call;

gao gui 告歸
go home on leave;

gao jia 告假
ask for leave of absence;

gao lao 告老
retire due to old age;

gao tui 告退
(1) resign;
(2) withdraw;

ge1 zhi 擱置
lay aside || fall into abeyance; hold in abeyance; in abeyance; keep in abeyance; lay on the shelf; leave in abeyance; pigeonhole; shelve;

ge zhi bu guan 擱置不管
lay aside / shelve / toss aside;

ge zhi bu yong 擱置不用
lie by / lie idle;

ge zhi dong yi 擱置動議
shelve a motion;

ge zhi nao hou 擱置腦後
off one's mind / put out of mind / throw to the winds;

ge2 chu 革出
dismiss / expel;

ge chu 革除
(1) abolish / do away with / get rid of;
(2) dismiss || dispel; excommunicate; expel; remove from office;

ge gu ding xin 革故鼎新
abolish the old and establish the new || abolish what is old and establish in its place the new order of things; discard the old and introduce the new; drop old habits and reform; reform the set rules to create sth new;

ge tui 革退
discharge / dismiss / fire;

ge xin 革新
innovate / reform / rennovate;

ge zhi 革職
discharge / dismiss / fire;

ge2 ge bu ru 格格不入
out of tune with || a round peg in a square hole; a square peg in a round hole; alien to; cannot get along with one another; feel out of one's element; go against sb's grain; ill-adapted to; incompatible with; jar with; like a square peg in a round hole; misfits; out of one's elements;

ge4 ren 個人
(1) individual;
(2) I / you;

ge ren chong bai 個人崇拜
personality cult;

ge ren se cai 個人色彩
personal touch;

ge ren zhu yi 個人主義
egoism / individualism;

ge xing 個性
individuality / one's character / one's personality;

ge xing chong tu 個性衝突
personality clash;

ge zi 個子
the build of a person;

geng1 nian qi 更年期
change of life / climacterium;
nan xing geng nian qi 男性更年期
male climacteric;
nü xing geng nian qi 女性更年期
female climacteric;
zao fa geng nian qi 早發更年期
climacterium praecox;

geng yi 更衣
change dresses / change one's clothes;

geng3 耿
(1) honest and just / upright;
(2) dedicated;

geng geng bu mei 耿耿不寐
lose sleep over sth / restless and unable to sleep because of uneasiness of mind;

geng3 si 梗死
infarction;
ji xing xin ji geng si 急性心肌梗死
acute myocardial infarction;
jia xing geng si 假性梗死
pseudoinfarction;
nang xing geng si 囊性梗死
cystic infarct;
pian tou tong xing geng si 偏頭痛性梗死
migrainous infarction;
pin xue xing geng si 貧血性梗死
anemic infarct;
xin ji geng si 心肌梗死
myocardial infarction;

geng zu 梗阻
obstruction;
jia xing geng zu 假性梗阻
pseudo-obstruction;

gong1 zuo 工作
work;

gong1 dao 公道
fair / impartial / just;

gong si bu fen 公私不分
make no distinction between public and private interests;

gong si fen ming 公私分明
scrupulous in distinguishing between public and private interests;

gong yun 公允
fair and proper;

gong zheng 公正
fair / impartial / just / without fear or favour;

gong1 cheng shen tui 功成身退
retire when the work is done;

gong neng xing ma bi 功能性麻痺
functional paralysis;

gong neng xing si wang 功能性死亡
functional death;

gong neng xing zhang ai 功能性障礙
functional disorder;

gong1 ji ben neng 攻擊本能
aggressive instinct;

gong1 躬
(1) body / person;
(2) in person / personally;
(3) bend;

gong feng qi sheng 躬逢其盛
be personally present at a grand occasion;

gong lin 躬臨
attend in person;

gong qin 躬親
in person / personally;

gong shen 躬身
bend the body in respect / bow;

gong xing 躬行
take action personally;

gong xing shi jian 躬行實踐
practise what one preaches;

gong yi 躬詣
call at another's house personally;

gong1 gong 觥觥
honest / straightforward / upright;

gong3 du xing zhen chan 汞毒性震顫
tremor mercurialis;

gou1 chu 勾出
check off;

gou da 勾搭
(1) gang up with;
(2) blandish / seduce;

gou gou da da 勾勾搭搭
flirt with ‖ gang up with; have illicit relations with; hitch up with; hobnob with; mix up with; stoop to secret dealings with; team up with; work hand in glove with; work in collusion with;

gou hun she po 勾魂攝魄
hook soul and arrest spirit ‖ do execution; have the power to make men crazy; summon spirits;

gou jie 勾結
collude with ‖ collaborate with; gang up with; hand and glove with; in league with; join in a plot; play footsie with // collusion;

gou liu 勾留
break one's journey at / stay / stop over;

gou tong 勾通
collude with ‖ join in a plot; secretly connected; work hand in glove with;

gou xiao 勾銷
cancel / wipe out / write off ‖ expunge; liquidate; strike out;

gou yin 勾引
seduce ‖ allure; entice; hook; lure; toll; tempt; undo // seduction / temptation;

gou yin nan ren 勾引男人
hook man;

gou1 tong 溝通
communicate / connect / link up / promote;

身體 *Body*

gou3 huo 苟活
live at the expense of one's honour / live at the expense of one's principle;

gou qie 苟且
(1) against one's principle;
(2) perfunctory;

gou qie tou an 苟且偷安
enjoy ease against one's principle / enjoy ease with a false sense of security;

gou qie tou sheng 苟且偷生
drag out an ignominious existence;

gou4 xian 構陷
frame sb up / make a false charge against sb;

gou4 購
buy / purchase;

gou mai 購買
buy;

gou wu 購物
do one's shopping / go shopping;

gou zhi 購置
buy / purchase;

gu1 xi 姑息
appease / indulge / tolerate;

gu xi qian jiu 姑息遷就
excessively accommodating / overlenient;

gu xi yang jian 姑息養奸
excessive indulgence breeds traitors || indulge the evildoers; lenient towards villains and let them grow; overindulgence nurtures evil; pardon makes offenders; to tolerate evil is to abet it; tolerant and indulgent;

gu xi yang jina, zong hu wei huan 姑息養奸，縱虎為患
indulge the evildoers and connive at their crimes;

gu1 du 孤獨
solitary;

gu ji 孤寂
lonely;

gu ku 孤苦
alone and helpless;

gu ku ling ding 孤苦伶仃
lonely and helpless;

gu ling 孤零
forlorn;

gu ling ling 孤零零
lonely;

gu pin 孤貧
lonely and poor;

gu te 孤特
isolated / unaided;

gu zhu yi zhi 孤注一擲
risk everything in one effort || a long shot gamble; all-or-nothing; ball the jack; bet all on a single throw; bet one's boots on; bet one's last dollar on; bet one's shirt on; bet one's bottom dollar on; cast the die; go for the gloves; go nap over; go the vole; have all one's eggs in one basket; kill or cure; make a last desperate effort; make a spoon or spoil a horn; make or break; make or mar; mend or mar; monkey with a buzz saw; neck or nothing; place one's efforts in a single thing; put all one's eggs in one basket; put the fate of ... at a stake; risk all on a single throw; risk everything on a single venture; shoot Niagara; shoot one's wad; shoot the works; sink or swim; stake all one's fortune in a single throw; stake all one has; stake everything on a cast of the dice; stake everything on one last throw; stake everything on one attempt; take a great risk; venture on a single chance; venture one's fortune on a single stake; vie money on the turn of a card; win the horse or lose the saddle; win the mare or lose the halter; throw the helve after the hatchet;

gu1 ming diao yu 沽名釣譽
fish for fame and reputation || angle for compliment; angle for praise; angle for undeserved fame; buy reputation and fish for praise; cater to publicity by sordid methods; chase fame; court publicity; fish for fame and compliments; strive for reputation;

gu1 fu 辜負
fail to live up to || disappoint; fall short of; let down; not come up to; unworthy of;

gu3 guai 古怪
eccentric / quaint / queer / strange;

gu guai xing wei 古怪行為
cranky behaviour / eccentric behaviour /

身體 *Body*

erratic behaviour / odd behaviour / strange behaviour;

gu3 chui 鼓吹
(1) advocate;
(2) preach || advertise; agitate; play up;

gu dao 鼓搗
(1) fiddle with / inker with;
(2) egg on / incite;

gu dong 鼓動
(1) actuate || agitate; arouse; promote; put up to; tickle;
(2) incite / instigate // instigation;

gu li 鼓勵
encourage || a pat on the back; comfort; foster; embolden; flatter; incite; pat sb on the back; poke; prompt; pull for; slap sb on the back; stimulate; urge;

gu qi 鼓起
pluck up || bag; balloon; blowup; call up; gather; muster up; puff; rally; swell; take heart;

gu qi yong qi 鼓起勇氣
pluck up one's courage || get up one's courage; look up; muster up one's courage; nerve oneself; pick oneself up; pluck up one's courage in both hands; screw up one's courage; summon up courage; take up one's courage in both hands;

gu wu 鼓舞
hearten / inspire || brace; embolden; fire; fortify; gladen; impulse; infuse; kindle; nerve; support; sustain // a shot in the arm;

gu wu dou zhi 鼓舞斗志
inspire the fighting spirit;

gu wu shi qi 鼓舞士氣
boost morale / enhance troop morale // a shot in the arm;

gu yi ba jin 鼓一把勁
marshal one's energies / put on a spurt;

gu zu gan jin 鼓足幹勁
exert the utmost efforts || do one's utmost; give full rein to one's energy; go all out; put forth one's energy; summon up one's energy;

gu zu yong qi 鼓足勇氣
pluck up one's courage / screw up one's courage;

gu3 蠱
bewitch / enchant;

gu huo 蠱惑
enchant / put under a spell;

gu mei 蠱媚
bewitch by sensual appeal / charm by sensual appeal;

gu4 nong xuan xu 故弄玄虛
deliberately mystifying || cast a mist before sb's eyes; deliberately to make things look mysterious; kick up a cloud of dust; make a mystery of; mystifying; play dishonest juggling tricks; puzzle people intentionally; use intrigues and tricks;

gu qu 故去
die / pass away;

gu shi 故世
die / pass away;

gu tai 故態
(1) one's former attitude;
(2) one's usual attitude;

gu tai fu meng 故態復萌
the old bad attitude is back / revert to one's old way of life;

gu zuo bu zhi 故作不知
play dumb / pretend ignorance;

gu4 痼
chronic disease;

gu ji 痼疾
chronic illness / intractable disease / malady / obstinate illness;

gu4 pi 痼癖
inveterate weakness;

gu xi 痼習
inveterate habit;

gu4 顧
(1) attend to / take into consideration;
(2) call on / visit;

gu bu de 顧不得
have to disregard / unable to take care of;

gu bu guo lai 顧不過來
unable to take care of;

gu bu liao 顧不了
unable to look after;

gu ci shi bi 顧此失彼
attend to one thing and lose sight of another || be put in a double squeeze; cannot attend to one thing without neglecting the other; care for this and lose that; unable to attend to everything at once; unable to hit one without losing hold of the other;

gu da ju, shi da ti 顧大局，識大體
bear the overall situation in mind and put the general interest above all;

gu dao 顧到
take sth into consideration;

gu de guo lai 顧得過來
able to take care of;

gu ji 顧及
attend to / give consideration to / take into account;

gu ji 顧忌
misgiving / qualm / scruple / stick;

gu quan da ju 顧全大局
consider the overall situation || act with the realization that one must always place the larger group-interests above private interests; bear the whole situation in mind; consider the situation as a whole; for the sake of the general good; for the sake of larger interest; give due consideration to the overall situation; mindful of the whole situation; out of consideration for the general interest; pay attention to the interests of the whole; take into consideration the situation as a whole; take the whole situation into consideration;

gua3 lou 寡陋
have narrow experience / have very little knowledge;

gua lou gua wen 寡陋孤聞
ignorant and ill-informed;

gua4 罣
hindrance / obstruction;

gua ai 罣礙
(1) hindrance / obstruction;
(2) block / hinder;

guai3 拐
(1) abduct / kidnap;
(2) driving / turn direction in walking;
(3) swindle;

guai dai 拐帶
abduct / kidnap;

guai mai 拐賣
abduct and sell;

guai pian 拐騙
(1) abduct / kidnap;
(2) swindle;

guai tao 拐逃
abscond with money;

guai4 怪
(1) strange || bewildering; odd; queer;
(2) find sth strange / wonder at;
(3) blame;

guai bing 怪病
strange disease;

guai zhang san, yuan li si 怪張三，怨李四
go around blaming everybody;

guan1 neng 官能
bodily functions / body functions;

guan neng zhang ai 官能障礙
functional disorder;

guan neng zheng 官能症
functional disease;

guan1 xi ai mei 關係曖昧
have a dubious relationship with sb;

guan1 li 觀禮
attend a celebration / attend a ceremony;

guan3 管
control / interfere;

guan bu liao 管不了
lack the capacity to control;

guan bu zhao 管不着
have no authority to interfere in;

guan bu zhu 管不住
incapable of controlling;

guan xian shi 管閒事
poke one's nose into others' business;

guang1 huo 光火
lose one's temper // in a rage / out of temper;

guang liu liu 光溜溜
naked;

guang luo 光裸
naked;

guang qian yu hou 光前裕後
win praises for one's ancestors and enrich one's posterity ‖ glorify one's forefathers and enrich one's posterity; glorify the before and enrich the behind; reflect lustre on one's ancestors and enrich one's posterity;

guang rong 光榮
credit / glory / honour // glorious / proud;

guang rong jiu yi 光榮就義
die a heroic death ‖ prefer death to disgrace; sacrifice one's life for the sake of righteousness;

guang yao 光耀
glorious / honourable;

guang yao duo mu 光耀奪目
dazzling;

guang yao men mei 光耀門楣
win honour and distinction for one's family ‖ bring honour to the family name; do honour to one's family;

guang yao men ting 光耀門庭
win honour and distinction for one's family ‖ bring honour to the family name; do honour to one's family;

guang zhe shen zi 光着身子
naked;

guang zong yao zu 光宗耀祖
bring honour to one's ancestors and the family name ‖ add lustre to one's ancestors and the family name; bring glory on one's ancesters; make one's ancestors illustrious;

guang4 逛
ramble / roam / stroll / wander about;

guang dang 逛蕩
loaf around / loiter about and do nothing;

guang jie 逛街
go window shopping / saunter along the street / stroll down the street;

guang yi guang 逛一逛
go for a saunter / go for a walk / take a stroll;

gui1 皈
follow;

gui yi 皈依
(1) be converted to Buddhism;
(2) the ceremony of proclaiming sb a Buddhist;

gui yi fo fa 皈依佛法
follow the laws of Buddha;

gui yi gui zhen 皈依歸真
become a Buddha after death;

gui yi san bao 皈依三寶
become a Buddhist;

gui yi zong jiao 皈依宗教
turn religious;

gui1 gui ju ju 規規矩矩
(1) gentlemanlike / honest / polite;
(2) well-behaved;

gui1 yi qi xing 瑰意琦行
extraordinary ideas and admirable action ‖ outstanding in thinking and action; praise of a man of high integrity;

gui1 jia 歸家
return home;

gui jiu 歸咎
ascribe to / impute / lay the blame on;

gui tian 歸天
pass away;

gui3 ba xi 鬼把戲
dirty trick / sinister plot;

gui gui sui sui 鬼鬼祟祟
furtive ‖ act secretively; behind one's back; behind the curtain; clandestinely; hole-and-corner; like a thief in the night; lurk and sneak around like a ghost; maliciously and secretly; on the cross; slinky; sneaky; stealthily; surreptitious; thievish; under the counter; up to some hanky-panky; with a hangdog expression;

gui hun 鬼混
fool around / hang around;

gui3 bing 詭病
dishonest practice;

gui jue 詭譎
crafty / cunning / treacherous;

gui li 詭戾
treacherous and perverse;

gui zha 詭詐
deceptive / dodgy / tricky // cunningness / deceit;

gun3 kai 滾開
get away / go away / naff off / scram;

guo3 duan 果斷
in a decisive manner / resolute;

guo4 bu lai 過不來
unable to come over;

guo bu qu 過不去
be hard on / unable to get through;

guo bu xia qu 過不下去
unable to live on;

guo cong 過從
associate / have friendly intercourse;

guo cong shen mi 過從甚密
on very intimate terms with ‖ in close association with; in constant and close contact with;

guo de qu 過得去
(1) not too bad / passable / tolerable;
(2) able to get through;

guo du fa yu 過度發育
macrophasia;

guo huo 過活
make a living;

guo lao 過勞
overwork / work too hard;

guo min fan ying 過敏反應
anaphylactic reaction;
quan shen xing guo min fan ying 全身性過敏反應
generalized anaphylaxis;

guo min xing xiu ke 過敏性休克
anaphylactic shock;

guo qian 過謙
too modest;

guo ri zi 過日子
live;

guo shi 過世
die / pass away;

hai2 zi qi 孩子氣
childish / infantile;

hai4 bing 害病
be taken ill / fall ill / get sick;

hai ren 害人
victimization;

hai ming 害命
commit murder;

hai ren bu qian 害人不淺
cause infinite harm to people ‖ cause deep injury to people; do people great harm; injure the people deeply; no small harm is done; very harmful to people;

hai ren fan hai ji 害人反害己
cut off one's nose to spite one's face / harm set, harm get / harm watch, harm catch;

hai ren hai ji 害人害已
he who bites others gets bitten himself ‖ bite off one's own head; curses come home to roost; harm set, harm get; harm watch, harm catch; injure both others and self;

hai ren li ji 害人利己
benefit self at the expense of another;

hai ren zhong hai ji 害人終害己
you will injure yourself in injuring others ‖ curses come home to roost; harm set, harm get; harm watch, harm catch; hoist with one's own petard; the damage recoils upon one's own head;

hai sao 害臊
bashful / shy;

hai xiu 害羞
bashful / shy;

han1 mian 酣眠
sleep soundly;

han ran ru shui 酣然入睡
fall into a deep sleep;

han shi 酣適
sound sleep;

han shui 酣睡
fall into a deep sleep || dead to the world; fast asleep; sleep like a log; sleep on both ears; sleep soundly;

han2 gou ren ru 含垢忍辱
eat dirt / endure disgrace and humiliation;

han ru 含辱
eat dirt / bear shame;

han yuan 含冤
be the victim of an unjust charge;

han yuan mo bai 含冤莫白
unable to clear oneself of a false accusation;

han2 suan 寒酸
look miserable and shabby;

han4 扞
(1) obstruct / oppose / resist;
(2) defend / guard / withstand;

han ge 扞格
conflict // incompatible;

han ge bu ru 扞格不入
contradict / disagree / do not mesh;

han ju 扞拒
oppose / resist / withstand;

han wei 扞衛
defend / guard;

han yu 扞禦
guard against / keep back;

han4 悍
(1) bold / brave;
(2) ferocious / fierce;

han ran 悍然
brazenly / flagrantly / outrageously;

han ran bu gu 悍然不顧
fly in the face of || fly in the teeth of; so audacious as to turn a deaf ear to; so rude and arrogant as to take no heed of;

han4 捍
defend / guard;

han ge 捍格
conflict // incompatible;

han ge bu ru 捍格不入
do not mesh // conflicting / mutually conflicting / obstructed;

han wei 捍衛
defend / guard || protest; safeguard; take up the cudgels for; uphold;

han4 撼
shake;

han dong 撼動
rock / shake / vibrate;

hao2 bu 毫不
not in the least || devoid of; not...at all; not the least bit; nothing; without the slightest;

hao bu dong yao 毫不動搖
not to waver in the least || impregnable; sit tight; unshaken in one's conviction; unwavering; without vacillating;

hao bu fei li 毫不費力
without the slightest effort || as slick as a whistle; effortless; like a dream; no sweat; with a wet finger; without a blow; without striking a blow;

hao bu han hu 毫不含糊
unequivocal || clear-cut; explicit; in no uncertain terms; in terms; unambiguous; unmistakable; well-defined;

hao bu ju shu 毫不拘束
not in the least feeling restrained;

hao bu qi nei 毫不氣餒
without flagging;

hao bu shi ruo 毫不示弱
not giving any impression of weakness / not taking sth lying down;

hao bu xiang gan 毫不相干
have nothing to do with || have nothing to say to; irrelevant;

hao bu xiang rong 毫不相容
utterly incompatible with;

hao bu xun se 毫不遜色
with the best of them;

hao bu yan shi 毫不掩飾
make no bones about || make no secret of; not to mince words; totally undisguised; undisguisedly;

hao bu yin hui 毫不隱諱
outspokenly / with great candour / without any reservation;

hao bu you yu 毫不猶疑
without the least hesitation || every time; straight away; straight off; unhesitatingly;

hao bu zai hu 毫不在乎
not to care a bit || completely unperturbed; do not mind at all; like it's going out of style; make nothing of; not care a snap; not give a snap; not to care a bean; not to care a cuss; not to care a hang; not to care a pin; not to care a row of beans; not to care a stiver; not to care at all; not to give a damn; think little of; without the slightest compunction;

hao bu zu qi 毫不足奇
not at all strange || there is no surprise; there is nothing strange;

hao wu jian shu 毫無建樹
have nothing to show for;

he2 bu lai 合不來
cannot get along with sb or others;

he de lai 合得來
get along well;

he li 合力
join forces / make a concerted effort / pool efforts;

he li tong xin 合力同心
with concerted effort || make a united effort; unite in a concerted effort; work in full co-operation and with unity of purpose; work together with one will;

he mou 合謀
conspire / plot together // conspiracy;

he mou bu gui 合謀不軌
engage conspiratorial activities together / plot sedition together;

he qing he li 合情合理
entirely reasonable || fair and resasonable; fair and sensible; in a reasonable manner; in all reason; make sense; perfectly logical and reasonable; reasonable and just; seemly and fitting; understandable;

he shen 合身
fit sb;

he zhu 合住
live together / muck in with;

he2 ai 和藹
affable / amiable / genial / kind // geniality;

he ai ke qin 和藹可親
pleasantly agreeable;

he mu xiang chu 和睦相處
live in amity / live together in a friendly way / live in harmony || keep in with; live side by side peacefully and friendly; live together in peace; live together in unity; on friendly terms; smoke the calumet together; smoke the pipe of peace together;

he qi sheng cai 和氣生財
harmony brings wealth || amiability attract riches; an even temper brings wealth; friendliness is conducive to business success; peace breeds wealth;

he qi xiang qia 和氣翔洽
a pervasive spirit of peace and harmony;

he qi zhi xiang 和氣致祥
good-naturedness leads to propitiousness / peaceful disposition brings blessing;

he2 er meng 荷爾蒙
hormone;
nan xing he er meng 男性荷爾蒙
androgen;
nü xing he er meng 女性荷爾蒙
female sex hormone;

hei1 liu 黑瘤
melanoma;

hen3 ming 狠命
make a desperate effort / use all the strength;

heng2 chen 橫陳
lie down with limbs fully stretched;

heng dao duo ai 橫刀奪愛
take away another's woman by force;

heng tang shu wo 橫躺豎臥
lying in total disorder;

heng xing 橫行
on a rampage / run amuck / run wild;

heng xing ba dao 橫行霸道
play the tyrant || act against law and reason,

like a tyrant; act in a tyrannous manner; act like an overlord; act outrageously and ferociously; act unreasonably; be unbridled in one's truculence; lord it over; play the bully; ride roughshod; run wild; swagger about; trample on; tyrannize over;

heng xing bu fa 橫行不法
violent and lawless // act against law and reason / act illegally;

heng xing jie shi 橫行介士
one who walks sideways — another name for the crab;

heng xing wu ji 橫行無忌
act outrageously without scruples / run amuck / run wild;

heng xing yi shi 橫行一時
run amuck at for a certain time / run wild for a time;

heng yue 橫越
overstep / traverse;

heng4 si 橫死
(1) violent death;
(2) die a violent death / meet with a sudden death;

heng yao 橫夭
unnatural death;

heng zao bu xing 橫遭不幸
a sudden misfortune / suffer a sudden misfortune;

heng zao xie po 橫遭脅迫
be unduly influenced by;

hong2 弘
great / magnanimous;

hong2 yang 宏揚
disseminate;

hong2 xing chu qiang 紅杏出牆
commit adultery by a married woman / a married woman having a lover;

hou4 ci bo bi 厚此薄彼
give too much to one and too little to another / treat with partiality || biased; discriminate against one and favour the other; discrimnate against some and favour others; favour one and be prejudiced agginst the other; give handsome treatment to one and niggardly treatment to the other; give royal welcome to one and cold reception to the other; liberal to one and stingy to another; make chalk of one and cheese of the other; make fish of one and flesh of another; make invidious distinctions; partial to one while neglecting the other; say turkey to one and buzzard to another; the treatment accorded to one is out of all proportion to that accorded to the other; treat one warmly and another coldly;

hou4 ban sheng 後半生
the later half of one's life;

hou tian mian yi 後天免疫
acquired immunity;

hou tui 後退
retreat / retrocede / withdraw // retreat / retrocedence / withdrawal;

hu2 chan 胡纏
harass;

hu gao 胡攪
mess things up;

hu hua luan yong 胡花亂用
spend money extravagantly;

hu hun 胡混
fool around / loaf around;

hu lai 胡來
fool with // recklessly and without thought;

hu luan 胡亂
mess about with // at will // recklessly;

hu nao 胡鬧
cut didoes / horse around // monkey business / prank / reckless actions;

hu wei 胡為
act recklessly;

hu zuo fei wei 胡作非為
act absurdly || act wildly; behave unscrupulously; break the law; commit all kinds of outrages; commit all manner of evil; commit evil acts; commit foolish acts; cut didoes / do all kinds of evil; do wrong; infamous conduct; misbehaviour; misconduct; misdeed; perpetrate whatever evil one pleases; play gangster; run amuck in society;

hu2 kou 糊口
eke out a living || eke out one's livelihood; keep body and soul together; make a living to feed the family;

hu kou mou sheng 糊口謀生
earn one's daily bread / eke out one's livelihood / eke out the barest of living / keep body and soul together / make a living / try to keep the pot boiling;

hu kou zhi dao 糊口之道
means to live by;

hu nong 糊弄
(1) cheat / deceive / fool;
(2) do sth lackadaisically / go through the motions;

hu3 ren 唬人
bluff / cheat / deceive / frighten;

hua1 zhao 花招
game / hype / trick;

hua2 ji 滑稽
amusing / comical / funny / hilarious;

hua4 liao 化療
chemotherapy;
ju bu hua liao 局部化療
regional chemotherapy;

hua shen 化身
(1) incarnate // incarnation;
(2) embodiment / manifestitation;

huai4 ju 壞疽
gangrene;
tang niao bing huai ju 糖尿病壞疽
diabetic gangrene;
wai shang xing huai ju 外傷性壞疽
traumatic gangrene;
ya po xing huai ju 壓迫性壞疽
pressure gangrene;
yan xing huai ju 炎性壞疽
inflammatory gangrene;
yuan fa xing huai ju 原發性壞疽
primary gangrene;

huai ju xing huai si 壞疽性壞死
gangrenous necrosis;

huai ju xing kui yang 壞疽性潰瘍
cancrum;

huai ju xing niu dou 壞疽性牛痘
vaccinia gangrenosa;

huai pi qi 壞脾氣
ill-humoured / ill-tempered / narky // ill humour / ill nature / nasty temper;

huai si 壞死
necrosis;
bo san xing huai si 播散性壞死
diaspironecrosis;
bo san xing jian jin xing huai si 播散性漸進性壞死
diaspironecrobiosis;
dong mai huai si 動脈壞死
arterionecrosis;
gan huai si 肝壞死
hepatic necrosis;
gu huai si 骨壞死
osteonecrosis;
gu ju xing huai si 骨疽性壞死
carionecrosis;
huai ju xing huai si 壞疽性壞死
gangrenous necrosis;
jian jin xing huai si 漸進性壞死
bionecrosis;
jin xing xing huai si 進行性壞死
necrosis progrediens;
ju bu huai si 局部壞死
local death;
mei du xing huai si 梅毒性壞死
syphilitic necrosis;
nong du xing huai si 膿毒性壞死
septic necrosis;
quan bu huai si 全部壞死
total necrosis;
que xue xing huai si 缺血性壞死
avascular necrosis;
xiao dong mai huai si 小動脈壞死
arteriolonecrosis;
ya po xing huai si 壓迫性壞死
pressure necrosis;
ya huai si 牙壞死
odontonecrosis;
zhen xing huai si 疹性壞死
exanthematous necrosis;

zhi fang huai si 脂肪壞死
adiponecrosis;

zhou wei xing huai si 周圍性壞死
peripheral necrosis;

huan1 du 歡度
spend an occasion joyfully;

huan ying 歡迎
welcome || greet; meet;

huan2 ji 還擊
counter-attack / fight back / hit back;

huan jia 還價
haggle over a price;

huan li 還禮
(1) return a salute;
(2) send a present in return;

huan qian 還錢
pay back a debt / return money;

huan qing 還情
repay a favour;

huan xiang 還鄉
return to one's hometown;

huan zhai 還債
repay a debt;

huan3 ban 緩辦
delay action / put off a project;

huan bu ji ji 緩不濟急
slow action cannot save a critical situation;

huan ji xiang zhu 緩急相助
help each other in case of need;

huan qi 緩氣
get a breathing space / take a breather;

huan yi kou qi 緩一口氣
get a breathing space / take a breather;

huan4 bing 患病
fall sick / get sick / suffer from an illness // ill;

huan bing lü 患病率
morbidity;

huan bu 患部
the infected part / the wounded part;

huan chu 患處
the infected part / the wounded part;

huan4 瘓
paralysis;

huang1 dan 荒誕
absurd / fantastic / incredible / unbelievable;

huang dan bu jing 荒誕不經
most absurd and irrational || absurd; fantastic; nonsensical; preposterous; wild and fanciful;

huang dan wu ji 荒誕無稽
absurd / absurd and groundless / fantastic / incredible / preposterous;

huang1 miu 荒謬
grossly absurd / preposterous / ridiculous;

huang miu jue lun 荒謬絕倫
absurd in the extreme;

huang tang 荒唐
absurd / fantastic / ludicrous / outrageous / preposterous;

huang tang bu jing 荒唐不經
absurd and unreasonable / fantastic / unbelievable // wild legend;

huang tang gu shi 荒唐故事
cock-and-bull stories / old wives' tales;

huang tang ke xiao 荒唐可笑
absurd and ridiculous // how absurd;

huang tang tou ding 荒唐透頂
absolutely ridiculous || cap the climax of absurdity; most illogcial; preposterous to the extreme; utterly absurd;

huang tang wu ji 荒唐無稽
most absurd || frivolous and unfounded; out of thin air;

hui2 bai 回拜
pay a return visit;

hui fang 回訪
pay a return visit;

hui lai 回來
come back / return;

hui2 bi 迴避
avoid / dodge / evade;

hui3 bai 毀敗
destroy / ruin;

hui hai 毀害
damage / injure;

hui huai 毀壞
damage / destroy / injure;

hui mie 毀滅
demolish / destroy / ruin;

hui qi 毀棄
abrogate / dissolve / repeal / rescind;

hui shang 毀傷
damage / injure;

hui xun 毀損
damage / injure;

hui4 賄
bribe;

hui lu 賄賂
bribe ‖ buy over; buy sb off; cross sb's hand; cross sb's palm; give a bribe to sb; grease sb's hand; grease sb's palm; hand out a bribe to sb; offer a bribe to sb; oil sb's palm; pay off;

hui lu cheng feng 賄賂成風
bribery has become a common practice;

hui lu gong xing 賄賂公行
bribery is openly practised ‖ bribery is practised in public; bribes are openly employed; corruption is rife; give and take bribes openly; practise bribery publicly; practise open bribery;

hui mai 賄賣
buy over;

hui shang mai xia 賄上賣下
bribe men high and low / send bribes to the upper and lower officials;

hui tuo 賄托
ask sb to do sth for a consideration;

hui xuan 賄選
get elected by bribery / practise bribery at an election;

hui4 ji ji yi 諱疾忌醫
hide one's sickness for fear of treatment ‖ conceal a malady for fear of taking medicine; conceal one's ailment and refuse to consult the doctor; refuse to face harsh reality;

hui mo ru shen 諱莫如深
avoid mentioning sth completely / keep as a top secret;

hui shi 諱飾
conceal the truth;

hui4 ming 穢名
notorious reputation;

hun1 shui bing 昏睡病
sleeping sickness / sleepy sickness;

hun1 婚
marry;

hun jia 婚嫁
marriage;

hun2 dan 渾蛋
bastard / blackguard / scoundrel / skunk / wretch;

hun hou 渾厚
simple and honest;

hun shen 渾身
all over / from head to foot;

hun shen da zhan 渾身打戰
shiver all over / shiver convulsively / shiver from head to foot / tremble like leaves;

hun shen duo suo 渾身哆嗦
feel one's skin creeping // all in a tremble / in a tremble / on the tremble;

hun shen fa dou 渾身發抖
tremble all over ‖ all of a dither; all of a shake; tremble from head to foot; tremble in every limb; tremble like an aspen leaf;

hun shen fa leng 渾身發冷
a chill comes creeping over one;

hun shen gao su 渾身縞素
dressed in the white robes of mourning;

hun shen jie shu 渾身解數
use all one's skill ‖ all one's skill; employ all one's skill to; every means of solution; exert oneself to the utmost to; try every means of solution;

hun shen qing zi 渾身青紫
be beaten black and blue;

hun shen rou chan 渾身肉顫
feel one's skin creeping;

hun shen shang hen 渾身傷痕
all one's body is covered with bruises;

hun shen shi tou 渾身濕透
be drenched / be soaked || be soaked to the skin; be wet to the skin; be wet through; get a thorough souse; have not a dry thread on; wet as a drowned rat; wet to the skin;

hun shen shi jin 渾身是勁
alive every fibre / brimming with energy;

hun shen shi shang 渾身是傷
be covered with wounds;

hun shen su guo 渾身素裹
be dressed all in white;

hun shen suan ruan 渾身酸軟
ache all over;

hun shen suan tong 渾身酸痛
ache all over / the whole body aches;

hun shen teng tong 渾身疼痛
have pains all over;

hun4 bu guo qu 混不過去
unable to fool others;

hun bu xia qu 混不下去
cannot to stay on the job any loner;

hun fan chi 混飯吃
drift along aimlessly / just to make a living;

hun he xing jing luan 混合性痙攣
mixed spasm;

hun he xing ma bi 混合性麻痺
mixed paralysis;

hun ri zi 混日子
fiddle about / fool about / fool around / muck about / muck around / muddle along;

hun shen duo suo 混身哆嗦
tremble all over;

huo1 ming 豁命
at the expense of one's life / risk one's life;

huo2 bu liao 活不了
cannot live longer / unlikely to survive;

huo bu xia qu 活不下去
cannot live on;

huo dao lao xue bu liao 活到老學不了
there is still much to learn after one has grown old;

huo dao lao xue dao lao 活到老學到老
live and learn || a person should study till their dying day; it is never too old to learn; keep on learning as long as you live; never too old to learn; one is never too old to learn;

huo de bu nai fan 活得不耐煩
getting tired of living;

huo li 活力
vitality;

huo ming 活命
live / survive;

huo po 活潑
lively;

huo si ren 活死人
living dead person;

huo3 bao 火爆
hot-tempered;

huo mao san zhang 火冒三丈
be furious with rage / fly into a rage // in a dudgeon / in high dudgeon;

huo qi 火氣
anger / fury;

huo tou shang 火頭上
in a fit of anger;

huo xing zi 火性子
hot-tempered;

huo4 bu dan xing 禍不單行
misfortunes never come singly || an evil chance seldom comes alone; an Illiad of woes; bad events rarely come singly; disasters do not come alone; disasters pile up on one another; it never rains but it pours; misery loves company; one misfortune calls upon another; one misfortune comes on the neck of another; one woe doth tread upon another's heels; when it rains it pours; when sorrows come, they come not single spies, but in battalions;

huo bu wang zhi 禍不妄至
disaster never strikes without cause / woes never come without reason;

huo4 luan 霍亂
cholera;

huo ran quan yu 霍然痊愈
suddenly one recovers from an illness;

huo4 獲
(1) capture / catch;
(2) obtain / reap / win;

huo de 獲得
achieve / acquire / earn / gain / obtain / win;

huo jiu 獲救
be rescued or saved from death;

huo li 獲利
make a profit ‖ earn profit; get profit; obtain profit; reap profits;

huo qu 獲取
achieve / gain / obtain;

huo sheng 獲勝
triumph / win victory;

huo shi 獲釋
be released / get off / set free;

huo xi 獲悉
learn of an event;

huo zhi 獲知
learn;

ji1 ti 肌體
human body / organism;

ji1 li 激勵
encourage / impel / inspire / put spurs to / set spurs to / spur / urge;

ji1 hui xing gan ran 機會性感染
opportunistic infection;

ji1 ban 緝辦
arrest and punish;

ji bu 緝捕
search and arrest;

ji huo 緝獲
arrest / capture / seize;

ji jiu 緝究
investigate and prosecute;

ji li 緝理
set in order;

ji na 緝拿
arrest / apprehend;

ji1 de 積德
accumulate virtue;

ji shui 積水
hydrops;
er ji shui 耳積水
hydrotis;
guan jie ji shui 關節積水
hydrarthrosis;
ji fa xing nao ji shui 繼發性腦積水
secondary hydrocephalus;
jia xing ji shui 假性積水
hydrops spuris;
mi lu ji shui 迷路積水
labyrinthine hydrops;
nao ji shui 腦積水
hydrocephalus;
shen yu ji shui 腎盂積水
nephrydrosis;

ji1 bai 擊敗
beat / defeat / vanish;

ji1 shen 躋身
work one's way up into a special rank;

ji1 羈
(1) bridle / headstall;
(2) control / restrain;
(3) delay / detain / stay;

ji ban 羈絆
fetters / trammels / yoke;

ji liu 羈留
(1) stay / stop over;
(2) detain / keep in custody;

ji lü 羈旅
live in a strange land / stay long in a strange place;

ji ya 羈押
detain / take into custody;

ji2 xing biao yan 即興表演
improvise;

ji2 bing 急病
acute disease;

ji bu ke dai 急不可待
very anxious;

ji bu xia ze 急不暇擇
cannot make a wise choice under pressure / too urgent to make a wise choice;

ji gong jin li 急功近利
eager for quick success and instant benefit;

ji huai 急壞
anxious but powerless;

ji ji 急急
hastily / hurriedly / in a rush;

ji ji mang mang 急急忙忙
in great haste / in a great hurry;

ji jin 急進
forge ahead vigorously;

ji mang 急忙
hurriedly / in haste;

ji qi zhi zhui 急起直追
try to catch up in great haste;

ji xing gao shan bing 急性高山病
acute altitude sickness / acute mountain sickness;

ji zheng 急症
emergency case;

ji2 疾
(1) disease / illness / sickness;
(2) difficulty / suffering;
(3) abhor / hate;

ji bing 疾病
disease / illness / sickness;
chuan ran xing ji bing 傳染性疾病
infection;
ju bu xing ji bing 局部性疾病
local disease;
quan shen xing ji bing 全身性疾病
systemic disease;
xi tong xing ji bing 系統性疾病
systemic disease;
xi jun xing ji bing 細菌性疾病
bacteriosis;
yin xing ji bing 隱性疾病
pseudodisease;
zhou qi xing ji bing 周期性疾病
periodic disease;

ji bing chan shen 疾病纏身
be eaten up with diseases;

ji bing cong sheng 疾病叢生
be infested with diseases;

ji huan 疾患
ailment / disease / illness;

ji ku 疾苦
suffering;

ji3 shen 己身
oneself;

ji3 擠
(1) jostle / push;
(2) press / squeeze / twist / wring;
(3) cram / crowd / pack / throng;

ji bu dong 擠不動
unable to budge because of crowdedness;

ji jin ji chu 擠進擠出
squeeze in and out;

ji lai ji qu 擠來擠去
jostle / push about;

ji shang qu 擠上去
force oneself up;

ji xian 擠陷
do harm intentionally;

ji4 ju 寄居
live temporarily // temporary abode;

ji shen 寄身
live away from one's home for the time being;

ji sheng chong gan ran 寄生蟲感染
parasitization;

ji sheng wu gan ran 寄生物感染
parasitism;

ji4 yu 際遇
(1) chance / opportunity;
(2) what one has experienced;

ji4 濟
(1) aid / relieve;
(2) benefit;

ji e 濟惡
help an evil cause;

ji ji 濟急
aid the people in urgent need;

ji ni 濟溺
help others in great difficulty;

ji pin 濟貧
aid the poor;

ji ren zhi ji 濟人之急
relieve others in urgent need;

ji ren zhi kun 濟人之困
save people from their difficulties;

ji ruo fu qing 濟弱扶傾
help the weak and aid the needy;

ji si 濟私
benefit one's own end / serve a selfish purpose;

ji wei 濟危
aid the needy;

ji4 fa gan jue 繼發感覺
secondary sensation;

ji fa gan ran 繼發感染
secondary infection;

jia1 jin nu li 加緊努力
put one's socks up;

jia1 zu xing zhen chan 家族性震顫
familial tremour;

jia3 xing liu gan 甲型流感
influenza A;

jia3 bing 假病
pseudodisease;

jia chong 假充
counterfeit / pretend;

jia fei da 假肥大
false hypertrophy / pseudohypertrophy;

jia gan jue 假感覺
pseudoesthesia;

jia mei 假寐
catnap / doze / drowse;

jia niu dou 假牛痘
pseudocowpox;

jia shui zhong 假水腫
pseudoedema;

jia si 假死
feign death / play dead / sham death;

jia xing fan ying 假性反應
pseudoreaction;

jia xing fei da 假性肥大
pseudohypertrophy;

jia xing ji shui 假性積水
hydrops spuris;

jia xing ma bi 假性麻痺
false paralysis;

jia xing nang zhong 假性囊腫
pseudocyst;

jia xing tian hua 假性天花
varioloid;

jia zhao zi 假招子
affected gestures;

jia zhong feng 假中風
pseudoapoplexy;

jia4 嫁
(1) marry / marry off;
(2) impute blame to another;

jia bu chu qu 嫁不出去
be left on the shelf / be on the shelf;

jia huo 嫁禍
impute blame to another;

jia huo yu ren 嫁禍於人
put the blame on sb else;

jia ji sui ji, jia gou sui gou 嫁雞隨雞，嫁狗隨狗
a woman follows her husband no matter what his lot is;

jia qu 嫁娶
marriage;

jia ren 嫁人
get married / marry / take a husband;

jian1 姦
(1) adultery / debauchery / licentiousness;
(2) attack a woman sexually;

jian wu 姦污
debauchery / rape;

jian wu fu nü 姦污婦女
rape a woman;

jian yin 姦淫
(1) adultery / illicit sexual relations;
(2) rape / seduce;

jian yin lu lüe 姦淫擄掠
rape and loot;

jian yin shao sha 姦淫燒殺
commit rape, arson and murder / engage in rape, arson and murder / rape, burn and kill;

jian1 ren 兼任
serve concurrently as…;

jian zhi 兼職
have part-time jobs;

jian1 chi 堅持
adhere to / hold by / insist / nail one's colours to the mast / perseverate / persist / pin one's colours to the mast // perseverance / persistence;

jian chi bu xie 堅持不懈
persistent / unremitting // perseverance;

jian chi bu yu 堅持不渝
persistant;

jian chi dao di 堅持到底
follow through / go through with it / stick it out;

jian chi ji jian 堅持己見
hold on to one's own views;

jian chi yuan ze 堅持原則
adhere to one's principle;

jian ding bu yi 堅定不移
stand fast // steadfast;

jian jue fan dui 堅決反對
adamantly oppose / resolutely oppose / set one's face against;

jian shou 堅守
defend resolutely;

jian shou li chang 堅守立場
stand by one's guns / stick to one's guns;

jian ren 堅認
firmly admit;

jian yi 堅毅
fortitude;

jian yi bu ba 堅毅不拔
hardbitten;

jian3 fei 減肥
lose flesh / lose weight / reduce weight // weight-loss;

jian ya 減壓
reduce pressure || decompress; pressure reduction; relax the pressure;

jian ya bing 減壓病
decompression sickness;

jian3 fu 儉腹
ignorant;

jian pu 儉樸
lead a simple and thrifty life;

jian shen 儉省
economical / frugal / thrift;

jian yong 儉用
careful in spending;

jian3 cha 檢查
check up on || check on; check out; check over; examine; go over; go through; inspect; look at; take a view of;

jian cha shen ti 檢查身體
have a check-up;

jian4 kang 健康
health // healthy;

jian mei 健美
(1) healthy and handsome;
(1) vigorous and graceful;

jian quan 健全
in good condition / in good order;

jian wang 健旺
healthy and vigorous;

jian zai 健在
alive / alive and kicking // in good health;

jian zhuang 健壯
strong and robust // in good health;

jian4 jin xing huai si 漸進性壞死
bionecrosis;

jian4 lü 踐履
fulfill a pledge;

jian yue 踐約
fulfill a promise / honour an agreement;

jiang1 gong bu guo 將功補過
make amends for one's faults by good deeds;

jiang gong shu zui 將功贖罪
atone for mistakes by meritorious service;

jiang ji jiu ji 將計就計
adopt one's scheme to that of the opponent;

jiang1 僵
(1) lie flat;
(2) at a stalmate;

jiang chi 僵持
at a stalmate;

jiang si 僵死
dead;

jiang wo 僵臥
lie still at full length;

jiang ying 僵硬
rigid / stiff;

jiang3 pai chang 講排場
display riches;

jiang qiu 講求
strive for;

jiang qiu wai biao 講求外表
pay special attention to appearances;

jiao1 cha chuan ran 交叉傳染
cross infection;

jiao cha fan she 交叉反射
crossed reflex;

jiao cha gan ran 交叉感染
cross infection;

jiao e 交惡
on unfriendly terms;

jiao hao 交好
be on good terms with / on friendly terms;

jiao hao yun 交好運
have good luck // lucky;

jiao she 交涉
negotiate;

jiao tao hua yun 交桃花運
be successful in romantic affairs;

jiao wang 交往
have friendly relations / rub shoulders with;

jiao you 交遊
one's circle of friends;

jiao you 交友
make friends;

jiao yun 交運
have everything going one's way;

jiao3 tong 絞痛
colic;
bian mi jiao tong 便秘絞痛
stercoral colic;
chang jiao tong 腸絞痛
intestinal angina; tormina;
dan jiao tong 膽絞痛
billary colic;
fu jiao tong 腹絞痛
angina abdominis / cramps;
lan wei jiao tong 闌尾絞痛
appendicular colic;
ru chong xing jiao tong 蠕蟲性絞痛
verminous colic;
tong jiao tong 銅絞痛
copper colic;
wei jiao tong 胃絞痛
gastric colic;
xiao hua bu liang xing jiao tong 消化不良性絞痛
angina dytspeptica;
xin jiao tong 心絞痛
angina pectoris;
zi gong jiao tong 子宮絞痛
uterine colic;
zu jiao tong 足絞痛
angina cruris;

jiao3 jian 矯健
strong and vigorous;

jiao jie 矯捷
agile / brisk / vigorous and nimble;

jiao rou zao zuo 矯揉造作
affected / hokey // affectation;

jiao wang guo zheng 矯枉過正
lean over backwards // overstrict in correcting mistakes;

jiao xing 矯形
orthopaedic / reshaping;

jie1 hui wu ji 嗟悔無及
too late for regrets and lamentations;

jie1 接
(1) meet / welcome;
(2) receive;

jie ban 接班
take one's turn on duty;

jie chu chuan ran 接觸傳染
contagion;

jie chu chuan ran bing 接觸傳染病
contagious disease / infectious disease;

jie dai 接待
receive a guest;

jie guo lai 接過來
receive / take over;

jie jian 接見
receive a guest;

jie shou 接受
accept;

jie2 ran yi shen 孑然一身
living alone;

jie2 劫
(1) plunder / rob;
(2) coerce / compel;

jie chi 劫持
abduct / hijack / hold under duress / kidnap;

jie duo 劫奪
seize by force;

jie lüe 劫掠
loot / plunder;

jie2 jue 拮据
in financial straits;

jie2 shi 結石
calculus / stone;
niao lu jie shi 尿路結石
lithangiuria;
niao suan jie shi 尿酸結石
urate calculus;
pang guang jie shi 膀胱結石
vesical calculus / bladder stone;
pi fu jie shi 皮膚結石
skin stone;

jie shi bing 結石病
calculosis;
niao suan jie shi bing 尿酸結石病
uric acid lithiasis;
pang guang jie shi bing 膀胱結石病
cystolithiasis;

jie2 duan xing ma zui 節段性麻醉
segmental anesthesia;

jie jian 節儉
frugal / thirfty // economize / practise austerity // fruality / thirft;

jie yong 節用
cut down expenses / economize / practise economy;

jie yue 節約
frugal / thrifty // scrimp / thrift;

jie2 jin 竭盡
do all one can / do one's utmost || exhaust; spare no effort; to the best of one's ability; use up;

jie jin mian li 竭盡棉力
do one's best to / do one's utmost;

jie jin neng shi 竭盡能事
leave no chance untried;

jie jin quan li 竭盡全力
do one's utmost / give one's all || at full strain; at strain; by all one's might and main; by might and main; do all at one's command; do all in one's full strength; do all in one's power to; do everything one can; do one's damnedest; do one's level best; do sth with all one's ability and with all one's might; exert all one's energy; exert all one's powers; exert every effort; exert one's full strength; exert one's utmost; go all lengths; go all out; go to any lengths; hammer and tongs; make all possible efforts; make every effort to; move heaven and earth; on the strain; pool one's efforts; pull all the stops out; pull out all the stops; put every ounce of strength into the effort; put one's best foot forward; shoot the works; spare no efforts; strain every nerve; strain one's efforts; strain oneself; strain oneself to the limit; strive tooth and

nail to; strive to the utmost of one's strength; strive with all one's might; with all one's might and main; take all measures in one's power; to the best of one's ability; try all one knows; with all one's might; with might and main; work full out; work to the best of one's ability;

jie jin suo neng 竭盡所能
exhaust all that one is able to do / make every effort;

jie li 竭力
do one's best / do one's utmost / exert one's utmost strength / exert oneself;

jie2 pi 潔癖
mysophobia;

jie3 jue 解決
(1) resolve / settle / solve / tackle;
(2) dispose of / finish off;

jie jue kun nan 解決困難
overcome difficulties;

jie wei 解危
head off danger;

jie wei 解圍
come to one's rescue / save others from embarrassment;

jie4 ru 介入
get involved / interfere with;

jie4 戒
(1) admonish / warn;
(2) give up;
(3) avoid / guard against;

jie bei 戒備
on guard;

jie bu diao 戒不掉
try in vain to give up a bad habit;

jie chu 戒除
abstain from / give up;

jie diao 戒掉
give up a bad habit;

jie du 戒賭
give up gambling;

jie4 gu 借故
find an excuse;

jie ti fa hui 借題發揮
make use of the subject under discussion to express one's own opinions;

jin3 yi shen mian 僅以身免
have a narrow escape || be saved only by the skin of one's teeth; escape by a hair's breadth; escape with one's bare body; escape with the skin of one's teeth; have a hairbreadth escape from being killed; narrowly escape with one's life;

jin3 殣
starve to death;

jin3 fang 謹防
guard carefully against / take precautions against;

jin fang an jian 謹防暗箭
guard against a hidden arrow;

jin fang jia mao 謹防假冒
beware of fakes;

jin fang pa shou 謹防扒手
beware of pickpockets;

jin jie 謹戒
prevent with the utmost care and caution;

jin4 bu 進步
improve / progress // improvement / progression;

jin jian 進見
call on a superior;

jin qu 進取
aggressive / pushy;

jin tui 進退
(1) advance and retreat;
(2) sense of propriety;

jin tui liang nan 進退兩難
in a dilemma || between the devil and the deep blue sea; between two fires; find it difficult to advance or to retreat; get into a nice hobble; have a wolf by the ears; have sb in a bind; hold a wolf by the ears; in a bind; in a box; in a cleft stick; in a fix; in a nice hobble; in a quandary; in an awkward predicament; in chancery; on the horn of a dilemma; place sb in a dilemma; put sb into a dilemma; up a gum tree; up a stump; up a tree; up the pole;

jin tui mo jue 進退莫決
not knowing what course of action to take;

jin tui shi ju 進退失據
difficult either to advance or to retreat || be kept in the air; equally difficult to go on or retreat; in a box; in a cleft stick; in a fix;

jin tui wei gu 進退維谷
in a dilemma || be locked in the horns of a dilemma; between Scylla and Charybdis; between the devil and the deep sea; find oneself in an awkward predicament whether to go forward or not; get into the hat; in a box; in a fix; in the hat; on the horn of a dilemma; stand at a nonplus; up a gum tree; up a tree;

jin tui wu men 進退無門
between two stools / in straits;

jin tui yu gong 進退與共
cast one's lot with another person;

jin tui zi ru 進退自如
free to advance or retreat // have room for manoeuvre / proceed or step back freely;

jin xing 進行
carry out / conduct / proceed;

jin xing xing huai si 進行性壞死
necrosis progrediens;

jin zhi 進止
proceed or stop // a course of action;

jin4 ben fen 盡本分
do one's bit / play one's proper role;

jin li 盡力
do one's utmost || all one's knows; as best one can; as far as in me lies; as far as possible; at full stretch; at pains to do sth; be going all out; break one's neck; do all in one's power to do sth; do all one can; do everything in one's power; do one's best; do one's damnedest to do sth; do one's endeavour; do one's level best; do sth with all one's might; exert oneself to do sth; lay oneself out; leave no stones unturned; make an all-out effort; make every effort; make great efforts; make the most of one's chance to…; move heaven and earth; put one's back into sth; spare no efforts; spare no pains; take great pains in doing sth; take the trouble; to the best of one's ability / abilities; to the full; to the top of one's bent; tooth and nail; try every means; try one's best; try one's hardest to do sth; with all one's energy; with all one's might;

jin li er wei 盡力而為
do one's utmost || contribute according to one's ability; do everything in one's power; do everything one can; do one's best; do sth to the best of one's capacities; do whatever lies in one's power; exert one's utmost; make the best of one's way; on one's mettle; shoot one's best;

jin ming 盡命
sacrifice one's own life;

jing1 li 經歷
experience / go through / live / undergo;

jing shang 經商
go into business;

jing1 han 精悍
strong and unyielding;

jing li 精力
energy / vigour;

jing li bu zu 精力不足
deficient in energy;

jing li chong pei 精力充沛
full of vitality || be going strong; full of beans; full of go; full of vigour; glow with energy; have a great deal of dash; very energetic;

jing li wang sheng 精力旺盛
very energetic and vigorous;

jing lian 精練
skillful and experienced / smart and capable;

jing min 精敏
keen and active;

jing ming qiang gan 精明強幹
able and efficient / hard-nosed / shrewd and capable;

jing pi li juan 精疲力倦
flake out / run out of oomph // worn-out;

jing qin 精勤
dedicated and diligent / devoted and industrious;

身體 *Body*

jing4 luan 痙攣
spasm || convulsion; cramp;

chang jing luan 腸痙攣
enterospasm;

hun he xing jing luan 混合性痙攣
mixed spasm;

ju bu jing luan 局部痙攣
idiospasm;

mian ji jing luan 面肌痙攣
mimetic convulsion;

mian jing luan 面痙攣
facial spasm;

pian ce jing luan 偏側痙攣
hemispasm;

shen jing xing jing luan 神經性痙攣
neurospasm;

shou ji jing luan 手肌痙攣
cheirospasm;

shou jing luan 手痙攣
cheirospasm;

shou zu jing luan 手足痙攣
carpopedal spasm;

shu xie jing luan 書寫痙攣
chirospasm;

tong kong jing luan 瞳孔痙攣
pupillary athetosis;

tong xing jing luan 痛性痙攣
algospasm;

yin dao jing luan 陰道痙攣
colpospasm;

ying er jing luan 嬰兒痙攣
infantile spasm;

zhen fa jing luan 陣發痙攣
clonospasm;

zhi chang jing luan 直腸痙攣
proctospasm;

zhi jing luan 指痙攣
dactylospasm;

zhi jing luan 趾痙攣
dactylospasm;

zhong du xing jing luan 中毒性痙攣
toxic spasm;

zi gong jing luan 子宮痙攣
hysterospasm;

jing4 hou 靜候
await quietly;

jiong3 kuang 窘況
in an inextricable predicament || embarrassed;

jiu1 chan 糾纏
involve / quibble / tangle // entanglement;

jiu jie 糾結
band together / collaborate;

jiu miu 糾謬
correct a blunder / correct a mistake;

jiu pian 糾偏
correct an error;

jiu sheng 糾繩
correct / discipline;

jiu zheng 糾正
check / correct / put right / rectify;

jiu3 si yi sheng 九死一生
close shave / narrow escape from death / narrow squeak // survive all perils;

jiu3 hou 久候
wait for a long time;

jiu liu 久留
stay for a long time;

jiu3 jing zhong du 酒精中毒
alcohol intoxication;

te ying xhing jiu jing zhong du 特應性酒精中毒
alcohol idiosyncratic intoxication;

jiu se 酒色
wine and women;

jiu se guo du 酒色過度
excessive indulgence in sensual pleasures;

jiu se cai qi 酒色財氣
wine, women, wealth and power;

jiu yi 酒意
tipsy feeling;

jiu zui 酒醉
drunkenness;

jiu4 fan 就範
be subdued / come to terms / yield;

jiu qin 就寢
go to bed;

jiu ren 就任
take office;

jiu wei 就位
take one's seat;

jiu xue 就學
go to school / receive schooling;

jiu ye 就業
get a job / get employment;

jiu yi 就醫
receive medical treatment;

jiu yi 就義
become a martyr;

jiu zuo 就座
take one's seat;

jiu4 bing fu fa 舊病復發
have a relapse of an old ailment;

ju1 gong 居功
take credit;

ju gong zi ao 居功自傲
claim credit for oneself and become arrogant;

ju liu 居留
reside;

ju shen 居身
one's way of life;

ju zhi 居止
stay and live;

ju zhu 居住
dwell / live / reside;

ju1 拘
arrest / detain;

ju jian 拘檢
restricted and restrained;

ju jin 拘謹
restrained and cautious;

ju na 拘拿
arrest;

ju pu 拘捕
arrest / detain;

ju qian 拘牽
restrain / restrict;

ju ya 拘押
put under arrest / take into custody;

ju1 gong 鞠躬
bow;

ju gong jin cui 鞠躬盡瘁
devote oneself to state affairs body and soul;

ju gong jin cui, si er hou yi 鞠躬盡瘁，死而後已
devote oneself to state affairs body and soul until one's death;

ju yu cheng ren 鞠育成人
rear to manhood;

ju2 bu fan she 局部反射
local reflex;

ju bu hua liao 局部化療
regional chemotherapy;

ju bu huai si 局部壞死
local death;

ju bu jing luan 局部痙攣
idiospasm;

ju bu ma bi 局部麻痺
local paralysis;

ju bu ma zui 局部麻醉
local anesthesia;

ju bu tong 局部痛
topalgia;

ju bu xing ji bing 局部性疾病
local disease;

ju xian xing shui zhong 局限性水腫
circumscribed oedema;

ju2 cu 侷促
restless;

ju cu bu an 侷促不安
nervous / restless / uneasy // like a cat on a hot tin roof / like a cat on hot bricks;

ju3 dong 舉動
action / movement;

ju qi bu ding 舉棋不定
unable to make up one's mind;

ju qi 舉起
hold up / lift / raise;

ju4 ren 巨人
giant;

ju ren zheng 巨人症
gigantism / hypersomia;

ju zhi 巨肢
macromelia;

ju4 拒
(1) defend / resist / ward off;
(2) refuse / reject;

ju bu 拒捕
resist arrest;

ju jian shi fei 拒諫飾非
refuse to listen to counsels and cover up one's faults;

ju jue 拒絕
decline / deny / refuse / reject / turn down;

ju4 聚
assemble / collect / come together / get together;

ju can 聚餐
get together for a meal;

ju du 聚賭
assemble for gambling;

ju he 聚合
assemble / come together / gather;

ju hui 聚會
assemble / come together / get together;

ju ji 聚集
assemble / gather / teem with;

ju ji 聚積
accumulate;

ju ju 聚居
live together;

ju lian 聚斂
amass illegally / amass immorally;

ju long 聚攏
assemble / come together / gather;

ju qi 聚齊
all present at a gathering;

ju san 聚散
meeting and parting;

ju san wu chang 聚散無常
meetings and departings are irregular;

ju4 fan dao shan 遽返道山
die suddenly / die unexpectedly;

juan3 ru 捲入
be drawn into / be involved in / become embroiled in;

juan ru xuan wo 捲入漩渦
get involved in a conflict;

juan4 dai 倦怠
languid / languorous / tired // languidness / languor / tireness;

jue2 ming 絕命
die // death;

jue zheng 絕症
incurable disease / fatal illness;

jue2 覺
sense;
mi lu jue 迷路覺
labyrinthine sense;

kai1 fang shi ma zui 開放式麻醉
open anesthesia;

kai fang xing chuang shang 開放性創傷
open wound;

kang1 fu 康復
be restored to health / convalesce / recover from illness / recuperate / rehabilitate // recovery / recuperation / rehabilitation;

kang fu zhi liao 康復治療
rehabilitation therapy;

kang4 抗
(1) oppose / resist;
(2) defy / rebuke / refute / reject;

kang bu 抗捕
resist arrest;

kang chen zou su 抗塵走俗
on constant run for worldly pursuit;

kang heng 抗衡
compete / contend / match;

kang ji 抗擊
beat back / resist;

kang ju 抗拒
oppose / resist;

kang ming 抗命
disobey orders;

kang wei 抗違
disobey / oppose;

kang zheng 抗爭
contend / oppose / resist;

kang zhi 抗直
straightforward and upright;

kang zhi bu qu 抗志不屈
adhere to high purposes and not submit to threats;

kao3 da 拷打
flog / torture / whip;

kao4 bu zhu 靠不住
not dependable / not reliable / not to be trusted;

kao de zhu 靠得住
can be trusted / dependable / reliable;

ke1 cha 苛察
relentless faultfinding;

ke dai 苛待
treat harshly / treat severely;

ke ke 苛刻
cold-hearted / harsh / merciless / pitiless / relentless / unkind;

ke nüe 苛虐
maltreat / treat cruelly;

ke qiu 苛求
very exacting;

ke1 瞌
tired and doze off;

ke shui 瞌睡
doze off while sitting;

ke2 sou xing zhen chan 咳嗽性震顫
tussive fremitus;

ke3 chi 可耻
disgraceful / ignominious / shameful;

ke4 fu 克服
overcome;

ke nan 克難
overcome difficulties;

ke zhi 克制
control oneself / exercise restrain / restrain;

ke4 qi 客氣
courteous / polite / respectful;

ke4 du 刻毒
wicked;

ke ku 刻苦
(1) assiduous / hardworking;
(2) simple and frugal;

ke ku cheng jia 刻苦成家
build up a family by hard work and frugality;

ke ku nai lao 刻苦耐勞
work hard without complaint;

ke xue 刻削
exploit ruthlessly;

ke4 ran chang shi 溘然長逝
die suddenly;

ke shi 溘世
die suddenly;

ke shi 溘逝
die suddenly;

ke xie 溘謝
die suddenly;

ken3 肯
agree / consent to // willing;

ken bu ken 肯不肯
willing or not willing;

ken gan 肯幹
indefatigable / willing to put in hard work;

kong1 qi chuan ran 空氣傳染
airborne infection;

kong3 wu you li 孔武有力
very strong and brave;

kong4 gao 控告
accuse / sue sb in court;

kong yu 控御
control and direct;

kong zhi 控制
control;

kou4 mao zi 扣帽子
put a label on sb;

ku3 dou 苦鬥
hard fight / hard struggle // fight desperately;

ku gan 苦幹
(1) make a strenuous effort / toil // toilsome;
(2) do sth against great odds;

ku gong 苦工
hard work / toil;

ku gong fu 苦工夫
painstaking effort;

ku gong 苦功
hard work / painstaking effort;

ku li 苦力
hard work / strenuous efforts;

ku ming 苦命
hard lot;

ku nan 苦難
adversity / hardship / privation / suffering / trials;

ku qiong 苦窮
desperately poor;

ku se 苦澀
agonized / anguished / pained;

ku shang jia ku 苦上加苦
bring additional pain;

ku tong 苦痛
discomfort / misery / pain / suffering;

ku xin 苦辛
adversity / hardship / suffering;

ku zhong zuo le 苦中作樂
enjoy in adversity / find joy amid hardship;

kuan3 dai 款待
entertain with courtesy and warmth // hospitality;

kuan jie 款接
entertain guests / receive visitors;

kuan ke 款客
entertain guests / entertain visitors;

kuang4 gong 曠工
play hookey;

kuang ke 曠課
play truant;

kui4 yang 潰瘍
ulcer;

ai xing kui yang 癌性潰瘍
cancerous ulcer / carcinelcosis;

bai hou xing kui yang 白喉性潰瘍
diphtheritic ulcer;

beng shi xing kui yang 崩解性潰瘍
perambulating ulcer;

bian yuan xing kui yang 邊緣性潰瘍
marginal ulcer;

chang kui yang 腸潰瘍
enterelcosis;

chuan kong xing kui yang 穿孔性潰瘍
perforating ulcer / diabrosis;

chuan tong xing kui yang 穿通性潰瘍
perforating ulcer;

chuan tou xing kui yang 穿透性潰瘍
penetrating ulcer;

dan chun xing kui yang 單純性潰瘍
simple ulcer;

huai ju xing kui yang 壞疽性潰瘍
cancrum;

jiao mo kui yang 角膜潰瘍
corneal ulcer;

kong chang kui yang 空腸潰瘍
jejunal ulcer;

kou chuang xing kui yang 口瘡性潰瘍
aphthous ulcer;

lang chuang yang kui yang 狼瘡樣潰瘍
lupoid ulcer;

lü pao xing kui yang 濾泡性潰瘍
follicular ulcer;

niao lu kui yang 尿路潰瘍
urelcosis;

pi kui yang 脾潰瘍
splenelcosis;

qian lie xian kui yang 前列腺潰瘍
prostatelcosis;

re dai kui yang 熱帶潰瘍
veldt sore;

re dai xing kui yang 熱帶性潰瘍
tropical ulcer;

身體 *Body*

ru fang kui yang 乳房潰瘍
masthelcosis;
shen jing yuan xing kui yang 神經源性潰瘍
neurogenic ulcer;
shen kui yang 腎潰瘍
nephrelcosis;
shi er zhi chang kui yang 十二指腸潰瘍
duodenal ulcer;
tang niao bing xing kui yang 糖尿病性潰瘍
diabetic ulcer;
tong feng xing kui yang 痛風性潰瘍
gouty ulcer;
wai yin kui yang 外陰潰瘍
cancrum pudendi;
xiao hua xing kui yang 消化性潰瘍
peptic ulcer;
xing kui yang 性潰瘍
venereal ulcer;
ya li xing kui yang 壓力性潰瘍
pressure ulcer;
yin bu kui yang 陰部潰瘍
pudendal ulcer;
ying yang bu liang xing kui yang 營養不良性潰瘍
trophic ulcer;
ying yang shen jing xing kui yang 營養神經性潰瘍
trophoneurotic ulcer;
ying ji xing kui yang 應激性潰瘍
stress ulcer;
zheng zhuang xing kui yang 症狀性潰瘍
symptomatic ulcer;
zhi jian kui yang 指間潰瘍
ulcus interdigitale;
zhi jian kui yang 趾間潰瘍
interdigital ulcer;
zu di kui yang 足底潰瘍
plantar ulcer;

kun4 fa 困乏
(1) impoverished;
(2) fatigued / tired / weary;

kun juan 困倦
tired / weary;

kun jue 困覺
go to bed;

kun qiong 困窮
poverty-stricken;

kun dun 困頓
(1) exhausted / fatigued / tired;
(2) in financial straits;

kuo4 bie 闊別
separated for a long time;

kuo chuo 闊綽
extravagant / lavish;

kuo qi 闊氣
lavish;

kuo4 zhang 擴張
dilation;
chang kuo zhang 腸擴張
enterectasis;
dan guan kuo zhang 膽管擴張
cholangiectasis;
dan nang kuo zhang 膽囊擴張
cholecystectasia;
jiao mo kuo zhang 角膜擴張
keratoectasia;
lin ba guan kuo zhang 淋巴管擴張
lymphangiectasis;
pang guang kuo zhang 膀胱擴張
megabladder;
shen kuo zhang 腎擴張
nephrectasia;
wei xue guan kuo zhang 微血管擴張
telangiectasis;
wei kuo zhang 胃擴張
dilatation of stomach;

la1 chu qu 拉出去
drag out / pull out;

la dao 拉倒
pull down;

la guan xi 拉關係
establish connections with the rich or powerful for one's own interest;

la guo lai 拉過來
drag here;

la hui 拉回
pull back;

la jia dai kou 拉家帶口
have a family burden;

la jia 拉架
mediate in a street fight / stop a brawl by separating the disputants;

la jiao qing 拉交情
try to seek friendship of influential persons;

la jin 拉緊
(1) pull tight;
(2) hang on firmly;

la jin 拉進
draw close / draw near;

la kai 拉開
pull away / pull off / pull part;

la ke 拉客
solicit patrons forcibly;

la long 拉攏
(1) draw sb over to one's side;
(2) make two persons or parties become friends;

la ma 拉馬
act as a pimp;

la mai mai 拉買賣
solicit business;

la nong 拉弄
pull apart;

la pi tiao 拉皮條
act as a pimp;

la ping 拉平
draw / end up in a draw / even up;

la qi 拉起
draw back / pull up;

la sheng yi 拉生意
solicit business;

la xia 拉下
pull down;

la xia shui 拉下水
drag sb into the mire;

la zhang 拉賬
run into debt;

la zhu gu 拉主顧
solicit customers;

la zhu 拉住
hold on firmly;

la4 shou 辣手
cruel / ruthless;

la zao 辣燥
hot-tempered and ruthless;

lai2 來
come;

lai fang 來訪
come to visit;

lai4 bu diao 賴不掉
cannot be denied / cannot be repudiated;

lai chuang 賴床
lie in;

lai de yi gan er jing 賴得一乾二淨
deny completely / repudiate completely;

lai hun 賴婚
break a marriage contract;

lai pi 賴皮
shameless;

lai xue 賴學
evade study at school / play truant;

lai zhai 賴債
repudiate a debt;

lai zhang 賴賬
(1) repudiate accounts;
(2) go back on one's word;

lan2 攔
bar / block / hinder / hold back / impede / obstruct;

lan bu zhu 攔不住
cannot be stopped / cannot stop / incapable of impeding;

lan che 攔車
stop a vehicle;

lan dang 攔擋
block / hinder / impede / obstruct;

lan ji 攔擊
intercept and attack;

lan lu 攔路
block the way;

lan zhu 攔住
block / hinder / obstruct / stop;

lan zu 攔阻
block / hinder / impede / obstruct / stop;

lang2 chuang yang kui yang 狼瘡樣潰瘍
lupoid ulcer;

lang4 man 浪漫
romantic;

lang mang 浪莽
unrestrained;

lang meng 浪孟
dejected / discouraged;

lao2 cui 勞瘁
tired out / worn out;

lao juan 勞倦
tired out;

lao ku 勞苦
work hard;

lao ku gong gao 勞苦功高
work hard and make a great contribution;

lao lei 勞累
overworked;

lao lu 勞祿
toil and moil // work hard;

lao3 cheng 老成
experienced / sophisticated;

lao cheng chi zhong 老成持重
experienced and cautious;

lao cheng diao xie 老成凋謝
the experienced and accomplished person has passed away;

lao lai qiao 老來俏
becomes more attractive as a woman gets older;

lao lian 老練
experienced / skilled / veteran;

lao ling hua 老齡化
aging;

lao nian 老年
old age / senium;

lao nian xing fan she 老年性反射
senile reflex;

lao nian xing wei suo 老年性萎縮
senile atrophy;

lao nian xing xiao shou 老年性消瘦
geromarasmus;

lao qi 老氣
experienced air;

lao qi heng qiu 老氣橫秋
arrogant on account of one's seniority;

lao qu 老去
grow old;

le4 suo 勒索
blackmail / extort;

le zha 勒詐
defraud;

le4 yu zhu ren 樂於助人
love to help others / ready to help others // obliging;

lei1 si 勒死
strangle;

lei4 累
(1) implicate / involve;
(2) owe;
(3) fatigue // tired / weary;

lei bing le 累病了
become sick owing to hard work;

lei de huang 累得慌
very tired;

lei huai le 累壞了
tired out;

lei ji 累及
implicate / involve;

lei ji ta ren 累及他人
implicate others / involve others;

lei ji wu gu 累及無辜
involve the innocent;

lei ji le 累極了
dead tired / dog-tired;

lei le 累了
tired;

lei ren 累人
tiresome / tiring;

lei si 累死
very tired;

leng3 bing bing 冷冰冰
cold as ice;

leng dan 冷淡
indifferent // give sb the cold shoulder;

leng ku 冷酷
grim / unfeeling;

leng luo 冷落
leave out in the cold / treat coldly;

leng mo 冷漠
cold and detached / indifferent;

leng nuan 冷暖
ways of the world;

leng nuan zi zhi 冷暖自知
know what it is like without being told;

leng re wu chang 冷熱無常
blow hot and cold;

leng ruo bing shuang 冷若冰霜
cold in manner / touch-me-not;

li2 bing 罹病
fall ill / suffer from disease;

li huo 罹禍
meet disaster;

li jiu 罹咎
incur punishment;

li nan 罹難
(1) die in a disaster / die in an accident;
(2) be murdered;

li yang 罹殃
meet a disaster;

li2 hun 離婚
bust up / divorce // the bust-up of marriage;

li jia 離家
away from home // depart from home / leave home;

li kai 離開
get away / leave;

li yi 離異
divorce / separate;

li3 hui 理會
pay attention to;

li kui 理虧
in the wrong / on the wrong side;

li se 理塞
in the wrong // have no excuse;

li suo dang ran 理所當然
as a matter of course / naturally;

li zhi qi zhuang 理直氣壯
say with perfect assurance;

li3 xian xia shi 禮賢下士
be courteous to one's staff;

li4 bu sheng ren 力不勝任
be unequal to one's task;

li4 shen chu shi 立身處世
conduct oneself in society || get on in life; get on in the world; ways of conducting oneself in society;

li shen yang ming 立身揚名
gain fame and position;

li4 勵
encourage / incite;

li xing 勵行
practise with determination;

li zhi 勵志
pursue a goal with determination;

lian2 gun dai pa 連滾帶爬
roll and crawl;

lian ren 連任
be reappointed / be reelected;

lian3 cai 斂財
collect wealth illegally or immorally;

lian4 da 練達
experienced / sophisticated;

liang2 si 良死
die a natural death;

liang xing zhong liu 良性腫瘤
benign tumour;

liang2 de 涼德
very little virtue;

liang3 bian dao 兩邊倒
sway / waver;

liang bian tao hao 兩邊討好
please both sides;

liang mian guang 兩面光
play a double game / please both parties;

liang mian san dao 兩面三刀
double-dealing;

liang mian tao hao 兩面討好
run with the hare and hunt with the hounds;

liang4 xiang 亮相
make an appearance / show up;

liao2 lai 聊賴
sth to live for / sth to rely on;

liao lang 聊浪
dissipated / unrestrained;

liao sheng 聊生
make a living;

liao2 撩
(1) incite / provoke / stir up / tease;
(2) confused / disorderly;

liao bo 撩撥
entice / provoke;

liao dou 撩逗
entice / provoke;

liao li 撩慄
dismal / dreary;

liao ren 撩人
make one excited;

liao3 ci can sheng 了此殘生
end this miserable life;

lie4 ming 獵名
after fame / hunt for a good reputation;

lie qu 獵取
chase after / hunt / pursue;

lie yan 獵艷
chase after pretty women;

lin2 bing xing zhong zhang 淋病性腫脹
blennorrhagic swelling;

lin2 bie 臨別
at the time of parting / on departure;

lin hua 臨畫
copy a painting;

lin ji ying bian 臨機應變
act according to what the circumstances dictate;

lin ming 臨命
before death / on the point of breathing one's last;

lin nan 臨難
beset by disasters / beset by troubles // at difficult times;

lin nian 臨年
at an advanced age;

lin si 臨死
at one's deathbed // just before dying;

lin wei bu ju 臨危不懼
remain calm in the face of dangers;

lin xing 臨行
on the point of departure // just before leaving;

lin zhen tuo tao 臨陣脱逃
absent oneself when one's presence counts;

lin zhong 臨終
just before dying // at one's deathbed // breathe one's last;

lin4 se 吝嗇
close-fisted / mean / mingy / miserly / niggard / parsimonious / penny-pinching / penurious / stingy / tight-fisted / ungenerous // parsimony;

ling2 ru 凌辱
(1) insult;
(2) assault;

ling3 dao 領導
guide / lead // leader / leadership;

ling dao you fang 領導有方
wise leadership;

ling yang 領養
adopt a child;

身體 *Body*

ling4 ren fan yan 令人煩厭
irksome;

ling ren sheng yan 令人生厭
irksome;

liu2 留
(1) remain / stay // at a standstill;
(2) detain / keep;
(3) preserve / reserve;
(4) leave;

liu bie 留別
give sth to a friend as a souvenir of parting;

liu bu zhu 留不住
unable to make sb stay / unable to retain;

liu lian 留連
reluctant to leave;

liu lian wang fan 留連忘返
so enchanted as to forget about home;

liu ming 留名
leave behind a good reputation;

liu nan 留難
make things difficult for sb / put obstacles in sb's way;

liu nian 留念
as a keepsake / as a souvenir;

liu2 gan 流感
influenza;
di fang xing liu gan 地方性流感
endemic influenza;
jia xing liu gan 甲型流感
influenza A;
qin liu gan 禽流感
Avian Flu;

liu xing bing 流行病
epidemic;

liu xing xing ban zhen shang han 流行性斑疹傷寒
epidemic typhus;

liu xing xing gan mao 流行性感冒
influenza;

liu xing xing shui zhong 流行性水腫
epidemic dropsy;

liu xing xing zhen chan 流行性震顫
epidemic tremour;

lou4 shen 鏤身
tattoo the body;

lu3 擄
capture / take captive;

lu huo 擄獲
capture / take captive;

lu jie 擄劫
pillage / plunder / rob;

lu lüe 擄掠
pillage / plunder / rob;

lu4 bi 路斃
die on the roadside;

lu4 勠
(1) unite;
(2) kill / slay;

lu li 勠力
unite efforts;

lu4 ti 露體
in the altogether / in the nude / naked;

lü4 ji 律己
(1) be strict with oneself / discipline oneself;
(2) self-discipline / self-restraint;

lü4 pao xing kui yang 濾泡性潰瘍
follicular ulcer;

lüe4 掠
(1) plunder / rob / take by force;
(2) skim over / sweep past;
(3) flog / whip;

lüe duo 掠奪
seize by force;

lüe guo 掠過
flicker across / skim over;

lüe mei 掠美
take credit for what has been done by sb else;

lüe qu 掠取
rob / take by force;

lun4 gong shou shang 論功受賞
be rewarded in recognition of one's services;

lun gong xing shang 論功行賞
award people according to their contribution;

luo3 裸
bare // naked / nude;

luo3 lu shen ti 裸露身體
bare the body;

luo tan 裸袒
bare // naked;

luo ti 裸體
naked / nude || in a state of nature; in one's birthday suit; in the altogether; in the buff; in the raw; in the rude // nudity;
ban luo ti 半裸體
half-naked;

luo4 luo da fang 落落大方
dignified manners / natural and self-confident;

luo luo gua he 落落寡合
unsociable / standoffish;

luo nan 落難
suffer a misfortune;

luo tuo 落托
uninhibited / unrestrained and unhampered;

luo tuo 落拓
uninhibited / unrestrained and unhampered;

ma2 bi 麻痺
paralysis;
bai hou xing ma bi 白喉性麻痺
diphtheritic paralysis;
biao qing ji ma bi 表情肌麻痺
mimetic paralysis;
chun ma bi 唇麻痺
labial paralysis;
da nao ma bi 大腦麻痺
cerebral paralysis;
gan jue ma bi 感覺麻痺
sensory paralysis;
gong neng xing ma bi 功能性麻痺
functional paralysis;
hou ma bi 喉麻痺
laryngoplegia;
hun he xing ma bi 混合性麻痺
mixed paralysis;
jia xing ma bi 假性麻痺
false paralysis;
ju bu ma bi 局部麻痺
local paralysis;
pian tan hou ma bi 偏癱後麻痺
posthemiplegic paralysis;
qian du xing ma bi 鉛毒性麻痺
lead paralysis;
quan ma bi 全麻痺
general paralysis;
que xue xing ma bi 缺血性麻痺
ischemic paralysis;
sheng dai ma bi 聲帶麻痺
vocal cord paralysis;
shui mian hou ma bi 睡眠後麻痺
postdormital paralysis;
shui mian qian ma bi 睡眠前麻痺
predormital paralysis;
shui mian xing ma bi 睡眠性麻痺
sleep paralysis;
si zhi ma bi 四肢麻痺
tetraplegia;
xiao shou xing ma bi 消瘦性麻痺
wasting paralysis;
ya po xing ma bi 壓迫性麻痺
compression paralysis;
ying er ma bi 嬰兒麻痺
infantile paralysis;
zhen chan ma bi 震顫麻痺
shaking palsy;
zhi ma bi 肢麻痺
acroparalysis;
zhi chang ma bi 直腸麻痺
proctoparalysis;
zhou qi xing ma bi 周期性麻痺
periodic paralysis;
zhou wei xing ma bi 周圍性麻痺
peripheral paralysis;

ma bi fa zuo 麻痺發作
ictus paralyticus;

ma bi zheng 麻痺症
paralysis;
xiao er ma bi zheng 小兒麻痺症
infantile paralysis / polio;

ma mu 麻木
numbness;
pian shen ma mu 偏身麻木
unilateral anesthesia;
si zhi ma mu 四肢麻木
acroanesthesia;

ma zui 麻醉
anesthesia;
chuan dao ma zui 傳導麻醉
conduction anesthesia;
jie duan xing ma zui 節段性麻醉
segmental anesthesia;
ju bu ma zui 局部麻醉
local anesthesia;
kai fang shi ma zui 開放式麻醉
open anesthesia;
quan shen ma zui 全身麻醉
general anesthesia;
xiang dui xing ma zui 相對性麻醉
relative analgesia;

mai4 ben shi 賣本事
show off one's feat;

mai chun 賣春
prostitution;

mai guai 賣乖
show off one's cleverness;

mai hao 賣好
curry favour with / ingratiate oneself with;

mai jing 賣勁
exert all one's strength;

mai lao 賣老
capitalize on one's age;

mai li 賣力
do all one can / exert oneself to the utmost ‖ do one's very best; exert all one's strength; spare no effort; work hard;

mai li qi 賣力氣
(1) do one's very best ‖ exert all one's strength; exert oneself to the utmost; spare no effort; strain every nerve;
(2) live by the sweat of one's brow / make a living by manual labour;

mai ming 賣名
capitalize on one's reputation;

mai ming qi 賣名氣
capitalize on one's reputation;

mai ming 賣命
work oneself to the bone for sb;

mai nong 賣弄
coquet / flaunt / show off;

mai nong feng qing 賣弄風情
flirt and coquet // coquetry;

mai qian 賣錢
sell for money;

mai qiao 賣俏
flirt / coquet;

mai ren qing 賣人情
do sb a favour for personal consideration;

mai shen 賣身
(1) sell oneself;
(2) sell one's body / sell one's soul;

mai shen qiu rong 賣身求榮
sell one's soul for self-advancement;

mai shen tou kao 賣身投靠
barter away one's honour for sb's patronage ‖ hire oneself and throw in one's lot with; hire oneself out to; sell oneself for support;

mai wen 賣文
make a living by writing;

mai yi 賣藝
earn a living by entertaining others;

mai yin 賣淫
prostitution ‖ accost; cruise; fast life; get the rent; have apartments to let; hustling; Mrs. Warren's profession; on the battle; on the game; on the stroll; see company; sit for company; sit at show windows; social service; street of shame; street of sin; streetwalking; the oldest profession; the social evil; the trade; vice; walk the streets; work for herself;

mai you 賣友
betray a friend;

man1 顢
careless, ignorant and stupid;

man han 顢頇
(1) careless;
(2) ignorant and stupid;

man2 瞞
deceive / hide the truth;

man bu liao ren 瞞不了人
cannot deceive others / cannot hide the truth from others;

man de guo 瞞得過
can be concealed / can be hidden;

man hong 瞞哄
deceive and cheat;

man pian 瞞騙
deceive and lie;

man shang qi xia 瞞上欺下
hide the truth from higher authorities and oppress the people;

man tian guo hai 瞞天過海
very clever and daring in deceiving others;

man2 bu jiang li 蠻不講理
impervious to reason / unreasonable / savage;

man gan 蠻幹
go ahead without considering the consequences;

man heng 蠻橫
barbarous / savage / unreasonable;

man li qi 蠻力氣
great strength;

man xing bu gai 蠻性不改
one's wild disposition is unalterable;

man3 bu zai hu 滿不在乎
not care in the least / nonchalant;

man shen 滿身
be covered all over with / be covered from head to toe || have one's body covered with;

man shen shi zhai 滿身是債
up to one's neck in debt;

man shen tong chou 滿身銅臭
filthy rich / stinking with money;

man shen you ni 滿身油膩
cover all over with grime;

man zhao sun, qian shou yi 滿招損，謙受益
one loses by pride and gains by modesty || self-satisfaction incurs losses, modesty receives benefit;

man4 bo shui mian 慢波睡眠
slow wave sleep;

man dao 慢到
arrive late;

man dong zuo 慢動作
small motion;

man man 慢慢
(1) leisurely / slowly / unhurriedly;
(2) by and by / gradually;

man teng teng 慢騰騰
at a leisurely pace / unhurriedly;

man tiao si li 慢條斯理
unhurried / without haste;

man tun tun 慢吞吞
exasperatingly slow / irritatingly slow;

man xing bing 慢性病
chronic disease;

man xing gao shan bing 慢性高山病
chronic mountain sickness;

man xing nong zhong 慢性膿腫
chronic abscess;

man xing yan 慢性炎
chronic inflammation;

man xing zi 慢性子
phelgmatic temperament;

man yi 慢易
inconsiderate;

man4 you 漫遊
travel about for pleasure;

man you yuan jin 漫遊遠近
roam over;

mang2 忙
(1) busy;
(2) hurried;

mang bu die 忙不迭
do sth with alacrity;

mang de bu ke kai jiao 忙得不可開交
have one's hands full // on the hop;

mang de hen 忙得很
very busy;

mang ge bu ting 忙個不停
on the hump;

mang he 忙合
assist / help;

mang li tou xian 忙裏偷閑
snatch leisure from a busy life;

mang lu 忙碌
be busy / bustle about // on the jump / on the trot;

mang luan 忙亂
busy and flustered;

mang mang dao dao 忙忙叨叨
very busy;

mang mang lu lu 忙忙碌碌
very busy // on the jump;

mang yu 忙於
busy doing sth;

mang zhong you cuo 忙中有錯
haste makes waste;

mang2 cong 盲從
follow blindly;

mang dong 盲動
act blindly / act rashly;

mao4 fan 冒犯
give offene / offend a superior;

mao huo 冒火
blow one's top / get angry;

mao jin 冒進
advance rashly;

mao mei 冒昧
take the liberty of / venture;

mao ming 冒名
assume another's name / go under sb's name;

mao ming ding ti 冒名頂替
assume the identity of;

mao sha qi 冒傻氣
act like a fool;

mao sheng ming wei xian 冒生命危險
risk one's life / risk one's neck;

mao shi 冒失
pert / rash / temerarious / thoughtless // temerity;

mao si 冒死
risk death;

mao xian 冒險
risk one's life / risk one's neck / stick one's neck out / take risks;

mei2 chi cun 沒尺寸
rash and thoughtless;

mei da mei xiao 沒大沒小
show no respect for one's elders || impertinent; impolite to an elder; imprudent;

mei jia zi 沒架子
unassuming;

mei jiao yang 沒教養
ill-bred;

mei jing da cai 沒精打彩
dispirited / listless;

mei lai 沒來
fail to show up / have not come;

mei ming 沒命
die;

mei qing mei zhong 沒輕沒重
without manners;

mei qu 沒去
did not go;

mei shen mei qian 沒深沒淺
ignorant and rash / impudent and thoughtless;

mei yong 沒用
useless;

mei zhi qi 沒志氣
without ambition;

mei zhong 沒種
cowardly;

mei2 du xing huai si 梅毒性壞死
syphilitic necrosis;

mei du xing nong zhong 梅毒性膿腫
syphilitic abscess;

mei3 de 美德
virtue;

mei de wu jia 美德無價
virtue is priceless;

mei e 美惡
good and bad / right and wrong;

mei ju 美舉
praiseworthy deed;

mei yu 美譽
fame / glory honour;

mei4 媚
(1) fawn on;
(2) please;
(3) love;
(4) attractive / seductive;
(5) coax;

mei gu 媚骨
obsequiousness;

mei ren yi 媚人意
seek to please another;

mei shi 媚世
fawn on others;

mei tai 媚態
(1) seductive gestures of a girl;
(2) fawning manner;

mei4 li 魅力
attractiveness / charisma / charm / glamour / sexiness;

meng1 pian 蒙騙
diddle / fool with the intention to cheat / hoodwink;

meng1 矇
cheat / deceive;

meng hun 矇混
fake and cheat;

meng pian 矇騙
deceive and cheat;

meng zhu 矇住
hide the truth and deceive others;

meng2 bi 蒙蔽
deceive / fool / swindle;

meng hong 蒙哄
cheat / deceive / hoodwink / swindle;

meng hun 蒙混
deceive and swindle / hoodwink;

meng mei 蒙昧
ignorant and stupid;

meng mei wu zhi 蒙昧無知
stupid and ignorant;

meng shang 蒙上
deceive one's superior;

meng shou 蒙受
suffer / sustain;

meng shou chi rou 蒙受耻辱
be humiliated;

meng xiu 蒙羞
suffer insult / suffer shame // ignominous;

meng yang 蒙養
educate young children;

meng zai gu li 蒙在鼓裏
be kept completely in the dark;

meng zhi 蒙稚
childish / ignorant / naïve;

meng3 ji 猛擊
wallop;

meng jin 猛進
press ahead / press forward / press on;

meng3 gu zheng 蒙古症
mongolism;

meng4 you zheng 夢遊症
somnambulism / sleepwalking;

meng4 lang 孟浪
rash / rough / rude;

mi2 lu ji shui 迷路積水
labyrinthine hydrops;

mi lu jue 迷路覺
labyrinthine sense;

mi2 man xing nong zhong 彌漫性膿腫
diffuse abscess;

mi man xing yan 彌漫性炎
diffuse inflammation;

mian3 chu zhi wei 免除職位
depose;

mian yi 免疫
immunity;
bao hu xing mian yi 保護性免疫
protective immunity;
hou tian mian yi 後天免疫
acquired immunity;

mian yi xing 免疫性
immunity from infection;

mian3 勉
(1) encourage;
(2) make efforts to / strive;

mian li 勉力
make efforts;

mian li er wei 勉力而為
do it as best as one can;

mian li 勉勵
encourage / urge;

mian qiang 勉強
(1) grudgingly / reluctantly;
(2) barely;
(3) unconvincing;

mian wei qi nan 勉為其難
force oneself to do a hard job;

min3 gan 敏感
allergic;

min li 敏力
apply oneself diligently;

ming2 wang 名望
fame / reputation;

ming zao yi shi 名噪一時
make a noise in the world;

ming4 gen zi 命根子
breath of life;

ming zhong zhu ding 命中注定
predoom;

mo1 摸
(1) feel out / try to find out;
(2) seek after / try to get at;

mo bu qing 摸不清
do not understand;

mo yu 摸魚
idle / loaf on a job;

mo2 ding fang zhong 摩頂放踵
fear no hardships ‖ rub smooth one's whole body from the crown to the heel; sacrifice oneself to save others; wear oneself out from head to foot to help others;

mo2 fang 摹仿
ape / copy / imitate / mimic / model after / pattern after;

mo2 lian 磨鍊
discipline / train // through the mill;

mo4 ai 默哀
stand in silent tribute;

mo zuo 默坐
sit in silence;

mou2 cai hai ming 謀財害命
commit murder out of greed / murder sb for his money;

mou qiu 謀求
seek / try to get;

mou qu 謀取
obtain / seek / try to gain;

mou sha 謀殺
murder;

mou sheng 謀生
get a livelihood / keep the pot boiling / make a living / make the pot boil;

mou shi 謀食
make a living / seek food;

mou shi 謀事
(1) manage business;
(2) scheme for an affair;
(3) look for a job;

mu3 xing 母性
maternal instinct;

mu4 yu 沐浴
(1) have a bath / take a bath;
(2) bathe / immerse;

mu4 睦
friendly / amiable / on friendly terms;

mu qin 睦親
close relatives;

mu yi 睦誼
cordiality;

mu4 ling 暮齡
closing years of one's life / declining years / old age;

mu nian 暮年
closing years of one's life / declining years / old age;

na2 da 拿大
pretend to be superior / put on airs;

na mao 拿毛
ask for trouble / look for trouble;

na4 fu 納福
enjoy oneself / have a good time / live in comfortable circumstances;

na hui 納賄
(1) offer bribes;
(2) receive bribes;

na jiao 納交
befriend / make friends with;

na liang 納涼
enjoy the cool air;

na qie 納妾
take a concubine;

na shui 納稅
pay taxes;

na xin 納新
take in the fresh;

nai4 耐
bear / endure / resist / stand;

nai bu jiu 耐不久
unable to endure long / unable to last long;

nai bu zhu 耐不住
unable to bear / unable to endure / unable to stand;

nai fan 耐煩
patient;

nai jiu 耐久
durable;

nai jiu li 耐久力
durability / endurance;

nai lao 耐勞
able to endure hardwork;

nai li 耐力
endurance / staying power;

nai ren xun wei 耐人尋味
intriguing / perplexing / puzzling // providing food for thought;

nai xing 耐性
patience / perseverance;

nan2 xing bing 男性病
andropathy;

nan xing geng nian qi 男性更年期
male climacteric;

nan xing he er meng 男性荷爾蒙
androgen;

nan xing mei li 男性魅力
masculine appeal;

nan2 ban 難辦
difficult to manage / difficult to operate;

nan chan 難纏
hard to deal with;

nan da jiao dao 難打交道
difficult to get along with / hard to deal with;

nan yi ren shou 難以忍受
insufferable / intolerable;

nan yi xiang chu 難以相處
hard to get along with;

nan zhi 難治
difficult to cure;

nang2 xing geng si 囊性梗死
cystic infarct;

nang xing xi rou 囊性息肉
cystic polyp;

nang zhong 囊腫
cyst;

chu xue xing nang zhong 出血性囊腫
bemorrhagic cyst;

jia xing nang zhong 假性囊腫
pseudocyst;

nong qi nang zhong 膿氣囊腫
pyopneumocyst;

nong xing nang zhong 膿性囊腫
pyocyst;

zhen xing nang zhong 真性囊腫
true cyst;

zhi qi guan nang zhong 支氣管囊腫
brochocele;

nao2 qu 撓屈
give way / submit / yield;

nao xing 撓性
(1) pliant;
(2) flexibility;

nao4 bing 鬧病
fall ill / get sick;

nao fan 鬧翻
fall out with sb;

nao fan tian 鬧翻天
raise a rumpus;

nao luan zi 鬧亂子
create disturbances / start trouble;

nao qi 鬧氣
go into a temper;

nao qiong 鬧窮
in lack of money;

nao shi 鬧事
cause trouble / cause uproar / raise hell;

nao xing zi 鬧性子
go into a temper;

nao yi jian 鬧意見
sulk;

nei4 fen mi 內分泌
endocrine / glandular excretion / internal secretion;

nei fen mi bing 內分泌病
endocrinopathy / endocrine disorders;

nei fen mi xi tong 內分泌系統
the internal system;

nei fen mi xing wei suo 內分泌性萎縮
endocrine atrophy;

nei shang 內傷
internal injury;

nei yuan xing fei pang 內源性肥胖
endogenous obesity;

nei yuan xing gan ran 內源性感染
endogenous infection;

nei zai mei 內在美
inner beauty;

neng2 能
can / able to // capability / competence;

neng bu 能不
how can one not;

neng bu neng 能不能
can or cannot / may or may not;

neng fou 能否
can or cannot / may or may not;

neng gan 能幹
able / capable / very competent and efficient // on the ball / worth one's salt;

neng li 能力
ability / capability;

neng nai 能耐
ability / capability / endurance;

neng qu neng shen 能屈能伸
adaptable / flexible;

neng wen neng wu 能文能武
gifted in both intellectual and martial arts;

ni2 怩
(1) shy;
(2) blush;

ni4 匿
conceal / hide;

ni bi 匿避
run away to escape capture;

ni fu 匿伏
hide oneself to escape capture / lie in hiding;

ni4 si 溺死
be drowned;

ni ying 溺嬰
infanticide;

ni yu jiu se 溺於酒色
indulge in wine and women;

nian1 hua re cao 拈花惹草
fool around with women / womanizing;

nian qing pa zhong 拈輕怕重
prefer the light to the heavy;

nian2 fu li qiang 年富力強
in the prime of one's life;

nian gao de shao 年高德劭
advance in years and virtue;

nian hua 年華
(1) age;
(2) years;

nian hua xu du 年華虛度
have spent one's best years without any achievements;

nian ji 年紀
age;

nian ji da 年紀大
long in the tooth;

nian li jiu shuai 年力就衰
aging and feeble;

nian ling 年齡
age;

nian mai 年邁
aged;

nian mao 年貌
age and appearance of a person;

nian qing 年輕
young / youthful // youth;

nian shao 年少
young;

nian shi 年事
age of a person;

nian sui 年歲
age of a person;

nian you wu zhi 年幼無知
ignorance for being young;

nian yu bu huo 年逾不惑
have passed forty;

nian2 ye shui zhong 黏液水腫
myxedema;

nian3 bi 輾斃
be run over by a vehicle and got killed;

nian3 攆
(1) drive / expel / oust;
(2) catch up;

nian bu kai 攆不開
try in vain to drive sb away;

nian chu qu 攆出去
drive sb away / throw sb out;

nian pao le 攆跑了
has driven sb away;

nian zhu 攆逐
drive sb away;

nian zou 攆走
drive sb away;

niang4 huo 釀禍
brew mischief;

niao3 嬲
dally with / flirt with;

niao4 du zheng hun mi 尿毒症昏迷
uremic coma;

nie1 bing 揑病
feign illness;

nie kong 揑控
fabricate a charge;

nie nong 揑弄
(1) fabricate / trump up;
(2) bring together;

nie zao 揑造
concoct / cook up / fabricate / invent / make up / trump up // concoction / fabrication;

nie zhe 揑着
hold with fingers;

ning4 si 寧死
would rather die;

niu2 dou 牛痘
smallpox;
huai ju xing niu dou 壞疽性牛痘
vaccinia gangrenosa;
jia niu dou 假牛痘
pseudocowpox;

niu pi qi 牛脾氣
bullheaded / grumpy / obstinate / stubborn;

niu3 扭
(1) turn / twist / wrench;
(2) grasp / seize;

niu da 扭打
grapple with sb / have a grapple;

niu da niu da 扭搭扭搭
swiveling from side to side / turning from side to side;

nong2 du xing huai si 膿毒性壞死
septic necrosis;

nong du xing xiu ke 膿毒性休克
septic shock;

nong qi nang zhong 膿氣囊腫
pyopneumocyst;

nong xing nang zhong 膿性囊腫
pyocyst;

nong zhong 膿腫
abscess;

bian tao ti zhou wei nong zhong 扁桃體周圍膿腫
peritonsillar abscess;

dan dao nong zhong 膽道膿腫
biliary abscess;

er yuan xing nao nong zhong 耳原性腦膿腫
otogenic brain abscess;

fei nong zhong 肺膿腫
lung abscess / suppuration of the lung;

gan nong zhong 肝膿腫
liver abscess;

hou nong zhong 喉膿腫
laryngeal abscess;

jing bu nong zhong 頸部膿腫
cervical abscess;

lan wei nong zhong 闌尾膿腫
appendiceal abscess;

man xing nong zhong 慢性膿腫
chronic abscess;

mei du xing nong zhong 梅毒性膿腫
syphilitic abscess;

mi man xing nong zhong 彌漫性膿腫
diffuse abscess;

nao nong zhong 腦膿腫
abscess;

pi nong zhong 脾膿腫
splenic abscess;

ru chong xing nong zhong 蠕蟲性膿腫
verminous abscess;

shen nong zhong 腎膿腫
kidney abscess;

wu tong nong zhong 無痛膿腫
indolent abscess;

ya cao nong zhong 牙槽膿腫
alveolar abscess;

yan hou nong zhong 咽後膿腫
retropharyngeal abscess;

yin nong zhong 齦膿腫
parulis;

you zou xing nong zhong 游走性膿腫
wandering abscess;

zhuan yi xing nong zhong 轉移性膿腫
metastatic abscess;

nong4 chu shi lai 弄出事來
get into trouble as a result of doing sth;

nong cuo 弄錯
commit an error / make a mistake;

nong gui 弄鬼
play tricks behind the scenes;

nong hao 弄好
(1) put into shape;
(2) do well;

nong huai 弄壞
bungle / spoil;

nong jiang 弄僵
bring to a deadlock;

nong qian 弄錢
raise money;

nong qiao cheng zhuo 弄巧成拙
bungle an ingenious scheme;

nong quan 弄權
abuse one's power;

nong xu zuo jia 弄虛作假
employ deceit / resort to deception;

nong zang 弄髒
smear / smirch / smudge / soil / stain;

nong zao 弄糟
bungle / make a mess of / mess up / spoil;

nong zi 弄姿
act coquettishly;

nu3 li 努力
exert oneself / work hard // diligent // diligence;

nu li gong zuo 努力工作
put one's shoulder on the wheel / put one's shoulder to the wheel / work hard;

nü3 xing geng nian qi 女性更年期
female climacteric;

nü xing he er meng 女性荷爾蒙
female sex hormone;

nüe4 dai 虐待
abuse / ill-treat / maltreat / torture // ill-treatment;

ou3 yu 偶遇
meet up / run into;

pa2 爬
(1) crawl / creep / grabble;
(2) clamber / climb;

pa bu dong 爬不動
unable to climb / unable to crawl;

pa bu qi lai 爬不起來
unable to get up;

pa chu lai 爬出來
climb out;

pa de gao die de zhong 爬得高跌得重
the higher one climbs, the harder one falls;

pa qi lai 爬起來
crawl up / get up;

pa shan 爬山
climb a mountain;

pa shan yue ling 爬山越嶺
over hills and crests;

pa shang 爬上
clamber up / climb up;

pa xia 爬下
climb down;

pa xing 爬行
crawl / creep;

pai1 ma pi 拍馬屁
flatter;

pai2 徘
move around / walk to and fro;

pai hui 徘徊
walk to and fro;

pai2 chu 排除
eliminate / get rid of / remove;

pai chu wan nan 排除萬難
overcome all difficulties;

pai chu yi ji 排除異己
expel the outsiders;

pai dui 排隊
fall in formation / fall in line / queue up for / stand in a queue;

pai fan 排飯
set the table;

pai jie 排解
make peace / resolve disputes;

pai kai 排開
spread out;

pai lian 排練
rehearse;

pai lie 排列
arrange in series;

pai men 排悶
dispel boredom / kill time;

pai ming 排命
tell sb's fortune;

pai nan jie fen 排難解紛
mediate a quarrel / reconcile a dispute;

pai2 pai zuo 排排坐
sit in rows;

pai tou 排頭
stand first in the line;

pan1 攀
(1) clamber / climb / hang on / hold to;
(2) involve;

pan che 攀扯
drag into an affair / implicate;

pan deng 攀登
climb / scale;

pan fu 攀附
attach oneself to power etc. / hang on;

pan lian 攀連
implicate / involve;

pan2 le 般樂
have fun without being conscious of time;

pan you 般遊
play without conscious of time;

pan4 ming 拌命
risk one's life;

pan qi 拌棄
abandon;

pan4 拚
(1) go all out / try very hard to;
(2) at the risk of / disregard;
(3) abandon / discard / reject;

pan cai 拚財
make rash speculations;

pan ming 拚命
go all out for a cause even at the risk of one's life;

pan qi 拚棄
abandon / reject;

pao1 duo 拋躲
abandon a lover;

pao qi 拋棄
abandon / cast off / give up / throw away / throw over;

pao4 niu 泡妞
gallanting / womanizing;

pei2 bu qi 賠不起
cannot afford to pay for compensation;

pei bu shi 賠不是
apologize;

pei huan 賠還
repay;

pei qian 賠錢
make a pecuniary compensation;

pei xiao xin 賠小心
make apologies;

pei4 佩
wear;

pei dai 佩帶
carry / wear;

pei fu 佩服
admire;

peng1 抨
assail by words / attack by words / censure / impeach;

peng he 抨劾
censure / impeach;

peng ji 抨擊
assail by words / attack by words / censure / impeach / jump down sb's throat;

peng4 dao 踫到
come upon;

peng jian 踫見
meet || bump into; fall in with; knock against; measure noses; nose to nose; run across; run against; run into; run up against;

pi1 yi 披衣
throw on clothes;

pi2 疲
exhausted / fatigued / tired / weary;

pi bei 疲憊
fatigued / tired / weary;

pi bei bu kan 疲憊不堪
about to collapse from exhaustion // dog-tired / extremely tired;

pi dun 疲頓
slothful from exhaustion / weary and slow;

pi fa 疲乏
exhausted / tired / weary;

pi juan 疲倦
fatigued / tired / weary // lassitude;

pi lao 疲勞
fatigue / tiredness // gruelling / tired;
ci ji xing pi lao 刺激性疲勞
stimulation fatigue;
sheng dai pi lao 聲帶疲勞
vocal fatigue;

pi lao guo du 疲勞過度
excessive fatigue;

pi lao re 疲勞熱
fatigue fever;

pi lao zheng 疲勞症
apokamnosis;

pi long 疲癃
humpback / hunchback;

pi ruan 疲軟
tired and feeble;

pi ruo 疲弱
weak from exhaustion / weary and weak;

pi ta 疲塌
negligent / slack;

pi wan 疲玩
negligent / not alert / remiss;

pi yu ben ming 疲於奔命
tired from running around;

pi2 qi 脾氣
temper / temperament;

pi qi bao zao 脾氣暴躁
have a bad temper / have a fierce disposition / have a hot temper // choleric / grumpy / hot-tempered / short-tempered;

pi qi bu hao 脾氣不好
bad-tempered / disagreeable / grumpy;

pi qi hao 脾氣好
good-tempered;

pi qi ji zao 脾氣急躁
impetuous in one's temper / irritable;

pi qi sui he 脾氣隨和
good-tempered || easy to get along with ; easygoing; unassuming // have an amiable disposition;

pi nong zhong 脾膿腫
splenic abscess;

pi xing 脾性
make / nature / of one's make / temperament;

pian1 ce fa yu bu liang 偏側發育不良
hemihypoplasia;

pian ce fa yu bu quan 偏側發育不全
hemihypoplasia;

pian ce fa yu guo du 偏側發育過度
hemihyperplasia;

pian ce fa yu zhang ai 偏側發育障礙
hemidystrophy;

pian ce fei da 偏側肥大
hemihypertrophy;

pian ce fei pang 偏側肥胖
hemiobesity;

pian ce gan jue chi dun 偏側感覺遲鈍
hemidysesthesia;

pian ce gan jue guo min 偏側感覺過敏
hemihyperesthesia;

pian ce gan jue que shi 偏側感覺缺失
hemianesthesia;

pian ce gan jue yi chang 偏側感覺異常
hemiparesthesia;

pian ce jing luan 偏側痙攣
hemispasm;

pian ji 偏激
radical;

pian kuang 偏狂
monomania;

pian lao 偏勞
let one person take on the work of the entire group or team;

pian shen fei pang 偏身肥胖
hemiobesity;

pian shen ma mu 偏身麻木
unilateral anesthesia;

pian shen zhen chan 偏身震顫
hemitremor;

pian tan 偏癱
hemiparalysis;

pian tan hou ma bi 偏癱後麻痺
posthemiplegic paralysis;

pian tan 偏袒
be partial toward;

pian tou tong xing geng si 偏頭痛性梗死
migrainous infarction;

pian xiang 偏向
to be inclined to;

pian xin xing wei suo 偏心性萎縮
eccentric atrophy;

pian zhi zheng 偏執症
paranoia;

pian zhong 偏重
give undue emphasis to;

pian4 騙
(1) cheat / deceive / fool / hoodwink;
(2) cheat sb of sth / get sth by fraud / swindle sb of sth;

pian qu 騙取
scrounge / wangle;

piao1 xie 剽竊
plagiarize;

piao1 dang 飄蕩
drift about with no fixed lodging place / wander;

piao piao ran 飄飄然
tread on air / walk on air;

piao piao yu xian 飄飄欲仙
the heaven of heavens / the seventh heaven;

piao po 飄泊
drift about with no fixed lodging place / wander;

pin1 dao di 拼到底
fight to the bitter end;

pin ming 拼命
(1) risk one's life;
(2) do one's utmost / exert the utmost strength / give one's all to a task;

pin ming gong zuo 拼命工作
slog one's guts out / sweat one's guts out / work like fury / work one's guts out;

pin si 拼死
fight desperately / risk one's life;

pin2 xue xing geng si 貧血性梗死
anemic infarct;

ping2 an 平安
safe and sound;

ping yong 平庸
commonplace / without talent;

ping yun 平允
fair and proper / just and appropriate;

po4 bu de yi 迫不得已
compelled by circumstances / have no alternative;

po bu ji dai 迫不及待
so urgent that there is no time for waiting / too impatient to wait;

po cong 迫從
compel to submit / force to comply;

po cu 迫促
pressed for time / urgent;

po hai 迫害
oppress cruelly / persecute;

po ling 迫令
demand forcibly;

po shi 迫使
force sb to do sth;

po xie 迫脅
coerce / force;

po4 shang feng 破傷風
tetanus;

pu3 bian xing shui zhong 普遍性水腫
hyposarca;

pu tong tian hua 普通天花
ordinary smallpox;

pu4 guang 曝光
expose / lay bare / make public;

qi1 si ba huo 七死八活
at death's door / on the verge of death;

qi1 攲
incline / lean / slant;

qi ce 攲側
incline / lurch / slant;

qi dao 攲倒
slant and fall;

qi qing 攲傾
incline slant;

qi wei 攲危
tottering;

qi wo 攲臥
lie in a reclined position;

qi xie 攲斜
incline / lurch / slant;

qi1 shen 棲身
dwell / live || live under sb's roof; obtain shelter; sojourn; stay; stay temporarily;

qi shen hu xue 棲身虎穴
take shelter in a place of danger;

qi shen zhi chu 棲身之處
a mere place of shelter / a refuge for the night / a roof over one's head;

qi1 欺
(1) cheat / deceive / swindle;
(2) disregard the dictates of one's own conscience;
(3) bully / insult;

qi dan 欺誕
cheat by exaggerating;

qi fu 欺負
bully / oppress / take sb high-handedly;

qi ling 欺淩
bully / insult / mistreat;

qi man 欺瞞
cheat / deceive / dupe / hoodwink / pull the wool over one's eyes;

qi pian 欺騙
cheat / deceive || be done; be done in by; beguile; cajoke; come around; come over sb; come round; cozen; cross sb up; defraud; delude; diddle; do; do sb down; do sb in the eye; do the dirty on sb; draw the wool over sb's eyes; dupe; fool; fraud; get over sb; give a flap with a foxtail; gum; have a game with sb; have sb on; have sb over sth; hocus; hocus-pocus; hoodwink; impose on sb; imposture; lead sb up the garden path; make a fool of; play a trick on sb; play sb false; play the old soldier over sb; play upon; pluck; practise on sb; pull a fast one over; pull the wool over sb's eyes; put it across on sb; put on sb; put upon sb; rope along sb; see sb coming; sell sb down the river; set one's cap; string along sb; swindle; take advantage of; take in; take sb for a ride; trick; throw dust in the eyes of; throw mud into the eyes of; throw sb a curve; wheedle;

qi pian xing wei 欺騙行為
imposture;

qi ren tai shen 欺人太甚
bully sb beyond the limit;

qi ren zi qi 欺人自欺
cheat oneself and others;

qi sheng 欺生
bully strangers;

qi shi dao ming 欺世盜名
win fame by cheating the world;

qi wang 欺罔
cheat;

qi wu 欺侮
bully / insult / ridicule;

qi ya 欺壓
cheat and oppress;

qi zha 欺詐
cheat / defraud / swindle;

qi2 nian shuo de 耆年碩德
aged and virtuous;

qi2 xing 琦行
admirable conduct;

qi3 lai 起來
(1) rise / sit up / stand up;
(2) get up;

qi4 xing shui zhong 氣性水腫
gaseous oedema;

qi du 氣度
appearance / bearing / manner / mien;

qi zhi 氣質
(1) disposition / temperament;
(2) makings / one's mental make / qualities;

qian1 xin wan ku 千辛萬苦
suffer many hardships;

qian1 che 牽扯
involve;

qian she 牽涉
be implicated in / concern / drag in / involve;

qian1 du xing ma bi 鉛毒性麻痺
lead paralysis;

qian zhong du 鉛中毒
lead poisoning;

qian1 慳
niggardly / parsimonious / stingy;

qian fan 慳煩
avoid making trouble;

qian jian 慳儉
frugal;

qian li 慳力
sparing of one's strength;

qian lin 慳吝
miserly / niggardly / stingy;

qian2 ban sheng 前半生
the first half of one's life;

qian qi ai 前期癌
precancer;

qian2 fu gan ran 潛伏感染
latent infection;

qian zai chuang shang 潛在創傷
potential trauma;

qian zai di yi 潛在敵意
latent hostility;

qian zai gan jue 潛在感覺
cryptesthesia;

qian zai xing gan ran 潛在性感染
latent infection;

qian4 shen 欠身
bend toward sb (as a gesture of courtesy);

qiang1 嗆
foolish / stupid;

qiang2 jian 強健
as right as nails / sturdy;

qiang shen 強身
invigorate the body;

qiang3 duo 搶奪
loot / nab / rob;

qiang jie 搶劫
rob;

qiang jing tou 搶鏡頭
outshine others / steal the show;

qiang pao 搶跑
take away by force;

qiao3 yu 巧遇
chance encounter;

qiao4 wei ba 翹尾巴
cocky / get stuck-up;

qie1 shen 切身
(1) directly affecting a person / of immediate concern to oneself;
(2) first-hand / one's own / personal;

qie shen gan shou 切身感受
personal impressions and experience;

qie shen li yi 切身利益
one's immediate interests / one's vital interests;

qie shen ti hui 切身體會
first-hand experience || direct experience; have intimate experience of; intimate experience; intimate knowledge; keenly aware of; one's own experience; personal understanding;

qie shen zhi tong 切身之痛
sorrow which hits close at home;

qie4 er bu she 鍥而不捨
do sth with persistence / perseverate // perseverance;

qin1 shen 親身
in person / personally;

qin shen jing li 親身經歷
first-hand experience / personal experience;

qin zi 親自
in person / personally;

qin zi chu ma 親自出馬
go out and take care of sth in person;

qin2 勤
hardworking / industrious;

qin fen 勤奮
assiduous / diligent / hardworking / industrious // assiduity / diligence / industry;

qin jian 勤儉
diligent and frugal;

qin jian chi jia 勤儉持家
diligent and frugal in managing a family;

qin jin 勤謹
diligent and prudent;

qin ken 勤懇
diligent and conscientious;

qin ku 勤苦
diligent / hardworking / industrious;

qin lao 勤勞
diligent / hardworking / industrious;

qin li 勤力
diligent / hardworking / industrious;

qin mian 勤勉
industrious / sedulous;

qin pu 勤樸
industrious and frugal;

qin xue 勤學
study diligently;

qin2 liu gan 禽流感
Avian Flu;

qing1 chun qi 青春期
adolescence / puberty / teens;

qing shao nian xi rou 青少年息肉
juvenile polyp;

qing1 bai 清白
unblemished;

qing gao 清高
morally lofty;

qing han 清寒
poor but clean and honest;

qing ku 清苦
poor but clean and honest;

qing jian 清減
lose weight;

qing lian 清廉
free from corruption // incorruptible;

qing pin 清貧
poor and virtuous;

qing shou 清瘦
thin and lean;

qing1 shang 輕傷
minor wound / slight injury;

qing shen 輕身
(1) make light of one's life;
(2) without a burden;

qing sheng 輕生
commit suicide;

qing tan 輕癱
paresis;

qing tian hua 輕天花
modified smallpox;

qing tui 輕推
nudge;

qing wu 輕侮
insult;

qing2 sha 情殺
crime of passion / murder caused by love entanglement;

qing shang 情商
ask for a favour as a friend;

qing si 情死
commit suicide for the sake of love;

qing3 ke 請客
stand treat;

qing4 shen 罄身
nakedness / nudity;

qiong2 kun liao dao 窮困潦倒
down-and-out;

qiu2 囚
imprison;

qiu2 jiao 求教
seek advice / seek instruction;

qiu jiu 求救
ask for rescue / seek relief;

qu1 屈
(1) bend / bow;
(2) humble / humiliate;
(3) injustice / wrong;

qu cong 屈從
bend / give way to / submit to / yield // passive obedience;

qu da cheng zhao 屈打成招
confess under torture to a crime one hasn't committed;

qu fu 屈服
bow down to / knock under / submit / succumb / yield // passive obedience;

qu1 趨
(1) go quickly / hasten / hurry;
(2) follow / tend;

qu bai 趨拜
hurry on to pay respects to;

qu feng 趨奉
hasten to please;

qu1 軀
(1) body / trunk;
(2) child in the womb;

qu gan 軀幹
body / trunk;

qu qiao 軀殼
body / human body / outer form;

qu ti 軀體
body / human body;

qu ti bing 軀體病
somatopathy;

qu3 dai 取代
replace / substitute / take the place of;

qu dao 取道
go by way of;

qu de 取得
acquire / attain / earn / gain / get / obtain;

qu le 取樂
make merry;

qu liang 取涼
enjoy the cool air;

qu nuan 取暖
warm oneself;

qu she 取捨
make a choice;

qu xiang 取向
orientation;

qu xin yu ren 取信於人
establish credibility among others;

qu yue 取悅
please;

qu4 shi 去世
die / pass away || depart from life; leave the world;

qu zhi 去職
be removed from office / resign from office;

quan1 nong 圈弄
frame up sb / trap sb;

quan2 bu gan jue 全部感覺
panesthesia;

quan bu huai si 全部壞死
total necrosis;

quan di fang bing 全地方病
holoendemic disease;

quan fan she 全反射
total reflection;

quan li 全力
with all-out effort;

quan li yi fu 全力以赴
do one's damnedest / go the whole hog / put one's best foot forward / put one's shoulder on the wheel / put one's shoulder to the wheel / spare no efforts / strain every nerve / strain oneself // at full strain / at full stretch / at strain / in high gear / in top gear / into high gear / into top gear / on the strain / with all the stops;

quan ma bi 全麻痺
general paralysis;

quan shen 全身
the whole body || all over the body; flesh and fell; to the teeth;

quan shen ma zui 全身麻醉
general anesthesia;

quan shen shui zhong 全身水腫
hyposarca;

quan shen tong 全身痛
pantalgia;

quan shen wei suo 全身萎縮
panatrophy;

quan shen xing fei pang 全身性肥胖
adiposis universalis;

quan shen xing guo min fan ying 全身性過敏反

應
generalized anaphylaxis;

quan shen xing ji bing 全身性疾病
systemic disease;

quan shen xing shui zhong 全身性水腫
anasarca;

quan shen ying yang bu liang 全身營養不良
pantatrophia;

quan2 痊
cured / healed / recovered from illness;

quan ke 痊可
cured / healed / recovered from illness;

quan yu 痊癒
cured / healed / recovered from illness;

quan4 he 勸和
reconcile a quarrel;

quan jia 勸架
mediate a quarrel;

quan jie 勸解
mediate / negotiate peace;

quan jie 勸戒
admonish;

quan juan 勸捐
ask for contribution;

quan zhi 勸止
dissuade sb from doing sth;

quan zu 勸阻
dissuade sb from doing sth;

que1 xian 缺陷
defect / handicap / inadequacy / shortcoming;

que1 xue xing huai si 缺血性壞死
avascular necrosis;

que xue xing ma bi 缺血性麻痺
ischemic paralysis;

que4 bing 卻病
prevent a disease;

qun1 逡
move backward / retreat / withdraw;

qun tui 逡退
retire from office when nothing could be accomplished;

qun xing 逡行
shrink;

qun xun 逡巡
hesitate / shrink back / waver;

qun xun bu qian 逡巡不前
hesitate / waver // reluctant to move ahead;

ran3 bing 染病
catch a disease / fall ill / get infected;

ran du 染毒
(1) be infected with venereal disease;
(2) use narcotics;

rang2 chu 攘除
eliminate / dispel / rid;

rang duo 攘奪
take by force;

rao2 ming 饒命
spare a life;

rao3 擾
(1) agitate / disturb / harass / trouble;
(2) trespass on sb's hospitality;

rao dong 擾動
agitate / disturb;

rao hai 擾害
harass and injure;

rao luan 擾亂
agitate / disrupt / disturb / harass;

re3 惹
bring upon oneself / cause / incur / offend / provoke / rouse / stir up / trifle with;

re bu qi 惹不起
(1) not daring to provoke;
(2) too powerful or vicious to be provoked or offended;

re de qi 惹得起
dare to provoke;

re huo shao shen 惹火燒身
bring trouble upon oneself;

re huo 惹禍
bring calamity upon oneself / bring disaster / stir up trouble;

re luan zi 惹亂子
bring trouble;

re ma fan 惹麻煩
excite trouble / get into trouble / invite trouble;

re qi 惹起
incite / incur / provoke;

re qi 惹氣
incur wrath / provoke one to anger;

re qian 惹嫌
incur hatred / provoke dislike;

re ren tao yan 惹人討厭
make a nuisance of oneself // obnoxious;

re yan 惹厭
incur dislike;

re shi 惹事
create trouble;

re shi fei 惹是非
incur unnecessary trouble / stir up trouble;

re shi sheng fei 惹是生非
incur unnecessary trouble / stir up trouble;

re4 bing 熱病
fever;

re dai kui yang 熱帶潰瘍
veldt sore;

re dai xing kui yang 熱帶性潰瘍
tropical ulcer;

re qing 熱情
ardour / enthusiasm / warmth / zeal;

re shuai jie 熱衰竭
heat exhaustion;

ren2 bi ren, qi si ren 人比人，氣死人
comparisons are odious;

ren ji guan xi 人際關係
human relations / person-to-person relations;

ren ming 人命
human life;

ren ming guan tian 人命關天
human life is most important;

ren ming you guan 人命攸關
a matter of life and death;

ren pin 人品
one's character / one's personality;

ren quan 人權
human rights;

ren shen 人身
(1) human body;
(2) personal liberty;

ren shen an quan 人身安全
personal safety / security of person;

ren shen bao hu ling 人身保護令
habeas corpus;

ren shen gong ji 人身攻擊
personal attack || assault and battery; attacks concerning personal matters; personal abuse;

ren shen zi you 人身自由
personal freedom || freedom of person; personal liberty;

ren ti 人體
human body;

ren xing 人性
human nature;

ren yuan 人緣
relations with others;

ren zhi chang qing 人之常情
way of the world;

ren3 gou 忍垢
live in disgrace / live in shame;

ren rang 忍讓
forbear;

ren shi 忍事
put up with adversities;

ren si 忍死
hold on to life;

ren3 rou 荏弱
fragile / soft / weak;

ren4 da 任達
unrestrained;

ren lao ren yuan 任勞任怨
do sth without complaint;

ren xing 任性
hoity-toity / unrestrained / wayward;

ren4 shen zhong du 妊娠中毒
gestosis;

ren4 bei 認背
resign oneself to one's fate;

ren cuo 認錯
admit a fault / admit a mistake;

ren ming 認命
accept fate / resign oneself to destiny;

ren zhen 認真
earnest / serious;

rong2 rang 容讓
give in / make a concession / yield;

rong ren 容忍
endure / put up with / stand / tolerate;

rong shen 容身
shelter oneself;

rong shen zhi di 容身之地
a place to stay;

rong shen wu di 容身無地
no place to set oneself in / no place to stay;

rong shou 容受
bear / endure / put up with;

rong xu 容許
admit of / allow / brook / permit;

rou4 gan 肉感
sexy / voluptuous;

rou liu 肉瘤
sarcoma;
gu rou liu 骨肉瘤
osteosarcoma;
lin ba rou liu 淋巴肉瘤
lymphosarcoma;
nian ye rou liu 黏液肉瘤
myxosarcoma;

rou liu bing 肉瘤病
sarcosis;

rou ma 肉麻
disgusting / revolting;

rou shen 肉身
physical body;

rou ti 肉體
flesh and blood / human body;

rou ti mei 肉體美
physical beauty;

rou ya liu 肉芽瘤
granulation tumour;

rou ya zhong 肉芽腫
granulation tumour;

rou ya zhong bing 肉芽腫病
granulomatosis;

ru2 chong gan ran 蠕蟲感染
invermination;

ru chong xing jiao tong 蠕蟲性絞痛
verminous colic;

ru chong xing nong zhong 蠕蟲性膿腫
verminous abscess;

ru3 lin 辱臨
condescend to come to such a humble place;

ru ming 辱命
fail to accomplish a mission;

ru shen 辱身
disgrace oneself;

ru4 shui 入睡
fall asleep / go to sleep;

ru yu 入獄
be imprisoned / be put into prison / be sent to jail / put behind bars;

ruan3 hua 軟化
softening up;
chuang shang xing gu ruan hua 創傷性骨軟化
malacia traumatica;
chuang shang xing ji sui ruan hua 創傷性脊髓軟化
spondylomalacia traumatica;
fei ruan hua 肺軟化
pneumomalacia;
gong mo ruan hua 鞏膜軟化
scleromalacia;
gu ruan hua 骨軟化
halisteresis;
ji sui ruan hua 脊髓軟化
spondylomalacia;
jia gu ruan hua 假骨軟化
pseudo-osteomalacia;
jian ban ruan hua 瞼板軟化
tarsomalacia;

jiao mo ruan hua 角膜軟化
keratomalacia;

nao ruan hua 腦軟化
softening of the brain;

shen jing ruan hua 神經軟化
neuromalacia;

shen ruan hua 腎軟化
nephromalcia;

ruan jin 軟禁
put under house arrest;

ruan ying jian shi 軟硬兼施
a carrot-and-stick approach;

ruo4 yao ren bu zhi, chu fei ji mo wei 若要人不知，除非己莫為
what is done by night appears by day;

sa1 bo 撒潑
behave rudely / in a tantrum;

sa bo da gun 撒潑打滾
fly into a tantrum;

sa feng sa chi 撒瘋撒癡
reckless;

sa jian 撒姦
play dirty tricks;

sa jiao 撒嬌
pretend to be displeased;

sa lai 撒賴
behave like a rascal;

sa qi 撒氣
vent anger;

sa ye 撒野
act boorishly / behave atrociously;

sa3 tang 灑湯
bungle / fail;

sai4 che 賽車
car race;

sai chuan 賽船
run a boat race;

sai ma 賽馬
horse-racing;

sai pao 賽跑
run a race on foot;

san1 da de 三達德
the three virtues of wisdom, benevolence, and courage;

san sheng 三生
the three incarnations of the past, present, and future;

san sheng you xing 三生有幸
a fortune in the three incarnations of the past, present, and future;

san wei 三圍
the vital statistics of a woman;

san zai ba nan 三災八難
suffer from one ailment after another in one's childhood;

sang4 ming 喪命
die / lose one's life || dispirited; downcast; feel disheartened; forfeit one's life; get killed; lose heart; meet one's death; meet one's end;

sang ou 喪偶
be deprived of one's spouse;

sang shen 喪身
lose one's life;

sao1 rao 騷擾
harass / molest // harassment;

se4 嗇
miserly / stingy;

sha1 hai 殺害
kill / murder;

sha ren 殺人
kill a person / murder;

sha ren bu jian xue 殺人不見血
kill with subtle means;

sha ren bu zha yan 殺人不眨眼
hardhearted;

sha ren yue huo 殺人越貨
kill and rob;

sha shang 殺傷
kill and wound;

sha shen cheng ren 殺身成仁
die a martyr to a noble cause || die to achieve virtue; die for a just cause; fulfil justice at the cost of one's own life; sacrifice one's life to preserve one's virtue intact;

sha shen zhi huo 殺身之禍
fatal disaster / lethal misfortune;

sha si 殺死
kill || account for; bump off; carry off; destroy; dispatch; dispose of; do for; eliminate; erase; execute; finish; finish off; fix; frag; get rid of; give sb the business; knock off; lay low; lay out; make away with; murder; obliterate; off; puff out; put an end to sb; put away; put down; put sb on the spot; put out; put sb out of their misery; put out of way; put sb to silence; put sb to sleep; remove; rub out; send sb up the Green River; send west; silence; slay; snuff out; take; take care of; take sb for a ride; take off; terminate; touch off; waste; wipe out; zap;

shan3 shen 閃身
(1) dodge;
(2) sideways;

shan4 善
(1) good;
(2) kind;
(3) good at;

shan liang 善良
kind-hearted;

shang1 傷
(1) injury;
(2) cut;
(3) grief;
(4) impede;
(5) hurt;
(6) make sick;

shang feng 傷風
catch cold / have a cold;
zhong shang feng 重傷風
serious cold;

shang feng bai su 傷風敗俗
corrupt public morals;

shang hai 傷害
hurt;

shang han 傷寒
typhoid;

shang han re 傷寒熱
typhoid fever;

shang ren 傷人
hurt people;

shang shen 傷身
harmful to the health / injurious to health;

shang sheng 傷生
bring injury to one's life;

shang tian hai li 傷天害理
commit crimes;

shang tong 傷痛
mourn;

shang wang 傷亡
casualities;

shang zhong shen wang 傷重身亡
die of a mortal wound;

shang1 殤
(1) die young;
(2) national mourning;

shang4 ban 上班
(1) go to work;
(2) go on duty;

shang ban shen 上半身
the upper half of the body / the upper part of the body // above the waist;

shang cai 上菜
place a dish on the table;

shang chang 上場
(1) go on stage;
(2) enter the field;

shang chuang 上床
go to bed / turn in;

shang che 上車
get on a vehicle;

shang chuan 上船
board a ship;

shang dang 上當
be fooled / be taken in;

shang diao 上吊
commit suicide by hanging / hang oneself;

shang fang 上訪
visit the capital by the common people;

shang gong 上工
begin work;

shang ke 上課
(1) attend class;
(2) conduct class;

shang jie 上街
(1) go on the street;
(2) go shopping;

shang lai 上來
come up;

shang lou 上樓
go upstairs;

shang lu 上路
start a journey;

shang men 上門
call / visit;

shang nian ji 上年紀
getting on in years // over the hill;

shang qi bu jie xia qi 上氣不接下氣
out of breath / short of breath;

shang qian 上前
come forward;

shang qu 上去
ascend / go up;

shang ren 上任
take up an appointment;

shang san 上山
go up a hill;

shang shen 上身
upper part of the body;

shang shou 上壽
advanced age;

shang shu 上書
present a petition;

shang su 上訴
appeal to a higher court;

shang suo 上鎖
lock;

shang tai 上臺
go on the stage;

shang ti 上體
upper part of the body;

shang yin 上癮
be addicted to / get into the habit of;

shang yu 上愚
the most stupid;

shang zhen 上陣
(1) play in the game;
(2) go to battle;

shang zhi 上肢
upper limbs;

shao1 si 燒死
burn to death;

she3 ben zhu mo 捨本逐末
concentrate on details but forget the main purpose;

she ji cong ren 捨己從人
give up one's views and follow those of another person;

she ming 捨命
give up one's life;

she4 shi 涉世
get along in the world / make one's way through the world;

she shi wei shen 涉世未深
inexperienced in affairs of the world;

she4 fa 設法
cast about / devise a way / find a way / go to the trouble / manage / take the trouble / think up a way / try / work out a way;

she li 設立
establish / set up;

she shen chu di 設身處地
put oneself in another's position;

shen1 bai ming lie 身敗名裂
lose both one's fortune and honour;

shen bing ti lei 身病體羸
ill and weak // physical wreck;

shen bu you ji 身不由己
do sth not of one's own free will ‖ helpless; incapable of resistance; involuntarily; lose control of oneself; one's limbs no longer obey one; unable to act according to one's own will; unable to contain oneself; under compulsion;

身體 *Body*

shen bu you zhu 身不由主
do sth not of one's own free will ‖ helpless; incapable of resistance; involuntarily; lose control of oneself; one's limbs no longer obey one; unable to act according to one's own will; unable to contain oneself; under compulsion;

shen can zhi bu can 身殘志不殘
broken in health but not in spirit;

shen can zhi jian 身殘志堅
broken in body but firm in spirit;

shen chang 身長
(1) height / stature;
(2) length;

shen chuan 身穿
be dressed in / wear ‖ attire oneself in; be attired in; be clad in; be clothed in; dress oneself in; have on;

shen chuan gao su 身穿縞素
be dressed entirely in white / be dressed in mourning white;

shen duan 身段
(1) figure / physique;
(2) postures;

shen fen 身分
one's capacity / one's identity / one's status;

shen fen bu ming 身分不明
of unknown identity ‖ one's legal identity not clarified; one's standing is not clear; unidentified;

shen fen xiang zheng 身分象徵
status symbol;

shen fu quan ze 身負全責
take up the whole responsibility / undertake the whole management;

shen fu zhong ren 身負重任
be charged with important tasks / shoulder an important task;

shen fu zhong shang 身負重傷
be badly wounded / be seriously injured;

shen gao 身高
stature ‖ a person of...metres; have a height of ... metres; height; ...metres in height; ... metres tall; stand...metres; top...metres;

shen gao qi shi 身高歧視
heightism;

shen gu 身故
die;

shen hou 身後
after one's death;

shen hou ming 身後名
posthumous fame;

shen hou shi 身後事
funeral affairs;

shen hou wu chu 身後無出
die without children / die without issue / without progeny after one's death;

shen hou xiao tiao 身後蕭條
die without leaving progeny behind / without money after one's death / without progeny after one's death;

shen jia 身家
ancestry / family background / pedigree;

shen jia bu qing 身家不清
of mean descent / of mean parentage;

shen jia nan bao 身家難保
live in great danger;

shen jia qing bai 身家清白
come of a decent family / of respectable descent;

shen jia xing ming 身家性命
one's life and family possessions;

shen jia bai bei 身家百倍
one's position and reputation shoot up hundredfold ‖ a meteoric rise in social status; come up in the world; find oneself substantially elevated in fame and status; have a sudden rise in social status; receive a tremendous boost in one's prestige; rise in the world; rise to high note;

shen jia 身價
(1) one's social status;
(2) the selling price of a slave;

shen jia shi bei 身價十倍
one's value increases tenfold ‖ go up in the world; the marketprice of sth has suddenly shot up tenfold;

shen jian shu zhi 身兼數職
hold several posts simultaneously;

shen jian zhong ren 身肩重任
bear a heavy burden / shoulder heavy responsibilities;

shen jiao 身教
teach by personal example / teach others by one's own example;

shen jiao sheng yu yan jiao 身教勝於言教
example is better than precept ‖ a good example is the best sermon; examples move more than words; the example of good man is visible philosophy;

shen jiao yan chuan 身教言傳
instruct sb not only in words, but by deeds / teach by precept and example;

shen jing bai lian 身經百煉
have gone through the mill;

shen jing bai zhan 身經百戰
seasoned fighter ‖ have experienced many battles; have fought countless battles; veteran of many wars;

shen liang 身量
one's height / one's physical dimensions;

shen lin qi jing 身臨其境
on the spot in person ‖ as though one were there in person; being there in person; experience personally; visit the place in person; watch the scene in person;

shen qiang li zhuang 身強力壯
physically strong ‖ be possessed of health; hale and strong; in fine feather; sturdy; tough;

shen qing ru yan 身輕如燕
with a body as light as a swallow's ;

shen qing ru ye 身輕如葉
one's body is as light as a leaf;

shen qing yan wei 身輕言微
when one's position is low, one's words carry little weight ‖ in my humble position, my word does not carry much weight;

shen qu 身軀
one's body / one's bulk / one's person / one's stature;

shen ru ku mu, xin ru si hui 身如枯木，心如死灰
with one's body like a withered tree and one's spirit like dying embers — without warm feelings;

shen ru hou men 身入侯門
marry into the purple;

shen ru ling yu 身入囹圄
be thrown into prison ‖ be committed to prison; be sent to goal; behind prison bars;

shen shang 身上
(1) on one's body;
(2) on one / with one;

shen shang fa guang, du li fa huang 身上發光，肚裏發慌
silks and satins put out the fire in the kitchen / silks and satins put out the kitchen-fire;

shen shi 身世
experiences in one's lifetime / one's life / one's life experience / one's lot;

shen shi qi liang 身世淒涼
sad life // lead a miserable and dreary life;

shen shou 身手
(1) skills / talent;
(2) agility / dexterity;

shen shou 身首
the trunk and the head;

shen shou yi chu 身首異處
be beheaded ‖ be dismembered; sever the head from the trunk;

shen shou 身受
(1) experience personally;
(2) accept personally / receive in person;

shen shou zhong chuang 身受重創
severely wounded;

shen si yi guo 身死異國
die in an alien land;

shen si yi xiang 身死異鄉
die in a strange place;

shen ti 身體
(1) body;
(2) health;
duan lian shen ti 鍛鍊身體
exercise the body;

luo lu shen ti 裸露身體
bare the body;
wan qu shen ti 彎曲身體
bend the body;
zi bu shen ti 滋補身體
nourish the body;

shen ti an kang 身體安康
alive and well / in good health;

shen ti bu shu fu 身體不舒服
not feel like anything // indisposed / off-colour // one degree under;

shen ti cha 身體差
in poor health / in poor nick;

shen ti fa yu bu liang 身體發育不良
hyposomia;

shen ti fa yu bu quan 身體發育不全
hyposomia;

shen ti jian cha 身體檢查
physical check-up / medical check-up || physical examination;

shen ti jian kang 身體健康
alive and well / as fit as a fiddle / in fine feather / in good feather / in good health / in good nick / in grand feather / in high feather / in very good nick;

shen ti li xing 身體力行
practise what one preaches || carry out by actual efforts; earnestly practise what one advocates; set an example by personally taking part;

shen ti qiang zhuang 身體強壯
able-bodied / sturdy;

shen ti yao bai 身體搖擺
body rocking;

shen ti ying lang 身體硬朗
be going strong;

shen ti yu yan 身體語言
body language;

shen tong 身痛
bodily pain;

shen wai zhi wu 身外之物
mere worldly possessions / things that are not part of one's body — external things / worldly goods;

shen wu chang wu 身無長物
have only bare necessities || have no personal superfluities; have no valuable things; have nothing;

shen wu fen wen 身無分文
without a penny in one's pocket || broke to the wide; flat broke; impecunious; not a penny; not a shot in one's locker; not a shot in the locker; not have a penny to bless oneself with; not have half-pennies to rub together; not have two pennies to rub together; not to have a bean; penniless; stone-broke; with empty pockets; without a bean; without a cash in one's pocket;

shen wu ji chu 身無己出
have no children of one's own;

shen xian shi zu 身先士卒
lead the charge || charge at the head of one's subordinates; in the van of one's officers and men;

shen xian jue jing 身陷絕境
be caught in a hopeless situation / get one's back to the wall / have one's back to the wall / land oneself in an impasse;

shen xian ling yu 身陷囹圄
be shut up in jail / be thrown into prison;

shen xin 身心
body and mind;

shen xin bu ning 身心不寧
feel uneasy in body and mind || on pins and needles;

shen xin chun jie 身心純潔
pure in mind and body;

shen xin huang hu 身心恍惚
ill at ease and somehow confused;

shen xin jian kang 身心健康
physically and mentally healthy / sound in body and mind;

shen xin jiao cui 身心交瘁
be mentally and physically exhausted // in a state of complete bodily and mental prostration // physical and mental fatigue;

shen xin pi lao 身心疲勞
weary in body and mind // physical and

mental fatigue;

shen xin shu tai 身心舒泰
body and mind at ease / there is peace in one's body and brain;

shen xin yi zhi 身心一致
body and mind accord / body and soul are in harmony;

shen xin yu kuai 身心愉快
feeling well both physically and mentally;

shen xing 身形
frame;

shen ying 身影
figure / form / person's silhouette;

shen yun 身孕
pregnancy;

shen zai fu zhong bu zhi fu 身在福中不知福
not to appreciate the happy life one enjoys / take one's good fortune for granted;

shen zai wu yan xia, zen gan bu di tou 身在屋檐下，怎敢不低頭
being under the eaves, dare one not lower one's head;

shen zai xin chi 身在心馳
the body is present but the spirit is far away;

shen zheng bu pa ying zi xie 身正不怕影子斜
a clean conscience laughs at false accusations / a righteous person fears no criticisms / just stand straight and never mind if shadow inclines;

shen zi 身子
(1) body / trunk;
(2) pregnancy;

shen1 bu gan jue 深部感覺
deep sensibility;

shen bu gan jue chi dun 深部感覺遲鈍
bathyhypesthesia;

shen bu gan jue guo min 深部感覺過敏
bathyhyperesthesia;

shen bu gan jue que shi 深部感覺缺失
bathyanesthesia;

shen ceng fan she 深層反射
deep reflex;

shen2 jing xing jing luan 神經性痙攣
neurospasm;

shen jing yuan xing kui yang 神經源性潰瘍
neurogenic ulcer;

shen jing yuan xing xiu ke 神經源性休克
neurogenic shock;

shen tai 神態
bearing / expression / manner / mien;

shen zhi hun luan 神志昏亂
delirious // delirium;

shen4 xing shui zhong 腎性水腫
renal oedema;

shen xue guan ying hua 腎血管硬化
nephroangiosclerosis;

sheng1 bing 生病
be ill ‖ be taken bad; be taken ill; be taken sick; fall ill; fall sick; get sick; have an illness; take ill; take sick;

sheng bu ru si 生不如死
a fate worse than death;

sheng huo fu hua 生活腐化
life corruption;

sheng huo you yu 生活優裕
live in affluence;

sheng li ji neng 生理機能
physiological function;

sheng li que xian 生理缺陷
physical defect;

sheng li xing fei da 生理性肥大
physiologic hypertrophy;

sheng ming 生命
life;

sheng ming li 生命力
vitality;

sheng qi 生氣
(1) angry / angry about sb / angry at sb / get angry at sb / get angry with sb ‖ annoyed; be fed up; be fed up to the eyelids; be fed up to the gills; be fed up to the teeth; be filled with fury; be incensed against; be incensed at; be incensed by; be incensed with sb; be offended with sb; become angry; become livid; beside oneself with anger; blow a fuse; blow a

gasket; blow off steam; blow one's cool; blow one's top; blow one's stack; bluster oneself into anger; boil over; boil with rage; bridle with anger; bristle with anger; buck up rough; burn; burn with anger; burn with wrath; bust a blood vessel; call sb down; create a scene; cross; cross as two sticks; cross with sb; cut up rough; down on sb; enraged; exasperated; fall into a rage; fire up; flare up; flip one's lid; flip one's raspberry; fly into a fury; fly into a passion; fly into a rage; fly into a temper; fly off the handle; foam at the mouth; fretful; fumed; furious; get a miff; get back at; get cross with sb; get hot under the collar; get into a huff; get into a passion; get mad with sb; get on one's nerves; get one's back up; get one's bristles up; get one's dander up; get one's Irish up; get one's monkey up; get one's own back; get one's quills up; get one's rag out; get out of bed on the wrong side; get someone; get someone's goat; get under sb's skin; give provocation; give sb a fit; give someone a piece of one's mind; give someone curry; give someone Larry Dooley; go crook at sb; go into a huff; go off the deep end; go off the handle; go off the top; go to market; grab for altitude; grow hot under the collar; have a fit; have a hemorrhage; have a miff; heat; huff; in a huff; in a passion; in a pet; in a rage with sb; in a stew; in a temper; in a thundering rage; in a tiff; in one of one's furies; in temper; in the sulks; incense; indignant at sth; irritate; kick up a row; kick up a shindy; kick up rough; lay out in lavender; lay someone out; let sb have it; livid; lock horns; look black; lose control; lose one's rag; lose one's temper; mad about; mad with sb; make a scene; make angry; make one's blood boil; miff; one's back is up; out of temper; peevish; pitch into; play sb up; put one's back up; put one's hackles up; put one's Irish up; put sb into a huff; raise Cain; rattle; red in the face; red with anger; rub sb with wrong way; ruffle one's feathers; ruffled; see red; seethe; set one's back up; set one's teeth on edge; show one's wrath on sb; sizzle; slip off the handle; spit nails; spitfire; spleen; stick in sb's crop; take a miff; take a pigue against sb; take amiss; take huff; take offence; take offence at; take sth amiss; take the pet; take umbrage; tell someone off; throw a scene; thunder at a person; tick off; touch one home; under provocation; vent one's wrath on sb; vexed; white with anger; white with rage;

(2) liveliness / vitality;

sheng xing 生性

natural disposition;

sheng xing ao man 生性傲慢

immodest personality / imperious by nature;

sheng xing gu zhi 生性固執

pertinacious / stubborn by nature;

sheng1 hua 聲華

good reputation;

sheng jia 聲價

fame of a person / popularity of a person;

sheng ming 聲名

fame / reputation;

sheng ming lang ji 聲名狼藉

disreputable / infamous / notorious // disrepute / infamy / notoriety / notorious reputation // one's name is dirt / one's name is mud;

sheng wang 聲望

fame / prestige / renown / reputation;

sheng wei 聲威

fame and the influence that goes with it;

sheng wen 聲聞

reputation;

sheng wen 聲問

(1) reputation;

(2) information;

sheng xi xiang wen 聲息相聞

keep in touch with each other;

sheng yu 聲譽

fame / reputation;

sheng yu zhuo zhu 聲譽卓着

famous / widely known;

shi1 chong 失寵

fall from favour / fall from grace / fall into disfavour / fall into disgrace / in disgrace / out of favour // one's nose is out of joint;

shi li 失禮

(1) impolite / rude;

(2) impropriety;

shi mian 失眠
insomnia;
chu qi shi mian 初期失眠
initial insomnia;
yuan fa xing shi mian 原發性失眠
primary insomnia;
zhong qi shi mian 中期失眠
middle insomnia;

shi mian zheng 失眠症
insomnia;

shi shen 失身
(1) lose one's chastity / lose one's virginity;
(2) incur danger;

shi shen fen 失身份
do sth beneath one's dignity;

shi tai 失態
misbehaviour;

shi zong 失踪
missing;

shi1 屍
carcass / corpse / dead body;

shi gu 屍骨
skeleton;

shi gu cheng dui 屍骨成堆
corpses are piled up high;

shi gu wei han 屍骨未寒
hardly cold in the grave / sb's remains are scarely cold yet;

shi heng bian ye 屍橫遍野
the field is strewn with corpses || a field littered with corpses; be literally strewn with enemy corpses; be littered with enemy corpses; be littered with the bodies of enemy dead; dead bodies scatter over the wilderness;

shi heng xue ran 屍橫血染
dead bodies lie in the streets and blood stains the road;

shi ji ru shan 屍積如山
the corpses lie about in heaps / the corpses are heaped up like mountains;

shi jian 屍諫
admonish at the cost of one's own life;

shi ju yu qi 屍居餘氣
at one's last gasp || a little breath is left in the body — dying; a living corpse; at the point of death; critically ill with a weak breath; more dead than alive;

shi shen 屍身
corpse / dead body / remains;

shi ti 屍體
corpse / dead body / remains;

shi1 jia ya li 施加壓力
put the heat on / put the screws on sb / tighten the screws on sb / turn the heat on // turn of the screw;

shi jiao 施教
educate / instruct / teach;

shi jiu 施救
rescue and resuscitate;

shi li 施禮
make a bow / salute;

shi wei 施威
impress with force;

shi wei 施為
action / behaviour / conduct;

shi yao 施藥
dispense medicine free of charge;

shi1 yi 施醫
give free medical service;

shi1 tou 濕透
soak through;

shi2 fan 拾翻
turn upside down;

shi2 shi qiu shi 實事求是
practical and realistic / seek truth from facts || be true to facts;

shi zhi shui zhong 實質水腫
solid oedema;

shi3 jing 使勁
exert effort;

shi ming 使命
mission;

shi ming gan 使命感
a sense of calling;

身體 *Body*

shi pi qi 使脾氣
get one's dander up / lose one's temper;

shi xing zi 使性子
indulge in one's temper / lose one's temper;

shi4 qi 士氣
morale;

shi4 gu 世故
experienced / knowing / sophiscated / worldly;

shi4 侍
serve / wait on;

shi feng 侍奉
attend on / serve;

shi li 侍立
in attendance;

shi4 bi gong qin 事必躬親
attend to everything personally;

shi4 shi 逝世
die / pass away;

shi4 li 勢利
dicty / snobbish / snooty // snobbery;

shi4 嗜
addict / be fond of / delight in / relish;

shi hao 嗜好
one's hobby / one's liking;

shi pi 嗜癖
(1) hobby;
(2) special liking for sth;

shi sha 嗜殺
be fond of killing;

shi4 弒
kill one's parent / kill one's superior;

shi fu 弒父
(1) commit patricide;
(2) patricide;

shi mu 弒母
(1) commit matricide;
(2) matricide;

shi xiong 弒兄
(1) commit fatricide;
(2) fatricide;

shi4 奭
in a free manner;

shi4 si 誓死
dare to die / pledge one's life;

shi si bu qu 誓死不屈
vow that one would rather die than yield;

shi4 ying 適應
adapt / adjust to;

shou1 收
(1) collect;
(2) accept;
(3) receive;

shou cang 收藏
collect / collect and keep / store;

shou cang pi 收藏癖
collectomania;

shou gong 收工
call it a day / call it a night / knock off;

shou yang 收養
adopt;

shou3 守
(1) defend / guard / protect;
(2) abide by;

shou chang 守常
stick to tradition;

shou cheng 守成
keep what has been accomplished;

shou cheng bu bian 守成不變
stick to tradition without making changes;

shou fa 守法
abide by the law;

shou gua 守寡
remain in widowhood;

shou hou 守候
wait;

shou hu 守護
guard / protect;

shou jiu 守舊
conservative;

shou mi mi 守秘密
keep a secret / keep one's mouth shut;

shou shen 守身
behave oneself correctly;

shou shen ru yu 守身如玉
keep one's chastity ‖ keep one's integrity; keep oneself as pure as jade — take heed of one's virtue;

shou shi 守時
punctual;

shou shi 守勢
defensive;

shou wang 守望
keep watch;

shou xin 守信
keep promises;

shou yue 守約
honour a pledge / keep a promise;

shou zhong li 守中立
maintain neutrality;

shou zhuo 守拙
happy to remain down to earth;

shou4 bing 受病
catch a disease;

shou cuo 受挫
suffer a setback;

shou fa 受罰
be fined / be punished;

shou hai 受害
suffer;

shou han 受寒
be damaged;

shou hui 受惠
benefit from;

shou hui 受賄
accept bribes / take bribes;

shou ku 受苦
suffer;

shou lei 受累
be put to trouble;

shou liang 受涼
catch cold;

shou ming 受命
(1) accept an order / receive an appointment;
(2) be given an order;

shou nan 受難
suffer calamities;

shou nüe kuang 受虐狂
masochism;

shou nüe pi 受虐癖
masochism;

shou nüe zheng 受虐症
masochism;

shou pian 受騙
be deceived / be fooled;

shou qi 受氣
suffer indignities;

shou qu 受屈
be wronged;

shou ru 受辱
be humiliated;

shou shang 受傷
be injuried / get hurt / hurt / injure;

shou shang 受賞
be awarded;

shou tuo 受託
be entrusted with;

shou xun 受訓
receive training;

shou yong 受用
get the benefit;

shou zui 受罪
suffer hardships;

shou4 授
(1) teach;
(2) give;
(3) give up;

shou ke 授課
teach;

shou ming 授命
give up one's life / sacrifice one's life;

shou tu 授徒
teach students;

shou yu 授與
confer / give;

shou4 ying 瘦硬
fine and forceful;

shou4 ming 壽命
life / life-span / natural life;

shou4 xing 獸行
atrocities / bestial conduct;

shou xing 獸性
bestiality;

shou xing da fa 獸性大發
raise one's animal disposition;

shu1 紓
(1) mitigate / relax / slacken / slow down;
(2) extricate from / free from / remove;

shu ge 紓革
get rid of evil;

shu huan 紓緩
slacken;

shu huo 紓禍
extricate from the grip of misfortune or catastrophe;

shu kun 紓困
provide financial relief;

shu nan 紓難
extricate from danger / extricate from trouble / free from difficulties / give relief in time of distress;

shu1 chang 舒暢
comfortable / pleasant;

shu fu 舒服
comfortable / cosy;

shu huan 舒緩
leisurely // relaxed;

shu san 舒散
leisurely // relaxed;

shu shi 舒適
comfortable / cosy;

shu tai 舒泰
happy and healthy;

shu tan 舒坦
comfortable / happy / in good health;

shu xu 舒徐
leisurely;

shu1 dang 疏宕
carefree / free and easy / open-minded;

shu fang 疏放
careless / lax / loose;

shu hu 疏忽
careless / inadvertent / negligent;

shu kuo 疏闊
cold / distant;

shu lan 疏懶
idle / lazy / loose;

shu lüe 疏略
neglect inadvertently;

shu man 疏慢
neglect inadvertently;

shu shen 疏神
careless / inadvertent;

shu shi 疏失
at fault / negligent / remiss;

shu shuai 疏率
careless and rash / heedless;

shu xie 疏懈
idle / lazy / neglectful / negligent;

shu ye 疏野
impolite / rude;

shu yuan 疏遠
alienate / drift apart / estrange / grow apart;

shu4 hou gan jue yi chang 術後感覺異常
postoperative paresthesia;

shu hou xiu ke 術後休克
postoperative shock;

shua3 耍
(1) play;
(2) play tricks;
(3) play with;
(4) display / show off;

shua ba xi 耍把戲
play tricks;

shua da pai 耍大牌
act like a top-billing actor or actress;

shua hua zhao 耍花招
play tricks;

shua lai 耍賴
act shamelessly // unreasonable;

shua lan 耍懶
loaf / loiter;

shua nao 耍鬧
frolic / sport;

shua nong 耍弄
deceive / make a fool of;

shua pi qi 耍脾氣
get angry / get one's dander up / lose one's temper;

shuai1 lao 衰老
senile // senility;

shuai ruo 衰弱
asthenia / feeble / weak;

zhou qi xing shuai ruo 周期性衰弱
periodic asthenia;

shuai ruo zheng 衰弱症
wasting disease;

shuai1 摔
fall down / lose one's balance / tumble;

shuai dao 摔倒
fall / lose one's balance / throw off one's balance / tumble;

shuai jiao 摔跤
fall down / suffer a fall / trip and fall / tumble;

shuang3 de 爽德
depart from virtue / forfeit one's virtue / lose virtue;

shuang fa 爽法
break regulations / disregard the law / violate the law;

shuang li 爽利
agile / alert / speedy;

shuang yue 爽約
break an appointment / fail to keep a promise;

shui3 zhong 水腫
oedema;

fei shui zhong 肺水腫
oedema pulmonary / pulmonary;

feng shi xing shui zhong 風濕性水腫
rheumatismal oedema;

gu mo shui zhong 骨膜水腫
periosteodema;

ji e xing shui zhong 飢餓性水腫
hunger swelling;

jia shui zhong 假水腫
pseudoedema;

jian shui zhong 瞼水腫
hydrohlepharon;

ju xian xing shui zhong 局限性水腫
circumscribed oedema;

liu xing xing shui zhong 流行性水腫
epidemic dropsy;

nian ye shui zhong 黏液水腫
myxedema;

pu bian xing shui zhong 普遍性水腫
hyposarca;

qi xing shui zhong 氣性水腫
gaseous oedema;

quan shen shui zhong 全身水腫
hyposarca;

quan shen xing shui zhong 全身性水腫
anasarca;

shen xing shui zhong 腎性水腫
renal oedema;

shi zhi shui zhong 實質水腫
solid oedema;

tai er shui zhong 胎兒水腫
fetal hydrops;

tai pan shui zhong 胎盤水腫
placental oedema;

te fa xing shui zhong 特發性水腫
idiopathic oedema;

wei suo xing shui zhong 萎縮性水腫
atrophedema;

xin xing shui zhong 心性水腫
cardiac oedema;

xin yuan xing shui zhong 心源性水腫
cardiac oedema;

yan xing shui zhong 炎性水腫
inflammatory oedema;

yin nang shui zhong 陰囊水腫
hydrocele;
yin xing shui zhong 隱性水腫
invisible oedema;
ying yang bu liang xing shui zhong 營養不良性水腫
alimentary oedema;
zan shi xing shui zhong 暫時性水腫
oedema fugax;
zhi fang shui zhong 脂肪水腫
lipedema;
zhi shui zhong 趾水腫
dactyledema;
zhong mo qi shui zhong 終末期水腫
terminal oedema;
zhong du xing shui zhong 中毒性水腫
toxic oedema;
zhou qi xing shui zhong 周期性水腫
periodic oedema;
zu shui zhong 足水腫
podedema;

shui zhong bing 水腫病
oedema disease;

shui zhong du 水中毒
water intoxication;

shui4 睡
sleep;

shui bu hao 睡不好
have a bad night;

shui de hao 睡得好
have a good night;

shui fa xing teng tong 睡發性疼痛
hypnalgia;

shui jiao 睡覺
go to bed / hit the sack / kip / pound one's ear / sleep // kip / shut-eye;

shui lan jiao 睡懶覺
get up late / lie-in / sleep in;

shui meng 睡夢
in sleep / in one's dreams;

shui meng xing gan jue guo min 睡夢性感覺過敏
oneiric hyperesthesia;

shui mian 睡眠
sleep / slumber;
man bo shui mian 慢波睡眠
slow wave sleep;
zhen fa xing shui mian 陣發性睡眠
paroxysmal sleep;

shui mian bing 睡眠病
sleeping disease / sleeping sickness;

shui mian bu zu 睡眠不足
insufficient sleep / want of sleep;

shui mian fa sheng 睡眠發生
hypnogenesis;

shui mian fan she 睡眠反射
hypnic jerks;

shui mian guo du 睡眠過度
hypersomnolence;
yuan fa xing shui mian guo du 原發性睡眠過度
primary hypersomnia;

shui mian hou ma bi 睡眠後麻痺
postdormital paralysis;

shui mian qian ma bi 睡眠前麻痺
predormital paralysis;

shui mian xing ma bi 睡眠性麻痺
sleep paralysis;

shui mian zhang ai 睡眠障礙
dyssomnia / sleep disorder;

shui mo 睡魔
extreme sleepiness;

shui shang jiao 睡晌覺
take a nap after lunch;

shui shu 睡熟
sleep soundly;

shui wu jiao 睡午覺
take an afternoon nap;

shui xing 睡醒
wake up from sleep;

shui yi 睡意
drowsiness / sleepiness;

shui you bing 睡遊病
somnambulism;

shui zhao 睡着
have fallen asleep;

shun4 shui ren qing 順水人情
a favour done at little cost to oneself;

si1 ben 私奔
elope / run away with;

si1 wen bai lei 斯文敗類
polished scoundrels;

si wen sao di 斯文掃地
the decadenc of the intellectuals;

si1 廝
each other;

si ban 廝伴
keep sb company;

si bing 廝併
fight desperately;

si chan 廝纏
tangle with each other;

si da 廝打
fight;

si hui 廝會
meet each other;

si hun 廝混
(1) mingle / mix each other;
(2) fool around together;

si ren 廝認
recognize each other;

si sha 廝殺
fight at close quarters;

si shou 廝守
take care of each other;

si3 死
(1) dead / die / die for;
(2) to the death;
(3) extremely / to death;
(4) deadly / implacable;

si bie 死別
be parted by death;

si bu hui gai 死不悔改
unrepentant;

si bu liao 死不了
cannot die / will not die;

si bu ren cuo 死不認錯
stubbornly refuse to admit one's guilt or mistake;

si bu zu xi 死不足惜
death is not to be regretted;

si de qi suo 死得其所
die a worthy death;

si ming 死命
cause to die;

si qian 死前
before death;

si qu huo lai 死去活來
half death;

si wang 死亡
die / pass away || all over with sb; all up with sb; among the immortals; an old floorer; answer the final summons; answer the last roll call; answer the last muster; asleep in Jesus; asleep in the Arms of God; asleep in the valley; at peace; at rest; be all washed up; be blown across the creek; be blown away; be blown creek; be brought to one's last home; be called to one's account; be called to one's long account; be called home; be called to God; be called to the beyond; be called to the Great Beyond; be cast into outer darkness; be cleaned out of the deck; be cut off; be done for; be gathered to one's fathers; be gathered to sb's people; be gone; be gone to Davy Jones's locker; be knocked out; be promoted to glory; be removed to the divine bosom; be rocked to sleep; be salted away; be sent to one's account; be shuffled; be taken to paradise; be translated into higher sphere; be trumped; be washed out; be written off; bite the dust; black out; blow sb away; bow off; bow out; breathe one's last; buy a one-way ticket; buy the farm; call it quits; cancel one's account; cash in; cash in one's chips; cease to be; cease to exist; cease to live; check in; check out; close one's career; close one's days; close one's eyes; close one's life; close up one's account; close upon; close upon the world; coil up one's ropes; come to an end; conk out; count daisies; croak; cross over; cross over the Great Divide; cross over the

River Jordan; cross the bar; cross the Bar; cross the great divide; cross the River Styx; cut; cut adrift; cut one's cable; cut one's stick; dangle in the sheriff's picture depart; decease; demise; depart; depart from life; depart from this life; depart from this world; depart to God; depart to the world of shadows; die in one's boots; dissolution; do one's bit; down for good; draw one's last breath; drop hooks; drop off the hooks; drop off the twig; drop the cue; drop the curtain; end; end in one's death; expire; fade away; fade out; fall; fall on sleep; final sleep; fire one's last shot; flunk out; fold up; frame; free; give up the breath; give up the ghost; give up the soul; give up the spirit; go beyond; go blooey; go down to the shades; go flooey; go forth; go hence; go home; go home in a box; go off; go off the hooks; go out; go out of the world; go out of this world; go the way of all flesh; go the way of all nature; go to a better world; go to the way of all the earth; go to Davy Jones's locker; go to heaven; go to hell; go to Jordan's banks; go to meet one's maker; go to one's account; go to one's doom; go to one's grass; go to one's last home; go to one's long home; go to one's own place; go to one's resting place; go to one's reward; go to sleep; go to the hereafter; go to the land of heart's desire; go to the last roundup; go to the mansions of rest; go to the races; go up salt river; go west; God rest his soul; grounded for good; hand in one's account; hand in one's dinner pail; hang up one's harness; hang up one's hat; hang up one's tackle; have fallen asleep; have fallen asleep in the Lord; have fallen by the wayside; have found rest; have gone to a better land; have gone to a better life; have gone to a better place; have gone to a better world; have gone to the Great Adventure; have gone to the happy hunting ground; have gone under; have one's name inscribed in the book of life; he is coming home; hide one's name under daisies; hit the rocks; home and free; hop off one's twig; hop the last rattler; hop the twig; in Abraham's bosom; in Davy Jones's locker; in heaven; in one's coffin; in the dust; in the grand secret; in the hereafter; in the undiscovered country; it's taps; join in the immortals; join one's ancesters; join the angelic choirs; join the angels; join the feathered choir; join the heavenly choir; join the invisible choir; join the ever increasing majority; join the Great majority; join the silent majority; jump the last hurdle; kick in; kick off; kick the bucket; last rest; launch into eternity; lay down life's burden; lay down one's knife and fork; lay down one's life; lay down one's pen; lay down one's shovel and hoe; leave this world; lie asleep; lose one's life; lose the decision; make an end of sb; make away with sb; make one's final exit; make the ultimate sacrifice; meet one's death; meet one's end; meet one's fate; mortal; move off; negative patient care outcome; never-ending sleep; no longer with us; no more; off the hooks; one's eternal rest; one's eyes are closed; one's heavenly rest; one's hard-earned rest; one's last taboo; out of pain; out of the game; out of the running; over the creek; pale horse; pass in one's alley; pass into stillness; pass on; pass out; pass out of the picture; pass over the Jordan; pass to the other side; pay Charon; pay day; pay one's fee; pay one's harp; pay one's last debt; pay saint Peter a visit; pay the debt of nature; peg out; perish; permit the water of life to run out; pop off; pop off the hooks; pop out; present at the last roll call; present at the last muster; pull the plug; push the clouds around; push up daisies; put sb out of his misery; put sb out of his pain; quit it; quit the scene; rest; rest in Abraham's bosom; rest in peace; return to dust; return to earth; ride into sunset; ring off; ring out; run one's course; run one's race; safe anchorage at last; safe in the arms of Jesus; say hello to Charon; say the last good-bye; see Confucius; settle all scores; settle one's account; shuffle off this mortal coil; shut up shop; sleep; sleep in the grave; sleep one's final sleep; sleep one's last sleep; sleep the big sleep; sleep the eternal sleep; sleep the final sleep; sleep the long sleep; sleep the never-ending sleep; sleep the sleep of death; sleep the sleep that knows no breaking; sleep the sleep that knows no waking; sleep with one's fathers; slip into outer darkness; slip off; slip off the hooks; slip one's cable; slip one's ropes; slip the cable; snuff it; step off; stick one's spoon in the wall; stop living; strike out; succumb to; suffer death; sup with Pluto; surcease; switch out the lights; take a count; take one's departure; take one's last sleep; take one's rest; take one-way ride; take the count; take the big jump; the big jump; the call of God; the curtain call; the end of the ball game; the eternal sleep; the final curtain; the final department; the final kick off; the final summons; the great leveller; the great whipper; the grim reaper; the last bow; the last call; the last getaway; the last great change; the last send-off; the last sleep; the last voyage; the long sleep; the remains; throw up the cards; throw sixes; toss in one's marbles; turn up one's toes to daisies; under the daisies; wink out; with God; with the angels; with their Father; write the last chapter; yield up the breath; yield up the ghost; yield up the soul; yield up the spirit;

gong neng xing si wang 功能性死亡
functional death;

wo chuang si wang 臥床死亡
cot death;

yi chuan si wang 遺傳死亡
genetic death;

si wang kong bu 死亡恐怖
thanatophobia;

si wang wang xiang 死亡妄想
necromimesis;

si4 zhi 四肢
all fours / arms and legs / the four limbs;

si zhi bai hai 四肢百骸
all the limbs and bones;

si zhi bing 四肢病
acropathy / illness of all four limbs;

si zhi bu quan 四肢不全
peromelia;

si zhi fa da, tou nao jian dan 四肢發達，頭腦簡單
have well-developed limbs but a moronic head;

si zhi ma bi 四肢麻痺
tetraplegia;

si zhi ma mu 四肢麻木
acroanesthesia;

si zhi tan huan 四肢癱瘓
quadriplegia;

si zhi wu li 四肢無力
feel weak in one's limbs;

si4 cha 伺察
investigate / spy;

si ji 伺機
wait for one's chance / wait for the opportunity;

si ji er dong 伺機而動
play a waiting game / play a winning game / wait for a chance to make a move;

si tan 伺探
investigate seretly / spy;

si4 nüe 肆虐
(1) indulge in atrocities / do damage unhinderedly;
(2) rampant / reckless and oppressive;

si wu ji dan 肆無忌憚
indulgent and reckless;

si xing 肆行
indulge;

si ying 肆應
good at dealing with varied matters properly;

si zong 肆縱
indulgent and without restraint;

song1 bang 鬆綁
undo / unfasten / untie;

song kai 鬆開
loosen;

song san 鬆散
slack off;

song4 bie 送別
see out / see sb off;

song bin 送殯
attend a funeral;

song jian 送餞
give a farewell party;

song jiao 送交
deliver to / hand over to;

song jiu ying xin 送舊迎新
bid farewell to the old and welcome the new;

song ke 送客
escort a visitor on his way out / show out;

song li 送禮
send gifts;

song ming 送命
lose one's life;

song sang 送喪
attend a funeral;

song si 送死
bring death upon oneself;

song wang ying lai 送往迎來
escort the parting and welcome the coming;

song xin 送信
deliver letters;

song xing 送行
bid sb farewell / see sb off;

song zang 送葬
attend a funeral;

sou1 shen 搜身
frisk;

sou3 擻
flutter / quake / shake / tremble;

sou dou dou 擻抖抖
shivering / trembling;

su1 xing 甦醒
come back to life;

su2 bu ke nai 俗不可耐
unbearably vulgar;

su qi 俗氣
(1) in poor taste // tarty / vulgar;
(2) hackneyed;

su4 pin 素貧
in a chronic state of poverty;

su xing 素行
daily conduct;

su4 宿
(1) stay overnight;
(2) long-cherished;

su liu 宿留
stay overnight;

suan1 zhong du 酸中毒
oxyosis;

tang niao bing xing suan zhong du 糖尿病性酸中毒
diabetic acidosis;

sui2 he 隨和
amiable / easygoing / unassuming;

sui ji ying bian 隨機應變
rise to the occasion;

sui shen 隨身
carry about / carry sth with one / take sth with one;

sun3 損
(1) damage;
(2) lose;
(3) decrease / reduce;

sun de 損德
cause damage to one's virtue;

sun hai 損害
damage / impair;

sun ren 損人
cause damage to others;

sun shang 損傷
damage / hurt / injure;

tan1 wu 貪污
embezzle / practise graft // embezzlement / graft;

tan wu fu hua 貪污腐化
graft and corruption;

tan zang 貪贓
practise graft / take bribes;

tan zang wan fa 貪贓枉法
prevert justice for a bribe / take bribes and bend the law;

tan1 huan 癱瘓
paralysis;

ban tan huan 半癱瘓
semiparalysis;

si zhi tan huan 四肢癱瘓
quadriplegia;

xue guan tan huan 血管癱瘓
vasoparesis;

zhou qi xing tan huan 周期性癱瘓
periodic paralysis;

tan huan fa zuo 癱瘓發作
paralytic stroke;

tan4 ju 炭疽
anthrax;

tan4 bing 探病
visit the sick;

tan fang 探訪
visit;

tan jiu 探究
investigate;

tan qin 探親
visit one's relatives;

tan qiu 探求
look into / seek;

tan shen zi 探身子
bend forward;

tan suo 探索
explore / look into / probe / search for / seek;

tan wang 探望
(1) visit;
(2) look about;

tan you 探友
visit friends;

tang2 se 搪塞
do sth perfunctorily / fob off / give sb the run-around / prevaricate / stall sb off // run-around;

tang2 niao bing hun mi 糖尿病昏迷
diabetic coma;

tang niao bing xing hun mi 糖尿病性昏迷
diabetic coma;

tang niao bing xing kui yang 糖尿病性潰瘍
diabetic ulcer;

tang niao bing xing suan zhong du 糖尿病性酸中毒
diabetic acidosis;

tang3 躺
in a lying position / lie down;

tang dao 躺倒
lie down;

tang xia 躺下
lie down;

tang zhe 躺着
in a lying position;

tao2 qi 淘氣
impish / mischievous / naughty;

tao2 逃
(1) escape / flee / run away;
(2) avoid / dodge / evade / shirk;

tao ben 逃奔
flee / run away;

tao bi 逃避
dodge / evade / run away from / shirk;

tao bi ren wu 逃避任務
flinch from a task;

tao bi ze ren 逃避責任
evade a responsibility / flee responsibility / shirk responsibility;

tao bu liao 逃不了
unable to escape;

tao chu chong wei 逃出重圍
break out from a heavy siege;

tao cuan 逃竄
disperse and flee / run away;

tao dun 逃遁
escape / flee / run away;

tao jia 逃家
run away from home;

tao li 逃離
run away / run away from;

tao ming 逃命
flee for one's life;

tao nan 逃難
seek refuge from calamities;

tao ni 逃匿
flee to a hiding place;

tao pao 逃跑
escape / flee / run away;

tao san 逃散
flee in all directions;

tao sheng 逃生
flee for one's life;

tao shi 逃世
go into seclusion / run away from the world;

tao shui 逃稅
avoid tax payment // tax evasion;

tao tuo 逃脱
escape from / free oneself from;

tao wang 逃亡
escape / flee / run away;

tao wang 逃往
flee toward;

tao xue 逃學
cut class / cut school / play hookey / play truant / truant;

tao yi 逃逸
break loose and get away / escape;

tao yin 逃隱
flee into seclusion;

tao zhai 逃債
run away from the creditor;

tao zhi yao yao 逃之夭夭
escape without leaving a single trace behind;

tao zou 逃走
escape / flee / fly / run away;

tao zui 逃罪
escape punishment;

tao ye xing qing 陶冶性情
mold one's temperament / shape one's spirit;

tao3 fan 討飯
beg for food;

tao hao 討好
curry favour / fawn on / ingratiate oneself with sb / make up to / please // ingratiation;

tao hao mai guai 討好賣乖
curry favour with / toady to;

tao huan 討還
get sth back;

tao jian 討賤
ask for insult;

tao jiu 討究
study and find the truth;

tao mei qu 討沒趣
ask for an insult;

tao pian yi 討便宜
seek undue advantage;

tao qi 討乞
beg;

tao qian 討錢
ask for money;

tao qiao 討巧
try to gain advantage with little effort;

tao qin 討親
take a wife;

tao qiu 討求
beg / demand;

tao qu 討取
ask for sth / demand;

tao rao 討饒
ask for leniency / ask for mercy;

tao ren pian yi 討人便宜
look for advantage of another;

tao sheng huo 討生活
make a living;

tao xi 討喜
likeable;

tao zhai 討債
demand repayment of a loan;

tao zhang 討賬
ask for the repayment of a loan;

te4 fa xing shui zhong 特發性水腫
idiopathic oedema;

te ying xhing jiu jing zhong du 特應性酒精中毒
alcohol idiosyncratic intoxication;

teng2 tong 疼痛
pain;
gu jie teng tong 骨節疼痛
arthralgia;
hun shen teng tong 渾身疼痛
have pains all over;
jing shen xing teng tong 精神性疼痛
psychalgia;
shui fa xing teng tong 睡發性疼痛
hypnalgia;

teng tong chan sheng 疼痛產生
algogenesia;

teng tong fa sheng 疼痛發生
algogenesia;

teng tong fan ying 疼痛反應
pain reaction;

teng tong kong bu 疼痛恐怖
algophobia;

teng tong zhang ai 疼痛障礙
pain disorder;

jing shen xing teng tong zhang ai 精神性疼痛障礙
psychogenic pain disorder;

ti1 fu 擿伏
bring a secret to light / expose evil;

ti3 體
body;

ti gao 體高
height (of a person);

ti ge 體格
physique;

ti ge jian zhuang 體格健壯
sturdy // of a vigorous and healthy constitution;

ti li 體力
physical strength / stamina;

ti li lao dong 體力勞動
manual labour / physical labour;

ti mian 體面
dignity / face / honour;

ti neng 體能
physical agility;

ti po 體魄
human body as the source of strength;

ti ruo 體弱
infirm;

ti tai 體態
carriage;

ti tie 體貼
considerate / kind / thoughtful;

ti wen 體溫
body temperature;

ti xian 體癬
ringworm of the body;

ti xing 體形
physique;

ti zhi 體質
bodily constitution / health / physique;

zeng qiang ti zhi 增強體質
build up one's body;

ti zhong 體重
body weight;

tian1 cai 天才
innate talent / natural talent;

tian fu 天賦
inborn talents / natural endowments;

tian hua 天花
smallpox;

bao fa xing tian hua 爆發型天花
fulminant smallpox;

bian ping tian hua 扁平天花
flat smallpox;

chu xue xing tian hua 出血性天花
hemorrhagic smallpox;

e xing tian hua 惡性天花
malignant smallpox;

jia xing tian hua 假性天花
varioloid;

pu tong tian hua 普通天花
ordinary smallpox;

qing tian hua 輕天花
modified smallpox;

tian sheng 天生
by nature / inborn / inbred / inherent / innate / natural-born;

tian sheng que xian 天生缺陷
birth defect;

tian tian guo nian 天天過年
hold Spring Festival-like celebrations every day;

tiao qie 佻竊
pinch / steal;

tiao2 jie 調解
mediate;

tiao xi 調戲
flirt with women;

tiao yang 調養
nurse one's health;

tiao yang she sheng 調養攝生
nurse and recuperate oneself;

tiao zhi 調治
undergo medical treatment and recuperation;

tiao zhi su ji 調治宿疾
attend and cure an old illness;

tiao3 bo 挑撥
foment dissension / incite / instigate / sow discord / stir up;

tiao bo li jian 挑撥離間
drive a wedge between / forment dissension / sow discord || forment disunity and dissension; incite one against the other; play one off against the other;

tiao dou 挑逗
arouse amorous desires / seduce;

tiao nong 挑弄
tease;

tiao nong shi fei 挑弄是非
stir up one side against the other;

tiao qing 挑情
make amorous advances;

tie1 shen 貼身
(1) next to the skin;
(2) personal;

ting1 tian you ming 聽天由命
at the mercy of fate;

ting2 停
(1) stop;
(2) suspend;

ting liu 停留
stay for a time;

ting xie 停歇
stop for a rest;

ting3 li 挺立
stand upright;

ting shen 挺身
straighten one's back;

ting shen er chu 挺身而出
thrust oneself forward to face a challenge || bell the cat; bolster oneself up; come forward courageously; come out boldly; stand up and volunteer to help; step forth bravely; step forward boldly; step forward bravely;

ting shen fan kang 挺身反抗
stand up and fight / stand up to an enemy;

ting shen ying fu 挺身應付
desperate;

ting zhu 挺住
stick it out;

tong1 痌
aching / painful;

tong1 da ren qing 通達人情
understanding and considerate;

tong da shi li 通達事理
understand ways of doing business;

tong li 通力
concerted efforts;

tong li he zuo 通力合作
make concerted efforts / work in concert;

tong quan da bian 通權達變
exercise one's discretion;

tong tuo 通脫
unconventional and carefree;

tong2 bing xiang lian 同病相憐
partake in each other's grief;

tong gan gong ku 同甘共苦
partake in each other's joys and sorrows / stick together through thick and thin;

tong ju 同居
live together;

tong2 jiao tong 銅絞痛
copper colic;

tong zhong du 銅中毒
copper poisoning;

tong4 痛
ache / pain;

bei tong 背痛
back pain / backache;

bi tong 臂痛
brachialgia;

bi tong 鼻痛
rhinalgia;

chang tong 腸痛
enterodynia;
chi xu tong 持續痛
continuous pain;
chuo tong 戳痛
piercing pain;
ci tong 刺痛
sharp pain;
dun tong 鈍痛
dull pain;
fang she tong 放射痛
radiating pain;
ji tong 激痛
severe pain;
jiao tong 絞痛
colic;
jing shen xing tong 精神性痛
algopsychalia;
jing luan tong 痙攣痛
crampy pain;
ju bu tong 局部痛
topalgia;
kui lan tong 潰爛痛
sore pain;
lie tong 烈痛
tearing pain;
qing tong 輕痛
slight pain;
quan shen tong 全身痛
pantalgia;
shan tong 疝痛
colic;
shao tong 燒痛
burning pain;
wan tong 頑痛
persistent pain;
ya tong 壓痛
pressing pain;

tong bu yu sheng 痛不欲生
grieve to the extent of wishing to die;

tong dian 痛點
pain spot;

tong feng 痛風
gout;

tong feng xing kui yang 痛風性潰瘍
gouty ulcer;

tong ji 痛擊
give a hard blow / light into;

tong jue 痛覺
algesthesia / pain sense;

tong jue guo du 痛覺過度
hyperpathia;

tong jue guo min 痛覺過敏
hyperalgia;

tong jue jian tui 痛覺減退
hypoalesia;

tong jue que shi 痛覺缺失
analgia;

tong jue yi chang 痛覺異常
paralgesia;

tong ou 痛毆
beat savagely;

tong xing fei pang 痛性肥胖
adiposis dolorosa;

tong xing gan jue que shi 痛性感覺缺失
anesthesia dolorosa;

tong xing jing luan 痛性痙攣
algospasm;

tong xing ying yang bu liang 痛性營養不良
algodystrophy;

tou1 偷
filch / pilfer / pinch / snitch / steal;

tou an 偷安
seek temporary ease // temporary peace / temporary stability;

tou dao 偷盜
steal // on the game;

tou dong xi 偷東西
steal // on the game;

tou han zi 偷漢子
a married woman having an affair with a man / adultress;

tou huo 偷活
live in disgrace;

tou kong 偷空
snatch a moment / take time off;

tou lan 偷懶
dodge the column / loaf on a job / mike // mike;

tou qie 偷竊
steal;

tou qie kuang 偷竊狂
kleptomania;

tou qie pi 偷竊癖
kleptomania;

tou sheng 偷生
lead an ignoble existence;

tou sheng pa si 偷生怕死
cowardly / timid // lack courage;

tou tou 偷偷
furtively / slinky / stealthily;

tou tou mo mo 偷偷摸摸
hole-and-corner / slinky / stealthily;

tou zou 偷走
make away with / make off with / run off with;

tou2 bao 投保
take out an insurance policy;

tou ben 投奔
(1) flee;
(2) seek employment from sb;

tou kao 投靠
go and seek refuge with sb / join and serve;

tou ming 投命
give one's life to;

tou shen 投身
give oneself to / join || plunge into; throw oneself into;

tou shen ge ming 投身革命
join in the revolution / join the revolutionary ranks;

tu2 lao 徒勞
futile effort / wasted effort;

tu lao wu gong 徒勞無功
flog a dead horse / labour in vain // to no avail;

tu lao wu yi 徒勞無益
ineffectual;

tuan2 zuo 團坐
sit around in circle;

tui1 推
(1) look into;
(2) shirk;
(3) elect;
(4) extend;

tui bing 推病
feign sickness;

tui dai 推戴
support a leader;

tui dang 推宕
delay / procrastinate;

tui dong 推動
propel;

tui fu 推服
admire / respect;

tui gu 推故
make excuses;

tui guang 推廣
popularize / promote / propagate / spread;

tui ji ji ren 推己及人
put oneself in another's position;

tui jian 推薦
recommend;

tui jin 推進
advance / move forward / push on;

tui qian 推遷
make excuses and delay / procrastinate;

tui que 推卻
decline an offer;

tui tuo 推託
make excuses / shirk;

tui xiao 推銷
promote sales / sell;

tui xie 推卸
irresponsible // shirk one's responsibility;

tui xie ze ren 推卸責任
opt out of responsibility / shirk one's responsibility;

tui xing 推行
carry out / implement / promote / pursue;

tui zun 推尊
admire and respect;

tui3 yun 頹運
declining fortune;

tui4 bi 退避
keep out of the way / withdraw and avoid;

tui hua 退化
degenrate / deteriorate // retrogradation;
lao nian xing tui hua 老年性退化
senile involution;

tui shao 退燒
reduce fever;

tui suo 退縮
blench / flinch / recoil / shrink;

tui xiu 退休
go into retirement / retire;

tui xue 退學
drop out from school;

tui yin 退隱
go into retirement / retire from public life;

tui yue 退約
break off an agreement;

tui zhi 退職
resign from office / retire;

tuo1 bing 托病
on the pretext of sickness / use sickness as an excuse;

tuo ci 托辭
(1) put forth a false reason / make excuses;
(2) excuse / pretext;

tuo fu 托付
charge / consign / entrust;

tuo gu 托故
rely on a pretext / use an excuse;

tuo lai 托賴
be indebted to / owe sth to;

tuo ming 托名
to do sth in the name of sb else;

tuo ren qing 托人情
gain one's ends through connections;

tuo shen 托身
have a place to live in / have a place to work in;

tuo1 ren xia shui 拖人下水
implicate another intentionally;

tuo shi jian 拖時間
stall for time;

tuo1 ban 託辦
consign / do sth entrusted by others;

tuo1 bing 託病
use illness as an excuse;

tuo da 託大
conceited / self-important // act arrogantly;

tuo fu 託付
commission / entrust to;

tuo gu 託故
find a pretext / make an excuse;

tuo ji 託疾
use poor health as an excuse;

tuo ren 託人
ask sb to do sth for oneself / entrust to sb;

tuo1 bu de shen 脫不得身
cannot disengage oneself / cannot get away;

tuo guang 脫光
denude / strip nude;

tuo kong 脫空
(1) work hard without success;
(2) lie;

tuo lan 脫懶
escape from duty;

tuo li guan xi 脫離關係
sever relations;

tuo li xian shi 脫離現實
be divorced from reality;

tuo qu 脫去
(1) peel off / strip / take off / throw off;
(2) vindicate;

tuo shen 脫身
extricate oneself ‖ escape; get away from; get free; leave; shake off;

tuo shen zhi ji 脫身之計
a plan of escape / a plan that helps one to slip

away;

tuo xia 脱下
drop / shed / take off;

tuo xian 脱險
escape from danger // out of danger;

tuo xie 脱鞋
remove shoes / take off shoes;

tuo xie 脱卸
relinquish one's responsibility / shirk one's responsibility;

tuo yi 脱衣
disrobe / take off one's clothes / unclothe / undress // undraped;

tuo ying er chu 脱穎而出
come from nowhere / come to the fore;

tuo zui 脱罪
exonerate sb from a charge;

wai4 biao 外表
mien;

wai4 shang 外傷
external injuries;

wai shang xing huai ju 外傷性壞疽
traumatic gangrene;

wai shang xing xiu ke 外傷性休克
traumatic shock;

wai yin xing zhong du 外因性中毒
exogenic toxicosis;

wai yin kui yang 外陰潰瘍
cancrum pudendi;

wai yuan xing fei pang 外源性肥胖
exogenous obesity;

wai yuan xing gan ran 外源性感染
exogenous infection;

wai zheng 外症
surface diseases;

wai zhou xing gan jue que shi 外周性感覺缺失
peripheral anesthesia;

wan1 qu shen ti 彎曲身體
bend the body;

wan2 ba xi 玩把戲
juggle / play with tricks;

wan bu dong 玩不動
too exhausted to play / too weak to play;

wan er ming 玩兒命
play with one's life at stake / toy with one's life;

wan hu zhi shou 玩忽職守
be derelict in one's duties / remiss // dereliction / neglect of duty / remissness;

wan hua yang 玩花樣
play tricks;

wan huo 玩火
play with fire;

wan huo zi fen 玩火自焚
whoever plays with fire will get burnt;

wan ming 玩命
gamble with one's life / play with one's life at stake / toy with one's life;

wan nong 玩弄
toy with;

wan shou duan 玩手段
manipulate / resort to scheming;

wan shua 玩耍
have fun / play;

wan2 zheng 頑症
chronic and obstinate disease / persistent ailment;

wang3 hou zou 往後走
turn back and proceed;

wang you guai 往右拐
turn right;

wang you zhuan 往右轉
turn right;

wang zuo guai 往左拐
turn left;

wang zuo zhuan 往左轉
turn left;

wang3 枉
(1) useless;
(2) crooked;
(3) be wronged / wrong;

wang duan 枉斷
decide unfairly;

wang fa 枉法
abuse law / twist law to suit one's own purpose;

wang fa cong si 枉法從私
bend the law to suit private interests;

wang fei gong fu 枉費工夫
spend time and work in vain / waste time and energy;

wang nao 枉橈
fail to carry out justice;

wang si 枉死
die through injustice;

wei1 危
dangerous;

wei du 危篤
critical / dying;

wei hai 危害
endanger;

wei ji 危急
pressing / urgent;

wei tai 危殆
in a critical condition / in a serious condition;

wei xian 危險
dangerous;

wei zuo 危坐
sit rigidly;

wei1 威
(1) dignity / majesty;
(2) authority / power;
(3) awe // awe-inspiring;

wei bi 威逼
coerce / intimidate;

wei bi li you 威逼利誘
threaten and bribe;

wei feng shao di 威風掃地
suffer a drastic fall in one's prestige;

wei fu 威服
coerce / overawe;

wei she 威懾
submit sb to power and threat;

wei sheng 威聲
prestige;

wei xia 威嚇
awe / frighten / intimidate / threaten;

wei xie 威脅
intimidate / menace / threaten // intimidation / menace / threat;

wei xin 威信
one's prestige;

wei yan 威嚴
(1) sterness;
(2) awe-inspiring air;

wei zhong 威重
dignified and awe-inspiring;

wei1 偎
(1) cuddle / embrace;
(2) lean on;

wei bao 偎抱
cuddle / hug;

wei bang 偎傍
stay close together;

wei tie 偎貼
snuggle close to;

wei yi 偎倚
cuddle to / curl to / lean close to / snuggle up to;

wei1 shang 微傷
slightly injured;

wei yang 微恙
indisposed / slightly unwell;

wei2 ming shi cong 惟命是從
always do as one is told;

wei2 e 為惡
do evil;

wei er bu you 為而不有
do sth but not to claim possession of it;

wei fei zuo dai 為非作歹
do evil / perpetrate outrages;

wei fu bu ren 為富不仁
rich but immoral / wealthy but unkind;

wei huan 為患
a cause of trouble // bring trouble;

wei li 為力
endeavour / make efforts / strive;

wei ren 為人
conduct oneself;

wei ren jing ming 為人精明
be no fool / be nobody's fool;

wei ren qian bo 為人淺薄
of a shallow character;

wei ren zai shi 為人在世
live in this world;

wei shan 為善
do good;

wei shan zui le 為善最樂
doing good is the greatest source of happiness;

wei suo yu wei 為所欲為
do as one pleases / have one's way;

wei xue 為學
engage in studies;

wei2 chi 維持
guard and support / keep / maintain / preserve / sustain;

wei chi ti mian 維持體面
keep up appearances;

wei chi xian zhuang 維持現狀
maintain the present condition / maintain the status quo;

wei hu 維護
preserve / protect / safeguard / uphold;

wei xi 維繫
keep / maintain / make secure and bind together;

wei3 dun 委頓
broken down / tired down / wearied / worn-out;

wei guo 委過
shift blame;

wei jiu 委疚
shift blame to others;

wei qi 委棄
abandon / give up / throw away;

wei qu 委曲
make concessions;

wei qu qiu quan 委曲求全
make concessions to accomplish sth;

wei shen 委身
(1) become the wife of;
(2) consign oneself to sb;

wei tuo 委託
commission / delegate;

wei yi zhong ren 委以重任
entrust sb with an important task;

wei3 da 偉大
extraordinary / great;

wei3 jun zi 偽君子
hypocrite;

wei shan 偽善
hypocritical / smooth-faced;

wei zhuang 偽裝
camouflage / disguise / feign / pretend;

wei3 suo 萎縮
atrophy;
chuang shang hou gu wei suo 創傷後骨萎縮
posttraumatic atrophy of bone;
gan wei suo 肝萎縮
hepatatrophia;
gao wan wei suo 睪丸萎縮
atrophia testiculi;
gu wei suo 骨萎縮
bone atrophy; osteanabrosis;
ji wei suo 肌萎縮
muscular atrophy;
lao nian xing wei suo 老年性萎縮
senile atrophy;
nao wei suo 腦萎縮
cerebral atrophy;
nei fen mi xing wei suo 內分泌性萎縮
endocrine atrophy;
pian xin xing wei suo 偏心性萎縮
eccentric atrophy;
quan shen wei suo 全身萎縮
panatrophy;
sheng li xing wei suo 生理性萎縮
physiologic atrophy;
wei wei suo 胃萎縮
gastric atrophy;

ya po xing wei suo 壓迫性萎縮
compression atrophy;

yan xing wei suo 炎性萎縮
inflammatory atrophy;

yan wei suo 眼萎縮
ophthalmatrophia;

ying yang bu liang xing wei suo 營養不良性萎縮
metatrophy;

ying yang shen jing xing wei suo 營養神經性萎縮
trophoneurotic atrophy;

zhi xing wei suo 脂性萎縮
fatty atrophy;

zhong du xing wei suo 中毒性萎縮
toxic atrophy;

zi gong wei suo 子宮萎縮
metratrophia;

wei suo xing shui zhong 萎縮性水腫
atrophedema;

wei suo zheng 萎縮症
atrophy;

wei3 痿
impotent / paralysis;

wei4 wang 位望
one's social status and prestige;

wei4 suo 畏縮
cower / falter / lose one's nerve / quail;

wei4 zui 畏罪
afraid of punishment;

wei zui zi sha 畏罪自殺
kill oneself from fear of punishment;

wei4 guo juan qu 為國捐軀
sacrifice one's life for the motherland;

wei guo xiao ming 為國效命
pursue the country's end regardless of one's own life;

wei guo zheng guang 為國爭光
struggle for the glory of one's country;

wei min chu hai 為民除害
destroy a public enemy / eliminate a public scourge / remove the evils from the people;

wei min qing ming 為民請命
appeal for the people / plead for the people;

wei ming wei li 為名為利
for fame and for wealth;

wei ren 為人
for others' interest / for the sake of others;

wei si 為私
for one's personal interest;

wei wo 為我
egoistic / selfish;

wei xiao shi da 為小失大
lose a pound in trying to save a penny;

wen1 瘟
epidemic / plague;

wen yi 瘟疫
epidemic / plague;

wen2 ru qi ren 文如其人
style is the man himself / the style is the man;

wen2 shen 紋身
tattoo / tattoo the body;

wen3 zha wen da 穩扎穩打
do sth slow and sure;

wo4 bing 臥病
bedridden on account of illness;

wo chuang 臥床
lie in bed;

wo qi 臥起
sleep and get up;

wo4 quan 握權
in authority / in command / in power;

wu1 hu 嗚呼
die;

wu2 chi 無恥
brazen / impudent / shameless;

wu li 無禮
ill breeding // impolite;

wu rong shen zhi di 無容身之地
there is no place for one in society ‖ no room for; nowhere to lay one's head; with no place to hide;

身體 *Body*

wu suo bu wei 無所不為
stop at nothing;

wu suo shi shi 無所事事
do nothing / twiddle one's thumbs // at a loose end / at loose ends // idle;

wu suo zuo wei 無所做為
attempt nothing and accomplish nothing;

wu tong nong zhong 無痛膿腫
indolent abscess;

wu wei 無畏
fearless / intrepid / undaunted;

wu yang 無恙
well // in good health;

wu3 nei ru fen 五內如焚
(1) very anxious;
(2) grief-stricken;

wu ti 五體
the five body constituents — tendon, vessel, muscle, hair and skin, and bone;

wu ti tou di 五體投地
prostrate oneself in admiration || admire sb from the bottom of one's heart; kneel at the feet of; prostrate oneself on the ground; throw oneself down at sb's feet;

wu zang 五臟
entrails / the five internal organs of the heart, liver, spleen, lungs and kidneys;

wu3 侮
(1) bully;
(2) disgrace / humiliate / insult;

wu man 侮慢
(1) humiliate;
(2) haughty and rude;

wu mie 侮蔑
disgrace / slight;

wu nong 侮弄
make a fool of sb;

wu ru 侮辱
humiliate / insult / mortify // humiliation / mortification;

wu3 bi 舞弊
irregularities / malpractice / misconduct;

wu4 dao 誤導
misguide / mislead // misguided / misleading;

wu fan 誤犯
offend unintentionally / violate unintentionally;

wu ren wu ji 誤人誤己
harm both others and oneself;

wu sha 誤殺
unintentional homicide;

wu shang 誤傷
hurt by mistake;

wu shi 誤事
bungle matters;

xi1 rou 息肉
polyp;
ai xing xi rou 癌性息肉
carcinopolypus;
bi xi rou 鼻息肉
nasal polyp;
er xi rou 耳息肉
aural polyp / otopolyus;
gong jing xi rou 宮頸息肉
cervical polyp;
hou xi rou 喉息肉
laryngeal polyp;
hou bi kong xi rou 後鼻孔息肉
choanal polyp;
nang xing xi rou 囊性息肉
cystic polyp;
qing shao nian xi rou 青少年息肉
juvenile polyp;
yan xing xi rou 炎性息肉
inflammatory polyp;
you nian xing xi rou 幼年性息肉
juvenile polyp;
zeng sheng xing xi rou 增生性息肉
hyperplastic polyp;
zhi chang xi rou 直腸息肉
polyp of rectum;

xi rou bing 息肉病
polyposis;
you nian xing xi rou bing 幼年型息肉病
juvenile polyposis;

xi1 悉
be familiar with / know;

xi li 悉力
with all one's strength / with might and main;

xi1 yi 熙怡
amiable and cordial;

xi1 nao 嬉鬧
frolic / romp;

xi nong 嬉弄
rollicksome // romp;

xi shua 嬉耍
play games with;

xi xi 嬉戲
frolic / make merry / play / romp;

xi1 sheng 犧牲
lay down one's life / sacrifice;

xi2 jian li jie 席間禮節
table manners;

xi2 fei 習非
be accustomed to wrongdoing;

xi fei cheng shi 習非成是
through practice the wrong becomes the right;

xi guan 習慣
(1) custom / habit / practice / use;
(2) be accustomed to / get used to;

xi guan cheng zi ran 習慣成自然
habit is second nature;

xi qi 習氣
bad custom / bad habit;

xi ran 習染
be corrupted by evil practices;

xi shan mie e 習善滅惡
learn good and forsake evil;

xi xing 習性
disposition / idosyncrasy / temperament;

xi yi wei chang 習以為常
fall into a habit;

xi4 tong xing ji bing 系統性疾病
systemic disease;

xi tong xing ying hua 系統性硬化
systemic sclerosis;

xi tong xing ying hua bing 系統性硬化病
systemic sclerosis;

xi4 bao 細胞
cell;
bian ping xi bao 扁平細胞
pavement cell;
gan jue xi bao 感覺細胞
seensory cell;
xing xi bao 性細胞
germ cell;

xi bao bi 細胞壁
cell wall;

xi bao fen lie 細胞分裂
cellular fission / cytiduerersus;

xi bao guo duo 細胞過多
hypercellularity;

xi bao guo shao 細胞過少
hypocellularity;

xi bao he 細胞核
cell nucleus;

xi bao jian shao 細胞減少
cyhtoreduction;

xi bao mo 細胞膜
cell membrane;

xi bao pei yang 細胞培養
cell culture;

xi bao po lie 細胞破裂
plasmatorrhexis;

xi bao si wang 細胞死亡
cell death;

xi bao ti 細胞體
cell body;

xi bao ye 細胞液
cell sap;

xi bao zeng zhi 細胞增殖
cell multiplication;

xi bao zhi 細胞質
cellularity / cytoplasm;

xi bao zu zhi 細胞組織
cellular tissuee;

xi jun xing ji bing 細菌性疾病
bacteriosis;

xi4 nong 戲弄
kid / make fun of / play a practical joke on / play a trick on / tease;

xi xi 戲嬉
merrymaking / play;

xia2 ling 遐齡
advanced age / long life / longevity;

xia qi 遐棄
(1) cast away / reject;
(2) desert one's post;

xia4 bai 下拜
bow;

xia ban 下班
check off / knock off / leave office after working hours;

xia ban bei zi 下半輩子
the latter half of one's life / the rest of one's life;

xia ban shen 下半身
the lower half of the body / the lower part of the body;

xia bei zi 下輩子
the next life;

xia bu lai 下不來
(1) cannot get down;
(2) be embarrassed;

xia bu liao tai 下不了台
be put on the spot;

xia che 下車
get off a vehicle;

xia chu 下廚
go to the kitchen / prepare food;

xia chuan 下船
get ashore;

xia chuang 下牀
get up;
(2) leave a sickbed;

xia da ming ling 下達命令
issue orders;

xia di 下地
(1) go to the fields;

xia di yu 下地獄
go to hell;

xia du 下毒
poison / put poison into sth;

xia gong 下工
knock off / leave office after working hours;

xia gong fu 下功夫
devote time and effort to a task;

xia hai 下海
turn professional;

xia jia 下嫁
marry sb beneath her station;

xia jian 下賤
cheap / degrading / lowly;

xia ke 下課
(1) get out of class;
(2) after class // finish class;

xia lai 下來
come down;

xia ling 下令
give orders;

xia liu 下流
low / mean / mucky / scurrilous;

xia liu hua 下流話
vulgar language / warm language;

xia liu xing wei 下流行為
immodest behaviour;

xia lou 下樓
go downstairs;

xia luo 下落
whereabouts;

xia ma 下馬
(1) dismount from a horse;
(2) discontinue;

xia ma wei 下馬威
deal sb a head-on blow at the first encounter;

xia ming ling 下命令
give orders;

xia pin 下聘
present betrothal gifts;

xia qi 下棋
play chess;

xia qu 下去
(1) go down;
(2) go on;

xia shan 下山
descend a mountain / go down a mountain;

xia shen 下身
lower part of the body;

xia shi 下世
die / pass away;

xia ta 下榻
stay;

xia tai 下臺
(1) be out of power / be relieved from office;
(2) get off stage;

xia tang 下堂
to be divorced by one's husband;

xia xiang 下鄉
go to the country;

xia xue 下學
leave school;

xia yao 下藥
put in poison;

xia yu 下獄
be imprisoned / put into jail;

xia zang 下葬
bury;

xia zhan shu 下戰書
deliver a challenge in writing;

xia zhi 下肢
the lower limbs;

xia zhi tong 下肢痛
melosalgia;

xia zhu ke ling 下逐客令
ask an unwelcome guest to leave;

xian1 tian 先天
congenital / innate;

xian tian bu zu 先天不足
inborn deficiency;

xian tian que xian 先天缺陷
birth defect;

xian1 shi 仙逝
die / pass away;

xian you 仙遊
die / pass away;

xian2 痃
bubo;

xian2 ju 閑居
lead a quiet life / lead a retired life;

xian shua 閑耍
amuse oneself / kill time;

xian2 bu zhu 閒不住
unable to remain idle;

xian dang 閒蕩
bugger about / fool about / fool around / gad / lie about / loaf about / loaf around / loiter / saunter / stroll;

xian de wu liao 閒得無聊
twiddle one's thumbs;

xian guang 閒逛
bugger about / fool about / fool around / gad / lie about / loaf about / loaf around / loiter / ramble / saunter / stroll;

xian san 閒散
unoccupied // with nothing to do;

xian yi 閒逸
carefree / leisurely;

xian zuo 閒坐
sit idle;

xian3 zheng 險症
serious disease / severe illness;

xian3 shen shou 顯身手
show one's paces;

xian4 hai 陷害
frame / snare;

xian ru kun jing 陷入困境
drive sb into a corner / drive sb to the wall / get into hot water / get sb cornered / push sb to the wall;

xian4 mei 獻媚
curry favour / toady;

xian shen 獻身
devote oneself to a cause;

xian yin qin 獻殷勤
flatter / ingratiate;

xiang1 an wu shi 相安無事
at peace with each other;

xiang chi bu xia 相持不下
at a stalemate;

xiang chu 相處
get along with / live together / spend time together;

xiang da 相打
have a fight;

xiang dui xing ma zui 相對性麻醉
relative analgesia;

xiang fan 相煩
ask for a favour / trouble sb with a request;

xiang feng 相逢
come across / meet each other / run into sb;

xiang hui 相會
meet each other / meet together;

xiang jian hen wan 相見恨晚
regret having not met earlier;

xiang jiao 相交
make friends with each other;

xiang jiu 相救
help out of difficulty;

xiang qin xiang ai 相親相愛
kind to each other and love each other;

xiang qiu 相求
ask for a favour / entreat;

xiang shan 相善
on friendly terms / on good terms;

xiang shi 相識
acquaintance with sb;

xiang xiang 相像
take after;

xiang yao 相邀
invite;

xiang yi 相依
depend on each other // interdependent;

xiang yi wei ming 相依為命
rely upon each other for life;

xiang yu 相遇
meet each other;

xiang yue 相約
make an appointment / reach an agreement;

xiang zheng 相爭
argue vehemently / fight each other over sth / quarrel;

xiang zhu 相助
help / help each other;

xiang zhuang 相撞
collide with each other;

xiang zuo 相左
at odds with / conflict with each other / differ / disagree;

xiang3 fu 享福
enjoy happiness and prosperity;

xiang le 享樂
seek pleasure;

xiang qing fu 享清福
live off the fat of the land / live on the fat of the land;

xiang shou 享受
enjoy / treat;

xiang yong 享用
enjoy the use of;

xiang3 ying 響應
echo in support / respond favourably / rise in support;

xiang4 yang 像樣
presentable;

xiao1 fei 消費
consume;

xiao hua bu liang xing jiao tong 消化不良性絞痛
angina dytspeptica;

xiao mo 消磨
while away time;

xiao mo jing li 消磨精力
fritter away one's energy;

xiao mo shi jian 消磨時間
kill time / pass the time;

xiao qi 消氣
allay one's anger / stroke sb down;

xiao shou 消瘦
emanciation;

lao nian xing xiao shou 老年性消瘦
geromarasmus;

mian rong xiao shou 面容消瘦
look emaciated;

xiao shou bing 消瘦病
pine;

ying yang bu liang xing xiao shou bing 營養不良性消瘦病
nutritional marasmus;

xiao xian 消閒
kill the leisure time;

xiao zhong 消腫
reduce a swell / remove a swell;

xiao1 yao 逍遙
loiter about / saunter about;

xiao yao fa wai 逍遙法外
remain out of law's reach;

xiao yao zi zai 逍遙自在
enjoy a free and leisurely life;

xiao3 cai da yong 小才大用
give great responsibility to a person of common ability;

xiao dong mai huai si 小動脈壞死
arteriolonecrosis;

xiao dong zuo 小動作
little tricks / petty action;

xiao er ma bi zheng 小兒麻痺症
infantile paralysis / polio;

xiao shi cong ming, ta shi hu tu 小事聰明，大事糊塗
penny wise and pound foolish;

xiao ti da zuo 小題大做
make a mountain out of a molehile / make much of a trifle;

xiao4 孝
filial piety;

xiao dao 孝道
the way of filial piety;

xiao jin 孝謹
show filial piety for one's parents with great care;

xiao jing 孝敬
(1) show filial piety and respect for one's parents;
(2) present one's parents or superiors with presents;

xiao shun 孝順
show filial obedience for one's parents;

xiao yang 孝養
serve one's parents with material needs;

xiao yi 孝義
devotion to one's parents and loyalty to one's friends;

xiao you 孝友
filial piety and brotherly love;

xie1 ban 歇班
have time off // off duty;

xie gong 歇工
stop work;

xie liang 歇涼
enjoy the cool in some shade / take a rest in a cool place;

xie xi 歇息
take a rest;

xie xie er 歇歇兒
take a little rest;

xie yi xie 歇一歇
lay on one's oars / rest one's oars / take a break / take a rest;

xie2 邪
depraved / evil / heretical / mean / vicious / wicked;

xie mei 邪媚
fawning;

xie2 協
assist / help;

xie li 協力
work in cooperation;

xie shang 協商
bargain / do a deal with / negotiate;

xie zhu 協助
assist;

xie2 tang 斜躺
recline;

xie2 諧
(1) harmonious;
(2) come to an agreement / settle;

xie fu 諧附
compromise and follow;

xie he 諧和
concordant / harmonious // accord / agreement / harmony;

xie qu 諧趣
fun / humour / pleasantry;

xie yi 諧易
humorous and easygoing;

xie4 ren 卸任
quit an office;

xie ze 卸責
(1) lay down one's responsibilities;
(2) shirk one's responsibility;

xie4 褻
(1) treat with irreverence;
(2) indecent / obscene;

xie du 褻瀆
blaspheme / profane;

xie man 褻慢
dally with / treat with disrespect;

xie wan 褻玩
dally with;

xie4 hou 邂逅
meet accidentally / meet by chance / pick up;

xin1 chou 辛臭
acrid and stinking;

xin chu 辛楚
sad / sorrowful;

xin ku 辛苦
(1) laborious / toilsome;
(2) go through hardships / work hard;

xin lao 辛勞
great effort / pains;

xin qin 辛勤
diligent / hardworking / industrious;

xin suan 辛酸
bitters of life / hardships;

xin xin ku ku 辛辛苦苦
laborious // with great efforts // take great pains;

xin1 chen dai xie 新陳代謝
metabolism;

xing1 feng zuo lang 興風作浪
cause trouble / cause unrest / fan the flames of disorder / incite trouble / make trouble / make waves / stir up trouble;

xing2 bu de 行不得
(1) cannot be done / should not be done;
(2) cannot go / should not go;

xing bu kai 行不開
confined / restricted // unable to act as one sees fit / unable to act freely;

xing bu tong 行不通
(1) block / unable to pass;
(2) get nowhere / won't work;
(3) impracticable / infeasible;

xing bu you jing 行不由徑
do not take shortcuts;

xing dong 行動
(1) act / make a move / move / take action;
(2) get about / proceed;
(3) action / movement / operation;

xing dong zi ru 行動自如
move freely / move without impairment;

xing dong zi you 行動自由
freedom of movements;

xing hui 行賄
bribe / grease sb's palm / grease the palm of sb / offer a bribe;

xing jian 行姦
commit adultery;

xing jiang jiu mu 行將就木
nearing death;

xing jie 行劫
loot / rob;

xing jing 行徑
one's actions / one's behaviour / one's conduct;

xing le 行樂
make merry / play;

xing nian 行年
at the age of;

xing pian 行騙
cheat / deceive / swindle;

xing qi 行棋
play chess;

xing qie 行竊
steal;

xing shan 行善
do good deeds;

xing wei 行為
act / action / behaviour / conduct / deed;

xing wei biao xian 行為表現
performance;

xing wei bu dang 行為不當
ill-behaved;

xing wei fan she 行為反射
behaviour reflex;

xing wei jiao zheng 行為矯正
behaviour modification;

xing wei shi kong 行為失控
dyscontrol;

xing wei wu li 行為無禮
ill-mannered;

xing wei zhang ai 行為障礙
behaviour disorder;

xing yi 行誼
conduct and virtues;

xing yi zhi nan 行易知難
to do is easier than to know;

xing zha 行詐
cheat / deceive / swindle;

xing zong 行蹤
whereabouts of a person;

xing zong bu ming 行蹤不明
whereabouts unknown;

xing zong piao hu 行蹤飄忽
have no fixed whereabouts;

xing zong wu ding 行蹤無定
have no fixed abode;

xing2 ying bu li 形影不離
always together as body and shadow;

xing4 xi bao 性細胞
germ cell;

xing4 yun 幸運
lucky // luck;

xiong1 兇
cruel / ferocious / fierce / violent;

xiong bao 兇暴
cruel and violent;

xiong e 兇惡
evil / ferocious;

xiu1 ke 休克
shock;
chuang shang xing xiu ke 創傷性休克
traumatic shock;
guo min xing xiu ke 過敏性休克
anaphylactic shock;
ji fa xing xing xiu ke 繼發性休克
secondary shock;
nong du xing xiu ke 膿毒性休克
septic shock;
shen jing yuan xing xiu ke 神經源性休克
neurogenic shock;
shu hou xiu ke 術後休克
postoperative shock;
wai shang xing xiu ke 外傷性休克
traumatic shock;
xin xing xiu ke 心性休克
cardiac shock;
xin yuan xing xiu ke 心源性休克
cardiogenic shock;
xing xiu ke 性休克
shock;

xiu1 de 修德
cultivate virtue;

xiu lian 修煉
practise asceticism;

xiu shen 修身
cultivate oneself ‖ cultivate one's moral character; practise moral culture;

xiu shen qi jia 修身齊家
cultivate oneself and put family in order ‖ cultivate one's moral character and manage the family's affairs well; cultivate one's moral character and put one's family affairs in order;

xiu shen zhi bang 修身止謗
correct one's own ways in order to stop gossip / stop slander by correcting one's own ways;

xiu shen zi xing 修身自省
look after one's conduct by self-examination;

xuan4 yao 炫耀
dangle / flaunt / show off // show-off;

xue2 踅
hang about / loiter around;

xue men liao hu 踅門瞭戶
loiter and chat at friends' houses;

xue shen 踅身
turn around / turn the body;

xue2 學
learn / study;

xue shi yuan bo 學識淵博
erudite / learned / omniscient / well read;

xue xi 學習
learn / study;

xun2 徇
profit;

xun si 徇私
profit oneself // favouritism;

xun si wu bi 徇私舞弊
play favouritism and commit irregularities // corrupt practices;

xun2 duan jian 尋短見
commit suicide;

xun fang 尋訪
try to find / try to locate;

xun huan zuo le 尋歡作樂
gallivant // seek pleasure and make merry // merrymaking;

xun le 尋樂
seek amusement;

xun qiu 尋求
seek;

xun shi 尋事
pick a fight / pick a quarrel;

xun shi sheng fei 尋事生非
make trouble / seek a quarrel;

xun si 尋死
commit suicide;

xun si mi huo 尋死覓活
attempt suicide repeatedly;

xun4 dao 殉道
die a martyr's death / die for the right cause;

xun jiao 殉教
die for a religious cause;

xun jie 殉節
die to protect one's virtue;

xun li 殉利
die for money;

xun ming 殉名
win fame at the expense of one's life;

xun nan 殉難
die for one's country;

xun shen 殉身
die for a cause;

xun zhi 殉職
die at one's post / die on one's job;

ya1 li xing kui yang 壓力性潰瘍
pressure ulcer;

ya po xing huai ju 壓迫性壞疽
pressure gangrene;

ya po xing huai si 壓迫性壞死
pressure necrosis;

ya po xing ma bi 壓迫性麻痺
compression paralysis;

ya po xing wei suo 壓迫性萎縮
compression atrophy;

ya4 迓
go out to meet / go out to receive;

ya4 shang 軋傷
run over and injure;

ya si 軋死
run over and kill;

yan1 yan yi xi 奄奄一息
dying;

yan1 si 淹死
drown;

yan2 nian yi shou 延年益壽
prolong life / promise longevity // life-prolonging / macrobiotic;

yan2 炎
inflammation;
dan chun xing yan 單純性炎
simple inflammation;
man xing yan 慢性炎
chronic inflammation;
mi man xing yan 彌漫性炎
diffuse inflammation;

yan xing huai ju 炎性壞疽
inflammatory gangrene;

yan xing shui zhong 炎性水腫
inflammatory oedema;

yan xing wei suo 炎性萎縮
inflammatory atrophy;

yan xing xi rou 炎性息肉
inflammatory polyp;

yan zheng 炎症
inflammation;

yan2 jin 嚴謹
well-knit;

yan jun 嚴峻
severe / stern;

yan4 宴
(1) feast;
(2) comfort / ease;

yan an 宴安
live in idle comfort;

yan ju 宴居
lead a leisurely life;

yan ke 宴客
entertain guests at a meal;

yan4 fan 厭煩
bored;

yan juan 厭倦
weary of;

yan qi 厭棄
get rid of / give up;

yang2 佯
pretend / sham;

yang bing 佯病
pretend to be ill;

yang kuang 佯狂
feign madness;

yang si 佯死
feign death / pretend to be dead;

yang2 feng yin wei 陽奉陰違
pretend to observe;

yang2 揚
(1) praise;
(2) display / expose / make known;
(3) scatter / spread;
(4) get excited / stir;

yang chang er qu 揚長而去
stalk off;

yang qi 揚棄
discard / renounce;

yang shan 揚善
make known others' good deeds;

yang3 bing 養病
convalesce / nurse a disease / recuperate // convalescence / recuperation;

yang cheng xi guan 養成習慣
acquire a habit / cultivate a habit / fall into the habit of / form a habit / nuture a habit;

yang huo 養活
(1) support sb or a family;
(2) bring up / rear;

yang jia 養家
support one's family;

yang jia huo kou 養家活口
look after one's family and a living to earn;

yang jing xu rui 養精蓄鋭
nourish and discipline one's stamina / nurse one's strength;

yang jing 養靜
cultivate mental calm;

yang shang 養傷
nurse one's injuries / nurse one's wounds;

yang shen 養身
keep one's body fit / nourish one's body;

yang shen han xin 養身涵心
take good care of one's health;

yang xing 養性
discipline one's temperament;

yang yu 養育
raise and educate / rear;

yang zun chu you 養尊處優
enjoy high position and live in ease and comfort / live in clover / mollycoddle oneself;

yao1 夭
die young;

yao shi 夭逝
die young;

yao shou 夭壽
die young;

yao wang 夭亡
die young;

yao zhe 夭折
die prematurely / die young // early grave;

yao2 shen yi bian 搖身一變
by a sudden metamorphosis || change one's identity; give oneself a shake and change into another form; suddenly change; take the form of...with a shake; up to the trick of a volte-face; with a twist of the body, one makes a sudden change;

yi1 ba zhua 一把抓
(1) take everything into one's own hands;
(2) try to tackle all problems at once;

yi bei 一輩
a generation;

yi bei zi 一輩子
a lifetime / from the cradle to the grave // cradle-to-grave;

yi bing bu qi 一病不起
fall ill and never recover || die of illness; fall ill and die; take to one's bed and never leave it again;

yi bing shen wang 一病身亡
die of serious illness / fall ill and die;

yi bu pa ku, er bu pa si 一不怕苦，二不怕死
fear neither hardship nor death;

yi bu zuo, er bu xiu 一不做，二不休
in for a penny, in for a pound;

yi de zhi gong 一得之功
a minor success;

yi dong 一動
(1) a move;
(2) move once;

yi dong bu ru yi jing 一動不如一靜
taking no action is better than taking any;

yi fan chang tai 一反常態
act out of one's character;

yi ge yang 一個樣
alike / of the same sort;

yi gu sha jin 一股傻勁
great enthusiasm;

yi gu zuo qi 一鼓作氣
at a burst / at one burst / at one go // press on without letting up one's effort;

yi lao yong yi 一勞永逸
make an effort to accomplish sth once and for all;

yi li 一力
do all one can / do one's best;

yi li cheng quan 一力成全
spare no effort in helping sb to accomplish sth;

yi li dang xian 一力當先
try one's utmost to be ahead of others;

yi ming gui xi 一命歸西
die / pass away;

yi ming gui yin 一命歸陰
die / pass away;

yi mo yi yang 一模一樣
be a copy of sb / look identical;

身體 *Body*

yi qi 一氣
(1) without stop;
(2) get angry;

yi qi he cheng 一氣呵成
(1) flow smoothly;
(2) accomplish sth at one sitting;

yi qi zhi xia 一氣之下
in a fit of anger / in a fury;

yi qu bu fu fan 一去不復返
gone forever;

yi qu bu hui 一去不回
leave for good;

yi shen 一身
(1) the whole body || all over the body;
(2) a single person / a solitary person / all alone / concerning one person only;

yi shen chou han 一身臭汗
stink with perspiration;

yi shen chou ming 一身臭名
earn a very bad name for oneself;

yi shen dan dang 一身擔當
face everything oneself;

yi shen er ren 一身二任
hold two positions concurrently / hold two posts simultaneously;

yi shen gao su 一身縞素
be dressed in mourning white;

yi shen guo qiu 一身裹裘
be wrapped in furs from top to toe;

yi shen huan ran 一身煥然
be arrayed in finery from head to foot;

yi shen liang yi 一身兩役
hold two jobs at the same time / serve in a dual capacity;

yi shen ling luo 一身綾羅
be dressed in silks and satins;

yi shen qing 一身輕
free-hearted;

yi shen rong yao 一身榮耀
be loaded with honours;

yi shen sao 一身臊
have one's goodwill taken for ill intent;

yi shen shi bing 一身是病
be afflicted by several ailments / be burdened with illness // full of infirmities;

yi shen shi zai 一身是債
deep in debt || be burdened down with debts; head over heels in debt; up to one's neck in debt;

yi shen su guo 一身素裹
be dressed all in white;

yi shen tong chou 一身銅臭
the whole body smelling of copper — covetous;

yi shen tong zhong 一身痛重
general pain and heaviness;

yi shen yong zhong 一身臃腫
be heavily padded;

yi shen zhong xiao 一身重孝
in full mourning;

yi sheng 一生
a lifetime / all one's life;

yi sheng kan ke 一生坎坷
a lifetime of frustrations // have hard luck all one's life;

yi sheng liao dao 一生潦倒
be a failure all one's life / remain poor all one's life;

yi sheng piao dang 一生飄蕩
go hither and thither all one's life;

yi sheng shou yong 一生受用
enjoy the benefit all one's life;

yi sheng xin lao 一生辛勞
a life of hardship;

yi shi 一世
a lifetime / all one's life;

yi shi wu cheng 一事無成
accomplish nothing / achieve nothing / get nowhere;

yi si bu gua 一絲不掛
without a stitch of clothing || as naked as a needle; as naked as a worm; as naked as I was born; as naked as my mother bore me; completely nude; have not a stitch on; have nothing on; in a state of nature; in nature's garb; in one's birthday suit; in one's skin;

in the altogether; in the nude; naked; not have a stitch on; not to have a rag to one's back; nude; stark naked; strip to the buff; unclothed; wearing one's birthday clothes; without a shred of clothing on;

yi si bai liao 一死百了
death pays all scores / death quits all scores / death squares all accounts / he that dies, pays all debts;

yi si liao zhi 一死了之
end one's troubles by death;

yi ta heng chen 一榻橫陳
lie in bed;

yi ta hu tu 一塌糊塗
in a great mess / in a muddle / in utter disorder;

yi wang zhi qian 一往直前
go ahead bravely without looking back;

yi xi shang cun 一息尚存
as long as one is alive;

yi xi zhi ge 一息之隔
a heartbeat away;

yi yong er ru 一擁而入
pile in / pile into;

yi yong er shang 一擁而上
rush up in a crowd;

yi zhao qian gu 一朝千古
die suddenly;

yi zhi qian jin 一擲千金
spend money like water / throw away money like dirt;

yi1 依
(1) depend on / rely on;
(2) follow;

yi bang 依傍
(1) depend on / rely on;
(2) follow / model after / pattern after;

yi fu 依附
(1) depend on / rely on;
(2) submit to;

yi kao 依靠
depend on / lean on / rely on;

yi lai 依賴
depend on / lean on / rely on;

yi ping 依憑
depend on / lean on / rely on;

yi wei 依偎
snuggle;

yi zhang 依仗
depend on / rely on;

yi1 醫
cure / treat;

yi bing 醫病
cure a disease / treat a patient;

yi liao 醫療
medical treatment;

yi zhi 醫治
cure a disease // medical treatment;

yi2 ren 宜人
agreeable;

yi2 痍
bruise / sore / wound;

yi2 chuan 遺傳
heredity;

yin xing yi chuan 隱性遺傳
recessive inheritance;

yi chuan bing 遺傳病
heredopathia;

yi chuan chuan ran 遺傳傳染
heredoinfection;

yi chuan ji bing 遺傳疾病
genetic disease;

yi chuan si wang 遺傳死亡
genetic death;

yi2 yang 頤養
keep fit / nourish / recuperate / take care of oneself;

yi3 qi ren zhi dao huan zhi qi ren zhi shen 以其人之道還治其人之身
beat sb at his own game / give sb a dose of one's own medicine / give sb a taste of one's own medicine;

yi shen shi fa 以身試法
dare to violate the law || defy the law; test the

law in one's own person;

yi shen xiang xu 以身相許
have sexual relations with one's beloved / pledge to marry sb;

yi shen xu guo 以身許國
dedicate oneself to the country's cause;

yi shen xun zhi 以身殉職
die at one's post / die on one's duties / give one's life in the course of performing one's duty;

yi shen zuo ze 以身作則
set an example for others to follow || hit the nail on the head; live what one teaches; make oneself an example; make oneself serve as an example to others; play an exemplary role; practise what one preaches; set oneself up as an example;

yi4 疫
epidemic;

yi bing 疫病
epidemic;

yi bing chuan ran 疫病傳染
contagion;

yi zheng 疫症
epidemic;

yi4 ju 逸居
be comfortably lodged / live in idleness / live in retirement;

yi le 逸樂
enjoyment of an easy life;

yi4 zhi 義肢
artificial limb;

yi4 詣
call on / visit;

yi men 詣門
visit sb;

yi ye 詣謁
pay a visit to;

yi4 縊
hang / strangle;

yi sha 縊殺
hang / strangle to death;

yi si 縊死
hang oneself;

yi4 殪
(1) die;
(2) kill;

yi4 譯
translate;

yin1 bing 因病
because of illness / due to illness;

yin bing xia yao 因病下藥
apply medicine according to indications;

yin3 jiu 引咎
take the blame on oneself;

yin jiu ci zhi 引咎辭職
take the blame on oneself and resign;

yin you 引誘
entice / induce / lure / seduce / tempt // seduction / temptation;

yin3 ji 隱疾
ailments one wants to keep to oneself;

yin ju 隱居
live in seclusion / retire from public life;

yin man 隱瞞
conceal / cover up / hide / keep … from;

yin mo 隱沒
disappear;

yin ni 隱匿
conceal / hide;

yin tong 隱痛
hidden pain / hidden sorrow;

yin tui 隱退
retire // retirement;

yin xing ai 隱性癌
hidden cancer / occult cancer;

yin xing fan she 隱性反射
concealed reflex;

yin xing gan ran 隱性感染
latent infection;

yin xing ji bing 隱性疾病
pseudodisease;

yin xing shui zhong 隱性水腫
invisible oedema;

yin xing yi chuan 隱性遺傳
recessive inheritance;

yin yin zuo tong 隱隱作痛
dull pain;

yin yuan xing gan ran 隱源性感染
cryptogenic infection;

ying1 nian zao shi 英年早逝
die an untimely death / die in one's prime / die young // early grave;

ying1 er cu si 嬰兒猝死
cot death;

ying er ma bi 嬰兒麻痺
infantile paralysis;

ying1 攖
(1) irritate / offend;
(2) disturb / stir up;

ying bing 攖病
be attacked by disease;

ying2 he 迎合
cater to;

ying hou 迎候
go out to await sb;

ying ji 迎擊
meet and attack;

ying jie 迎接
greet / receive / welcome;

ying song 迎送
greet the newcomers and bid farewell to the leavers;

ying ya 迎迓
greet / receive / welcome;

ying2 yan bing 營養病
trophonosis;

ying yang bu liang 營養不良
dystrophy / innutrition / malnutrition // malnourished;

chuang shang hou ying yang bu liang 創傷後營養不良
wound dystrophy;

e xing ying yang bu liang 惡性營養不良
malignant malnutrition;

quan shen ying yang bu liang 全身營養不良
pantatrophia;

tong xing ying yang bu liang 痛性營養不良
algodystrophy;

zhi zhi ying yang bu liang 脂質營養不良
lipodystrophy;

ying yang bu liang xing kui yang 營養不良性潰瘍
trophic ulcer;

ying yang bu liang xing shui zhong 營養不良性水腫
alimentary oedema;

ying yang bu liang xing wei suo 營養不良性萎縮
metatrophy;

ying yang bu liang xing xiao shou bing 營養不良性消瘦病
nutritional marasmus;

ying yang bu zu 營養不足
oligotrophy;

ying yang guo du 營養過度
hypernutrition;

ying yang guo du bing 營養過度病
hyperalimentosis;

ying yang guo huan 營養過緩
bradytrophia;

ying yang guo shao 營養過少
oligotrophy;

ying yang liang hao 營養良好
eutrophia;

ying yang ping heng 營養平衡
nutritive equilibrium;

ying yang que fa bing 營養缺乏病
deficiency disease / deprivation disease;

ying yang que fa zheng 營養缺乏症
deficiency disease / deprivation disease;

ying yang shen jing xing kui yang 營養神經性潰瘍
trophoneurotic ulcer;

ying yang shen jing xing wei suo 營養神經性萎縮
trophoneurotic atrophy;

ying yang xing bing bian 營養性病變
trophic lesion;

ying yang yi chang 營養異常
anomalotrophy;

ying yang yin shi 營養飲食
nutraceutical diet;

ying yang zhang ai 營養障礙
dystrophia;

ying2 贏
(1) win;
(2) gains / profits;

ying de 贏得
win;

ying qian 贏錢
win money by gambling;

ying4 ai 硬癌
scirrhous cancer;

ying hua 硬化
sclerosis;
nei zang ying hua 內臟硬化
splanchnosclerosis;
pi ying hua 脾硬化
splenokeratosi;
shen xiao qiu ying hua 腎小球硬化
glomerulosclerosis;
shen xue guan ying hua 腎血管硬化
nephroangiosclerosis;
shen ying hua 腎硬化
nephroscerosis;
xi tong xing ying hua 系統性硬化
systemic sclerosis;
xiao dong mai ying hua 小動脈硬化
arteriolar sclerosis;
xin nei mo ying hua 心內膜硬化
endocardial sclerosis;
xue guan ying hua 血管硬化
angiosclerosis / sclerosis vascularis;

ying hua bing 硬化病
sclerosis;
xi tong xing ying hua bing 系統性硬化病
systemic sclerosis;

ying4 應
(1) answer / echo / react to / respond to;
(2) comply with / grant;
(3) cope with / deal with;
(4) assent to;

ying bian 應變
(1) adapt oneself to changes;
(2) prepare oneself to change;

ying fu 應付
(1) cope with / deal with / handle;
(2) do sth perfunctorily;
(3) make do with;

ying men 應門
answer the door;

ying pin 應聘
accept an offer of employment;

ying ji xing kui yang 應激性潰瘍
stress ulcer;

yong1 dai 擁戴
support a leader;

yong hu 擁護
advocate / back / endorse / support;

yong ru 擁入
crowd into;

yong shang lai 擁上來
well up;

yong3 bei zi 永輩子
for life / forever;

yong bao qing chun 永保青春
remain youthful forever;

yong bie 永別
die / part for good;

yong bu fen li 永不分離
never to be separated;

yong chui bu xiu 永垂不朽
be remembered forever by posterity;

yong jue 永訣
be gone forever / die;

yong ming 永命
a long life / longevity;

yong nian 永年
a long life / longevity;

yong sheng 永生
eternal life;

yong xiang 永享
enjoy forever;

yong4 gong fu 用工夫
practise diligently / study hard / work hard;

yong gong 用功
study diligently / study hard / work hard;

yong jin 用勁
exert oneself / put forth one's strength;

yong jin 用盡
exhaust;

yong jin fang fa 用盡方法
resort to every possible means;

yong li 用力
exert oneself / make an effort / put forth one's strength;

yong li guo du 用力過度
exert oneself too strenuously;

yong qian 用錢
spend money;

yong qian ru shui 用錢如水
spend money like water;

you1 優
excellent / good;

you dai 優待
give special treatment;

you2 yang bing bian 疣樣病變
verruca;

you zhuang zeng sheng 疣狀增生
verrucous hyperplasia;

you2 dang 遊蕩
lie about / loaf about / loiter;

you zou xing nong zhong 游走性膿腫
wandering abscess;

you2 guang 遊逛
gad about / roam about / stroll;

you xi 遊息
play and rest;

you3 ba wo 有把握
confident of success;

you ban fa 有辦法
(1) know how to do sth;
(2) resourceful;

you ben ling 有本領
capable / resourceful / talented;

you bing 有病
feeling unwell / ill / sick;

you qian 有錢
be made of money / have money to burn // loaded / moneyed / rich / wealthy / well off / well-heeled // in the money // well-off;

you suo jian shu 有所建樹
have sth to show for;

you zhong 有種
have guts;

you4 nian 幼年
childhood;

you nian xing xi rou bing 幼年型息肉病
juvenile polyposis;

you nian xing fan she 幼年性反射
juvenile reflex;

you nian xing xi rou 幼年性息肉
juvenile polyp;

you4 guai 誘拐
abduct / kidnap;

you huo 誘惑
(1) entice;
(2) attract // attractive;

you jian 誘姦
statutory rape;

you pian 誘騙
beguile / cajole / induce by deceit / inveigle;

you ren fan zui 誘人犯罪
induce others to break the law;

you ren wei e 誘人為惡
seduce others to evil;

you sha 誘殺
trap and kill;

you xie 誘脅
tempt and threaten;

身體 *Body*

you ye 誘掖
guide and encourage;

you yin 誘引
lure / seduce;

yu1 dan 迂誕
absurd / preposterous;

yu fu 迂腐
hackneyed / pedantic / stale / trite;

yu kuo 迂闊
impractical / unrealistic;

yu lou 迂陋
hackneyed / stale;

yu yuan 迂遠
impractical / unrealistic;

yu zhi 迂直
impractical and artless;

yu zhuo 迂拙
impractical and clumsy;

yu1 ti 紆體
bend one's body / bow down / crouch;

yu zun 紆尊
deign;

yu zun jiang gui 紆尊降貴
condescend / deign to;

yu3 ren fang bian 與人方便
accommodate others / give sb convenience;

yu ren wei shan 與人為善
help others;

yu ren wu wu 與人無忤
have no discord with others;

yu shi chang ci 與世長辭
depart from the world for good / pass away;

yu shi fu chen 與世浮沉
rise and sink with the rest of the world;

yu shi tui yi 與世推移
change with the times;

yu shi wu zheng 與世無爭
in harmony with the rest of the world;

yu shi yan yang 與世偃仰
rise and sink with the rest of the world;

yu3 zhong bu tong 與眾不同
different from other people;

yu4 ti 玉體
(1) your esteemed health / your person / yourself;
(2) the nude body of a girl;

yu ti heng chen 玉體橫陳
the beautiful nude body lying in full view;

yu ti wei he 玉體違和
sorry to learn that you are indisposed;

yu4 ci 遇刺
be assassinated;

yu dao 遇到
come across / meet with / run into;

yu hai 遇害
be assassinated / be murdered;

yu jian 遇見
bump into / come across / come upon / encounter / meet with / run into;

yu jiu 遇救
be rescued / be saved;

yu nan 遇難
get killed in an accident;

yu ren bu shu 遇人不淑
marry the wrong person;

yu shi sheng feng 遇事生風
stir up trouble;

yu xian 遇險
meet with danger // in danger / in distress;

yuan2 qi 元氣
vitality and constitution;

yuan2 fa ai 原發癌
primary cancer;

yuan fa xing shui mian guo du 原發性睡眠過度
primary hypersomnia;

yuan wei ai 原位癌
preinvasive cancer;

yue1 qing 約請
invite;

yue shu 約束
restrain;

yue4 fen 越分
go beyond one's proper position;

yue gui 越軌
go beyond what is proper;

yue gui xing wei 越軌行為
impermissible behaviour;

yue quan 越權
act without authorization;

yun3 允
(1) allow / consent;
(2) faithful;

yun xu 允許
allow / permit;

yun3 mie 隕滅
meet one's death / perish;

yun ming 隕命
die;

yun3 ming 殞命
die / meet one's death / perish;

yun mo 殞沒
die / perish;

yun4 dong 運動
motion;

yun dong bing 運動病
motion sickness;

yun dong bu neng 運動不能
acinesia;

yun dong bu neng zheng 運動不能症
akinesia;

yun dong chi huan 運動遲緩
bradykinesia;

yun dong dao cuo 運動倒錯
paracinesia;

yun dong gan 運動感
kinesthesia;

yun dong gan jue 運動感覺
kinesthetic sense;

yun dong gong neng jian tui 運動功能減退
hypocinesia;

yun dong gong neng kang jin 運動功能亢進
hypercinesia;

yun dong guo du 運動過度
hypercinesia;

yun dong guo huan 運動過緩
bradycinesia;

yun dong guo qiang 運動過強
hypermotility;

yun dong hou pi fa 運動後疲乏
postactivation exhaustion;

yun dong jian ruo 運動減弱
hypomotility;

yun dong jian shao 運動減少
hypokinesia;

yun dong neng li 運動能力
kinetism;

yun dong pin fa 運動貧乏
poverty of movement;

yun dong shi tiao 運動失調
parakinesia;

yun dong tong 運動痛
kinesalgia;

yun dong zhang ai 運動障礙
dyscinesia;

yun dong zheng chang 運動正常
eukinesia;

yun yong bu neng 運用不能
apraxia;

yun yong zhang ai 運用障礙
dyspraxia;

za2 fan wan 砸飯碗
lose one's job;

zai4 hang 在行
professional // in the know;

zai4 hun 再婚
remarry;

zai jia 再嫁
remarry;

zai lai 再來
come again;

zai qu 再娶
remarry;

身體 *Body*

zan3 qian 攢錢
hoard money;

zan4 shi xing shui zhong 暫時性水腫
oedema fugax;

zan shi xing zhong zhang 暫時性腫脹
fugitive swelling;

zan4 cheng 贊成
agree with / go along with // in favour;

zang1 zheng 髒症
venereal disease;

zang4 mai 葬埋
bury the dead;

zang shen 葬身
be buried;

zang shen huo hai 葬身火海
be engulfed in sea of flames;

zang shen huo ku 葬身火窟
be buried in flames / become food for flames;

zang shen yi yu 葬身異域
be buried in a foreign country / die in a foreign country;

zang shen yu fu 葬身魚腹
be swept to a watery grave / feed the fish || become food for fish — be drowned; get drowned; go to Davy Jone's locker; in Davy's locker;

zang shen zhi di 葬身之地
burial ground / come to a bad end;

zang yu mai xiang 葬玉埋香
(1) bury a beauty;
(2) the untimely death of a beauty;

zao1 bian 遭變
hit by a great misfortune;

zao feng bu xing 遭逢不幸
meet with misfortune;

zao hai 遭害
be assassinated / be murdered;

zao jie 遭劫
meet with disaster;

zao nan 遭難
meet with difficulty (misfortune or death);

zao yang 遭殃
meet with disaster / meet with misfortune;

zao zai 遭災
encounter disaster;

zao1 hui 糟毀
damage by rough treatment;

zao jian 糟踐
(1) debase / degrade / ruin / waste;
(2) insult / libel;

zao ta 糟蹋
affront / insult;

zao3 fa geng nian qi 早發更年期
climacterium praecox;

zao lao 早老
presenility;

zao lao zheng 早老症
progeria;

zao3 shen 澡身
take a bath;

zao4 fan 造反
revolt / rise up against // uprising;

zao fu 造福
benefit / bring benefit to;

zao ni 造孽
do evil things;

zao ni zuo e 造孽作惡
commit crime and do evil;

zao yi 造詣
one's scholastic attainment;

zeng1 sheng 增生
hyperplasia;
gu zhi zeng sheng 骨質增生
hyperplasia;
lu gu zeng sheng 顱骨增生
hyperostosis cranli;
nei pi zeng sheng 內皮增生
endotheliosis;
qian lie xian zeng sheng 前列腺增生
prostatic hyperplasia;
you zhuang zeng sheng 疣狀增生
verrucous hyperplasia;

zeng sheng xing xi rou 增生性息肉
hyperplastic polyp;

zha4 痄
scrofulous swellings and sores;

zha sai 痄腮
mumps;

zha4 詐
(1) fake;
(2) cheat / deceive;
(3) trick into;

zha bai 詐敗
feign defeat;

zha bing 詐病
malinger / pretend to be ill;

zha hu 詐唬
bluff / bluster;

zha pian 詐騙
defraud / swindle;

zha qi 詐欺
cheating / fraud / imposture;

zha qi lian cai 詐欺斂財
obtain money under false pretences;

zha si 詐死
fake death / feign death / play dead / pretend to be dead;

zha wei 詐偽
artful / cunning / deceitful // falsehood;

zha xiang 詐降
fake surrender;

zha xuan 詐諼
artful and crafty / dishonest / unfaithful;

zhan1 guang 沾光
ride on sb's coattails to success;

zhan hua re cao 沾花惹草
fool around with women;

zhan pian yi 沾便宜
take advantage of a person;

zhan ran 沾染
become addicted to;

zhan ran shi su 沾染世俗
be corrupted by worldly ways;

zhan ran xi qi 沾染習氣
be corrupted by prevailing bad practices;

zhan3 輾
roll over / turn over;

zhan zhuan 輾轉
roll about / toss;

zhan zhuan fan ce 輾轉反側
toss about in bed;

zhan4 pian yi 佔便宜
take advantage of a person;

zhan shang feng 佔上風
have the upper hand;

zhang1 li 張力
tension;

zhang li bu deng 張力不等
heterotonia;

zhang li guo di 張力過低
hypotonia;

zhang li guo gao 張力過高
hypertonia;

zhang li guo qiang 張力過強
hypertonus;

zhang li jian tui 張力減退
hypotonus;

zhang li que fa 張力缺乏
abirritation;

zhang li que shi 張力缺失
atonia;

zhang li shi chang 張力失常
dystonia;

zhang li yi chang 張力異常
paratonia;

zhang li zheng chang 張力正常
normotonia;

zhang3 ai 長癌
get cancer;

zhang cheng 長成
(1) grow to manhood;
(2) grow into;

zhang da 長大
grow up / mature;

zhang jin 長進
make progress;

zhang4 ai 障礙
disorder;
fa yu zhang ai 發育障礙
developmental disorder;
gong neng xing zhang ai 功能性障礙
functional disorder;

zhao1 cheng 招承
confess // confession;

zhao hu 招呼
(1) accost / beckon / call / greet;
(2) receive / take care of;
(3) engage in a fight;

zhao huo 招禍
invite disasters / invite troubles;

zhao ji 招集
gather together;

zhao jia 招架
defend / hold one's own / resist / ward off blows;

zhao jia bu zhu 招架不住
no match for sb / unable to hold off;

zhao jiu 招咎
invite troubles;

zhao lan 招攬
(1) collect / gather together;
(2) solicit customers;

zhao lan gu ke 招攬顧客
solicit customers;

zhao leng 招冷
catch cold;

zhao qin 招親
take a husband;

zhao quan na hui 招權納賄
abuse one's power and take bribes;

zhao re 招惹
incur / provoke;

zhao ren 招認
confess // confession;

zhao shi 招事
bring trouble upon oneself / invite trouble;

zhao xie 招攜
recruit deserters and traitors;

zhao yao 招邀
invite / request sb to come;

zhao yao 招搖
act ostentatiously;

zhao yao guo shi 招搖過市
swagger down the streets;

zhao zai 招災
bring disasters upon oneself / invite disasters;

zhao zai re huo 招災惹禍
court disasters / invite troubles;

zhao zhi 招致
bring about / incur / induce / invite / result in;

zhao1 feng 着風
expose to wind;

zhao liang 着涼
catch a chill / catch cold;

zhao yu 着雨
get wet in the rain;

zhao3 找
(1) find / look for / search for / seek;
(2) return change;

zhao bing 找病
ask for trouble;

zhao bu zhao 找不着
look in vain / search in vain;

zhao dui xiang 找對象
look for a partner in marriage;

zhao ma fan 找麻煩
(1) ask for trouble;
(2) find fault / pick on sb;

zhao men lu 找門路
look for employment by seeking help from the right connections;

zhao qian 找錢
give change;

zhao shi 找事
(1) look for jobs;
(2) look for trouble;

zhao si 找死
invite death / seek death;

zhao4 gu 照顧
care for / keep an eye on / look after / see after / watch over;

zhe1 折
(1) fall head over heels / somersault / turn upside down;
(2) pour all out;

zhe teng 折騰
(1) fall head over heels / somersault / turn upside down;
(2) squander away / waste // extravagantly;
(3) pull about / suffer from / toss about;

zhen1 xing fei da 真性肥大
true hypertrophy;

zhen xing nang zhong 真性囊腫
true cyst;

zhen1 cha 偵查
investigate;

zhen3 xing huai si 疹性壞死
exanthematous necrosis;

zhen3 診
diagnose / examine;

zhen bing 診病
examine a patient;

zhen cha 診察
examine and observe;

zhen duan 診斷
diagnose a disease // diagnosis;

zhen hou 診候
examine and diagnose / treat a patient;

zhen liao 診療
diagnose and treat;

zhen qie 診切
examine a person's pulse;

zhen shi 診視
examine a patient;

zhen zhi 診治
diagnose and treat;

zhen4 fa xing shui mian 陣發性睡眠
paroxysmal sleep;

zhen4 振
(1) arouse to action / raise / rise;
(2) pull up / relieve / save;
(3) shake;
(4) restore to order;

zhen ba 振拔
free oneself from a predicament and brace oneself up for action;

zhen zuo qi lai 振作起來
cheer up / recollect oneself;

zhen4 chan 震顫
tremour;
gong du xing zhen chan 汞毒性震顫
tremor mercurialis;
jia zu xing zhen chan 家族性震顫
familial tremour;
ke sou xing zhen chan 咳嗽性震顫
tussive fremitus;
liu xing xing zhen chan 流行性震顫
epidemic tremour;
pian shen zhen chan 偏身震顫
hemitremor;
yu yin zhen chan 語音震顫
vocal fremitus;

zhen chan bing 震顫病
trembles;

zhen chan ma bi 震顫麻痺
shaking palsy;

zhen4 tong 鎮痛
(1) ease pain;
(2) analgesia;

zheng1 chang jing duan 爭長競短
squabble over trifles;

zheng dou 爭鬭
conflict / contend / struggle;

zheng duo 爭奪
compete for / contend for / fight for / scramble for / struggle for / vie for;

zheng fen duo miao 爭分奪秒
race against time;

zheng feng chi cu 爭風吃醋
fight for the affection of a man or woman / quarrel from jealousy;

zheng gong 爭功
contend for credit;

zheng guang 爭光
win glory;

zheng heng 爭衡
scramble for advantage / vie for superiority;

zheng jing 爭競
compete / vie;

zheng ming duo li 爭名奪利
struggle for fame and wealth;

zheng qi 爭氣
bring credit / make a good showing / strive to excel / try to win credit for;

zheng qiang 爭強
struggle for supremacy;

zheng qu 爭取
fight for / strive for / try to get / win over;

zheng quan duo li 爭權奪利
fight for selfish gains / scramble for personal gains;

zheng sheng 爭勝
contend for the upper hand / struggle for the upper hand;

zheng xian 爭先
try to be the first to do sth;

zheng yi kou qi 爭一口氣
strive for a vindication;

zheng zhi 爭執
argue obstinately / contest / wrangle;

zheng zhi bu xia 爭執不下
each sticks to his own stand;

zheng1 掙
(1) make efforts / strive;
(2) get free from;

zheng zha 掙扎
strive / struggle;

zheng3 拯
(1) deliver / save;
(2) lift up / raise;

zheng jiu 拯救
deliver / rescue / save;

zheng xu 拯恤
save and help the poor or needy;

zheng3 ren 整人
fix sb / give sb a hard time;

zheng yi 整衣
adjust one's clothes;

zheng4 zhi 正直
fair-minded / honest / upright // probity;

zheng zuo 正坐
sit straight;

zheng4 症
(1) disease / ailment;
(2) symptoms of a disease;

zheng zhuang xing kui yang 症狀性潰瘍
symptomatic ulcer;

zheng4 掙
(1) struggle;
(2) earn money;

zheng fan chi 掙飯吃
earn a living;

zheng jia li ye 掙家立業
establish a home and make achievements;

zheng kai 掙開
get free with effort;

zheng ming 掙命
fight for one's life;

zheng qian 掙錢
earn money;

zheng tuo 掙脱
break away with force / shake off;

zheng tuo jia suo 掙脱枷鎖
throw off the shackles;

zhi1 chi 支持
(1) back / champion / side with / support;
(2) bear / hold / sustain;

zhi1 肢
the four limbs of a person;

ju zhi 巨肢
macromelia;

zhi duan fei da zheng 肢端肥大症
acromegalia / acromegaly;

zhi duan tan huan 肢端癱瘓
acroparesthesia;

身體 *Body*

zhi duan tong zheng 肢端痛症
acrodynia;

zhi duan ying hua bing 肢端硬化病
acrosclerosis;

zhi gan 肢感
acrognosis;

zhi jie 肢解
dismember || pull sb limb from limb; tear sb limb from limb;

zhi ma bi 肢麻痺
acroparalysis;

zhi tan huan 肢癱瘓
acroparalysis;

zhi ti 肢體
(1) limbs;
(2) limbs and trunk / the body;

zhi ti yu yan 肢體語言
body language;

zhi tong 肢痛
melagra;

zhi tong bing 肢痛病
acromelalgia;

zhi tong zheng 肢痛症
acrodynia;

zhi1 fang 脂肪
fat;

zhi fang bian 脂肪變
fatty change;

zhi fang dai xie 脂肪代謝
lipometabolism;

zhi fang fa sheng 脂肪發生
adipogenesis;

zhi fang fen jie 脂肪分解
lipophagy;

zhi fang guo duo 脂肪過多
hyperliposis;

zhi fang guo duo zheng 脂肪過多症
lipomatosis;

zhi fang guo shao 脂肪過少
hypoliposis;

zhi fang huai si 脂肪壞死
adiponecrosis;

zhi fang jian shao 脂肪減少
lipopenia;

zhi fang li 脂肪痢
stearrhea;

zhi fang liu 脂肪瘤
adipose tumour / fatty tumour;

zhi fang que fa bing 脂肪缺乏病
fat-deficiency disease;

zhi fang rou liu 脂肪肉瘤
liposarcoma;

zhi fang shan 脂肪疝
fat hernia;

zhi fang sheng cheng 脂肪生成
lipogenesis;

zhi fang shui zhong 脂肪水腫
lipedema;

zhi fang tong 脂肪痛
adiposalgia;

zhi fang tu chu 脂肪突出
adipocele;

zhi fang zeng duo 脂肪增多
lipotrophy;

zhi fang zeng sheng 脂肪增生
lipohypertrophy;

zhi fen qi 脂粉氣
sissy;

zhi ji liu 脂肌瘤
lipomyoma;

zhi liu 脂瘤
fatty tumour;

zhi liu bing 脂瘤病
steatomatosis;

zhi xing wei suo 脂性萎縮
fatty atrophy;

zhi yi bing 脂溢病
seborrhea;

zhi zhi ying yang bu liang 脂質營養不良
lipodystrophy;

zhi1 shen 隻身
all by oneself / alone / by oneself;

zhi2 li 直立
stand erect;

zhi2 xing 執行
execute;

zhi2 ye bing 職業病
occupational disease;

zhi3 tong 止痛
kill pain / stop pain;

zhi3 zui jin mi 紙醉金迷
indulge in a wanton life;

zhi4 si 至死
till death / to the death / to the last;

zhi si bu bian 至死不變
unswerving till death;

zhi si bu qu 至死不屈
stick to one's principle till death;

zhi si bu yu 至死不渝
remain faithful until death;

zhi4 bing 治病
treat a disease;

zhi bing jiu ren 治病救人
cure the disease and save the patient;

zhi gong 治躬
cultivate oneself;

zhi guo 治國
govern a nation;

zhi jia 治家
manage a family;

zhi liao 治療
cure / treat a disease;

zhi sheng 治生
make a living;

zhi zui 治罪
bring to justice;

zhi4 ai 致癌
cancer-causing / carcinogenic;

zhi ai wu 致癌物
cancer-causing agent / carcinogen / carcinogenic substance;

zhi dian 致電
give sb a call;

zhi fu 致富
acquire wealth / become rich;

zhi he 致賀
extend congratulations / offer congratulations;

zhi jing 致敬
pay homage / pay respects / pay tribute to / salute;

zhi li 致力
devote oneself to;

zhi ming 致命
fatal;

zhi ming shang 致命傷
(1) mortal wound;
(2) weak point;

zhi shen 致身
dedicate one's life to a cause;

zhi xie 致謝
offer thanks / thank;

zhi4 shen 置身
place oneself / stay;

zhi shen du wai 置身度外
keep oneself from getting involved;

zhi shen ju wai 置身局外
refrain from getting involved || keep aloof from; keep out of; not to be drawn into; remain aloof from;

zhi shen qi jian 置身其間
put oneself in the midst of — be involved;

zhi shen shi wai 置身事外
refuse to be drawn into the matter || detach oneself from; have nothing to do with; keep out of the business; keep out of the affair; not to get involved in; remain aloof from the affair; stay aloof from the affair; stay away from an affair;

zhi zhi bu li 置之不理
wave aside;

zhong1 bao si nang 中飽私囊
feather one's own nest / line one's purse / sweep everything into one's net;

身體 *Body*

zhong nian 中年
mid-life / middle age // middle-aged;

zhong nian fa fu 中年發福
middle-age spread;

zhong nian wei ji 中年危機
mid-life crisis;

zhong qi shi mian 中期失眠
middle insomnia;

zhong1 lao 終老
throughout one's life / until death;

zhong mo qi shui zhong 終末期水腫
terminal oedema;

zhong qi yi sheng 終其一生
throughout one's life;

zhong shen 終身
all one's life / lifelong / the whole life;

zhong shen ban lü 終身伴侶
lifelong companion;

zhong shen bu jia 終身不嫁
remain unmarried all one's life;

zhong shen da shi 終身大事
marriage || a great event affecting one's whole life; the important affair of a final settlement in life; the main affair of one's life;

zhong shen gu yong 終身僱傭
permanent employment;

zhong shen jiao yu 終身教育
lifelong education;

zhong shen shi ye 終身事業
lifelong career / one's lifework;

zhong shen shou gu 終身受僱
life employment;

zhong shen you kao 終身有靠
can depend on sb all one's life;

zhong shen zhi jiao 終身之交
lifelong friends;

zhong shen zhi 終身職
job for life / lifetime job / office for life;

zhong shen zhi 終身制
lifelong tenure / system of life tenure;

zhong sheng 終生
the whole life / throughout one's life;

zhong3 da 腫大
intumesce;

zhong kuai 腫塊
tumour;

zhong liu 腫瘤
tumour;

ai yang zhong liu 癌樣腫瘤
cancerous tumour / cancroid tumour;

e xing zhong liu 惡性腫瘤
malignant tumour;

gao wan zhong liu 睾丸腫瘤
orchiocele;

hou e xing zhong liu 喉惡性腫瘤
malignant tumour of larynx;

hou liang xing zhong liu 喉良性腫瘤
benign tumour of larynx;

liang xing zhong liu 良性腫瘤
benign tumour;

nang xing zhong liu 囊性腫瘤
cystoma;

nao zhong liu 腦腫瘤
brain tumour;

pi zhong liu 脾腫瘤
splenoma;

yan e xing zhong liu 咽惡性腫瘤
malignant tumour of pharynx;

yan liang xing zhong liu 咽良性腫瘤
benign tumour of pharynx;

zhong liu bing 腫瘤病
oncosis;

zhong liu fa sheng 腫瘤發生
tumorigenesis;

zhong qi lai 腫起來
swell up;

zhong shang 腫瘍
painful swellings;

zhong tong 腫痛
swollen and inflamed;

zhong zhang 腫脹
swelling;

lin bing xing zhong zhang 淋病性腫脹
blennorrhagic swelling;

zan shi xing zhong zhang 暫時性腫脹
fugitive swelling;

zhong4 du 中毒
intoxication / poisoning / toxicosis;

bing li xing zhong du 病理性中毒
pathological intoxication;

jiu jing zhong du 酒精中毒
alcohol intoxication;

qian zhong du 鉛中毒
lead poisoning;

ren shen zhong du 妊娠中毒
gestosis;

shui zhong du 水中毒
water intoxication;

suan zhong du 酸中毒
oxyosis;

tong zhong du 銅中毒
copper poisoning;

wai yin xing zhong du 外因性中毒
exogenic toxicosis;

wai yuan xing zhong du 外源性中毒
exogenic toxicosts;

zhong du xing jing luan 中毒性痙攣
toxic spasm;

zhong du xing shui zhong 中毒性水腫
toxic oedema;

zhong du xing wei suo 中毒性萎縮
toxic atrophy;

zhong feng 中風
apoplexy ‖ paralytic stroke; suffer from a stroke of paralysis;

jia zhong feng 假中風
pseudoapoplexy;

zhong feng fa zuo 中風發作
apoplectic fit;

zhong han 中寒
be attacked by cold / catch cold;

zhong shu 中暑
get a sunstroke // heat stroke / heated exhaustion / thermoplegia;

zhong4 chuang 重創
inflect a severe blow on (the enemy);

zhong shang 重傷
serious injury;

zhong shang feng 重傷風
serious cold;

zhong yong 重用
give sb an important assignment;

zhou1 qi xing ji bing 周期性疾病
periodic disease;

zhou qi xing ma bi 周期性麻痺
periodic paralysis;

zhou qi xing shuai ruo 周期性衰弱
periodic asthenia;

zhou qi xing shui zhong 周期性水腫
periodic oedema;

zhou qi xing tan huan 周期性癱瘓
periodic paralysis;

zhou shen 周身
all over the body / the whole body;

zhou shen da liang 周身打量
look sb over from head to foot / stare sb up and down / survey sb from top to toe;

zhou shen duan xiang 周身端詳
eye sb from head to toe;

zhou wei xing huai si 周圍性壞死
peripheral necrosis;

zhou wei xing ma bi 周圍性麻痺
peripheral paralysis;

zhou wei yan 周圍炎
periarthritis;

lan wei zhou wei yan 闌尾周圍炎
periappendicitis;

dan nang zhou wei yan 膽囊周圍炎
perichlecystitis;

yin dao zhou wei yan 陰道周圍炎
pericolpitis;

zhi chang zhou wei yan 直腸周圍炎
paraproctitis;

zhou you 周遊
tour to places;

zhu1 ru 侏儒
drawf / midget / pygmy;

zhu ru zheng 侏儒症
drawfism / nanism;

zhu1 誅
(1) execute / kill;
(2) punish;

zhu chu 誅除
eliminate / root out;

zhu jian 誅奸
punish the traitorous;

zhu jiu 誅求
demand greedily;

zhu jiu wu yi 誅求無已
make endless exorbitant demands;

zhu lu 誅戮
kill / slaughter;

zhu lun 誅論
sentence to death;

zhu mie 誅滅
eliminate / eradicate;

zhu2 chu 逐出
drive out / expel / kick out;

zhu li 逐利
pursue material gains;

zhu4 住
dwell / inhabit / live;

zhu4 he 祝賀
congratulate sb on / felicitate sb on / slap on the back // a slap on the back;

zhu4 cheng da cuo 鑄成大錯
commit a serious mistake / make a gross error;

zhuan3 shen 轉身
face about / spin round / turn about / turn around / turn the body // turnaround;

zhuan yi xing nong zhong 轉移性膿腫
metastatic abscess;

zhuan4 qian 賺錢
earn money / make a profit;

zhuan ren 賺人
cheat sb;

zhuang1 bing 裝病
fabricate illness / feign illness / feign oneself sick / malinger / pretend illness // simulation;

zhuang ban 裝扮
disguise;

zhuang feng mai sha 裝瘋賣傻
play the fool / pretend to be crazy and stupid;

zhuang jia 裝假
feign / pretend;

zhuang men mian 裝門面
adorn for the sake of face / keep up appearances / put up a front // for show;

zhuang mo zuo yang 裝模作樣
act affectedly / act with affected manners // affectation;

zhuang qiang 裝腔
affect certain airs;

zhuang qiang zuo shi 裝腔作勢
affected / niminy-piminy / pretentious // keep up one's act;

zhuang shui 裝睡
feign sleep / pretend to be asleep;

zhuang si 裝死
feign death / play dead / sham death // necromimesis;

zhuang suan 裝蒜
affected / pretentious;

zhuang yang zi 裝樣子
do sth for appearance's sake / put on an act;

zhuang zui 裝醉
pretend to be drunken;

zhuang4 壯
strong;

zhuang lie 壯烈
courageous;

zhuang lie xi sheng 壯烈犧牲
die as a martyr;

zhuang nian 壯年
the prime of one's life;

zhuang4 tai 狀態
condition / state of affairs;

zhuang tai bu jia 狀態不佳
in bad form / off form / off one's stroke / out of form;

zhuang4 撞
(1) bump / collide / dash / strike;
(2) bump into / meet by chance / run into;

zhuang dao 撞倒
knock down by bumping;

zhuang ge man huai 撞個滿懷
bump into one another;

zhuang huai 撞壞
damage by bumping;

zhuang jian 撞見
run into;

zhuang kai 撞開
knock away by bumping;

zhuang pian 撞騙
swindle;

zhuang ru 撞入
burst into / thrust into;

zhuang shang 撞傷
injure by bumping;

zhuang si 撞死
kill by bumping;

zhui2 gan 追趕
run after;

zhui jiu 追究
investigate and punish;

zhui qiu 追求
(1) go after / pursue / run after / seek;
(2) court a woman / make up to // courtship;

zhui ren 追認
approve afterward / confirm / ratify;

zhui zong 追蹤
trace / trail;

zhun3 xu 准許
allow / permit;

zi1 孜
unwearied and diligent;

zi zi bu juan 孜孜不倦
peg away at / work with diligence and without fatigue // sedulous;

zi1 shi 姿勢
posture;

zi shi fan she 姿勢反射
postural reflex;

zi1 bu shen ti 滋補身體
nourish the body;

zi1 bing 訾病
find fault with;

zi li 訾厲
disease / illness;

zi4 bi huan xiang 自閉幻想
autistic fantasy;

zi bi 自斃
destroy oneself // self-destruction;

zi bian 自貶
self-abasement;

zi bian 自便
as one wishes;

zi bu liang li 自不量力
do sth beyond one's ability / not to recognize one's own limited strength;

zi cai 自裁
commit suicide;

zi chu 自處
where to place oneself;

zi fu 自負
conceited / pretentious / toploafty // conceit / vanity;

zi gao fen yong 自告奮勇
volunteer;

zi gong 自供
confess;

zi gu bu xia 自顧不暇
have trouble even in taking care of oneself;

zi gu zi 自顧自
(1) selfish;
(2) mind one's business;
(3) everyone for himself;

zi hao 自好
self-esteem / self-respect;

zi jian 自薦
introduce oneself / recommend oneself /

volunteer;

zi jin 自盡
commit suicide / kill oneself;

zi jing 自經
(1) hang oneself;
(2) commit suicide;

zi jing 自剄
commit suicide by cutting the throat;

zi jiu 自救
self-salvation;

zi jue fen mu 自掘墳墓
dig one's own grave;

zi jue 自絕
(1) isolate oneself;
(2) seek self-destruction;

zi ku 自苦
give oneself unnecessary pains / look for trouble;

zi kuang 自況
compare oneself with another person;

zi lü 自律
control oneself // self-control / self-discipline;

zi qian 自遣
amuse oneself / cheer oneself / comfort oneself / console oneself;

zi qiang 自戕
abuse oneself / harm oneself / inflict injuries on oneself;

zi qiang 自強
strengthen oneself;

zi qiang bu xi 自強不息
continuous self-strengthening;

zi qing zi jian 自輕自賤
belittle oneself and debase oneself;

zi qu 自取
of one's own doing;

zi qu qi jiu 自取其咎
receive punishment through one's own fault;

zi qu qi ru 自取其辱
ask for an insult / invite humiliation;

zi ren 自認
(1) believe;
(2) accept adversity with resignation;

zi ren hui qi 自認晦氣
accept bad luck without complaint / grin and bear it;

zi sha 自殺
commit suicide / kill oneself ‖ be going without a passport; bring about one's own destruction; court destruction; cut one's own throat; die by one's own hand; do a Dutch act; do away with oneself; do oneself harm; do the Dutch act; douse the light; drain the cup of life; drink the waters of Lethe; Dutch act; end it all; end one's days; end one's own life; fall on one's sword; find a way out; go to Lethe; gorge out; happy dispatch; have a fatal accident; lay violent hands on oneself; lover's leap; make the great leap; planned termination; quaff the cup; self-deliverance; self-destruction; self-execution; self-immolation; self-termination; self-violence; solitaire; susanside; take one's own life; take the coward's way out; take the easy way out; take the pipe; take the road of one's doom;

jing shen xing zi sha 精神性自殺
psychic suicide;

zi sha wei sui 自殺未遂
attempted suicide;

zi shang 自傷
(1) inflict injury on oneself;
(2) feel sorrow for oneself / pity oneself;

zi shen 自身
oneself / self;

zi shen nan bao 自身難保
unable to protect oneself ‖ can hardly survive; cannot even be sure of one's own safety; hardly be able to save oneself; hard to protect one's own self; one's own life is in danger; risk one's head; unable even to fend for oneself;

zi shi qi guo 自食其果
suffer the consequences of one's own doing;

zi shi qi li 自食其力
live by one's own exertion / live on one's hump;

zi shou 自首
surrender oneself to the authorities;

zi shu 自贖
atone for one's crime / redeem oneself;

zi shu 自署
sign one's name;

zi tou luo wang 自投羅網
put one's head in a noose / put one's neck in the noose;

zi wei 自衛
defend oneself // self-defence;

zi wen 自刎
commit suicide by cutting one's own throat;

zi wo fang zong 自我放縱
self-abandon // self-abandonment;

zi wo ke zhi 自我克制
self-abnegation / self-control;

zi wo ken ding 自我肯定
self affirmation;

zi wo shen cha 自我審查
self-censorship;

zi wo xi sheng 自我犧牲
self-sacrifice;

zi wo xin shang 自我欣賞
self-appreciation;

zi wo yue shu 自我約束
self-discipline;

zi wo zhe mo 自我折磨
self-torture;

zi wu 自誤
cause damage to one's own interest;

zi wu wu ren 自誤誤人
compromise the interest of oneself and that of others;

zi xi 自習
learn and practise by oneself;

zi xin 自新
self-renewal;

zi xin 自信
self-confident // self-confidence;

zi xing qi shi 自行其是
act as one thinks proper / go one's own way;

zi xiu 自修
learn and practise by oneself;

zi xu 自許
regard oneself as // conceited / pretentious;

zi xuan 自衒
show off;

zi xue 自學
study independently / study on one's own / teach oneself;

zi xun si lu 自尋死路
invite one's own destruction;

zi yi wei shi 自以為是
self-approbation;

zi yi 自縊
hang oneself;

zi you zi zai 自由自在
carefree / comfortable and at ease;

zi yu 自娛
amuse oneself;

zi ze 自責
blame oneself // self-abuse / self-accusation / self-reproach;

zi zhao ma fan 自找麻煩
ask for trouble / look for trouble;

zi zhong 自重
self-esteem / self-respect;

zi zun 自尊
self-esteem / self-respect;

zi zuo nie 自作孽
bring disaster to oneself;

zi zuo zhu zhang 自作主張
decide for oneself / take the law into one's own fists / take the law into one's own hands;

zi zuo zi shou 自作自受
stew in one's own juice / take one's medicine;

zi4 bing 漬病
catch a disease / fall ill / get infected;

zong3 lan da quan 總攬大權
in full power // have overall authority;

zong4 guan 綜管
in overall charge // arrange and manage everything;

zong lan 綜攬
in overall charge // arrange and manage everything;

zong li 綜理
in overall charge // arrange and manage everything;

zong4 heng chi cheng 縱橫馳騁
move about freely and swiftly / sweep through the length and breath of;

zong huo 縱火
commit arson;

zong shen 縱身
jump / leap;

zu3 lan 阻攔
bar the way / hold back / obstruct / stop;

zu rao 阻撓
obstruct / stand in the way / thwart;
bai ban zu nao 百般阻撓
create all sorts of obstacles;

zuan1 kong zi 鑽空子
exploit an advantage;

zuan yan 鑽研
dig into / study thoroughly;

zuan yang 鑽仰
seek the truth and stick to it;

zuan ying 鑽營
(1) seek advantage for oneself by all means;
(2) study and scrutinize thoroughly;

zun1 尊
honour / respect / revere;

zun chong 尊崇
hold in reverence / revere / venerate;

zun lao 尊老
respect the aged;

zun sheng 尊生
respect life;

zun shi zhong dao 尊師重道
respect the teacher and his teachings;

zun yan 尊嚴
dignity / honour;

zun zhong 尊重
esteem / respect // obeisance;

zun1 shou 遵守
abide by / comply with / follow / observe;

zun shou xie yi 遵守協議
abide by the agreement;

zun3 撙
(1) comply with;
(2) economize / save;

zun jie 撙節
(1) follow rule and order / restrain;
(2) economize;

zun shen 撙省
economize;

zuo3 pi qi 左脾氣
stubbornly peevish temper;

zuo you wei nan 左右為難
at the horn of a dilemma / in a dilemma / in an awkward predicament // be hard put / be torn between / feel caught in the middle;

zuo4 坐
(1) sit;
(2) take;

zuo bu wen 坐不穩
cannot sit steady;

zuo bu zhu 坐不住
cannot sit still;

zuo dai 坐待
sit back and wait;

zuo deng 坐等
sit back and wait;

zuo di 坐地
sit on the ground;

zuo ding 坐定
to be seated;

zuo lao 坐牢
be imprisoned;

zuo leng ban deng 坐冷板凳
(1) hold a position with little power;
(2) be out in the cold;

zuo li bu an 坐立不安
restless;

zuo wo bu ning 坐臥不寧
feel restless and uneasy;

zuo xia 坐下
sit down;

zuo yi dai bi 坐以待斃
await one's doom;

zuo4 an 作案
commit a crime;

zuo ban 作伴
keep sb company;

zuo bie 作別
bid farewell / take one's leave;

zuo dong 作東
stand treat;

zuo dui 作對
act against;

zuo e 作惡
do evil;

zuo e duo duan 作惡多端
indulge in all sorts of evildoing;

zuo fa zi bi 作法自斃
be caught by one's own device;

zuo feng 作風
one's way of doing things;

zuo geng 作梗
hamper / hinder / obstruct;

zuo gu 作古
die / pass away;

zuo guai 作怪
play tricks;

zuo kuo 作闊
show off;

zuo le 作樂
have fun / make merry;

zuo luan 作亂
raise an uprising / rebel;

zuo mei 作媒
act as a go-between;

zuo nie 作孽
do evil;

zuo nong 作弄
make a fool of / play a trick on / tease;

zuo pei 作陪
accompany / escort;

zuo tai 作態
strike an attitude;

zuo tong 作痛
ache / cause pain;

zuo wei zuo fu 作威作福
throw one's weight around // bossy;

zuo wei 作為
(1) behaviour / conduct;
(2) accomplish;
(3) look upon as / regard as;

zuo4 做
(1) do / work;
(2) act;
(3) become;

zuo ban 做伴
keep sb company;

zuo fen nei shi 做分內事
do one's stuff;

zuo gong 做工
work;

zuo hao zuo dai 做好做歹
play the good or crook;

zuo huo 做活
earn a living / work;

zuo jia 做假
cheat;

zuo ke 做客
to be a guest;

zuo kuo 做闊
show off one's wealth / splash one's wealth around;

zuo ren 做人
conduct oneself;

zuo ren qing 做人情
do sb a favour;

zuo wen zhang 做文章
(1) write an essay;
(2) make an issue of;

zuo xi 做戲
(1) act in a play;

(2) playact / put on a show;

zuo yang zi 做樣子
pretend to do sth;

zuo za huo 做雜活
potter;

zuo zhu 做主
be master of / decide / take charge;

Appearance and Manners 樣子和態度

ai3 矮
short;

ai cuo 矮矬
short;

ai du du 矮篤篤
dumpy / pudgy / stumpy;

ai dun dun 矮墩墩
dumpy / pudgy / stumpy;

ai ge zi 矮個子
short person;

ai pang 矮胖
dumpy / pudgy / roly-poly / short and fat / short and stout // tubbiness;

ai ren 矮人
pyknic / short person;

ai xiao 矮小
short and small / short-statured / undersized;

ai xiao bing 矮小病
runt disease;

ai xiao zong he zheng 矮小綜合症
short stature syndrome;

an4 ran 岸然
in a solemn manner;

ang2 cang 昂藏
tall and imposing;

ang cang qi chi zhi qu 昂藏七尺之軀
manly man / tall strapping man;

bai3 guan jia zi 擺官架子
put on the airs of an official;

bai jia zi 擺架子
put on airs / put on side // self-important and pretentious;

bai kuo 擺闊
make a parade of one's wealth;

bai kuo qi 擺闊氣
make a parade of one's wealth;

bai men mian 擺門面
ostentatious // flaunt one's wealth / put up an impressive front / show off;

bai yang zi 擺樣子
do sth for show / put on for appearance's sake // for appearance's sake;

bian3 di 貶低
belittle / downplay;

bin1 彬
intelligent, refined and gentle;

bin bin 彬彬
handsome and solid / refined / urbane;

bin bin jun zi 彬彬君子
refined gentleman;

bin bin you li 彬彬有禮
courteous / genial / refined and courteous / unbane / well-mannered // with a good grace // gentility;

bing1 xue cong ming 冰雪聰明
brilliant / very bright / very clever;

bu4 mei 不美
not beautiful / not pretty;

bu xiu bian fu 不修邊幅
(1) be sloppily dressed;
(2) look unkempt;

bu ya 不雅
inelegant;

chan3 諂
cringe / fawn on / flatter;

chan guan qi min 諂官欺民
curry favour with the officials and oppress the people;

chan mei 諂媚
fawn on / flatter / toady;

chan mei feng cheng 諂媚奉承
stoop to flattery;

chan shang ao xia 諂上傲下
pay too much respect to one's superiors and

despise those who are of lower ranks;

chan shang qi xia 諂上欺下
be servile to one's superiors and tyrannical to one's subordinates / fawn on those above and bully those below;

chan yu 諂諛
flatter;

cheng3 逞
(1) flaunt / show off;
(2) carry out an evil design / succeed in a scheme;
(3) give free rein to / indulge;

cheng neng 逞能
act up / parade one's ability / show off one's skill;

cheng qiang 逞強
flaunt one's superiority // cocky;

cheng qiang hao sheng 逞強好勝
flaunt one's superiority and seek to pull others down / parade one's superiority and strive to outshine others;

cheng wei feng 逞威風
lord it over / show off one's strength / swagger about;

cheng xing wang wei 逞性妄為
act recklessly / act on impulse / behave unscrupulously;

cheng xiong 逞凶
act violently;

cheng xiong ba dao 逞凶霸道
throw one's weight about;

cheng ying xiong 逞英雄
play the hero / pose as a hero;

cheng zhi zuo wei 逞志作威
intimidate people as one pleases without any scruples;

chi2 cai ao wu 持才傲物
proud of one's talent and regard things with contempt;

chong2 shang 崇尚
advocate / uphold;

chong shang qin jian 崇尚勤儉
advocate industry and thrift / uphold hardworking and thrift;

chong shang zheng yi 崇尚正義
uphold justice;

chong yang 崇洋
worship the foreign;

chong yang fu gu 崇洋復古
worship the foreign and revive the ancient;

chong yang mei wai 崇洋媚外
worhsip foreign things and fawn on foreign powers || be crazy about foreign things and obsequious to foreigners; be subservient to foreigners; worship and fawn on foreigners; worhsip foreign things and toady to foreign powers;

chou4 jia zi 臭架子
high and mighty airs / nauseating airs / the ugly mantle of pretentiousness;

chou pi qi 臭脾氣
foul temper // narky;

chu3 shi 處世
conduct oneself in society;

chu shi fang zheng 處世方正
conduct oneself in society in an upright manner / draw a straight furrow // fair and square in all dealings;

chu shi li shen 處世立身
ways of conducting oneself in society // begin the world with / behave oneself;

chu shi 處事
deal with affairs;

chu shi chi zhong 處事持重
prudent and steady in attending to business;

chu shi du cheng 處事篤誠
honest in one's dealings;

chu shi gong ping 處事公平
play fair / play the game;

chu shi gong zheng 處事公正
candid about the matter;

chu shi ji jing 處事機警
know what's what;

chu shi jing ming 處事精明
clever and smart in attending to business;

chu zhi tai ran 處之泰然
take sth in good part ‖ bear sth with equanimity; face... with equqnimity; maintain...with a quiet attitude; not to bat an eyelid; not to stir an eyelid; remain unruffled; take it easy; take things calmly // equanimous / impassive;

chu zhi tan ran 處之坦然
preserve one's equanimity / take sth undisturbedly;

chu zhi tian ran 處之恬然
remain unruffled / take sth unperturbedly;

chu3 chu 楚楚
delicate;

chu chu dong ren 楚楚動人
delicate and attractive / moving the heart of all those around her;

chu chu ke lian 楚楚可憐
delicate and touching / miserable;

chuo4 yue 綽約
graceful;

chuo yue duo zi 綽約多姿
charmingly delicate / graceful and attractive;

da4 ge zi 大個子
hulk;

dian3 ya 典雅
elegant / refined;

dian ya da fang 典雅大方
elegant and graceful;

dou4 ren 逗人
amuse / tease / tickle;

dou ren xi ai 逗人喜愛
crack sb up / get a laugh from a person;

duan1 zhuang 端莊
demure / dignified / sedate;

duan3 xiao 短小
short / short and small / small;

duan xiao jing han 短小精悍
not of imposing stature but strong and capable ‖ dapper and little; short and sweet; small and perfectly formed; small, compactly built, and very capable; very alert and agile;

feng1 丰
(1) good-looking / buxom;
(2) appearance and carriage of a person;

feng cai 丰采
dashing appearance // good-looking;

feng shen 丰神
manners;

feng yun 丰韻
charming appearance or carriage / graceful poise;

feng zi 丰姿
agreeable manners;

feng zi chuo yue 丰姿綽約
agreeable manners;

feng1 cai 風采
elegant appearance / elegant demeanour / graceful bearing;

feng cai bu jian dang nian 風采不減當年
as good-looking as ever;

feng cai dong ren 風采動人
cut a fine figure;

feng cai yi ran 風采依然
one's elegance remains as before;

feng cai yun xiu 風采韻秀
of a most refined and prepossessing appearance;

feng du 風度
bearing / demeanour / mien;

feng du bu fan 風度不凡
have an imposing appearance;

feng du da fang 風度大方
have an easy manner;

feng du pian pian 風度翩翩
graceful bearing;

feng hua 風華
elegance and talented;

feng hua jue dai 風華絕代
unsurpassed beauty of a generation ‖ indescribably beautiful and striking; really a most unusual and individual beauty; unparalleled manner and deportment;

feng hua zheng mao 風華正茂
in one's prime ‖ at life's full flowering; at the height of one's youth and vigour;

feng qing 風情
amorous feelings / flirtatious expressions;

feng qing wan zhong 風情萬種
(of a woman) exceedingly fascinating and charming;

feng sao 風騷
coquettish;

feng yun 風韻
charm / graceful bearing;

feng yun yi jiu 風韻依舊
as charming as before / look still attractive / one's majesty and charm still remain;

feng yun you cun 風韻猶存
keep one's charm / still look attractive;

feng zi 風姿
charm / graceful bearing;

feng zi chuo yue 風姿綽約
charming appearance and personality / graceful figure // charming in manner;

feng zi e nuo 風姿婀娜
graceful manner;

feng zi juan xiu 風姿娟秀
her deportment and air are refined and attractive — said of a beautiful woman;

feng1 yi 豐儀
elegant demeanour;

feng ying 豐盈
(1) have a full figure;
(2) plentiful;

feng yu 豐腴
full and round / have a full figure / well-developed;

fu4 yong feng ya 附庸風雅
mingle with men of letters and pose as a lover of culture;

gan1 shou 乾瘦
bony / skinny;

guo2 se 國色
national beauty;

guo se tian xiang 國色天香
celestial beauty ‖ national beauty and heavenly fragrance;

guo se tian zi 國色天姿
a woman of great beauty ‖ celestial beauty; possess surpassing beauty;

han1 tai 憨態
silly appearance;

han tai ke ju 憨態可掬
charmingly naive;

he4 li ji qun 鶴立雞群
stand head and shoulders above others ‖ a crane among a brood of chickens — a distinguished man in a common crowd; a giant among dwarfs; a triton among minnows; like a crane standing among chickens — stand head and shoulders above others; stand out like a stork in a flock of fowls; the flower of the flock;

hui4 zhong xiu wai 慧中秀外
clever in mind and beautiful in appearance / intelligent within and beautiful without // have both brains and beauty;

jia3 ban 假扮
disguise;

jia dong zuo 假動作
deceiving move;

jia gong ji si 假公濟私
act in the public service for one's own ends ‖ abuse the public trust; gain private ends in a public cause; jobbery; promote one's private interests under the guise of serving the public; utilizing public means to satisfy private ends;

jia hun mi 假昏迷
pseudocoma;

jia mao 假冒
pass off as sb else;

jia ren jia yi 假仁假義
hypocrisy;

jia zheng jing 假正經
hypocritical;

jia zhuang 假裝
pretend ‖ assume; fake sth; feign; have an affectation; let on; look through one's fingers

at; make as if; make a pretence of...; make believe; pose as; put on; simulate;

jia zhuang zheng jing 假裝正經
put on the appearance of honesty || assume an air of modesty; assume the guise of a person of integrity; feign a correct posture; pose as a person of high morals; pretend to be a cultivated person; pretend to be a saint;

jia4 zi 架子
(1) framework / outline / skeleton;
(2) airs / haughty manner / posture / stance;

jia zi da 架子大
assume an air of importance;

jia zi shi zu 架子十足
on one's high horse // overbearing // put on airs of greatness;

jiao1 嬌
(1) beautiful / lovely;
(2) coddled / pampered / spoiled;

jiao chi 嬌痴
lovely and innocent;

jiao di di 嬌滴滴
beautiful / charming;

jiao mei 嬌美
beautiful and graceful;

jiao mei 嬌媚
beautiful;

jiao nuo 嬌娜
graceful / winsome;

jiao qi 嬌氣
delicate;

jiao rao 嬌嬈
seductive and charming;

jiao ruo 嬌柔
delicate and charming;

jiao tai 嬌態
delicate and beautiful;

jiao xiao 嬌小
dainty and small;

jiao xiao ling long 嬌小玲瓏
delicate and refined;

jiao xiu 嬌羞
bashful;

jiao yan 嬌艷
delicate and charming;

jiao3 佼
attractive / beautiful / charming / handsome / pretty;

jiao hao 佼好
pleasant / pretty;

jiao jiao 佼佼
good-looking;

jiao ren 佼人
a beauty;

jin4 zhi yong rong 進止雍容
dignified in carriage;

ju3 zhi 舉止
bearing / behaviour / carriage / deportment / manner;

ju zhi cu su 舉止粗俗
crass behaviour;

ju zhi da fang 舉止大方
have a dignified air / have poise;

ju zhi you ya 舉止優雅
graceful;

ju zhi zhao yao 舉止招搖
have flashing manners;

juan1 娟
attractive / good-looking / graceful / pretty;

juan juan 娟娟
beautiful / elegant / lovely;

juan xiu 娟秀
beautiful / elegant / good-looking / lovely;

jun4 俊
(1) handsome;
(2) talented;

jun ba 俊拔
uncommon;

jun mei 俊美
handsome;

jun qiao 俊俏
good-looking and smart;

jun ya 俊雅
handsome and elegant;

ke3 ai 可愛
adorable / likeable / lovable / lovely;

kua1 姱
elegant / good-looking / pretty;

kui2 wu 魁梧
husky / tall and robust;

lou4 mian 露面
appear in public / make an appearance / show one's face / show up;

mei3 li 美麗
beautiful / pretty;

mei li dong ren 美麗動人
personable;

mei xiu 美秀
beautiful and intelligent;

mei4 ren 媚人
attractive;

mi2 ren 迷人
charming ‖ alluring; appealing; beautiful; bewitching; dazzling; delightful; enchanting; fascinating; gorgeous; loving; ravishing; stunning;

mi ren shen cai 迷人身材
delectable body;

mu2 yang 模樣
appearance;

nian2 qing mao mei 年輕貌美
young and pretty;

niao3 嬝
delicate / graceful;

niao niao 嬝嬝
appealingly slender and delicate;

niao nuo 嬝娜
slender and delicate;

ning2 chou xiang mao 獰醜相貌
having a repulsive ugly appearance;

ning wu ke bu 獰惡可怖
fierce and terrifying;

nü3 se 女色
woman's charms;

pang4 胖
chubby / fat / plump;

pang bai you qu 胖白有趣
plump / stout;

pang bing 胖病
obesity;

pang dun dun 胖墩墩
plump / stout;

pang hu hu 胖呼呼
chubby / plump / pudgy / strutty;

pang zhong 胖腫
general swelling over the body;

piao4 liang 漂亮
beautiful / pretty;

ping1 娉
charming / good-looking;

ping ting 娉婷
graceful and charming / slender and elegant;

ping ting yu mao 娉婷玉貌
a slender, beautiful figure;

qi1 chi zhi qu 七尺之軀
the human adult body ‖ a manly body; a virile body;

qi2 mao bu yang 其貌不揚
physically unattractive / ugly in appearance;

qiao4 俏
pretty and cute;

qiao li 俏麗
good-looking / pretty;

shen1 cai 身材
stature ‖ figure; physical build; physique;
zhong deng shen cai 中等身材
of middling height;

shen cai ai xiao 身材矮小
short and slight // microsomia ‖ of short stature; of small bulk; short and slight in figure; short and slight in stature; short in stature; small and slight in person; small in stature;

shen cai duan xiao 身材短小
microsoma;

身體 *Body*

shen cai feng man 身材豐滿
fleshy;

shen cai gao da 身材高大
of great stature // strapping;

shen cai kui wu 身材魁梧
of great height and powerful build / of imposing stature // strapping / tall and sturdy;

shen cai miao tiao 身材苗條
have a slender figure // of slight make;

shen cai shou xiao 身材瘦小
slight of figure / slight of stature // of slight make // slim figure;

shen cai yao tiao 身材窈窕
have very graceful figure // her stature is gentle and graceful;

shen cai yun chen 身材勻稱
of proportional build;

shou4 瘦
(1) emaciated / slim / thin;
(2) lean;
(3) tight;
(4) lose flesh;

shou ba 瘦巴
lean / skinny;

shou chang 瘦長
lanky || gangling; long and rangy; long and thin; rangy; skinny and tall; tall and lean; tall and thin;

shou gu lin xun 瘦骨嶙峋
raw-boned / thin and bony || a bag of bones; as lean as a rake; as thin as a lath; become as emaciated as a fowl; very skinny;

shou gu ling ding 瘦骨伶仃
thin and weak / skinny and scrawny;

shou ji 瘦瘠
emaciated / thin;

shou ruo 瘦弱
thin and frail || emaciated; emaciated and frail; thin and weak;

shou xiao 瘦小
puny / thin and small;

shou xue 瘦削
slim / grunt / very thin;

ti3 mao 體貌
figure and face;

ting2 婷
attractive / graceful / pretty;

ting ting 婷婷
attractive / graceful / pretty;

tu3 li tu qi 土裏土氣
countrified / rustic || hillbilly; hob-nailed; stupid and uncouth; unsophisticated;

tu qi 土氣
countrified / rustic || hillbilly; hob-nailed; stupid and uncouth; unsophisticated;

wai4 zai mei 外在美
physical beauty / physical charm;

wan3 婉
(1) agreeable / amiable;
(2) beautiful / good-looking;

wan wan 婉婉
amiable / graceful;

wei feng 威風
awe-inspiring;

wei feng lin lin 威風凜凜
awe-inspiring;

wei yi 威儀
one's dignity of demeanour;

wei3 an 偉岸
tall and robust;

wo1 xiao zheng 倭小症
dwarfism;

wu3 嫵
attractive / lovely;

wu mei 嫵媚
lovely / very attractive;

xuan1 ang 軒昂
dignified / lofty;

xuan ang qi yu 軒昂氣宇
dignified / exalted;

xuan xiu 軒秀
distinguished / eminent / prominent;

xuan xuan 軒軒
(1) complacent / smug;
(2) outstanding;

ya3 guan 雅觀
graceful and elegant in appearance // propriety in conduct;

yan2 妍
(1) beautiful / good-looking / pretty;
(2) coquettish / seductive;

yan li 妍麗
beautiful / charming;

ye3 rong 冶容
charming;

ye yan 冶艷
beautiful;

yi2 儀
appearance / deployment;

yi biao 儀表
appearance / deployment;

yi tai 儀態
bearing / demeanour / deployment;

yi tai wan qian 儀態萬千
charming poises and exquisite bearing;

yi3 mao qu ren 以貌取人
judge a person by their looks / judge sb by appearances only;

ying1 jun 英俊
handsome;

ying ming 英明
intelligent / perspicacious / sagacious;

ying wu 英武
brave and strong / gallant / valiant / valorous;

ying zi 英姿
dashing appearance;

yong1 rong 雍容
graceful appearance;

yong rong hua gui 雍容華貴
graceful and poised / regal;

yong rong zi de 雍容自得
poised // in the peace of mind;

you4 ai you pang 又矮又胖
dumpy / short and fat;

you ai you shou 又矮又瘦
short and thin;

you ai you xiao 又矮又小
short and small;

you shou you ben 又瘦又笨
lanky;

you shou you fa 又瘦又乏
lean and weakly;

you shou you xiao 又瘦又小
short and slight;

zhang3 pang 長胖
become fat / gain weight || flesh out; flesh up; gain flesh; get fat; get flesh; make flesh; pick up flesh; put on flesh; put on weight;

zhang4 fu qi gai 丈夫氣概
manliness;

zheng yan dou yan 爭妍鬭艷
contend in beauty and fascination;

zhuang4 jian 壯健
strong and healthy;

zi1 姿
(1) bearing / carriage;
(2) looks;

zi mao 姿貌
a woman's looks;

zi mei 姿媚
elegant and graceful manners;

Personality and Abilities 個性和能力

ai4 ban nong shi fei 愛搬弄是非
talebearing;

ai bao yuan 愛抱怨
querulous;

ai cai 愛財
avaricious / covetous / greedy for money;

ai cai ru ming 愛財如命
love money as much as one's life / love money as one loves one's life / regard wealth as one's life // greedy for money / stingy;

ai jiang jiu 愛講究
pernickety;

ai tai gang 愛抬杠
love to dispute for its own sake / love to have a crow to pick with sb / love to have high words with sb;

ai xiang shou 愛享受
be a lover of pleasure;

ai xiao 愛小
keen on getting petty advantages // go after petty advantages;

ai xu rong 愛虛榮
vainglorious;

ai zhan xiao pian yi 愛佔小便宜
keen on getting petty advantages // go after petty advantages;

an1 fen 安分
know one's place;

an fen shou ji 安分守己
keep one's place;

an1 ming 安命
accept one's lot / be content with one's lot;

an ming shou fen 安命守分
come to terms with one's existence;

an pin le dao 安貧樂道
content with poverty, caring for one's principles;

an pin le jian 安貧樂賤
happy to lead a simple and virtuous life;

an zhi ruo su 安之若素
handle difficulties and unexpected happenings as calmly as dealing with ordinary things / regard wrong views or wrongdoing with indifference;

ao4 傲
(1) arrogant / haughty;
(2) despise / look down on;

ao an 傲岸
haughty / proud;

ao man 傲慢
arrogant / haughty / haughty and overbearing / hauteur / high-hat / hoity-toity / imperious / impudent / insolent / presumptuous / proud-hearted // arrogance / contumely / hubris;

ao man wu li 傲慢無禮
contumelious / discourteous / insolent / presumptuous;

ao qi 傲氣
air of arrogance / haughtiness;

ao ran 傲然
loftily / proudly / unyieldingly;

ao wu 傲物
contemptuous / haughtily distainful / supercilious;

ao xing 傲性
proud temperament;

ba1 mian guang 八面光
worldly sophiscated;

ba mian ling long 八面玲瓏
slick and foxy / smooth and tactful;

ba mian wei feng 八面威風
commanding presence;

ba1 jie 巴結
butter up / curry favour with / fawn on / flatter / make up to / please / suck around / suck up / toady to;

ba2 hu 跋扈
bossy / bullying / domineering / rampant;

ba4 dao 霸道
(1) domineering;
(2) bullying;

ba qi 霸氣
domineering;

bai3 ban bi hu 百般庇護
shelter by all possible means;

bai ban di lai 百般抵賴
deny by every means;

bai ban diao nan 百般刁難
create all sorts of difficulties / obstruct by all possible means;

bai ban fu wei 百般撫慰
try to soothe in every possible way;

bai ban zu nao 百般阻撓
create all sorts of obstacles / obstruct by all means;

bai3 yi bai shun 百依百順
be all obedience / agree with sb in everything;

bai zhe bu hui 百折不回
advance bravely and never withdraw || keep on fighting in spite of all setbacks; pushing forward despite repeated frustrations; with indomitable fortitude;

bai zhe bu nao 百折不撓
keep on fighting in spite of all setbacks ‖ assiduous in; bob up like a cork; indomitable; never say die; persistent efforts; put up a stiff resistance against great odds; unbending; undaunted by repeated setbacks; unflinching despite repeated setbacks; unrelenting; unremitting; unshakable; unswerving; unyielding despite reverses;

bai zhe bu nao, zai jie zai li 百折不撓，再接再勵
indomitable / through one's dauntless and persistent efforts;

bai4 de 敗德
evil conduct / licentious behaviour;

bai er bu nei 敗而不餒
be undismayed by failure / not be discouraged by failure;

bai huai 敗壞
corrupt / ruin ‖ debase; deteriorate; ruin; spoil; undermine;

bai huai men mei 敗壞門楣
disgrace one's family;

bai huai ming yu 敗壞名譽
damage the reputation of / defame / discredit;

ban1 men nong fu 班門弄斧
show off one's slight skill in the presence of an expert ‖ a foolish display of axe before the master carpenter's home; offer to teach fish to swim; preach to be wise; show off one's proficiency with the axe before Lu Ban, the master carpenter; teach a dog to bark; teach one's grandmother to suck eggs; wielding an axe before the door of Lu Ban the master carpenter — showing off in the presence of an expert;

ban3 zhi 板直
(1) inflexible and straightforward;
(2) solemn;

bei1 卑
(1) low;
(2) base / inferior / mean;
(3) humble / modest;

bei bi 卑鄙
base / mean ‖ contemptible; crooked; deliquent; depraved; despicable;

bei bi bu kan 卑鄙不堪
contemptible for one's meanness;

bei bi gou dang 卑鄙勾當
dirty deal;

bei bi shou duan 卑鄙手段
contemptible means / dirty tricks;

bei bi wo chuo 卑鄙齷齪
base / foul / mean / sordid;

bei bi wu chi 卑鄙無恥
mean and having no sense of shame / mean and vulgar;

bei bi xing jing 卑鄙行徑
sordid conduct;

bei bo 卑薄
poor and barren;

bei bu zu dao 卑不足道
too inferior to be worth mentioning ‖ beneath discussion; beneath mention; not worth mentioning; inconsiderable; insignificant; too insignificant to be worth mentioning; trivial;

bei ci hou li 卑詞厚禮
humble words and handsome gifts / sweet words and lavish gifts;

bei gong qu xi 卑躬屈膝
bow and scrape ‖ act servilely; cap in hand; cringe; eat dirt; eat humble pie; grovel in the dirt; grovel in the dust; hat in hand; humble oneself in serving a master; humiliate oneself in serving; kiss the ground; kowtow to; make a great show of obedience and courtesy; menial; on one's knees;

bei jian 卑賤
(1) humble / lowly;
(2) mean and low;

bei lie 卑劣
base / depraved / despicable / mean;

bei lie shou fa 卑劣手法
despicable trick / mean trick;

bei lie xing jing 卑劣行徑
base conduct / dishonourable behaviour;

bei lou 卑陋
(1) humble / lowly;
(2) degrading / inferior / low / mean / vulgar;

bei qie 卑怯
abject / mean and cowardly;

bei qu 卑屈
obsequiously submissive;

bei rang 卑讓
defer / yield with courtesy;

bei ruo 卑弱
delicate / docile / meek / weak;

bei wei 卑微
humble / inferior / lowly;

bei wu 卑污
despicable and filthy / foul;

bei xia 卑下
base / humble / low / mean / petty and low;

bei xing 卑行
of the lower generation;

bei yi zi mu 卑以自牧
keep modest so as to cultivate one's moral character;

bei4 ban 悖叛
rebel / revolt;

bei de 悖德
immoral;

bei li 悖理
contrary to reason / irrational ‖ absurd; unreasonable;

bei li 悖禮
contrary to etiquette / impolite / uncivil;

bei li shi jian 悖禮失檢
contrary to decorum and lacking in care;

bei li 悖戾
deviate from accepted rules or standards // perverse;

bei luan 悖亂
rebellion / revolt / sedition;

bei lun 悖論
dilemma / paradox;

bei man 悖漫
arrogantly impolite / disrespectful // show irreverence;

bei miu 悖謬
absurd / irrational / preposterous / unreasonable;

bei ni 悖逆
disloyal / treasonable;

bei ni bu dao 悖逆不道
break accepted morals ‖ defy all laws; offensive to all established values;

bei pan 悖叛
rebel / revolt;

bei qi 悖棄
turn away from sth in revolt;

bei qing 悖情
against human nature;

bei ru bei chu 悖入悖出
evil begets evil // ill-spent;

ben4 笨
(1) dull / stupid;
(2) awkward / clumsy;

ben de yao ming 笨得要命
as stupid as an owl / as stupid as they make them;

ben ru dai lü 笨如呆驢
as stupid as an ass;

ben shou ben jiao 笨手笨腳
all thumbs / clumsy ‖ acting clumsily; awkward; cach-handed; gawky; ham-fisted; have a hand like a foot; have one's fingers all thumbs; heavy-handed; one is awkward with one's hands;

bi3 鄙
(1) base / despicable / low / mean / rustic / vulgar;
(2) despise / disdain / look down / scorn;
(3) shallow / superficial;

bi3 bo 鄙薄
(1) base / low / mean / vulgar;
(2) ignorant and shallow / shallow / superficial;
(3) despise / have contempt for / have disdain for / loathe / scorn;

bi jian 鄙賤
(1) base / humble lowly / mean;
(2) despise / disdain / look down on;

身體 *Body*

bi li 鄙俚
coarse / crude / philistine / uneducated / vulgar;

bi lie 鄙劣
inferior / mean;

bi lin 鄙吝
(1) mean / miserly / niggardly / stingy;
(2) philistine / vulgar;

bi lin fu meng 鄙吝復萌
vulgar ideas reemerge in one's mind;

bi lou 鄙陋
(1) base / mean;
(2) shallow / superficial;

bi lou ping yong 鄙陋平庸
shallow and mediocre;

bi lou wu zhi 鄙陋無知
shallow and ignorant;

bi qi 鄙棄
despise / disdain / feel contempt for / loathe / scorn / spurn;

bi shi 鄙視
despise / disdain / have a contempt for / hold in contempt / look down on / make light of / set little store by sth / slight;

bi su 鄙俗
low / philistine / vulgar;

bi yi 鄙夷
contempt / despise / have a contempt for / look down on / scorn;

bi zha 鄙詐
deceitful / despicably untruthful;

bi4 愎
obstinate / perverse / self-willed / stubborn;

bi4 gong bi jing 必恭必敬
extremely deferential / reverent and respectful;

bi4 gong bi jing 畢恭畢敬
in a most respectful attitude ‖ cap in hand; extremely deferential; hat in hand; in humble reverence; reverent and respectful; with all courtesy and respect; with excessive courtesy; with the utmost deference;

bian1 zao gu shi 編造故事
trump up a story;

bing3 gong wu si 秉公無私
handle affairs justly;

bing xing geng zhi 秉性耿直
candid / upright by nature;

bing zheng 秉正
just / upright;

bing zhi 秉直
(1) frank and honest;
(2) adhere to correct principles;

bing3 fu 稟賦
natural endowment;

bing fu cong ming 稟賦聰明
be gifted with keen intelligence;

bing fu guo ren 稟賦過人
possess original talents superior to other people / surpass many others in natural endowment;

bing xing 稟性
natural disposition / natural temperament;

bing xing an ruo 稟性闇弱
naturally weak;

bing xing chun liang 稟性純良
simple and honest by nature;

bing xing gang bi 稟性剛愎
have a perverse temper / perverse in temper;

bing xing shan liang 稟性善良
frank by nature // the milk of human kindness;

bing xing shuang zhi 稟性爽直
frank by nature;

bu4 bei bu kang 不卑不亢
neither humble nor arrogant ‖ neither cringing nor arrogant; neither haughty nor humble; neither haughty nor pushy; neither servile nor overbearing;

bu cheng shi 不誠實
dishonest / mendacious // dishonesty / mendacity;

bu hao ke 不好客
inhospitable // inhospitality;

bu he qun 不合群
asocial;

bu kang bu bei 不亢不卑
neither proud nor humble || in a happy medium between pride and humility; neither haughty nor humble; neither overbearing nor servile; neither supercilious nor obsequious;

bu lao shi 不老實
dishonest // dishonesty;

cheng2 du 誠篤
honest;

cheng jing 誠敬
sincere and respectful;

cheng pu 誠樸
honest and simple;

cheng shi 誠實
honest / trustworthy / upright / veracious // veracity;

cheng shi ke kao 誠實可靠
honest and reliable;

cheng shi zheng zhi 誠實正直
clean-living;

cheng zhi 誠摯
cordial / sincere;

chun2 du 純篤
honest and devoted;

chun jie 純潔
chaste / clean and honest / innocent / pure and clean / sincere and faithful / virginal;

chun jie wu xia 純潔無瑕
as pure as a lily;

chun liang 純良
honest / kind;

chun pu 純樸
simple and sincere / unsophisticated;

chun pu dun hou 純樸敦厚
simple and honest;

chun pu shuang lang 純樸爽朗
honest and frank;

chun zhen 純真
pure || genuine; sincere; sincere and faithful; unsophisticated;

chun zhen wu xie 純真無邪
pure and innocent;

chun2 淳
honest / pure;

chun he 淳和
simple and gentle;

chun he tong qing 淳和通情
agreeable and reasonable;

chun hou 淳厚
pure and honest / simple and kind;

chun jie 淳潔
pure and clean;

chun jie wu xia 淳潔無瑕
pure and flawless;

chun liang 淳良
pure, simple and honest;

chun pu 淳樸
honest / simple / unsophiscated;

chun3 蠢
dull / foolish / silly / stupid;

chun ben 蠢笨
foolish / stupid;

chun ben yu wan 蠢笨愚頑
stupid and stubborn;

chun chun yu dong 蠢蠢欲動
restless and about to start some move || eager for action; be going to start sth; itch for action; on the move; ready for action;

chun lou 蠢陋
stupid and uncultured;

chun xing 蠢行
foolery;

cu1 bao 粗暴
brutal / crude / rough / rude / violent;

cu ben 粗笨
(1) awkward / clumsy;
(2) bulky / cumbersome / heavy / unwieldy;

cu bi 粗鄙
coarse / vulgar;

cu fang 粗放
bold and unrestrained;

cu guang 粗獷
(1) boorish / rough / rude;
(2) bold and unconstrained / rugged / straightforward and uninhibited;

cu hao 粗豪
forthright / straightforward;

cu lu 粗魯
boorish / rough / rude;

cu lu ben zhuo 粗魯笨拙
outlandish / rude and clumsy;

cu man 粗蠻
rough / rude / unrefined;

cu mang 粗莽
reckless / rude;

cu qian 粗淺
(1) coarse and shallow / shallow;
(2) simple / superficial;

dai1 ban 呆板
(1) boring;
(2) stiff;

dai ben 呆笨
dull / stupid / unintelligent;

dai mu 呆木
dazed and numb;

dai4 怠
idle / lazy / remiss / slack;

dai duo 怠惰
idle / indolent / inert / lazy / slothful;

dai fei 怠廢
idle;

dai hu 怠忽
neglect / remiss;

dai huan 怠緩
idle and lax / procrastinating;

dai huang 怠荒
idle and waste time;

dai huang 怠遑
indolence;

dai juan 怠倦
lax and tired;

dai man 怠慢
cold-shoulder / remiss / slight;

dai qi 怠棄
idly abandon;

dai san 怠散
remiss, lax and negligent;

dai xi 怠息
idle and rest;

dan4 bo 淡泊
do not seek fame and fortune / lead a tranquil life without worldly desires;

dan bo ming li 淡泊名利
indifferent to fame and wealth;

dan bo ming zhi 淡泊明志
live a simple and honest life / show high ideals by simple living;

dan mo 淡漠
indifferent;

dan4 澹
calm / quiet;

dan bo 澹泊
not seek fame and wealth;

dan bo ming li 澹泊名利
indifferent towards fame and wealth;

dan bo ming zhi 澹泊明志
live a simple life, showing one's true goal in life;

dan bo zi gan 澹泊自甘
tranquil and satisfied;

dan ran 澹然
cool / indifferent;

dan ya 澹雅
quiet and refined;

diao1 e 刁惡
rascally brutal;

diao han 刁悍
cunning and fierce;

diao hua 刁滑
crafty / wily;

diao man 刁蠻
obstinate / stubborn;

diao pi 刁脾
naughty;

diao wan 刁頑
obstinate / stubborn;

diao zha 刁詐
crafty / dishonest / knavish;

diao zuan 刁鑽
crafty / wily;

diao zuan gu guai 刁鑽古怪
cranky;

die2 dang 跌宕
bold and unconstrained / free and easy;

die dang bu ji 跌宕不羈
unrestrained and reckless;

ding3 tian li di 頂天立地
of indomitable spirit and morals || most respectable; of gigantic stature;

du2 duan 獨斷
arbitrary / dictatorial;

du duan du xing 獨斷獨行
go one's own way / take one's own way;

du duan zhuan xing 獨斷專行
make dictatorial decisions and act dictatorially || a law unto oneself; act arbitarily; act dictatorially; act personally in all matters; decide and act arbitrarily; decide and act alone; decide and act on one's own way; indulge in arbitrary decisions and preemptory actions; paddle one's way on one's own canoe; take arbitrary action; take one's own course; wheel and deal;

du duan zhuan xing, fa hao shi ling 獨斷專行，發號施令
decide and act arbitrarily and issue orders left and right / make dictatorial decisions and order others about;

du lan 獨攬
arrogate / monopolize;

du lan da quan 獨攬大權
grasp at authority by oneself / arrogate all power to oneself;

du3 hou 篤厚
sincere and magnanimous;

du shi 篤實
(1) honest and sincere;
(2) solid / sound;

du shi guang hui 篤實光輝
sincere and glorious;

dun1 dun shi shi 敦敦實實
cordial / honest / sincere / upright;

dun hou 敦厚
honest and simple / honest and sincere;

dun mian 敦勉
honest and diligent;

dun mu 敦睦
promote friendly relations;

dun pu 敦樸
honest / sincere / upright;

dun shi 敦實
solid / stocky;

dun shi chun pu 敦實淳樸
stocky and honest;

fang4 dan 放誕
wile in speech and behaviour;

fang dan bu ji 放誕不羈
dissipated and unrestrained || dissolute in conduct; reckless and dissipated in behaviour and speech;

fang dan bu jing 放誕不經
absurd / fantastic;

fang dan feng liu 放誕風流
reckless and dissipated in behaviour and speech;

fang dan wu li 放誕無禮
guilty of a liberty;

fang dang 放蕩
(1) dissipated / dissolute / jaded / profligate;
(2) unconventional;

fang dang bu ji 放蕩不羈
on the loose || have full swing; have one's fling; lead a fast life; licentious in conduct; run riot; sow one's wild oats; take the bit between one's teech; take one's swing; tear around; throw off restraint and become dissolute; unconventional and unbridled; unconventional and unrestrained; uninhibited;

fang lang 放浪
debauch / dissipate;

fang lang xing hai 放浪形骸
abandon oneself to a debauched life;

fang si 放肆
run wild || get wise; unbridled; wanton;

fang si wu ji 放肆無忌
throw all restraint to the winds / unbridled and run amuck;

fang si wu li 放肆無禮
guilty of taking liberties;

fang zi 放恣
proud and self-indulgent / proud and undisciplined;

fang zi shi yi 放恣失儀
debauched and impolite;

fang zong 放縱
connive at / indulge / let sb have their own way;

fang zong bu ji 放縱不羈
uninhibited;

fei1 yang ba hu 飛揚跋扈
throw one's weight around || act like overlords; arrogant and domineering; domineer; lord it over; powerful and arrogant;

feng1 gu 風骨
strength of character;

feng liu 風流
(1) distinguished and admirable;
(2) talented and romantic;
(3) amorous / dissolute / loose;

feng liu ru ya 風流儒雅
cultured, talented and refined;

feng liu sou ze 風流藪澤
the marshy place of lewdness — brothels;

feng liu ti tang 風流倜儻
casual and elegant bearing;

feng liu xiao sa 風流瀟灑
gay and light-hearted / graceful but not showy;

feng liu yun jie 風流蘊藉
graceful but not showy / urbanely charming;

fu2 bo 浮薄
flippant / frivolous;

fu hua 浮華
ostentatious || flashy; foppish rococo; showy; vain;

fu hua lang rui 浮華浪蕊
frivolous;

fu kua 浮誇
boastful / exaggerate / fuddy-duddy;

gan1 she 干涉
interfere / intervene / intrude / meddle / put in one's oar / stick in one's oar;

gang1 bi 剛愎
head-strong / self-willed / stubborn;

gang bi zi yong 剛愎自用
self-willed and conceited || headstrong; obstinate and adhere to one's own judgement; obstinate and self-opinionated; set in one's ways; wayward; wrong-headed;

gang jian 剛健
energetic / robustic / vigorous;

gang jian zhi pu 剛健質樸
vigorous and simple;

gang jin 剛勁
bold / sturdy / vigorous;

gang lie 剛烈
tough and vehement;

gang qiang 剛強
firm / staunch / unyielding;

gang qiang bu ba 剛強不拔
steely fortitude;

gang qiang guo duan 剛強果斷
firm and resolute;

gang rou bing ji 剛柔並濟
couple hardness with softness || exercise a combination of inflexibility and yielding; temper severity with mercy; temper toughness with gentleness; use both tough and gentle methods;

gang yi 剛毅
resolute and steadfast;

gang yi guo jue 剛毅果決
resolute and daring;

gang yi jing shen 剛毅精神
fortitude;

gang zheng 剛正
principled / upright // rectitude;

gang zheng bu e 剛正不阿
frank and straightforward ‖ neither bribes nor pressure from above can deflect sb from administering the law justly;

gang zhi 剛直
upright and outspoken;

gao1 ao 高傲
arrogant ‖ haughty; insolent; stiff-backed; supercilious;

gao ao zi da 高傲自大
arrogant and self-important ‖ be stuck up; get a swollen head; have a big head; have a swelled head; too big for one's breeches;

gao feng 高風
noble character;

gao feng liang jie 高風亮節
noble character and sterling integrity ‖ exemplary conduct and nobility of character; have a strong sense of integrity; high and upright character;

gao shang 高尚
noble ‖ high; high-minded; lofty; respectable; sublimate;

gao shang xian ya 高尚嫻雅
grace / noble and refined;

gao ya 高雅
elegant / noble and graceful / refined;

geng3 耿
honest and just / upright;

geng geng 耿耿
dedicated / devoted;

geng jie ba su 耿介拔俗
straightforward and outstanding — not like ordinary men;

geng zhi 耿直
fair and just / honest and frank / straightforward / upright;

geng3 xing 梗性
obstinate in disposition;

geng zhi 梗直
straight and honest;

geng3 zheng 骾正
straightforward and upright;

geng zhi 骾直
honest / outspoken / straightforward;

gu1 ao 孤傲
proud and aloof;

gu fang 孤芳
narcissistic;

gu fang zi shang 孤芳自賞
indulge in self-admiration;

gu fen 孤憤
cynical;

gu pi 孤僻
idiosyncratic;

gu3 ban 古板
square;

gu4 zhi 固執
(1) bullheaded / hard-headed / obstinate / pertinacious / stubborn / unbending // pertinacity / stiff neck;
(2) cling to / persist in;

gua3 lian xian chi 寡廉鮮恥
have no sense of dishonour and disgrace ‖ as bold as brass; be dead to shame; be destitute of shame; be lost to all sense of shame; brazen-faced; have no sense of shame; shameless; unscrupulous and shameless;

guai1 乖
(1) obedient / well-behaved;
(2) perverse / obstinate / sulky;
(3) crafty / cunning;

guai li 乖戾
perverse;

guai miu 乖謬
absurd / unusual;

guai pi 乖僻
eccentric / perverse / unreasonable;

guai qiao 乖巧
(1) cute / lovely;
(2) clever / quick;

guai yi 乖異
eccentric / strange;

guai zhang 乖張
eccentric and unreasonable;

guai4 dan 怪誕
absurd / strange / weird;

guai dan bu jing 怪誕不經
weird and uncanny || crazy; droll; fantastic; supernatural and unreasonable;

guai dan xing wei 怪誕行為
antics;

guai li guai qi 怪裡怪氣
eccentric / queer / strange;

guai mo guai yang 怪模怪樣
queer appearance and manner;

guai pi qi 怪脾氣
(1) oddity;
(2) tetchy;

guai pi 怪僻
crankery / eccentric / kink;

guai pi 怪癖
eccentric behaviour / strange hobbies;

guai tai 怪態
affected and disgusting manners;

guai te 怪特
strange and peculiar;

guai yi 怪異
strange / unusual || monstrous;

guang1 ming lei luo 光明磊落
open and aboveboard || aboveboard; completely open; frank and forthright; on the up-and-up; open and upright; plain dealing; plainly and squarely;

guang ming zheng da 光明正大
aboveboard and straightforward || abovebroad; entirely aboveboard; fair and square; frank and righteous; just and honourable; on the square; open and aboveboard; openly and honestly; plain dealing; sporting; upright;

guo3 gan 果敢
do sth without hesitation / unflinching;

guo jue 果決
daring and determined;

guo yi 果毅
determination and fortitude;

han1 憨
(1) foolish / silly;
(2) naive || simple and honest; straightforward;

han chi 憨痴
idiotic;

han hou 憨厚
simple and honest / straightforward and good-natured;

han shi 憨實
(1) stalwart / sturdy;
(2) simple-hearted;

han zhi 憨直
honest and straightforward / honest and upright;

hao4 chu feng tou 好出風頭
fond of the limelight / like to get into the limelight;

hao da xi gong 好大喜功
crave after greatness and success || ambitious for great achievements; attempt to do sth overambitious and unrealistic; be ambitious; flamboyant; have a fondness for the grandiose; like to do grandiose things to impress people;

hao dou 好鬥
aggressively hostile / bellicose / belligerent;

hao fa huo 好發火
apt to lose one's temper easily;

hao gao wu yuan 好高騖遠
reach for what is beyond one's grasp || aim at the moon; aim too high; be a flier; bite off more than one can chew; crave after sth high and out of reach; hitch one's wagon to a star; run after far-off things; try to run before one can walk;

hao guan xian shi 好管閒事
fond of meddling in other people's business || enjoy having one's finger in every pie; have an oar in very man's boat; like poke and pry; meddlesome; pose one's nose in other people's affairs;

hao jiao ji 好交際
clubable / clubby;

hao jie cheng pi 好潔成癖
excessive fondness for cleanliness;

hao ke 好客
hospitable // keep open house;

hao se 好色
fond of women // salacious;

hao shan le shi 好善樂施
always glad to give to charities ‖ always ready to help in a worthy cause; be interested in charities; do good naturally and happily; happy in doing good; love to do philanthropic work; prodigal of benefactions;

he2 ai ke qin 和藹可親
kind and amiable ‖ affable; amiable; courteous and accessible; genial;

he qi 和氣
(1) gentle / kind / polite;
(2) amiable / friendly / harmonious;

he shan 和善
genial / good-natured;

heng4 bao 橫暴
perverse and tyrannical;

heng man 橫蠻
harsh and unreasonable / perverse;

heng man wu li 橫蠻無理
arrogant and high-handed ‖ become high-handed in one's behaviour towards; truculent and unreasonable;

heng ni 橫逆
effrontery / insult / unreasonable;

hong2 da 弘大
great / magnanimous;

hong liang 弘量
generous / liberal / magnanimous;

hong yi 弘毅
having a broad and strong mind;

hong2 liang 宏量
great generosity;

hou4 dao 厚道
considerate / kind / kind-hearted;

huang1 yin 荒淫
debauched / dissolute / licentious;

huang yin fu xiu 荒淫腐朽
lead a depraved and dissolute life / live in wanton luxury;

huang yin wu chi 荒淫無恥
dissipated and unashamed ‖ licentious and decadent; profligate and shameless; shameless dissipation; shamelessly dissipated;

huang yin wu dao 荒淫無道
be profligate and devoid of principles;

huang yin wu du 荒淫無度
be vicious beyond measures ‖ indulge in sensual excesses; excessive indulgence in lewdness; given to sexual pleasures; immeasurably dissolute;

hui4 zhong 慧中
intelligent inside;

hui4 zhi 蕙質
good and pure quality of a person;

huo4 da 豁達
generous / magnanimous / open-minded;

huo da da du 豁達大度
generous / magnanimous / open-minded;

huo dang 豁蕩
carefree / unrestrained;

ji2 xing zi 急性子
(1) of impatient disposition / short-temper // short-tempered;
(2) impetuous person;

ji zao 急躁
(1) hotheaded / irascible / irritable / testy;
(2) impatient / impetuous / rash;

ji zao mao jin 急躁冒進
impetuous and rash // rush things through;

ji2 e ru chou 疾惡如仇
abhor evils as deadly foes ‖ abhor evils as if they were one's personal enemies; hate evil as much as one hates an enemy; hate injustice like poison; hate the wicked like enemies;

jian1 zha 奸詐
crafty / deceitful ‖ fraudulent; on the crook; treacherous // guile / treachery;

jian zha yin xian 奸詐陰險
deceitful and designing;

jian3 yue 儉約
thrifty and temperate;

jian3 jian 謇謇
faithful / loyal;

jian3 man 簡慢
inhospitable / negligent;

jiang1 shan yi gai, ben xing nan yi 江山易改，本性難移
it is easier to move a mountain than change a man's character || a fox may grow grey but never good; a leopard cannot change its spots; a sow, when washed, returns to the muck; clipping a tiger's claws never makes him lose his taste for blood; it is easy to move rivers and mountains, but difficult to change a person's nature; the wolf may lose its teeth, but never his nature; what is bred in the bone will come out of the flesh; you can change mountains and rivers but not a person's nature; you cannot make a crab walk straight;

jiao1 ao 驕傲
proud || arrogant; big-headed; cock-a-hoop; cock-sure; cocky; conceited; get uppish; get too big for one's breeches; have a big head; pride oneself on; snooty; stuck up; take pride in; too big for one's shoes; uppish; uppity; vain of;

jiao ao bi bai 驕傲必敗
pride will cause a fall;

jiao ao jin kua 驕傲矜誇
haughty and boastful;

jiao ao zi da 驕傲自大
conceited and arrogant || be bloated with pride; be puffed up; be swollen with pride; cocky; feel high and mighty; have a swelled head; get a swelled head; give oneself airs; self-important; stuck-up;

jiao ao zi man 驕傲自滿
arrogant and complacent || be inflated with pride; big with pride; conceit and self-complacency; conceited;

jiao ao zi shi 驕傲自恃
over-confidence and conceit;

jiao heng 驕橫
arrogant and high-handed / high and mighty;

jiao jian 驕蹇
proud and disrespectful;

jiao jin 驕矜
conceited / haughty / proud / self-important;

jiao man 驕慢
arrogant / haughty / supercilious;

jiao qi 驕氣
arrogance / overbearing airs;

jiao she 驕奢
pride and extravagance;

jiao she yin yi 驕奢淫逸
pride, extravagance, lust and self-indulgence;

jiao tai 驕態
haughty manner / overbearing attitude / proud bearing;

jiao xia 驕狎
treat with haughty disrespect;

jiao yi 驕易
treat with disrespect;

jiao ying 驕盈
proud and self-complacent;

jiao zi 驕恣
proud and unruly;

jiao zong 驕縱
proud and unruly;

jiao3 hua 狡猾
artful / crafty / cunning / sly // cunningness;

jie1 shi 結實
strong / sturdy;

jie2 ji 潔己
keep oneself free from immorality;

jie ji feng gong 潔己奉公
clean oneself and perform a duty;

jie lian 潔廉
clean / incorruptible;

jie shen zi ai 潔身自愛
lead an honest and clean life || exercise self-control so as to protect oneself from immorality; keep one's integrity and refuse to swin with the stream; mind one's own business in order to keep out of trouble; preserve one's purity; refuse to be contaminated by evil influence; refuse to soil

one's hands;

jin1 chi 矜持
carry oneself with dignity and reserve / conduct oneself with circumspection;

jin da 矜大
arrogant and exaggerative / proud and bragging;

jin fa 矜伐
arrogant due to one's accomplishments;

jin zhong 矜重
dignified / self-esteem;

ju1 ni 拘泥
be tied down by conventions / go strictly by the book;

ju ni bu tong 拘泥不通
slow-witted, stubborn, and stupid;

ju ni xiao jie 拘泥小節
punctilious;

ju4 倨
arrogant / haughty / rude;

ju ao 倨傲
arrogant / haughty / rude;

jue2 jiang 倔強
obstinate / stubborn;

kan3 侃
frank / open / straightforward;

kan zhi 侃直
resolute and honest;

ke4 ji 克己
overcome one's desires;

ke ji feng gong 克己奉公
put the interest of the public above one's own;

ke qin ke jian 克勤克儉
diligent and frugal;

ke4 ji dai ren 刻己待人
self-sacrificing;

kuan1 hong da liang 寬宏大量
broad-minded / clement / magnanimous // have a large heart;

kuan hou 寬厚
benign / benignant // bengnity;

kuang2 ao 狂傲
improperly domineering / unreasonably haughty;

kuang bao 狂暴
brutal / ferocious / fierce / furious / wild;

kuang bei 狂悖
abandoned / licentious;

kuang dang 狂蕩
debauch / dissipate;

kuang fang 狂放
unrestrained / wild;

kuang luan 狂亂
frantic / frenzied / frenzy / mad / wild;

kuang wang 狂妄
(1) bumptious / crazy / irrational / pretentious / wild // out of one's right mind // hubris;
(2) extremely conceited;

kuang wang wu zhi 狂妄無知
conceited and ignorant;

kuang wang zi da 狂妄自大
arrogant and conceited / pretentious;

kuang zi 狂恣
dissolute / uninhibited / unrestrained;

kuang4 da 曠達
broad-minded / free / unrestrained;

kuang fang 曠放
free and composed;

kuang yi 曠逸
unrestrained;

kuo4 da 闊達
broad-minded;

lao3 shi 老實
honest;

lao shi ba ba 老實巴巴
honest;

lian2 廉
incorrupt;

lian cha 廉察
examine / inspect / investigate;

lian chi 廉耻
incorruptibility and a sense of honour;

身體 *Body*

lian jie 廉節
frugal / thrifty;

lian jie 廉潔
honest / incorrupt // probity;

lian jie 廉介
incorrupt and uncompromising;

lian yu 廉隅
punctilious / scrupulous;

lian zhi 廉直
honest and upright;

lin3 ruo bing shuang 凜若冰霜
cold as ice;

lu3 mang 魯莽
(1) discourteous / disrespectful / ill-mannered / rude / uncivil;
(2) careless / imprudent / rash / reckless;

ma2 fan 麻煩
bother / hassle / trouble // troublesome;

ma mu bu ren 麻木不仁
numbed / paralyzed / unfeeling / unsympathetic;

ming2 wan 冥頑
stubborn;

ming wan bu ling 冥頑不靈
stupid and obstinate;

miu4 li 謬
stubbornly unreasonable;

miu wang 謬罔
absurd and reckless;

nei4 xiang 內向
indrawn / introverted // inwardness;

nei xiang xing ge 內向性格
introverted character / withdrawn personality;

ni4 lai shun shou 逆來順受
accept adversity philosophically / be resigned to one's fate // meek;

ning2 si bu qu 寧死不屈
would rather die than submit;

pin3 品
character / personality;

pin de 品德
personal character;

pin ge 品格
one's moral character;

pin mao 品貌
one's personality and appearance;

pin wei 品味
one's taste;

pin xing 品行
behaviour / one's moral character and performance;

pin xing duan zheng 品行端正
of good character;

pin xue 品學
one's moral character and learning;

ping2 yi jin ren 平易近人
easy to approach / easy to get along with // affable;

pu2 樸
honest / simple / sincere;

pu dun 樸鈍
dull / slow / stupid;

pu hou 樸厚
simple and sincere;

pu pu shi shi 樸樸實實
honest / simple in taste / sincere;

pu ye 樸野
rustic / simple;

pu zhi 樸直
honest / simple-minded;

pu zhi 樸質
unadorned;

pu zhuo 樸拙
simple and naïve;

qi1 ruan pa ying 欺軟怕硬
bully the weak and fear the strong;

qi shan pa e 欺善怕惡
oppress the good and timid and fear the wicked;

qi shang man xia 欺上瞞下
cheat one's superiors and defraud one's subordinates;

qi4 器
(1) magnanimity;

(2) ability / capacity / talent;

qi ju 器局
one's intellectual and moral capacity;

qi liang 器量
magnanimity / tolerance;

qi shi 器識
one's magnanimity and intellectual outlook;

qi yu 器宇
one's physical appearance;

qi yu quan ang 器宇軒昂
of dignified bearing;

qi zhi xing ren ge zhang ai 器質性人格障礙
organic personality disorder;

qian1 謙
humble / modest || retiring; self-effacing; unassuming;

qian bei 謙卑
humble / modest / self-depreciating // humility;

qian bei xun shun 謙卑遜順
humble and retiring;

qian chong 謙沖
modest / unassuming;

qian gong 謙恭
modest and courteous / modest and polite / respectful / unassuming // humility;

qian gong you li 謙恭有禮
modest and polite;

qian guang 謙光
shining modesty;

qian he 謙和
modest and amiable / modest and gentle / modest and good-natured / sauve;

qian ke 謙克
humble and self-controlled;

qian qian jun zi 謙謙君子
a hypocritically modest person / a modest, cautious gentleman;

qian qian you rong 謙謙有容
modest and tolerable;

qian rang 謙讓
modestly decline / modestly yield precedence to others / yield from modesty;

qian shou yi, man zhao sun 謙受益，滿招損
one gains by modesty and loses by pride || benefit goes to the humble, while failure awaits the arrogant; modesty brings benefit while pride leads to loss; the modest receive benefit, while the conceited reap failure;

qian shun 謙順
modest and differential / submissive;

qian tui 謙退
modest and retiring / reserved;

qian xu 謙虛
(1) humble / modest / self-effacing / unassuming // modesty;
(2) make modest remarks;

qian xu jin shen 謙虛謹慎
humble and cautious / modest and prudent;

qian xun 謙遜
humble and unpresumptuous || humble; lowly; modest; unassuming // humility;

qiao4 pi 俏皮
pretty and cute;

qing1 xiang 傾向
proclivity / propensity / tendency;

qing1 bo 輕薄
(1) flippant / frivolous;
(2) insult;

qing cai hao yi 輕財好義
generous and philanthropic;

qing1 di 輕敵
underestimate the enemy;

qing fu 輕浮
flippant / frivolous / giddy / hoity-toity;

qing hu 輕忽
ignore / neglect / slight;

qing jian 輕賤
base / mean;

qing jie 輕捷
agile / nimble;

qing jue wang dong 輕舉妄動
act rashly and blindly;

qing kuai 輕快
(1) agile / brisk / nimble;
(2) light-hearted;

qing kuang 輕狂
flippant / frivolous;

qing man 輕慢
disrespectful / insolent / irreverent;

qing mie 輕蔑
despise / disdain / scorn / slight;

qing shuai 輕率
(1) ignore / make light of / neglect / slight;
(2) careless / harebrained / imprudent / indiscreet / reckless / temerarious // indiscretion / temerity;

qing shuang 輕爽
comfortable / easy / relax;

qing song 輕鬆
(1) lighten / relax;
(2) comfortable / easy / light;

qing tiao 輕佻
flippant / frivolous / hoity-toity;

qing tuo 輕脫
frivolous;

qiu2 fu mian huo 求福免禍
seek happiness and avoid calamity;

qiu ming qiu li 求名求利
seek fame and fortune / seek fame and wealth;

qu1 jie 屈節
compromise one's integrity;

qu ru 屈辱
(1) disgrace / humiliation;
(2) suffer an insult;

qu wang 屈枉
falsely accuse;

qu zun 屈尊
condescension;

qu1 fu quan gui 趨附權貴
a hanger-on of ranking officials;

qu ji bi xiong 趨吉避凶
pursue good fortune and shun the course of calamity;

qu yan fu shi 趨炎附勢
hang on to men of influence;

ren2 ge 人格
personality / personhood;
shuang chong ren ge 雙重人格
double personality / dual personality;

ren2 ge zhang ai 人格障礙
personality disorder;
qi zhi xing ren ge zhang ai 器質性人格障礙
organic personality disorder;

rou2 ruo 柔弱
delicate / namby-pamby / weak;

ru2 ya 儒雅
scholarly and refined;

sa3 luo 灑落
casual and elegant;

sa tuo 灑脫
casual and carefree;

sha3 傻
(1) foolish / stupid;
(2) naïve;

sha he he 傻呵呵
simple-minded;

sha qi 傻氣
silly manners;

shou3 zhen 守真
keep one's original character;

shou zheng bu e 守正不阿
stick to justice despite pressure;

shuai4 xing 率性
(1) one's natural disposition;
(2) act according to the dictates of one's conscience;

shuai xing tian zhen 率性天真
simple and innocent // naivete;

shuai zhen 率真
candid / frank / honest;

shuai zhi 率直
candid / frank / honest / straight;

shuang1 chong ren ge 雙重人格
double personality / dual personality;

si1 si wen wen 斯斯文文
cultured / elegant / gentle / refined;

su4 pu 素樸
plain and simple;

su xing 素性
one's true disposition / one's true temperament;

su ya 素雅
simple but elegant / unadorned and in good taste;

sui2 yu er an 隨遇而安
feel at ease under all circumstances;

tai4 ran 泰然
composed / unperturbed;

tai4 態
(1) attitude / position;
(2) bearing / carriage / manner;

tai du 態度
(1) attitude / position / stand;
(2) manner / way;

tai du ai mei 態度曖昧
ambiguous attitude;

tai du hao 態度好
courteous / elegant / well-behaved / well-mannered;

tai du he ping 態度和平
amicable / friendly // a peaceful attitude;

tai du huai 態度壞
discourteous / ill-mannered / impolite;

tai du leng dan 態度冷淡
cool / indifferent // give sb the cold shoulder / give short shrift to sb;

tai du xian ya 態度嫻雅
have refined manners;

tan3 bai 坦白
candid / frank / honest / straightforword;

tan cheng 坦誠
frank / heart-to-heart / open-hearted / sincere;

tan ran 坦然
fully at ease;

tan ran zi ruo 坦然自若
calm and confident;

tan shuai 坦率
bluff / blunt / frank / straight from the shoulder / straightforword;

tao1 guang 韜光
conceal one's talents;

tao guang yang hui 韜光養晦
conceal one's abilities and bide one's time;

tao hui 韜晦
hide one's true capacities;

tao hui yin ju 韜晦隱居
hide one's light and live in seclusion;

ti4 倜
unrestrained;

ti dang 倜儻
unconventional / untrammeled;

ti dang bu ji 倜儻不羈
unconventional / untrammeled;

tian1 zhen 天真
dewy-eyed / ingenuous / innocent / naïve // ingenuousness / naivete;

tian zhen lan man 天真爛漫
innocent and carefree;

tian zhen wu xie 天真無邪
dewy-eyed / ingenuous / innocent / naïve // ingenuousness;

tian zi 天姿
natural beauty;

tian zi 天資
natural endowments;

tiao1 佻
frivolous / imprudent;

tiao bo 佻薄
frivolous / giddy / not dignified / skittish;

tiao qiao 佻巧
frivolous and tricky;

tiao tuo 佻脱
frivolous and careless;

tiao2 pi 調皮
(1) naughty;
(2) tricky / unruly;

ting1 hua de 聽話的
biddable;

tui2 fang 頹放
cynical / slovenly / unconventional;

tui fei 頹靡
crestfallen / dejected / downcast;

tui fei 頹廢
(1) decadent / ruined;
(2) depressed / low-spirited;

tui ran 頹然
pliant / submissive;

tui sang 頹喪
beaten / discouraged / ruined;

tui sang bu zhen 頹喪不振
dejected after defeat;

wan2 shi bu gong 玩世不恭
take everything lightly;

wan2 dun 頑鈍
dull / foolish / stupid;

wan geng 頑梗
foolishly obstinate / foolishly stubborn / perverse / pigheaded;

wan geng bu hua 頑梗不化
obstinate and unchangeable;

wan gu 頑固
(1) head-strong / obstinate / pertinacious / stubborn // obstinateness / pertinacity;
(2) ultraconservative;

wan kang 頑抗
resist stubbornly;

wan lie 頑劣
stubborn and stupid;

wan pi 頑皮
impish / mischievous / naughty;

wan qiang 頑強
obstinate / pertinacious / stubborn / tenacious;

wei1 wu 威武
awe-inspiring display of military power;

wei wu bu qu 威武不屈
not to be subdued by force;

wei wu xiong zhuang 威武雄壯
full of power and grandeur;

wei3 猥
lewd / licentious / low / vulgar / wanton;

wei bi 猥鄙
base / despicable / mean;

wei jian 猥賤
low and vulgar;

wei lie 猥劣
base / mean;

wei suo 猥瑣
low and petty;

wei xie 猥褻
lewd / obscene // obscenity;

wei xie xing wei 猥褻行為
obscene acts / indecent acts;

wen1 rou 溫柔
warm and tender;

wen rou dun hou 溫柔敦厚
tender and gentle;

wen run 溫潤
beautiful and tender;

wen run ke qin 溫潤可親
lovable and approachable;

wen shun 溫順
tractable;

wen wan 溫婉
gentle / obedient;

wen wen 溫文
genial / gentle and polite / urbane;

wen wen er ya 溫文爾雅
genial / gentle and graceful // gentle mien;

wen ya 溫雅
genial / gentle and graceful;

wen2 jing 文靜
gracefully quiet;

wen mao 文貌
civility / courtesy / politeness;

wen ruo 文弱
effeminate and soldierly;

wen ya 文雅
graceful / polished / refined / suave;

wen zhi bin bin 文質彬彬
elegant and refined in manner;

wo3 xing wo su 我行我素
go one's own gait / go one's way;

wu4 ao 兀傲
proud;

xian2 mei 閑媚
quiet and charming;

xian shu ren ci 閑淑仁慈
reserved, modest and gracious;

xian2 賢
(1) capable / talented;
(2) virtuous / worthy;
(3) admire / esteem / praise;

xian de 賢德
good conduct / virtuous;

xian hui 賢慧
virtuous and intelligent;

xian ming 賢明
capable and virtuous;

xian neng 賢能
talented and virtuous;

xian shu 賢淑
virtuous and understanding;

xian2 嫻
gracious / refined;

xian jing 嫻靜
quiet and refined;

xian ya 嫻雅
cultured / polished / refined;

xian3 e 險惡
devious / diabolic / mean / sinister;

xian jue 險譎
crafty and mean / cunning and vivious;

xian zha 險詐
sinister and crafty / treacherous // treachery;

xiao1 囂
arrogant / haughty / proud;

xiao fu 囂浮
frivolous;

xiao ran 囂然
(1) sad;
(2) hungry;

xiao zhang 囂張
arrogant / bossy / haughty / rampant;

xiao3 qi 小氣
close-fisted / costive / mingy / narrow-minded / niggard / parsimonious / penny-pinching / petty-minded / small-minded / ungenerous // parsimony;

xing4 ge 性格
character / disposition / nature / temperament;

xing ge jian yi 性格堅毅
firm in character // firmness of character;

xing ge nei xiang 性格內向
introvert / withdrawn personality;

xing ge wai xiang 性格外向
extrovert;

xuan1 嬛
frivolous;

xuan bo 嬛薄
frivolous;

xuan4 lu 衒露
show off one's talent;

xuan nong 衒弄
flaunt / show off;

xuan qiao 衒俏
show off one's charms;

xuan yao 衒耀
boast / brag / flaunt / show off;

xuan yi 衒異
show off one's talents;

xuan yi lu cai 衒異露才
show off and expose ability;

xue4 xing 血性
strong sense of righteousness;

yan2 ku 嚴酷
ruthless / severe;

yan yi lü ji, kuang yi dai ren 嚴以律己，寬以待人
be strict with oneself and tolerant with others;

yan zheng 嚴正
solemn;

yi2 訑
assuming / overbearing / self-satisfaction;

yi yi 訑訑
arrogant;

yi2 zhi qi shi 頤指氣使
order about // extremely bossy;

yi4 軼
(1) excel / surpass;
(2) be scattered / go loose;

yi dang 軼蕩
unrestrained;

yi lun 軼倫
outstanding;

yi qun 軼群
excel the rest;

yi4 qun 逸群
head and shoulders above others / outstanding;

yi xiu 逸秀
head and shoulders above others / outstanding;

yi4 毅
(1) firm / resolute;
(2) endurance / fortitude;

yi li 毅力
determination / perseverance / resoluteness;

yi ran 毅然
courageous // firmly;

yi yong 毅勇
firm courage / fortitude;

yi zhi 毅志
ambition / determination;

yin1 chen 陰沈
quiet and designing;

yin xian 陰險
crafty / cunning / deceitful / sinister;

yin yang guai qi 陰陽怪氣
eccentric / queer;

yin zha 陰詐
crafty / cunning / deceitful;

yin1 諲
respect / venerate;

ying1 yong 英勇
brave / courageous / heroic / gallant / valiant / valorous;

ying3 hui 穎慧
bright / clever / intelligent;

ying tuo 穎脫
distinguish oneself in performance;

ying wu 穎悟
unusually intelligent;

ying xiu 穎秀
outstandingly talented;

yong3 勇
bold / brave / fearless / valiant;

yong gan 勇敢
brave / courageous / daring / spunky / valiant;

yong han 勇悍
brave and fierce;

yong meng 勇猛
brave and fierce;

yong qi 勇氣
bravery / courage;

yong wang zhi qian 勇往直前
go straight ahead fearlessly;

you1 rong 優容
treat with magnanimity;

you xian 優閒
carefree;

you yue gan 優越感
a sense of superiority;

yuan2 hua 圓滑
tactful;

zao4 躁
(1) hot-tempered / irritable;
(2) restless / uneasy;

zao dong 躁動
agitation;

zao ji 躁急
impatient / uneasy;

zao jin 躁進
impatient to rise in the world;

zao jing 躁競
eager to grab power from others / impatient to excel others;

zao kuang 躁狂
irritable and unrestrained;

zao kuang fa zuo 躁狂發作
manic episode;

zao kuang zheng 躁狂症
mania;

zao li 躁戾
irritable and cruel;

zao lü 躁率
impatient and careless;

zao nao 躁鬧
cause a disturbance;

zao qie 躁切
anxious / impatient;

zao rao 躁擾
annoy / trouble;

zao tiao 躁佻
frivolous / rash;

zao wang 躁妄
impetuous;

zao yu 躁鬱
manic-depressive;

zao yu zheng 躁鬱症
mania;

zhen1 bai 貞白
chastity / integrity;

zhen gu 貞固
stick to righteousness and virtue;

zhen jie 貞潔
chaste and pure / virtuous;

zhen shu 貞淑
pure and chaste;

zhen1 cheng 真誠
genuine / sincere / true;

zhen4 jing 鎮靜
calm / cool / self-composed // have nerves of iron / have nerves of steel;

zhi2 pi qi 直脾氣
frank / outspoken;

zhi shuai 直率
candid / frank / outspoken / straightforward;

zhi shuang 直爽
forthright / frank / straightforward;

zhi4 zhi 質直
simple and honest / solid and straightforward;

zhong1 deng shen cai 中等身材
of middling height;

zhong1 hou 忠厚
honest and tolerant;

zhong xiao liang quan 忠孝兩全
both loyal to one's country and filial to one's parents;

zhong4 yi qi 重義氣
particular about loyalty to friends;

zhong yi qing li 重義輕利
value justice above material gains;

zhou1 dao 週到
considerate / thoughtful;

zhuan1 heng 專橫
despotic / dictatorial / domineering / high-handed / imperious / tyrannical;

zhuan heng ba hu 專橫跋扈
despotic and imperious;

zhuang1 yan 莊嚴
dignified / solemn;

zhuang zhong 莊重
dignified / sedate / solemn / stately;

zhuo2 拙
poor / stupid;

zhuo ben 拙笨
clumsy / stupid;

zhuo shi 拙實
raw and sturdy;

zhuo xing 拙性
clumsy // stupidity;

zi4 bao zi qi 自暴自棄
abandon oneself to a dissipated life / have no ambition at all / self-abandon // self-abandonment;

zi gan duo luo 自甘墮落
abandon oneself to wanton ways;

zi gao zi da 自高自大
arrogant / conceited / pompous / self-

important // with one's nose in the air;

zi hao 自豪
feel proud of / pride oneself on / take pride in;

zi man 自滿
complacent;

zi ming qing gao 自鳴清高
consider oneself morally superior to others;

zi ming 自命
consider oneself / regard oneself as;

zi ming bu fan 自命不凡
delusions of grandeur / self-glorification / swelled head;

zi qian 自謙
self-debasement;

zi si 自私
selfish // selfishness;

zi si zi li 自私自利
egocentric / selfish;

zong4 lang 縱浪
uninhibited / unrestrained;

zong tuo 縱脱
uninhibited / unrestrained;

zong yi 縱逸
dissolute / uninhibited / unrestrained;

Shen jing 神經 Nerve

ai2 kong bu 癌恐怖
cancerphobia;

ai xing duo shen jing bing 癌性多神經病
carcinomatous polyneuropahty;

an1 shen 安神
calm the nerves / soothe the nerves / steady one's nerves;

bai2 hou xing duo shen jing bing 白喉性多神經病
diphtheritic polyneuropahty;

bai4 xing 敗興
disappointed / disillusioned;

bi4 shen jing 臂神經
brachial nerve;

bian1 yuan xing jing shen fen lie zheng 邊緣性精神分裂症
borderline schizophrenia;

bu4 sui yi shen jing xi tong 不隨意神經系統
involuntary nervous system;

can2 liu xing jing shen fen lie zheng 殘留型精神分裂症
residual schizophrenia;

can liu xing jing shen fen lie zheng 殘留性精神分裂症
residual schizophrenia;

can zhi shen jing tong 殘肢神經痛
stump neuralgia;

can zhi xing shen jing liu 殘肢性神經瘤
stump neroma;

chan3 hou jing shen bing 產後精神病
postpartum psychosis;

chi3 shen jing 尺神經
cubital nerve / ulnar nerve;

chuan1 pi shen jing 穿皮神經
perforating cutaneous nerve;

chuan2 chu shen jing 傳出神經
efferent nerve;

chuan ru shen jing 傳入神經
afferent nerve;

chuang4 shang xing shen jing bing 創傷性神經

病
traumatic neuropathy;

chuang shang xing shen jing liu 創傷性神經瘤
traumatic neuroma;

dan1 chun xing jing shen fen lie zheng 單純型精神分裂症
simple schizophrenia;

dan shen jing bing 單神經病
mononeuropathy;

dan shen jing yan 單神經炎
mononeuritis;

di4 fang xing duo shen jing yan 地方性多神經炎
endemic polyneuritis;

di4 ba nao shen jing 第八腦神經
eighth cranial nerve;

di ba shen jing 第八神經
eight nerve;

di er nao shen jing 第二腦神經
second cranial nerve;

di er shen jing 第二神經
second nerve;

di jiu nao shen jing 第九腦神經
ninth cranial nerve;

di jiu shen jing 第九神經
ninth nerve;

di liu nao shen jing 第六腦神經
sixth cranial nerve;

di liu shen jing 第六神經
sixth nerve;

di qi nao shen jing 第七腦神經
seventh cranial nerve;

di qi shen jing 第七神經
seventh nerve;

di san nao shen jing 第三腦神經
third cranial nerve;

di san shen jing 第三神經
third nerve;

di shi er nao shen jing 第十二腦神經
twelfth cranial nerve;

di shi er shen jing 第十二神經
twelfth nerve;

di shi nao shen jing 第十腦神經
seventh cranial nerve;

di shi shen jing 第十神經
seventh nerve;

di shi yi nao shen jing 第十一腦神經
eleventh cranial nerve;

di shi yi shen jing 第十一神經
eleventh nerve;

di si nao shen jing 第四腦神經
fourth cranial nerve;

di si shen jing 第四神經
fourth nerve;

di wu nao shen jing 第五腦神經
fifth cranial nerve;

di wu shen jing 第五神經
fifth nerve;

di yi nao shen jing 第一腦神經
first cranial nerve;

di yi shen jing 第一神經
first nerve;

dian1 顛
lunatic / mad;

dian dian chi chi 顛顛痴痴
crazy and silly;

dian kuang 顛狂
crazy / lunatic / mad;

ding4 shen 定神
get one's act together;

dong4 yan shen jing 動眼神經
oculomotor nerve;

duo1 fa xing shen jing yan 多發性神經炎
polyneuritis;

duo shen jing bing 多神經病
polyneuropahty;

ai xing duo shen jing bing 癌性多神經病
carcinomatous polyneuropahty;

bai hou xing duo shen jing bing 白喉性多神經病
diphtheritic polyneuropahty;

niao du zheng xing duo shen jing bing 尿

毒症性多神經病
uremic polyneuropathy;
pin xue xing duo shen jing bing 貧血性多神經病
anemic polyneuropathy;
ying yang xing duo shen jing bing 營養性多神經病
nutritional polyneuropathy;

duo shen jing yan 多神經炎
polyneuritis;
di fang xing duo shen jing yan 地方性多神經炎
endemic polyneuritis;
pi fu duo shen jing yan 皮膚多神經炎
dermatopolyneuritis;
pin xue xing duo shen jing yan 貧血性多神經炎
anemic polyneuritis;

fa1 feng 發瘋
go crazy || around the bend; become insane; drive sb crazy; go daft; go mad; go out of one's mind; insane; inside oneself; lose one's mind; lose one's reason; lose one's senses; nutty; off one's butt; off one's head; out of one's head; out of one's mind; round the bend; round the twist; run mad;

fa huang 發慌
feel nervous / get panic || become confused; get flustered;

fa kuang 發狂
become mad / flip out / go crazy / go mad / run mad // delirium;

fa leng 發愣
in a daze / in a trance // stare blankly;

fa shen jing 發神經
go mad;

fan3 ying xing jing shen fen lie zheng 反應性精神分裂症
reactive schizophrenia;

fei2 chang shen jing 腓腸神經
sural nerve;

fei shen jing 腓神經
peroneal nerve;

feng1 瘋
(1) bonkers / crackers // crazy / insane / mad;
(2) spindle;

feng dian 瘋癲
crazy / insane / mad;

feng feng dian dian 瘋瘋顛顛
lunatic || act like a lunatic; as daft as a brush; balmy on the crumpet; barmy on the crumpet; bats; be mentally deranged; behave in a crazy manner; batty; flighty; gesticulate wildly; go gaga; have a bee in one's bonnet; have a screw loose; have a screw missing; have bats in one's belfry; have rats in the garret; off one's crumpet; off one's head; out of one's head; out of one's senses; queer in one's garret; screwy; wrong in one's garret;

feng kuang 瘋狂
(1) insane;
(2) frenzied / unbridled;

fu4 jiao gan shen jing 副交感神經
parasympathetic nerve;

fu shen jing 副神經
accessory nerve;

gan3 jue shen jing 感覺神經
sensory nerve;

gong1 neng xing jing shen bing 功能性精神病
functional psychosis;

gu3 shen jing 股神經
femoral nerve;

guan1 jie shen jing 關節神經
articular nerve;

guan jie shen jing tong 關節神經痛
arthroneuralgia;

hua2 che shen jing 滑車神經
trochlear nerve;

hun2 魂
soul / spirit;

hun bu fu ti 魂不附體
be frightened out of one's wits;

hun fei po san 魂飛魄散
be frightened out of one's senses / be frightened out of one's wits;

hun fei tian wai 魂飛天外
be frightened out of one's senses / be frightened out of one's wits;

hun ling 魂靈
soul / spirit;

hun po 魂魄
soul;

hun xiao 魂銷
bewitched / infatuated / spellbound;

ji3 shen jing 脊神經
the spinal nerve;

ji sui shen jing 脊髓神經
spinal nerve;

jiao1 gan shen jing 交感神經
sympathetic nerve;

jiao4 覺
nap / sleep;

jie2 duan xing shen jing yan 節段性神經炎
segmental neuritis;

jin3 zhang 緊張
be strung up / be tensed up / key up // nervous / tense / strained // tension / tonus;

jin zhang bing 緊張病
nervousness;

jin zhang bu an 緊張不安
fluster;

jin zhang fan she 緊張反射
tonic reflex;

jin zhang guo du 緊張過度
overstressed;

jin zhang zheng 緊張症
catatonia / stress disease;

jin4 xing xing jing shen fen lie zheng 進行性精神分裂症
process schizophrenia;

jing1 兢
(1) fear;
(2) cautious;

jing jing 兢兢
(1) cautious;
(2) strong;

jing jing ye ye 兢兢業業
with caution and fear;

jing1 shen 精神
essence / gist / mind / soul / spirit;

jing shen bao man 精神飽滿
bright-eyed and bushy-tailed / in high spirits / vigorous and energetic;

jing shen beng kui 精神崩潰
mental breakdown / nervous breakdown;

jing shen bing 精神病
mental disease / mental disorder / mental illness / psychosis;

chan hou jing shen bing 產後精神病
postpartum psychosis;

gong neng xing jing shen bing 功能性精神病
functional psychosis;

jiu du xing jing shen bing 酒毒性精神病
alcoholic psychosis;

lao nian qi jing shen bing 老年期精神病
senile psychosis;

lao nian xing jing shen bing 老年性精神病
senile psychosis;

qi zhi xing jing shen bing 器質性精神病
organic psychosis;

qing gan xing jing shen bing 情感性精神病
affective psychosis;

wang xiang xing jing shen bing 妄想性精神病
delusional psychosis;

yuan fa jing shen bing 原發精神病
primary mental disorder;

zhong du xing jing shen bing 中毒性精神病
toxic psychosis;

jing shen bu si 精神不死
the spirit of a heroic person will never die;

jing shen cuo luan 精神錯亂
demented / deranged // over the edge // aberration / amentia / dementia / mental aberration;

jing shen fa xie 精神發泄
abreaction;

yun dong xing jing shen fa xie 運動性精神發泄
motor abreaction;

jing shen fa yu 精神發育
psychogenesis;

jing shen fen lie zheng 精神分裂症
schizophrenia / schizophrenosis;
bian yuan xing jing shen fen lie zheng 邊緣性精神分裂症
borderline schizophrenia;
can liu xing jing shen fen lie zheng 殘留型精神分裂症
residual schizophrenia;
can liu xing jing shen fen lie zheng 殘留性精神分裂症
residual schizophrenia;
dan chun xing jing shen fen lie zheng 單純型精神分裂症
simple schizophrenia;
fan ying xing jing shen fen lie zheng 反應性精神分裂症
reactive schizophrenia;
jin zhang xing jing shen fen lie zheng 緊張性精神分裂症
catatonic schizophrenia / catatonic disorder;
jin xing xing jing shen fen lie zheng 進行性精神分裂症
process schizophrenia;
qing chun qi jing shen fen lie zheng 青春期精神分裂症
hebephrenia;
yin xing jing shen fen lie zheng 隱性精神分裂症
latent schizophrenia;

jing shen gan ran 精神感染
psychic contagion;

jing shen gan ying 精神感應
telepathy;

jing shen gan zhao 精神感召
be moved to emulate an example;

jing shen guan neng zheng 精神官能症
neurosis;

jing shen huang hu 精神恍惚
absent-minded;

jing shen ji huan 精神疾患
mental disorder / mental illness;

jing shen jian quan 精神健全
compos mentis / sanity;

jing shen jin zhang 精神緊張
tension;

jing shen jue shuo 精神矍鑠
hale and hearty / healthy and spry;

jing shen kuang luan 精神狂亂
phrenetic;

jing shen que xian 精神缺陷
incompetence;

jing shen shen jing bing 精神神經病
psychoneurosis;

jing shen sheng huo 精神生活
moral life / spiritual life;

jing shen shi chang 精神失常
psychosis // insane;

jing shen shi tiao 精神失調
psychataxia;

jing shen shi liang 精神食糧
spiritual nourishment;

jing shen shuai ruo 精神衰弱
psychasthenia;

jing shen wen luan 精神紊亂
insane // insanity;

jing shen xing teng tong 精神性疼痛
psychalgia;

jing shen xing teng tong zhang ai 精神性疼痛障礙
psychogenic pain disorder;

jing shen xing tong 精神性痛
algopsychalia;

jing shen xing zi sha 精神性自殺
psychic suicide;

jing shen xing zi dian 精神性紫癜
psychogenic purpura;

jing shen yi yu 精神抑鬱
mental depression;

jing shen zhang ai 精神障礙
mental aberration;
qi zhi xing jing shen zhang ai 器質性精神障礙
organic mental aberration;
wang xiang xing jing shen zhang ai 妄想性精神障礙
delutional disorder;

jing shen zheng chang 精神正常
orthophrenia;

jing shen zhi liao 精神治療
psychotherapy;

jing shen zhuang tai 精神狀態
mental condition;

jing1 dao 驚倒
collapse from fright;

jing dong 驚動
(1) alarm / alert / astonish / startle / stir up;
(2) bother / disturb / trouble;

jing hai 驚駭
frightened / terrified / terror-stricken;

jing hun 驚魂
frightened mind;

jing hun wei ding 驚魂未定
not yet recovered from astonishment;

jing jue 驚厥
(1) faint due to emotional upset / faint from fear;
(2) convulsions;

jing qi 驚奇
be surprised / marvel;

jing rao 驚擾
cause trouble to others / disturb;

jing xia 驚嚇
alarm suddenly / frighten / scare;

jing xing 驚醒
wake up with a start;

jing ya 驚訝
be amazed / be surprised / knock for six / marvel;

jing3 shen jing 頸神經
cervical nerve;

jing4 shen jing 脛神經
tibial nerve;

jiu3 du xing jing shen bing 酒毒性精神病
alcoholic psychoses;

jiu jing xing shen jing bing 酒精性神經病
alcoholic neuropathy;

jiu jing xing shen jing yan 酒精性神經炎
alcoholic nerritis;

jiu jing yi yu zheng 酒精抑鬱症
alcoholic depression;

ju3 sang 沮喪
dejected / despondent / downcast / downhearted / heartsick / low-spirited // dejection // eat one's heart out // in low spirits / out of heart;

jue2 覺
(1) senses;
(2) feel;
(3) conscious of / sense;

jue cha 覺察
aware of / detect / realize / sense;

jue de 覺得
(1) realize / sense;
(2) feel;
(3) think;

jue leng 覺冷
feel cold;

jue re 覺熱
feel hot;

jue tong 覺痛
feel the sensation of pain;

jue xing 覺醒
wake up;

jue yang 覺癢
feel itchy;

kong3 an zheng 恐暗症
scotophobia;

kong bu 恐怖
fear / morbid fear / phobia // spine-chilling;
pu bian xing kong bu 普遍性恐怖
panphobia;

kong bu zheng 恐怖症
phobia;

kong chu zheng 恐觸症
hapephobia;

kong du zheng 恐毒症
fear of poison;

kong fei zheng 恐飛症
fear of flying / flight phobia;

kong gao zheng 恐高症
acrophobia;

kong hong zheng 恐紅症
erythrophobia;

kong huang 恐慌
panic;

kong huang bing 恐慌病
panic disorder;

kong huo zheng 恐火症
pyrophobia;

kong ju 恐懼
horror;

kong kuang zheng 恐曠症
agoraphobia;

kong ma zheng 恐馬症
equinophobia;

kong man zheng 恐蟎症
acarophobia;

kong mao zheng 恐猫症
ailurophobia;

kong qian zheng 恐犬症
cynophobia;

kong sheng zheng 恐聲症
acousticophobia;

kong shi zheng 恐時症
chronophobia;

kong shui zheng 恐水症
aquaphobia;

kong si zheng 恐死症
thanatophobia;

kong suo zheng 恐縮症
koro;

kong tong zheng 恐痛症
algophobia;

kong xue zheng 恐血症
hemophobia;

lao3 nian qi jing shen bing 老年期精神病
senile psychosis;

lao nian xing jing shen bing 老年性精神病
senile psychosis;

lao nian xing shen jing bing 老年性神經病
senile neuropathy;

lei4 jian shen jing 肋間神經
intercostal nerve;

lian4 fu qing jie 戀父情結
Electra complex;

lian ji pi 戀己癖
narcissism;

yuan fa xing lian ji pi 原發性戀己癖
primary narcissism;

lian mu qing jie 戀母情結
Oedipus complex;

lian shi kuang 戀屍狂
necromania;

lian shi pi 戀屍癖
necrophily;

lian shou yu 戀獸慾
zoolagnia;

lian tong pi 戀童癖
pedophilia;

lian wu pi 戀物癖
fetishism;

lian wu zheng 戀物症
fetishism;

luan3 chao shen jing tong 卵巢神經痛
ovariodysneuria;

mei2 du xing shen jing yan 梅毒性神經炎
syphilitic nertitis;

mi2 zou shen jing 迷走神經
vagus;

mi zou shen jing qie chu 迷走神經切除
vagotomy;

mi4 han shen jing 泌汗神經
sudomotor nerves;

mian4 shen jing 面神經
facial nerve;

mian shen jing tong 面神經痛
opalgia;

nao3 shen jing 腦神經
cranial nerve;

di er nao shen jing 第二腦神經
second cranial nerve;

di jiu nao shen jing 第九腦神經
ninth cranial nerve;

di liu nao shen jing 第六腦神經
sixth cranial nerve;

di qi nao shen jing 第七腦神經
seventh cranial nerve;

di san nao shen jing 第三腦神經
third cranial nerve;

di shi er nao shen jing 第十二腦神經
twelfth cranial nerve;

di shi nao shen jing 第十腦神經
seventh cranial nerve;

di shi yi nao shen jing 第十一腦神經
eleventh cranial nerve;

di si nao shen jing 第四腦神經
fourth cranial nerve;

di wu nao shen jing 第五腦神經
fifth cranial nerve;

di yi nao shen jing 第一腦神經
first cranial nerve;

nei4 zang shen jing 內臟神經
splanchnic nerve;

nei zang shen jing jie 內臟神經節
splanchnic ganglion;

niao4 du zheng xing duo shen jing bing 尿毒症性多神經病
uremic polyneuropathy;

nong2 du xing shen jing yan 膿毒性神經炎
septineuritis;

pang2 guang shen jing tong 膀胱神經痛
cystoneuralgia;

pi2 fu duo shen jing yan 皮膚多神經炎
dermatopolyneuritis;

pin2 xue xing duo shen jing bing 貧血性多神經病
anemic polyneuropathy;

pin xue xing duo shen jing yan 貧血性多神經炎
anemic polyneuritis;

pu3 bian xing kong bu 普遍性恐怖
panphobia;

pu tong gan jue shen jing 普通感覺神經
nerve of general sensibility;

qi4 zhi xing jing shen bing 器質性精神病
organic psychosis;

qi zhi xing jing shen zhang ai 器質性精神障礙
organic mental aberration;

qian1 du xing shen jing bing 鉛毒性神經病
lead neuropathy;

qian du xing shen jing yan 鉛毒性神經炎
lead neuritis;

qian zhong du xing shen jing bing 鉛中毒性神經病
lead neuropathy;

qian zhong du xing shen jing yan 鉛中毒性神經炎
lead neuritis;

qian2 ting shen jing 前庭神經
vestibular nerve;

qian ting shen jing jie 前庭神經節
ganglion vestibulare;

qian ting shen jing yan 前庭神經炎
vestibular neritis;

qing1 chun qi jing shen fen lie zheng 青春期精神分裂症
hebephrenia;

qing2 gan xing jing shen bing 情感性精神病
affective psychosis;

que1 xue xing shen jing bing 缺血性神經病
ischemic neuropathy;

rao2 shen jing 橈神經
radial nerve;

san1 cha shen jing 三叉神經
trigeminal nerve;

san cha shen jing jie 三叉神經節
trigeminal ganglion;

san cha shen jing tong 三叉神經痛
trigeminal neuralgia;

she2 shen jing 舌神經
lingual nerve;

she xia shen jing 舌下神經
hypoglossal;

she yan shen jing 舌咽神經
glossopharyngeal nerve;

shen2 hun dian dao 神魂顛倒
be infatuated / moonstruck / moony;

shen jing 神經
nerve;
bi shen jing 臂神經
brachial nerve;
chi shen jing 尺神經
cubital nerve / ulnar nerve;
chuan pi shen jing 穿皮神經
perforating cutaneous nerve;
chuan chu shen jing 傳出神經
efferent nerve;
chuan ru shen jing 傳入神經
afferent nerve;
di er shen jing 第二神經
second nerve;
di jiu shen jing 第九神經
ninth nerve;
di liu shen jing 第六神經
sixth nerve;
di qi shen jing 第七神經
seventh nerve;
di san shen jing 第三神經
third nerve;
di shi er shen jing 第十二神經
twelfth nerve;
di shi shen jing 第十神經
seventh nerve;
di shi yi shen jing 第十一神經
eleventh nerve;
di si shen jing 第四神經
fourth nerve;
di wu shen jing 第五神經
fifth nerve;
di yi shen jing 第一神經
first nerve;
dong yan shen jing 動眼神經
oculomotor nerve;
fei chang shen jing 腓腸神經
sural nerve;
fei shen jing 腓神經
peroneal nerve;
fu jiao gan shen jing 副交感神經
parasympathetic nerve;
fu shen jing 副神經
accessory nerve;
gan jue shen jing 感覺神經
sensory nerve;
gu shen jing 股神經
femoral nerve;
guan jie shen jing 關節神經
articular nerve;
hua che shen jing 滑車神經
trochlear nerve;
ji shen jing 脊神經
the spinal nerve;
ji sui shen jing 脊髓神經
spinal nerve;
jiao gan shen jing 交感神經
sympathetic nerve;
jing shen jing 頸神經
cervical nerve;
jing shen jing 脛神經
tibial nerve;
lei jian shen jing 肋間神經
intercostal nerve;
mi zou shen jing 迷走神經
vagus;
mian shen jing 面神經
facial nerve;
nao shen jing 腦神經
cranial nerve;
nei zang shen jing 內臟神經
splanchnic nerve;
pu tong gan jue shen jing 普通感覺神經
nerve of general sensibility;
qian ting shen jing 前庭神經
vestibular nerve;
rao shen jing 橈神經
radial nerve;
san cha shen jing 三叉神經
trigeminal nerve;
she xia shen jing 舌下神經
hypoglossal;
she yan shen jing 舌咽神經
glossopharyngeal nerve;

shi shen jing 視神經
optic nerve;

ting shen jing 聽神經
auditory nerve / acoustic nerve;

wei shen jing 味神經
nerve of taste;

xiang xin shen jing 向心神經
afferent nerve;

xiong shen jing 胸神經
thoracic nerve;

xiu shen jing 嗅神經
olfactory nerve;

ye shen jing 腋神經
axillary nerve;

yin dao shen jing 陰道神經
vaginal nerve;

ying yang shen jing 營養神經
trophic nerve;

yun dong shen jing 運動神經
motor nerve;

zhan shen jing 展神經
abducent nerve;

zuo gu shen jing 坐骨神經
sciatic nerve;

shen jing beng kui 神經崩潰
nervous breakdown;

shen jing bing 神經病
mental disorder / nervous disease / neuropathy / neurosis // neurotic;

chuang shang xing shen jing bing 創傷性神經病
traumatic neuropathy;

jing shen shen jing bing 精神神經病
psychoneurosis;

jiu jing xing shen jing bing 酒精性神經病
alcoholic neuropathy;

lao nian xing shen jing bing 老年性神經病
senile neuropathy;

qian du xing shen jing bing 鉛毒性神經病
lead neuropathy;

qian zhong du xing shen jing bing 鉛中毒性神經病
lead neuropathy;

que xue xing shen jing bing 缺血性神經病
ischemic neuropathy;

tang niao bing shen jing bing 糖尿病神經病
diabetic neuropathy;

wai shang xing shen jing bing 外傷性神經病
traumatic neuropathy;

ya po xing shen jing bing 壓迫性神經病
compression neuropathy;

ying yang bu liang xing shen jing bing 營養不良性神經病
dystrophoneurosis;

yun dong xing shen jing bing 運動性神經病
kinesioneurosis;

zhong du xing shen jing bing 中毒性神經病
toxic neuropahty;

zhou wei shen jing bing 周圍神經病
peripheral neuropathy;

zhou zhou xing shen jing bing 軸周性神經病
periaxial neuropathy;

shen jing bu zheng chang 神經不正常
nervous disorder // one’s nerves are out of kilter;

shen jing chuang shang 神經創傷
neurotrauma;

shen jing cuo luan 神經錯亂
nervous disorder || beside oneself; blow one’s top; mental disorder; take leave of one’s senses;

shen jing gan 神經幹
nerve trunk;

shen jing gen 神經根
nerve root;

shen jing gen bing 神經根病
radiculopathy;

shen jing gen tong 神經根痛
radiculalgia;

shen jing gong 神經弓
neural arch;

shen jing gou 神經溝
neural groove;

神經 *Nerve*

shen jing guan neng zheng 神經官能症
neurosis;

shen jing guo min 神經過敏
nervous irritability ‖ have a fit of nerves; jimjams; jumpy; neurotic; oversensitive; react nervously; thin-skinned; too nervous;

shen jing ji neng bing 神經機能病
nerosis;

shen jing jian cha 神經檢查
neurological examination;

shen jing jie 神經節
ganglion;
qian ting shen jing jie 前庭神經節
ganglion vestibulare;
san cha shen jing jie 三叉神經節
trigeminal ganglion;
shen shang shen jing jie 腎上神經節
suprapenal ganglion;
shen shen jing jie 腎神經節
ganglia renalia;
ting shen jing jie 聽神經節
auditory ganglion;

shen jing jin zhang 神經緊張
nervous ‖ be a bag of nerves; be a bundle of nerves; be all nerves; get on sb's nerves; one's nerves are high-strung; one's nerves are on edge; set sb's nerves on edge;

shen jing liu 神經瘤
nerve tumour / neuroma;
can zhi xing shen jing liu 殘肢性神經瘤
stump neuroma;
chuang shang xing shen jing liu 創傷性神經瘤
traumatic neuroma;
ting shen jing liu 聽神經瘤
acoustic nerve tumour;
zhen xing shen jing liu 真性神經瘤
true neuroma;

shen jing mo shao 神經末梢
nerve endings;

shen jing ruan hua 神經軟化
neuromalacia;

shen jing shi chang 神經失常
nervous breakdown // mentally deranged // have bats in one's belfry;

shen jing shuai ruo 神經衰弱
nervous breakdown / nervous debility / nervous prostration ‖ neurasthenia; panasthenia;

shen jing tong 神經痛
neuralgia;
can zhi shen jing tong 殘肢神經痛
stump neuralgia;
guan jie shen jing tong 關節神經痛
arthroneuralgia;
luan chao shen jing tong 卵巢神經痛
ovariodysneuria;
pang guang shen jing tong 膀胱神經痛
cystoneuralgia;
pian tou tong xing shen jing tong 偏頭痛性神經痛
migrainous neuralgia;
te fa xing shen jing tong 特發性神經痛
idiopathic neuralgia;
zhou wei shen jing tong 周圍神經痛
peripheral neuralgia;
zu shen jing tong 足神經痛
pododynia;

shen jing xi bao 神經細胞
nerve cell;

shen jing xi tong 神經系統
nervous system;
bu sui yi shen jing xi tong 不隨意神經系統
involuntary nervous system;
zhong shu shen jing xi tong 中樞神經系統
central nervous system;
zhou wei shen jing xi tong 周圍神經系統
peripheral nervous system;

shen jing xing fen 神經興奮
nerve impulse;

shen jing yan 神經炎
neuritis;
duo fa xing shen jing yan 多發性神經炎
polyneuritis;
jie duan xing shen jing yan 節段性神經炎
segmental neuritis;
jiu jing xing shen jing yan 酒精性神經炎
alcoholic nerritis;

mei du xing shen jing yan 梅毒性神經炎
syphilitic nertitis;
nong du xing shen jing yan 膿毒性神經炎
septineuritis;
qian du xing shen jing yan 鉛毒性神經炎
lead neuritis;
qian zhong du xing shen jing yan 鉛中毒性神經炎
lead neuritis;
qian ting shen jing yan 前庭神經炎
vestibular neritis;
yin shi xing shen jing yan 飲食性神經炎
dietetic neuritis;
you zou xing shen jing yan 游走性神經炎
migrating neuritis;
zhong du xing shen jing yan 中毒性神經炎
toxic neuritis;
zhou wei shen jing yan 周圍神經炎
peripheral neuritis;
zhou zhou xing shen jing yan 軸周性神經炎
periaxial neuritis;
zuo gu shen jing yan 坐骨神經炎
sciatic neuritis;

shen jing zheng 神經症
neurosis;
shi yan xing shen jing zheng 實驗性神經症
experimental neurosis;
yi bing xing shen jing zheng 疑病性神經症
hypochondriacal neurosis;
zhen xing shen jing zheng 真性神經症
actual neurosis;

shen jing zhi 神經質
nervosity / nervous temperament;

shen jing zhong shu 神經中樞
nerve centre;

shen4 shang shen jing jie 腎上神經節
suprapenal ganglion;

shi2 yan xing shen jing zheng 實驗性神經症
experimental neurosis;

shi4 shen jing 視神經
optic nerve;

shi shen jing que sun 視神經缺損
coloboma of optic nerve;

tang2 niao bing shen jing bing 糖尿病神經病
diabetic neuropathy;

te4 fa xing shen jing tong 特發性神經痛
idiopathic neuralgia;

ting1 shen jing 聽神經
acoustic nerve / auditory nerve;

ting shen jing jie 聽神經節
auditory ganglion;

ting shen jing liu 聽神經瘤
acoustic nerve tumour;

tun2 shang pi shen jing 臀上皮神經
superior cluneal nerve;

tun shang shen jing 臀上神經
superior gluteal nerve;

tun shen jing 臀神經
gluteal nerves;

tun xia pi shen jing 臀下皮神經
inferior cluneal nerve;

tun xia shen jing 臀下神經
inferior gluteal nerve;

tun zhong pi shen jing 臀中皮神經
middle cluneal nerve;

tun zhong shen jing 臀中神經
middle gluteal nerve;

wai4 er dao shen jing 外耳道神經
nerve of external acoustic meatus;

wai shang xing shen jing bing 外傷性神經病
traumatic neuropathy;

wang4 xiang xing jing shen bing 妄想性精神病
delusional psychosis;

wang xiang xing jing shen zhang ai 妄想性精神障礙
delutional disorder;

wei4 shen jing 味神經
nerve of taste;

wu1 jing da cai 無精打彩
lackadaisical // lassitude;

xiang4 xin shen jing 向心神經
afferent nerve;

xiong1 shen jing 胸神經
thoracic nerve;

xiu4 shen jing 嗅神經
olfactory nerve;

ya1 po xing shen jing bing 壓迫性神經病
compression neuropathy;

yan3 魘
nightmare;

yan mei 魘魅
kill by magic / kill by witchcraft;

yang3 shen 養神
have mental relaxation;

ye4 shen jing 腋神經
axillary nerve;

yi2 bing xing shen jing zheng 疑病性神經症
hypochondriacal neurosis;

yi4 yu zheng 抑鬱症
depression;

yin1 bu shen jing 陰部神經
pudendal nerve;

yin bu shen jing he 陰部神經核
nucleus of pudendal nerve;

yin dao shen jing 陰道神經
vaginal nerve;

yin3 shi xing shen jing yan 飲食性神經炎
dietetic neuritis;

yin3 xing jing shen fen lie zheng 隱性精神分裂症
latent schizophrenia;

ying2 yang bu liang xing shen jing bing 營養不良性神經病
dystrophoneurosis;

ying yang shen jing 營養神經
trophic nerve;

ying yang xing duo shen jing bing 營養性多神經病
nutritional polyneuropathy;

you1 bi kong bu zheng 幽閉恐怖症
claustrophobia;

you2 zou xing shen jing yan 游走性神經炎
migrating neuritis;

yuan2 fa jing shen bing 原發精神病
primary mental disorder;

yuan fa xing lian ji pi 原發性戀己癖
primary narcissism;

yun1 暈
(1) faint;
(2) giddy and dizzy;

yun dao 暈倒
faint and fall / swoon;

yun guo qu 暈過去
faint / pass out;

yun jue 暈厥
faint / syncope;

yun4 dong shen jing 運動神經
motor nerve;

yun dong shen jing bing 運動神經病
motor neuropathy;

yun dong shen jing gen 運動神經根
motor nerve root;

yun dong xing jing shen fa xie 運動性精神發泄
motor abreaction;

yun dong xing shen jing bing 運動性神經病
kinesioneurosis;

zhan3 shen jing 展神經
abducent nerve;

zhen1 xing shen jing liu 真性神經瘤
true neuroma;

zhen xing shen jing zheng 真性神經症
actual neurosis;

zhong1 shu shen jing xi tong 中樞神經系統
central nervous system;

zhong4 du xing jing shen bing 中毒性精神病
toxic psychosis;

zhong du xing shen jing bing 中毒性神經病
toxic neuropahty;

zhong du xing shen jing yan 中毒性神經炎
toxic neuritis;

zhou1 wei shen jing bing 周圍神經病
peripheral neuropathy;

zhou wei shen jing xi tong 周圍神經系統
peripheral nervous system;

zhou wei shen jing yan 周圍神經炎
peripheral neuritis;

zhou2 zhou xing shen jing bing 軸周性神經病
periaxial neuropathy;

zhou zhou xing shen jing yan 軸周性神經炎
periaxial neuritis;

zu2 shen jing tong 足神經痛
pododynia;

zuo4 gu shen jing 坐骨神經
sciatic nerve;

zuo gu shen jing tong 坐骨神經痛
sciatic nerve pain / sciatica;

zuo gu shen jing yan 坐骨神經炎
sciatic neuritis;

Shen 腎 Kidney

bian4 xing shen yan 變性腎炎
degenerative nephritis;

bu3 shen zhuang yang 補腎壯陽
invigorate the kidney and strengthen maculinity;

chong1 xue shen 充血腎
congested kidney;

chu1 xue xing shen bing shen yan 出血性腎病腎炎
hemorrhagic nephrosonephritis;

diao1 gan zhuo shen 雕肝琢腎
exhaust physical and mental energy;

du2 xing shen bing 毒性腎病
toxic nephrosis;

e4 xing shen ying hua 惡性腎硬化
malignant nephroscerosis;

fan3 liu xing shen bing 返流性腎病
reflux nephropathy;

fu2 you shen zheng 浮游腎症
floating kidney;

hou4 qi shen 後期腎
metanephros;

hou shen 後腎
hind-kidney;

hou shen guan 後腎管
metanephric duct;

huai4 si xing shen bing 壞死性腎病
necrotizing nephrosis;

ji2 xing shen bing 急性腎病
acute nephrosis;

ji xing shen shuai jie 急性腎衰竭
acute renal failure;

ji xing shen yan 急性腎炎
acute nephritis;

ji xing shen yan zong he zheng 急性腎炎綜合症
acute nephritic syndrome;

ji xing shen yu shen yan 急性腎盂腎炎
acute pyelonephritis;

ji4 fa xing shen jie shi 繼發性腎結石
secondary renal calculus;

ji fa xing shen shang xian gong neng bu quan 繼發性腎上腺功能不全
secondary adrenal insufficiency;

jie2 shi xing shen yan 結石性腎炎
lithonephritis;

jie shi xing shen yu yan 結石性腎盂炎
calcipyelitis;

kong1 pao xing shen bing 空泡性腎病
vacuolar nephrosis;

kong pao yang shen bing 空泡樣腎病
hydropic nephrosis;

lang2 chuang shen xiao qiu shen yan 狼瘡腎小球腎炎
lupus glomerulonephritis;

lang chuang shen yan 狼瘡腎炎
lupus nephritis;

lao3 nian xing shen ying hua 老年性腎硬化
senile nephrosclerosis;

liang2 xing shen ying hua 良性腎硬化
benign nephroscerosis;

liu2 xing xing shen bing 流行性腎病
epidemic nephrosis;

man4 xing niao suan shen bing 慢性尿酸腎病
chronic uric acid nephropathy;

man xing shen bing 慢性腎病
chronic nephrosis;

man xing shen shang xian pi zhi ji neng jian tui zheng 慢性腎上腺皮質機能減退症
Addison's disease;

man xing shen shuai jie 慢性腎衰竭
chronic renal failure;

man xing shen xiao qiu shen yan 慢性腎小球腎炎
chronic glomerulonephritis;

mei2 du xing shen yan 梅毒性腎炎
syphilitic nephritis;

mei2 jun xing shen bing 霉菌性腎病
mycotic nephrosis;

mo2 xing shen bing 膜性腎病
membranous nephropathy;

mo xing shen xiao qiu shen yan 膜性腎小球腎炎
membranous glomerulonephritis;

nang2 xing shen yan 囊性腎炎
capsular nephritis;

nang xing shen yu yan 囊性腎盂炎
pyelitis cystica;

niao4 suan shen bing 尿酸腎病
uric acid nephropathy;

man xing niao suan shen bing 慢性尿酸腎病
chronic uric acid nephropathy;

nong2 shen 膿腎
pyonephrosis;

nong xing shen ji shui 膿性腎積水
pyohydronephrosis;

nong xing shen yan 膿性腎炎
pyonephritis;

pan2 zhuang shen 盤狀腎
disk kidney;

pang2 guang shen yu shen yan 膀胱腎盂腎炎
cystopyelonephritis;

pang guang shen yu yan 膀胱腎盂炎
cystopyelitis;

qi4 xing shen yu shen yan 氣性腎盂腎炎
emphysematous pyelonephritis;

qian1 du xing shen yan 鉛毒性腎炎
saturnine nephritis;

qian2 qi shen 前期腎
pronephros;

qian shen 前腎
forekidney;

qing1 lian xing shen bing 輕鏈型腎病
light-chain nephropathy;

que1 xue xing shen bing 缺血性腎病
ischemic nephropathy;

ren4 shen qi shen yan 妊娠期腎炎
nephritis of pregnancy;

ren shen qi shen yu yan 妊娠期腎盂炎
pyelitis gravidarum;

ren shen shen yu yan 妊娠腎盂炎
encyopyelitis;

ren shen xing shen yu shen yan 妊娠性腎盂腎炎
pyelonephritis of pregnancy;

rou4 ya zhong xing shen yu yan 肉芽腫性腎盂炎
pyelitis granulosa;

shen4 腎
(1) kidney;
(2) testicles;
chong xue shen 充血腎
congested kidney;
hou qi shen 後期腎
metanephros;
hou shen 後腎
hind-kidney;
nong shen 膿腎
pyonephrosis;
pan zhuang shen 盤狀腎
disk kidney;
qian qi shen 前期腎
pronephros;
qian shen 前腎
forekidney;
xi shen 洗腎
dialysis;

shen bian ying 腎變硬
nephrosclerosis;

shen bing 腎病
kidney disease;
du xing shen bing 毒性腎病
toxic nephrosis;
fan liu xing shen bing 返流性腎病
reflux nephropathy;
huai si xing shen bing 壞死性腎病
necrotizing nephrosis;
ji xing shen bing 急性腎病
acute nephrosis;
kong pao xing shen bing 空泡性腎病
vacuolar nephrosis;
kong pao yang shen bing 空泡樣腎病
hydropic nephrosis;
liu xing xing shen bing 流行性腎病
epidemic nephrosis;
man xing shen bing 慢性腎病
chronic nephrosis;
mei jun xing shen bing 霉菌性腎病
mycotic nephrosis;
mo xing shen bing 膜性腎病
membranous nephropathy;
niao suan shen bing 尿酸腎病
uric acid nephropathy;
qing lian xing shen bing 輕鏈型腎病
light-chain nephropathy;
que xue xing shen bing 缺血性腎病
ischemic nephropathy;
shen xiao qiu shen bing 腎小球腎病
glomerulonephropathy;
shen yu shen bing 腎盂腎病
pyelonephrosis;
tang niao bing shen bing 糖尿病腎病
diabetic nephropathy;
tong feng shen bing 痛風腎病
gouty nephropathy;
tong feng xing shen bing 痛風性腎病
gouty nephropathy;
yin xing shen bing 隱性腎病
larval nephrosis;
zhi xing shen bing 脂性腎病
lipid nephrosis;
zhong mo qi shen bing 終末期腎病
end-stage renal disease;
zhong du xing shen bing 中毒性腎病
toxic nephrosis;

shen bing bian 腎病變
nephropathy;
shen tou xing shen bing bian 滲透性腎病變
osmotic nephrosis;
zhi xing shen bing bian 脂性腎病變
liponephrosis;

shen bing shen yan 腎病腎炎
nephrosonephritis;
chu xue xing shen bing shen yan 出血性腎病腎炎
hemorrhagic nephrosonephritis;

shen chong xue 腎充血
nephrohemia;

shen chu xue 腎出血
nephrorrhagia;

shen dong mai 腎動脈
renal artery;

shen fa yu bu liang 腎發育不良
renal dysplasia;

shen fa yu bu quan 腎發育不全
renal dysplasia;

shen fei da 腎肥大
nephromegaly;

shen gong neng bu quan 腎功能不全
renal insufficiency;

shen guan bi 腎關閉
renal shutdown;

shen ji shui 腎積水
hydronephrosis;

nong xing shen ji shui 膿性腎積水
pyohydronephrosis;

shen jie he 腎結核
renal tuberculosis;

shen jie shi 腎結石
renal calculus ‖ calculus renalis; kidney stone; nephrolithus;

ji fa xing shen jie shi 繼發性腎結石
secondary renal calculus;

yuan fa xing shen jie shi 原發性腎結石
primary renal calculus;

shen jie shi bing 腎結石病
lithiasis;

shen jie shi yan 腎結石炎
nephrolithiasis;

shen kong 腎孔
nephrostoma;

shen kou 腎口
nephrostoma;

shen kui 腎虧
asthenia of kidney;

shen kui yang 腎潰瘍
nephrelcosis;

shen kuo zhang 腎擴張
nephrectasia;

shen liu 腎瘤
kidney tumour / nephroma;

shen men 腎門
hilum of kidney;

shen nang 腎囊
capsulae renis;

shen nong zhong 腎膿腫
kidney abscess;

shen pang guang yan 腎膀胱炎
nephrocystitis;

shen po lie 腎破裂
kidney fracture;

shen qie chu 腎切除
nephrectomy;

shen ruan hua 腎軟化
nephromalcia;

shen shan 腎疝
nephrocele;

shen shang xian 腎上腺
adrenal gland;

shen shang xian gong neng bu quan 腎上腺功能不全
adrenal insufficiency;

ji fa xing shen shang xian gong neng bu quan 繼發性腎上腺功能不全
secondary adrenal insufficiency;

shen shang xian su 腎上腺素
adrenaline;

shen shen jing jie 腎神經節
ganglia renalia;

shen shi 腎石
kidney stone;

shen shi qie chu 腎石切除
nephrolithotomy;

shen shuai jie 腎衰竭
renal failure;

ji xing shen shuai jie 急性腎衰竭
acute renal failure;

man xing shen shuai jie 慢性腎衰竭
chronic renal failure;

shen tong 腎痛
nephralgia;

shen xia chui 腎下垂
nephroptosia;

shen xiao nang 腎小囊
renal capsule;

shen xiao qiu 腎小球
glomerules;

shen xiao qiu bing 腎小球病
glomerulopathy;

tang niao bing xing shen xiao qiu bing 糖尿病性腎小球病
diabetic glomerulopathy;

wei xian xing shen xiao qiu bing 萎陷性腎小球病
collapsing glomerulopathy;

shen xiao qiu shang pi 腎小球上皮
glomerular epithelium;

shen xiao qiu shen bing 腎小球腎病
glomerulonephropathy;

shen xiao qiu shen yan 腎小球腎炎
glomerulonephritis;

lang chuang shen xiao qiu shen yan 狼瘡腎小球腎炎
lupus glomerulonephritis;

man xing shen xiao qiu shen yan 慢性腎小球腎炎
chronic glomerulonephritis;

mo xing shen xiao qiu shen yan 膜性腎小球腎炎
membranous glomerulonephritis;

shen xiao qiu yan 腎小球炎
glomerulitis;

shen xiao qiu ying hua 腎小球硬化
glomerulosclerosis;

tang niao bing xing shen xiao qiu ying hua 糖尿病性腎小球硬化
diabetic glomerulosclerosis;

shen xu yang wei 腎虛陽痿
impotence due to kidney asthenia;

shen yan 腎炎
nephritis;

bian xing shen yan 變性腎炎
degenerative nephritis;

chu xue xing shen yan 出血性腎炎
hemorrhagic nephritis;

ji xing shen yan 急性腎炎
acute nephritis;

jie shi xing shen yan 結石性腎炎
lithonephritis;

lang chuang shen yan 狼瘡腎炎
lupus nephritis;

mei du xing shen yan 梅毒性腎炎
syphilitic nephritis;

nang xing shen yan 囊性腎炎
capsular nephritis;

nong xing shen yan 膿性腎炎
pyonephritis;

qian du xing shen yan 鉛毒性腎炎
saturnine nephritis;

ren shen qi shen yan 妊娠期腎炎
nephritis of pregnancy;

shen chu xing shen yan 滲出性腎炎
exudative nphritis;

shi zhi xing shen yan 實質性腎炎
parenchymatous nephritis;

shu xue xing shen yan 輸血性腎炎
transfusion nephritis;

shui zhong xing shen yan 水腫性腎炎
dropsical nephritis;

tong xing shen yan 痛性腎炎
nephritis dolorosa;

xi jun xing shen yan 細菌性腎炎
bacterial nephritis;

xing hong re shen yan 猩紅熱腎炎
scarlatinal nephritis;

ying jie xing shen yan 硬結性腎炎
indurative nephritis;

zeng sheng xing shen yan 增生性腎炎
productive nephritis;

shen yan zong he zheng 腎炎綜合症
nephritic syndrome;

ji xing shen yan zong he zheng 急性腎炎綜合症
acute nephritic syndrome;

shen ying hua 腎硬化
nephroscerosis;

e xing shen ying hua 惡性腎硬化
malignant nephroscerosis;

lao nian xing shen ying hua 老年性腎硬化
senile nephrosclerosis;

liang xing shen ying hua 良性腎硬化
benign nephroscerosis;
xiao dong mai xing shen ying hua 小動脈性腎硬化
arteriolar nephrosclerosis;

shen yu 腎盂
pelvis of ureter;

shen yu bing 腎盂病
pyelopathy;

shen yu ji shui 腎盂積水
nephrydrosis;

shen yu shen bing 腎盂腎病
pyelonephrosis;

shen yu shen yan 腎盂腎炎
nephropyelitis;
ji xing shen yu shen yan 急性腎盂腎炎
acute pyelonephritis;
pang guang shen yu shen yan 膀胱腎盂腎炎
cystopyelonephritis;
qi xing shen yu shen yan 氣性腎盂腎炎
emphysematous pyelonephritis;
ren shen xing shen yu shen yan 妊娠性腎盂腎炎
pyelonephritis of pregnancy;

shen yu yan 腎盂炎
pyelitis;
jie jia xing shen yu yan 結痂性腎盂炎
encrusted pyelitis;
jie shi xing shen yu yan 結石性腎盂炎
calcipyelitis;
nang xing shen yu yan 囊性腎盂炎
pyelitis cystica;
pang guang shen yu yan 膀胱腎盂炎
cystopyelitis;
ren shen qi shen yu yan 妊娠期腎盂炎
pyelitis gravidarum;
ren shen shen yu yan 妊娠腎盂炎
encyopyelitis;
rou ya zhong xing shen yu yan 肉芽腫性腎盂炎
pyelitis granulosa;
xian xing shen yu yan 腺性腎盂炎
pyelitis glandularis;

shen zang 腎臟
kidney;

shen zang bing 腎臟病
kidney disease;

shen zang jie shi 腎臟結石
kidney stone;

shen zang yan 腎臟炎
nephritis;

shen4 chu xing shen yan 滲出性腎炎
exudative nphritis;

shen tou xing shen bing bian 滲透性腎病變
osmotic nephrosis;

shi2 zhi xing shen yan 實質性腎炎
parenchymatous nephritis;

shu1 xue xing shen yan 輸血性腎炎
transfusion nephritis;

shui3 zhong xing shen yan 水腫性腎炎
dropsical nephritis;

tang2 niao bing shen bing 糖尿病腎病
diabetic nephropathy;

tang niao bing xing shen xiao qiu bing 糖尿病性腎小球病
diabetic glomerulopathy;

tang niao bing xing shen xiao qiu ying hua 糖尿病性腎小球硬化
diabetic glomerulosclerosis;

tong4 feng shen bing 痛風腎病
gouty nephropathy;

tong feng xing shen bing 痛風性腎病
gouty nephropathy;

tong xing shen yan 痛性腎炎
nephritis dolorosa;

tou2 shen 頭腎
head kidney;

tuan2 kuai shen 團塊腎
lump kidney;

wei3 suo shen 萎縮腎
atrophic kidney;

wei xian xing shen xiao qiu bing 萎陷性腎小球病
collapsing glomerulopathy;

xi3 shen 洗腎
dialysis;

xi4 jun xing shen yan 細菌性腎炎
bacterial nephritis;

xian4 xing shen yu yan 腺性腎盂炎
pyelitis glandularis;

xiao3 dong mai xing shen ying hua 小動脈性腎硬化
arteriolar nephrosclerosis;

xing1 hong re shen yan 猩紅熱腎炎
scarlatinal nephritis;

yin3 xing shen bing 隱性腎病
larval nephrosis;

ying4 jie xing shen yan 硬結性腎炎
indurative nephritis;

you2 zou shen 游走腎
hypermobile kidney;

yuan2 fa xing shen jie shi 原發性腎結石
primary renal calculus;

yuan shen 原腎
protonephron;

zeng1 sheng xing shen yan 增生性腎炎
productive nephritis;

zhi1 fang shen 脂肪腎
fatty kidney;

zhi xing shen bing 脂性腎病
lipid nephrosis;

zhong1 qi shen 中期腎
mesonephros;

zhong shen 中腎
middle kidney;

zhong shen liu 中腎瘤
mesonephroma;

zhong1 mo qi shen bing 終末期腎病
end-stage renal disease;

zhong4 du xing shen bing 中毒性腎病
toxic nephrosis;

Shou 手 Hand

ai2 yi dun quan tou 挨一頓拳頭
be punched / get a punch;

ai yi quan 挨一拳
get a punch / have it;

ai zou 挨揍
take a beating;

ai4 bu shi shou 愛不釋手
be so fond of sth that one cannot take one's hands off it / be too fond of sth as not to let go of it / love sth so much that one cannot bear to part with it / love sth so much that one is loathe to part with it;

ai4 shou 礙手
hindrance // in the way;

ai shou ai jiao 礙手礙腳
hinder the movement of sb's hand and feet / stand in the way // drag / nuisance // cumbersome;

ai shou jiao 礙手腳
hinder the movement of sb's hand and feet / stand in the way // drag / nuisance // cumbersome;

an1 fang 安放
place safely / put in a proper manner;

an4 按
(1) press down ‖ depress; place the hand on; press; press with one's hand; push; push down; ring;
(2) put aside ‖ lay by; leave aside; push aside; put away; repress; set aside; shelve;
(3) keep a tight grip on / keep one's hand on;

an jian 按劍
grasp one's sword;

an mai 按脈
feel the pulse / take the pulse;

an mo 按摩
massage;
kong qi an mo 空氣按摩
pneumatic massage;

an xia qu 按下去
press down;

an ya 按壓
press;

an zhu 按住
press down and not to let go;

ao3 拗
bend or twist so as to break;

ao duan 拗斷
break into two / break off / snap;

ao hua zhi 拗花枝
pluck a flowery branch;

ao sui 拗碎
break in pieces;

ao wan 拗彎
twist;

ao zhe 拗折
break by twisting;

ba1 zhang 巴掌
hand / palm;

ba1 扒
(1) claw ‖ strip off; take off;
(2) climb / scale;
(3) dig up ‖ dig; pull down; rake;
(4) hold on to ‖ catch hold of; cling to;
(5) pull down ‖ demolish; tear down;

ba de gao die de zhong 扒得高跌得重
the higher one climbs, the harder one falls;

ba la 扒拉
(1) push lightly;
(2) remove;

ba pi 扒皮
skin / strip off the skin;

ba zhu 扒住
cling to / hold on to;

ba2 拔
(1) pull out ‖ pull up; remove; uproot;
(2) draw ‖ suck out;
(3) destroy ‖ eradicate; smash up;
(4) pick ‖ choose; select;
(5) lift / raise;
(6) attack and take / capture / seize;
(7) cool sth in water;

ba cao 拔草
pull up weeds / weed;

ba cao yin she － zi tao ku chi 拔草引蛇——自討苦吃
plucking weeds to stir the snakes － suffer from one's own actions;

ba chu 拔出
draw out / extract / pull out;

ba chu 拔除
pull out / weed out ‖ eradicate; pluck; remove; uproot; wipe out;

ba chu za cao 拔除雜草
weed out the rank grass;

ba dao xiang xiang 拔刀相向
draw one's sword against / draw upon sb / pull a knife on sb;

ba dao xiang zhu 拔刀相助
draw a sword and render help ‖ help another for the sake of justice; take up the cudgels against an injustice;

ba ding zi 拔釘子
pull out nails;

ba gen 拔根
uproot;

ba jian 拔劍
draw a sword / whip out a sword;

ba jian zi wen 拔劍自刎
draw one's sword to slay oneself;

ba mao 拔錨
haul in an anchor / weigh anchor;

ba qu 拔取
choose / draw off / select;

ba shen 拔身
escape;

ba3 把
(1) grasp / hold / hold in hand / take hold of;
(2) carry / handle;

ba jiu 把酒
raise one's wine up ‖ drink; fill a wine cup for sb; hold a wineglass;

ba jiu jie feng 把酒接風
pour out the wine of welcome;

ba jiu xiao chou 把酒消愁
drown one's worries in drink / take to drinking to forget one's sorrows;

ba jiu yan huan 把酒言歡
take up the wine cup and chat merrily — union of friends;

ba juan 把卷
hold a book in one's hand to read;

ba shou 把手
hold hands;

ba wan 把玩
fondle / hold and play with;

ba zhan 把盞
hold up in hand;

ba zhuo 把捉
(1) grasp;
(2) assess;

ba4 bi 罷筆
stop writing;

ba shou 罷手
give up || discontinue an action; pause; stay one's hand; stop;

bai1 掰
break off with the hands;

bai kai 掰開
pull apart with hands;

bai wan zi 掰腕子
hand wrestling;

bai2 shou 白手
empty-handed // with bare hands;

bai shou xing jia 白手興家
become rich from scratch / start empty-handed || build up from nothing; build up one's fortune from scratch; from rags to riches; lift oneself by one's own bootstraps; rise from poverty; rise in life by one's own efforts; run up from a shoestring; self-made; start from scratch; start on a shoestring;

bai3 捭
(1) open / spread out;
(2) strike with both hands;

bai3 擺
(1) arrange / display / place / put / set...in order;
(2) wave;

bai bu kai 擺不開
there is no room to place it;

bai chu lai 擺出來
(1) take out for display;
(2) assume / put on;

bai dong 擺動
flicker / sway / swing;

bai fan 擺飯
lay the table for a meal;

bai shou 擺手
wave one's hand;

bai fan 擺飯
lay the table for a meal;

bai fang 擺放
lay || deposit; leave; place; put;

bai hao 擺好
place properly / set properly;

bai kai 擺開
place in order;

bai lie 擺列
display in neat rows / place in order;

bai nong 擺弄
(1) fiddle with / play with / toy with;
(2) make fun of / trick;
(3) manipulate / order about;

bai qi 擺齊
place in neat order;

bai shang 擺上
put up;

bai shou 擺手
swing one's arms / wave one's hand;

bai xia 擺下
(1) put down;
(2) arrange;

bai zhuo zi 擺桌子
set the table;

ban1 扳
pull / switch / turn;

ban kai 扳開
pull open;

ban1 nong 搬弄
move by hand;

ban4 拌
mix / mix and stir;

ban he 拌和
mix and stir;

ban yun 拌勻
mix evenly;

bang1 shou 幫手
give a hand / help / lend a hand;

bang3 綁
tie || bind; bind sb's hands behind him; fasten; tie up;

bang fu 綁縛
bind / tie up / truss up;

bang qi lai 綁起來
tie up;

bang za 綁紮
(1) bind up / wrap up;
(2) bundle up / pack / tie up;

bao1 包
wrap;

bao za 包紮
pack || bind up; dress; pack up; wrap up;

bao3 yi lao quan 飽以老拳
strike sb hard with the fist || dust sb's jacket; give sb a proper pummelling; give sb a sound beating; give sb bellyfuls of fisticuffs; hit sb full in the face; whale away at sb with both fists;

bao4 抱
carry in the arms / hold in the arms || embrace; hug; take in the arms;

bao quan 抱拳
salute with hands folded and raised in front of one's face;

bao quan zhi li 抱拳致禮
salute with hands folded and raised in front of one's face;

bei4 zhe shou 背着手
with one's hands clasped behind one's back;

ben4 shou ben jiao 笨手笨腳
all thumbs // clumsy || acting clumsily; awkward; be all fingers and thumbs; bungle; cach-handed; have a hand like a foot; heavy-handed; one is awkward with one's hands;

bi3 比
gesticulate / gesture / hand gesture;

bi bi hua hua 比比劃劃
gesticulate as one talks // with lively gesticulations;

bi hua 比劃
(1) gesticulate / gesture;
(2) come to blows;

bi shou hua jiao 比手劃腳
make lively gestures / talk with the help of gestures;

bian1 鞭
flog / lash / whip;

bian chi 鞭笞
flog / lash;

bian chu 鞭楚
flagellate / flog / whip;

bian da 鞭打
flagellate / flog / lash / thrash / whip;

bian ta 鞭撻
castigate / lash;

bian3 ping shou 扁平手
flat hand / manus plana;

bian4 抃
applaud / cheer / clap one's hands;

bian wu 抃舞
cheer and dance / dance for joy / make merry;

bian yue 抃悅
cheer / clap one's hands for joy;

bian yong 抃踊
cheer and dance;

bian zhang 抃掌
clap one's hands;

bin4 擯
discard / expel / get rid of / oust / reject;

bin chu 擯除
dispense with / eliminate / expel / oust;

bin qi 擯棄
cast away / discard / relinquish / set away;

bing4 zhi 併指
losyndactyly;
ju bing zhi 巨併指
megalosyndactyly;

bo1 剝
peel / shell / skin / strip;

bo de jing guang 剝得精光
strip bare / strip to the skin;

bo kai 剝開
strip the covering off;

bo qu 剝去
strip / take off;

bo1 撥
(1) poke / stir / tune in / turn;
(2) allocate / appropriate / set aside;

bo biao 撥錶
set the watch;

bo chong 撥充
appropriate sth for;

bo chu 撥出
(1) dial-out;
(2) appropriate;

bo dian hua 撥電話
dial the telephone;

bo fa 撥發
allocate / appropriate for / issue to;

bo fu 撥付
appropriate / make payment;

bo gei 撥給
appropriate;

bo huo 撥火
poke a fire;

bo jiao 撥交
appropriate / issue to;

bo kai 撥開
push aside;

bo nong 撥弄
(1) fiddle with / toy with;
(2) move to and fro;
(3) pluck;

bo xian 撥絃
pluck the strings;

bo2 搏
(1) pounce on;
(2) arrest / catch / grasp / seize;
(3) box / strike;

bo ji 搏擊
fight with hands / strike;

bo4 擘
(1) thumb;
(2) break / tear apart;

bo hua 擘畫
make arrangements for / plan / scheme;

bo kai 擘開
break off / break open / open;

bo lie 擘裂
cleave / hew apart / rend apart / split;

bo zhang 擘張
draw a bow;

bu4 kan yi ji 不堪一擊
cannot withstand a single blow;

ca1 擦
(1) chafe / rub / rub away / scrape;
(2) scour / wipe / wipe away;
(3) apply / paint / put on / spread on;
(4) brush / mop / polish / shave;
(5) scrape into shreds;
(6) pass along quickly;

ca chu 擦除
abrade / scrape off;

ca diao 擦掉
erase / rub off / rub out / wipe out;

ca gan 擦乾
dry / swab up / wipe dry;

ca liang 擦亮
shine;

ca qu 擦去
wipe off;

ca shi 擦拭
clean / cleanse / scrub / wipe;

ca sun 擦損
be damaged by friction or rubbing;

ca xi 擦洗
rinse / scrub;

ca you 擦油
apply pomade / coat with oil / oil / polish;

ca zao 擦澡
take a sponge bath / rub oneself down with a wet towel;

ca zhi mo fen 擦脂抹粉
paint rouge and power;

cai3 採
gather / pick / pluck;

cai ji 採集
collect / gather;

cai qu 採取
adopt / assume / resort to / take;

cai qu xing dong 採取行動
take action;

cai qu zhu dong 採取主動
take the initiative;

cai xuan 採選
pick / select;

cai yong 採用
adopt / apply / take and use / use;

cai ze 採擇
pick / select;

cai zhai 採摘
select and pick;

cai zhi 採製
collect and process;

cang1 bai zhi 蒼白指
white finger;

cao1 操
grasp / hold;

cao lao 操勞
look after / take care;

cao zuo 操作
manipulate / operate;

cha1 shou 叉手
fold hands in salute;

cha shou gong li 叉手拱立
stand forking one's hands together;

cha1 插
insert / put in / stick into;

cha dui 插隊
jump the queue / nip in the queue // queue-jump / queue-jumping;

cha jin 插進
thrust into ‖ dip; interject; let in; stick in; work in;

cha ru 插入
plug in ‖ break in; dig; implant; infix; inlay; insert; intercalate; interpose; intervene; run in;

cha shang yi shou 插上一手
get one's finger into the pie / have a hand in / poke one's nose into;

cha shou 插手
(1) lend a hand / take part;
(2) meddle in ‖ get into the act; have a hand in; poke one's nose into;

cha shou qi jian 插手其間
have a hand in / meddle in / place oneself in;

cha2 搽
apply / put sth on the skin;

cha fen 搽粉
powder;

cha yao 搽藥
rub on some external medicine;

cha you 搽油
apply ointment;

cha zhi mo fen 搽脂抹粉
apply cosmetics ‖ paint and powder one's face; paint and powder oneself; rub on the rouge and daub the paint;

chai1 拆
open / take apart / tear open;

chai chu 拆除
dismantle and get rid of;

chai huai 拆壞
damage / destroy;

chai hui 拆毀
damage / demolish / destroy;

chan1 攙
(1) support sb with one's hand;

(2) mingle / mix;
(3) add;

chan fu 攙扶
support sb with one's hand;

chan he 攙合
blend / mingle / mix;

chan qi 攙起
help sb stand up by giving him a hand;

chan za 攙雜
mingle / mix;

chan2 fu 纏縛
bind / wrap;

chan guo 纏裹
cover tightly / wrap up;

chan shou 纏手
hard to deal with // troublesome;

chan zhu 纏住
wind around / wrap tightly;

chan3 剷
(1) shovel;
(2) level off / raze to the ground / shovel;

chan chu 剷除
eradicate / root out;

chan ping 剷平
level / level to the ground;

chan3 鏟
scoop / shovel;

chan chu 鏟除
clear off / eliminate / uproot;

chao1 抄
(1) copy / transcribe;
(2) plagiarize;

chao na 抄拿
grab / seize;

chao xi 抄襲
copy off / plagiarize;

chao xie 抄寫
copy / transcribe;

che3 扯
(1) tear;
(2) drag / pull;
(3) lump;

che bu dong 扯不動
cannot be torn / cannot tear;

che che la la 扯扯拉拉
pull and push;

che po 扯破
tear to pieces / tear to shreds;

che tuo 扯脱
break loose;

che zhu 扯住
grasp firmly;

che2 撦
tear;

che po 撦破
tear open;

che4 掣
(1) pull / tug;
(2) draw;
(3) snatch away;

chen1 抻
(1) lengthen / stretch;
(2) drag out / draw out;

chen chang 抻長
lengthen;

cheng2 棖
touch;

cheng bo 棖撥
push aside with hand;

cheng chu 棖觸
(1) touch sth, moving it slightly;
(2) move sb / stir up sb's feelings;

chi2 持
(1) grasp / hold;
(2) keep / maintain;

chi bi 持筆
hold the pen;

chi dao 持刀
hold a knife;

chi you 持有
hold;

chi4 shou kong quan 赤手空拳
bare-handed || have only empty hands; unarmed; with bare hands; with naked fists;

chou1 抽
(1) take out;
(2) obtain by drawing;
(3) lash / thrash / whip;

chou da 抽打
lash / whip // lashing;

chou qian 抽簽
draw lots || ballot; cast lots; draw cuts;

chou4 da 臭打
sound beating / sound thrashing;

chou zou 臭揍
sound beating / sound thrashing;

chu1 shou 出手
spend money;

chu shou kuo chuo 出手闊綽
free-handed;

chu4 mo 觸摸
touch || contact; feel; fumble; grope; put one's hand on; stroke;

chuai1 揣
(1) conceal sth in the bosom;
(2) hold and support;

chuai zai huai li 揣在懷裏
hold in the bosom;

chuan2 傳
pass / pass on;

chui2 shou 垂手
(1) obtain sth with hands down / within easy reach;
(2) let the hands hang by the sides / stand with one's hands hanging by the sides;

chui shou er li 垂手而立
stand with one's hands hanging by the sides / stand with the hands down;

chui shou ke de 垂手可得
get sth without lifting a finger || acquire a thing easily; acquire sth with a wet finger; at one's fingertips; easy to come by; easy to win; win sth with hands down; within easy reach;

chui2 捶
beat / pound / thump;

chui bei 捶背
pound sb's back;

chui chuang dao zhen 捶牀搗枕
beat wildly with one's fists on the bed and the pillows;

chui da 捶打
beat / thump;

chui gu 捶鼓
beat a drum;

chui ji 捶擊
thrash / thump;

chui le yi xia 捶了一下
give sb a thump;

chui ping 捶平
flatten by pounding;

chui zhuo pai yi 捶桌拍椅
pound the table and slap the chair;

chui2 椎
beat / hammer / hit / strike;

chui2 搥
beat / pound / strike with a fist / strike with a stick;

chuo1 戳
(1) jab / poke / stab;
(2) blunt / sprain;
(3) erect / stand sth on end;
(4) back up / support;

chuo chuan 戳穿
(1) pierce through / puncture;
(2) explode / expose / lay bare;

chuo shang 戳傷
stab / stab wound;

chuo4 醊
pour wine in a libation;

cou4 shou 凑手
at hand / within easy reach;

cu1 shou ben jiao 粗手笨腳
clumsy || awkward; maladroit; with a heavy hand;

cuan1 攛
(1) fling / throw;
(2) persuade / urge;
(3) do in a hurry;

cuan duo 攛掇
egg on / induce / persuade / urge;

cuan gan 攛趕
hurry;

cuan nong 攛弄
induce / persuade / urge;

cuan2 攢
assemble / bring together / collect / gather;

cui4 jia zheng 脆甲症
fragilitas unguium;

cuo1 搓
(1) twist;
(2) rub / rub with the hands / scrub;

cuo ban er 搓板兒
flat-chested girl / skinny person;

cuo ma jiang 搓麻將
play mahjong;

cuo nong 搓弄
rub with the hands;

cuo rou 搓揉
knead / rub;

cuo shou 搓手
(1) rub one's hands together;
(2) wring one's hands (in despair or disappointment);
(3) wash one's hands with invisible soap and imperceptible water;

cuo shou dun jiao 搓手頓腳
rub one's hands and stamp one's feet in exasperation / wring one's hands and stamp one's feet;

cuo shou qu nuan 搓手取暖
rub one's hands together to warm them;

cuo sui 搓碎
rub into bits;

cuo zuo yi tuan 搓作一團
roll into a ball;

cuo1 撮
(1) take with fingers;
(2) bring together / gather;
(3) gather up / scoop up;
(4) extract / summarize;

cuo tu 撮土
scoop up rubbish with a dustbin;

cuo tu wei xiang 撮土為香
burn incense in the dust in memory of;

cuo4 措
(1) place;
(2) arrange / collect / handle;
(3) abandon / renounce;
(4) make plans;

cuo shou 措手
deal with / manage;

cuo shou bu ji 措手不及
be caught unprepared ‖ at a loss; attack before sb knows it; be caught unawared; be taken by surprise; cannot make an adequate defence; catch sb napping; catch sb on the wrong foot; catch sb with his pants down; have sb over the barrel; make a surprise attack on sb; put sb off his guard; spring a surprise on sb; take sb napping; throw sb off his guard; too late to do anything about it;

cuo zhi 措置
arrange / execute / manage;

cuo zhi de dang 措置得當
be handled properly;

cuo zhi shi dang 措置失當
mismanage;

da1 搭
carry / lift sth up;

da ba shou 搭把手
lend me a hand;

da shou 搭手
help sb / render sb a service;

da3 打
(1) attack / beat / fight;
(2) break / smash;
(3) hit / knock / strike;
(4) build / construct;
(5) forge / make;

(6) beat / mix / stir;
(7) pack / tie up;

da ba 打靶
target practice;

da bai 打敗
(1) beat / defeat / worst;
(2) be defeated / suffer a defeat;

da bai zhang 打敗仗
be defeated in battle / suffer a defeat;

da bao 打包
pack;

da bu kai 打不開
cannot be opened;

da bu huan shou 打不還手
not to strike back when attacked;

da bu si 打不死
try in vain to beat to death;

da bu tong 打不通
the line is engaged;

da cha 打叉
cross;

da de ban si 打得半死
beat sb half dead / beat sb until they are half dead / beat sb within an inch of their life / beat to a mummy;

da de luo hua liu shui 打得落花流水
beat sb into fits || beat sb to sticks; blow into smithereens; break into smithereens; cut to ribbons; dash into smithereens; inflict telling blows; knock into smithereens; knock sb into fits; knock the stuffing out of; rout; shatter to pieces; smash to smithereens; smite hip and thigh; sweep every bit into the dust;

da de pi kai rou zhan 打得皮開肉綻
be beaten till one's flesh is laid bare / be bruised and lacerated;

da de si qu huo lai 打得死去活來
beat sb to a frazzle / beat within an inch of his life;

da de tou po xue liu 打得頭破血流
beat sb black and blue || badly battered; badly trounced; maul and cut up;

da gou 打鈎
tick;

da gou kan zhu ren 打狗看主人
in beating a dog you must consider who is the owner || in beating a dog regard must be paid to the status of its master;

da gou qi zhu 打狗欺主
to beat the dog is to bully its owner / to humiliate the protected is to humiliate the protector;

da gu 打鼓
(1) beat a drum;
(2) feel nervous / feel uncertain;

da huo jie 打活結
tie a fast knot;

da huo 打火
strike a light;

da kai 打開
(1) open / unfold / untie / unwrap;
(2) switch on / turn on;
(3) break through;
(4) broaden / open up / spread / widen;

da ma 打罵
beat and scold;

da pai zi 打拍子
beat time;

da pai 打牌
(1) play cards;
(2) play mahjong;
(3) (mahjong) discard a tile;

da pi gu 打屁股
beat on the buttocks / get punished / receive punishment / spank;

da po 打破
break;

da pu ke 打撲克
(1) play poker;
(2) play cards;

da pu gai 打鋪蓋
set up a bed;

da qiang 打槍
fire with a pistol;

da qiao pai 打橋牌
play a bridge game;

da quan 打拳
box || practise boxing; shadow boxing;

da san 打傘
hold an umbrella;

da shou shi 打手勢
gesticulate / make a gesture;

da sui 打碎
smash || batter; break into pieces; pound;

da zi 打字
type / typewrite;

da4 mu zhi 大拇指
thumb;

da shou da jiao 大手大腳
extravagant;

da zhi 大指
thumb;

dai4 ren zhuo dao 代人捉刀
ghostwrite for others / write sth for sb else;

dan1 chun zhi jia fei da 單純指甲肥大
hyperonychia;

dang3 擋
block / get in the way of / impede / obstruct / resist / stop / ward off;

dang bu zhu 擋不住
incapable of blocking;

dang feng 擋風
keep off the wind;

dang zhu 擋住
block / hinder / impede / obstruct;

dao3 搗
beat / pound;

dao hui 搗毀
destroy / smash;

dao lan 搗爛
pound sth until it becomes pulp;

dao sui 搗碎
pound to pieces;

dao3 擣
(1) beat / pound;
(2) attack;
(3) disturb / harass;

dao gui 擣鬼
do mischief / play tricks;

dao luan 擣亂
disturb sb / make trouble;

dao xu 擣虛
launch a surprise attack;

dao4 shou 到手
come into one's hands;

dao4 cha 倒茶
fill the cup with tea / pour tea;

dao bei shou 倒背手
with one's hands behind one;

di1 提
hold / take in hand;

di liu 提溜
hold / take in hand;

di2 滌
(1) cleanse / wash;
(2) sweep;

di chu 滌除
do away with / eliminate / wash away;

di chu xia hui 滌除瑕穢
purge away the stains;

di dang 滌蕩
cleanse / get rid of / wash away / wipe out;

di dang wu yu 滌蕩無餘
rinse off without leaving a remainder;

di lü xi xin 滌慮洗心
sweep away anxieties and wash the heart;

di xia dang hui 滌瑕蕩穢
get rid of the stains / remove the flaw and wash away the dirt;

di4 er wan gu 第二腕骨
second carpal bone;

di er zhi 第二指
second finger;

di4 遞
(1) give / hand over / pass;
(2) in the proper order / successively;

di cha jing yan 遞茶敬煙
serve tea and offer cigarettes to guests;

di jiao 遞交
deliver / hand over / present / submit;

di jin 遞進
go forward one by one;

di song 遞送
deliver / send;

dian1 掂
weigh in the hand;

dian liang 掂量
weigh in the hand;

dian suan 掂算
consider / estimate / ponder / weigh;

diao4 掉
(1) turn / turn around;
(2) come off / drop / fall / shed;
(3) lose / miss;
(4) change / swap;
(5) drop behind / fall behind / lag behind;
(6) move / shake / wag;

diao dong 掉動
(1) move / stir;
(2) change / exchange;

diao guo lai 掉過來
turn around;

diao huan 掉換
change / exchange / invert / substitute;

diao xia lai 掉下來
fall down;

diao zhuan 掉轉
turn around / turn back;

diu1 丟
(1) cast away / throw;
(2) put aside;

diu bu kai shou 丟不開手
cannot keep one's hands off;

diu diao 丟掉
cast away / throw away;

diu kai 丟開
throw away;

diu qu 丟去
cast away;

diu shou 丟手
give up / wash one's hands of;

diu xia 丟下
throw down;

dong4 bi 動筆
start writing;

dong shou 動手
(1) get to work / start work;
(2) handle / touch;

dong shou dong jiao 動手動腳
(1) take liberties with sb || fresh with a girl; get fresh with sb; let one's hand and foot take too great liberties;
(2) make motions to start a fight / put out hand and foot to fight;

dong zhe da ma 動輒打罵
beat sb and swear at him on the least pretext;

du2 da 毒打
beat cruelly / beat savagely / beat sb up;

duan3 zhi 短指
brachydactyly;

duo1 shou 多手
like to try one's hand at things;

duo4 剁
chop / mash / mince;

duo rou 剁肉
mash meat / mince meat;

duo sui 剁碎
mash / mince;

e2 shou 額手
raise the hand to the forehead;

e shou cheng qing 額手稱慶
congratulate each other by raising the hand to the brow || overjoyed; place one's hands over one's forehead in jubilation; praise oneself on one's luck; salute each other in a gesture of greeting; thank one's lucky stars;

e4 扼
(1) control / repress / restrain;
(2) clutch / grasp / grip;

e wan 扼腕
seize one's wrist;

en4 摁
(1) press;
(2) delay / hold;

er4 mu zhi 二拇指
the index finger;

fan1 shou wei yun fu shou wei yu 翻手為雲，覆手為雨
play fast and loose || blow hot and cold; change and change about; chop and change;

fan3 shou 反手
backhand;

fan zhang 反掌
a turn of one's hand;

fang4 bu xia shou 放不下手
cannot stop doing sth;

fang kai 放開
let go / lose hold of / quit hold of / relieve from restrictions / remove restrictions / set free // free from rein;

fang kai shou jiao 放開手腳
have one's hands and feet unfettered;

fang ping 放平
(1) put sth flat on the ground;
(2) knock sb down;

fang shou 放手
(1) let go / loosen the grasp / loosen the hold;
(2) give up;
(3) have a free hand;

fang shou fang jiao 放手放腳
with hands and feet unfettered;

fang shou qu zuo 放手去做
do sth with a free hand;

fang xia 放下
lay down / put down;

fang xia tu dao 放下屠刀
lay down the butcher's knife – repent and reform;

fang xia tu dao, li di cheng fo 放下屠刀，立地成佛
a wrongdoer may become a man of virtue once he does good;

fang zhi 放置
lay aside / lay up / place;

fei2 hou zhi 肥厚指
blubber finger;

fei4 shou jiao 費手腳
take much time and energy || take much handwork and footwork; take much physical labour;

fen1 shou 分手
break up || be separated; drift apart; part; part company; say goodbye to; separate; split up with sb;

fu2 拂
(1) stroke;
(2) flick / whisk;
(3) go against;

fu chen 拂塵
shake off dust;

fu chu 拂除
brush off / wipe off;

fu qu 拂去
flick away / flip / whisk;

fu shi 拂拭
whisk off / wipe off;

fu xiu 拂袖
shake one's sleeve;

fu xiu er qu 拂袖而去
leave in displeasure;

fu2 縛
bind / tie;

fu jin 縛緊
tie or bind tightly;

fu shou fu jiao 縛手縛腳
unable to act freely / with too many constraints;

fu3 拊
(1) pat / touch with hand lightly;
(2) slap / tap;

fu zhang 拊掌
clap hands;

fu3 撫
(1) comfort / console;

(2) foster / nurture;
(3) stroke;

fu ai 撫愛
fondle ‖ caress; cop a feel on sb; fondle sb sexually; touch sb sexually;

fu mo 撫摸
stroke;

fu nong 撫弄
fondle / stroke;

fu zhang 撫掌
clap one's hands;

fu zhang da xiao 撫掌大笑
clap one's hands and laugh aloud / laugh loud and clap one's hands;

fu4 shou 覆手
turn one's palm;

gao1 tai gui shou 高抬貴手
will you do me a favour;

ge1 割
cut / sever;

ge1 擱
(1) lay / leave / put;
(2) file / keep;
(3) delay / put aside / shelve;

ge bu xia 擱不下
unable to forget / unable to lay down;

ge bu zhu 擱不住
(1) not fit to be kept long;
(2) cannot stand;

ge de xia 擱得下
capable of putting aside / capable of putting down;

ge qi 擱起
delay / hold up;

ge zhi 擱置
shelve;

gong3 拱
(1) fold hands across one's chest;
(2) encircle with one's hands;

gong bao 拱抱
encircle sth or sb with two arms;

gong bie 拱別
bid farewell by holding one's hands together in an up-and-down motion;

gong shou 拱手
(1) fold one's hands in a bow;
(2) submissively;

gong shou cheng xie 拱手稱謝
join one's hands together in salute and thank;

gong shou chu rang 拱手出讓
give away sth to sb with both hands;

gong shou er bie 拱手而別
bid farewell in a respectful manner / take leave by saluting with both hands folded and raised in front;

gong shou rang ren 拱手讓人
give up sth to others without putting up a fight ‖ give away sth to sb with both hands; hand over sth on a silver platter; hand over with a bow; surrender sth submissively;

gong shou zhi li 拱手致禮
salute with joined hands / salute with the handed folded;

gu1 zhang nan ming 孤掌難鳴
cannot clap with one hand ‖ a single palm cannot clap; alone and helpless; it is difficult to accomplish sth without the help of others; those who stand alone have no power;

gu3 zhang 鼓掌
applaud / clap one's hands;

gu zhang he cai 鼓掌喝彩
applaud with the hands / clap the hands in applause;

gu zhang huan hu 鼓掌歡呼
clap one's hands and cheer / rejoice over;

gua4 掛
hang / hang up / suspend;

gua bu xia 掛不下
there is no room to hang it;

gua bu zhu 掛不住
cannot be hung;

gua ming 掛名
in name / nominally;

guan4 摜
fling down / throw to the ground;

guan chu 摜出
throw off;

guan4 盥
(1) wash hands;
(2) wash;

guan xi 盥洗
wash one's hands and face;

guang1 shou 光手
bare-handed;

guo2 摑
slap another on his face;

guo4 shou 過手
handle;

han4 撼
joggle / jolt / rock / shake;

han dong 撼動
rock / shake;

han dun 撼頓
shake / stagger / totter;

han luo 撼落
shake down;

han yao 撼搖
joggle / jolt / rock / shake;

he1 shou 呵手
breathe on one's hands to warm them;

he2 shi 合十
put the palms together;

he shi qian cheng 合十虔誠
put one's hands together in prayer;

hong1 shou 烘手
warm hands by the fire;

hua1 quan 花拳
exhibition boxing;

hua quan xiu tui 花拳繡腿
fancy boxing;

hua2 quan 划拳
play the finger-guessing game;

hua4 劃
draw;

huan1 bian 歡忭
clap hands as a result of joy;

huan2 shou 還手
hit back / strike back;

huan4 換
alter / change / substitute;

huan qu 換取
change / exchange;

huan shang 換上
change into / make changes / substitute;

huan ti 換替
(1) alternately / by turns;
(2) replace;

huang1 le shou jiao 慌了手腳
be thrown into a panic ‖ be greatly alarmed; be seized with a panic; be thrown off one's balance; become panicky;

huang shou huang jiao 慌手慌腳
in a great flurry;

hui1 zhi jia 灰指甲
leuconychia;

hui1 揮
(1) brandish / flick / shake / wave / wield;
(2) wipe away;
(3) scatter / sprinkle;
(4) swing;

hui dao 揮刀
brandish a sword;

hui dong 揮動
wield sth;

hui huo 揮霍
fritter away one's money / splurge on // improvident / prodigal / spendthrift;

hui huo wu du 揮霍無度
abuse money without limit;

hui quan 揮拳
swing fists;

hui shou 揮手
wave / wave one's hand;

hui shou gao bie 揮手告別
wave goodbye to sb ‖ wave away; wave farewell; wave off; wave one's hand to bid sb

farewell; wave one's hands on departure;

hui shou zhi yi 揮手致意
wave greetings to / wave to sb in acknowledgement;

hui wu 揮舞
brandish / wave / wield;

hui2 jing yi quan 回敬一拳
return a blow;

hui shou 回手
return a blow for a blow;

huo2 quan 豁拳
finger-guessing game;

huo4 擭
catch / seize;

ji2 shou 棘手
knotty / troublesome // a hard nut to crack / a tough egg to crack;

ji2 擊
(1) beat / hit / strike;
(2) assault / attack;

ji dao 擊倒
knock down;

ji jie 擊節
beat time;

ji jie zan shang 擊節讚賞
clap and applaud / clap one's hands in admiration / clap the hands in applause;

ji shang 擊賞
show appreciation by clapping hands;

ji sui 擊碎
knock to pieces / smash to pieces;

ji zhang 擊掌
clap hands;

ji zhong tong chu 擊中痛處
hit sb on a tender place / hit sb squarely in a sore spot / hit sb to the quick;

ji zhong yao hai 擊中要害
hit sb's vital point ‖ come home; cut to the quick; get home; go home; have hit at the nub of; hit close to home; hit home; hit sb where it hurts; hit the point; shoot home; strike at the root of; strike home; touch sb's tender spot;

ji3 掎
drag / draw aside / pull;

jia3 shou 假手
do sth by means of an agent;

jia shou ta ren 假手他人
do sth by another hand;

jia shou yu ren 假手於人
make sb else do the work ‖ make a cat's paw of sb; put into another's hand; use the hand of;

jian3 剪
cut / trim;

jian zhi jia 剪指甲
trim one's nails;

jian3 揀
(1) choose / pick / select;
(2) pick up;

jian bie 揀別
distinguish;

jian chu 揀出
pick out;

jian dao pian yi 揀到便宜
get the better of a bargain;

jian fei tiao shou 揀肥挑瘦
very choosy;

jian xuan 揀選
choose / pick / select;

jian ze 揀擇
choose / select;

jian3 撿
collect / gather / pick up;

jian qi lai 撿起來
pick up;

jiao1 交
hand in / hand over;

jiao cha shuang shou 交叉雙手
fold one's hands;

jiao chu 交出
hand over / surrender;

jiao shou 交手
exchange blows;

jiao3 撟
put right / set right;

jiao3 攪
(1) stir / mix;
(2) agitate / annoy / disturb;

jiao ban 攪拌
mix / stir;

jiao dong 攪動
churn / mix / stir;

jiao he 攪和
(1) mix evenly by stirring to mingle;
(2) confuse / mix up;

jie1 接
(1) connect;
(2) take over;
(3) answer / receive;

jie bu shang 接不上
(1) cannot be connected;
(2) cannot catch up with;

jie bu zhu 接不住
cannot catch it;

jie dao 接到
receive;

jie he 接合
assemble / connect;

jie shou 接受
accept;

jie tong 接通
put through;

jie zhu 接住
catch;

jie1 揭
(1) lift off / lift up / raise high;
(2) expose / take off / tear off / uncover / unearth / unveil;

jie chuan 揭穿
expose / lay bare / show up / unmask;

jie fa 揭發
bring to light / expose / lay open / peach against sb / reveal / take the lid off;

jie kai 揭開
(1) pull apart;
(2) open / uncover;

jie po 揭破
expose / uncover;

jie ren shang ba 揭人傷疤
turn the knife in the wound / twist the knife;

jie3 nang 解囊
open one's purse to help sb generously with money;

jin3 wo 緊握
clasp / grasp firmly / take a tight hold of sth // hold fast;

jin zhua 緊抓
clutch firmly / grasp firmly / hold on to;

jin4 zai shou bian 近在手邊
close at hand;

jing1 shou 經手
attend a matter personally / deal with / handle;

jing1 shen xing shi xie zheng 精神性失寫症
mental agraphia;

jiu1 揪
(1) clutch / grab / grasp with one's hand / hold fast / seize;
(2) drag / pull;
(3) pick on;

jiu chu 揪出
ferret out / uncover;

jiu niu 揪扭
grapple / seize by hand;

jiu zhu 揪住
seize with force;

ju1 掬
hold in both hands;

ju shui 掬水
scoop up with water with the hands;

ju3 舉
hold up / lift / raise;

ju bei 舉杯
lift the cup;

ju shou 舉手
raise one's hand;

ju shou biao jue 舉手表決
take a vote by a show of hands / vote by a show of hands / vote by raising hands // show of hands;

ju shou da ren 舉手打人
raise one's hand to a person;

ju shou fa shi 舉手發誓
hold up one's hand and pledge;

ju shou ke de 舉手可得
within one's grasp;

ju shou tou xiang 舉手投降
raise one's arms in surrender;

ju shou xuan shi 舉手宣誓
hold up one's hand and take a solemn oath;

ju shou zan cheng 舉手贊成
approve sth with a show of hands;

ju shou zhi lao 舉手之勞
lift a finger;

ju4 bing zhi 巨併指
megalosyndactyly;

ju shou 巨手
cheiromegaly;

ju zhi 巨指
macrodactyly;

ju zhi jia 巨指甲
megalonychia;

juan3 捲
(1) roll up;
(2) curl hair;

juan qi 捲起
roll up;

jue2 抉
(1) choose / pick / select;
(2) dig / gouge;

jue ti 抉剔
choose / pick out / select;

jue ze 抉擇
choose;

jue2 掘
dig / excavate;

jue chuan 掘穿
dig through;

jue dong 掘洞
dig a hole;

jue jin 掘金
dig for gold;

jue jing 掘井
dig a well;

jue kai 掘開
dig;

jue keng 掘坑
dig a pit;

jue2 攫
seize / snatch / take hold of;

jue duo 攫奪
grab / seize / snatch;

jue qu 攫取
grab / seize;

jun4 捃
collect / gather / pick up;

jun shi 捃拾
collect / gather / pick up;

kai1 揩
clean / rub / scrub / wipe;

kai gan jing 揩乾淨
wipe clean;

kan3 sha 砍殺
chop and kill / hack to death;

kan shang 砍傷
wound by cutting / wound by hacking;

kan si 砍死
hack to death;

kang4 shou 抗手
raise one's hand as a salute;

kao3 shou 烤手
warm the hands;

kong1 qi an mo 空氣按摩
pneumatic massage;

kong quan 空拳
bare-handed // hold nothing in the hand;

kong quan chi shou 空拳赤手
a hollow fist and bare hands — relying on no one; bare-handed;

kong shou 空手
empty-handed;

kong shou cheng jia 空手成家
build up one's fortune from scratch;

kong shou er gui 空手而歸
come back empty-handed / return empty;

kong shou qi jia 空手起家
from rags to riches / make a fortune starting from nothing;

kou1 摳
(1) raise;
(2) grope for;
(3) delve into / inquire into;
(4) dig with fingers;

kou po 摳破
injure by scratching;

kou3 qiao shou zhuo 口巧手拙
glib in tongue and clumsy in hands / those who are good at making excuses will be good at nothing else;

kou wen shou xie 口問手寫
ask questions and take notes;

kou4 扣
(1) rap / tap;
(2) buckle / fasten;

kou jin 扣緊
fasten tightly;

kou lao 扣牢
fasten / tie securely;

kou men 扣門
knock at a door;

ku1 刳
cut apart;

kuai3 擓
(1) scratch;
(2) carry on the arm;

kuai po 擓破
break by scratching;

kuai4 shou 快手
deft hand / nimble-handed person / quick worker;

kuai shou kuai jiao 快手快腳
nimble of hands and fast of feet || agile; do things quickly; do things with alacrity; nimble;

kuan3 men 款門
knock at the door;

kun3 捆
(1) bind / bundle up / hogtie / tie / truss;
(2) bundle / sheaf / truss;

kun bang 捆綁
bind / tie up / truss up;

kun fu 捆縛
bind / bound / tie up;

kun qi lai 捆起來
tie up;

kun shang 捆上
bind up;

kun zhu shou jiao 捆住手腳
bound hand and foot / hogtie;

kuo4 括
(1) embrace / include / sum up;
(2) ransack / search for / seek;
(3) bound / tie;
(4) restrain;

la1 拉
(1) drag / draw / hold / pull / seize;
(2) elongate / lengthen;

la bu chu lai 拉不出來
(1) cannot pull out;
(2) constipated;

la bu dong 拉不動
unable to make it move by pulling;

la bu kai 拉不開
cannot pull it open;

la shou 拉手
(1) hold hands / join hands;
(2) grab sb by the hand / pull by the hands;

la4 shou 辣手
difficult to handle;

lan3 攬
(1) in full possession of;
(2) take into one's arms;

(3) take on / undertake;
(4) grasp / monopolize;

lan qu 攬取
get hold of;

lan quan 攬權
arrogate power to oneself / grasp full authority;

lao3 quan 老拳
fists;

le4 捋
gather in the fingers / pluck;

lei2 擂
beat / hit;

lei gu 擂鼓
beat a drum;

lian2 shou 聯手
gang up / join hands;

lian3 shou 斂手
refrain from doing sth;

liang3 shou 兩手
dual tactics;

liang shou cha bei 兩手叉背
with one's hands behind one's back;

liang shou cha yao 兩手叉腰
with arms akimbo ‖ akimbo; with one's hands on one's hips;

liang shou chan dou 兩手顫抖
one's hands quivering;

liang shou jiao bi 兩手交臂
have one's arms folded;

liang shou kong kong 兩手空空
empty-handed ‖ be left with nothing whatsoever; nothing is gained;

liang shou yi tan 兩手一攤
spread one's two hands in despair;

liang shou zhun bei 兩手準備
have two strings to one's bow / prepare oneself for both eventualities;

liao3 ru zhi zhang 了如指掌
know sth thoroughly ‖ be conversant with; have sth at one's fingertips; know like the back of one's hand; know sth like a book; know sth like the palm of one's hand; quite up on; read sth like a book;

liao4 撂
(1) lay down / put down;
(2) leave behind;

liao shou 撂手
give up / pocket one's hands;

liao xia 撂下
lay down / put down;

lie4 捩
(1) twist with hands;
(2) rip apart / tear apart;

ling1 拎
carry / lift;

liu4 zhi 六指
hexagactyly;

lou1 摟
(1) hold / tuck;
(2) collect / gather up;

lou lan 摟攬
monopolize;

lou suan 摟算
calculate;

lou3 摟
drag / drag away / pull;

lou4 yi shou 露一手
make an exhibition of one's ability / skills;

luan2 qi shou zu 攣其手足
hands and feet crooked;

luan4 le shou jiao 亂了手腳
be thrown into chaos;

luan pao 亂拋
throw about / throw around;

luan reng 亂扔
throw about / throw around;

lun1 掄
(1) turn with hands;
(2) brandish / wave;

lun dao 掄刀
swing a knife;

lun gun 掄棍
swing a stick;

lun quan 掄拳
swing a fist;

lun2 掄
choose / select;

lun xuan 掄選
select;

lun yuan 掄元
come out first in examinations;

luo1 攞
pull / tuck;

luo qi yi fu 攞起衣服
tuck up the skirt of a garment;

mao2 shou mao jiao 毛手毛腳
rough-handed || brash and clumsy; careless; clumsily; recklessly;

men2 捫
(1) feel or touch with hands / hold;
(2) search;

meng3 la 猛拉
hoick;

mo1 摸
(1) caress / feel lightly with fingers / grabble / touch lightly with fingers;
(2) grope;

mo mo 摸摸
have a feel;

mo suo 摸索
feel about / grabble / grope;

mo2 zhang 魔掌
in evil hands / in the devil's clutches;

mo3 抹
(1) mop / rub / wipe;
(2) apply to / smear;
(3) blot out;

mo gan 抹乾
wipe dry;

mo gan jing 抹乾淨
wipe clean;

mo qu 抹去
blot out / cross out / erase / obliterate / wipe out;

mu3 拇
(1) thumb;
(2) the big toe;

mu zhi 拇指
(1) thumb;
(2) the big toe;
er mu zhi 二拇指
the index finger;

na2 拿
(1) bring / fetch / get / hold in one's hand / grasp / take;
(2) arrest / capture / take;
(3) in / with;

na bu chu shou 拿不出手
not presentable;

na bu dong 拿不動
too heavy to take it;

na bu liao 拿不了
too many to take it;

na bu qi lai 拿不起來
(1) too heavy to raise it;
(2) cannot control;

na bu wen 拿不穩
cannot hold it steadily;

na bu zhu 拿不住
cannot keep in possession / too slippery to grasp it;

na da ding 拿大頂
stand on one's own hands;

na de dong 拿得動
able to take it;

na de liao 拿得了
able to take it;

na de zhu 拿得住
able to hold it steadily;

na guo lai 拿過來
bring it here / take it here;

na kai 拿開
take it away;

na qu 拿去
take it away;

na wen 拿穩
hold steadily;

na4 捺
press down / press hard with hands;

nang3 攮
stab / thrust;

nei4 fan zhi 內翻指
digitus varus;

nei pian shou 內偏手
manus vara;

nen4 shou 嫩手
raw hand;

nian1 拈
(1) pick up with the thumb and one and two fingers / take or hold with fingers;
(2) draw lots;

nian bi 拈筆
pick up a pen to write / take a pen;

nian nong 拈弄
finger and play / fondle;

nian3 捻
(1) nip with fingers;
(2) twist;

nian3 撚
toy with / twist with fingers;

nian zhi jian 撚指間
at the snap of one's fingers – in an instant;

nie1 捏
(1) knead / pinch / squeeze with fingers;
(2) mold;
(3) fabricate / make up / trump up;

nie shou nie jiao 捏手捏腳
with light steps and soft movements of one's hands || let one's hand and foot take too great liberties; move around lightly; walk gingerly; walk on tiptoe; walk with light steps;

nie1 捻
pinch with the fingers;

nie hua 捻花
pluck flowers;

nie shou nie jiao 捻手捻腳
stealthily;

nie4 shou nie jiao 躡手躡腳
with light steps and soft movements of one's hands || do things stealthily; make one's way noiselessly to; tiptoe; walk gingerly; walk on tiptoe;

niu3 duan 扭斷
twist and break sth;

niu gan 扭乾
wring sth dry;

niu jie 扭結
tangle / twist together;

niu qu 扭曲
twist;

niu yi niu 扭一扭
give a twist;

nuan3 shou 暖手
warm the hands;

nuo2 挼
(1) fondle / rub / stroke;
(2) crumple;

nuo sa 挼挲
fondle / rub / stroke;

nuo cuo 挼搓
crumple;

nuo2 挪
move / shift / transfer;

nuo bu dong 挪不動
cannot move it;

nuo bu kai 挪不開
cannot move away;

nuo dong 挪動
move;

nuo yi 挪移
move;

nuo yong 挪用
embezzle / misappropriate;

ou1 毆
beat / hit;

ou bi 毆斃
beat to death;

ou da 毆打
beat up / hit;

ou ji 毆擊
beat sb with fists;

ou ru 毆辱
beat and insult;

ou sha 毆殺
beat to death;

ou shang 毆傷
injure by beating;

pa2 扒
(1) gather up / rake up;
(2) braise / stew;
(3) claw / scratch;

pa qie 扒竊
pick pockets and steal;

pai1 拍
pat || beat; bounce; clap; flap; slap; tap; swat; take;

pai ba zhang 拍巴掌
clap hands;

pai da 拍打
pat / slap lightly;

pai ji 拍擊
slap / strike;

pai men 拍門
knock at the door;

pai shou 拍手
clap hands || applaud; clap one's hands;

pai shou cheng kuai 拍手稱快
clap one's hands for joy || clap and cheer; clap in high glee; clap one's hands with satisfaction; hail gleefully;

pai shou da xiao 拍手大笑
clap one's hands and laugh aloud / clap one's hands and roar with laughter;

pai shou he ge 拍手和歌
clap one's hands and join in the chorus;

pai shou he cai 拍手喝彩
clap hands and applaud;

pai shou jiao hao 拍手叫好
applaud with hand clap / clap one's hands and applaud;

pai shou zan cheng 拍手贊成
clap one's hands in approval;

pai zhang 拍掌
applaud / clap one's hands;

pai zhang cheng kuai 拍掌稱快
clap one's hands in applause / clap one's hands with satisfaction;

pai zhao 拍照
take a photo;

pai zhuo zi 拍桌子
pound the table;

pai2 排
(1) arrange / fall in line / put in order;
(2) reject;

pan1 zhai 攀摘
pick from trees;

pan zhe 攀折
break branches || pick; pluck; pull down and break off;

pan4 shi 拌石
throw a stone;

pao1 拋
hurl / throw || cast; chuck; fling; toss;

pao chu 拋出
cast away / throw out;

pao zhi 拋擲
cast / hurl / throw;

peng3 捧
hold sth by both hands;

peng zhu 捧住
hold firmly and securely;

pi1 披
(1) unroll;
(2) disperse / spread out;
(3) throw on;

pi3 shou 劈手
thrust forth the hand;

pi4 擗
beat the breast;

pian2 shou zhi zu 胼手胝足
toil and moil // with hand and feet becoming callous;

pie1 撇
(1) abandon / cast away / neglect / throw away;
(2) skim;

pie diao 撇掉
cast away / throw away;

pie kai 撇開
set aside;

pie qi 撇棄
abandon / cast away / discard / give up;

pin1 拼
incorporate / join together / make a whole / put together;

pin cou 拼凑
(1) put bits together to make a whole;
(2) raise money here and there;

pou2 抔
scoop up with both hands;

pou2 掊
collect taxes / exact;

pou ke 掊克
exact high taxes from people;

pou3 掊
attack / break / cudgel / cut / strike;

pou ji 掊擊
break / strike;

pu1 扑
beat / strike;

pu ji 扑擊
hit / strike;

pu ta 扑撻
flog / lash / whip;

pu1 撲
(1) beat / pound / strike;
(2) dash / smash;
(3) spring at / throw oneself on;

pu da 撲打
beat / pat;

pu guo lai 撲過來
come in a dash;

pu pu 撲撲
throb;

qi1 shou ba jiao 七手八腳
with everybody lending a hand ‖ all flurry and confusion; all lend a hand to; all pitching in; bustle about; great hurry and bustle; helter-skelter; hurriedly; in a bustle; in great haste; many people doing sth at the same time in a disorganized manner; serve hand and foot; several people engaged in a scuffle; take all together; too many cooks spoil the broth; with many people taking part; with seven hands and eight feet;

qi3 zhi 枝指
additional finger / forked finger;

qia1 掐
(1) dig the nail into;
(2) cut with fingernails / nip / pinch;
(3) clutch / grasp / hold;

qia ba 掐把
hold fast;

qia duan 掐斷
break / nip;

qia hua er 掐花兒
pluck flowers with fingernails;

qia si 掐死
choke to death by strangling with hands;

qia zhi yi suan 掐指一算
calculate / count;

qia zhu 掐住
grasp / hold / seize;

qian1 扦
penetrate / pick / pierce;

qian1 牽
lead by a rope, leash, or hand;

qian shou 牽手
lead by the hand;

qian1 掔
drag along / pull;

qian1 搴
pluck up / pull;

qian2 拑
grasp / hold;

qiao1 敲
beat / hit / knock / rap / strike / tap;

qiao da 敲打
beat / knock / rap / tap;

qiao ji 敲擊
beat / knock;

qiao men 敲門
knock at the door;

qiao po 敲破
shatter / smash;

qiao qiao da da 敲敲打打
beat drums continuously;

qiao sui 敲碎
beat to pieces / knock to pieces;

qiao1 撬
lift / raise;

qiao3 shou 巧手
dab hand / expert / skilful person;

qiao4 撬
pry;

qiao bu dong 撬不動
incapable of prying;

qiao bu kai 撬不開
incapable of prying open;

qiao men 撬門
pry a door open;

qin1 ru shou zu 親如手足
as dear to each other as brothers ‖ as close as brothers; cozy;

qin ru shou zu, xiu qi xiang guan 親如手足，休戚相關
kindred like brothers, with our joys and sorrows interconnected;

qin shou 親手
with one's own hands // personally;

qin2 擒
arrest / capture / seize;

qin bu 擒捕
arrest / capture;

qin huo 擒獲
arrest / capture;

qin na 擒拿
arrest / capture;

qin zhu 擒住
succeed in capturing;

qin4 揿
press down ‖ press with the hand; push; push down;

qin ling 揿鈴
push a bell;

qin ya 揿壓
press down / push down;

qing1 er yi ju 輕而易舉
easy to accomplish // with one's eyes closed / with one's eyes shut // pushover;

qing fang 輕放
put down gently;

qing pai 輕拍
pat / tap;

qing shou qing jiao 輕手輕腳
light-handed and light-footed ‖ cautiously without any noise; do sth gently; gently; nimble-fingered and light-heeled; on tiptoe; softly;

qing2 tong shou zu 情同手足
affectionate to each other like brothers ‖ be attached to each other like brothers; brotherly friendship; close like brothers; have the same affection for each other as though they were brothers; kindred like brothers; like born brothers; love another as one does one's brothers; regard each other as brothers; with brotherly love for each other;

qing2 擎
lift / prop up / support;

qing qi 擎起
lift up;

qing shou 擎手
raise one's hands — stop doing sth;

qu1 zhi 屈指
count on one's fingers;

qu zhi ke shu 屈指可數
can be counted on one's fingers ‖ be numbered; count on one's fingers; few and far between; not very many; one can count them on one's fingers; only a few to count; very few;

qu zhi yi suan 屈指一算
reckon on one’s fingers;

qu3 取
acquire / fetch / get / take;

quan2 拳
(1) fist;
(2) box / punch || give a punch; strike;
(3) boxing / pugilism / the art of boxing;

quan bang 拳棒
fighting feats;

quan bu li shou, qu bu li kou 拳不離手，曲不離口
boxing cannot dispense with the hand, nor songs the mouth || keep one’s eye in; keep one’s hand in; no day without a line; one cannot strike without the hand, nor sing without the mouth; practice makes perfect; the boxer’s fist must stick to its task, and the singer’s mouth no rest must ask;

quan da 拳打
strike with fists;

quan da jiao ti 拳打腳踢
give sb a good beating || beat and kick; beat up; box and kick; cuff and kick; strike and kick;

quan ji 拳擊
(1) boxing / pugilism;
(2) strike with fist;

quan jiao 拳腳
Chinese boxing;

quan jiao jiao jia 拳腳交加
beat up with fists and kicks // violent beating;

quan lai jiao qu 拳來腳去
exchange blows / give tit for tat;

quan ru yu xia 拳如雨下
blows fall fast and thick || a storm of blows; lay into; rain blows upon; strike sb repeatedly with one’s fist;

quan tou 拳頭
fist;

quan tou da tiao zao 拳頭打跳蚤
hit a flea with one’s fist || break a butterfly on a wheel;

quan wo 拳握
hold in the fist;

quan zu jiao jia 拳足交加
give sb both punches and kicks / hit sb by kicks and blows of the fists / strike and kick;

que1 zhi 缺指
ectrodactyly;

que4 推
knock / strike;

ran3 zhi 染指
come in for a share || encroach on; have a hand in; take a share of sth one is not entitled to;

ran zhi jia 染指甲
paint fingernails;

ran zhi ze fei 染指擇肥
dip one’s finger in the pie and claim the lion’s share;

re4 lie gu zhang 熱烈鼓掌
applaud wildly / clad enthusiastically / clap with all one’s might;

ren2 duo shou za 人多手雜
too many cooks spoil the broth;

ren shou 人手
(1) human hand;
(2) manpower;

ren shou bu zu 人手不足
short of hands // shorthanded / understaffed;

ren shou yi ce 人手一冊
everybody has a copy // in everybody’s hand;

reng1 扔
(1) cast / flip / hurl / throw;
(2) abandon / discard / litter;

reng diao 扔掉
cast away / chuck away / chuck out / throw away;

reng guo qu 扔過去
chuck / throw over;

reng kai 扔開
throw off;

reng qi 扔棄
chuck out / discard / get rid of / throw away;

reng xia 扔下
leave behind / put aside / throw down;

rou2 揉
(1) knead / rub;
(2) crumble by hand / roll into;
(3) massage;
(4) make peaceful / make smooth / subdue;

rou ba 揉巴
crumple / knead / rub;

rou cuo 揉搓
(1) knead / massage / rub;
(2) play jokes on / tease;

rou sui 揉碎
crumble to pieces;

rou4 bo 肉搏
hand-to-hand combat;

ru2 shou ru zu 如手如足
like brothers;

ru4 shou 入手
start with / take as the point of departure || begin with; get under way; proceed from; put one's hand to;

ruo2 挼
(1) crumple;
(2) rub / stroke;

ruo cuo 挼搓
crumple / knead / rub;

ruo suo 挼挲
fondle / rub / stroke;

sa1 撒
(1) ease / relax;
(2) loosen / unleash;
(3) display / exhibit / show;

sa fang 撒放
release / unleash;

sa kai 撒開
(1) get away;
(2) part;
(3) let go / release;

sa shou 撒手
(1) leave hold of || let go; let go one's hold; relax the grasp; relax the hold; relinguish one's hold;
(2) abandon / give up || wash one's hands off the matter;

sa shou bu gan 撒手不幹
chuck up one's job;

sa shou bu guan 撒手不管
refuse to have anything more to do with the matter || refuse to take any further part in; relinquish one's hold on; take no further interest in; wash one's hands of the business;

sa shou chen huan 撒手塵寰
die / leave this mortal world / pass away;

sa shou gui xi 撒手歸西
die / pass away || go to the western Heaven; go west; pay one's debt of nature;

sa shou jian 撒手鐧
one's best card / one's trump card;

san1 cha shou 三叉手
trident hand;

san mu zhi 三拇指
middle finger;

san quan di bu guo si shou 三拳敵不過四手
three fists are no match of four hands — the few cannot fight the many; be outnumbered;

san quan liang jiao 三拳兩腳
a few cuffs and kicks;

san zhi shou 三隻手
pickpocket;

sao1 搔
scratch lightly;

sao dao yang chu 搔到癢處
scratch where it itches || say sth right to the point; scratch at the place that itches — touch the exact point; scratch where it itches — hit the nail on the head;

sao hu tou, nong hu xu 搔虎頭，弄虎鬚
offend the mighty and powerful;

sao pa 搔爬
scratch lightly;

sao yang 搔癢
scratch an itch / scratch the itching place // titillation;

sao3 掃
(1) clear away / sweep with a broom;

(2) exterminate / weed out / wipe away / wipe out;

sao chen 掃塵
sweep clean;

sao chu 掃除
clean / eliminate / eradicate / sweep up;

sao di 掃地
sweep the floor;

sao gan jing 掃乾淨
sweep clean;

shan1 搧
(1) fan;
(2) incite / stir up;
(3) slap on the face;

shan dong 搧動
agitate / incite / stir up;

shang4 xia qi shou 上下其手
distort facts to suit one's private ends ‖ act in collusion with; get up to tricks; in collusion with sb; league together for some evil end; manoeuvre for some evil end; practise fraud; work hand in glove with sb;

shao1 捎
(1) carry;
(2) brush over lightly;

shao dai 捎帶
carry;

shen1 伸
(1) extend / stick out / straighten / stretch;
(2) report;

shen chang 伸長
elongate / extend / lengthen / prolongate;

shen chu shou lai 伸出手來
hold out one's hand;

shen shou 伸手
hold out one's hand / reach out one's hand / stretch out one's hand;

shen shou bu jian wu zi 伸手不見五指
pitch darkness ‖ darkness visible; Egyptian darkness; so dark that you can't see your hand in front of you;

shen shou ke ji 伸手可及
at arm's length;

sheng4 shou 聖手
master;

shi1 shou 失手
accidentally drop / fluff / slip;

shi xie zheng 失寫症
agraphia;
jing shen xing shi xie zheng 精神性失寫症
mental agraphia;
ting jue xing shi xie zheng 聽覺性失寫症
acoustic agraphia;
yi wang xing shi xie zheng 遺忘性失寫症
agraphia amnemonica;
yun dong xing shi xie zheng 運動性失寫症
motor agraphia;
za luan xing shi xie zheng 雜亂性失寫症
jargon agraphia;

shi2 ge zhi tou you chang duan 十個指頭有長短
even the ten fingers cannot be of equal length — men are not all perfect / fingers are unequal in length — you can't expect everybody to be the same;

shi shou suo zhi 十手所指
be condemned by all / target of public condemnation ‖ what ten fingers point to — everybody knows;

shi zhi lian xin 十指連心
the nerves of the fingertips are linked with the heart;

shi zhi xian xian 十指纖纖
one's delicate bamboo-shoot fingertips;

shi2 zhi 食指
first finger / forefinger / index / index finger;

shi zhi hao fan 食指浩繁
many mouths to feed;

shi2 拾
(1) collect / pick up;
(2) put away;

shi de 拾得
find / pick up;

shi duo 拾掇
arrange in order / tidy up;

手 *Hand*

shi huang 拾荒
glean and collect scraps;

shi qi 拾起
pick up;

shi qu 拾取
collect / pick up;

shi4 拭
(1) rub / wipe;
(2) clean / dust;

shi fu 拭拂
wipe, dust and clean;

shi jing 拭淨
wipe and clean;

shi4 shou 釋手
loosen one's grip / relax the hold;

shou3 手
(1) hand;
(2) have in one's hand / hold;
(3) convenient / handy;
bian ping shou 扁平手
flat hand / manus plana;
ju shou 巨手
cheiromegaly;

shou bei 手背
back of the hand / opisthenar;

shou bian 手邊
at hand / on hand;

shou bo 手搏
fight with bare hands;

shou bu chuo bi 手不輟筆
write without stopping;

shou bu lao shi 手不老實
have sticky fingers;

shou bu shi juan 手不釋卷
(1) diligent reader;
(2) studious;

shou bu ting hui 手不停揮
write without rest;

shou bu wen 手不穩
light-fingered / thievish;

shou bu ying xin 手不應心
one's hand could no longer act as one's heart directed;

shou chao 手抄
copy by hand;

shou chui zheng 手垂症
carpoptosis;

shou dao bing chu 手到病除
illness departs at a touch of the hand / sickness retires at one's touch / the disease is cured as soon as one sets his hand to it;

shou dao qin lai 手到擒來
capture sb easily;

shou duan 手段
means / measure / medium / method;

shou duan gao ming 手段高明
play one's cards well;

shou duan zhuo lie 手段拙劣
hanky-panky tactics;

shou fa 手法
(1) skill / technique;
(2) gimmick / trick;

shou fa gao ming 手法高明
play a good game;

shou fa zhuo lie 手法拙劣
play a poor game / play a wretched game;

shou fa yu bu liang 手發育不良
atelocheiria;

shou fa yu bu quan 手發育不全
atelocheiria;

shou gao shou di 手高手低
small difference;

shou hua 手滑
do sth at will;

shou hui mu song 手揮目送
shake with the hand and follow with the eye — in bidding farewell;

shou ji jing luan 手肌痙攣
cheirospasm;

shou ji yan kuai 手急眼快
act dexterously // deft of hand and quick of eye // neat-handed and sharp-sighted;

shou jiao 手腳
(1) motion / movement of hands or feet;

(2) trick / underhand method;

shou jiao bu gan jing 手腳不幹淨
in the habit of stealing || hands are not too clean; light-fingered; questionable in money matters; seek minor illicit gains; sticky-fingered; sticky-handed; with dirty hands;

shou jiao gan jing 手腳幹淨
clean hands;

shou jiao li luo 手腳利落
dexterous || agile; deft; numble; not to make a hash of;

shou jin 手緊
(1) short of money;
(2) thrifty;

shou jing luan 手痙攣
cheirospasm;

shou kou xiang ying 手口相應
action and words are in correspondence;

shou kuai 手快
deft of hand / quick in action // nimble;

shou la shou 手拉手
hand in hand // holding hands;

shou la 手辣
ruthless;

shou man 手慢
slow in action // slow-moving;

shou mang jiao luan 手忙腳亂
be thrown into confusion / in disorderly haste || act with confusion; all in a hustle of excitement; frantically busy; helter-skelter; in a flurry; in a frantic rush; in a great bustle; in a great hurry and amid confusion; in a muddle; running around in circles;

shou na 手拿
hold in hand / take by hand;

shou pian zu zhi 手胼足胝
calluses found both on one's hands and feet — working hard;

shou qi dao luo 手起刀落
cut down / raise one's sword and make a cut;

shou qi 手氣
luck at gambling etc.;

shou qi bu jia 手氣不佳
luck goes against one;

shou qi hao 手氣好
all one touches turns to gold / have the Midas touch;

shou qiao 手巧
deft / dexterous / skilful with one's hands;

shou qin 手勤
diligent / hardworking / industrious;

shou qin jiao kuai 手勤腳快
keen and quick in one's work;

shou qiu yuan zhang 手球員掌
handball palm;

shou ren 手刃
kill with one's own hand / stab sb to death;

shou ruan 手軟
irresolute when firmness is needed / soft-hearted;

shou shang 手上
in one's hands;

shou sheng 手生
lack practice and skill // out of practice;

shou shi 手勢
gesture / sign;

shou shu 手書
(1) write in one's own hand;
(2) personal letter;

shou song 手鬆
spending money freely;

shou ti 手提
carry with a hand // portable;

shou tong 手痛
cheiralgia;

shou tong feng 手痛風
cheiragra;

shou tou 手頭
(1) at hand || on hand; right beside one;
(2) one's financial condition at the moment;

shou tou bu bian 手頭不便
short of cash || hard up; have little money to spare;

shou tou hao 手頭好
deft / dexterous;

shou tou jie ju 手頭拮据
in hard need of money ‖ at low-water mark; feel the draught; hard-pressed; in low water; low in pocket; out of cash; out of pocket; pinched for money; pushed for money; short of funds; uptight; when the chips are down;

shou tou jin 手頭緊
(1) short of money;
(2) closefisted;

shou tou kuan yu 手頭寬裕
well off at the moment ‖ in easy circumstances; in the bucks; with plenty of money to spend;

shou tou kun fa 手頭困乏
hard up for money ‖ in great straits; in straitened circumstances; on the rocks;

shou tou kuo chuo 手頭闊綽
free of hand;

shou tou qiao 手頭巧
deft / dexterous;

shou tou song 手頭鬆
in easy circumstances;

shou wan zi 手腕子
wrist;

shou wen 手紋
handprint;

shou wu cun tie 手無寸鐵
with no weapon in one's hand // barehanded / defenceless / unarmed;

shou wu fu ji zhi li 手無縛雞之力
not to have strength enough in one's hands to tie a chicken fast ‖ cannot play pew; cannot punch one's way out of a paper bag; lack the strength to truss a chicken — physically very weak;

shou wu zu dao 手舞足蹈
dance with excitement ‖ cut a caper; dance for joy; dance with joy; flourish; gesticulate merrily; gesticulate with hands and feet; kick up one's heels; shake one's hands and stamp one's feet; wave one's arm and beat time with one's feet; wave one's arms and stamp one's feet in joy; with vigorous movements of hands and feet;

shou xia 手下
(1) under / under the leadership of;
(2) at hand;
(3) at the hands of sb;
(4) lackey;

shou xia liu qing 手下留情
pull one's punches / show mercy // lenient;

shou xian 手癬
fungus infection of the hand / tinea manuum;

shou xin 手心
(1) palm / palm of the hand;
(2) control // in the hands of sb;

shou yan kuai 手眼快
nimble / quick in action;

shou yan tong tian 手眼通天
exceptionally adept in trickery;

shou yang 手癢
(1) one's fingers itch;
(2) have an itch to do sth;

shou yin 手淫
masturbation ‖ hand job; do-it-yourself; fluff one's duff; jerk off;

shou yu 手語
sign language;

shou zhang 手掌
palm;

shou zhi 手指
finger;

shou zhi bei mian 手指背面
facies digitales dorsales manus;

shou zhi feng er 手指縫儿
space between two fingers;

shou zhi jia 手指甲
fingernail;

shou zhi jiao cha 手指交叉
chiasm of digits of hand;

shou zhi tou 手指頭
(1) fingertips;
(2) fingers;

shou zhong 手重
heavy-handed;

shou zu 手足
(1) brothers / members;
(2) hands and feet;

shou zu guo chang 手足過長
acrodolichomelia;

shou zu jing luan 手足痙攣
carpopedal spasm;

shou zu kou bing 手足口病
hand-foot-and-mouth disease;

shou zu qing shen 手足情深
the love between brothers is deep;

shou zu tong 手足痛
cheiropodalgia;

shou zu wu cuo 手足無措
at a loss what to do || all in a fluster; at a loss how to act; bewildered; disconcerted; feel completely at a loss; lose oneself; panic-stricken; perplexed;

shou zu xiang can 手足相殘
fraternal strifes;

shou zu zhi qing 手足之情
brotherhood || brotherly affection; fraternal tie; the yoke of brotherhood;

shou3 qu yi zhi 首屈一指
the best || bear the palm; come first on the list; come out first; second to none; stand highest in esteem; the best one; the foremost; the top;

shou4 授
give / hand over to;

shou shou 授受
give and receive;

shu1 xie 書寫
writing;

shu xie biao da zhang ai 書寫表達障礙
disorder of written expression;

shu xie bu neng 書寫不能
agraphia;

shu xie cuo luan 書寫錯亂
graphorrhea;

shu xie dao cuo 書寫倒錯
paragraphia;

shu xie jing luan 書寫痙攣
chirospasm;

shu xie kun nan 書寫困難
dysgraphia;

shu xie ma bi 書寫麻痺
scriveners' palsy;

shu4 fu shou jiao 束縛手腳
bind sb hand and foot / hamper the initiative of / tie sb's hands;

shu shou 束手
have one's hands tied // helpless;

shu shou dai bi 束手待斃
wait for death with tied hands || die without a fight; fold one's hands and await destruction; fold one's hands and wait for death; fold one's hands and wait to be slain; resign oneself to extinction; wait for death with hands bound up; wait helplessly for death;

shu shou jiu fu 束手就縛
allow oneself to be bound without putting up a fight || be captured; just to stand still to be bound;

shu shou jiu qin 束手就擒
allow oneself to be seized without putting up a fight || allow oneself to be arrested without offering any resistance; resign oneself to being held as a prisoner; submit to arrest with folded arms;

shu shou shou fu 束手受縛
wait calmly to be put into bonds;

shu shou shu jiao 束手束腳
be bound hand and foot // overcautiousness; undue caution;

shu shou wu ce 束手無策
at a loss what to do || have one's hands tie; helpless; no way out; up a stump;

shu4 qi 豎起
erect / hoist / hold up;

shu qi da mu zhi 豎起大拇指
hold up one's thumb in approval / thumbs up;

shua1 刷
brush / scrub;

shuai1 摔
break / fling / throw to the ground;

shuai diao 摔掉
cast off / dash away / throw away;

shuai po 摔破
break sth by dashing it on the ground;

shuai sui 摔碎
break into pieces after falling to the ground;

shuai3 shou 甩手
(1) swing one's arms;
(2) ignore ‖ refuse to do; take no heed; wash one's hands of;

shuan1 拴
fasten / tie up;

shuan fu 拴縛
tie up with a rope;

shuan kun 拴捆
bind / tie up;

shuan ma 拴馬
tie up a horse;

shuan shang 拴上
fasten;

shuan shu 拴束
pack / tie up;

shuan zhe 拴着
fastened / tied up;

shuan zhu 拴住
make fast / tie up;

shuang1 quan nan di si shou 雙拳難敵四手
not even Hercules could contend against two;

shuang shou 雙手
both hands / the two hands;

shuang shou feng shang 雙手奉上
present respectfully with both hands;

shuang shou gong rang 雙手拱讓
give away sth to sb with both hands;

shuang shou he shi 雙手合十
put one's palms together devoutly;

shuang shou shuang jiao 雙手雙腳
all fours;

shuang shou zan cheng 雙手贊成
raise both hands in approval ‖ all for it; support fully;

shun4 shou 順手
(1) smoothly / without difficulty;
(2) conveniently / without extra trouble;
(3) do sth as a natural sequence;
(4) convenient and easy to use / handy;

shun shou qian yang 順手牽羊
go off with sth near at hand ‖ go on the scamp; lead away the sheep offhand — pick up sth in passing; steal sth in passing; walk away with sth;

si1 撕
rip / tear;

si da 撕打
beat up / maul;

si diao 撕掉
tear off / tear up;

si hui 撕毀
destroy by tearing;

si kai 撕開
rip open / tear open;

si lan 撕爛
rip to pieces / tear to shreds;

si po 撕破
rip / tear;

si qu 撕去
tear away / tear off;

si sui 撕碎
rip to pieces / tear to pieces;

si xia lai 撕下來
tear off;

si3 bu fang shou 死不放手
hold on like grim death;

si4 zhi 四指
tetradactyly;

song1 shou 鬆手
let go the hands / relax the hold;

su4 shou 素手
(1) white and tender hands;
(2) empty-handed;

sui2 shou 隨手
at hand ‖ conveniently; immediately; readily; without extra trouble;

sui shou guan men 隨手關門
close the door behind one / shut the door after you;

suo1 抄
feel with hands / touch;

suo1 shou 縮手
(1) draw back one's hand;
(2) shrink from doing sth;

suo shou pang guan 縮手旁觀
watch from the sideline without interferring;

suo shou suo jiao 縮手縮腳
become irresolute and passive ‖ have cold feet; overcautious; shrink from doing sth; shrink with cold; timid and fliching;

suo shou wu ce 縮手無策
fold one's hands helplessly;

ta4 撻
chastise / flog / strike / whip;

ta ru 撻辱
beat and disgrace;

tai2 擡
carry / lift / raise;

tai bu dong 擡不動
incapable of being lifted / incapable of lifting;

tai shou dong jiao 擡手動腳
manner / personal behavour;

tan2 zhi 彈指
a short moment;

tan zhi ke dai 彈指可待
can be accomplished in a very brief space of time ‖ during the snapping of the fingers; in a twinkling;

tan zhi ke de 彈指可得
can take it with a flick of the fingers;

tan zhi yi hui 彈指一揮
with a mere snap of the fingers;

tan zhi zhi jian 彈指之間
at the snap of a finger ‖ in a flash; in a moment; in a short moment; in a twinkling of an eye; in an instant; instantly;

tan zou 彈奏
play / pluck / strum;

tang4 shou 燙手
(1) scald one's hand;
(2) difficult to manage;

tao1 掏
(1) pull out / take out;
(2) dig / scoop out;
(3) steal from sb's pocket;

tao chu lai 掏出來
draw out / pull out;

tao qian 掏錢
spend money / take out money;

tao yao bao 掏腰包
shell out / spend one's own money;

tao1 搯
pull out / take out;

ti2 提
(1) lift by hand / pull up / raise;
(2) obtain;
(3) control / manage;

ti bu qi lai 提不起來
unable to lift;

ti gao 提高
lift / raise;

ti shou nie jiao 提手躡腳
walk on tiptoe;

ti4 剃
shave;

tiao1 挑
(1) choose / pick / select;
(2) pick by pitchfork;

tiao chu 挑出
pick out;

tiao fei jian shou 挑肥揀瘦
pick and choose;

tiao jian 挑揀
choose / pick / select;

tiao qu 挑取
choose / pick / select;

tiao san jian si 挑三揀四
pick and choose;

tiao ti 挑剔
find fault with sb / find fault with sth / niggle

about / nitpick // fastidious / hypercritical / particular about / picky;

tiao xuan 挑選
choose / pick / select // choice / selection;

tiao3 xin 挑衅
provoke;

tie3 wan 鐵腕
iron fist / iron hand;

ting1 jue xing shi xie zheng 聽覺性失寫症
acoustic agraphia;

tong4 da 痛打
beat soundly ‖ give a severe thrashing; lash out at sb; make hamburger out of sb; skin alive; stoush;

tong da yi dun 痛打一頓
give sb a good beating / give sb a sound thrashing / lash out at sb;

tou2 投
(1) hurl / pitch / throw / toss;
(2) lodge / stay;

tou jin qu 投進去
throw in / throw into;

tou zhi 投擲
hurl / throw / throw away;

tu2 徒
bare-handed / empty-handed;

tu bo 徒搏
hand-to-hand combat;

tu shou 徒手
bare-handed / empty-handed / unarmed;

tu shou bo dou 徒手搏鬭
fight bare-handed;

tu shou qi jia 徒手起家
become rich bare-handed / make a fortune starting from scratch;

tu shou zhi fu 徒手致富
start out empty-handed and become rich later;

tuan2 摶
roll round with the hand;

tui1 推
push / shove;

tui bu chu 推不出
unable to push out;

tui bu dong 推不動
be unable to move by pushing;

tui bu kai 推不開
unable to push away;

tui chu 推出
push out;

tui dao 推倒
(1) overturn / push over / topple;
(2) shove;

tui dong 推動
move / promote / propel / push;

tui kai 推開
push away / push off;

tun4 shou 褪手
hide one's hands in sleeves;

tuo1 拖
(1) drag along;
(2) delay / procrasinate;
(3) implicate;

tuo chang 拖長
(1) lengthen;
(2) drag on;

tuo kua 拖垮
be torn down;

tuo1 shou 脱手
(1) slip out of the hand;
(2) dispose of ‖ dishoard; get off one's hands; sell;

tuo4 shou ke de 唾手可得
acquire sth easily ‖ acquire sth with a wet finger; extremely easy to come at; get sth without great effort; get...without lifting a finger;

wa1 挖
(1) dig out / scoop out;
(2) cut / gouge;

wa chu lai 挖出來
dig out / excavate / gouge out;

wa dong 挖洞
dig out a hole;

wa ni 挖泥
dredge up mud;

wan1 剜
scoop out;

wan3 挽
(1) draw / pull;
(2) seize;
(3) restore;

wan shou 挽手
hold hands // arm in arm;

wan zhu 挽住
hold back;

wan4 腕
wrist;

wan dai 腕帶
bracelet;

wan gu 腕骨
carpal bone;
di er wan gu 第二腕骨
second carpal bone;

wan zi 腕子
wrist;

wang3 shang la 往上拉
pull up;

wang xia tui 往下推
push down;

wen3 cao sheng quan 穩操勝券
be certain to win / have full assurance of success / have the game in one's own hands;

wen4 抆
wipe;

wen shi 抆拭
wipe away;

wen4 揾
(1) wipe out;
(2) press down with fingers;

wo4 握
(1) clench one's fist / grasp / hold fast / make a fist;
(2) a handful;

wo bi 握筆
hold a pen;

wo bie 握別
shake hands at parting;

wo jin 握緊
clench / grapple / grasp firmly / hold fast;

wo juan 握卷
hold a book;

wo quan 握拳
bunch a fist / clench one's fist / make a fist;

wo shou 握手
clasp hands / shake hands // handgrip;

wo shou cheng jiao 握手成交
give one's hand on a bargain / shake hands on the bargain;

wo shou gao bie 握手告別
shake hands with sb in farewell;

wo shou xi bie 握手惜別
grasp a person's hand in farewell;

wo shou yan huan 握手言歡
shake hands to show affection || bury the hatchet; give us your fist; greet sb with a hearty handshake; hold hands and chat cheerfully; shake hands and make up;

wo zhua 握抓
hold;

wu2 ming zhi 無名指
ring finger;

wu shou 無手
achiria;

wu suo cuo shou zu 無所措手足
at a loss what to do || find no place to put one's hands and feet; have nowhere to put hand or foot — at a loss to know how to conduct oneself; not to know what to do;

wu3 zhi 五指
the five fingers — the thumb, the index finger, the middle finger, the ring finger, and the little finger;

wu3 捂
conceal / cover / hide;

wu bu zhu 捂不住
cannot be concealed;

wu gai 捂蓋
cover up / hide;

wu qi lai 摀起來
imprison;

wu3 shou nong jiao 舞手弄腳
play gestures;

xi1 zhi shi zhang 惜指失掌
stint a finger only to lose the whole hand — try to save a little only to lose a lot;

xi3 shou 洗手
(1) wash one's hands;
(2) stop doing evil and reform oneself;
(3) wash one's hands of sth;

xi shou bu gan 洗手不幹
wash one's hand of it once and for all ‖ clear one's skirts; hang up one's axe; never to do such a thing again; quit committing crimes; through with; throw up; wash one's hands; wash one's hands of the matter; wash one's hands of the whole affair;

xia1 mo 瞎摸
fumble;

xia4 bi 下筆
start writing;

xia bi cheng zhang 下筆成章
write quickly and effortlessly;

xia du shou 下毒手
lay violent hands on sb;

xia shou 下手
put one's hand to ‖ lay one's hand on; set about; set to; start; start doing sth;

xian1 xia shou wei qiang 先下手為強
to take the initiative is to gain the upper hand ‖ he who strikes first gains the advantage; he who strikes first prevails; it's always advantageous to make the first move; offence is the best defence; the best defence is offence; the early bird gets the worm; the first blow is half the battle; whoever strikes the first blow has the advantage;

xian xia shou wei qiang, hou xia shou zao yang 先下手為強，後下手遭殃
he who strikes first prevails, he who strikes late fails;

xian1 掀
(1) lift with the hands / raise;
(2) cause / rise / stir / stir up;

xian bu dong 掀不動
unable to lift it;

xian bu kai 掀不開
cannot lift it;

xian dong 掀動
lift / stir up;

xian kai 掀開
open / uncover / unveil;

xian qi 掀起
stir up / surge;

xian1 shou 孅手
delicate hands;

xian shou xi yao 纖手細腰
tender hands and slender waist;

xian xian yu shou 纖纖玉手
fine and slim hands of a young woman;

xiang3 yi lao quan 餉以老拳
give sb a taste of one's fist — give sb a punch;

xiao3 mu zhi 小姆指
one's little finger;

xiao shou xiao jiao 小手小腳
(1) mean / miserly / stingy;
(2) timid;

xiao zhi 小指
little finger / microdactyly;

xiao zhi wan qu 小指彎曲
streptomicrodactyly;

xie1 shou 歇手
stop doing sth;

xie2 挾
(1) hold under the arm;
(2) embrace;

xie chi 挾持
(1) grasp sb on both sides by the arms;
(2) hold sb under duress;

xie dai 挾帶
(1) carry under arms;
(2) smuggle;

xie2 擷
collect / gather / pick;

xie cai 擷采
cull / gather / pick;

xie fang 擷芳
pick flowers;

xie ju jing hua 擷取精華
pick the best;

xie2 攜
(1) carry / take;
(2) help / lead;

xie bao 攜抱
carry in one's arms;

xie dai 攜帶
carry with oneself / take along;

xie shou 攜手
hand in hand / hold each other's hand;

xie shou bing jin 攜手並進
advance hand in hand / join hands and advance together / march forward hand in hand;

xie shou tong xing 攜手同行
go hand in hand / walk with arms linked;

xie tong 攜同
bring along;

xie you 攜幼
take one's young children along;

xie3 寫
draw / sketch / write;

xin1 shou 新手
new hand / greenhorn / novice / tender foot;

xin4 shou 信手
at random;

xin shou nian lai 信手拈來
get without effort;

xiu1 zhi jia 修指甲
(1) trim fingernails;
(2) manicure fingernails;

xiu4 shou pang guan 袖手旁觀
look on without even lifting a finger / stand by / watch with folded arms;

xuan1 揎
(1) pull up the sleeves and show the arms;
(2) fight with bare hands;

xuan ji 揎擊
hit with bare fists;

xuan quan lu xiu 揎拳擄袖
pull up the sleeves and get ready to fight;

xun2 撏
pick / pluck / take;

xun che 撏撦
pick here and there;

ya4 揠
pull out / pull up;

ya miao zhu zhang 揠苗助長
pull up the seedling in the hope of making it grow faster;

yan3 掩
(1) conceal / cover / cover with one's hand;
(2) close / shut;

yan bu zhu 掩不住
cannot shut out / unable to cover / unable to hide;

yan gai 掩蓋
conceal / cover up;

yan shang 掩上
shut;

yan3 揜
(1) rob / take by force;
(2) conceal / cover up;
(3) shut;

yang2 揚
raise;

yao2 搖
shake / wave;

yao bai 搖擺
oscillate / sway / swing to and fro;

yao dong 搖動
rock / shake / sway;

yao huang 搖晃
falter / shake / sway / swing to and fro;

yao lai yao qu 搖來搖去
swing to and fro;

yao shou 搖手
(1) handle;
(2) shake one's hand in admonition or

disapproval / wave one's hand;

yao yao 搖搖
shaky;

yao yao bai bai 搖搖擺擺
swagger / swing;

ye1 掖
(1) conceal / tuck away;
(2) fold / roll up;

ye ye gai gai 掖掖蓋蓋
stealthily;

yi1 ba chang 一巴掌
slap;

yi ba 一把
handful;

yi ba shou 一把手
good hand;

yi chu ji fa 一觸即發
imminent;

yi chu ji kui 一觸即潰
collapse at the first encounter;

yi ge ba zhang pai bu xiang 一個巴掌拍不響
it takes two to start an argument || one hand alone can't clap — it takes two to make a quarrel / you can't clap with one hand;

yi hui er jiu 一揮而就
finish writing an article or drawing a painting very quickly;

yi quan lai, yi jiao qu 一拳來，一腳去
a blow for a blow / a Roland for an Oliver / retaliation equal to its provocation / retort equal to its provocation;

yi quan yi jiao 一拳一腳
with a blow of one's fist and a kick from one's foot;

yi shou 一手
(1) good at / proficiency / skill;
(2) move / trick;
(3) single-handed || all alone; all by oneself;

yi shou bao ban 一手包辦
(1) undertake sth alone || be manipulated by sb single-handedly; do sth all by oneself; keep everything in one's own hands; single-handedly; take everything on oneself;
(2) arbitrary / dictatorial;

yi shou ce hua 一手策劃
engineer sth single-handedly;

yi shou de lai, yi shou shi qu 一手得來，一手失去
lose on the swings what one makes on the roundabout;

yi shou du pai sui ji wu sheng 一手獨拍雖疾無聲
no matter how capable a person is, they need the help of others to do things better;

yi shou jiao qian, yi shou jiao huo 一手交錢，一手交貨
cash on delivery || give me the cash, and I'll give you the goods; transaction in cash; with one hand I take the money, with the other I release the goods;

yi shou nan zhua liang tou man 一手難抓兩頭鰻
if you run after two hares, you will catch neither || he that hunts two hares oft loseth both;

yi shou pao zhi 一手炮製
concoct sth single-handed;

yi shou qing tian 一手擎天
hold up the sky with one hand / lift up the sky with one hand / prop up the sky with a single hand;

yi shou yan jin tian xia ren er mu 一手掩盡天下人耳目
hide from public knowledge the errors committed by sb;

yi shou yi zu 一手一足
one hand and one foot;

yi shou ying yi shou ruan 一手硬一手軟
promote one thing and neglect another thing at the same time;

yi shou zai pei 一手栽培
bring sb up single-handed / raise sb all by oneself;

yi shou zao cheng 一手造成
be solely responsible for sth || be fomented single-handedly by;

yi shou zhe tian 一手遮天
hoodwink the public || hide the truth from

the masses; pull the wool over the eye of the public;

yi shou zhi kuan 一手之寬
a hand's breadth;

yi zhen zhang sheng 一陣掌聲
a round of applause;

yi zhi shou pai bu xiang 一隻手拍不響
it takes two to make a quarrel;

yi1 揖
bow with hands folding in front;

yi bai 揖拜
make a bow with hands folding in front;

yi bie 揖别
bid farewell by bowing with hands folding in front;

yi xie 揖謝
bow in thanks;

yi2 bing 疑病
hypochondriasis;

yi2 wang xing shi xie zheng 遺忘性失寫症
agraphia amnemonica;

yi3 shou jia e 以手加額
exhibit gratification || fold one's hands upon one's forehead; place one's hand over one's forehead;

yi shou zhe lian 以手遮臉
veil one's face with one's hand;

yi4 抑
(1) press / press down;
(2) force to / restrain;

yi4 ru fan zhang 易如反掌
as easy as turning over one's hand || a piece of cake; as easy as ABC; as easy as child's play; as easy as damn it; as easy as falling off a log; as easy as my eye; as easy as pot; as easy as shelling peas; as easy as turning one's palm over; as easy as winking; at a hand's turn // like a duck takes to water;

yi ru zhi zhang 易如指掌
as easy as pointing at a palm || a piece of cake; as easy as ABC; as easy as child's play; as easy as damn it; as easy as falling off a log; as easy as my eye; as easy as pot; as easy as shelling peas; as easy as turning one's palm over; as easy as winking; at a hand's turn // like a duck takes to water;

yi shou 易手
change hands;

yi4 挹
decant wine;

yi zhuo 挹酌
pour out wine;

yi4 shou 義手
artificial hand;

ying4 shou 應手
smoothly / without a hitch;

yong1 擁
(1) embrace / hold / hug;
(2) have / possess;
(3) follow / support;

yong bao 擁抱
embrace / hold in one's arms / hug;

yong you 擁有
have / possess / own;

you2 shou hao xian 游手好閒
idle about || eat the bread of idleness; fool; in the street; keep one's hands in one's pockets; live in idleness; loaf about; loaf around; loitering about and doing nothing; mess around doing nothing; not to do a stitch of work; on the loaf; rogue; shilly-shally; squander one's time;

you4 da you ma 又打又罵
beat and curse at the same time;

you4 shou 右手
right hand;

yu2 揄
(1) draw out / scoop out;
(2) hang;

yu mei 揄袂
walk with hands swinging in one's sleeves;

yu2 li 餘力
energy to spare / strength to spare;

yu nian 餘年
remaining years of one's life;

yu sheng 餘生
remaining years of one's life;

yu2 chi 踰侈
too extravagant / too luxurious;

yu fen 踰分
go beyond one's proper function / go beyond one's proper position;

yu ju 踰矩
transgresss the bounds of correctness;

yu xian 踰閑
break decorum / break moral conventions;

yu4 jian 玉尖
tapering fingers of a beautiful woman;

yu nu qian shou 玉奴纖手
the slender fingers of a girl;

yu shou xian xian 玉手纖纖
the slender hands of a pretty young woman;

yu wan 玉腕
the wrist and forearm of a beautiful woman;

yu xian xiu mei 玉纖秀美
the fingers of a beauty are graceful;

yuan2 shou 援手
extend a helping hand || aid; rescue; save;

yun4 dong xing shi xie zheng 運動性失寫症
motor agraphia;

za2 luan xing shi xie zheng 雜亂性失寫症
jargon agraphia;

zha1 shou 扎手
(1) prick the hand;
(2) difficult to handle / thorny;

zha shou wu jiao 扎手舞腳
make exaggerated gestures;

zha1 揸
grasp by hand / pick up with fingers;

zha2 扎
strive / struggle;

zha zheng 扎掙
strive / struggle;

zha zheng bu zhu 扎掙不住
struggle or strive in vain;

zhai1 摘
(1) pick / pluck / take off;
(2) choose / select;
(3) jot down;

zhai chu 摘除
excise;

zhai diao 摘掉
pick off / take off;

zhai hua 摘花
pluck flowers;

zhai que 摘取
pick / select / take;

zhai xia 摘下
pick off / take off;

zhai xuan 摘選
select;

zhan1 shou 沾手
(1) touch with the hand;
(2) have a finger in the pie / play a role in sth;

zhan3 斬
(1) cut;
(2) behead / kill;

zhan cao chu gen 斬草除根
remove weed by rooting it out;

zhan huo 斬獲
score a victory on the battlefield;

zhan3 搌
(1) bind;
(2) wipe;

zhang1 shou 張手
open one's hands;

zhang3 掌
(1) the palm of the hand;
(2) slap with one's hand || smack; strike with the palm of the hand;
(3) control || in charge of; supervise; wield;

zhang fan she 掌反射
palmar reflex;

zhang shang ming zhu 掌上明珠
one's dear daughter || a pearl on the palm — a beloved daughter; the apple of one's eye;

zhang sheng 掌聲
applause / clapping / the sound of clapping;

zhang sheng lei dong 掌聲雷動
thunderous applause || a round of applause; a storm of applause set the rafters ringing;

applaud to the echo; burst into thunderous applause; the applause is deafening; the applause raises the roof;

zhang wen 掌紋
hand lines / palm prints;

zhang wo 掌握
in one's grasp ‖ grasp; grip; in sb's hand; know well; master; within one's power;

zhang wo fen cun 掌握分寸
act properly ‖ behave oneself; exercise sound judgement; handle appropriately; speak properly;

zhang wo ju shi 掌握局勢
have the situation under control / have the situation well in hand;

zhang wo yao ling 掌握要領
grasp the essentials;

zhang wo zhi zhong 掌握之中
within one's grasp ‖ have...in one's pocket; in one's hands; in sb's clutches; lie at sb's mercy; under the control of;

zhang wo zhu dong quan 掌握主動權
have the initiative in one's hands;

zhang xia 掌頰
slap sb's face;

zhang xin 掌心
centre of the palm;

zhang yin 掌印
in power // keep the seal;

zhang zui 掌嘴
slap sb in the face;

zhao1 shou 招手
beckon with the hand / wave a hand / wave one's hand;

zhao shou zhi yi 招手致意
wave in acknowledgement ‖ wave back in acknowledgement; wave one's greetings;

zhe2 折
(1) break / snap;
(2) fold;
(3) destroy / tear into halves;
(4) fold;

zhe ban 折半
reduce by half / reduce to half;

zhe die 折疊
fold;

zhe duan 折斷
break / snap;

zhe2 摺
fold / plait;

zhe die 摺疊
fold up / plait together;

zhen1 斟
(1) fill a cup with (tea / wine);
(2) pour into a cup;

zhen cha 斟茶
fill a cup with tea;

zhen jiu 斟酒
pour wine into a cup;

zhen man 斟滿
fill a cup to the brim;

zhen4 揕
stab / strike / thrust;

zhi1 shou 隻手
single-handed;

zhi shou bu neng zhe tian 隻手不能遮天
one hand cannot cover the sky;

zhi2 執
(1) grasp / hold;
(2) maintain;

zhi bi 執筆
write;

zhi shou 執手
hold hands;

zhi shou tong xing 執手同行
walk together;

zhi shou tong you 執手同游
saunter holding each other's hand;

zhi shou wei li 執手為禮
shake hands;

zhi2 摭
collect / pick up from the ground / take up;

zhi cai 摭採
collect;

zhi shi 摭拾
collect / pick;

zhi3 指
(1) finger;
(2) direct / point;
(3) indicate / mean / refer to;
bing zhi 併指
losyndactyly;
ju zhi 巨指
macrodactyly;

zhi bi zhi zhu 指臂之助
mutual assistance || the assistance of finger and forearm;

zhi bu sheng qu 指不勝屈
too many to be counted || a great many; countless; innumerable; more than can be counted on one's fingers; too many for the fingers to calculate;

zhi chi 指斥
denounce / reprove;

zhi chu 指出
point out || a sign of; lay one's finger on; show clearly;

zhi dian 指點
instruct || advise; give directions; give pointers; show how; teach;

zhi dian mi jin 指點迷津
show sb how to get on the right path || Ariadne's thread; point out the right way to sb when he goes astray;

zhi dong da xi, zhi nan da bei 指東打西，指南打北
hit on every side / point east and strike west, point south and strike north;

zhi dong hua xi 指東話西
mislead with talk || irrelevant; point to east and west; talk nonsense;

zhi dong ji xi 指東擊西
aim at east and hit west / point to the east and strike west — make a feint;

zhi dong shuo xi 指東説西
make a concealed reference to sth / make insinuations;

zhi fa 指法
fingering;

zhi fan she 指反射
digital reflex;

zhi fei da 指肥大
pachydactyly;

zhi fu wei hun 指腹為婚
prenatal betrothal || propose a marriage by pointing to the stomach — an old practice of marriage;

zhi gu 指骨
bones of fingers;

zhi gu guo duan 指骨過短
brachyphalangia;

zhi gu que shi 指骨缺失
ectrophalangia;

zhi gu tou 指骨頭
head of phalanx of fingers;

zhi gu yan 指骨炎
phalangitis;

zhi gu zhi jian 指顧之間
before you turn your back / in a short while;

zhi hei dao bai 指黑道白
call black white / point to black and say it is white;

zhi ji ma gou 指雞罵狗
scold a person indirectly || abuse one over the shoulder of another; make oblique accusations; point at one thing and abuse another; point at the chicken and curse the dog;

zhi3 jia 指甲
fingernail;
ju zhi jia 巨指甲
megalonychia;

zhi jia fei da 指甲肥大
onychauxis;
dan chun zhi jia fei da 單純指甲肥大
hyperonychia;

zhi jia guo xiao 指甲過小
micronychia;

zhi jia ying yang bu liang 指甲營養不良
onychodystrophy;

zhi jia ying hua 指甲硬化
scleronychia;

zhi jian 指尖
fingertip;

zhi jian bi 指間襞
interdigital fold;

zhi jian kui yang 指間潰瘍
ulcus interdigitale;

zhi jie 指節
knuckle;

zhi jing luan 指痙攣
dactylospasm;

zhi kuo zhang 指擴張
digital dilation;

zhi lu wei ma 指鹿為馬
call a stag a horse ‖ call white black; distort facts; talk black into white;

zhi mi 指迷
show the way ‖ give advice; give guidance; indicate the way;

zhi ming 指名
mention by name / name / single out by name;

zhi ming dao xing 指名道姓
mention sb's name ‖ identify by name the person; name names;

zhi ming ru ma 指名辱罵
call a person names / insult someone by using bad names;

zhi mo 指模
fingerprint;

zhi mo xue 指模學
dactylography;

zhi po mi jin 指破迷津
point out where one has gone astray from right path;

zhi sang dao huai 指桑道槐
name the lime tree but really mean the acacia — hidden allusions and innuendoes;

zhi sang ma huai 指桑罵槐
make oblique accusations / veiled abuse ‖ abuse a person by ostensibly pointing to someone else; abuse one over the shoulder of another; curse one thing while pointing to another; mock the locust on behalf of the mulberry tree; scold the locust while pointing at the mulberry;

zhi shou hua jiao 指手劃腳
(1) gesticulate / make gestures ‖ wave the hands and throw the feet about;
(2) point right and left ‖ carp and cavil; make indiscreet remarks or criticisms; order people about;

zhi suan 指算
count by fingers;

zhi tian hua di 指天劃地
behave without regard to decorum ‖ fling one's arms about; point right and left;

zhi tian shi ri 指天誓日
call heaven to witness / swear by the heaven and sun as witness / take an oath under heaven;

zhi tou 指頭
finger;

zhi tou jian er 指頭尖兒
fingertip;

zhi tuo luo 指脫落
dactylolysis;

zi fa xing zhi tuo luo 自發性指脫落
dactylolysis spontanea;

zhi wan qu 指彎曲
clinodactyly;

zhi wen 指紋
fingerprint;

zhi yan 指炎
dactylitis;

zhi yin 指印
fingerprint;

zhi ze 指責
accuse ‖ attack; censure; charge; condemn; criticize; disparage; find fault with; impugn; rebuke // stricture;

zhi zhang 指掌
fingers and palms;

zhi zhi dian dian 指指點點
(1) gesticulating / waving one's hands about;
(2) indicate / point / point out;

zhi4 shou zhi jiao 窒手窒腳
obstructing hand and foot // troublesome;

zhi4 擲
cast / throw;

zhi di 擲地
throw to the ground;

zhi jiao 擲交
hand over;

zhong1 zhi 中指
middle finger;

zhu4 shou 住手
stop || cut it out; hands off; hold; stay one's hand;

zhua1 抓
(1) scratch;
(2) catch / clutch / grab / grasp / grip / seize / snatch / take;

zhua bu qi lai 抓不起來
incapable of taking;

zhua gong fu er 抓功夫兒
steal time for idling;

zhua jin 抓緊
(1) grapple / grasp firmly;
(2) pay close attention to;

zhua kong 抓空
use leisure moments;

zhua lao 抓牢
grasp;

zhua nao 抓撓
(1) scratch;
(2) scramble;
(3) conflict / struggle;
(4) hustle / make hastily;

zhua po 抓破
injure skin by scratching;

zhua qu 抓取
take by grasping;

zhua quan 抓權
grasp power;

zhua ren 抓人
(1) dragoon people;
(2) arrest;

zhua xun 抓尋
look for / search for;

zhua yi ba 抓一把
take a handful;

zhua zei 抓賊
catch a thief;

zhua zhu 抓住
(1) catch on / clutch / grab / grasp / grip;
(2) hold / keep from going away;

zhua zhua nao nao 抓抓撓撓
hurriedly;

zhua1 撾
beat / strike;

zhua gu 撾鼓
beat a drum;

zhuai1 拽
fling / hurl;

zhuai4 拽
(1) drag after / trail;
(2) pull / drag;

zhuan3 shou 轉手
change hands || fall into another's hands; pass on; sell what one has bought;

zhuan shou bian gua 轉手變卦
change one's mind at the last moment;

zhuan shou cheng kong 轉手成空
lose all quickly;

zhuan shou dao mai 轉手倒賣
buy sth and resell it at a profit;

zhuan4 撰
compose / write;

zhuan gao 撰稿
write an article;

zhuan shu 撰述
write an account of;

zhuan xie 撰寫
compose / write;

zhuan zhu 撰著
write;

zhuo1 捉
(1) catch / grasp / seize;
(2) arrest;

zhuo jin jian zhou 捉襟見肘
cannot make ends meet || hard up; have to many difficulties to cope with; have too many problems to tackle; in straitened circumstances; on one's uppers; out at elbows;

zhuo mo bu ding 捉摸不定
mercurial;

zhuo na 捉拿
arrest;

zhuo zei 捉賊
catch thieves;

zhuo zhu 捉住
catch / seize;

duo1 掇
(1) collect / gather;
(2) pluck / select;

duo cai 掇採
gather / pluck / select;

duo nong 掇弄
(1) stir up conflicts;
(2) gather up / repair;
(3) deal with sth;

duo shi 掇拾
collect / select;

zhuo2 斫
chop / cut;

zhuo duan 斫斷
chop off / cut off;

zhuo mu 斫木
chop wood;

zhuo sha 斫殺
kill with an ax / sword;

zhuo zhan 斫斬
chop / cut / hew;

zhuo2 shou 着手
put one's hand to || launch out; set about; set one's hand to; start doing sth;

zhuo shou cheng chun 着手成春
have admirable skill in curing diseases || cure every patient treated; have miraculous skill in treating patients; sickness retreats at one's touch;

zhuo2 擢
(1) extract / pick out / pull out / select / take out;
(2) promote / raise;

zhuo yin 擢引
pick and promote;

zhuo yong 擢用
pick and promote;

zi4 fa xing zhi tuo luo 自發性指脱落
dactylolysis spontanea;

zi jue fen mu 自掘墳墓
dig one's own grave;

zou4 揍
(1) beat || hit hard; slug;
(2) break;

zou ren 揍人
slug a person;

zou yi dun 揍一頓
beat / give a sound beating;

zuan4 捘
grip || clench; clutch; hold or seize with the hand;

zuan quan tou 捘拳頭
clench one's fist;

zuan4 攥
clutch / grasp / grip;

zuan jin quan tou 攥緊拳頭
clench one's fist;

zui4 quan 醉拳
drunkard boxing;

zuo2 捽
(1) grasp / hold with hands / seize;
(2) pull up;

zuo3 shou 左手
(1) left hand;
(2) left-hand side;

zuo you shou 左右手

(1) left and right hands;

(2) right-hand man / valuable assistant;

zuo4 shou jiao 做手腳

mess about with / play a trick / tamper with sth;

zuo shou shi 做手勢

gesticulate // gesticulation;

Tou 頭 Head

ang2 shou 昂首

hold up one's head / raise one's head high;

ang shou kuo bu 昂首闊步

march forward with one's head high ‖ galumph; keep one's head high and march ahead; prance about; step along in high spirits; stride forward proudly; stride forward with head held high; stride forward with one's chin up; stride proudly ahead; walk in a proud, self-important manner;

ang shou ting xiong 昂首挺胸

chin up and chest up / fling back one's head / hold up one's head and throw out one's chest;

ba1 tou tan nao 巴頭探腦

peep furtively from behind / stretch one's head in search;

bai2 shou 白首

grey-haired / hoary head;

bai shou qiong jing 白首窮經

continue to study even in old age;

bai tou 白頭

(1) grey hair / hoary head;

(2) old age;

bai tou ru xin 白頭如新

maintain an old acquaintanceship having no real understanding with each other;

bai tou xie lao 白頭偕老

remain a devoted couple to the end of their lives ‖ live to a ripe old age as husband and wife; live to a ripe old age in conjugal bliss; stick to each other till the hair turns grey; stick to each other to the end of their lives;

bai3 tou 擺頭

shake one's head in disapproval;

ban1 bai 斑白

grey-headed;

ban4 tou 半頭

half a head;

bao3 chi tou nao qing xing 保持頭腦清醒

keep one's head / know if one is coming or going;

bao chi zhen jing 保持鎮靜
keep cool / remain calm || keep face; keep one's calm / keep one's cool / keep one's countenance; keep one's hair on; keep one's head; keep one's shirt on; keep one's wig on; keep one's wool on;

bao4 shou er dun 抱首而遁
hide one's face and beat a retreat;

bao tou da ku 抱頭大哭
embrace and sob bitterly;

bao tou shu cuan 抱頭鼠竄
cover one's head and creep away || be frightened away; cover the head and scurry away like a rat back to its hole; flee helter-skelter; flee in a panic; flee with arms covering one's head; run away frightened like a rat; run away like rats; run off like a rat; run wildly like cornered rats; scamper off like a rat; scurry away like a frightened rat; throw one's arms over one's head and run away;

bao tou tong ku 抱頭痛哭
throw into each other's arms and cry one's heart out || cry in each other's arm; embrace one another's head and weep; fall upon one another's shoulders and weep; hang on sb's neck and weep out; wail sorrowfully; weep in each other's arm;

bao4 tou huan yan 豹頭環眼
round eyes and well-formed forehead;

bi2 yuan tou tong 鼻淵頭痛
sinus headache;

bian3 lu 扁顱
platycrania;

bian4 ya xing xuan yun 變壓性眩暈
alternobaric vertigo;

bu4 kan hui shou 不堪回首
cannot bear to look back;

bu mo tou 不摸頭
not acquainted with the situation;

cang2 shou na wei 藏首納尾
hide one's head and pull in one's tail — play down one's massive image;

cang tou lu wei 藏頭露尾
give a partial account of || act equivocately; show the tail but hide the head — tell part of the truth but not all of it;

chong1 xue xing tou tong 充血性頭痛
congestive headache / hyperremic headache;

chou1 chu xing yun jue 抽搐性暈厥
convulsive snycope;

chu1 tou lu mian 出頭露面
appear in public;

chuang4 shang hou tou tong 創傷後頭痛
posttraumatic headache;

chuang shang hou xuan yun 創傷後眩暈
posttraumatic vertigo;

chui2 shou tie er 垂首帖耳
docile and obedient;

chui tou 垂頭
hang one's head;

chui tou sang qi 垂頭餒氣
become dejected and despondent || blue about the gills; bury one's head in dejection; down at the mouth; down in the chops; down in the dumps; down in the hips; down in the mouth; downcast; hang one's head; have one's tail down; in low spirits; in the dumps; look downcast; mope oneself; off the hinges; one's crest fall; out of heart; out of spirits; out of sorts; sing the blues; take the heart out of sb;

chui tou zheng 垂頭症
kubisgari;

cong2 tou dao jiao 從頭到腳
from face to foot / from head to foot / from head to toe / from the sole of the foot to the crown of the head / from top to toe;

cuan2 tou jie er 攢頭接耳
put heads together / whisper;

da1 la zhe nao dai 耷拉着腦袋
droop one's head / hang one's head;

da4 tou chao xia 大頭朝下
(1) head over heels // upside down;
(2) handstand;

da tou zheng 大頭症
bighead;

dai4 戴
put on / wear;

頭 *Head*

dai gao mao zi 戴高帽子
(1) flatter / lay it on thick;
(2) wear a tall paper hat;

dai lü mao zi 戴綠帽子
wear a green hat // a husband whose wife has an affair with other men / a cuckhold;

dai mao zi 戴帽子
(1) put on one's hat / wear one's hat;
(2) be branded as / be labelled / pin the label of ...on sb / put labels on sb;

dang1 tou 當頭
(1) head on / right on sb's head / right over head;
(2) imminent;

dang tou bang he 當頭棒喝
give a timely warning / issue a strong warning;

dang tou yi ji 當頭一擊
one for his nob;

dao3 guo tou lai 倒過頭來
turn the other way round;

dao tou 倒頭
lie down;

dao tou bian shui 倒頭便睡
fall asleep as soon as one goes to bed;

dao4 zai cong 倒栽蔥
fall head over heels / fall headlong;

di1 shou 低首
lower one's head;

di shou bu yu 低首不語
bow one's head and keep silent / hang down the head without uttering a word / hang one's head in silence;

di shou xia xin 低首下心
bow one's head in humility ‖ bow and scrape; give oneself up; humble oneself; obsequiously submissive; submit; yield;

di tou 低頭
(1) bend one's head / bow one's head / cast down one's head; hang one's head; lower one's head;
(2) submit / yield;

di tou bu da 低頭不答
bend one's head and do not reply / bend one's head down and make no answer / cast down one's head and do not reply;

di tou bu yu 低頭不語
lower one's head and keep quiet;

di tou ha yao 低頭哈腰
humble oneself in serving a master;

di tou ren zui 低頭認罪
hang one's head and admit one's guilt / plead guilty;

di tou tan xi 低頭歎息
hang one's head and sigh;

di tou wu yan 低頭無言
bow and be silent / lower one's head and say nothing;

di tou xun si 低頭尋思
bend one's head and try hard to remember / lower one's head in thought // with bowed head in deep thought;

di xia tou 低下頭
lower one's head;

dian3 xing pian tou tong 典型偏頭痛
classic migraine;

dian3 shou 點首
nod;

dian tou 點頭
give permission / nod / nod assent / nod one's head / noddle;

dian tou cheng shan 點頭稱善
nod and express approval;

dian tou gao bie 點頭告別
nod one's farewell;

dian tou ha yao 點頭哈腰
bow and scrape / nod and bow;

dian tou huan ying 點頭歡迎
nod sb a welcome / welcome sb with a nod;

dian tou hui yi 點頭會意
nod in understanding ‖ catch on and nod; nod understandingly; nod with understanding;

dian tou peng you 點頭朋友
nodding acquaintance;

dian tou shi yi 點頭示意
give a nod as a signal / signal by nodding;

dian tou tong yi 點頭同意
agree with a nod / show approval by nodding;

dian tou yi xiao 點頭一笑
nod with a smile;

dian tou yun nuo 點頭允諾
nod acceptance / nod acquiescence / nod agreement;

dian tou zan tong 點頭贊同
nod in approval / nod in consent;

dian tou zhao hu 點頭招呼
nod to sb as a greeting;

dian tou zhi jiao 點頭之交
bowing acquaintance / casual acquaintance / incidental acquaintance / passing acquaintance / speaking acquaintance // have a nodding acquaintance with sb;

dian tou zhi zhi yi 點頭致意
nod a greeting / nod in acknowledgement / nod in salutation;

diao4 guo tou lai 掉過頭來
turn around / turn back / turn one's head;

diao tou 掉頭
turn about / turn round || change direction;

diao tou er qu 掉頭而去
fling off;

diao tou jiu zou 掉頭就走
turn away and leave / turn one's head and walk away;

diao4 dao jiu pao 調頭就跑
double back;

e2 額
forehead;

e gu 額骨
frontal bone;

e jiao 額角
temples;

e tou 額頭
forehead;

fa1 re xing tou tong 發熱性頭痛
pyrexial headache;

fang1 lian tu e 方臉突額
have a prominent forehead and a broad face;

fei2 tou da er 肥頭大耳
large head and big ears — signs of a prosperous man;

fei tou da lian 肥頭大臉
a great fullness of face;

fei tou pang er 肥頭胖耳
large head and big ears — signs of a prosperous man;

fen3 mian you tou 粉面油頭
powder the face and anoint the head / the fair sex / the ladies;

fu3 俯
bow one's head;

fu shou 俯首
bend one's head / bow one's head;

fu shou jiu fan 俯首就範
bend one's head and sbumit to control / bow the head and conform to the rule — meekly submitting;

fu shou jiu fu 俯首就縛
bend the head and be tied / droop one's head and allow oneself to be bound — give no resistance;

fu shou jiu lu 俯首就戮
bow before the butcher's knife;

fu shou qu xi 俯首屈膝
kneel down humbly;

fu shou tie er 俯首帖耳
submissive and obedient || all obedience and servility; docile and obedient; docilely obey; in complete obedience; obey with servility; servile like a dog; subservient to;

fu shou ting ming 俯首聽命
bow down to obey submissively || at sb's beck and call; be submissive; bend one's neck; obey sb's order with all due submission; obey with bent head; submissively hear and obey;

fu shou wu yan 俯首無言
bend one's head in silence;

fu yang 俯仰
bending of the head / lifting of the head || simple action; simple move;

fu yang wu kui 俯仰無愧
feel not disgraceful in looking down and up — having a clear conscience;

fu yang zhi jian 俯仰之間
in a flash / in a short span / in a twinkling / in an instant / in the twinkling of an eye;

fu yang you ren 俯仰由人
be at others' beck and call ‖ be twisted round others' finger; submit oneself to others' whims and fancies;

fu yang zi de 俯仰自得
contented and happy wherever one may be;

gai3 tou huan mian 改頭換面
disguise in a different garb ‖ camouflage; change only the appearance; change the outside only; disguise; dish up in a new form; in a disguised form; make only superficial changes; refurnish; rehash;

gong1 neng xing tou tong 功能性頭痛
functional headache;

guang1 tou 光頭
(1) bareheaded;
(2) shaven head // shaven-headed;

guang tou tu e 光頭禿額
with balding hair and shining forehead;

gui3 ti tou 鬼剃頭
balding disease;

gui tou gui nao 鬼頭鬼腦
stealthy ‖ crafty and sinister; furtive; hiding and peeping; peeping and prying; secretive; thievish;

gui tou ha ma yan 鬼頭蛤蟆眼
furtive / stealthy;

han2 xiao dian tou 含笑點頭
nod with a smile;

han4 頷
nod;

han shou 頷首
nod;

han shou hui yi 頷首會意
nod one's comprehension;

han shou shi yi 頷首示意
give a nod as a signal;

han shou wei xiao 頷首微笑
nod smilingly;

han shou zhi jiao 頷首之交
a nodding acquaintance;

hao4 shou 皓首
hoary head;

hao shou qiong jing 皓首窮經
a hoary head does research in the classics // continue to study even in old age / live and learn;

hui1 tou tu mian 灰頭土面
dusty and dirty in appearance;

hui2 shou 回首
(1) turn one's head / turn round;
(2) call to mind / look back / recollect;

hui shou qian chen 回首前塵
look back upon the past / recall past events;

hui tou 回頭
turn about / turn one's head / turn round;

hui tou jian 回頭見
cheerio / see you later;

hui tou shi an 回頭是岸
repentance is salvation ‖ it is never too late to mend; just repent and salvation is at hand; never too late to mend; repentance is never too late; repentance never comes too late; the shore is just behind you; there is yet time for you to mend your ways; to repent is the only way out; turn back and you are ashore; turn back to safety; turn from one's evil ways; turn the head and the shore is at hand — to repent and be saved;

hui tou yi kan 回頭一看
glance over one's shoulder / look back / turn one's head and look;

hui tou yi xiang 回頭一想
on a second thought;

hun1 tou hun nao 昏頭昏腦
addle-headed ‖ absent-minded; addle-brained; be infatuated; forgetful; muddleheaded; not to know if one is on one's head or one's heels;

hun tou zhuan xiang 昏頭轉向
confused and dizzy // with a swirling head;

頭 *Head*

hun2 tou hun nao 渾頭渾腦
addleheaded || absent-minded; addlebrained; be infatuated; forgetful; muddle-headed; not to know if one is on one's head or one's heels;

ji2 shou cu e 疾首蹙額
frown in disgust || with abhorrence; with aching head and knitted brows;

ji shou tong xin 疾首痛心
with an aching head and a broken heart;

jia3 xuan yun 假眩暈
pseudovertigo;

jiao1 tou jie er 交頭接耳
speak in each other's ears || bill and coo; exchange confidential whispers; head to head; heads together and ears stretched out; secret conversations; talk confidentially; talk mouth to ear; whisper into each other's ears; whisper to each other; whispering;

jin3 zhang xing tou tong 緊張性頭痛
tension headache;

ju3 shou 舉首
raise one's head;

ju4 tou 巨頭
megalocephaly;

ju tou zheng 巨頭症
cephalonia;

ju4 shou 聚首
get together / meet;

jue4 tou jue nao 倔頭倔腦
blunt in manner and gruff of speech;

kan3 tou 砍頭
behead / decapitate / hack off one's head;

kang2 tou 扛頭
raise one's head in a gesture of disdain;

ke1 tou 磕頭
kowtow;

ke tou li bai 磕頭禮拜
make obeisance and perform the rites of courtesy;

ke tou pei zui 磕頭賠罪
give sb a grand knowtow and apologize;

ke tou peng nao 磕頭碰腦
bump against things on every side / push and bump against one another;

ke tou zuo yi 磕頭作揖
kowtow and bow;

ke2 sou xing tou tong 咳嗽性頭痛
cough headache;

ke sou yun jue 咳嗽暈厥
cough syncope;

kou shou 叩首
kowtow;

kou4 tou 叩頭
kowtow;

kou tou li bai 叩頭禮拜
kneel down in prayer;

kou tou pei zui 叩頭賠罪
give sb a grand kowtow and apologize;

kou tou qiu rao 叩頭求饒
beat one's forehead on the ground and whine for mercy;

kou tou ru ni 叩頭如泥
repeatedly kowtow by touching the ground with one's forehead;

kou tou ru yi 叩頭如儀
knock one's head on the floor as ceremony / kowtow as custom required;

kou tou xie zui 叩頭謝罪
hit one's forehead on the ground and acknowledge one's guilt;

kou tou zuo yi 叩頭作揖
kowtow and bow with a great show of respect;

kui4 頍
raise one's head;

la4 li 瘌痢
favus of the scalp;

la li tou 瘌痢頭
a person affected with favus on the head;

leng3 shui jiao tou 冷水澆頭
like a bucket of cold water thrown over sb || feel as if a basin of cold water has been poured over one's head; feel as if doused with cold water;

leng4 tou ke nao 愣頭瞌腦
(1) stupid;
(2) rash;

leng4 tou leng nao 愣頭愣腦
(1) rash / reckless;
(2) stupid / stupid-looking;

lian2 lian dian tou 連連點頭
nod again and again / nod repeatedly / nod vigorously;

liu2 xing xing xuan yun 流行性眩暈
epidemic vertigo;

lou1 tou 摟頭
head-on;

lu2 顱
cranium / skull;
bian lu 扁顱
platycrania;

lu bing 顱病
craniopathy;

lu fa yu bu liang 顱發育不良
atelocephaly;

lu fa yu bu quan 顱發育不全
atelocephaly;

ma2 bi xing xuan yun 麻痺性眩暈
paralytic vertigo;

mai2 shou yu 埋首於
be engrossed in ‖ hammer away at; immerse oneself in;

mai tou 埋頭
be engrossed in / immerse oneself in ‖ drown in; duck; give up to;

mai tou du shu 埋頭讀書
bury oneself in books / grind away;

mai tou gong zuo 埋頭工作
give oneself wholly to one's work;

mai tou ku gan 埋頭苦幹
immerse oneself in hard work ‖ bring one's nose to the grindstone; complete absorption in arduous work; engage oneself in unostentatious hard work; have one's shoulder to the collar; hold one's nose to the grindstone; keep one's nose to the grindstone; put one's nose to the grindstone; quietly immerse oneself in hard work; quietly put one's shoulder to the wheel; work doggedly in silence; work very energetically; work with quiet hard application;

mai tou ye wu 埋頭業務
engross oneself in vocational work;

mai tou yong gong 埋頭用功
be buried in study;

mai4 tou mai jiao 賣頭賣腳
sell one's head and feet / show one's face in public;

man3 tou da han 滿頭大汗
with sweat all over one's face ‖ all of a sweat; be covered with sweat; one's face is bathed in sweat; sweat drips from one's face; sweat streams down one's face; sweat trickles down one's face;

man tou han zhu 滿頭汗珠
on one's forehead stands great beads of perspiration;

mao2 tou mao nao 毛頭毛腦
impetuous / rash;

meng2 tou gai lian 蒙頭蓋臉
cover one's head and face // with face covered;

mi2 lu xing xuan yun 迷路性眩暈
labyrinthine vertigo;

mi tou 迷頭
confused / mixed up / stupid;

mo1 tou 摸頭
know the real situation / learn the ropes;

mo tou bu zhao 摸頭不着
all at sea ‖ unable to find the proper approach or order in the whole thing; unable to make anything out of;

mo4 tou 抹頭
turn round / turn the body;

na2 ding 拿頂
stand on one's head;

nao2 tou 撓頭
scratch one's head;

pao1 tou lu, sa re xue 拋頭顱，灑熱血
shed one's blood and lay down one's life;

pao tou lu mian 抛頭露面
appear in public / show oneself in public // in the limelight;

peng2 shou gou mian 蓬首垢面
with unkempt hair and a dirty face ‖ filthy appearance; unkempt; with dishevelled hair and grimy face;

peng tou gou mian 蓬頭垢面
with dishevelled hair and a dirty face ‖ dishevelled hair and dirty face; unkempt appearance; with uncombed hair and dirty face;

peng tou san fa 蓬頭散髮
with dishevelled hair // shock-head // shockheaded;

peng4 tou 碰頭
meet sb;

pi1 tou 劈頭
right in the face / straight on the head;

pi tou gai lian 劈頭蓋臉
right in the face ‖ a vicious assault on a person; direct to one's head and face; scold sb to his face;

pian1 tan xing pian tou tong 偏癱性偏頭痛
hemiplegic migraine;

pian tou tong 偏頭痛
blind headache / migraine / migraine headache / sick headache;
dian xing pian tou tong 典型偏頭痛
classic migraine;
pian tan xing pian tou tong 偏癱性偏頭痛
hemiplegic migraine;
shen jing xing pian tou tong 神經性偏頭痛
neurologic migraine;

ping2 tou zheng lian 平頭正臉
neat appearance // well-featured;

ping2 tou lun zu 評頭論足
carp at;

qi1 qiao 七竅
seven apertures in the human head — eyes, ears, nostrils and mouth;

qi qiao liu xue 七竅流血
bleeding from the seven apertures in the human head;

qi qiao sheng yan 七竅生煙
smoke belches out from the seven apertures in the human head;

qi2 zai tou shang 騎在頭上
ride on the backs of ‖ lord it over; ride roughshod over; sit on the backs of;

qi zai tou shang, la shi la niao 騎在頭上，拉屎拉尿
ride on the back of the people and piss and shit on them;

qi zai tou shang, zuo wei zuo fu 騎在頭上，作威作福
ride roughshod on the back of;

qi3 稽
bow to the ground / kowtow;

qi sang 稽顙
kowtow with one's forehead touching the ground;

qi shou 稽首
kowtow;

qi4 zhi xing tou tong 器質性頭痛
organic headache;

qi zhi xing xuan yun 器質性眩暈
organic vertigo;

qian2 e 前額
forehead;

qian tou 前頭
in front ‖ ahead; take their place in the van;

qiao2 shou 翹首
raise one's head and look;

qiao shou er wang 翹首而望
raise one's head and look ‖ lift up one's head in expectation; on the tiptoe of expectation; raise the head and stand on tiptoe expecting; raise one's head in hope;

qiao shou kang zu 翹首抗足
raise one's head and stand on tiptoe in admiration;

qiao shou qi zu 翹首企足
crane one's neck and stand on tiptoe in pleasurable expectation / raise one's head and stand on tiptoe to look eargerly ahead;

qiao shou xing kong 翹首星空
lift up one's eyes to the starry sky / look up at

頭 *Head*

the starry sky;

qiao shou yi dai 翹首以待
raise one's head and look forward to // on the tiptoe of expectation;

qie4 tou qie nao 怯頭怯腦
nervous and clumsy, timid and unsophisticated;

san1 tou er mian 三頭二面
cunning / double-faced / two-faced;

san tou liu bi 三頭六臂
a resourceful and capable man ‖ an extraordinarily able person; three heads and six arms — superhuman;

sao1 sao tou pi 搔搔頭皮
scratch one's head;

sao shou 搔首
scratch one's head;

sao shou chi chu 搔首踟躕
at a loss as to what to do ‖ hesitate; in a dilemma; in perplexity; scratch one's head in great perplexity; scratch one's head in hesitation; undecided;

sao shou nong zi 搔首弄姿
stroke one's hair while flirting ‖ affected in manner; coquettish; flirt; giggle and flirt; posture and preen oneself; stroke one's hair in coquetry — the seductive act of a woman;

sao tou 搔頭
scratch one's head;

sao tou mo er 搔頭摸耳
hesitating / undecided;

sha1 tou 殺頭
behead / decapitate;

sha3 tou sha nao 傻頭傻腦
(1) foolish-looking;
(2) muddleheaded ‖ cloddish; clumsy and stupid; foolish; off one's dot; silly;

she2 tou shu wei 蛇頭鼠尾
sneaky, crafty look;

she tou shu yan 蛇頭鼠眼
a snake's head and a rat's eyes / crafty / cunning / wily;

shen1 tou tan nao 伸頭探腦
crane one's neck to watch / poke one's head to peek at / stretch the neck in an effort to find out;

shen2 jing xing pian tou tong 神經性偏頭痛
neurologic migraine;

sheng4 liu xing xuan yun 剩留性眩暈
residual vertigo;

shi2 bu jiu hui tou 十步九回頭
look back nine times every ten steps // hesitating / wavering;

shou3 ken 首肯
nod one's head in approval;

shou4 tou shou nao 壽頭壽腦
stupid looking;

suo1 tou suo nao 縮頭縮腦
hesitant / timid;

suo tou tu she 縮頭吐舌
shrug and stick out the tongue;

tai2 qi tou 擡起頭
lift up one's head / raise one's head;

tai tou 擡頭
(1) lift up one's head / raise one's head;
(2) upsurge;

tai tou jian xi 擡頭見喜
raise one's head and see bliss;

tai tou ting xiong 擡頭挺胸
chin up and chest out — full of confidence;

tai tou wen 擡頭紋
wrinkles on one's forehead;

tan4 tou tan nao 探頭探腦
poke out one's head to peek at ‖ act stealthily; crane one's neck to peer; peep furtively from behind; pop one's head in and look about; probe furtively;

tan tou zhang wang 探頭張望
crane one's neck and look around;

ti4 剃
shave;

ti guang tou 剃光頭
shave the head bald;

ti ping tou 剃平頭
have a crew cut;

ti tou 剃頭
(1) have one's head shaved / shave the head;
(2) have a haircut / have one's hair cut;

tian1 ting 天庭
forehead;

tong2 tou tie e 銅頭鐵額
brass head iron forehead — courageous and cruel;

tou2 頭
head;
ju tou 巨頭
megalocephaly;

tou bing 頭病
cephalopathy;

tou bu 頭部
head / top;

tou bu bing 頭部病
cephalopathy;

tou ding 頭頂
top of one's head;

tou e 頭額
one's forehead;

tou guo duan 頭過短
hyperbrachycephaly;

tou hun 頭昏
dizzy / giddy;

tou hun mu xuan 頭昏目眩
feel dizzy;

tou hun nao zhang 頭昏腦脹
feel dizzy and have a headache ‖ feel one's head swimming; get very dizzy and one's head begins to ache; make sb's head swim;

tou hun yan hua 頭昏眼花
with head giddy and eyes dazzled ‖ cutting out paper dolls; dazed; dizzy; feel dizzy and with eyesight dimmed; light-headed; mentally confused; one's head begins to swim and one's eyes are misted; punck-drunk; see stars; slap-happy;

tou lu 頭顱
head / skull;

tou pi 頭皮
epicranium / scalp;

tou pi xie 頭皮屑
dandruff;

tou po xue liu 頭破血流
with one's head broken and bleeding;

tou shang 頭上
on the head / on top;

tou shang an tou 頭上安頭
fit on a head where there is a head — superfluous;

tou shang zhang chuang, jiao di liu nong 頭上長瘡，腳底流膿
rotten to the core // with boils on the head and feet running with pus — rotten from head to foot;

tou shi 頭虱
bug / head louse;

tou shi bing 頭虱病
pediculosis capillitii;

tou teng 頭疼
headache;

tou teng nao re 頭疼腦熱
headache and slight fever / slight illness;

tou tong 頭痛
cephalalgia / headache // ache in one's head / have a headache;
bi yuan tou tong 鼻淵頭痛
headache of nasosinusitis;
chong xue xing tou tong 充血性頭痛
congestive headache ‖ hyperremic headache;
chuan ci xing tou tong 穿刺性頭痛
puncture headache;
chuang shang hou tou tong 創傷後頭痛
post-traumatic headache;
fa re xing tou tong 發熱性頭痛
pyrexial headache;
gong neng xing tou tong 功能性頭痛
functional headache;
jin zhang xing tou tong 緊張性頭痛
tension headache;
ke sou xing tou tong 咳嗽性頭痛
cough headache;
pin xue xing tou tong 貧血性頭痛
anemic headache;

qi zhi xing tou tong 器質性頭痛
organic headache;
wai shang hou tou tong 外傷後頭痛
post-traumatic headache;
xiang xian tou tong 象限頭痛
quadrantal cephalalgia;
zheng zhuang xing tou tong 症狀性頭痛
symptomatic headache;
zhong du xing tou tong 中毒性頭痛
toxic headache;

tou tong fa re 頭痛發熱
have a headache and fever / have a headache and high temperature;

tou tong nao re 頭痛腦熱
a headache and slight fever / a headache or a sore throat / slight illness;

tou tong yi tou, jiao tong yi jiao 頭痛醫頭，腳痛醫腳
cure only the symptoms || a defensive stopgap measure; sporadic and piecemeal steps; take only palliative measures for one's illness; treat the head when the head aches, treat the foot when the foot hurts — treat symptons but not the disease; treat the head when there's a headache, and the foot when there's a footache — apply palliative remedies;

tou tu 頭突
head process;

tou xie 頭屑
dandruff;

tou xuan 頭癬
favus of the scalp;

tou yao leng, xin yao re 頭要冷，心要熱
cool in the head but warm at heart;

tou yun 頭暈
dizzy / giddy;

tou yun mu xuan 頭暈目眩
dizzy of head and dim of eyes || be afflicted with vertigo; dizzy; eyes swim in one's head; have a dizzy spell; light in the head; light-headed; rocky;

tou yun nao zhang 頭暈腦脹
feel dizzy and have a headache;

tou yun yan hua 頭暈眼花
dizzy head and blurred eyes || dizzy; dizzy of head and dim of sight; one's head begins to swim and one's eyes are misted;

tou zhang 頭脹
feel heavy in the head;

tou zhong jiao qing 頭重腳輕
top-heavy || one's head grows heavy and one's feet grow light; weigh down;

tou zu dao zhi 頭足倒置
turn everything upside down;

tu2 shou 徒首
bareheaded;

tu3 tou tu nao 土頭土腦
countrified / rustic || hillbilly; hob-nailed; jungli; stupid and uncouth; unsophisticated;

wai4 shang hou tou tong 外傷後頭痛
posttraumatic headache;

wai zhou xing xuan yun 外周性眩暈
peripheral vertigo;

wei1 tu de tou ding 微禿的頭頂
the balding crown of one's head;

wei4 bing xing xuan yun 胃病性眩暈
stomachal vertigo;

wei xing xuan yun 胃性眩暈
gastric vertigo;

xia4 hun le tou 嚇昏了頭
be struck dumb / be stunned;

xiang4 xian tou tong 象限頭痛
quadrantal cephalalgia;

xie2 tou 斜頭
plagiocephaly;

xin1 xing yun jue 心性暈厥
cardiac syncope;

xiu1 de tai bu qi tao lai 羞得抬不起頭來
hide one's face;

xiu4 ding 秀頂
bald head // baldheaded;

xuan4 yun 眩暈
vertigo;
bian ya xing xuan yun 變壓性眩暈
alternobaric vertigo;

頭 *Head*

chuang shang hou xuan yun 創傷後眩暈
posttraumatic vertigo;
jia xuan yun 假眩暈
pseudovertigo;
liu xing xing xuan yun 流行性眩暈
epidemic vertigo;
ma bi xing xuan yun 麻痺性眩暈
paralytic vertigo;
mi lu xing xuan yun 迷路性眩暈
labyrinthine vertigo;
qi zhi xing xuan yun 器質性眩暈
organic vertigo;
sheng liu xing xuan yun 剩留性眩暈
residual vertigo;
wai zhou xing xuan yun 外周性眩暈
peripheral vertigo;
wei bing xing xuan yun 胃病性眩暈
stomachal vertigo;
wei xing xuan yun 胃性眩暈
gastric vertigo;
ya li xing xuan yun 壓力性眩暈
pressure vertigo;
yan bing xing xuan yun 眼病性眩暈
ocular vertigo;
ye fa xing xuan yun 夜發性眩暈
nocturnal vertigo;
yuan fa xing xuan yun 原發性眩暈
primary vertigo;
zhen fa xing xuan yun 陣發性眩暈
paroxysmal vertigo;
zhi li xing xuan yun 直立性眩暈
vertical vertigo;
zhong du xing xuan yun 中毒性眩暈
toxic vertigo;
zi fa xing xuan yun 自發性眩暈
essential vertigo;
zu zhong xing xuan yun 卒中性眩暈
apoplectic vertigo;

ya1 li xing xuan yun 壓力性眩暈
pressure vertigo;

yan3 bing xing xuan yun 眼病性眩暈
ocular vertigo;

yang3 qi tou 仰起頭
lift up one's head;

yang shou da xiao 仰首大笑
throw one's head back and laugh;

yang shou shen mei 仰首伸眉
with one's chin up and eyebrows dancing — look of exultation;

yao2 shou 搖首
shake one's head in disapproval;

yao tou 搖頭
shake one's head;

yao tou bai shou 搖頭擺手
wag the head and wave the hand;

yao tou bai wei 搖頭擺尾
shake the head and wag the tail — assume an air of complacency / toss one's head and tail;

yao tou huang nao 搖頭晃腦
wag one's head ‖ nod one's head — assume an air of self-approbation; wag one's head — look pleased with oneself;

yao tou tai xi 搖頭太息
shake one's head and heave a deep sigh / shake the head and utter a deep sigh;

yao yao tou 搖搖頭
shake one's head;

ye4 fa xing xuan yun 夜發性眩暈
nocturnal vertigo;

yi1 tou 一頭
a head;

yi tou wu shui 一頭霧水
be totally confused // in bewilderment / in confusion // not knowing what is the matter;

yi4 shou 抑首
lower one's head;

ying2 tou 迎頭
directly / head-on;

ying tou er shang 迎頭而上
face sth directly / meet it head-on;

ying tou gan shang 迎頭趕上
catch up forthwith / come up from behind / try hard to catch up;

ying tou tong ji 迎頭痛擊
deal head-on blows ‖ a hard knock at the head; a head-on hammer-blow; deal a severe blow; give a good hiding; give sb a bad

knock on the head; knock sb on the head; make a frontal attack; meet head-on; score a hard, direct hit;

ying4 zhe tou pi 硬着頭皮
brace oneself to do sth || brazen it out; brazen it through; force oneself; put a bold face on it; steel oneself; summon up courage; toughen one's scalp;

ying zhe tou pi ding zhu 硬着頭皮頂住
brace oneself and bear with it / hold out tenaciously;

you2 tou fen mian 油頭粉面
pomaded hair and powdered face;

you tou hua nao 油頭滑腦
flippant / slick;

you3 tou you mian er 有頭有面兒
(1) honoured / respected;
(2) presentable;

yuan2 fa xing xuan yun 原發性眩暈
primary vertigo;

yun1 暈
areola;

yun che 暈車
riders' vertigo;

yun che bing 暈車病
car sickness;

yun chuan 暈船
sea sickness;

yun ji 暈機
aviation sickness;

yun jue 暈厥
faint / syncope;
chou chu xing yun jue 抽搐性暈厥
convulsive syncope;
ke sou yun jue 咳嗽暈厥
cough syncope;
xin xing yun jue 心性暈厥
cardiac syncope;

yun tou 暈頭
(1) blockhead;
(2) feel dizzy;

yun tou ba nao 暈頭巴腦
feel dizzy and giddy;

yun tou zhuan xiang 暈頭轉向
(1) feel dizzy and giddy;
(2) so confused that one doesn't know what to do or say;

zei2 tou zei nao 賊頭賊腦
behave stealthily like a thief || a mean look; act suspiciously; every inch of him a thief; furtive; thief-like; villainous-looking;

zhan3 shou 斬首
behead;

zhan shou shi zhong 斬首示眾
behead a criminal and exhibit the severed head to the public as a warning to would-be offenders;

zhe1 gen tou 折跟頭
somersault // fall head over heels;

zhe1 tou gai mian 遮頭蓋面
act stealthily / cover one's head and face;

zhen4 fa xing xuan yun 陣發性眩暈
paroxysmal vertigo;

zheng4 zhuang xing tou tong 症狀性頭痛
symptomatic headache;

zhi2 li xing xuan yun 直立性眩暈
vertical vertigo;

zhong4 du xing tou tong 中毒性頭痛
toxic headache;

zhong du xing xuan yun 中毒性眩暈
toxic vertigo;

zhua1 tou 抓頭
scratch the head;

zhuan3 tou 轉頭
turn one's head;

zhuo2 tou 斫頭
behead / decapitate;

zi4 fa xing xuan yun 自發性眩暈
essential vertigo;

zu2 zhong xing xuan yun 卒中性眩暈
apoplectic vertigo;

Tun 臀 Buttocks

bi4 髀
(1) buttocks;
(2) hipbone / innominate bone;

bi gu 髀骨
hipbone / innominate bone;

ca1 pi gu 擦屁股
clear up the mess left by sb else / patch up sth others have not done well;

da3 pi gu 打屁股
(1) slap on the buttocks;
(2) criticize sharply;

da zuo 打坐
sit in meditation;

fu3 bi 拊髀
slap one's own buttocks in excitement or despair;

fu bi xing tan 拊髀興歎
slap one's own buttocks to lament one's own inability to resume work;

gan3 lan pi gu — zuo bu zhu 橄欖屁股 —— 坐不住
the bottom of a Chinese olive — cannot sit firmly // cannot sit still // hyperactive;

guang1 pi gu 光屁股
stark-naked // in the nude;

nü3 tun guo fei 女臀過肥
an extreme accumulation of fat on the buttocks in women / steatopygia;

pai1 bi 拍髀
pat the thigh;

pi4 gu 屁股
buttocks ‖ backside; behind; boff; butt; hunker; one's bottom; one's bum; the cheeks; the chuff;

pi gu dan 屁股蛋
buttocks;

tu2 zuo 徒坐
sit in leisure / sit without doing anything;

tun2 臀
buttocks ‖ clunis; behind; bottom; hunkers; rump;

tun bu 臀部
buttocks / haunch / hunkers / posteriors;

tun fan she 臀反射
gluteal reflex;

tun gou 臀溝
gluteal furrow;

tun lie 臀裂
gluteal cleft;

tun shang lin ba jie 臀上淋巴結
superior gluteal lymph nodes;

tun tong 臀痛
pygalgia;

tun xia lin ba jie 臀下淋巴結
inferior gluteal lymph nodes;

wu2 tun 無臀
abrachia;

wu4 zuo 兀坐
sit upright;

Xi 膝 Knee

bai4 gui 拜跪
kneel and kowtow;

bao4 xi er zuo 抱膝而坐
sit with one's arms about one's knees;

bei1 gong qu xi 卑躬屈膝
bow and scrape || act servilely; cap in hand; cringe; eat dirt; eat humble pie; genuflect; grovel in the dirt; grovel in the dust; hat in hand; humble oneself in serving a master; humiliate oneself in serving; kiss the ground; kowtow to; make a great show of obedience and courtesy; meek; on one's knees // subservient;

bin4 臏
kneecap;

bin gu 臏骨
kneecap;

bin4 髕
kneecap / kneepan;

bin fan she 髕反射
patellar reflex;

bin gu 髕骨
patella;

bin jiao 髕腳
cutting off the kneecap (ancient punishment);

cu4 xi 促膝
sit very close to each other;

cu xi tan xin 促膝談心
sit close to each other and have a heart-to-heart talk / talk intimately;

ding3 bai 頂拜
kneel down and kowtow;

fa2 gui 罰跪
keep a person kneeling as punishment;

fu3 shou qu xi 俯首屈膝
kneel down humbly;

gui4 跪
fall on one's knees / go down on one's knees / grovel on one's kneels / kneel;

gui bai 跪拜
kowtow / worship on bended knees;

gui dao 跪倒
throw oneself on one's knees || grovel; prostrate oneself;

gui dao jiao xia 跪倒腳下
throw oneself at sb's feet;

gui dao pa qi 跪倒爬起
kneel on the ground again and again;

gui dao zai di 跪倒在地
go down on one's knees / kneel on the ground;

gui di 跪地
grovel on one's kneels / kneel on the ground;

gui di ai qiu 跪地哀求
kneel on the ground crying for mercy;

gui di qi ming 跪地乞命
lie in the dust pleading for one's life;

gui di qi rao 跪地乞饒
prostrate oneself before sb and beg for mercy and forgiveness / throw oneself on the ground and plead for mercy;

gui fu 跪伏
couch;

gui luo 跪落
knee drop;

gui ru zhi en 跪乳之恩
filial piety;

gui song 跪送
bid farewell in a kneeling position;

gui xia 跪下
drop to one's knees / kneel;

gui xia qiu rao 跪下求饒
fall to one's knees, begging for mercy / kneel down begging for pardon;

gui xie 跪謝
express thanks on one's knees;

gui ying 跪迎
greet in a kneeling position / receive in a kneeling position;

gui zai ren qian 跪在人前
fall on one's knees before sb / kneel at sb's feet;

gui zi 跪姿
kneeling position;

ji4 跽
kneel for a long time;

jie1 xi 接膝
knee to knee – sit close to each other;

jie xi jiao yan 接膝交言
sit close to each other and talk;

nei4 fan xi 內翻膝
genu introsum;

nong2 du xing xi guan jie yan 膿毒性膝關節炎
septic knee;

nu2 yan bi xi 奴顏婢膝
bow and scrape like slaves to // abject submission ‖ bend one's knees before; bow low and humiliate oneself; bow low and sweep the ground with one's cap; lick sb's boots; make a great show of obedience and courtesy;

nü3 pu xi bing 女僕膝病
housemaid's knee;

pai1 xi er ge 拍膝而歌
sing, beating time on one's knees;

pan2 xi er zuo 盤膝而坐
sit cross-legged / sit tailor-fashion / sit with the legs crossed;

qu1 xi 屈膝
bend one's knees ‖ drop on one's knees; fall on one's knees; genuflect; give in; go down on one's knees; kneel down; knuckle down; succumb;

qu xi gui bai 屈膝跪拜
genuflection;

qu xi li bai 屈膝禮拜
bend the knees in worship;

qu xi qiu he 屈膝求和
bow the knees to... and sue for peace;

qu xi qiu rao 屈膝求饒
capitulate to...and beg for mercy;

qu xi tou xiang 屈膝投降
bend and surrender to ‖ bow and surrender to; fall on one's knees to surrender; give in and surrender to; go down on one's knees in surrender; kneel down in capitulation; knuckle under; submit and surrender to; throw oneself at the feet of;

qu xi xing li 屈膝行禮
bow a courtesy / drop a courtesy;

rao4 xi cheng huan 繞膝承歡
stay with one's parents in order to make them happy;

rong2 xi zhi di 容膝之地
a place just big enough to get the knees in / a tiny spot;

san1 gui jiu kou 三跪九叩
kneel three times with the head touching the ground nine times;

tiao4 yuan yun dong yuan xi 跳遠運動員膝
jumper's knee;

xi1 膝
geniculum / knee;

xi bu 膝步
walk on knees;

xi fan qu 膝反屈
back knee;

xi fan she 膝反射
knee jerk / knee reflex / patellar;

xi gai 膝蓋
knee;

xi gai gu 膝蓋骨
kneecap / patella;

xi guan jie 膝關節
knee joint;

xi jian fan she 膝腱反射
knee jerk;

xi liu 膝瘤
gonyoncus;

xi nei fan 膝內翻
gonyectyposis;

xi qian qu 膝前區
anterior region of knee;

xi qian wan 膝前彎
sprung knee;

xi qu 膝區
knee region;

xi tan 膝袒
walk on knees and bare one's breast;

xi tong 膝痛
gonalgia;

xi wai fan 膝外翻
gonycrotesis;

xi wan qu 膝彎曲
gonycampsis;

xi xia 膝下
children;

xi xia cheng huan 膝下承歡
please one's parents by living with them;

xi xia er nü 膝下兒女
children surrounding parents' knees — children living with their parents;

xi xia you xu 膝下猶虛
have no children // still childless;

xi xing 膝行
walk on knees;

xi yang sao bei 膝癢搔背
scratch the back while the knee is itching — irrelevant;

xi zhong 膝腫
knee-gall;

xia4 gui 下跪
go down on one's knees / kneel down;

Xian 腺 Gland

chan3 hou jia zhuang xian yan 產後甲狀腺炎
postpartum thyroiditis;

chang2 xian 腸腺
enteraden;

chang xian yan 腸腺炎
enteradenitis;

dan1 chun xing lin ba guan liu 單純性淋巴管瘤
simple lymphangioma;

dan xing xing xian liu 單形性腺瘤
monomorphic adenoma;

dan3 guan xian 膽管腺
glands of bile duct;

dan guan xian liu 膽管腺瘤
bile duct adenoma;

dan guan yan 膽管炎
cholangitis;

ying hua xing dan guan yan 硬化性膽管炎
scerosing cholangitis;

di1 fang xing jia zhuang xian zhong 地方性甲狀腺腫
endemic goiter;

e4 xing lin ba liu 恶性淋巴瘤
malignant tumor;

er3 xia xian 耳下腺
parotid gland;

fu4 jia zhuang xian 副甲狀腺
parathyroid;

han4 xian 汗腺
sweat gland;

han xian yan 汗腺炎
hidradenitis;

hua nong xing han xian yan 化膿性汗腺炎
purulent hidradenitis;

hua4 nong xing han xian yan 化膿性汗腺炎
purulent hidradenitis;

ji2 xing yi xian huai si 急性胰腺壞死
acute pancreatic necrosis;

ji xing yi xian yan 急性胰腺炎
acute pancreatitis;

jia3 zhuang xian 甲狀腺
thyroid gland;
fu jia zhuang xian 副甲狀腺
parathyroid;

jia zhuang xian ai 甲狀腺癌
thyroid carcinoma;
lü pao xing jia zhuang xian ai 濾泡性甲狀腺癌
follicular thyroid carcinoma;

jia zhuang xian du zheng 甲狀腺毒症
thyrotoxicosis;

jia zhuang xian ji neng bu quan 甲狀腺機能不全
thyropenia;

jia zhuang xian qie chu 甲狀腺切除
thyroidectomy;

jia zhuang xian yan 甲狀腺炎
thyroiditis;
chan hou jia zhuang xian yan 產後甲狀腺炎
postpartum thyroiditis;
man xing jia zhuang xian yan 慢性甲狀腺炎
chronic thyroiditis;
rou ya zhong xing jia zhuang xian yan 肉芽腫性甲狀腺炎
granulomatous thyroiditis;
wei suo xing jia zhuang xian yan 萎縮性甲狀腺炎
atrophic thyroiditis;
ying hua xing jia zhuang xian yan 硬化性甲狀腺炎
sclerosing thyroiditis;

jia zhuang xian zhong 甲狀腺腫
goitre;
di fang xing jia zhuang xian zhong 地方性甲狀腺腫
endemic goiter;
lü pao xing jia zhuang xian zhong 濾泡性甲狀腺腫
follicular goiter;
mi man xing jia zhuang xian zhong 彌漫性甲狀腺腫
diffuse goiter;
nang xing jia zhuang xian zhong 囊性甲狀腺腫
cystic goiter;
shi zhi xing jia zhuang xian zhong 實質性甲狀腺腫
parenchymatous goiter;

jie2 jie zhuang lin ba liu 結節狀淋巴瘤
nodular lymphoma;

jie shi xing yi xian yan 結石性胰腺炎
calcareous pancreatitis;

jie2 mao xian 睫毛腺
ciliary glands;

jie xian 睫腺
ciliary glands;

jing1 nang xian 精囊腺
glandula vesiculosa / seminal gland;

jing nang xian pai xie guan 精囊腺排泄管
excretory duct of seminal gland;

jing nang xian wai mo 精囊腺外膜
tunica adventitia glandulae vesiculosae;

jing3 lin ba jie he 頸淋巴結核
tuberculosis of the cervical lymph nodes;

ju2 xian xing lin ba jie yan 局限性淋巴結炎
regional lymphadenitis;

kui4 yang xing lin ba guan yan 潰瘍性淋巴管炎
ulcerative lymphangitis;

lei4 xian 淚腺
lacriminal gland;

lei xian dong mai 淚腺動脈
lacrimal artery;

lei xian tong 淚腺痛
dacryoadenalgia;

lei xian yan 淚腺炎
dacryoadenitis;

lin2 ba 淋巴
lymph;

lin ba ai 淋巴癌
lymphoma;

lin ba bing 淋巴病
lymphopathia;
xing bing xing lin ba bing 性病性淋巴病
lymphopathia venerea;

lin ba fa sheng 淋巴發生
lymphogenesis;

lin ba fa yu bu liang 淋巴發育不良
alymphoplasia;

lin ba fa yu bu quan 淋巴發育不全
alymphoplasia;

lin ba guan 淋巴管
lymphatic ducts;

lin ba jie 淋巴結
lymph node;
dan nang lin ba jie 膽囊淋巴結
cystic lymph node;
fei men lin ba jie 肺門淋巴結
hilar lymph nodes;
lan wei lin ba jie 闌尾淋巴結
appendicular lymph nodes;
mian lin ba jie 面淋巴結
facial lymph nodes;
pi lin ba jie 脾淋巴結
splenic lymph nodes;
she lin ba jie 舌淋巴結
nodi lymphoidei linguales;
tun shang lin ba jie 臀上淋巴結
superior gluteal lymph nodes;
tun xia lin ba jie 臀下淋巴結
inferior gluteal lymph nodes;

lin ba jie bing 淋巴結病
lymphadenopathy;
pi fu lin ba jie bing 皮膚淋巴結病
dermatopathic lymphadenopathy;

lin ba jie jie he 淋巴結結核
tuberculosis of lymph nodes;

lin ba jie qie chu 淋巴結切除
lymphadenectomy;

lin ba jie yan 淋巴結炎
lymphadenitis;
ju xian xing lin ba jie yan 局限性淋巴結炎
regional lymphadenitis;

lin ba jie zhong da 淋巴結腫大
enlargement of the lymph nodes;

lin ba liu 淋巴瘤
lymphoma;
e xing lin ba liu 惡性淋巴瘤
malignant tumor;
jie jie zhuang lin ba liu 結節狀淋巴瘤
nodular lymphoma;
lü pao xing lin ba liu 濾泡性淋巴瘤
follicular lymphoma;
mi man xing lin ba liu 彌漫性淋巴瘤
diffuse lymphoma;
pi fu lin ba liu 皮膚淋巴瘤
lymphoma cutis;

lin ba qiu 淋巴球
lymphocyte;

lin ba rou liu 淋巴肉瘤
lymphosarcoma;

lin ba xi bao 淋巴細胞
lymphocyte;

lin ba xian 淋巴腺
lymphatic gland;

lin ba xian ai 淋巴腺癌
cancer of the lymph glands;

lin ba xian jie he 淋巴腺結核
lymphadenitis tuberculosis;

lin ba xian yan 淋巴腺炎
lymphadenitis;

lin ba zhu zhi 淋巴組織
lymphoid tissue;

liu2 xing xing sai xian yan 流行性腮腺炎
epidemic parotitis;

lü4 pao xing jia zhuang xian ai 濾泡性甲狀腺癌
follicular thyroid carcinoma;

lü pao xing jia zhuang xian zhong 濾泡性甲狀腺腫
follicular goiter;

lü pao xing lin ba liu 濾泡性淋巴瘤
follicular lymphoma;

man4 xing jia zhuang xian yan 慢性甲狀腺炎
chronic thyroiditis;

man xing yi xian yan 慢性胰腺炎
chronic pancreatitis;

mi2 man xing jia zhuang xian zhong 彌漫性甲狀腺腫
diffuse goiter;

mi man xing lin ba liu 彌漫性淋巴瘤
diffuse lymphoma;

mi4 chou xian 泌臭腺
cryptae odoriferae;

mo4 xing xian liu 膜性腺瘤
membranous adenoma;

nang2 xing jia zhuang xian zhong 囊性甲狀腺腫
cystic goiter;

nei4 fen mi xian 內分泌腺
endocrine gland;

nian2 ye xian 黏液腺
mucous gland;

nian ye xian ai 黏液腺癌
mucinous adenocarcinoma;

nong2 xing sai xian yan 膿性腮腺炎
parotitis plegmonosa;

pi2 zhi xian liu 皮質腺瘤
cortical adenomas;

pi zhi xian 皮脂腺
sebaceous gland;

pi2 lin ba jie 脾淋巴結
splenic lymph nodes;

qian2 lie xian 前列腺
prostate gland;

qing1 chun xian 青春腺
reproductive glands;

ren4 shen xian 妊娠腺
pregnancy gland;

rou4 ya zhong xing jia zhuang xian yan 肉芽腫性甲狀腺炎
granulomatous thyroiditis;

ru3 xian 乳腺
mammary gland;

ru xian bing 乳腺病
mastopathy;

ru xian chu xue 乳腺出血
mastorrhagia;

ru xian fei da 乳腺肥大
hypermastia;

ru xian guo xiao 乳腺過小
hypomastia;

ru xian tong 乳腺痛
mastalgia;

ru xian wei suo 乳腺萎縮
mastatrophy;

ru xian yan 乳腺炎
mastitis;
shi zhi xing ru xian yan 實質性乳腺炎
glandular mastitis;

sai1 xian 腮腺
parotid gland;

sai xian guan 腮腺管
parotid duct;

sai xian yan 腮腺炎
parotitis;
liu xing xing sai xian yan 流行性腮腺炎
epidemic parotitis;
nong xing sai xian yan 膿性腮腺炎
parotitis plegmonosa;
shu hou sai xian yan 術後腮腺炎
postoperative parotitis;

sha1 yan xian 沙眼腺
trachoma gland;

she2 lin ba jie 舌淋巴結
nodi lymphoidei linguales;

shen4 shang xian 腎上腺
adrenal gland;

shen shang xian bing 腎上腺病
adrenopathy;

shen shang xian gong neng bing 腎上腺功能病
adrenalism;

shen shang xian gong neng bu zu 腎上腺功能不足
adrenal insufficiency;
yuan fa xing shen shang xian gong neng bu zu 原發性腎上腺功能不足
primary adrenal insufficiency;

shen xian ai 腎腺癌
adenocarcinoma of kidney;

shen xian liu 腎腺瘤
adenomas of kidney;

sheng1 zhi xian 生殖腺
genital gland / gonad;

sheng zhi xian fa sheng 生殖腺發生
gonadogenesis;

sheng zhi xian fa yu bu quan 生殖腺發育不全
gonadal dysgenesis;

shi2 zhi xing jia zhuang xian zhong 實質性甲狀腺腫
parenchymatous goiter;

shi zhi xing ru xian yan 實質性乳腺炎
glandular mastitis;

shu4 hou sai xian yan 術後腮腺炎
postoperative parotitis;

tuo4 ye xian 唾液腺
salivary gland;

tuo ye xian bing 唾液腺病
salivary gland disease;

tuo ye xian lou 唾液腺瘻
salivary fistula;

tuo ye xian yan 唾液腺炎
sialadenitis;

tuo ye xian zhong da zheng 唾液腺腫大症
sialosis;

wei3 suo xing jia zhuang xian yan 萎縮性甲狀腺炎
atrophic thyroiditis;

wei4 xian 胃腺
gastric gland;

wei xian liu 胃腺瘤
gastric adenoma;

wei xian yan 胃腺炎
gastradenitis;

xi1 rou yang xian ai 息肉樣腺癌
polypoid adenocarcinoma;

xian4 腺
gland;

xian ai 腺癌
glandular cancer;

han xian ai 汗腺癌
syringocarcinoma;

jia zhuang xian ai 甲狀腺癌
thyroid carcinoma;

lin ba xian ai 淋巴腺癌
cancer of the lymph glands;

nian ye xian ai 黏液腺癌
mucinous adenocarcinoma;

qian lie xian ai 前列腺癌
cancer of the prostate gland;

shen xian ai 腎腺癌
adenocarcinoma of kidney;

xi rou yang xian ai 息肉樣腺癌
polypoid adenocarcinoma;

xian bing 腺病
adenopathy;

xian chui ti 腺垂體
adenohypophysis;

xian liu 腺瘤
adenoma / glandular tumour;

dan xing xing xian liu 單形性腺瘤
monomorphic adenoma;

dan guan xian liu 膽管腺瘤
bile duct adenoma;

lü pao xing xian liu 濾泡性腺瘤
follicular adenoma;

mo xing xian liu 膜性腺瘤
membranous adenoma;

pi zhi xian liu 皮質腺瘤
cortical adenomas;

shen xian liu 腎腺瘤
adenomas of kedney;

zhi fang xian liu 脂肪腺瘤
lipoadenoma;

xian rou liu 腺肉瘤
adenosarcoma;

xian ti 腺體
gland;

xian yan 腺炎
adenitis;

bao pi xian yan 包皮腺炎
tysonitis;

chang xian yan 腸腺炎
enteradenitis;

er xia xian yan 耳下腺炎
mumps;

han xian yan 汗腺炎
hydradenitis;

腺 *Gland*

lei xian yan 淚腺炎
dacryoadenitis;
sai xian yan 腮腺炎
parotiditis;
tuo ye xian yan 唾液腺炎
sialadenitis;
wei xian yan 胃腺炎
gastradenitis;
yi xian yan 胰腺炎
pancreatitis;
yin dao xian yan 陰道腺炎
adenosis vaginae;
ying hua xing xian yan 硬化性腺炎
scleradenitis;

xian ying hua 腺硬化
adenosclerosis;

xian zeng da 腺增大
hyperadenosis;

xian zhou yan 腺周炎
periadenitis;

xiao3 chang xian 小腸腺
glands of small intestine;

xing4 bing xing lin ba bing 性病性淋巴病
lymphopathia venerea;

xing xian 性腺
sex gland;

xing xian bing 性腺病
gonadopathy;

xing xian fa sheng 性腺發生
gonadogenesis;

xing xian fa sheng bu quan 性腺發生不全
gonadal dysgenesis;

xing xian fa yu bu quan 性腺發育不全
gonadal dysgenesis;

xiu4 xian 臭腺
scent glands;

yan2 xian 涎腺
salivary gland;

yi2 xian huai si 胰腺壞死
pancreatic necrosis;
ji xing yi xian huai si 急性胰腺壞死
acute pancreatic necrosis;

yi xian yan 胰腺炎
pancreatitis;
ji xing yi xian yan 急性胰腺炎
acute pancreatitis;
jie shi xing yi xian yan 結石性胰腺炎
calcareous pancreatitis;
man xing yi xian yan 慢性胰腺炎
chronic pancreatitis;

yin1 dao xian 陰道腺
vaginal gland;

yin dao xian yan 陰道腺炎
adenosis vaginae;

ying4 hua xing dan guan yan 硬化性膽管炎
scerosing cholangitis;

ying hua xing jia zhuang xian yan 硬化性甲狀腺炎
sclerosing thyroiditis;

ying hua xing xian yan 硬化性腺炎
scleradenitis;

yuan2 fa xing shen shang xian gong neng bu zu 原發性腎上腺功能不足
primary adrenal insufficiency;

zeng1 zhi xian 增殖腺
adenoid;

zeng zhi xian bing 增殖腺病
adenoidism;

zeng zhi xian yan 增殖腺炎
adenoiditis;

zhi1 fang xian liu 脂肪腺瘤
lipoadenoma;

Xin 心 Heart

ai1 ai 哀哀
deeply grieved / very sad // in deep grief;

ai ai yu jue 哀哀欲絕
be overcome by grief / be overwhelmed by grief / be so distressed as if one's heart would break / be so grieved as if one's heart would break;

ai bu yu sheng 哀不欲生
becomes so sad that one wants to end one's life;

ai chou 哀愁
lamentation / sadness / sorrow // grieved / sad / sorrowful;

ai chuang 哀愴
grieved / sad / sorrowful || grief;

ai dao 哀悼
mourn over sb's death || condole with sb upon the death of...; express one's condolences on the death of sb; grieve; grieve over sb's death; lament; lament sb's death; mourn; mourn for the dead; mourn over sb's death; wail the dead // condolence / mourning;

ai diao 哀吊
(1) grieve over sb's death;
(2) express deeply sympathy for;

ai er bu shang 哀而不傷
mournful but not distressing || deeply felt but not sentimental; in moderation; modest; sorrow without self-injury; temperate; the cap fits; to a nicety; within the limits;

ai gan 哀感
grief / sadness;

ai jin 哀矜
commiserate with / feel compassion for / feel pity for / pity / sympathize;

ai jin wu gu 哀矜無辜
pardon the innocent;

ai jin wu xi 哀矜勿喜
feel compassion for and not be happy about sb or sth;

ai ken 哀懇
beg / entreat / implore;

ai ku 哀苦
grievous;

ai ku wu yi 哀苦無依
helpless and grievous / miserable;

ai lian 哀憐
pity || commiserate; feel compassion for; have compassion for; have pity; have sympathy for;

ai liang 哀涼
desolate / mournful / sad;

ai min 哀憫
pity || commiserate with; feel compassion for; feel pity for;

ai mo da yu xin si 哀莫大於心死
no sorrow is greater than despair || despair is the greatest sorrow; he begins to die that quits his desires; nothing gives greater cause for sorrow than despair; nothing gives so much cause for sorrow as the death of one's heart; nothing is more lamentable than a dead heart; the greatest pity is the death of the human heart; there is no poverty like the poverty of spirit; there is nothing worse than apathy; tine heart, tine all;

ai mo da yu xin si, er ren si yi ci zhi. 哀莫大於心死，而人死亦次之。
no sorrow is greater than despair, even a man's death comes next to it.

ai qi 哀淒
melancholy / mournful / sad / sad and wretched;

ai qi 哀戚
grief || be overcome with sorrow; grievous; look woeful; sadness; sorrow; woe;

ai qi bu xing 哀其不幸
feel sorry for sb's misfortune || have pity on sb for their misfortune;

ai qie 哀切
sad and wretched;

ai qiu 哀求
obsecration;

ai shang 哀傷
sad || distressed; feel grief; feel sorrow; grieve; mourn; mournful; sorrowful;

ai4 愛
(1) be affectionate to sb / be affectionate with sb / love / have affection for;
(2) cherish / hold dear / treasure / value;
(3) be fond of / be keen on / like;
(4) apt to / in the habit of;

ai chu feng tao 愛出風頭
be fond of the limelight;

ai dai 愛戴
love and esteem / love and support;

ai guo 愛國
(1) love one's country;
(2) patriotic;

ai hu 愛護
cherish / take good care of / treasure;

ai lian 愛憐
conceive great affection for / show fondness for / show love for / show tender affection for // love and pity;

ai lian 愛戀
be in love with / feel deeply attached to // feelings of love;

ai mu 愛慕
(1) love and envy;
(2) admire / adore;

ai qing 愛情
love;

ai qing zhuan yi 愛情專一
steadfast in love;

ai shang 愛上
fall in love with sb / give one's heart to;

ai xin 愛心
loving heart || affection; compassion; love;

ai zeng 愛憎
love and hate;

ai zeng fen ming 愛憎分明
be clear about what to love or hate / understand what to love and what to hate;

ai zhong 愛重
love and respect;

an1 ding ren xin 安定人心
set people's minds at rest / quiet the public sentiment / reassure the public;

an fu 安伏
calm a person down / comfort / console;

an fu 安撫
appease / calm down / comfort / console / sooth;

an fu ren xin 安撫人心
appease the public;

an quan gan 安全感
sense of security;

an ren 安忍
endure patiently;

an wei 安慰
comfort / console;

an xin 安心
(1) be relieved / feel relieved;
(2) put sb's mind at ease / put sb's mind at rest / set one's mind at rest;

an4 na 按捺
control || hold back; press down firmly; repress; restrain; withhold;

an na bu zhu 按捺不住
cannot control oneself || beside oneself; cannot contain oneself; unable to hold back; unable to repress;

an na bu zhu ji dong de xin qing 按捺不住激動的心情
unable to hold back one's excitement;

an zhu 按住
keep under control || hold up; press down and not let go; repress; restrain; withhold;

an4 ji 暗記
learn by heart || bear in mind; commit to memory; get by heart; memorize;

an li 暗裏
in one's heart / inwardly / secretly;

an shi 暗示
allude to / hint at || drop a hint of; drop a hint to; drop sb a hint; fall a hint of; give a hint of; give a hint to; give sb a hint; give sb an inkling of; give sb the cue; give sb to know; give sb to understand; hint; hint about; hint of; hint to sb; implicit; imply; insinuate; intimate sth; intimate to sb; let a hint of; put a bug in sb's ear; put a flea in sb's ear; suggest;

suggestive of;

an suan 暗算
plot against || secret plot; treachery // attack by treachery; plot; plot in secret; secretly plot against;

an xi 暗喜
feel secretly delighted / feel secretly happy;

an zhi 暗指
hint / imply || give a hint unknown to others; insinuate;

an zi 暗自
inwardly / secretly / to oneself;

an zi qing xing 暗自慶幸
congratulate oneself / consider oneself lucky / rejoice in secret;

an4 song 闇誦
commit to memory / recite in silence;

an4 ran 黯然
dejected / depressed / downcast / low-spirited / sad;

an ran gao bie 黯然告別
say goodbye with a heavy heart;

an ran shen shang 黯然神傷
downhearted || down; down in the mouth; feel dejected; feel depressed; feeling low;

an ran xiao hun 黯然銷魂
very gloomy || be plunged in grief; dumb with grief; grief-stricken; sorrow at parting; sorrow-stricken; sorrowful;

ang2 fen 昂奮
exited || earnest; enthusiastic; fervent; zealous;

ang ran 昂然
proud and bold;

ang ran zi de 昂然自得
be upright and pleased with oneself || be elated; walk on air;

ao1 nao 熬惱
unhappy and dejected;

ao xin 熬心
annoying / unhappy / vexing;

ao4 nu 拗怒
suppress anger;

ao4 懊
(1) regretful / remorseful;
(2) angry / annoyed / vexed;

ao hen 懊恨
resentful;

ao hui 懊悔
feel remorse || regret; repent; reproach oneself; upset // regretful / rueful;

ao men 懊悶
eat one's heart out / pine away;

ao nao 懊惱
feel remorseful and angry || chagrin; be chagrined; feel annoyed; upset; vexed;

ao nao wan fen 懊惱萬分
much to one's annoyance / much to one's chagrin;

ao sang 懊喪
dejected / depressed / despondent / sorrowfully;

ba1 wang 巴望
hope anxiously for || await anxiously; eager to; expect; look forward to;

ba xiang 巴想
await anxiously / hope anxiously;

ba3 xin tao chu lai 把心掏出來
open up one's heart / pour out all one's sincerity;

ba xin yi heng 把心一橫
harden one's heart;

bai2 fei xin ji 白費心機
make plans to no avail / scheme in vain;

bai3 ban ai qiu 百般哀求
resort to every means to entreat;

bai ban ai quan 百般哀勸
admonish strongly and sadly;

bai gan jiao ji 百感交集
a multitude of feelings surge up || a hundred emotions crowd into the heart; a multitude of feelings welling up; all sorts of feelings well up in one's heart; be moved by a mixture of feelings; fill one's mind with a myriad of thoughts; run the gamut of emotions; with mingled feelings; with mixed emotions;

bai ren bai xin, bai ren bai xing. 百人百心，百

人百性。
different people think and behave differently / people differ in mind and in character;

bai ren 百忍
great endurance / great forbearance;

bai wu liao lai 百無聊賴
feel extremely bored || be overcome with boredom; bored; bored stiff; bored to death; find time hang heavy on one's hands; idle along; in dreary and cheerless circumstances; suffer from boredom; the day is long to him who knows not how to use it; thoroughly bored; while away one's time aimlessly;

bai you 百憂
all sorrows / all worries;

bai zong qian sui 百縱千隨
yield to all the wishes;

bai3 mi hun zhen 擺迷魂陣
lay out a scheme to bewitch sb / set a trap;

bai nong 擺弄
(1) fiddle with || move back and forth; play with; toy with;
(2) manipulate / order about;
(3) make fun of / trick;

bai tuo 擺脫
break away from || break from; break loose; break off; cast off; clear of; clear off; clear sb of sth; cut loose from; do away with; extricate oneself from; find freedom from; free from; free of; free oneself from; free sth of; get out; get over; get rid of; get sth off one's hands; give sb a miss; give sb the go-by; give sth a miss; give sth the go-by; rid; rid of; rid oneself of; see the back of sb; shake off; wash one's hands of;

bai tuo kun jing 擺脫困境
escape from a predicament || above water; extricate oneself from a predicament; get sb off the hook; out of hot water;

bai tuo yi lai 擺脫依賴
shake off dependence on;

bai4 dao 拜倒
fall on one's knees / grovel / prostrate oneself;

bai dao shi liu qun xia 拜倒石榴裙下
fall head over heels for a woman || at one's feet; throw oneself at sb's feet;

bai fu 拜服
greatly admire;

bai4 huai ren xin 敗壞人心
corrupt people's minds || deprave; perversion of one's mind;

ban4 xin ban yi 半心半意
half-hearted || lukewarm; not with all one's heart;

ban xin ban yi 半信半疑
half in doubt || half believe; half believe, half doubt; half-believing, half-doubting; not quite convinced; take sth with a grain of salt; with a pinch of salt;

bao1 cang 包藏
conceal / contain / harbour;

bao cang huo xin 包藏禍心
harbour evil intentions || cover up one's sinister motives; entertain a vicious scheme in mind; harbour malicious intent; hide a malicious intent;

bao rong 包容
forgive / tolerate;

bao rong li 包容力
capacity for taking in people;

bao1 yu wei huai 胞與為懷
treat all creatures like one's brothers;

bao3 shou xu jing 飽受虛驚
suffer from nervous fears;

bao3 ai 寶愛
lovely dearly / treasure;

bao4 bei guan 抱悲觀
feel pessimistic // pessimistic;

bao can han xiu 抱慚含羞
be overcome by shame;

bao ding jue xin 抱定決心
hold on to one's determination // determined;

bao fu 抱負
ambition / aspiration;

bao fu bu fan 抱負不凡
have great life ambition || ambitious; cherish

aspirations out of the common; entertain high aspirations;

bao han 抱憾
deplore / regret / repent of / sorry about;

bao han zhong sheng 抱憾終生
regret sth to the end of one's days || harbour a lifetime remorse; have a remorse of a lifetime; have a secret regret for life;

bao hen 抱恨
have a gnawing regret;

bao hen zhong sheng 抱恨終生
regret sth to the end of one's days || bitterly lament the nonfulfilment of one's mission; cherish hatred all one's life; feel remorse for the rest of one's life; harbour an eternal sorrow; regret all one's life; regret forever; with a feeling of bitter frustration;

bao hen zhong tian 抱恨終天
regret sth to the end of one's days || bitterly lament the nonfulfilment of one's mission; cherish hatred all one's life; feel remorse for the rest of one's life; harbour an eternal sorrow; regret all one's life; regret forever; with a feeling of bitter frustration;

bao jiu 抱疚
have compunction about;

bao kui 抱愧
feel ashamed // abashed;

bao kui ren cuo 抱愧認錯
blush at one's mistake / blush scarlet and apologize;

bao le guan 抱樂觀
feel optimistic // optimistic;

bao qian 抱歉
feel apologetic / feel sorry / regret / sorry;

bao qian zhi zhi 抱歉之至
feel very sorry / very sorry;

bao qu 抱屈
bear a grudge / feel wronged / harbour resentment;

bao qu han yuan 抱屈含冤
be wronged and aggrieved / bear a deep grudge;

bao tong xi he 抱痛西河
feel sorrow over the loss of one's son / mourn over the death of one's son / suffer the sorrow of losing one's son;

bao yuan 抱怨
complain / grumble about || air one's grievances; blame; blow off; carp at; chew the rag about; complain; complain about; complain of; grouch; grouse about; grumble; grumble at; kick against; kick at; make a fuss; murmur against; murmur at; mutter against; mutter at; natter on about; quarrel with; rail against; rail at;

bao zui 抱罪
conscious of guilt / feel guilty;

bao4 nu 暴怒
furious / rabid anger // blow one's top / fly into a rage / fly into a temper || fury; great fury; rage; violently raging;

bei1 bao fu 背包袱
weigh on one's mind || become a burden on one's mind; carry a bundle on one's back; have a load on one's mind; have a weight on one's mind; take on a mental burden;

bei1 悲
(1) sad || doleful; melancholy; mournful; rueful; sorrowful; woeful;
(2) deplore || lament; mourn; pity; sympathize;

bei ai 悲哀
grief || down in the blues; down in the mouth; grieve; grieved; look blue; mourn; mourning; sad; sadness; sorrow; sorrow over; sorrowful; woe; woeful;

bei bei qie qie 悲悲切切
sad and touching // full of grief;

bei bu zi sheng 悲不自勝
abandon oneself to grief / be overcome with grief || be transported with grief; unable to restrain one's grief;

bei can 悲慘
miserable / tragic;

bei ce 悲惻
sad / sorrowful;

bei chou 悲愁
heavy-hearted / low-spirited / sad;

bei cong zhong lai 悲從中來
feel sadness welling up;

bei dao 悲悼
grieve over sb's death / mourn;

bei fen 悲憤
grief and indignation || despair and resent an injustice;

bei fen jiao ji 悲憤交集
with mixed feelings of grief and indignation;

bei fen tian ying 悲憤填膺
be filled with grief and indignation || burning with indignation; in righteous indignation; one's breast is full of grief and anger;

bei fen yu jue 悲憤欲絕
be torn by grief / give oneself up to grief;

bei gan 悲感
a sense of sadness;

bei guan 悲觀
pessimistic;

bei guan qing xu 悲觀情緒
pessimism / pessimistic emotion;

bei guan shi wang 悲觀失望
abandon oneself to despair / become disheartened / lose faith in;

bei guan yan shi 悲觀厭世
pessimism and world-weariness;

bei huai 悲懷
sad feelings / sorrowful mood;

bei huan li he 悲歡離合
the sorrow of parting and the joy of meeting;

bei lian 悲憐
take pity on sb;

bei liang 悲涼
desolate / dismal / sad and dreary;

bei min 悲憫
pity || have compassion for; have sympathy for;

bei qi 悲淒
sorrowful;

bei qi 悲戚
doleful / mournful / rueful;

bei qi 悲泣
weep with grief;

bei qie 悲切
mournful;

bei shang 悲傷
sad / sorrowful;

bei suan 悲酸
sad and bitter;

bei tian min ren 悲天憫人
be concerned over the destiny with mankind || bemoan the state of the universe and pity the fate of mankind; bewail the times and pity the people; lament the miserable state of affairs and feel pity for the suffering of all mankind;

bei tong 悲痛
grieved / sorrowful // deep sorrow;

bei tong wan fen 悲痛萬分
be deeply grieved / be far gone in grief;

bei tong yu jue 悲痛欲絕
be torn with deep sorrow // the anguish of grief / eat one's heart out || abandon oneself to grief; go to pieces; wring one's heart to the very core;

bei tong 悲慟
weep loudly from sorrow;

bei xi jiao ji 悲喜交集
mixed feelings of grief and joy || alternate between joy and grief; be joyful and sorrowful at the same time; grief and joy intermingled; have mixed feelings; overcome partly with sorrow and partly with joy; with mingled feelings of sorrow and joy;

bei zhuang 悲壯
tragically heroic;

bei4 背
commit to memory / learn by heart || learn by rote; recite from memory; remember by rote;

bei4 悖
go against / go counter to / revolt against // contrary to;

bei ban 悖叛
rebel / revolt;

bei de 悖德
immoral;

bei li 悖戾
perverse;

bei luan 悖亂
(1) revolt;
(2) rebellion;

bei qi 悖棄
turn away from sth in revolt;

bei ru bei chu 悖入悖出
evil begets evil;

bei4 yi wang 被遺忘
pass into silence;

bei4 憊
exhausted / tired / weary;

bei juan 憊倦
exhausted / fatigued / tired / weary;

bei lan 憊懶
tired and indolent;

bei lei 憊累
exhausted / tired / weary;

ben3 xin 本心
original intention;

ben yi 本意
original intention;

ben4 tou ben nao 笨頭笨腦
muddleheaded || dead from the neck up; have a thick skull; with a wooden head;

ben zhuo 笨拙
awkward / clumsy / slow-witted / stupid / unskilled;

bi4 si zhi xin 必死之心
with one's back to the wall;

bi4 愎
obstinate / perverse / self-willed / stubborn;

bi4 愊
(1) honest / sincere;
(2) depressed / melancholy;

bi4 xue dan xin 碧血丹心
loyal-hearted // deep patriotism;

bian3 di 貶低
abase / belittle || cry down; denigrate; depreciate; detract from; disparage; play down; run down;

bian yi 貶抑
belittle / depreciate;

bian3 褊
narrow-minded;

bian lou 褊陋
narrow-minded and ignorant;

bian qian 褊淺
narrow-minded and shallow;

bian xia 褊狹
narrow-minded;

bian xin 褊心
narrow-minded and impatient;

bian yi 褊隘
narrow-minded and impatient;

bian4 忭
delighted / overjoyed / pleased;

bian he 忭賀
celebrate / congratulate with joy;

bian huan 忭懽
pleased and delighted;

bian song 忭頌
be pleased to offer best wishes;

bian yue 忭躍
leap with joy // great joy / tremendous pleasure;

bian4 xin 變心
break faith / cease to be faithful / cease to love one's spouse / jilt a lover // change of heart;

biao3 表
announce / demonstrate / express / manifest / show;

biao bai 表白
bare one's heart / lay bare || clarify; clear up; explain; express clearly; state clearly;

biao bai xin ji 表白心跡
bare one's true intentions / unbosom oneself / unburden one's heart;

biao da 表達
convey / demonstrate / express / make known / present / voice;

biao da neng li 表達能力
ability of expression;

biao lu 表露
expose / express / make plain / reveal / show / voice;

biao lu gan qing 表露感情
wear one's heart on one's sleeve;

biao ming 表明
indiciate / make clear / make known / state clearly;

biao ming guan dian 表明觀點
express one's viewpoint || lay down one's cards; lay one's cards on the table; place one's cards on the table; put one's card on the table; show one's cards; show one's colours; show one's hand;

biao ming li chang 表明立場
declare one's stand / make known one's position;

biao ming xin ji 表明心跡
lay bare one's true feeling / show clearly one's mind;

biao qing da yi 表情達意
convey one's ideas or feelings;

biao shi 表示
express / indicate / manifest / show;

biao shi fan dui 表示反對
indicate one's opposition / turn thumbs down;

biao shi jing yi 表示敬意
show respect;

biao shi man yi 表示滿意
express satisfaction;

biao shi qing he 表示慶賀
express one's congratulations;

biao shi tong yi 表示同意
express approval / indicate one's approval;

biao shi xie yi 表示謝意
express one's gratitude / show one's appreciation;

biao tong qing 表同情
commiserate / express one's sympathy;

bie1 憋
(1) suppress the inner feelings with efforts;
(2) feel oppressed;

bie bu zhu 憋不住
cannot help / cannot suppress;

bie bu zhu qi 憋不住氣
cannot hold one's anger any longer / ready to burst;

bie de huang 憋得慌
intolerably depressing;

bie men 憋悶
depressed / melancholy;

bie niu 憋扭
(1) of contrary opinion;
(2) awkward / clumsy;

bie qi 憋氣
(1) suffer breathing obstruction;
(2) choke with resentment;

bie qu 憋屈
aggrieved // nurse a grievance;

bie zhu qi 憋住氣
(1) hold one's breath;
(2) smolder with resentment;

bie2 chu xin cai 別出心裁
ingenious;

bie jiu qing shu 別久情疏
far from eye, far from heart / long absent, soon forgotten;

bie ju hui xin 別具慧心
have a special understanding;

bie ju jiang xin 別具匠心
have originality / show ingenuity;

bie ju si xin 別具私心
have an axe to grind;

bie wang xin li qu 別往心裏去
not take…to heart || hope you don't mind; just forget it; think nothing of it;

bie xu 別緒
the sorrow of parting;

bie you yong xin 別有用心
have a hidden purpose / have an axe to grind || have an ulterior motive; have ulterior motives;

bie2 jiao 蹩腳
dejected / uncomfortable;

bing1 xin 冰心
(1) chaste / virtuous;
(2) not enthusiastic / somewhat indifferent;

bo2 ran 泊然
calm and at rest;

bo2 nu 勃怒
break into a rage / lose one's temper suddenly;

bo ran da nu 勃然大怒
burst into a fit of temper / flare up ‖ be apoplectic with rage; blow a fuse; blow a gasket; blow one's lid; blow one's stack; blow one's top; bluster oneself into anger; burst into anger; explode with lyric wratch; fall into a rage; flame forth; flame out; flame up; fly into a passion; fly into a rage; fly off the handle; foam at the mouth; get up on one's ear; go off like a rocket; go off like a Roman candle; go off on one's ear; go off the top; go through the roof; hasty indignation; have a mad on; hit the ceiling; hit the roof; in a flaming temper; in an awful bate; livid; one's anger flames out; one's anger flames up; one's temper flames out; raise the roof; take pepper in the nose // outburst of fury;

bo2 ai 博愛
universal love;

bo qu huan xin 博取歡心
curry favour;

bo qu tong qing 博取同情
enlist sb's sympathy / seek sb's sympathy / win sympathy;

bo4 qing 薄情
fickle ‖ disloyal to one's love; heartless; inconstant in love; unfaithful; ungrateful;

bo qing wu yi 薄情無義
heartless;

bo xing 薄倖
fickle // inconstant in love;

bo xing wu qing 薄倖無情
inconstant in love;

bu4 an 不安
disturbed / disquieting / intranquil / restless / uneasy / uncomfortable / unpeaceful / unstable // discomfort / perturbation;

bu chen yi 不稱意
do not match one's expectation;

bu cun xin 不存心
do not intend // unintentional;

bu dan 不憚
not fear / not afraid of / not mind;

bu dan qi fan 不憚其煩
not mind taking the trouble / patient;

bu dao Huang He xin bu si 不到黄河心不死
refuse to give up until one's goal is achieved / refuse to yield until all hope is gone;

bu de ren xin 不得人心
unpopular ‖ contrary to the will of the people; fail to gain popular support; fall into disfavour among the people; go against the will of the people; have no popular support; not enjoy popular support; unable to win popular support;

bu de ren yi 不得人意
deep in one's black books / really in one's black books;

bu dong xin 不動心
show no interest;

bu er qi xin 不貳其心
not be disloyal;

bu fang xin 不放心
anxious for / feel worried about;

bu gan xin 不甘心
not reconciled to / not resigned to;

bu guo yi 不過意
feel sorry;

bu hai pa 不害怕
unafraid;

bu han er li 不寒而慄
trembling with fear;

bu hao guo 不好過
feeling miserable;

bu huai hao yi 不懷好意
ill-intended ‖ after no good; bear ill-will; harbour evil designs; harbour malicious intentions; have bad intentions; not to

have good intentions; not with the best of intentions; up to no good; with bad intentions;

bu jie feng qing 不解風情
do not understand implications in love affair;

bu jie yi 不介意
do not mind;

bu jin ren qing 不近人情
inconsiderate / unreasonable;

bu jing yi 不經意
carelessly;

bu kai xin 不開心
(1) displeased / unhappy // in low spirits / out of humour;
(2) feel under the weather / indisposed / out of sorts;

bu ke yuan liang 不可原諒
inexcusable;

bu kuai 不快
(1) displeased / unhappy // in low spirits / out of humour;
(2) feel under the weather / indisposed / out of sorts;

bu kuai le 不快樂
unhappy;

bu kui 不愧
deserve to be called / prove oneself to be / worthy of;

bu kui bu zuo 不愧不怍
have neither shame nor blush;

bu nai fan 不耐煩
be impatient;

bu neng ren shou 不能忍受
unbearable;

bu neng yuan liang 不能原諒
unforgivable / unpardonable;

bu nian jiu e 不念舊惡
forget past grudges;

bu qing yuan 不情願
not willing to // grudging;

bu ren 不忍
cannot bear to do sth;

bu ren zhi xin 不忍之心
a heart of mercy;

bu ren zuo shi 不忍坐視
cannot bear to sit and watch without doing anything / cannot bear to stand idly by;

bu si xin 不死心
unwilling to give up;

bu tong yi 不同意
disagree;

bu wei suo dong 不為所動
remain unmoved;

bu wen ding xing xin jiao tong 不穩定型心絞痛
unstable angina pectoris;

bu xiang 不想
do not want / do not wish;

bu xiao de 不曉得
do not know;

bu xie 不懈
indefatigable / untiring;

bu yi wei ran 不以為然
do not approve;

bu yi 不意
unexpectedly;

bu yuan yi 不願意
(1) loath / not willing;
(2) be disposed / feel indisposed / loathe / not want to // indisposition;

bu yue 不悅
displeased / unhappy // displeasure;

bu zai yi 不在意
(1) couldn't care less / not care / not care a damn / pay no attention to;
(2) careless / negligent;

bu zhong yi 不中意
not to one's liking;

bu zhuan xin 不專心
unabsorbed;

bu zuo chi xiang 不作此想
have no intention to do sth;

bu4 怖
frightened / terrified // frighten / threaten;

bu hai 怖駭
alarmed / frightened / scared;

bu huo 怖禍
adversity / calamity / great disaster / great misfortune;

bu ju 怖懼
fear / scare;

bu li 怖慄
trembling with fear;

bu she 怖懾
scared and faint-hearted;

bu wei 怖畏
be afraid / be scared / dread;

cai1 ji 猜忌
suspicious and jealous || envious; envy; jealous of; suspicious; suspicious of and resent;

can2 ren 殘忍
brutal / cruel / heartless;

can2 慚
ashamed / humiliated / mortified;

can de 慚德
ashamed of being defective in morality;

can huang 慚惶
ashamed and bewildered / embarrassed;

can ju 慚沮
ashamed and depressed;

can kui 慚愧
ashamed;

can song 慚悚
affected with shame and fear;

can zuo 慚怍
feel ashamed / feel shame;

can3 慘
(1) miserable / sad / sorrowful / tragic;
(2) brutal / cruel / merciless;
(3) dark / dull / gloomy;
(4) disastrously;

can ce 慘惻
anguished / grieved;

can chuang 慘愴
anguished / grieved;

can da 慘怛
grieved / heavy-hearted / sad;

can ju 慘沮
despondent in one's soul / miserable in heart;

can ku 慘酷
cruel and sadistic / merciless / pitiless;

can li 慘慄
bitterly cold;

can nüe 慘虐
extremely cruel;

can qie 慘切
heartbreaking / pathetic / sad / tragic;

can ran 慘然
grieved / sad / saddened;

can tong 慘痛
agonizing / bitter / very painful;

can zhong 慘重
disastrous / grievous / heavy;

can3 憯
grieved / sad / sorrowful;

cang2 nu 藏怒
harbour wrath in one's mind / lay up anger;

cao1 xin 操心
take pains / take trouble / worry;

cao3 慅
anxious / apprehensive / uneasy;

ce4 惻
feel anguish // sad / sorrowful;

ce ce 惻惻
in anguish // sad / sorrowful;

ce chuang 惻愴
grieved / mournful / sad;

ce da 惻怛
sad and worried;

ce ran 惻然
grieved / sorrowful;

ce yin 惻隱
compassion / pity;

ce yin zhi xin 惻隱之心
heart of compassion || sense of pity; the milk of human kindness;

cha4 yi 詫異
be surprised;

chan2 mian 纏綿
tenderly attached to each other // affectionate;

chan mian fei ce 纏綿悱惻
exceedingly sentimental / very pathetic;

chan mian xiang si 纏綿鄉思
be tormented by homesickedness;

chan re 纏惹
be annoyed;

chan4 懺
confess one's sin / repent;

chan hui 懺悔
repent one's sin;

chan hui zi xin 懺悔自新
repent and turn over a new leaf;

chang3 kai xin fei 敞開心扉
open one's heart to;

chang4 悵
disappointed / dissatisfied / frustrated;

chang chang 悵悵
disappointed / upset;

chang chang bu le 悵悵不樂
heavy-hearted ‖ disconsolate; feel dissatisfied; feeling gloomy; in low spirit;

chang hen 悵恨
melancholy and resentful;

chang ran 悵然
disappointed / upset;

chang ran er fan 悵然而返
return sorrowfully home ‖ come away disappointed;

chang ran ruo shi 悵然若失
become lost in a deep reverie ‖ feel lost; in a despondent mood;

chang ran yu huai 悵然於懷
feel dissatisfied in one's soul;

chang wan 悵惋
regret sorrowfully;

chang wang 悵惘
distracted / listless;

chang wang 悵望
long pensively;

chang yang 悵怏
disappointed;

chang4 huai 暢懷
comfortable and joyful // to one's heart's content;

chang shu ji jian 暢舒己見
express one's views freely ‖ air one's view fully; assert without any restraint; speak one's mind;

chang suo yu wei 暢所欲為
do exactly as the mind dictates / do whatever one wants;

che4 wu 徹悟
have a thorough enlightenment;

che4 wu 澈悟
have a thorough enlightenment;

chen1 嗔
(1) be angry // fly into a temper;
(2) be annoyed with;

chen kuang 嗔狂
deranged;

chen nu 嗔怒
be annoyed / get angry / get in a temper;

chen2 忱
(1) sincere;
(2) rely on;

chen kun 忱悃
sincere sentiments;

chen2 men 沈悶
depressed / heavy at heart;

chen tong 沈痛
(1) deep feeling of grief or remorse;
(2) bitter / deeply felt;

chen tong ai dao 沈痛哀悼
mourn over sb's death with deep grief;

chen2 xin 塵心
worldly desires;

chen4 xin 趁心
have as one wishes;

心 Heart

chen4 xin 稱心
find sth satisfactory // gratified;

chen xin ru yi 稱心如意
to one's heart's desire || after one's heart; be well satisfied in accord with one's wishes; desirable; to one's liking; to one's taste; very gratifying and satisfactory;

chen yi 稱意
agreeable / satisfactory;

chen yuan 稱願
just as one wishes;

cheng1 xian 稱羡
envy / express one's admiration;

cheng xian bu yi 稱羡不已
express profuse admiration;

cheng2 xin 成心
intentionally / on purpose / with deliberate intent;

cheng xin zuo dui 成心作對
purposely antagonize sb;

cheng2 誠
cordial / honest / sincere;

cheng du 誠篤
cordial / sincere;

cheng fu 誠服
obey willingly / submit willingly;

cheng huang cheng kong 誠惶誠恐
in fear and trepidation || be struck with awe; with reverence and awe;

cheng ken 誠懇
sincere;

cheng ken dai ren 誠懇待人
treat others with earnestness;

cheng pu 誠樸
honest / sincere and simple;

cheng shi 誠實
honest;

cheng shi ke kao 誠實可靠
honest and dependable / honest and reliable // all wool and a yard wide;

cheng xin 誠心
sincere desire / wholeheartedness;

cheng xin cheng yi 誠心誠意
with sincerity / with the whole heart;

cheng yi 誠意
good faith / sincerity;

cheng yi zheng xin 誠意正心
sincere thought and righteous heart;

cheng zhi 誠摯
cordial / sincere;

cheng2 qi si lü 澄其思慮
purify one's thoughts;

cheng xin 澄心
calm one's mind;

cheng xin qing yi 澄心清意
purify the heart and clean the mind;

cheng2 懲
chastise / punish / reprimand / reprove / warn;

cheng chu 懲處
penalize / punish;

cheng e quan shan 懲惡勸善
punish wickedness and encourage virtue;

cheng fa 懲罰
chastise / penalize / punish;

cheng jie 懲戒
discipline / punish / reprimand;

cheng quan 懲勸
reward and punishment;

cheng3 e 逞惡
presume on powerful connections in doing evil;

cheng xin 逞心
do as one pleases;

cheng yi 逞意
act as one pleases;

cheng yuan 逞願
make one's wish fulfilled;

cheng zhi 逞志
indulge oneself / satisfy oneself;

cheng3 騁
give free rein to;

cheng huai 騁懷
give free rein to one's thoughts and feelings;

chi1 cu 吃醋
jealous;

chi jing 吃驚
be astonished / be taken aback || alarmed; amazed; astound; be filled with wonder; freeze; give a start; in astonishment; in surprised; marvel at; marvel over; strike with wonder; suprised; take alarm at; take sb by surprise; to one's astonishment; with astonishment; with surprise;

chi xin 吃心
exhaust one's mentality;

chi1 mi 痴迷
infatuated;

chi qing 痴情
all-absorbing passion / infatuation;

chi xin 痴心
all-absorbing passion / infatuation;

chi xin wang xiang 痴心妄想
be infatuated with and indulge in vain hopes || aspire after the impossible; be obsessed with wild ideas; cry for the moon; fond dream; wishful thinking;

chi1 癡
crazy / foolish / idiotic / insane / senseless / silly / stupid;

chi mi 癡迷
besotted / infatuated;

chi xin 癡心
(1) blind love / blind passion / infatuation;
(2) silly wish;

chi xin wang xiang 癡心妄想
silly and fantastic notions || daydreaming;

chi4 cheng 赤誠
absolute sincerity / singleness of heart;

chi cheng dai ren 赤誠待人
treat people with absolute sincerity;

chi dan zhong xin 赤膽忠心
wholehearted dedication || a red heart of complete dedication; ardent loyalty; loyalty; true devotion; utter devotion;

chi xin 赤心
wholehearted devotion || a sincere heart; genuine sincerity; sincere;

chi xin xiang dai 赤心相待
treat sb with all sincerity;

chi zi zhi xin 赤子之心
the heart of a newborn baby — utter innocence;

chong1 man yuan qi 充滿怨氣
be filled with anger / be filled with spleen;

chong xue xing xin ji bing 充血性心肌病
congestive cardimyopathy;

chong xue xing xin li shuai jie 充血性心力衰竭
congestive heart failure;

chong1 忡
anxious / uneasy / worried;

chong chong 忡忡
careworn / laden with anxiety;

chong zheng 忡怔
feeling anxious and unsettled;

chong1 憧
(1) indecisive / irresolute;
(2) aspire / yearn;

chong chong 憧憧
indecisive / irresolute;

chong jing 憧憬
long for / look forward to;

chong2 wen jiu meng 重溫舊夢
indulge again in one's pipe-dream || recall the past sweet experience; recapture the dtreams one has lost; relive an old experience; renew one's old romance; renew the ecstasies of sensual delight; revive an old dream; seek once more what one experienced in a dream;

chong wen jiu qing 重溫舊情
renew an old friendship / revive the old affection;

chong zhen xin xin 重振信心
restore one's confidence;

chong3 寵
bestow favour on / dote on / pamper / spoil;

chong ai 寵愛
cosset / dote on / make a pet of sb;

chong huai 寵壞
spoil;

chong lian 寵憐
loving and compassionate;

chong ru 寵辱
in favour or out of favour;

chong ru bu jing 寵辱不驚
remain indifferent whether favoured or humiliated || remain indifferent whether granted favours or subjected to humiliation; unmoved by official honour or disgrace;

chong ru ruo jing 寵辱若驚
be terrified whether granted favours or subjected to humiliation;

chong shan zhuan fang 寵擅專房
be unusually favoured by a husband — said of a concubine;

chong xin 寵信
favour and trust;

chong xing 寵幸
show special favour to a lady;

chong yu 寵遇
treat as a favourite;

chou2 仇
enmity / hatred;

chou hen 仇恨
enmity / hatred / hostility / old grudge;

chou hen man xiong 仇恨滿胸
be filled with bitter hatred;

chou hen nan xiao 仇恨難消
one's hatred and grief are undying;

chou huo zhong shao 仇火中燒
inflame sb's anger // flames of hatred blazes in one's heart / one's heart is aflame with hatred;

chou sha 仇殺
kill in revenge;

chou xi 仇隙
bitter quarrel / feud;

chou yuan 仇怨
enmity / hatred / hostility;

chou2 惆
regretful / rueful;

chou chang 惆悵
regretful / rueful;

chou chang ruo shi 惆悵若失
in a despondent mood;

chou ran 惆然
regretful / wistful;

chou wan 惆惋
regretful / wistful;

chou2 愁
be anxious / worry;

chou can 愁慘
be mournfully grieved;

chou cheng 愁城
realm of sorrow;

chou fan 愁煩
worried // worry;

chou hai 愁海
a sea of sorrows / a sea of worries;

chou huai 愁懷
sad feelings / sadness;

chou ku 愁苦
distressful // anxiety / distress;

chou lü jiao zhi 愁慮交織
intense sorrow and concern are mixed in one's heart;

chou men 愁悶
be depressed / in low spirits || distress; feel gloomy; glum;

chou ran 愁然
sorrowfully;

chou si 愁思
feelings of anxiety / sad thoughts || deep longing; forlornness; melancholy;

chou xu 愁緒
feeling of sadness || gloomy mood; skein of sorrow;

chou xu man huai 愁緒滿懷
one's breast is filled with melancholy thoughts || be distracted with worries; have the weight of the world on one's shoulders;

chou yi 愁意
a touch of sorrow;

chou yun 愁雲
depressing clouds || a cloud of sorrow; heavy clouds;

chou yun can wu 愁雲慘霧
a cloud of sorrow / gathering clouds and rolling mists;

chou yun man bu 愁雲滿佈
clouded with worry;

chou zi wei 愁滋味
taste of sorrow;

chu1 kou qi 出口氣
vent one's anger / vent one's spleen / work off one's feeling;

chu yu hao yi 出於好意
out of good intentions || mean well; out of a good heart; out of good will; well-intended; with the best of intentions;

chu1 lian 初戀
calf love / first love / puppy love;

chu xin 初心
one's original intention;

chu zhi 初志
one's original ambition;

chu zhong 初衷
one's original aspiration;

chu3 xin ji lü 處心積慮
brood over a matter for a long time || deliberately plan; have long schemed to; incessantly scheme; intrigue all the time; rack one's brains; scheme and use every kind of trick; scheme day and night; seek by all means; set one's mind on; work hard and deliberately at;

chu4 怵
(1) afraid / frightened / scared / timorous;
(2) entice / induce;

chu chang 怵場
stage fright;

chu mu jing xin 怵目驚心
be shocked at the sight of / strike the eye and rouse the mind;

chu ran 怵然
scared // look frightened;

chu ti 怵惕
scared and cautious;

chu4 dong xin xian 觸動心弦
touch a string / touch sb on a tender string / touch the right chord;

chu ji ling hun 觸及靈魂
touch sb to his very soul / touch sb to the quick / touch sb to their soul / touch sb's innermost being;

chu jing qing shen 觸景情深
stir one's deep feelings when beholding the view // the present scene moves one to the depths;

chu jing shang qing 觸景傷情
be moved by what one sees || feel very depressed at the prospect; memories revive at the sight of familiar places; recall old memories at familiar sights; the circumstances excite one's feelings; the scene brings back memories; the scene stirs up the feelings; the sight strikes a chord in one's heart;

chu jing sheng qing 觸景生情
be moved by what one sees || be touched with memories awakened by the scene; memories revive at the sight of familiar places; recall old memories at familiar sights; stir one's deep feelings when beholding the view; the circumstances excite one's feelings; the scene brings back memories; the scene evokes memories of the past; the scene moves him to the depths; the scene touches a chord in one's heart; the sight strikes a chord in one's heart; what meets one's eye awakens a feeling of affection;

chu jue 觸覺
feel / touch || feeling; sense of touch; tactile sensation; touch reception;

chu jue chi dun 觸覺遲鈍
amblyaphia;

chu jue guo min 觸覺過敏
hyperaphia;

chu jue jian dui 觸覺減退
hypopselaphesia;

chu jue que shi 觸覺缺失
anaphia;

chu nu 觸怒
enrage || comb sb's hair the wrong way; get

sb's back up; infuriate; make angry; peeve; put sb's back up; rub sb's hair the wrong way; set sb's back up; stroke sb's hair the wrong way;

chuan2 qing 傳情
flirt;

chuang4 愴
mournful / sad / sorrowful;

chuang ce 愴惻
grieved / sad / sorrowful;

chuang chuang yu jue 愴愴欲絕
distressed to the utmost;

chuang lang 愴悢
sad / sorrowful;

chuang ran 愴然
sorrowful;

chui2 ai 垂愛
show gracious concern for sb;

chui lian 垂憐
have sympathy on sb;

chui nian 垂念
so gracious as to remember me;

chui2 xin qi xue 椎心泣血
deep sorrow / extreme grief;

chui xin tong ku 椎心痛哭
cry one's heart out;

chun1 chou qiu si 春愁秋思
spring longings and autumn thoughts;

chun qing 春情
longing for love / stirrings of love;

chun xin 春心
desire for love / longing for love / stirrings of love / thoughts of love;

chun xin dang yang 春心蕩漾
the surging of lustful desire;

chun2 lu zhi si 蓴鱸之思
homesickness ‖ the intention of retiring from office and going back home;

chun3 chun 踳踳
disappointed / frustrated / unhappy;

chuo4 惙
doleful / gloomy / melancholy / mournful;

chuo chuo 惙惙
gloomy / melancholy;

chuo da 惙怛
doleful / mournful / rueful / sorrowful;

ci2 慈
benevolent / benignant / charitable / kind / loving / merciful;

ci ai 慈藹
kind and amiable;

ci ai 慈愛
affection / kindness / love / loving-kindness / maternal love;

ci bei 慈悲
(1) benevolent;
(2) mercy;

ci bei le shan 慈悲樂善
merciful and benevolent;

ci bei wei ben 慈悲為本
compassion is the principle of life;

ci hang 慈航
merciful ferry / way of salvation;

ci hang pu du 慈航普渡
salvation through charity to others;

ci he 慈和
kind and amiable;

ci he xiang chu 慈和相處
live on friendly terms;

ci mu duo bai er 慈母多敗兒
a fond mother spoils the son;

ci mu yan fu 慈母嚴父
a kind mother and a severe father;

ci shan 慈善
benevolent / charitable / philanthropic;

ci shan wei huai 慈善為懷
cherish charity;

ci shan xin 慈善心
philanthropy;

ci xiang 慈祥
amicable / benevolent / kind;

ci you 慈幼
love the young;

ci you yang lao 慈幼養老
love the young and care for the old;

ci4 xin zhi yan 刺心之言
words that pierce the heart;

cong1 xin di 從心底
deep down;

cong xin kan li 從心坎裏
from the privacy of one's thoughts;

cong xin suo yu 從心所欲
do as one pleases / follow one's heart's desire // free-wheeling;

cu1 xin 粗心
careless / inadvertent / negligent / thoughtless;

cu xin da yi 粗心大意
careless ‖ inadvertent; incautious; negligent; remiss; scatter-brain; slipshod; thoughtless; want of care // inadvertence / negligence;

cu xin fu qi 粗心浮氣
unthoughtful and rash;

cu4 醋
jealousy;

cu hai fan bo 醋海翻波
turn with jealousy;

cu hai sheng bo 醋海生波
a storm of jealousy / disturbance due to jealousy;

cu tan zi 醋罈子
jealous person;

cu xin 醋心
acid reflex / belching of acid from stomach / dyspepsia;

cu yi 醋意
feeling of jealousy;

cu yi chi lie 醋意熾烈
burning with jealousy;

cui4 bao ren qing 脆薄人情
thin and brittle human feeling;

cui4 悴
(1) haggard / tired out / worn-out;
(2) sad / worried;

cui bo 悴薄
enfeebled / impoverished / weakened;

cui jian 悴賤
needy and lowly;

cun2 nian 存念
keep sth as a memento;

cun wei 存慰
send a messenger to express sympathy to sb;

cun xin 存心
(1) cherish certain intentions;
(2) deliberately / intentionally / on purpose;

cun xin bu liang 存心不良
have wicked intentions ‖ cherish evil designs; cherish evil thoughts; evil-minded; harbour evil intentions; have ulterior motives; ill-disposed; mean ill; with evil intent;

cun xin diao nan 存心刁難
purposely to make difficulties for sb;

cun xin po ce 存心叵測
cherish unscrupulous intentions / harbour evil intent // with concealed intentions;

cun xin zuo dui 存心作對
antagonize sb on purpose;

cun xu 存恤
give comfort and relief;

cun yi 存疑
leave a question unanswered;

cun3 忖
consider / suppose;

cun duo 忖度
consider / suppose;

cun liang 忖量
(1) consider;
(2) conjecture;

cun si 忖思
imagine / wonder;

cun xiang 忖想
imagine / wonder;

cun4 cao chun hui 寸草春暉
great parental love // owe an eternal debt of gratitude to our parents;

cun duan 寸斷
be torn to pieces;

cun xin 寸心
feelings;

cun xin bu wang 寸心不忘
bear in mind forever / never forget;

cuo1 huo 搓火
feel impatient / get angry / worry;

cuo4 yi 措意
look out / mind / pay attention to // careful;

cuo4 ai 錯愛
misplaced favour;

cuo e 錯愕
astonished / startled;

cuo yi 錯疑
suspect because of misunderstanding;

da1 qiao shou shu 搭橋手術
coronary artery bypass grafting;

da2 怛
(1) distressed / grieved;
(2) alarmed / shocked / surprised;
(3) striving and toiling;

da da 怛怛
toiling and striving;

da hua 怛化
(1) dead / die;
(2) don't be shocked by death;

da shang 怛傷
distressed / grieved;

da3 dong 打動
arouse one's feelings / move / sink deep into one's mind / touch;

da4 chi yi jing 大吃一驚
be greatly shocked ‖ be astounded at; be given quite a turn; be greatly surprised; be knocked into the middle of next week; be startled at; be struck all of a heap; be taken aback; be taken completely by surprise; be thunderstruck; get a shock; jump out of one's skin; take fright at;

da ci da bei 大慈大悲
all loving and merciful / charitable / infinitely merciful;

da de ren xin 大得人心
enjoy great popularity / have high prestige among the people;

da fa ci bei 大發慈悲
for mercy's sake / have pity on / show mercy;

da fa shan xin 大發善心
become extremely benevolent;

da kuai ren xin 大快人心
fill people's hearts with great happiness ‖ cause great rejoicing among the masses of the people; cause popular rejoicing; it gladdens people's hearts; this cheers the people greatly; to the satisfaction of the masses;

da nu 大怒
foam at the mouth // in great anger;

da shi suo wang 大失所望
be greatly disappointed ‖ a body blow; extremely disappointed; lose great popularity; to one's great disappointment;

da wei jing kong 大為驚恐
be seized with terror / be struck with panic / in a funk;

da wei nao huo 大為惱火
fume with rage;

da wei zhen nu 大為震怒
become furious / fly into a rage / foam at the mouth;

da xi 大喜
great rejoicing;

da xi guo wang 大喜過望
be overjoyed ‖ be delighted that things are better than one expected; be pleased beyond expectation; rejoice beyond all expectations;

da xi que yue 大喜雀躍
joyful like a bird dancing;

da xi ri zi 大喜日子
a red-letter day / one's wedding-day;

da xi ruo kuang 大喜若狂
go crazy with joy / in an ecstasy of joy;

da yi 大意
(1) the general idea;
(2) careless / negligent;

dai3 歹
bad / evil;

dai xin 歹心
evil intent;

dai yi 歹意
evil intention / malicious intent;

dai4 怠
(1) idle / remiss / lax / negligent;
(2) treat coldly;

dai qing yang xing 怠情養性
renounce aggressiveness and practise relaxation;

dai4 li bu li 待理不理
treat coolly ‖ give the cold shoulder to sb; listen to sb; half-heartedly; show sb the cold shoulder;

dan1 xin 耽心
be worried;

dan you 耽憂
worry;

dan1 xin 躭心
apprehensive / worried;

dan1 lian 單戀
one-sided love / unrequited love;

dan si 單思
unrequited love;

dan xiang si 單相思
one-sided love / unrequited love;

dan xin shi 單心室
single ventricle;

dan1 jing shou pa 擔驚受怕
be in a state of anxiety ‖ afraid and on edge; feel alarmed; remain in a state of apprehension;

dan xin 擔心
be anxious / worry ‖ care about; entertain apprehension of; feel anxious; have apprehensions for; under the apprehension // misgivings;

dan you 擔憂
be anxious / worry;

dan1 xin 殫心
devote one's entire mind;

dan4 yuan 但願
hope / wish // if only;

dan yuan ru ci 但願如此
be it so ‖ I hope so; I hope that's right; I only hope it is so; I simply wish it to be so; I wish it were true; let it be so; let's hope so; so be it;

dan4 chou 淡愁
slight grief;

dan mo 淡漠
(1) apathetic / indifferent / nonchalant;
(2) dim / faint / hazy;

dan mo shi zhi 淡漠視之
look at ...nonchalantly;

dan mo wu qing 淡漠無情
indifferent and merciless / sternly cool and unmoved;

dan ran 淡然
cool / indifferent;

dan ran chu zhi 淡然處之
take things coolly ‖ give the cold shoulder to; regard coolly; take it with indifference; treat with indifference; turn the cold shoulder on;

dan ran zhi zhi 淡然置之
take things coolly ‖ give the cold shoulder to; regard coolly; take it with indifference; treat with indifference; turn the cold shoulder on;

dan4 憚
fear / shirk;

dan dan 憚憚
worry and fear;

dan fan 憚煩
afraid of trouble / dislike taking trouble;

dan fu 憚服
submit from awe;

dan gai 憚改
afraid to correct errors / afraid to reform;

dan lao 憚勞
avoid trouble / shrink from toils;

dan4 憺
(1) content and stable;
(2) fear;

dan ran 憺然
contented / satisfied;

dang1 xin 當心
be careful / be cautious / have a care / keep nix / take care / watch out / watch out for;

dang xin huo che 當心火車
beware of trains;

dang xin pa shou 當心扒手
beware of pickpockets;

dang4 qi hui chang 蕩氣迴腸
deeply affects one's emotions // heartrending / soulstirring / thrilling;

dang ran wu cun 蕩然無存
reduce to nothing || all gone; have nothing left; nothing remaining; there is nothing left;

dang ren xin shen 蕩人心神
play havoc with one's feelings;

dang yang 蕩漾
agitated // ripple / undulate;

dang yi ping xin 蕩意平心
allay the thought and quiet the mind;

dao1 忉
distressed / grieved;

dao da 忉怛
distressed / grieved / sad / worried;

dao dao 忉忉
distressed / worried;

dao4 悼
grieve / lament / mourn / regret;

dao nian 悼念
grieve / grieve over / lament for / mourn;

dao shang 悼傷
remember the deceased with sorrow;

dao tong 悼痛
mourn in anguish;

dao wang 悼亡
be bereaved of one's wife;

dao xi 悼惜
deplore / lament;

dao4 de 道德
morality / virtue // moral / virtuous;

dao de xing 道德心
sense of morality;

de2 chang su yuan 得償夙願
have fulfilled one's long-cherished wish / realize one's long-cherished hope;

de ren xin 得人心
be beloved and supported by the people / win the favour of the people // popular;

de xin ying shou 得心應手
(1) with high proficiency || in a masterly way; what the heart wishes one's hand accomplishes; with facility;
(2) handy / serviceable;

de yi 得意
complacent;

de yi wang xing 得意忘形
get dizzy with success || become highly conceited; dizzy with success; elated to the degree of forgetting one's form; go wild with joy; have one's head turned by success; lose all bearings in a moment of pride and satisfaction; on cloud nine; puffed up with pride;

de yi yang yang 得意洋洋
feel oneself highly flattered || be immensely proud; cheerful and confident; elevate one's crest; elevated exulting; flushed; glowing with pride; have one's nose in the air; have one's tail up; in the skies; jubilant; look triumphant; on cloud nine; on cloud seven; on the high ropes; pleased with oneself; tread on air; walk on air; with evident pride; with smug satisfaction;

de zhi 得志
have one's ambition fulfilled;

de zui 得罪
offend sb / upset sb;

de2 gao wang zhong 德高望重
of noble character and standing;

di1 liu zhe xin 提溜着心
anxious, worried and nervous;

di2 kai 敵愾
enmity / hatred toward the enemy / hostility;

di kai tong chou 敵愾同仇
hate a common enemy and fight against him

together;

di yi 敵意
antagonism / enmity / hostility / ill will;

di4 zeng xing xin jiao tong 遞增型心絞痛
crescendo angina;

dian3 xing xing xin jiao tong 典型性心絞痛
typical angina;

dian4 惦
be concerned about / remember with concern;

dian gua 惦掛
be concerned about / worry about;

dian huai 惦懷
look back fondly on / remember nostalgically;

dian ji 惦記
be concerned about / keep thinking about / remember with concern;

dian nian 惦念
anxious about / keep thinking about / worry about;

diao4 yi qing xin 掉以輕心
take sth lightly ‖ let down one's guard; lower one's guard; take a casual attitude;

die2 惵
afraid / fearful / terrified;

die die 惵惵
afraid / fearful / terrified;

die xi 惵息
holding breath from fear;

ding4 qing 定情
(1) get married;
(2) fall in love;

ding shen 定神
(1) compose oneself / pull oneself together;
(2) concentrate one's attention;

ding xin 定心
free of worries;

diu1 hun shi po 丟魂失魄
distracted;

dong4 恫
fear;

dong he 恫嚇
frighten / intimidate / scare / threaten;

dong yi xu he 恫疑虛喝
threaten loudly;

dong4 huo 動火
flare up / get angry / lose one's temper;

dong nu 動怒
flare up / get angry / get one's dander up / lose one's temper;

dong qi 動氣
become angry / get angry / get one's dander up / lose one's temper / take offense;

dong qing 動情
(1) become excited / get worked up;
(2) become enamoured ‖ have more than a fleeting interest in a woman; have one's sexual passions aroused;

dong ren 動人
moving / touching;

dong ren fei fu 動人肺腑
touch sb's heart ‖ come home to sb's heart; heartening; move sb deeply; touch sb to the depths of his soul;

dong ren ting wen 動人聽聞
excite one to hear about // exciting to hear;

dong ren xin xian 動人心弦
strike a chord in the heart of sb ‖ deeply moving; pull at sb's heartstrings; rouse one's tender emotions; stir up one's inmost feelings; strike a deep chord in the heart of sb; touch sb's feeling; touch the right chord; tug at one's heartstrings;

dong xin 動心
(1) be moved // one's desire is aroused;
(2) show interest;

dong yao jun xin 動搖軍心
demoralize the army / shake the army's morale;

dong yao ren xin 動搖人心
sway people's mind;

dong zhe fa nu 動輒發怒
get angry easily / get into a huff / go into a huff / prone to anger / take offence at trifles // huffy / touchy;

du2 chu xin cai 獨出心裁
unique in one's planning and design;

du ju jiang xin 獨具匠心
have an inventive mind / have great originality / show ingenuity;

du3 xin 堵心
feel badly;

du3 ai 篤愛
deep affection;

du zhi 篤志
firm determination;

du4 xin 杜心
give up all hope // despair;

du4 妒
envious of / jealous of;

du hen 妒恨
envy and resent;

du huo zhong shao 妒火中燒
burn with envy / burn with jealousy / inflame sb's jealousy ‖ be consumed with envy; green with envy;

du ji 妒忌
envious of / jealous of;

du xian ji liang 妒賢嫉良
envy the virtuous and wise;

du xian ji neng 妒賢嫉能
envious of the worthy and able ‖ envy someone better or abler than oneself; envy the good and be jealous of men of ability; jealous and envious of capable men;

du xin 妒心
jealous mind;

du yi 妒意
jealous;

dui4 憝
(1) wicked person;
(2) hate;

dui4 懟
hate / rancor / resent;

dun1 惇
generous / kind / sincere;

dun dun 惇惇
generous / kind / sincere;

dun hui 惇惠
benign / benignant;

dun hui 惇誨
teach kindly;

dun4 ran hui wu 頓然悔悟
be suddenly awakened to one's errors / suddenly realize one's error and show repentance;

dun wu 頓悟
sudden enlightenment;

dun wu qian fei 頓悟前非
suddenly recalls to mind a previous fault;

duo1 chou shan gan 多愁善感
sentimental ‖ always in sorrow and melancholy; always melancholy and moody; hearts and flowers; oversensitive; womanish sentiment;

duo qing 多情
emotional / passionate;

duo xin 多心
groundlessly suspicious / oversensitive;

duo2 ren xin mu 奪人心目
grasp one's heart and dazzle one's eyes;

e4 惡
(1) bad / evil / wicked;
(2) ferocious / fierce;

e de 惡德
corruption / immorality / vice;

e du 惡毒
malicious / venomous / vicious;

e fan 惡煩
boring / nauseating / tedious;

e gan 惡感
enmity / ill blood / ill feeling / ill will / malice;

e hen hen 惡狠狠
ferocious;

e la 惡辣
knavish / villainous;

e nian 惡念
evil intent / evil intentions;

e ren e xin gan 惡人惡心肝
a vicious person has a vicious heart;

e ren xin bu an 惡人心不安
a wicked person is their own hell;

e yi 惡意
evil intentions / ill will / malice // malicious / malignant / vicious;

e yi gong ji 惡意攻擊
bad mouth // bad-mouth;

e yi zhong shang 惡意中傷
do sb dirt;

e you e bao 惡有惡報
evil will be recompensed with evil;

e4 愕
astounded / startled / stunned;

e e 愕愕
amazed / astonished / astounded / startled;

e ran 愕然
astounded / stunned;

e4 yu 遏慾
curb one's passions;

en1 恩
benevolence / charity / favour / grace / gratitude / kindness / mercy;

en ai 恩愛
affectionate // conjugal love;

en ai fu qi bu dao tou 恩愛夫妻不到頭
an affectionate couple often cannot live together to the end of their lives;

en bi tian da 恩比天大
one's kindness and benevolence is as great as heaven;

en bi tian gao 恩比天高
one's concern is higher than the sky;

en chou 恩仇
debt of gratitude and of revenge / love and hatred;

en chou fen ming 恩仇分明
make a clear distinction between kindness and wrongs done by others;

en chou wei bao 恩仇未報
have not settled old accounts with sb;

en ci 恩賜
(1) bestow;
(2) charity / favour;

en ci guan dian 恩賜觀點
the attitude of bestowing ...as a favour;

en de 恩德
favour / grace / kindness;

en dian 恩典
benevolence / favour / grace / kindness;

en duo cheng yuan 恩多成怨
too much kindness will eventually engender grudge;

en hui 恩惠
bounty / favour / grace / kindness;

en jiang chou bao 恩將仇報
bite the hand that feeds one || quit love with hate; repay kindness with ingratitude; repay love with hate; requite kindness with enmity; return evil for good; return kindness with ingratitude; treat one's benefactor as one's enemy;

en li you jia 恩禮有加
shower sb with favours and courtesy;

en nian 恩念
kind thoughtfulness;

en qing 恩情
great kindness / love / loving-kindness;

en ren 恩人
benefactor;

en shen si hai 恩深似海
such mercy is deeper than the deepest sea;

en shen yi zhong 恩深義重
deep favour and weighty righteousness / the spiritual debt is deep and great;

en shi 恩師
one's respected teacher;

en tong yu lu 恩同雨露
one's grace is like rain and dew;

en tong zai zao 恩同再造
a favour tantamount to giving sb a new lease of life || as merciful as if one had rebuilt sb's character; one's goodness has made sb a new man;

en wei bing yong 恩威並用

apply the carrot and stick judiciously / employ both kindness and severity;

en wei jian shi 恩威兼施

alternate kindness with severity / employ both kindness and severity / temper justice with mercy;

en xin 恩信

favour and trust;

en yi 恩義

gratitude / spiritual debt;

en yuan 恩怨

feelings of gratitude / feelings of resentment / grievances / old scores / resentment;

en yuan fen ming 恩怨分明

discriminate between love and hate / make a clear distinction between kindness and hatred // kindness and hatred are clearly distinguished;

en ze 恩澤

bounties bestowed by a monarch;

en zhong ru shan 恩重如山

favours weighty as a mountain // a great debt of gratitude;

er4 xin 二心

disloyalty / half-heartedness;

er4 xin 貳心

disloyalty / half-heartedness;

fa1 chou 發愁

become sad / worry // anxious / sullen / vexed;

fa men 發悶

(1) feel suffocated;

(2) depressed;

fa nu 發怒

get angry || act up; be miffed; do one's nut; fit to be tied; flare up; fly into a rage; get into a huff; go into a huff; have a black dog on one's shoulder; have one's gorge rise; lose one's rag; lose one's temper; miff; see red;

fa xie gan qing 發洩感情

relieve one's feelings / uncork one's emotion;

fa zi nei xin 發自內心

from the bottom of one's heart // of one's own will;

fan1 ran 幡然

come to a sudden realization // suddenly;

fan ran hui wu 幡然悔悟

determined to make a clean break with one's past / see the error of one's ways and repent;

fan ran hui wu, gai xian geng zhang 幡然悔悟，改弦更張

repent and mend one's ways;

fan ran gui wu 幡然歸悟

make determined effort to make amends for past misdeeds || be determined to make a clean break with one's past; make an effort to atone for one's misdeeds; see the error of one's ways and repent; quickly wake up to one's error;

fan1 hui 翻悔

disavow a promise;

fan ran hui wu 翻然悔悟

repent and mend one's ways;

fan2 xin 凡心

desires of the flesh / worldly desires;

fan2 men 煩悶

malcontented;

fan nao 煩惱

cares / vexation / worries // vexatious / vexed / worried;

fan rao 煩擾

(1) bother / disturb;

(2) feel disturbed;

fan xiang 煩想

worries;

fan xin 煩心

trouble the mind;

fan zao 煩躁

agitated / annoyed and impatient / irritable / restive / vexed // fidgety // in a fret;

fan zao bu an 煩躁不安

agitated / annoyed and impatient / short-tempered / vexed // have the fidgets / set one's nerves on edge // dysphoria;

fan3 gan 反感

antipathy / aversion / habitual dislike / repulsion / revulsion // hacked-off;

fan4 yi 犯疑
suspicious;

fan yi 犯意
criminal intent;

fang1 xin 芳心
affection of a young lady / heart of a young lady;

fang xin wu zhu 芳心無主
(said of a lady) not knowing what to do;

fang4 bu xia xin 放不下心
cannot stop worrying / ill at ease / not quite trust sb;

fang huai 放懷
(1) to one's heart's content;
(2) free from anxiety;

fang xin 放心
set one's mind at rest || at ease; breathe easy; do not worry; feel relieved; free from cares; have one's heart at ease; put one's heart at ease; put sb's mind at ease; put sb's mind at rest; rest assured; rest one's heart;

fang xin bu xia 放心不下
be kept in suspense || feel anxious; in daily suspense;

fang zai xin li 放在心裏
bear in mind / keep in mind;

fei3 悱
(1) unable to give vent to one's emotion;
(2) at a loss for words // not to know what to say;

fei ce 悱惻
affected by sorrow / laden with sorrow / sad at heart // sorrowful;

fei fen 悱憤
sadness kept to oneself;

fei4 怫
(1) inarticulate / unable to give vent to one's emotion;
(2) deeply sad / sorrowful;

fei fen 怫憤
sadness kept to oneself;

fei4 fu 肺腑
from the bottom of one's heart;

fei4 jin xin ji 費盡心機
exhaust all mental efforts || beat one's brains about; cudgel one's brains; exert one's powers of thought to the utmost; exhaust one's abilities; rack one's brains; rack one's wits; ransack; take great pains to; tax one's ingenuity;

fei jin xin xue 費盡心血
expend all one's energies // with much ado;

fei xin 費心
give a lot of care / take a lot of trouble;

fei xin lao li 費心勞力
take a lot of trouble;

fen1 xin 分心
(1) give some attention;
(2) fail to pay full attention;
(3) distract the attention of sb // distraction;
(4) distracted;

fen you 分憂
help sb to get over a difficulty / share sb's cares and burdens;

fen you dai lao 分憂代勞
share sb's sorrow and toil / share sb's worry and relieve him of work;

fen you gong huan 分憂共患
share sb's sorrows and misfortunes;

fen you jie chou 分憂解愁
relieve sb of the daily worries / share and lessen worry;

fen4 忿
indignant // strong displeasure at sth considered unjust // fury / indignation / resentment;

fen fen bu ping 忿忿不平
indignant and disturbed;

fen fen er qu 忿忿而去
go away burning with rage / go away in ill humour / leave in a state of great anger;

fen hen 忿恨
fury / indignation / resentment / wrath;

fen huo 忿火
the flames of anger;

fen li 忿戾
angry and perverse;

fen li cu bao 忿厲粗暴
angry, fierce and rough;

fen men 忿懣
anger / indignation;

fen men 忿悶
angry and complaining;

fen nu 忿怒
fury / indignation / wrath;

fen yuan 忿怨
harbour a grudge;

fen zheng 忿爭
argue in anger;

fen4 憤
anger / indignation / resentment;

fen bu yu sheng 憤不欲生
so angry that one does not wish to live / would end life in a fit of bitterness;

fen fen bu le 憤憤不樂
upset and displeased;

fen fen bu ping 憤憤不平
feel aggrieved / nurse a grievance // indignant / resentful;

fen hen 憤恨
detest / indignantly resent // resentment;

fen hui 憤恚
deeply resentful;

fen ji 憤激
excitement / fury / vehemence;

fen ji ruo kuang 憤激若狂
wild with excitement;

fen kai 憤慨
indignation / strong displeasure at sth considered unjust;

fen men 憤懣
depressed and discontented / resentful;

fen nu 憤怒
blow hot coals // anger / indignation / outrage / wrath;

fen qie 憤切
grind the teeth with anger;

fen ran 憤然
angrily / with strong resentment;

fen ran li qu 憤然離去
leave in anger / shake the dust off one's feet / walk off in a huff;

fen ran zuo se 憤然作色
cynical || detest the world and its ways; feel resentful and disgusted at the living reality of society;

fen shi ji su 憤世嫉俗
destest the world and its ways / highly critical of society // misanthropic;

fen wan 憤惋
resentful and regretful;

feng1 bi xin fei 封閉心扉
close one's mind to;

feng1 qing yue zhai 風情月債
love affairs between man and woman;

fu2 rong qi mian, she xie qi xin 芙蓉其面，蛇蝎其心
have a fair face, but a foul heart;

fu2 怫
angry / depressed and discontented;

fu er bu shi 怫而不釋
unable to get rid of one's anxiety;

fu ran 怫然
abruptly / angrily;

fu ran bu yue 怫然不悦
be very much offended by / show an angry expression / show a sign of displeasure;

fu yu 怫鬱
depressed and discontented;

fu2 lü 拂慮
drive away cares and worries // carefree;

fu ni 拂逆
disagreeable;

fu yi 拂意
feel thwarted / run counter to one's ideas;

fu2 zhi xin ling 福至心靈
when luck comes it brings astuteness || when fortune comes, one's mind is alert — luck brings wisdom; when good luck comes, one has good ideas;

fu3 yang wu kui 俯仰無愧
have not done anything to make one feel

ashamed;

fu3 cun 撫存
comfort and relieve;

fu wei 撫慰
comfort / console / soothe // propitiatory // propitiation;

fu xu 撫恤
comfort and compensate a bereaved family / relieve;

fu4 jiu 負疚
have a guilty conscience / regret // uneasy in heart;

fu xin 負心
heartless / ungrateful;

fu xin bo xing 負心薄倖
ungrateful and lacking in right feelings;

gai3 bian zhu yi 改變主意
change one's mind // a change of heart;

gai hui 改悔
repent;

gan1 xin 甘心
(1) readily / willingly;
(2) be reconciled / content with / resign oneself to;

gan xin fu shou 甘心俯首
content to bow one's head and yield to;

gan xin le yi 甘心樂意
of one's free will / perfectly happy;

gan xin ming mu 甘心瞑目
die at peace / die content / die without dissatisfaction;

gan xin qing yuan 甘心情願
act entirely of one's own free will // perfectly willing / willingly and gladly;

gan yuan 甘願
readily / willingly;

gan yuan xiao lao 甘願效勞
render readily a service to sb || exert oneself voluntarily in the service of another; glad to do sth for sb; glad to offer one's services; willingly serve;

gan zhi ru yi 甘之如飴
content even in adversity;

gan3 bu fu xin 敢不腹心
make a frank statement without reservations / speak boldly from the depth of one's heart;

gan nu er bu gan yan 敢怒而不敢言
feel indignant but not dare to speak out || be forced to keep one's resentment to oneself; furious but not dare to say anything; choke with silent fury; not dare to express one's inner anger or discontent; suppress one's rage;

gan3 感
(1) feel / sense;
(2) affect / move / touch;
(3) grateful / obliged;
(4) be affected;
(5) feeling / sense;

gan chu 感觸
feelings / thoughts and feelings;

gan dao 感到
become aware of / feel / perceive / sense;

gan dong 感動
be moved / be touched / move / touch;

gan dong luo lei 感動落淚
be moved to tears || be melted into tears; in a melting mood;

gan en 感恩
feel grateful / thankful;

gan en bu jin 感恩不盡
everlastingly grateful;

gan en dai de 感恩戴德
be overwhelmed with gratitude || bear a debt of gratitude; bear a debt of gratitude for past kindness; feel a debt of gratitude for some kind act; feel grateful for; grateful for favour; grateful for sb's kindness; thankful for sb's goodness; with one's heart overflowing with gratitude;

gan en fei qian 感恩非淺
esteem it a great favour;

gan en mo ming 感恩莫名
do not know how to express one's gratitude;

gan en tu bao 感恩圖報
feel grateful for a kind act and plan to repay it || grateful for sb and seek ways to return his kindness; owe a debt of gratitude and hope to

requite it;

gan en zhong sheng 感恩終生
grateful to sb as long as one lives;

gan fen 感奮
be fired with enthusiasm / be moved and inspired;

gan fen bu yi 感奮不已
be greatly moved and inspired;

gan fen 感憤
feel aggrieved / feel indignant;

gan hua 感化
help sb to change by education and persuasion;

gan huai 感懷
(1) recall with emotion;
(2) recollections / reflections / thoughts;

gan huai wang shi 感懷往事
be moved to think of the past affairs / recall past events with deep feeling;

gan ji 感激
feel grateful / feel indebted / thankful;

gan ji bu jin 感激不盡
exceedingly thankful || extremely grateful; have no way to express all one's gratitude; owe sb a debt of endless gratitude;

gan ji mo ming 感激莫名
more grateful for this than words can tell || my gratitude beggars description; not to know how to express one's gratitude;

gan ji ti ling 感激涕零
be moved to tears of gratitude || bring sb to tears of gratitude; shed grateful tears; shed tears of joy and thank sb; so grateful as to shed tears; thank sb with tears in one's eyes; with tearful gratitude;

gan jue 感覺
(1) feeling / sensation / sense perception;
(2) become aware of / feel / perceive;

gan kai 感慨
sigh with emotion;

gan kai liu ti 感慨流涕
be moved to tears;

gan kai wan duan 感慨萬端
all sorts of feelings well up in one's mind // with great feeling;

gan kai wan qian 感慨萬千
be filled with a thousand regrets / be filled with painful recollections;

gan kui jiao ji 感愧交集
both grateful and shameful || be moved and ashamed simultaneously; feel grateful and uneasy at the same time;

gan nian 感念
recall with deep emotion / remember with gratitude;

gan qing 感情
affection / emotion / feeling / sentiment;

gan qing chong dong 感情衝動
act on a momentary impulse || be carried away by one's emotions; emotional impulse; impulsive;

gan qing fan chang 感情反常
emotional abnormality;

gan qing mi du 感情彌篤
have an ever deeper affection for each other;

gan qing po lie 感情破裂
fall out;

gan qing yong shi 感情用事
do sth in an emotional manner || abandon oneself to emotion; act according to one's sentiment; act impetuous; allow emotion to sway one's judgment; be swayed by emotions; give oneself over to blind emotions; give way to one's feelings; let emotions hold sway; under the sway of emotions;

gan ran 感染
(1) be infected / infect // infectious;
(2) affect / influence;

gan ren 感人
moving / touching;

gan ren fei fu 感人肺腑
touch sb to the heart || be deeply moved by; bring home to sb's heart; come home to sb's heart; fill sb with a deep emotion; go to sb's heart; move sb deeply; pull at sb's heartstrings; touch sb deeply in the heart;

touch sb to the depths of his soul; touch the chords of sb's heart;

gan ren zhi shen 感人至深
move people deeply;

gan shang 感傷
sentimental // have tender emotions;

gan shou 感受
be affected by / experience / feel;

gan tong shen shou 感同身受
appreciate it as a personal favour || be deeply affected by ... as if one had experienced it oneself; count it as a personal favour; feel indebted as if it were received in person; I shall count it as a personal favour; I would consider it as a personal favour to me;

gan wu shang huai 感物傷懷
be deeply affected at seeing sth — touch to the heart;

gan xiang 感想
impressions / reflections / thoughts;

gan xie 感謝
thank / gratitude;

gan xing 感性
perceptual;

gan zhao 感召
impel / move and inspire;

ge1 ai 割愛
give up what is dear to one's heart;

ge2 mian ge xin 革面革心
repent and reform oneself inside out;

ge xin 革心
repent;

ge2 xin 格心
correct one's heart;

geng3 geng ci xin 耿耿此心
devoted // this loyal heart;

geng geng yu huai 耿耿於懷
take sth to heart || bear sb a grudge; brood on an injury; uneasy heart;

geng geng zhong xin 耿耿忠心
be dedicated heart and soul // dogged adherence to;

gong1 de xin 公德心
public-mindedness // public-spirited;

gong1 jie 攻訐
accuse / charge;

gong xin 攻心
attempt to demoralize sb || make a psychological attack; try to persuade an offender to confess;

gong xin wei shang 攻心為上
it is better to win the hearts of the people || psychological offense is the best of tactics; the winning of a person's friendship is a greater achievement;

gong1 恭
deferential / respectful / reverent;

gong mo 恭默
reverent and quiet;

gong qian 恭謙
respect and modesty;

gong xi 恭喜
congratulations;

gou1 qing 勾情
flirt with sb;

gou xin dou jiao 勾心鬥角
intrigue against each other / mind struggles mind / scheme and plot against one another || conspire against each other; each trying to outwit the other; engage in a battle of wits; engage in petty intrigue and try to get the better of each other; jockey for position; scheme against each other;

gou1 xin dou jiao 鉤心鬥角
intrigue against each other;

gu1 en 辜恩
show ingratitude to a person;

gu en bei yi 辜恩背義
have no sense of gratitude and justice / ungrateful to kindness;

gu3 yuan 賈怨
invite complaints / invite grudges;

gu3 wu ren xin 鼓舞人心
gladden the people's hearts || heartening; inspiring; set the hearts of the people aflame;

gu3 huo 蠱惑
enchant / poison and bewitch;

gu huo ren xin 蠱惑人心
befog the minds of the people || agitate people by demagogy; beguile people out of the right way; confuse and poison people's minds; confuse public opinion; hoodwink people with demagogy; instil poisonous suspicions into people's minds; resort to demagogy; spread false doctrines to undermine the people's morale; undermine popular morale by spreading unfounded rumours;

gu4 yi 故意
deliberate / intentional / mean / on purpose // deliberately / designedly / intentionally / willfully;

gu yi liu nan 故意留難
make difficult for sb;

gu zuo duo qing 故作多情
drippy / mawkish;

gu4 ji 顧忌
misgivings / scruples;

gu lü 顧慮
show concern about // scruples;

gu nian 顧念
(1) be worried about / care for;
(2) think of with affection;

gu xu 顧恤
care for / sympathize with;

gua3 duan 寡斷
indecisive / irresolute;

gua en 寡恩
showing little favour / unkind;

gua huan 寡歡
unhappy;

gua qing 寡情
cold-hearted / heartless / unfeeling;

gua yu 寡欲
have few desires;

gua yu qing xin 寡欲清心
have few desires and cleanse the heart;

gua4 du qian chang 掛肚牽腸
be deeply concerned / be much worried about / cause deep personal concern;

gua huai 掛懷
miss || lie at sb's heart; think of; worry about sb who is absent;

gua lü 掛慮
anxious about / worried;

gua nian 掛念
miss || have on one's mind; lie at sb's heart; think of; worry about sb who is absent;

gua xin 掛心
be concerned about / bear in mind / have on one's mind / keep in mind;

gua yi 掛意
mind;

gua zai xin shang 掛在心上
bear in mind / have on one's mind / have sth at heart / keep sth in mind;

gua4 nian 罣念
concerned / worried;

guan1 huai 關懷
care / concern / show solicitude for;

guan huai bei zhi 關懷備至
be deeply concerned with || give meticulous care to sb; show every concern for sb; show the utmost solicitude;

guan xin 關心
care about || be concerned about; be concerned for; be concerned with; be interested in; care for; concern oneself about; concern oneself with; display deep concern for; display one's concern for; express great concern for; express one's concern for; feel concerned about; feel concerned for; give first place to; have a concern for; have a thought for; have...at heart; have ...in one's heart; make over; make the most of; show concern for; show consideration for; show one's concern for; solicitous for; solitude; surround sb with love and care; take...to one's heart; think of; thoughtful about;

guan xin ji ku 關心疾苦
care about sb's troubles;

guan xin min mo 關心民瘼
look after the suffering of the people;

guan4 xin bing 冠心病
coronary disease / coronary heart disease;

gui1 xin 歸心
the idea of returning home;

gui xin si jian 歸心似箭
anxious to go back home || anxious to return home as soon as possible; eager to dart homeward; impatient to get back; long to return home; return with the swiftness of an arrow;

gui3 mi xin qiao 鬼迷心竅
be obsessed / be possessed;

guo4 du jiao lü zheng 過度焦慮症
overanxious disorder;

guo lü 過慮
overanxious;

guo min xing xin ji yan 過敏性心肌炎
hypersensitivity myocarditis;

guo yi 過意
feel offended;

guo yi bu qu 過意不去
(1) very much obliged;
(2) feel sorry;

hai4 pa 害怕
afraid of / fear || afraid for sth; be frightened; be overcome by fear; be overcome with fear; be scared of; can't say boo to a goose; dread; dreadful; fearful; fly the white feather; for fear of; frighten; frightful; get cold feet; have a dread of; have cold feet; in dread of sb; in dread of sth; in fear of; make one's blood run cold; make one's hair stand on end; mount the white feather; quail; shake in one's boots; show the white feather; strike fear into; tremble in one's shoes;

hai4 駭
astonished / shocked;

hai cha wu si 駭詫無似
in incomparable amazement;

hai e 駭愕
be amazed / be flabbergasted;

hai e wan fen 駭愕萬分
amazing to the greatest degree;

hai guai 駭怪
astonished / shocked;

hai pa 駭怕
frightened / scared;

hai ran 駭然
gasping with astonishment // be struck dumb with amazement;

hai wan 駭惋
marvel;

hai yi 駭異
astonished / shocked;

han1 chang lin li 酣暢淋漓
heartily / to one's heart's content;

han1 憨
(1) foolish / silly / stupid;
(2) naïve / straightforward;

han hou 憨厚
simple and honest;

han tou han nao 憨頭憨腦
with a stupid head and a dull brain || doltish; foolhardy; foolish; silly;

han zhi 憨直
honest and straightforward;

han2 bei 含悲
exercise restraint over grief;

han hen 含恨
cherish resentment;

han nu 含怒
in anger;

han qing mai mai 含情脈脈
full of tenderness;

han2 xin 寒心
(1) be bitterly disappointed;
(2) feel the blood running cold || afraid; fearful;

han4 撼
dissatisfaction // regret / remorse;

han dong ren xin 撼動人心
move one's heart / shake people's faith;

han hen 撼恨
chagrin / feeling of vexation // be marked by disappointment;

han shi 撼事
regrettable thing / matter for regret;

han yuan 撼怨
chagrin;

hao2 bu guan xin 毫不關心
totally indifferent || apathetic; care nothing for; express no concern; glacial indifference; indifferent; let things go hang; nonchalant; not care a brass farthing; not care a button; not care a damn; not care a fart; not care a fuck; not care a monkey's fuck; not care a toss; not care a tuppenny; not care two hoots; not give a brass farthing; not give a button; not give a damn; not give a fart; not give a fuck; not give a hoot; not give a monkey's fuck; not give a toss; not give a tuppenny; not give two hoots; take a casual attitude; unconcerned;

hao bu jie yi 毫不介意
not care at all || don't care a fig; don't mind; not matter a farthing; not to care a straw; pay no attention to; take no notice of;

hao bu li ji, yi xin wei gong 毫不利己，一心為公
be dedicated to serving the public without any thought of oneself;

hao bu liu qing 毫不留情
relentlessly || act in cold blood; give no quarter; give...no mercy; in spades; show...no mercy; take off the gloves to; with the gloves off; without gloves;

hao bu rong qing 毫不容情
without making any allowance || make absolutely no allowance; mercilessly; not to pull any punches;

hao bu wei ju 毫不畏懼
dauntless / without a trace of fear;

hao bu zai yi 毫不在意
not to care a bit || not to care a dump; not to care a rap; not to care a whoop;

hao bu zhi chi 毫不知恥
have the impudence to / lose all sense of shame;

hao bu zu guai 毫不足怪
not at all surprising;

hao2 fang 豪放
vigorous and unrestrained;

hao fang bu ji 豪放不羈
vigorous and unrestrained;

hao mai 豪邁
generous and open-minded / straightforward and carefree;

hao mai qi gai 豪邁氣概
heroic spirit / unrestrained spirit;

hao mai xing qing 豪邁性情
magnanimous disposition;

hao qi 豪氣
undaunted spirit;

hao qing 豪情
lofty sentiments;

hao qing man huai 豪情滿懷
be filled with boundless pride // full of pride and enthusiasm / full of spirit;

hao qing zhuang zhi 豪情壯志
lofty sentiments and aspirations / lofty spirit and soaring determination;

hao shuang 豪爽
bold and generous // virile vigour;

hao zi 豪恣
unbridled / unrestrained;

hao3 gan 好感
favourable impression / take a fancy to;

hao xin 好心
good intentions // good-hearted;

hao xin chang 好心腸
good-hearted;

hao xin hao yi 好心好意
goodwilled and well-intentioned || for the best; have one's heart in the right place; kind-hearted; with good intentions; with goodwill;

hao xin you hao bao 好心有好報
good-heartedness often meets with recompense / your charity would be rewarded;

he2 hu qing li 合乎情理
reasonable;

he qing he li 合情合理
fair and reasonable;

he yi 合意
agreeable // to one's liking;

he4 奭
angry;

hei1 xin 黑心
(1) black heart / evil heart;
(2) black-hearted / cruel / sinister;

hen3 du 狠毒
atrocious / brutal / cruel / malicious;

hen li 狠戾
atrocious / cruel / vicious;

hen xin 狠心
cruel / heartless / merciless / pitiless;

hen4 恨
(1) hate / resent // hatred / resentment;
(2) regret;

hen du 恨毒
malicious hatred;

hen e 恨惡
loathe;

hen hai 恨海
deep hatred;

hen nu 恨怒
animosity;

hen zhi ru gu 恨之入骨
hate sb to the marrow || be consumed with hatred for; bear a bitter hatred for; cherish bitter hatred; harbour an intense hatred; hate sb like poison; hate sb to the core; hate sb's guts; hate sth like poison; hate with all one's soul; nurse an inveterate hatred for;

heng2 xin 恒心
perseverance;

heng2 le xin 横了心
steel one's heart;

heng xia xin lai 横下心來
harden the heart || become case-hardened; case-hardened towards; dead determined to; steel oneself to do sth;

heng xin 横心
become desperate / steel one's heart;

hong2 yuan 弘願
great ambition;

hong2 da 宏達
intelligent / knowledgeable;

hong fang 宏放
broad-minded and unrestrained;

hong yuan 宏願
ambition;

hou4 hui 後悔
regret / remorse / repent;

hou hui bu yi 後悔不已
be overcome with regret;

hou hui mo ji 後悔莫及
too late to repent || cry over spilled milk; it is too late for regrets;

hou hui shi yan 後悔失言
bite off one's tongue / bite one's tongue off;

hou hui wu yi 後悔無益
cry over spilled milk / repentance is of no avail;

hou4 ai 厚愛
great kindness;

hou yi 厚意
good intention;

hu1 hu bu le 忽忽不樂
be discouraged and unhappy;

hu1 惚
absent-minded / entranced // in a trance;

hu2 觳
shrink and tremble in fear;

hu su 觳觫
shrink and tremble in fear;

hu4 怙
rely on / presume on;

hu e ling ren 怙惡凌人
intimidate and oppress others;

hu guo 怙過
show no repentance for one's wrong-doings;

hu yi 怙依
things or persons that one relies on;

huai2 懷
(1) harbour / hold;
(2) recollect / think of;
(3) mind;

huai cai bu yu 懷才不遇
have talent but no opportunity to use it;

huai fu 懷服
give in / submit / yield;

huai hen 懷恨
bear a grudge / harbour resentment / nurse a hatred for;

huai hen zai xin 懷恨在心
harbour resentment in one's heart || bear sb a grudge; bear sb a spite; cherish a secret resentment against; entertain a feeling against; full of rancour against sb; harbour a grudge against; have a spite against; have resentment rankling on one's mind; nourish feeling of hatred; nurse hatred in one's heart; nurse rancour against; rancorous;

huai jiu 懷舊
(1) remember the good old days / think of the bygone days with yearning;
(2) think of old friends;

huai lian 懷戀
think fondly of;

huai nian 懷念
cherish memories / have a sweet memory of / long / miss / remember with longing / remember with nostalgia / think of;

huai xiang 懷鄉
homesick;

huai xie 懷邪
harbour evil;

huai yi 懷疑
disbelieve / doubt / question / suspect;

huai you 懷憂
be concerned / be worried;

huai4 liang xin 壞良心
depraved conscience // heartless;

huai zhu yi 壞主意
wicked ideas;

huan1 懽
glad / happy / joyous;

huan1 bian 歡忭
happy / joyful;

huan chang 歡暢
elated / thoroughly delighted;

huan kuai 歡快
cheerful and lighthearted;

huan le 歡樂
gaiety / happiness / joy;

huan tian xi di 歡天喜地
overjoyed || be filled with great joy; be greatly pleased; dance for joy; elated and happy; extremely delighted; full of joy; go into raptures; in an ecstasy of joy; in high glee; in raptures; in the seventh heaven; one's happiness knows no bounds; tread on air; wild with joy; with boundless joy;

huan xi 歡喜
(1) delighted / happy / joyful;
(2) delight in / fond of / like;

huan xi que yue 歡喜雀躍
skipping and jumping about with joy / tread on air;

huan xi ruo kuang 歡喜若狂
frantic with joy || gloat over; tread on air; gleefully;

huan xin 歡心
favour / liking / love;

huan xin 歡欣
be filled with joy // elated // jubilation;

huan xin gu wu 歡欣鼓舞
be filled with exultation || be gladdened; buck up; dance with pleasure; elated and inspired; exult; gladden and inspire; jubilant over; jump for joy;

huan yu 歡愉
happy / joyful;

huang1 慌
(1) confused / flurried / flustered / panic;
(2) awfully / unbearably;

huang huang mang mang 慌慌忙忙
hurriedly / in a rush;

huang huang zhang zhang 慌慌張張
in a flurried manner || be covered with confusion; hastily; helter-skelter; in a flurry; in an abrupt manner;

huang li huang zhang 慌裏慌張
in a hurried and confused manner || all in a fluster; higgledy-piggledy; in a rush; lose one's head; on the rush;

huang luan 慌亂
hurry and confusion // alarmed and bewildered; flurried;

huang mang 慌忙
hurriedly || in a flurry; in a great rush; rush to;

huang zhang 慌張
confused / flurried / flustered / higgledy-piggledy / hurry-scurry // trepidation;

huang zuo yi tuan 慌作一團
be thrown into utter confusion || be struck all of a heap; crouch with fear; in a flap; in a flutter; in great excitement;

huang2 惶
(1) anxiety / fear / trepidation;
(2) anxious / uneasy;
(3) flurried / hurried;

huang huang 惶惶
in a state of anxiety || alarmed; disquieted; on tenterhooks;

huang huang bu an 惶惶不安
live in terror and uncertainty || be greatly upset; fear and panic; go hot and cold; in a state of anxiety; on tenterhooks // perturbation;

huang huang bu ke zhong ri 惶惶不可終日
in a constant state of anxiety || be kept in a state of constant nervousness; be kept perpetually in a state of tension; on edge and alarmed all day; on tenderhoods all the time; sit on thorns;

huang huang ru sang jia zhi quan 惶惶如喪家之犬
as frightened as a stray cur / panic like homeless curs;

huang huang wu zhu 惶惶無主
panicky and not know what to do;

huang huo 惶惑
apprehensive / perplexed and alarmed;

huang huo bu an 惶惑不安
in a state of great agitation || be lost and ill at ease; perplexed and uneasy;

huang ji wan zhuang 惶急萬狀
in great urgency;

huang ju 惶遽
frightened / scared;

huang kong 惶恐
frightened / panic-stricken / scared / terrified // trepidation;

huang kong bu an 惶恐不安
be greatly alarmed || be terrified and uneasy; fear and panic; great alarm; heebie-jeebies; in a state of alarm; in a state of trepidation; panic-stricken; with one's heart going pit-pat;

huang kong wan zhuang 惶恐萬狀
be frightened out of one's senses / be seized with fear;

huang kong wu cuo 惶恐無措
up a stump // panicky and not know what to do;

huang rao 惶擾
agitate / perturb;

huang3 怳
(1) dejected / despondent;
(2) mad;

huang3 恍
absent-minded / unconscious;

huang hu 恍惚
absent-minded / unconscious;

huang ran da wu 恍然大悟
come to understand suddenly;

huang ran ruo shi 恍然若失
feel as if one has lost one's bearings;

hui1 xin 灰心
lose courage / lose heart // disappointed / discouraged / disheartened;

hui xin duan nian 灰心斷念
throw up one's cards;

hui xin lan yi 灰心懶意
disheartened and reluctant;

hui xin sang qi 灰心喪氣
utterly disheartened || despondent; discouraged; lose heart; yield to despair;

hui2 xin zhuan yi 回心轉意
change one's mind || a change of heart; change one's views; come round; correct one's thinking and attitude; repent;

hui3 悔
regret / repent;

hui ai 悔艾
change one's behaviour / change one's habits / decide to turn over a new leaf;

hui bu dang chu 悔不當初
regret a previous mistake || kick oneself; regret having done sth;

hui gai 悔改
repent and mend one's ways;

hui guo 悔過
repent one's error // repentance; penitence;

hui guo cong shan 悔過從善
acknowledge one's errors and become a good person;

hui guo zi xin 悔過自新
repent and turn over a new leaf || express one's repentance and determination to turn over a new leaf; repent and make a fresh start; repent and start anew; repent and start with a clean slate;

hui hen 悔恨
bitterly remorseful / regret deeply // remorse;

hui hen jiao jia 悔恨交加
mixed feelings of remorse and shame / regret mingled with self-reproach;

hui hen mo ji 悔恨莫及
cry over spilled milk;

hui hen zhong shen 悔恨終身
have a secret regret for life / nurse a secret regret all one's life / regret all one's life;

hui huo 悔禍
hope the disaster would not happen again / wish the disaster would not be repeated;

hui ju 悔懼
repentant and fearful of the consequence;

hui kui 悔愧
regret and shame;

hui kui jiao zhi 悔愧交織
be torn by self-recrimination and repentance;

hui lai 悔賴
renege on a promise;

hui qi 悔氣
bad luck;

hui wu 悔悟
awake from sin / contrite / regret / repent;

hui xie 悔謝
regret and admit a fault;

hui xin 悔心
penitence;

hui zhi wu ji 悔之無及
too late to repent || rue it in vain; too late for remorse; useless to repent now;

hui zhi wu yi 悔之無益
repentance is of no avail / there is no point in repenting;

hui zhi yi wan 悔之已晚
it is now too late to repent || it is no use regretting it now; repentance is too late; there is no sense crying over spilled milk; too late for regrets; too late to regret;

hui zui 悔罪
show penitence / show repentance;

hui4 恚
anger / rage;

hui fen 恚憤
be enraged / indignant;

hui hen 恚恨
hate vehemently;

hui nu 恚怒
be enraged // furious / indignant;

hui yuan 恚怨
resent bitterly;

hui4 惠
(1) benevolent / gracious / kind;
(2) gentle and yielding;

hui yu 惠育
care for with tenderness;

hui ze 惠澤
benevolence / favour / kindness;

hui4 wu 會悟
realize / understand;

hui xin 會心
knowing / understanding // meeting of minds;

hui xin wei xiao 會心微笑
smile a smile of understanding // an understanding smile;

hui yi 會意
meeting of ideas;

hui4 慧
intelligent / bright / wise;

hui gei 慧給
intelligent and eloquent;

hui min 慧敏
sagacious / shrewd;

hui xin 慧心
clear and alert mind;

hui xing 慧性
intelligence;

hui ye 慧業
natural and intelligent;

hui4 xin 蕙心
pure heart;

hui zhi lan xin 蕙質蘭心
pure heart and spirit;

hun1 惛
(1) confused;
(2) senile;

hun bei 惛憊
muddleheaded;

hun hun 惛惛
(1) confused in mind;
(2) absorbed / entranced;

hun mao 惛眊
senile // senility;

hun mao 惛耄
senile;

hun mi 惛迷
confused;

hun nao 惛怓
turmoil / uproar;

hun4 慁
(1) distress / disturb / upset;
(2) disgrace;
(3) worry;

huo4 惑
(1) beguile / confuse / delude / misguide / mislead;
(2) doubt / suspect;

huo luan 惑亂
confuse / delude / puzzle;

huo ni 惑溺
indulge in;

huo nong 惑弄
befool / beguile / delude;

huo shu 惑術
deceitful tricks;

huo yu mei se 惑於美色
be taken by a bewitching face;

huo zhi 惑志
doubt / suspicion;

huo zhong 惑眾
confuse people / delude people;

huo4 ran da nu 霍然大怒
fly into a rage || bluster oneself into anger; burst into a passion; flare up; foam at the mouth; one's anger flares up; suddenly burst into a fit of temper; suddenly grow very angry;

ji1 xin 機心
shrewd and cunning;

ji1 ang 激昂
impassioned;

ji dong ren xin 激動人心
arouse sb's feelings // soul-stirring;

ji fen 激憤
indignant / wrathful;

ji nu 激怒
enrage / get on sb's nerves / get one's hackles up / infuriate / irritate / make sb's hackles rise / raise sb's hackles / raise the hackles of sb / stroke sb the wrong way / stroke sb's hair the wrong way;

ji qing 激情
enthusiasm / passion;

ji1 yuan 積怨
accumulated rancor / deep-rooted grudge /

grudge;

ji1 hen 齎恨

entertain a grudge / harbour hatred;

ji2 急

(1) urgent;

(2) anxious;

ji ba ba 急巴巴

very anxious;

ji ji 急激

radical / vehement;

ji xing xin ji geng si 急性心肌梗死

acute myocardial infarction;

ji2 嫉

(1) envious / jealous;

(2) detest / hate;

ji du 嫉妒

envy // jealous of;

ji e ru chou 嫉惡如仇

have an abhorrence of evil;

ji hen 嫉恨

envy and hate / hate out of jealousy;

ji xian du neng 嫉賢妒能

jealous of capable people;

ji2 jin xin li 極盡心力

put one's body and soul into a task / work to the best of one's ability;

ji4 忌

(1) envy // jealous / jealous of;

(2) dread / fear / scruple / shun;

(3) abstain from / avoid / shun;

(4) give up / quit;

(5) the death anniversary of one's parents or grandparents;

ji cai 忌才

jealous of other people's talent // resent people more able than oneself;

ji dan 忌憚

dread / fear / scruple;

ji du 忌妒

envy // jealous;

ji hen 忌恨

envy and hate;

ji ke 忌刻

jealous and malicious / jealous and mean;

ji4 nian 紀念

commemorate / mark / remember;

ji4 gua 記掛

be concerned about / keep thinking about / miss;

ji4 liao 寂寥

lonesome;

ji mo 寂寞

lonely / lonesome;

ji4 huai 寄懷

express one's feeling;

ji qing 寄情

give expression to one's feelings;

ji qing shan shui 寄情山水

abandon oneself to nature;

ji qing shi jiu 寄情詩酒

abandon oneself to poetry and wine;

ji yi 寄意

send one's regards;

ji4 悸

fear / palpitate / palpitate from nervousness / throb with terror // palpitation of the heart;

ji dong 悸動

palpitate from nervousness / palpitate with terror;

ji li 悸慄

palpitate from nervousness / throb with terror / tremble with fear;

ji4 冀

hope;

ji qiu 冀求

hope to get / seek for;

ji wang 冀望

hope / hope for / long for / look forward to;

ji4 xing 覬幸

hope to get sth by good chance;

ji yu 覬覦

covet / desire sth belonging to others;

ji4 chou 羈愁

a traveler's sorrow;

ji xin **羈心**
the melancholy feeling during travel;

jia2 **恝**
indifferent / unconcerned / unworried;

jia ran **恝然**
indifferent / unconcerned / unworried;

jia zhi **恝置**
disregard / ignore / neglect;

jia3 ci bei **假慈悲**
pretend to be kind-hearted / shed crocodile tears;

jia xin jia yi **假心假意**
hypocritical show of friendship / tongue-in-cheek // pretend to;

jia xin jiao tong **假心絞痛**
pseudoangina;

jia yi **假意**
hypocritic / insincere // hypocrisy / insincerity;

jia zhuang duo qing **假裝多情**
make a pretence of affection;

jia4 yuan **嫁怨**
imput blame to another;

jian1 xin bi lu **奸心畢露**
reveal one's entire scheme;

jian1 ai **兼愛**
love without discrimination / love without judging;

jian1 ding xin nian **堅定信念**
impregnable belief;

jian shou xin nian **堅守信念**
follow the courage of one's opinions / have the courage of one's convictions / stick to one's convictions;

jian1 xin **煎心**
very worried;

jian3 **譾**
mentally shallow;

jian lou **譾陋**
mentally shallow;

jian lou wu neng **譾陋無能**
shallowly experienced and incapable;

jiang1 xin bi xin **將心比心**
judge another person's feeling by one's own || compare one's feelings with another's; feel for others; have to see things through other people's eyes;

jiang xin jiang yi **將信將疑**
skeptical;

jiang4 xin **匠心**
ingenuity / inventiveness / originality;

jiang xin du ju **匠心獨具**
display great originality / have great originality / show ingenuity;

jiang xin du yun **匠心獨運**
display one's ingenuity / exercise one's inventive mind / show one's own ingenuity;

jiang xin jing ying **匠心經營**
take great pains to create;

jiang4 xin xiang cong **降心相從**
subject one's own will to the dictate of others / submit to others against one's will;

jiao1 qing **交情**
friendship;

jiao xin **交心**
be frank with others / lay one's heart bare / open hearts to each other / open one's heart to;

jiao1 ji **焦急**
anxious / / worried // in deep anxiety / on one's toes;

jiao ji bu an **焦急不安**
flutter // in a swivel / on the anxious seat;

jiao ji wan zhuang **焦急萬狀**
one's anxiety is at its height // restless with anxiety;

jiao jie **焦竭**
worried and exhausted;

jiao ke **焦渴**
very anxous;

jiao ku **焦苦**
miserable;

jiao lao **焦勞**
worried and worn down by hard work;

jiao lü 焦慮
feel anxious / have worries and misgivings // extremely anxious;

jiao lü bu an 焦慮不安
be racked with anxiety || fret and fume; in a flutter of excitement; in a way; nail-biting; on the rack; on tenderhooks; on thorns; tear one's hair; toss about;

jiao men 焦悶
harassed / worried and anxious;

jiao si 焦思
deep worry;

jiao tou lan e 焦頭爛額
be bruised and battered || badly battered; be scorched and burned; be scorched by the flames; beat sb's head off; in a sorry plight; in a terrible fix; smash heads and scorch brows; utterly exhausted from overwork;

jiao xin 焦心
feel terribly worried;

jiao xin ku lü 焦心苦慮
deeply anxious // in deep anxiety;

jiao zao 焦躁
getting restless because of anxiety // worried, anxious and getting impatient;

jiao zhuo 焦灼
deeply worried / very anxious;

jiao1 憍
arrogant / self-conceited;

jiao1 bo 澆薄
rash and perfidious / faithless and ungrateful;

jiao chou 澆愁
wash away sorrows with wine;

jiao1 xin fan zao 燋心煩躁
being distressed and harassed;

jiao3 xin 絞心
(1) suffer in one's heart;
(2) rack one's brains;

jiao3 qing 矯情
affectedly unconventional;

jie2 bu jie chou 結不解仇
become a sworn enemy;

jie bu jie yuan 結不解緣
be united by an ironclad bond;

jie nian 結念
remember;

jie tong xin 結同心
of one mind;

jie yuan 結寃
contract enmity / contract ill will;

jie yuan 結緣
form ties of affection;

jie yuan 結怨
arouse ill will / incur hatred;

jie2 ai 節哀
restrain grief;

jie ai shun bian 節哀順變
retrain grief and accept the change;

jie2 cheng 竭誠
wholeheartedly / with all sincerity;

jie jin xin li 竭盡心力
work to the best of one's ability || exert one's heart and strength to the utmost; exhaust one's mental abilities; put one's body and soul into a task; with all one's mind and energy;

jie lü 竭慮
devote one's mental energy to the full;

jie3 hen 解恨
slake one's hatred;

jie huo 解惑
remove doubts;

jie men 解悶
dispel loneliness / get rid of boredom / kill time;

jie qi 解氣
ease anger / pacify / placate;

jie tuo 解脱
extricate / disentangle / free oneself from worldly worries / get rid of shackles;

jie wu 解悟
realize / understand;

jie you 解憂
alleviate sorrow / relieve worries;

jie4 huai 介懷
mind;

jie yi 介意
(1) brood on sth unpleasant;
(2) mind;

jie4 xin 戒心
alertness / vigilance / wariness;

jin1 矜
commiserate with / feel sorry for / pity / sympathize with // compassionate;

jin lian 矜憐
commiserate with / feel sorry for / pity;

jin min 矜憫
pity / sympathize // compassionate;

jin xi 矜惜
treasure / value;

jin xue 矜恤
have pity on / sympathize with;

jin1 襟
ambition / aspiration / mental outlook;

jin bao 襟抱
ambition / aspiration;

jin duo 襟度
mental outlook and capacity for tolerance;

jin duo kuang hong 襟度寬宏
broad-minded;

jin duo xia xiao 襟度狹小
narrow-minded;

jin huai 襟懷
one's ambitions / one's feelings;

jin ling 襟靈
ambition / aspiration;

jin qing 襟情
feelings buried deep in one's heart;

jin qu 襟曲
the true feelings deep in one's heart;

jin yun 襟韻
one's aspirations and manners;

jin3 shen 謹慎
cautious / chary / circumspect / prudent // prudence // play for safety;

jin xiao shen wei 謹小慎微
circumspect / overcautious;

jin yuan 謹願
honest / sincere;

jin4 qu qing jie 進取情結
achievement complex;

jin qu xin 進取心
aggressiveness / enterprising spirit;

jin4 qing 盡情
to one's heart's content || as much as one likes; to the full;

jin qing fa hui 盡情發揮
bring into full play;

jin qing fang zong 盡情放縱
have one's fling;

jin qing huan le 盡情歡樂
make merry to one's heart's content;

jin qing liu lu 盡情流露
give free vent to;

jin qing tu lu 盡情吐露
free one's heart / wear one's heart upon one's sleeve;

jin qing xiang gao 盡情相告
make a clean breast of things to sb / unbosom oneself to sb;

jin xin 盡心
put one's heart and soul into // with all one's heart;

jin xin bao guo 盡心報國
devote one's energies entirely to the service of the state / do one's best for the country;

jin xin jie li 盡心竭力
do one's best || do one's level best; exert one's heart and strength to the utmost; go to great lengths; heart and soul; put one's heart and soul into; strain every nerve; use one's best efforts; with all one's heart and all one's might;

jin yi 盡意
to one's heart's content;

jin zhong 盡忠
do one's duty as a subject;

jin zhong bao guo 盡忠報國
devote oneself to one's country;

jing1 xin 經心
painstaking / very careful and attentive;

jing yi 經意
advertent / attentive / careful;

jing1 cheng 精誠
purity and sincerity // earnest and sincere;

jing cheng suo zhi, jin shi wei kai 精誠所至，金石為開
where wholehearted dedication is directed, the whole world will step aside to let you by;

jing cheng tuan jie 精誠團結
consolidate with faith and dedication / solidate with dedication and honesty;

jing xin 精心
carefully / elaborately / meticulously / painstakingly // put all one's mind in;

jing xin ce hua 精心策劃
carefully calculated / carefully plan / deliberately design / elaborately plan / painstakingly engineer;

jing xin hu li 精心護理
nurse with the best of care;

jing xin jie zuo 精心傑作
masterpiece;

jing xin pao zhi 精心炮製
be carefully dished up / be done with meticulous care / rack one's brains to make sth;

jing xin pei yu 精心培育
take meticulous care of;

jing xin tiao li 精心調理
nurse sb with the best care;

jing xin zhao liao 精心照料
take precious good care of;

jing xin zhi liao 精心治療
give meticulous treatment;

jing xin zhi zuo 精心製作
elaboration;

jing1 cha 驚詫
amazed / astonished / surprised;

jing e 驚愕
be astonished / be astounded / be dumbfound;

jing guai 驚怪
be amazed and puzzled / marvel;

jing huang 驚慌
be frightened and confused / lose one's head from terror / panic;

jing huang shi se 驚慌失色
lose countenance;

jing huang shi cuo 驚惶失措
be out of countenance / lose one's head from fear // panic;

jing ji 驚悸
quickened heartbeat due to fear;

jing ju 驚懼
afraid / fearful / scared;

jing kong 驚恐
afraid / fearful / scared;

jing kong wan fen 驚恐萬分
horror-struck;

jing pa 驚怕
afraid / fearful / scared;

jing xi 驚悉
be shocked to learn;

jing xi 驚喜
pleasantly surprised;

jing xin 驚心
be frightened / be shaken;

jing xin diao dan 驚心掉膽
be frightened out of one's wits;

jing xin dong po 驚心動魄
soul-stirring and breathtaking;

jing xin po dan 驚心破膽
heart startled and gallbladder broken — be extremely frightened;

jing yi 驚疑
afraid and anxious / fearful and apprehensive;

jing3 mu 景慕
admire and respect;

jing yang 景仰
admire and respect / look up to;

jing3 憬
awake / come to understand / realize;

jing ran 憬然
aware / knowing;

jing wu 憬悟
become aware of / come to see the truth / come to understand / realize;

jing3 ti 警惕
guard against / watch out for // on guard against / on one's guard / on the alert // vigilant / wary;

jing4 xin xiu shen 淨心修身
cleanse one's heart and order one's behaviour;

jing4 敬
(1) esteem / honour / respect / revere;
(2) offer / present;

jing ai 敬爱
respect and love;

jing fu 敬服
respect unreservedly;

jing jin 敬謹
deferentially / respectfully;

jing lao 敬老
respect the old;

jing ling 敬領
accept with respect;

jing mu 敬慕
respect and admire;

jing pei 敬佩
admire / esteem / respect / think highly;

jing qian 敬虔
devout / pious;

jing wei 敬畏
hold in awe / revere / stand in awe of / venerate;

jing yang 敬仰
admire / esteem / respect;

jing yi 敬意
respects;

jing zhong 敬重
esteem / have high regard for / revere / respect;

jing4 xin 靜心
calm one's mind // peaceful mind;

jiu1 xin 揪心
(1) unable to set one's mind at rest;
(2) anxious / nervous / worried;

jiu4 疚
(1) prolonged illness;
(2) mental discomfort;

jiu huai 疚懷
ashamed;

jiu xin 疚心
ashamed;

jiu4 e 舊惡
old grudges / past feud;

jiu en 舊恩
past kindness;

jiu hen xin chou 舊恨新愁
sorrows old and new;

jiu qing 舊情
former affection;

ju1 xin 居心
harbour evil intentions;

ju xin bu liang 居心不良
harbour evil intentions || harbour hostile designs; have some dirty trick up one's sleeve; with bad intentions;

ju xin bu shan 居心不善
ill-disposed // one's heart is bent on evil;

ju xin he zai 居心何在
what is the motive behind all this || what is sb up to; what is sb's intention;

ju xin po ce 居心叵測
with ulterior motives || cherish dark designs; harbour evil intention towards; have evil designs; with concealed intentions; with hidden intent;

ju xin xian e 居心險惡
of a malicious disposition // vicious in one's motives;

ju xin yin xian 居心陰險
of a malicious disposition;

ju xian xing xin bao yan 局限性心包炎
localized pericarditis;

ju2 cu 局促
feel constraint / show constraint;

ju cu bu an 局促不安
ill at ease / not know where to put oneself;

ju4 懼
(1) dread / fear / in fear of;
(2) frighten;

ju gao zheng 懼高症
acrophobia;

ju nei 懼內
henpecked;

ju pa 懼怕
be afraid of / dread / fear;

ju qie 懼怯
afraid / timid;

ju shui zheng 懼水症
fear of water / hydrophobia;

juan4 悁
angry / indignant / irritable;

juan fen 悁忿
angry / enraged / indignant;

juan ji 悁急
anxious / impatient / irritable;

juan juan 悁悁
(1) sad / unhappy / worried;
(2) angry / irritable;

juan4 yi 倦意
sleepiness / tiredness / weariness;

juan4 眷
(1) care for;
(2) admire / love;

juan ai 眷愛
care for / love / regard with affection;

juan gu 眷顧
care for;

juan huai 眷懷
cherish the memory of / remember;

juan juan 眷眷
remember with tender feelings;

juan lian 眷戀
admire / be attached to sb;

juan nian 眷念
remember with affection / think of with affection;

juan you 眷佑
care for and assist;

juan zhu 眷注
care for / concern with affection;

jue2 xin 決心
determined / resolved / stout-hearted // determination / resolution / stout heart;

xia ding jue xin 下定決心
come to a resolution / make a firm resolve to do sth / make up one's mind;

xia jue xin 下決心
come to a resolution / make a firm resolve to do sth / make up one's mind;

jue yi 決意
decide / make up one's mind / resolve;

jue2 wang 絕望
hopeless // give up hope // despair;

jue2 wu 覺悟
aware / come to understand / realize;

jue2 懼
(1) respectful;
(2) awe-struck;

jue ran 懼然
awe-struck // surprisingly;

kai1 huai 開懷
happy / joyful / jubilant // to one's heart's content;

kai kai xin 開開心
relax and enjoy oneself;

kai xin 開心
happy // feel happy || bucked; delighted; full of glee; get a kick; in high glee; make joy; rejoice; take joy;

kai xin jian cheng 開心見誠
talk from the heart, with nothing concealed || expose one's feelings; wear one's heart upon one's sleeve;

kai3 愷
gentle / good / joyful / kind;

kai ce 愷惻
graciousness;

kai qie 愷切
gently and sincerely;

kai ti 愷悌
amiable / friendly / happy and easygoing;

kai3 慨
(1) regret;
(2) generous / magnanimous;

kai fen 慨憤
angry / indignant;

kai hen 慨恨
angry / indignant;

kai ran 慨然
generous / magnanimous;

kai xi 慨惜
regret;

kai4 愒
idle away time;

kai ri 愒日
idle away the days;

kai shi 愒時
idle away the time;

kai4 愾
anger / enmity / hatred / wrath;

kai fen 愾憤
angry // show wrath;

kai ran 愾然
sigh with deep feelings;

kang1 慷
(1) ardent / impassioned;
(2) generous / liberal / magnanimous / unselfish;

kang kai 慷慨
(1) ardent / impassioned;
(2) generous / liberal / magnanimous / munificent / open-handed / unselfish // generosity / liberality / open-handedness;

kang kai bei fen 慷慨悲憤
impassioned by lamentation and indignation;

kang kai ji ang 慷慨激昂
arousing / impassioned;

kang kai jiu yi 慷慨就義
die a martyr's death;

kang4 fen 亢奮
excited / stimulated;

ke3 wu 可惡
detestable;

ke xin ru yi 可心如意
things that are after one's heart || congenial; find sth satisfactory; to one's heart's content;

ke4 bo 刻薄
cold-hearted / mean / unfeeling;

ke bo gua en 刻薄寡恩
cold-hearted without generosity;

ke gu ming xin 刻骨銘心
imprint on sb's mind;

ke yi 刻意
careful and diligent // painstakingly;

ke4 恪
respectful / reverent;

ke qin 恪勤
cautious and industrious;

ke shen 恪慎
respectful and cautious;

ke shou dao de 恪守道德
straight and narrow;

ke zun 恪遵
obey orders with respect;

ken3 懇
cordial / earnest / sincere;

ken chi 懇辭
decline earnestly;

ken en 懇恩
beg a favour;

ken qi 懇乞
ask earnestly / beg / beseech / entreat / implore;

ken qie 懇切
earnest / very sincere;

ken qiu 懇求
beseech / entreat / implore / plead // entreaty / obsecration;

ken zhi 懇摯
eager / earnest / sincere;

kong1 悾
candid / sincere;

kong kong 悾悾
(1) candid / sincere;
(2) simple-minded;

kong kuan 悾款
candid / sincere;

kong3 huai 孔懷
think very much of each other;

kou3 bu ying xin 口不應心
words not agreeing with the heart ‖ carry fire in one hand and water in the other; not to have the courage of one's opinion; profess one thing, but mean another;

kou kuai xin zhi 口快心直
what the heart thinks, the tongue speaks ‖ blunt, outspoken, but honest; free from affectation and hesitation; open-hearted; wear one's heart on one's sleeve;

kou song xin wei 口誦心惟
read sth while pondering its meaning;

kou tian xin la 口甜心辣
honey on the lips and viciousness in the heart;

kou xin ru yi 口心如一
one means what one says / what one says is indeed what one thinks;

kou xiong xin ruan 口兇心軟
one's bark is worse than one's bite;

kou4 ren xin xian 扣人心弦
grip the hearts of sb ‖ carry one away; cliff-hanging; play on sb's heartstrings; pull at sb's heartstrings; soul-stirring; thrilling; touch one's feelings; touch sb to the heart; tug at one's heartstrings;

ku3 chu 苦楚
pain / suffering;

ku da chou shen 苦大仇深
suffer bitterly and harbour deep hatred;

ku ku ai qiu 苦苦哀求
implore / piteously entreat;

ku le 苦樂
comfort and discomfort / joys and sorrows;

ku lei 苦累
adversity / hardship / privation / toil / trials;

ku lian 苦戀
unrequited love;

ku men 苦悶
bored / dejected / depressed / distressed / low-spirited // boredom;

ku nao 苦惱
distress / misery / trouble;

ku xin 苦心
pains // take trouble to;

ku xin gu yi 苦心孤詣
make extraordinarily painstaking efforts / take great pains;

ku xin jing ying 苦心經營
work out with unsparing efforts ‖ elaborative in the undertaking; manage painstakingly; mastermind with painstaking effort; take great pains to build up an enterprise;

ku xin pin cou 苦心拼湊
painstakingly piece together / take great pains to rig up;

ku xin si suo 苦心思索
puzzle over;

ku xin zhi zhi 苦心致志
by faithful devotion and constancy of purpose;

ku zhong 苦衷
a reason for doing sth not easily understood by others;

ku4 ai 酷愛
very fond of sth;

kuai4 gan 快感
pleasant feeling;

kuai le 快樂
cheerful / happy;

kuai shi 快適
happy and contented / pleased and satisfied;

心 Heart

kuai wei 快慰
happy / pleased;

kuai xin 快心
be pleased / feel happy;

kuai yi 快意
pleasing / satisfying;

kuan1 da 寬大
lenient / magnanimous;

kuan da wei huai 寬大為懷
forgiving / magnanimous / tolerant;

kuan dai 寬待
treat generously;

kuan hong da liang 寬宏大量
broad-minded / magnanimous / open-hearted;

kuan hou 寬厚
tolerant and generous;

kuan rao 寬饒
forgive / show mercy;

kuan rong 寬容
forgive / pardon;

kuan shu 寬恕
forgive / pardon;

kuan wei 寬慰
comfort / console / soothe;

kuan xin 寬心
feel relieved ‖ at ease; feel at rest; feel free from anxiety; find relief; relaxed; relieved; set one's mind at ease;

kuan yan 寬嚴
lenity and severity;

kuan zong 寬縱
benignly kind / benignly permissive / indulgent;

kuang1 恇
afraid / fearful / timid;

kuang hai 恇駭
fearful / frightened;

kuang ju 恇懼
afraid / fearful;

kuang qie 恇怯
timid;

kuang rao 恇擾
harass // confusedly scared;

kuang2 nu 狂怒
apoplectic fury / convulsive rage / fury / great fury // fly into a rage / fly into a temper // livid // in an awful bate;

kuang xi 狂喜
be in raptures / go into raptures / rejoice with great excitement / show wild joy // ecstatic // ecstasy / rapture;

kui1 悝
deride / make fun of / ridicule;

kui1 xin 虧心
go against conscience / have a guilty conscience;

kui xin shi 虧心事
sth that gives one a guilty conscience ‖ a deed that weighs on one's conscience; a discreditable affair; a matter of remorse; a thing which conscience condemns;

kui4 愧
abashed / ashamed / shameful;

kui bu gan dang 愧不敢當
not deserve to have sth;

kui hen 愧恨
remorseful // shame and remorse;

kui hui 愧悔
feel mortified and remorseful;

kui jiu 愧疚
feel the discomfort of shame // compulsion;

kui xin 愧心
feeling of shame;

kui4 憒
confused in one's mind / muddleheaded;

kui kui 憒憒
confused / muddleheaded;

kui luan 憒亂
at a loss / confused in one's mind / dazed;

kui mao 憒眊
dull-witted / muddleheaded;

kun3 悃
honest / sincere;

kun bi wu hua 悃愊無華
honest and simple;

kun cheng 悃誠
earnest / free of deceit / genuine / sincere;

kun kuan 悃款
(1) single-minded;
(2) earnest / free of deceit / genuine / sincere;

kun shi 悃實
simple and sincere;

kun4 huo 困惑
bemused / bewildered / confused / get licked / perplexed / puzzled // perplexity;

kun ku nan kan 困苦難堪
suffer unbearble hardships;

kun nao 困惱
annoy / be vexed / irritate / vex;

kun rao 困擾
bewildered / confused / perplexed / puzzled;

lan2 婪
covetous / greedy;

lan lan 婪婪
covetous / greedy;

lan3 懶
disinclined / idle / indolent / lazy / listless;

lan duo 懶惰
indolent / lazy / sluggish;

lan san 懶散
inactive / indolent / slothful / sluggish // slackness / sloth;

lan tai 懶怠
disinclined / idle / indolent / lazy / listless / slothful;

lan yang yang 懶洋洋
indolent / sluggish;

lan yu 懶於
too lazy to do sth;

lao2 chou 牢愁
sad / sorrowful / unhappy;

lao2 xin 勞心
(1) labour mentally // brain-work;
(2) be worried;

lao3 nian xing xin zang bing 老年性心臟病
presbycardia;

lao xiu cheng nu 老羞成怒
angry as a result of embarrassment;

lao4 憦
feel remorse / regret;

le4 樂
(1) delighted / elated / happy / joyful / pleased;
(2) agreeable / comfortable / enjoyable / pleasant / pleasing;

le bu ke zhi 樂不可支
beside oneself with happiness / on cloud nine / on cloud seven;

le he he 樂呵呵
buoyant / happy and gay;

le huai le 樂壞了
very happy;

le shan hao shi 樂善好施
willing to do good and give help to the poor;

le tao tao 樂陶陶
cheerful / happy / joyful;

le tian 樂天
be contented with one's lot;

le tian zhi ming 樂天知命
be contented with one's lot // happy-go-lucky;

le xi xi 樂嘻嘻
cheerful / happy / joyful;

le yi wang you 樂以忘憂
seek pleasure in order to free oneself from care;

le yi 樂意
(1) willing;
(2) pleased;

le yu 樂於
like doing sth / love doing sth;

le zi zi 樂滋滋
contented / pleased;

leng3 ku wu qing 冷酷無情
cold-blooded / hard-hearted / heartless / merciless / obdurate / ruthless / unfeeling // as cold as ice;

leng xin 冷心
apathetic / uninterested;

leng4 愣
(1) dumbfounded / stupefied;
(2) irresponsible / rash / reckless / rude;
(3) outspoken;

leng gan 愣幹
do things recklessly;

li2 chou 離愁
parting sorrows / sad feelings at separation;

li hen 離恨
parting grief;

li qing bie xu 離情別緒
parting sorrows / sad feelings at separation;

li xin li de 離心離德
disaffection;

li3 悝
grieved / sad / worried;

li3 kui xin xu 理虧心虛
feel apprehensive because one is in the wrong;

li4 bu chong xin 力不從心
lacking the ability to do what one wishes;

li yu yuan wei 力與願違
unable to do what one wishes;

li4 yu xun xin 利慾熏心
be blinded by greed ‖ avarice and lust becloud one's heart; be lured by profits; be obsessed with the desire for gain; be overcome by covetousness; be possessed by greed for gain; be possessed with a lust for gain; money-grabbing; on the make; put profit above conscience; reckless with greed; sordid;

li4 慄
shudder / tremble;

li li 慄慄
(1) fearful / frightful / terrified / timorous;
(2) chilly / cold;

li lie 慄冽
bone-chilly / chilly;

lian2 怜
pity / sympathize;

lian2 xin 連心
meeting of minds // be deeply attached to each other;

lian2 憐
(1) commiserate / pity / sympathize;
(2) feel tender regard for;
(3) touching;

lian ai 憐愛
feel pity and love for / have tender regard for;

lian min 憐憫
commiserate / pity / take compassion on;

lian pin 憐貧
commiserate the poor / pity the poor;

lian xi 憐惜
feel tender regard for;

lian xiang xi yu 憐香惜玉
have a tender heart for the fair sex;

lian xu 憐恤
help out of compassion;

lian3 yuan 斂怨
accumulate hatred;

lian4 qiu jun xing xin yan 鏈球菌性心炎
streptococcal carditis;

lian4 戀
(1) love sb / love sth;
(2) have a persistent attachment;

lian ai 戀愛
be in love;

lian fu qing jie 戀父情結
Electra complex;

lian mu qing jie 戀母情結
Oedipus complex;

lian mu 戀慕
lose one's heart to / pine for;

liang2 xin 良心
better feelings / conscience;

liang xin bu an 良心不安
have an uneasy conscience;

liang xin fa xian 良心發現
be strung by conscience // one's better nature asserts itself;

liang xin qian ze 良心遣責
one's conscience pricks one ‖ pricks of conscience; the strings of conscience;

liang xin you kui 良心有愧
guilty conscience // conscience-stricken;

liang xin sang jin 良心喪盡
utterly conscienceless;

liang xin ze bei 良心責備
have a guilty conscience ‖ have compunctions; one's own conscience rebukes one; prickings of conscience;

liang xing zhong liu 良性腫瘤
benign tumour;

liang3 qing qian quan 兩情繾綣
deeply in love with each other;

liang tiao xin 兩條心
in fundamental disagreement / not of one mind;

liang xiang qing yuan 兩相情願
both parties are willing;

liang4 jie 諒解
forgive // understanding;

liao2 biao cun xin 聊表寸心
as a small token of my feelings ‖ it's a mere proof of my regard; just to show my appreciation; just to show my gratitude;

liao yi jie you 聊以解憂
a crumb of comfort;

liao yi zi wei 聊以自慰
just to console oneself / take comfort in;

liao2 憀
disappointed / sad;

liao3 憭
clear / intelligible;

lin2 nan bu ju 臨難不懼
calm in the face of danger;

lin3 懍
(1) awe-stricken;
(2) fearful / inspiring awe;

lin li 懍慄
fearful // trembling with awe;

lin lin 懍懍
(1) awe-struck;
(2) inspiring fear;

lin ran 懍然
(1) awe-struck;
(2) inspiring fear;

ling2 伶
cute / pleasing;

ling li 伶俐
agile / cute / pleasing;

ling2 xin hui xing 靈心慧性
intelligent and talented;

ling xing 靈性
intelligence;

ling4 ren fan gan 令人反感
offensive / repulsive;

ling ren han xin 令人寒心
bitterly disappointing // cast a chill over sb;

ling ren huai yi 令人懷疑
cause suspicion;

ling ren jing xin dong po 令人驚心動魄
make sb stirred to the soul / shake sb to the core;

ling ren kong bu 令人恐怖
horrendous / horrific;

ling ren qing xin 令人傾心
carry sb off her feet / sweep sb off his feet;

ling ren tong xin 令人痛心
cut one to the heart;

ling ren xin fu 令人心服
carry conviction;

ling ren xin han 令人心寒
cast a chill over one;

ling ren xin suan 令人心酸
cause sb's heart to ache / make sb want to cry out of pity;

ling ren xin sui 令人心碎
break a person's heart ‖ break sb's heartstrings; break the heartstrings of sb; heartbreaking; heartrending;

ling ren xin tong 令人心痛
heartrending;

ling ren xin wei 令人欣慰
heartwarming;

ling ren yan wu 令人厭惡
disgusting / loathsome;

liu2 lian 留戀
(1) be reluctant to leave;
(2) recall with nostalgia;

liu nian 留念
accept as a souvenir / keep as a souvenir;

liu shen 留神
be careful;

liu xin 留心
be careful / keep an eye open for / keep an eye out for / keep one's ears open for / keep one's eyes open / keep one's eyes peeled / keep one's eyes skinned / mind / see about / take care // with one's eyes open;

liu yi 留意
exercise caution / pay attention to / take care // careful;

lou4 gu ming xin 鏤骨銘心
engrave on the bones and imprint on the heart — remember forever with gratitude / wholeheartedly grateful to sb;

lou xin ke gu 鏤心刻骨
inscribe a debt of gratitude on one's mind;

lu4 li tong xin 戮力同心
make concerted efforts ‖ all exert themselves as one person; all work with a singleness of purpose and unity of effort; of one mind; pull together and work hard as a team; unite in a concerted effort; work together in a coalition;

lü4 慮
be concerned about / worry about;

lü huan 慮患
apprehensive of trouble;

mai3 fu ren xin 買服人心
win the heart of the masses;

mai4 en 賣恩
do sb a favour with a view to earning his gratitude;

mai ren qing 賣人情
do sb a favour for personal consideration;

man2 xin mei ji 瞞心昧己
against one's conscience // blot out one's conscience / deceive oneself;

man3 huai 滿懷
a heart full of;

man qiang 滿腔
have one's bosom filled with;

man qiang bei fen 滿腔悲憤
unutterable sadness fills one's heart;

man qiang chou hen 滿腔仇恨
be filled with an inveterate hatred / burn with hatred / see things with hatred;

man qiang chou men 滿腔愁悶
full of care;

man qiang ji qing 滿腔激情
one's breast is filled with emotion;

man qiang ku shui 滿腔苦水
full of grievances;

man qiang nu huo 滿腔怒火
anger flames in one's heart // be filled with boiling anger / be filled with fury / boil with fury;

man qiang re chen 滿腔熱忱
with warmth and enthusiasm ‖ be filled with ardour and sincerity; feel warmth towards; full of enthusiasm; full of zealous and sincere feelings; in all earnestness; in the fullness of one's heart; show warmth towards sb; with great enthusiasm; with zeal;

man qiang re qing 滿腔熱情
full of enthusiasm ‖ ardently; enthusiastically; fervently; full of warmth; make a warmhearted effort; show earnest concern; warmheartedly; wholehearted enthusiasm; wholeheartedly;

man qiang re xue 滿腔熱血
one's heart is filled with enthusiasm ‖ full of patriotic fervour; full of sympathetic feelings; full of zeal; in the fullness of one's heart;

man qiang tong qing 滿腔同情
brim over with sympathy;

man xin 滿心
have one's heart filled with sth;

man xin fen nu 滿心憤怒
in a towering rage;

man xin huan xi 滿心歡喜
with heartfelt delight || delighted; full of joy; very pleased;

man xin you lü 滿心憂慮
one's heart is full of grief;

man yi 滿意
chuffed / content / happy / satisfied;

man4 bu jing xin 漫不經心
in a careless way || absent; absent-minded; inadvertent; inattentive; indifferently; insouciant; let slide; negligent; pay no heed to; remiss; totally unconcerned; wanting in care;

man4 xing xin lü shi chang 慢性心律失常
chronic arrhythmia;

mao2 dun xin li 矛盾心理
ambivalence;

mei2 liang xin 沒良心
heartless / ungrateful / without conscience;

mei xin chang 沒心腸
no heart for / not interested in;

mei xin gan 沒心肝
heartless / ungrateful;

mei xin mei fei 沒心沒肺
inattentive / wanting in care;

mei xin yan er 沒心眼兒
mindless || candid; careless; frank; lack of calculation;

mei3 gan 美感
sense of beauty;

mei yi 美意
goodwill / kind intention;

mei4 ji man xin 昧己瞞心
deceive oneself / do evil against one's conscience / play treacherous tricks against one's conscience;

mei liang xin 昧良心
disregard one's conscience;

mei xin 昧心
against one's conscience;

mei zhe liang xin 昧着良心
against one's conscience;

mei4 liang xin 滅良心
go against conscience;

mei xin 滅心
go against conscience;

mei4 huo 魅惑
bedevil / bewitch / captivate;

men1 悶
shut oneself indoors;

men ren 悶人
stifling;

men2 xin 捫心
examine one's conscience / feel one's heart by hand;

men xin wu kui 捫心無愧
feel no qualms upon self-examination || feel that one has not done anything wrong; have a good conscience; one's heart is in the right place;

men xin zi wen 捫心自問
examine oneself // introspection;

men4 懣
resentful / sulky / sullen;

meng3 懵
ignorant;

meng kui 懵憒
unaware / uncomprehending / dull-witted;

meng meng wu zhi 懵懵無知
quite ignorant;

meng ran 懵然
ignorant / lacking in knowledge / unaware / uninformed;

mi2 hu hu 迷忽忽
(1) muddleheaded // confused mind;
(2) unconscious;

mi hu 迷糊
unconscious;

mi huo 迷惑
confuse / delude / misguide / mislead / nonplus // bewildered / confused / puzzled;

mi huo ren xin 迷惑人心
confuse the masses || befuddle public opinion; pull the wool over people's eyes; throw dust in the eyes of the public;

mi le xin qiao 迷了心竅
be obsessed with || be captivated by; be possessed with; under an obsession of;

mi lian 迷戀
in blind love with // be infatuated with / be stuck on // spoony;

mi ren 迷人
bewitching / charming / enchanting / fascinating;

mi wang 迷惘
(1) mentally stupefied;
(2) bemused;

mi zhu 迷住
bewitch / captivate / charm / enchant / infatuate / spellbind;

mian2 si meng xiang 眠思夢想
think day and night;

mian3 愐
(1) give thought to / remember;
(2) shy;

mian huai 愐懷
cherish the memory of / recall / remember / think of;

mian3 huai 緬懷
cherish the memory of / recall / remember / think of;

mian xiang 緬想
remember with affection / think of fondly;

min3 gan 敏感
sensitive;

min hui 敏慧
clever / keen / quick in understanding / sharp-witted;

min wu 敏悟
quick to understand;

min3 愍
commiserate / pity;

min ce 愍惻
have sympathy with / show sympathy for;

min lian 愍憐
pity;

min xu 愍恤
feel pity;

min3 憫
(1) commiserate / feel concerned over / pity;
(2) grieve / sorrow;

min ce 憫惻
pity;

min xi 憫惜
have compassion on / pity;

min xue 憫恤
pity and help;

ming2 gan 銘感
remember with gratitude;

ming ji yu xin 銘記於心
be engraved on sb's heart || be engraved on the mind; be enshrined in the heart; be implanted in sb's bosom; be impressed on sb's memory; bear in mind; embalm in the memory; enshrine in one's memory; imprint on one's mind; sink into sb's mind; store up in one's heart; treasure up in one's memory;

ming ke yu xin 銘刻於心
be enthroned in the hearts / be imprinted on one's heart;

ming pei 銘佩
remember with admiration;

ming xin 銘心
always remember / be imprinted on one's mind / never forget;

ming xin ke gu 銘心刻骨
be imprinted on one's bones and in one's heart || always remember; be imprinted on one's bones and in one's heart — bear in mind forever; engrave on the heart;

miu4 ai 謬愛
undeserved favour / undeserved kindness;

miu mao 謬耄
feeble-minded and senile;

mo3 le liang xin 抹了良心
blot out all the moral sense // unconscionable;

mo4 ni yu xin 莫逆於心
finding each other congenial / with complete mutual understanding;

mo4 bu guan xin 漠不關心
totally indifferent ‖ apathetic; care nothing for; express no concern; glacial indifference; indifferent; let things go hang; nonchalant; not care a brass farthing; not care a button; not care a damn; not care a fart; not care a fuck; not care a monkey's fuck; not care a toss; not care a tuppenny; not care two hoots; not give a brass farthing; not give a button; not give a damn; not give a fart; not give a fuck; not give a hoot; not give a monkey's fuck; not give a toss; not give a tuppenny; not give two hoots; take a casual attitude; unconcerned // indifference / indifferentism / unconcern;

mo4 nian 默念
recite silently inside the mind;

mu3 ai 母愛
maternal love / mother love;

mu4 慕
(1) long for / yearn for;
(2) admire / adore;

mu fang 慕倣
imitate in admiration;

mu ming 慕名
(1) eager for fame;
(2) admire another's reputation;

mu ming li 慕名利
long for fame and fortune;

mu se shi 慕色勢
hanker afer women and influence;

mu si 慕思
think of one repeatedly;

mu xiao 慕效
imitate in admiration;

mu yi 慕義
admire righteousness / emulate a good action;

mu yong 慕用
employ one due to the admiration of one's virtue;

mu yue 慕悦
mutual liking;

na4 han 納罕
feel curious / feel surprised;

na men 納悶
(1) feel depressed // nonplussed;
(2) feel curious / wonder;

nai4 fan 耐煩
bearing sth with fortitude and calmness // patient;

nai xin 耐心
patience / perseverance;

nan2 yi wang hui 難以忘懷
indelible / unforgettable;

nao2 怓
confused / wild;

nao3 惱
(1) annoy / exasperate / irritate / trouble / vex;
(2) angered / annoyed / offended / vexed;

nao ba ba 惱巴巴
angry / annoyed / cross;

nao fan 惱犯
anger / annoy / enrage / infuriate;

nao hen 惱恨
hate / resent;

nao huo 惱火
annoy / irritate / vex;

nao luan 惱亂
disturb / trouble;

nao men 惱悶
grieved and sad / troubled in the mind;

nao nu 惱怒
angry / furious / indignant / snuffy // get the needle / have the needle / heat up // on one's ear;

nao qi 惱氣
anger / indignation / irritation / rage;

nao ren 惱人
annoying / irritating / niggling / trying;

nao ren chun se 惱人春色
suffering from love in spring;

nao xin 惱心
irritated state of mind;

nao xiu cheng nu 惱羞成怒
lose one's temper from embarrassment || become angry and red-faced; become angry from embarrassment; become angry from shame; fly into a rage with shame; fly into a shameful rage;

nao yi 惱意
the feeling of anger;

nao4 qing xu 鬧情緒
in a bad mood / in a low spirit;

nao yi qi 鬧意氣
sulk;

nei4 jiu 內疚
compunction / guilty conscience;

nei xin 內心
heart / innermost being / the bottom of one's heart;

nei xin chong tu 內心衝突
intrapsychic conflict;

nei xin du bai 內心獨白
soliloquy;

nei xin fan teng 內心翻騰
one's heart is in a tumult;

nei xin shen chu 內心深處
at the bottom of one's heart || cockles of the heart; in one's heart of hearts; in the depth of one's heart; in the privacy of one's thoughts;

nei xin shi tiao 內心失調
intrapsychic ataxia;

nei xin shi jie 內心世界
one's inner world / the inner world of the heart;

nei xin you kui 內心有愧
have a guilty conscience;

ni4 惄
pensive / worried;

ni4 yuan 匿怨
bear a secret grudge;

nian2 lian xing xin bao 黏連性心包
adherent pericardium;

nian lian xing xin bao yan 黏連性心包炎
adhesive pericarditis;

niao4 du zheng xin bao yan 尿毒症心包炎
uremic pericarditis;

ning2 xin 寧心
calm one's mind and spirit;

ning xin ding qi 寧心定氣
quiet the mind and still the passion nature;

ning yuan 寧願
prefer / would rather;

niu3 忸
(1) be inclined to;
(2) ashamed / bashful;

niu ni 忸怩
bashful / coyly;

nong2 chou 濃愁
deep anxiety / deep grief;

nong qing 濃情
affectionate regard / passionate feeling;

nong qing mi yi 濃情蜜意
strong affection and deep love;

nong2 du xing xin nei mo yan 膿毒性心內膜炎
septic endocarditis;

nong qi xing xin bao yan 膿氣性心包炎
pyopneumopericardium;

nong xing xin bao yan 膿性心包炎
pyopericarditis;

nu4 怒
(1) anger / rage;
(2) angry / furious;
(3) forceful and vigorous;

nu bu ke e 怒不可遏
beside oneself in anger // in uncontrollable fury;

nu e 怒惡
wrath and spite;

nu hen 怒恨
full of anger and spite;

nu huo 怒火
dander / flames of fury / fury;

nu huo zhong shao 怒火中燒
be inflamed with anger / boil with fury;

nu qi 怒氣
anger / dander / fury / rage / wrath;

nu qi chong chong 怒氣沖沖
angry / furious // in an awful bate / in a great rage / with one's hackles up;

nu yi 怒意
anger / dander / wrath;

nü4 恧
ashamed;

nü suo 恧縮
recoil on account of shame;

nuo4 懦
cowardly / timid / weak;

nuo dun 懦鈍
weak and dull;

nuo qie 懦怯
coward / timid;

nuo ruo 懦弱
cowardly / weak;

ou3 gan 偶感
(1) feel suddenly;
(2) feel occasionally;

ou3 xin 嘔心
exert one's utmost effort;

ou xin li xue 嘔心瀝血
make painstaking efforts || exhaust one's lifeblood; shed one's heart's blood; spare no pains; strain one's heart and mind; take infinite pains; through painstaking effort; throw all one's energy into; with one's heart-blood; work one's heart out;

ou4 慪
annoy / irritate;

ou qi 慪氣
become exaperated // difficult and sulky;

ou ren 慪人
disgusting / exasperating;

pa4 怕
dread / fear;

pa lao po 怕老婆
be intimidated by one's wife / be scared of one's wife // browbeaten / henpecked;

pa leng 怕冷
dread cold weather;

pa sao 怕臊
bashful / shy;

pa shi 怕事
timid and overcautious;

pa si 怕死
fear death // afraid of death;

pa xiu 怕羞
shy;

pan4 mu 盼慕
admire;

pan nian 盼念
hope / long for;

pan wang 盼望
hope / wish;

pan xiang 盼想
hope;

pang2 徬
agitated / anxious / indecisive;

pang huang 徬徨
anxious, agitated and not knowing what to do;

peng1 怦
anxious / eager / impulsive;

peng peng 怦怦
(1) eager and anxious to do sth;
(2) become excited;

peng ran 怦然
with a sudden shock;

peng ran xin dong 怦然心動
eager with excitement / palpitate with excitement;

pi1 huai 披懷
harbour no secret / open one's heart // very frank;

pi huo 披豁
open one's heart in perfect frankness / talk without reserve;

pi lu xin fu 披露心腹
disclose a secret / tell one's innermost thoughts;

pi lu xin qu 披露心曲
lay bare one's heart / tell one's innermost thoughts || disburden one's conscience; disclose one's pent-up feelings; open one's mind; tell a piece of one's mind; unburden one's mind;

pi xin 披心
open and show one's heart;

pian1 ai 偏愛
have a penchant / have a preference for // predilection / preference;

pian xin 偏心
(1) decentration;
(2) bias / partiality;

ping2 chang xin 平常心
calmness / composure;

ping xin jing qi 平心靜氣
be calm and fair in settling a dispute;

ping2 憑
(1) rely on;
(2) lean on;
(3) be based on;
(4) basis;

ping liang xin 憑良心
as one's conscience dictates;

ping yi 憑依
be based on / depend on / rely on;

po2 xin 婆心
kind and compassionate heart / soft;

pou1 bai xin ji 剖白心跡
lay bare one's true feelings / lay one's heart bare;

pou xin 剖心
bare one's heart / bare one's soul;

pou xin lu gan 剖心露肝
bare one's heart / open one's heart to sb;

pou xin zi bai 剖心自白
open one's heart and clear one's reputation;

pu2 sa xin chang 菩薩心腸
have a heart of gold || great kind heart; kind-hearted and merciful;

qi1 qing 七情
the seven emotions of pleasure, anger, sorrow, joy, love, hate, and desire;

qi qing liu yu 七情六慾
the seven emotions of pleasure, anger, sorrow, joy, love, hate, and desire and the six sensory pleasures derived from the eyes, ears, nose, tongue, body and mind;

qi1 悽
(1) afflicted / grieved / sorrowful;
(2) grievous / pathetic / pitiful / tragic;

qi can 悽慘
heartrending / tragic;

qi ce 悽惻
sad / sorrowful;

qi chu 悽楚
grievous / pathetic / pitiful / saddening;

qi chuang 悽愴
(1) grievous / pathetic / pitiful / saddening;
(2) cold / desolate / dreary;

qi huang 悽惶
(1) sorrowful and apprehensive;
(2) in a hurry;

qi ku 悽苦
tragic suffering;

qi li 悽戾
sorrowful;

qi liang 悽涼
desolate / dreary;

qi qi 悽戚
tragically unhappy;

qi qi 悽悽
grievous / pathetic / pitiful;

qi qie 悽切
grievous / pathetic / pitiful / saddening;

qi ran 悽然
sad / sorrowful;

qi shang 悽傷
sad / sorrowful;

qi wan 悽婉
pathetic / pitiful / plaintive;

qi wang 悽惘
sad and dejected;

qi1 xin 欺心
disregard the dictates of one's own conscience;

qi1 慼
(1) mournful / woeful;
(2) ashamed;

qi qi 慼慼
rueful / sad / sorrowful;

qi you 慼憂
sad and depressed;

qi2 qing ke min 其情可憫
one's case deserves sympathy;

qi xin ke zhu 其心可誅
condemnable in intention // devious in intention / evil-minded / malicious in motive;

qi2 xin 齊心
of one heart / of one mind;

qi xin xie li 齊心協力
work in full cooperation and with unity of purpose || all of one mind; bend their efforts in a single direction; hang together; join forces in an effort; join hands; make concerted efforts; of one heart; of one mind; pull all together; pull together; put forth a united effort; rally round; shoulder to shoulder; with one heart; with one mind and one heart; with united effort; work as one person; work in concert; work in harmony; work together as one man;

qi xin yi zhi 齊心一致
united and of one mind;

qi3 pan 企盼
hope with eagerness;

qi3 qing 綺情
tender feeling;

qi4 xu xin tiao 氣吁心跳
out of breath and with a fast-beating heart;

qi4 zhi xing qiao lü zheng 器質性憔慮症
organic anxiety disorder;

qi4 憩
repose / rest;

qi xi 憩息
rest / take a rest;

qian1 dong ren xin 牽動人心
affect sb's feeling;

qian gua 牽掛
be concerned for / feel anxious about / worry about;

qian nian 牽念
be concerned for / feel anxious about;

qian xin gua chang 牽心掛腸
very worried;

qian1 愆
fault / misdemeanor / mistake;

qian guo 愆過
fault / mistake;

qian te 愆忒
fault / mistake / sin / transgression;

qian you 愆尤
fault / mistake / offense;

qian2 cheng 虔誠
devout / pious // piety / sincerity;

qian jing 虔敬
reverent // reverently;

qian ke 虔恪
reverent / respectful;

qian xin 虔心
piety / sincere reverence;

qian2 xin 潛心
devote oneself to sth || do sth with great concentration; have a quiet concentrated mind;

qian xin yan jiu 潛心研究
devote oneself to the study of sth;

qian3 huai 遣懷
dispel one's sorrow in writing on the spur of the moment;

qian men 遣悶
drive away melancholy / kill time;

qian yi 遣意
dispel one's sorrow in writing as relaxation;

qian you 遣憂
dispel sadness;

qian3 quan 繾綣
make tender love;

qian quan qing yi 繾綣情意
entangled relations between lovers;

qian quan rou qing 繾綣柔情
tender affection;

qian quan zhi qing 繾綣之情
deep attachment / sentimental attachment;

qian4 qing 欠情
owe favours;

qian4 慊
resent;

qian qian 慊慊
resentful and discontented;

qian4 yi 歉意
regrets / apologies;

qiao1 qiao di 悄悄地
in a clandestine way / quietly / secretly / stealthily;

qiao2 憔
emaciated || haggard; thin; wane; withered; worn;

qiao cui 憔悴
(1) haggard / thin and pallid / wan and sallow;
(2) withered;

qiao cui ku gao 憔悴枯槁
haggard from anxiety and dried like a stalk;

qiao lü 憔慮
impatient and anxious;

qiao lü zheng 憔慮症
anxiety disorder;
qi zhi xing qiao lü zheng 器質性憔慮症
organic anxiety disorder;

qiao3 悄
quiet;

qiao ran 悄然
(1) quietly;
(2) sorrowly;

qie4 怯
(1) cowardly / timidly;
(2) nervous;

qie chang 怯場
stage fright;

qie nuo 怯懦
cowardly / gutless // cowardice / gutlessness;

qie qu 怯懼
fear / gutless / nervous out of fear;

qie ruo 怯弱
timid and cowardly;

qie yi 怯疑
timid and vacillating;

qie zheng 怯症
(1) impotent;
(2) fear and nervousness caused by poor health;

qie4 愜
cheerful / contented / satisfied;

qie huai 愜懷
contented / satisfied;

qie qing 愜情
contented / satisfied;

qie xin 愜心
contented / pleased / satisfied;

qie yi 愜意
contented / satisfied;

qie4 慊
contented / gratified / pleased / satisfied;

qie4 qu ren xin 竊取人心
steal away sb's heart;

qin1 欽
admire / respect;

qin chi 欽遲
admire / look up to;

qin chong 欽崇
admire / adore;

qin jing 欽敬
admire and respect;

qin mu 欽慕
admire / look up to;

qin pei 欽佩
admire / respect;

qin yang 欽仰
admire and respect / look up to;

qin yi 欽挹
admire and respect / look up to;

qin2 懃
cordial / hearty;

qin qin ken ken 懃懃懇懇
cordial and sincere;

qin4 ren fei fu 沁人肺腑
mentally refreshing || gladden the heart; refreshing; seep into one's heart; touch one's heart;

qin ren xin pi 沁人心脾
refreshing the mind || affect people deeply; exhilarating; gladden people's hearts; gladdening the heart and refreshing the mind; gratifying; mentally refreshing; touch one's heart;

qing1 pi qin fei 清脾沁肺
the coolness sinks into the heart;

qing xin 清心
clear away heart-fire;

qing xin gua yu 清心寡欲
purify one's heart and diminish one's passions || a pure heart and few desires; cleanse one's heart and limit one's desires; purge one's mind of desires and ambitions; remove worries and control one's desires;

qing xin xiu shen 清心修身
cleanse one's heart and temper one's behaviour;

qing xin yang xing 清心養性
purify one's heart and cultivate one's moral character;

qing1 傾
be fascinated by / admire;

qing dao 傾倒
be infatuated by / fall for;

qing mu 傾慕
admire;

qing xin 傾心
(1) admire / be bent on / be enamoured with sb / fall for / fall in love with / fix one's affections upon / lose one's heart to / set one's affections on;
(2) cordial / heart-to-heart / intimate and candid / warm and sincere;

qing xin jie li 傾心竭力
exert oneself to the uttermost / exhaust every effort to;

qing xin jiao tan 傾心交談
have a heart-to-heart chat / have a heart-to-heart talk;

qing xin tu dan 傾心吐膽
lay bare one's heart || make a clean breast of; open one's heart wide and lay bare one's thoughts; open one's mind; pour out one's heart; speak one's mind; speak out everything that is in one's heart; tell all that is in one's heart; unbosom oneself; unburden one's mind;

qing xin zhe fu 傾心折服
submit cordially / submit with admiration;

qing1 lian mi ai 輕憐蜜愛
tender love between a couple in love;

qing2 情
(1) emotions / feelings / sentiments;
(2) affection / love / passion;

qing ai 情愛
love (between man and woman);

qing bu zi jin 情不自禁
be seized with an impulse;

qing cao gao shang 情操高尚
high-minded;

qing chang 情長
lasting affection for sb;

qing chang 情場
the arena of love;

qing chang shi yi 情場失意
be frustrated in love;

qing chang 情腸
loving heart;

qing dou chu kai 情竇初開
first awaking of love;

qing dou wei kai 情竇未開
before puberty;

qing fen 情分
(1) friendship;
(2) good intentions / good will / solicitude;

qing gan 情感
emotions / feelings / sentiments;

qing gan chong dong 情感衝動
outburst of emotion;

qing huai 情懷
feelings;

qing huo 情火
flames of love;

qing ji 情急
desperate // desperation;

qing ji zhi sheng 情急智生
hit on a good idea in a moment of desperation;

qing lei 情累
the burden of love;

qing nong 情濃
strong affection;

qing shen xi hai 情深似海
love that is as deep as the sea;

qing su 情愫
innermost feelings;

qing tian 情天
the realm of love;

qing tian hen hai 情天恨海
the deep love or regret between man and woman;

qing tian 情田
one's heart;

qing tong shou zu 情同手足
be attached to each other like brothers;

qing tou yi he 情投意合
congenial // agree in tastes and temperament;

qing wang 情網
love trap / the snare of love;

qing xin 情心
compassion;

qing xu 情緒
emotion / feeling / mood / sentiment;

qing xu bing 情緒病
emotional illness;

qing xu di luo 情緒低落
depressed / down at the mouth / down in the mouth / mopy // sunken spirits;

qing xu ji ang 情緒激昂
in an emotive state / in high spirits;

qing xu ji dong 情緒激動
be heated with passion;

qing yi 情誼
friendly relations;

qing yi 情意
feeling / sentiment;

qing yi mian mian 情意綿綿
long-lasting love // lovey-dovey;

qing you ke yuan 情有可原
excusable / pardonable;

qing you suo zhong 情有所鍾
have a lover in one's heart;

qing yu 情慾
passion / sensual desire;

qing yuan 情願
be disposed to // inclined / willing;

qing zhi yi jin 情至義盡
with entire sincerity;

qiong2 惸
(1) distressed / worried;
(2) brotherless / friendless;

qiong du 惸獨
friendless / helpless and lonely;

qiong qiong 惸惸
anxious / distressed / worried;

qiong2 chou 窮愁
dejection caused by poverty and sorrow;

qiong chou liao dao 窮愁潦倒
crack up under the strain of poverty and sorrow;

qiong kai xin 窮開心
enjoy moments of happiness even in poverty;

qiu2 ai 求愛
court / woo;

qu1 xin 屈心
have a guilty conscience;

quan1 悛
reform / repent;

quan gai 悛改
reform oneself / repent one's sin;

quan xin 悛心
repentant heart;

quan yi 悛懌
reform oneself / repent one's sin;

quan2 wu xin gan 全無心肝
totally heartless || absolutely ungrateful; completely without scruples; dead to all feeling; totally unconscionable;

quan xin quan yi 全心全意
wholeheartedly || body and soul; complete devotion; have one's heart and soul; heart and soul; put one's heart and soul into; unstinted support; up to the handle; with all one's heart; with all one's heart and soul; with heart and hand; with wholehearted devotion // full-hearted / wholehearted;

quan xin yan 全心炎
pancarditis;

quan2 惓
candid / sincere;

quan quan 惓惓
candid / sincere;

quan quan yu huai 惓惓於懷
remember sb at heart constantly;

quan2 mi xin qiao 權迷心竅
be obsessed by a lust for power // power-happy;

que1 de 缺德
deficient in the sense of morality;

que han 缺憾
defect / flaw / shortcoming;

que xue xing xin ji bing 缺血性心肌病
ischemic cardiomyopathy;

que xue xing xin zang bing 缺血性心臟病
ischemic heart disease;

que4 愨
honest / prudent;

rao2 shu 饒恕
forgive / pardon;

re3 nao 惹惱
annoy / get in sb's hair / get into sb's hair / get on sb's nerves / irritate / make sb angry / offend / peeve / provoke;

re4 qing 熱情
gusto / zest;

re xin 熱心
enthusiastic || ardent; avid; eager; earnest; warmhearted;

re xin chang 熱心腸
warm heart // warmheartedness;

re xin gong yi 熱心公益
make earnest efforts to promote public good;

ren2 da xin da 人大心大
become gradually more assertive as one grows older / grow in independence of mind;

ren duo xin za 人多心雜
many men, many minds / too many people, too many ideas || there are as many minds as there are men; too many people to have the same opinion;

ren lao xin bu lao 人老心不老
old in age, but young in mind || man grows old in years, but his heart does not grow old; one is old in years but not old at heart; though old in age, yet young at heart;

ren qing 人情
(1) human emotion;
(2) favours asked or done;

ren tong ci xin, xin tong ci li 人同此心，心同此理
everybody feels the same about this || on this matter people feel and think alike; the sense of justice and rationality is the same with everybody; this is the general feeling shared by all;

ren xin 人心
public feeling || human emotion; human feeling; human heart; human will; morale; popular feeling; the will of the people;

ren xin bu gu 人心不古
public morality is not what it used to be || human hearts are not what they were in the old days; men are not what they were in the times of long ago; people are not so honest as their ancestors were;

ren xin bu tong, ge ru qi mian 人心不同，各如其面

the hearts of people differ as much as their faces || individual thinking is as varied as individual looks; people's hearts differ just as their faces do; several people, several minds; so many heads, so many opinions; so many people, so many minds;

ren xin bu zu, de long wang shu 人心不足，得隴望蜀

no person is content || desire hath no rest; those who are allowed more liberty than is reasonable will desire more than is allowed;

ren xin bu zu she tun xiang 人心不足蛇吞象

no man is content with his lot || a man whose heart is not content is like a snake which tries to swallow an elephant — insatiable desire; no man is content;

ren xin da kuai 人心大快

the people are all jubilant / the public sentiment is satisfied;

ren xin ge yi, you ru qi mian 人心各異，猶如其面

men's hearts differ just as their faces do / not all bread is baked in one oven / several man, several minds;

ren xin gui xiang 人心歸向

the feelings of the people are for... / the inclination of the hearts of the people;

ren xin huan san 人心渙散

divided in public opinion / people being not of one mind;

ren xin huang huang 人心惶惶

people are agitated || everyone is jittery; jittery; panicky;

ren xin mo ce 人心莫測

the human heart is a mystery // inscrutable;

ren xin po ce 人心叵測

harbour an evil heart || man's heart is incomprehensible; one's heart is past finding out; the heart of man is past finding out;

ren xin qi, qun shan yi 人心齊，群山移

when people are of one heart, they can move mountains || if we all pull together, we can move the highest mountain;

ren xin sang jin 人心喪盡

completely forfeit the confidence of the people / lose all popular sympathy;

ren xin si bian 人心思變

people are longing for change / all are hoping for a change;

ren xin suo xiang 人心所向

the feelings of the people || in terms of popular support; popular feelings; the common aspiration of the people; the desire of the people; the direction of popular sentiment; what is unanimously supported by the people;

ren xin wei wei 人心惟危

human hearts are evil || human hearts are unfathomable;

ren xin xiang bei 人心向背

the feelings of the people || whether the people are for or against; whether the public attitude for or against; who commands popular sympathy; with whom popular sympathy lies;

ren xin zhen fen 人心振奮

the people are filled with enthusiasm;

ren2 ai 仁愛

humane;

ren ci 仁慈

benevolent / humane / merciful;

ren xin 仁心

kind heart;

ren3 忍

(1) bear / endure / put up with / stand / tolerate;

(2) check / forbear / refrain from / repress;

ren nai 忍耐

patient;

ren ru 忍辱

bear disgrace and insults while discharging one's duties conscientiously;

ren ru fu zhong 忍辱負重

endure all disgrace and insults in order to accomplish a task;

ren ru han gou 忍辱含垢

eat humble pie;

ren shou 忍受
endure / lie down under / live with / put up with;

ren shou bu liao 忍受不了
sick and tired of;

ren tong 忍痛
suffer pain when giving up sth;

ren wu ke ren 忍無可忍
exhaust one's patience // beyond one's endurance;

ren xin 忍心
have the heart to || hard-hearted; merciless; steel one's heart; unfeeling;

ren xin hai li 忍心害理
commit a crime in cold blood || do a cruel thing in cold blood; so malicious as to violate justice; ruthless and devoid of human feelings;

ren xin pie kai 忍心撇開
have the heart to leave sb;

ren4 yi 任意
arbitrary / at will;

ri4 jiu jian ren xin 日久見人心
time reveals a person's heart || a long task proves the sincerity of a person; it takes time to know a person; time is a revealer of a person's sincerity; time will tell a true friend from a false one;

ri jiu sheng qing 日久生情
having been together for a long time, people come to have a tender feeling for each other;

rong2 qing 容情
excuse / forgive / pardon;

rong yue 容悅
curry favour with / flatter / please;

rou2 qing 柔情
soft and sentimental / the tender feeling of a lover;

rou qing si shui 柔情似水
tender and soft as water;

rou xin ruo gu 柔心弱骨
as mild as a dove by nature / tender conscience;

rou4 ya zhong xing xin ji yan 肉芽腫性心肌炎
granuomatous myocarditis;

ru2 xin 如心
contented / gratified / pleased / satisfied;

ru yi 如意
as one wishes;

ru yi suan pan 如意算盤
wishful thinking;

ru yuan 如願
as one wishes;

ru yuan yi chang 如願以償
have one's wish fulfilled;

ruan3 xin chang 軟心腸
soft-hearted / tender-hearted;

rui4 yi 銳意
determination / earnest intention / sharp will;

rui zhi 銳志
determination / earnest intention / sharp will;

run4 xin yang yan 潤心養眼
good to hear or see;

san1 xin liang yi 三心兩意
(1) have two minds // in two minds || change one's mind constantly; dilly-dally; hesitating; infirm of purpose; irresolute; of two minds; play the field; undecided; vacillating;
(2) half-hearted;

san4 xin 散心
let one's mind relax || carefree; drive away one's cares; ease up; enjoy a diversion; relieve boredom; take one's mind off oneself;

san xin jie men 散心解悶
divert the mind from boredom;

sang4 xin bing kuang 喪心病狂
act as if one were crazy || as mad as a March hare; be seized with crazy ideas; bereft of one's senses; frenzied; frantic; become frenzied; lose all balance of judgement; lose one's senses; out of one's right mind;

sha4 fei ku xin 煞費苦心
take great pains;

shan1 dong bu man 煽動不滿
incite discontent / foment discontent;

shan dong qing xu 煽動情緒
fan the flames;

shan huo ren xin 煽惑人心
incite people by demagogy || agitate people by demagogy; deceive and stir up people's mind; undermine popular morale by spreading unfounded rumour;

shan4 xin 善心
kind heart || benevolence; compassionate heart; good intention; kindhearted; kindness; mercy;

shan yi 善意
good intentions / goodwill // good-intentioned;

shang1 bei 傷悲
distress / grief;

shang dao 傷悼
mourn over the loss of a dear one;

shang gan 傷感
distressed;

shang gan qing 傷感情
hurt the feelings;

shang huai 傷懷
grief;

shang xin 傷心
sad || break one's heart; brokenhearted; grieved; heartsore; hurt one's feelings;

shang xin can mu 傷心慘目
break the heart and distress the eye || pitiful; too ghastly to look at; too horrible to look at; tragic;

shang xin luo lei 傷心落淚
shed sad tears / weep in grief;

shang xin yu jue 傷心欲絕
inconsolable;

shang3 xin 賞心
please the heart;

shang xin le shi 賞心樂事
a fair treat / a happy event that pleases everyone / pleasant things that one enjoys doing;

shang xin yue mu 賞心悦目
gladden the heart and please the eye || a feast for the eye; a perfect delight to the eye; cheerful and pleasing to the eye; find the scenery pleasing to both the eye and the mind; flatter the heart and please the eye; gladden the eyes and heart; let the eye take in the landscape and please the spirit; pleasant to look at; pleasant to the eye;

shang4 xia yi tiao xin 上下一條心
the leadership and the rank and file are of one mind || both the higher and lower levels are united as one; of one heart and mind;

shang xia yi xin 上下一心
of one heart and mind;

shao1 xin 燒心
anxious / apprehensive / fretful / uneasy;

she2 xie xin chang 蛇蠍心腸
have a murderous heart;

shen1 chou da hen 深仇大恨
deep-seated hatred;

shen de ren xin 深得人心
enjoy immense popular support || high in sb's favour; win the hearts of all;

shen en 深恩
great favours;

shen gan 深感
feel keenly;

shen hen 深恨
deep hatred;

shen lü 深慮
deep worry;

shen qie guan huai 深切關懷
be deeply concerned about / show great concern about;

shen qie huai nian 深切懷念
dearly cherish the memory of;

shen qing 深情
deep affection;

shen qing hou yi 深情厚誼
long and close relationship;

shen ru ren xin 深入人心
go deep into the hearts of the people || be deeply rooted among the people; find its way ever deeper into the hearts of the people; gain popularity; penetrate deeply into the people's mind; sink deep into people's heart; strike a

deeper chord in the hearts of the people;

shen shou ai dai 深受愛戴
be held in deep affection;

shen wu tong jue 深惡痛絕
have a great aversion to sth or sb;

shen xin 深心
deep in one's heart;

shen xin 深信
be firmly convinced;

shen xin bu yi 深信不疑
believe without a shadow of doubt;

shen you 深憂
deep worries;

shen3 shen 審慎
careful / cautious / scrupulous;

shen4 慎
careful / cautious / prudent / scrupulous;

shen du 慎獨
cautious when one is alone;

shen mi 慎密
careful / meticulous;

shen mo 慎默
cautious and reticent;

shen wei 慎微
careful about minute details;

shen wu 慎勿
be careful not to;

shen zhong 慎重
careful / cautious / discreet / prudent;

shen4 chu xing xin bao yan 滲出性心包炎
pericarditis with effusion;

sheng1 lian 生憐
have tender affection for;

sheng yi 生意
vitality;

sheng3 xin 省心
save worries;

sheng4 nu 盛怒
foam at the mouth // in great anger // wrath;

sheng qing 盛情
warmhearted;

sheng qing nan que 盛情難卻
it is hard to turn down the offer made with such warmheartedness;

sheng yi 盛意
generosity;

shi1 de 失德
loss of one's virtue;

shi lian 失戀
lose one's love // aborted love affair;

shi shen 失神
absent-minded;

shi shen 失慎
careless;

shi wang 失望
be disappointed;

shi xin feng 失心瘋
amnesia // being out of one's mind;

shi xin 失信
break one's promise;

shi yi 失意
frustrated;

shi1 en 施恩
give favours to others;

shi2 ren shi xin 十人十心
many people, many minds;

shi2 xin 實心
(1) honest / sincere;
(2) in a serious manner;

shi xin shi yi 實心實意
honest and sincere;

shi yi 實意
sincerity;

shi3 xin 豕心
avaricious / greedy;

shi4 dao ren xin 世道人心
the ways of the world and the heart of human beings;

shi4 ai 示愛
show one's tender feeling to one of the opposite sex;

shi yi 示意
indicate one's intention;

shi4 jiu jian ren xin 事久見人心
a long task proves a person's heart;

shi4 fei zhi xin 是非之心
one's conscience / the instinct to tell right from wrong;

shi fei zhi xin, ren jie you zhi 是非之心，人皆有之
every person has a sense of right and wrong;

shi4 yu 嗜慾
sensual desires;

shi4 bu er xin 誓不二心
swear to be loyal forever;

shi4 yi 適意
as desired // agreeable / comfortable;

shi4 han 釋憾
dispel a grudge / dispel hatred;

shi men 釋悶
chase gloom / disperse melancholy;

shi yi 釋疑
dispel doubt / settle uncertainties;

shou1 mai ren xin 收買人心
win popular support;

shou suo xing xin li shuai jie 收縮性心力衰竭
systolic heart failure;

shou xin 收心
(1) bring one's mind back from || concentrate on more serious things; get into the frame of mind for work;
(2) have a change of heart;

shou xin gui zheng 收心歸正
get into the right frame of mind / give up evil ways and return to the right path;

shou3 xin yang xing 守心養性
cultivate one's mind and preserve its original good nature;

shou4 yi 授意
do sth by giving a hint;

shou4 xin 獸心
bestiality;

shou yu 獸慾
carnal desire / lust;

shu1 抒
(1) express / give expression to;
(2) ease / lighten / relieve / unburden;

shu fa 抒發
express / give expression to;

shu huai 抒懷
relieve the heart of emotions;

shu nian 抒念
be relieved of thoughts burdening one's mind;

shu qing 抒情
express one's feelings;

shu yi 抒意
express one's ideas;

shu1 you 紓憂
remove worries;

shu1 xin 淑心
pure heart;

shu1 huai 舒懷
free the mind from tension / set the mind at rest;

shu xin 舒心
agreeable / pleasant;

shu1 攄
make known to / vent;

shu cheng 攄誠
frank;

shu fen 攄憤
vent one's indignation;

shu huai 攄懷
give vent to one's emotion;

shu yi 攄意
give expression to one's feelings;

shu4 恕
(1) excuse / forgive;
(2) benevolence / charitableness / goodwill;

shu guo 恕過
forgive a fault / pardon a mistake;

shu you 恕宥
excuse / forgive;

shua3 xin yan er 耍心眼兒
exercise one's wits for personal gains;

shuai4 huai 率懷
follow one's bent / follow one's heart's desire;

shuai wu 率悟
realize quickly // quick in understanding;

shuai yi 率意
(1) act on the spur of the moment / follow one's inclination;
(2) with all one's sincerity;

shuan1 bu zhu xin 拴不住心
(1) unable to hold a person's heart;
(2) unable to keep one's mind fixed;

shuang3 hui 爽慧
agile / intelligent;

shuang lang 爽朗
open-minded / straightforward;

shuang ran 爽然
dejected / disappointed / discouraged;

shuang ran ruo shi 爽然若失
dejected as if one had made a mistake;

shuang xin 爽心
cheerful / gratified / pleased / satisfied;

shuang xin yue mu 爽心悅目
refreshing to the heart and pleasing to the eye ‖ entertaining;

shuang zhi 爽直
frank / open-hearted / straightforward;

shui3 qi ling xin 水氣凌心
heart attacked by retention of fluid;

shun4 xin 順心
gratifying / satisfactory;

si1 fen 私憤
personal spite;

si nian 私念
selfish motives;

si qing 私情
(1) private feelings;
(2) illicit love;

si xin 私心
selfish motives / selfishness;

si xin za nian 私心雜念
selfish consideration / selfish ideas and personal considerations;

si xin zi yong 私心自用
selfish and self-satisfied;

si yuan 私怨
personal grudge;

si zhong 私衷
personal wish;

si1 re qing qian 思惹情牽
admire sb deeply;

si yi 思憶
cherish the memory of;

si3 xin 死心
drop the idea forever / give up the idea forever ‖ give up one's hope for good; have no more illusions about the matter; think no more of sth;

si xin ta di 死心塌地
unreservedly ‖ dance obediently; dead set on; head over heels; hell-bent on; wholeheartedly;

si xin yan er 死心眼兒
stubborn ‖ as obstinate as a mule; be bent on one purpose; obstinate and simple-minded; too pig-headed;

si ye an xin 死也安心
one will die in peace;

si ye gan xin 死也甘心
willing even to die;

si4 yi 肆意
at will / without any restraint;

si zhi 肆志
be puffed up with pride;

song1 xie 鬆懈
relax efforts;

song xin 鬆心
carefree;

song3 悚
fearful / frightened / terrified;

song ran 悚然
terror-strickened // in terror;

song song 悚悚
dread / fear // fright / scare;

song3 竦
(1) respectful;
(2) awed;

song que 竦懼
tremble with fear;

song ran 竦然
fearful / scared;

song3 ju 聳懼
frightened / shocked / terrified;

song yong 聳恿
egg on / urge;

song4 qing 送情
convey one's feelings;

song ren qing 送人情
do another person a favour at no great cost to oneself;

song4 慫
incite / instigate;

su4 hui 夙慧
inborn intelligence;

su yuan 夙願
long-cherished wish;

su zhi 夙志
long-cherished ambition;

su4 ai 素愛
what has been loved;

su huai 素懷
long-cherished ambitions / long-cherished hopes;

su xin 素心
(1) simple and honest;
(2) one's conscience;

su yuan 素願
long-cherished ambitions / long-cherished aspirations / long-cherished hopes;

su zhi 素志
long-cherished ambitions / long-cherished aspirations;

su4 hen 宿恨
old grudge;

su yuan 宿願
long-cherished wish;

su zhi 宿志
long-cherished desire;

su4 愫
honesty / sincerity;

su4 觫
shrink and tremble in fear;

su4 愬
(1) complain;
(2) afraid / frightened / scared;

su su 愬愬
afraid / frightened / scared;

suan1 huai 酸懷
grief / sorrow;

suan xin 酸心
(1) grieved / heartbroken / sad;
(2) heartburn / indigestion;

sui2 xin suo yu 隨心所欲
do as one pleases || as one pleases; as one sees fit; at one's own discretion; at one's sweet will; at one's will; do anything one's heart dictates; do as one likes; do whatever one wants; follow one's bent; follow the heart's desire; have an entirely free hand in; have one's way; take one's own course // footloose;

sui yi 隨意
act as one pleases / have no restraint // according to one's wish / as one likes it;

sui4 xin 遂心
after one's own heart || fulfil one's desire; have one's own way; have one's will; to one's liking;

sui xin ru yi 遂心如意
after one's heart || one's wishes are met; perfectly satisfied;

sui xin suo yu 遂心所欲
follow what the heart desires || have one's will; satisfy one's desire; to one's liking;

sui yi 遂意
have everything going one's way;

ta1 shi 塌實
free from anxiety;

ta4 嗒
dejected / depressed / in low spirits;

心 Heart

ta sang 嗒喪
dejected / depressed / in low spirits;

tai4 xi 太息
lament / sigh;

tan1 de wu yan 貪得無厭
grabby / insatiable;

tan duo bi shi 貪多必失
all covet, all lose / grasp all, lose all;

tan lan 貪婪
acquisitive / avaricious / greedy / rapacious // avarcity / covetousness / cupidity / greed / rapacity // have an itching palm;

tan lian 貪戀
desire;

tan nian 貪念
covetous thoughts;

tan tu 貪圖
covet / desire / hanker after / hope / long for / wish;

tan tu fu gui 貪圖富貴
desire wealth and honour;

tan xin 貪心
avarious / greedy / insatiable / voracious || cupidity;

tan xin bu zu 貪心不足
greedy and dissatisfied // covetousness / insatiable desire / insatiable greed;

tan yu 貪慾
avarice / greed;

tan3 忐
(1) apprehensive / timid;
(2) cannot make up one's mind // indecisive;

tan te 忐忑
be mentally disturbed / be perturbed;

tan te bu an 忐忑不安
nervous and uneasy || all of a tremble; be overwhelmed with anxiety; feel troubled and uneasy; fidgety; fluttered; have palpitation of the heart from nervousness; in a flutter; in a tremble; in fear and trembling; in rather a nervous state; on nettles; on the anxious bench; on the anxious seat; on the tremble; restless; uneasy; unsettled and uneasy;

tang3 惝
discouraged / disheartened / dispirited;

tang huang 惝怳
discouraged / disheartened / dispirited;

tang huang wu ding 惝怳無定
dispirited and distracted;

tang ran 惝然
crestfallen / dejected / discouraged / disheartened / dispirited;

tao1 慆
(1) delighted / happy;
(2) doubtful / suspicious;

tao man 慆慢
idle and remiss;

tao xin 慆心
delight one's mind;

tao2 ran 陶然
cheerful / happy / joyous;

tao zui 陶醉
be inebriated / be intoxicated // greatly pleased / very happy;

tao3 kui 討愧
be ashamed;

tao qing 討情
ask for forgiveness / plead for leniency;

tao ren xi huan 討人喜歡
charming / cute / likeable / personable;

tao ren xian 討人嫌
incur disgust / incur dislike // annoying;

tao xian 討嫌
incur disgust / incur dislike // disgusting / repulsive / revolting;

tao yan 討厭
disgusting / odious / troublesome // disgust / dislike / incur / loathe / take against;

te4 忑
(1) apprehensive / nervous;
(2) indecisive;

te4 en 特恩
special favour / special kindness;

te fa xing xin bao yan 特發性心包炎
idiopathic pericarditis;

te fa xing xin ji bing 特發性心肌病
idiopathic cardiomyopathy;

te fa xing xin ji yan 特發性心肌炎
idiopathic myocarditis;

te yi xing xin ji bing 特異性心肌病
specific heart muscle disease;

te yi 特意
intentionally / on purpose;

te4 慝
evil / evil idea / inquity / vice;

ti2 xin diao dan 提心吊膽
cautious and anxious ‖ always on tenterhooks; be filled with anxiety; be haunted with fear; have one's heart in one's mouth; in a state of suspense; in great terror; live in constant fear; on tenterhooks; restless and anxious; scared;

ti xin zai kou 提心在口
cautious and anxious // have one's heart in one's mouth;

ti3 hui 體會
experience / feel / understand;

ti liang 體諒
considerate / sympathetic toward // understanding;

ti nian 體念
understanding;

ti xu 體恤
considerate of and sympathize with;

ti4 悌
show or respect brotherly love;

ti mu 悌睦
live at peace as brothers;

ti you 悌友
show brotherly love for friends;

ti4 惕
(1) careful / cautious / prudent // be on the alert;
(2) afraid;
(3) anxious;

ti li 惕厲
exercise caution and discipline;

ti ran 惕然
fearful of;

ti ti 惕惕
apprehensive / fearful;

ti xi 惕息
pant from fear or anxiety;

tian1 li liang xin 天理良心
conscience ‖ one's better feelings; the course of nature and one's conscience;

tian li ren qing 天理人情
reasonable;

tian liang 天良
one's conscience;

tian xing 天性
natural temperament;

tian2 恬
peaceful / quiet / undisturbed;

tian bu zhi chi 恬不知耻
brazen-faced / shameless / unashamed;

tian2 qing mi yi 甜情蜜意
tender affection between man and woman;

tian xin 甜心
sweetheart;

tiao1 恌
frivolous / self-indulgently carefree // lack a serious purpose;

tiao2 qing 調情
dally with / flirt / gallant with / make up to / mess about with / mess around with / play at love / play the gallant // flirtation;

tiao4 ta 跳踢
get angry furiously / lose temper fretfully;

tie1 怗
(1) compliant / observant / submissive;
(2) peaceful / quiet;

tie fu 怗服
compliant / resigned / submissive;

tie1 xin 貼心
close / intimate;

tie xin tie yi 貼心貼意
amiable and obliging;

tie3 shi xin chang 鐵石心腸
iron-hearted || a cold heart; a heart of flint; a heart of steel; a heart of stone; an unfeeling heart; as hard as a flint; as hard as a stone; as hard as nails; as tough as nails; callous; dead to all feelings; drop millstones; flint-hearted; hard-hearted; have a heart as hard as stone; have a heart as hard as iron; have a heart of stone; implacable; inexorable; obdurate; stony-hearted; sweep millstones;

tie xin 鐵心
have a heart of iron;

tong1 恫
disease / pain / sickness;

tong guan 恫瘝
hardship / illness;

tong guan zai bao 恫瘝在抱
show intimate concern over the people's hardships;

tong2 gan 同感
have the same feeling;

tong qing 同情
emphathize / sympathize // sympathetic // sympathy;

tong qing xin 同情心
emphathy / sympathy;

tong xin 同心
(1) with one heart || united at heart; united in common purpose;
(2) concentric / homocentric;

tong xin tong de 同心同德
be dedicated to the same cause; dedicate ourselves heart and soul to the same cause; of one heart and one mind; of one mind; with one heart and one mind;

tong xin xie li 同心協力
work together with one heart || hang together; have one heart to help each other; make a united effort; make concerted efforts; of one mind; pull together; shoulder to shoulder; unite in a concerted effort; unite in spirit and action; with concerted effort; with united strength; work in concert with sb; work in cooperation; work in full cooperation and with unity of purpose;

tong yi 同意
agree / agree with / concur in / fall in with / go along with / hold with / homologate;

tong2 xin 童心
childish heart / childishness / childlike innocence;

tong xin wei min 童心未泯
knock on woods / retain a childish heart;

tong4 ai 痛愛
love deeply / love passionately;

tong che fei fu 痛徹肺腑
cut sb to the heart // deep regret;

tong che xin gan 痛徹心肝
cut sb to the heart — deep grief;

tong dao 痛悼
grieve over the death of sb bitterly;

tong ding si tong 痛定思痛
recall the past with pangs in the heart;

tong gan 痛感
keenly felt;

tong hen 痛恨
detest / hate deeply;

tong hui 痛悔
repent bitterly;

tong jue 痛覺
sense of pain;

tong kuai 痛快
(1) delighted / very happy;
(2) to one's heart's content;

tong wu 痛惡
detest / hate bitterly;

tong xi 痛惜
regret deeply;

tong xin 痛心
distressed / grieved / heartbroken // heartache;

tong xin ji shou 痛心疾首
resent deeply || be filled with resentment; deplore greatly; feel bitter about; hate bitterly; hate deeply; with bitter hatred;

tong xin qie chi 痛心切齒
gnash one's teeth with anger / make sb burn with anger;

tong zi hui gai 痛自悔改
show deep repentance;

tong4 慟
extreme grief;

tou1 qing 偷情
have a clandestine love affair;

tu1 gan 突感
feel suddenly;

tu4 dan qing xin 吐膽傾心
pour out one's heart || open one's heart wide and lay bare one's thoughts; speak out everything that is in one's heart; unbosom oneself;

tui1 en 推恩
extend benevolence to others;

tui jin song bao 推襟送抱
bare one's heart to sb || disclose everything to sb; lay one's heart bare to sb; meet in all sincerity; open one's heart to sb; sincere in dealing with others; talk in all sincerity; treat sb with sincerity; unbosom oneself to;

tui nian 推念
miss sb distant / think of sb past;

tui xin zhi fu 推心置腹
open one's heart to sb || confide in sb; lay bare one's heart; pour out all one's inmost feeling; put every trust in; repose full confidence in sb;

tui zhong 推重
admire / hold in high esteem;

tuo1 ran 脫然
free / untrammeled;

tuo ran wu lei 脫然無累
without a worry in the world;

tuo sa 脫灑
easy and unrestrained / handsome in manner;

wa1 kong xin si 挖空心思
cudgel one's brains;

wan1 kong xin si 刓空心思
exhaust one's wits;

wan4 惋
(1) regret;
(2) be alarmed;

wan e 惋愕
be alarmed / be astonished;

wan hen 惋恨
acrimony / enmity / malice;

wan qi 惋悽
pathetic;

wan shang 惋傷
regret sorrowfully;

wan tan 惋歎
deplore / regret;

wan tong 惋慟
deplore / lament;

wan xi 惋惜
feel sorry for / regret;

wan4 zhong yi xin 萬眾一心
all of one heart || all for one and one for all; all have one heart; all unite in one purpose; millions of people unite as one man; unite as one; with one heart and one mind;

wang3 fei xin ji 枉費心機
cudgel one's brain in vain;

wang3 惘
feel lost || dejected; disappointed; discouraged; feel disappointed; feel frustrated; in a daze;

wang ran 惘然
at a loss || disappointed; frustrated; in a daze; stupefied;

wang ran ruo shi 惘然若失
feel lost || all adrift; feel disturbed as if having lost sth; look blank; look distracted; vacant;

wang wang wu zhu 惘惘無主
irresolute without decision;

wei1 ai 偎愛
be intimately in love;

wei1 yi 微意
a token of gratitude;

wei2 kong 惟恐
for fear that // the only fear is that;

wei kong tian xia bu luan 惟恐天下不亂
anxious to see trouble;

心 *Heart*

wei2 xin 惟心
spiritual;

wei2 xin 違心
against one's will / contrary to one's convictions;

wei xin zhi lun 違心之論
words uttered against one's conscience || insincere utterances; obviously insincere talk; statement contrary to one's inner belief; utterances which are contrary to right;

wei3 qu 委屈
feel aggrieved / feel very hard done by;

wei3 mi 萎靡
dispirited / listless;

wei mi bu zhen 萎靡不振
unable to pick oneself up // despondent / in a dejected state / in a state of mental doldrums / lethargic;

wei4 zhi da jing 為之大驚
be amazed;

wei zhi nan ran 為之赧然
blush with shame;

wei4 bi 畏避
evade because of fear;

wei dan 畏憚
have scruples about;

wei fu 畏服
submit from fear / yield from awe;

wei ji 畏忌
have scruples about;

wei jing 畏敬
stand in awe of;

wei ju 畏懼
dread / fear;

wei nan 畏難
fear difficulty;

wei pa 畏怕
dread / fear / stand in awe of;

wei qie 畏怯
be scared of / fear;

wei shou wei wei 畏首畏尾
have too many fears;

wei xi 畏葸
afraid / timid;

wei xi tui suo 畏葸退縮
recoil from fear;

wei4 慰
assuage / comfort / console / relieve / soothe;

wei an 慰安
comfort / soothe;

wei cun 慰存
comfort / show stympathy;

wei ji 慰藉
comfort / console / give solace / soothe;

wei jie 慰解
console by relieving one's pain;

wei lao 慰勞
entertain and cheer;

wei wen 慰問
express sympathy and solicitude;

wei yan 慰唁
condole with;

wen1 qing 溫情
warm feelings;

wo1 xin 窩心
suffer an insult which one is powerless to avenge;

wu2 dong yu zhong 無動於衷
aloof and indifferent / apathetic / callous / unconcerned / unmoved / untouched // get hardened;

wu kui yu xin 無愧於心
have a clear conscience;

wu qing wu yi 無情無義
heartless;

wu suo wei ju 無所畏懼
dauntless / fearless / undaunted;

wu suo yong xin 無所用心
without applying one's mind to anything good;

wu you wu lü 無憂無慮
carefree / insouciant // without a worry and care in the world;

wu3 忤
(1) disobedient / recalcitrant / stubbornly defiant / uncongenial;
(2) blunder / mistake / wrong;

wu ni 忤逆
(1) recalcitrant / stubbornly defiant;
(2) disobedient to one's parents / unfilial;

wu wu 忤物
disagree with others // at odds with others;

wu3 憮
disappointed / regretful;

wu ran 憮然
disappointedly / regretfully;

wu4 nian 勿念
do not worry;

wu4 bo qing hou 物薄情厚
the gift is of small value but the thoughtfulness behind it is immense;

wu4 悟
awake to / become aware of / comprehend / enlighten / realize;

wu xing 悟性
the capacity for understanding;

wu4 xin 惡心
cheese off / make sb sick // disgust;

xi1 希
desire / hope / long / wish;

xi mu 希慕
long for // desirous of;

xi qi 希冀
desire / wish for;

xi tu 希圖
hope and scheme for;

xi wang 希望
desire / hope / look forward to / wish;

xi1 恓
frightened and worried;

xi huang 恓惶
frightened and worried;

xi1 息
rest;

xi fen 息忿
quit one's anger;

xi nu 息怒
appease sb's anger / let one's anger cool off;

xi xin 息心
set one's heart at rest;

xi1 xin 悉心
devote all one's attention || take the utmost care; with concentrated effort; with one's whole heart;

xi xin yan jiu 悉心研究
devote oneself to the study of sth;

xi xin zhao liao 悉心照料
coddle / take the utmost care of sb;

xi1 惜
(1) feel sorry for sb / pity / regret / sympathize;
(2) value highly;
(3) grudge / spare;

xi bie 惜別
reluctant to part company;

xi fu 惜福
make sparing use of one's wealth;

xi lao lian pin 惜老憐貧
pity the aged and the poor;

xi li 惜力
be sparing of one's energy // energy-conserving;

xi yu lian xiang 惜玉憐香
be tender toward pretty girls;

xi3 xin di lü 洗心滌慮
purify the heart and do away with cares || cleanse one's heart and order one's behaviour; cleanse the heart from sin; make a thorough reformation; reform oneself thoroughly; repent genuinely; start life anew;

xi xin ge mian 洗心革面
cleanse one's heart and order one's behaviour || change one's heart and reform; cleanse the heart from sin; reform oneself thoroughly; start life anew; turn over a new leaf;

xi3 喜
(1) joy;

(2) like;

xi ai 喜愛
affect / be partial to;

xi bu zi sheng 喜不自勝
be delighted beyond measure / be entranced with joy / ecstatic;

xi hao 喜好
be fond of / be partial to / like / delight in;

xi huan 喜歡
(1) care for / fond of / have one's eyes on / like / love / prefer;
(2) delightful / happy;

xi le 喜樂
joy / pleasure;

xi nu ai le 喜怒哀樂
feelings of joy, anger, sorrow, and delight;

xi nu wu chang 喜怒無常
moody / unpredictable temper;

xi qi yang yang 喜氣洋洋
(1) festive mood;
(2) cheerful look;

xi yue 喜悅
delight / gratification / joy;

xi zai xin tou 喜在心頭
feel joyous / feel jubilant;

xi zi zi 喜孜孜
joyful // looking pleased;

xi3 憙
delighted / glad / happy / joyful / pleased;

xi4 nian 系念
anxious about / be concerned / feel concerned about / worry about;

xi4 jun xing xin bao yan 細菌性心包炎
bacterial pericarditis;

xi jun xing xin ji yan 細菌性心肌炎
bacterial myocarditis;

xi xin 細心
attentive / careful / circumspective;

xi xin chuai mo 細心揣摩
think of it carefully;

xi4 gua 繫掛
be concerned about;

xi huai 繫懷
have one's heart drawn by;

xi lian 繫戀
inextricably in love with;

xi nian 繫念
have constantly on one's mind;

xia2 xin 遐心
(1) thought of keeping aloof;
(2) wish to abandon;
(3) desire to live in retirement;

xia4 ding jue xin 下定決心
come to a resolution / make a firm resolve to do sth / make up one's mind to do sth;

xia jue xin 下決心
come to a resolution / make a firm resolve to do sth / make up one's mind to do sth;

xia4 嚇
frighten / intimidate / scare;

xia hu 嚇唬
freigten / intimidate / scare;

xia ren 嚇人
(1) frighten people;
(2) freightening / horrible;

xian2 jing 閑靜
peaceful and calm in mind;

xian2 qing yi zhi 閒情逸致
peaceful and comfortable mood;

xian xin 閒心
unburdened mind || a peaceful mood; free, leisurely mood;

xian2 嫌
(1) detest / dislike;
(2) doubt / mistrust / suspect;
(3) complain;

xian cai 嫌猜
dislike and suspicion;

xian ci 嫌疵
criticize / dislike;

xian ji 嫌忌
doubt / mistrust / suspect;

xian pa 嫌怕
be afraid of / be scared of;

xian qi 嫌棄
abandon / give up in disgust;

xian wu 嫌惡
detest / hate / loathe;

xian yan 嫌厭
dislike / loathe;

xian yi 嫌疑
doubt / mistrust / suspect;

xian yuan 嫌怨
enmity / hatred;

xian zeng 嫌憎
dislike / hate;

xian2 en 銜恩
cherish gratitude;

xian hen 銜恨
harbour grudges;

xian xu 銜恤
(1) nurse a sorrow;
(2) suffer the death of parents;

xian4 zhi xing xin ji bing 限制性心肌病
restrictive cardiomyopathy;

xiang1 ai 相愛
love each other;

xiang si 相思
in love with each other / miss each other;

xiang si bing 相思病
lovesickness;

xiang1 chou 鄉愁
homesickness;

xiang si 鄉思
homesickness;

xiang3 想
(1) miss / remember with longing;
(2) expect / hope;

xiang nian 想念
miss sb / miss sth;

xiao1 chou jie men 消愁解悶
quench sorrow and dissipate worry;

xiao chu you lü 消除憂慮
hush one's anxiety;

xiao3 qi 小器
close-minded / narrow-minded;

xiao xin 小心
careful / cautious || beware of; guard against; mind; pay attention to; take care;

xiao xin jin shen 小心謹慎
careful || buck one's ideas up; cautious; circumspect; discreet; discretion; easy does it; gingerly; prudent; with great care;

xiao xin wei miao 小心為妙
you cannot be too careful;

xiao xin xing shi 小心行事
act cautiously || handle matters carefully; play it cozy;

xiao xin yan er 小心眼兒
petty-minded || extremely sensitive; narrow-minded;

xiao xin yi yi 小心翼翼
with great care || cautiously; in a gingerly fashion; play it safe; run scared; tiptoe; tread on eggs; very carefully; very gingerly; very scrupulous; very timidly; warily; wary; watchful and reverent; with caution; with kid-gloves; with the greatest care; with the greatest circumspection;

xiao4 ai 孝愛
filial love;

xiao ci 孝慈
filial piety and parental tenderness;

xiao xin 孝心
filial heart / love toward parents;

xiao4 cheng 效誠
faithful / sincere;

xiao zhong 效忠
loyal to / pledge allegiance to;

xie1 xin 歇心
not to care / not to worry || not to indulge in desire; not to indulge in fancy; peaceful and carefree; relaxed;

xie2 nian 邪念
evil thoughts / wicked ideas;

xie xin 邪心
evil intentions || bad intentions; evil thoughts; wicked ideas;

xie2 li tong xin 協力同心
make concerted efforts || all of one mind; cooperate with one heart; of one heart; unite together in a common effort; with one heart; work as one man; work in full cooperation and with unity of purpose;

xie4 fen 泄憤
vent one's anger;

xie4 yi 屑意
care / mind;

xie4 懈
inattentive / negligent / relaxed / remiss;

xie chi 懈弛
relax;

xie man 懈慢
neglectful / negligent;

xie tai 懈怠
neglect / relax / slack;

xie yi 懈意
inactivity / indolence;

xie4 chen 謝忱
sincere gratitude / thankfulness;

xie en 謝恩
express thanks for great favours;

xie yi 謝意
appreciation / gratitude;

xin1 心
(1) heart;
(2) mind // mental;
(3) intention;

xin an 心安
peace of mind || calmness of emotion; carefree;

xin an ji fu 心安即福
peace of mind is a blessing;

xin an li de 心安理得
feel at ease and justified || feel no qualm; happy and at peace; have an easy conscience; peace of conscience; with mind at rest and conscience clear;

xin an shen xian 心安神閒
one's heart is at rest and one's spirit at ease / the mind is at peace and free from anxiety;

xin ban mo 心瓣膜
cardiac valve;

xin ban mo yan 心瓣膜炎
cardiovalvulitis;

xin bao 心包
pericardium;
nian lian xing xin bao 黏連性心包
adherent pericardium;

xin bao dou 心包竇
pericardial sinus;

xin bao yan 心包炎
pericarditis;
ai xing xin bao yan 癌性心包炎
carcinomatous pericarditis;
bing du xing xin bao yan 病毒性心包炎
viral pericarditis;
chu xue xing xin bao yan 出血性心包炎
hemorrhagic pericarditis;
chuang shang xing xin bao yan 創傷性心包炎
traumatic pericarditis;
feng shi xing xin bao yan 風濕性心包炎
rheumatic pericarditis;
ji nong xing xin bao yan 積膿性心包炎
purulent pericarditis;
ji shui xing xin bao yan 積水性心包炎
pericarditis with effusion;
ju xian xing xin bao yan 局限性心包炎
localized pericarditis;
nian lian xing xin bao yan 黏連性心包炎
adhesive pericarditis;
niao du zheng xin bao yan 尿毒症心包炎
uremic pericarditis;
nong qi xing xin bao yan 膿氣性心包炎
pyopneumopericardium;
nong xing xin bao yan 膿性心包炎
pyopericarditis;
shen chu xing xin bao yan 滲出性心包炎
pericarditis with effusion;
te fa xing xin bao yan 特發性心包炎
idiopathic pericarditis;
xi jun xing xin bao yan 細菌性心包炎
bacterial pericarditis;

xin ji xin bao yan 心肌心包炎
myopericarditis;
xin nei mo xin bao yan 心內膜心包炎
endopericarditis;
zhong liu xing xin bao yan 腫瘤性心包炎
neoplastic pericarditis;

xin bi tian gao 心比天高
one's heart is loftier than the sky || very ambitious;

xin bing 心病
(1) anxiety / mental disorder / worry;
(2) secret trouble / sore point;
(3) heart disease / mental disorder;

xin bing hai xu xin yao yi 心病還須心藥醫
heartsickness needs heart medicine for a cure || in sickness of the heart, it is the medicine of love that can effect a cure; no herb will cure love; no doctor can cure love sickness; where love is in the case, the doctor is an ass;

xin bo 心搏
heartbeat;

xin bo guo su 心搏過速
tachyrhythmia;

xin bo ting dun 心搏停頓
cardiac standstill;

xin bo ting zhi 心搏停止
asystolia;

xin bo xu huan 心搏徐緩
bradycardia;

xin bu you zhu 心不由主
cannot control one's mind || lose mental control; lose self-control; unable to control the mind;

xin bu zai yan 心不在焉
absent-minded // absence of mind || in an absent way; in brown study; in the clouds; inattentive; jump the track; nobody home; one's heart is no longer in it; one's mind is not in it; one's mind is occupied with other things; one's wits go woolgathering; out to lunch; preoccupied with sth else; unabsorbed; with an abstracted air; with one's mind wandering; with one's thoughts elsewhere; woolgathering;

xin cai 心裁
conception / idea / mental plan;

xin chang 心腸
(1) heart / intention;
(2) mood / state of mind;

xin chang hao 心腸好
have a good heart / have a kind heart / have an emphathetic heart;

xin chang ruan 心腸軟
have a soft heart // soft-hearted / tender-hearted;

xin chao 心潮
surging thoughts and emotions / the tidal surge of emotions;

xin chao fan gun 心潮翻滾
thoughts tumble through one's mind like tides || one's mind is confused and excited; one's mind is in a tumult; one's mind is racing;

xin chao ji dang 心潮激蕩
thoughts surging in one's mind;

xin chao peng pai 心潮澎湃
one's thoughts surge like the tide || feel an upsurge of emotion; full of excitement; one's mind is flooded with memories; one's mind is racing;

xin chao qi fu 心潮起伏
the tide in one's heart rises and falls || one's heart seems to rise and fall like the waves; one's hopes rise and ebb;

xin chi shen wang 心馳神往
have a deep longing for / one's thoughts fly to...;

xin ci 心慈
kind / kindhearted / softhearted;

xin ci mian ruan 心慈面軟
kind heart and soft countenance / tender-hearted and unable to turn down others' requests;

xin ci shou la 心慈手辣
have a hand of iron but a heart of gold;

xin ci shou ruan 心慈手軟
kindhearted and irresolute || faint of heart and hesitant in action; faint-hearted and hesitant

in action; show mercy to sb; softhearted;

xin cu 心粗

careless / thoughtless;

xin cu qi fu 心粗氣浮

not sober and cool-headed;

xin cun jie di 心存芥蒂

bear someone a grudge / have a grudge against / nurse a grievance;

xin cun wei que 心存魏闕

undying loyalty to one's own country while living on a strange land;

xin dan 心膽

(1) heart and gallbladder;

(2) courage / guts / will and courage;

xin dan ju lie 心膽俱裂

be frightened out of one's wits / strike terror into the hearts of // terror-stricken;

xin dang shen chi 心蕩神馳

be transported with || fall head over heels for; lose control of one's mind and will;

xin de 心得

what one has learned from work, study, practice, etc.;

xin di 心底

(1) base of heart;

(2) heart / innermost being;

xin di 心地

the true nature of a person || a person's character; a person's mind; a person's moral nature; character; conscience;

xin di guang ming 心地光明

clear conscience / upright;

xin di shan liang 心地善良

kind-hearted || good-natured; have a heart of gold; one's heart is in the right place;

xin di xia zhai 心地狹窄

narrow-minded || have a heart that is very narrow; have a mean heart; not of a generous disposition;

xin dong 心動

(1) the palpitation of the heart;

(2) become interested in sth;

xin dong guo huan 心動過緩

bradycardia;

zi fa xing xin dong guo huan 自發性心動過緩

essential bradycardia;

xin dong guo su 心動過速

tachyrhythmia;

zhi li xing xin dong guo su 直立性心動過速

orthostatic tachycardia;

xin du 心毒

evil heart / wicked heart;

xin du kou la 心毒口辣

vicious with a sharp, quick tongue;

xin du shou la 心毒手辣

vicious and ruthless || callous and cruel; cold-blooded; merciless at heart and in deeds;

xin duan 心段

cardiac segment;

xin duo 心多

over-suspicious;

xin fa yu bu liang 心發育不良

atelocardia;

xin fa yu bu quan 心發育不全

atelocardia;

xin fan 心煩

perturbed || annoyed; fretful; piqued; upset; vexed;

xin fan ji yang 心煩技癢

(1) itchy and restless;

(2) the desire to display that in which one excels / the desire to show off;

xin fan yi luan 心煩意亂

confused and worried || confused in mind; distracted; eat at sb; get hot under the collar; get on sb's nerves; have a troubled breast; in an emotional turmoil; off one's top; perturbed; set sb's nerves on edge; terribly upset; with troubled and distorted thoughts;

xin fan she 心反射

heart reflex;

xin fang 心房

auricle;

xin fang fei da 心房肥大
atriomegaly;

xin fang fen li 心房分離
atrial dissociation;

xin fang geng si 心房梗死
atrial infarction;

xin fang kuo da 心房擴大
dilation of heart;

xin fang qi po 心房起搏
atrial pacing;

xin fang shou suo 心房收縮
atrial systole;

xin fang ting dun 心房停頓
atrial standstill;

xin fang zeng da 心房增大
atrial enlargement;

xin fei 心非
the mind disagrees with what is said;

xin fei 心扉
door of one's heart / heart of hearts / way of thinking;

xin fei da 心肥大
cardiomegaly;

xin fei zheng 心肺症
cor pulmonale;

xin fu 心服
(1) acknowledge one's defeat sincerely;
(2) genuinely convinced ‖ admire sincerely and willingly; have one's heart won;

xin fu kou fu 心服口服
admit sb's superiority with sincerity ‖ fully convinced; genuinely convinced; sincerely convinced;

xin fu 心浮
unsettled and short-tempered ‖ flighty and impatient; restless and fretful; unstable;

xin fu qi zao 心浮氣燥
unsettled and short-tempered;

xin fu 心腹
(1) bosom friend ‖ confidant; henchman; reliable agent; trusted subordinate;
(2) faith / loyalty;

xin fu da huan 心腹大患
mortal malady;

xin fu peng you 心腹朋友
bosom friend / sworn friend / very intimate friend / one's self half;

xin fu ren 心腹人
confidant / trusted subordinate;

xin fu shi 心腹事
one's innermost secrets;

xin fu zhi huan 心腹之患
mortal malady / the threat from within;

xin fu zhi jiao 心腹之交
bosom friend / very intimate friend;

xin gan qing yuan 心甘情願
most willing to / perfectly happy to / willingly ‖ with a good grace; with good cheer; without protest;

xin gan 心肝
(1) darling / dear / honey / sweetheart;
(2) conscience / sense of justice;

xin gan bao bei 心肝寶貝
darling baby;

xin gan zhong da 心肝腫大
cardiohepatomegaly;

xin gao qi ao 心高氣傲
proud and arrogant;

xin gao zhi da 心高志大
have high ambitions;

xin gong neng bu quan 心功能不全
cardiac insufficiency;

xin guang ti pan 心廣體胖
liberal in mind and stout of body ‖ a clear conscience contributes to physical well-being; a liberal mind and a well-nourished body; carefree and contented; fit and happy; hale and hearty; of wide girth and ample heart;

xin han 心寒
be bitterly disappointed;

xin han chi leng 心寒齒冷
chill the heart ‖ bitterly disappointed; cast a chill over one;

心 *Heart*

xin han dan qie 心寒膽怯
shuddering and fearful / trepidation;

xin han mao shu 心寒毛豎
the heart shudders and the hair stands on end;

xin hei shou la 心黑手辣
black-hearted and cruel;

xin hen 心狠
hardhearted || callous; flinty; heartless; unfeeling;

xin hen shou la 心狠手辣
wicked and merciless || black-hearted and cruel; cruel and evil;

xin hong si huo 心紅似火
one's heart is as red as fire / with a heart red as fire;

xin hua nu fang 心花怒放
brimming with joy / burst with joy / wild with joy || cheer the cockles of one's heart; delight the cockles of one's heart; elated; enraptured; exult; feel exuberantly happy; gladden the cockles of one's heart; highly delighted; in an extremely happy mood; one's heart is gladdened; one's heart melts away; one's heart sings with joy; rejoice the cockles of one's heart;

xin huai 心懷
(1) cherish / entertain / harbour;
(2) intention / purpose;
(3) mood / state of mind;

xin huai bu gui 心懷不軌
harbour dark designs / have evil intentions;

xin huai bu man 心懷不滿
be filled with resentment / feel discontented || harbour quiet resentment; nurse a grievance; store up resentment // disaffected / disgruntled / hacked-off;

xin huai bu ping 心懷不平
feel aggrieved / have a grievance against;

xin huai bu shan 心懷不善
cherish evil thoughts / harbour ill intent;

xin huai chou hen 心懷仇恨
nurse hatred in one's heart;

xin huai di yi 心懷敵意
have an enmity against / hostile to;

xin huai e yi 心懷惡意
have designs on / have evil intentions towards;

xin huai er yi 心懷二意
harbour disloyal sentiments / have two faces;

xin huai gui tai 心懷鬼胎
have ulterior motives || conceive mischief; entertain dark schemes; have evil intentions; have sinister motives; with misgivings in one's heart;

xin huai po ce 心懷叵測
cherish evil designs || entertain rebellious schemes; harbour dark designs; harbour evil intentions; have an axe to grind; have an evil intent towards; have some dirty tricks up one's sleeve; nurse evil intentions;

xin huang 心慌
(1) nervous || flustered; get alarmed; panicky; shaken and perturbed;
(2) palpitate;

xin huang yi luan 心慌意亂
nervous and flustered || alarmed and nervous; all in a fluster; all in the wind; be confused and uncertain as to what to do; fall into a flutter; lose one's balance; lose one's presence of mind; lose one's wits totally; mentally confused; one's mind is in a tumult; shaken and perturbed;

xin hui yi lan 心灰意懶
feel disheartened || a broken spirit; discouraged; disheartened; dispirited; downcast and disappointed; downhearted; extremely discouraged; lose heart; one's heart dies within one; out of heart;

xin hui yi leng 心灰意冷
downhearted || dispirited; feel discouraged and hopeless; pessimistic and dejected;

xin hui yi zhuan 心回意轉
change one's mind || a change of heart; alter one's mind; change one's views; come around; repent; start a new life;

xin huo er ruan 心活耳軟
easily moved // of a credulous nature;

xin huo 心火
(1) internal heat;
(2) hidden anger;

xin ji 心肌
cardiac muscle;

xin ji bing 心肌病
cardiomyopathy;
chong xue xing xin ji bing 充血性心肌病
congestive cardimyopathy;
que xue xing xin ji bing 缺血性心肌病
ischemic cardiomyopathy;
te fa xing xin ji bing 特發性心肌病
idiopathic cardiomyopathy;
te yi xing xin ji bing 特異性心肌病
specific heart muscle disease;
xian zhi xing xin ji bing 限制性心肌病
restrictive cardiomyopathy;

xin ji cuo shang 心肌挫傷
myocardial contusion;

xin ji duan lie 心肌斷裂
fragmentation of myocardium;

xin ji geng se 心肌梗塞
myocardial infarction;
ji xing xin ji geng se 急性心肌梗塞
acute myocardial infarction;

xin ji geng si 心肌梗死
myocardial infarction;
ji xing xin ji geng si 急性心肌梗死
acute myocardial infarction;

xin ji gong neng bu quan 心肌功能不全
myocardial insufficiency;

xin ji gong neng sang shi 心肌功能喪失
myocardial stunning;

xin ji xin bao yan 心肌心包炎
myopericarditis;

xin ji yan 心肌炎
myocarditis;
bai hou xing xin ji yan 白喉性心肌炎
diphtheritic myocarditis;
bing du xing xin ji yan 病毒性心肌炎
viral myocarditis;
feng shi xing xin ji yan 風濕性心肌炎
rheumatic myocarditis;
guo min xing xin ji yan 過敏性心肌炎
hypersensitivity myocarditis;
ji xing xin ji yan 急性心肌炎
acute myocarditis;
man xing xin ji yan 慢性心肌炎
chronic myocarditis;
rou ya zhong xing xin ji yan 肉芽腫性心肌炎
granuomatous myocarditis;
te fa xing xin ji yan 特發性心肌炎
idiopathic myocarditis;
xi jun xing xin ji yan 細菌性心肌炎
bacterial myocarditis;
yuan chong xing xin ji yan 原蟲性心肌炎
protozoal myocarditis;
zhong du xing xin ji yan 中毒性心肌炎
toxic myocarditis;

xin ji 心機
craftiness / scheming / thinking;

xin ji 心急
impatient / short-tempered;

xin ji huo liao 心急火燎
burning with impatience / in a nervous state;

xin ji kou kuai 心急口快
impatient and outspoken / outspoken;

xin ji qing qie 心急情切
impatience and eagerness;

xin ji ru fen 心急如焚
burning with anxiety // one's heart is torn with anxiety;

xin ji ru huo 心急如火
afire with impatience || burn with impatience; one's mind is tense with a great sense of urgency;

xin ji shui bu kai 心急水不開
a watched pot is long in boiling / a watched pot never boils;

xin ji tui man 心急腿慢
the more impatient, the slower the movement;

xin ji 心疾
(1) illness caused by deep worries;
(2) mental ailment;

xin ji 心悸
palpitation of the heart;

心 Heart

xin ji 心跡
innermost feelings / real intentions;

xin jian 心尖
cardiac apex;

xin jian ru shi 心堅如石
one's heart is as constant as stones / one's heart is firm as a rock;

xin jian shi chuan 心堅石穿
when one's heart is single-minded even rocks are riven / with a strong will power, nothing is impossible;

xin jiang 心匠
a welding of ideas into plans;

xin jiao 心交
close friend;

xin jiao 心焦
anxious / impatient / very eager / vexed / worried;

xin jiao qi ao 心驕氣傲
arrogant at heart and haughty in manner;

xin jiao tong 心絞痛
angina pectoris;
bu wen ding xing xin jiao tong 不穩定型心絞痛
unstable angina pectoris;
di zeng xing xin jiao tong 遞增型心絞痛
crescendo angina;
dian xing xing xin jiao tong 典型性心絞痛
typical angina;
jia xin jiao tong 假心絞痛
pseudoangina;

xin jiao tong kong bu 心絞痛恐怖
anginophobia;

xin jin 心勁
(1) idea / thought;
(2) analytic ability;

xin jing 心旌
fluttering heart / unsettled state of mind;

xin jing dan zhan 心驚膽戰
tremble with fright || all of a jump; be deeply alrmed; quake with fear; shake with fright;

xin jing rou tiao 心驚肉跳
one's heart leaps into one's throat || be filled with apprehension; feel nervous and apprehensive; have one's heart in one's mouth; have the jitters to palpitate with anxiety and fear; jumpy; in a state of trepidation; make one's flesh creep; nervous and feel creepy and shivery; sudder with fear; tremble with fear;

xin jing 心淨
at ease / be cleared of worries;

xin jing 心境
mood || frame of mind; mental state; state of mind;

xin jing bu jia 心境不佳
in a bad mood;

xin jing e lie 心境惡劣
dysphoria;

xin jing zhang ai 心境障礙
mood disorders;

xin jing 心靜
a mind free of worries and cares / calm;

xin jing zi ran liang 心靜自然涼
so long as one keeps calm, one doesn't feel the heat too much;

xin kan 心坎
(1) bottom of one's heart / the heart's chord;
(2) bosom / dear to the heart;

xin ken 心肯
acceptance in the heart / inner approval / inner assent;

xin kong 心孔
intellectual capacity;

xin kou 心口
(1) precordium;
(2) bosom / pit of the stomach;
(3) one's utterance and what one really thinks;

xin kou bu yi 心口不一
speak contrary to one's thought / speak one way and think another;

xin kou ru yi 心口如一
say what one thinks || faithful to one's words; frank and unreserved; honest and straightforward; speak from the heart; speak one's mind; the mouth agrees with the mind; what one says is indeed what one thinks;

xin kou tong 心口痛
precordialgia;

xin kuan 心寬
light-hearted || carefree; feeling at peace with the world; not lend oneself to worry and anxiety; open-minded; optimistic;

xin kuan ti pan 心寬體胖
light-hearted and well-built || broad-mindedness brings health; laugh and grow fat; laughter will make one fat; liberal mind brings health; when the mind is at ease, the body becomes fat; when the mind is enlarged, the body is at ease;

xin kuang shen yi 心曠神怡
carefree and happy || feel on top of the world; feel way above par; free of mind and happy of heart; of good cheer; refresh and gladden sb's heart; relax and happy;

xin kui 心虧
guilty conscience;

xin kui li qie 心虧理怯
have a guilty conscience and an unjust case;

xin kuo zhang 心擴張
cardiectasis;

xin lao li zhuo 心勞力拙
feel tired in mind and exhausted in strength;

xin lao ri zhuo 心勞日拙
fare worse and worse for all one's scheming / go from bad to worse for all one's pains / make tiring and useless pretentions;

xin li 心理
mentality / mind / psychology;

xin li bian tai 心理變態
psychopathy;

xin li bing tai 心理病態
mental abnormality;

xin li gan ran 心理感染
psychic contagion;

xin li jian kang 心理健康
mental health;

xin li shi chang 心理失常
aberration;

xin li wei sheng 心理衛生
mental hygiene;

xin li zhang ai 心理障礙
mental disorder;

xin li 心裏
at heart / in mind / in the heart;

xin li an xiao 心裏暗笑
laugh in one's sleeve;

xin li bei tong 心裏悲痛
sore at heart;

xin li bie niu 心裏別扭
feel all wrong;

xin li bu an 心裏不安
not feel at ease / pertinacious // pertinacity;

xin li chen zhong 心裏沉重
weigh heavily on one's heart;

xin li da gu 心裏打鼓
feel diffident / have butterflies in the stomach;

xin li fa mao 心裏發毛
feel nervous / feel scared // panic-stricken;

xin li fa men 心裏發悶
feel constriction in the area of the heart;

xin li fan men 心裏煩悶
sick at heart;

xin li hai pa 心裏害怕
afraid at heart;

xin li hua 心裏話
one's innermost thoughts and feelings;

xin li ming bai 心裏明白
clear in one's mind;

xin li nan guo 心裏難過
one's heart is filled with pain;

xin li pan suan 心裏盤算
turn things over in one's mind;

xin li pao bu kai 心裏拋不開
cannot put it out of one's mind;

xin li qi shang ba xia 心裏七上八下
agitated / perturbed;

xin li ta shi 心裏踏實
feel at ease;

xin li yi zheng 心裏一怔
one's heart misses a beat;

xin li you gui 心裏有鬼
be up for some trick / have a bellyful of tricks / have an ulterior object in view;

xin li you shu 心裏有數
aware of sth without speaking out / know very well in one's heart;

xin li yu men 心裏鬱悶
feel blue / feel depressed / feel low;

xin li yue pa gui yue lai 心裏越怕鬼越來
the more afraid you are, the more likely the devil is to come;

xin li zha gen 心裏扎根
strike roots in one's heart / take deep roots in the heart of sb / take root in one's self;

xin li 心力
mental and physical efforts / mental power;

xin li bu zu 心力不足
bypodynamia cordis;

xin li jiao cui 心力交瘁
both the mind and strength are worn out ‖ mentally and physically exhausted; physically and mentally tired; tire oneself out both mentally and physically;

xin li shuai jie 心力衰竭
cardiac failure / heart failure;
chong xue xing xin li shuai jie 充血性心力衰竭
congestive heart failure;
shou suo xing xin li shuai jie 收縮性心力衰竭
systolic heart failure;

xin lian xin 心連心
heart linked to heart ‖ of one mind with; one's heart beats with the heart of sb;

xin liang ban jie 心涼半截
be stricken to the heart;

xin ling 心靈
(1) clear / intelligent / quick-witted;
(2) heart / mental / mind / spirit / spiritual / soul;

xin ling gan ying 心靈感應
telepathy;

xin ling shou min 心靈手敏
clever in mind and quick of action / nimble;

xin ling shou qiao 心靈手巧
clear and deft / ingenious / quick-witted and nimble-fingered // ingenuity // the mind is clever as the hands are numble;

xin ling 心領
(1) understand without verbal exchange // understanding;
(2) appreciate;

xin ling shen hui 心領神會
take the hint / understand tacitly ‖ appreciate sb's thought; enter into; know without being told; mental conception; readily take a hint; secret understanding;

xin lu 心路
(1) scheme / the process of thinking / wit;
(2) mindedness / tolerance;

xin lü bu qi 心律不齊
arrhythmia;

xin lü guo huan 心律過緩
bradyrhythmia;

xin lü shi chang 心律失常
arrhythmia;
man xing xin lü shi chang 慢性心律失常
chronic arrhythmia;
qing nian qi xin lü shi chang 青年期心律失常
juvenile arrhythmia;
yong jiu xing xin lü shi chang 永久性心律失常
perpetual arrhtythmia;

xin luan 心亂
confused and perturbed;

xin luan ru ma 心亂如麻
extremely confused and disturbed ‖ have one's mind all in a tangle; have one's mind as confused as a tangled hemp; in a stew; off the hooks; terribly upset; utterly confused and disconcerted;

xin man yi zu 心滿意足
to one's heart's content ‖ complacent; contented; feel very pleased with; fully contented; fully satisfied; in the pride of one's heart; on top of the world; perfectly content; rest satisfied; solid satisfaction; unwilling to call the king one's cousin; very contented; would not call the king one's cousin;

xin mang 心盲
mental blindness / psychic blindness;

xin mi 心迷
be confused of mind / puzzled;

xin miao 心苗
decisions / ideas / intentions / opinions;

xin ming ru jing 心明如鏡
one's mind is as clear as a mirror;

xin ming yan liang 心明眼亮
sharp-eyed and clearheaded || able to see everything clearly and correctly; see and think clearly; with one's mind clear and eyes sharp;

xin mu 心目
mind's eye || inward eye; mental view; mind;

xin mu zhong 心目中
(1) in one's mind || in one's eye; in one's heart; in one's mental view; in one's mind's eye;
(2) in one's memory;

xin mu shou zhui 心慕手追
what one's heart admires the hands follow || imitate laboriously;

xin nei mo 心內膜
endocardium;

xin nei mo bing 心內膜病
endocardiopathy;

xin nei mo xin bao yan 心內膜心包炎
endopericarditis;

xin nei mo yan 心內膜炎
endocarditis;
nong du xing xin nei mo yan 膿毒性心內膜炎
septic endocarditis;

xin nei mo ying hua 心內膜硬化
endocardial sclerosis;

xin nei ya 心內壓
endocardial pressure;

xin ping qi he 心平氣和
ataraxia || become gentle with; calmly and relaxedly; even-tempered and good-humoured; in a calm mood; in a placid mood; in cold blood; in one's sober senses; of a peaceful disposition; peace of mind; without losing one's temper;

xin po lie 心破裂
cardiorrhexis;

xin qi yi tuan 心起疑團
arouse one's suspicion;

xin qi 心氣
(1) intention / motive;
(2) frame of mind / state of mind;
(3) ambition / aspiration;

xin qi bu ning 心氣不寧
intranquility of heart energy;

xin qian yi cheng 心虔意誠
with pious wishes;

xin qiang 心腔
chambers of the heart;

xin qiao ling long 心竅玲瓏
very bright-minded;

xin qing 心情
mood || feeling tone; frame of mind; state of mind;

xin qing bu jia 心情不佳
feel out of one's plate / in bad mood / in low spirits;

xin qing chang kuai 心情暢快
have ease of mind;

xin qing chen men 心情沉悶
feel depressed;

xin qing chen zhong 心情沉重
heavy heart / with a heavy heart // heavy-hearted;

xin qing huan chang 心情歡暢
be filled with joy / in high spirits;

xin qing huo da 心情豁達
in an open-minded frame of mind // liberal in affection;

xin qing ji dong 心情激動
excited / thrilled;

xin qing ji fen 心情激憤
be filled with indignation;

xin qing shu chang 心情舒暢
ease of mind || a mind at ease; enjoy ease of mind; feel happy; good-humoured; have

one's mind at ease; in good humour; in a merry mood;

xin qing ya yi 心情壓抑
feel constrained;

xin qing yu kuai 心情愉快
in a good mood || have a light heart; in a cheerful frame of mind;

xin qiu 心球
bulb of the heart;

xin qu 心曲
(1) heart / innermost being / mind;
(2) sth weighing on one's mind;

xin qu ren nan liu 心去人難留
when one's heart is gone, it is difficult to keep his body;

xin ru bing tan 心如冰炭
heartless and cold as ice;

xin ru chao yong 心如潮湧
one's thoughts surge like the tide;

xin ru dao ci 心如刀刺
feel as if a knife were piercing one's heart || feel as if one's heart were pierced by daggers; feel as though a knife were sticking into one's heart;

xin ru dao ge 心如刀割
feel as if a knife were piercing one's heart || be cut to the quick; feel as if one's heart were stabbed by a knife; feel as though a knife has been plunged into one's heart; feel greatly distressed like one's heart suffers a knife cut; like a dagger cuts deep into one's heart; one's heart contracts in pain as if stabbed by a knife; one's heart feels as if transfixed with a dagger;

xin ru dao ge, lei ru yu xia 心如刀割，淚如雨下
one's heart breaks and one's tears cascade;

xin ru dao jiao 心如刀絞
be cut to the quick / feel as if a knife were being twisted in one's heart;

xin ru dao zha 心如刀扎
one's heart seems pierced with a knife;

xin ru gu jing 心如古井
call forth no response in sb's breast // one's heart is as tranquil as an old well;

xin ru gun chao 心如滾潮
like tossing waves in one's heart / one's mind is in a tumult;

xin ru huo fen 心如火焚
burning with impatience / one's heart is afire / torn by anxiety;

xin ru jin shi jian 心如金石堅
the heart is as constant as metals and stones are durable;

xin ru lei kuai 心如累塊
be weighed down by anxious cares;

xin ru she xie 心如蛇蝎
have the heart of a devil / one's heart is as poisonous as any viper or scorpion;

xin ru shi chen 心如石沉
one's heart sinks like a stone;

xin ru si hui 心如死灰
one's heart is like dead ashes — utterly dispirited;

xin ru tie shi 心如鐵石
have a heart of stone || inexorable; keep one's heart as hard as the nether millstone; one's heart is like iron or stone; with a steelcold heart;

xin ru xuan jing 心如懸旌
one's heart flutters like a pennant in the wind;

xin ru xuan zhong 心如懸鐘
the heart is like a hanging bell;

xin ru zhen zha 心如針扎
feel as if needles were pricking one's heart / feel greatly distressed as though one's heart pricks;

xin ru zhi shui 心如止水
a mind tranquil as still water / one's mind settles as still water / the heart is like still water;

xin ruan 心軟
kind-hearted / soft-hearted / tender-hearted;

xin sang qi ju 心喪氣沮
the heart mourns and spirit spoils;

xin shan 心善
kind heart // kind-hearted;

xin shan mian leng 心善面冷
has a heart of gold although one seldom

smiles;

xin shang 心上
at heart / in one's heart / in one's mind / in the heart;

xin shang ren 心上人
lover / sweetheart;

xin shen bing 心身病
psychosomatic illness;

xin shen zhang ai 心身障礙
psychosomatic disorder;

xin shen 心神
mood / state of mind;

xin shen bu an 心神不安
feel uneasy ‖ feel perturbed; fidgety; have the fidgets; ill at ease; not to feel easy in one's mind; suffer from the fidgets / uneasy // pertinacity / unease;

xin shen bu ding 心神不定
feel restless ‖ a confused state of mind; a restless mood; agitated; an unstable mood; anxious and preoccupied; distracted; have no peace of mind; ill at ease; in a state of discomposure; indisposed; out of sorts; wandering in thought;

xin shen bu ji 心神不羈
difficult to concentrate one's mind on sth / with one's mind running wild;

xin shen bu ning 心神不寧
inquietude;

xin shen dian dao 心神顛倒
go off into raptures // utterly confused;

xin shen huang hu 心神恍惚
ill at ease and full of dread / perturbed in mind // in a trance;

xin sheng yi ji 心生一計
hit upon an idea ‖ a good idea occurs to sb; a scheme comes to one's mind;

xin sheng 心聲
the heart's desire ‖ aspirations; heartfelt wishes; intentions; thinking; thoughts;

xin sheng 心盛
enthusiastic // in high spirit;

xin shi 心室
ventricle;

dan xin shi 單心室
single ventricle;

you xin shi 右心室
right ventricle;

zuo xin shi 左心室
left ventricle;

xin shi fei da 心室肥大
ventricular hypertrophy;

xin shi gong neng 心室功能
ventricular function;

xin shi 心實
honest / truthful;

xin shi 心事
sth weighing on one's mind ‖ a load on one's mind; secrets in one's mind; worry;

xin shi chong chong 心事重重
sth weighing heavily on one's mind ‖ be cumbered with care; be laden with anxiety; be preoccupied by some troubles; be weighed down with care; gloomy with worry; there are too many problems on one's mind; with a heavy heart;

xin shou xiang ying 心手相應
as the mind wills, the hand responds ‖ at one's finger's end; mind and hand in accord;

xin shu 心術
designs / intentions / schemes;

xin shu bu zheng 心術不正
harbour evil intentions ‖ lack of sincerity; not have one's heart in the right place; one's intention is not right;

xin si 心思
(1) ideas / intelligence / thoughts;
(2) thinking / thoughts;
(3) mood / state of mind;

xin si 心死
in a state of stupour // abandoned / heartless;

xin suan 心酸
grief-stricken / grieved / heartsick / heartsore // feel sad / sadden;

xin suan 心算
mental arithmetic;

xin sui 心髓
innermost beings / innermost feelings;

xin sui 心碎
brokenhearted / heartbroken // broken heart / heartbreak;

xin tai 心態
mentality;

xin teng 心疼
(1) love dearly;
(2) make one's heart ache / feel sorry / the heart bleeds;

xin tian 心田
(1) one's heart;
(2) one's disposition / one's intentions;

xin tian qi he 心恬氣和
a pleasant peaceful frame of mind;

xin tiao 心跳
(1) heartbeat / heartthrob;
(2) the palpitation of the heart caused by fear or anxiety;

xin tong 心痛
cardiodynia / cardiac pain // feel the pangs of the heart;

xin tong che bei 心痛徹背
chest pain radiating to the back;

xin tong ru jiao 心痛如絞
have an excruciating pain in the chest;

xin tong yu sui 心痛欲碎
one's heart is breaking and aches so badly with sorrow;

xin tou yi he 心投意合
in perfect agreement ‖ hit it off perfectly; in rapport; of the same opinion;

xin tou 心頭
heart / intentions / mind;

xin tou hen 心頭恨
ranking hatred;

xin tou huo qi 心頭火起
one's mind is inflamed with passion ‖ angry; flare up in anger; infuriated; one's heart burns;

xin tou rou 心頭肉
sb dear to the heart / the apple of one's eye;

xin tou shi luo 心頭石落
as if a heavy stone has been removed from the pit of one's stomach;

xin tou xiao lu 心頭小鹿
one's heart beats wildly / one's heart goes pit-a-pat // with a throbbing heart;

xin wang shen chi 心往神馳
let one's thoughts fly to a person / let one's thoughts fly to a place // long for;

xin wang yi chu xiang, jin wang yi chu shi 心往一處想，勁往一處使
think and work with one heart and one mind / with everyone's thoughts and efforts directed towards one goal;

xin wei xing yi 心為形役
the heart is being put to toil by the body;

xin wo 心窩
(1) in one's heart;
(2) precordium / the region between the ribs;

xin wu er yong 心無二用
one cannot keep one's mind on two things at the same time ‖ one can't do two things at once; one should concentrate one's attention on one thing at a time; one's mind could not work on two things together; the mind cannot be devoted to two things at one time;

xin wu pang wu 心無旁騖
single-minded // without distraction;

xin wu zhu jian 心無主見
weak-willed;

xin xi 心細
careful / cautious;

xin xian 心弦
heartstrings / the heart's cord;

xin xian 心險
crafty and evil-minded;

xin xiang 心香
devotion / piety / sincerity;

xin xiang 心想
expect / figure / think;

xin xiang 心象
mental image;

xin xie xing hui 心邪形穢
when the mind is filthy, the appearance will not be any better;

xin xin nian nian 心心念念
anxiously longing for / keep in mind always / keep thinking about / remember always;

xin xin xiang lian 心心相連
be closely attached to each other / be linked in their hearts;

xin xin xiang yin 心心相印
a complete meeting of minds || all of one mind; both of the same mind; have identical feelings and views; have mutual affinity; hearts and feelings find a perfect response; in complete rapport; in mutual understanding; in perfect harmony with; kindred spirits; mind acts on mind; mutually attached to each other; share the feelings of; share the same feelings; the communion of heart with heart; their love is reciprocal;

xin xing 心性
constitution of the mind / disposition / temperament;

xin xing shui zhong 心性水腫
cardiac eodema;

xin xing xiu ke 心性休克
cardiac shock;

xin yuan xing shui zhong 心源性水腫
cardiac oedema;

xin yuan xing xiu ke 心源性休克
cardiogenic shock;

xin zang xing cu si 心臟型猝死
sudden cardiac death;

xin xiong 心胸
(1) in the depth of one's heart;
(2) breadth of mind || ambition; aspiration; capacity for tolerance;

xin xiong huo da 心胸豁達
broad-minded / large-minded // with a great heart;

xin xiong kai kuo 心胸開闊
broad-minded / large-minded / unprejudiced;

xin xiong xia zhai 心胸狹窄
narrow-minded / small-minded / intolerant;

xin xiu 心秀
intelligent without seeming so;

xin xu 心虛
(1) guilty conscience || afraid of being found out; with a guilty conscience;
(2) diffident / lacking in self-confidence;

xin xu dan qie 心虛膽怯
apprehensive and cowardly // have a guilty conscience;

xin xu 心許
a tacit acceptance / a tact approval // acclaim without words;

xin xu mu cheng 心許目成
convey love by exchanging longing glances;

xin xu 心緒
mood / state of mind;

xin xu bu ning 心緒不寧
in a disturbed state of mind || flutter; in a bad mood; in a flutter; in a state of agitation; nerve-racking; one's state of mind is not at ease;

xin xu fei teng 心緒沸騰
one's heart is in a tumult;

xin xu fan luan 心緒煩亂
emotionally upset / in an emotional turmoil;

xin xu liao luan 心緒繚亂
be emotionally upset // in a confused state of mind / in an emotional turmoil;

xin xuan liang di 心懸兩地
a mind concerned within two places / have worries at two places at the same time;

xin xue 心學
study of the mind;

xin xue 心血
painstaking care / painstaking efforts;

xin xue guan bing 心血管病
cardiovascular disease;

xian tian xing xin xue guan bing 先天性心血管病
congenital cardiovascular disease;

xin xue lai chao 心血來潮
be prompted by a sudden impulse || a whim; be seized by a whim; have a brainstorm; hit upon a sudden idea; in an impulsive moment; on the spur of the moment;

xin xue lai chao, wang hu suo yi 心血來潮，忘

乎所以

be carried away by a sudden impulse ‖ be carried away by one's whims and act recklessly; forget oneself in a moment of excitement; forget oneself in an impulsive moment; lose one's head in a moment of excitement;

xin yan 心炎

carditis;

feng shi xing xin yan 風濕性心炎

rheumatic carditis;

lian qiu jun xing xin yan 鏈球菌性心炎

streptococcal carditis;

quan xin yan 全心炎

pancarditis;

you xing xin yan 疣性心炎

verrucous carditis;

xin yan er 心眼兒

(1) heart / mind;

(2) intention;

(3) cleverness / intelligence;

(4) unfounded doubts / unnecessary misgivings;

xin yan er duo 心眼兒多

full of unnecessary misgivings // oversensitive // too much attention to details;

xin yan er hao 心眼兒好

generous / generous and kind-hearted / good-natured / kind-hearted;

xin yan huo fan 心眼活泛

have a supple mind // quick-witted;

xin yang 心癢

itching heart;

xin yang nan sao 心癢難搔

itch in the heart but unable to scratch it — too happy to know what to do;

xin yang 心漾

one's heart is aroused by desires;

xin yao 心藥

psychological treatment;

xin yi 心儀

admire in the heart / feel drawn to sb;

xin yi qi ren 心儀其人

admire a particular person;

xin yi 心意

(1) kindly feelings / regard;

(2) decisions / ideas / intentions / opinions / purposes;

xin ying 心影

impression / mental image;

xin ying 心硬

callous / stony-hearted / unfeeling;

xin ying hua 心硬化

cardiosclerosis;

xin you ling xi yi dian tong 心有靈犀一點通

hearts which beat in unison are linked / hearts which have a common beat are linked / telepathy;

xin you pang wu 心有旁騖

have sth else to go after // preoccupied;

xin you wei gan 心有未甘

somewhat dissatisfied;

xin you yu er li bu zu 心有餘而力不足

more than willing but lacking the power to ‖ one is willing, yet unable; one's ability falls short of one's wishes; one's mind is willing, but the body is weak; the spirit is willing, but the flesh is weak; willing but lacking the power to do; willing but unbale;

xin you yu jing 心有餘悸

have a lingering fear ‖ one's heart still fluttering with fear; shudder in retrospect; sufficient alarm; there is still a certain trepidation; with unforgotten trepidation;

xin yu li zhuo 心餘力拙

unable to do what one wants very much to do ‖ bite more than one can chew; more than willing but lacking the power to; the spirit is willing, but the flesh is weak;

xin yuan yi ma 心猿意馬

restless and whimsical ‖ a heart like a capering monkey and a mind like a galloping horse — restless; capricious; fanciful and fickle; perturbed; scatter-brained; unsettled in mind; wavering in purpose; with the heart of an ape and the mind of a horse — in a restless and jumpy mood;

xin yuan 心願

aspiration / cherished desire / one's heart's desire;

xin yuan li wei 心願力違
the spirit is willing, but the flesh is weak;

xin yue cheng fu 心悅誠服
admire sb from the heart ‖ be completely convinced; concede willingly; feel a heartfelt admiration; submit willingly;

xin zang 心臟
cardiac / heart / ticker;

xin zang bing 心臟病
cardiac disease / heart disease / heart trouble;
feng shi xing xin zang bing 風濕性心臟病
rheumatic heart disease;
lao nian xing xin zang bing 老年性心臟病
presbycardia;
que xue xing xin zang bing 缺血性心臟病
ischemic heart disease;

xin zang bing fa zuo 心臟病發作
heart attack;

xin zang fei da 心臟肥大
cardiomegaly;

xin zang kuo zhang 心臟擴張
dilatation of the heart;

xin zang qi po 心臟起搏
cardiac pacing;

xin zang shuai jie 心臟衰竭
cardiac failure;
chong xue xing xin zang shuai jie 充血性心臟衰竭
congestive failure;

xin zang xia chui 心臟下垂
cardioptosis;

xin zang xiu ke 心臟休克
cardiac shock;

xin zang yan 心臟炎
carditis;

xin zang zeng da 心臟增大
cardiac enlargement;

xin zhai 心窄
narrow-minded;

xin zhao 心照
have an understanding / understand without being told;

xin zhao bu xuan 心照不宣
tacit agreement / tacit understanding // have a tacit understanding / take wordless counsel // be tacitly understood;

xin zhe 心折
admire without reservations / have one's heart won;

xin zheng bu pa xie 心正不怕邪
if the heart is upright, there need not be any apprehension of depravity;

xin zhi 心知
consciousness / intelligence / mind;

xin zhi kou kuai 心直口快
frank and outspoken ‖ frank and sincere; frank by nature with a ready tongue; honest and outspoken; speak one's mind freely; wear one's heart on one's sleeve;

xin zhi bi geng 心織筆耕
the pen labours on the ideas of the mind;

xin zhi 心志
fortitude / will power;

xin zhong 心中
at heart / in one's heart / in one's mind / in the heart / in the mind;

xin zhong an xi 心中暗喜
be secretly pleased ‖ rejoice in one's heart; secretly feel pleased;

xin zhong bu fu 心中不服
a lack of hearty support / mutinous in one's heart;

xin zhong hu yi 心中狐疑
with one's stomach heaving with torturing doubts;

xin zhong huai nu 心中懷怒
nourish anger in one's heart;

xin zhong na men 心中納悶
be grieved and disappointed;

xin zhong pan suan 心中盤算
debate in one's mind / debate with oneself;

xin zhong qiu he 心中丘壑
obstinate to one's own ideas;

xin zhong wu shu 心中無數
not to know for certain / not to know one's own mind / not too sure / without clear aims;

xin zhong yi yu 心中抑鬱
one's mind is depressed;

xin zhong you gui 心中有鬼
have a bellyful of tricks / have sth to hide / have ulterior designs;

xin zhong you kui 心中有愧
feel ashamed / have a guilty conscience / have sth on one's conscience;

xin zhong yu shu 心中有數
have a clear idea about || feel sure of; have a good idea of how things stand; have a pretty good idea of; know at heart; know fairly well; know one's own mind; know the score; know what's what;

xin zui 心醉
be charmed / be enchanted / be fascinated;

xin zui shen mi 心醉神迷
be thrown into ecstacies // in an ecstasy of delight / in ecstasies over;

xin1 忻
delight / happy;

xin xin 忻忻
pleased and satisfied;

xin1 欣
delighted / glad / happy / joyful;

xin bian 欣忭
delight / joy;

xin ran 欣然
gladly / with pleasure;

xin ran cong ming 欣然從命
obey with alacrity;

xin shang 欣賞
admire / appreciate / enjoy / like;

xin wei 欣慰
comforted / contented / delighted / gratified / satisfied;

xin xi 欣喜
delight / happy / joyful;

xin xi ruo kuang 欣喜若狂
beside oneself with joy;

xin xian 欣羨
admire / envy;

xin xin ran 欣欣然
complacent / happy / joyful;

xin xing 欣幸
joyful and thankful;

xin yue 欣悅
delighted / glad / happy / joyous;

xin yue 欣躍
dancing with glee;

xin1 訢
joy // happy;

xin ran 訢然
happy / very pleased;

xin xin 訢訢
joyfully;

xin1 chou 新愁
fresh sorrows;

xin1 mu 歆慕
cherish;

xin xian 歆羨
admire / envy;

xin yan 歆艷
admire / envy;

xin4 xin 信心
confidence;

xing1 fen 興奮
excited / stimulated;

xing2 chou xin shan 形醜心善
have a rough look but a good heart;

xing xiang 形相
appearance / facial look / form;

xing3 wu 省悟
awake to;

xing3 wu 醒悟
come to one's senses // disillusion;

xing4 性
disposition / temper;

xing lie 性烈
fiery disposition;

xing qi 性氣
disposition / personality / temperament;

xing qing 性情
disposition / habitude / temper / temperament;

xing qing bao zao 性情暴躁
irascible / irritable // have an irascible temperament;

xing qing bu he 性情不合
uncongenial;

xing qing ping he 性情平和
have a calm temper;

xing qing sui he 性情隨和
carefree temper;

xing qing wen he 性情溫和
mild disposition;

xing4 悻
angry / enraged / indignant;

xing zhi 悻直
bluff / blunt / brusque;

xing4 gao cai lie 興高采烈
cheerful / elated / high-spirited / jubilant // as merry as the maids / full of cheer and good spirits // in high spirits / over the moon // cut round;

xing zhi 興致
eagerness / enthusiasm / interest;

xing zhi bo bo 興致勃勃
ebullient // full of enthusiasm // feel one's oats;

xiong1 huai 胸懷
ambition / aspiration;

xiong huai lei luo 胸懷磊落
frank / honest;

xiong huai tan bai 胸懷坦白
frank / open-minded;

xiong huai huo da 胸懷豁達
open-minded;

xiong huai xia zhai 胸懷狹窄
narrow-minded;

xiong jin 胸襟
breadth of mind / mind;

xiong jin huo da 胸襟豁達
broad-minded / open-minded // have a large breadth of mind / have largeness of mind;

xiong jin kai kuo 胸襟開闊
broad-minded / large-minded / liberal in outlook / unprejudiced;

xiong2 jian 雄健
heroic;

xiong xin 雄心
ambition / great ambition / lofty aspiration;

xiong xin bo bo 雄心勃勃
ambitious ‖ a flight of ambition; with breathless eagerness to; with determination and ardour;

xiong xin wei si 雄心未死
undying ambition ‖ not willing to give up; still full of ambition;

xiong xin zhuang zhi 雄心壯志
great ideals and lofty aspirations ‖ a high aspiring mind; great and lofty aspirations; high ambitions; high hopes and great ambitions; lofty ambitions; lofty aspirations and high aims; lofty ideals and high aspirations; magnificent and heroic aims;

xiu1 xin du xing 修心篤行
become pure in heart and good in behaviour;

xiu xin yang xing 修心養性
cultivate one's mind and improve one's character ‖ cultivate one's original nature; enjoy obscurity for the sake of self-improvement;

xiu1 羞
(1) abashed / ashamed;
(2) bashful / shy;
(3) disgrace / insult / shame;

xiu1 chan 羞慚
abashed / ashamed / humiliated / mortified;

xiu chi 羞恥
sense of shame;

xiu chi zhi xin 羞恥之心
sense of shame;

xiu da da 羞答答
bashful / shy;

xiu fen 羞憤
ashamed and angry;

xiu gui 羞愧
disgraced / mortified / shamed;

心 *Heart*

xiu nao 羞惱
humiliated and indignant;

xiu nao cheng nu 羞惱成怒
become angry from shame;

xiu qie 羞怯
shy and nervous;

xiu ren 羞人
feel ashamed / feel embarrassed;

xiu ren da da 羞人答答
abashed / ashamed / bashful;

xiu ru 羞辱
insult / disgrace / humiliate // humiliation / shame;

xiu wu 羞惡
ashamed of evil deeds;

xiu wu zhi xin 羞惡之心
feeling of shame / moral sense / sense of shame;

xiu yu wei wu 羞與為伍
ashamed to associate with sb;

xu1 huai 虛懷
humble / open-minded;

xu huai ruo gu 虛懷若谷
open-minded;

xu qie 虛怯
timid;

xu qing jia yi 虛情假意
hypocritical;

xu rong xin 虛榮心
vainglory / vanity;

xu xin 虛心
modest / open-minded / with an open mind;

xu xin hao xue 虛心好學
modest and eager to learn;

xu xin qiu jiao 虛心求教
ready to listen to advice / willing to take advice;

xu xin ting qu 虛心聽取
listen patiently / listen with an open mind;

xu xin xia qi 虛心下氣
humble and meek;

xu4 恤
(1) give relief / help / relieve;
(2) pity / sympathize;

xu bing 恤病
show sympathy for the sick;

xu kui 恤匱
relieve the distressed;

xu li 恤嫠
relieve widows;

xu pin 恤貧
give relief to the poor;

xu ran 恤然
astonished / startled;

xu4 qing 敘情
bare one's heart;

xu4 勗
encourage;

xu mian 勗勉
encourage;

xu4 慉
bring up / raise;

xu jie 慉結
depressed / melancholy;

xu4 hen 蓄恨
long pent-up hatred;

xu yi 蓄意
premeditated;

xu yi tiao yin 蓄意挑釁
premeditated provocation;

xu zhi 蓄志
long-conceived aspiration;

xuan1 qu 軒渠
cheerful / laughing / merry;

xuan ran 軒然
delighted / smiling;

xuan xuan zi de 軒軒自得
delighted and satisfied with oneself;

xuan2 xin 懸心
concern about sb / concern about sth;

xuan xin diao dan 懸心吊膽
on tenderhooks // be filled with anxiety / be

filled with fear;

xuan yi 懸疑
suspense;

xuan4 huo 眩惑
confuse and cheat / mislead;

xue3 chi 雪恥
avenge humiliation;

xue hen 雪恨
avenge / avenge one's grudge;

xue yuan 雪冤
vindicate oneself / wipe out grievances;

xue4 chen 血忱
loyalty / sincerity;

xue chou 血仇
blood feud;

xue guan cheng xing shu 血管成形術
angioplasty;

xue hai shen chou 血海深仇
intense and deep-seated hatred;

xue xin 血心
loyalty / sincerity;

xun2 恂
(1) have faith in / trust;
(2) sincere;
(3) afraid / scared;

xun da 恂達
intelligent;

xun li 恂慄
awe-inspiring / scared;

xun ran 恂然
sincerely;

xun shi 恂實
sincerely honest;

xun zhi 恂直
frank and sincere;

xun4 qing 殉情
die for love;

ya3 huai 雅懷
generous heart;

yan1 懨
(1) in poor health;
(2) peaceful / tranquil;

yan yan 懨懨
(1) in poor health;
(2) peaceful / tranquil;

yan4 hen 厭恨
hate / loathe;

yan wu 厭惡
be disgusted with / detest / dislike / disrelish / loathe // revulsion;

yang2 yang de yi 洋洋得意
elated / in high spirits / proud and happy / walk on air;

yang yang zi de 洋洋自得
self-satisfied;

yang2 yang de yi 揚揚得意
exult over / smug and complacent / walk on air;

yang yang zi de 揚揚自得
complacent / smug;

yang3 xin 養心
cultivate mental calm / nourish the heart / nourish the mind;

yang xin shou zhuo 養心守拙
keep to one's primitive simplicity;

yang xin yi shen 養心怡神
refresh one's spirit by keeping quiet;

yang4 怏
discontented / disheartened / dispirited;

yang ran 怏然
discontent / unhappy;

yang yang 怏怏
discontented / dispirited / sad;

yang yi 怏悒
discontent / melancholy / sad;

yang yu 怏鬱
gloom / pensiveness;

yang4 恙
(1) disease;
(2) worry;

ye3 xin 野心
(1) ambition / wild ambition;
(2) greediness;

ye xin bo bo 野心勃勃
full of ambition || a flight of ambition; be obsessed with ambition; be overweeningly ambitious; burn with ambition; highflying; indulge oneself in ambition; lust for;

ye xin bu si 野心不死
cling to one's ambitious designs // one's personal ambitions are unsatisfied;

yi1 e 一愕
be taken aback;

yi ge xin yan er 一個心眼兒
(1) have one's heart set on sth;
(2) of one mind;

yi nu er qu 一怒而去
leave in anger;

yi pian bing xin 一片冰心
a pure state of mind;

yi pian cheng xin 一片誠心
in all sincerity // straight from one's heart;

yi pian chi xin 一片痴心
sheer infatuation / strong affection;

yi pian dan xin 一片丹心
a heart of pure loyalty / a leaf of red heart / a loyal heart / a piece of loyalty;

yi pian hao xin 一片好心
with the best of intentions;

yi pian po xin 一片婆心
kind heart / motherly feeling;

yi pian xiao xin 一片孝心
show one's filial piety;

yi pian zhen xin 一片真心
straight from one's heart || from the bottom of one's heart; in all sincerity; true heart;

yi shi chong dong 一時衝動
on the spur of the moment;

yi shi ji dong 一時激動
in the heat of the moment;

yi tiao xin 一條心
be at one // of one mind;

yi wang qing shen 一往情深
fall deeply in love;

yi xiang qing yuan 一廂情願
wishful thinking;

yi xin 一心
(1) heart and soul / wholeheartedly;
(2) at one / of one mind;

yi xin bu neng er yong 一心不能二用
no man can do two things at once || a man cannot spin and reel at the same time; a man cannot whistle and drink at the same time;

yi xin er yong 一心二用
keep one eye on;

yi xin wei gong 一心為公
be utterly devoted to public interests / set one's heart on the common good // wholehearted devotion to the public interest;

yi xin xiang wang 一心向往
give all one's heart to / give one's heart completely to;

yi xin yi de 一心一德
of one heart and one mind || at one; wholeheartedly and faithfully; with united will;

yi xin yi yi 一心一意
(1) wholeheartedly || at one; have one's heart in sth; heart and soul; intent on; of one heart and mind; one-minded; put one's whole heart into; single-hearted; single-minded; singleness of purpose; undivided attention; with all one's heart and mind; with body and soul; with one heart and one mind; with wholehearted devotion;
(2) be bent on;

yi yi 一意
(1) with complete devotion;
(2) stubbornly;

yi yi gu xing 一意孤行
do sth against the advice of others || act arbitrarily; be bent on having one's own way; cling obstinately to one's course; dead set on having one's own way; do one's own thing; follow one's bigoted course; go one's own way; have everything one's own way; hell-bent on having one's own way; insist on having one's own way; persist in one's course; persist in wilfully and arbitrarily; self-assertion; self-opinionated; self-willed;

take one's own course; wheel and deal; wilfully cling to one's own course;

yi zhao zhi fen 一朝之忿
a sudden burst of anger / momentary anger;

yi1 lian 依戀
be emotionally attached to sb;

yi mu 依慕
adore;

yi yi 依依
reluctant to part;

yi yi bu she 依依不捨
unwilling to part with sb;

yi1 de 醫德
medical ethics;

yi2 怡
pleasure;

yi le 怡樂
pleasures;

yi qing yang xing 怡情養性
contribute to one's peace of mind and inner tranquility;

yi qing yue xing 怡情悦性
please one's mind and delight one's spirit;

yi ran 怡然
pleasant and contented / satisfied and happy;

yi ran zi de 怡然自得
happy and contented;

yi shen 怡神
inspire peace and harmony in one's mind;

yi yi 怡怡
take delight in;

yi2 qing 移情
empathize // empathy;

yi qing bie lian 移情別戀
transfer one's affections to sb else;

yi2 dou 疑竇
doubt / suspicion;

yi huo 疑惑
(1) doubt;
(2) suspicion;
(3) puzzle;

yi ji 疑忌
suspicious and jealous;

yi lü 疑慮
anxiety / apprehension / misgivings;

yi tuan 疑團
a maze of suspicions;

yi xin 疑心
doubt / suspect // suspicion;

yi xin bing 疑心病
hypochondria;

yi xin sheng an gui 疑心生暗鬼
a supicious heart will see imaginary ghosts / he that has a great nose thinks everybody is speaking of it / suspicions create fantastic fears;

yi xin zi wu 疑心自誤
make one's own mistakes for being suspicious;

yi xin can ban 疑信參半
half in belief and half in doubt;

yi2 ai 遺愛
the love left behind by a dead person;

yi han 遺憾
feel sorry / pity / regret // regrettable;

yi hen 遺恨
feel sorry / regret // regrettable;

yi3 xiao ren zhi xin, duo jun zi zhi fu 以小人之心，度君子之腹
gauge the heart of a gentleman with one's own mean measure || like a dwarf plumbing the heart of a giant with his midget sounding rod; like the knave who uses his own yardstick to measure the motives of upright men; measure the mind of an upright man by the yardstick of a knave; measure the stature of great men by the yardstick of small men; with the heart of the mean trying to estimate what's in the heart of the great;

yi xin chuan xin, bu li wen zi 以心傳心，不立文字
the Buddhist dharma is taught through the mind, not through the written word;

yi xin huan xi 以心換心
confidence begets confidence;

yi4 e 抑遏
coerce / curb / restrain / suppress;

yi le 抑勒
repress and restrain;

yi se 抑塞
(1) give no chance to / reject;
(2) dejection / despondency;

yi ya 抑壓
coerce / curb / restrain;

yi yi 抑抑
cautious and grave;

yi yu 抑鬱
depressed / gloomy / sad and melancholy // depression / despondency;

yi zhi 抑止
check / restrain / stop / suppress;

yi zhi 抑制
control / repress / restrain;

yi zhi ji qing 抑制激情
curb one's passions;

yi zhi nu huo 抑制怒火
check one's anger / restrain one's fury;

yi4 nu 易怒
crotchety / huffy / irascible / irritable / peevish / querulous / short-tempered / snuffy / spiky / touchy // have an inflammable temper / short temper;

yi4 悒
troubled in the mind / unhappy;

yi fen 悒憤
resent / unhappy with anger;

yi men 悒悶
depressed / low-spirited;

yi yang 悒怏
dejected / depressed / grieved / sad / unhappy;

yi yi 悒悒
depressed / grieved / sad / worried / unhappy;

yi yu 悒鬱
disconsolate / melancholy / unhappy;

yi4 xin 異心
dishonesty / infidelity / insincerity;

yi4 意
inclination / intention;

yi biao 意表
expectations;

yi hui 意會
sense;

yi jing 意境
conception / frame of mind;

yi lan xin hui 意懶心灰
greatly discouraged;

yi liao 意料
expectations;

yi nian 意念
idea;

yi qi 意氣
emotion / heart / spirits;

yi qi chong tian 意氣衝天
high-spirited;

yi qi feng fa 意氣風發
high-spirited and vigorous;

yi qi ju sang 意氣沮喪
crestfallen / dejected / depressed / disheartened / dispirited // in a dejected state / in low spirits;

yi qi xiang tou 意氣相投
congenial;

yi qi yang yang 意氣揚揚
elated / in high spirits;

yi qi yong shi 意氣用事
act on impulse;

yi qi zhi zheng 意氣之爭
quarrel over a matter of emotion;

yi qi zi de 意氣自得
easy and dignified;

yi shi 意識
consciousness;

yi si 意思
(1) meaning;
(2) desire / intention / wish;

yi tai 意態
air / bearing / manner;

yi tu 意圖
design / intent / intention;

yi wai 意外
accidental / surprising / unexpected / unforeseen // accident / surprise;

yi xiang bu dao 意想不到
beyond expectation / unexpected // unexpectedly;

yi xiang 意向
inclinations / intentions;

yi xing 意興
enthusiasm / interest;

yi xing lan shan 意興闌珊
feel dispirited;

yi xu 意緒
(1) threads of thought;
(2) mood / state of mind;

yi you wei jin 意猶未盡
wish to continue doing sth one has done for a long time;

yi zhi 意旨
intent / meaning / will / wish;

yi zhi 意指
drive at;

yi zhi 意志
volition / will / will power;

yi zhi bo ruo 意志薄弱
weak-willed // have a feeble mind / have a weak character / have a weak will // feeble-minded;

yi zhi jian ding 意志堅定
firm in character / hardbitten / tough-minded // have an inflexible will;

yi zhi xiao chen 意志消沉
dejected / depressed / low-spirited / pessimistic;

yi zhuan xin hui 意轉心回
change one's mind;

yi4 fen 義憤
moral indignation / righteous anger;

yi fen tian xiong 義憤填胸
be filled with righteous indignation / feel indignant at the injustice;

yi fen tian ying 義憤填膺
be filled with righteous indignation / feel indignant at the injustice;

yi4 憶
bear in mind / recall / recollect / remember;

yi ji 憶及
call to mind / recollect / remember;

yi jiu 憶舊
recall the bygone days with nostalgia / recollect the past;

yi ku si tian 憶苦思甜
recall one's past misfortune and think over one's present happiness;

yi nian 憶念
nostalgic memory / recollection;

yi qi 憶起
call to mind / recall / remember;

yi xi 憶昔
recall the bygone days with nostalgia / recollect the past;

yi4 懌
delighted / glad / happy / pleased;

yi yue 懌悅
delighted / glad / happy / pleased;

yi4 懿
(1) fine / good / virtuous;
(2) chaste;

yi de 懿德
fine virtue;

yi wang 懿望
good reputation;

yin1 yu 陰鬱
depressed / dismal / gloomy;

yin1 愔
composed / serene / peaceful;

yin1 慇
(1) mournful / sorrowful;
(2) respectful;

yin qin 慇懃
attentive / civil / courteous / polite;

yin xin 慇心
feel for;

yin yin 殷殷

melancholy / mournful / sad / sorrowful;

yin you 殷憂

deep grief / distress / sorrow;

yin2 xin 淫心

immoral thoughts / sexual desire;

yin yu 淫慾

sexual desire / wanton desire;

yin yu guo du 淫慾過度

abandon oneself to the passion;

yin3 ce 隱惻

commiseration / sympathy;

yin ren 隱忍

bottle up one's resentment / forbear;

yin you 隱憂

latent worries;

yin zhong 隱衷

hidden and unspoken feelings;

yin4 慭

(1) willing;

(2) cautious;

ying1 ren xin 攖人心

disturb peace of mind / disturb people's hearts;

ying4 xin chang 硬心腸

hard-hearted // heart of stone;

yong1 慵

idle / indolent / lazy;

yong duo 慵惰

idle / inactive / indolent / lazy;

yong kun 慵困

tired and indolent;

yong3 ji zai xin 永記在心

remain forever in one's heart and spirit;

yong jiu xing xin lü shi chang 永久性心律失常

perpetual arrhtythmia;

yong mu 永慕

remember forever;

yong zhi bu wang 永誌不忘

bear in mind forever / remember forever;

yong3 shang xin lai 湧上心來

come up in the mind like a ground swell;

yong xiang xin tou 湧向心頭

crowd on one's mind / rise in the mind / well up in one's mind;

yong3 慂

persuade / urge;

yong4 qing 用情

appeal to emotion / feel serious about a love affair;

yong qing bu zhuan 用情不專

frivolous in the affairs of the heart;

yong xin 用心

diligently || attentively; exercise caution; pay attention; take care; with concentrated attention;

yong xin jie li 用心竭力

attentively and diligently // exhaust one's brain and energy;

yong xin liang ku 用心良苦

cudgel one's brains / lay oneself out;

yong xin si suo 用心思索

do some hard thinking / think hard;

yong xin xian e 用心險惡

have vicious ulterior motives // with malicious intent;

yong yi 用意

intention;

you1 悠

meditative / pensive / sad;

you hu 悠忽

lazy and idle;

you ran 悠然

in a leisurely manner / unhurried;

you xian 悠閒

leisurely // unhurried / unrestrained;

you you 悠悠

leisurely // slow / unhurried;

you you hu hu 悠悠忽忽

(1) spending time idly;

(2) in a trance;

you zai you zai 悠哉悠哉
free from restraint // carefree;

you1 憂
(1) grieved / mournful / pensive / sad;
(2) anxiety;
(3) worry about;
(4) anxious / apprehensive;

you chou 憂愁
melancholy / mournful / sad;

you fen 憂憤
grieved and indignant;

you guo you min 憂國憂民
be concerned about one's country and one's people;

you huan 憂患
distress / hardship / misery / suffering / trouble / worry;

you huan yu sheng 憂患餘生
survive countless worries and distresses;

you jian 憂煎
in agonies of worry;

you ju 憂懼
anxious and fearful / worried and apprehensive;

you ju wan zhuang 憂懼萬狀
extremely anxious and fearful;

you lao cheng ji 憂勞成疾
lose one's health because of care;

you le xiang gong 憂樂相共
share worries and blessings;

you lü 憂慮
anxious / apprehensive / carking / worried // anxiety / disquietude / worry;

you men 憂悶
depressed / low-spirited;

you qi 憂慼
sad and worried;

you shang 憂傷
worried and grieved;

you tian min ren 憂天憫人
worry about the destiny of mankind;

you xin 憂心
anxiety / sad heart / worry;

you xin chong chong 憂心忡忡
have a heart loaded with worry || anxiety-ridden; be oppressed by tormenting anxieties; care-laden; care-ridden; deeply grieved in heart; full of anxiety; have kittens; heavy-hearted; in dismay; laden with anxiety; sick at heart; weigh down with anxieties; with a troubled heart; worry a great lot; worry to death;

you xin lie lie 憂心烈烈
burn with sorrow;

you xin ru fen 憂心如焚
burning with anxiety || anxiety gnaws at one's heart; be killed by grief; deeply worried; devour one's heart; eat one's heart out; eat out one's heart; in a stew; sorrow-stricken; very anxious; worry oneself to death;

you xin ru jian 憂心如煎
one's heart burns with melancholy so that the pain is like that of boiling oil in one;

you yi 憂悒
cheerless / dejected / depressed / dispirited / melancholy;

you yu 憂鬱
careworn / cheerless / dejected / depressed / dispirited / melancholy;

you yu zheng 憂鬱症
bypochondriac / melancholiac;

you2 zhong 由衷
from the depth of one's heart;

you2 xing xin yan 疣性心炎
verrucous carditis;

you2 xin 遊心
think deeply into sth;

you3 gan er fa 有感而發
make a comment out of personal feeling;

you xin 有心
have a mind to / have an intention / set one's mind on;

you xin xiong 有心胸
ambitious / independent-minded;

you xin yan er 有心眼兒
shrewd / vigilant;

you yi 有意
(1) have a mind / intend;
(2) be interested / be inclined to;

you yi wu yi zhi jian 有意無意之間
consciously or unconsciously;

you4 jing you xi 又驚又喜
both alarmed and delighted;

you4 xin 右心
right heart;

you xin fang 右心房
right atrium;

you xin shi 右心室
right ventricle;

you4 宥
forgive / pardon;

you guo 宥過
excuse a mistake;

you shu 宥恕
excuse / forgive / pardon;

you4 huo ren xin 誘惑人心
tempt the hearts of the people;

yu1 xin bu an 於心不安
not to be set at rest // pertinacity;

yu xin bu ren 於心不忍
against one's conscience / can't bear to / not to have the heart to;

yu xin he ren 於心何忍
how can one bear it in one's heart / how can one bear to do it / how can one have the heart to do it;

yu xin wu kui 於心無愧
feel no compunction / have a good conscience / have nothing on one's conscience;

yu xin you kui 於心有愧
feel ashamed / have a guilty conscience / have sth on one's conscience // ashamed in the heart;

yu1 yu 紆鬱
melancholy / sad;

yu2 愉
contented / happy / pleased;

yu kuai 愉快
cheerful / delighted / happy / pleased;

yu le 愉樂
pleased and joyful;

yu yi 愉逸
happy and leisurely;

yu yue 愉悦
glad / happy / joyful // mirth;

yu2 愚
(1) foolish / silly / stupid / unintelligent / unwise;
(2) cheat / deceive / fool;

yu ben 愚笨
foolish / maladroit / stupid // folly;

yu chun 愚蠢
foolish / stupid || daft; damfool; dead from the neck up // folly;

yu chun xing wei 愚蠢行為
an act of folly;

yu dai 愚呆
blockheaded / dull / slow to learn;

yu dun 愚鈍
dull / dull-witted / obtuse / stupid;

yu mei 愚昧
benighted / ignorant / stupid;

yu nong 愚弄
have a game with sb / make a fool of sb;

yu wan 愚頑
stupid and obstinate;

yu wang 愚妄
stupid and rash;

yu2 fen wei ping 餘忿未平
one's anger is not appeased;

yu ji 餘悸
lingering fear / lingering shock;

yu nu wei xiao 餘怒未消
feel the lingering anger;

yu2 覦
strong desire for possession // covet;

yu xin chi qi 覦心熾起
covetous desires blazing up;

yu4 xin 玉心
a heart as pure as jade;

yu xin jiao jie 玉心皎潔
a pure heart is unsullied;

yu4 ai 欲愛
passion-love;

yu wang 欲望
desires / longings;

yu xiang 欲想
desires for wealth and women;

yu xin 欲心
one's desires;

yu yuan 欲願
desire / wish;

yu4 yi 寓意
moral of a story;

yu yi shen ke 寓意深刻
be pregnant with meaning;

yu4 慾
appetite / desire / greed / lust / passion;

yu hai 慾海
the sea of passion;

yu huo 慾火
passion / the fire of lust;

yu huo fen shen 慾火焚身
the fire of lust is consuming the body;

yu ling zhi hun 慾令智昏
greed can benumb reason;

yu nian 慾念
craving / desire / longing;

yu wang 慾望
appetence / aspirations / craving / desire / longing // urge;

yu4 chen chen 鬱沈沈
dejected / depressed / despondent / low-spirited;

yu ji 鬱積
pent-up feelings // smolder;

yu jie 鬱結
suffer from pent-up feelings;

yu men 鬱悶
have pent-up emotions / have pent-up thoughts;

yu tao 鬱陶
melancholy / pensive / sad // anxiously;

yu yi 鬱伊
melancholy / pensive / sad;

yu yu 鬱紆
melancholy depressed;

yu yu bu le 鬱鬱不樂
dejected / depressed / despondent / low-spirited;

yu yu gua huan 鬱鬱寡歡
feel low / mope // saturnine;

yuan1 冤
grievance;

yuan qu 冤屈
grievance;

yuan wang 冤枉
do injustice to sb / wrong sb;

yuan2 chong xing xin ji yan 原蟲性心肌炎
protozoal myocarditis;

yuan liang 原諒
excuse / forgive / pardon;

yuan4 怨
(1) hatred / resentment;
(2) complain;

yuan chou 怨仇
old enemy;

yuan du 怨毒
hatred / malice;

yuan dui 怨懟
hatred / ill will;

yuan fen 怨忿
grudge / ill will;

yuan hen 怨恨
enmity / ill will / resentment;

yuan jie 怨結
pent-up hatred;

yuan ming 怨命
blame one's fate;

yuan mu 怨慕
dissatified and full of earnest desire;

yuan qi 怨氣
dissatisfaction / resentment;

yuan tian you ren 怨天尤人
impute all faults and wrongs to others;

yuan wang 怨望
ill will;

yuan4 愿
faithful / honest / sincere / virtuous;

yuan yi 願意
(1) ready / willing;
(2) hope / want / wish;

yue4 悦
(1) delight / gratify / please;
(2) delighted / glad / gratified / happy / pleased;

yue fu 悦服
concede willingly / submit willingly;

yue le 悦樂
pleasure;

yue ren 悦人
delightful / pleasant / pleasing;

yue xin 悦心
gladden;

yue yi 悦意
(1) pleasantness;
(2) expression of happiness;

yue yu 悦豫
delighted / happy / pleased;

yue ze 悦澤
pleasantly bright;

yun4 惲
consider / deliberate;

yun mou 惲謀
plan / scheme;

yun4 慍
angry / displeased / irritated / vexed;

yun dui 慍懟
resent;

yun hen 慍恨
indignation / rancor / resentment;

yun hui 慍恚
feel resentment // rancorous;

yun nu 慍怒
angry / chagrin / displeased / irritated / mumpish;

za2 gan 雜感
random thoughts;

za nian 雜念
distracting thoughts;

zang1 xin 髒心
dirty mind / impure heart;

zang xin lan fei 髒心爛肺
dirty in character;

zao1 xin 糟心
(1) annoyed / dejected / vexed;
(2) unlucky;
(3) get into a mess;

zao4 慥
kindhearted / sincere;

zao zao 慥慥
sincere and honest / wholeheartedly;

zao4 燥
impatient / restless;

zao yu zheng 燥鬱症
bipolar;

zei2 xin 賊心
crooked mind / evil designs / evil intentions / wicked and suspicious mind / wicked heart;

zei xin bu si 賊心不死
not to give up one's gangster designs / refuse to give up one's evil designs;

zeng1 憎
abominate / detest / hate / loathe;

zeng du 憎妒
bear a jealous hatred for;

zeng hen 憎恨
abhor / abominate / detest / hate / hold a grudge against / loathe;

zeng ji 憎嫉
feel a jealous hatred for;

zeng wu 憎惡
(1) abhor / abominate / detest / execrate / hate / loathe;
(2) hate evil;

zeng xian 憎嫌
dislike / hate;

zeng yuan 憎怨
bear a grudge against / feel bitterness for;

zha1 xin 扎心
heartbreaking;

zhai1 xin 齋心
purify the mind;

zhai2 xin 宅心
intention;

zhai xin ren hou 宅心仁厚
of a kindly disposition // settle the mind with benevolence and honesty;

zhan1 zhan zi xi 沾沾自喜
complacent / smug and complacent;

zhao1 ji 招嫉
invite jealousy;

zhao yuan 招怨
incur animosity / incur grudges / inspire hatred;

zhao yuan shu di 招怨樹敵
incur animosity and make enemy;

zhao1 huang 着慌
anxious / jittery / worried;

zhao ji 着急
anxious / worried;

zhao mang 着忙
anxious / nervous / panicky;

zhe2 慴
fearful / frightened / terrified;

zhe fu 慴伏
submit out of fear;

zhe2 懾
awe-struck / fearful;

zhe fu 懾服
submit because of fear / yield from fear;

zhe xi 懾息
hold one's breath in fear;

zhe zhe 懾慴
lose one's courage in fear;

zhen1 ai 真愛
genuine affection / genuine love / true love;

zhen qing 真情
true feelings;

zhen xin 真心
sincere ‖ actual intention; from the bottom of one's heart; heartfelt; real intention; true intention; wholehearted;

zhen xin cheng yi 真心誠意
with all one's heart ‖ have one's heart in the right place; in earnest; in good faith;

zhen xin hao yi 真心好意
good intentions;

zhen xin hui gai 真心悔改
sincerely repent and earnestly reform oneself;

zhen xin shan yi 真心善意
with sincerity and good intentions ‖ open and true-hearted; sincerely and with good intentions;

zhen xin shi yi 真心實意
truly and wholeheartedly ‖ genuine and sincere; genuinely and sincerely; in earnest; in good faith; sincerely; with one's whole heart;

zhen xin zhen yi 真心真意
wholehearted ‖ from the bottom of one's heart; have a sincere desire; heartfelt; honest; with all one's soul;

zhen yi 真意
true intent;

zhen1 ai 珍愛
hold dear / love dearly / treasure;

zhen1 chen 斟愖
hesitate // hesitating;

zhen3 dao 軫悼
mourn deeply;

zhen huai 軫懷
remember with deep emotion;

zhen mu 軫慕
remember with deep emotion;

zhen nian 軫念
remember with deep emotion;

zhen xi 軫惜
have pity on / mourn with deep regret;

zhen xu 軫恤
pity deeply;

zhen you 軫憂
worried and grieved;

zhen4 bu 振怖
alarm;

zhen fei 振靡
awaken the weak and enervated;

zhen fen 振奮
(1) arouse to action;
(2) encouraging / heartening;

zhen fen ren xin 振奮人心
inspire popular morale ‖ encouraging; exciting; fill people with enthusiasm; heartening; heart-stirring; inspire people; inspiring; invigorating;

zhen4 dao 震悼
be shocked and grieved;

zhen dong ren xin 震動人心
make a great impact on people;

zhen hai 震駭
greatly shocked / greatly stunned / greatly terrified;

zhen han 震撼
shake // shaken;

zhen han ren xin 震撼人心
soul-stirring ‖ have a great impact on; stirring; thrilling;

zhen ji 震悸
shocked / terrified;

zhen jing 震驚
greatly surprised;

zhen ju 震懼
in trepidation / terrified;

zhen kong 震恐
be shocked;

zhen li 震慄
trembling from fear;

zhen nu 震怒
great infuriated // rage / wrath;

zhen she 震慴
be frightened;

zhen she 震懾
awe / frighten;

zheng1 怔
scared / stunned / terrified;

zheng ying 怔營
scared and nervous;

zheng zhong 怔忪
frightened / scared and nervous;

zheng4 xin 正心
rectification of the mind;

zheng yi gan 正義感
sense of justice / sense of righteousness;

zheng zhong xia huai 正中下懷
after sb's heart / just what one hopes for;

zhi1 xin 知心
(1) intimate // understanding;
(2) bosom friend;

zhi xin huan ming 知心換命
stick together through thick and thin;

zhi xin peng you 知心朋友
bosom friend / intimate friend;

zhi xin ren 知心人
bosom friend;

zhi1 fang xin 脂肪心
fatty heart;

zhi2 jue 直覺
intuition;

zhi li xing xin dong guo su 直立性心動過速
orthostatic tachycardia;

zhi liang 直諒
honest and understanding;

zhi2 mi bu wu 執迷不悟
hold on to sth wrong stubbornly;

zhi yi 執意
be bent on / be determined to / insist on;

zhi3 du 止妒
suppress jealousy;

zhi nu 止怒
stop anger / check anger;

zhi4 cheng 至誠
the greatest sincerity;

zhi xin 至心
the most sincere heart;

zhi yi 至意
the best and sincerest intention;

zhi4 志
(1) determination;
(2) be bent on doing sth;

zhi da cai shu 志大才疏
have high aspirations but little ability;

zhi de yi man 志得意滿
fully satisfied;

zhi qi 志氣
ambition / determination / will;

zhi qu 志趣
purpose and interest;

zhi qu xiang tou 志趣相投
people of similar purpose and interest // like-minded;

zhi tong dao he 志同道合
sharing the same ambition and purpose;

zhi yuan 志願
ambition / aspiration;

zhi4 忮
(1) jealous // jealousy;
(2) dislike;

zhi qiu 忮求
jealous and greedy;

zhi xin 忮心
jealousy;

zhi4 懥
angry / enraged / indignant / resentful;

zhong1 忪
(1) agitated;
(2) frightened;

zhong1 忠
(1) faithful / loyal;
(2) devoted / honest;

zhong cheng 忠誠
faithful and honest // be devoted to;

zhong shi 忠實
(1) loyal and faithful;
(2) reliable;

zhong shu 忠恕
magnanimity;

zhong shun 忠順
loyal and obedient;

zhong xin 忠心
loyal // devotion / faithfulness / loyalty / sincerity;

zhong xin bao guo 忠心報國
repay one's country with loyalty / work for the country heart and soul;

zhong xin chi dan 忠心赤膽
wholehearted devotion;

zhong xin geng geng 忠心耿耿
loyal and devoted ‖ faithful and conscientiously; infinitely loyal; loyal, faithful and true; most faithful and true; single-hearted; single-minded; staunch and standfast;

zhong xin wei guo 忠心為國
true and loyal to the state;

zhong xin 忠信
faithful and honest;

zhong yi 忠義
faithful and virtuous;

zhong zhen 忠貞
faithful and true;

zhong zhen bu er 忠貞不貳
loyal to sb to the end of one's life / remain faithful and true in spite of all trials;

zhong zhi 忠直
faithful and upright;

zhong1 chang 衷腸
innermost feelings;

zhong huai 衷懷
innermost feelings;

zhong qu 衷曲
inner feelings / voice of one's heart;

zhong xin 衷心
cordial / heartfelt / wholehearted;

zhong xin ai dai 衷心愛戴
love sb from the bottom of one's heart / love wholeheartedly / love with all one's heart;

zhong xin gan xie 衷心感謝
express one's sincere thanks to / thank sb from the bottom of one's heart / thank sincerely;

zhong xin man yi 衷心滿意
be sincerely satisfied with;

zhong xin yong hu 衷心擁護
give wholehearted support / support wholeheartedly;

zhong xin zhe fu 衷心折服
admire from the heart;

zhong xin zhu yuan 衷心祝願
congratulate sb heartily / sincerely wish;

zhong1 shen bu wang 終身不忘
keep in memory throughout one's life span;

zhong shen yi han 終身遺憾
one's lifelong regret;

zhong shen zhi hen 終身之恨
lifelong sorrow / one's eternal remorse;

zhong3 liu xing xin bao yan 腫瘤性心包炎
neoplastic pericarditis;

zhong4 du xing xin ji yan 中毒性心肌炎
toxic myocarditis;

zhong yi 中意
to one's liking ‖ agreeable; catch one's fancy; satisfied; suit one's fancy;

zhong4 qing 重情
attach importance to affection;

zhu3 yi 主意
idea / suggestion;

zhu4 xin 注心
concentrate attention / focus attention;

zhu yi 注意
give an eye to / mind out / pay attention to / take note of;

zhu yi li 注意力
attention;

zhuan1 xin 專心
be absorbed / concentrate one's attention / give one's mind to / put one's mind to / set one's mind to // attentive / wholehearted;

zhuan xin yi yi 專心一意
be bound up in // undivided attention;

zhuan xin yi zhi 專心一志
concentrate one's attention on;

zhuan xin zhi zhi 專心致志
do sth with all one's heart ‖ apply one's mind to; be absorbed in; be attached to sth; be bent on; be bound up in; be engrossed in; be preoccupied with; be steeped in; bend one's mind to; buckle down; bury oneself in; busy at; commit oneself to; concentrate one's attention on; deep in; devote one's attention to; devote one's mind to; devote oneself to; eager to; focus one's attention on; give one's mind to; have a good mind to do sth; keep one's mind on; mad for; occupy oneself with; peg away; put one's back into; put one's heart into; put one's life into; put one's mind into; put one's mind to; put one's whole heart and soul into; set one's heart on; set one's mind to; single-minded; steep oneself in; throw oneself heart and soul into; throw oneself into; with rapt attention; with single-hearted devotion;

zhuan yi 專一
concentrate one's attention on // single-minded // singleness;

zhuan zhu 專注
concentrate one's attention on;

zhuan4 xi wei bei 轉喜為悲
laugh on the other side of one's face / laugh on the wrong side of one's face;

zhuan xin 轉心
harbour evil thoughts / hold evil thoughts in the mind;

zhuang4 戇
simple-minded;

zhuang zhi 戇直
blunt and tactless / simple and honest / simple and upright;

zhui1 dao 追悼
commemorate the dead;

zhui hui 追悔
regret afterward / repent;

zhui hui mo ji 追悔莫及
too late to regret;

zhui nian 追念
remember with gratitude / remember with nostalgia;

zhui xiang 追想
remember nostalgically;

zhui yi 追憶
call to memory / look back / remember;

zhui1 xin qi xue 椎心泣血
deep sorrow / excruciating pains / extreme grief;

zhui4 惴
afraid / anxious / apprehensive / worried;

zhui ju 惴懼
anxious and worried / in fear and trembling;

zhui kong 惴恐
dread / fear;

zhui li 惴慄
shudder / tremble with fear;

zhui zhui 惴惴
afraid / apprehensive / fearful / timorous // feel apprehensive;

zhuo2 yi 着意
pay attention to;

zi1 jian 孜煎
fret / grieve / worry;

zi4 ai yu 自愛慾
narcissism;

zi ao qing jie 自傲情結
superiority complex;

zi bi 自卑
despise oneself / slight oneself / underestimate oneself // self-abasement / self-contempt;

zi bi gan 自卑感
inferiority complex / sense of inferiority;

zi bi qing jie 自卑情結
inferiority complex;

zi can jiu zhuo 自慚鳩拙
feel ashamed of one's lack of creative talent;

zi can xing hui 自慚形穢
feel inferior to others;

zi fa xing xin dong guo huan 自發性心動過緩
essential bradycardia;

zi jiu 自咎
blame oneself / rebuke oneself // self-reproach;

zi kuan 自寬
comfort oneself // self-consolation;

zi lian 自戀
narcissism;

zi ming de yi 自鳴得意
pleased with what one has done / pleased with what one has achieved / smug;

zi shi 自恃
presume on one's wealth or connections // hubris;

zi wei 自慰
comfort oneself // self-consolation;

zi wo zeng wu 自我憎惡
self-abhorrence;

zi xun fan nao 自尋煩惱
look for trouble;

zi yuan zi yi 自怨自艾
blame and censure oneself / complain about oneself;

zi4 恣
debauch / dissipate / throw off restraint;

zi qing 恣情
abandon oneself to passion / give rein to passion;

zi si 恣肆
licentious / wilful;

zi xing wu ji 恣行無忌
behave recklessly / throw off all restraint;

zi xing 恣性
unrestrained behaviour;

zi yi 恣意
unbridled / unscrpulous;

zi yi wang wei 恣意妄為
act wilfully;

zi yu 恣欲
give rein to lust;

zi zong 恣縱
(1) having no regard for rules;
(2) licentious / morally unrestrained;

zong4 qing 縱情
act without self-control / do as one pleases / follow one's inclinations // to one's heart's content;

zong qing xiang le 縱情享樂
glut oneself with pleasures;

zong xing 縱性
do as one pleases;

zong yin 縱淫
abandon oneself to carnal desire // debauched / dissolute;

zong yu 縱慾
abandon oneself to carnal desire // debauched / dissolute / oversexed;

zong yu wu du 縱慾無度
indulge in carnal pleasure without restraint // oversexed;

zong zi 縱恣
behave wthout restrain / give free rein to the passions;

zong zi qing yu 縱恣情慾
give rein to lust;

zui4 xin 醉心
be addicted to / be bent on / be infatuated with / be preoccupied with / be wrapped up in;

zuo3 xin 左心
left heart;

zuo xin fang 左心房
left atrium;

zuo xin shi 左心室
left ventricle;

zuo4 huai bu luan 坐懷不亂
be immune from femine charms;

zuo4 怍
(1) shame;
(2) blush;

zuo se 怍色
(1) be ashamed;
(2) blush / colour;

zuo yi 怍意
be ashamed / feel ashamed;

zuo4 zei xin xu 做賊心虛
have a guilty conscience || he that has a great nose thinks everybody is speaking of it;

Xing qi guan 性器官 Sex Organ

an1 quan qi 安全期
safe period;

an quan qi bi yun fa 安全期避孕法
rhythm method;

bai2 dai 白帶
leukorrhoea / white vaginal discharge / whites;

bai dai guo duo 白帶過多
leukorrhagia;

bai hou xing yin dao yan 白喉性陰道炎
diphtheritic vaginitis;

bao1 pi 包皮
foreskin / phimosis / prepuce;

wu bao pi 無包皮
aposthia;

bao pi gou 包皮垢
smegma;

bao pi guo chang 包皮過長
redundant prepuce;

bao pi jie shi 包皮結石
preputial calculus;

bao pi xian 包皮腺
glandulae preputiales;

bao pi xian yan 包皮腺炎
tysonitis;

bao pi yan 包皮炎
acrobystitis;

beng1 lou dai xia 崩漏帶下
uterine bleeding and vaginal discharge;

beng shi xing yang jing tou yan 崩蝕性陽莖頭炎
phagedenic balanitis;

bi1 屄
cunt / vagina / vulva;

bi1 jian 逼姦
rape;

bi liang wei chang 逼良為娼
force girls of good families to be prostitutes ‖ compel a female to engage in prostitution; force young girls of good families to prostitute themselves;

bi4 jing 閉經
amenorrhea;

chuang shang xing bi jing 創傷性閉經
traumatic amenorrhea;

chui ti xing bi jing 垂體性閉經
pituitary amenorrhea;

luan chao xing bi jing 卵巢性閉經
ovarian amenorrhea;

sheng li xing bi jing 生理性閉經
physiologic amenorrhea;

xiang dui xing bi jing 相對性閉經
relative amenorrhea;

ying yang xing bi jing 營養性閉經
dietary amenorrhea;

yuan fa bi jing 原發閉經
primary amenorrhea;

bi4 yun 避孕
avoid pregnancy // conception control / contraception;

bian4 xing 變性
degeneration / denaturation / sex change;

chuang shang xing bian xing 創傷性變性
traumatic degeneration;

ji fa xing bian xing 繼發性變性
secondary degeneration;

lao nian xing bian xing 老年性變性
senile degeneration;

shui zhong xing bian xing 水腫性變性
hydropic degeneration;

wai shang xing bian xing 外傷性變性
traumatic degeneration;

yi chuan xing bian xing 遺傳性變性
heredodegeneration;

ying hua bian xing 硬化變性
sclerotic degeneration;

bo2 qi 勃起
erection;

wan quan bo qi 完全勃起
telotism;

bo qi gong neng zhang ai 勃起功能障礙
erection dysfunction;

bu4 quan she jing 不全射精
ejaculatio deficiens;

bu wan quan xing jiao 不完全性交
coitus interruptus;

bu yu 不育
sterility;
nan xing bu yu 男性不育
male sterility;
nü xing bu yu 女性不育
atocia;

bu yu zheng 不育症
sterility;

chan3 luan 產卵
oviposition;

chi3 gu 恥骨
(1) pubic bone / pubis;
(2) sidebone;

chi mao 恥毛
one's brush / pubic hair;

chong1 xue xing tong jing 充血性痛經
congestive dysmenorrhea;

chou4 jing 臭經
bromomenorrhea;

chou wei yue jing 臭味月經
bromomenorrhea;

chu1 xue xing shu luan guan yan 出血性輸卵管炎
hemorrhagic salpingitis;

chu1 jing qi 初經期
menarche;

chu qi mei du 初期梅毒
primary syphilis;

chu3 nü 處女
virgin;

chu nü mo 處女膜
hymen || cherry; hymenal membrane; maidenhead; virginal membrane;

chu nü mo bi suo 處女膜閉鎖
imperforate hymen;

chu nü mo yan 處女膜炎
hymenitis;

chuang1 shang xing bi jing 創傷性閉經
traumatic amenorrhea;

chuang shang xing bian xing 創傷性變性
traumatic degeneration;

chuang shang xing gao wan yan 創傷性睪丸炎
traumatic orchitis;

chuang2 di zhi jian 牀第之間
in bed or in its intimacies;

chuang di zhi qing 牀第之情
conjugal affection;

chui2 ti xing bi jing 垂體性閉經
pituitary amenorrhea;

chun1 qing 春情
sexual desire;

chun yao 春藥
aphrodisiac / philter;

ci4 yang wei 次陽痿
secondary impotence;

cui1 qing yao 催情藥
philter;

dan1 gao wan 單睪丸
monorchism;

dan gao zheng 單睪症
monorchia;

dan4 dan er fa 旦旦而伐
have sexual intercourse every night;

di1 chong xing yin dao yan 滴蟲性陰道炎
trichomonas vaginitis;

di4 fang xing mei du 地方性梅毒
endemic syphilis;

di4 er qi mei du 第二期梅毒
secondary syphilis;

di san qi mei du 第三期梅毒
tertiary syphilis;

di si qi mei du 第四期梅毒
quaternary syphilis;

di yi qi mei du 第一期梅毒
primary syphilis;

dun1 lun 敦倫
sexual act between husband and wife;

duo1 gao zheng 多睪症
polyorchidism;

e4 xing mei du 恶性梅毒
luesmalign;

fan2 yan ben neng 繁衍本能
sexual drive;

fan zhi li 繁殖力
uberty;

fang2 lao guo du 房勞過度
excess of sexual intercourse;

fei1 xing bing mei du 非性病梅毒
nonvenereal syphilis;

fei2 hou xing gao wan qiao mo yan 肥厚性睪丸鞘膜炎
plastic vaginalitis;

fei hou xing shu luan guan yan 肥厚性輸卵管炎
hypertrophic salpingitis;

fu4 gao 附睪
epididymis;

fu gao qie chu 附睪切除
epidiclymectomy;

fu gao yan 附睪丸
epididymitis;

fu jian yan 附件炎
adnexitis;

fu4 gao wan 副睪丸
epididymis;

fu gao wan yan 副睪丸炎
epididymitis;

fu4 nü lin bing 婦女淋病
baptothecorrhea;

gang1 jiao 肛交
sodomy;

gao1 wan 睪丸
testis || achers; acres; apples; balls; ballocks; bollocks; the clappers; the clusters; the cobblers; the cods; the danglers; the dusters; the family jewels; the flowers; the gollies; the knackers; the marbles; the pills; the plums; testicles; the wedding kit; the wedding tackle;

fu gao wan 副睪丸
epididymis;

shou zu gao wan 受阻睪丸
obstructed testis;

you zou xing gao wan 游走性睪丸
retractile testis;

gao wan ai 睪丸癌
cancer of the testis;

gao wan bing 睪丸病
orchiopathy;

gao wan dong mai 睪丸動脈
arteria testicularis;

gao wan liu 睪丸瘤
testicular tumour;

gao wan mo 睪丸膜
tunicae testis;

gao wan qiao mo yan 睪丸鞘膜炎
vaginalitis;

fei hou xing gao wan qiao mo yan 肥厚性睪丸鞘膜炎
plastic vaginalitis;

nian lian xing gao wan qiao mo yan 黏連性睪丸鞘膜炎
periorchitis adhaesiva;

gao wan su 睪丸素
testosterone;

gao wan tong 睪丸痛
didymalgia;

gao wan tu chu 睪丸突出
orchiocele;

gao wan wei jiang 睪丸未降
undescended testis;

gao wan wei suo 睪丸萎縮
atrophia testiculi;

gao wan xia chui 睪丸下垂
orchidoptosis;

gao wan yan 睪丸炎
orchitis;

chuang shang xing gao wan yan 創傷性睪丸炎
traumatic orchitis;

fu gao wan yan 副睪丸炎
epididymitis;

zhuan yi xing gao wan yan 轉移性睪丸炎
metastatic orchitis;

gao wan ying bian 睪丸硬變
orchioscirrhus;

gao wan zheng 睪丸症
orchidism;

ju gao wan zheng 巨睪丸症
macro-orchidism;

gao wan zhong liu 睪丸腫瘤
orchiocele;

ge1 bao pi 割包皮
circumcision;

gong1 neng xing yang wei 功能性陽痿
functional impotence;

gou3 he 苟合
illicit sexual act;

gui1 tou 龜頭
glans penis;

gui tou yan 龜頭炎
balanitis;

guo4 chang bao pi 過長包皮
redundant prepuce;

hai3 mian ti 海綿體
corpus cavernosum and spongiosum;

hao4 se 好色
fond of pleasures of flesh // lascivious / lickerish / prurient;

hou4 qi mei du 後期梅毒
late syphilis;

hua1 liu bing 花柳病
venereal disease;

hua zhu ye yang wei 花燭夜陽痿
wedding night impotence;

huai2 chun 懷春
(1) become sexually awakened;
(2) begin to think of love // in love;

huan4 xing 換性
transsexual;

ji1 fu zhi qin 肌膚之親
intimacy arising from sexual intercourse;

ji2 xing wai yin kui yang 急性外陰潰瘍
ulcus vulvae acutum;

ji4 fa xing bian xing 繼發性變性
secondary degeneration;

ji fa xing tong jing 繼發性痛經
secondary dysmenorrhea;

ji fa xing xing xiu ke 繼發性休克
secondary shock;

ji fa xing yang wei 繼發性陽痿
secondary impotence;

ji fa xing yin jing yi chang bo qi 繼發性陰莖異常勃起
secondary priapism;

jia3 lin bing 假淋病
pseudogonorrhea;

jia yue jing 假月經
pseudomenstruation;

jiao1 gou 交媾
copulation / sexual intercourse || bonk; coitus; screw;

jiao gou kun nan 交媾困難
dyspareunia;

jiao gou zhong duan 交媾中斷
onanism;

jiao he 交合
sexual intercourse;

jie1 jie xing shu luan guan yan 結節性輸卵管炎
nodular salpingitis;

jie4 se 戒色
abstain from carnal pleasure;

jing1 bi 經閉
amenorrhea;

jing jue qi 經絕期
menopause;

jing qian jin zhang 經前緊張
premenstrual tension;

jing tong 經痛
menstrual pain;

jing1 guan 精管
seminal duct;

jing nang 精囊
gonecystis / seminal vesicle;

jing nang hua nong 精囊化膿
gonecystopyosis;

jing nang ji nong 精囊積膿
pyovesiculosis;

jing nang shi 精囊石
gonecystolith;

jing nang yan 精囊炎
spermatocystitis;
shu jing guan jing nang yan 輸精管精囊炎
vasovesicalitis;

jing nang zhou yan 精囊周炎
perivesiculitis;

jing shen xing yang wei 精神性陽痿
psychic impotence;

jing ye 精液
semen / sperm;
nong xing jing ye 膿性精液
pyospermia;

jing ye bing 精液病
spermatopathia;

jing ye guo duo 精液過多
polyspermia;

jing ye jiang 精液漿
seminal plasma;

jing ye li 精液粒
seminal granules;

jing ye lou 精液瘻
spermatic fistula;

jing ye que fa 精液缺乏
aspermia;

jing ye sheng cheng 精液生成
gonepoiesis;

jing ye yi chang 精液異常
dysspermia;

jing zi 精子
sperm;

jing zi bao nang 精子包囊
spermatophore;

jing zi fa sheng 精子發生
spermatogenesis;

jing zi fang chu 精子放出
spermiation;

jing zi guo shao 精子過少
spermacrasia;

jing zi jian shao 精子減少
oligozoospermatism;

jing zi nang zhong 精子囊腫
spermatocyst;

jing zi pai fang 精子排放
spermiation;

jing zi po huai 精子破壞
spermatolysis;

jing zi que fa 精子缺乏
spermacrasia;

jing zi rong jie 精子溶解
spermatolysis;

jing zi sheng cheng 精子生成
spermatogenesis;

jing zi xing cheng 精子形成
spermateliosis;

jing zi yi chang 精子異常
dysspermia;

jing4 luan xing tong jing 痙攣性痛經
spasmodic dysmenorrhea;

ju4 gao wan zheng 巨睪丸症
macro-orchidism;

ju yin di 巨陰蒂
megaloclitoris;

ju yin jing 巨陰莖
macrophallus;

jue2 jing 絕經
menopause;
zao fa jue jing 早發絕經
menopause praecox;

kou3 jiao 口交
oral sex ‖ a blow job; a gob job; a head job; a skull job; blow sb; felatio; give head; gobble sb; lip service; plate sb;

kui4 yang xing wai yin yan 潰瘍性外陰炎
ulcerative vulvitis;

lai2 yue jing 來月經
come around / come round;

lan4 jiao 濫交
sleep around // promiscuous // promiscuity;

lao3 nian xing bian xing 老年性變性
senile degeneration;

lao nian xing yin dao yan 老年性陰道炎
senile vaginitis;

lin2 bing 淋病
gonorrhea / the clap;
jia lin bing 假淋病
pseudogonorrhea;

lou4 jing 漏精
spermatorrhea;

lou4 yin pi 露陰癖
exhibitionism;

lou yin zheng 露陰症
exhibitionism;

luan3 chao xing bi jing 卵巢性閉經
ovarian amenorrhea;

luan chao xing tong jing 卵巢性痛經
ovarian dysmenorrhea;

luo4 hong 落紅
bleed during the first sexual intercourse;

mei2 du 梅毒
lues / lues venerea / syphilis;
chu qi mei du 初期梅毒
primary syphilis;
di fang xing mei du 地方性梅毒
endemic syphilis;
di er qi mei du 第二期梅毒
secondary syphilis;
di san qi mei du 第三期梅毒
tertiary syphilis;
di si qi mei du 第四期梅毒
quaternary syphilis;
di yi qi mei du 第一期梅毒
primary syphilis;
e xing mei du 惡性梅毒
luesmalign;
fei xing bing mei du 非性病梅毒
nonvenereal syphilis;
hou qi mei du 後期梅毒
late syphilis;
qian fu mei du 潛伏梅毒
latent syphilis;
shi zhi xing mei du 實質性梅毒
parenchymatous syphilis;
shou zhang mei du 手掌梅毒
palmar syphilis;
xian tian xing mei du 先天性梅毒
congenital syphilis;
yi chuan mei du 遺傳梅毒
heredolues;
zao qi mei du 早期梅毒
early syphilis;
zao qi qian fu mei du 早期潛伏梅毒
early latent syphilis;
zu di mei du 足底梅毒
plantar syphilid;

mei du jie jie 梅毒結節
syphilitic node;

mei du liu 梅毒瘤
gummy tumour;

mei du zhen 梅毒疹
syphilid;

mei2 jun xing yin dao yan 霉菌性陰道炎
colpitis mycotica;

meng4 li hua jing 夢裏滑精
nocturnal emission;

mi2 lan xing wai yin yan 糜爛性外陰炎
erosive vulvitis;

mi lan xing yin jing tou yan 糜爛性陰莖頭炎
erosive balanitis;

mo4 yang tong jing 膜樣痛經
membranous dysmenorrhea;

nan2 xing bing 男性病
andropathy;

nan xing bo qi zhang ai 男性勃起障礙
male erection disorder;

nan xing bu yu 男性不育
male sterility;

nan xing sheng zhi qi 男性生殖器
male genital organs;

nan zi lin bing 男子淋病
bapturethrorrhea;

nei4 fen mi xing yang wei 內分泌性陽痿
endocrine impotence;

nian2 lian xing gao wan qiao mo yan 黏連性睾

丸鞘膜炎
periorchitis adhaesiva;

nian lian xing yin dao yan 黏連性陰道炎
adhesive vaginitis;

nong2 xing jing ye 膿性精液
pyospermia;

nü3 sheng zhi qi 女生殖器
muliebria;

nü xing bu yu 女性不育
atocia;

nü xing tong xing lian 女性同性戀
lesbianism;

nü xing xing leng gan 女性性冷感
frigidity;

nü yin 女陰
cunnus;

nü yin lang chuang 女陰狼瘡
esthiomene;

nü yin lie 女陰裂
vulval cleft;

nü yin sao yang 女陰瘙癢
pruritus vulvae;

pai2 luan 排卵
ovulate;

pin1 姘
illicit intercourse;

pin shi 姘識
have illicit intercourse with sb;

po4 shen 破身
the first sexual intercourse of a man or woman;

qi4 zhong xing yin dao yan 氣腫性陰道炎
colpitis emphysematosa;

qi4 zhi xing yang wei 器質性陽痿
organic impotence;

qian2 fu mei du 潛伏梅毒
latent syphilis;

qing2 jian 情姦
adultery from mutual attraction;

qing yu 情慾
sensual desire / sexual passion;

que1 jing 缺精
aspermic;

re4 bing shang jing 熱病傷精
consumption of body fluid caused by febrile diseases;

ren2 gong shou jing 人工受精
artificial insemination;

ren gong shou yun 人工受孕
artificial insemination;

rou4 yu 肉慾
corporeal appetites;

se4 qing 色情
lust / sexual passion // saucy / sexy;

se qing kuang 色情狂
sex maniac;

se yu 色慾
lust / sexual desire / sexual passion;

shao3 jing ye zheng 少精液症
oligospermia;

shao jing zheng 少精症
oligozoospermatism;

shao jing zi zheng 少精子症
oligospermatism;

she4 jing 射精
ejaculation ‖ ejaculation of semen; gonobolia; spermatization;

bu quan she jing 不全射精
ejaculatio deficiens;

she jing chi huan 射精遲緩
ejaculatio retardata;

she ging guo huan 射精過緩
bradyspermatism;

she jing guo zao 射精過早
ejaculatio praecox / premature ejaculation;

she jing xu huan 射精徐緩
bradyspermatism;

she jing zhang ai 射精障礙
defective ejaculation;

shen2 jing yuan xing xing zao shu 神經源性性早熟
neurogenic precocious puberty;

shen jing yuan xing yang wei 神經源性陽痿
neurogenic impotence;

sheng1 li xing bi jing 生理性閉經
physiologic amenorrhea;

sheng zhi 生殖
procreation;

sheng zhi guan 生殖管
gonaduct;

sheng zhi li 生殖力
fecundity;

sheng zhi qi 生殖器
genital organs / genitals / reproductive organs;
nan xing sheng zhi qi 男性生殖器
male genital organs;
nü sheng zhi qi 女生殖器
muliebria;
wu sheng zhi qi 無生殖器
agenosomia;

sheng zhi qi fa yu bu quan 生殖器發育不全
agenosomia;

sheng zhi qi fa yu guo du 生殖器發育過度
hypergenitalism;

sheng zhi qi fa yu zhang ai 生殖器發育障礙
dysgenitalism;

sheng zhi qi guan 生殖器官
reproductive organ;

sheng zhi qi guo xiao 生殖器過小
microgenitalism;

shi1 zhen xing wai yin yan 濕疹型外陰炎
eczematiform vulvitis;

shi2 zhi xing mei du 實質性梅毒
parenchymatous syphilis;

shi zhi xing shu luan guan yan 實質性輸卵管炎
parenchymatous salpingitis;

shou3 yin 手淫
masturbate / wank // masturbation;

shou zhang mei du 手掌梅毒
palmar syphilis;

shou4 jing 受精
(1) fecundation / insemination;
(2) impregnate;
ren gong shou jing 人工受精
artificial insemination;

shou jing luan 受精卵
amphicytula;

shou yun 受孕
(1) conception / insemination / pregnancy;
(2) impregnate;
ren gong shou yun 人工受孕
artificial insemination;

shou zu gao wan 受阻睪丸
obstructed testis;

shou4 jing 授精
insemination;

shu1 jing guan 輸精管
deferent duct;

shu jing guan jie zha 輸精管結紮
ligation of spermatic duct;

shu jing guan jing nang yan 輸精管精囊炎
vasovesicalitis;

shu luan guan 輸卵管
oviduct;

shu luan guan yan 輸卵管炎
salpingitis;
chu xue xing shu luan guan yan 出血性輸卵管炎
hemorrhagic salpingitis;
fei hou xing shu luan guan yan 肥厚性輸卵管炎
hypertrophic salpingitis;
jie jie xing shu luan guan yan 結節性輸卵管炎
nodular salpingitis;
shi zhi xing shu luan guan yan 實質性輸卵管炎
parenchymatous salpingitis;
yi liu xing shu luan guan yan 溢流性輸卵管炎
salpingitis profluens;

shui3 zhong xing bian xing 水腫性變性
hydropic degeneration;

si1 chu 私處
private parts;

sui2 yi xing jiao 隨意性交
casual sex;

tang2 niao bing xing wai yin yan 糖尿病性外陰炎
diabetic vulvitis;

tang niao bing xing yang wei 糖尿病性陽痿
diabetic impotence;

tang niao bing xing yin jing tou yan 糖尿病性陰莖頭炎
diabetic balanitis;

tao1 yin 慆淫
live a licentious life;

te4 fa xing xing zao shu 特發性性早熟
idiopathic precocious puberty;

ting2 jing 停經
menolipsis;

tong1 jian 通姦
commit adultery / fornicate / have illicit sexual intercourse // adultery / conjugal infidelity / marital infidelity;

tong2 xing lian 同性戀
homoerotism / homosexuality;

tong xing xing yu 同性性慾
homoerotism;

tong xing xing zao shu 同性性早熟
isosexual precocious puberty;

tong4 jing 痛經
dysmenorrhea;

chong xue xing tong jing 充血性痛經
congestive dysmenorrhea;

ji fa xing tong jing 繼發性痛經
secondary dysmenorrhea;

jing luan xing tong jing 痙攣性痛經
spasmodic dysmenorrhnea;

luan chao xing tong jing 卵巢性痛經
ovarian dysmenorrhea;

mo yang tong jing 膜樣痛經
membranous dysmenorrhea;

yan xing tong jing 炎性痛經
inflammatory dysmenorrhea;

yuan fa xing tong jing 原發性痛經
primary dysmenorrhea;

zi fa xing tong jing 自發性痛經
essential dysmenorrhea;

tuo1 xie xing yin dao yan 脫屑性陰道炎
desquamative inflammatory vaginitis;

wai4 shang xing bian xing 外傷性變性
traumatic degeneration;

wai yin bai ban zheng 外陰白斑症
leukoplakia vulvae;

wai yin bing 外陰病
vulvopathy;

wai yin kui yang 外陰潰瘍
ulcus vulvae;

ji xing wai yin kui yang 急性外陰潰瘍
ulcus vulvae acutum;

wai yin lie 外陰裂
vulval cleft;

wai yin sao yang 外陰瘙癢
pruitus vulvae;

wai yin yan 外陰炎
vulvitis;

kui yang xing wai yin yan 潰瘍性外陰炎
ulcerative vulvitis;

mi lan xing wai yin yan 糜爛性外陰炎
erosive vulvitis;

shi zhen xing wai yin yan 濕疹型外陰炎
eczematiform vulvitis;

tang niao bing xing wai yin yan 糖尿病性外陰炎
diabetic vulvitis;

wei suo xing wai yin yan 萎縮性外陰炎
atrophic vulvitis;

wai yin yin dao yan 外陰陰道炎
vulvovaginitis;

wai zhu jun yin dao yan 外珠菌陰道炎
candidal vaginitis;

wei3 suo xing wai yin yan 萎縮性外陰炎
atrophic vulvitis;

wei suo xing yin dao yan 萎縮性陰道炎
atrophic vaginitis;

wan2 quan bo qi 完全勃起
telotism;

wu2 bao pi 無包皮
aposthia;

wu gao 無睪
eunuchism;

wu gao wan 無睪丸
anorchia;

wu gao zheng 無睪症
anorchidism;

wu luan chao 無卵巢
anovarism;

wu luan xing yue jing 無卵性月經
nonovulational menstruation;

wu pai luan 無排卵
anovulation;

wu pai luan xing yue jing 無排卵性月經
nonovulational menstruation;

wu sheng zhi qi 無生殖器
agenosomia;

wu3 se dai 五色帶
multicoloured vaginal discharge;

xi4 jun xing yin dao bing 細菌性陰道病
bacterial vaginosis;

xia4 bu 下部
the private parts;

xia gan 下疳
venereal ulver;

xia shen 下身
the privates;

xia ti 下體
(1) the privates;
(2) genitals;

xian1 tian xing mei du 先天性梅毒
congenital syphilis;

xiang1 dui xing bi jing 相對性閉經
relative amenorrhea;

xiao3 yin chun 小陰唇
nympha;

xiao yin chun yan 小陰唇炎
nymphitis;

xiao yin jing 小陰莖
microphallus;

xie2 yin 邪淫
lewdness / licentiousness // lustful;

xing2 fang 行房
have sexual relations with one's legal spouse;

xing jing 行經
in the period;

xing4 性
sex;

xing ai 性愛
sexual love;

xing ben neng 性本能
sexual instinct;

xing bian tai 性變態
sex perversion;

xing bie 性別
gender / sex || sexual distinction; sexuality;

xing bie kong zhi 性別控制
sex control;

xing bing 性病
vernereal disease;

xing bing chuang 性病瘡
venereal sore;

xing bo xue 性剝削
sexploitation;

xing chong dong 性衝動
sex impulse / sexual drive / sexual impulse;

xing dao cuo 性倒錯
sexopathy;

xing fan she 性反射
sexual reflex;

xing fan zui 性犯罪
sexual offence;

xing gan 性感
sex appeal // dishy / sexy;

xing gan que shi 性感缺失
anorgasmy;

xing gao chao 性高潮
climax || come; come off; cum; orgasm;

xing gong neng zhang ai 性功能障礙
sexual disorder / sexual dysfunction;

性器官 *Sex Organ*

xing he er meng 性荷爾蒙
sex hormone;

xing ji su 性激素
sex hormone;

xing jiao 性交
copulation / sexual intercourse ‖ act of love; action; amorous congress; amorous rites; aphrodisia; approach; art of pleasure; balling; caress; carnal acquaintance; carnal connection; carnal engagement; carnal enjoyment; carnal knowledge; carnalize; coitus; compress; concubitus; congress; conjugal relations; conjugal rites; conjugal visit; conjugate; connection; consummation; conversation; conpulate; conpulation; crouch with; deed of kind; do a kindness to; do it; do some good for oneself; do the chores; effect intromission; enjoy a woman; familiar with; federate; fix her plumbing; foraminate; foregather; fruit that made men wise; funch; game; get into; get it on; get one's oats; go all the way; go the limit; go the whole route; go to bed with; gratification; grease the wheel; greens; have a bit; have carnal knowledge of; have one's will of a woman; have relations; improper intercourse; in Abraham's bosom; in bed; intercourse; intimate with; jump; keeping company; larks in the night; last favours; lewd infusion; lie with; life one's leg; light the lamp; love life; lovemaking; make it; make love; make someone; make out; make time with; marital duty; matinee; meaningful relationships; night work; on the make; pareunia; perform; play; play at in-and-out; play doctor; please; pluck; possess carnally; rites of love; scale; score; see; service; sex experience; sexual intimacy; sleep together; switch; the bee is in the hive; the facts of life; tie the true lover's knot; union; venereal act; what Eve did with Adam; work;

bu wan quan xing jiao 不完全性交
coitus interruptus;

sui yi xing jiao 隨意性交
casual sex;

xing jiao kong bu 性交恐怖
coitophobia;

xing jiao xing wei 性交行為
sex act;

xing jiao lü 性焦慮
gender dysphoria;

xing jiao yu 性教育
sex education / sexual education;

xing jie chu 性接觸
sexual intercourse;

xing jin ji 性禁忌
sex taboo;

xing kui yang 性潰瘍
venereal ulcer;

xing leng gan 性冷感
frigidity;

nü xing xing leng gan 女性性冷感
frigidity;

xing leng gan zheng 性冷感症
frigidity;

xing mei li 性魅力
sex appeal;

xing neng li 性能力
potency;

xing nüe dai 性虐待
sexual abuse;

xing nüe dai kuang 性虐待狂
sadism;

xing pi 性癖
idiosyncrasy / one's peculiar likes and dislikes;

xing qi 性器
sexual organs;

xing qi guan 性器官
sexual organs ‖ genitals; reproductive organs;

xing qing xiang 性傾向
sexual proclivity;

xing sao rao 性騷擾
sexual harassment // be molested / be physically molested / be sexually harassed;

xing sheng huo 性生活
sex life / sexual life;

xing wei sheng 性衛生
sexual hygiene;

xing wu neng 性無能
impotent;

xing xiang **性向**
disposition;

xing xin li fa yu **性心理發育**
psychosexual development;

xing xin li zhang ai **性心理障礙**
psychosexual disorder;

xing xing wei **性行為**
sex instinct act / sexual behaviour;

xing xiu ke **性休克**
shock;

ji fa xing xing xiu ke **繼發性休克**
secondary shock;

xing xuan zhe **性選擇**
apolegamy;

xing xue **性學**
sexology;

xing yu **性慾**
lust / sexual appetite / sexual desire / sexual urge;

tong xing xing yu **同性性慾**
homoerotism;

you er xing yu **幼兒性慾**
infantile sexuality;

xing yu chong dong **性慾衝動**
sexual impulse;

xing yu dao cuo **性慾倒錯**
paraphilia;

xing yu fa sheng **性慾發生**
erotogenesis;

xing yu gao chao **性慾高潮**
orgasm;

xing yu jian tui **性慾減退**
hyposexuality;

xing yu yi chang **性慾異常**
sexopathy;

xing yu zhang ai **性慾障礙**
sexual desire disorder;

xing zao shu **性早熟**
sexual precocity;

shen jing yuan xing xing zao shu **神經源性性早熟**
neurogenic precocious puberty;

te fa xing xing zao shu **特發性性早熟**
idiopathic precocious puberty;

tong xing xing zao shu **同性性早熟**
isosexual precocious puberty;

zhen xing xing zao shu **真性性早熟**
true precocious puberty;

xing zhang ai **性障礙**
sexual disorder;

yan2 xing tong jing **炎性痛經**
inflammatory dysmenorrhea;

yang2 jing **陽莖**
aedeagus;

yang jin bo qi **陽莖勃起**
hard-on;

yang jing tou yan **陽莖頭炎**
balanitis;

beng shi xing yang jing tou yan **崩蝕性陽莖頭炎**
phagedenic balanitis;

yang ju **陽具**
dick || jigger; joy-stick; kidney-wiper; middle leg; mole; nudger; padlock; tadger; tail; third leg; three-piece suit; tinkler; todger; wanger; weapon; wee man; wick; wille; willy; winkie; winky; yard; John Thomas; Mr Sausage; necessaries; one's old fellow; one's peter; one's sexing-piece; corey; dangler; donger; male reproductive organ; Percy; short arm;

yang wei **陽痿**
impotence;

ci yang wei **次陽痿**
secondary impotence;

gong neng xing yang wei **功能性陽痿**
functional impotence;

hua zhu ye yang wei **花燭夜陽痿**
wedding night impotence;

ji fa xing yang wei **繼發性陽痿**
secondary impotence;

jing shen xing yang wei **精神性陽痿**
psychic impotence;

nei fen mi xing yang wei **內分泌性陽痿**
endocrine impotence;

qi zhi xing yang wei **器質性陽痿**
organic impotence;

shen jing yuan xing yang wei **神經源性陽**

痿
neurogenic impotence;
tang niao bing xing yang wei 糖尿病性陽痿
diabetic impotence;
yuan fa xing yang wei 原發性陽痿
primary impotence;

yang wu 陽物
penis;

ye4 jian yin jing bo qi 夜間陰莖勃起
nocturnal penile tumescence;

yi1 ye qing 一夜情
one-night stand;

yi2 chuan mei du 遺傳梅毒
heredolues;

yi chuan xing bian xing 遺傳性變性
heredodegeneration;

yi jing 遺精
gonacratia / seminal emission || emission;

yi jing zao xie 遺精早泄
emission and premature ejaculation;

yi4 xing pi 易性癖
transsexualism;

yi4 liu xing shu luan guan yan 溢流性輸卵管炎
salpingitis profluens;

yin1 bu 陰部
vagina / the private part || fanny; fudd; front bottom; front passage; grumble and grunt; hole; little man in the boat; minge; mole-catcher; mott; muff; pussy; quim; slit; slot; sluice; tenuc; the private parts; twam; twammy; twim; twot; winker; yoni;

yin1 bu kui yang 陰部潰瘍
pudendal ulcer;

yin bu lie 陰部裂
pudendal fissure;

yin bu shan 陰部疝
pudendal hernia;

yin chun 陰唇
labia / lips of the vulva;
xiao yin chun 小陰唇
nympha;

yin chun lian he 陰唇連合
comissura labiorum pudendi;

yin chun long qi 陰唇隆起
labial swelling;

yin chun shan 陰唇疝
labial hernia;

yin dao 陰道
vagina;

yin dao bi 陰道襞
vaginal fold;
zhi chang yin dao bi 直腸陰道襞
rectovaginal fold;

yin dao bing 陰道病
vaginosis;
xi jun xing yin dao bing 細菌性陰道病
bacterial vaginosis;

yin dao chu xue 陰道出血
vaginal hemorrhage;

yin dao gan zao 陰道乾燥
colpoxerosis;

yin dao ge 陰道隔
vaginal septum;
zhi chang yin dao ge 直腸陰道隔
rectovaginal septum;

yin dao ji ceng 陰道肌層
tunica muscularis vaginae;

yin dao ji ceng yan 陰道肌層炎
myocolpitis;

yin dao ji nong 陰道積膿
pyocolpos;

yin dao ji qi 陰道積氣
aerocolpos;

yin dao ji shui 陰道積水
hydrocolpos;

yin dao ji xue 陰道積血
hematocolpos;

yin dao jing luan 陰道痙攣
colpospasm;

yin dao kou 陰道口
vaginal orifice;

yin dao kuo zhang 陰道擴張
colpectasia;

yin dao lou 陰道瘻
vaginal fistula;
zhi chang yin dao lou 直腸陰道瘻
rectovaginal fistula;

yin dao pang guang yan 陰道膀胱炎
colpocystitis;

yin dao pang yan 陰道旁炎
paravaginitis;

yin dao qiang 陰道腔
vaginal canal;

yin dao shan 陰道疝
vaginal hernia;
zhi chang yin dao shan 直腸陰道疝
rectovaginal hernia;

yin dao tong 陰道痛
colpodynia / vaginal pain;

yin dao tuo chui 陰道脫垂
colpoptosis;

yin dao xia zhai 陰道狹窄
colpostenosis;

yin dao yan 陰道炎
vaginal inflammation / vaginitis;
bai hou xing yin dao yan 白喉性陰道炎
diphtheritic vaginitis;
di chong xing yin dao yan 滴蟲性陰道炎
trichomonas vaginitis;
fei hou xing yin dao yan 肥厚性陰道炎
pachyvaginitis;
gong jing yin dao yan 宮頸陰道炎
cervicovaginitis;
ke li zhuang yin dao yan 顆粒狀陰道炎
granular vaginitis;
lao nian xing yin dao yan 老年性陰道炎
senile vaginitis;
mei jun xing yin dao yan 霉菌性陰道炎
colpitis mycotica;
nian lian xing yin dao yan 黏連性陰道炎
adhesive vaginitis;
nian zhu jun yin dao yan 念珠菌陰道炎
candidal vaginitis;
qi zhong xing yin dao yan 氣腫性陰道炎
colpitis emphysematosa;
tuo xie xing yin dao yan 脱屑性陰道炎
desquamative inflammatory vaginitis;
wai yin yin dao yan 外陰陰道炎
vulvovaginitis;
wei suo xing yin dao yan 萎縮性陰道炎
atrophic vaginitis;

yin dao zhou wei yan 陰道周圍炎
pericolpitis;

yin di 陰蒂
clitoris;
ju yin di 巨陰蒂
megaloclitoris;

yin di bao pi 陰蒂包皮
preputium clitoridis;

yin di fei da 陰蒂肥大
clitorimegaly;

yin di ti 陰蒂體
corpus clitoridis;

yin di tou 陰蒂頭
glans clitoridis;

yin di yan 陰蒂炎
clitoritis;

yin he 陰核
the clitoris;

yin hu 陰戶
vagina / the female reproductive organ;

yin jing 陰莖
dick / penis;
ju yin jing 巨陰莖
macrophallus;
xiao yin jing 小陰莖
microphallus;

yin jing bao pi 陰莖包皮
prepuce;

yin jing bei 陰莖背
dorsum penis;

yin jing bo qi 陰莖勃起
penile tumescence;
ye jian yin jing bo qi 夜間陰莖勃起
nocturnal penile tumescence;

yin jing chu xue 陰莖出血
phallorrhagia;

yin jing fan she 陰莖反射
penis reflex;

yin jing gen 陰莖根
radix penis;

yin jing jiao 陰莖腳
crus penis;

yin jing jing 陰莖頸
cervix glandis;

yin jing lie 陰莖裂
penischisis;

yin jing qiu 陰莖球
bulb of penis;

yin jing tong 陰莖痛
phallalgia;

yin jing tou 陰莖頭
head of penis;

yin jing tou yan 陰莖頭炎
balanitis;

mi lan xing yin jing tou yan 糜爛性陰莖頭炎
erosive balanitis;

tang niao bing xing yin jing tou yan 糖尿病性陰莖頭炎
diabetic balanitis;

yin jing tui suo 陰莖退縮
phallocrypsis;

yin jing wan qu 陰莖彎曲
phallocampsis;

yin jing yan 陰莖炎
penitis;

yin jing yi chang bo qi 陰莖異常勃起
priapism;

ji fa xing yin jing yi chang bo qi 繼發性陰莖異常勃起
secondary priapism;

yin jing zhong 陰莖腫
phalloncus;

yin mao 陰毛
public hair ‖ feathers; pubis; short hairs; short-and-curlies; turf;

yin men 陰門
vaginal orifice / vulva;

yin nang 陰囊
scrotum;

yin nang liu 陰囊瘤
oscheoma;

yin nang long qi 陰囊隆起
scrotal swelling;

yin nang shan 陰囊疝
scrotal hernia;

yin nang shui zhong 陰囊水腫
hydrocele;

yin nang yan 陰囊炎
oscheitis;

yin nang zhong da 陰囊腫大
oscheocele;

yin wei 陰痿
impotence;

yin2 淫
(1) dissolute / lascivious / lewd / licentious;
(2) obscene / pornoqraphic;
(3) debauch / seduce;

yin ben 淫奔
elope;

yin dang 淫蕩
lewd and libidinous / licentious;

yin fang 淫放
give free rein to the passion;

yin hui 淫穢
dirty / obscene;

yin le 淫樂
carnal pleasures;

yin luan 淫亂
debauchery;

yin luan zheng 淫亂症
nymphomania;

yin wei 淫猥
indecent / obscene / pornographic;

yin xi 淫戲
sexual intercourse;

yin yi du ri 淫逸度日
pass days with luxurious ease;

yin3 gao zheng 隱睾症
cryptorchidism / cryptorchismus;

yin xing yue jing 隱性月經
cryptomenorrhea;

ying2 yang xing bi jing 營養性閉經
dietary amenorrhea;

ying4 hua bian xing 硬化變性
sclerotic degeneration;

you2 zou xing gao wan 游走性睾丸
retractile testis;

you4 er xing yu 幼兒性慾
infantile sexuality;

yuan2 fa bi jing 原發閉經
primary amenorrhea;

yuan fa xing tong jing 原發性痛經
primary dysmenorrhea;

yuan fa xing yang wei 原發性陽痿
primary impotence;

yue4 jing 月經
menstruation || beno; bloody Mary; blue days; courses; cramps; discharge; domestic afflictions; effluvium; the flowers; her time; holy week; little friend; menses; monthlies; monthly courses; mother-nature; periods; problem days; roses; show; terms; the curse; the female complaint; the female disorder; the female problem; the female trouble; the flowers; the illness; the thing; wallflower week;

chou wei yue jing 臭味月經
bromomenorrhea;

jia yue jing 假月經
pseudomenstruation;

wu luan xing yue jing 無卵性月經
nonovulational menstruation;

wu pai luan xing yue jing 無排卵性月經
nonovulational menstruation;

yin xing yue jing 隱性月經
cryptomenorrhea;

zheng chang yue jing 正常月經
eumenorrhea;

yue jing bi zhi 月經閉止
absence of menses / amenorrhea;

yue jing bing 月經病
emmeniopathy;

yue jing bu tiao 月經不調
menoxenia / irregular menses;

yue jing guo duo 月經過多
excessive menstruation / hypermenorrhea;

yue jing guo pin 月經過頻
epimenorrhea;

yue jing guo pin guo duo 月經過頻過多
epimenorrihagia;

yue jing guo shao 月經過少
hypomenorrhea / scanty menstrual flow;

yue jing jian shao 月經減少
relative amenorrhea;

yue jing lai chao 月經來潮
menstruate // menstruation;

yue jing lin li 月經淋漓
menostaxis;

yue jing liu chu 月經流出
menorrhea;

yue jing pin duo 月經頻多
menometrorrhagia;

yue jing pin fa 月經頻發
polymenia;

yue jing pin shao 月經頻少
polyhypomenorrhea;

yue jing qi 月經期
menstrual cycle / menstrual period / period;

yue jing qi kou chu xue 月經期口出血
stomatomenia;

yue jing ting zhi 月經停止
amenorrhea / cessation of menses;

yue jing xi fa 月經稀發
oligomenorrhea;

yue jing xi shao 月經稀少
infrequent menstruation;

yue jing zhang ai 月經障礙
paramenia;

yue jing zhou qi 月經周期
menstrual cycle;

zao3 fa jue jing 早發絕經
menopause praecox;

zao qi mei du 早期梅毒
early syphilis;

zao qi qian fu mei du 早期潛伏梅毒
early latent syphilis;

zao xie 早泄
premature ejaculation / prospermia;

zhen1 xing xing zao shu 真性性早熟
true precocious puberty;

zheng4 chang yue jing 正常月經
eumenorrhea;

zhi2 chang yin dao ge 直腸陰道隔
rectovaginal septum;

zhi chang yin dao lou 直腸陰道瘻
rectovaginal fistula;

zhi chang yin dao shan 直腸陰道疝
rectovaginal hernia;

zhi4 膣
vagina;

zhi yan 膣炎
vaginal inflammation;

zhuan3 yi xing gao wan yan 轉移性睾丸炎
metastatic orchitis;

zhuang4 yang 壯陽
stimulate male virility / strengthen maculinity;

zhuang yang ji 壯陽劑
aphrodisiac;

zhuang yang yao 壯陽藥
pet pill / philter;

zi4 fa xing tong jing 自發性痛經
essential dysmenorrhea;

zu2 di mei du 足底梅毒
plantar syphilid;

zuo4 ai 做愛
make love ‖ a bit of meat; a Donald Duck; a leg-over; a meat injection; a navel engagement; a quick snort; a quickie; a ride; at it; bill and coo; boff sb; boffing; bonk sb; bump tummies; cattle; cattle truck; cut off a slice; diddle; dip one's wick; do the business; dunk; end to end; fuck; get a bit; get a jump; get it on; get off with sb; get one's leg over; get one's oats; give it to sb; grind; have a bit; have a bit off with sb; have a jump; have a quickie; have a roll; have it with sb; have it away with sb; have it off with sb; have sex; have sexual relations; horizontal exercise; jig-a-lig; jiggady-jig; jump; make a baby; make babies; make it with; mush; naughty; nookie; perform sexual intercourse; play bouncy-bouncy; play hide the sausage; poke; pole; porking; push in the truck; put-and-take; ride sb; rumpy-pumpy; rumpty-tumpty; score with; screw; screw the arse off sb; shaft; shag; shagging; slip it to sb; slip sb a fatty; slip sb a length; stuff sb; tear off a piece; thread the needle; tummy-tickling; tup with sb;

zuo ai qian zou 做愛前奏
foreplay;

Xiong bu, xiong tang 胸部、胸膛 Breast and Chest

ao1 xiong 凹胸
foveated chest / funnel chest;

bian3 ping xiong 扁平胸
flat chest;

bo2 dong xing nong xiong 搏動性膿胸
pulsating empyema;

chi1 nai 吃奶
suck the breast;

chu1 xue xing xiong mo yan 出血性胸膜炎
hemorrhagic pleuritis;

chu4 jue ru tou 觸覺乳頭
tactile papilla;

chui2 xiong da ku 捶胸大哭
beat one's breast and weep / cry one's heart out / hit one's chest and cry;

chui xiong da tong 捶胸大慟
beat one's breast and cry bitterly / clasp one's bosom in deep sorrow;

chui xiong die zu 捶胸跌足
pound one's chest and stamp the ground / smite one's breast and stamp one's foot in despair / stamp one's feet, beating one's breast;

chui xiong du zhou 捶胸賭咒
swear / thumping one's chest;

chui xiong dun zu 捶胸頓足
beat one's breast and stamp one's feet / beat the breast and stamp;

chui xiong pai an 捶胸拍案
beat the breast and pound the table;

dan1 ru xiong 單乳胸
amazon thorax;

di1 xiong 低胸
low-cut;

fei2 hou xing xiong mo yan 肥厚性胸膜炎
pachypleuritis;

fu3 xin 拊心
slap one's chest;

hua4 nong xing xiong mo yan 化膿性胸膜炎
suppurative pleurisy;

huai4 si xing ru tou yan 壞死性乳頭炎
necrotizing papillitis;

ji2 xing ru fang yan 急性乳房炎
acute mastitis;

jia3 ru fang 假乳房
pseudomamma;

jia xiong mo yan 假胸膜炎
pseudomeningitis;

jie2 he xing xiong mo yan 結核性胸膜炎
tuberculous pleuritis;

jie kuai ru fang 結塊乳房
caked breast;

ju2 xian xing xiong mo yan 局限性胸膜炎
circumscribed pleurisy;

ju4 ru fang 巨乳房
gigantomastia;

lang2 chuang xing xiong mo yan 狼瘡性胸膜炎
lupus pheuritis;

lian4 qiu jun xing nong xiong 鏈球菌性膿胸
streptococcal empyema;

liang3 lei 兩肋
both sides of the chest;

liang lei cha dao 兩肋插刀
help at the loss of one's life;

ling2 xing xiong 菱形胸
tetrahedron chest;

liu2 xing xing xiong tong 流行性胸痛
epidemic pleurodynia;

long2 ru 隆乳
breast inplant;

long xiong 隆胸
breast inplant;

ma2 bi xiong 麻痺胸
paralytic chest;

mi2 man xing xiong mo yan 彌漫性胸膜炎
diffuse pleurisy;

mo4 xiong chui bei 抹胸捶背
rub one's chest and massage one's back;

nan2 ru fang 男乳房
mamma masculina;

nai3 奶
breasts of a woman;

nai bang zi 奶膀子
breasts;

nai tou 奶頭
nipples / teats;

nai zi 奶子
breasts;

nian2 lian xing xiong mo yan 黏連性胸膜炎
adhesive pleurisy;

nian ye ru tou liu 黏液乳頭瘤
myxopapilloma;

niao4 du zheng xing xiong mo yan 尿毒症性胸膜炎
uremic pleuritis;

nong2 qi xiong 膿氣胸
pneumoempyema;

nong xiong 膿胸
empyema / pyothorax;

bo dong xing nong xiong 搏動性膿胸
pulsating empyema;

lian qiu jun xing nong xiong 鏈球菌性膿胸
streptococcal empyema;

qian fu xing nong xiong 潛伏性膿胸
latent empyema;

nu4 man xiong tang 怒滿胸膛
one's breast is filled with anger;

nu qi tian xiong 怒氣填胸
one's breast is filled with anger;

nuan3 su 暖酥
the warm and soft breasts of a girl;

pi1 xiong 劈胸
right against the chest;

qian2 fu xing nong xiong 潛伏性膿胸
latent empyema;

ru3 乳
breasts / nipple;

ru ai 乳癌
breast cancer / mammary cancer;

ru fang 乳房
breast ‖ diddies; the apples; the bangles; the bazoombas; the bazungas; the beef curtains; the blobs; the boobs; the bosoms; the bouncers; the bubbies; the bumpers; the charlies; the chestnuts; the dairies; the easts and wests; the fainting fits; the female breasts; the funbags; the jamboree bags; the jugs; the knobs; the knockers; the love blobs; the milk-jugs; the milk-bars; the shock absorbers; the stonkers; the tits; the titties; the udders; the wammers; whammers;

jia ru fang 假乳房
pseudomamma;

jie kuai ru fang 結塊乳房
caked breast;

ju ru fang 巨乳房
gigantomastia;

nan ru fang 男乳房
mamma masculina;

song chui ru fang 鬆垂乳房
pendulous breasts;

wu ru fang 無乳房
amastia;

ru fang bing 乳房病
mastopathy;

ru fang chao hong 乳房潮紅
breast flush;

ru fang guo xiao 乳房過小
micromastia;

ru fang kui yang 乳房潰瘍
masthelcosis;

ru fang qie chu 乳房切除
mastectomy;

ru fang tong 乳房痛
mammalgia;

ru fang xia chui 乳房下垂
mastoptosis;

ru fang yan 乳房炎
mastitis;

ji xing ru fang yan 急性乳房炎
acute mastitis;

ru fang zeng da 乳房增大
breast augmentation;

ru gou 乳溝
cleavage;

ru mi xiong 乳糜胸
chylothorax;
wai shang xing ru mi xiong 外傷性乳糜胸
traumatic chylothorax;

ru tong zheng 乳痛症
mastodynia;

ru tou 乳頭
diddies / mammilla / nipple / teat;
chu jue ru tou 觸覺乳頭
tactile papilla;
sai xian ru tou 腮腺乳頭
parotid papilla;
shen jing ru tou 神經乳頭
neurothele;
wu ru tou 無乳頭
athelia;
yuan zhui ru tou 圓錐乳頭
papillae conicae;

ru tou chu xue 乳頭出血
thelorrhagia;

ru tou liu 乳頭瘤
papilloma;
nian ye ru tou liu 黏液乳頭瘤
myxopapilloma;

ru tou peng zhang 乳頭膨脹
thelerethism;

ru tou tong 乳頭痛
thelalgia;

ru tou tu 乳頭突
mamelon;

ru tou yan 乳頭炎
thelitis;
huai si xing ru tou yan 壞死性乳頭炎
necrotizing papillitis;
ying hua xing ru tou yan 硬化性乳頭炎
sclerosing mastoiditis;

ru xian 乳腺
mammary glands;

ru xiong 乳胸
thorax;
dan ru xiong 單乳胸
amazon thorax;

ru xiu wei gan 乳臭未乾
one's mouth is full of pap / smell of the baby // not dry behind the ears / unfledged / very young and inexperienced like a sucking child;

ru yun 乳暈
areola mammae;
ru yun yan 乳暈炎
areolitis;

ru zhi guo duo 乳汁過多
hypergalactia;

ru zhi jian shao 乳汁減少
hypogalactia;

sai1 xian ru tou 腮腺乳頭
parotid papilla;

shen1 bu xiong ji bing 深部胸肌病
deep pectoral myopathy;

shen2 jing ru tou 神經乳頭
neurothele;

shen4 chu xing xiong mo yan 滲出性胸膜炎
exudative pleurisy;

shun3 ru 吮乳
suck the breast;

song1 chui ru fang 鬆垂乳房
pendulous breasts;

su1 xiong 酥胸
the soft and smooth skin of a woman's bosom;

tan3 xiong lu bei 坦胸露背
expose chest and back;

tan xiong lu fu 坦胸露腹
bare-chested;

tan xiong lu pu 坦胸露脯
bare one's breast;

tan3 xi 袒裼
bare one's breast and arms || take off one's jacket and expose part of the body; with one's breast and arms bare;

tan xiong lu bei 袒胸露背
expose one's chest and back;

tan xiong lu bi 袒胸露臂
bare one's chest and expose one's arms / lay bare one's bosom and arms // with chest exposed and arms bare;

tan xiong lu pu 袒胸露脯
air the dairy / bare one's breast;

tang2 膛
breast / chest;

tian3 zhe xiong pu 腆着胸脯
stick out one's chest;

ting2 ru 停乳
delactation;

ting3 qi xiong tang 挺起胸膛
stand straight in gesture of self-confidence / stick out one's chest;

ting xiong 挺胸
square one's shoulders / throw out one's chest / thrust out one's chest;

ting xiong tu du 挺胸突肚
a high breast and big belly || puff up one's chest; stand straight in a gesture of self-confidence; stick out one's chest; stretch the chest and expand the belly; with one's chest stuck out;

tong1 ru 通乳
lactogenesis;

wai4 shang xing ru mi xiong 外傷性乳糜胸
traumatic chylothorax;

wu2 ru fang 無乳房
amastia;

wu ru tou 無乳頭
athelia;

xiong1 胸
(1) bosom / breast / bust / chest / throax;
(2) heart / mind;
bian ping xiong 扁平胸
flat chest;
ma bi xiong 麻痺胸
paralytic chest;

xiong bi tong 胸壁痛
pleurodynia;

xiong bu 胸部
bosom / breast / bust / chest;

xiong bu bing 胸部病
thoracopathy;

xiong bu feng man de 胸部豐滿的
bosomy / buxom / chesty;

xiong fu 胸腹
chest and belly;

xiong gu 胸骨
breastbone / sternum;

xiong guan 胸管
ductus thoracicus;

xiong huai 胸懷
ambition / aspiration / breast / heart / mind;

xiong huai da zhi 胸懷大志
cherish high aspirations in one's mind || aim high; cherish high ideals; cherish lofty designs in one's bosom; entertain great ambitions; fly a high pitch; fly at high game; fly at higher game; fly high; have lofty aspirations; hitch one's wagon to a star;

xiong huai kuan guang 胸懷寬廣
broad-minded / large-minded // have largeness of mind;

xiong huai lei luo 胸懷磊落
open-hearted and upright || frank; harbour no evil thought; honest;

xiong huai quan ju 胸懷全局
have the overall situation in mind / keep the whole situation in mind;

xiong huai ruo gu 胸懷若谷
one's broad-mindedness is vast as the ocean;

xiong huai shi jie 胸懷世界
bear the whole world in mind / one's heart embraces the whole world;

xiong huai tan bai 胸懷坦白
frank and open || free heart; largeness of mind; open-hearted;

xiong huai tao lüe 胸懷韜略
one's bosom hides a strategy;

xiong huai xia zhai 胸懷狹窄
narrow-minded / small-minded;

xiong ji 胸肌
chest muscle / muscles in the area of one's chest;

xiong ji bing 胸肌病
pectoral myopathy;
shen bu xiong ji bing 深部胸肌病
deep pectoral myopathy;

xiong ji 胸脊
thoracic vertebrae;

xiong kou 胸口
middle of the chest / the pit in the upper part of the stomach;

xiong kuo 胸廓
thorax;

xiong kuo qie kai 胸廓切開
thoracotomy;

xiong le mo 胸肋膜
pleura costalis;

xiong mao 胸毛
chest hair;

xiong mo 胸膜
pleurae;

xiong mo yan 胸膜炎
pleurisy / pleuritis;

chu xue xing xiong mo yan 出血性胸膜炎
hemorrhagic pleuritis;

fei hou xing xiong mo yan 肥厚性胸膜炎
pachypleuritis;

hua nong xing xiong mo yan 化膿性胸膜炎
suppurative pleuritis;

jia xiong mo yan 假胸膜炎
pseudomeningitis;

jie he xing xiong mo yan 結核性胸膜炎
tuberculous pleuritis;

ju xian xing xiong mo yan 局限性胸膜炎
circumscribed pleurisy;

lang chuang xing xiong mo yan 狼瘡性胸膜炎
lupus pheuritis;

mi man xing xiong mo yan 彌漫性胸膜炎
diffuse pleurisy;

nian lian xing xiong mo yan 黏連性胸膜炎
adhesive pleurisy;

niao du zheng xing xiong mo yan 尿毒症性胸膜炎
uremic pleuritis;

shen chu xing xiong mo yan 滲出性胸膜炎
exudative pleurisy;

ying jie xing xiong mo yan 硬結性胸膜炎
indurative pleurisy;

zeng sheng xing xiong mo yan 增生性胸膜炎
proliferating pleurisy;

xiong pu 胸脯
chest;

xiong tang 胸膛
bosom / breast / chest / thorax;

xiong tong 胸痛
have a pain in the chest;

liu xing xing xiong tong 流行性胸痛
epidemic pleurodynia;

xiong wu cheng fu 胸無城府
have nothing hidden in one's mind || artless; frank; honest; open and unreserved; simple and candid; unrestrained and frank in nature;

xiong wu da zhi 胸無大志
unambitious // with no ambition at all / with no ideals;

xiong wu dian mo 胸無點墨
completely illiterate || cannot read or write; ignorant; illiterate; unlearned; unlettered;

xiong wu jie di 胸無芥蒂
no grudge in the mind || no enmity; nothing at all on the mind;

xiong wu su wu 胸無宿物
never to bear sb a grudge / nothing concealed in a straightforward man's mind;

xiong you cheng zhu 胸有成竹
know what to do in one's mind || every step is thought out in advance; have a card up one's sleeve; have a well-thought-out plan;

xiong you cheng fu 胸有城府
scheming || calculating; mental reservation; reticence;

xiong you miao suan 胸有妙算
have smart ideas up one's sleeve / have some tricks up one's sleeve;

xiong yu 胸宇
one's ambition / one's aspiration;

xiong zhong qiu he 胸中丘壑
a mind's intricate thoughts;

xiong zhong wu shu 胸中無數
have no idea as to how things stand || feel unsure of sth; have no figures in one's head; not to know what's what;

xiong zhong you shu 胸中有數
have a good idea of how things stand || feel sure of sth; have a head for figures; know quite well how things stand; know the true state of affairs;

yi4 xiong 義胸
falsies;

ying4 hua xing ru tou yan 硬化性乳頭炎
sclerosing mastoiditis;

ying jie xing xiong mo yan 硬結性胸膜炎
indurative pleurisy;

you2 nai bian shi niang 有奶便是娘
whoever suckles me is my mother || he that serves God for money will serve the devil for better wages; obey anyone who feeds one; lick the hand of anyone who throws one a few crumbs; submit oneself to anyone who feeds one; submit to whoever feeds one;

yuan2 zhui ru tou 圓錐乳頭
papillae conicae;

zeng1 sheng xing xiong mo yan 增生性胸膜炎
proliferating pleurisy;

Xue 血 Blood

ai1 xing A 型
Group A;

ai2 xing xin bao yan 癌性心包炎
carcinomatous pericarditis;

ai xue zheng 癌血症
carcinemia;

ai yang xue guan liu 癌樣血管瘤
canceroderm;

an1 zhuang xue shuan 鞍狀血栓
saddle embolism;

bai2 hou xing xin ji yan 白喉性心肌炎
diphtheritic myocarditis;

bai se xue kuai 白色血塊
white clot;

bai xue bing 白血病
leukaemia;
ji xing bai xue bing 急性白血病
acute leukemia;
jia bai xue bing 假白血病
pseudoleukemia;
man xing bai xue bing 慢性白血病
chronic leukemia;
pi fu bai xue bing 皮膚白血病
leukemia cutis;

bai xue qiu 白血球
leucocyte / white blood cell / white cell;

bai xue qiu zeng duo 白血球增多
leucocytosis;

bai4 xue 敗血
poisonous blood;

bai xue bing 敗血病
blood poisoning / septicemia;
nong du bai xue bing 膿毒敗血病
septicopyemia;
yin xing bai xue bing 隱性敗血病
cryptogenic septicemia;

bai xue nong du zheng 敗血膿毒症
septicopyemia;

bai xue xing xiu ke 敗血性休克
septic shock;

bai xue zheng 敗血症
septicemia / vanquished blood;
chan hou bai xue zheng 產後敗血症
puerperal septicemia;
chu xue xing bai xue zheng 出血性敗血症
hemorrhagic septicemia;
nong du bai xue zheng 膿毒敗血症
septicopyemia;
zhuan yi xing bai xue zheng 轉移性敗血症
metastasizing septicemia;

bao3 tai 保胎
prevent a miscarriage / secure the foetus;

bi1 xing B 型
Group B;

bian4 ying xing xue guan yan 變應性血管炎
hypersensitivity angiitis;

bing4 du xing xin bao yan 病毒性心包炎
viral pericarditis;

bing du xing xin ji yan 病毒性心肌炎
viral myocarditis;

bo2 dong xing xue zhong 搏動性血腫
pulsating hematoma;

bu2 wen ding xing gao xue ya 不穩定型高血壓
labile hypertension;

bu wen ding xue hong dan bai 不穩定血紅蛋白
unstable hemoglobins;

bu3 xue 補血
enrich the blood;

bu xue an tai 補血安胎
enrich the blood and calm the fetus;

can1 hou xing di xue tang zheng 餐後性低血糖症
postprandial hypoglycemia / reactive hypoglycemia;

cang1 bai xue shuan 蒼白血栓
pale thrombus;

cao3 suan zhong du xing tong feng 草酸中毒性痛風
oxalic gout;

chan3 hou bai xue zheng 產後敗血症
puerperal septicemia;

chan hou chu xue 產後出血
postpartum hemorrhage;

chan hou xue shuan xing cheng 產後血栓形成
puerperal thrombosis;

chan shi chu xue 產時出血
intrapartum hemorrhage;

chong1 xue 充血
congestion / engorgement;
fei chong xue 肺充血
pulmonary congestion;
gong neng xing chong xue 功能性充血
functional congestion;
pi chong xue 脾充血
splenemphraxis;
sheng li xing chong xue 生理性充血
physiologic congestion;
yan bu chong xue 咽部充血
congested throat;
yun dong xing chong xue 運動性充血
exercise hyperemia;

chong xue xing xin zang shuai jie 充血性心臟衰竭
congestive failure;

chou1 xue 抽血
drawing blood;

chu1 xue 出血
bleeding / hemorrhage // plunk down / shed blood;
chan hou chu xue 產後出血
postpartum hemorrhage;
chan shi chu xue 產時出血
intrapartum hemorrhage;
hong mo chu xue 虹膜出血
iridemia;
hou chu xue 喉出血
laryngorrhagia;
hou bi chu xue 後鼻出血
posterior epistaxis;
jie chang chu xue 結腸出血
colonorrhagia;
nei chu xue 內出血
internal bleeding / internal hemorrhage;
pi chu xue 脾出血
splenorrhagia;

qi guan chu xue 氣管出血
tracheorrhagia;

qian bi chu xue 前鼻出血
anterior epistaxis;

qian chu xue 潛出血
occult bleeding;

ru tou chu xue 乳頭出血
thelorrhagia;

shen chu xing chu xue 滲出性出血
diapedesis;

shi zhi xing chu xue 實質性出血
parenchymatous hemorrhage;

wai chu xue 外出血
external bleeding / external hemorrhage;

xia ji chu xue 夏季出血
summer bleeding;

chu xue bing 出血病
bleeding disease;

chu xue re 出血熱
hemorrhagic fever;

liu xing xing chu xue re 流行性出血熱
epidemic hemorrhagic fever;

chu xue xing bai xue zheng 出血性敗血症
hemorrhagic septicemia;

chu xue xing huai xue bing 出血性壞血病
hemmorrhagic scurvy;

chu xue xing pin xue 出血性貧血
hemorrhagic anemia;

chu xue xing xin bao yan 出血性心包炎
hemorrhagic pericarditis;

chuan2 bo xing xue shuan 傳播性血栓
propagated thrombus;

chuang3 shang xing xin bao yan 創傷性心包炎
traumatic pericarditis;

chuang shang xing xue shuan 創傷性血栓
traumatic thrombus;

da4 chu xue 大出血
massive hemorrhage / profuse bleeding;

da nao xue guan yan 大腦血管炎
cerebral vasculitis;

rou ya zhong xing da nao xue guan yan 肉芽腫性大腦血管炎
granulomatous cerebral vasculitis;

dan1 chun xing xue guan liu 單純性血管瘤
hemangioma simplex;

dan3 gu chun 膽固醇
cholesterol;

di1 xue tang 低血糖
hypoglycemia;

di xue tang zheng 低血糖症
hypoglycemia;

can hou xing di xue tang zheng 餐後性低血糖症
postprandial hypoglycemia; reactive hypoglycemia;

fan ying xing di xue tang zheng 反應性低血糖症
reactive hypoglycemia;

ying yang xing di xue tang zheng 營養性低血糖症
alimentary hypoglycemia;

di xue ya 低血壓
hypotension;

zhi li xing di xue ya 直立性低血壓
orthostatic hypotension;

di4 zhong hai pin xue 地中海貧血
Mediterranean anemia;

qing xing di zhong hai pin xue 輕型地中海貧血
thalassemia minor;

dian3 xing tong feng 典型痛風
regular gout;

dian xing xue you bing 典型血友病
classical hemophilia;

die2 xue 喋血
bloodbath / bloodshed;

die xue sha chang 喋血沙場
the shedding of blood in battlefields;

dong4 mai chu xue 動脈出血
arterial bleeding;

dong mai ying hua zheng 動脈硬化症
artero sclerosis;

du2 xue zheng 毒血症
toxaemia;

duo1 xue 多血
hyperemia;

quan shen duo xue 全身多血
panhyperemia;

duo xue zheng 多血症
plethora;

e4 xing gao xue ya 惡性高血壓
malignant hypertension;

e xing pin xue 惡性貧血
pernicious anemia;

qing shao nian e xing pin xue 青少年惡性貧血
juvenile pernicious anemia;

fan3 ying xing di xue tang zheng 反應性低血糖症
reactive hypoglycemia;

fang1 xue 放血
bloodletting;

fei1 dian xing tong feng 非典型痛風
irregular gout;

fei2 da xing xue guan liu 肥大性血管瘤
hypertrophic angioma;

gao1 dan gu chun 高膽固醇
hypercholestero;

gao dan gu chun xue zheng 高膽固醇血症
hypercholesterolemia;

jia zu xing gao dan gu chun xue zheng 家族性高膽固醇血症
familial hypercholesterolemia;

gao xue tang 高血糖
hyperglycosemia;

gao xue tang zheng 高血糖症
hyperglycemia;

gao xue ya 高血壓
high blood pressure / hypertension;

bu wen ding xing gao xue ya 不穩定型高血壓
labile hypertension;

e xing gao xue ya 惡性高血壓
malignant hypertension;

ji jin xing gao xue ya 急進性高血壓
accelerated hypertension;

ji fa xing gao xue ya 繼發性高血壓
secondary hypertension;

jia gao xue ya 假高血壓
pseudohypertension;

shen xing gao xue ya 腎形高血壓
renal hypertension;

shen xue guan xing gao xue ya 腎血管性高血壓
renovascular hypertension;

te fa xing gao xue ya 特發性高血壓
idiopathic hypertension;

yuan fa xing gao xue ya 原發性高血壓
primary hypertension;

zheng zhuang xing gao xue ya 症狀性高血壓
symptomatic hypertension;

zi fa xing gao xue ya 自發性高血壓
essential hypertension;

gong1 neng xing chong xue 功能性充血
functional congestion;

guo4 min xing xue guan yan 過敏性血管炎
hypersensitivity vasculitis;

han2 xue pen ren 含血噴人
cast malicious words to injure sb ‖ do wrong to sb; fling mud at; make slanderous accusations; make slanderous charges against others; make vicious attacks; mud-slinging; sling mud at; slur sb's good name; smite with the tongue; spit poison; throw dirt at sb; throw mud at;

hong2 bai xue bing 紅白血病
erythroleukemia;

ji xing hong bai xue bing 急性紅白血病
acute erythroleukemia;

hong xue qiu 紅血球
erythrocyte / red blood cell / red cell;

hong xue qiu zeng duo zheng 紅血球增多症
polycythaemia;

huai4 si xing xue guan yan 壞死性血管炎
necrotizing angiitis;

huai xue bing 壞血病
scurvy;

chu xue xing huai xue bing 出血性壞血病
hemmorrhagic scurvy;

ying er huai xue bing 嬰兒壞血病
infantile scurvy;

huai xue bing kou yan 壞血病口炎
stomatitis scorbutica;

huai xue bing xing pin xue 壞血病性貧血
scorbutic anemia;

huai xue zheng 壞血症
scurvy;

huan4 xue 換血
blood exchange transfusion;

hun2 shen shi xue 渾身是血
be covered all over with blood;

huo2 xue 活血
invigorate the blood circulation;

ji1 hua xue shuan 機化血栓
organized thrombus;

ji1 nong xing xin bao yan 積膿性心包炎
purulent pericarditis;

ji shui xing xin bao yan 積水性心包炎
pericarditis with effusion;

ji2 jin xing gao xue ya 急進性高血壓
accelerated hypertension;

ji xing hong bai xue bing 急性紅白血病
acute erythroleukemia;

ji xing xin ji geng se 急性心肌梗塞
acute myocardial impaction;

ji xing xin ji yan 急性心肌炎
acute myocarditis;

ji4 sheng chong xing ka xue 寄生蟲性咯血
parasitic hemoptysis;

ji sheng chong xing xue shuan 寄生蟲性血栓
parasitic thrombus;

ji4 fa xing gao xue ya 繼發性高血壓
secondary hypertension;

ji fa xing tong feng 繼發性痛風
secondary gout;

jia1 zu xing gao dan gu chun xue zheng 家族性高膽固醇血症
familial hypercholesterolemia;

jia3 bai xue bing 假白血病
pseudoleukemia;

jia gao xue ya 假高血壓
pseudohypertension;

jia ka xue 假咯血
pseudohemoptysis;

jia tong feng 假痛風
pseudogout;

jia xing tong feng 假性痛風
pseudogout;

jia xue niao 假血尿
pseudohematuria;

jia xue you bing 假血友病
pseudohemophilia;

jian4 xue 濺血
splash with drops of blood;

jie2 jie xing xue guan yan 結節性血管炎
nodular vasculitis;

ju4 xue xiao ban 巨血小板
giant platelet;

juan1 xue 捐血
blood donation;

ka3 xue 咯血
cough up blood // hematemesis / hemoptysis / spitting of blood;
ji sheng chong xing ka xue 寄生蟲性咯血
parasitic hemoptysis;
jia ka xue 假咯血
pseudohemoptysis;
xin xing ka xue 心性咯血
cardiac hemoptysis;

lao3 nian xing xue guan liu 老年性血管瘤
senile angiomas;

leng3 xue 冷血
cold-blooded;

liang2 xue 涼血
(1) cool the blood;
(2) cold-blooded;

liang2 xue ya 量血壓
take sb's blood pressure;

liu2 xing xing chu xue re 流行性出血熱
epidemic hemorrhagic fever;

liu xue 流血
bleed / shed blood;

liu xue cheng he 流血成河
bloody fighting / massacre;

liu xue chong tu 流血衝突
bloody conflict / sanguiary conflict;

liu xue xi sheng 流血犧牲
at the cost of one's blood and sacrifices // shed one's blood and lay down one's life;

man4 xing bai xue bing 慢性白血病
chronic leukemia;

mao2 xi xue guan 毛細血管
blood capillary;

mo4 xue 沫血
blood flowing in one's face // bleeding face;

nan2 zhi xing pin xue 難治性貧血
refractory anemia;

nei4 chu xue 內出血
internal bleeding / internal hemorrhage;

nong2 xue zheng 濃血症
anhydremia;

nong2 du bai xue bing 膿毒敗血病
septicopyemia;

nong du bai xue zheng 膿毒敗血症
septicopyemia;

nong xue 膿血
pus and blood;

ou1 xing O 型
Group O;

ou3 xue 嘔血
vomitting blood;

pi2 fu bai xue bing 皮膚白血病
leukemia cutis;

pi xia chu xue 皮下出血
subcutaneous ecchymoma;

pi2 pin xue 脾貧血
splenic anemia;

pin2 xue 貧血
anemia;

chu xue xing pin xue 出血性貧血
hemorrhagic anemia;

di zhong hai pin xue 地中海貧血
Mediterranean anemia;

e xing pin xue 恶性貧血
pernicious anemia;

huai xue bing xing pin xue 壞血病性貧血
scorbutic anemia;

nan zhi xing pin xue 難治性貧血
refractory anemia;

pi pin xue 脾貧血
splenic anemia;

que tie xing pin xue 缺鐵性貧血
iron deficiency anemia;

rong xue xing pin xue 溶血性貧血
hemolytic anemia;

sheng li xing pin xue 生理性貧血
physiologic anemia;

ying yang que fa xing pin xue 營養缺乏性貧血
deficiency anemia;

zhong du xing pin xue 中毒性貧血
toxanemia;

qi4 xue 泣血
weep blood;

qi xue ji sang 泣血稽顙
weep blood and knock one's head on the ground;

qi4 de ou xue 氣得嘔血
one is so incensed that one literally coughs up blood;

qi xue shi tiao 氣血失調
disorder of vital energy and blood;

qian1 du xing tong feng 鉛毒性痛風
saturnine gout;

qian zhong du xing tong feng 鉛中毒性痛風
lead gout;

qian2 chu xue 潛出血
occult bleeding;

qian fu xing tong feng 潛伏性痛風
latent gout;

qian xue 潛血
occult blood;

qing1 ban xue guan yan 青斑血管炎
livedo vasculitis;

qing shao nian e xing pin xue 青少年恶性貧血
juvenile pernicious anemia;

qing xue zheng 青血症
cyanemia;

qing1 xing di zhong hai pin xue 輕型地中海貧血
thalassemia minor;

quan2 shen duo xue 全身多血
panhyperemia;

quan xue guan yan 全血管炎
panangiitis;

que1 tie xing pin xue 缺鐵性貧血
iron deficiency anemia;

que xue 缺血
ischemia;

que xue xing fan she 缺血性反射
ischemic reflex;

re4 ru xue shi 熱入血室
heat-evil attacking the blood chamber;

re xue 熱血
fervent ‖ fiery-spirited; hot-blooded; righteous ardour; warm blood; zealous;

re xue fei teng 熱血沸騰
burning with righteous indignation ‖ have a boiling passion; in warm blood; one's blood boils with indignation; one's hot blood is boiling; seethe with fervour; with heart afire;

ren2 zao xue guan 人造血管
artificial blood vessel;

ren4 shen xue qing 妊娠血清
pregnancy serum;

rong2 xue xing pin xue 溶血性貧血
hemolytic anemia;

rou4 ya zhong xing da nao xue guan yan 肉芽腫性大腦血管炎
granulomatous cerebral vasculitis;

san4 xue 散血
promote blood circulation;

shang1 kou chu xue 傷口出血
wound bleeding;

shen4 xing gao xue ya 腎形高血壓
renal hypertension;

shen xue guan xing gao xue ya 腎血管性高血壓
renovascular hypertension;

shen4 chu xing chu xue 滲出性出血
diapedesis;

sheng1 li xing chong xue 生理性充血
physiologic congestion;

sheng li xing pin xue 生理性貧血
physiologic anemia;

shi1 xue 失血
lose blood;

shi xue zhi si 失血致死
bleeding to death;

shi2 zhi xing chu xue 實質性出血
parenchymatous hemorrhage;

shi zhi xing xue zhong 實質性血腫
parenchymatous hematoma;

shi4 xue 嗜血
bloodsucking / bloodthirsty;

shu1 xue 輸血
blood transfusion;

gong nei shu xue 宮內輸血
intrauterine transfusion;

shu xue fan ying 輸血反應
transfusion reaction;

shu xue guo duo 輸血過多
overtransfusion;

si1 xue guan 絲血管
silk blood vessel;

sou1 xue 溲血
hematuria;

te4 fa xing gao xue ya 特發性高血壓
idiopathic hypertension;

te fa xing xue niao 特發性血尿
essential hematuria;

tu4 xue 吐血
spit blood / spit out blood / vomit blood;

wai4 chu xue 外出血
external bleeding / external hemorrhage;

wei1 xue guan chu xue 微血管出血
capillary hemorrhage;

wei xue guan kuo zhang 微血管擴張
telangiectasis;

xi1 xue 吸血
suck blood;

xi4 tong xing xue guan yan 系統性血管炎
systemic vasculitis;

xia4 ji chu xue 夏季出血
summer bleeding;

xian1 tian xing xin xue guan bing 先天性心血管病
congenital cardiovascular disease;

xian1 xue 鮮血
blood / fresh blood;

xian xue beng liu 鮮血迸流
the blood is flowing in streams / the fresh blood flows out;

xian xue jian fei 鮮血濺飛
the red blood flows;

xian xue lin li 鮮血淋漓
fresh blood is streaming out ‖ drench with blood; drip with blood; the blood oozes out;

xin1 xing ka xue 心性咯血
cardiac hemoptysis;

xu4 xue 蓄血
syndrome of accumulation of stagnant blood;

xue4 血
(1) blood;
(2) blood relationship / related by blood;

xue ai 血癌
leukaemia;

xue an 血案
(1) bloody incident;
(2) murder case;

xue an ru shan 血案如山
with a long list of bloody crimes;

xue ban 血斑
blood stains;

xue beng 血崩
menorrhagia;

xue beng zheng 血崩症
metrorrhagia;

xue bi shui nong 血比水濃
blood is thicker than water;

xue bi shui nong, shu bu jian qin 血比水濃，疏不間親
blood is thicker than water;

xue bing 血餅
blood clot / coagulated blood;

xue chen 血塵
blood dust / hemoconia;

xue chen bing 血塵病
hemoconiosis;

xue chen 血沉
erythrocytic sedimentation rate;

xue chong 血蟲
bloodworm;

xue dian 血點
blood splashes / blood spots / drops of blood;

xue du zheng 血毒症
blood poisoning;

xue guan 血管
blood vessel;

mao xi xue guan 毛細血管
blood capillary;

ren zao xue guan 人造血管
artificial blood vessel;

xue guan geng se 血管梗塞
infarct;

xue guan jing luan zheng 血管痙攣症
vascular spasm;

xue guan liu 血管瘤
angioma / hemangioma / vascular tumour;

ai yang xue guan liu 癌樣血管瘤
canceroderm;

dan chun xing xue guan liu 單純性血管瘤
hemangioma simplex;

fei da xing xue guan liu 肥大性血管瘤
hypertrophic angioma;

lao nian xing xue guan liu 老年性血管瘤
senile angiomas;

ying hua xing xue guan liu 硬化性血管瘤
sclerosing hemangioma;

xue guan tan huan 血管癱瘓
vasoparesis;

xue guan yan 血管炎
angiitis;

bian ying xing xue guan yan 變應性血管炎
hypersensitivity angiitis;

da nao xue guan yan 大腦血管炎
cerebral vasculitis;
guo min xing xue guan yan 過敏性血管炎
hypersensitivity vasculitis;
huai si xing xue guan yan 壞死性血管炎
necrotizing angiitis;
jie jie xing xue guan yan 結節性血管炎
nodular vasculitis;
pi fu xue guan yan 皮膚血管炎
angiodermatitis;
qing ban xue guan yan 青斑血管炎
livedo vasculitis;
quan xue guan yan 全血管炎
panangiitis;
xi tong xing xue guan yan 系統性血管炎
systemic vasculitis;
xue shuan xing xue guan yan 血栓性血管炎
thromboagiitis;

xue guan ying hua 血管硬化
angiosclerosis / sclerosis vascularis;

xue guo duo 血過多
plethora;

xue han 血汗
blood and sweat / sweat and toil;

xue han suo de 血汗所得
be earned by the sweat and blood of sb;

xue hong 血紅
as red as blood / blood red / scarlet;

xue hong dan bai 血紅蛋白
haemoglobin;
bu wen ding xue hong dan bai 不穩定血紅蛋白
unstable hemoglobins;

xue hua 血花
blood splashes / bloodstains;

xue ji 血跡
bloodstain;

xue ji ban ban 血跡斑斑
all covered with bloodstains / be besmeared with blood // blood-soaked / bloodstained;

xue jiang 血漿
blood plasma;

xue kou pen ren 血口噴人
attack sb with most malicious words || curse and slander; make false accusations against others; make unfounded and malicious attacks upon sb; smite with the tongue; venomously slander;

xue ku 血庫
blood bank;

xue kuai 血塊
blood clot;
bai se xue kuai 白色血塊
white clot;

xue kui 血虧
anemia;

xue kui bi jing 血虧閉經
amenorrhoea due to deficiency of blood;

xue lei 血淚
blood and tears — extreme sorrow;

xue lei ban ban 血淚斑斑
full of blood and tears / with spots of tears and blood;

xue lei chou 血淚仇
vengeful feelings nurtured by blood and tears;

xue liang 血量
blood volume;

xue lin lin 血淋淋
(1) bloody;
(2) naked facts;

xue liu cheng he 血流成河
blood flows in rivers || blood is flowing over the ground like water; shed blood like water;

xue liu cheng qu 血流成渠
blood flows in streams || the blood fills the water courses; the ground is covered with streams of blood;

xue liu piao chu 血流漂杵
blood flows so as to float a pestle || so much blood being shed as to float the pestles — great massacre;

xue liu ru zhu 血流如注
shed blood like water || a stream of blood; bleed like a pig; bleed like a struck hog; bleed profusely; blood streaming down; the

blood gushes in torrents;

xue lu 血路

blood vessel;

xue lu lu 血淥淥

blood dripping all around / sanguinary;

xue mai 血脈

(1) large and small blood vessels;

(2) blood relationship;

xue mai liu tong 血脈流通

blood circulation;

xue niao 血尿

blood urine;

jia xue niao 假血尿

pseudohematuria;

te fa xing xue niao 特發性血尿

essential hematuria;

yuan fa xing xue niao 原發性血尿

primary hematuria;

zi fa xing xue niao 自發性血尿

essential hematuria;

xue nong yu shui 血濃於水

blood is thicker than water;

xue pen da kou 血盆大口

large and fierce-looking mouth;

xue qi 血氣

(1) one's disposition;

(2) sap / vigour;

(3) courage and uprightness;

xue qi fang gang 血氣方剛

in one's raw youth || easily excited; full of animal spirits; full of sap; full of vigour and vitality; full of vim and vigour; hot-tempered; in one's salad days; in the green;

xue qi xu ruo 血氣虛弱

frail // weak constitution;

xue qi zhi yong 血氣之勇

brute courage / foolhardiness;

xue qin 血親

consanquinity / blood relation / blood relatives;

xue qing 血清

blood serum / serum;

ren shen xue qing 妊娠血清

pregnancy serum;

xue qing bing 血清病

serum disease;

xue qiu 血球

blood cell / blood corpuscle;

xue rou 血肉

flesh and blood;

xue rou heng fei 血肉橫飛

blood and flesh flying in every direction;

xue rou mo hu 血肉模糊

badly mutilated / mutilated beyond recognition;

xue rou xiang lian 血肉相連

link together as flesh and blood || as close as flesh and blood; be linked by flesh-and-blood ties; be related by flesh and blood; bone of the bone and flesh of the flesh; flesh of its flesh and blood of its blood; maintain flesh-and-blood ties; ties of flesh and blood;

xue rou xiang lian, xiu qi yu gong 血肉相連，休戚與共

flesh and blood relationship // with common joys and sorrows;

xue rou zhi qin 血肉之親

blood relationship;

xue rou zhi qu 血肉之軀

flesh and blood / the human body;

xue ru quan yong 血如泉湧

blood gushes forth in fountains / blood gushes out like a fountain;

xue shu 血書

letter written in one's own blood;

xue shuan 血栓

thrombus;

an zhuang xue shuan 鞍狀血栓

saddle embolism;

cang bai xue shuan 蒼白血栓

pale thrombus;

chuan bo xing xue shuan 傳播性血栓

propagated thrombus;

chuang shang xing xue shuan 創傷性血栓

traumatic thrombus;

ji hua xue shuan 機化血栓
organized thrombus;
ji sheng chong xing xue shuan 寄生蟲性血栓
parasitic thrombus;
yuan fa xue shuan 原發血栓
primary thrombus;

xue shuan qie chu 血栓切除
thrombectomy;

xue shuan xing cheng 血栓形成
thrombosis;
chan hou xue shuan xing cheng 產後血栓形成
puerperal thrombosis;

xue shuan xing xue guan yan 血栓性血管炎
thromboagiitis;

xue shuan zheng 血栓症
thrombosis;

xue shui 血水
(1) blood;
(2) bloodstained water;

xue si chong 血絲蟲
filaria;

xue si chong bing 血絲蟲病
filariasis;

xue tang 血糖
blood sugar;

xue tong 血統
blood lineage || blood relationship; lineage; of a certain stock; pedigree;

xue wu 血污
blood-smeared / bloodstained;

xue xi chong bing 血吸蟲病
schistosomiasis / snail fever;

xue xiao ban 血小板
blood platelet;
ju xue xiao ban 巨血小板
giant platelet;

xue xiao ban jian shao zheng 血小板減少症
thrombocytopenia;

xue xiao ban rong jie 血小板溶解
thrombocytolysis;

xue xin 血心
loyalty / sincerity;

xue xing 血腥
bloody / sanguinary;

xue xing 血型
blood group / blood type;
ai xing A 型
Group A;
bi xing B 型
Group B;
ou xing O 型
Group O;

xue xing 血性
strong sense of righteousness;

xue xiong 血胸
hemothorax;

xue xu 血虛
anemia / blood deficiency;

xue xu bu yun 血虛不孕
sterility due to deficiency of blood;

xue xun huan 血循環
blood circulation;

xue ya 血壓
blood pressure;
di xue ya 低血壓
hypotension;
liang xue ya 量血壓
take sb's blood pressure;
zheng chang xue ya 正常血壓
orthoarteriotony;

xue ya di 血壓低
low blood pressure;

xue ya gao 血壓高
high blood pressure;

xue ye 血液
blood;

xue ye bing 血液病
blood disease;

xue ye ning gu 血液凝固
blood coagulation;

xue ye tou xi 血液透析
hemodialysis;

xue ye xun huan 血液循環
blood circulation;

xue you bing 血友病
bleeder disease / hemophilia;
dian xing xue you bing 典型血友病
classical hemophilia;
jia xue you bing 假血友病
pseudohemophilia;

xue yu xing feng 血雨腥風
a foul wind and a rain of blood;

xue yuan 血緣
blood relationship / kin / ties of blood;

xue zhai 血債
debt of blood;

xue zhai lei lei 血債累累
have a mountain of blood debts // a record of sanguinary crimes / heavy blooddebts;

xue zhai xue huan 血債血還
the debt in blood must be repaid with blood || blood demands blood; blood for blood; blood must atone for blood; blood will have blood; debts of blood must be paid in blood; demand blood for blood; make sb pay blood for blood; the blood debts must be repaid in kind;

xue zhan 血戰
bathe in blood / bloody battle;

xue zhan dao di 血戰到底
fight to the bitter end / fight to the finish / fight to the last drop of one's blood;

xue zhong 血腫
hematoma;
bo dong xing xue zhong 搏動性血腫
pulsating hematoma;
shi zhi xing xue zhong 實質性血腫
parenchymatous hematoma;

xue zhong du 血中毒
blood poisoning;

xue zhi 血脂
blood lipoids;

yan4 xue 驗血
blood analysis / blood test;

yang3 xue 養血
nourish blood;

yi1 di xue 一滴血
a drop of blood;

yi zhen jian xue 一針見血
exactly right / hit the nail on the head / to the point;

yi3 xue xi xue 以血洗血
blood must atone for blood || blood will have blood; demand blood for blood; slaughter for slaughter; the blood debt must be repaid in kind;

yin3 xing bai xue bing 隱性敗血病
cryptogenic septicemia;

ying1 er huai xue bing 嬰兒壞血病
infantile scurvy;

ying2 yang que fa xing pin xue 營養缺乏性貧血
deficiency anemia;

ying yang xing di xue tang zheng 營養性低血糖症
alimentary hypoglycemia;

ying4 hua xing xue guan liu 硬化性血管瘤
sclerosing hemangioma;

you3 xue you rou 有血有肉
true to life / vivid;

yu1 xue 淤血
blood clot;

yu1 瘀
hematoma;

yu nong 瘀膿
pus;

yu rou 瘀肉
gangrene;

yu shang 瘀傷
bruise;

yu xue 瘀血
blood stasis / hematoma;

yu4 xue 郁血
stagnation of blood / stasis of blood;

yu4 xue 浴血
bathed in blood // bloody;

yuan2 fa xing gao xue ya 原發性高血壓
primary hypertension;

yuan fa xing xue niao 原發性血尿
primary hematuria;

yuan fa xue shuan 原發血栓
primary thrombus;

yun4 dong xing chong xue 運動性充血
exercise hyperemia;

zheng4 chang xue ya 正常血壓
orthoarteriotony;

zheng4 zhuang xing gao xue ya 症狀性高血壓
symptomatic hypertension;

zhi2 li xing di xue ya 直立性低血壓
orthostatic hypotension;

zhi3 xue 止血
hemostasis // stanch bleeding / stop bleeding;

zhong4 du xing pin xue 中毒性貧血
toxanemia;

zhuan3 yi xing bai xue zheng 轉移性敗血症
metastasizing septicemia;

zhui1 xin qi xue 椎心泣血
deep sorrow / excruciating pains / extreme grief;

zi4 fa xing gao xue ya 自發性高血壓
essential hypertension;

zi fa xing xue niao 自發性血尿
essential hematuria;

Ya 牙 Tooth

ao2 ya 聱牙
jaw-breaking;

ba2 ya 拔牙
extract a tooth / pull out a tooth;
xuan ze xing ba ya 選擇性拔牙
selected extraction;

ba ya hou chu xue 拔牙後出血
hemorrhage following tooth extraction;

ban3 ya 板牙
front tooth;

bao4 ya 暴牙
buck teeth / goofy teeth / projecting teeth / protruding teeth;

bian1 yuan xing ya zhou yan 邊緣性牙周炎
marginal periodontitis;

bing4 sheng ya 併生牙
gemination;

bing4 li xing ya yi wei 病理性牙移位
pathologic tooth wandering;

bing ya 病牙
affected tooth;

bo1 tuo xing yin yan 剝脫性齦炎
desqamative gingivitis;

bu3 ya 補牙
fill a tooth / have a tooth stopped;

bu4 chi 不齒
condemn / despise;

bu zu gua chi 不足掛齒
not worth mentioning ‖ beneath notice; not worthy of mention; nothing to speak of; of no importance;

bu4 fen tuo ya 部分托牙
partial denture;

bu fen wu ya 部份無牙
partial anodontia;

cao2 ya 槽牙
front tooth;

chang2 guan ya 長冠牙
taurodontism;

chen4 chi 齔齒
shed milk teeth for the new teeth;

cheng2 ren ya zhou yan 成人牙周炎
adult periodontitis;

chi2 chu ya 遲出牙
dentia tarda;

chi yan 遲牙
dens sorotinus;

chi3 齒
(1) tooth;
(2) tooth-like part of anything;
jie chi 潔齒
clean the teeth;

chi de ju zun 齒德俱尊
honourable both in age and virtue;

chi du 齒蠹
tooth decay;

chi fa 齒髮
one's tooth and hair;

chi feng 齒縫
embrasure;

chi gen 齒根
gums / root of a tooth;

chi gou 齒垢
tartar;

chi guan 齒冠
crown of a tooth;

chi han 齒寒
suffer due to failure of the other;

chi ji 齒擊
clatter the teeth in trembling;

chi ji 齒及
mention;

chi jian liu xiang 齒間留香
leave a sweet taste in one's mouth;

chi jue 齒決
bite off with the teeth;

chi kong 齒孔
dental foramina;

chi leng 齒冷
show contempt by grinning;

chi liu 齒瘤
odontoma;

chi qiang 齒腔
dental cavity / gum of the tooth;

chi qu 齒齲
tooth decay;

chi ru pian bei 齒如編貝
very beautiful teeth;

chi sui 齒髓
pulp of the tooth;

chi sui yan 齒髓炎
pulpitis;

chi tong 齒痛
toothache;

chi wang she cun 齒亡舌存
the soft and flexible lasts longer than the hard / the hard is lost, while the weak and soft endure;

chi wen 齒吻
teeth and lips;

chi yin 齒齦
gum of the tooth / tooth-ridge;

chi yin kui yang 齒齦潰瘍
gumboil;

chi yin yan 齒齦炎
gingivitis;

chi zhi 齒質
dentine;

chong2 ya 蟲牙
carious tooth;

chu1 xue xing yin yan 出血性齦炎
hemorrhagic gingivitis;

chu ya 出牙
teethe // dentia / teething / tooth eruption;

chu ya bu liang 出牙不良
dysodontiasis;

chu ya guo zao 出牙過早
precocious dentition;

chu ya kun nan 出牙困難
dysodontiasis;

chu ya yan chi 出牙延遲
retarded dentition;

chun2 hong chi bai 唇紅齒白
red lips and white teeth;

ci1 齹
irregular teeth / uneven teeth;

da4 ban ya 大板牙
protruding tooth / snag;

da ya 大牙
molar teeth;

dan1 chun xing ya zhou yan 單純性牙周炎
simple periodontitis;

dao3 ya 倒牙
set one's teeth on edge;

diao4 ya 掉牙
a tooth drops off;

du2 ya 毒牙
poison fang / venom fang;

du ya bi lou 毒牙畢露
bare one's poison fangs;

e2 wai ya 額外牙
supernumerary teeth;

e4 齶
roof of the mouth;

fen1 ya 分牙
separation;

gao1 wei ya 高位牙
supraversion;

gong1 neng xing yan ben zhi 功能性牙本質
functional dentin;

gua4 chi 掛齒
mention;

guan4 zhou yan 冠周炎
pericoronitis;

hang2 kong ya tong 航空牙痛
aero-odontodynia;

hao4 chi e mei 皓齒蛾眉
white teeth and pretty eyebrows;

hao chi zhu chun 皓齒朱唇
have pearly white teeth and crimson lips // one's teeth are very white and one's lips vermillion // white teeth and red lips;

he2 zu gua chi 何足掛齒
don't mention it;

hen4 de ya yang 恨得牙癢
gnash one's teeth with hatred;

heng2 ya 恒牙
permanent tooth / second teeth;

hou4 ya 後牙
buccal teeth / posterior teeth;

hua4 nong xing ya zhou yan 化膿性牙周炎
purulent periodontitis;

huai4 si xing ya sui 壞死性牙髓
necrotic pulp;

huai si ya sui 壞死牙髓
dead pulp;

huai xue bing xing yin yan 壞血病性齦炎
scorbutic gingivitis;

huan4 ya 換牙
grow permanent teeth;

ji2 jin xing ya zhou yan 急進性牙周炎
rapidly progressive periodontitis;

ji4 fa xing ya ben zhi 繼發性牙本質
secondary dentin;

jia2 chi 頰齒
cheek teeth;

jia ya 頰牙
cheek teeth;

jia3 ya 假牙
artificial tooth / false tooth / store teeth;

jian1 ya 尖牙
canine tooth / cynodont / eye tooth;

jie2 chi 潔齒
clean the teeth;

jie ya 潔牙
clean the teeth;

jiu4 chi 臼齒
back teeth / molar / molar teeth;

ju1 chi 駒齒
milk teeth;

ju3 jue ya 咀嚼牙
morsal teeth;

ju3 齟
irregular teeth;

ju yu 齟齬
in disagreement;

ju4 ya 巨牙
macrotooth;

ju ya zheng 巨牙症
macrodontia;

kai1 fang xing ya sui yan 開放性牙髓炎
open pulpitis;

ke1 ya 磕牙
chat / gossip;

ke4 嗑
crack sth between the teeth;

lao3 diao ya 老掉牙
(1) very old;
(2) obsolete / old-fashioned / outdated;

li4 zui hua ya 利嘴花牙
have a ready tongue // saponaceous;

lian4 qiu jun xing yin yan 鏈球菌性齦炎
streptococcal gingivitis;

liao2 ya 獠牙
buckteeth / fangs / long protruding teeth;

lie4 chi 裂齒
carnassial tooth;

ling2 ya li chi 伶牙俐齒
silver-tongued || fluent; have a silver tongue; very good at speaking and talking;

ling2 齡
age / years;

ling4 ren chi leng 令人齒冷
arouse sb's scorn / invite contempt;

lou4 chi 露齒
expose one's teeth;

lou chi er xiao 露齒而笑
grin / toothpaste smile;

ma3 chi ri zeng 馬齒日增
become older daily // long in the tooth;

ma chi tu zeng 馬齒徒增
accomplish nothing despite one's advanced age || old and unfit for anything; outgrow one's usefulness;

ma chi yi zhang 馬齒已長
advanced in age / old // one is old;

mei3 chi 美齒
beautiful teeth;

men2 chi 門齒
front tooth / incisor;

mo2 ya 磨牙
(1) argue endlessly / talk nonsense;
(2) idle away time / kill time;
(3) crack sth between the teeth / grind one's teeth / grit one's teeth;

mo ya zheng 磨牙症
bruxism;

mo4 chi 沒齒
to the end of one's life;

mo chi bu wang 沒齒不忘
never forget as long as one lives / grateful to sb until the last tooth falls out of one's head / remember as long as one lives / remember for the rest of one's life;

mo chi nan wang 沒齒難忘
never forget as long as one lives / grateful to sb until the last tooth falls out of one's head / remember as long as one lives / remember for the rest of one's life;

mo chi wu yuan 沒齒無怨
without any complaint to the end of one's life;

nan2 yu qi chi 難於啟齒
difficult to speak out one's mind // have a bone in the throat;

nian2 chi 年齒
age of a person;

nie4 齧
bite / gnaw;

nie duan 齧斷
bite off;

nie he 齧合
clench the teeth;

nu4 mu qie chi 怒目切齒
intense hatred;

pai2 ya 排牙
tooth arrangement;

pao4 zhen xing yin yan 疱疹性齦炎
herpetic gingivitis;

pie3 chi la zui 撇齒拉嘴
wear a contemptuous expression;

qi3 chi 啟齒
open one's mouth to say sth || bring up; mention; start to talk about sth;

qian2 mo ya 前磨牙
premolar tooth;

qie1 chi 切齒
(1) incisor;
(2) gnash one's teeth / grind the teeth in anger / grit one's teeth;

qie chi fu xin 切齒腐心
gnash one's teeth in hatred / hate with all one's soul // in deep hatred and anger;

qie chi ren shou 切齒忍受
grin and bear it;

qie chi tong hen 切齒痛恨
gnash one's teeth in hatred || grind one's teeth in a spurt of hatred; hate bitterly; hate with gnashing teeth; hate with particular venom; have a bitter hatred for; strong indignation;

qie chi zhi chou 切齒之仇
bitter hatred that makes one gnash the teeth;

qie chi zhi hen 切齒之恨
extreme hatred // grinding hatred;

qie chi zhou ma 切齒咒罵
curse with clenched teeth / grind one's teeth and heap curses on;

qing1 chun qi qian ya zhou yan 青春期前牙周炎
prepubertal periodontitis;

qing shao nian xing ya zhou yan 青少年型牙周炎
juvenile periodontitis;

qu3 齲
rotten teeth / tooth decay;

qu chi 齲齒
(1) caries / dental caries;
(2) carious tooth / decayed tooth;
yuan fa xing qu chi 原發性齲齒
primary dental caries;

qu du 齲蠹
rotten teeth;

quan2 kou tuo ya 全口托牙
complete denture / full denture;

quan3 ya 犬牙
canine tooth / eye tooth;

que1 ya 缺牙
missing tooth;

ren2 zao guan 人造冠
artificial crown;

ren4 shen xing yin yan 妊娠性齦炎
pregnancy gingivitis;

ren shen yin yan 妊娠齦炎
gingivitis gravidarum;

rou4 ya zhong xing ya yin liu 肉芽腫性牙齦瘤
epulis granulomatosa;

ru3 chi 乳齒
calf's teeth / deciduous teeth / milk teeth;

ru ya 乳牙
milk tooth / primary teeth;

sai1 ya 塞牙
food stuck between the teeth;

san1 jian ya 三尖牙
tricuspid tooth;

shang4 jian ya 上尖牙
eyetooth;

shang quan ya 上犬牙
eyetooth;

she4 yu qi chi 赦於啟齒
feel shy to speak;

shi2 ren ya hui 拾人牙慧
pick up what others say || offer another's ideas as one's own; pick up phrases from sb and pass them off as one's own; plagiarize; steal others' ideas; take up and adopt others' thoughts instead of using one's own;

shua1 ya 刷牙
brush the teeth;

shuang1 jian ya 雙尖牙
premolar tooth;

tai1 sheng ya 胎生牙
natal tooth;

牙 *Tooth*

ti1 ya 剔牙
pick the teeth;

tiao2 齠
shed the milk teeth;

tiao chen 齠齔
shed the milk teeth;

ting1 chi 聽齒
auditory teeth;

tuo1 ya 托牙
denture;

bu fen tuo ya 部分托牙
partial denture;

quan kou tuo ya 全口托牙
complete denture / full denture;

tuo1 ya 脱牙
dedentition;

wu2 ya 無牙
anodontia;

bu fen wu ya 部份無牙
partial anodontia;

xi4 jun xing ya sui yan 細菌性牙髓炎
anachoretic pulpitis;

xia4 chen ya 下沉牙
submerged tooth;

xian2 ke ya 閑磕牙
leisure conversation about nothing in particular;

xian2 ke da ya 閒磕打牙
chat without a purpose;

xiang1 ya 鑲牙
crown a tooth / fill in an artificial tooth;

xiao3 ya 小牙
denticle;

xiao ya zheng 小牙症
microdontia;

xin1 sheng er ya 新生兒牙
neonatal tooth;

xin sheng er yin liu 新生兒齦瘤
epulis of newborn;

xiu1 yu qi chi 羞於啟齒
too shy to speak out one's mind;

xuan3 ze xing ba ya 選擇性拔牙
selected extraction;

ya2 牙
(1) teeth;
(2) tooth-like thing;

jie ya 潔牙
clean the teeth;

ju ya 巨牙
macrotooth;

ya bai kou qing 牙白口清
able to speak articulately;

ya ben zhi 牙本質
dentin;

gong neng xing yan ben zhi 功能性牙本質
functional dentin;

ji fa xing ya ben zhi 繼發性牙本質
secondary dentin;

yuan fa xing ya ben zhi 原發性牙本質
primary dentin;

ya cao 牙槽
socket of the tooth;

ya cao chu xue 牙槽出血
odontorrhagia;

ya cao gu sui yan 牙槽骨髓炎
alveolar osteomyelitis;

ya cao nong lou 牙槽膿漏
pyorrhoea;

ya cao nong zhong 牙槽膿腫
alveolar abscess;

ya cao yan 牙槽炎
alveolar / alveolitis;

ya chi 牙齒
tooth;

ya chi bao jian 牙齒保健
dental health;

ya chi da zhan 牙齒打戰
make sb's teeth chatter;

ya chi qin shi zheng 牙齒侵蝕症
dental erosion;

ya chi yao he bu zheng 牙齒咬合不正
malocclusion;

ya chuang 牙牀
gums / jawbone;

ya fa sheng 牙發生
odontogenesis;

ya fa sheng bu quan 牙發生不全
odotogenesis imperfecta;

ya fa yu bu liang 牙發育不良
hypodontia;

ya fen 牙粉
tooth powder;

ya feng er 牙縫兒
space between the teeth;

ya gen 牙根
base of the teeth / fang / root;

ya gen fa suan 牙根發酸
put sb's teeth on edge / set sb's teeth on edge;

ya gou 牙垢
tartar on the teeth;

ya gu zhi 牙骨質
tooth bone || cement; crusta petrosa;

ya guan 牙關
mandibular joint;

ya guan jin bi 牙關緊閉
lockjaw // with jaws shut tight;

ya guan jin suo zheng 牙關緊鎖症
trismus;

ya guan 牙冠
crown;

ya guo duo 牙過多
hyperdontia;

ya guo xiao 牙過小
microdontism;

ya huai si 牙壞死
odontonecrosis;

ya hui 牙慧
what others have said;

ya jian 牙尖
dental cusp;

ya jiao wai lu 牙腳外露
root exposed;

ya li bu qi 牙列不齊
malalignment;

ya rou shou su 牙肉收縮
gingival recession;

ya shen jing tong 牙神經痛
odontoneuralgia;

ya song 牙鬆
looseness of the tooth;

ya sui 牙髓
dental pulp / pulp;
huai si xing ya sui 壞死性牙髓
necrotic pulp;
huai si ya sui 壞死牙髓
dead pulp;

ya sui yan 牙髓炎
pulpitis;
kai fang xing ya sui yan 開放性牙髓炎
open pulpitis;
xi jun xing ya sui yan 細菌性牙髓炎
anachoretic pulpitis;
zeng sheng xing ya sui yan 增生性牙髓炎
hyperplastic pulpitis;

ya ting 牙挺
elevator;

ya tong 牙痛
toothache;
hang kong ya tong 航空牙痛
aero-odontodynia;
zhen fa xing ya tong 陣發性牙痛
grinding toothache;

ya tuo luo 牙脫落
exfoliation;

ya xing 牙型
tooth form;

ya yan 牙炎
odontitis;

ya yao dong 牙搖動
vacillation of the tooth;

ya yi wei 牙移位
tooth migration;
bing li xing ya yi wei 病理性牙移位
pathologic tooth wandering;

ya yin 牙齦
gum;

ya yin hong zhong 牙齦紅腫
redness and swelling of the gum;

ya yin kou yan 牙齦口炎
gingivostomatitis;

ya yin lie 牙齦裂
gingival cleft;

ya yin liu 牙齦瘤
epulides;
rou ya zhong xing ya yin liu 肉芽腫性牙齦瘤
epulis granulomatosa;

ya yin yan 牙齦炎
gingivitis;

ya you zhi 牙釉質
enamel / encaustum;

ya zhe lie 牙折裂
odontoclasis;

ya zhi 牙質
dentine;

ya zhou bing 牙周病
periodontal disease / periodontic / periodontosis;

ya zhou yan 牙周炎
periodontitis;
bian yuan xing ya zhou yan 邊緣性牙周炎
marginal periodontitis;
cheng ren ya zhou yan 成人牙周炎
adult periodontitis;
dan chun xing ya zhou yan 單純性牙周炎
simple periodontitis;
hua nong xing ya zhou yan 化膿性牙周炎
purulent periodontitis;
ji jin xing ya zhou yan 急進性牙周炎
rapidly progressive periodontitis;
qing chun qi qian ya zhou yan 青春期前牙周炎
prepubertal periodontitis;
qing shao nian xing ya zhou yan 青少年型牙周炎
juvenile periodontitis;
yin ya zhou yan 齦牙周炎
gingivoperiodontitis;

yao3 chi jiao chun 咬齒嚼唇
grind one's teeth and bite one's lips;

yao jin ya guan 咬緊牙關
grit one's teeth || bite the bullet; carry a stiff upper lip; clench one's jaws; endure with dogged will; keep a stiff upper lip; set one's teeth;

yao ya 咬牙
(1) grit one's teeth;
(2) grind one's teeth;

yao ya qie chi 咬牙切齒
clench one's teeth / gnash one's teeth / grind one's teeth / set one's teeth;

yi2 ya huan ya 以牙還牙
a tooth for a tooth || answer blows with blows; fight fire with fire; give as good as one gets; like for like; repay evil with evil; return blow for blow; return like for like; strike back; tit for tat; tooth for tooth;

yi ya huan ya, yi yan huan yan 以牙還牙，以眼還眼
an eye for an eye and a tooth for a tooth || eye for eye, tooth for tooth; measure for measure; meet force by force; serve sb with the same sauce; serve the same sauce to sb;

yi4 chi 義齒
artificial teeth;

yin2 齗
gum of the tooth;

yin2 bao ya 齦包牙
odontoclamis;

yin bi 齦壁
gingival wall;

yin chu xue 齦出血
ulorrhagia;

yin liu 齦瘤
epulis;
xin sheng er yin liu 新生兒齦瘤
epulis of newborn;

yin nong zhong 齦膿腫
parulis;

yin ya zhou yan 齦牙周炎
gingivoperiodontitis;

yin yan 齦炎
gingivitis;
bo tuo xing yin yan 剥脱性齦炎
desqamative gingivitis;
chu xue xing yin yan 出血性齦炎
hemorrhagic gingivitis;
huai xue bing xing yin yan 壞血病性齦炎
scorbutic gingivitis;
lian qiu jun xing yin yan 鏈球菌性齦炎
streptococcal gingivitis;
pao zhen xing yin yan 疱疹性齦炎
herpetic gingivitis;
ren shen xing yin yan 妊娠性齦炎
pregnancy gingivitis;
ren shen yin yan 妊娠齦炎
gingivitis gravidarum;

ying4 hua ya 硬化牙
sclerotic teeth;

yong3 jiu chi 永久齒
permanent teeth;

yuan2 fa xing qu chi 原發性齲齒
primary dental caries;

yuan fa xing ya ben zhi 原發性牙本質
primary dentin;

zan4 ya 暫牙
temporary teeth;

zao3 chu ya 早出牙
dentia praecox;

zao shu ya 早熟牙
premature teeth;

zeng1 sheng ya 增生牙
nupernumerary tooth;

zeng sheng xing ya sui yan 增生性牙髓炎
hyperplastic pulpitis;

zan4 chi 暫齒
milk tooth / tempory tooth;

zhang1 ya lu chi 張牙露齒
show one's teeth;

zhang ya wu zhao 張牙舞爪
sabre rattling ‖ bare fangs and brandish claws — make threatening gestures; bare one's fangs and open one's claws — make threatening gestures like a beast of prey; bare one's teeth; indulge in sabre rattling; put out a claw; show one's claws; show one's fangs and claws; snap and claw; with bared fangs; with one's fangs bared and one's claws sticking out;

zhang3 ya 長牙
cut a tooth / cut one's teeth / cut teeth / grow teeth;

zhen4 fa xing ya tong 陣發性牙痛
grinding toothache;

zhi4 chi 智齒
wisdom tooth;

zhi ya 智牙
wisdom tooth;

zhong1 qie ya 中切牙
central incisor;

zhu1 chun hao chi 朱唇皓齒
red lips and white teeth / rosy lips and ivory white teeth;

zhu4 chi 蛀齒
decayed teeth / dental caries;

zhu ya 蛀牙
(1) caries / dental caries;
(2) carious tooth / decayed tooth;

zi1 齜
(1) open the mouth and show the teeth;
(2) uneven teeth;

zi ya 齜牙
open the mouth and show the teeth;

zi ya deng yan 齜牙瞪眼
gnash the teeth and stare in anger;

zi ya lie zui 齜牙咧嘴
(1) look fierce / show one's teeth;
(2) contort one's face in agony / grimace in pain;

zu3 sheng ya 阻生牙
impacted tooth;

Yan 眼 Eye

ai2 yan 癌眼
cancer eye;

ai4 hu shi li 愛護視力
take good care of one's eyesight;

ai hu yan jing 愛護眼睛
protect one's eyes;

ai4 mu 礙目
eyesore;

ai yan 礙眼
offend the eye // unpleasant to look at / unpleasant to the eye;

an4 qi 暗泣
weep behind others' backs / weep without uttering sound;

an shi 暗視
scotopia;

an shi jue 暗視覺
scotopic vision / twilight vision;

an song qiu bo 暗送秋波
(1) cast coquettish glances at || cast sheep's eyes at; make eyes at; make goo-goo eyes at; ogle at; secretly cast flirtatious looks at; send sb the glad eye; stealthily give sb the glad eye;
(2) make secret overtures to || flirt; leer at; stealthily send speechless messages;

an4 ran xia lei 黯然下淚
grieve to the shedding of tears;

ao1 yan 凹眼
(1) sunken eyes;
(2) celophthalmia;

ao4 ni 傲睨
look down on || despise; regard with disdain;

ao shi 傲視
regard with disdain || scorn; turn up one's nose at;

ba1 zi mei 八字眉
slanted eyebrows;

ba1 ang yan 巴昂眼
bungeye;

ba gao wang shang 巴高望上
seek advancement;

ba wang 巴望
hope for anxiously;

ba1 la yan 疤瘌眼
scarred eyelids;

ba la yan er zhao jing zi — zi zhao nan kan 疤瘌眼兒照鏡子——自找難看
a person with a scarred eyelid looking into a mirror — exposing one's own defects;

ba3 wu 把晤
meet / see each other;

bai2 白
stare at sb with contempt;

bai mei chi yan 白眉赤眼
white-browed and red-eyed;

bai nei zhang 白內障
cataract;
chu fa bai nei zhang 初發白內障
incipient cataract;
chu qi bai nei zhang 初期白內障
incipient cataract;
chuang shang xing bai nei zhang 創傷性白內障
traumatic cataract;
di gai xue xing bai nei zhang 低鈣血性白內障
hypocalcemic cataract;
guo shu bai nei zhang 過熟白內障
hypermature cataract / overripe cataract;
hei se bai nei zhang 黑色白內障
black cataract;
ji fa xing bai nei zhang 繼發性白內障
secondary cataract;
lan ban bai nei zhang 藍斑白內障
blue dot cataract;
lan se bai nei zhang 藍色白內障
blue cataract;
lao nian bai nei zhang 老年白內障
senile cataract;
lao nian xing bai nei zhang 老年性白內障
senile cataract;
mo xing bai nei zhang 膜性白內障
membranous cataract;

nang xing bai nei zhang 囊性白內障
capsular cataract;
pi zhi xing bai nei zhang 皮質性白內障
cortical cataract;
qing guang yan xing bai nei zhang 青光眼性白內障
glaucomatous cataract;
quan bai nei zhang 全白內障
total cataract;
tang niao bing bai nei zhang 糖尿病白內障
diabetic cataract;
tang niao bing xing bai nei zhang 糖尿病性白內障
diabetic cataract;
te ying xing bai nei zhang 特應性白內障
atopic cataract;
wai shang xing bai nei zhang 外傷性白內障
traumatic cataract;
wan quan bai nei zhang 完全白內障
complete cataract;
yan zheng hou bai nei zhang 炎症後白內障
postinflammatory cataract;
ying yang que fa xing bai nei zhang 營養缺乏性白內障
nutritional deficiency cataract;
you nian xing bai nei zhang 幼年型白內障
juvenile cataract;
yuan fa xing bai nei zhang 原發性白內障
primary cataract;
zao chan er bai nei zhang 早產兒白內障
cataracts of prematurity;
zao lao xing bai nei zhang 早老性白內障
presenile cataract;
zhong zhang qi bai nei zhang 腫脹期白內障
intumescent cataract;
zhong du xing bai nei zhang 中毒性白內障
toxic cataract;

bai xue bing xing shi wang mo bing 白血病性視網膜病
leukemic retinophathy;

bai xue bing xing shi wang mo yan 白血病性視網膜炎
leukemic retinitis;

bai yan 白眼
(1) the whites of the eyes;
(2) contemptuous look / supercilious look;
(3) contempt / disdain;
zao ren bai yan 遭人白眼
be treated with disdain ‖ be held in disdain; receive a cold disdainful look; receive a cold stare;

bai yan kan ren 白眼看人
look upon people with disdain / treat people superciliously;

bai yan xiang kan 白眼相看
despise / look down on / turn up the whites of one's eyes upon;

bai yan zhu 白眼珠
the white of the eye;

bai zhou shi jue 白晝視覺
day vision;

bai3 kan bu yan 百看不厭
be at all time a great pleasure to see ‖ be worth reading a hundred times; be worth watching a hundred times; never get tired to reading; never tire of seeing;

bai wen bu ru yi jian 百聞不如一見
seeing is believing ‖ a thousand words of hearsay are not worth a single glance at the reality; better seeing once than hearing a hundred times; hearsays are no substitutes for seeing with one's own eyes; it is better to see sth once than hear about it a hundred times; seeing for oneself is a hundred times better than hearing from others; seeing for oneself is better than all hearsays; there is nothing like seeing for oneself; to see is to believe; to see it once is better than to hear a hundred times;

bai3 dong xing yan zhen 擺動性眼震
pendular nystagmus;

bai4 du 拜讀
have the honour to read / read with respect;

bai du da zuo 拜讀大作
have the honour to read / have the pleasure of perusing your work / read with respect your work;

bai jian 拜見
(1) call to pay respect / pay a formal visit;

(2) meet one's senior or superior;

ban4 mang 半盲
hemianopsia / partial blindness;

bao3 du 飽讀
be well-read;

bao du shi shu 飽讀詩書
be well-read in the classics;

bao kan 飽看
feast one's eyes on / read to one's heart's content;

bao xiang yan fu 飽享眼福
enjoy the sight to one's great satisfaction / feast one's eyes on;

bao yan fu 飽眼福
feast one's eyes on;

bao4 tou huan yan 豹頭環眼
round eyes and well-formed forehead;

bao4 tu 暴突
bulge / protrude / stick out;

bei4 yan 背眼
not easily seen;

beng4 lei 迸淚
tears pouring out;

bi1 shi 逼視
(1) look at from close-up / stare down / stare out / watch intently;
(2) stare at sternly;

bi3 shi 鄙視
disdain / dispise / look down on / look down upon / scorn / slight / turn up one's nose;

bi4 mu he jing 閉目合睛
shut one's eyes;

bi mu ku zuo 閉目枯坐
block one's ears and shut one's eyes to sth / close one's eyes and sit doing nothing;

bi mu se ting 閉目塞聽
shut one's eyes and stop up one's ears‖out of touch with reality; turn a blind eye and a deaf ear to;

bi mu yang sheng 閉目養神
close one's eyes for a rest / close the eyes and give the mind a brief rest;

bi shang yan 閉上眼
close one's eyes / shut one's eyes;

bi4 睥
(1) scornful look;
(2) look askance;

bi ni 睥睨
look askance;

bi4 yan 碧眼
blue-eyed;

bi4 mu 蔽目
blindfold / cover the eyes;

bi4 er bu jian 避而不見
avoid meeting sb / evade a meeting with sb;

bian1 yuan xing yan jian yan 邊緣性眼瞼炎
blear eye;

bian3 xing yan 扁形眼
platymorphia;

bian4 guan 徧觀
see everything;

bie1 zhu yan lei 憋住眼淚
fight back tears;

bie2 ju zhi yan 別具隻眼
have an original view;

bo2 lan qun shu 博覽群書
go far afield in one's reading;

bu4 chi bu long 不痴不聾
blind and deaf / indifferent // pretend not to see and hear;

bu chou bu cai 不瞅不睬
completely ignore‖give sb a cold shoulder; neither look nor give attention; not to notice sb; pay no attention;

bu da yan 不打眼
unattractive;

bu gu 不顧
disregard / take no account of;

bu jian 不見
(1) have not met / have not seen;
(2) disappear / missing;

bu jian bu san 不見不散
don't leave until we are all there / not to leave without seeing each other;

bu jian guan cai bu luo lei 不見棺材不落淚
not to shed tears until one sees the coffin — refuse to repent until one is faced with complete defeat;

bu jian tian ri 不見天日
in total darkness;

bu jin luo lei 不禁落淚
cannot help shedding tears / cannot help weeping;

bu jue yu er 不絕於耳
can be heard without end / linger in one's ears;

bu kan hui shou 不堪回首
cannot bear to look back / find it unbearable to recall / too sad to reflect;

bu kan ru mu 不堪入目
intolerable to the eye / not fit to be seen;

bu qi yan 不起眼
inconspicuous;

bu ren zheng shi 不忍正視
hate the sight of / heartbreaking to look at;

bu ren zu du 不忍卒睹
cannot bear to see / hate the sight of;

bu ren zuo shi 不忍坐視
cannot bear to sit and watch without doing anything / cannot bear to stand idly by;

bu shun yan 不順眼
disagreeable to the eye || an eye sore; cannot bear the sight of; get tired of; incurring dislike; look odd;

bu xie yi gu 不屑一顧
not worth sb's notice || be taken as beneath notice; beneath one's notice; cock a snook at; fob off; not to deign to take a glance; not worth a single glance; shrug off; snap one's fingers at; turn up one's nose; will not spare a glance for; wave aside;

bu ya guan 不雅觀
unbecoming;

bu zai yan li 不在眼裏
beneath one's notice / treat with disdain || have no respect for; show one's contempt for; snap one's fingers at; think nothing of;

bu zhi yi gu 不值一顧
not worth a single glance || beneath contempt; beneath notice; not worth notice; nothing to make a song about; out of court;

ca1 liang yan jing 擦亮眼睛
sharpen one's vigilance || become more clear-sighted; heighten one's viligance; keep one's eyes skinned; keep one's eyes wide open; on the outlook; remove the scales from one's eyes; wide the dust from one's eyes;

cai3 睬
(1) look / watch;
(2) notice / pay attention to;

can1 jian 參見
call on (a superior);

can kan 參看
refer to;

can3 bu ren du 慘不忍睹
so miserable that one cannot bear seeing it || could not bear the sight; extremely tragic or cruel; so appalling that one could hardly bear the sight of it; so horrible that one could hardly bear to look at it; too deplorable to see; too horrible to look at;

can4 lan duo mu 燦爛奪目
dazzling || brilliant; the lustre dazzles the eye;

cao3 cao guo mu 草草過目
cast a running glance at / give a cursory reading / read through roughly / skim through;

ce4 mu 側目
(1) sidelong glance;
(2) cause raised eyebrows;

ce mu er shi 側目而視
cast a sidelong glance / give sb a sidelong glance / look askance at sb / look with a sidelong glance;

ce mu kui shi 側目窺視
cast a sidelong glance at;

ce mu zhu shi 側目注視
give sb a sidelong glance / look at sb with a sidelong glance;

ce shi 側視
side-looking;

cen2 涔
tearful;

cen cen 涔涔
tearful;

cen cen lei xia 涔涔淚下
in tears // tearful;

cha2 kan 查看
check / examine / have a look || look about; look at; look into; look over; look up; make sure; see; see about;

cha2 kan 察看
check / inspect / look carefully at / observe / see over / watch;

cha yuan guan se 察言觀色
gather another's frame of mind through his words and expressions;

chai1 yue 拆閱
open and read a letter or document;

chan2 yan kong 饞眼孔
lecherous look at women;

chang2 jian 常見
see or be seen frequently;

chen1 瞋
open the eyes;

chen mu 瞋目
(1) angry eyes;
(2) open one's eyes wide;

chen mu er shi 瞋目而視
stare angrily || glare; glare at sb in anger; stare at sb angrily;

chen shi 瞋視
look angrily at / look with angry eyes;

cheng1 瞠
stare;

cheng hu qi hou 瞠乎其後
be left far behind || a far cry from sb; consider oneself inferior to another; fail to secure a leading place; far behind, without any hope of catching up; feel one is not another's equal; lag far behind; nowhere; unable to catch up;

cheng mu 瞠目
wide-eyed;

cheng mu chi jing 瞠目吃驚
wide-eyed with horror;

cheng mu er shi 瞠目而視
stare at with wide eyes;

cheng mu jie she 瞠目結舌
stare tongue-tied || be struck dumb; be wide-eyed and unable to speak; gape with astonishment; stare dumbfounded; stare tongue-tied; wide-eyed and tongue-tied;

cheng mu zhi shi 瞠目直視
wild-eyed with surprise;

cheng shi 瞠視
stare at;

cheng3 mu 騁目
look into the distance;

cheng mu si gu 騁目四顧
gaze in four directions / look around;

cheng mu yuan tiao 騁目遠眺
scan distant horizons;

cheng wang 騁望
look as far as one can see;

chi1 bai yan 吃白眼
be given the cold shoulder / be looked down on;

chi1 眵
caking of eye secretions;

chi mu hu 眵目糊
caking of eye secretions;

chi4 眙
(1) look in the face / stare;
(2) look in astonishment;

chong1 xue xing qing guang yan 充血性青光眼
congestive glaucoma;

chou1 qi 抽泣
snivel / sob / whimper;

chou2 shi 仇視
look upon with hatred || hostile to; regard as an enemy;

chou2 mei 愁眉
knitted brows / worried look;

chou mei bu zhan 愁眉不展
with knitted brows || a cloud upon one's

brow; bend the brows; gloom hangs upon one's brow; have a gloomy countenance; knit the brows; look blue; lower one's eyebrows; with a worried frown; with brows knit in deep thought // dusky frown;

chou mei cu e 愁眉蹙額
gloomy eyebrows and wrinkled forehead — knit the brows;

chou mei gu lian 愁眉苦臉
a face of woe ‖ a face shaded with melancholy; down in the dumps; down in the mouth; draw a long face; frown of dismay; gloomy face; have a face as long as a fiddle; have a face like a fiddle; have a worried look; look blue; look melancholy; make a long face; mops and mows; pull a long face; put on a long face; wear a glum countenance; with a long face;

chou mei suo yan 愁眉鎖眼
knit one's brows and cast down one's eyes in despair / knit one's brows in despair;

chou2 shi 讎視
regard with hostility // hostile to;

chou3 瞅
gaze / look at / see;

chou bu de 瞅不得
not worth seeing / should not be seen;

chou bu jian 瞅不見
look but unable to see / unable to see;

chou cai 瞅睬
look / notice;

chou jian 瞅見
see / catch a glimpse of sth or sb;

chou le yi yan 瞅了一眼
take a look at;

chu1 ti 出涕
shed tears;

chu xue xing qing guang yan 出血性青光眼
hemorrhagic glaucoma;

chu xue xing shi wang mo bing 出血性視網膜病
hemorrhagic retinopathy;

chu1 fa bai nei zhang 初發白內障
incipient cataract;

chu qi bai nei zhang 初期白內障
incipient cataract;

chu3 chu ke guan 楚楚可觀
being clear and distinct, it is worth seeing;

chu4 mu jing xin 怵目驚心
be shocked at the sight of ‖ be shocked to witness; strike the eye and rouse the mind;

chu4 mu 觸目
(1) meet the eye;
(2) attracting attention / conspicuous / shocking / startling;

chu mu jie shi 觸目皆是
be seen everywhere ‖ a common sight; be everywhere in evidence; can be seen everywhere;

chu mu jing xin 觸目驚心
strike the eye and rouse the mind ‖ horrid; shocking; startling;

chu ran xing yan yan 觸染性眼炎
contagious ophthalmia;

chu yan 觸眼
conspicuous / eye-catching;

chuan2 guan 傳觀
pass on for reading;

chuan ran xing yan yan 傳染性眼炎
infectious ophthalmia;

chuan yue 傳閱
circulate for perusal / pass round for perusal;

chuang1 shang xing bai nei zhang 創傷性白內障
traumatic cataract;

chuang shang xing qing guang yan 創傷性青光眼
traumatic glaucoma;

chuang shang xing ruo shi 創傷性弱視
traumatic amblyopia;

chuang4 jian 創見
new ideas;

chuang4 ran lei xia 愴然淚下
burst into sorrowful tears;

chui1 hu zi deng yan jing 吹鬍子瞪眼睛
blow a fuse / scowl and growl ‖ blow a gasket; browbeat; fall into a rage; froth at the

mouth and glare with rage; fume with rage; snort and stare in anger;

chui2 lei 垂淚
shed tears / weep;

chui qi 垂泣
shed tears / weep;

chui ti 垂涕
shed tears / weep;

chui xia yan jian 垂下眼瞼
lower one's eyes;

chun1 ji yan yan 春季眼炎
spring ophthalmia;

chuo4 qi 啜泣
sob;

ci2 mei shan mu 慈眉善目
benevolent and kind countenance / benignant look;

ci4 ji xing tong kong suo xiao 刺激性瞳孔縮小
irritative miosis;

ci mu 刺目
dazzling / irritating to the eye // hurt sb's eyes;

ci yan 刺眼
dazzling / irritating to the eye // hurt sb's eyes;

cong2 chang yuan lai kan 從長遠來看
in the long haul / in the long run / over the long haul;

cu1 mei da yan 粗眉大眼
bushy eyebrows and big eyes || coarse features; thick-eyebrowed and big eyed;

cu4 蹙
knit one's brows;

cu an 蹙頞
knit the brows / look distressed;

cu e 蹙額
frown / knit one's brows;

cu e zhou mei 蹙額縐眉
frown / knit the brows / wrinkle one's brows;

cu mei 蹙眉
frown / knit one's brows / pucker one's eyebrows;

cuan2 mei 攢眉
frown / knit one's brows;

cuan mei cu e 攢眉蹙額
bend the brows / contract the brows / frown / knit the brows;

cui1 mei zhe yao 摧眉折腰
bow and scrape / bow unctuously;

cui3 can duo mu 璀璨奪目
with dazzling brightness || bright-coloured and dazzling; dazzling; dazzling splendour; its elegance ravishes the eyes; resplendent; shine with dazzling brilliance; the dazzling brightness blinds the eyes; the lustre dazzled the eye;

cuo4 fan yan pi 錯翻眼皮
turn a wrong eyelid;

da3 liang 打量
(1) look sb up and down || look over; measure with the eye; size up; take the measure of sb;
(2) reckon || suppose; think;

da yan 打眼
(1) attract attention / catch the eye;
(2) beautiful / good-looking;

da4 bao yan fu 大飽眼福
feast one's eyes / glut one's eyes;

da kai yan jie 大開眼界
eye-opening // feed one's sight on / get an eyeful / have an eyeful / widen one's horizon // eye-opener;

da song qiu bo 大送秋波
give sb the glad eye / make eyes at / make sheep's eyes at / send speechless messages from the eyes;

da yan qiu 大眼球
macrophthalmia;

da you ke guan 大有可觀
quite impressive / worthwhile seeing;

da zhang jian wen 大長見聞
a great eye-opener to sb;

dai4 yan jing 戴眼鏡
wear spectacles;

dan1 眈
look downward;

dan dan 眈眈
eyeing gloatingly / look at greedily;

dan1 chun jin shi san guang 單純近視散光
simple myopic astigmatism;

dan chun xing jie mo yan 單純性結膜炎
simple conjunctivitis;

dan chun xing jin shi 單純性近視
primary myopia / simple myopia;

dan chun xing qing guang yan 單純性青光眼
simple glaucoma;

dan chun xing shi wang mo yan 單純性視網膜炎
simple retinitis;

dan chun yuan shi san guang 單純遠視散光
simple hyperopic astigmatism;

dan se jue yan 單色覺眼
monochromatic eye;

dan se shi jue 單色視覺
monochromatism;

dan yan 單眼
ocellus;

dan yan duo shi 單眼多視
polyopia monophthalmica;

dan yan duo shi zheng 單眼多視症
polyopia monophthalmica;

dan yan fu shi 單眼複視
polyopia monophthalmica;

dan yan pi 單眼皮
single-fold eyelids;

dan yan shi jue 單眼視覺
monocular vision;

dan yan shi li 單眼視力
monocular vision;

dan4 sao e mei 淡掃蛾眉
apply a light makeup / finish pencilling one's eyebrows slightly;

dang3 yan 擋眼
obstruct one's view;

de2 kui quan bao 得窺全豹
able to see a sample of sth in its entirety / able to see the entire thing;

de kui yi ban 得窺一斑
able to see a segment of a whole;

deng3 liang qi guan 等量齊觀
draw a parallel between / put on a par;

deng xian shi zhi 等閒視之
regard it as of no importance;

deng zhe qiao 等着瞧
wait and see;

deng4 瞪
glare / gorgonize / stare at;

deng da yan jing 瞪大眼睛
open one's eyes wide;

deng mu 瞪目
(1) open one's eyes wide;
(2) glare / glower at sb / gorgonize / stare;

deng mu ning shi 瞪目凝視
stare with wide eyes;

deng shi 瞪視
glower at sb / goggle / stare sb in the face;

deng yan 瞪眼
(1) glare / goggle / gorgonize / open one's eyes wide / stare;
(2) get angry with sb / glower and glare at sb;
(3) goggle-eyed;

deng yan nu shi 瞪眼怒視
scowl down / stare and scowl at;

di1 gai xue xing bai nei zhang 低鈣血性白內障
hypocalcemic cataract;

di mei 低眉
lower one's eyebrows;

di2 shi 敵視
regard with hostility;

di2 覿
meet / see each other;

di mian 覿面
meet / see each other;

di4 睇
(1) take a casual look at;
(2) cast a sidelong glance / look askance / look sideways;

di bu ru yan 睇不入眼
look at but what is seen does not please the

眼 *Eye*

eyes;

di4 yan se 遞眼色
dart a meaning look at sb / hint with the eyes / tip sb the wink / wink at sb;

di4 shi 諦視
look attentively;

diao4 jing 吊睛
slant-eyed;

diao4 lei 掉淚
come to tears / tears falling;

diao qian yan er li 掉錢眼兒裏
calculating / money-hungry;

diao xia 掉下
(1) fall;
(2) drop;

diao xia lei lai 掉下淚來
tears roll down one's cheeks;

die2 眣
squinting eyes;

ding1 盯
affix the eye on sb / fix one's eyes on / gaze at;

ding shao 盯梢
shadow sb / tail sb;

ding shi 盯視
stare;

ding zhe 盯着
keep an eye on || affix the eye on sb; fix one's eyes on; gaze at; glue one's eyes on; keep a close watch on; stare at;

ding zhe dian er 盯着點儿
keep an eye on;

ding zhu 盯住
affix the eye on sb / keep a close watch on;

ding4 jing 定睛
fix one's eyes on;

ding jing xi kan 定睛細看
give sb a good look / give sth a good look;

diu1 ge yan se 丢個眼色
give a hint with the eyes / tip sb the wink;

diu yan se 丢眼色
wink at sb || give a hint with the eyes; give sb a wink; tip sb the wink;

dong1 qiao xi wang 東瞧西望
gaze this way and that || stare about; watch out furtively to the east and west;

dong zhang xi wang 東張西望
gaze around || gaze right and left; glance this way and that; look all round; peer around; peer in all directions;

dong4 jian 洞見
see very clearly;

dong jian zheng jie 洞見症結
discern clearly the crucial reason / get to the heart of the problem / see clearly the crux of the matter;

dong ruo guan huo 洞若觀火
as clear as looking at fire || as clear as day; as plain as a pikestaff; observe things as clearly as if looking at a fire; see sth as clearly as blazing fire;

dong4 mu 動目
(1) look attentively;
(2) attract one's attention;

dong ren er mu 動人耳目
make one's ears and eyes tingle;

dou4 ji yan 鬭雞眼
crossed eyes;

dou yan 鬭眼
bow-eye / cross-eye;

du2 ju hui yan 獨具慧眼
can see what others cannot / discern what others don't / have mental discernment;

du yan 獨眼
cyclopia / one-eyed;

du yan long 獨眼龍
one-eyed person;

du yan long kan shu — yi mu liao ran 獨眼龍看書——一目瞭然
a one-eyed person reading a book — taking everything at a glance;

du yan long xiang qin — yi mu liao ran 獨眼龍相親——一目瞭然
a one-eyed person sizing up his prospective wife — taking everything at a glance;

du3 睹
gaze at / look at / see;

du er bu jian 睹而不見
look without seeing / turn a blind eye to;

du jing shang qing 睹景傷情
be moved by what one sees || feel depressed at the sight of the scene; the scene evokes bitter memories of the past; the sight strikes a chord in one's chord;

du wu sheng qing 睹物生情
the sight of familiar objects fills one with infinite melancholy — think of the dead;

du wu si ren 睹物思人
seeing the thing one thinks of the person — the thing reminds one of its owner;

duan1 liang 端量
look a person up and down;

duan shi 端視
look steadily;

duan xiang 端詳
look at closely;

duan xiang 端相
look at carefully;

duan3 jian 短見
(1) shallow knowledge / short-sighted;
(2) suicide;

duan jian gua wen 短見寡聞
of limited experience // short sight and rare hearing;

duan shi 短視
(1) myopia / near-sightedness;
(2) lack foresight // short-sighted;

dui4 yan 對眼
(1) cross-eye / internal strabismus;
(2) to one's liking / to one's taste;

dun3 盹
doze;

dun er 盹兒
doze / nap;

dun shui 盹睡
doze / nap / nod;

duo1 jian bo wen 多見博聞
have extensive knowledge / have seen and heard much // widely experienced;

duo jian bu guai 多見不怪
use lessens marvel;

duo jian duo ting 多見多聽
see more and hear often;

duo jian duo wen 多見多聞
experienced;

duo kan shao shuo 多看少說
keep your mouth shut and your eyes open;

duo wen duo jian 多聞多見
have seen the elephant // widely experienced;

duo2 kuang er chu 奪眶而出
brim over / start from one's eyes;

duo mu 奪目
dazzle the eyes;

duo ren xin mu 奪人心目
grasp one's heart and dazzle one's eyes;

e2 mei 娥眉
beautiful eyebrows — a beautiful girl / girl;

e4 mei e yan 惡眉惡眼
fierce look;

e xing qing guang yan 惡性青光眼
malignant glaucoma;

e xing tu yan 惡性突眼
malignant exophthalmos;

e yan xiang xiang 惡眼相向
cast an evil eye on sb;

e4 ku 愕顧
look in amazement;

e ran si gu 愕然四顧
look around in astonishment;

e shi 愕視
stare in amazement;

fa3 yan 法眼
discerning eyes;

fan1 bai yan 翻白眼
(1) show the whites of one's eyes;
(2) in a dying situation;

fan kan 翻看
leaf through;

fan yue 翻閱
browse / glance over / leaf through / look over / thumb through;

fan2 mu 凡目
worldly viewpoints;

fan yan 凡眼
mortal eyesight;

fan3 gu 反顧
look back;

fan mu 反目
fall out // at odds;

fan mu cheng chou 反目成仇
fall out and become enemies / quarrel with sb and then become enemies with each other;

fan4 guan 泛觀
a quick and general glance;

fan lan 泛覽
a quick and general glance;

fang4 yan 放眼
scan widely / take a broad view;

fang yan shi jie 放眼世界
open one's eyes to the whole world || have the whole world in view; keep the whole world in view;

fei4 yan 費眼
strain the eye / waste eyesight;

fu3 kan 俯瞰
look down at / overlook;

fu shi 俯視
look down at / overlook;

fu3 shi tong ku 撫尸慟哭
stroke the corpse and cry bitterly || cry over sb's body; mourn loudly over sb's remains; weep bitterly over sb's corpse; weep over the corpse;

fu4 shi 複視
diplopia;
dan yan fu shi 單眼複視
polyopia monophthalmica;
sheng li xing fu shi 生理性複視
physiological diplopia;
tong ce fu shi 同側複視
homonymous diplopia;

gan1 deng yan 乾瞪眼
look on in despair || look on helplessly; stand by anxiously, unable to help;

gan ku wu lei 乾哭無淚
howl without tears / wail a few times without shedding tears;

gan yan zheng 乾眼症
xerophthalmia;

gao1 shi kuo bu 高視闊步
carry oneself proudly || prance; stalk; strut like a turkey-cock; with one's head in the air;

gao yan 高眼
keen foresight / vision;

gao zhan yuan zhu 高瞻遠矚
see far and wide || far-sighted; from the most commanding height and with the greatest vision; look far ahead and aim high; show great foresight; standhigh and see far; stand on a high vantage point and have a farsighted view; take a broad and long view; transcendent views; with clear vision; with great foresight;

ge1 bi wa yan 割鼻挖眼
cut off the nose and gouge out the eyes;

ge4 chi ji jian 各持己見
each sticks to his own views;

ge shu ji jian 各抒己見
each airs his own views;

gong1 neng xing mang 功能性盲
functional blindness;

gong1 du 恭讀
read respectfully;

gong3 mo 鞏膜
external covering of the eyeball / sclera;

gong mo guan 鞏膜管
scleral canal;

gong mo hong mo yan 鞏膜虹膜炎
scleroiritis;

gong mo ruan hua 鞏膜軟化
scleromalacia;

gong mo yan 鞏膜炎
scleritis;

huai si xing gong mo yan 壞死性鞏膜炎
scleritis necroticans;
jiao mo gong mo yan 角膜鞏膜炎
keratoscleritis;
jie jie xing gong mo yan 結節性鞏膜炎
nodular scleritis;

gou3 yan kan ren 狗眼看人
judge people by wealth and power / treat people with snobbish attitude;

gou yan kan ren di 狗眼看人低
act like a snob / judge sb by wealth and power / look down on sb // snobbish;

gu3 瞽
blind;

gu4 zhi ji jian 固執己見
stick to one's opinions // assertive;

gu4 顧
look at / turn round and look at;

gu mian 顧眄
turn one's head and look around;

gu pan 顧盼
look around;

gu pan shen fei 顧盼神飛
in one's eyes there is a look of quick intelligence and soft refinement;

gu pan sheng zi 顧盼生姿
look around charmingly;

gu pan zi ru 顧盼自如
gaze round as one wishes / gaze round to one's heart's content;

gu pan zi xiong 顧盼自雄
gaze round with great airs || as proud as a peacock; look about complacently; look about in a haughty manner; preen oneself; struct about pleased with oneself;

gu ying zi lian 顧影自憐
look at one's image in the mirror and pity oneself || admire oneself in the mirror; feel self-pity when looking at one's own shadow; look at one's reflection and admire oneself; look at one's shadow and lament one's lot; pity oneself at the sight of one's shadow; self-affection;

gu zhi zhi jian 顧指之間
the moment of glancing back and moving a finger — instantly;

gua1 mu xiang kan 刮目相看
look at sb with new eyes || have a completely new appraisal of sb; hold sb in greater esteem; hold sb in high esteem; keep eyes polished; make the town sit up and take notice; regard sb with special esteem; set a higher value on sb; see sb in a new light; sit up and take notice; treat sb with increased respect;

gua3 jian shao wen 寡見少聞
ignorant and ill-informed // have limited knowledge / have seen few and heard little;

gua yan 寡言
taciturn;

guan1 觀
(1) look at / observe / watch;
(2) sight / view;
(3) concept / outlook;

guan ce 觀測
observe / view;

guan ce qi xiang 觀測氣象
make weather observations;

guan cha 觀察
examine / inspect || observe; perceive; study; survey; watch;

guan cha dong jing 觀察動靜
watch what is going on;

guan cha feng xiang 觀察風向
find out which way the wind blows || find out how the wind blows; see how the gander hops; see how the land lies; see which way the cat jumps; wait for the cat to jump;

guan cha xing shi 觀察形勢
examine the situation / observe the situation;

guan chao 觀潮
view a tide;

guan guang 觀光
go sightseeing / tour / visit;

guan hai 觀海
look at the sea;

guan huo 觀火
see the fire;

guan ju 觀劇
watch a stage show;

guan kan 觀看
behold / view / watch;

guan mo 觀摩
inspect and learn from each other's work / view and emulate;

guan mo yan chu 觀摩演出
performance before fellow artists for the purpose of discussion and emulation;

guan qi xing er zhi qi ren 觀其行而知其人
a man is known by his behaviour / a tree is known by its fruit;

guan qi you, zhi qi ren 觀其友，知其人
a man is known by the company he keeps;

guan qi bu yu zhen jun zi 觀棋不語真君子
a true gentleman should keep silent while watching a chess game;

guan ren lian se 觀人臉色
read a person's face;

guan se cha yan 觀色察言
observe another's countenance and examine his utterance;

guan shang 觀賞
enjoy the sight of / see and enjoy / view and admire;

guan wang zhi lai 觀往知來
study the past and foretell the future changes;

guan wang 觀望
look on / wait and see;

guan wang bu qian 觀望不前
hesitate and make no move || hesitate; look about and make no move; undecided;

guan wang tai du 觀望態度
take a wait-and-see attitude;

guan wang xing shi 觀望形勢
wait for the cat to jump;

guan wei zhi ju 觀微知巨
a straw shows which way the wind blows;

guan xiang zhi ren 觀相知人
studying a man's physiognomy reveals his character;

guan yun zhi tian 觀雲知天
watch clouds and know signs in the sky;

guan zhan 觀瞻
sight / view || the appearance of a place and the impressions it leaves;

guan3 jian 管見
my humble opinion / my limited understanding;

guan jian suo ji 管見所及
in my humble opinion || as far as I can see; as my humble view could reach; in my apprehension; in the light of my limited experience;

guan kui 管窺
have a restricted view || look at sth through a bamboo tube;

guan kui kuang ju 管窺筐舉
limited outlook;

guan kui li ce 管窺蠡測
be restricted in vision and shallow in understanding || benighed; look at the sky through a tube and measure the sea with an oyster shell — a metaphor for a man of small experience; view the sky through a bamboo tube and measure the sea with a calabash — be restricted in vision and shallow in understanding;

guan kui suo ji 管窺所及
in my humble opinion;

guan kui zhi jian 管窺之見
the view through a tube — limited outlook / what has been seen through a tube — one's narrow views;

guan zhong kui bao 管中窺豹
have a limited view of sth || look at a leopard through a bamboo tube — have a limited view of sth; peep at a leopard through a tube — have a small field of vision;

guan zhong kui bao, ke jian yi ban 管中窺豹，可見一斑
you may know by a handful the whole sack || conjure up the whole thing through seeing a part of it; from his claw you may know the lion; from his foot you may know Hercules; look at one spot on a leopard and

you can visualize the whole animal; one may see day at a little hole;

guang1 cai duo mu 光彩奪目
dazzling with brilliance;

guang3 kai yan jie 廣開眼界
broaden one's field of vision / widen one's horizon // one's field of vision is vastly enlarged;

gui1 ze san guang 規則散光
regular astigmatism;

gui4 er jian mu 貴耳賤目
easily accept others' words and decline to see with one's own eyes / trust one's ears rather than one's eyes — rely on hearsay;

guo4 du lao shi 過度老視
hyperpresbyopia;

guo min xing jiao mo yan 過敏性角膜炎
anaphylactic;

guo min xing jie mo yan 過敏性結膜炎
anaphylactic conjunctivitis;

guo mu 過目
go over / look over;

guo mu bu wang 過目不忘
have a retentive memory ‖ gifted with an extraordinarily retentive memory; once seen it is always remembered;

guo mu cheng song 過目成誦
able to recite sth after reading it over once;

guo shu bai nei zhang 過熟白內障
hypermature cataract / overripe cataract;

guo yan 過眼
(1) pass before the eyes;
(2) take a glance;

hai4 yan 害眼
have eye trouble;

han2 lei 含淚
with tears in the eyes;

han lei ai qiu 含淚哀求
implore with tears;

han qi tun sheng 含泣吞聲
choke down one's tears;

han yan zhong tian 含眼終天
die unavenged;

han zhe yan lei 含着眼淚
have tears in one's eyes // in tears / with tears in one's eyes;

han3 jian 罕見
rare / rarely seen / seldom seen;

hao1 mu 蒿目
gaze far / gaze into the distance;

hao mu shi jian 蒿目時艱
look with anxiety at the world's ills ‖ foresee and worry about worldly troubles; survey the country's situation with concern; survey the world with concern;

hao3 kan 好看
(1) good-looking / goodly / handsome / nice-looking // look nice / look pretty;
(2) interesting;
(3) be honoured / do credit to / honour;
(4) deliberately embarrass sb // in a fix / in an embarrassing situation / on the spot;

hao4 chi e mei 皓齒蛾眉
white teeth and pretty eyebrows;

he2 yan 合眼
close the eyes;

he2 yi jian de 何以見得
what makes you think that;

hei1 mei wu zui 黑眉烏嘴
dark / filthy;

hei meng 黑朦
amaurosis;

hei mou 黑眸
black pupil of the eye;

hei se bai nei zhang 黑色白內障
black cataract;

hen4 shi 恨視
glare with anger;

heng2 mei 橫眉
frown / scowl;

heng mei deng yan 橫眉瞪眼
look angrily;

heng mei nu mu 橫眉怒目
raise one's eyebrows and stare in anger ‖ dart fierce looks of hate; face others with frowning brows and angry eyes; straighten

the eyebrows and raise the eyes — angry looks;

heng mei shu yan 橫眉豎眼
put on a fierce look;

heng mu 橫目
angry eyes // look angrily at;

heng mu xie ni 橫目斜睨
cross the eyes and look askance / leer / leer at;

heng tiao bi zi shu tiao yan 橫挑鼻子豎挑眼
find faults in a petty manner ‖ look for flaws; nit-pick; pick faults right and left; pick faults with sb in various ways; pick holes in;

heng2 shi 衡視
look horizontally;

hong3 mo 虹膜
iris;

hong mo bi suo 虹膜閉鎖
atresia iridis;

hong mo bing 虹膜病
iridopathy;

hong mo chu xue 虹膜出血
iridemia;

hong mo fei hou 虹膜肥厚
iridauxesis;

hong mo jiao 虹膜角
angulus iridis;

hong mo jiao mo yan 虹膜角膜炎
iridokeratitis;

hong mo si lie 虹膜撕裂
iridorhexis;

hong mo tong 虹膜痛
iridalgia / pain in the iris of the eye;

hong mo yan 虹膜炎
inflammation of the iris of the eye / iritis;

jiao mo hong mo yan 角膜虹膜炎
corneoiritis;

lü pao xing hong mo yan 濾泡性虹膜炎
follicular iritis;

qiu zhen xing hong mo yan 丘疹性虹膜炎
iritis papulosa;

tang niao bing xing hong mo yan 糖尿病性虹膜炎
diabetic iritis;

tong feng hong mo yan 痛風虹膜炎
gouty iritis;

hong2 lei 紅淚
tears of sadness / tears with blood;

hong se mang 紅色盲
protanopia / red blindness;

hong shi zheng 紅視症
erythropia;

hong yan 紅眼
(1) blood-shot eye / pinkeye;
(2) jealous of sb;
(3) become infuriated / see red;

hong yan bing 紅眼病
(1) pinkeye / red eye disease;
(2) jealousy / resentment;

hou4 gu 後顧
(1) turn back;
(2) look back on the past;

hou gu mang mang 後顧茫茫
the look into the future is uncertain;

hou gu qian shan 後顧前瞻
look back to the past and ahead into the future / look behind and before;

hou gu wu you 後顧無憂
looking behind, there is no anxiety;

hou gu zhi you 後顧之憂
fear of disturbance in the rear ‖ cares at home; fear of attack from behind; family considerations that cause delay in decision;

hou shi jue 後視覺
aftervision;

hu1 jian 忽見
see suddenly;

hu shi 忽視
disregard / give a cold shoulder / ignore / neglect / overlook / slight;

hu2 wang 鵠望
eagerly look forward to;

hu3 shi 虎視
(1) glare fiercely and covetously / watch sb with hungry eyes;

(2) gaze augustly;

hu shi dan dan 虎視眈眈
eye with hostility / watch sb with hungry eyes // hungry watchfulness;

hua1 yan 花眼
far-sightedness / presbyopia;

hua4 mei 畫眉
blacken eyebrows;

huai4 si xing gong mo yan 壞死性鞏膜炎
scleritis necroticans;

huan2 gu 環顧
look about / look around;

huan gu si zhou 環顧四周
look about / look all around / look around;

huan gu zuo you 環顧左右
look to the left and right;

huan mu 環目
afraid to look at sb straight in the face due to fear;

huan shi 環視
look about / look around;

huan4 shi 幻視
vision / visual hallucination;
lan guang huan shi 藍光幻視
cyanophose;
lan huan shi 藍幻視
indicophose;
zhen dong huan shi 振動幻視
oscillopsia;

huang1 liang man mu 荒涼滿目
waste and destitution meet the eyes;

huang2 hun mang 黃昏盲
twilight blindness;

huang2 huang yu lei 惶惶欲淚
close to tears / tears are very near to one's eyes;

hui1 lei 揮淚
flick a tear / shed tears;

hui lei er bie 揮淚而別
part in tears / wipe one's tears and leave;

hui lei er du 揮淚而讀
read...through flowing tears;

hui lei ru yu 揮淚如雨
in a storm of tears;

hui2 gu 回顧
look back / retrospect / review;

hui gu guo qu 回顧過去
look back on the past / review the past;

hui mou 回眸
glance back;

hui mou yi xiao 回眸一笑
look back at sb with a smile || give a smile, glancing back prettily;

hui3 lei 悔淚
tears of regret;

hui4 mang 晦盲
see nothing because of darkness;

hui4 jian 會見
interview / meet with;

hui wu 會晤
meet;

hui4 mu 慧目
discerning eyes;

hui yan 慧眼
discerning eyes;

hui yan du ju 慧眼獨具
can see what others cannot;

hui yan shi ren 慧眼識人
develop a sharp eye for discovering able people;

hui yan shi ying xiong 慧眼識英雄
discorning eyes can tell greatness from mediocrity;

hun1 hua 昏花
dim-sighted;

hun1 meng 惛懵
dim-eyed;

hun4 he san guang 混合散光
mixed astigmatism;

hun xiao shi ting 混淆視聽
throw dust in sb's eyes || call black white; confuse the people; confuse the public; confuse public opinion; lead the public opinion astray; mislead the people; mislead the public;

huo3 shao mei mao 火燒眉毛
imminent;

huo yan jin jing 火眼金睛
penetrating insight / piercing eye;

huo4 zai yan qian 禍在眼前
misfortune is before one's very eyes;

ji2 lei 急淚
sudden tears;

ji ru ran mei 急如燃眉
as urgent as if the eyebrows are burning;

ji yan 急眼
(1) get angry / lose one's temper;
(2) feel restless and uneasy;
(3) urgent;

ji2 mu 極目
look as far as the eye can see;

ji mu si tiao 極目四眺
survey all that is spread before one / take a panoramic view from some vantage point;

ji mu yuan tiao 極目遠眺
gaze into the distance / look far into the distance / strain one's eyes to look at the distance;

ji3 mei nong yan 擠眉弄眼
make eyes || give sb a surreptitious wink now and then; lift one's eyebrows and wink as signals to sb; make faces; ogle; signal to each other by glance; wink and cast a glance as a signal; wink and leer; wink at each other;

ji yan er 擠眼兒
wink at;

ji4 yu 覬覦
cast greedy eyes on / cast one's covetous eyes on;

ji4 fa xing bai nei zhang 繼發性白內障
secondary cataract;

ji fa xing jiao mo yan 繼發性角膜炎
secondary keratitis;

ji fa xing qing guang yan 繼發性青光眼
secondary glaucoma;

ji fa xing yan zhen 繼發性眼震
secondary nystagmus;

ji fa yan 繼發眼
secondary eye;

ji4 ran mei zhi ji 濟燃眉之急
help meet an urgent need;

jia3 sha yan 假沙眼
pseudotrachoma;

jia xing jin shi 假性近視
pseudomyopia;

jia xing xie shi 假性斜視
pseudosrrabismus;

jia yan 假眼
artificial eye / ocular prosthesis;

jia yan zhen 假眼震
pseudonystagmus;

jia zhuang bu jian 假裝不見
look through one's fingers at;

jian1 gu 兼顧
look after both sides;

jian1 shi 監視
keep watch on || guard; keep a lookout over; monitor;

jian3 shi 檢視
view;

jian3 瞼
eyelid;
ju jian 巨瞼
macroblepharia;

jian ban 瞼板
tarsus;

jian ban mo 瞼板膜
tarsal membrane;

jian ban ruan hua 瞼板軟化
tarsomalacia;

jian fei hou 瞼肥厚
blepharopachynsis;

jian fen liu 瞼粉瘤
blepharoatheroma;

jian jiao yan 瞼角炎
blepharitis angularis;

jian jing luan 瞼痙攣
blepharism;
zheng zhuang xing jian jing luan 症狀性瞼

痙攣
symptomatic blepharospasm;
zi fa xing jian jing luan 自發性瞼痙攣
essential blepharospasm;

jian nei fan 瞼內翻
entropion;
jing luan xing jian nei fan 痙攣性瞼內翻
spastic entropion;

jian ruan gu 瞼軟骨
ciliary cartilages;

jian shui zhong 瞼水腫
hydrohlepharon;

jian wai fan 瞼外翻
ectropion;
lao nian xing jian wai fan 老年性瞼外翻
senile ectropion;
ma bi xing jian wai fan 麻痺性瞼外翻
paralytic ectropion;

jian xian yan 瞼腺炎
sty;

jian yan 瞼炎
palpebritis;

jian yuan yan 瞼緣炎
blepharitis;
zhi yi xing jian yuan yan 脂溢性瞼緣炎
seborrheic blepharitis;

jian3 mei 繭眉
beautiful eyebrows;

jian4 bu de 見不得
(1) not to be exposed to / unable to stand;
(2) not fit to be seen or revealed // unpresentable;

jian bu de ren 見不得人
cannot bear the light of day / cannot stand scrutiny / too ashamed to show up in public;

jian bu de tian ri 見不得天日
cannot bear the light of day;

jian bu zhao 見不着
cannot see / unable to meet;

jian cai qi yi 見財起意
at the sight of money evil ideas rise in one's head / think of stealing on seeing sb's money;

jian ci wang bi 見此忘彼
observe this and neglect that;

jian da shi mian 見大世面
get a glimpse of the great world;

jian dao 見到
see;

jian duo shi guang 見多識廣
have wide experience and extensive knowledge ‖ be richly equipped with general knowledge; experienced and knowledgeable; have a wide range of experience; have great experience; know a thing or two; know one's way round; up to a thing or two; with wide experience;

jian feng jiu shi yu 見風就是雨
accept sth as true after one has only seen the slightest sign or heard some hearsay;

jian feng shi duo 見風使舵
find out how the wind blows ‖ jump on the bandwagon; sail with every shift of wind; see how the wind blows; see which way the cat jumps; trim one's sails; wait for the cat to jump;

jian feng cha zhen 見縫插針
make full use of every opportunity ‖ avail oneself of every opportunity; make use of every single space; seize every opportunity to do sth; stick in a pin wherever there's room — make use of every bit of time;

jian gao di 見高低
contest and see who is better / fight for mastery / see who is better;

jian ge gao xia 見個高下
contest and see who is better / fight for mastery / see who is better;

jian guai 見怪
blame / give offence / mind / take offence;

jian guai bu guai, qi guai zi bai 見怪不怪——其怪自敗
become inured to the unusual ‖ facing the fearful without fear — its fearfulness disappears; what once seemed bewildering will no longer be so;

jian guan luo lei 見棺落淚
tears start to flow from one's eyes as one sees the coffin;

jian guan 見慣
be accustomed to seeing sth;

jian guo 見過
have met / have seen;

jian guo shi mian 見過世面
have experienced life / have seen much of life / have seen the world;

jian ji 見機
as befits the occasion ‖ according to circumstances; as the opportunity arises;

jian ji er zuo 見機而作
take advantage of an opportunity that comes one's way;

jian ji xing shi 見機行事
act according to circumstances ‖ act as circumstances dictate; act as the occasion demands; act on seeing an opportunity; adapt oneself to circumstnaces; do as one sees fit; play to the score; profit by the occasion; see one's chance and act; use one's own judgment and do what one deemed best;

jian jie 見解
idea / opinion / view / way of thinking;

jian jie tong da 見解通達
hold sensible views / show good sense;

jian jing shang qing 見景傷情
become beset with memories in one's old haunts and fall into one's melancholy condition again;

jian jing sheng qing 見景生情
be moved by what one sees ‖ memories revive at the sight of familiar places; the circumstances excite one's feelings; the scene evokes memories of the past;

jian li qi yi 見利棄義
sell one's birthright for a mess of pottage;

jian li si yi 見利思義
think of righteousness on seeing gain;

jian li wang wei 見利妄為
lose sight of everything else in view of a present advantage / stop at nothing to gain profit;

jian li wang yi 見利忘義
disregard moral principles in pursuit of profit / forget all moral principles at the sight of profits / forget friendship for profit / forget honour at the prospect of profits;

jian lie xin xi 見獵心喜
thrill to see one's favourite sport and itch to have a go ‖ at seeing the hunters one feels delighted; anxious to display one's skill;

jian mao bian se 見貌辨色
quick to see which way the wind blows;

jian mian 見面
(1) meet / meet sb in the face / see;
(2) contact / link;

jian mian fen yi ban 見面分一半
get half of it on seeing it;

jian mian li 見面禮
a gift presented to sb at the first meeting;

jian mu bu jian lin 見木不見林
not to see the wood for the trees / note only the details but not the overall situation;

jian qian xin dong 見錢心動
be tempted by money;

jian qian yan kai 見錢眼開
open one's eyes wide at the sight of money — greedy of money ‖ be moved at the sight of money; be tempted by money; care for nothing but money; one's eyes grow round with delight at the sight of money;

jian qing 見情
feel grateful to sb for his kindness;

jian ren 見人
meet people;

jian ren shuo ren hua, jian gui shuo gui hua 見人説人話，見鬼説鬼話
scratch sb where he feels an itch // double-cross / double-faced;

jian ren zhi shi, zhi ji zhi shi 見人之失，知己之失
do not ask for whom the bells toll, they may toll for you;

jian ren jian zhi 見仁見智
different people, different views / different people have different views / each according to his lights / opinions differ;

jian shi 見識
(1) enrich one's experience / widen one's

knowledge;
(2) experience / knowledge / sensibleness;

jian shi duan qian 見識短淺
lacking knowledge and experience // shallow;

jian shi guang bo 見識廣博
have extensive experience // wide in experience;

jian shi mian 見世面
enrich one's experience / get a look at the elephant / see life / see the elephant / see the world;

jian shi sheng feng 見事生風
stir up trouble with very little cause || arouse trouble with very little cause; create disturbance under a slight excuse;

jian shi bu miao 見勢不妙
find the situation unfavourable || realize the situation is going against; see bad weather ahead; see that matters are in a bad way;

jian shu bu jian lin 見樹不見林
cannot see the wood for the trees / fail to see the wood for the trees;

jian si bu jiu 見死不救
do nothing to save sb from dying || bear to see sb die without trying to save him; do nothing to save sb from ruin; fold one's arms and see sb die; fold one's hands and see sb die; leave one to sink; leave one to swim; leave sb in the lurch; not to help a dying man; not to rescue those in mortal danger; rufuse to help sb in real trouble; see sb in mortal danger without lifting a finger to save him; shut one's eyes to people who are dying; stand by when sb is in peril; stand calmly by while another is drowning;

jian si bu ju 見死不懼
fearless in face of death / not be dismayed at the prospect of death;

jian suo wei jian 見所未見
see what one has never seen before || see things of which one has hitherto been unaware;

jian tou zhi wei 見頭知尾
as soon as one perceives the head of ... he knows what the tail is;

jian tu gu quan 見兔顧犬
take instant advantage of an opportunity that comes only once in a long while || it is not too late to snatch the opportunity at once; turn to order a dog to pursue and capture the hare after having seen it;

jian wei shou ming 見危受命
be entrusted with one's mission at a critical and difficlt moment / receive an appointment in sight of danger;

jian wei zhi zhu 見微知着
a straw shows which way the wind blows || from one small clue one can see what is to come; from the first small beginnings one can see how things will develop; one may see day at a little hole; recognize the world through observation of the part;

jian wen 見聞
what one sees and hears // information / knowledge;

jian wen bu guang 見聞不廣
have only limited knowledge;

jian wen guang bo 見聞廣博
have extensive knowledge // well-informed;

jian wu bu jian ren 見物不見人
ignore the human factor and see only the material factor || see things but not people — see only material factors to the neglect of human ones;

jian wu shang qing 見物傷情
the sight of familiar objects fills one with infinite melancholy // grief-stricken at the sight of things;

jian wu si ren 見物思人
seeing the thing, one thinks of the person — the thing reminds one of its owner;

jian xian si qi 見賢思齊
emulate those better than oneself / when one sees another better than oneself, try to equal him;

jian xiao bu jian da 見小不見大
fail to see the wood for the trees / strain at a gnat and swallow a camel;

jian yi si qian 見異思遷
change one's mind as one sees sth new || a rolling stone; change about; change one's

mind the moment one sees sth new; fickle; inconstant; vagaries of the mind; whimsical;

jian yi si qian, yi shi wu cheng 見異思遷，一事無成

a rolling stone gathers no moss;

jian yi yong wei 見義勇為

act bravely for a just cause || do boldly what is righteous; help a lame dog over a stile; never hesitate where good is to be done; ready to take up the cudgels for a just cause;

jian yuan bu jian jin 見遠不見近

much water runs by the mill than the miller knows of;

jian zheng 見證

witness;

jian4 xie xing xie shi 間歇性斜視

intermittent strabismus;

jian4 mei 劍眉

straight eyebrows slanting upwards and outwards;

jian4 shi 賤視

regard with contempt;

jiao1 jie 交睫

close eyes;

jiao3 mo 角膜

cornea;

ju jiao mo 巨角膜

macrocornea;

ying hua xing jiao mo 硬化性角膜

sclerocornea;

jiao mo bai ban 角膜白斑

keratoleukoma;

nian lian xing jiao mo bai ban 黏連性角膜白斑

adherent leukoma;

jiao mo ban 角膜斑

epicauma;

jiao mo bing 角膜病

keratonosus;

jiao mo bing bian 角膜病變

keratopathy;

jiao mo ding 角膜頂

vertex corneae;

jiao mo fan she 角膜反射

corneal reflex;

jiao mo gan zao zheng 角膜乾燥症

xerosis corneae;

jiao mo gong mo yan 角膜鞏膜炎

keratoscleritis;

jiao mo hong mo yan 角膜虹膜炎

corneoiritis;

jiao mo jie mo yan 角膜結膜炎

keratoconjunctivitis;

liu xing xing jiao mo jie mo yan 流行性角膜結膜炎

epidemic kerato-conjunctivitis;

jiao mo kui yang 角膜潰瘍

corneal ulcer;

jiao mo kuo zhang 角膜擴張

keratoectasia;

jiao mo lao 角膜癆

phthisis cornease;

jiao mo lie 角膜裂

corneal cleft;

jiao mo lou 角膜瘻

fistula cornease;

jiao mo pao zhen 角膜疱疹

herpes corneae;

jiao mo ruan hua 角膜軟化

keratomalacia;

jiao mo tong 角膜痛

keratalgia;

jiao mo yan 角膜炎

keratitis;

guo min xing jiao mo yan 過敏性角膜炎

anaphylactic;

ji fa xing jiao mo yan 繼發性角膜炎

secondary keratitis;

kui yang xing jiao mo yan 潰瘍性角膜炎

ulcerative keratitis;

pan zhuang jiao mo yan 盤狀角膜炎

disciform keratitis;

pao xing jiao mo yan 泡性角膜炎

phlyctenular keratitis;

shen ceng jiao mo yan 深層角膜炎

deep keratitis;

shi zhi xing jiao mo yan 實質性角膜炎
parenchymatous keratitis;
ying hua xing jiao mo yan 硬化性角膜炎
scleosing keratitis;

jie2 jie xing gong mo yan 結節性鞏膜炎
nodular scleritis;

jie jie xing jie mo yan 結節性結膜炎
nodular conjunctivitis;

jie jie xing yan yan 結節性眼炎
ophthalmia nodosa;

jie mo 結膜
conjunctiva;

jie mo fan she 結膜反射
conjunctival reflex;

jie mo gan zao 結膜乾燥
xeroma;

jie mo huang ban 結膜黃斑
pinguicula;

jie mo jie shi 結膜結石
lithiasis conjunctivae;

jie mo yan 結膜炎
conjunctivitis;
dan chun xing jie mo yan 單純性結膜炎
simple conjunctivitis;
guo min xing jie mo yan 過敏性結膜炎
anaphylactic conjunctivitis;
jiao mo jie mo yan 角膜結膜炎
keratoconjunctivitis;
jie jie xing jie mo yan 結節性結膜炎
nodular conjunctivitis;
jie shi xing jie mo yan 結石性結膜炎
calcareous conjunctivitis;
ke li xing jie mo yan 顆粒性結膜炎
granular conjunctivitis;
lin bing xing jie mo yan 淋病性結膜炎
gonorrheal conjunctivitis;
lin qiu jun xing jie mo yan 淋球菌性結膜炎
gonococcal conjunctivitis;
liu xing xing jie mo yan 流行性結膜炎
epidemic conjunctivitis;
lü pao xing jie mo yan 濾泡性結膜炎
follicular conjunctivitis;
niu dou xing jie mo yan 牛痘性結膜炎
vaccinial conjunctivitis;
nong yi xing jie mo yan 膿溢性結膜炎
blennorrheal conjunctivitis;
pao xing jie mo yan 泡性結膜炎
phlyctenular conjunctivitis;
pi fu jie mo yan 皮膚結膜炎
dermatoconjunctivitis;
shi zhen xing jie mo yan 濕疹性結膜炎
eczematous conjunctivitis;
te ying xing jie mo yan 特應性結膜炎
atopic conjunctivitis;
ying er nong xing jie mo yan 嬰兒膿性結膜炎
infantile purulent conjunctivitis;
you yong chi jie mo yan 游泳池結膜炎
swimming pool conjunctivitis;

jie shi xing jie mo yan 結石性結膜炎
calcareous conjunctivitis;

jie2 睫
cilium / eyelash;

jie mao 睫毛
cilia / eyelash;

jie mao tuo luo 睫毛脱落
madarosis;

jie xian 睫癬
tinea ciliorum;

jin1 yu yan 金魚眼
pop-eyed;

jin3 suo shuang mei 緊鎖雙眉
contract the eyebrows / knit the eyebrows // one's eyebrows are knit in a frown / one's brows furrow;

jin ya xing shi wang mo 緊壓性視網膜
coarctate retina;

jin zhang xing tong kong 緊張性瞳孔
tonic pupil;

jin4 shi 近視
myopia / near-sightedness / short sight / short-sightedness // short-sighted;
dan chun xing jin shi 單純性近視
simple myopia / primary myopia;
e xing jin shi 惡性近視
malignant myopia / pernicious myopia;

jia xing jin shi 假性近視
pseudomyopia;
jin xing xing jin shi 進行性近視
progressive myopia;
lao nian jin shi 老年近視
gerontopia;
qu du xing jin shi 曲度性近視
curvature myopia;

jin shi fan she 近視反射
myopic reflex;

jin shi san guang 近視散光
myopic astigmatism;
dan chun jin shi san guang 單純近視散光
simple myopic astigmatism;

jin xing xing jin shi 進行性近視
progressive myopia;

jin zai mei jie 近在眉睫
close at hand / very near as if located right before one's eyelash;

jin zai yan qian 近在眼前
right before one's eyes || at hand; imminent; right here under one's nose;

jin4 qing tong ku 盡情痛哭
cry one's eyes out / cry one's heart out;

jin shou yan di 盡收眼底
have a panoramic view;

jing1 睛
eye-ball / pupil of the eye;

jing qiu 睛球
eyeball / pupil of the eye;

jing zhu 睛珠
eyeball / pupil of the eye;

jing1 shen xing mang 精神性盲
psychic blindness;

jing1 hong yi pie 驚鴻一瞥
have a fleeting glimpse of a beauty;

jing shi 驚視
look at in surprise;

jing4 luan xing jian nei fan 痙攣性瞼內翻
spastic entropion;

jing luan xing tong kong kuo da 痙攣性瞳孔擴大
spasmodic mydriansis;

jing4 guan 靜觀
observe quietly;

ju3 mu 舉目
look / raise the eyes;

ju mu jie shi 舉目皆是
can be seen everywhere || be found everywhere; meet the eye everywhere;

ju mu si wang 舉目四望
look around;

ju mu wu qin 舉目無親
a stranger in a strange land || be left alone, with no relative near; be stranded far away from one's folks; cannot find anybody whom one knows; find no kin to turn to; find oneself alone and kinless; have neither friend nor relation; have no one to turn to; have none of one's relations near one;

ju mu yuan tiao 舉目遠眺
look into the distance;

ju4 jian 巨瞼
macroblepharia;

ju jiao mo 巨角膜
macrocornea;

ju kuang 巨眶
megaseme;

ju yan 巨眼
macrophthalmia;

juan4 眷
look back;

juan4 睠
look back;

jue2 mu 抉目
gouge out an eye or eyes;

jue yan 抉眼
gouge out an eye or eyes;

jue2 mu 絕目
as far as one's eyes can reach;

jue2 瞿
watch in fright // scared;

jue jue 瞿瞿
look without paying attention;

jue ran 矍然
looking around in fear;

kai1 kuo yan jie 開闊眼界
broaden one's outlook / broaden one's horizons / widen one's field of vision;

kai yan 開眼
open one's eyes || add to one's expereince; broaden one's mind; broaden one's view; enrich one's experience; open one's mental horizon; see new things; see the world; widen one's horizons; widen one's view;

kai yan jie 開眼界
enrich one's experience / see the world / widen one's horizon / widen one's vision;

kai1 yan lei 揩眼淚
wipe away tears;

kan4 看
behold / clap eyes on / eye / look / look at / see / set eyes on / view / watch;

kan bing 看病
(1) see a doctor;
(2) see a patient;

kan bu chu 看不出
unable to see;

kan bu de 看不得
(1) should not see;
(2) not worth seeing;

kan bu guan 看不慣
detest / disdain;

kan bu lai 看不來
(1) not willing to see;
(2) unable to see;

kan bu qi 看不起
despise / look down on / scorn;

kan bu shang 看不上
not up to one's standard;

kan bu tou 看不透
unable to see through;

kan bu xia qu 看不下去
unable to continue seeing;

kan cheng 看成
look upon as;

kan cheng 看承
attend to / look after;

kan chu 看出
see / make out;

kan chuan 看穿
see through (a trick);

kan dai 看待
look upon / regard / treat;

kan dao 看到
catch sight of / see // at sight;

kan de guo 看得過
presentable;

kan de lai 看得來
worth seeing;

kan de qi 看得起
have a good opinion of / think highly of;

kan de shang 看得上
to one's taste;

kan de tou 看得透
able to see through;

kan fa 看法
point of view / way of looking at things / way of thinking;

kan fa yi zhi 看法一致
go along with / go with sb / see eye to eye;

kan feng se 看風色
find out how the wind blows / see how things stand / see which way the wind blows;

kan feng tou 看風頭
find out how the wind blows / see how things stand / see which way the wind blows;

kan feng shi duo 看風使舵
adapt oneself to circumstances / sail with the wind / see how the cat jumps / take one's cue from changing conditions;

kan feng zhuan duo 看風轉舵
adapt oneself to circumstances / sail with the wind / see how the cat jumps / take one's cue from changing conditions;

kan ge bao 看個飽
see to one's heart's content;

kan gu 看顧
look after;

kan guan 看慣
used to seeing;

kan jian 看見
catch sight of / clap eyes on / make out / see;

kan kan 看看
take a look at;

kan lai 看來
it looks as if;

kan le yi yan 看了一眼
give sth or sb a look / throw one's eye on;

kan po 看破
see through;

kan po hong chen 看破紅塵
see through the vanity of life;

kan qing 看輕
despise / hold cheap / underestimate;

kan qing chu 看清楚
make out / open sb's eyes / see clearly;

kan qing zhen xiang 看清真相
remove the scales from sb's eyes;

kan qing xing 看情形
depending on circumstances;

kan ren mei jie 看人眉睫
subservient // watch sb's look;

kan shang 看上
take a fancy to;

kan tou 看透
see through;

kan wang 看望
call on;

kan yi kan 看一看
take a gander / take a look;

kan zai yan li 看在眼裏
notice sth out of the corner of one's eye / watch sth with the tail of one's eye;

kan zai yan li, ji zai xin li 看在眼裏，記在心裏
bear in mind what one sees / see and heed;

kan zhong 看中
have one's eyes on / settle on;

kan zhong 看重
value;

kan4 瞰
(1) look far away / watch;
(2) watch from above;

kan lin 瞰臨
overlook / watch from above;

kan wang 瞰望
look from above / overlook;

kan4 矙
(1) watch;
(2) look downward / overlook;

ke1 li xing jie mo yan 顆粒性結膜炎
granular conjunctivitis;

ke li xing yan yan 顆粒性眼炎
granular ophthalmia;

ke3 ge ke qi 可歌可泣
very moving / very touching;

ke guan 可觀
be worth seeing;

ke jian 可見
(1) that can be seen;
(2) to be perceived;

ke wang er bu ke ji 可望而不可即
can be looked at but not touched;

kou1 lou 摳摟
sunken;

kuang4 眶
rim of the eye / socket of the eye;
ju kuang 巨眶
megaseme;

kuang bing 眶病
orbitopathy;

kui1 ce 窺測
watch and assess;

kui cha 窺察
spy on / watch;

kui jian 窺見
get a glimpse of;

kui shi 窺視
peek / peep at / watch secretly;

kui si 窺伺
watch and wait;

kui2 睽
stare at;

kui kui 睽睽
stare / staring;

kui4 yang xing jiao mo yan 潰瘍性角膜炎
ulcerative keratitis;

kui4 nan jian ren 愧難見人
ashamed to be seen in public;

lai4 睞
(1) glance / look at;
(2) squint // cockeyed;

lai zhe yan 睞着眼
blinking one's eyes;

lan2 ban bai nei zhang 藍斑白內障
blue dot cataract;

lan guang huan shi 藍光幻視
cyanophose;

lan huan shi 藍幻視
indicophose;

lan huang se mang 藍黃色盲
blue-yellow blindness;

lan se bai nei zhang 藍色白內障
blue cataract;

lan se mang 藍色盲
blue blindness;

lan shi zheng 藍視症
cyanopsia;

lan3 覽
(1) look at / sightsee;
(2) read;
(3) listen to;

lan sheng 覽勝
see a scenic spot;

lao3 hua yan 老花眼
old-age hyperopia / presbyopia;

lao lei heng liu 老淚橫流
tears flowing from the aged eyes;

lao lei zong heng 老淚縱橫
tears flow from aged eyes / the old man weeps bitterly / the old man's face is covered with tears;

lao mao 老眊
dim sight of the aged;

lao nian bai nei zhang 老年白內障
senile cataract;

lao nian jin shi 老年近視
gerontopia;

lao nian xing bai nei zhang 老年性白內障
senile cataract;

lao nian xing jian wai fan 老年性瞼外翻
senile ectropion;

lao yan guang 老眼光
old views / old ways of looking at things;

lao yan hun hua 老眼昏花
dim-sighted from old age;

lei4 淚
lacrima / tear;

lei bie 淚別
tearful farewell;

lei cen cen 淚涔涔
tears falling down abundantly;

lei di 淚滴
teardrops;

lei fan she 淚反射
lacrimal reflex;

lei gan chang duan 淚乾腸斷
weeping one's eyes out and heartbroken;

lei gan sheng jie 淚乾聲竭
one's tears dry up and one's voice fails one;

lei guang 淚光
glistening teardrops;

lei hen 淚痕
tear stains / traces of tear;

lei hen ban ban 淚痕斑斑
wet with tears || be bathed in tears; cover with grease spots; tear-stained;

lei hen man mian 淚痕滿面
the face is covered with traces of tears // with a tear-stained face;

lei hen wei gan 淚痕未乾
tears are not yet dry;

lei hua 淚花
tears in one's eye;

lei hua jing ying 淚花晶瑩
one's eyes sparkle with tears;

lei liu man mian 淚流滿面
one's face is covered with tears / tears course down one's cheeks;

lei liu ru zhu 淚流如注
one's eyes are streaming with tears;

lei liu shuang jia 淚流雙頰
tears course down one's cheeks / tears run down the cheeks / tears trickle down one's cheeks;

lei luo ru dou 淚落如豆
tears as big as peas roll down one's cheeks;

lei nang 淚囊
lachrymal sac;

lei ru bu gan 淚濡不乾
be drowned in tears;

lei ru quan yong 淚如泉湧
tears gush from one's eyes || a deluge of tears; a flood of tears; a stream of tears; burst into a flood of tears; tears gush forth in floods; tears gush out like a bubbling spring; tears well up in one's eyes; tears well up like a fountain; the tears flow in streams;

lei ru yu xia 淚如雨下
one's tears fall like rain || a banquet of brine; an inundation of tears; burst into a flood of tears; in a flood of tears; one's eyes rain tears; one's tears flow fast; shed a flood of tears; tears trickle down like rain;

lei sa tao sai 淚灑桃腮
her tears fall like pearls and beans / the pearly tears never cease to roll down her peach-like cheeks;

lei shi yi jin 淚濕衣襟
tears bedew one's coat / tears stain one's clothes / wet the front part of one's garment with tears;

lei shi yi xiu 淚濕衣袖
wet one's sleeve with tears;

lei shui 淚水
teardrops / tears;

lei ti jiao liu 淚涕交流
one's eyes and nose are flooded / tears and snivel run down the face;

lei wang wang 淚汪汪
eyes brimming with tears || tearful; with watery eyes;

lei xia zhan jin 淚下沾襟
wet the front part of one's garment with tears;

lei xian 淚腺
lachrymal gland;

lei yan 淚眼
moist eyes / tearful eyes;

lei yan jing ying 淚眼晶瑩
tears dim one's eyes and sparkle on one's eyelashes // with a brilliant sparkle in one's eyes;

lei yan mi meng 淚眼迷濛
one's eyes are blurred with tears / one's eyes are dim with tears / one's eyes become dim by tears;

lei yan mo hu 淚眼模糊
eyes blurred by tears;

lei ye 淚液
tears;

lei yong shuang mu 淚湧雙目
tears come into one's eyes / tears start to the eyes;

lei zhan shan xiu 淚沾衫袖
wet one's sleeves with tears;

lei zhan yi jin 淚沾衣襟
tears bedew one's coat / tears wet the jacket;

lei zhan zhen qin 淚沾枕衾
the pillow is wet with tears;

lei zhu 淚珠
teardrop;

lei zhu gun gun 淚珠滾滾
the pearly tears roll down the cheeks || tears as big as peas rain down one's checks; tears course down one's cheeks; tears run down one's cheeks like pearls from a broken thread; tears trickle down one's face;

lei zhu su su 淚珠簌簌
tears trickle down from one's eyes;

leng3 yan 冷眼
(1) cool detachment;
(2) cold-shoulder;
(3) cold stare;

leng yan kan ren 冷眼看人
give sb the eye / look coldly upon sb;

leng yan pang guan 冷眼旁觀
look on coldly || look coldly from the sidelines; look on as a disinterested bystander; look on unconcerned; look on with a cold eye; see it from the side; stand aloof and look on with cold indifference; stay aloof; take a detached point of view; watch indifferently;

leng yan re xin 冷眼熱心
affected indifference / outward indifference but inward fervency;

leng yan xiang kan 冷眼相看
look at coldly / look coldly upon;

li4 mei li yan 立眉立眼
get angry / become furious;

li4 mu er shi 厲目而視
look with severe glare;

li4 li zai mu 歷歷在目
remain vivid in one's mind's eye || come clearly into view; leap to the eyes; leap up vividly before one's eyes; present to the mind; remain clear and distinct in one's mind; remember clearly to this day; still vivid in one's mind; visible before the eyes;

liang3 gu xiang fu 兩瞽相扶
two blind men support each other — neither one will lead;

liang lei cen cen 兩淚涔涔
two lines of tears keep on rolling down one's cheeks;

liang lei jiao liu 兩淚交流
with two streams of tears running down one's face;

liang lei ru ma 兩淚如麻
one's tears are scattered near and far;

liang lei wang wang 兩淚汪汪
eyes brimming with tears;

liang yan chao le tian 兩眼朝了天
drop dead / kick the bucket;

liang yan fa hei 兩眼發黑
all has turned black before one's eyes / everything turns dark before one's eyes;

liang yan fan bai 兩眼翻白
show the whites of one's eyes;

liang yan mao huo 兩眼冒火
one's eyes flashing;

liang yan wang chuan 兩眼望穿
wear out one's eyes watching for sb;

liang yan yuan zheng 兩眼圓睜
one's eyes nearly start from his head // with wide-open eyes;

liang yan zhi ding 兩眼直盯
keep one's eyes fixed on || fix a steady gaze upon; fix one's eyes on; keep one's eyes glued to; rivet one's eyes on;

liao4 瞭
look down from a higher place;

liao wang 瞭望
look down from a higher place;

lie4 yan 裂眼
angry look;

lin2 bing xing jie mo yan 淋病性結膜炎
gonorrheal conjunctivitis;

lin bing xing yan yan 淋病性眼炎
gonorrheal ophthalmia;

lin qiu jun xing jie mo yan 淋球菌性結膜炎
gonococcal conjunctivitis;

lin2 lang man mu 琳琅滿目
a feast for the eyes || a multitude of beautiful things dazzle the eyes; a superb collection of beautiful things; the eyes are fully filled with the sparkling of gems — resplendent with a multitude of beautiful things;

lin2 瞵
(1) look at / stare at;
(2) (eyes) clear and bright;

lin pan 瞵盼
look around;

ling4 ren luo lei 令人落淚
bring tears to one's eyes / make the angels

weep;

ling4 yan kan dai 另眼看待
devote special attention to / give sb a special treatment / keep an eye on / treat sb with special respect;

ling yan xiang kan 另眼相看
(1) look at sb with quite different eyes || pay special regard to; regard sb with special respect; regard with special attention;
(2) look at sb in a different light || see sb in a new light; treat sb with special consideration; view a person in quite a different light than one does the rest of the people; view sb in a new, more favourable light;

liu1 yan 溜眼
cast a glance to hint;

liu2 lan 流覽
(1) survey;
(2) skim over / read through;

liu lei 流淚
shed tears;

liu mian 流眄
turn the eyes;

liu xing xing jiao mo jie mo yan 流行性角膜結膜炎
epidemic kerato-conjunctivitis;

liu xing xing jie mo yan 流行性結膜炎
epidemic conjunctivitis;

liu2 lan 瀏覽
glance over / pass one's eyes over / skim through / thumb through;

liu3 mei 柳眉
arch eyebrows || the eyebrows of a beautiful woman;

liu mei dao shu 柳眉倒豎
her willow-leaf shaped eyebrows rise;

liu mei shuang suo 柳眉雙鎖
she knits her beautiful eyebrows;

liu mei xing yan 柳眉杏眼
graceful eyebrows and large eyes;

long2 mei feng mu 龍眉鳳目
have eyebrows like a dragon's and eyes like those of a phoenix / have long eyebrows and long slit eyes;

long mei hao fa 龍眉皓髮
with white hair and white eyebrows;

lü3 jian bu xian 屢見不鮮
not rare / nothing new / of ordinary occurrence;

lü4 se mang 綠色盲
deuteranopia;

lü se rou 綠色弱
deuteranomaly;

lü shi zheng 綠視症
chloropia;

lü4 pao xing hong mo yan 濾泡性虹膜炎
follicular iritis;

lü pao xing jie mo yan 濾泡性結膜炎
follicular conjunctivitis;

luan4 shi 亂視
astigmatism;

luo2 覶
see carefully;

luo4 lei 落淚
cry / shed tears / weep;

ma2 bi xing jian wai fan 麻痺性瞼外翻
paralytic ectropion;

ma bi xing tong kong kuo da 麻痺性瞳孔擴大
paralytic mydriasis;

ma bi xing tong kong suo xiao 麻痺性瞳孔縮小
paralytic miosis;

ma bi xing xie shi 麻痺性斜視
paralytic strabismus;

man2 瞞
dim-sighted;

man3 mu 滿目
meet the eye on every side;

man mu chuang yi 滿目瘡痍
everywhere a scene of devastation meets the eye || be covered all over with wounds and scars; distress and suffering can be seen everywhere; in a state of bad devastation; misery and suffering greets the eyes everywhere; see evidence of people's distress everywhere; the sight of the wounded meets the eye everywhere — the country is full of suffering and distress; wherever one looks,

there is devastation;

man mu han lei 滿目含淚

one's eyes are filled with tears / one's eyes are full of tears;

man mu huang liang 滿目荒涼

a scene of desolation meets the eye on every side — the sight of a war-worn area;

man mu qi liang 滿目淒涼

all one can see is grief — full of grief everywhere / desolation all round / desolation spreads as far as the eyes can reach;

man mu xiao ran 滿目蕭然

a melancholy and solitary aspect as far as the eyes can see;

man mu xiao suo 滿目蕭索

a melancholy and solitary aspect as far as the eyes can see;

man yan 滿眼

(1) have one's eyes filled with;

(2) meet the eyes on every side;

man yan hong si 滿眼紅絲

with bloodshot eyes;

man yan lei shui 滿眼淚水

an eyeful of tears;

man yan xiong guang 滿眼兇光

there is a murderous gleam in one's eyes;

man4 xing qing guang yan 慢性青光眼

chronic glaucoma;

mang2 盲

blindness;

gong neng xing mang 功能性盲

functional blindness;

jing shen xing mang 精神性盲

psychic blindness;

pi zhi xing mang 皮質性盲

cortical blindness;

quan mang 全盲

total blindness;

ri shi mang 日蝕盲

eclipse blindness;

ri shi xing mang 日蝕性盲

eclipse blindness;

zhen dang xing mang 震蕩性盲

concussion blindness;

mang mu 盲目

blind;

mang mu bu mang 盲目不盲

blind in the eye but not in the mind;

mang mu chong bai 盲目崇拜

blind worship;

man mu xing shi 盲目行事

follow one's nose;

mao4 眊

dim-sighted;

mao kui 眊聵

dim-sighted and hard of hearing;

mao mao 眊眊

unable to see clearly;

mao4 瞀

dim-sighted;

mei2 jian guo shi mian 沒見過世面

green and inexperienced;

mei jian shi 沒見識

inexperienced and ignorant;

mei kai guo yan 沒開過眼

have seen little of the world;

mei2 眉

brow / eyebrow // superciliary;

jian mei 劍眉

straight eyebrows slanting upwards and outwards;

mei dai 眉黛

painted eyebrows / pretty eyebrows;

mei fei se wu 眉飛色舞

one's eyebrows dancing || a look of exultation; beam with joy; brighten up with joy; exultant; smack one's lips;

mei gao yan di 眉高眼低

adopt different attitudes and measures under different circumstances;

mei huan yan xiao 眉歡眼笑

with one's eyebrows arched and laughter in one's eyes || all smiles; beam all over one's face; beam with joy; feel happy and smile; grin all over; grin from ear to ear; one's face melts in smiles; smile happily; with beaming face;

mei ji 眉急
very urgent;

mei jie 眉睫
(1) the eyebrows and eyelashes;
(2) imminent / urgent;

mei jie zhi huo 眉睫之禍
imminent disaster;

mei jie zhi jian 眉睫之間
in close proximity;

mei jie zhi li 眉睫之利
small immediate interests;

mei jie zhi nei 眉睫之內
in close proximity;

mei kai yan xiao 眉開眼笑
smile happily from ear to ear || a beaming countenance; all smiles; beam with delight; beam with joy; face melting in smiles; feel happy and smile; grin all over; grin from ear to ear; look cheerful; one's eyes kindle with joy; one's face melts in smiles; one's shining eyes dance with joy; very happy;

mei lai yan qu 眉來眼去
cast sheep's eyes at sb / exchange amorous glances || exchange love glances with sb; flirt with each other; flirting glances between sexes; leer at sb; make eyes at each other; wink at each other;

mei mao 眉毛
eyebrows // superciliary;

mei mao hu zi yi ba zhua 眉毛鬍子一把抓
try to grasp the eyebrows and the beard all the same time || all is fish that comes to his net; all is flour that comes to his mill; take things all of a lump; try to attend to big and small matters all at once;

mei mu 眉目
features / looks;

mei mu bu qing 眉目不清
not well organized in one's writing / the details are not at all clear;

mei mu chuan qing 眉目傳情
send messages of love to sb with one's brows || an ocular intercourse; cast arch glances at; flash amorous glances; make eyes at; send speechless messages of love; send speechless messages from the eyes; throw the eye at;

mei mu han qing 眉目含情
her eyes wear an expression of coquetry;

mei mu ru hua 眉目如畫
as pretty as a picture;

mei qing mu xiu 眉清目秀
one's eyebrows are well shaped and one's eyes beautiful || beautiful eyes and brows; have beautiful eyes; have delicate features; look clean and pretty;

mei ru mo hua 眉如墨畫
one's eyebrows seem as if painted on with India ink;

mei ru xin yue 眉如新月
one's eyebrow is like the crescent moon / one's eyebrows are curved like the sickle of the new moon;

mei shao 眉梢
tip of the brow;

mei shu mu zhan 眉舒目展
unknit one's eyebrows || a pleased expression; feel happy at success;

mei si qing shan 眉似青山
one's brows are arched like lines of distant hills || her eyebrows are curved like the graceful contours of distant hills;

mei tou 眉頭
one's brows;

mei tou bu zhan 眉頭不展
with knitted brows;

mei tou bai jie 眉頭百結
with knitted brows;

mei tou jin suo 眉頭緊鎖
one's brows knit / one's eyebrows knit in a frown;

mei tou shen suo 眉頭深鎖
furrow one's brow;

mei tou yi zhou, ji shang xin lai 眉頭一皺，計上心來
knit the brows and a stratagem comes to mind / knit the brows and you will hit upon a stratagem;

mei xin 眉心
the space between the eyebrows;

mei yan chuan qing 眉眼傳情
cast amorous glances;

mei yan er zuo gei xia zi kan 眉眼兒作給瞎子看
waste good acts on sb who won't understand;

mei yan gao di 眉眼高低
adopt different attitudes under different circumstances;

mei yu 眉宇
forehead;

mei yu mu chuan 眉語目傳
speaking with one's eyebrows and giving a hint;

mei yue 眉月
crescent-shaped eyebrows;

mei2 du xing shi wang mo yan 梅毒性視網膜炎
syphilitic retinitis;

mei3 guan 美觀
beautiful to look at / pleasant to the eye;

mei guan da fang 美觀大方
beautiful and dignified;

mei mian 美眄
captivating glance;

mei mu 美目
beautiful eyes;

mei mu liu pan 美目流盼
the bewitching glance of a beauty;

mei pan 美盼
charming glance;

mei4 shi 昧視
watch in secret;

mei4 眛
dim-sighted;

mei yu 昧於
blind to;

mei4 yan 媚眼
come-hither eyes / goo-goo eyes / ogling eyes / soft glance;

meng2 瞢
dim-sighted;

meng2 矇
blind;

meng kui 矇聵
blind and deaf;

meng mei 矇昧
dim-sighted;

meng mei bu cha 矇昧不察
blind in one's view;

meng meng 矇矇
obscure and dim;

mi1 瞇
(1) close the eyes;
(2) narrow the eyes;

mi feng 瞇縫
narrow one's eyes;

mi feng yan er 瞇縫眼兒
slit-eyed;

mi shang yan jing 瞇上眼睛
close one's eyes;

mi zhe yan xiao 瞇着眼笑
smile at someone through half-closed eyes;

mi2 lu xing yan zhen 迷路性眼震
labyrinthine nystagmus;

mi ren yan mu 迷人眼目
confuse the eyes of the people || fool people; pull the wool over sb's eyes; throw dust in sb's eyes;

mi3 眯
close one's eyes into narrow slits;

mian2 mu jing si 眠目靜思
close the eyes and meditate;

mian3 眄
(1) look askance / ogle;
(2) look;

mian lai 眄睞
looking concerned;

mian mian 眄眄
(1) looking askance;
(2) looking dull;

mian ni 眄睨
look askance;

miao2 瞄
look at attentively;

miao zhun 瞄準
aim at / take aim / take sight;

miao3 shi 藐視
look down on ‖ despise; treat with contempt;

miao shi yi qie 藐視一切
despise everything;

mie2 shi 蔑視
contemn / despise / disdain / hold cheap / hold in contempt / scorn / set at naught / show contempt for;

ming2 cha qiu hao 明察秋毫
see through a brick wall;

ming mou hao chi 明眸皓齒
have bright eyes and white teeth;

ming mou shan lai 明眸善睞
the enticing glances of a beauty ‖ clear eyes with a winning look; shining eyes and attractive looks; the fond gazing of a beauty;

ming mou xiu mei 明眸秀眉
the enticing glances of a beauty ‖ clear-eyes with a winning look; the fond gazing of a beauty;

ming mu zhang dan 明目張膽
in a barefaced manner ‖ before one's very eye; brazen; daringly; fearlessly; in a flagrant way; openly and wantonly; without caring for any on-lookers;

ming2 瞑
close the eyes;

ming ming 瞑瞑
look but see nothing;

ming mu 瞑目
close one's eyes in death / die content;

ming mu chang mian 瞑目長眠
rest in peace — said of a dead man;

ming mu chang shi 瞑目長逝
close one's eyes forever;

ming mu er shi 瞑目而逝
close one's eyes and die;

ming mu jiu quan 瞑目九泉
may one's soul rest in peace;

mo2 xing bai nei zhang 膜性白內障
membranous cataract;

mo3 lei 抹淚
wipe away one's tears;

mo4 mo 脈脈
affectionately / amorously / lovingly;

mo mo han qing 脈脈含情
eyes quietly sending the message of love;

mo4 shi 漠視
ignore / overlook ‖ brush aside; pay no attention to; show no concern for; treat with indifference;

mou2 眸
pupil of the eye;

mou zi 眸子
eye / pupil of the eye;

mu4 目
(1) eye;
(2) look;

mu bo 目波
glances as bright as dancing waves;

mu bu ji jie 目不及接
too busy for the eyes to see / too many things to be seen;

mu bu jian jie 目不見睫
can't see the lashes in one's own eye — not to know oneself / the eye can't see its lashes — lack self-knowledge;

mu bu jiao jie 目不交睫
cannot close one's eyes to sleep ‖ have one's eyes open throughout the night; not a wink of sleep; not to sleep a wink;

mu bu kui yuan 目不窺園
never to take a peep into the garden — bury oneself in one's studies / not to cast one's eyes at the garden — absolute concentration on studies;

mu bu pang gu 目不旁顧
without even letting one's eyes wander;

mu bu ren du 目不忍睹
cannot bear the sight of / one's eyes cannot bear the scene;

mu bu shi ding 目不識丁

totally illiterate ‖ a battledoor; a bull's foot; not to know A from B; not to know a single word; not to know B from a battledore; unable to recognize a single written character;

mu bu xia ji 目不暇給

there are too many things for the eye to take in ‖ have no time to take in the scene as a whole; have too much to watch; the eye cannot take it all in; too much for the eye to feast on;

mu bu xie shi 目不斜視

look neither right nor left / not to look sideways / refuse to be distracted;

mu bu xie shi, er bu pang ting 目不斜視，耳不旁聽

deaf and blind to everything going on around — concentrate on sth totally;

mu bu zhuan jing 目不轉睛

not to look sideways ‖ all eyes for; fasten one's eyes on; gaze fixedly; gaze with fixed eyes; have one's eyes glued on; keep one's gaze fixed upon; look at intently without winking; look intently at; look with fixed gaze; not to take one's eyes off; regard with rapt attention; stare continuously; staringly; watch with the utmost concentration; watch without a blink; with staring eyes;

mu deng kou dai 目瞪口呆

stare open-mouthed ‖ be struck dumb; be dumbfounded; be dumbstruck; gape; gaping; knock dead; knock sideways; stand aghast; stare in mute amazement; stare with astonishment; strike sb dumb; stunned; stupefied;

mu deng kou dai, mian mian xiang qu 目瞪口呆，面面相覷

look blankly into each other's faces in bewilderment;

mu dong 目動

the eyes moving about;

mu du 目睹

see with one's own eyes / witness;

mu guang 目光

(1) sight / view / vision;

(2) gaze / look;

mu guang dai zhi 目光呆滯

with a dull look in one's eyes ‖ one's eyesight is restrained; with heavy leaden eyes // fishy eyes / stony stare;

mu guang duan qian 目光短淺

shortsighted ‖ blinkered; myopic; never to see the end of one's nose; not to see beyond one's nose;

mu guang jiao liu 目光交流

eye language;

mu guang jie chu 目光接觸

eye contact;

mu guang jiong jiong 目光炯炯

with flashing eyes ‖ have eyes with a piercing pleam; eyes bright and shining; one's eyes flash like lightning;

mu guang lao lian 目光老練

have an experienced eye;

mu guang qian jin 目光淺近

short-sighted;

mu guang ru dian 目光如電

one's eyes flash like lightning;

mu guang ru dou 目光如豆

narrow-visioned / short-sighted ‖ as blind as a bat; as blind as a beetle; as blind as a mole; one's circle of vision is as small as a bean — narrow-visioned; short-sighted;

mu guang ru ju 目光如炬

farsighted ‖ eyes blazing like torches — blazing with anger; look ahead with wisdom; with flashing eyes;

mu guang rui li 目光鋭利

sharp-sighted ‖ eagle-eyed; have an experienced eye; have sharp eyes; have the eye of a sailor; hawk-eyed; see through a millstone; sharp-eyed;

mu guang tan lan 目光貪婪

with a covetous eye on;

mu guang xi li 目光犀利

look sharply at / one's eyesight is sharp;

mu guang xiang jie 目光相接

meet one's eye;

mu guang yuan da 目光遠大

far-sighted ‖ have a broad vision; have a

great insight; have farsightedness; have large vies; show great foresight; one's eyesight is extensive — farseeing;

mu guang zhuo zhuo 目光灼灼
with keen, sparkling eyes;

mu ji 目擊
see with one's own eyes / witness;

mu ji er wen 目擊耳聞
what one sees and hears || fall under one's observation; have seen with one's own eyes and heard with one's own ears; what is seen and heard;

mu jian 目見
see for oneself;

mu jie zhi lun 目睫之論
superficial view;

mu ju 目距
eye-distance;

mu kong yi qie 目空一切
look with scorn at everybody and everything || as proud as Lucifer; consider everybody and everything beneath one's notice; full of oneself; look down on everyone else; on one's high horse; with one's nose in the air;

mu kuang 目眶
eye sockets;

mu li 目力
eyesight / vision;

mu li suo li 目力所及
as far as the eye can reach;

mu mi wu se 目迷五色
be dazzled by a riot of colours / be bewildered by a complicated situation;

mu ming ru ying 目明如鷹
as sharp-sighted as an eagle;

mu ru dian qi 目如點漆
one's eyes shine like lacquer;

mu shi 目視
visual;

mu shi wu shen 目視無神
dull eyes;

mu shu mei zhan 目舒眉展
one's frown fades;

mu si ming xing 目似明星
one's eyes are like lustrous stars;

mu song 目送
follow sb with one's eyes / gaze after / watch sb go;

mu song di ying 目送睇迎
receive and part with the eyes respectively;

mu song shou hui 目送手揮
hands and eyes acting in coordination;

mu tao 目逃
look away in awe / look away in shame;

mu tiao xin zhao 目挑心招
seduce sb by attractive looks;

mu ting 目聽
hear with the eyes;

mu ting er shi 目聽耳視
hear with the eyes and see with the ears;

mu wu fa ji 目無法紀
disregard for law and discipline || act in utter disregard of law and discipline; bid defiance to the law; defy the law; disregard the law; flout law and discipline; have no regard for laws; to one's eyes there are no laws and rules; set the law at defiance; show contempt for the law;

mu wu guang ze 目無光澤
dull eyes // one's eyes are without lustre;

mu wu zun zhang 目無尊長
show no respect to elders and superiors // with no regard for one's elders and betters;

mu xiao 目笑
cast a derisive look;

mu xu xia chen 目無下塵
look down on the masses // conceited and arrogant / supercilious;

mu xuan 目眩
dazed / dazzled / dizzy;

mu xuan yan hua 目眩眼花
dazed and blurred;

mu yu 目語
communicate with the eyes;

mu zhi qi shi 目指氣使
order people about by gesture ‖ give order by look or glance — bossy to others; order people about by gesture — insufferably arrogant;

mu zhong wu ren 目中無人
look down on everyone else ‖ care for nobody; consider everyone beneath one's notice; contemptuous of others; haughty; have no respect for anyone; look down one's nose at everybody; on the high horse; overweening; snooty; supercilious; too big for one's shoes; too big for one's trousers; with one's nose in the air;

nan2 kan 難看
bad-looking / not pleasant to the eye / offensive / repulsive / ugly;

nang2 xing bai nei zhang 囊性白內障
capsular cataract;

nei4 fen mi tu yan 內分泌突眼
endocrine exophthalmos;

nei gu 內顧
look after domestic affairs;

nei gu zhi you 內顧之憂
worry for domestic troubles;

nei xie shi 內斜視
cross-eye / esotropia;

nei xie yan 內斜眼
crossed eyes;

neng2 jian du 能見度
visibility;

ni4 du 逆覩
foresee / see beforehand;

ni4 睨
look askance;

nian2 lian xing jiao mo bai ban 黏連性角膜白斑
adherent leukoma;

niao4 du zheng xing ruo shi 尿毒症性弱視
uremic amblyopia;

ning2 mou 凝眸
fix one's eyes on / focus one's eyes upon;

ning mou er shi 凝眸而視
behold with a fixed gaze — stare at;

ning shen xi shi 凝神細視
look hard;

ning shi 凝視
gaze at / gaze fixedly / peer / stare;

ning3 mei deng yan 擰眉瞪眼
raise one's eyebrows and stare in anger;

niu2 dou xing jie mo yan 牛痘性結膜炎
vaccinial conjunctivitis;

nong2 mei 濃眉
bushy eyebrows / thick eyebrows // beetle-browed;

nong2 mei da yan 濃眉大眼
bushy eyebrows and big eyes / heavy features // with big eyes and thick eyebrows / with bushy eyebrows and big eyes;

nong2 xing yan yan 膿性眼炎
ophthalmoblennorrhea;

nong yi xing jie mo yan 膿溢性結膜炎
blennorrheal conjunctivitis;

nu3 zhe yan 努着眼
with bulging eyes;

nu4 mu 怒目
fierce stare / glaring eyes;

nu mu di shi 怒目諦視
look angrily at;

nu mu er shi 怒目而視
stare angrily ‖ glare angrily at; glare furiously; glare with rage; look daggers at; scowl at; shoot angry glances at;

nu mu qie chi 怒目切齒
intense hatred;

nu mu xiang xiang 怒目相向
glare defiance at each other ‖ flash fire; gaze upon with animosity; glare at; glower at; look daggers at; stare angrily;

nu shi 怒視
glare at / glower at / scowl at;

pai2 hui guan wang 徘徊觀望
wait and see;

pan2 zhuang jiao mo yan 盤狀角膜炎
disciform keratitis;

pan zhuang shi wang mo yan 盤狀視網膜炎
disciform retinitis;

pan4 盼
look;

pan qian 盼倩
enchanting appeal in the look;

pang2 guan 旁觀
look on / watch on the sideline;

pang2 guan 傍觀
look on / watch on the sideline;

pang2 mei hao fa 龐眉皓髮
shaggy eyebrows and hoary head — a healthy, aged person / with white hair and white eyebrows;

pao1 xing jiao mo yan 泡性角膜炎
phlyctenular keratitis;

pao xing jie mo yan 泡性結膜炎
phlyctenular conjunctivitis;

pao xing yan yan 泡性眼炎
phlyctenular ophthalmia;

pao1 mei yan 抛媚眼
flutter one's eyelashes at / make eyes at sb;

pi1 lan 披覽
open and read / peruse;

pi1 yue 披閱
read;

pi2 fu yan yan 皮膚眼炎
dermato-ophthalmitis;

pi zhi xing bai nei zhang 皮質性白內障
cortical cataract;

pi zhi xing mang 皮質性盲
cortical blindness;

pian1 ce ruo shi 偏側弱視
hemiamblyopia;

pian ce se mang 偏側色盲
hemiachromatopsia;

pian jian 偏見
bias / prejudice;

pian mang 偏盲
blind in one eye / hemianopia;
tong ce pian mang 同側偏盲
homonymous hemianopia;
wan quan pian mang 完全偏盲
absolute hemianopia;
xiang dui xing pian mang 相對性偏盲
relative hemianopia;
xiang xian pian mang 象限偏盲
quadrant hemianopia;

pian mang xing tong kong fan ying 偏盲性瞳孔反應
hemiopic pupillary reaction;

pian shi 偏視
anorthopia;

pian xie 偏斜
deviation;
yuan fa xing pian xie 原發性偏斜
primary deviation;

pian xie yan 偏斜眼
deviating eye;

piao3 瞟
look askance at;

pie1 瞥
glance one's eyes at / have a casual and brief glance / have a quick peek at / peek / take a peek into;

pie jian 瞥見
catch a glimpse of / catch sight of / peek / take a peek into;

pie le yi yan 瞥了一眼
cast a look at / catch a momentary glance / have a quick peek at / peek / snatch a momentary glance / take a peek into;

pie shi 瞥視
glance one's eyes at / glance one's eyes over / have a quick peek at / peek / take a peek into;

pie yan 瞥眼
in a twinkling of an eye;

pin2 顰
frown / knit one's brows;

pin cu 顰蹙
knit the brows;

pin mei cu e 顰眉蹙額
contract one's brows in a frown / knit the brows / make a wry face;

pin xiao bu gou 顰笑不苟
do not frown or smile to order // natural;

ping2 tiao 憑眺
look far from an eminence;

po4 zai mei jie 迫在眉睫
imminent || approaching; extremely urgent; hang over sb's head; hard-pressed; immediate; impending; likely to come in no time; pressing; stare sb in the face; urgent;

pu1 su lei xia 撲簌淚下
one's tears pour down;

pu2 sa di mei 菩薩低眉
kind-looking // with a kind expression on one's face;

qi2 guan 奇觀
a spectacular sight;

qi2 jian 歧見
conflicting ideas / different views;

qi shi 歧視
discriminate against;

qi2 mei 齊眉
respect between husband and wife;

qi4 泣
(1) burst into tears / come to tears / give way to tears / shed tears / sob / weep;
(2) cause to weep;
(3) come to tears without crying // tears;

qi bie 泣別
part in tears;

qi jian 泣諫
counsel in tears;

qi su 泣訴
tell one's grievances in tears;

qi ti 泣涕
come to tears / weep;

qi xia ru yu 泣下如雨
tears falling down like rain;

qian1 li yan 千里眼
far-sightedness;

qian2 suo wei jian 前所未見
have never seen before;

qian2 fu xing xie shi 潛伏性斜視
latent strabismus;

qiao2 瞧
(1) glance at / look / look at / see;
(2) glance quickly / steal a glance;

qiao bing 瞧病
(1) consult a doctor / see a doctor;
(2) examine a patient / see a patient;

qiao bu de 瞧不得
not worth seeing / should not be seen / unnecessary to see;

qiao bu guan 瞧不慣
not used to seeing cruel scenes;

qiao bu guo 瞧不過
not hard-hearted enough to see sth to its brutal end;

qiao bu qi 瞧不起
look down on || have no regard for; hold cheap; hold in contempt; hold in low esteem; look down one's nose at; look down upon; turn up one's nose at sb;

qiao bu shang yan 瞧不上眼
not worth so much a look at || be held cheap; beneath notice; consider beneath one's notice; not at all appealing to the eye; not up to one's taste; turn one's nose up at; turn up one's nose at;

qiao bu tou 瞧不透
not able to understand / unable to see through;

qiao de qi 瞧得起
have a high regard for || esteem; hold in high esteem; look up to; respect; see much in; think much of; think well of; value;

qiao de shang 瞧得上
good enough to suit one's taste;

qiao de tou 瞧得透
(1) see through;
(2) understand thoroughly;

qiao jian 瞧見
catch sight of / see;

qiao ni de 瞧你的
let's see what you can do;

qiao re nao er 瞧熱鬧兒
(1) go and see where the fanfare is;
(2) a bystander in fights;

qiao shang 瞧上
set eyes on sth and wish to have it;

qiao wo de 瞧我的
you just watch how I do it;

qiao yi qiao 瞧一瞧
take a look;

qiao zhe 瞧着
(1) while looking;
(2) let's see;

qiao zhe ban 瞧着辦
let's wait and see what happens and plan our strategy then;

qie4 kan 竊看
look at sth stealthily / peep;

qie kui 竊窺
peep / steal a glance / watch stealthily;

qie shi 竊視
peep;

qin1 jian 親見
have seen in person / see with one's own eyes;

qin jian qin wen 親見親聞
see with one's own eyes and hear with one's own ears;

qin yan 親眼
see with one's own eyes;

qin yan kan jian 親眼看見
see with one's own eyes / witness;

qin yan mu du 親眼目睹
live to see / see with one's own eyes;

qing1 bai yan 青白眼
esteem or look down;

qing guang yan 青光眼
glaucoma;

chong xue xing qing guang yan 充血性青光眼
congestive glaucoma;

chu xue xing qing guang yan 出血性青光眼
hemorrhagic glaucoma;

chuang shang xing qing guang yan 創傷性青光眼
traumatic glaucoma;

dan chun xing qing guang yan 單純性青光眼
simple glaucoma;

e xing qing guang yan 恶性青光眼
malignant glaucoma;

ji fa xing qing guang yan 繼發性青光眼
secondary glaucoma;

man xing qing guang yan 慢性青光眼
chronic glaucoma;

nang xing qing guang yan 囊性青光眼
capsular glaucoma;

qing shao nian xing qing guang yan 青少年型青光眼
juvenile glaucoma;

rong xue xing qing guang yan 溶血性青光眼
hemolytic glaucoma;

wai shang xing qing guang yan 外傷性青光眼
traumatic glaucoma;

yan xing qing guang yan 炎性青光眼
inflammatory glaucoma;

ying er xing qing guang yan 嬰兒性青光眼
infantile glaucoma;

yuan fa xing qing guang yan 原發性青光眼
primary glaucoma;

zai ti xing qing guang yan 甾體性青光眼
steroid glaucoma;

zu zhong xing qing guang yan 卒中性青光眼
apoplectic glaucoma;

zu se xing qing guang yan 阻塞性青光眼
obstructive glaucoma;

qing guang yan ban 青光眼斑
glaukomflecken;

qing guang yan mang 青光眼盲
glaucosis;

qing guang yan xing bai nei zhang 青光眼性白內障
glaucomatous cataract;

qing guang yan yun 青光眼暈
glaucomatous halo;

qing mang 青盲
(1) green-blindness;

(2) amaurosis / loss of sight;

qing nei zhang 青內障
glaucoma;

qing shao nian xing qing guang yan 青少年型青光眼
juvenile glaucoma;

qing yan 青眼
favour / high regard / preference;

qing1 shi 輕視
look down on / take lightly || belittle; bridle at sth; cock a snoot at; cock one's nose; condemn; contemptuous; cry down; curl one's lip; despise; disdain; disdainful; disparage; feel contempt for; give sb the go-by; give sth the go-by; hold in contempt; hold in scorn; in contempt of; look down on; look down one's nose at; look down upon; make light of; make light of sb; make little account of; make little of; mocking; pooh-pooh; regard lightly; scorn; scornful of; set at naught; set light by sb; set little of; set little store by sb; set little store by sth; set no store by sb; set no store by sth; set not much store by; show scorn; slight; snap one's fingers at; sneeze at; take no account of; think light of; think little of; think nothing of; think scorn of; treat with contempt; trifle with; turn one's nose up at sb; underestimate; underrate;

qing shi ao man 輕視傲慢
(1) contempt and pride;
(2) dispise and be haughty;

qing shi kun nan 輕視困難
make light of difficulties;

qiong2 mu 窮目
see as far as one can;

qiu1 zhen xing hong mo yan 丘疹性虹膜炎
iritis papulosa;

qiu1 bo 秋波
the bewitching eyes of a beautiful woman;

qiu bo an song 秋波暗送
send silent and endearing messages with bewitching eyes;

qiu bo chuan qing 秋波傳情
give a loving glance || cast sheep's eyes; give sb the glad eye; make eyes at sb; throw amorous glances at sb;

qiu bo liu mei 秋波流媚
glance at sb coquettishly;

qiu bo wei zhuan 秋波微轉
a slight turn of the bewitching eyes of a beautiful woman / eloquent eyes that send a silent message;

qiu bo ying ying 秋波盈盈
the coquettish glances of a beautiful woman;

qiu3 jian 求見
seek an interview;

qu1 du xing jin shi 曲度性近視
curvature myopia;

qu du yuan shi 曲度遠視
curvature hyperopia;

qu4 覷
gaze / look / spy on / watch;

qu ji hui 覷機會
watch for a chance / watch for an opportunity;

qu kui 覷窺
peep at;

qu zhe yan 覷着眼
narrow one's eyes and gaze at sth with great attention;

quan2 bai nei zhang 全白內障
total cataract;

quan mang 全盲
total blindness;

quan se mang 全色盲
complete colour blindness;

quan yan ji shui 全眼積水
hydrophthalmos totalis;

quan yan qiu yan 全眼球炎
panophthalmitis;

ran2 mei 燃眉
very dangerous / urgently critical;

ran mei zhi ji 燃眉之急
as pressing as a fire singeing one's eyebrows || a burning necessity; a matter of utmost urgency; a pressing danger; a pressing need; as urgent as one's burning eyebrows need attention; imminent danger; impending; it is extremely urgent; of great urgency; sth extremely urgent; sth that brooks not a

moment's delay; sth that calls for immediate attention;

re2 ren zhu mu 惹人注目
attract attention;

re4 lei gun gun 熱淚滾滾
warm tears streaming down one's face;

re lei ying kuang 熱淚盈眶
hot tears well up in one's eyes ‖ eyes moistening; in the melting mood; one's eyes brim with warm tears; one's eyes fill with hot tears; one's eyes are suffused with warm tears; tearful; tears of excitement fill one's eyes and nearly brim over; tears of joy spring to one's eyes; the warm tears gush from one's eyes;

re lei zong heng 熱淚縱橫
shed hot tears / weep bitter tears;

ren2 duo yan za 人多眼雜
four eyes see more than two / the more people, the more eyes;

ren jian ren ai 人見人愛
be loved by all;

ren3 lei 忍淚
choke back one's tears / hold back one's tears;

ren lei tun sheng 忍淚吞聲
choke down one's tears;

ren ti 忍涕
hold back one's tears;

ren xiao 忍笑
hold back laughter / stifle a laugh;

ren4 shen xing shi wang mo yan 妊娠性視網膜炎
gravidic retinitis;

ri4 guang xing shi wang mo yan 日光性視網膜炎
solar retinitis;

ri shi mang 日蝕盲
eclipse blindness;

ri shi xing mang 日蝕性盲
eclipse blindness;

ri shi xing shi wang mo yan 日蝕性視網膜炎
solar retinitis;

rong2 xue xing qing guang yan 溶血性青光眼
hemolytic glaucoma;

rou2 yan jing 揉眼睛
rub one's eyes;

rou4 yan 肉眼
naked eye;

rou yan fan tai 肉眼凡胎
short-sighted and good-for-nothing person;

rou yan neng jian 肉眼能見
visible to the naked eye // can see sth without the aid of instruments;

rou yan wu zhu 肉眼無珠
blind as a mole;

ru4 yan 入眼
pleasing to the ear;

rui4 yan 鋭眼
sharp eyes;

run4 xin yang yan 潤心養眼
good to hear or see;

ruo4 shi 弱視
amblyopia;
chuang shang xing ruo shi 創傷性弱視
traumatic amblyopia;
niao du zheng xing ruo shi 尿毒症性弱視
uremic amblyopia;
pian ce ruo shi 偏側弱視
hemiamblyopia;
wai shang xing ruo shi 外傷性弱視
traumatic amblyopia;
ye fa xing ruo shi 夜發性弱視
nocturnal amblyopia;
ying yang que fa xing ruo shi 營養缺乏性弱視
deficiency amblyopia;
zhong du xing ruo shi 中毒性弱視
toxic amblyopia;

ruo shi xing yan zhen 弱視性眼震
amblyopic nystagmus;

ruo shi yi chuan 弱視遺傳
recessive inheritance;

sa3 lei 灑淚
shed tears;

sa lei er bie 灑淚而別
part in tears || as one said farewell, the tears run down one's cheeks; bid each other farewell with tears in one's eyes; in tears to bid each other farewell; take their leave of each other, shedding tears;

sa lei gao bie 灑淚告別
part in tears / pay one's last respects with tears / take a tearful leave;

san1 zhi yan 三隻眼
clear-sighted;

san3 guang 散光
astigmia;
gui ze san guang 規則散光
regular astigmatism;
hun he san guang 混合散光
mixed astigmatism;
sheng li xing san guang 生理性散光
physiological astigmatism;

sao3 mei 掃眉
paint eyebrows;

se4 mang 色盲
colour blindness / parachomatoblepsia;
bu fen se mang 部份色盲
chromatopsia;
lan huang se mang 藍黃色盲
blue-yellow blindness;
lan se mang 藍色盲
blue blindness;
pian ce se mang 偏側色盲
hemiachromatopsia;
quan se mang 全色盲
complete colour blindness;
yi wang xing se mang 遺傳性色盲
amnesic colour blindness;

se mi mi de yan guang 色迷迷的眼光
lewd glances;

se ruo 色弱
colour weakness;

se shi jue 色視覺
colour vision;

sha1 yan 沙眼
trachoma;
jia sha yan 假沙眼
pseudotrachoma;

sha1 yan 砂眼
trachoma;

sha1 kan 傻看
gawp;

sha yan 傻眼
be dumbfounded / be stunned;

sha4 yan 霎眼
wink;

shan1 潸
tears flowing / weep;

shan ran 潸然
tears falling;

shan ran lei xia 潸然淚下
drop a few silent tears || shed silent tears; tears trickling down one's cheeks;

shan shan 潸潸
weep continually;

shan xuan 潸泫
tears flowing / weeping;

shang4 yan 上眼
be worth looking at;

shao3 jian 少見
rare / seldom seen;

shao jian duo guai 少見多怪
a man who has seen little regards many things as strange || comment excitedly on a commonplace thing; consider sth remarkable simply because one has not seen it before; having seen little, one gets excited easily; he who has little experience has many surprises; ignorant people are easily surprised; kick up a fuss; the less a man has seen the more he has to wonder at; things rarely seen are regarded as strange; things seldom seen seem strange; wonder at what one has not seen; wonder is the daughter of ignorance;

shen2 jing xing shi pi lao 神經性視疲勞
nervous asthenopia;

shen3 yue 審閱
check and approve / examine / review;

shen4 xing shi wang mo bing 腎性視網膜病
renal retinopathy;

shen xing shi wang mo yan 腎性視網膜炎
renal retinitis;

shen4 chu xing shi wang mo bing 滲出性視網膜病
exudative retinopahty;

shen chu xing shi wang mo yan 滲出性視網膜炎
exudative retinitis;

sheng1 li xing fu shi 生理性複視
physiological diplopia;

sheng li xing san guang 生理性散光
physiological astigmatism;

sheng1 lei ju xia 聲淚俱下
cry while speaking;

sheng3 眚
eye disease;

shi1 ming 失明
become blind / go blind / lose one's sight // blind;

shi1 yi yan se 施以眼色
give sb the wink ‖ shoot at sb a meaningful glance; shoot sb a warning glance;

shi1 yan 詩眼
the mind's eye of a poet;

shi1 zhen xing jie mo yan 濕疹性結膜炎
eczematous conjunctivitis;

shi zhen xing yan yan 濕疹性眼炎
ophthalmia eczematosa;

shi2 zhi xing jiao mo yan 實質性角膜炎
parenchymatous keratitis;

shi3 yan se 使眼色
make eyes at ‖ say sth with eyes; shoot sb a warning glance; tip sb the ink; wink;

shi4 lei 拭淚
wipe tears;

shi4 mu yi dai 拭目以待
wait and see;

shi4 視
(1) look at / see;
(2) look upon ‖ consider; look upon as; regard; regard as; take it for;
(3) inspect / observe / watch;
(4) imitate / take as a model;

shi cha 視差
parallax;
tong ce shi cha 同側視差
homonymous parallax;

shi cha 視察
inspect / observe;

shi chang 視唱
sightsinging;

shi dong xing yan zhen 視動性眼震
opticokinetic nystagmus;

shi er bu jian 視而不見
look without seeing ‖ absent-minded; ignore; look at but pay no attention to; look at but pretend not to see; observe but not to pay attention to; see it without taking any notice; shut one's eyes to; turn a blind eye to; turn one's blind eye on; wink at; with unseeing eyes;

shi er bu jian, ting er bu wen 視而不見，聽而不聞
look at but pay no attention to, and listen to but hear nothing ‖ look but see not, listen but hear not; see and hear it without taking any notice;

shi guan 視官
organ of vision;

shi jie 視界
eyeshot / field of view / field of vision / range of vision;

shi jue 視覺
sense of sight / vision / visual sense;
bai zhou shi jue 白晝視覺
day vision;
dan yan shi jue 單眼視覺
monocular vision;
wu se shi jue 無色視覺
achromatic vision;

shi jue jiao dian 視覺焦點
eye-catcher;

shi jue kong jian 視覺空間
visual space;

shi jue min rui 視覺敏銳
visual acuity;

shi jue yin xiang 視覺印象
visual impression;

shi jue zhong shu 視覺中樞
visual centre;

shi li 視力
eyesight / sight / the power of vision / vision;
ai hu shi li 愛護視力
take good care of one's eyesight;
dan yan shi li 單眼視力
monocular vision;

shi li shuai tui 視力衰退
failing eyesight;

shi neng 視能
function of eyesight;

shi pi lao 視疲勞
asthenopia;
shen jing xing shi pi lao 神經性視疲勞
nervous asthenopia;

shi ru bi xi 視如敝屣
cast aside sth or sb as worthless || regard as worn-out shoes — cast aside as worthless; regard as worthless as worn-out shoes — have the greatest contempt for;

shi ru cao jie 視如草芥
treat sb like dirt || hold sth as grass — regard as if of no importance; regard as worthless; regard sth or sb as worthless;

shi ru fen tu 視如糞土
treat sb like dirt / treat sth as mud || consider as beneath contempt; look upon as dirt; look upon as filth and dirt; treat sth as the mud beneath one's feet;

shi ru ji chu 視如己出
treat sb as one's own child || regard sb almost as one's own child; treat a child as if he were one's own;

shi ru kou chou 視如寇仇
regard sb as one's enemy;

shi ru she xie 視如蛇蝎
regard with great detestation || deem to be snakes and scorpions; have a great aversion to;

shi ru wan wu 視如玩物
be treated as playthings;

shi ru zhen bao 視如珍寶
hold sth in high esteem || care for as precious stones — hold sth in high esteem; regard sb or sth as a jewel of the greatest value;

shi ruo er xi 視若兒戲
consider it as mere child's play || treat as a trifle; trifle with;

shi ruo jin luan 視若禁臠
regard her as an inaccessible woman / regard sth as a forbidden slice of meat;

shi ruo wei tu 視若畏途
look upon it as an objectionable pursuit / think of it as a dangerous road;

shi ruo wu du 視若無睹
take no notice of what one sees || be undisturbed by what one has seen; ignore; show no concern for; shut one's eyes to; turn a blind eye to;

shi ruo wu wu 視若無物
gaze at it as nothing / regard as nothing;

shi ruo zhi bao 視若至寶
hold sth in high esteem / regard as priceless;

shi shan wen qin 視膳問寢
wait on one's parents and attend to their meals and rest;

shi shi 視事
assume office / attend to business after assuming office;

shi si ru guai 視死如歸
look upon death as nothing || defy death; face death unflinchingly; go to one's death as if one were going home; look death calmly in the face; look on death without flinching; make no more of dying than of going home; regard death as going home; unafraid of death;

shi ting 視聽
(1) knowledge and experience / what one sees and hears;
(2) public opinion;

shi ting yan dong 視聽言動
see, hear, talk, and move;

shi tong er xi 視同兒戲
consider as child's play || not to take seriously; regard it as unimportant; take it

lightly; treat a serious matter as a trifle; trifle;

shi tong ju wen 視同具文
regard as mere empty words;

shi tong lu ren 視同路人
treat sb as a passer-by stranger || make a stranger of; regard sb as a stranger; treat as outsiders; treat as strangers; treat sb like a stranger;

shi tong mo lu 視同陌路
treat sb as if he were a complete stranger || cut sb dead; give sb the go-by;

shi tong shen ming 視同神明
look upon sb as superhuman;

shi tong shou zu 視同手足
treat sb as one's own brother;

shi tong yi lü 視同一律
consider all as alike / identify with;

shi tong yi ti 視同一體
accord the same treatment to all || impartial; look as an integral whole; make no distinction;

shi tong zhen bao 視同珍寶
hold sth in high esteem / look upon sth as a treasure;

shi wang mo 視網膜
retina;

jin ya xing shi wang mo 緊壓性視網膜
coarctate retina;

shi wang mo bing 視網膜病
retinitis;

bai xue bing xing shi wang mo bing 白血病性視網膜病
leukemic retinophathy;

chu xue xing shi wang mo bing 出血性視網膜病
hemorrhagic retinopathy;

shen xing shi wang mo bing 腎性視網膜病
renal retinopathy;

shen chu xing shi wang mo bing 滲出性視網膜病
exudative retinopahty;

tang niao bing shi wang mo bing 糖尿病視網膜病
diabetic retinopathy;

tang niao bing xing shi wang mo bing 糖尿病性視網膜病
diabetic retinopathy;

zao chan er shi wang mo bing 早產兒視網膜病
retinopathy of prematurity;

zeng sheng xing shi wang mo bing 增生性視網膜病
proliferative retinopathy;

shi wang mo fa yu bu liang 視網膜發育不良
retinal dysplasia;

shi wang mo fa yu bu quan 視網膜發育不全
retinal aplasia;

shi wang mo tuo li 視網膜脫離
detached retina;

shi wang mo yan 視網膜炎
retinitis;

bai xue bing xing shi wang mo yan 白血病性視網膜炎
leukemic retinitis;

dan chun xing shi wang mo yan 單純性視網膜炎
simple retinitis;

mei du xing shi wang mo yan 梅毒性視網膜炎
syphilitic retinitis;

niao du zheng xing shi wang mo yan 尿毒症性視網膜炎
uremic retinitis;

pan zhuang shi wang mo yan 盤狀視網膜炎
disciform retinitis;

ren shen xing shi wang mo yan 妊娠性視網膜炎
gravidic retinitis;

ri guang xing shi wang mo yan 日光性視網膜炎
solar retinitis;

ri shi xing shi wang mo yan 日蝕性視網膜炎
solar retinitis;

shen xing shi wang mo yan 腎性視網膜炎
renal retinitis;

shen chu xing shi wang mo yan 滲出性視網膜炎
exudative retinitis;

tang niao bing xing shi wang mo yan 糖尿病性視網膜炎
diabetic retinitis;

zeng sheng xing shi wang mo yan 增生性視網膜炎
proliferating retinitis;

zhuan yi xing shi wang mo yan 轉移性視網膜炎
metastatic retinitis;

zu zhong xing shi wang mo yan 卒中性視網膜炎
apoplectic retinitis;

shi wang mo yi zhi 視網膜移植
retina transplant;

shi wei 視為
consider as / regard as;

shi wei jin luan 視為禁臠
regard as one's exclusive domain || regard sth as a forbidden slice of meat — regard her as an inaccessible woman;

shi wei ju wen 視為具文
regard as mere empty words || consider as a mere form of words; look to as a mere form; regard the law as a dead letter;

shi wei wei tu 視為畏途
regard it as a dangerous road to take || afraid to undertake; look upon it as an objectionable pursuit; regard as a road full of dangers — regard as an undertaking full of difficulties; regard as dangerous;

shi wei zhi ji 視為知己
look upon sb as one's best friend / treat sb as a bosom friend;

shi wei zhi bao 視為至寶
regard as priceless / set great store by;

shi xian ru yi 視險如夷
regard a hazardous location as level ground — no fear of danger and difficulties;

shi xian 視線
eyesight;

shi ye 視野
eyeshot / field of vision / horizon;

shi zuo deng xian 視作等閒
regard as a light matter / treat lightly;

shi zuo hong shui meng shou 視作洪水猛獸
regard sth as dangerous as floods and wild beasts;

shi4 li yan 勢利眼
(1) snobbish attitude;
(2) snob;
(3) judge a person by wealth and power;

shou1 kan 收看
watch (television);

shou lei 收淚
stop crying;

shou4 ren zhu mu 受人矚目
come into prominence / come to prominence;

shu1 mei 舒眉
relax the brows to show pleasure;

shu mei zhan yan 舒眉展眼
lift one's eyebrows and open one's eyes || beam with joy; relax the brows and stretch the eyes to show pleasure;

shu2 shi 熟視
look carefully and for a long time / scrutinize;

shu shi wu du 熟視無睹
pay no attention to a familiar sight || care nothing for; close one's eyes to; fail to notice; ignore; indifferent to; look at but pay no attention to; not to see sth right under one's nose; regard as of no consequence; take no notice; turn a blind eye to;

shu3 mu 鼠目
(1) small, protruding eyes;
(2) short-sighted;

shu mu cun guang 鼠目寸光
lack of foresight || lack of vision and prevision; not to be able to see beyond one's nose; not to see an inch beyond one's nose; see no further than one's nose; see only what is under one's nose; short-sighted;

shu yan 鼠眼
(1) small, protruding eyes;
(2) lack of foresight;

shu4 mei deng mu 豎眉瞪目
raise one's brows and one's dilated pupils flashed with anger / raise one's eyebrows and stare in anger;

shu yan 豎眼
angry looks;

shuang1 mei jin suo 雙眉緊鎖
one's brows furrow / one's brows knit together / one's brows tightly knit;

shuang mu 雙目
one's eyes;

shuang mu jiong jiong 雙目炯炯
one's eyes are piercingly bright;

shuang mu shen xian 雙目深陷
the eyes wax hollow;

shuang mu shi ming 雙目失明
blind in both eyes || become blind; go blind in both eyes; lose one's eyesight; lose the sight of both eyes;

shuang mu wu shen 雙目無神
lacklustre in one's eyes // one's eyes are lustreless;

shuang tong jian shui 雙瞳翦水
clear, beautiful eyes of a pretty girl;

shuang yan pi 雙眼皮
double-fold eyelids;

shuang yan qing zi 雙眼青紫
contused eyeballs;

shui4 睡
rest with eyes closed;

shui yan meng long 睡眼矇矓
bleary-eyed / sleepy-eyed;

shui yan xing song 睡眼惺忪
have a drowsy look // bleary-eyed;

shun4 yan 順眼
please the eye // agreeable in one's eyes / pleasant to the eye;

shun4 瞬
blink / wink;

shun mu 瞬目
(1) winking;
(2) palpebrate;

shun mu fan she 瞬目反射
blink reflex;

shun xi 瞬息
twinkling;

shun xi wan bian 瞬息萬變
under myriad changes in the twinkling of an eye;

shun xi zhi jian 瞬息之間
in the twinkling of an eye;

shuo4 jian bu xian 數見不鮮
a common occurrence || be encountered with many times; not uncommon; nothing new; nothing uncommon; what is frequently seen is not strange;

si1 kong jian guan 司空見慣
commonplace || a common enough thing; a common occurrence; a common sight; a matter of common occurrence; a matter of common practice; a matter of repeated occurrence; be accustomed to seeing such things; it is quite common for...; the order of the day;

si1 lei 絲淚
little teardrops;

si1 jian 廝見
see each other;

si3 bu ming mu 死不瞑目
die without closing one's eyes || cannot die in peace; die discontent; die dissatisfied; die with everlasting regret; die with injustice unredressed; turn in one's grave;

si mei deng yan 死眉瞪眼
(1) with a straight face // a wooden expression that infuriates;
(2) inanimate;

si4 gu 四顧
look around;

si gu mang ran 四顧茫然
see nothing but emptiness all around;

si gu wu ren 四顧無人
look around to find nobody anywhere;

si4 mu 肆目
stretch one's eyes as far as one can see;

song3 dong shi ting 聳動視聽
create a sensation;

song4 qiu bo 送秋波
throw amorous glances / flutter one's eyelashes at / make eyes at;

sou3 瞍
have eyes without pupils // blind;

su2 yan 俗眼
mortal eyes;

sui1 睢
raise one's eyes;

sui2 yi xing yan zhen 隨意性眼震
voluntary nystagmus;

suo3 wen suo jian 所聞所見
what one sees and hears;

suo3 mei 鎖眉
frown / knit one's brows;

tan2 lei suo ti 彈淚索涕
sniff and blink away one's tears;

tan4 wei guan zhi 歎為觀止
the most magnificent sight of all || a sight never to be forgotten; acclaim a work of art as the acme of perfection; be lost in wonder; hold it to be the best; take one's breath away in astonishment;

tang2 niao bing bai nei zhang 糖尿病白內障
diabetic cataract;

tang niao bing shi wang mo bing 糖尿病視網膜病
diabetic retinopathy;

tang niao bing xing bai nei zhang 糖尿病性白內障
diabetic cataract;

tang niao bing xing shi wang mo bing 糖尿病性視網膜病
diabetic retinopathy;

tang niao bing xing shi wang mo yan 糖尿病性視網膜炎
diabetic retinitis;

tang3 yan lei 淌眼淚
shed tears;

tang yan mo lei 淌眼抹淚
cry / weep;

tao2 sai xing yan 桃腮杏眼
peach cheeks and almond-shaped eyes / rosy cheeks and almond eyes;

te4 ying xing bai nei zhang 特應性白內障
atopic cataract;

te ying xing jie mo yan 特應性結膜炎
atopic conjunctivitis;

ti2 ku 啼哭
cry / wail;

ti qi 啼泣
sob / wail;

ti4 涕
tears;

ti lei 涕淚
tears;

ti lei jiao liu 涕淚交流
cry with a flood of tears || shed streams of tears and snivel; tears and snivel fall down at the same time;

ti lei ju xia 涕淚俱下
tears and snivel flowing down together;

ti lei zong heng 涕淚縱橫
with tears streaming down one's face;

ti ling 涕零
shed tears;

ti ling ru yu 涕零如雨
tears streaming down like rain drops;

ti qi 涕泣
cry / weep;

ti qi zhan jin 涕泣沾襟
wet the front part of one's garment with tears;

ti si 涕泗
tears and snivel;

ti si heng liu 涕泗橫流
tears and snivel flowing down rapidly;

ti si jiao liu 涕泗交流
tears and snivel fall down at the same time;

ti si pang tuo 涕泗滂沱
be drenched with tears and snivel || a flood of tears; tears and snivel run abundantly down one's face;

ti ti 涕洟
tears and snivel;

tiao1 yan 挑眼
find fault / pick flaws;

tiao2 jie xing xie shi 調節性斜視
accommodative strabismus;

tiao4 眺
look far away / take a look at faraway things;

tiao wang 眺望
look far away || espy; look into the distance from a high place; overlook; survey;

tong1 mei 通眉
have joined eyebrows;

tong2 ce fu shi 同側複視
homonymous diplopia;

tong ce pian mang 同側偏盲
homonymous hemianopia;

tong ce shi cha 同側視差
homonymous parallax;

tong2 xie yan yan 銅屑眼炎
chalkitis;

tong2 瞳
pupil of the eye;

tong kong 瞳孔
pupil of the eye;

jin zhang xing tong kong 緊張性瞳孔
tonic pupil;

tong kong bi he 瞳孔閉合
coreclisis;

tong kong fan she 瞳孔反射
pupillary reflex;

tong kong fan ying 瞳孔反應
pupillary reflex;

pian mang xing tong kong fan ying 偏盲性瞳孔反應
hemiopic pupillary reaction;

tong kong jing luan 瞳孔痙攣
pupillary athetosis;

tong kong kuo da 瞳孔擴大
mydriasis;

jing luan xing tong kong kuo da 痙攣性瞳孔擴大
spasmodic mydriansis;

ma bi xing tong kong kuo da 麻痺性瞳孔擴大
paralytic mydriasis;

tong kong san da 瞳孔散大
mydriasis;

tong kong suo xiao 瞳孔縮小
miosis;

ci ji xing tong kong suo xiao 刺激性瞳孔縮小
irritative miosis;

ma bi xing tong kong suo xiao 麻痺性瞳孔縮小
paralytic miosis;

tong kong xia xiao 瞳孔狹小
stenocoriasis;

tong kong yi chang 瞳孔異常
dyscoria;

tong zi 瞳子
pupil of the eye;

tong4 feng hong mo yan 痛風虹膜炎
gouty iritis;

tong ku 痛哭
cry bitterly / wail / weeply bitterly;

tong ku liu ti 痛哭流涕
cry and shed bitter tears || cry bitterly; cry one's heart out; set one's eyes at flow; shed tears in bitter sorrow; shed tears of anguish; weep bitter tears; weep bitterly;

tong ku shi sheng 痛哭失聲
be choked with tears / lose one's voice after weeping;

tong ku yi chang 痛哭一場
give free vent to one's sorrow with many tears and loud laments / have a good cry;

tong ku yu jue 痛哭欲絕
cry one's heart out;

tong4 ku 慟哭
wail / weep bitterly;

tou1 kan 偷看
cast a furtive glance / peek / steal a glance / steal a look / take a furtive glance;

tou kan yi yan 偷看一眼
cast a furtive glance / peek / steal a glance / steal a look / take a furtive glance;

tou yan 偷眼
cast a furtive glance / peek / steal a glance / take a furtive glance;

tou4 shi 透視
see through;

tu1 yan 突眼
exophthalmos / protuberant eyes;
bo dong xing tu yan 搏動性突眼
pulsating exophthalmos;
e xing tu yan 惡性突眼
malignant exophthalmos;
nei fen mi tu yan 內分泌突眼
endocrine exophthalmos;

wa1 yan jing 挖眼睛
gouge out eyes;

wai4 shang xing bai nei zhang 外傷性白內障
traumatic cataract;

wai shang xing qing guang yan 外傷性青光眼
traumatic glaucoma;

wai shang xing ruo shi 外傷性弱視
traumatic amblyopia;

wan2 quan bai nei zhang 完全白內障
complete cataract;

wan quan pian mang 完全偏盲
absolute hemianopia;

wan4 mu kui kui 萬目睽睽
all eyes are staring / all eyes centre on // under the glare of the public;

wang3 qian kan 往前看
look ahead / look forward;

wang3 jian 罔見
fail to see;

wang4 望
(1) gaze into the distance / look far ahead;
(2) call on / visit;
(3) expect / hope / look forward to;

wang bu jian 望不見
incapable of being seen / incapable of seeing;

wang chuan qiu shui 望穿秋水
aspire earnestly || await with great anxiety; gaze with eager expectation; keep gazing anxiously till one's eyes are strained;

wang chuan shuang yan 望穿雙眼
wear out one's eyes by gazing anxiously;

wang er que bu 望而卻步
shrink back at the sight of sth || direct the eyes upon...and step back; flinch; halt in face of;

wang er sheng wei 望而生畏
be awed by the sight of || awe-inspiring; be daunted at the sight of; be terrified by the sight of sb; hold sb in awe; inspire awe even from a distance; stand in awe of;

wang feng 望風
keep watch // on the lookout;

wang feng bu ying 望風捕影
be taken in by rumours || on a false scent; on a wrong scent; on the wrong track; pursue a phantom;

wang feng er lai 望風而來
come from all directions;

wang feng er tao 望風而逃
flee at the mere sight of the oncoming force || flee before sb; run away at the rumour of the approach of; turn tail at the mere rustle of a leaf;

wang feng er xiang 望風而降
everyone surrenders at the mere rumour of sb's coming;

wang feng pi mi 望風披靡
flee helter-skelter at the mere sight of the oncoming force || flee pell-mell before sb; melt away at the mere whisper of sb's coming;

wang feng pu ying 望風撲影
give a wild-goose chase / launch a witch hunt / search without any clue;

wang feng yin ling 望風引領
gaze at the wind and stretch out the neck — anxiously expecting sb;

wang jian 望見
catch sight of / descry / see;

wang shi 望視
look upwards;

wang wang 望望
look distracted;

wang wen wen qie 望聞問切
look, listen, question and feel the pulse — four ways of diagnosis;

wang yan yu chuan 望眼欲穿
aspire earnestly / gaze anxiously till one's eyes are overstrained ‖ have long been looking forward with eager expectancy; look for with impatient expectancy; look on with longing eyes; wear out one's eyes looking for; one's expecting eyes are going to be worn out; one's eyes are worn out watching for sb;

wang yang xing tan 望洋興歎
lament one's littleness before the vast ocean ‖ gaze at the ocean and complain of its infinitude — feel utterly helpless in face of a task beyond one's capability;

wei4 jian 未見
have not seen;

wei jian qi ren, xian wen qi sheng 未見其人，先聞其聲
sb who is not yet here, but his voice has already been heard;

wei4 guang 畏光
photophobia;

wen1 rou mu guang 溫柔目光
tender-eyed;

wen4 lei 抆淚
wipe one's tears away;

wen4 lei 搵淚
wipe off tears;

wo4 can mei 臥蠶眉
arched eyebrows;

wu1 嗚
sob / weep;

wu ye 嗚咽
sob / weep / whimper;

wu2 fa yu jian 無法預見
unforeseeable / unforeseen;

wu se shi jue 無色視覺
achromatic vision;

wu shi 無視
shut one's eyes to;

wu shi xian shi 無視現實
bury one's head in the sand / hide one's head in the sand;

wu3 shi 忤視
look defiantly at;

wu3 shang yan jing 捣上眼睛
cover up one's eyes;

wu4 晤
interview / meet / see / see face to face;

wu dui 晤對
meet face to face;

wu mian 晤面
meet / see / see each other;

wu shang 晤商
face-to-face negotiation // discuss in an interview;

wu tan 晤談
converse / have a talk / interview / meet and talk;

wu yan 晤言
meet and talk;

xi1 lei 嬉淚
tears of joy;

xi2 jian 習見
frequently seen / often seen;

xi3 shang mei shao 喜上眉梢
happiness appears on the eyebrows // look very happy // radiant with joy;

xi yi mei shao 喜溢眉梢
one's delight appears on the end of the eyebrow ‖ kindle with joy; illuminate with joy; light up with joy;

xi yi mei yu 喜溢眉宇
eyes kindled with joy ‖ joy diffused the face; radiant; radiant with joy;

xi4 盻
look in anger;

xi shi chou ren 盻視仇人
glare at the foe;

xi4 kan 細看
examine in detail / look at carefully;

xia1 瞎
blind;

xia le 瞎了
be blinded / lose one's vision;

xia yan 瞎眼
blind;

xia2 tiao 遐眺
stretch one's sight as far as it can reach;

xia4 de mu deng kou dai 嚇得目瞪口呆
strike sb speechless || be paralysed with terror; be scared stiff; strike sb dumb;

xian1 du wei kuai 先睹為快
all eagerness to see it // consider it a pleasure to be among the first to read it;

xian jian 先見
foresight;

xian jian zhi ming 先見之明
ability to discern what is coming || a long head; able to anticipate; able to predict; ability to foresee; far-sightedness; foresight; prescience; prevision; prophetic vision; second sight; show foresight;

xian ru zhi jian 先入之見
preconception;

xian1 mei liang yan 鮮眉亮眼
distinct eyebrows and bright eyes — a good-looking face;

xian yan duo mu 鮮艷奪目
dazzlingly beautiful || attractively bright-coloured; resplendent; splendour blinds the eyes;

xian3 er yi jian 顯而易見
appparently / evidently;

xian yan 顯眼
conspicuous / eye-catching / striking;

xiang1 dui er qi 相對而泣
look into each other's eyes and weep / mingle tears;

xiang dui xing pian mang 相對性偏盲
relative hemianopia;

xiang dui yuan shi 相對遠視
relative hyperopia;

xiang gu shi se 相顧失色
look at each other in dismay;

xiang kan 相看
look at each other;

xiang qu 相覷
look at each other;

xiang shi 相視
look at each other;

xiang shi er xiao 相視而笑
smile at each other;

xiang shi mo ni 相視莫逆
regard each other as intimate friends;

xiang4 qian kan 向前看
forward-looking;

xiang yu er qi 向隅而泣
be left to grieve and weep all alone in the corner;

xiang4 xian pian mang 象限偏盲
quadrant hemianopia;

xiao3 kan 小看
look down upon || belittle; despise; feel contempt for sth; set at naught;

xiao qiao 小瞧
look down on || belittle; despise; feel contempt for sth; set at naught;

xiao shi 小視
look down upon || belittle; despise; feel contempt for sth; set at naught;

xiao yan 小眼
nanophthalmos;

xiao yan qiu 小眼球
microphthalmia;

xie2 mu ji yu 邪目覬覦
cast a covetous eye on // one's shifty eyes squint right and left;

xie2 bai yan 斜白眼
wall-eye // wall-eyed;

xie ni 斜睨
despise / leer at / look askance / look down on;

xie shi 斜視
strabismus || askance; cast a sidelong glance; cockeyed; leer at; look sideways; skew; skew-eyed; slant; squint-eyed;

jia xing xie shi 假性斜視
pseudostrabismus;
jian xie xing xie shi 間歇性斜視
intermittent strabismus;
ma bi xing xie shi 麻痺性斜視
paralytic strabismus;
nei xie shi 內斜視
cross-eye;
qian fu xing xie shi 潛伏性斜視
latent strabismus;
tiao jie xing xie shi 調節性斜視
accommodative strabismus;
zhou qi xing xie shi 周期性斜視
cyclic strabismus;

xie yan 斜眼
(1) strabismust;
(2) cross-eye / squint-eye;
(3) cross-eyed / sloe-eyed / squint-eyed;

xie yan tou kan 斜眼偷看
see sb out of the corner of one's eye;

xie yan yi piao 斜眼一瞟
look askance at / throw sb a sidelong glance;

xie4 ti 泄涕
come to tears / cry;

xin1 sheng er yan yan 新生兒眼炎
adenologaditis;

xing1 mou 星眸
bright eyes / starry eyes;

xing3 shi 省視
examine / inspect;

xing3 mu 醒目
eye-catching || attract attention; catch the eye; striking;

xing yan 醒眼
catch the eye || attract attention; refreshing;

xing4 yan 杏眼
almond-eyed // almond eyes / apricot-like eyes;

xing yan liu yao 杏眼柳腰
apricot-like eyes and soft waistline of a beauty;

xing yan tao sai 杏眼桃腮
almond-shaped eyes and peach cheeks / large eyes and rosy cheeks;

xing yan xiu mei 杏眼秀眉
with almond-shaped eyes and long eyebrows;

xing yan yuan zheng 杏眼圓睜
with eyes distended with fury;

xiu4 mei 秀眉
long hairs in the eyebrows of an aged person;

xiu mei da yan 秀眉大眼
big eyes and slender eyebrows / fine eyebrows and large eyes;

xiu4 shou pang guan 袖手旁觀
look on without even lifting a finger / watch with folded arms;

xu1 盱
(1) open the eyes wide;
(2) anxious / uneasy / worried;

xu heng 盱衡
(1) look with eyes wide open;
(2) make a general survey;

xu heng dang shi 盱衡當世
have open eyes and know what is going on / have the knowledge of the time;

xu heng li se 盱衡厲色
gaze in stern countenance;

xu heng ren wu 盱衡人物
open eyes on people and things;

xu xi 盱闟
frown / knit one's brows;

xu xu 盱盱
(1) stare with eyes wide open;
(2) proud and haughty;

xuan1 mei tu qi 軒眉吐氣
air of pride and satisfaction;

xuan4 mu 炫目
dazzle the eyes;

xuan ren er mu 炫人耳目
confuse the ears and eyes of the people;

xuan4 ba 眩巴
blink;

xuan ba yan er 眩巴眼兒
wink one's eyes in quick succession;

xuan huang 眩晃
dazzled;

xuan xuan 眩眩
look / see;

xuan yan 眩眼
wink;

xuan yan jian 眩眼間
a very short time / in the twinkling of an eye;

xuan yun 眩暈
dizziness;

xue3 mang zheng 雪盲症
snow blindness;

xue yan yan 雪眼炎
ophthalmia nivialis;

xue4 lei 血淚
blood and tears — extreme sorrow;

xue lei ban ban 血淚斑斑
full of blood and tears // with spots of tears and blood;

xue lei chou 血淚仇
vengeful feelings nurtured by blood and tears;

xun2 mu 恂目
at the twinkling of an eye / in a wink;

xun2 尋
look around;

xun liu 尋溜
look around as to seek sth;

xun lou 尋摟
look around as to seek sth;

xun mo 尋摸
look around as to seek sth;

yan2 xing qing guang yan 炎性青光眼
inflammatory glaucoma;

yan zheng hou bai nei zhang 炎症後白內障
postinflammatory cataract;

yan2 jian 延見
grant an interview with sb;

yan3 眼
(1) eye;
(2) glance / look;

ba ang yan 巴昂眼
bungeye;

jia yan 假眼
ocular prosthesis;

ju yan 巨眼
macrophthalmia;

lai zhe yan 睞着眼
blinking one's eyes;

yan ai 眼癌
eye cancer;

yan ba ba 眼巴巴
(1) with steady gaze;
(2) anxiously / eagerly / expectantly;
(3) helplessly;

yan bai 眼白
white of the eye;

yan bai hua bing 眼白化病
ocular albinism;

yan bai mo 眼白膜
albuginea oculi;

yan bao du ji 眼飽肚飢
although one's eyes feast, one's belly starves;

yan bing 眼病
ophthalmopathy;

yan bing xing yan zhen 眼病性眼震
ocular nystagmus;

yan bo 眼波
bright-eyed // eyesight / vision;

yan bu guan xie 眼不觀邪
turn eyes away from evils;

yan bu jian wei jing 眼不見為淨
what the eye sees not, the heart rues not || out of sight, out of mind; what eyes do not see is regarded as clean; what the eye doesn't see, the heart doesn't grieve over;

yan bu jian, xin bu fan 眼不見，心不煩
one who avoids seeing trouble does not have to worry about trouble / what the eye doesn't see the heart doesn't grieve;

yan bu jian, xin bu xiang 眼不見，心不想
far from eye, far from heart / out of sight, out of mind;

yan cha 眼岔
mistake one for another;

yan chan 眼饞
covet / envious;

yan chan chan 眼饞饞
watch enviously;

yan chan du bao 眼饞肚飽
the eye is bigger than the belly;

yan chi 眼眵
gum;

yan chuan 眼穿
anxiously awaiting / eagerly expecting;

yan da xin fei 眼大心肥
proud and arrogant;

yan dai 眼袋
pouch;

yan dao shou dao 眼到手到
take down notes while reading;

yan di 眼底
fundus oculi;

yan di xia 眼底下
(1) right before one's eyes;
(2) at present;

yan er 眼兒
(1) eye;
(2) orifice / tiny hole;

yan fu 眼福
a feast to the eye || delight to the eye; joy to the eye; the good fortune of seeing sth rare or beautiful;

yan fu bu qian 眼福不淺
lucky enough to see // not a shallow delight to the eye;

yan gan zao 眼乾燥
scheroma / xerophtalmia;

yan gan zao zheng 眼乾燥症
xerophthalmia;

yan gao shou di 眼高手低
have great aims but poor ability / have sharp eyes but clumsy hands || conceited but incompetent; fastidious but incompetent; have grandiose aims but puny abilities; have high ambition but low ability; have high standards but little ability; high in aim but lowrate in execution; one's ability doesn't match one's high goal; pursue an aim far beyond one's reach;

yan gao xin ao 眼高心傲
have a haughty look and a proud heart;

yan guan bi, bi guan xin 眼觀鼻，鼻觀心
sit quietly without looking sideways;

yan guan liu lu 眼觀六路
keep one's eyes over;

yan guan liu lu, er ting ba fang 眼觀六路，耳聽八方
have sharp eyes and keen ears || keep one's eyes and ears open — extraordinarily alert; observant and alert;

yan guang 眼光
(1) eye / foresight / insight / sight / vision;
(2) the way of looking at things // view;
(3) acumen;

yan guang duan qian 眼光短淺
short-sighted;

yan guang min rui 眼光敏銳
acute eyesight;

yan guang shui ping 眼光水平
eye-level;

yan guang yuan da 眼光遠大
far-sighted // have a broad vision;

yan guo du kai da 眼過度開大
hypereuryopia;

yan han lei hua 眼含淚花
tears sparkle in one's eyes / have swimming eyes / one's eyes dim with tears;

yan hei 眼黑
avarice / greedy;

yan hong 眼紅
(1) covet / envious / jealous;
(2) angry / furious;
(3) red-eyed;

yan hua 眼花
be dazzled / dazzle one's eyes || dim of sight; dizzy; giddy; have blurred vision; have dim eyesight;

yan hua er 眼花兒
darling / the apple of one's eye;

yan hua liao luan 眼花繚亂
be dazzled / dazzle one's eyes || in a daze; see things in a blur;

yan hua xin luan 眼花心亂
one's eyes are not clear and one's heart confused;

yan ji 眼肌
eye muscles;

yan ji bing 眼肌病
ocular myopathy;

yan ji tan huan 眼肌癱瘓
ophtalmoplegia;

yan ji yan 眼肌炎
ophthalmomyositis;

yan ji shui 眼積水
hydrophthalmos;
quan yan ji shui 全眼積水
hydrophthalmos totalis;

yan ji shou kuai 眼疾手快
sharp eyes and agile hands;

yan ji zui kuai 眼疾嘴快
quick of eye and deft of beak;

yan ji dong 眼急動
saccade;

yan jian 眼尖
quick of sight / sharp-eyed;

yan jian 眼瞼
eyelid;

yan jian gong neng bu quan 眼瞼功能不全
insufficiency of the eyelids;

yan jian jing luan 眼瞼痙攣
blepharospasm;

yan jian yan 眼瞼炎
blepharitis;
bian yuan xing yan jian yan 邊緣性眼瞼炎
blear eye;

yan jian de 眼見得
it is evident;

yan jian mu du 眼見目睹
see with one's own eyes;

yan jian wei shi 眼見為實
seeing is believing / what you see is true;

yan jian 眼腱
tendo oculi;

yan jian yan 眼腱炎
ophthalmodesmitis;

yan jiao 眼角
canthus / the corner of the eye;

yan jiao han qing 眼角含情
gaze at sb with tenderness;

yan jie mao 眼睫毛
eyelashes;

yan jie 眼界
one's field of vision / one's outlook;

yan jie gao 眼界高
have one's standard set high;

yan jing 眼睛
eyes;
ai hu yan jing 愛護眼睛
protect one's eyes;

yan jing ao xian 眼睛凹陷
hollow-eyed;

yan jing ao hong 眼睛熬紅
one's eyes are bloodshot from lack of sleep;

yan jing bai deng 眼睛白瞪
roll one's eyes in fury;

yan jing fa ding 眼睛發定
with staring eyes;

yan jing fan bai 眼睛翻白
turn up the whites of one's eyes;

yan jing hong hong 眼睛紅紅
with blood-shot eyes;

yan jing ku hong 眼睛哭紅
one's eyes are red from crying;

yan jing ku zhong 眼睛哭腫
cry one's eyes out;

yan jing mao huo 眼睛冒火
one's eyes flashing fire — in an angry mood;

yan jing mi feng 眼睛眯縫
laugh till one's eyes are slits;

yan jing pi lao 眼睛疲勞
eyestrain;

yan jing xiang xia 眼睛向下
cast one's sights on the masses;

yan jing xue liang 眼睛雪亮
have a discerning eye;

yan jing yi shun 眼睛一瞬
a twinkling of the eye / in the twinkling of an eye;

yan jing zhang zai tou ding shang 眼睛長在頭頂上
with one's eyes at the top of one's head — too haughty;

yan ju tong 眼劇痛
ophthalmagra;

yan kai yan bi 眼開眼閉
close one's eyes to / pretend not to see / purposely overlook / turn a blind eye to;

yan kan 眼看
(1) imminent / in a moment / soon;
(2) see sth happening;
(3) look on passively / watch helplessly;

yan kong si hai 眼空四海
consider everyone and everything beneath one's notice / look down on everyone else // supercilious;

yan kong 眼孔
eyelet / orifice;

yan kuai shou ji 眼快手疾
quick of eye and deft of hand;

yan kuan ren shu 眼寬人熟
sociable;

yan kuang 眼眶
(1) eye socket / orbit;
(2) rim of the eye;

yan lei 眼淚
eyedrops / tears;

yan lei bao 眼淚包
be easily reduced to tears;

yan lei bi ti 眼淚鼻涕
shed streams of tears and mucus / the waterworks begin to play // weeping and sniffling;

yan lei cen cen 眼淚涔涔
drip with tears // in a flood of tears // one's eyes water;

yan lei heng liu 眼淚橫流
stream with tears;

yan lei ku gan 眼淚哭乾
cry until one has no more tears to shed / weep until one's tears run dry;

yan lei man kuang 眼淚滿眶
the tears are filling one's eyes;

yan lei mi meng 眼淚迷蒙
one's eyes are dim with tears / one's eyes are misted with tears;

yan lei ru yu 眼淚如雨
one's tears fall like rain;

yan lei shang yong 眼淚上湧
tears come into one's eyes / tears gush to one's eyes / tears rise to one's eyes / tears start to come into one's eyes;

yan lei su su 眼淚簌簌
one's tears fall fast / tears streaming down;

yan lei wang wang 眼淚汪汪
with tearful eyes || eyes brimming with tears; full of tears; having eyes damp with tears; in tears; one's eyes are moist with tears; one's eyes drown in tears; one's eyes are filled with tears; one's eyes swim in tears; tears well up in one's eyes; with eyes swimming in tears;

yan lei xi mian 眼淚洗面
one's face is bathed in tears || tears rain down one's cheeks; wash one's face with tears; with tears all over one's face;

yan lei xiao chu 眼淚笑出
laugh till one's tears come;

yan lei yan mian 眼淚淹面
be bathed in tears;

yan lei ying kuang 眼淚盈眶
tears fill the eyes || one's eyes fill with tears; tears gush from one's eyes; tears spring into one's eyes; tears standing in the eyes; tears suffuse one's eyes;

yan lei yong yong 眼淚湧湧
dash the tears from one's eyes;

yan lei yu di 眼淚欲滴
tears are very near to one's eyes / tears well from one's eyes / tears well up in one's eyes;

yan lei zhi tang 眼淚直淌
burst into a flood of tears / tears are welling from one's eyes;

yan li 眼離
optical illusion;

yan li 眼力
(1) eyesight / vision;
(2) discerning ability / discrimination / judgment / power of judgment;

yan li bu cuo 眼力不錯
have good taste and good eyes;

yan li 眼裏
in one's eyes / within one's vision;

yan lian 眼簾
iris;

yan liang 眼亮
clear-sighted / sharp-sighted;

yan lu jing yi 眼露驚異
there is a startled look in one's eyes;

yan lu sha qi 眼露殺氣
a wicked light shines in one's eyes;

yan lun za ji 眼輪匝肌
orbicularis oculi;

yan mao jin xing 眼冒金星
one's eyes flame with fury || see stars; sparks flow before one's eyes; stars dance before one's eyes;

yan mao nu huo 眼冒怒火
one's eyes flash with rage;

yan mei 眼眉
brow;

yan mian qian de shi 眼面前的事
daily things / everyday events;

yan ming shou kuai 眼明手快
sharp of sight and quick of hand || clearly discerning, swift-handed; nimble; one's eye is clear and one's hand swift; quick of eye and deft of hand; see things clearly and act speedily; sharp-eyed and quick-moving;

yan ming xin liang 眼明心亮
sharp-eyed and clearheaded // see and think clearly;

yan mu 眼目
(1) eyes;
(2) serve as the eye of another / spy;

yan nei ya 眼內壓
intraocular pressure;

yan pao 眼泡
upper eyelid;

yan pi 眼皮
eyelids;
dan yan pi 單眼皮
single-fold eyelids;
shuang yan pi 雙眼皮
double-fold eyelids;

yan pi di xia 眼皮底下
under one's eyes / under the nose of sb;

yan pi lao 眼疲勞
asthenopia / eyestrain;

yan qian 眼前
(1) before one's eyes;
(2) at present / at the moment / now;

yan qian yi liang 眼前一亮
one's eyes are suddenly brightened;

yan qiu 眼球
eyeball;

yan qiu tu chu 眼球突出
protopsis;
bo dong xing yan qiu tu chu 搏動性眼球突出
pulsating exophthalmos;

yan qiu yan 眼球炎
ophthalmitis;
quan yan qiu yan 全眼球炎
panophthalmitis;

yan quan fa hei 眼圈發黑
have dark circles beneath one's eyes;

yan quan zi 眼圈子
eye socket / rim of the eye;

yan re 眼熱
covet / envious;

yan ru liu xing 眼如流星
one's eyes are like glittering stars;

yan ru qiu shui 眼如秋水
bright-eyed // one's eyes are like autumn water — as clear as water;

yan ruo qiu shui, mu ru han xing 眼若秋水，目如寒星
with a pair of eyes like the autumn water and stars of a wintry night;

yan ru shui xing 眼如水杏
one's eyes are like almonds swimming in water;

yan se 眼色
wink || a cue given with the eyes; a hint given with the eyes; meaningful glance; the expression of one's eyes;

yan shen 眼神
(1) expression in one's eyes / gleams of the eyes / light;
(2) eyesight;

yan shen bu ji 眼神不濟
have poor eyesight;

yan sheng 眼生
look unfamiliar // unfamiliar by sight;

yan shi 眼屎
gum / gum in the eyes / secretions of the eyes;

yan shu 眼熟
look familiar || seem to know; seemingly familiar by sight;

yan shu mu heng 眼豎目橫
stare in anger / stare in contempt;

yan si qiu bo 眼似秋波
bright-eyed || in her eyes lay the gleam of the autumn wave; one's eyes glisten with the shine of autumn waves;

yan tiao 眼跳
twitching of the eyelid;

yan tiao xin jing 眼跳心驚
eyes leaping and heart trembling — nervous apprehension;

yan tong 眼同
together with;

yan tong 眼痛
ophthalmodynia;

yan wai xie 眼外斜
abtorsion;

yan wei suo 眼萎縮
ophthalmatrophia;

yan wo 眼窩
eye socket / orbit;

yan wo ao xian 眼窩凹陷
have sunken eyes;

yan xia 眼下
at the moment;

yan ya 眼壓
intraocular pressure;

yan yan 眼炎
ophthalmia;
chu ran xing yan yan 觸染性眼炎
contagious ophthalmia;
chuan ran xing yan yan 傳染性眼炎
infectious ophthalmia;
chun ji yan yan 春季眼炎
spring ophthalmia;
jie jie xing yan yan 結節性眼炎
ophthalmia nodosa;
ke li xing yan yan 顆粒性眼炎
granular ophthalmia;
lin bing xing yan yan 淋病性眼炎
gonorrheal ophthalmia;
nong xing yan yan 膿性眼炎
ophthalmoblennorrhea;
pao xing yan yan 泡性眼炎
phlyctenular ophthalmia;
pi fu yan yan 皮膚眼炎
dermato-ophthalmitis;
shi zhen xing yan yan 濕疹性眼炎
ophthalmia eczematosa;
tong xie yan yan 銅屑眼炎
chalkitis;
xin sheng er yan yan 新生兒眼炎
adenologaditis;
zhou qi xing yan yan 周期性眼炎
periodic ophthalmia;
zhuan yi xing yan yan 轉移性眼炎
metastatic ophthalmia;

yan yu 眼語
eye-talk;

yan yun 眼暈
(1) halo;
(2) feel dizzy;
qing guang yan yun 青光眼暈
glaucomatous halo;

yan zhen 眼震
nystagmus;
bai dong xing yan zhen 擺動性眼震
pendular nystagmus;
ji fa xing yan zhen 繼發性眼震
secondary nystagmus;
jia yan zhen 假眼震
pseudonystagmus;
mi lu xing yan zhen 迷路性眼震
labyrinthine nystagmus;
ruo shi xing yan zhen 弱視性眼震
amblyopic nystagmus;
shi dong xing yan zhen 視動性眼震
opticokinetic nystagmus;
sui yi xing yan zhen 隨意性眼震
voluntary nystagmus;
yan bing xing yan zhen 眼病性眼震
ocular nystagmus;
yin xing yan zhen 隱性眼震
latent nystagmus;
zhen dong xing yan zhen 振動性眼震
vibratory nystagmus;
zi fa xing yan zhen 自發性眼震
spontaneous nystagmus;

yan zheng zheng 眼睜睜
(1) right before one's eyes ‖ in broad daylight; openly; publicly;
(2) unfeelingly // watch helplessly;
(3) attentively / watchful;

yan zhong ding 眼中釘
a thorn in the flesh / eyesore;

yan zhong ding, rou zhong ci 眼中釘，肉中刺
a thorn in one's flesh;

yan zhong han lei 眼中含淚
one's eyes are swimming with tears;

yan zhong ren 眼中人
the loved one / the person after one's heart;

yan zhong wu ren 眼中無人
having no respect for anyone ‖ arrogant; haughty; too big for one's boots;

yan zhong 眼腫
baggy-eyed;

yan zhu 眼珠
eyeball;

yan zhu zi 眼珠子
eyeball;

yan zhuo 眼拙
dim-sighted;

yan3 mu bu que 掩目捕雀
catch birds with eyes closed — self-deceit / close the eyes to catch a bird — self-deception;

yan ren er mu 掩人耳目
deceive others / hoodwink people;

yan4 li duo mu 艷麗奪目
of dazzling beauty;

yang2 mei tu qi 揚眉吐氣
proud and elated ‖ blow off steam in rejoicing; elated; feel proud; feel proud and elated after one suddenly comes to fame, wealth or good luck; happy and proud; hold one's head high; stand up with head high;

yang3 tian chui lei 仰天垂淚
gaze up at the sky and let the tears roll down one's cheeks;

yang wang 仰望
(1) look up at;
(2) rely on;

yang3 mu run xin 養目潤心
please the eye and gladden the heart — good to see or hear;

yao2 jian 遙見
see at a distance;

yao wang 遙望
look at a distant place / look into the distance / take a distant look;

yao4 mu 耀目
dazzle;

yao yan 耀眼
dazzling / lurid / scintillating;

yao yan zeng guang 耀眼增光
dazzling;

ye4 fa xing ruo shi 夜發性弱視
nocturnal amblyopia;

ye mang 夜盲
night blindness;

ye mang zheng 夜盲症
night blindness;

ye shi 夜視
night sight;

yi1 bao yan fu 一飽眼福
enjoy watching sth to the full / feast one's eyes on sth / feed one's sight / glut one's eyes;

yi du wei kuai 一睹為快
enjoy the pleasure of sb's acquaintance / glad to see sb;

yi jian gao di 一見高低
fight it out / fight with sb to victory or defeat;

yi jian qing xin 一見傾心
fall in love at first sight / love at first sight;

yi jian ru gu 一見如故
become fast friends at the first meeting || become intimate at the first meeting; become old acquaintances at the first meeting; hit it off well right from the start; like old friends from the start; strike up a friendship with sb at the first meeting; they hit it off immediately;

yi jian wei kuai 一見為快
enjoy the pleasure of sb's acquaintance / glad to see sb;

yi jian zhong qing 一見鍾情
love at first sight || fall in love at first sight; fall in love with sb the first time one sets one's eyes on sb; take an instant fancy to;

yi kan bian zhi 一看便知
see at a glance / readily see;

yi kan er bang 一看二幫
first to observe, and second to give help / observe and help;

yi kan jiu dong 一看就懂
see at a glance || be apprehended at a glance; learn by merely reading it once over; see with half an eye;

yi kong zhi jian 一孔之見
a narrow view || a limited view; a peephole view; a very limited outlook; glimpses of the truth; short-sighted;

yi lan 一覽
bird's-eye view / general survey;

yi lan wu yu 一覽無餘
a single glance takes in all || command the whole view of; cover all at one glance; in full view; panoramic view; take in everything at one glance; unobstructed;

yi lan zai mu 一覽在目
bird's-eye view / commanding view;

yi ming bu shi 一瞑不視
die / pass away // dead;

yi mu liao ran 一目了然
understand fully at a glance || able to tell its own story; as clear as the day; as plain as the nose on one's face; carry on its face; clear at a glance; easily comprehensible; he who runs may read; leap to the eye / eyes; meet one's eye; see at a glance; see with half an eye; stick out a mile; open-and-shut // an open book;

yi mu shi hang 一目十行
read ten lines of writing with one single glance || learn ten lines at a glance; take in ten lines at a glance — read rapidly;

yi pie 一瞥
(1) a glance / a glimse;
(2) take a glance at / take a glimpse at;

yi pie mei mao 一撇眉毛
brow;

yi ri bu jian, ru ge san qiu 一日不見，如隔三秋
a day apart is like three years;

yi shi tong ren 一視同仁
even-handed / impartial / without discrimination;

yi shou yan jin tian xia ren er mu 一手掩盡天下人耳目
hide from public knowledge the errors committed by sb;

yi shun 一瞬
the twinkling of an eye;

yi wang er zhi 一望而知
know all at a single glance || it needs no ghost to tell us; it's written all over one's face; see with half an eye;

yi wang wu ji 一望無際
a boundless expanse of || an uninterrupted stretch of; command an extensive view; spread out far beyond the horizon; stretch to the horizon; wide stretches of;

yi wang wu ya 一望無涯
stretch far off into the distance and out of sight || boundless; stretching beyond the horizon;

yi wang wu yin 一望無垠
stretch as far as the eye can see || stretch beyond the horizon; interminable; unbounded; vast in extent;

yi xin er mu 一新耳目
a fresh look / a new look // present a new appearance;

yi yan 一眼
glance;

yi yan bian zhi 一眼便知
can see it with half an eye / can tell at a glance;

yi yan kan chuan 一眼看穿
see through at a glance / see through with a discerning eye;

yi yan kan qu 一眼看去
(1) take a sweeping look;
(2) at first glance;

yi yan kan zhong 一眼看中
become infatuated with sb at first sight;

yi ye zhang mu, bu jian Tai Shan 一葉障目，不見泰山
what is important is overshadowed by the trivial;

yi zha yan 一眨眼
in a wink;

yi zha yan gong fu 一眨眼工夫
in a twinkling / in a wink / in the twinkling of an eye / on the instant;

yi zhan feng cai 一瞻豐采
have a look at sb's beautiful appearance;

yi zhen lei shui 一陣淚水
a torrent of tears;

yi zhuan yan 一轉眼
in a wink of the eye;

yi zi yi lei 一字一淚
a teardrop for each word;

yi2 眱
stare at sb for a long time without talking;

yi2 wang xing se mang 遺傳性色盲
amnesic colour blindness;

yi3 jiu ran mei 以救燃眉
meet a pressing need;

yi lei xi mian 以淚洗面
one's face is bathed in tears || cry with abandon; tears bathe the cheeks; wash one's face with tears — weep bitterly;

yi mu chuan qing 以目傳情
cast affectionate glances / convey a betwitching gleam;

yi mu dai gang 以目代綱
use the secondary to replace the primary;

yi mu shi yi 以目示意
give a hint with the eyes || give sb a meaningful look; give sb the wink; make a sign with the eyes; make eyes at; throw the eye at; tip sb the wink;

yi yan huan yan 以眼還眼
an eye for an eye / eye for eye;

yi yu yan mu 以娛眼目
please the eye;

yi zheng shi ting 以正視聽
so as to clarify matters to the public || ensure a correct understanding of the facts; in order to ensure a correct understanding of the facts; so that the public may know the facts;

yi3 shi 蟻視
despise;

yi shi yi qie 蟻視一切
regard everything with contempt;

yi4 瞖
cataract;

yin2 mu 淫目
lascivious looks;

yin shi 淫視
lascivious looks;

yin3 ren zhu mu 引人注目
attract sb's attention || attract the gaze of people; become the centre of attention; catch the eye; conspicuous; eye-catching; notable; noticeable; remarkable; protuberant; spectacular; strike the eye; striking;

yin3 xing yan zhen 隱性眼震
latent nystagmus;

yin xing yuan shi 隱性遠視
latent hyperopia;

ying1 xiong suo jian lüe tong 英雄所見略同
great minds think alike / great wits jump;

ying1 er nong xing jie mo yan 嬰兒膿性結膜炎
infantile purulent conjunctivitis;

ying er xing qing guang yan 嬰兒性青光眼
infantile glaucoma;

ying2 di 迎睇
meet with the eye;

ying jian 迎見
receive visitors;

ying2 kuang 盈眶
one's eyes filled with tears;

ying2 yang que fa xing bai nei zhang 營養缺乏性白內障
nutritional deficiency cataract;

ying yang que fa xing ruo shi 營養缺乏性弱視
deficiency amblyopia;

ying4 ru yan lian 映入眼簾
come into sight / come into view / greet the eye / leap to the eyes / meet the eye / strike the eye;

ying yan 映眼
dazzling / glaring;

ying4 hua xing jiao mo 硬化性角膜
sclerocornea;

ying hua xing jiao mo yan 硬化性角膜炎
scleosing keratitis;

yong4 yan shi yi 用眼示意
hint by the eye;

you2 chi guan zhi 由此觀之
judging from this / looking at the matter from this viewpoint;

you chi ke jian 由此可見
thus it can be seen;

you2 mu cheng huai 游目騁懷
rejoice one's eyes and heart || let the eye take in the landscape and please the spirit; let the eye travel over the great scene and let fancy free;

you yong chi jie mo yan 游泳池結膜炎
swimming pool conjunctivitis;

you2 guan 遊觀
travel and see the sights;

you lan 遊覽
sight-seeing;

you3 ai guan zhan 有礙觀瞻
unsightly || an eyesore; leave a bad impression to the beholder; offend the eye; repugnant to the eye;

you mei mu 有眉目
about to materialize / begin to take shape;

you mu gong du 有目共睹
everyone can see that || it is clear to all that; obvious to all; obvious to everyone; obvious to people; perfectly obvious; plain; plain for everybody to judge for himself; visible to the eye;

you mu gong shang 有目共賞
appeal to all alike || evoke the admiration of the beholders; evoke the appreciation of the beholders; have a universal appeal; win high praise from anyone who sees it;

you mu wu zhu 有目無珠
eye without pupil — as blind as a bat;

you yan bu shi tai shan 有眼不識泰山
fail to recognize a great person;

you yan wu zhu 有眼無珠
as blind as a bat || eyes and no eyes; have eyes but fail to see; have eyes without eyeballs — have eyes but see not; have two slits for eyes but cannot see; lack discerning power;

you4 ku you xiao 又哭又笑
cry and laugh at the same time;

you4 yan 右眼
right eye;

you4 nian xing bai nei zhang 幼年型白內障
juvenile cataract;

you4 yu cheng wen 囿於成見
be bound by prejudice;

you yu jian wen 囿於見聞
be handicapped by lack of knowledge and experience;

you yu su jian 囿於俗見
be blinded by current biases;

yu1 jian 迂見
absurd view / impractical opinion;

yu2 wei wen 魚尾紋
crow's-foot;

yu2 mu 娛目
please the eye;

yu2 mu 隅目
(1) angry eyes;
(2) furious;

yu4 lei 雨淚
tears pouring down like rain;

yu4 ku wu lei 欲哭無淚
one feels like weeping but has no tears / one wants to cry but has no tears;

yu4 mu 寓目
gaze / look over / stare;

yu4 jian 預見
anticipate / envision / foresee // foresight / prevision;

yuan2 fa xing bai nei zhang 原發性白內障
primary cataract;

yuan fa xing pian xie 原發性偏斜
primary deviation;

yuan fa xing qing guang yan 原發性青光眼
primary glaucoma;

yuan fa xing shi mian 原發性失眠
primary insomnia;

yuan fa yan 原發眼
primary eye;

yuan3 jian 遠見
foresight / far-sightedness / long-headedness;

yuan shi 遠視
far-sighted / long-sighted // far-sightedness / hyperopia;

qu du yuan shi 曲度遠視
curvature hyperopia;

xiang dui yuan shi 相對遠視
relative hyperopia;

yin xing yuan shi 隱性遠視
latent hyperopia;

yuan shi san guang 遠視散光
hypermetropic astigmatism;

dan chun yuan shi san guang 單純遠視散光
simple hyperopic astigmatism;

yuan shi yan 遠視眼
far-sighted // hypermetropia / hyperopia;

yuan tiao 遠眺
take a distant look;

yuan wang fu ji 遠望弗及
looking from afar but cannot reach it;

yuan zhu 遠矚
look far ahead / take a look at faraway places;

yue4 mu 悅目
easy on the eye / good-looking / pleasant to the eye / pleasing to the eye // titillate the eye;

yue4 du 閱讀
read;

yue du guo huan 閱讀過緩
bradylexia;

yue du xu huan 閱讀徐緩
bradylexia;

yue du zhang ai 閱讀障礙
reading disorder;

yun2 yan guo yan 雲煙過眼
clouds and smoke that float past the eyes;

yun3 si 隕泗
shed tears;

yun ti 隕涕
tears falling;

zai1 ti xing qing guang yan 甾體性青光眼
steroid glaucoma;

zai4 jian 再見
good-bye || bye; bye-bye; cheerio; see you; see you again; so long;

zao1 ren bai yan 遭人白眼
be treated with disdain || be held in disdain; receive a cold disdainful look; receive a cold stare;

zao3 chan er bai nei zhang 早產兒白內障
cataracts of prematurity;

zao chan er shi wang mo bing 早產兒視網膜病
retinopathy of prematurity;

zao lao xing bai nei zhang 早老性白內障
presenile cataract;

zei2 mei shu yan 賊眉鼠眼
thievish-looking || mean look; have a sneaky look; look like a thief // shifty-eyed // with furtive eyes and sullen look;

zei mei zei yan 賊眉賊眼
have a shifty look / roguish looks;

zei yan 賊眼
furtive glance / shifty eyes;

zei yan ji yu 賊眼覬覦
one's shifty eyes squinted right and left;

zei yan yi liu 賊眼一溜
cast a furtive look at sth;

zeng1 sheng xing shi wang mo bing 增生性視網膜病
proliferative retinopathy;

zeng sheng xing shi wang mo yan 增生性視網膜炎
proliferating retinitis;

zha1 yan 扎眼
(1) dazzling / offending to the eye;
(2) offensively conspicuous;

zha3 眨
blink / wink;

zha ba 眨巴
blink;

zha ba yan er 眨巴眼兒
wink one's eyes in quick succession;

zha yan 眨眼
nictitation // twinkle / wink;

zha yan fan ying 眨眼反應
blink response;

zha yan guo pin 眨眼過頻
palpebration;

zha yan jian 眨眼間
in the twinkling of an eye;

zha4 jian 乍見
(1) meet for the first time;
(2) see suddenly;

zha kan qi lai 乍看起來
at first glance / at the first face;

zha kan shang qu 乍看上去
at first appearance;

zha yan yi kan 乍眼一看
at first appearance / at first sight;

zhan1 瞻
look / look up;

zhan gu 瞻顧
look ahead and behind;

zhan qian gu hou 瞻前顧後
look forward and backward;

zhan shi 瞻視
behold / look / look up to;

zhan wang 瞻望
look forward to a faraway place / raise one's head and look far ahead;

zhan3 wang 展望
envision // general view of the future;

zhang1 mu 張目
(1) open one's eyes wide;
(2) boost sb's arrogance / help publicize an unworthy cause;

zhang wang 張望
(1) peep through a crack;
(2) look about / look around / look into the distance;

zhang yan 張眼
open one's eyes;

zhang1 zhang zai mu 彰彰在目
clear for all to see;

zhang1 tou shu mu 獐頭鼠目
rat-eyed and buck-headed || facial features

suggesting cunning and meanness; with head like deer, eyes like rats — contemptibly ugly; with the head of a buck and the eyes of a rat — repulsively ugly and sly-looking;

zhang3 zhen yan 長針眼
have a sty;

zhao1 deng 招瞪
invite a stare;

zhao yan 招眼
conspicuous || attractive; in limelight; make oneself conspicuous;

zhao yan du 招眼毒
cause jealousy;

zhao1 zhao zai mu 昭昭在目
clear in the people's eyes;

zhao2 yan 着眼
direct one's attention to / eye with attention / have sth in mind;

zhao yan dian 着眼點
starting point / the point to watch;

zhao4 kan 照看
attend to / keep an eye on / look after / see after / watch over;

zhe1 ren er mu 遮人耳目
pull the wool over the eyes of the people / throw dust in people's eyes;

zhe yan fa 遮眼法
camouflage;

zhen4 dong huan shi 振動幻視
oscillopsia;

zhen dong xing yan zhen 振動性眼震
vibratory nystagmus;

zhen4 dang xing mang 震蕩性盲
concussion blindness;

zheng1 睜
open the eyes;

zheng da yan jing 睜大眼睛
open one's eyes wide;

zheng kai yan jing 睜開眼睛
open the eyes;

zheng mu nu mei 睜目怒眉
dart fierce looks of hate;

zheng yan 睜眼
open the eyes;

zheng yan bu guan 睜眼不管
look on with folded arms;

zheng yan xia zi 睜眼瞎子
illiterate person || a man who can neither read nor write; a man unable to write or read;

zheng yi zhi yan, bi yi zhi yan 睜一隻眼，閉一隻眼
turn a blind eye to sth || pretend not to see; purposely overlook; wink at sth;

zheng zhe yan jing shuo xia hua 睜着眼睛說瞎話
tell a bare-faced lie;

zheng4 shi 正視
face squarely / look straight in the eye || face up to; look at sth without bias; look sb in the eye; look squarely at;

zheng shi kun nan 正視困難
face difficulties squarely / face up to difficulties;

zheng shi xian shi 正視現實
face reality squarely / look reality in the face;

zheng4 zhuang xing jian jing luan 症狀性瞼痙攣
symptomatic blepharospasm;

zhi1 mei 芝眉
dignified eyebrows;

zhi1 yi xing jian yuan yan 脂溢性瞼緣炎
seborrheic blepharitis;

zhi1 yan 隻眼
(1) one-eyed;
(2) fresh view / original idea;

zhi2 mei deng yan 直眉瞪眼
stare blankly || be stupefied; fume; in a daze; look angry; stare in anger;

zhi shi 直視
look steadily at;

zhi3 jian 祇見
(1) see only;
(2) behold;

zhong1 kan 中看
good to look at;

zhong3 zhang qi bai nei zhang 腫脹期白內障
intumescent cataract;

zhong4 du xing bai nei zhang 中毒性白內障
toxic cataract;

zhong du xing ruo shi 中毒性弱視
toxic amblyopia;

zhong4 shi 重視
take sth seriously || attach importance to; consider important; hold dear; make account of; make much account of; pay attention to; set store by; take account of; take into account; take sth seriously; think highly of; think the world of; value;

zhong4 mu gong du 眾目共睹
what every eye sees / what everyone can see;

zhong mu kui kui 眾目睽睽
in the full glare of publicity || in the face of the world; in the full blaze of publicity; under the public gaze; under the watchful eyes of the people; with a crowd of people watching; with everybody watching;

zhong mu suo jian 眾目所見
be seen by all / what every eye sees / what everyone can see;

zhong mu suo shi 眾目所視
be seen by all / what every eye sees / what everyone can see;

zhong mu zhao zhang 眾目昭彰
be seen clearly by everyone // clear to all;

zhou1 qi xing xie shi 周期性斜視
cyclic strabismus;

zhou qi xing yan yan 周期性眼炎
periodic ophthalmia;

zhou4 mei 皺眉
frown || bend one's brows; contract one's brows; knit the brows; lour;

zhou mei cu e 皺眉蹙額
draw the brows together into wrinkes || contract one's brows in a frown; frown; knit one's brows; one's eyebrows knit in a frown; with knitted brows; wrinkle one's brows;

zhou mei tou 皺眉頭
frown || contract one's brows; contract one's brows in a frown; knit one's brows; lour;

zhu1 lei 珠淚
tears;

zhu lei gun gun 珠淚滾滾
tears pour down one's cheeks || one's tears fall like pearls and beans; the tears run from one's eyes in torrents;

zhu lei su su 珠淚簌簌
tears trickle down one's cheeks || big tears trickle down from one's eyes; one's tears fall like pearls; the tears run down one's face like water dropping through a sieve;

zhu lei ying kuang 珠淚盈眶
tears like pearls fill the eyes;

zhu3 guan 主觀
one's subjective view;

zhu3 jue 矚爵
look steadily || gaze; observe carefully; pay attention; watch;

zhu mu 矚目
fix one's eyes on / focus one's attention on;

zhu wang 矚望
(1) look forward to;
(2) gaze at / look long and steadily upon;

zhu wang yi jiu 矚望已久
have been eagerly looking forward to it for a long time;

zhu4 mu 注目
fix one's eyes on / focus one's look on / gaze at / look attentively at / stare at;

zhu shi 注視
contemplate / focus one's look on / gaze at / glue / have one's eyes on / look attentively at / watch;

zhuan3 pan 轉盼
turn the eyes;

zhuan shun 轉瞬
turn the eyes;

zhuan yan 轉眼
in the twinkling of an eye || a moment; an instant; in a flash; in an instant;

zhuan yan bian wang 轉眼便忘
out of sight, out of mind;

zhuan yan bu jian 轉眼不見
cease to exist in the twinkling of an eye;

zhuan yan cheng kong 轉眼成空
vanish in the twinkling of an eye;

zhuan yan zhi jian 轉眼之間
in the twinkling of an eye || as swift as a wink; before you can say Jack Robinson; before you know where you are; in a flash; in a jiffy; in a trice; in a twinkling; in a wink; in an instant; in jig time; in no time; in the turn of a hand; on the instant;

zhuan yi shi xian 轉移視線
(1) divert public attention / divert sb's attention / draw attention to some other matter;
(2) divert the line of sight / turn the gaze;

zhuan yi xing shi wang mo yan 轉移性視網膜炎
metastatic retinitis;

zhuan yi xing yan yan 轉移性眼炎
metastatic ophthalmia;

zhuo2 jian 灼見
excellent views;

zhuo2 jian 卓見
excellent views;

zi4 fa xing jian jing luan 自發性瞼痙攣
essential blepharospasm;

zi fa xing yan zhen 自發性眼震
spontaneous nystagmus;

zi shi 自視
consider oneself / image oneself / think oneself;

zi shi guo gao 自視過高
think too highly of oneself // hoity-toity;

zi shi kan ran 自視欿然
be dissatisfied with oneself;

zi shi shen gao 自視甚高
think highly of oneself;

zi4 眥
eye socket;

zi lie 眥裂
open eyes wide, as in anger;

zi mu 眥目
open eyes wide;

zong1 guan 綜觀
view generally;

zong lan 綜覽
view generally;

zong4 guan 縱觀
take a free, wide look / take a sweeping look;

zong guan quan ju 縱觀全局
take a panoramic view of the situation;

zong lan 縱覽
look freely and extensively;

zong mu 縱目
look as far as one's eyes can see;

zong mu si wang 縱目四望
gaze far into the distance / turn one's eyes in all directions and take in as much as one can in that single sweep;

zong tiao 縱眺
look far and wide;

zou3 ma guan hua 走馬觀花
look at flowers while riding on horse back / make a cursory investigation of the situation;

zu2 zhong xing qing guang yan 卒中性青光眼
apoplectic glaucoma;

zu zhong xing shi wang mo yan 卒中性視網膜炎
apoplectic retinitis;

zu3 se xing qing guang yan 阻塞性青光眼
obstructive glaucoma;

zui4 yan 醉眼
drunken eyes;

zui yan hun hua 醉眼昏花
indistinct drunken eyes;

zui yan meng long 醉眼朦朧
bleary-eyed due to drunkenness;

zui yan xing song 醉眼惺忪
have one's eyes blurred with drinking;

zun1 jian 尊見
your opinion;

zuo3 gu 左顧
look to the left;

zuo gu you pan 左顧右盼

(1) cast glances about / gaze round || glance left and right; inattentive; lack of concentration; look around; look left and right;

(2) flirtatious;

zuo jian 左見

bias / prejudice;

zuo yan 左眼

left eye;

zuo4 jing guan tian 坐井觀天

short-sightedness;

zuo shi 坐視

sit by and watch / keep hands off || sit tight and look on; watching without extending a helping hand;

zuo shi bu guan 坐視不管

sit watching;

zuo shi bu jiu 坐視不救

sit idly by without lending a helping hand || sit and look on unconcerned; sit back and watch without going to the rescue; sit still and not try to save; sit there and make no effort to save;

zuo shi bu li 坐視不理

look on with folded arms / sit by idly and remain indifferent;

zuo shi wu du 坐視無睹

sit with arms folded;

zuo bi shang guan 作壁上觀

watch a fight with detachment;

zuo4 yan 做眼

gather intelligence;

Yao 腰 Waist

ba2 gen han mao, bi bie ren yao cu 拔根汗毛，比別人腰粗。

one hair from one's body is thicker than sb's waist;

bai4 dao zai di 拜倒在地

be bowed to the ground;

cha1 yao 叉腰

rest the arms on the hips / stand with arms akimbo;

cha1 yao 扠腰

akimbo;

cheng1 yao 撐腰

back up / bolster up / give backing to sb / support;

cheng yao da qi 撐腰打氣

bolster and support || bolster and pep up; in an effort to back up;

chu3 yao 楚腰

slender waist;

chui2 yao 搥腰

massage the waist by light pounding;

cui1 mei zhe yao 摧眉折腰

bow and scrape / bow unctuously;

da3 chi bo 打赤膊

bare the upper body / strip to the waist;

da qi cheng yao 打氣撐腰

brace and bolster / encourage and support;

di1 yao 低腰

long waist;

feng1 yao xue jian 蜂腰削肩

have a supple waist like a wasp and round, gently sloping shoulders / have a supple wasplike waist and slender shoulders;

gong1 yao 弓腰

curve one's body backward like an arch;

ha1 yao 哈腰

(1) bend one's back / stoop;

(2) bow slightly in greeting;

ha yao qu bei 哈腰曲背

humble oneself in serving a master;

hu3 bei xiong yao 虎背熊腰
of a stocky and imposing build || boxer's sinuous posture; strong as a bear in the hips and with a back supple as a tiger's strapping; thick, powerful back and shoulders; tiger-backed and bear-loined — stalwart;

kua4 髂
waist bone;

lan2 yao 攔腰
by the waist;

lan3 yao 懶腰
stretch;

liang3 shou cha yao 兩手叉腰
with arms akimbo || akimbo; with one's hands on one's hips;

liu3 yao 柳腰
slender waist / willowy waist;

luan2 yao 攣腰
crooked back;

nian2 lao yao wan 年老腰彎
be bent with age;

niu3 yao 扭腰
twist the waist;

que1 xue xing yao tong 缺血性腰痛
ischemic lumbago;

shan3 yao 閃腰
strain a muscle on the waist;

shen1 lan yao 伸懶腰
stretch and yawn;

shen yao 伸腰
straighten one's back / straighten oneself up / stretch oneself;

shen3 yao 沈腰
slender waist;

shu4 yao 束腰
girdle one's waist;

tan3 bo 袒膊
bare oneself to the waist and bind one's hands at the back / bare to the waist / strip to the waist;

tan fu qing ming 袒膊請命
begging for life by baring the shoulder and tying the arms behind;

tuo1 bo 脫膊
bare from the waist up / strip to the waist;

wan1 yao 彎腰
bend down / stoop / stoop down;

xi4 yao 細腰
(1) slender waist;
(2) slim-waisted wasp;

xi yao xue jian 細腰削肩
with an ell-like figure and narrow, sloping shoulders;

xian1 yao 纖腰
slender waist;

xian yao xiu xiang 纖腰秀項
have a slender waist and a beautiful neck;

yao1 腰
(1) midriff / waist;
(2) kidney;

yao ban bo ying 腰板脖硬
rigid in movements / stiff in movements;

yao ban er 腰板兒
back of the midriff / waist and the back;

yao bu 腰部
waist;

yao fan she 腰反射
lumbar reflex;

yao gu 腰骨
pelvic bones;

yao ji lao sun 腰肌勞損
strain of lumbar muscles;

yao kua 腰胯
hip / hip joint;

yao ru xian liu 腰如纖柳
her waist is as slender as the willow;

yao san jiao 腰三角
lumbar triangle;

yao shan 腰疝
lumbar hernia;

yao shen 腰身
waist;

yao suan bei tong 腰酸背痛
a sore waist and an aching back || an ache in one's waist and back; have a backache; have

a pain in the back; one's back is aching;

yao suan tui teng 腰酸腿疼
aching back and legs;

yao teng 腰疼
low back pain / lumbago;

yao tong 腰痛
lumbago;
que xue xing yao tong 缺血性腰痛
ischemic lumbago;

yao tui 腰腿
nimbleness of one's waist and legs;

yao wei 腰圍
waistlines;

yao xi ru feng 腰細如蜂
have a slender waist like a wasp;

yao yuan 腰圓
kidney-shaped / oval-shaped;

yao zhan 腰斬
chop in two at the waist;

yao zhi 腰肢
waistline;

yao zi 腰子
kidney;

zhang4 yao zi 仗腰子
back up sb;

zhe2 yao 折腰
bow / humble oneself;

zhi2 zhi yao er 直直腰兒
give the waist a stretch;

Zi gong 子宮 Womb

an1 xing zi gong 鞍型子宮
saddle-shaped uterus;

bao1 yi 胞衣
afterbirth / placenta;

bi4 yun 避孕
contraception;

bi yun shi bai 避孕失敗
contraceptive failure;

bo1 tuo xing zi gong nei mo yan 剝脫性子宮內膜炎
exfoliative endometritis;

bu4 ren 不妊
infecundity / sterility;

bu ren zheng 不妊症
infecundity / sterility;

bu yu 不育
infecundity;
ji fa xing bu yu 繼發性不育
secondary sterility;
xiang dui xing bu yu 相對性不育
relative sterility;
yuan fa xing bu yu 原發性不育
primary sterility;

bu yu zheng 不育症
infertilitas;

bu yun 不孕
infertility;
ji fa bu yun 繼發不孕
secondary infertitility;
yuan fa bu yun 原發不孕
primary infertility;

bu yun zheng 不孕症
infertility;
chu fa xing bu yun zheng 初發性不孕症
primary infertility;

chan3 hou tong 產後痛
afterpains;

chan hou zi gong nei mo yan 產後子宮內膜炎
puerperal endometritis;

chan hou zi gong yan 產後子宮炎
lochiometritis;

chu1 fa xing bu yun zheng 初發性不孕症
primary infertility;

chu4 ran xing liu chan 觸染性流產
contagious abortion;

chuan2 ran xing liu chan 傳染性流產
infectious abortion;

chuang4 shang xing gong jing yan 創傷性宮頸炎
traumatic cervicitis;

cui1 chan 催產
expedite child delivery / hasten parturition;

cui sheng 催生
expedite child delivery / hasten child delivery / hasten parturition;

da3 tai 打胎
have an abortion;

da4 du zi 大肚子
pregnant;

dai4 shen zi 帶身子
become pregnant;

dan1 tai ren shen 單胎妊娠
monocyesis;

di1 sheng yu li 低生育力
hypofertility;

diao4 tai 掉胎
(1) abort / miscarry;
(2) abortion / miscarriage;

duo1 bao tai 多胞胎
multiple birth;

duo tai yun ren 多胎孕妊
multiple pregnancy;

duo4 tai 墮胎
(1) aborticide / feticide / induced abortion;
(2) have an induced abortion;

fei1 fa liu chan 非法流產
illegal abortion;

fen1 mian 分娩
childbearing / childbirth;
guo qi fen mian 過期分娩
delayed labour;
guo shu fen mian 過熟分娩
postmature delivery;
ji su fen mian 急速分娩
oxytocia;
qiang cu fen mian 強促分娩
accouchement force;
yin dao fen mian 陰道分娩
vaginal delivery;
zheng chang fen mian 正常分娩
eutocia;
zi ran fen mian 自然分娩
natural childbirth;

fen mian guo huan 分娩過緩
bradytocia;

fen mian qi tong 分娩期痛
expulsive pains;

gong1 xing zi gong 弓形子宮
uterus arcuatus;

gong1 jiao ren shen 宮角妊娠
cornual pregnancy;

gong jing 宮頸
cervix;

gong jing fa yu bu liang 宮頸發育不良
cervical dysphlasia;

gong jing fa yu bu quan 宮頸發育不全
cervical dysphlasia;

gong jing guan 宮頸管
cervical tunnels;

gong jing ji xue 宮頸積血
hematotrachelos;

gong jing lie 宮頸裂
cervical clefts;

gong jing lou 宮頸瘻
cervical fistula;

gong jing ren shen 宮頸妊娠
cervical pregnancy;

gong jing xi rou 宮頸息肉
cervical polyp;

gong jing yan 宮頸炎
cervicitis;
chuang shang xing gong jing yan 創傷性宮頸炎
traumatic cervicitis;
rou ya zhong xing gong jing yan 肉芽腫性

宮頸炎
granulomatous cervicitis;

wai shang xing gong jing yan 外傷性宮頸炎
traumatic cervicitis;

gong jing yin dao yan 宮頸陰道炎
cervicovaginitis;

qi zhong xing gong jing yin dao yan 氣腫性宮頸陰道炎
cervicocolpitis emphysematosa;

gong nei fa yu chi huan 宮內發育遲緩
intrauterine growth retardation;

gong nei fei yan 宮內肺炎
intrauterine pneumonia;

gong nei gu zhe 宮內骨折
intrauterine fracture;

gong nei shu xue 宮內輸血
intrauterine transfusion;

gong nei tuo wei 宮內脫位
intrauterine dislocation;

gong suo 宮縮
uterine contraction;

gong suo wu li 宮縮無力
inertia uteri;

gong wai ren shen 宮外妊娠
extrauterine pregnancy;

gong wai yun 宮外孕
ectopic pregnancy / extrauterine pregnancy;

gong wai yun tai 宮外孕胎
exterogestate;

gui3 tai 鬼胎
dark scheme / evil plot;

guo4 qi fen mian 過期分娩
delayed labour;

guo qi ren shen 過期妊娠
post-term pregnancy;

guo shu fen mian 過熟分娩
postmature delivery;

hai4 xi 害喜
pregnant;

huai2 tai 懷胎
conceive / conceive a child // in the family way / pregnant;

huai yun 懷孕
pregnant ‖ a hole out in one; a waiting woman; an accident; an expectant mother; anticipating; awkward; be caught; be caught out; be expecting; be gone; become impregnated; become pregnant; beget; break one's ankle; clucky; conceive a child; eating for two; enceinte; expecting; fall; far gone; female irregularity; fragrant; full of heir; gestate; gestation; have a hump in the front; have a little tax deduction; have a white swelling; have one watermelon on the vine; have one on the way; heavy with child; in a bad shape; in a certain condition; in a delicate condition; in a familiar way; in a particular condition; in an interesting condition; in her time; in the club; in the family way; in the pudding club; in trouble; in young; infanticipating; Irish toothache; knitting; lady-in-waiting; mother-to-be; mum-to-be; on the nest; preparing the bassinet; rattle shopping; rehearsing lullabies; ring the stork bell; ruin a woman's shape; spoil a woman's shape; swallow a watermelon seed; wear the apron high; with child; with young;

huan4 xiang ren shen 幻想妊娠
phantom pregnancy;

huan yun 幻孕
phantom pregnancy;

ji1 tai 畸胎
abnormity;

ji tai ai 畸胎癌
teratocarcinoma;

ji tai liu 畸胎瘤
dysembryoma;

ji2 su fen mian 急速分娩
oxytocia;

ji4 fa bu yun 繼發不孕
secondary infertitility;

ji fa xing bu yu 繼發性不育
secondary sterility;

jia3 ren shen 假妊娠
pseudogestation;

jin3 po liu chan 緊迫流產
imminent abortion;

jue2 yu 絕育
sterilization;

lin2 chan 臨產
in childbirth // about to give birth to a child;

lin chan zhen tong 臨產陣痛
birth pangs / labour pains;

lin pen 臨盆
childbirth / parturition;

lin yue 臨月
the month when the childbirth is due;

liu2 chan 流產
abort / fall through / miscarry // abortion / miscarriage;

chu ran xing liu chan 觸染性流產
contagious abortion;

chuan ran xing liu chan 傳染性流產
infectious abortion;

jin po liu chan 緊迫流產
imminent abortion;

nan mian liu chan 難免流產
inevitable abortion;

nong du xing liu chan 膿毒性流產
septic abortion;

te fa xing liu chan 特發性流產
idiopathic abortion;

wan quan liu chan 完全流產
complete abortion;

xian zhao liu chan 先兆流產
threatened abortion;

liu chan gan ran 流產感染
septic abortion;

luan3 chao 卵巢
oophoron;

luan chao bing 卵巢病
oophoropathy;

luan chao liu 卵巢瘤
oophoroma;

luan chao tong 卵巢痛
oophoralgia;

luan chao yan 卵巢炎
oophoritis;

ying hua xing luan chao yan 硬化性卵巢炎
sclero-oophoritis;

luo4 tai 落胎
abort / effort an abortion;

mian3 娩
give birth to a child;

mian chu 娩出
be delivered of a child / give birth to;

mian chu si tai 娩出死胎
abort;

mian tong 娩痛
labour pains;

mo2 xing ren shen 膜性妊娠
membranous pregnancy;

mo xing zi gong nei mo yan 膜性子宮內膜炎
membranous endometritis;

nan2 chan 難產
dystocia;

nan mian liu chan 難免流產
inevitable abortion;

nian2 lian tai pan 黏連胎盤
adherent placenta;

niang2 tai 娘胎
mother's womb;

nong2 du xing liu chan 膿毒性流產
septic abortion;

nong xing zi gong yan 膿性子宮炎
pyometritis;

nong4 wa 弄瓦
give birth to a daughter;

nong zhang 弄璋
give birth to a son;

pai2 luan 排卵
ovulate // ovulation;

pai luan guo shao 排卵過少
oligo-ovulation;

pai luan qi 排卵期
period of ovulation;

pan2 zhuang tai pan 盤狀胎盤
placenta discoidea;

pin3 tai 品胎
triplets;

qi1 tai 七胎
septuplet;

qi4 zhong xing gong jing yin dao yan 氣腫性宮頸陰道炎
cervicocolpitis emphysematosa;

qiang2 cu fen mian 強促分娩
accouchement force;

qing1 chun qi zi gong 青春期子宮
pubescent uterus;

ren4 shen 妊娠
pregnancy;
dan tai ren shen 單胎妊娠
monocyesis;
gong jiao ren shen 宮角妊娠
cornual pregnancy;
gong jing ren shen 宮頸妊娠
cervical pregnancy;
gong wai ren shen 宮外妊娠
extrauterine pregnancy;
guo qi ren shen 過期妊娠
post-term pregnancy;
huan xiang ren shen 幻想妊娠
phantom pregnancy;
jia ren shen 假妊娠
pseudogestation;
mo xing ren shen 膜性妊娠
membranous pregnancy;
shen jing xing ren shen 神經性妊娠
nervous pregnancy;
zheng chang ren shen 正常妊娠
encyesis;

ren shen nang 妊娠囊
gestation sac;

ren shen ou tu 妊娠嘔吐
vomiting of pregnancy;

ren shen pao zhen 妊娠疱疹
herpes gestationis;

ren shen zi gong 妊娠子宮
gravid uterus;

rou4 ya zhong xing gong jing yan 肉芽腫性宮頸炎
granulomatous cervicitis;

san1 bao tai 三胞胎
triplets;

shen1 huai liu jia 身懷六甲
pregnant || be expecting; heavily pregnant / heavy with child; in a certain condition; in a delicate condition; in a particular condition; in a family way; in an interesting condition; in the family way;

shen1 娠
pregnant;

shen2 jing xing ren shen 神經性妊娠
nervous pregnancy;

shen4 xing tai pan 腎形胎盤
placenta reniformis;

sheng1 er yu nü 生兒育女
bear children and rear them;

shou4 tai 受胎
be impregnated;

shou tai lü 受胎率
conception rate;

shou yun 受孕
be impregnated / become pregnant;

shuang1 bao tai 雙胞胎
twins;

si3 tai 死胎
dead fetus / stillbirth;

si4 bao tai 四胞胎
quadruplets;

tai1 胎
(1) embryo / foetus;
(2) birth;

tai bao 胎胞
embryo / fetus / placenta;

tai dong 胎動
fetal movement;

tai dong bu an 胎動不安
excessive fetal movement;

tai dong gan 胎動感
quickening;

tai er 胎兒
embryo / fetus / unborn baby;

tai er bing 胎兒病
fetopathy;

tai er fa yu 胎兒發育
fetation;

tai er hu xi 胎兒呼吸
fetal respiration;

tai er shui zhong 胎兒水腫
fetal hydrops;

tai fen 胎糞
meconium;

tai fen xi ru 胎糞吸入
meconium aspiration;

tai gou 胎垢
smegma embryonum;

tai ji 胎記
birthmark;

tai mao 胎毛
lanugo hair;

tai mo 胎膜
fetal membrane;

tai pan 胎盤
embryo / fetus / placenta;
pan zhuang tai pan 盤狀胎盤
placenta discoidea;
shen xing tai pan 腎形胎盤
placenta reniformis;

tai pan bing 胎盤病
placentopathy;

tai pan liu 胎盤瘤
placentoma;

tai pan shui zhong 胎盤水腫
placental oedema;

tai qi 胎氣
fetus-energy;

tai pan xing cheng 胎盤形成
placentation;

tai si fu zhong 胎死腹中
death in the womb;

tai wei 胎位
position of a fetus;

tai xing zi gong 胎性子宮
fetal uterus;

tai yi 胎衣
embryo / fetus / placenta;

te2 fa xing liu chan 特發性流產
idiopathic abortion;

tou2 tai 投胎
get into the cycle of reincarnation;

tou2 tai 頭胎
firstborn;

tuo1 tai 脱胎
be born out of / emerge from the womb of;

tuo tai huan gu 脱胎換骨
change oneself inside out;

wai4 shang xing gong jing yan 外傷性宮頸炎
traumatic cervicitis;

wai zi gong jing 外子宮頸
exocervix;

wan2 quan liu chan 完全流產
complete abortion;

wei3 suo luan 萎縮卵
blighted ovum;

wu2 zi gong 無子宮
ametria;

wu3 bao tai 五胞胎
quintuplets;

wu4 sheng 寤生
give birth to a baby while asleep;

xian4 xing zi gong nei mo yan 腺性子宮內膜炎
glandular endometritis;

xiang1 dui xing bu yu 相對性不育
relative sterility;

xiao3 chan 小產
abortion / have a miscarriage / suffer a miscarriage // abortion / miscarriage;

xin1 xing zi gong 心形子宮
uterus cordiformis;

yi1 ju de nan 一舉得男
get a son as one's first child;

yi luan shuang bao tai 一卵雙胞胎
identical twins;

yi suo de nan 一索得男
produce a male heir by first childbirth;

yi tai duo zi 一胎多子
multiparous;

yi tai san zi 一胎三子
give birth to triplets;

yin1 dao fen mian 陰道分娩
vaginal delivery;

ying4 hua xing luan chao yan 硬化性卵巢炎
sclero-oophoritis;

you3 shen 有身
pregnant;

you xi 有喜
pregnant;

yuan2 fa bu yun 原發不孕
primary inferitlity;

yuan fa xing bu yu 原發性不育
primary sterility;

yun4 孕
conceive // pregnant;

yun ling 孕齡
gestational age;

yun qi 孕期
gestation / pregnancy;

yun tu 孕吐
vomiting during pregnancy;

yun yu 孕育
be pregnant with ‖ breed; foster; nourish; nurse; nurture;

zao3 chan 早產
premature birth;

zhen4 tong 陣痛
labour pangs / pangs of childbirth;

zheng4 chang fen mian 正常分娩
eutocia;

zheng chang ren shen 正常妊娠
encyesis;

zhong4 shen zi 重身子
pregnant;

zhu1 tai 珠胎
human embryo in a woman's body;

zhu tai an jie 珠胎暗結
a human embryo is formed in the woman's body // pregnant;

zhui4 tai 墜胎
abort // abortion;

zi3 gong 子宮
uterus / womb;

an xing zi gong 鞍型子宮
saddle-shaped uterus;

qing chun qi zi gong 青春期子宮
pubescent uterus;

ren shen zi gong 妊娠子宮
gravid uterus;

xin xing zi gong 心形子宮
uterus cordiformis;

zi gong ai 子宮癌
cancer of the uterus / cancer of the womb / uterine cancer;

zi gong bai dai 子宮白帶
metroleukorrhea;

zi gong bi 子宮襞
arbor vitae uteri;

zi gong bing 子宮病
hysteropathy / metropathy / uterine disease;

zi gong chu xue 子宮出血
endometrorrhagia / metrorrhagia / uterine bleeding;

zi gong fa yu bu quan 子宮發育不全
uterine hypoplasia;

zi gong gong neng bu liang 子宮功能不良
dysfunction of uterus;

zi gong gong neng bu quan 子宮功能不全
uterine insufficiency;

zi gong ji liu 子宮肌瘤
hysteromyoma;

zi gong ji shui 子宮積水
hydrometra;

zi gong ji xue 子宮積血
hematometra;

zi gong jiao tong 子宮絞痛
uterine colic;

zi gong jing 子宮頸
cervix / cervix of womb / uterine cervix;
wai zi gong jing 外子宮頸
exocervix;

zi gong jing ai 子宮頸癌
cancer of the cervix / cervical cancer;

zi gong jing mi lan 子宮頸糜爛
cervical erosion;

zi gong jing yan 子宮頸炎
cervicitis;

zi gong jing luan 子宮痙攣
hysterospasm;

zi gong kou 子宮口
ostium uteri;

zi gong nei mo 子宮內膜
endometrium;

zi gong nei mo yan 子宮內膜炎
endometritis;
bo tuo xing zi gong nei mo yan 剝脫性子宮內膜炎
exfoliative endometritis;
chan hou zi gong nei mo yan 產後子宮內膜炎
puerperal endometritis;
mo xing zi gong nei mo yan 膜性子宮內膜炎
membranous endometritis;
xian xing zi gong nei mo yan 腺性子宮內膜炎
glandular endometritis;

zi gong sai 子宮塞
vaginal pessary;

zi gong shan 子宮疝
hysterocele;

zi gong shou suo 子宮收縮
uterine contraction;

zi gong tong 子宮痛
hysterodynia;

zi gong tuo chui 子宮脫垂
metroptosis / prolapse of uterus;

zi gong wai yun 子宮外孕
ectopic pregnancy / extrauterine pregnancy;

zi gong wei suo 子宮萎縮
metratrophia;

zi gong wu li 子宮無力
metratonia;

zi gong xia chui 子宮下垂
hysteroptosia;

zi gong yan 子宮炎
hysteritis / metritis / uteritis;
chan hou zi gong yan 產後子宮炎
lochiometritis;
nong xing zi gong yan 膿性子宮炎
pyometritis;

zi gong ying hua 子宮硬化
uterosclerosis;

zi4 ran fen mian 自然分娩
natural childbirth;

General Index

a

b

c

d

e

f

g

h

j

k

l

m

n

o

p

q

r

S

t

W

X

y

Z